Irwin Shaw

FOUR COMPLETE NOVELS

Rich Man, Poor Man

Beggarman, Thief

Nightwork

Evening in Byzantium

AVENEL BOOKS · NEW YORK

CONTENTS

Rich Man, Poor Man

To My Son

Part One

CHAPTER 1

1945

I

MR. DONNELLY, THE track coach, ended the day's practice early because Henry Fuller's father came down to the high-school field to tell Henry that they had just got a telegram from Washington announcing that Henry's brother had been killed in action in Germany. Henry was the team's best shot-putter. Mr. Donnelly gave Henry a chance to go in and change his clothes alone and go home with his father, then whistled to gather the whole squad in a group and said they could all go home, as a gesture of respect.

The baseball team was practicing on the diamond, but nobody on the baseball team had lost a brother that afternoon, so they kept on practicing.

Rudolph Jordache (two-twenty low hurdles) went into the locker room and took a shower, although he hadn't run enough to work up a sweat. There never was enough hot water at home and when he could he showered at the gym. The high school had been built in 1927, when everybody had money, and the showers were roomy and with plenty of hot water. There was even a swimming pool. Usually, Rudolph took a swim too, after practice, but he didn't today, out of respect.

The boys in the locker room spoke in low tones and there was none of the usual horsing around. Smiley, the captain of the team, got up on a bench and said he thought that if there was a funeral service for Henry's brother, they all ought to chip in and buy a wreath. Fifty cents a man would do it, he thought. You could tell by the looks on the boys' faces who could spare the fifty cents and who couldn't. Rudolph couldn't spare it, but he made a conscious effort to look as though he could. The boys who agreed most readily were the ones whose parents took them down to New York City before the school term to buy the year's clothes for them. Rudolph bought his clothes in town, in Port Philip, at Bernstein's Department Store.

He was dressed neatly, though, with a collar and tie and a sweater under a leather windbreaker, and brown pants, from an old suit whose jacket had gone through at the elbows. Henry Fuller was one of the boys who got his clothes in New York, but Rudolph was sure Henry wasn't getting any pleasure from the fact this afternoon.

Rudolph got out of the locker room quickly because he didn't want to walk home with any of the other fellows and talk about Henry Fuller's brother. He wasn't particularly friendly with Henry, who was rather stupid, as the weight men were likely to be, and he preferred not to pretend to any excessive sympathy.

The school was in a residential part of the town, to the north and east of the business center, and was surrounded by semi-detached one-family houses that had been built at about the same time as the school, when the town was expanding. They were all the same originally, but through the years their owners had painted the trim and doors in different colors and here and there had added a bay window or a balcony in forlorn attempts at variety.

Carrying his books, Rudolph strode along the cracked sidewalks of the neighborhood. It was a windy early spring day, although not very cold, and he had a sense of well-being and holiday because of the light workout and the short practice. Most of the trees had already put out their leaves and there were buds everywhere.

The school was built on a hill and he could see the Hudson River below him, still looking cold and wintry, and the spires of the churches of the town, and in the distance to the south, the chimney of the Boylan Brick and Tile Works, where his sister Gretchen worked, and the tracks of the New York Central, along the river. Port Philip was not a pretty town, although once it had been, with big white Colonial houses mingled with solid Victorian stone. But the boom in the 1920's had brought a lot of new people into town, working people whose homes were narrow and dark, spreading out into all neighborhoods. Then the Depression had thrown almost everybody out of work and the jerry-built houses had been neglected, and as Rudolph's mother complained, the entire town had become a single slum. This wasn't absolutely true. The northern part of the town still had many fine big houses and wide streets and the houses had been kept up through everything. And even in the neighborhoods that were run down there were big houses that families had refused to leave and were still presentable behind generous lawns and old trees.

The war had brought prosperity once again to Port Philip and the Brick and Tile Works and the cement plant were going full blast and even the tannery and the Byefield Shoe Factory had started up again with Army orders. But with the war on, people had other things to do than worry about keeping up appearances and, if possible, the city looked more dilapidated than ever.

With the town spread before him like that, planless and jumbled in the windy afternoon sun, Rudolph wondered if anybody would give his life to defend it or to take it, as Henry Fuller's brother had given his life to take some nameless town in Germany.

Secretly, he hoped that the war would last another two years, although it didn't look now as though it would. He was going to be seventeen years old soon and another year after that he could enlist. He saw himself with a lieutenant's silver bars, taking an enlisted man's salute, waving a platoon to follow him under machine-gun fire. It was the sort of experience a man ought to have. He was sorry there was no more cavalry. That must have been something—waving a saber, at a full gallop, charging the despicable foe.

He didn't dare mention anything like this around the house. His mother became hysterical when anybody as much as suggested that perhaps the war would last and her Rudolph would be taken. He knew that some boys lied about their age to enlist—there were stories about fifteen-year-old boys, even fourteen-year-olds, who were in the Marines and who had won medals—but he couldn't do anything like that to his mother.

As usual he made a detour to pass the house where Miss Lenaut lived. Miss Lenaut was his French teacher. She was nowhere in sight.

Then he walked down to Broadway, the main street of the town, which ran parallel to the river and which was also the through highway from New York to Albany. He dreamed of having a car, like the ones he saw speeding through town. Once he had a car he would go down to New York every weekend. He wasn't quite sure what he would do in New York, but he would go there.

Broadway was a nondescript thoroughfare, with shops of all kinds mixed together, butcher shops and markets next to quite large stores that sold women's clothes and cheap jewelry and sporting goods. He stopped, as he often did, before the window of the Army and Navy Store, which had fishing equipment displayed along with work shoes and chino pants and shirts and flashlights and penknives. He stared at the fishing rods, thin and elegant, with their expensive reels. He fished in the river and, when the season was on, in the trout streams that were open to the public, but his equipment was primitive.

He went down another short street and turned to his left on Vanderhoff Street, where he lived. Vanderhoff Street ran parallel to Broadway and seemed to be trying to emulate it, but doing it badly, like a poor man in a baggy suit and scuffed shoes pretending he had arrived in a Cadillac. The shops were small and the wares in their windows were dusty, as though the owners knew there really was no use. Quite a few of the shop fronts were still boarded up, having closed down in 1930 or 1931. When new sewer lines were laid down before the war the WPA had felled all the trees which had shaded the sidewalks and nobody had bothered to plant new ones. Vanderhoff was a long street and as he approached his own house the street became shabbier and shabbier, as though just the mere act of going south was somehow spiritually a decline.

His mother was in the bakery, behind the counter, with a shawl around her shoulders, because she was always cold. The building was on a corner, so there were two big windows and his mother kept complaining that with all that glass there was no way of keeping the shop warm. She was putting a dozen hard rolls in a brown paper bag for a little girl. There were cakes and tarts displayed in the front window, but they were no longer baked in the cellar. At the start of the war, his father, who did the baking, had decided that it was more trouble than it was worth and now a truck from a big commerical bakery stopped every morning to deliver the cakes and pastries and Axel confined himself to baking the bread and rolls. When pastries had remained in the window three days, his father would bring them upstairs for the family to eat.

Rudolph went in and kissed his mother and she patted his cheek. She always looked tired and was always squinting a little, because she was a chain smoker and the smoke got into her eyes.

"Why so early?" she asked.

"Short practice today," he said. He didn't say why. "I'll take over here. You can go upstairs now."

"Thank you," she said. "My Rudy." She kissed him again. She was very affectionate with him. He wished she would kiss his brother or his sister once in a while, but she never did. He had never seen his mother kiss his father.

"I'll go up and make dinner," she said. She was the only one in the family who called supper dinner. Rudolph's father did the shopping, because he said his wife was extravagant and didn't know good food from bad, but most of the time she did the cooking.

She went out the front door. There was no door that opened directly from the bakery to the hallway and the staircase that led up to the two floors above, where they lived, and he saw his mother pass the show window, framed in pastry and shivering as the wind hit her. It was hard for him to remember that she was only a little over forty years old. Her hair was graying and she shuffled like an old lady.

He got out a book and read. It would be slow in the shop for another hour. The book he was reading was Burke's speech *On Conciliation With the Colonies*, for his English class. It was so convincing that you wondered how all those supposedly smart men in Parliament hadn't agreed with him. What would America have been like if they had listened to Burke? Would there have been earls and dukes and castles? He would have liked that. Sir Rudolph Jordache, Colonel in the Port Philip Household Guards.

An Italian laborer came in and asked for a loaf of white bread. Rudolph put down Burke and served him.

The family ate in the kitchen. The evening meal was the only one they all ate together because of the father's hours of work. They had lamb stew tonight. Despite rationing, they always had plenty of meat because Rudolph's father was friendly with the butcher, Mr. Haas, who didn't ask for ration tickets because he was German, too. Rudolph felt uneasy about eating black market lamb on the same day that Henry Fuller had found out his brother had been killed, but all he did about it was ask for a small portion, mostly potatoes and carrots, because he couldn't talk to his father about fine points like that.

His brother, Thomas, the only blond in the family, besides the mother, who really couldn't be called blonde anymore, certainly didn't seem to be worried about anything as he wolfed down his food. Thomas was just a year younger than Rudolph, but was already as tall and much stockier than his brother. Gretchen, Rudolph's older sister, never ate much, because she worried about her weight. His mother just picked at her food. His father, a massive man in shirt-sleeves, ate enormously, wiping his thick, black moustache with the back of his hand from time to time.

Gretchen didn't wait for the three-day-old cherry pie that they had for dessert, because she was due at the Army hospital just outside town where she worked as a volunteer nurse's aide five nights a week. When she stood up, the father made his usual joke. "Be careful," he said. "Don't let those soldiers grab you. We don't have enough rooms in this house to set up a nursery."

"Pa," Gretchen said reproachfully.

"I know soldiers," Axel Jordache said. "Just be careful."

Gretchen was a neat, proper, beautiful girl, Rudolph thought, and it pained him that his father talked like that to her. After all, she was the only one in the family who was contributing to the war effort.

When the meal was over, Thomas went out, too, as he did every night. He never did any homework and he got terrible marks in school. He was still a freshman in the high school, although he was nearly sixteen. He never listened to anybody.

Axel Jordache went into the living room up front to read the evening newspaper before going down to the cellar for the night's work. Rudolph stayed in the kitchen to dry the dishes after his mother had washed them. If I ever get married, Rudolph thought, my wife will not have to wash dishes.

When the dishes were done, the mother got out the ironing board and Rudolph went upstairs to the room he shared with his brother, to do his homework. He knew that if ever he was going to escape from eating in a kitchen and listening to his father and wiping dishes it was going to be through books, so he was always the best prepared student in the class for all examinations.

II

Maybe, Axel Jordache thought, at work in the cellar, I ought to put poison in one of them. For laughs. For anything. Serve them right. Just once, just one night. See who gets it.

He drank the blend straight out of the bottle. By the end of the night the bottle would be almost gone. There was flour all the way up to his elbows and flour on his face, where he had wiped away the sweat. I'm a goddamn clown, he thought, without a circus.

The window was open to the March night and the weedy Rhenish smell of the river soaked into the room, but the oven was cooking the air in the basement. I am in hell, he thought, I stoke the fires of hell to earn my bread, to make my bread. I am in hell making Parker House rolls.

He went to the window and took a deep breath, the big chest muscles, age-ridged, tightening against his sweaty skivvy shirt. The river a few hundred yards away, freed now of ice, carried the presence of North with it like the rumor of passing troops, a last cold marching threat of winter, spreading on each side of its banks. The Rhine was four thousand miles away. Tanks and cannon were crossing it on improvised bridges. A lieutenant had run across it when a bridge had failed to blow up. Another lieutenant on the other side had been court-martialed and shot because he had failed to blow the bridge as ordered. Armies. Die Wacht am Rhein. Churchill had pissed in it recently. Fabled river. Jordache's native water. Vineyards and sirens. Schloss Whatever. The cathedral in Cologne was still standing. Nothing much else. Jordache had seen the photographs in the newspapers. Home sweet home in old Cologne. Bulldozed ruins with the ever-remembered stink of the dead buried under collapsed walls. It couldn't have happened to a nicer city. Jordache thought dimly of his youth and spat up and out of the window in the direction of the other river. The invincible German Army. How many dead? Jordache spat again and licked his black moustache that drooped down at the corners of his mouth. God bless America. He had killed to get there. He took one last breath of the river's presence and limped back to work.

His name was on view on the window of the shop above the basement. BAKERY, A. Jordache, Pro. Twenty years ago, when the sign had been put up, it had read A. Jordache, Prop., but one winter the *p* had fallen off and he hadn't bothered to have it put back on. He sold just as many Parker House rolls without the *p*.

The cat lay close to the oven staring at him. They had never bothered to give the cat a name. The cat was there to keep the mice and rats out of the flour. When Jordache had to address it, he said, "Cat." The cat probably thought its name was Cat. The cat watched him steadily all night, every night. She lived on one bowl of milk a day and all the mice and rats she could catch. The way the cat looked at him, Jordache was sure the cat wished she was ten times bigger than she was, as big as a tiger, so she could spring on him one night and have one real meal.

The oven was hot enough now and he limped over and put in the first tray of the night. He grimaced when he opened the oven door and the heat hit him.

III

Upstairs, in the narrow room he shared with his brother, Rudolph was looking up a word in an English-French dictionary. He had finished his homework. The word he was looking for was longing. He had already looked up hints and visions. He was writing a love letter in French to his French teacher, Miss Lenaut. He had read *The Magic Mountain*, and while most of the book had bored him, with the exception of the chapter about the seance, he had been impressed by the fact that the love scenes were in French and had painfully translated them for himself. To make love in French seemed to him to be distinguished. One sure thing, there was no other sixteen-year-old boy writing a love letter in French that night anywhere in the whole Hudson Valley.

"*Enfin*"—he wrote, in a carefully fashioned, almost printed script that he had developed over the last two years—"*enfin, je dois vous dire, chère Madame, quand je vous vois par hasard dans les couloirs de l'école ou se promenant dans votre manteau bleuclair dans les rues, j'ai l'envie*"—that was the closest he could get to longing—"*très profond de voyager dans le monde d'où vous êtes sortie et des visions délicieuses de flâner avec vous à mes côtés sur les boulevards de Paris, qui vient d'être libéré par les braves soldats de votre pays et le mien. Votre cavalier servant*, Rudolph Jordache (French 32b)."

He reread the letter, then read it in the English in which he had first written it. He had tried to make the English as much like French as possible. "Finally, I must tell you, Dear Madame, that when I see you by accident in the hallways of the school or walking along in your light-blue coat on the street, I have a deep longing to travel in the world you came from and wonderful visions of strolling arm in arm with you along the boulevards of Paris, which has just been liberated by the brave soldiers of your country and mine."

He read the French version again with satisfaction. There was no doubt about it. If you wanted to be elegant, French was the language for it. He liked the way Miss Lenaut pronounced his name, correctly, Jordahsh, making it soft and musical, not Jawdake, as some people said it, or Jordash.

Then, regretfully, he tore both letters into small pieces. He knew he was never going to send Miss Lenaut any letters. He had already written her six letters and torn them up because she would think he was crazy and would probably tell the principal. And he certainly didn't want his father or mother or Gretchen or Tom to find any love letters in any language in his room.

Still, the satisfaction was there. Sitting in the bare little room above the bakery, with the Hudson flowing a few hundred yards away, writing the letters was like a promise to himself. One day he would make long voyages, one day he would sail the river and write in new languages to beautiful women of high character, and the letters would actually be mailed.

He got up and looked at himself in the wavy little mirror above the battered oak dresser. He looked at himself often, searching his face for the man he wanted to be. He was very careful with his looks. His straight, black hair was always perfectly brushed; occasionally he plucked two or three bits of dark fuzz from the space between his eyebrows; he avoided candy so that he would have a minimum of pimples; he remembered to smile, not laugh aloud, and even that not frequently. He was very conservative with the colors he chose to wear and had worked on the way he walked, so that he never seemed hurried or exuberant, but walked in an easy gliding motion with his shoulders squared. He kept his nails filed and his sister gave him a manicure once a month and he kept out of fights because he didn't want to have his face marred by a broken nose or his long, thin hands twisted by swollen knuckles. To keep in shape, there was the track team. For the pleasures of nature and solitude he fished, using a dry fly when somebody was watching, worms at other times.

"*Votre cavalier servant*," he said into the mirror. He wanted his face to look French when he spoke the language, the way Miss Lenaut's face suddenly looked French when she addressed the class.

He sat down at the little yellow oak table he used for a desk and pulled a piece of paper toward him. He tried to remember exactly what Miss Lenaut looked like. She was quite tall, with flat hips and full breasts always prominently propped up, and thin, straight legs. She wore high heels and ribbons and a great deal of lipstick. First he drew her with her clothes on, not achieving much of a likeness but getting the two curls in front of her ears and making the mouth convincingly prominent and dark. Then he tried to imagine what she might look like without any clothes. He drew her naked, sitting on a stool looking at herself in a hand-mirror. He stared at his handiwork. *O, God, if ever!* He tore up the naked drawing. He was ashamed of himself. He deserved to live over a bakery. If they ever found out downstairs what he thought and did upstairs . . .

He began to undress for bed. He was in his socks, because he didn't want his mother, who slept in the room below, to know that he was still awake. He had to get up at five o'clock every morning to deliver the bread in the cart attached to a bicycle and his mother kept after him for not getting enough sleep.

Later on, when he was rich and successful, he would say, I got up at five o'clock in the morning, rain or shine, to deliver rolls to the Depot Hotel and the Ace Diner and Sinowski's Bar and Grill. He wished his name wasn't Rudolph.

IV

At the Casino Theater Errol Flynn was killing a lot of Japs. Thomas Jordache was sitting in the dark at the rear of the theater eating caramels from a package that he had taken from the slot machine in the lobby with a lead slug. He was expert at making lead slugs.

"Slip me one, Buddy," Claude said, making it sound tough, like a movie gangster asking for another clip of 45 cartridges for his rod. Claude Tinker had an uncle who was a priest and to overcome the damaging implications of the relationship he tried to sound tough at all times. Tom flipped a caramel in the air and Claude caught it and started chewing on it loudly. The boys were sitting low on their spines, their feet draped over the empty seats in front of them. They had sneaked in as usual, through a grating that they had pried loose last year. The grating protected a window in the men's room in the cellar. Every once in a while, one or the other of them would come up into the auditorium with his fly open, to make it look for real.

Tom was bored with the picture. He watched Errol Flynn dispose of a platoon of Japs with various weapons. "Phonus bolonus," he said.

"What language you speaking, Professor?" Claude said, playing their game.

"That's Latin," Tom said, "for bullshit."

"What a command of tongues," Claude said.

"Look," Tom said, "Down there to the right. That GI with his girl."

A few rows in front of them a soldier and a girl were sitting, entwined. The theater was half-empty and there was nobody in the row they were in or in the rows behind them. Claude frowned. "He looks awful big," Claude said. "Look at that neck on him."

"General," Tom said, "we attack at dawn."

"You'll wind up in the hospital," Claude said.

"Wanna bet?" Tom swung his legs back from the chair in front of him and stood up and started toward the aisle. He moved silently, his sneakered feet light on the worn carpet of the Casino floor. He always wore sneakers. You had to be sure-footed and ready to make the fast break at all times. He hunched his shoulders, bulky and easy under his sweater, and tucked in his gut, enjoying the hard, flat feeling under the tight belt. Ready for anything. He smiled in the darkness, the excitement beginning to get him, as it always did at these preliminary choosing moments.

Claude followed him, uneasily. Claude was a lanky, thin-armed boy, with a long-nosed squirrely wedge of a face and loose, wet lips. He was nearsighted and wore glasses and that didn't make him look any better. He was a manipulator and behind-the-scenes man and slid out of trouble like a corporation lawyer and conned teachers into giving him good marks although he almost never opened a school book. He wore dark suits and neckties and had a kind of literary stoop and shambled apologetically when he walked and looked insignificant, humble, and placating. He was imaginative, his imagination concentrating on outrages against society. His father ran the bookkeeping department of the Boylan Brick and Tile Works and his mother, who had a degree from St. Anne's College for Women, was the president of the draft board, and what with all that and the priest-uncle besides, and his harmless and slightly repulsive appearance, Claude maneuvered with impunity through his plot-filled world.

The two boys moved down the empty row and sat directly behind the GI and his girl. The GI had his hand in the girl's blouse and was methodically squeezing her breast. The GI hadn't removed his overseas cap and it peaked down steeply over his forehead. The girl had her hand somewhere down in the shadows between the soldier's legs. Both the GI and the girl were watching the picture intently. Neither of them paid any attention to the arrival of the boys.

Tom sat behind the girl, who smelled good. She was liberally doused with a flowery perfume which mingled with the buttery, cowlike aroma from a bag of popcorn they had been eating. Claude sat behind the soldier. The soldier had a small head, but he was tall, with broad shoulders, and his cap obscured most of the screen from Claude, who had to squirm from side to side to glimpse the film.

"Listen," Claude whispered, "I tell you he's too big. I bet he weighs one seventy, at least."

"Don't worry," Tom whispered back. "Start in." He spoke confidently, but he could feel little shivers of doubt in his fingertips and under his armpits. That hint of doubt, of fear, was familiar to him and it added to his expectation and the beauty of the final violence. "Go ahead," he whispered harshly to Claude. "We ain't got all night."

"You're the boss," Claude said. Then he leaned forward and tapped the soldier on the shoulder. "Pardon me, Sergeant," he said. "I wonder if you'd be so kind as to remove your cap. It's difficult for me to see the screen."

"I ain't no sergeant," the soldier said, without turning. He kept his cap on and continued watching the picture, squeezing the girl's breast.

The two boys sat quietly for more than a minute. They had practiced the tactic of provocation so often together that there was no need for signals. Then Tom leaned forward and tapped the soldier heavily on the shoulder. "My friend made a polite request," he said. "You are interfering with his enjoyment of the picture. We will have to call the management if you don't take your cap off."

The soldier swiveled a little in his seat, annoyedly. "There's two hundred empty seats," he said. "If your friend wants to see the picture let him sit someplace else." He turned back to his two preoccupations, sex and art.

"He's on the way," Tom whispered to Claude. "Keep him going."

Claude tapped the soldier on the shoulder again. "I suffer from a rare eye disease," Claude said. "I can only see from this seat. Everywhere else it's a blur. I can't tell whether it's Errol Flynn or Loretta Young up there."

"Go to an eye doctor," the soldier said. The girl laughed at his wit. She sounded as though she had drunk some water the wrong way when she laughed. The soldier laughed, too, to show that he appreciated himself.

"I don't think it's nice to laugh at people's disabilities," Tom said.

"Especially with a war on," Claude said, "with all those crippled heroes."

"What sort of an American are you?" Tom asked, his voice rising patriotically. "That's the question I would like to ask, what sort of an American are you?"

The girl turned. "Get lost, kids," she said.

"I want to remind you, sir," Tom said, "that I hold you personally responsible for anything your lady friend says."

"Don't pay them no mind, Angela," the soldier said. He had a high, tenor voice.

The boys sat in silence again for a moment.

"Marine, tonight you die," Tom said in a high falsetto, in his Japanese imitation. "Yankee dog, tonight I cut off your balls."

"Watch your goddamn language," the soldier said, turning his head.

"I bet he's braver than Errol Flynn," Tom said. "I bet he's got a drawer full of medals back home but he's too modest to wear them."

The soldier was getting angry now. "Why don't you kids shut up? We came here to see a movie."

"We came to make love," Tom said. He caressed Claude's cheek elaborately. "Didn't we, hotpants?"

"Squeeze me harder, darrrling," Claude said. "My nipples're palpitating."

"I am in ecstasy," Tom said. "Your skin is like a baby's ass."

"Put your tongue in my ear, honey," Claude said. "Ooooh—I'm coming."

"That's enough," the soldier said. Finally he had taken his hand out of the girl's blouse. "Get the hell out of here."

He had spoken loudly and angrily and a few people were turning around up front and making shushing noises.

"We paid good money for these seats," Tom said, "and we're not moving."

"We'll see about that." The soldier stood up. He was about six feet tall. "I'm going to get the usher."

"Don't let the little bastards get your goat, Sidney," the girl said. "Sit down."

"Sidney, remember I told you I hold you personally responsible for your lady friend's language," Tom said. "This is the last warning."

"Usher!" the soldier called across the auditorium, to where the lone attendant, dressed in frayed gold braid, was sitting in the last row, dozing under an exit light.

"Ssh, sssh!" came from spots all over the theater.

"He's a real soldier," Claude said. "He's calling for reinforcements."

"Sit down, Sidney." The girl tugged at the soldier's sleeve. "They're just snotty kids."

"Button your shirt, Angela," Tom said. "Your titty's showing." He stood up, in case the soldier swung.

"Sit down, please," Claude said politely, as the usher came down the aisle toward them, "this is the best part of the picture and I don't want to miss it."

"What's going on here?" the usher asked. He was a big weary-looking man of about forty who worked in a furniture factory during the day.

"Get these kids out of here," the soldier said. "They're using dirty language in front of this lady."

"All I said was, please take your hat off," Claude said. "Am I right, Tom?"

"That's what he said, sir," Tom said, sitting down again. "A simple polite request. He has a rare eye disease."

"What?" the usher asked, puzzled.

"If you don't throw them out," the soldier said, "there's going to be trouble."

"Why don't you boys sit someplace else?" the usher said.

"He explained," Claude said. "I have a rare eye disease."

"This is a free country," Tom said. "You pay your money and you sit where you want to sit. Who does he think he is— Adolf Hitler? Big shot. Just because he's wearing a soldier suit. I bet he never got any nearer to the Japs than Kansas City, Missouri. Coming here, giving a bad example to the youth of the country, screwing girls in public. In uniform."

"If you don't throw them out, I'm going to clout them," the soldier said thickly. He was clenching and unclenching his fists.

"You used bad language," the usher said to Tom. "I heard it with my own ears. Not in this theater. Out you go."

By now most of the audience was booing. The usher leaned over and grabbed Tom by his sweater. By the feel of the big hand on him Tom knew there was no chance with the man. He stood up. "Come on, Claude," he said. "All right, Mister," he said to the usher. "We don't want to cause any disturbance. Just give us our money back and we'll leave."

"Fat chance," the usher said.

Tom sat down again. "I know my rights," he said. Then very loudly, so that his voice rang through the entire auditorium over the sound of the gunfire from the screen, "Go ahead and hit me, you big brute."

The usher sighed. "Okay, okay," he said. "I'll give you your money back. Just get the hell out of here."

The boys stood up. Tom smiled up at the soldier. "I warned you," he said. "I'll be waiting for you outside."

"Go get your ma to change your diapers," the soldier said. He sat down heavily.

In the lobby, the usher gave them each thirty-five cents out of his own pocket, making them sign receipts to show to the owner of the theater. Tom signed the name of his algebra teacher and Claude signed the name of the president of his father's bank. "And I don't want to see you ever trying to get in here again," the usher said.

"It's a public place," Claude said. "You try anything like that and my father'll hear about it."

"Who's your father?" the usher said, disturbed.

"You'll find out," Claude said menacingly. "In due time."

The boys stalked deliberately out of the lobby. On the street they clapped each other on the back and roared with laughter. It was early and the picture wouldn't end for another half hour, so they went into the diner across the street and had a piece of pie and some coffee with the usher's money. The radio was on behind the counter and a newscaster was talking about the gains the American Army had made that day in Germany and about the possibility of the German high command falling back into a redoubt in the Bavarian Alps for a last stand.

Tom listened with a grimace twisting his round baby face. The war bored him. He didn't mind the fighting, it was the crap about sacrifice and ideals and our brave boys all the time that made him sick. It was a cinch they'd never get *him* in any army.

"Hey, lady," he said to the waitress, who was buffing her nails behind the counter, "can't we have some music?" He got enough patriotism at home, from his sister and brother.

The waitress looked up languidly. "Ain't you boys interested in who's winning the war?"

"We're Four F," Tom said. "We have a rare eye disease."

"Oh, my rare eye disease," Claude said, over his coffee. They burst into laughter again.

They were standing in front of the Casino when the doors opened and the audience began to stream out. Tom had given Claude his wristwatch to hold so that it wouldn't get broken. He stood absolutely still, purposely controlling himself, his hands hanging loosely at his sides, hoping that the soldier hadn't left before the end of the picture. Claude was pacing up and down nervously, his face sweating and pale from excitement. "You're sure now?" he kept saying. "You're absolutely sure? He's an awful big sonofabitch. I want you to be *sure*."

"Don't you worry about me," Tom said. "Just keep the crowd back so I have room to move. I don't want him grappling me." His eyes narrowed. "Here he comes."

The soldier and his girl came out onto the sidewalk. The soldier looked about twenty-two or twenty-three. He was a little pudgy, with a heavy, sullen face. His tunic bulged over a premature paunch, but he looked strong. He had no hash marks on his sleeve and no ribbons. He had his hand possessively on the girl's arm, steering her through the stream of people. "I'm thirsty," he was saying. "Let's go get ourselves a coupla beers." Tom went over to him and stood in front of him, barring his way.

"You here again?" the soldier said, annoyed. He stopped for a moment. Then he started moving again, pushing Tom with his chest.

"You better stop pushing," Tom said. He grabbed the soldier's sleeve. "You're not going anywhere."

The soldier stopped in surprise. He looked down at Tom, who was at least three inches shorter than he, blond and cherubic looking in his old blue sweater and basketball sneakers. "You sure are perky for a kid your size," the soldier said. "Now get out of my way." He pushed Tom to one side with his forearm.

"Who do you think you're pushing, Sidney?" Tom said and jabbed sharply at the soldier's chest with the heel of his hand. By now people were stopping around them and looking on curiously. The soldier's face reddened in slow anger. "Keep your hands to yourself, kid, or you'll get hurt."

"What's the matter with you, boy?" the girl said. She had redone her mouth before coming out of the theater but there were still lipstick smears on her chin and she was uncomfortable at all the attention they were getting. "If this is some kind of joke, it's not funny."

"It's not a joke, Angela," Tom said.

"Stop that Angela crap," the soldier said.

"I want an apology," Tom said.

"That's the least," Claude said.

"Apology? Apology for what?" The soldier appealed to the small crowd that by now had collected around them. "These kids must be nuts."

"Either you apologize for the language your lady friend used to us in there," Tom said, "or you take the consequences."

"Come on, Angela," the soldier said, "let's go get that beer." He started to take a step, but Tom grabbed his sleeve and pulled. There was a tearing noise and a seam broke open at the shoulder.

The soldier twisted around to view the damage. "Hey you little sonofabitch, you tore my coat."

"I told you you weren't going nowhere," Tom said. He backed away a little, his arms crooked, his fingers outspread.

"Nobody gets away with tearing my coat," the soldier said. "I don't care who he is." He swung with his open hand. Tom moved in and let the blow fall on his left shoulder. "Ow!" he screamed, putting his right hand to his shoulder and bending over as though he were in terrible pain.

"Did you see that?" Claude demanded of the spectators. "Did you see that man hit my friend?"

"Listen, soldier," a gray-haired man in a raincoat said, "you can't beat up on a little kid like that."

"I just gave him a little slap," the soldier turned to the man apologetically. "He's been dogging me all . . . "

Suddenly Tom straightened up and hitting upward, with his closed fist, struck the soldier, not too hard, so as not to discourage him, along the side of the jaw.

There was no holding the soldier back now. "Okay, kid, you asked for it." He began to move in on Tom.

Tom retreated and the crowd pushed back behind him.

"Give them room," Claude called professionally. "Give the men room."

"Sidney," the girl called shrilly, "you'll kill him."

"Nah," the soldier said, "I'll just slap him around a little. Teach him a lesson."

Tom snaked in and hit the soldier with a short left hook to the head and went in deep to the belly with his right. The soldier let the air out of his lungs with a large, dry sound, as Tom danced back.

"It's disgusting," a woman said. "A big oaf like that. Somebody ought to stop it."

"It's all right," her husband said. "He said he'd only slap him a couple of times."

The soldier swung a slow, heavy right hand at Tom. Tom ducked under it and dug both his fists into the soldier's soft middle. The soldier bent almost double in pain and Tom hooked both hands to the face. The soldier began to spurt blood and he waved his hands feebly in front of him and tried to clinch. Contemptuously, Tom let the soldier grapple him but kept his right hand free and clubbed at the soldier's kidneys. The soldier slowly went down to one knee. He looked up blearily at Tom through the blood that was flowing from his cut forehead. Angela was crying. The crowd was silent. Tom stepped back. He wasn't even breathing hard. There was a little glow under the light, blond fuzz on his cheeks.

"My God," said the lady who had said that somebody ought to stop it, "he looks just like a baby."

"You getting up?" Tom asked the soldier. The soldier just looked at him and swung his head wearily to get the blood out of his eyes. Angela knelt beside him and started using her handkerchief on the cuts. The whole thing hadn't taken more than thirty seconds.

"That's all for tonight, folks," Claude said. He was wiping sweat off his face.

Tom strode out of the little circle of watching men and women. They were very quiet, as though they had seen something unnatural and dangerous that night, something they would like to be able to forget.

Claude caught up to Tom as they turned the corner. "Boy, oh boy," Claude said, "You worked fast tonight. The combinations, boy, oh boy, the combinations."

Tom was chuckling. "Sidney, you'll kill him," he said, trying to imitate the girl's voice. He felt wonderful. He half-closed his eyes and remembered the shock of his fists against skin and bone and against the brass buttons of the uniform. "It was okay," he said. "Only it didn't last long enough. I should have carried him a while. He was just a pile of shit. Next time let's pick somebody that can *fight*."

"Boy," Claude said, "I really enjoyed that. I sure would like to see that fella's face tomorrow. When you going to do it again?"

Tom shrugged. "When I'm in the mood. Good night." He didn't want Claude hanging around him anymore. He wanted to be alone and remember every move of the fight. Claude was used to these sudden rejections and treated them respectfully. Talent had its prerogatives. "Good night," he said. "See you tomorrow."

Tom waved and turned off down the avenue for the long walk toward his house. They had to be careful to go to other parts of town when Tom wanted to fight. He was too well known in his own neighborhood. Everybody avoided him when they sensed one of his moods coming on.

He walked swiftly toward home down the dark street toward the smell of the river, dancing a little around a lamppost here and there. He'd shown them, he'd shown them. And he was going to show them a lot more. *Them.*

As he turned the last corner, he saw his sister Gretchen approaching the house from the other end of the street. She was hurrying and she had her head down and she didn't see him. He slipped into a doorway across the street and waited. He didn't want to have to talk to his sister. She hadn't said anything that he wanted to hear since he was eight years old. He watched her almost run up to the door next to the bakery window and get her key out of her bag. Maybe once he would follow her and really find out what she did with her nights.

Gretchen opened the door and went in. Tom waited until he was sure that she was safely upstairs and in her room, then crossed the street and stood in front of the weathered gray frame building. Home. He had been born in that house. He had come unexpectedly, early, and there had been no time to get his mother to the hospital. How many times he had heard *that* story. Big deal, being born at home. The Queen did not leave the Palace. The Prince first saw the light of day in the royal bedchamber. The house looked desolate, ready to be torn down. Tom spat again. He stared at the building, all exhilaration gone. There was the usual light from the basement window, where his father was working. The boy's face hardened. A whole life in a cellar. What do they know? he thought. Nothing.

He let himself in quietly with the key and climbed to the room he shared with Rudolph on the third floor. He was careful on the creaky stairs. Moving soundlessly was a point of honor with him. His exits and entrances were his own business. Especially on a night like this. There was some blood on the sleeve of his sweater and he didn't want anybody coming in and howling about it.

He could hear Rudolph breathing steadily, asleep, as he closed the door quietly behind him. Nice, proper Rudolph, the perfect gentleman, smelling of toothpaste, right at the head of his class, everybody's pet, never coming home with blood on him, getting a good night's sleep, so he wouldn't miss a good morning, Ma'am, or a trigonometry problem the next day. Tom undressed in the dark, throwing his clothes carelessly over a chair. He didn't want to answer any questions from Rudolph, either. Rudolph was no ally. He was on the other side. Let him be on the other side. Who cared?

But when he got into the double bed, Rudolph awoke. "Where you been?" Rudolph asked sleepily.

"Just to the show."

"How was it?"

"Lousy."

The two brothers lay still in the darkness. Rudolph moved a bit toward the other side of the bed. He thought it was degrading to have to sleep in the same bed with his brother. It was cold in the room, with the window open and the wind coming off the river. Rudolph always opened the window wide at night. If there was a rule, you could bet Rudolph would obey it. He slept in pajamas. Tom just stripped to his shorts for sleeping. They had arguments about that twice a week.

Rudolph sniffed. "For Christ's sake," he said, "you smell like a wild animal. What've you been doing?"

"Nothing," Tom said. "I can't help the way I smell." If he wasn't my brother, he thought, I'd beat the shit out of him.

He wished he'd had the money to go to Alice's behind the railroad station. He'd lost his virginity there for five dollars and he'd gone back several times after that. That was in the summer. He had had a job on a dredge in the river and he told his father he made ten dollars a week less than he actually did. That big dark woman, that Florence girl, up from Virginia, who had let him come twice for the same five dollars because he was only fourteen and he was cherry, that would have really finished the night off. He hadn't told Rudolph about Alice's either. Rudolph was still a virgin, that was for sure. He was above sex or he was waiting for a movie star or he was a fairy or something. One day, he, Tom, was going to tell Rudolph everything and then watch the expression on his face. Wild animal. Well, if that's what they thought of him, that's what he was going to be—a wild animal.

He closed his eyes and tried to remember what the soldier looked like, down on one knee on the pavement with the blood leaking all over his face. The image was clear, but there was no pleasure in it any more.

He started to tremble. The room was cold, but that wasn't why he was trembling.

V

Gretchen sat in front of the little mirror which was propped up on the dressing table against the wall of her room. It was an old kitchen table she had bought at a junk sale for two dollars and painted pink. There were some cosmetic jars on it and a silver-backed brush she had gotten as a present on her eighteenth birthday and three small bottles of perfume and a manicure set all neatly laid out on a clean towel. She had on an old bathrobe. The worn flannel was warm against her skin and gave her some of the same feeling of coziness she used to have when she came in out of the cold and put it on before bedtime as a young girl. She needed what comfort she could find tonight.

She scrubbed the cold cream off her face with a piece of Kleenex. Her skin was very white, a heritage from her mother, like her blue, shading-to-violet eyes. Her straight, black hair was like her father's. Gretchen was beautiful, her mother said, just as she had been when she was Gretchen's age. Her mother was constantly imploring her not to allow herself to decay, as she had done. Decay was the word her mother used. With marriage, her mother intimated, decay set in immediately. Corruption lay in the touch of a man. Her mother did not lecture her about men; she was sure of what she called Gretchen's virtue (that was another word she used freely), but she used her influence to get Gretchen to wear loose clothes that did not show off her figure. "There's no sense in seeking out trouble," her mother said. "It comes finding you out soon enough. You have an old-fashioned figure, but your troubles will be strictly up-to-date."

Her mother had once confided to Gretchen that she had wanted to be a nun. There was a bluntness of sensibility there that disturbed Gretchen when she thought about it. Nuns had no daughters. She existed, aged nineteen, seated in front of a mirror on a March night in the middle of the century because her mother had failed to live up to her destiny.

After what had happened to her tonight, Gretchen thought bitterly, she herself would be tempted to enter a nunnery. If only she believed in God.

She had gone to the hospital as usual after work. The hospital was a military one on the outskirts of town, full of soldiers convalescing from wounds received in Europe. Gretchen was a volunteer worker five nights a week, distributing books and magazines and doughnuts, reading letters to soldiers with eye wounds and writing letters for soldiers with hand and arm injuries. She wasn't paid anything, but she felt it was the least she could do. Actually she enjoyed the work. The soldiers were grateful and docile, made almost childlike by their wounds, and there was none of the tense sexual parading and reconnoitering that she had to endure in the office all day. Of course, many of the nurses and some of the other volunteers slipped off with the doctors and the more active officer-wounded, but Gretchen had quickly shown that she wasn't having any of that. So many girls were available and willing, that very few of the men persisted. To make it all easier, she had arranged to be assigned to the crowded enlisted men's wards, where it was almost impossible for a soldier to be alone with her for more than a few seconds at a time. She was friendly and easy with men conversationally, but she couldn't bear the thought of any man touching her. She had been kissed by boys from time to time, of course, at parties and in cars after dances, but their clumsy gropings had seemed meaningless to her, unsanitary and vaguely comic.

She never was interested in any of the boys who surrounded her in school and she scorned the girls who had crushes on football heroes or boys with cars. It all seemed so *pointless*. The only man she had ever speculated about in that way was Mr. Pollack, the English teacher, who was an old man, maybe fifty, with tousled gray hair, and who spoke in a low, gentlemanly voice and read Shakespeare aloud in class. "'To-morrow, and to-morrow, and to-morrow, creeps in this petty pace from day to day . . . '" She could imagine herself in his arms, and his poetic and mournful caresses, but he was married and had daughters her age and never remembered anyone's name. As for her dreams . . . She forgot her dreams.

Something enormous was going to happen to her, she was sure, but it wasn't going to be this year or in this town.

As she went on her rounds in the loose, gray smock provided by the hospital, Gretchen felt motherly and useful, making up in a small way for what these courteous, uncomplaining young men had suffered for their country.

The lights were low in the wards and all the men were supposed to be in bed. Gretchen had made her usual special visit to the bedside of a soldier named Talbot Hughes, who had been wounded in the throat and couldn't speak. He was the youngest soldier in the ward and the most pitiful and Gretchen liked to believe that the touch of her hand and her good-night smile made the long hours before dawn more bearable for the boy. She was tidying the common room, where the men read and wrote letters, played cards and checkers and listened to the phonograph. She stacked the magazines neatly on the center table, cleared off a chessboard and put the pieces in their box, dropped two empty Coca-Cola bottles into a waste-basket.

She liked the little housewifely end of the night, conscious of the hundreds of young men sleeping around this central, warm core of the hospital block, young men saved from death, acquitted of war, young men healing and forgetting fear and agony, young men one day nearer to peace and home.

She had lived in small, cramped quarters all her life and the spaciousness of the common room, with its pleasant light-green walls and deep upholstered chairs, made her feel almost like a hostess in her own elegant home, after a successful party. She was humming as she finished her work and was just about to turn out the light and start for the locker room to change her clothes when a tall young Negro in pajamas and the Medical Corps maroon bathrobe limped in.

"Evening, Miss Jordache," the Negro said. His name was Arnold. He had been in the hospital a long time and she knew him fairly well. There were only two Negroes in the block and this was the first time Gretchen had seen one without the other. She always made a particular point of being agreeable to them. Arnold had had his leg smashed when a shell hit the truck he was driving in France. He came from St. Louis, he had told her, and had eleven brothers and sisters, and had finished high school.

He spent many hours reading and wore glasses while doing so. Although he seemed to read at random, comic books, magazines, the plays of Shakespeare, anything that happened to be lying around, Gretchen had decided that he was ripe for literature. He did look bookish, like a brilliant, lonely student from an African country, with his Army-issue glasses. From time to time Gretchen brought him books, either her own or her brother Rudolph's, or sometimes from the public library in town. Arnold read them promptly and returned them conscientiously, in good condition, without ever offering any comment on them. Gretchen felt that he was silent out of embarrassment, not wanting to pretend to be an intellectual in front of the other men. She read a great deal herself, but omnivorously, her taste guided in the last two years by Mr. Pollack's catholic enthusiasms. So she had through the months offered Arnold such disparate works as *Tess of the D'Urbervilles*, the poems of Edna St. Vincent Millay and Rupert Brooke, and *This Side of Paradise*, by F. Scott Fitzgerald.

She smiled as the boy came into the room. "Good evening, Arnold," she said. "Looking for something?"

"Naw. Just wanderin'. Couldn't get to sleep, somehow. Then I saw the light in here and I say to myself, 'I'll go in and visit with that pretty li'l Miss Jordache, pass the time of day.'" He smiled at her, his teeth white and perfect. Unlike the other men, who called her Gretchen, he always used her last name. His speech was somehow countrified, as though his family had carried the burden of their Alabama farm with them when they had migrated north. He was quite black, gaunt in the loose bathrobe. It had taken two or three operations to save his leg, Gretchen knew, and she was sure she could see the lines of suffering around his mouth.

"I was just going to put the light out," Gretchen said. The next bus passed the hospital in about fifteen minutes and she didn't want to miss it.

Pushing off his good leg, Arnold bounced up onto the table. He sat there swinging his legs. "You don't know the pleasure a man can get," Arnold said, "just looking down and seeing his own two feet. You just go on home, Miss Jordache, I imagine you got some fine young man waiting outside for you and I wouldn't like him to be upset your not coming on time."

"Nobody's waiting for me," Gretchen said. Now she felt guilty that she had wanted to hustle the boy out of the room just to catch a bus. There'd be another bus along. "I'm in no hurry."

He took a package of cigarettes out of his pocket and offered her one. She shook her head. "No, thank you. I don't smoke."

He lit his cigarette, his hand very steady, his eyes narrowed against the smoke. His movements were all deliberate and slow. He had been a football player in high school in St. Louis before he was drafted, he had told her, and the athlete remained in the wounded soldier. He patted the table next to him. "Why don't you set awhile, Miss Jordache?" he said. "You must be weary, on your feet all night, running around the way you do for us."

"I don't mind," Gretchen said. "I sit most of the day in the office." But she hoisted herself up to the table beside him, to show that she was not anxious to leave. They sat side by side, their legs hanging over the side of the table.

"You got pretty feet," Arnold said.

Gretchen looked down at her sensible, low-heeled, brown shoes. "I suppose they're all right," she said. She thought she had pretty feet, too, narrow and not too long, and slender ankles.

"I became an expert on feet in this man's army," Arnold said. He said it without self-pity, as another man might have said, "I learned how to fix radios in the Army," or, "The Army taught me how to read maps." His absence of compassion for himself made her feel a rush of pity for the soft-spoken, slow-moving boy. "You'll be all right," she said. "The nurses tell me the doctors've done wonders for your leg."

"Yeah." Arnold chuckled. "Just don't bet on old Arnold gaining a lot of ground from here on in."

"How old are you, Arnold?"

"Twenty-two. You?"

"Nineteen."

He grinned. "Good ages, huh?"

"I suppose so. If we didn't have a war."

"Oh, I'm not complaining," Arnold said, pulling at his cigarette. "It got me out of St. Louis. Made a man of me." There was the tone of mockery in his voice. "Ain't a dumb kid no more. I know what the score is now and who adds up the numbers. Saw some interesting places, met some interesting folk. You ever been in Cornwall, Miss Jordache? That's in England."

"No."

"Jordache," Arnold said. "That a name from around these parts?"

"No," Gretchen said. "It's German. My father came over from Germany. He was wounded in the leg too. In the First War. He was in the German army."

Arnold chuckled. "They get a man coming and going, don't they?" he said. "He do much running, your pa?"

"He limps a little," Gretchen spoke carefully. "It doesn't seem to interfere too much."

"Yeah, Cornwall." Arnold rocked back and forth a little on the table. He seemed to have had enough of talk about wars and wounds. "They got palm trees, little old towns, make St. Louis look like it was built the day before yesterday. Big, wide beaches. Yeah. Yeah, England. Folk're real nice. Hospitable. Invite you to their homes for Sunday dinner. They surprised me. Always felt the English were uppity. Anyway, that was the general impression about 'em in the circles in which I moved in St. Louis as a young man."

Gretchen felt he was making fun of her, gently, with the ironic formal pronouncement. "People have to learn about each other," she said stiffly, unhappy about how pompous she was sounding, but somehow put off, disturbed, forced on the defensive by the soft, lazy, country voice.

"They sure do," he agreed. "They sure enough do." He leaned on his hands and turned his face toward her. "What have I got to learn about you, Miss Jordache?"

"Me?" A forced little laugh was surprised out of her. "Nothing. I'm a small-town secretary who's never been anyplace and who'll never go anyplace."

"I wouldn't agree to that, Miss Jordache," Arnold said seriously. "I wouldn't agree to that at all. If ever I saw a girl that was due to rise, it's you. You got a neat, promising style of handling yourself. Why, I bet half the boys in this building'd ask you to marry them on the spot, you gave them any encouragement."

"I'm not marrying anyone yet," Gretchen said.

"Of course not." Arnold nodded soberly. "No sense in rushing, lock yourself in, a girl like you. With a wide choice." He stubbed his cigarette out in an ash tray on the table, then reached automatically into the package in the pocket of the bathrobe for a fresh one, which he neglected to light. "I had a girl in Cornwall for three months," he said. "The prettiest, most joyous, loving little girl a man could ever hope to see. She was married, but that made never no mind. Her husband was out in Africa somewhere since 1939 and I do believe she forgot what he looked like. We went to pubs together and she made me Sunday dinner when I got a pass and we made love like we was Adam and Eve in the Garden."

He looked thoughtfully up at the white ceiling of the big empty room. "I became a human being in Cornwall," he said. "Oh, yeah, the Army made a man out of little Arnold Simms from St. Louis. It was a sorrowful day in that town when the orders came to move to fight the foe." He was silent, remembering the old town near the sea, the palm trees, the joyous, loving little girl with the forgotten husband in Africa.

Gretchen sat very still. She was embarrassed when anybody talked of making love. She wasn't embarrassed by being a virgin, because that was a conscious choice on her part, but she was embarrassed by her shyness, her inability to take sex lightly and matter-of-factly, at least in conversation, like so many of the girls she had gone to high school with. When she was honest with herself, she recognized that a good deal of her feeling was because of her mother and father, their bedroom separated from hers by only a narrow hallway. Her father came clumping up at five in the morning, his slow footsteps heavy on the stairs, and then there would be the low sound of his voice hoarsened by the whiskey of the long night and her mother's complaining twitterings and then the sounds of the assault and her mother's tight, martyred expression in the morning.

And tonight, in the sleeping building, in the first really intimate conversation she had had alone with any of the men, she was being made a kind of witness, against her will, of an act, or the ghost and essence of an act, that she tried to reject from her consciousness. Adam and Eve in the Garden. The two bodies, one white, one black. She tried not to think about it in those terms, but she couldn't help herself. And there was something meaningful and planned in the boy's revelations—it was not the nostalgic, late-at-night reminiscences of a soldier home from the wars—there was a direction in the musical, flowing whispers, a target. Somehow, she knew the target was herself and she wanted to hide.

"I wrote her a letter after I was hit," Arnold was saying. "but I never got no answer. Maybe her husband come home. And from that day to this I never touched a woman. I got hit early on and I been in the hospital ever since. The first time I got out was last Saturday. We had an afternoon pass, Billy and me." Billy was the other Negro in the ward. "Nothin' much for two colored boys to do in this valley. It ain't Cornwall, I'll tell you that." He laughed. "Not even any colored folk around. Imagine that, being sent to maybe the one hospital in the United States that's in a town without any colored folk. We drank a couple of beers that we got in the market and we took the bus upriver a bit, because we heard there was a colored family up at the Landing. Turned out it was just an old man from South Carolina, living all by himself in an old house on the river, with all his family gone and forgotten. We gave him some beer and told him some lies about how brave we were in the war, and said we'd come back fishin' on our next pass. Fishin'!"

"I'm sure," Gretchen said, looking at her watch, "that when you get out of the hospital for good and go back home you'll find a beautiful girl and be very happy again." Her voice sounded prissy and false and nervous all at the same time and she was ashamed of herself, but she knew she had to get out of that room. "It's awfully late, Arnold," she said. "I've enjoyed our little talk, but now I'm afraid I . . . " She started to get off the table, but he held her arm in his hand, not hard, but firmly.

"It ain't all that late, Miss Jordache," Arnold said. "To tell you the truth, I been waiting for just such an occasion, all alone like this."

"I have to catch a bus, Arnold. I . . . "

"Wilson and me, we've been discussing you." Arnold didn't let go of her arm. "And we decided on our next pass, that's this Saturday, we would like to invite you to spend the day with us."

"That's very kind of you and Wilson," Gretchen said. She had difficulty trying to keep her voice normal. "But I'm terribly busy on Saturdays."

"We figured it wouldn't do to be seen in the company of two black boys," Arnold went on, his voice flat, neither manacing nor inviting, "being as how this is your town and they're not used to seeing things like that around here, and we're only enlisted men . . ."

"That really has nothing to do with . . . "

"You take the bus up to the Landing at twelve-thirty," Arnold continued, as though there had been no interruption. "We'll go earlier and give that old man five bucks to buy himself a bottle of whiskey and go to the show and we'll fix up a nice meal for the three of us in his house. You turn left directly at the bus stop and walk on about a quarter of a mile down to the river and it's the only house there, sitting real pretty on the bank, with nobody around to snoop or make a fuss, just the three of us, all folksy and friendly."

"I'm going home now, Arnold," Gretchen said loudly. She knew she would be ashamed to call out, but she tried to make him think she was ready to shout for help.

"A good meal, a couple of nice long drinks," Arnold said, whispering, smiling, holding her. "We been away a long time, Miss Jordache."

"I'm going to yell," Gretchen said, finding it hard to speak. How could he do it—be so polite and friendly in one breath and then . . . She despised herself for her ignorance of the human race.

"We have a high opinion of you, Miss Jordache, Wilson and me. Ever since I first laid eyes on you I can't think about anybody else. And Wilson says it's the same with him . . . "

"You're both crazy. If I tell the Colonel . . . " Gretchen wanted to pull her arm away, but if anybody happened to come in and saw them struggling, the explanations would be painful.

"As I said, our opinion is high," Arnold said, "and we're willing to pay for it. We got a lot of back pay accumulated, Wilson and me, and I been particularly lucky in the crap game in the ward. Listen careful, Miss Jordache. We got eight hundred dollars between us and you're welcome to it. Just for one little afternoon on the river . . . " He took his hand off her arm and unexpectedly, jumped down from the table, landing lightly on his good foot. He started limping out, his big body made clumsy by the floating maroon bathrobe. He turned at the door. "No need to say yes or no this minute, Miss Jordache," he said politely. "Think on it. Saturday's two days away. We'll be there at the Landing, from eleven A.M. on. You just come anytime you get your chores done, Miss Jordache. We'll be waiting on you." He limped out of the room, standing very straight and not holding onto the walls for support.

For a moment, Gretchen sat still. The only sound she heard was the hum of a machine somewhere in the basement, a sound she didn't remember ever having heard before. She touched her bare arm, where Arnold's hand had held it, just below the elbow. She got off the table and turned off the lights, so that if anybody came in, they wouldn't see what her face must look like. She leaned against the wall, her hands against her mouth, hiding it. Then she hurried to the locker room and changed into her street clothes and almost ran out of the hospital to the bus stop.

She sat at the dressing table wiping off the last of the cold cream from the delicately veined pale skin under her swollen eyes. On the table before her stood the jars and vials with the Woolworth names of beauty—Hazel Bishop, Coty. *We made love like Adam and Eve in the Garden.*

She mustn't think about it, she mustn't think about it. She would call the Colonel tomorrow and ask to be transferred to another block. She couldn't go back *there* again.

She stood up and took off her bathrobe and for a moment she was naked in the soft light of the lamp over the dressing table. Reflected in the mirror, her high, full breasts were very white and the nipples stood disobediently erect. Below was the sinister, dark triangle, dangerously outlined against the pale swell of her thighs. What can I do about it, what can I do about it?

She put on her nightgown and put out the light and climbed into the cold bed. She hoped that this was not going to be one of the nights that her father picked to claim her mother. There was just so much that she could bear in one night.

The bus left every half hour on the way upriver toward Albany. On Saturday it would be full of soldiers on weekend passes. All the battalions of young men. She saw herself buying the ticket at the bus terminal, she saw herself seated at the window looking out at the distant, gray river, she saw herself getting off at the stop for the Landing, standing there alone, in front of the gas station; under her high-heeled shoes she felt the uneven surface of the gravel road, she smelled the perfume she couldn't help but wear, she saw the dilapidated, unpainted frame house on the bank of the river, and the two dark men, glasses in their hands, waiting silently, knowing executioners, figures of fate, not rising, confident, her shameful pay in their pockets, waiting, knowing she was coming, watching her come to deliver herself in curiosity and lust, knowing what they were going to do together.

She took the pillow from beneath her head and put it between her legs and clamped it hard.

VI

The mother stands at the lace-curtained window of the bedroom staring out at the cindery back yard behind the bakery. There are two spindly trees there, with a board nailed between them, from which swings a scuffed, heavy, leather cylinder, stuffed with sand like the heavy bags prize fighters use to train on. In the dark enclosure, the bag looks like a hanged man. In other days in the back gardens on the same street, there were flowers and hammocks strung between the trees. Every afternoon, her husband puts on a pair of wool-lined gloves and goes out into the back yard and flails at the bag for twenty minutes. He goes at the bag with a wild, concentrated violence, as though he is fighting for his life. Sometimes, when she happens to see him at it, when Rudy takes over the store for her for awhile to let her rest, she has the feeling that it isn't a dead bag of leather and sand her husband is punishing, but herself.

She stands at the window in a green sateen bathrobe, soiled at the collar and cuffs. She is smoking a cigarette and the ash drifts down unnoticed onto the robe. She used to be the neatest and the most meticulous of girls, clean as a blossom in a glass vase. She was brought up in an orphanage and the Sisters knew how to inculcate strict habits of cleanliness. But she is a slattern now, loose-bodied and careless about her hair and skin and her clothes. The Sisters taught her a love of religion and affection for the ceremonies of the Church, but she has not been to Mass for almost twenty years. When her first child, her daughter, Gretchen, was born, she arranged with the Father for the christening, but her husband refused to appear at the font and forbade her then or ever again to give as much as a penny in contribution to the Church. And he a born Catholic.

Three unbaptized and unbelieving children and a blaspheming, Church-hating husband. Her burden to bear.

She had never known her father or mother. The orphanage in Buffalo had been her mother and father. She was assigned a name. Pease. It might have been her mother's name. When she thought of herself it was always as Mary Pease, not Mary Jordache, or Mrs. Axel Jordache. The Mother Superior had told her when she left the orphanage that it might well have been that her mother was Irish, but nobody knew for sure. The Mother Superior had warned her to beware of her fallen mother's blood in her body and to abstain from temptation. She was sixteen at the time, a rosy, frail girl with bright golden hair. When her daughter had been born she had wanted to name the baby Colleen, to memorialize her Irish descendance. But her husband didn't like the Irish and said the girl's name would be Gretchen. He had known a whore in Hamburg by that name, he said. It was only a year after the wedding, but he already hated her.

She had met him in the restaurant on the Buffalo lake front where she worked as a waitress. The orphanage had placed her there. The restaurant was run by an aging German-American couple named Mueller and the people at the orphanage had chosen them as employers because they were kindly and went to Mass and allowed Mary to stay with them in a spare room above their apartment. The Muellers were good to her and protected her and none of the customers dared to speak improperly to her in the restaurant. The Muellers let her off three times a week to continue her education at night school. She was not going to be a waitress in a restaurant all her life.

Axel Jordache was a huge, silent young man with a limp, who had emigrated from Germany in the early 1920's and who worked as a deckhand on the Lake steamers. In the winter, when the Lakes were frozen over, he sometimes helped Mr. Mueller in the kitchen as a cook and baker. He hardly spoke English then and he frequented the Muellers' restaurant so that he could have someone to talk to in his native tongue. When he had been wounded in the German army and couldn't fight any more they had made him into a cook at the hospital in Frankfurt.

Because, during another war, a young man had come out of a hospital alienated and looking for exile, she was standing tonight in a shabby room, over a shop in a slum, where every day, twelve hours a day, she had given up her youth, her beauty, her hopes. And no end in sight.

He had been most polite. He never as much as tried to hold her hand and when he was in Buffalo between voyages he would walk her to night school and wait to accompany her home. He had asked her to correct his English. Her English was a source of pride to her. People told her they thought she came from Boston when they heard her talk and she took it as a great compliment. Sister Catherine, whom she admired above all the teachers in the orphanage, came from Boston, and spoke crisply and with great precision and had the vocabulary of an educated woman. "To speak slovenly English," Sister Catherine had said, "is to live the life of a cripple. There are no aspirations denied a girl who speaks like a lady." She had modeled herself on Sister Catherine and Sister Catherine had given her a book, a history of Irish heroes, when she had left the orphanage. "To Mary Pease, my most hopeful student," was written in a bold, upright hand on the flyleaf. Mary had modeled her handwriting on Sister Catherine's too. Somehow, Sister Catherine's teaching had made her believe that her father, whoever he was, must have been a gentleman.

With Mary Pease coaching him in the silvery Back Bay accents of Sister Catherine, Axel Jordache had learned how to speak proper English very quickly. Even before they were married, he spoke so well that people were surprised when he told them that he had been born in Germany. There was no denying it, he was an intelligent man. But he used his intelligence to torment her, torment himself, torment everyone around him.

He hadn't even kissed her before he proposed to her. She was nineteen at the time, her daughter Gretchen's age, and a virgin. He was unfailingly attentive, always cleanly bathed and shaved and he always brought her small gifts of candy and flowers when he returned from his trips.

He had known her for two years before he proposed.

He hadn't dared to speak earlier, he said, because he was afraid she would reject him because he was a foreigner and because he limped. How he must have laughed to himself as he saw the tears come to her eyes at his modesty and his lack of confidence in himself. He was a diabolical man, weaving lifetime plots.

She said yes, conditionally. Perhaps she thought she loved him. He was a good-looking man, with that Indian head of black hair and a sober, industrious, thin face and clear, brown eyes that seemed soft and considerate when they looked at her. When he touched her it was with the utmost deceptive gentleness, as though she were made of china. When she told him she had been born out of wedlock (her phrase) he said he already knew it, from the Muellers, and that it didn't make any difference, in fact, it was a good thing, there wouldn't be any in-laws to disapprove of him. He himself was cut off from what remained of his family. His father had been killed on the Russian front in 1915 and his mother had remarried a year later and moved to Berlin from Cologne. There was a younger brother he had never liked, who had married a rich German-American girl who had come to Berlin after the war to visit relatives. The brother now lived in Ohio, but Axel never saw him. His loneliness was apparent and it matched her own.

Her conditions were stringent. He was to give up his job on the Lakes. She didn't want a husband who was away most of the time and who had a job that was no better than a common laborer's. And they were not to live in Buffalo, where everyone knew about her birth and the orphanage and where at every turn she would meet people who had seen her working as a waitress. And they were to be married in church.

He had agreed to everything. Oh, diabolical, diabolical. He had some money saved up and through Mr. Mueller he got in touch with a man who had a bakery in Port Philip whose lease was for sale. She made him buy a straw hat for the trip to Port Philip to conclude the deal. He was not to go wearing his usual cloth cap, that hangover from Europe. He was to look like a respectable American businessman.

Two weeks before the wedding, he took her to see the shop in which she was going to spend her life and the apartment above it in which she was going to conceive three children. It was a sunny day in May and the shop was freshly painted, with a large, green awning to protect the plate-glass window, with its array of cakes and cookies, from the sun. The street was a clean, bright one, with other little shops, a hardware store, a dry-goods store, a pharmacy on the corner. There was even a milliner's shop, with hats wreathed in artificial flowers on stands in the window. It was the shopping street for a quiet residential section that lay between it and the river. Large comfortable houses behind green lawns. There were sails on the river and a white excursion boat, up from New York, passed as they sat on a bench under a tree looking across the broad stretch of summer-blue water. They could hear the band on board playing waltzes. Of course, with his limp, they never danced.

Oh, the plans she had that sunny May waltzing rivery day. Once they were established, she would put in tables, redecorate the shop, put up curtains, set out candles, serve chocolate and tea, then, later, buy the shop next door (it was empty that first day she saw it) and start a little restaurant, not one like the Muellers', for working men, but for traveling salesmen and the better class of people of the town. She saw her husband in a dark suit and bow tie showing diners to their table, saw waitresses in crisp muslin aprons hurrying with loaded platters out of the kitchen, saw herself seated behind the cash register, smiling as she rang up the checks, saying, "I hope you enjoyed your dinner," sitting down with friends over coffee and cake when the day's work was over.

How was she to know that the neighborhood was going to deteriorate, that the people she would have liked to befriend would consider her beneath them, that the people who would have liked to befriend her she would consider beneath her, that the building next door was to be torn down and a large, clanging garage put up beside the bakery, that the millinery shop was to vanish, that the houses facing the river would be turned into squalid apartments or demolished to make place for junkyards and metal-working shops?

There were never any little tables for chocolate and cakes, never any candles and curtains, never any waitresses, just herself, standing on her feet twelve hours a day summer and winter, selling coarse loaves of bread to grease-stained mechanics and slatternly housewives and filthy children whose parents fought drunkenly with each other in the street on Saturday nights.

Her torment began on her wedding night. In the second-class hotel in Niagra Falls (convenient to Buffalo). All the fragile hopes of the timid, rosy, frail young girl who had been photographed smiling in bridal white beside her unsmiling, handsome groom just eight hours before disappeared in the blood-stained, creaking Niagra bed. Speared helplessly under the huge, scarred, demonically tireless, dark, male body, she knew that she had entered upon her sentence of life imprisonment.

At the end of her week of honeymoon she wrote a suicide note. Then she tore it up. It was an act she was to repeat again and again through the years.

During the day, they were like other honeymooning couples. He was unfailingly considerate, he held her elbow when they crossed the street, he bought her trinkets and took her to the theater (the last week in which he ever showed any generosity to her. Very soon she discovered she had married a fanatical miser). He took her into ice cream parlors and ordered huge whipped cream sundaes (she had a child's sweet tooth) and smiled indulgently at her like a favorite uncle as she spooned down the heaped confections. He took her for a ride on the river under the Falls and held her hand lovingly when they walked in the sunlight of the northern summer. They never discussed the nights. When he closed the door behind them after dinner it was as though two different and unconnected souls swooped down to inhabit their bodies. They had no vocabulary with which to discuss the grotesque combat in which they were engaged. The severe upbringing of the Sisters had left her inhibited and full of impossible illusions of gentility. Whores had educated him and perhaps he believed all women who were worthy of marriage lay still and terrified in the marriage bed. Or perhaps he thought all American women.

In the end, of course, after months had passed, he recognized that fatalistic, lifeless rejection for what it was, and it enraged him. It spurred him on, made his attacks wilder. He never went with other women. He never looked at another woman. His obsession slept in his bed. It was her misfortune that the one body he craved was hers and was at his disposal. For twenty years he besieged her, hopelessly, hating her, like the commander of a great army incredibly being held at bay before the walls of a flimsy little suburban cottage.

She wept when she discovered that she was pregnant.

When they fought it was not about this. They fought about money. She learned that she had a sharp and hurtful tongue. She became a shrew for small change. To get ten dollars for a new pair of shoes and, later on, for a decent dress for Gretchen to wear to school, took months of bitter campaigning. He begrudged her the bread she ate. She was never to know how much money he had in the bank. He saved like a lunatic squirrel for a new ice age. He had been in Germany when a whole population had been ruined and he knew it could happen in America, too. He had been shaped by defeat and understood that no continent was immune.

The paint was flaking off the walls of the shop for years before he bought five cans of whitewash and repainted. When his prosperous, garage-owning brother came from Ohio to visit him and offered him a share in a new automobile agency he was acquiring, for a few thousand dollars which he could borrow from his brother's bank, Axel threw his brother out of the house as a thief and schemer. The brother was chubby and cheerful. He took a two-week holiday in Saratoga every summer and went to the theater in New York several times a year with his fat, garrulous wife. He was dressed in a good wool suit and smelled nicely of bay rum. If Axel had been willing to borrow money like his brother, they would have lived in comfort all their lives, could have been freed from the slavery of the bakery, escaped from the slum into which the neighborhood was sinking. But her husband would not draw a penny from the bank or put his name on a note. The paupers of his native country, with their tons of worthless money, watched with gaunt eyes over every dollar that passed through his hands.

When Gretchen graduated from high school, although, like her brother Rudolph, she was always at the head of her class, there was no question of her going to college. She had to go to work immediately and hand half her salary over to her father every

Friday. College ruined women, turned them into whores. The Father has spoken. Gretchen would marry young, the mother knew, would marry the first man who asked her, to escape her father. Another life destroyed, in the endless chain.

Only with Rudolph was her husband generous. Rudolph was the hope of the family. He was handsome, well-mannered, well-spoken, admired by his teachers, affectionate. He was the only member of the family who kissed her when he left in the morning and returned in the evening. Both she and her husband saw the redemption of their separate failures in their older son. Rudolph had a talent for music and played the trumpet in the school band. At the end of the last school year Axel had bought a trumpet for him, a gleaming, golden instrument. It was the one gift to any of them that Axel had ever made. Everything else he had given to them had come as a result of ferocious bargaining. It was strange to hear the soaring, triumphant horn notes resounding through the gray, undusted apartment when Rudolph was practicing. Rudolph played club dates at dances and Axel had advanced him the money for a tuxedo, thirty-five dollars, an unheard-of outpouring. And he permitted Rudolph to hold onto the money he earned. "Save it," he said. "You'll be able to use it when you get to college." It was understood from the beginning that Rudolph was going to go to college. Somehow.

She feels guilty about Rudolph. All her love is for him. She is too exhausted to love anybody but her chosen son. She touches him when she can, she goes into his room when he is sleeping and kisses his forehead, she washes and irons his clothes when she is dizzy from fatigue so that his splendor will be clear to all eyes at every moment. She cuts out items from the school newspaper when he wins a race and pastes his report cards neatly in a scrapbook that she keeps on her dresser next to her copy of *Gone With the Wind*.

Her younger son, Thomas, and her daughter are inhabitants of her house. Rudolph is her blood. When she looks at him she sees the image of her ghostly father.

She has no hopes for Thomas. With his blond, sly, derisive face. He is a ruffian, always brawling, always in trouble at school, insolent, mocking, going his own way, without standards, sliding in and out of the house on his own secret schedule, impervious to punishment. On some calendar, somewhere, disgrace is printed in blood red, like a dreadful holiday, for her son Thomas. There is nothing to be done about it. She does not love him and she cannot hold out a hand to him.

So, the mother, standing on swollen legs at the window, surrounded by her family in the sleeping house. Insomniac, unfastidious, overworked, ailing, shapeless, avoiding mirrors, a writer of suicide notes, graying at the age of forty-two, her bathrobe dusted with ash from her cigarette.

A train hoots far away, troops piled into the rattling coaches, on their way to distant ports, on their way to the sound of the guns. Thank God Rudolph is not yet seventeen. She would die if they took him for a soldier.

She lights a last cigarette, takes off her robe, the cigarette hanging carelessly from her lower lip, and gets into bed. She lies there smoking. She will sleep a few hours. But she knows she will wake when she hears her husband coming heavily up the steps, rank with the sweat of his night's work and the whiskey he has drunk.

CHAPTER 2

THE OFFICE CLOCK stood at five to twelve. Gretchen kept typing. Since it was Saturday, the other girls had already stopped working and were making up, ready to depart. Two of them, Luella Devlin and Pat Hauser, had invited her to go out and have a pizza with them, but she was in no mood for their brainless gabble this afternoon. When she was in high school she had had three good friends, Bertha Sorel, Sue Jackson, Felicity Turner. They were the brightest girls in the school and they had made a small, superior, isolated clique. She wished all three of them or any one of them were in town today. But they all came from well-off families and had gone to college and she had found no one else to take their place in her life.

Gretchen wished that there were enough work to give her an excuse to remain at her desk the whole afternoon, but she was typing out the final items of the last bill of lading Mr. Hutchens had put on her desk and there was no way of dragging it out.

She hadn't gone to the hospital the last two nights. She had phoned in and said she was sick and had gone home directly after work and stayed there. She had been too restless to read and had fussed over her entire wardrobe, washing blouses that were already spotlessly clean, pressing dresses that didn't have a crease in them, washing her hair and setting it, manicuring her nails, insisting on giving Rudy a manicure, although she had given him one just the week before.

Late on Friday night, unable to sleep, she had gone down into the cellar where her father was working. He looked up at her in surprise as she came down the steps, but didn't say anything, even when she sat down on a chair and said, "Here, pussy, pussy," to the cat. The cat backed away. The human race, the cat knew, was the enemy.

"Pa," she said, "I've been wanting to talk to you."

Jordache didn't say anything.

"I'm not getting anywhere in this job I have," Gretchen said. "There's no chance of more money and no place to go. And once the war is over, they'll be cutting down and I'll be lucky if I can hang on."

"The war's not over yet," Jordache said. "There's still a lot of idiots waiting that have to be killed."

"I thought I ought to go down to New York and look for a real job there. I'm a good secretary now and I see ads for all sorts of jobs with twice the pay I'm getting now."

"You talk to your mother about this?" Jordache began to shape the dough into rolls, with quick little flips of his hand, like a magician.

"No," Gretchen said, "She's not feeling so well and I didn't want to disturb her."

"Everyone's so damn thoughtful in this family," Jordache said. "Warms the cockles."

"Pa," Gretchen said, "be serious."

"No," he said.

"Why not?"

"Because I said so. Be careful, you're going to get flour all over that fancy gown."

"Pa, I'll be able to send back a lot more money . . . "

"No," Jordache said. "When you're twenty-one, you can fly off anyplace you want. But you're not twenty-one. You're nineteen. You have to bear up under the hospitality of the ancestral home for two years. Grin and bear it." He took the cork out of the bottle and took a long swig of whiskey. With deliberate coarseness, he wiped his mouth with the back of his hand, leaving a smudge of flour across his face.

"I've got to get out of this town," Gretchen said.

"There are worse towns," Jordache said. "I'll see you in two years."

Five minutes past twelve, the clock read. She put the neatly typed papers in the drawer of her desk. All the other clerks were gone. She put the cover on her typewriter and went into the washroom and stared at herself in the mirror. She looked feverish. She dabbed some cold water on her forehead, then took out a vial of perfume from her bag and put a little on under each ear.

She went out of the building and through the main gate, under the big sign, "Boylan's Brick and Tile Works." The plant and the sign, with its ornate lettering that looked as though it advertised something splendid and amusing, had been there since 1890.

She looked around to see if Rudy was by any chance waiting for her. Sometimes he came by the Works and walked her home. He was the only one in the family she could talk to. If Rudy had been there, they could have had lunch in a restaurant and then perhaps splurged on a movie. But then she remembered that Rudy had gone with the high-school track team to a neighboring town for a meet.

She found herself walking toward the bus terminal. She walked slowly, stopping often to look into shop windows. Of course, she told herself, she was not going to take the bus. It was daytime now and the fantasies of night were safely behind her. Although it would be refreshing to drive along the river and get out somewhere and breathe a little country air. The weather had changed and spring was announcing itself. The air was warm and there were little white clouds high in the blue sky.

Before leaving the house in the morning, she had told her mother she was going to work in the hospital that afternoon to make up for the time she had lost. She didn't know why she had suddenly invented the story. She rarely lied to her parents. There was no need. But by saying she had to be on duty at the hospital, she avoided being asked to come and work in the store to help her mother handle the Saturday afternoon rush. It had been a sunny morning and the idea of long hours in the stuffy store had been distasteful to her.

A block from the terminal she saw her brother Thomas. He was pitching pennies in front of a drugstore with a gang of rowdyish-looking boys, a girl who worked in the office had been at the Casino Wednesday night and had seen the fight and told Gretchen about it. "Your brother," the girl said. "*He's scary*. A little kid like that. He's like a snake. I sure wouldn't like to have a kid like that in *my* family."

Gretchen told Tom that she knew about the fight. She had heard similar stories before. "You're a hideous boy," she said to Tom. He had just grinned, enjoying himself.

If Tom had seen her she would have turned back. She wouldn't have dared to go into the bus terminal with him watching. But he didn't see her. He was too busy pitching a penny at a crack in the sidewalk.

She drifted into the terminal. She looked at the clock. Twelve thirty-five. The bus upriver must have left five minutes ago and of course she wouldn't hang around there for twenty-five more minutes waiting for the next one. But the bus was late and she was still standing there. She went up to the ticket window. "One for King's Landing," she said.

She got into the bus and sat up front near the driver. There were a lot of soldiers on the bus, but it was still early in the day and they hadn't had time to get drunk yet and they didn't whistle at her.

The bus pulled out. The motion of the bus lulled her and she drowsed with her eyes open. Trees flashed by, newly budded; houses, stretches of river; there were glimpses of faces in a town. Everything seemed washed and beautiful and unreal. Behind her the soldiers sang, young men's voices blending together, in "Body and Soul." There was a Virginia voice among the others, a slow Southern tone, sweetening the song's lament. Nothing could happen to her. Nobody knew where she was. She was between event and event, choiceless, unchoosing, floating among soldiers' yearning voices.

The bus drew to a halt. "King's Landing, miss," the driver said.

"Thank you," she said and stepped down neatly onto the side of the road. The bus pulled away. Soldiers blew kisses at her through the windows. She kissed her fingers to the young men in return, smiling. She would never see them again. They knew her not, nor she them, and they could not guess her errand. Singing, their voices waining, they disappeared north.

She stood on the side of the empty road in the hushed Saturday afternoon sunlight. There was a gas station and a general store. She went into the store and bought herself a Coke from a white-haired old man in a clean, faded, blue shirt. The color pleased her eye. She would buy herself a dress that color, fine, clean, pale cotton, to wear on a summer evening.

She went out of the store and sat down on a bench in front of it to drink her Coke. The Coke was icy and sweet and stung the back of her mouth in little tart explosions. She drank slowly. She was in no hurry. She saw the graveled road leading away from the highway to the river. The shadow of a little cloud raced down it, like an animal running. It was silent from one coast to the other. The wood of the bench under her was warm. No cars passed. She finished her Coke and put the bottle down under the bench. She heard the ticking of the watch on her wrist. She leaned back, to catch the weight of the sun on her forehead.

Of course she wasn't going to go to the house on the river. Let the food go cold, let the wine go unpoured, let the suitors languish by the side of the river. Unknown to them, their lady is near, playing her single, teasing game. She wanted to laugh, but would not break the wilderness silence.

It would be delicious to push the game further. To go halfway down the gravel road between the stands of second-growth birch, white pencils in the woodshade. Go halfway and then return, in inner mirth. Or better still, weave through the forest, in and out of the shadows, Iroquois maiden, silent on her stockinged feet over last year's leaves, down to the river, and there, from the protection of the trees, spy out, Intelligence agent in the service of all virgins, and watch the two men, their lusty plans prepared, sitting waiting on the porch. And then steal back, her crisp dress flecked with bark and sticky buds, safe, safe, after the edge of danger, but feeling her power.

She stood up and crossed the highway toward the leafy entrance of the gravel-top road. She heard a car coming fast, from the south. She turned and stood there, as though she were waiting for a bus to take her in the direction of Port Philip. It wouldn't do to be seen plunging into the woods. Secrecy was all.

The car swept toward her, on the far side of the road. It slowed, came to a halt opposite her. She did not look at it, but kept searching for the bus she knew wouldn't appear for another hour.

"Hello, Miss Jordache." She had been named, in a man's voice. She could feel the blush rising furiously to her cheeks as she turned her head. She knew it was silly to blush. She had every right to be on the road. No one knew of the two black soldiers waiting with their food and liquor and their eight hundred dollars. For a moment she didn't recognize the man who had spoken, sitting alone at the wheel of a 1939 Buick convertible, with the top down. He was smiling at her, one hand, in a driving glove, hanging over the door of the car on her side. Then she saw who it was. Mr. Boylan. She had only seen him once or twice in her life, around the plant which bore his family's name. He was rarely there, a slender, blond, tanned, cleanly shaven man, with bristly blond eyebrows and highly polished shoes.

"Good afternoon, Mr. Boylan," she said, not moving. She didn't want to get close enough for him to be able to notice her blush.

"What in the world are you doing all the way up here?" Privilege his voice suggested. He sounded as though this unexpected discovery, the pretty girl alone in her high heels at the edge of the woods, amused him.

"It was such a lovely day." She almost stammered. "I often go on little expeditions when I have an afternoon off."

"All alone?" He sounded incredulous.

"I'm a nature lover," she said lamely. What a clod he must think I am, she thought. She caught him smiling as he looked down at her high-heeled shoes. "I just took the bus on the spur of the moment," she said, inventing without hope. "I'm waiting for the bus back to town." She heard a rustle behind her and turned, panic-stricken, sure that it must be the two soldiers, growing impatient and come to see if she had arrived. But it was only a squirrel, racing across the gravel of the side road.

"What's the matter?" Boylan asked, puzzled by her spasmodic movement.

"I thought I heard a snake." Oh, good-bye, she thought.

"You're pretty jittery," Boylan said gravely, "for a nature lover."

"Only snakes," she said. It was the stupidest conversation she had ever had in her life.

Boylan looked at his watch. "You know, the bus won't be along for quite some time," he said.

"That's all right," she said, smiling widely, as though waiting for buses in the middle of nowhere was her favorite Saturday afternoon occupation. "It's so nice and peaceful here."

"Let me ask you a serious question," he said.

Here it comes, she thought. He's going to want to know whom I'm waiting for. She fumbled for a serviceable short list. Her brother, a girl friend, a nurse from the hospital. She was so busy thinking, she didn't hear what he said, although she knew he had said something.

"I'm sorry," she said. "I missed that."

"I said, have you had your lunch yet, Miss Jordache?"

"I'm not hungry, really I . . . "

"Come." He gestured to her with his gloved hand. "I'll buy you lunch. I despise lunching alone."

Obediently, feeling small and childish, under adult orders, she crossed the road behind the Buick and stepped into the car, as he leaned over from his side to open the door for her. The only other person she had ever heard use the word "despise" in normal conversation was her mother. Shades of Sister Catherine, Old Teacher. "It's very kind of you, Mr. Boylan," she said.

"I'm lucky on Saturdays," he said as he started the car. She had no notion of what he meant by that. If he hadn't been her boss, in a manner of speaking, and old besides, forty, forty-five at least, she would have somehow managed to refuse. She regretted the secret excursion through the woods that now would never take place, the obscene, tantalizing possibility that perhaps the two soldiers would have glimpsed her, pursued her . . . Limping braves on tribal hunting grounds. Eight hundred dollars worth of war paint.

"Do you know a place called The Farmer's Inn?" Boylan asked as he started the car.

"I've heard of it," she said. It was a small hotel on a bluff above the river about fifteen miles farther on and supposed to be very expensive.

"It's not a bad little joint," Boylan said. "You can get a decent bottle of wine."

There was no more conversation because he drove very fast and the wind roared across the open car, making her squint against the pressure on her eyes and swirling her hair. The wartime speed limit was supposed to be only thirty-five miles an hour, to conserve gasoline, but of course a man like Mr. Boylan didn't have to worry about things like gasoline.

From time to time, Boylan looked over at her and smiled a little. The smile was ironical, she felt, and had to do with the fact that she was sure he knew she had been lying about her reasons for being alone so far from town, waiting senselessly for a bus that wouldn't arrive for another hour. He leaned over and opened the glove case and brought out a pair of dark Air Force glasses and handed it to her. "For your pretty blue eyes," he shouted, over the wind. She put the glasses on and felt very dashing, like an actress in the movies.

The Farmer's Inn had been a relay house in the post-colonial days when travel between New York and upstate had been by stagecoach. It was painted red with white trim and there was a large wagon wheel propped up on the lawn. It proclaimed the owner's belief that Americans liked to dine in their past. It could have been a hundred miles or a hundred years away from Port Philip.

Gretchen combed her hair into some sort of order, using the rear-view mirror. She was uncomfortable and conscious of Boylan watching her. "One of the nicest things a man can see in this life," he said, "is a pretty girl with her arms up, combing her hair. I suppose that's why so many painters have painted it."

She was not used to talk like that from any of the boys who had gone through high school with her or who hung around her desk at the office and she didn't know whether she liked it or not. It seemed to invade her privacy, talk like that. She hoped she wasn't going to blush any more that afternoon. She started to put on some lipstick, but he reached out and stopped her. "Don't do that," he said authoritatively. "You've got enough on. More than enough. Come." He leaped out of the car, with surprising agility, she thought, for a man that age, and came around and opened the door for her.

Manners, she noted automatically. She followd him from the parking lot, where there were five or six other cars ranged under the trees, toward the entrance to the hotel. His brown shoes, well they weren't really shoes (jodhpur boots, she was later to discover they were called), were highly shined, as usual. He was wearing a hounds-tooth tweed jacket, and gray flannel slacks, and a scarf at the throat of his soft wool shirt, instead of a tie. He's not real, she thought, he's out of a magazine. What am I doing with him?

Beside him, she felt dowdy and clumsy in the short-sleeved navy-blue dress that she had taken so much care to choose that morning. She was sure he was already sorry he had stopped for her. But he held the door open for her and touched her elbow helpfully as she passed in front of him into the bar.

There were two other couples in the bar, which was decorated like an eighteenth-century tap room, all dark oak and pewter mugs and plates. The two women were youngish and wore suede skirts with tight flat jerseys and spoke in piercing, confident voices. Looking at them, Gretchen was conscious of the gaudiness of her own bosom and hunched over to minimize it. The couples were seated at a low table at the other end of the room and Boylan guided Gretchen to the bar and helped her sit on one of the heavy, high, wooden stools. "This end," he said in a low voice. "Get away from those ladies. They make a music I can do without."

A Negro in a starched white jacket came to take their order. "Afternoon, Mr. Boylan," the Negro said soberly. "What is your pleasure, sir?"

"Ah, Bernard," Boylan said, "you ask the question that has stumped philosiphers since the beginning of time."

Phoney, Gretchen thought. She was a little shocked that she could think it about a man like Mr. Boylan.

The Negro smiled dutifully. He was as neat and spotless as if he were ready to conduct an operation. Gretchen looked at him sideways. I know two friends of yours not far from here, she thought, who aren't giving anybody any pleasure this afternoon.

"My dear," Boylan turned to her, "what do you drink?"

"Anything. Whatever you say." The traps were multiplying. How did she know what she drank? She never drank anything stronger than Coke. She dreaded the arrival of the menu. Almost certainly in French. She had taken Spanish and Latin in School. Latin!

"By the way," Boylan said, "you *are* over eighteen."

"Oh, yes," she said. She blushed. What a silly time to blush. Luckily it was dark in the bar.

"I wouldn't want to be dragged into court for leading minors into corruption," he said, smiling. He had nice, well-cared-for dentist's teeth. It was hard to understand why a man who looked like that, with teeth like that and such elegant clothes, and all that money, would ever have to have lunch alone.

"Bernard, let's try something sweet. For the young lady. A nice Daiquiri, in your inimitable manner."

"Thank you, sir," Bernard said.

Inimitable, she thought. Who uses words like that? Her sense of being the wrong age, wrongly dressed, wrongly made-up, made her hostile.

Gretchen watched Bernard squeeze the limes and toss in the ice and shake the drink, with expert, manicured black-and-pink hands. *Adam and Eve in the Garden*. If Mr. Boylan had had an inkling . . . There wouldn't be any of that condescending talk about corruption.

The frothy drink was delicious and she drank it like lemonade. Boylan watched her, one eye raised, a little theatrically, as the drink disappeared.

"Once again, please, Bernard," he said.

The two couples went into the dining room and they had the bar to themselves, as Bernard prepared the second round. She felt more at ease now. The afternoon was opening up. She didn't know why those were the words that occurred to her, but that's the way it seemed—*opening up*. She was going to sit at many dark bars and many kindly older men in peculiar clothes were going to buy her delicious drinks.

Bernard put the drink in front of her.

"May I make a suggestion, pet?" Boylan said. "I'd drink this one more slowly, if I were you. There *is* rum in them, after all."

"Of course," she said, with dignity. "I guess I was thirsty, standing out there in the hot sun."

"Of course, pet," he said.

Pet. Nobody had ever called her anything like that. She liked the word, especially the way he said it, in that cool, unpushy voice. She took little ladylike sips of the cold drink. It was as good as the first one. Maybe even better. She was beginning to feel that she wasn't going to blush anymore that afternoon.

Boylan called for the menu. They would order in the bar while they were finishing their drinks. The headwaiter came in with two large, stiff cards, and said, bowing a little, "Glad to see you again, Mr. Boylan."

Everybody was glad to see Mr. Boylan, in his shiny shoes.

"Should I order?" Boylan asked her.

Gretchen knew, from the movies, that gentlemen often ordered for ladies in restaurants, but it was one thing to see it on the screen and another thing to have it happen right in front of you. "Please do," she said. Right out of the book, she thought triumphantly. My, the drink was good.

There was a brief but serious discussion about the menu and the wine between Mr. Boylan and the headwaiter. The headwaiter disappeared, promising to call them when their table was ready. Mr. Boylan took out a gold cigarette case and offered her a cigarette. She shook her head.

"You don't smoke?"

"No." She felt that she was not living up to the level of the place and the rules of the situation by not smoking, but she had tried two or three times and it had made her cough and go red eyed and she had given up the experiment. Also, her mother smoked, day and night, and anything her mother did Gretchen didn't want to do.

"Good," Boylan said, lighting his cigarette with a gold lighter he took from his pocket and put down on the bar beside the monogrammed case. "I don't like girls to smoke. It takes away the fragrance of youth."

Fancy talk, she thought. But it didn't offend her now. He was putting himself out to please her. She was suddenly conscious of the odor of the perfume that she had dabbed on herself in the washroom at the office. She worried that it might seem cheap to him. "I must say," she said, "I was surprised you knew my name."

"Why?"

"Well, I don't think I've seen you more than once or twice at the Works. And you never come through the office."

"I've seen you," he said. "I wondered what a girl who looked like you was doing in a dreary place like Boylan's Brick and Tile Works."

"It isn't as awful as all that," she said defensively.

"No? I'm glad to hear that. I was under the impression that all my employees found it intolerable. I make it a point not to visit it more than fifteen minutes a month. I find it depresses me."

The headwaiter appeared. "Ready now, sir."

"Leave your drink, pet," Boylan said, helping her off her stool. "Bernard'll bring it in."

They followed the headwaiter into the dining room. Eight or ten of the tables were occupied. A full colonel and a party of young officers. Other tweedy couples. There were flowers on the polished fake-colonial tables and rows of shining glasses. There is nobody here who makes less than ten thousand dollars a year, she thought.

The conversation in the room dropped as they followed the headwaiter to a small table at the window, overlooking the river far below. She felt the young officers regarding her. She touched her hair. She knew what was going on in their minds. She was sorry Mr. Boylan wasn't younger.

The headwaiter held the chair for her and she sat down and put the large, creamy napkin demurely over her lap. Bernard came in with their unfinished Daiquiris on a tray and put them down on the table.

"Thank you, sir," he said as he backed off.

The headwaiter appeared with a bottle of red wine from France and the table waiter came up with their first course. There was no manpower shortage at The Old Farmer's Inn.

The headwaiter ceremoniously poured a little of the wine into a huge, deep glass. Boylan sniffed it, tasted it, looked up, squinting, at the ceiling, as he kept it for a moment in his mouth before swallowing. He nodded at the headwaiter. "Very good, Lawrence," he said.

"Thank you, sir," the headwaiter said. With all those thank you's, Gretchen thought, the bill was going to be horrendous.

The headwaiter poured the wine into her glass, then into Boylan's. Boylan raised his glass to her and they both sipped the wine. It had a strange dusty taste and was warm. Eventually, she was sure, she was going to learn to like that taste.

"I hope you like hearts of palm," Boylan said. "I developed the taste in Jamaica. That was before the war, of course."

"It's delicious." It tasted like a flat nothing to her, but she liked the idea that a whole noble palm tree had been cut down just to serve her one small, delicate dish.

"When the war is over," he said, picking at his plate, "I'm going to go down there and settle. Jamaica. Just lie on the white sand in the sun from year's end to year's end. When the boys come marching home this country's going to be impossible. A world fit for heroes to live in," he said mockingly, "is hardly fit for Theodore Boylan to live in. You must come and visit me."

"Sure," she said. "I'll rhumba on down on my salary from the Boylan Brick and Tile Works."

He laughed. "It is the proud boast of my family," he said, "that we have underpaid our help since 1887."

"Family?" she said. As far as she knew, he was the only Boylan existing. It was common knowledge that he lived alone in the mansion behind the stone walls of the great estate outside town. With servants, of course.

"Imperial," he said, "We are spread in our glory from coast to coast, from pine-clad Maine to orange-scented California. Aside from the Boylan Cement plant and the Boylan Brick and Tile Works in Port Philip, there are Boylan shipyards, Boylan oil companies, Boylan heavy-duty machinery plants throughout the length and breadth of this great land, each with a Boylan brother or uncle or cousin at its head, supplying the sinews of war at cost-plus to our beloved country. There is even a Major General Boylan who strikes shrewd blows in his nation's cause in the Service of Supply in Washington. Family? Let there be the sniff of a dollar in the air and there you will find a Boylan, first on the line."

She was not used to people running down their own families; her loyalties were simple. Her face must have showed her disappointment.

"You're shocked," Boylan said. Again that crooked look of amusement.

"Not really," she said. She thought of her own family. "Only people inside a family know how much love they deserve."

"Oh, I'm not all bad," Boylan said. "There's one virtue which my family has in abundance and I admire it without reservation."

"What's that?"

"They're rich. They're verrry, verrry rich." He laughed.

"Still," she said, hoping that he wasn't as bad as he sounded, that it was just a show-off lunchtime act that he was performing to impress an empty-headed girl, "still, you work. The Boylans've done a lot for this town . . . "

"They certainly have," he said. "They have bled it white. Naturally, they feel a sentimental interest in it. Port Philip is the most insignificant of the imperial posses-sions, not worth the time of a true, one hundred percent, up-and-at-em male Boylan, but they do not abandon it. The last and the least of the line, your humble servant, is delegated to the lowly home province to lend the magic of the name and the authority of the living family presence at least once or twice a month to the relic. I perform my ritual duties with all due respect and look forward to Jamaica when the guns have fallen silent."

He not only hates the family, she thought, he hates himself.

His quick, pale eyes noted the minute change in her expression. "You don't like me," he said.

"That isn't true," she said. "It's just that you're different from anyone I know."

"Different better or different worse?"

"I don't know," she said.

He nodded gravely. "I abide the question," he said. "Drink up. Here comes another bottle of wine."

Somehow, they had gone through the whole bottle of wine and they hadn't reached the main course yet. The headwaiter gave them fresh glasses and there was the ceremony of tasting once more. The wine had flushed her face and throat. The conversation in the rest of the restaurant seemed to have receded and came to her ears now in a regular, reassuring rhythm, like the sound of distant surf. She suddenly felt at home in the polished old room and she laughed aloud.

"Why are you laughing?" Boylan asked suspiciously.

"Because I'm here," she said, "and I could be so many other places instead."

"You must drink more often," he said. "Wine becomes you." He reached over and patted her hand. His hand was dry and firm on her skin. "You're beautiful, pet, beautiful, beautiful."

"I think so, too," she said.

It was his turn to laugh.

"Today," she said.

By the time the waiter brought their coffee she was drunk. She had never been drunk before in her life so she didn't know that she was drunk. All she knew was that all colors were clearer, that the river below her was cobalt, that the sun lowering in the sky over the faraway western bluffs was of a heartbreaking gold. All the tastes in her mouth were like summertime and the man opposite her was not a stranger and her employer, but her best and most intimate friend, his fine, tanned face kindly and marvelously attentive, the occasional touch of his hand on hers of a welcome calm dryness, his laugh an accolade to her wit. She could tell him anything, her secrets were his.

She told him anecdotes about the hospital—about the soldier who had been hit over the eye by a bottle of wine that an enthusiastic French woman had thrown to welcome him to Paris and who had been awarded the Purple Heart because he suffered from double vision incurred in the line of duty. And the nurse and the young officer who made love every night in a parked ambulance and who, one night, when the ambulance had been called out, had been driven all the way to Poughkeepsie stark naked.

As she spoke, it became clear to her that she was a unique and interesting person who led an incident-crammed, full life. She described the problems she had when she had played Rosalind in *As You Like It* in the school play in her senior year. Mr. Pollack, the director, who had seen a dozen Rosalinds, on Broadway and elsewhere, had said that it would be a crime if she wasted her talent. She had also played Portia the year before and wondered briefly if she wouldn't make a brilliant lawyer. She thought women ought to go in for things like that these days, not settle for marriage and babies.

She was going to tell Teddy (he was Teddy by dessert) something that she hadn't confided to a soul, that when the war was over she was going to go down to New York to be an actress. She recited a speech from *As You Like It*, her tongue lively and tripping from the Daiquiris, the wine, the two glasses of Benedictine.

"Come, woo me, woo me," she said, *"for now I am in a holiday humor, and like enough to consent. What would you say to me now, an I were your very, very Roslind?"*

Teddy kissed her hand as she finished and she accepted the tribute graciously, delighted with the flirtatious aptness of the quotation.

Warmed by the man's unflagging attention, she felt electric, sparkling, and irresistible. She opened the top two buttons of her dress. Let her glories be displayed. Besides, it was warm in the restaurant. She could speak of unmentionable things, she could use words that until now she had only seen scrawled on walls by naughty boys. She had achieved candor, that aristocratic privilege.

"I never pay any attention to them." She was responding to a question from Boylan about the men in the office.

"Squirming around like puppies. Small-town Don Juans. Taking you to the movies and an ice-cream soda and then necking in the back seat of a car, grabbing at you as though you're the brass ring on a merry-go-round. Making a noise like a dying elk and trying to put their tongues in your mouth. Not for me. I've got other things on my mind. They try it once and after that they know better. I'm in no hurry!" She stood up suddenly. "Thank you for a delicious lunch," she said. "I have to go to the bathroom." She had never before said to any of her dates that she had to go to the bathroom. Her bladder had nearly burst from time to time in movie houses and at parties.

Teddy stood up. "The first door in the hall to the left," he said. He was a knowing man, Teddy, informed on all subjects.

She sauntered through the room, surprised that it was empty. She walked slowly, knowing that Teddy was following her every step with his pale, intelligent eyes. Her back was straight. She knew that. Her neck was long and white under the black hair. She knew that. Her waist was slender, her hips curved, her legs long and rounded and firm. She knew all that and walked slowly to let Teddy know it once and for all.

In the ladies' room, she looked at herself in the mirror and wiped off the last of the lipstick from her mouth. I have a wide, striking mouth, she told her reflection. What a fool I was to paint it just like any old mouth.

She went out into the hall from the ladies' room. Teddy was waiting for her at the entrance to the bar. He had paid the bill and he was drawing on his left glove. He stared at her somberly as she approached him.

"I am going to buy you a red dress," he said. "A blazing red dress to set off that miraculous complexion and that wild, black hair. When you walk into a room, the men will drop to their knees."

She laughed, red her color. That was the way a man should talk.

She took his arm and they went out to the car.

He put the top up because it was getting cold and they drove slowly south, his bare right hand, thoughtfully ungloved, on hers on the seat between them. It was cosy in the car, with all the windows up. There was the flowery fragrance of the alcohol they had drunk, mixed with the smell of leather.

"Now," he said, "tell me. What were you *really* doing at the bus stop at King's Landing?"

She chuckled.

"That was a dirty chuckle," he said.

"I was there for a dirty reason," she said.

He drove without speaking for awhile. The road was deserted, and they drove through stripes of long shadows and pale sunshine down the tree-lined highway.

"I'm waiting," Teddy said.

Why not? she thought. All things could be said on this blessed afternoon. Nothing was unspeakable between them. They were above the trivia of prudery. She began to speak, first hesitantly, then more easily, as she got into it, of what had happened at the hospital.

She described what the two Negroes were like, lonely and crippled, the only two colored men in the ward, and how Arnold had always been so reserved and gentlemanly and had never called her by her first name, like the other soldiers, and how he read the books she loaned him and seemed so intelligent and sad, with his wound and the girl in Cornwall who had never written to him again. Then she told about the night he found her alone when all the other men were asleep and the conversation they had and how it led up to the proposition, the two men, the eight hundred dollars. "If they'd been white, I'd have reported them to the Colonel," she said, "but this way . . . "

Teddy nodded understandingly at the wheel, but said nothing, just drove a little faster down the highway.

"I haven't been back to the hospital since," she said. "I just couldn't. I begged my father to let me go to New York. I couldn't bear staying in the same town with that man, with his knowing what he said to me. But my father . . . There's no arguing with my father. And naturally, I couldn't tell him why. He'd have gone out to the hospital and killed those two men with his bare hands. And then, this morning—it was such a lovely day—I didn't *go* to the bus, I *drifted* into it. I knew I didn't want to go to that house, but I guess I wanted to know if they really were there, if there were men who actually acted like that. Even so, even after I got out of the bus, I just waited on the road. I had a Coke, I took a sunbath . . . I . . . Maybe I would have gone a bit down the road. Maybe all the way. Just to see. I knew I was safe. I could run away from them easily, even if they saw me. They can hardly move, with their legs . . . "

The car was slowing down. She had been looking down at her shoes, under the dashboard of the car, as she spoke. Now she glanced up and saw where they were. The gas station. The general store. Nobody in sight.

The car came to a halt at the entrance to the gravel road that led down to the river.

"It was a game," she said, "a silly, cruel, girl's game."

"You're a liar," Boylan said.

"What?" She was stunned. It was terribly hot and airless in the car.

"You heard me, pet," Boylan said. "You're a liar. It wasn't any game. You were going to go down there and get laid."

"Teddy," she said, gasping, "please . . . please open the window. I can't breathe."

Boylan leaned across her and opened the door on her side. "Go ahead," he said. "Walk on down, pet. They're still there. Enjoy yourself. I'm sure it'll be an experience you'll cherish all you life."

"Please, Teddy . . . " She was beginning to feel very dizzy and his voice faded in her ears and then came up again, harshly.

"Don't worry about transportation home," Boylan said. "I'll wait here for you. I have nothing better to do. It's Saturday afternoon and all my friends are out of town. Go ahead. You can tell me about it when you come back. I'll be most interested."

"I've got to get out of here," she said. Her head was expanding and contracting and she felt as though she were choking. She stumbled out of the car and threw up by the side of the road in great racking heaves.

Boylan sat immobile at the wheel, staring straight ahead of him. When she was finished and the throat-tearing convulsions had ceased, he said, curtly, "All right, come back in here."

Depleted and fragile, she crept back into the car, cold sweat on her forehead, holding her hand up to her mouth against the smell.

"Here, pet," Boylan said kindly. He gave her the large colored silk handkerchief from his breast pocket. "Use this."

She dabbed at her mouth, wiped the sweat from her face. "Thank you," she whispered.

"What do you *really* want to do, pet?" He asked.

"I want to go home," she whimpered.

"You can't go home in that condition," he said.

He started the car.

"Where're you taking me?"

"My house," he said.

She was too exhausted to argue and she lay with her head against the back of the seat, her eyes closed, as they drove swiftly south along the highway.

He made love to her early that evening, after she had rinsed her mouth a long time with a cinnamon-flavored mouthwash in his bathroom and had slept soddenly on his bed for two hours. Afterward, silently, he drove her home.

Monday morning, when she came into the office at nine o'clock, there was a long, white, plain envelope on her desk, with her name printed on it and "Personal" scribbled in one corner. She opened the envelope. There were eight one-hundred-dollar bills there.

He must have gotten up at dawn to drive all the way into town and get into the locked factory before anyone appeared for work.

CHAPTER 3

THE CLASSROOM WAS silent, except for the busy scratching of pens on paper. Miss Lenaut was seated at her desk reading, occasionally raising her head to scan the room. She had set a half-hour composition for her pupils to write, subject, "Franco-American Friendship." As Rudolph bent to his task at his desk toward the rear of the room, he had to admit to himself that Miss Lenaut might be beautiful, and undoubtedly French, but that her imagination left something to be desired.

Half a point would be taken off for a mistake in spelling or a misplaced accent, and a full point for any errors in grammar. The composition had to be at least three pages long.

Rudolph filled the required three pages quickly. He was the only student in the class who consistently got marks of over 90 on compositions and dictation, and in the last three tests he had scored 100. He was so good in the language that Miss Lenaut had grown suspicious and had asked him if his parents spoke French. "Jordache," she said. "It is not an American name." The imputation hurt him. He wanted to be different from the people around him in many respects, but not in his American-ness. His father was German, Rudolph told Miss Lenaut, but aside from an occasional word in that language, all Rudolph ever heard at home was English.

"Are you sure your father wasn't born in the Alsace?" Miss Lenaut persisted.

"Cologne," Rudolph said and added that his grandfather had come from Alsace-Lorraine.

"*Alors*," Miss Lenaut said. "It is as I suspected."

It pained Rudolph that Miss Lenaut, that incarnation of feminine beauty and worldly charm and the object of his feverish devotion, might believe, even for a moment, that he would lie to her or take secret advantage of her. He longed to confess his emotion and had fantasies of returning to the high school some years hence, when he was a suave college man, and waiting outside the school for her and addressing her in French, which would by that time be fluent and perfectly accented, and telling her, with an amused chuckle for the shy child he had been, of his schoolboy passion for her in his junior year. Who knew what then might happen? Literature was full of older women and brilliant young boys, of teachers and precocious pupils . . .

He reread his work for errors, scowling at the banality which the subject had imposed upon him. He changed a word or two, put in an accent he had missed, then looked at his watch. Fifteen minutes to go.

"Hey!" There was a tortured whisper on his right. "What's the past participle of *venir*?"

Rudolph turned his head slightly toward his neighbor, Sammy Kessler, a straight *D* student. Sammy Kessler was hunched in a position of agony over his paper, his eyes flicking desperately over at Rudolph. Rudolph glanced toward the front of the room. Miss Lenaut was engrossed in her book. He didn't like to break the rules in her class, but he couldn't be known by his comtemporaries as a coward or a teacher's pet.

"*Venu*," he whispered.

"With two *o*'s?" Kessler whispered.

"A *u*, idiot," Rudolph said.

Sammy Kessler wrote laboriously, sweating, doomed to his *D*.

Rudolph stared at Miss Lenaut. She was particularly attractive today, he thought. She was wearing long earrings and a brown, shiny dress that wrinkled skin-tight across her girdled hips and showed a generous amount of her stiffly armored bosom. Her mouth was a bright-red gash of lipstick. She put lipstick on before every class. Her family ran a small French restaurant in the theatrical district of New York and there was more of Broadway in Miss Lenaut than the Faubourg St. Honoré, but Rudolph was happily unaware of this distinction.

Idly, Rudolph began to sketch on a piece of paper. Miss Lenaut's face took shape under his pen, the easily identifiable two curls that she wore high on her cheeks in front of her ears, the waved, thick hair, with the part in the middle. Rudolph continued drawing. The earrings, the rather thick, beefy throat. For a moment, Rudolph hesitated. The territory he was now entering was dangerous. He glanced once more at Miss Lenaut. She was still reading. There were no problems of discipline in Miss Lenaut's class. She gave out punishments for the slightest infractions with merciless liberality. The full conjugation of the reflexive irregular verb *se taire*, repeated ten times, was the lightest of her sentences. She could sit and read with only an occasional lifting of her eyes to reassure herself that all was well, that there was no whispering, no passing of papers between desk and desk.

Rudolph gave himself to the delights of erotic art. He continued the line down from Miss Lenaut's neck to her right breast, naked. Then he put in her left breast. He was satisfied with the proportions. He drew her standing, three-quarter view, one arm extended, with a piece of chalk in her hand, at the blackboard. Rudolph worked with relish. He was getting better with each opus. The hips were easy. The mons veneris he drew from memory of art books in the library, so it was a bit hazy. The legs, he felt, were satisfactory. He would have liked to draw Miss Lenaut barefooted, but he was bad on feet, so he gave her the high-heeled shoes, with straps above the ankle, that she habitually wore. Since he had her writing on the blackboard, he decided to put some words on the blackboard. "*Je suis folle d'amour*," he printed in an accurate representation of Miss Lenaut's blackboard script. He started to shade Miss Lenaut's breast artistically. He decided that the entire work would be more striking if he drew it as though there were a strong light coming from the left. He shaded the inside of Miss

Lenaut's thigh. He wished there were someone he knew in school he could show the drawing to who would appreciate it. But he couldn't trust the boys on the track team, who were his best friends, to treat the picture with appropriate sobriety.

He was shading in the straps on the ankles when he became conscious of someone standing beside his desk. He looked up slowly. Miss Lenaut was glaring down at the drawing on his desk. She must have moved down the aisle like a cat, high heels and all.

Rudolph sat motionless. No gesture seemed worthwhile at the moment. There was fury in Miss Lenaut's dark, mascaraed eyes and she was biting the lipstick off her lips. She reached out her hand, silently. Rudolph picked up the piece of paper and gave it to her. Miss Lenaut turned on her heel and walked back to her desk, rolling the paper in her hands so that no one could see what was on it.

Just before the bell rang to end the class, she called out, "Jordache."

"Yes, ma'am," Rudolph said. He was proud of the ordinary tone he managed to use.

"May I see you for a moment after class?"

"Yes, ma'am," he said.

The bell rang. The usual chatter broke out. The students hurried out of the room to rush for their next classes. Rudolph, with great deliberation, put his books into his briefcase. When all the other students had quit the room, he walked up to Miss Lenaut's desk.

She was seated like a judge. Her tone was icy. "*Monsieur l'artiste*," she said. "You have neglected an important feature of your *chef d'oeuvre*." She opened the drawer of her desk and took out the sheet of paper with the drawing on it and smoothed it with a rasping noise on the blotter of the desk top. "It is lacking a signature. Works of art are notoriously more valuable when they are signed authentically by the artist. It would be deplorable if there were any doubts as to the origin of a work of such richness." She pushed the drawing across the desk toward Rudolph. "I will be much indebted to you, Monsieur," she said, "if you would have the kindness to affix your name. Legibly."

Rudolph took out his pen and signed his name on the lower right hand corner of the drawing. He did it slowly and deliberately and he made sure that Miss Lenaut saw that he was studying the drawing at the same time. He was not going to act like a frightened kid in front of her. Love has its own requirements. Man enough to draw her naked, he was man enough to stand up to her wrath. He underlined his signature with a little flourish.

Miss Lenaut reached over and snatched the drawing to her side of the desk. She was breathing hard now. "Monsieur," she said shrilly, "you will go get one of your parents immediately after school is over today and you will bring it back for a conversation with me speedily." When she was excited, there were little, queer mistakes in Miss Lenaut's English. "I have some important things to reveal to them about the son they have reared in their house. I will be waiting here. If you are not here with a representative of your family by four o'clock the consequences will be of the gravest. Is it understood?"

"Yes, ma'am. Good afternoon, Miss Lenaut." The "good afternoon" took courage. He went out of the room, neither more quickly nor more slowly than he usually did. He remembered his gliding motion. Miss Lenaut sounded as though she had just run up two flights of stairs.

When he reached home after school was over, he avoided going into the store where his mother was serving some customers and went up to the apartment, hoping to find his father. Whatever happened, he didn't want his mother to see that drawing. His father might whack him, but that was to be preferred to the expression that he was sure would be in his mother's eyes for the rest of her life if she saw that picture.

His father was not in the house. Gretchen was at work and Tom never came home until five minutes before supper. Rudolph washed his hands and face and combed his hair. He was going to meet his fate like a gentleman.

He went downstairs and into the shop. His mother was putting a dozen rolls into a bag for an old woman who smelled like a wet dog. He waited until the old woman had left, then went and kissed his mother.

"How were things at school today?" she asked, touching his hair.

"Okay," he said. "The usual. Pa around anywhere?"

"He's probably down at the river. Why?" The "Why?" was suspicious. It was unusual for anyone in the family to seek out her husband unnecessarily.

"No reason," Rudolph said carelessly.

"Isn't there track practice today?" she probed.

"No." Two customers came into the shop, the little bell over the door tingling, and he didn't have to lie any more. He waved and went out as his mother was greeting the customers.

When he was out of sight of the shop he began to walk quickly down toward the river. His father kept his shell in the corner of a ramshackle warehouse on the waterfront and usually spent one or two afternoons a week working on the boat there. Rudolph prayed that this was one of those afternoons.

When he reached the warehouse he saw his father out in front of it, sandpapering the hull of the one-man shell, which was propped, upside down, on two sawhorses. His father had his sleeves rolled up and was working with great care on the smooth wood. As Rudolph approached, he could see the ropy muscles of his father's forearms hardening and relaxing with his rhythmic movements. It was a warm day, and even with the wind that came off the river his father was sweating.

"Hi, Pa," Rudolph said.

His father looked up and grunted, then went back to his work. He had bought the shell in a half-ruined condition for practically nothing from a boys' school nearby that had gone bankrupt. Some river memory of youth and health from his boyhood on the Rhine was behind the purchase and he had reconstructed the shell and varnished it over and over again. It was spotless and the mechanism of the sliding seat gleamed with its coating of oil. After he had gotten out of the hospital in Germany, with one leg almost useless and his big frame gaunt and weak, Jordache had exercised fanatically to recover his strength. His work on the Lake boats had given him the strength of a giant and the grueling miles he imposed on himself sweeping methodically up and down the river had kept him forbiddingly powerful. With his bad leg he couldn't catch anybody, but he gave the impression of being able to crush a grown man in those hairy arms.

"Pa . . ." Rudolph began, trying to conquer his nervousness. His father had never hit him, but Rudolph had seen him knock Thomas unconscious with one blow of his fist just last year.

"What's the matter?" Jordache tested the smoothness of the wood, with broad, spatulate fingers. The back of his hands and his fingers were bristling with black hairs.

"It's about school," Rudolph said.

"You in trouble? *You*?" Jordache looked over at his son with genuine surprise.

"Trouble might be too strong a word," Rudolph said. "A situation has come up."

"What kind of situation?"

"Well," Rudolph said, "there's this French woman who teaches French. I'm in her class. She says she wants to see you this afternoon. Now."

"Me?"

"Well," Rudolph admitted, "she said one of my parents."

"What about your mother?" Jordache asked. "You tell her about this?"

"It's something I think it's better she doesn't know about," Rudolph said.

Jordache looked across the hull of the shell at him speculatively. "French," he said.

"I thought that was one of your good subjects."

"It is," Rudolph said. "Pa, there's no sense in talking about it, you've got to see her."

Jordache flicked a spot off the wood. Then he wiped his forehead with the back of his hand and began rolling down his sleeves. He swung his windjacket over his shoulder, like a workingman, and picked up his cloth cap and put it on his head, and started walking. Rudolph followed him, not daring to suggest that perhaps it would be a good idea if his father went home and put on a suit before the conversation with Miss Lenaut.

Miss Lenaut was seated at her desk correcting papers when Rudolph led his father into the room. The school building was empty, but there were shouts from the athletic field below the classroom windows. Miss Lenaut had put lipstick on at least three more times since Rudolph's class. For the first time, he realized that she had thin lips and plumped them out artificially. She looked up when they came into the room and her mouth set. Jordache had put his windjacket on before entering the school and had taken off his cap, but he still looked like a workman.

Miss Lenaut stood up as they approached the desk.

"This is my father, Miss Lenaut," Rudolph said.

"How do you do, sir?" she said, without warmth.

Jordache said nothing. He stood there, in front of the desk, chewing at his moustache, his cap in his hands, proletarian and subdued.

"Has your son told you why I asked you to come this afternoon, Mr. Jordache?"

"No," Jordache said, "I don't remember that he did." That peculiar, uncharacteristic mildness was in his voice, too. Rudolph wondered if his father was afraid of the woman.

"It embarrasses me even to talk about it." Miss Lenaut immediately became shrill again. "In all my years of teaching . . . The indignity . . . From a student who has always seemed ambitious and diligent. He did not say what he had done?"

"No," Jordache said. He stood there patiently, as though he had all day and all night to sort out the matter, whatever it turned out to be.

"*Eh, bien,*" Miss Lenaut said, "the burden devolves upon my shoulders." She bent down and opened the desk drawer and took out the drawing. She did not look at it, but held it down and away from her as she spoke. "In the middle of my classroom, when he was supposed to be writing a composition, do you know what he was doing?"

"No," said Jordache.

"*This!*" She poked the drawing dramatically in front of Jordache's nose. He took the paper from her and held it up to the light from the windows to get a better look at it. Rudolph peered anxiously at his father's face, searching for signs. He half expected his father to turn and hit him on the spot and wondered if he would have the courage to just stand there and take it without flinching or crying out. Jordache's face told him nothing. He seemed quite interested, but a little puzzled.

Finally, he spoke. "I'm afraid I can't read French," he said.

"That is not the point," Miss Lenaut said excitedly.

"There's something written here in French." Jordache pointed with his big index finger to the phrase, "*Je suis folle d'amour,*" that Rudolph had printed on the drawing of the blackboard in front of which the naked figure was standing.

"I am crazy with love, I am crazy with love." Miss Lenaut was now striding up and down in short trips behind her desk.

"What's that?" Jordache wrinkled his forehead, as though he was trying his best to understand but was out in waters too deep for him.

"That's what's written there." Miss Lenaut pointed a mad finger at the sheet of paper. "It's a translation of what your talented son has written there. 'I am crazy with love, I am crazy with love.'" She was shrieking now.

"Oh, I see," Jordache said, as though a great light had dawned on him. "Is that dirty in French?"

Miss Lenaut gained control of herself with a visible effort, although she was biting her lipstick again. "Mr. Jordache," she said, "have you ever been to school?"

"In another country," Jordache said.

"In whatever country you went to school, Mr. Jordache, would it be considered proper for a young boy to draw a picture of his teacher nude, in the classroom?"

"Oh!" Jordache sounded surprised. "Is this you?"

"Yes, it is," Miss Lenaut said. She glared bitterly at Rudolph.

Jordache studied the drawing more closely. "By God," he said, "I see the resemblance. Do teachers pose nude in high school these days?"

"I will not have you mock of me, Mr. Jordache," Miss Lenaut said with cold dignity. "I see there is no further point to this conversation. If you will be so good as to return the drawing to me . . ." She stretched out her hand. "I will say good day to you and take the matter up elsewhere, where the gravity of the situation will be appreciated. The office of the principal. I had wanted to spare your son the embarrassment of putting his obscenity on the principal's desk, but I see no other course is open to me. Now, if I may have the drawing please, I won't detain you further . . ."

Jordache took a step back, holding onto the drawing. "You say my son did this drawing?"

"I most certainly do," Miss Lenaut said. "His signature is on it."

Jordache glanced at the drawing to confirm this. "You're right," he said. "It's Rudy's signature. It's his drawing, all right. You don't need a lawyer to prove that."

"You may expect a communication from the principal," Miss Lenaut said. "Now, please return the drawing. I'm busy and I've wasted enough time on this digusting affair."

"I think I'll keep it. You youself said it's Rudy's," Jordache said placidly. "And it shows a lot of talent. A very good likeness." He shook his head in admiration. "I never guessed Rudy had it in him. I think I'll have it framed and hang it up back home. You'd have to pay a lot of money to get a nude picture as good as this one on the open market."

Miss Lenaut was biting her lips so hard she couldn't get a word out for the moment. Rudolph stared at his father, dumbfounded. He handn't had any clear idea of how his father was going to react, but this falsely innocent, sly, country-bumpkin performance was beyond any concept that Rudolph might ever have had of how his father would behave.

Miss Lenaut gave tongue. She spoke in a harsh whisper, leaning malevolently over her desk and spitting out the words at Jordache. "Get out of here, you low, dirty, common foreigner, and take your filthy son with you."

"I wouldn't talk like that, Miss," Jordache said, his voice still calm. "This is a taxpayer's school and I'm a taxpayer and I'll get out when I'm good and ready. And if you didn't strut around with your tail wiggling in a tight skirt and half your titties showing like a two dollar whore on a street corner, maybe young boys wouldn't be tempted to draw pictures of you stark-assed naked. And if you ask me, if a man took you out of all your brassieres and girdles, it'd turn out that Rudy was downright complimentary in his art work."

Miss Lenaut's face was congested and her mouth writhed in hatred. "I know about you," she said. "*Sale Boche.*"

Jordache reached across the desk and slapped her. The slap resounded like a small firecracker. The voices from the playing field had died down and the room was sickeningly silent. Miss Lenaut remained bent over, leaning on her hands on the desk, for another moment. Then she burst into tears and crumpled onto her chair, holding her hands to her face.

"I don't go for talk like that, you French cunt," Jordache said. "I didn't come all the way here from Europe to listen to talk like that. And if I was French these days, what with running like rabbits the first shot the dirty Boche fired at them, I'd think twice about insulting anybody. If it'll make you feel any better, I'll tell you I killed a

Frenchman in 1916 with a bare bayonet and it won't surprise you that I stuck it in his back while he was trying to run home to his Mama."

As his father talked, calmly, as though he were discussing the weather or an order for flour, Rudolph began to shiver. The malice in the words was made intolerable by the conversational, almost friendly, tone in which they were delivered.

Jordache was going on, inexorably. "And if you think you're going to take it out on my boy here, you better think twice about that, too, because I don't live far from here and I don't mind walking. He's been an *A* student in French for two years and I'll be here to ask some questions if he comes back at the end of the term with anything less. Come on, Rudy."

They went out of the room, leaving Miss Lenaut sobbing at her desk.

They walked away from the school without speaking. When they came to a trash basket on a corner, Jordache stopped. He tore the drawing into small pieces, almost absently, and let the pieces float down into the basket. He looked over at Rudolph. "You are a silly bastard, aren't you?" he said.

Rudolph nodded.

They resumed walking in the direction of home.

"You ever been laid?" Jordache said.

"No."

"That the truth?"

"I'd tell you."

"I suppose you would," Jordache said. He walked silently for awhile, with his rolling limp. "What're you waiting for?"

"I'm in no hurry," Rudolph said defensively. Neither his father nor his mother had ever mentioned anything about sex to him and this afternoon was certainly the wrong day to start. He was haunted by the sight of Miss Lenaut, dissolved and ugly, weeping on her desk, and he was ashamed that he had ever thought a silly, shrill woman like that worthy of his passion.

"When you start," Jordache said, "don't get hung up on one. Take 'em by the dozen. Don't ever get to feel that there's only one woman for you and that you got to have her. You can ruin you life."

"Okay," Rudolph said, knowing that his father was wrong, dead wrong.

Another silence as they turned a corner.

"You sorry I hit her?" Jordache said.

"Yes."

"You've lived all your life in this country," Jordache said. "You don't know what real hating is."

"Did you really kill a Frenchman with a bayonet?" He had to know.

"Yeah," Jordache said. "One of ten million. What difference does it make?"

They were nearly home. Rudolph felt depressed and miserable. He should have thanked his father for sticking up for him that way, it was something that very few parents would have done, and he realized that, but he couldn't get the words out.

"It wasn't the only man I killed," Jordache said, as they stopped in front of the bakery. "I killed a man when there was no war on. In Hamburg, Germany, with a knife. In 1921. I just thought you ought to know. It's about time you learned something about your father. See you at supper. I got to go put the shell under cover." He limped off, down the shabby street, his cloth cap squarely on top of his head.

When the final marks were posted for the term, Rudolph had an A in French.

CHAPTER 4

I

THE GYMNASIUM OF the elementary school near the Jordache house was kept open until ten o'clock five nights a week. Tom Jordache went there two or three times a week, sometimes to play basketball, sometimes merely to shoot the breeze with the boys and young men who gathered there or to play in the mild game of craps that occasionally was held in the boys' toilet, out of sight of the gym teacher refereeing the permanent game on the basketball court.

Tom was the only boy his age allowed in the crap game. He had gained entrance with his fists. He had found a place between two of the players in the ring and had kneeled on the floor one night and thrown a dollar into the pot and said, "You're faded," to Sonny Jackson, a boy of nineteen waiting to be drafted, and the guiding spirit of the group that congregated around the school. Sonny was a strong, stocky boy, pugnacious and quick to take offense. Tom had chosen Sonny purposely for his debut. Sonny had looked at Tom, annoyed, and pushed Tom's dollar bill back along the floor toward him. "Go way, punk," he said. "This game is for men."

Without hesitation, Tom had leaned across the open space and backhanded Sonny, without moving from his knees. In the fight that followed, Tom made his reputation. He had cut Sonny's eyes and lips and had finished by dragging Sonny into the showers and turning the cold water on him and keeping him there for five minutes before he turned the water off. Since then, whenever Tom joined the group in the gymnasium, they made room for him.

Tonight, there was no game in progress. A gangling twenty-year-old by the name of Pyle, who had enlisted early in the war, was displaying a samurai sword he said he had captured himself at Guadalcanal. He had been discharged from the Army after having malaria three times and nearly died. He was still alarmingly yellow.

Tom listened skeptically as Pyle described how he had thrown a hand grenade into a cave just for luck. Pyle said he heard a yell inside and had crawled in with his lieutenant's pistol in his hand to find a dead Jap captain, with the sword at his side. It sounded to Tom more like Errol Flynn in Hollywood than anybody from Port Philip in the South Pacific. But he didn't say anything, because he was in a peaceful mood and you couldn't beat up on a guy who looked that sick and yellow, anyway.

"Two weeks later," Pyle said, "I cut off a Jap's head with this sword."

Tom felt a tug at his sleeve. It was Claude, dressed in a suit and tie, as usual, and bubbling a little at the lips. "Listen," Claude whispered, "I got something to tell you. Let's get out of here."

"Wait a minute," Tom said. "I want to hear this."

"The island was secured," Pyle was saying, "but there were still Japs hiding out, coming out at night, and shooting up the area and knocking off guys. The C.O. got pissed off and he sent out patrols three times a day. He told us to clean every last one of the bastards out of the area.

"Well, I'm on one of those patrols and we see one of 'em trying to wade across a creek so we let him have it. He was hit but not bad and he's sitting up, holding his hands over his head, saying something in Jap. There wasn't no officers on the patrol, just a corporal and six other guys, and I says, 'Hey, listen, you guys, just hold him here and I'll go back to get my samurai sword and we'll have a regular execution.' The corporal was a little chicken about it, the orders were to bring in prisoners, but like I said, there were no officers present and after all, that's what the bastards did all the time to our guys, cut off their heads, and we took a vote and they tied the fucker up and I went back and got my samurai sword. We made him kneel down in the regular way and he did it just like he was used to it. It was my sword so I got to do the job. I picked it up way over my head and clunk! there was his head rolling on the ground like a coconut, with his eyes wide open. The blood spurted out, it must have been close to ten feet. I tell you," Pyle said, touching the edge of the weapon lovingly, "these swords are something."

"Horseshit," Claude said loudly.

"What's that?" Pyle asked, blinking. "What'd you say?"

"I said horseshit," Claude repeated. "You never cut off no Jap's head. I bet you bought that sword in a souvenir shop in Honolulu. My brother Al knows you and he told me you haven't got the guts to kill a rabbit."

"Listen, kid," Pyle said, "sick as I am, I'll give you the beating of your life, if you don't shut up and get out of here. Nobody says horseshit to me."

"I'm waiting," Claude said. He took off his glasses and put them in the breast pocket of his suit. He looked pathetically defenseless.

Tom sighed. He stepped in front of Claude. "Anybody wants to pick on my friend," he said, "he has to go through me first."

"I don't mind," Pyle began, handing the sword to one of the other boys. "You're young, but you're fresh."

"Knock it off, Pyle," said the boy who now was holding the sword. "He'll murder you."

Pyle looked uncertainly at the circling faces. There was something sobering that he saw there. "I didn't come back from fighting in the Pacific," he said loudly, "to get into arguments with little kids in my home town. Give me my sword, I'm due back at the house."

He beat a retreat. The others drifted off without a word, leaving Tom and Claude in possession of the boys' toilet.

"What'd you want to do that for?" Tom asked, irritated. "He didn't mean no harm. And you know they wouldn't let him take me on."

"I just wanted to see the expression on their faces," Claude said, sweating and grinning. "That's all. Power. Raw power."

"You're going to get me killed one day with your raw power," Tom said. "Now what the hell did you have to tell me?"

"I saw your sister," Claude said.

"Hooray for you, you saw my sister. I see her every day. Sometimes twice a day."

"I saw her in front of Bernstein's Department Store. I was riding around on the bike and I went around the block again to make sure and she was getting into a big convertible Buick and a guy was holding the door open for her. She was waiting for him in front of Bernstein's, that's for sure."

"So, big deal," Tom said. "She got a ride in a Buick."

"You want to know who was driving the Buick?" Behind his glasses, Claude's eyes were joyous with information. "You'll drop dead."

"I won't drop dead. Who?"

"Mr. Theodore Boylan, Esquire," Claude said. "That's who. How do you like that for moving up in class?"

"What time you see them?"

"An hour ago. I've been looking for you all over."

"He probably drove her to the hospital. She works in the hospital on week nights."

"She isn't in any hospital tonight, Buddy," Claude said. "I followed them part of the way on the bike. They took the road up the hill. Toward his place. You want to find your sister tonight, I advise you to look in on the Boyland estate."

Tom hesitated. It would have been different if Gretchen was with one of the fellows around her own age, off in a car to the lover's lane down near the river for a little simple necking. Tease her a little later on. *Hideous boy.* Get a little of his own back. But with an old man like Boylan, a big shot in the town . . . He would rather not have to get mixed up in it. You never knew where something like that could lead you.

"I'll tell you something," Claude said, "if it was my sister, I'd look into it. That Boylan has quite a reputation around town. You don't know some of the things I hear around the house when my father and uncle are talking and they don't know I'm listening. Your sister may be asking for a big load of trouble . . ."

"You got the bike outside?"

"Yeah. But we need some gas." The motorcycle belonged to Claude's brother Al, who had just been drafted two weeks before. Al had promised to break every bone in Claude's body if he came back and found that Claude had used the machine, but whenever his parents went out at night, Claude pushed it out of the garage, after siphoning off a little gas from the family's second car, and raced around town for an hour or so, avoiding the police, because he was too young to have a license.

"Okay," Tom said. "Let's see what's happening up the hill."

Claude had a length of rubber tubing slung on the motorcycle and they went behind the school, where it was dark, and opened the gas tank of a Chevy that was parked there and Claude put the tube in and sucked hard, then, as the gasoline came up, filled the tank of the motorcycle.

Tom got on behind and with Claude driving they spurted through back streets toward the outskirts of town and began to climb the long winding road that went up the hill to the Boylan estate.

When they got to the main gate, made of huge wrought-iron wings standing open and set into a stone wall that seemed to run for miles on each side, they parked the motorcycle behind some bushes. The rest of the way they'd have to go on foot, so as not to be heard. There was a gatekeeper's cottage, but since the war nobody had lived in it. The boys knew the estate well. For years, they had been jumping over the wall and hunting for birds and rabbits with BB guns. The estate had been neglected for years and it was more like a jungle than the meadowed park it had been originally.

They walked through the woods toward the main house. When they got near it, they saw the Buick parked in front. There were no lights on outside, but there was a gleam from a big French window downstairs.

They moved cautiously toward the flower bed in front of the window. The window came down almost to the ground. One side of it was ajar. The curtains had been drawn carelessly and with Claude kneeling in the loam and Tom standing astride him, they both could look inside at the same time.

As far as they could see, the room was empty. It was big and square, with a grand piano, a long couch, and big easy chairs and tables with magazines on them. A fire was going in the fireplace. There were a lot of books on the shelves along the walls. A few lamps did for the lighting. The double doors facing the window were open and Tom could see a hallway and the lower steps of a staircase.

"That's the way to live," Claude whispered. "If I had a joint like this, I'd have every broad in town."

"Shut up," Tom said. "Well, there's nothing doing here. Let's move."

"Come on, Tom," Claude protested. "Take it easy. We just got here."

"This isn't my idea of a big night," Tom said. "Just standing out in the cold looking at a room with nobody in it."

"Give it a chance to develop, for Christ's sake," Claude said. "They're probably upstairs. They can't stay there all night."

Tom knew that he didn't want to see anybody come into that room. Anybody. He wanted to get away from that house. And stay away. But he didn't want to look as though he was chickening out. "All right," he said, "I'll give it a couple of minutes." He turned away from the window, leaving Claude on his knees peering in. "Call me if anything happens," he said.

The night was very still. The mist rising from the wet ground was getting heavier and there were no stars. In the distance, below them, there was the faint glow of the lights of Port Philip. The Boylan grounds swept away from the house in all directions, a myriad of great old trees, the outline of the fence of a tennis court, some low buildings about fifty yards away that had once been used as stables. One man living in all that. Tom thought of the bed he shared with his brother. Well, Boylan was sharing a bed tonight, too. Tom spat.

"Hey!" Claude beckoned to him excitedly. "Come here, come here."

Slowly, Tom went back to the window.

"He just come in, down the stairs," Claude whispered. "Look at that. Just look at that, will you."

Tom looked in. Boylan had his back to the window, on the far side of the room. He was at a table with bottles, glasses and a silver ice container on it. He was pouring whiskey into two glasses. He was naked.

"What a way to walk around a house," Claude said.

"Shut up," Tom said. He watched as Boylan carelessly dropped some ice into the glasses and splashed soda from a siphon into the glasses. Boylan didn't pick up the glasses right away. He went over to the fireplace and threw another log on the fire, then went to a table near the window and opened a lacquered box and took out a cigarette. He lit it with a foot-long silver cigarette lighter. He was smiling a little.

Standing there, so close to the window, he was clearly outlined in the light of a lamp. Mussed, bright blond hair, skinny neck, pigeony chest, flabby arms, knobby knees, and slightly bowed legs. His dick hung down from the bush of hair, long, thick, reddened. A dumb rage, a sense of being violated, of being witness to an unspeakable obscenity, seized Tom. If he had had a gun he would have killed the man. That puny stick, that strutting, smiling, satisfied weakling, that feeble, pale, hairy slug of a body so confidently displayed, that long, fat, rosy instrument. It was worse, infinitely worse, than if he and Claude had seen his sister come in naked.

Boylan walked across the thick carpet, the smoke from his cigarette trailing over his shoulder, out into the hall. He called up the stairs. "Gretchen, do you want your drink up there or do you want to come down for it?" He listened. Tom couldn't hear the answer. Boylan nodded and came back into the room and picked up the two glasses. Then, carrying the whiskey, he went out of the room and up the stairs.

"Jesus, what a sight," Claude said. "He's built like a chicken. I guess if you're rich you can be built like the Hunchback of Notre Dame and the broads still come running."

"Let's get out of here," Tom said thickly.

"What the hell for?" Claude looked up at him in surprise, the light that came through the parted curtains reflecting damply on his eyeglasses. "The action is just beginning."

Tom reached down and grabbed Claude by the hair and jerked him savagely to his feet.

"Hey, for Christ's sake, watch what you're doing," Claude said.

"I said let's get out of here." Tom held Claude roughly by his necktie. "And you keep quiet about what you saw tonight."

"I didn't see anything," Claude whined. "What the hell did I see! A skinny crock with a dick on him like an old rubber hose. What's there to keep quiet about?"

"Just keep quiet, that's all," Tom said, his face close to Claude's. "If I ever hear a word from anyone, you'll get a beating you'll never forget. Got it?"

"Jesus, Tom," Claude said reproachfully, rubbing his sore scalp, "I'm your friend."

"Got it?" Tom said fiercely.

"Sure, sure. Anything you say. I don't know what there's to get so excited about."

Tom let him go and wheeled and strode across the lawn away from the house. Claude followed him, grumbling. "Guys tell me you're crazy," he said, as he caught up to Tom, "and I always tell them they're nuts, but now I'm beginning to see what they mean, I swear to God I do. Boy, are you temperamental."

Tom didn't answer. He was almost running as they neared the gate house. Claude wheeled out the bike and Tom swung on behind him. They drove into town without talking to each other.

II

Replete and drowsy, Gretchen lay in the wide soft bed, her hands behind her head, staring up at the ceiling. The ceiling reflected the fire that Boylan had lit before he had undressed her. The arrangements for seduction were planned meticulously and smoothly practiced up here on the hill. The house was hushed and luxurious, the servants were never in evidence, the telephone never rang, there was never any fumbling or hurrying. Nothing clumsy or unforeseen was allowed to intrude on their evening ritual.

Downstairs, a clock chimed softly. Ten o'clock. It was the hour the common room in the hospital emptied and the wounded men made their way, on crutches and in wheelchairs, back to the wards. These days Gretchen only went to the hospital two or three times a week. Her life was centered, with a single urgency, on the bed in which she lay. The days were passed in expectation of it, the nights away from it in its memory. She would make restitution to the wounded some other time.

Even when she had opened the envelope and seen the eight one-hundred-dollar bills, she had known she would return to this bed. If it was one of Boylan's peculiarities that he had to humiliate her, she accepted it. She would make the man pay for it later.

Neither Boylan nor she had ever spoken of the envelope on her desk. On Tuesday, as she was coming out of the office after work, the Buick was there, with Boylan at the wheel. He had opened the car door without a word and she had gotten in and he had driven to his house. They had made love and after that gone to The Farmer's Inn for dinner and after that had driven home and made love again. When he took her into town, toward midnight, he had dropped her off two blocks from her home and she had walked the rest of the way.

Teddy did everything perfectly. He was discreet—secrecy was to his taste; it was a necessity for her. Nobody knew anything about them. Knowledgeable, he had taken her to a doctor in New York to be fitted for a diaphragm, so that she didn't have to worry about *that*. He had bought her the red dress, as promised, on the same trip to New York. The red dress hung in Teddy's wardrobe. There would come a time when she would wear it.

Teddy did everything perfectly, but she had little affection for him and certainly didn't love him. His body was flimsy and unprepossessing; only when he was dressed in his elegant clothes could he be considered in any way attractive. He was a man without enthusiasms, self-indulgent and cynical, a confessed failure, friendless and shunted off by a mighty family to a crumbling shipwreck of a Victorian castle in which most of the rooms were permanently closed off. An empty man in a half-empty house. It was easy to understand why the beautiful woman whose photograph still stood on the piano downstairs had divorced him and run away with another man.

He was not a lovable or admirable man, but he had other uses. Having renounced the ordinary activities of the men of his class, work, war, games, friendship, he dedicated himself to one thing: he copulated with all his hoarded force and cunning. He demanded nothing of her except to be there, the material of his craft. His triumph was in his own performance. The battles he had declined elsewhere, he won in the face below his on the pillow. The fanfares of victory were her sighs of pleasure. For her part, Gretchen was not concerned with Boylan's profits and losses. She lay passively under him, not even putting her arms around the unimportant body, accepting, accepting. He was anonymous, nobody, the male principle, an abstract, unconnected priapus, for which she had been waiting, unknowing, all her life. He was a servant to her pleasures, holding a door open to a palace of marvels.

She was not even grateful.

The eight hundred dollars lay folded into the leaves of her copy of the works of Shakespeare, between Acts II and III of *As You Like it*.

A clock chimed somewhere and his voice floated into the room from downstairs. "Gretchen, do you want your drink up there or do you want to come down for it?"

"Up here," she called. Her voice was lower, huskier. She was conscious of new, subtler tonalities in it; if her mother's ear for such things had not been deafened by her own disaster, she would have known with one sentence that her daughter was sunnily sailing that dangerous sea in which she herself had foundered and drowned.

Boylan came into the room, naked in the firelight, bearing the two glasses. Gretchen propped herself up and took the glass from his hand. He sat on the edge of the bed, flicking ashes from his cigarette into the ash tray on the bed table.

They drank. She was developing a liking for Scotch. He leaned over and kissed her breast. "I want to see how it tastes with whiskey on it," he said. He kissed the other breast. She took another sip from her glass.

"I don't have you," he said. "I don't have you. There's only one time when I can make myself believe I have you—when I'm in you and you're coming. All the rest of the time, even when you're lying right beside me naked and I have my hand on you, you've escaped. *Do* I have you?"

"No," she said.

"Christ," he said. "Nineteen years old. What are you going to be like at thirty?"

She smiled. He would be forgotten by that year. Perhaps before. Much before.

"What were you thinking about up here while I was down getting the drinks?" he asked.

"Fornication," she said.

"Do you have to talk like that?" His own language was strangely prissy, some hangover fear of a domineering nanny quick with the kitchen soap to wash out the mouths of little boys who used naughty words.

"I never talked like that until I met you." She took a satisfying gulp of whiskey.

"I don't talk like that," he said.

"You're a hypocrite," she said. "What I can do, I can name."

"You don't do so damn much," he said, stung.

"I'm a poor little, inexperienced, small-town girl," she said. "If the nice man in the Buick hadn't come along that day and got me drunk and taken advantage, I probably would have lived and died a withered, dried-up old maid."

"I bet," he said. "You'd have been down there with those two niggers."

She smiled ambiguously. "We'll never know, now, will we?"

He looked at her thoughtfully. "You could stand some education," he said. Then he stubbed out his cigarette, as though he had come to a decision. "Excuse me." He stood up. "I have to make a telephone call." He put on a robe this time and went downstairs.

Gretchen sat, propped against the pillows, slowly finishing her drink. She had paid him off. For the moment earlier in the evening when she had delivered herself so absolutely to him. She would pay him off every time.

He came back into the room. "Get dressed," he said. She was surprised. Usually they stayed until midnight. But she said nothing. She got out of bed and put on her clothes. "Are we going somewhere?" she asked. "How should I look?"

"Look anyway you want," he said. Dressed, he was important and privileged again, a man to whom other men deferred. She felt diminished in her clothes. He criticized the things she wore, not harshly, but knowingly, sure of himself. If she weren't afraid of her mother's questions, she would have taken the eight hundred dollars out from between Acts II and III of *As You Like It* and bought herself a new wardrobe.

They went through the silent house and into the car and drove off. She asked no more questions. They drove through Port Philip and sped on down south. They didn't speak. She wouldn't give him the satisfaction of asking where they were going. There was a scorecard in her head in which she kept track of the points they gained against each other.

They went all the way to New York. Even if they turned back promptly, she wouldn't get home much before dawn. There probably would be hysterics from her mother. But she didn't remonstrate. She refused to show him that she allowed herself to be worried by things like that.

They stopped in front of a darkened four-story house on a street lined with similar houses on both sides of it. Gretchen had only come down to New York a few times in her life, twice with Boylan in the last three weeks, and she had no idea of what neighborhood they were in. Boylan came over to her side of the car, as usual, and opened the door for her. They went down three steps into a little cement courtyard behind an iron fence and Boylan rang a doorbell. There was a long wait. She had the feeling that they were being inspected. The door opened. A big woman in a white evening gown stood there, her dyed red hair piled heavily on her head. "Good evening, honey," she said. Her voice was hoarse. She closed the door behind them. The lights in the entrance hall were low and the house was hushed, as though it was heavily carpeted throughout and its walls hung with muffling cloth. There was a sense of people moving about it softly and carefully.

"Good evening, Nellie," Boylan said.

"I haven't seen you in a dog's age," the woman said, as she led them up a flight of steps and into a small pinkly lit living room on the first floor.

"I've been busy," Boylan said.

"So I see," the woman said, looking at Gretchen, appraising, then admiring. "How old are you, darling?"

"A hundred and eight," Boylan said.

He and the woman laughed. Gretchen stood soberly in the small, draped room hung with oil paintings of nudes. She was determined to show nothing, respond to nothing. She was frightened, but tried not to feel it or show it. In numbness there was safety. She noticed that all the lamps in the room were tasseled. The woman's white dress had fringes at the bosom and at the hem of the skirt. Was there a connection there? Gretchen made herself speculate on these matters to keep from turning and fleeing from the hushed house with its malevolent sense of a hidden population moving stealthily between rooms on the floors above her head. She had no notion of what would be expected of her, what she might see, what would be done with her. Boylan looked debonair, at ease.

"Everything is just about ready, I think, honey," the woman said. "Just a few more minutes. Would you like something to drink, while waiting?"

"Pet?" Boylan turned toward Gretchen.

"Whatever you say." She spoke with difficulty.

"I think a glass of champagne might be in order," Boylan said.

"I'll send a bottle up to you," the woman said. "It's cold. I have it on ice. Just follow me." She led the way out into the hall and Gretchen and Boylan climbed the carpeted stairs behind her up to a dim hallway on the second floor. The stiff rustling of the woman's dress sounded alarmingly loud as she walked. Boylan was carrying his coat. Gretchen hadn't taken off her coat.

The woman opened a door off the hallway and switched on a small lamp. They went into the room. There was a large bed with a silk canopy over it, an oversized maroon velvet easy chair, and three small gilt chairs. A large bouquet of tulips made a brilliant splash of yellow on a table in the center of the room. The curtains were drawn and the sound of a car passing on the street below was muffled. A wide mirror covered one wall. It was like a room in a slightly old-fashioned, once-luxurious hotel, now just a little bit déclassé.

"The maid will bring you your wine in a minute," the woman said. She rustled out, closing the door softly but firmly behind her.

"Good old Nellie," Boylan said, throwing his coat down on an upholstered bench near the door. "Always dependable. She's famous." He didn't say what she was famous for. "Don't you want to take your coat off, pet?"

"Am I supposed to?"

Boyland shrugged. "You're not supposed to do anything."

Gretchen kept her coat on, although it was warm in the room. She went over and sat on the edge of the bed and waited. Boylan lit a cigarette and sat comfortably in the easy chair, crossing his legs. He looked over at her, smiling slightly, amused. "This is a brothel," he said matter-of-factly. "In case you haven't guessed. Have you ever been in one before, pet?"

She knew he was teasing her. She didn't answer. She didn't trust herself to speak.

"No, I suppose not," he said. "Every lady should visit one. At least once. See what the competition is doing."

There was low knock on the door. Boylan went over to it and opened it. A frail middle-aged maid in a white apron over a short, black dress came in carrying a silver tray. On the tray there was a bucket of ice with a champagne bottle sticking out of it. There were two champagne glasses on the tray. The maid set the tray down on the table next to the tulips without speaking. There was no expression on her face. Her function was to appear not to be present. She began to pry open the cork. She was wearing felt slippers, Gretchen noticed.

She struggled with the cork, her face becoming flushed with the effort, and a strand of graying hair fell over her eyes. It made her look like the aging, slow-moving women with varicose veins, to be seen at early Mass, before the working day begins.

"Here," Boyland said, "I'll do that." He took the bottle from her hands.

"I'm sorry, sir," the maid said. She had betrayed her function. She was there, made noticeable by her failure.

Boylan couldn't get the bottle open, either. He pulled, he pushed at the cork with his thumbs, holding the bottle between his legs. He, too, began to get red in the face, as the maid watched him apologetically. Boylan's hands were slender and soft, useful only for gentler work.

Gretchen stood up and took the bottle. "I'll do it," she said.

"Do you open many bottles of champagne at the brick works?" Boylan asked.

Gretchen paid no attention to him. She grasped the cork firmly. Her hands were quick and strong. She twisted the cork. It popped and flew out of her hands and hit the ceiling. The champagne bubbled out and soaked her hands. She handed the bottle to Boylan. One more mark on the scorecard. He laughed. "The working classes have their uses," he said. He poured the champagne as the maid gave Gretchen a towel to dry her hands. The maid left in her felt slippers. Soft, mouselike traffic in the hallways.

Boylan gave Gretchen the glass of champagne. "The shipments are now steady from France, although they tell me the Germans made important inroads," he said. "Last year, I understand, was a mediocre one for the vintage." He was plainly angered by his fiasco with the bottle and Gretchen's success.

They sipped the champagne. There was a diagonal red line on the label. Boylan made an approving face. "One can always be assured of the best in Nellie's place," he said. "She would be hurt if she knew that I called her establishment a brothel. I think she thinks of it as a kind of salon where she can exercise her limitless sense of hospitality for the benefit of her many gentlemen friends. Don't think all whore houses are like this, pet. You'll only be in for a disappointment." He was still smarting from the tussle over the bottle and he was getting his own back. "Nellie's is one of the last hangovers from a more gracious era, before the Century of the

Common Man and Common Sex engulfed us all. If you develop a taste for bordellos ask me for the proper addresses, pet. You might find yourself in terribly sordid places otherwise, and we wouldn't want that, would we? Do you like the champagne?"

"It's all right," Gretchen said. She seated herself once more on the bed, holding herself together rigidly.

Without warning, the mirror lit up. Somebody had turned on a switch in the next room. The mirror was revealed as a one-way window through which Boylan and Gretchen could see what was going on next door to them. The light in the next room came from a lamp hanging from the ceiling, its brightness subdued by a thick silk shade.

Boylan glanced at the mirror. "Ah," he said, "the orchestra is tuning up." He took the bottle of champagne from the bucket and came over and sat down on the bed beside Gretchen. He set the bottle on the floor next to him.

Through the mirror, they could see a tall young woman with long blonde hair. Her face was pretty enough, with the pouting, greedy, starlet expression of a spoiled child. But when she threw off the pink, frilly negligee she was wearing, she revealed a magnificent body with long, superb legs. She never even glanced toward the mirror, although the routine must have been familiar to her, and she knew she was being watched. She threw back the covers on the bed and let herself fall back on it, all her movements harmonious and unaffected. She lay there, waiting, content to let hours go past, days, lazily allowing herself to be admired. Everything passed in utter silence. No sound came through the mirror.

"Some more champagne, pet?" Boylan asked. He lifted the bottle.

"No, thank you." Gretchen found it difficult to speak.

The door opened and a young Negro came into the other room.

Oh, the bastard, Gretchen thought, oh the sick, revengeful bastard. But she didn't move.

The young Negro said something to the girl on the bed. She waved a little in greeting and smiled a baby-beauty-contest-winner's smile. Everything happened on the other side of the mirror in pantomime and gave an air of remoteness, of unreality, to the two figures in the other room. It was falsely reassuring, as though nothing serious could happen there.

The Negro was dressed in a navy-blue suit and white shirt and a dotted red bow-tie. He had on sharply pointed light-brown shoes. He had a nice, young, smiling "Yes, suh" kind of face.

"Nellie has a lot of connections in night clubs up in Harlem," Boylan said as the Negro began to undress, hanging his jacket nearby on the back of a chair. "He's probably a trumpet player or something in one of the bands, not unwilling to make an extra buck of an evening, entertaining the white folk. A buck for a buck." He chuckled briefly at his own *mot*. "You sure you don't want some more to drink?"

Gretchen didn't answer. The Negro started to unbutton his pants. She closed her eyes.

When she opened her eyes the man was naked. His body was the color of bronze, with gleaming skin, wide, sloping muscular shoulders, a tapering waist, like an athlete at the height of training. The comparison with the man beside her made her rage.

The Negro moved across the room. The girl opened her arms to receive him. Lightly as a cat, he dropped down onto the long white body. They kissed, and her hands clutched at his back. Then he rolled over and she began to kiss him, first on the throat, then his nipples, slowly and expertly, while her hand caressed his mounting penis. The blonde hair tangled over the coffee-colored gleaming skin, went down lower as the girl licked the tight skin over the flat muscles of the man's belly and he tautened convulsively.

Gretchen watched, fascinated. She found it beautiful and fitting, a promise to herself that she could not formulate in words. But she could not watch it with Boylan at her side. It was too unjust, filthily unjust, that these two magnificent bodies could be bought by the hour, like animals in a stable, for the pleasure or perversity or vengeance of a man like Boylan.

She stood up, her back to the mirror. "I'll wait for you in the car," she said.

"It's just beginning, pet," Boylan said mildly. "Look what she's doing now. After all, this is really for your instruction. You'll be very popular with the . . ."

"I'll see you in the car," she said, and ran out of the room and down the stairs.

The woman in the white dress was standing near the hall doorway. She said nothing, although she smiled sardonically as she opened the door for Gretchen.

Gretchen went and sat in the car. Boylan came out fifteen minutes later, walking unhurriedly. He got into the car and started the motor. "It's a pity you didn't stay," he said. "They earned their hundred dollars."

They drove all the way back without a word. It was nearly light when he stopped the car in front of the bakery. "Well," he said after the hours of silence, "did you learn anything tonight?"

"Yes," she said. "I must find a younger man. Good night."

She heard the car turn around as she unlocked the door. As she climbed the stairs, she saw the light streaming from the open door of her parents' bedroom, across from hers. Her mother was sitting upright on a wooden chair, staring out at the hallway. Gretchen stopped and looked at her mother. Her mother's eyes were those of a madwoman. It could not be helped. Mother and daughter stared at each other.

"Go to bed," the mother said. "I'll call the Works at nine o'clock to say you're sick, you won't be in today."

She went into her room and closed the door. She didn't lock it because there were no locks on any of the doors in the house. She took down her copy of Shakespeare. The eight one-hundred-dollar bills were no longer between Acts II and III of *As You Like It*. Still neatly folded in the envelope, they were in the middle of Act V of *Macbeth*.

CHAPTER 5

I

THERE WERE NO lights on in the Boylan house. Everybody was downtown celebrating. Thomas and Claude could see the rockets and roman candles that arched into the night sky over the river and could hear the booming of the little cannon that was used at the high-school football games when the home team scored a touchdown. It was a clear, warm night and from the vantage point on the hill, Port Philip shimmered brightly, with every light in town turned on.

The Germans had surrendered that morning.

Thomas and Claude had wandered around town with the crowds, watching girls kissing soldiers and sailors in the streets and people bringing out bottles of whiskey. Throughout the day Thomas grew more and more disgusted. Men who had dodged the draft for four years, clerks in uniform who had never been more than a hundred miles away from home, merchants who had made fortunes off the black market, all kissing and yelling and getting drunk as though they, personally, had killed Hitler.

"Slobs," he had said to Claude, as he watched the celebrants. "I'd like to show 'em."

"Yeah," Claude said. "We ought to have a little celebration of our own. Our own private fireworks." He had been thoughtful after that, not saying anything, as he watched his elders cavorting. He took off his glasses and chewed on an earpiece, a habit of his when he was preparing a coup. Thomas recognized the signs, but braced himself against anything rash. This was no time for picking on soldiers and any kind of fight, even with a civilian, would be a wrong move today.

Finally, Claude had come up with his VE Day plan and Thomas conceded that it was worthy of the occasion.

So there they were on the Boylan hill, with Thomas carrying the can of gasoline and Claude the bag of nails and the hammer and the bundle of rags, making their way cautiously through the underbrush toward a dilapidated greenhouse standing on a bare knoll about five hundred yards from the main house. They had not come the usual way, but had approached the estate on a small dirt road that was on the inland side, away from Port Philip, and led to the rear of the house. They had broken in through a gardener's gate and left the bike hidden near an abandoned gravel pit outside the estate walls.

They reached the greenhouse on the knoll. Its glass panes were dusty and broken and a musty odor of rotten vegetation came from it. There were some long, dry planks along one side of the sagging structure, and a rusty shovel that they had noticed on other occasions when they had prowled the grounds. When Thomas began to dig, Claude selected two big planks and began to hammer them into a cross. They had perfected their plans during the day and there was no need for words.

When the cross was finished, Claude soaked the boards with gasoline. Then they both lifted it and jammed it into the hole that Thomas had dug. He put dirt around the base of the cross, and stamped it down hard with his feet and the back of the shovel, to keep everything firm. Claude soaked the rags he had been carrying with the rest of the gasoline. Everything was ready. The boom of the cannon floated up the hill from the high-school lawn and rockets glared briefly far off in the night sky.

Thomas was calm and deliberate in his movements. As far as he was concerned it wasn't anything very important that they were doing. Once more, in his own way, he was thumbing his nose at all those grown-up phoneys down there. With the extra pleasure of doing it on that naked prick Boylan's property. Give them all something to think about, between kisses and the "Star-Spangled Banner." But Claude was all worked up. He was gasping, as though he couldn't get any air in his lungs, and he was bubbling, almost drooling at the mouth, and he had to keep wiping his glasses off with his handkerchief because they kept clouding up. It was an act of huge significance for Claude, with an uncle who was a priest, and a father who made him go to Mass every Sunday and who lectured him daily on Mortal Sin, keeping away from loose Protestant women, and remaining pure in the eyes of Jesus.

"Okay," Thomas said softly, stepping back.

Claude's hands trembled as he struck a match and bent over and touched it to the gasoline-soaked rags at the base of the cross. Then he screamed and began to run, as the rags flared up. His arm was on fire and he ran blindly across the clearing, screaming. Thomas ran after him, yelling to him to stop, but Claude just kept running, crazily. Thomas caught up with him and tackled him, then rolled on Claude's arm, using his chest, which was protected by his sweater, to smother the flames.

It was over in a moment. Claude lay on his back, moaning, holding his burnt arm, and whimpering, unable to say anything.

Thomas stood up and looked down at his friend. Every drop of sweat on Claude's face could be clearly made out, in the light of the flaming cross. They had to get out of there fast. People were bound to arrive at any minute. "Get up," Thomas said. But Claude didn't move. He rolled a little from side to side, with his eyes staring, but that was all.

"Get up, you stupid son of a bitch." Thomas shook Claude's shoulder. Claude looked up at him, his face rigid with fear, dumb. Thomas bent over and picked Claude up and threw him over his shoulder and began to run down off the crown of the hill in the direction of the gardener's gate, crashing through underbrush, trying not to listen to Claude saying, "Oh, Jesus, oh, Jesus, oh, sweet Mother Mary."

There was a smell Thomas recognized, as he stumbled down the hill under the weight of his friend. It was the smell of broiling meat.

The cannon was still booming down in the town.

II

Axel Jordache rowed slowly out toward the center of the river, feeling the pull of the current. He wasn't rowing for exercise tonight. He was out on the river to get away from the human race. He had decided to take the night off, the first weekday night he had not worked since 1924. Let his customers eat factory bread tomorrow. After all, the German army only lost once every twenty-seven years.

It was cool on the river, but he was warm enough, in his heavy blue turtle-neck sweater, from his deckhand days on the Lakes. And he had a bottle with him to take the nip out of the air and to drink to the health of the idiots who had once more led Germany to ruin. Jordache was a patriot of no country, but he reserved his hatred for the land in which he was born. It had given him a life-long limp, had cut short his education, had exiled him, and had armed him with an utter contempt for all policies and all politicians, all generals, priests, ministers, presidents, kings, dictators, all conquests and all defeats, all candidates and all parties. He was pleased that Germany had lost the war, but he was not happy that America had won it. He hoped he'd be around twenty-seven years from now, when Germany would lose another war.

He thought of his father, a little, God-fearing, tyrannical man, a clerk in a factory office, who had gone marching off, singing, with a posy of flowers in his rifle barrel, a happy, militant sheep, to be killed at Tannenburg, proud to leave two sons who soon would be fighting for the *Vaterland,* too, and a wife who had remained a widow less than a year. Then at least she had had the wisdom to marry a lawyer who spent the war managing tenements behind the Alexander Platz in Berlin.

"Deutschland, Deutschland, über alles," Jordache sang mockingly, resting on his oars, letting the waters of the Hudson carry him south, as he lifted the bottle of bourbon to his lips. He toasted the youthful loathing with which he had regarded Germany when he had been demobilized, a cripple among cripples, and which had driven him across the ocean. America was a joke, too, but at least he was alive tonight as were his sons, and the house in which he lived was still standing.

The noise of the little cannon carried across the water and the reflections from the rockets twinkled in the river. Fools, Jordache thought, what're they celebrating about? They never had it so good in their whole lives. They'd all be selling apples on street corners in five years, they'd be tearing each other to pieces on the lines outside factories waiting for jobs. If they had the brains they were born with they'd all be in the churches tonight praying that the Japanese would hold out for ten years.

Then he saw the fire flare up suddenly on the hill outside the town, a small, clear spurt of flame which quickly defined itself as a cross, burning on the rim of the horizon. He laughed. *Business as usual and screw victory. Down with the Catholics, the Niggers, and the Jews, and don't forget it. Dance tonight and burn tomorrow. America is America. We're here and we're telling you what the score really is.*

Jordache took another drink, enjoying the spectacle of the flaming cross dominating the town, savoring in advance the mealy-mouthed lamentations that would appear tomorrow in the town's two newspapers on the subject of the affront to the memory of the brave men of all races and creeds who had died defending the ideals on which America was founded. And the sermons on Sunday! It would almost be worthwhile to go to a church or two to listen to what the holy bastards would say.

If I ever find out who put up that cross, Jordache thought, I'm going to shake their hands.

As he watched, he saw the fire spread. There must have been a building right near the cross, down wind from it. It must have been good and dry, because in no time at all the whole sky was lit up.

In a little while, he heard the bells of the fire engines racing through the streets of the town and up the hill.

Not a bad night, Jordache thought, all things considered.

He took a last drink and then started to row leisurely toward the river bank.

III

Rudolph stood on the steps of the high school and waited for the boys at the cannon to shoot it off. There were hundreds of boys and girls milling around on the lawn, shouting, singing, kissing. Except for the kissing, it was very much like the Saturday nights after the team had won a big football game.

The cannon went off. A huge cheer went up.

Then Rudolph put his trumpet to his lips and began to play, "America." First the crowd fell silent and the slow music rang out all alone, note by solemn note over their heads. Then they began to sing and in a moment all the voices joined in:

"*America, America, God shed His grace on thee, And crown thy good with brotherhood, From sea to shining sea . . .* "

There was a big cheer after the song was over and he began to play the "Stars and Stripes Forever." He couldn't stand still while playing the "Stars and Stripes Forever," so he began to march around the lawn. People fell in behind him and soon he was leading a parade of boys and girls, first around the lawn and then into the street, marching to the rhythm of his horn. The boys serving the cannon trundled it along at the head of the procession just behind him and at every intersection they stopped and fired it and the boys and girls cheered and grownups along the route applauded and waved flags at them.

Striding at the head of his army, Rudolph played "When the Caissons Go Rolling Along," and "Columbia the Gem of the Ocean," and the high-school hymn, and "Onward Christian Soldiers," as the parade wound its jubilant way through the streets of the town. He led them down toward Vanderhoff Street and stopped in front of the bakery and played, "When Irish Eyes Are Smiling," for his mother's sake. His mother opened the window upstairs and waved to him and he could see her dabbing at her eyes with a handkerchief. He ordered the boys at the cannon to give a salute to his mother and they fired the piece and the hundreds of boys and girls roared and his mother wept openly. He wished his mother had combed her hair before opening the window and it was too bad she never took the cigarette out of her mouth. There was no light from the cellar tonight, so he knew his father wasn't there. He wouldn't have known what to play for him. It would have been hard to choose the proper selection for a veteran of the Germany army on this particular night.

He would have liked to go out to the hospital and serenade his sister and her soldiers, but the hospital was too far away. With a last flourish for his mother, he led the parade toward the center of town, playing "Boola-Boola." Perhaps he would go to Yale when he finished school next year. Nothing was impossible tonight.,

He didn't really decide to do it, but he found himself on the street on which Miss Lenaut lived. He had stood outside the house often enough, hidden in the shadow of a tree across the street, looking up at the lighted window on the second floor which he knew was hers. The light was on now.

He stopped boldly in the middle of the street in front of the house, looking up at the window. The narrow street with its modest two-family dwellings and tiny lawns was packed with his followers. He felt sorry for Miss Lenaut, alone, so far from home, thinking of her friends and relatives joyously flooding the streets of Paris at this moment. He wanted to make amends to the poor woman, show that he forgave her, demonstrate that there were depths to him she had never guessed, that he was more than a dirty little boy with a foul-mouthed German father, who specialized in pornographic drawings. He put the trumpet to his lips and began to play the "*Marseillaise*." The complicated, triumphant music, with its memories of flags and battles, of desperation and heroism, rang in the shabby little street, and the boys and girls chanted along with it, without words, because they didn't know the words. By God, Rudolph thought, no high-school teacher in Port Philip ever had anything like this happen to her before. He played it through straight once, but Miss Lenaut didn't appear at the window. A girl with a blonde pigtail down her back came out of the house next door and stood near Rudolph, watching him play. Rudolph started all over again, but this time as a tricky solo, playing with the rhythm, improvising, now soft and slow, now brassy and loud. Finally, the window opened. Miss Lenaut stood there, in a dressing gown. She looked down. He couldn't see the expression on her face. He took a step so that the light of a street-lamp illuminated him clearly and pointed his trumpet directly up at Miss Lenaut and played loud and clear. She had to recognize him. For another moment she listened, without moving. Then she slammed the window down and pulled the blind.

French cunt, he thought, and finished the "*Marseillaise*" with a mocking sour note. He took the trumpet from his lips. The girl who had come out of the house next door was standing next to him. She put her arm around his neck and kissed him. The boys and girls around him cheered and the cannon went off. He grinned. The kiss was delicious. He knew the girl's address, too, now. He put the trumpet to his lips and began playing "Tiger Rag," as he marched, swinging, down the street. The boys and girls danced behind him in a gigantic swirling mass as they headed toward Main Street.

Victory was everywhere.

IV

She lit another cigarette. Alone in an empty house, she thought. She had closed all the windows, to mute the sounds from the town, the cheering and the noise of the fireworks and the blares of music. What did she have to celebrate? It was a night on which husbands turned to wives, children to parents, friends to friends, when even strangers embraced on street corners. Nobody had turned to her, she had been taken in no embrace.

She went into her daughter's room and turned on the light. the room was spotlessly clean, with the bedspread freshly ironed, a polished brass reading lamp, a brightly painted dressing table with jars and instruments of beauty. The tricks of the trade, Mary Jordache thought bitterly.

She went over to the small mahogany bookcase. The books were all neatly in place, carefully arranged. She took out the thick book of the works of Shakespeare. She opened it to where the envelope parted the pages of *Macbeth*. She peered into the envelope. The money was still there. Her daughter didn't even have the grace to try to hide it somewhere else, even knowing now that her mother knew. She took the envelope out of the Shakespeare and stuffed the book back carelessly on the shelf.

She took out another book at random, an anthology of English poetry Gretchen had used in her last year of high school. The fine food of her fine daughter's mind. She opened the book and put the envelope between the pages. Let her daughter worry about her money. If her father ever discovered there was eight hundred dollars in the house, she wouldn't find it just by going through her bookshelves.

She read a few lines.

Break, break, break,
On thy cold gray stones, O Sea!
And I would that my tongue could utter
The thoughts that arise in me.

Oh, fine, fine . . .

She put the book back in its place on the shelf. She didn't bother to turn out the light when she went out of the room.

She went into the kitchen. The pots and dishes that she had used for the dinner she had eaten alone that night lay unwashed in the sink. She doused her cigarette in a frying pan, half-filled with greasy water. She had had a pork chop for her dinner. Coarse food. She looked at the stove, turned on the gas in the oven. She dragged a chair over to the oven and opened the oven door and sat down and put her head in. The smell was unpleasant. She sat like that for a little while. Sounds of cheering in the town filtered in through the closed kitchen window. She had read somewhere that there were more suicides on holidays than at any other time, Christmas, New Year's. What better holiday would she ever find?

The smell of the gas grew stronger. She began to feel giddy. She took her head out of the oven and turned the gas off. There was no rush.

She went into the living room, mistress of the house. There was a faint smell of gas in the small room, with the four wooden chairs arranged geometrically around the square oak table in the center of the worn, reddish carpet. She sat down at the table, took a pencil out of her pocket and looked around for some paper, but there was only the student's exercise book in which she kept her daily accounts in the bakery. She never wrote letters and never received any. She tore several sheets of paper out of the back of the book and began to write on the ruled paper.

"Dear Gretchen," she wrote. "I have decided to kill myself. It is a mortal sin and I know it, but I can't go on any more. I am writing from one sinner to another. There is no need for me to say more. You know what I mean.

"There is a curse on this family. On me, on you, on your father and your brother Tom. Only your brother Rudolph may have escaped it and perhaps in the end he too will feel it. I am happy that I will not live to see that day. It is the curse of sex. I will tell you now something I have hidden from you all your life. I was an illegitimate child. I never knew my father or my mother. I cannot bear to think what sort of life my mother must have led and the degradation she must have wallowed in. That you should be following in her footsteps and have gone to the gutter should not surprise me. Your father is an animal. You sleep in the room next to ours, so you must know what I mean. He has crucified me on his lust for twenty years. He is a raging beast and there have been times when I was sure he was going to kill me. I have seen him nearly beat a man to death with his fists over an eight-dollar bakery bill. Your brother Thomas inherits from his father and it would not surprise me if he winds up in jail or worse. I am living in a cage of tigers.

"I am guilty, I suppose. I have been weak and I have permitted your father to drive me from the Church and to make heathens of my children. I was too worn out and beaten down to love you and protect you from your father and his influence. And you always seemed so neat and clean and well-behaved that my fears were put to sleep. With the results that you know better than I do."

She stopped writing and read what she had written with satisfaction. Finding her mother dead and this address from the grave on her pillow would poison the whore's guilty pleasures. Each time she allowed a man to put a hand on her, Gretchen would remember her mother's last words to her.

"Your blood is tainted," she wrote, "and it is now plain to me that your character is tainted too. Your room is clean and dainty but your soul is a stable. Your father should have married someone like you. You would have been fitting partners for each other. My last wish is for you to leave the house and go far away so that your influence cannot corrupt your brother Rudolph. If only one decent human being comes out of this terrible family, perhaps it will make a balance in God's eyes."

There was a confused sound of music and cheering growing stronger outside. Then she heard the trumpet, and recognized it. Rudolph was playing beneath the window. She got up from the table and opened the window and looked out. There he was, at the head of what looked like a thousand boys and girls, playing "When Irish Eyes Are Smiling," up to her.

She waved down at him, feeling the tears start. Rudolph ordered the boys with the cannon to fire a salute for her and the boom echoed along the street. She was crying frankly now and had to take out her handkerchief. With a last wave, Rudolph led his army down the street, his trumpet playing them on.

She went in and sat down at the table, sobbing. He has saved my life, she thought, my beautiful son has saved my life.

She tore up the letter and went into the kitchen and burned the scripts in the soup pot.

V

A good many of the soldiers were drunk. Everybody who could walk and get into a uniform had fled the hospital without waiting for passes as soon as the news had come over the radio, but some of them had come back with bottles and the common room smelled like a saloon as men in wheel chairs and on crutches reeled around the room, shouting and singing. The celebration had degenerated into destruction after supper and men were breaking windows with canes, tearing posters down from the walls, ripping books and magazines into handfuls of confetti, with which they conducted Mardi-gras battles amid drunken whoops of laughter.

"I am General George S. Patton," shouted a boy to no one in particular. He had a steel contraption around his shoulders that kept his shattered arm sticking out above his head. "Where's your necktie, soldier? Thirty years KP." Then he seized Gretchen with his good arm and insisted on dancing with her in the middle of the room to the tune of "Praise the Lord and Pass the Ammunition," which the other soldiers obligingly sang for him. Gretchen had to hold the boy tight to keep him from falling. "I'm the greatest, highest-class, one-armed 105-millimeter ballroom dancer in the world and I'm going to Hollywood tomorrow to waltz with Ginger Rogers. Marry me, baby, we'll live like kings on my total disability pension. We won the war, baby. We made the world safe for total disability." Then he had to sit down, because his knees wouldn't suppport him anymore. He sat on the floor and put his head between his knees and sang a verse of "Lili Marlene."

There was nothing Gretchen could do for any of them tonight. She kept a fixed smile on her face, trying to intervene when the confetti battles became too rough and looked as though they would become real fights. A nurse came to the door of the room and beckoned to Gretchen. Gretchen went over to her. "I think you'd better get out of here," the nurse said in a low, worried voice. "It's going to be wild in a little while."

"I don't really blame them," Gretchen said. "Do you?"

"I don't blame them," the nurse said, "but I'm staying out of their way."

There was a crash of glass from the room. A soldier had thrown an empty whiskey bottle through a window. "Fire for effect" the soldier said. He picked up a metal waste basket and hurled it through another window. "Put the mortars on the bastards, lieutenant. Take the high ground."

"It's a lucky thing they took their guns away from them before they came here," said the nurse. "This is worse than Normandy."

"Bring on the Japs," someone shouted. "I'll beat 'em to death with my first-aid kit. Banzai!"

The nurse tugged at Gretchen's sleeve. "Go on home," she said. "This is no place for a girl tonight. Come early tomorrow and help pick up the pieces."

Gretchen nodded and started toward the locker room to change, as the nurse disappeared. Then she stopped and turned back and went down the corridor from which the wards angled off. She went into the ward where the bad head and chest wounds were cared for. It was dimly lit here, and quiet. Most of the beds were empty, but here and there she could see a figure lying still under blankets. She went to the last bed in the corner, where Talbot Hughes lay, with the glucose dripping into his arm from the bottle rigged on its stand next to the bed. He was lying there with his eyes open, enormous and feverishly clear in the emaciated head. He recognized her and smiled. The shouting and singing from the distant common room sounded like the confused roar from a football stadium. She smiled down at him and sat on the edge of his bed. Although she had seen him only the night before he seemed to have grown ominously thinner in the last twenty-four hours. The bandages around his throat were the only solid thing about him. The doctor in the ward had told her Talbot was going to die within the week. There really was no reason for him to die, the wound was healing the doctor said, although he would never be able to speak again, of course. But by this time, by any normal calculation, he should have been taking nourishment and even walking around a little. Instead, he was fading quietly away day by day, politely and irresistibly insisting upon dying, making no fuss, a trouble to no one.

"Would you like me to read to you tonight?" Gretchen asked.

He shook his head on the pillow. Then he put out his hand toward hers. He grasped her hand. She could feel all the fragile birdlike bones. He smiled again and closed his eyes. She sat there, motionless, holding his hand. She sat like that for more than fifteen minutes, not saying anything. Then she saw that he was sleeping. She disengaged her hand gently, stood up, and walked softly out of the room. Tomorrow she would ask the doctor to tell her when he thought Talbot Hughes, victorious, was about to go. She would come and hold his hand, representative of his country's sorrow, so that he would not be alone when he died, twenty years old, everything unspoken.

She changed into her street clothes quickly and hurried out of the building.

As she went out the front door, she saw Arnold Simms leaning against the wall next to the door, smoking. This was the first time she had seen him since the night in the common room. She hesitated for a moment, then started toward the bus stop.

"Evenin', Miss Jordache." The remembered voice, polite, countrified.

Gretchen made herself stop. "Good evening, Arnold," she said. His face was bland, memoryless.

"The boys finally got themselves something to yell about, didn't they?" Arnold gestured with a little movement of his head toward the wing which contained the common room.

"They certainly did," she said. She wanted to get away, but didn't want to appear as if she were afraid of him.

"These little old Yoonited States went and did it," Arnold said. "'Twas a mighty fine effort, wouldn't you say?"

Now he was making fun of her. "We all should be very happy," she said. He had the trick of making her pompous.

"I'm very happy," he said. "Yes, indeed. Mighty happy. I got good news today, too. Special good news. That's why I waited on you out here. I wanted to tell you."

"What is it, Arnold?"

"I'm being discharged tomorrow," he said.

"That *is* good news," she said. "Congratulations."

"Yup," he said. "Officially, according to the Yoonited States Medical Corps, I can walk. Transportation orders to installation nearest point of induction and immediate processing of discharge from the service. This time next week I'll be back in St. Louis. Arnold Simms, the immediate civilian."

"I hope you'll be . . . " She stopped. She had nearly said happy, but that would have been foolish. "Lucky," she said. Even worse.

"Oh, I'm a lucky fella," he said "No one has to worry about l'il ole Arnold. Got some more good news this week. It was a big week for me, a giant of a week. I got a letter from Cornwall."

"Oh, isn't that nice." Prissy. "That girl you told me about wrote you." Palm trees. Adam and Eve in the Garden.

"Yep." He flicked away his cigarette. "She just found out her husband got killed in Italy and she thought I'd like to know."

There was nothing to say to this, so she kept quiet.

"Well, I won't be seeing you any more, Miss Jordache," he said, "unless you happen to be passin' through St. Louis. You can find me in the telephone book. I'll be in an exclusive residential district. I won't keep you no longer. I'm sure you got a victory ball or a country club dance to go to. I just wanted to thank you for everything you done for the troops, Miss Jordache."

"Good luck, Arnold." she said coldly.

"Too bad you didn't find the time to come on down to the Landing that Saturday," he said, drawling it out flately. "we got ourselves two fine chickens and roasted them and had ourselves quite a picnic. We missed you."

"I'd hoped you weren't going to talk about that, Arnold," she said. Hypocrite, hypocrite.

"Oh, God," he said, "you so beautiful I just want to sit down and cry."

He turned and opened the door to the hospital and limped in.

She walked slowly toward the bus stop, feeling battered. Victory solved nothing.

She stood under the light, looking at her watch, wondering if the bus drivers were also celebrating tonight. There was a car parked down the street in the shadow of a tree. The motor started up and it drove slowly toward her. It was Boylan's Buick. For a moment she thought of running back into the hospital.

Boylan stopped the car in front of her and opened the door. "Can I give you a lift, ma'am?"

"Thank you very much, no." She hadn't seen him for more than a month, not since the night they had driven to New York.

"I thought we might get together to offer fitting thanks to God for blessing our arms with victory," he said.

"I'll wait for the bus, thank you," she said.

"You got my letters, didn't you?" he asked.

"Yes." There had been two letters, on her desk at the office, asking her to meet him in front of Bernstein's Department Store. She hadn't met him and she hadn't answered the letters.

"Your reply must have been lost in the mail," he said. "The service these days is very hit and miss, isn't it?"

She walked away from the car. He got out and came up to her and held her arm.

"Come up to the house with me," he said harshly. "This minute."

His touch unnerved her. She hated him but she knew she wanted to be in his bed. "Let go of me," she said, and pulled her arm savagely out of his grasp. She walked back to the bus stop, with him following her.

"All right," he said. "I'll say what I came to say. I want to marry you."

She laughed. She didn't know why she laughed. Surprise.

"I said I want to marry you," he repeated.

"I'll tell you what," she said, "you go on down to Jamaica, as you planned, and I'll write you there. Leave your address with my secretary. Excuse me, here's my bus."

The bus rolled to a stop and she jumped up through the door as soon as it opened. She gave the driver her ticket and went and sat in the back by herself. She was trembling. If the bus hadn't come along, she would have said yes, she would marry him.

When the bus neared Port Philip she heard the fire engines and looked up the hill. There was a fire on the hill. She hoped it was the main building, burning to the ground.

VI

Claude hung on to him with his good arm, as Tom drove the bike down the narrow back road behind the Boylan estates. He hadn't had much practice and he had to go slowly and Claude moaned in his ear every time they skidded or hit a bump. Tom didn't know how bad the arm was, but he knew something had to be done about it. But if he took Claude to the hospital, they'd ask how he happened to get burned and it wouldn't take Sherlock Holmes to figure out the connection between the boy with the burned arm and the cross flaming on the Boylan hill. And Claude sure as hell wouldn't take the blame alone. Claude was no hero. He'd never die under torture with his secret forever clamped between his lips, that was for sure.

"Listen," Tom said, slowing the bike down so that they were hardly moving, "you got a family doctor?"

"Yeah," Claude said. "My uncle."

That was the kind of a family to have. Priests, doctors, there probably was a lawyer uncle, too, who would come in handy later on, after they were arrested.

"What's the address?" Tom asked.

Claude mumbled the address. He was so frightened he found it almost impossible to speak. Tom speeded up and keeping on back roads, found his way to the big house on the outskirts of the town, with the sign on the lawn that said, "Dr. Robert Tinker, M.D."

Tom stopped the bike and helped Claude off. "Listen," he said, "you're going in there alone, you understand, and no matter what you tell your uncle, you don't mention my name. And you better get your father to send you out of town tonight. There's going to be an awful mess in this town tomorrow and if anybody sees you walking around with a burned hand it'll take them just about ten seconds to come down on you like a load of bricks."

For answer, Claude moaned, and hung onto Tom's shoulder. Tom pushed him away. "Stand on your own two feet, man," Tom said. "Now get in there and make sure you see your uncle and nobody else. And if I ever find out that you gave me away I'll kill you."

"Tom," Claude whimpered.

"You heard me," Tom said. "I'll kill you. And you know I mean it." He pushed him toward the door of the house.

Claude staggered toward the door. He reached up his good hand and range the bell. Tom didn't wait to see him go in. He hurried off down the street. Above the town the fire was still blazing, lighting up the sky.

He went down to the river near the warehouse in which his father kept his shell. It was dark along the bank and here was the acid odor of rusting metal. He took off his sweater. It had the sick smell of burnt wool, like vomit. He found a stone and tied it into the sweater and heaved the bundle out into the river. There was a dull splash and he could see the little fountain of white water against the black of the current, as the sweater sank. He hated to lose the sweater. It was his lucky sweater. He had won a lot of fights while wearing it. But there were times when you had to get rid of things and this was one of them.

He walked away from the river toward home, feeling the chill of the night through his shirt. He wondered if he really was going to have to kill Claude Tinker.

CHAPTER 6

I

WITH HIS GERMAN food, Mary Jordache thought, as Jordache came in from the kitchen, carrying the roast goose on a platter with red cabbage and dumplings. Immigrant.

She didn't remember when she had seen her husband in such a high mood. The surrender of the Third Reich that week had made him jovial and expansive. He had devoured the newspapers, chuckling over the photographs of the German generals signing the papers at Rheims. Now, on Sunday, it was Rudolph's seventeenth birthday, and Jordache had decreed a holiday. No other birthday in the family was celebrated by more than a grunt. He had bought Rudolph a fancy fishing rod, God knew how much it cost, and had told Gretchen that she could keep half her salary from now on instead of the usual quarter. He had given Thomas the money for a new sweater to replace the one he said he lost. If the German army could be brought to surrender every week, life might be tolerable in the home of Axel Jordache.

"From now on," Jordache said, "we eat Sunday dinner together." The bloody defeat of his race, it seemed, had given him a sentimental interest in the ties of blood.

So they were all seated at the table, Rudolph self-consciously the focus of the occasion, wearing a collar and tie, and sitting very erect, like a cadet at table at West Point; Gretchen in a lacy, white shirtwaist looking as though butter wouldn't melt in her mouth, the whore; and Thomas, with his gambler's dodgy smile, all neatly washed and combed. Thomas had changed unaccountably since VE day, too, coming right home from school, studying all evening in his room, and even helping out in the shop for the first time in his life. The mother permitted herself the first glimmerings of timid hope. Perhaps by some unknown magic, the falling silent of the guns in Europe would make them a normal family.

Mary Jordache's idea of a normal American family was largely formed by the lectures of the nuns in the orphanage and later on by glances at the advertisements in popular magazines. Normal American families were always well-washed and fragrant and smiled at each other constantly. They showered each other with gifts for Christmas, birthdays, weddings, anniversaries, and Mother's Day. They had hale old parents who lived on farms in the country and at least one automobile. The sons called the father sir and the daughters played the piano and told their mothers about their dates and everybody used Listerine. They had breakfast, dinner, and Sunday lunch together and attended the church of their choice, and took holidays at the seashore en masse. The father commuted to business every day in a dark suit and had a great deal of life insurance. None of this was completely formulated in her mind, but it was the misty standard of reference against which she compared her own circumstances. Both too shy and too snobbish to mix with her own neighbors, the reality of the life of the other families who lived in the town was unknown to her. The rich were out of her reach and the poor were beneath her contempt. By her reckoning, hazy and unsystematic as it was, she, her husband, Thomas, and Gretchen, were not a family in any way that she could accept or that might give her pleasure. Rather they were an abrasive group collected almost at random for a voyage which none of them had chosen and during which the best that could be hoped for was that hostilities could be kept to a minimum.

Rudolph, of course, was excepted.

II

Axel Jordache put the goose down on the table with satisfaction. He had spent all morning preparing the meal, keeping his wife out of the kitchen, but without the usual insults about her cooking. He carved the bird roughly, but competently, and set out huge portions for all, serving the mother first, to her surprise. He had bought two bottles of California Riesling and he filled all their glasses ceremoniously. He raised his glass in a toast. "To my son Rudolph, on his birthday," he said huskily. "May he justify our hopes and rise to the top and not forget us when he gets there."

They all drank seriously, although the mother saw Thomas make a little grimace. Perhaps he thought the wine was sour.

Jordache did not specify just which top he expected his son to rise to. Specifications were unnecessary. The top existed, a place with boundaries, densities, privileges. When you got there you recognized it and your arrival was greeted with hosannahs and Cadillacs by earlier arrivals.

III

Rudolph ate the goose delicately. It was a little fatty to his taste and he knew that fact caused pimples. And he ate sparingly of the cabbage. He had a date later in the afternoon with the girl with the blonde pigtail who had kissed him outside Miss Lenaut's house and he didn't want to be smelling of cabbage when he met her. He only sipped at his wine. He had decided that he was never going to get drunk in his whole life. He was always going to be in full control of his mind and his body. He had also decided, because of the example of his mother and father, that he was never going to get married.

He had gone back to the house next to Miss Lenaut's the following day and loitered obviously across the street from it. Sure enough, after about ten minutes the girl had come out wearing blue jeans and a sweater and waved to him. She was just about his age, with bright-blue eyes and the open and friendly smile of someone who has never had anything bad happen to her. They had walked down the street together and in half an hour Rudolph felt that he had known her for years. She'd just moved into the neighborhood from Connecticut. Her name was Julie and her father had something to do with the Power Company. She had an older brother who was in the Army in France, and that was the reason she'd kissed him that night, to celebrate her brother's being alive in France with the war over for him. Whatever the reason, Rudolph was glad that she kissed him, although the memory of that first brush of the lips between strangers made him diffident and awkward for awhile.

Julie was crazy about music and liked to sing and thought he played a marvelous trumpet and he had half promised her that he would get his band to take her along with them to sing with them on their next club date.

She liked serious boys, Julie said, and there was no doubt about it, Rudolph was serious. He had already told Gretchen about Julie. He liked to keep saying her name. "Julie, Julie . . ." Gretchen had merely smiled, being a little bit too patronizingly grown-up for his taste. She had given him a blue-flannel blazer for his birthday.

He knew his mother would be disappointed that he wasn't going to take her for a walk this afternoon, but the way his father was behaving all of a sudden, the miracle might happen and his father might actually take her for a walk himself.

He wished he was as confident about getting to the top as his father and mother were. He was intelligent, but intelligent enough to know that intelligence by itself carried no guarantees along with it. For the kind of success his mother and father expected of him you had to have something special—luck, birth, a gift. He did not know yet if he was lucky. He certainly could not count upon his birth to launch him on a career and he was doubtful of his gifts. He was a connoisseur of others' gifts and an explorer of his own. Ralph Stevens, a boy in his class, could hardly make a *B* average overall, but he was a genius in mathematics and was doing problems in calculus and physics for fun while his classmates were laboring with elementary algebra. Ralph Stevens had a gift which directed his life like a magnet. He knew where he was going because it was the only way he could go.

Rudolph had many small talents and no definite direction. He wasn't bad on the horn, but he didn't fool himself that he was any Benny Goodman or Louis Armstrong. Of the four other boys who played in the band with him, two were better than he and the other two were just about as good. He listened to the music he made with a cool appreciation of what it was worth and he knew it wasn't worth much. And wouldn't be worth much more, no matter how hard he worked on it. As an athlete, he was top man in one event, the two-twenty hurdles, but in a big city high school, he doubted if he could even make the team, as compared with Stan O'Brien, who played fullback for the football team, and had to depend upon the tolerance of his teachers to get marks just good enough to keep him eligible to play. But on a football field O'Brien was one of the smartest players anybody had ever seen in the state. He could feint and find split-second holes and make the right move every time, with that special sense of a great ahtlete that no mere intelligence could ever compete with. Stan O'Brien had offers of scholarships from colleges as far away as California and if he didn't get hurt would probably make All-American and be set for life. In class, Rudolph did better on the English Literature tests than little Sandy Hopewood, who edited the school paper and who flunked all his science courses regularly, but all you had to do was read one article of his and you knew that nothing was going to stop Sandy from being a writer.

Rudolph had the gift of being liked. He knew that and knew that was why he had been elected president of his class three times in a row. But he felt it wasn't a real gift. He had to *plan* to be liked, to be agreeable to people, and seem interested in them, and cheerfully take on thankless jobs like running school dances and heading the advertising board of the magazine and working hard at them to get people to appreciate him. His gift of being liked wasn't a true gift, he thought, because he had no close friends and he didn't really like people himself very much. Even his habit of kissing his mother morning and evening and taking her for walks on Sundays was planned for her gratitude, to maintain the notion he knew she had of him as a thoughtful and loving son. The Sunday walks bored him and he really couldn't stand her pawing him when he kissed her, though, of course, he never showed it.

He felt that he was built in two layers, one that only he knew about and the other which was displayed to the world. He wanted to be what he seemed but he was doubtful that he could ever manage it. Although he knew that his mother and his sister and even some of his teachers thought he was handsome, he was uncertain about his looks. He felt he was too dark, that his nose was too long, his jaws too flat and hard, his pale eyes too light and too small for his olive skin, and his hair too lower-class dull black. He studied the photographs in the newspapers and the magazines to see how boys at good schools like Exeter and St. Paul's dressed and what college men at places like Harvard and Princeton were wearing, and tried to copy their styles in his own clothes and on his own budget.

He had scuffed white-buckskin shoes with rubber soles and now he had a blazer but he had the uneasy feeling that if he were ever invited to a party with a group of preppies he would stand out immediately for what he was, a small-town hick, pretending to be something he wasn't.

He was shy with girls and had never been in love, unless you could call that stupid thing for Miss Lenaut love. He made himself seem uninterested in girls, too busy with more important matters to bother with kid stuff like dating and flirting and necking. But in reality he avoided the company of girls because he was afraid that if he ever got really close to one, she would find out that behind his lofty manner he was inexperienced and clownish.

In a way he envied his brother. Thomas wasn't living up to anyone's estimate of him. His gift was ferocity. He was feared and even hated and certainly no one truly liked him, but he didn't agonize over which tie to wear or what to say in an English class. He was all of one piece and when he did something he didn't have to make a painful and hesitant selection of attitudes within himself before he did it.

As for his sister, she was beautiful, a lot more beautiful than most of the movie stars he saw on the screen, and that gift was enough for anybody.

"This goose is great, Pop," Rudolph said, because he knew his father expected him to comment on the meal. "It really is something." He had already eaten more than he wanted, but he held out his plate for a second portion. He tried not to wince when he saw the size of the piece that his father put on the plate.

IV

Gretchen ate quitcly. When am I going to tell them, what's the best moment? On Friday she had been given two weeks notice at the Works. Mr. Hutchens had called her into his office and after a little distracted preliminary speech about how efficient she was and conscientious and how her work was always excellent and how agreeable it was to have her in the office, he had come out with it. He had received orders that morning to give her notice, along with another girl in the office. He had gone to the manager to remonstrate, Mr. Hutchens said, his dry voice clicking with real distress, but the manager had said he was sorry, there was nothing he could do about it. With the end of the war in Europe there were going to be cutbacks on government contracts. A falling-off in business was expected and they had to economize on staff. Gretchen and the other girl were the last two clerks to be hired in Mr. Hutchens' department and so they had to be the first to go. Mr. Hutchens had been so disturbed that he had taken out his handkerchief several times while talking to her and blown his nose aridly, to prove to her that it was none of his doing. Three decades of working with paper had left Mr. Hutchens rather papery himself, like a paid bill that has been tucked away for many years and is brittle and yellowed and flaking at the edges, when it is brought out to be examined. The emotion in his voice as he spoke to her was incongruous, like tears from a filing cabinet.

Gretchen had to console Mr. Hutchens. She had no intention of spending the rest of her life working for the Boylan Brick and Tile Works, she told him, and she understood why the last to be hired had to be the first to go. She did not tell Mr. Hutchens the real reason why she was being fired and she felt guilty about the other girl, who was being sacrificed as camouflage to Teddy Boylan's act of vengeance.

She had not yet figured out what she was going to do and she hoped to be able to wait until her plans were set before telling her father about her dismissal. There was bound to be an ugly scene and she wanted to have her defenses ready. Today, though, her father was behaving like a human being for once, and perhaps at the end of the meal, ripened by wine and basking in his pleasure in the one child, he might prove to be lenient with another. With the dessert, she decided.

V

Jordache had baked a birthday cake and he came in from the kitchen carrying it, eighteen candles alight on the icing, seventeen and one to grow on, and they all actually were singing "Happy birthday to you, dear Rudolph," when the doorbell rang. The sound stopped the song in mid-verse. The doorbell almost never rang in the Jordache house. No one ever came to visit them and the mailman dropped the letters through a slot.

"Who the hell is that?" Jordache asked. He reacted pugnaciously to all surprises, as though anything new could only be an attack of one kind or another.

"I'll go," Gretchen said. She had the instantaneous certainty that it must be Boylan downstairs at the door, with the Buick parked in front of the shop. It was just the sort of demented thing he was liable to do. She was running down the stairs as Rudolph blew out the candles. She was glad that she was all dressed up and had done her hair that morning for Rudolph's party. Let Teddy Boylan mourn over what he was never going to get anymore.

When she opened the door, there were two men standing there. She knew them both, Mr. Tinker and his brother, the priest. She knew Mr. Tinker from the Works and everybody knew Father Tinker, a burly, red-faced man, who looked like a longshoreman who had made a mistake in his profession.

"Good afternoon, Miss Jordache," Mr. Tinker said, taking off his hat. His voice was sober, and his long, flabby face looked as though he had just discovered a terrible error in the books.

"Hello, Mr. Tinker. Father," Gretchen said.

"I hope we're not interrupting anything," Mr. Tinker said, his voice more ceremoniously churchly than that of his ordained brother. "But we have to speak to your father. Is he in?"

"Yes," Gretchen said. "If you'll come up . . . We're just at dinner, but . . . "

"I wonder if you'd be good enough to ask him to come down, child," said the priest. He had the round, assured voice of a man who inspried confidence in women. "We have a most important matter to discuss with him in private."

"I'll go get him," Gretchen said. The men came into the dark little hallway and shut the door behind them, as though unwilling to be observed from the street. Gretchen put the light on. She felt peculiar about leaving the two men standing crowded together in the dark. She hurried up the steps, knowing that the Tinker brothers were looking at her legs as she mounted.

Rudolph was cutting the cake as she went into the living room. Everybody looked at her inquiringly.

"What the hell was that about?" Jordache asked.

"Mr. Tinker's down there," Gretchen said. "With his brother, the priest. They want to speak to you, Pa."

"Well, why didn't you ask them to come up?" Jordache accepted a slice of cake on a plate from Rudolph and took a huge bite.

"They didn't want to. They said they had a most important matter to discuss with you in private."

Thomas made a little sucking sound, pulling his tongue over his teeth, as though he had a morsel of food caught between one tooth and another.

Jordache pushed back his chair. "Christ," he said, "a priest. You'd think the bastards would at least leave a man in peace on a Sunday afternoon." But he stood up and went out of the room. They could hear his heavy limping tread as he descended the staircase.

Jordache didn't greet the two men standing in the feeble light of the forty-watt bulb in the hallway. "Well, gentlemen," he said, "what the hell is so important that you've got to take a working man away from his Sunday dinner to talk about?"

"Mr. Jordache," Tinker said, "could we talk to you in private?"

"What's wrong with right here?" Jordache asked, standing above them on the last step, still chewing on his cake. The hallway smelled of the goose.

Tinker looked up the stairway. "I wouldn't like to be overheard," he said.

"As far as I can tell," Jordache said, "we got nothing to say to each other that the whole goddamn town can't hear. I don't owe you any money and you don't owe me none." Still, he took the step down into the hallway and opened the door to the street and unlocked the front door of the bakery with the key he always carried in his pocket.

The three men went into the bakery, its big window covered from within by a canvas blind for Sunday.

VI

Upstairs, Mary Jordache was waiting for the coffee to boil. Rudolph kept looking at his watch, worried that he'd be late for his date with Julie. Thoms sat slumped in his chair, humming tunelessly and tapping an annoying rhythm on his glass with his fork.

"Stop that, please," the mother said. "You're giving me a headache."

"Sorry," Thomas said. "I'll take up the trumpet for my next concert."

Never a courteous moment, Mary Jordache thought. "What's keeping them down there?" she asked querulously. "The one day we're having a normal family meal." She turned accusingly on Gretchen. "You work with Mr. Tinker," she said. "Have you done something disgraceful downtown?"

"Maybe they discovered I stole a brick," Gretchen said.

"Even one day," her mother said, "is too much for this family to be polite." She went into the kitchen to get the coffee, her back a drama of martyrdom.

There was the sound of Jordache coming up the staircase. He came into the living room, his face expressionless. "Tom," he said flatly, "come on downstairs."

"I got nothing to say to the Tinker family," Thomas said.

"They got something to say to you." Jordache turned and went out of the room and down the stairs again. Thomas shrugged. He pulled at his fingers, tugging with one hand against the other, the way he did before a fight, and followed his father.

Gretchen frowned. "Do you know what it's all about?" she asked Rudolph.

"Trouble," Rudolph said gloomily. He knew he was going to be late for Julie.

VII

In the bakery the two Tinkers, one in a navy-blue suit and the other in his shiny, black, priest's suit, looked like two ravens against the bare shelves and the gray marble counter. Thomas came in and Jordache closed the door behind him.

I'm going to have to kill him, Thomas thought. "Good afternoon, Mr Tinker," he said, smiling boyishly. "Good afternoon, Father."

"My son," the priest said portentously.

"Tell him what you told me," Jordache said.

"We know all about it, son," the priest said. "Claude confessed everything to his uncle, as was only right and natural. From confession flows repentance and from repentance forgiveness."

"Save that crap for Sunday school," Jordache said. He was leaning with his back against the door, as though to make sure nobody was going to escape.

Thomas didn't say anything. He was wearing his little prefight smile.

"The shameful burning of the cross," the priest said. "On a day consecrated to the memory of the brave young men who have fallen in the struggle. On a day when I celebrated a holy mass for the repose of their souls at the altar of my own church. And with all the trials and intolerance we Catholics have undergone in this country and our bitter efforts to be accepted by our bigoted countrymen. And to have the deed perpetrated by two Catholic boys." He shook his head sorrowfully.

"He's no Catholic," Jordache said.

"His mother and father were born in the Church," the priest said. "I have made inquiries."

"Did you do it or didn't you do it?" Jordache asked.

"I did it," Thomas said. That yellow, gutless son of a bitch Claude.

"Can you imagine, my son," the priest went on, "what would happen to your family and Claude's family if it ever became known who raised that flaming cross?"

"We'd be driven out of town," Mr. Tinker said excitedly. "That's what would happen. Your father wouldn't be able to *give* away a loaf of bread in this town. The people of this town remember you're foreigners, Germans, even if you'd like to forget it."

"Oh, Christ, now," Jordache said. "The red, white, and blue."

"Facts are facts," Mr. Tinker said. "You might as well face it. I'll give you another fact. If Boylan ever finds out who it was that set fire to his greenhouse he'll sue us for our lives. He'll get a smart lawyer that'll make that old greenhouse seem like the most valuable property between here and New York." He shook his fist at Thomas. "Your father won't have two pennies to rub against each other in his pocket. You're minors. *We're* responsible, your father and me. The savings of a lifetime . . . "

Thomas could see his father's hands working, as though he would like to put them around Thomas's neck and strangle him.

"Keep calm, John," the priest said to Tinker. "There's no sense in getting the boy too upset. We have to depend upon his good sense to save us all." He turned to Thomas. "I will not ask you what devilish impulse moved you to incite our Claude to do this awful dead . . . "

"He said it was my idea?" Thomas asked.

"A boy like Claude," the priest said, "growing up in a Christian home, going to Mass every Sunday, would never dream up a desperate scheme like that on his own."

"Okay," Thomas said. He sure as hell was going to be out looking for Claude.

"Luckily," the priest went on, in measured Gregorian tones, "when Claude visited his uncle, Dr. Robert Tinker, that awful night, with his cruelly wounded arm, Dr. Tinker was alone, He treated the boy and extracted the story from him and took him home in his own car. By the grace of God, he was not observed. But the burns are severe and Claude will be in bandages for at least three more weeks. It was not possible to keep him hidden at home safely until he was fully recovered. A maid might become suspicious, a delivery boy might get a glimpse of him, a school friend might pay a visit out of pity . . . "

"Oh, Christ, Anthony," Mr. Tinker said, "get out of the pulpit!" His face pale and working convulsively, his eyes bloodshot, he strode over to Thomas. "We drove the little bastard down to New York last night and we put him on a plane to California this morning. He's got an aunt in San Francisco and he'll be stashed away until he can get the bandages off and then he's going to military school and I don't care if he doesn't come back to this town before he's ninety. And if he knows what's good for him your father'd damn well better get you out of town, too. As far away as possible, where nobody knows you and nobody'll ask any questions."

"Don't worry, Tinker," Jordache said. "He'll be out of town by nightfall."

"He'd better be," Tinker said threateningly.

"All right now." Jordache opened the door. "I've had enough of the both of you. Get out."

"I think we ought to go now, John," the priest said. "I'm certain Mr. Jordache will do the proper thing."

Tinker had to get in the last word. "You're being let off easy," he said. "All of you." He marched out of the store.

"God forgive you, my son," the priest said, and followed his brother.

Jordache locked the door and faced Thomas. "You've hung a sword over my head, you little shit," he said. "You've got something coming to you." He limped toward Thomas and swung his fist. It landed high on Thomas's head. Thomas staggered and then, instinctively, hit back, going off the floor and catching his father flush on the temple with the hardest right hand he had ever thrown. Jordache didn't fall, but swayed a little, his hands out in front of him. He stared disbelieving at his son, at the blue eyes icy with hatred. Then he saw Thomas smile and drop his hands to his side.

"Go ahead and get it over with," Thomas said contemptuously. "Sonny boy won't hit his brave daddy any more."

Jordache swung once more. The left side of Thomas's face began to swell immediately and became an angry wine red, but he merely stood there, smiling.

Jordache dropped his hands. The one blow had been a symbol, nothing more. Meaningless, he though dazedly. Sons.

"Okay," he said. "That's over. Your brother's going to take you on the bus to Grafton. From there you'll take the first train to Albany. In Albany you'll change for Ohio. Alone. My brother'll have to take care of you. I'll call him today and he'll be expecting you. Don't bother packing. I don't want anybody to see you leaving town with a valise." He unlocked the bakery door. Thomas went out, blinking in the Sunday afternoon sunlight.

"You wait here," Jordache said. "I'll send your brother down. I don't fancy any farewell scenes with your mother." He locked the bakery door and limped into the house.

Only after his father was gone did Thomas touch the tender, swollen side of his jaw.

VIII

Ten minutes later, Jordache and Rudolph came down. Thomas was leaning against the bakery window, staring calmly across the street. Rudolph was carrying the jacket of Thomas's one suit; striped and greenish. It had been bought two years before and was too small for him. He couldn't move his shoulders freely when he put it on and his hands dangled far out of the tight sleeves.

Rudolph looked dazed and his eyes widened when he saw the welt on Thomas's cheek. Jordache had the appearance of a sick man. Under the naturally dark tint of his skin, there was a wash of pallid green and his eyes were puffy. One punch, Thomas thought, and look what happens to him.

"Rudolph knows what he has to do," Jordache said. "I gave him some money. He'll buy your ticket to Cleveland. Here's your uncle's address." He handed Thomas a slip of paper.

I'm moving up in class, Thomas thought, I have uncles for emergencies, too. Call me Tinker.

"Now get moving," Jordache said. "And keep your trap shut."

The boys stared down the street. Jordache watched, feeling the vein throb in his temple where Thomas had hit him and not seeing anything clearly. His sons moved off in a blur down the sunny empty slum street, the one tallish and slender and well dressed in the gray-flannel slacks and a blue blazer, the other almost as tall but wider and looking childish in the jacket that was too small for him. When the boys had disappeared around a corner, Jordache turned and walked in the opposite direction, toward the river. This was one afternoon he had to be alone. He would call his brother later. His brother and his wife were just slobs enough to take in the son of a man who had kicked them out of his house and hadn't even said thank you for the yearly Christmas card that was the only evidence that two men who had been born long ago in the same house in Cologne and who were living in different parts of America were, in fact, brothers. He could just hear his brother saying to his fat wife, in that ineradicable German accent, "After all, vat can ve do? Blut is thicker than vater."

"What the hell happened?" Rudolph asked as soon as they were out of their father's sight.

"Nothing," Thomas said.

"He hit you," Rudolph said. "Your jaw's a sight."

"It was a terrible blow," Thomas said mockingly. "He's next in line for a shot at the title."

"He came upstairs looking sick," Rudolph said.

"I clipped him one." Thomas grinned, remembering.

"You *hit* him?"

"Why not?" Thomas said. "What's a father for?"

"Christ! And you're still alive?"

"I'm alive," said Thomas.

"No wonder he's getting rid of you." Rudolph shook his head. He couldn't help being angry at Thomas. Because of Thomas he was missing his date with Julie. He would have liked to pass her house, it was only a few blocks out of the way to the bus station, but his father had said he wanted Thomas out of town immediately and with nobody knowing about it. "What the hell is the matter with you, anyway?"

"I'm a high-spirited, red-blooded, normal American boy," Thomas said.

"It must be real trouble," Rudolph said. "He gave me fifty bucks for the train fare. Anytime he shells out fifty bucks, it must be something enormous."

"I was discovered spying for the Japs," Thomas said placidly.

"Oh, boy, you're smart" Rudolph said, and they walked the rest of the way to the bus station in silence.

They got off the bus at Gratfon near the railroad station and Thomas sat under a tree in a little park across the square from the station while Rudolph went in to see about Thomas's ticket. The next train to Albany was in fifteen minutes and Rudolph bought the ticket from the wizened man with a green eyeshade behind the wicket. He didn't buy the ticket for the connection to Cleveland. His father had told him he didn't want anybody to know Thomas's final destination, so Thomas was going to have to buy the ticket himself at the station in Albany.

As he took the change, Rudolph had an impulse to buy another ticket for himself. In the opposite direction. To New York. Why should Thomas be the first one to escape? But of course, he didn't buy any ticket to New York. He went out of the station and past the dozing drivers waiting in their 1939 taxis for the arrival of the next train. Thomas was sitting on a bench under a tree, his legs sprawled out in a *V*, his heels dug into the scrubby lawn. He looked unhurried and peaceful, as though nothing was happening to him.

Rudolph glanced around to make sure nobody was watching them. "Here's your ticket," he said, handing it to Thomas, who looked at it lazily. "Put it away, put it away," Rudolph said. "And here's the change for the fifty dollars. Forty-two fifty. For your ticket from Albany. You'll have a lot left over, the way I figure it."

Thomas pocketed the money without counting it. "The old man must have shit blood," Thomas said, "when he took it out from wherever he hides his dough. Did you see where he keeps it?"

"No."

"Too bad. I could come back some dark night and lift it. Although I don't suppose you'd tell me, even if you knew. Not my brother Rudolph."

They watched a roadster drive up with a girl at the wheel and a lieutenant in the Air Force beside her. They got out of the car and went into the shade of the tiled overhang of the depot. Then they stopped and kissed. The girl was wearing a pale-blue dress and the summery wind twirled it around her legs. The lieutenant was tall and very tan, as though he had been in the desert. He had medals and wings on his green Eisenhower jacket and he was carrying a stuffed flight bag. Rudolph heard the roar of a thousand engines in foreign skies as he watched the couple. Again, he felt the pang because he had been born too late and missed the war.

"Kiss me, darling," Thomas said, "I bombed Tokyo."

"What the hell are you proving?" Rudolph said.

"You ever get laid?" Thomas asked.

The echo of his father's question the day Jordache hit Miss Lenaut disturbed Rudolph. "What's it to you?"

Thomas shrugged, watching the two people go through the open door of the station. "Nothing. I just thought I'm going to be away a long time, maybe we ought to have a heart-to-heart talk."

"Well, if you must know, I haven't," Rudolph said stiffly.

"I was sure of it," Thomas said. "There's a place called Alice's in town on McKinley, you can get a good piece of tail for five bucks. Tell them your brother sent you."

"I'll take care of myself my own way," Rudolph said. Although he was a year older than Thomas, Thomas was making him feel like a kid.

"Our loving sister is getting hers regularly," Thomas said. "Did you know that?"

"That's her business." But Rudolph was shocked. Gretchen was so *clean* and neat and politely spoken. He couldn't imagine her in the sweaty tangle of sex.

"Do you want to know who with?"

"No."

"Theodore Boylan," Thomas said. "How do you like that for class?"

"How do you know?" Rudolph was sure that Thomas was lying.

"I went up and watched through the window," Thomas said. "He came down into the living room bare-assed, with his thing hanging down to his knees, he's a regular horse, and made two whiskies and called up the stairs, 'Gretchen, do you want your drink up there or do you want to come down for it?' " Thomas simpered as he imitated Bolyan.

"Did she come down?" Rudolph didn't want to hear the rest of the story.

"No. I guess she was having too good a time where she was."

"So you didn't see whoever it was." Rudolph fell back on logic to preserve his sister. "It might have been anybody up there."

"How many Gretchens you know in Port Philip?" Thomas said. "Anyway, Claude Tinker saw them drive up the hill together in Boylan's car. She meets him in front of Bernstein's when she's supposed to be at the hospital. Maybe Boylan got wounded in a war, too. The Spanish-American War."

"Jesus," Rudolph said. "With an ugly old man like Boylan." If it had been with someone like the young lieutenant who had just gone into the station, she would still have remained his sister.

"She must be getting something out of it," Thomas said carelessly. "Ask her."

"You ever tell her you knew?"

"Nah. Let her screw in peace. It's not my cock. I just went up there for laughs," Thomas said. "She don't mean anything to me. La-di-da, la-di-da, where do babies come from, Mummy?"

Rudolph wondered how his brother could have perfected his hatred so young.

"If we were Italians or something," Thomas said, "or Southern gentlemen, we'd go up that hill and avenge the honor of the family. Cut off his balls or shoot him or something. I'm busy this year, but if you want to do it, I give you permission."

"Maybe you'll be surprised," Rudolph said. "Maybe I will do something."

"I bet," Thomas said. "Anyway, just for your information, I've already done something."

"What?"

Thomas looked consideringly at Rudolph. "Ask your father," he said, "he knows." He stood up. "Well, I better be getting along. The train's due."

They went out onto the platform. The lieutenant and the girl were kissing again. He might never come back, this might be the last kiss, Rudolph thought; after all, they were still fighting out in the Pacific, there were still the Japanese. The girl was weeping as she kissed the lieutenant and he was patting her back with one hand to comfort her. Rudolph wondered if there ever would be a girl who would cry on a station platform because he had to leave her.

The train came in with a whoosh of country dust. Thomas swung up onto the steps.

"Look," Rudolph said, "if there's anything you want from the house, write me. I'll get it to you somehow."

"There's nothing I want from that house," Thomas said. His rebellion was pure and complete. The undeveloped, childish face seemed merry, as if he were going to a circus.

"Well," Rudolph said lamely. "Good luck." After all, he was his brother and God knew when they would ever see each other again.

"Congratulations," Thomas said. "Now you got the whole bed to yourself. You don't have to worry about my smelling like a wild animal. Don't forget to wear your pajamas."

Giving nothing, right up to the last moment, he went into the vestibule and into the car without looking back. The train started and Rudolph could see the lieutenant standing at an open window waving to the girl, who was running along the platform.

The train gathered speed and the girl stopped running. She became conscious of Rudolph looking at her and her face closed down, erasing public sorrow, public love. She wheeled and hurried off, the wind whipping her dress about her body. Warrior's woman.

Rudolph went back to the park and sat on the bench again and waited for the bus back to Port Philip.

What a goddamn birthday.

IX

Gretchen was packing a bag. It was a big, frayed, yellow-stippled, cardboardish rectangle, studded with brass knobs, that had held her mother's bridal trousseau when she arrived in Port Philip. Gretchen had never spent a night away from home in her whole life so she had never had a valise of her own. When she had made her decision, after her father had come up from the conference with Thomas and the Tinkers, to announce that Thomas was going away for a long time, Gretchen had climbed to the narrow little attic where the few things that the Jordaches had collected and had no further use for were stored. She had found the bag and brought it down to her own room. Her mother had seen her with the bag and must have guessed what it meant, but had said nothing. Her mother hadn't talked to her in weeks, ever since the night she had come in at dawn after the trip to New York with Boylan. It was as though she felt that conversation between them brought with it the contagion of Gretchen's rank corruption.

The air of crisis, of hidden conflicts, the strange look in her father's eyes when he had come back into the living room and told Rudolph to come with him, had finally pushed Gretchen to action. There would never be a better day to leave than this Sunday afternoon.

She packed carefully. The bag wasn't big enough to take everything she might need and she had to choose deliberately, putting things in, then taking them out in favor of other things that might be more useful. She hoped that she could get out of the house before her father came back, but she was prepared to face him and tell him that she had lost her job and was going down to New York to look for another. There had been something in his face as he started downstairs with Rudolph that was passive and stunned and she guessed that today might be the one day she could walk past him without a struggle.

She had to turn almost every book upside down before she found the envelope with the money in it. That crazy game her mother played. There was a fifty-fifty chance that her mother would wind up in an asylum. Eventually, she hoped, she would be able to learn to pity her.

She was sorry that she was going without a chance to say good-bye to Rudolph but it was growing dark already and she didn't want to reach New York after midnight. She had no notion of where she was going to go in New York. There must be a Y.W.C.A. somewhere. Girls had spent their first nights in New York in worse places.

She looked around her stripped room without emotion. Her good-bye to her room was flippant. She took the envelope, now empty of money, and laid it squarely in the middle of her narrow bed.

She lugged the suitcase out into the hallway. She could see her mother sitting at the table, smoking. The remains of the dinner, the goose carcass, the cold cabbage, the dumplings jellied in slime, the stained napkins, had remained untouched all these hours on the table, as her mother had sat there, wordless, staring at the wall. Gretchen went into the room. "Ma," she said, "this is going-away day, I guess. I'm packed and I'm leaving."

Her mother turned her head slowly and blearily toward her. "Go to your fancy man," she said thickly. Her vocabulary of abuse dated from earlier in the century. She had finished all the wine and she was drunk. It was the first time Gretchen had seen her mother drunk and it made her want to laugh.

"I'm not going to anybody," she said. "I lost my job and I'm going to New York to look for another one. When I'm settled, I'll write you and let you know."

"Harlot," the mother said.

Gretchen grimaced. Who said harlot in 1945? It made her going unimportant, comic. But she forced herself to kiss her mother's cheek. The skin was rough and seamed with broken capillaries.

"False kisses," the mother said, staring. "The dagger in the rose."

What books she must have read as a young girl!

The mother pushed back a wisp of hair from her forhead with the back of her hand, in the gesture that had been weary since she was twenty-one years old. It occurred to Gretchen that her mother had been born worn out and that much should be forgiven her because of it. For a moment she hesitated, searching for some vestige of affection within her for the drunken woman sitting wearthed in smoke at the cluttered table.

"Goose," her mother said disdainfully. "Who eats goose?"

Gretchen shook her head hopelessly and went out into the hallway and picked up the bag and struggled down the staircase with it. She unlocked the door below and pushed the suitcase out over the sill into the street. The sun was just setting and the shadows on the street were violet and indigo. As she picked up the bag, the streetlamps went on, lemony and pale, doing premature and useless service.

Then she saw Rudolph hurrying down the street toward the house. He was alone. She put down her bag and waited for him. As he approached she thought how well the blazer fit him, how neat he looked, and was glad she had spent the money.

When Rudolph saw her, he broke into a run. "Where're *you* going?" he said as he came up to her.

"New York," she said lightly. "Come along?"

"I wish I could," he said.

"Help a lady to a taxi?"

"I want to talk to you," he said.

"Not here," she said, glancing at the bakery window. "I want to get away from here."

"Yeah," Rudolph said, picking up her bag. "This is for sure no place to talk."

They started down the street together to look for a taxi. Good-bye, good-bye, Gretchen sang to herself, as she passed the familiar names, good-bye Clancy's Garage, Body Work, good-bye Soriano's Hand Laundry, good-bye Bolton's Drug Store, good-bye Wharton's Paints and Hardware, good-bye Bruno's Barber Shop, good-bye Jardino's Fruits and Vegetables. The song inside her head was lilting as she walked briskly beside her brother, but there was a minor undertone in it. You leave no place after nineteen years without regrets.

They found a taxi two blocks father on and drove to the station. While Gretchen went over to the window to buy her ticket, Rudolph sat on the old-fashioned valise, thinking, I am spending my eighteenth year saying good-bye in every station of the New York Central railroad.

Rudolph couldn't help but feeling a little bruised by the rippling lightness in his sister's movements and the pinpoints of joy in her eyes. After all, she was not only leaving home, she was leaving *him*. He felt strange with her now, since he knew she had made love with a man. *Let her screw in peace.* He must find a more melodious vocabulary.

She touched him on the sleeve. "The train won't be along for more than a half hour," she said. "I feel like a drink. Celebrate. Put the valise in the baggage room and we'll go across the street to the Port Philip House."

Rudolph picked up the valise. "I'll carry it," he said. "It costs ten cents in the baggage room."

"Let's be big for once." Gretchen laughed. "Squander our inheritance. Let the dimes flow."

As he took a check for the valise, he wondered if she had been drinking all afternoon.

The bar of the Port Philip House was empty except for two soldiers who were moodily staring at glasses of wartime beer near the entrance. The bar was dark and cool and they could look out through the windows at the station, its lights now on in the dusk. They sat at a table near the back and when the bartender came over to them, wiping his hands on his apron, Gretchen said, firmly, "Two Black and White and soda, please."

The barman didn't ask whether or not they were over eighteen. Gretchen had ordered as if she had been drinking whiskey in bars all her life.

Actually, Rudolph would have preferred a Coke. The afternoon had been too full of occasions.

Gretchen poked at his check with two fingers. "Don't look so glum," she said. "It's your birthday."

"Yeah," he said.

"Why did Pa send Tommy away?"

"I don't know. Neither of them would tell me. Something happened with the Tinkers. Tommy hit Pa. I know *that*."

"Wooh . . . " Gretchen said softly. "Quite a day, isn't it?"

"It sure is," Rudolph said. It was a bigger day than she realized, he thought, remembering what Tom had told him earlier about her. The barman came over with their drinks and a siphon bottle. "Not too much soda, please," Gretchen said.

The barman splashed some soda in Gretchen's glass. "How about you?" He held the siphon over Rudolph's glass.

"The same," Rudolph said, acting eighteen.

Gretchen raised her glass. "To that well-known ornament to Port Philip society," she said, "the Jordache family."

They drank. Rudolph had not yet developed a taste for Scotch. Gretchen drank thirstily, as though she wanted to finish the first one fast, so that there would be time for another one before the train came in.

"What a family." She shook her head. "The famous Jordache collection of authentic mummies. Why don't you get on the train with me and come live in New York?"

"You know I can't do that," he said.

"I thought I couldn't do it, too," she said. "And I'm doing it."

"Why?"

"Why what?"

"Why're you going? What happened?"

"A lot of things," she said vaguely. She took a long swig of her whiskey. "A man mostly." She looked at him defiantly. "A man wants to marry me."

"Who? Boylan?"

Her eyes dilated, grew darker in the dim saloon. "How do you know?"

"Tommy told me."

"How does he know?"

Well, why not, he thought. She asked for it. Jealousy and shame for her made him want to hurt her. "He went up to the hill and looked in through a window."

"What did he see?" she asked coldly.

"Boylan. Naked."

"He didn't get much of a show, poor Tommy." She laughed. The laugh was metallic. "He's not much to look at, Teddy Boylan. Did he have the good luck to see me naked, too?"

"No."

"Too bad," she said. "It would have made his trip worthwhile." There was something hard and self-wounding in his sister that Rudolph had never seen in her before. "How did he know I was there?"

"Boylan called upstairs to ask you 'if you wanted to have your drink there."

"Oh," she said. "That night. That was a big night. Some time I'll tell you about it." She studied his face. "Don't look so stormy. Sisters have a habit of growing up and going out with fellas."

"But Boylan," he said bitterly. "That puny old man."

"He's not that old," she said. "And not that puny."

"You liked him," he said accusingly.

"I liked *it*," she said. Her face became very sober. "I liked it better than anything that ever happened to me."

"Then why're you running away?"

"Because if I stay here long enough, I'll wind up marrying him. And Teddy Boylan's not fit for your pure, beautiful little sister to marry. It's complicated, isn't it? Is your life complicated, too? Is there some dark, sinful passion you're nursing in your bosom, too? An older woman you visit while her husband's at the office, a . . . ?"

"Don't make fun of me," he said.

"Sorry." She touched his hand, then gestured toward the bartender. When he came over, she said, "One more, please." As the bartender went back to fill the order, she said, "Ma was drunk when I left. She finished all your birthday wine. The blood of the lamb. That's all that family needs—" She spoke as though they were discussing the idiosyncracies of strangers. "A drunken crazy old lady. She called me a harlot." Gretchen chuckled. "A last loving farewell to the girl going to the big city. Get out," She said harshly, "get out before they finish crippling you. Get out of that house where nobody has a friend, where the doorbell never rings."

"I'm not crippled," he said.

"You're frozen in an act, Brother." The hostility was out in the open now. "You don't fool me. Everybody's darling, and you don't give a good goddamn if the whole world lives or dies. If that's not being crippled, put me in a wheelchair any day."

The bartender came over and put her drink down in front of her and half filled the glass with soda.

"What the hell," Rudolph said, standing up, "If that's what you think of me, there's no sense in my hanging around any more. You don't need me."

"No, I don't," she said.

"Here's the ticket for your bag." He handed her the slip of paper.

"Thanks," she said woodenly. "You've done your good deed for the day. And I've done mine."

He left her sitting there in the bar, drinking her second whiskey, her lovely, oval face flushed at the cheek bones, her eyes shining, her wide mouth avid, beautiful, hungry, bitter, already a thousand miles removed from the dingy apartment above the bakery, removed from her father and mother, her brothers, her lover, on her way to a city that engulfed a million girls a year.

He walked slowly toward home, tears for himself in his eyes. They were right, they were right about him, his brother, his sister; their judgments on him were just. He had to change. How do you change, what do you change? Your genes, your chromosomes, your sign of the zodiac?

As he neared Vanderhoff Street, he stopped. He couldn't bear the thought of going home yet. He didn't want to see his mother drunk, he didn't want to see that stunned, hating look, like a disease, in his father's eyes. He walked down toward the river. There was a faint afterglow from the sunset and the river slid by like wet steel, with a smell like a deep, cool cellar in chalky ground. He sat on the rotting wharf near the warehouse in which his father kept his shell and looked out toward the opposite shore.

Far out, he could see something moving. It was his father's shell, the oars going in a fierce, even rhythm, biting the water, going upstream.

He remembered that his father had killed two men, one with a knife, one with a bayonet.

He felt empty and beaten. The whiskey he had drunk burned in his chest and there was a sour taste in his mouth.

I'll remember this birthday, he thought.

X

Mary Pease Jordache sat in the living room, in darkness and in the fumes of smoke from the roast goose. She was oblivious to them and to the vinegary aroma of the cabbage that lay cold on the disordered platter. Two of them gone, she though, the thug and the harlot. I have Rudolph alone now, she exulted drunkenly. If only a storm came up and swamped the shell, far, far out on the cold river, what a day it would be.

CHAPTER 7

I

A HORN BLEW outside the garage and Tom climbed out from under the Ford on which he was working in the grease pit, and wiping his hands on a rag, went out to where the Oldsmobile was standing next to one of the pumps.

"Fill'er up," Mr. Herbert said. He was a steady customer, a real estate man who had taken options on outlying properties near the garage at low, wartime prices, lying in wait for the post-war boom. Now that the Japanese had surrendered, his car passed the garage frequently. He bought all his gas at the Jordache station, using the black-market ration stamps Harold Jordache sold him.

Thomas unscrewed the tank cap and ran the gasoline in, holding onto the trigger of the hose nozzle. It was a hot afternoon and the fumes from the flowing gasoline rose in visible waves from the tank. Thomas turned his head, trying to avoid breathing in the vapor. He had a headache every night from this job. The Germans are using chemical warfare on me, he thought, now that the war is over. He thought of his uncle as German in a way that he didn't think of his father as German. There was the accent, of course, and the two pale-blonde daughters who were dressed in vaguely Bavarian fashion on holidays, and the heavy meals of sausage, smoked pork, and kraut, and the constant sound of people singing Wagner and Schubert *lieder* on the phonograph in the house, because Mrs. Jordache loved music. Tante Elsa, she asked Thomas to call her.

Thomas was alone in the garage. Coyne, the mechanic, was sick this week, and the second man was out on a call. It was two o'clock in the afternoon and Harold Jordache was still home at lunch. *Sauerbraten mit spetzli* and three bottles of Miller High Life and a nice snooze on the big bed upstairs with his fat wife to make sure they didn't overwork and have premature heart attacks. Thomas was just as glad that the maid gave him two sandwiches and some fruit in a bag for his lunch to eat at the garage. The less he saw of his uncle and his family, the better he liked it. It was enough he had to live in the house, in the minuscule room in the attic, where he lay sweating all night in the heat that had collected there under the roof in the summer sun during the day. Fifteen dollars a week. His Uncle Harold had made a good thing out of that burning cross in Port Philip.

The tank overflowed a little and Thomas hung up the hose and put on the cap and wiped away the splash of gasoline on the rear fender. He washed the windshield down and collected four dollars and thirty cents from Mr. Herbert, who gave him a dime tip.

"Thanks," Thomas said, with a good facsimile of gratitude, and watched the Oldsmobile drive off into town. The Jordache garage was on the outskirts of town, so they got a lot of transient traffic, too. Thomas went into the office and charged up the sale on the register and put the money into the till. He had finished the grease job on the Ford and for the moment he had nothing to do, although if his uncle were there, he would have no trouble finding work for him. Probably cleaning out the toilets or polishing the chrome of the shining hulks in the Used Car Lot. Thomas thought idly of cleaning out the cash register instead, and taking off somewhere. He rang the No Sale key and looked in. With Mr. Herbert's four dollars and thrity cents, there was exactly ten dollars and thirty cents in the drawer. Uncle Harold had lifted the morning's receipts when he went home for lunch, just leaving five one-dollar bills and a dollar in silver in case somebody had to have change. Uncle Harold hadn't become the owner of a garage and a Used Car Lot and a filling station and an automobile agency in town by being careless with his money.

Thomas hadn't eaten yet, so he picked up his lunch bag and went out of the office and sat tilted on the cracked wooden chair against the wall of the garage, in the shade, watching the traffic go by. The view was not unpleasant. There was something nautical about the cars in diagonal lines in the lot, with gaily colored banners overhead announcing bargains. Beyond the lumberyard diagonally across the road, there were the ochre and green of patches of the farmland all around. If you sat still, the heat wasn't too bad and just the absence of Uncle Harold gave Thomas a sense of well-being.

Actually, he wasn't unhappy in the town. Elysium, Ohio, was smaller than Port Philip, but much more prosperous, with no slums and none of the sense of decay that Thomas had taken as a natural part of his environment back home. There was a small lake nearby, with two hotels that were open for the summer, and holiday cottages owned by people who came there from Cleveland, so the town itself had some of the spruced-up air of a resort, with good shops, restaurants, and entertainments like horse shows and regattas for small sailboats on the lake. Everybody seemed to have money in Elysium and that was a real change from Port Philip.

Thomas dug into the bag and pulled out a sandwich. It was wrapped neatly in waxed paper. It was a bacon, lettuce, and tomato sandwich, with a lot of mayonnaise, on fresh, thinly cut rye bread. Recently, Clothilde, the Jordaches' maid, had begun to give him fancy sandwiches, different ones, every day, instead of the unrelieved diet of bologna on thick hunks of bread that he had had to make do with the first few weeks. Tom was a little ashamed, seeing his grease-stained hands with the black nails on the elaborate tea-shoppe sandwich. It was just as well that Clothilde couldn't see him as he ate her offerings. She was nice, Clothilde, a quiet French-Canadian woman of about twenty-five who worked from seven in the morning until nine at night, with every other Sunday afternoon off. She had sad, dark eyes and black hair. Her uniform somberness of coloring set her off as being ineluctably lower in the social scale than the aggressively blonde Jordaches, as though she had been born and marked specifically to be their servant.

She had taken to leaving a piece of pie out on the kitchen table for him, too, at night, when he left the house after dinner, to wander around the town. Uncle Harold and Tante Elsa couldn't keep him in the house at night any more than his own parents could. He had to wander. Nighttime made him restless. He didn't do much— sometimes he'd play in a pickup softball game under the lights in the town park or he'd go to a movie and have a soda afterward, and he'd found some girls. He had made no friends who might ask embarrassing questions about Port Philip and he'd been careful to be civil to everyone and he hadn't had a fight since he'd come to town. He'd had enough trouble for the time being. He wasn't unhappy. Being out from under his mother and father was a blessing and not living in the same house and sharing the same bed with his brother, Rudolph, was soothing to the nerves. And not having to go to school was a big improvement. He didn't mind the work at the garage, although Uncle Harold was a nuisance, always fussing and worrying. Tante Elsa clucked over him and kept giving him glasses of orange juice under the impression that his lean fitness was a sign of malnutrition. They meant well enough, even if they were slobs. The two little girls stayed out of his way.

Neither of the senior Jordaches knew why he had been sent away from home. Uncle Harold had pried, but Thomas had been vague and had merely said that he was doing badly at school, which was true enough, and that his father had thought it would be good for his character to get away from home and earn some money on his own. Uncle Harold was not one to underestimate the moral beauties of sending a boy out to earn money on his own. He was surprised, though, that Thomas never got any mail from his family and that after the first Sunday afternoon telephone call from Axel telling him that Thomas was on his way, there had been no further communication from Port Philip. Harold Jordache was a family man, himself, extravagantly affectionate with his two daughters and lavish with gifts for his wife, whose money it had been in the first place that had enabled him to take his comfortable place in Elysium. In talking about Axel Jordache to Tom, Uncle Harold had sighed over the differences in temperament between the brothers. "I think, Tom," Uncle Harold had said, "it was because of the wound. He took it very hard, your father. It brought out the dark side in him. As though nobody ever was wounded before."

He shared one conception with Axel Jordache. The German people, he believed, had a streak of childishness in them, which drove them into waging war. "Play a band and they march. What's so attractive about it?" he said. "Clumping around in the rain with a sergeant yelling at you, sleeping in the mud instead of a nice, warm bed with your wife, being shot at by people you don't know, and then, if you're lucky, winding up in an old uniform without a pot to piss in. It's all right for a big industrialist, the Krupps, making cannons and battleships, but for the small man—" He shrugged. "Stalingrad. Who needs it?" With all his Germanness, he had kept clear of all German-American movements. He liked where he was and what he was and he was not to be lured into any associations that might compromise him. "I got nothing against anybody," was one of the foundations of his policy. "Not against the Poles, or the French, or the English, or the Jews or anybody. Not even the Russians. Anybody who wants can come in and buy a car or ten gallons of gas from me and if he pays in good American money, he's my friend."

Thomas lived placidly enough in Uncle Harold's house, observing the rules, going his own way, occasionally annoyed at his uncle's reluctance to see him sitting down for a few minutes during the working day, but by and large more grateful than not for the sanctuary that was being offered him. It was only temporary. Sooner or later, he knew he was going to break away. But there was no hurry.

He was just about to dig into the bag for the second sandwich, when he saw the twins' 1938 Chevy approaching. It curved in toward the filling station and Tom saw that there was only one of the twins in it. He didn't know which one it was, Ethel or Edna. He had laid them both, as had most of the boys in town, but he couldn't tell them apart.

The Chevy stopped, gurgling and creaking. The twins' parents were loaded with money, but they said the old Chevy was good enough for two sixteen-year-old girls who had never earned a cent in their lives.

"Hi, twin," Tom said, to be on the safe side.

"Hi, Tom." The twins were nice-looking girls, well tanned, with straight, brown hair and plump little, tight asses. They had skin that always looked as if they had just come out of a mountain spring. If you didn't know that they had laid every boy in town, you'd be pleased to be seen with them anywhere.

"Tell me my name," the twin said.

"Aw, come on," Tom said.

"If you don't tell me my name," the twin said, "I'll buy my gas somewhere else."

"Go ahead," Tom said. "It's my uncle's money."

"I was going to invite you to a party," the twin said. "We're cooking some hot dogs down at the lake tonight and we have three cases of beer. I won't invite you if you don't tell me my name."

Tom grinned at her, stalling for time. He looked into the open Chevy. The twin was going swimming. She had a white bathing suit on the seat beside her. "I was only kidding you, Ethel," he said. Ethel had a white bathing suit and Edna had a blue one. "I knew it was you all the time."

"Give me three gallons," Ethel said. "For guessing right."

"I wasn't guessing," he said, taking down the hose. "You're printed on my memory."

"I bet," Ethel said. She looked around at the garage and wrinkled her nose. "This is a dumb old place to work. I bet a fellow like you could get something a lot better if he looked around. At least in an office."

He had told her he was nineteen years old and graduated from high school when he had first met her. She had come over to talk to him after he had spent fifteen minutes one Saturday afternoon down at the lake, showing off on the diving board. "I like it here," he said. "I'm an outdoor man."

"Don't I know," she said, chuckling. They had screwed out in the woods on a blanket that she kept in the rumble seat of the car. He had screwed her sister Edna in the same place on the same blanket, although on different nights. The twins had an easygoing family spirit of share and share alike. The twins did a lot toward making Tom willing to stay in Elysium and work in his uncle's garage. He didn't know what he was going to do in the winter, though, when the woods were covered in snow.

He put the cap back on the tank and racked up the hose. Ethel gave him a dollar bill, but no ration coupons. "Hey," he said, "where's the tickets?"

"Surprise, surprise," she said, smiling. "I'm all out."

"You got to have 'em."

She pouted. "After everything you and I are to each other. Do you think Antony asked Cleopatra for ration tickets?"

"She didn't have to buy gas from him," Tom said.

"What's the difference?" Ethel asked. "My old man buys the coupons from your uncle. In one pocket and out the other. There's a war on."

"It's over."

"Only just."

"Okay," Tom said. "Just because you're beautiful."

"Do you think I'm prettier than Edna?" she asked.

"One hundred per cent."

"I'll tell her you said that."

"What for?" Tom said. "There's no sense in making people unhappy." He didn't relish the idea of cutting his harem down by half by an unnecessary exchange of information.

Ethel peered into the empty garage. "Do you think people ever do it in a garage?"

"Save it for tonight, Cleopatra," Tom said.

She giggled. "It's nice to try everything once. Do you have the key?"

"I'll get it sometime." Now he knew what to do in the winter.

"Why don't you just leave this dump and come on down to the lake with me? I know a place we can go skinny bathing." She wriggled desirably on the cracked leather of the front seat. It was funny how two girls in the same family could be such hot numbers. Tom wondered what their father and mother thought when they started out to church with their daughters on Sunday morning.

"I'm a working man," Tom said. "I'm essential to industry. That's why I'm not in the Army."

"I wish you were a captain," Ethel said. "I'd love to undress a captain. One brass button after another. I'd unbuckle your sword."

"Get out of here," Tom said, "before my uncle comes back and asks me if I collected your ration tickets."

"Where should I meet you tonight?" she asked, starting the motor.

"In front of the Library. Eight-thirty okay?"

"Eight-thirty, Lover Boy," she said. "I'll lay out in the sun and think about you all afternoon and pant." She waved and went off.

Tom sat down in the shade on the broken chair. He wondered if his sister, Gretchen, talked like that to Theodore Boylan.

He reached into the lunch bag and took out the second sandwich and unwrapped it. There was a piece of paper, folded in two, on the sandwich. He opened up the paper. There was writing on it in pencil. "I love you," in careful, schoolgirlish script. Tom squinted at the message. He recognized the handwriting. Clothilde wrote out the list of things she had to phone for in the market every day and the list was always in the same place on a shelf in the kitchen.

Tom whistled softly. He read aloud. "I love you." He had just passed his sixteenth birthday but his voice was still adolescently high. A twenty-five-year-old woman to whom he'd hardly ever spoken more than two words. He folded the paper carefully and put it in his pocket and stared out at the traffic sweeping along the road toward Cleveland for a long time before he began eating the bacon, lettuce, and tomato sandwich, soaked in mayonnaise.

He knew he wasn't going out to the lake tonight, for any old weeny roast.

II

The River Five played a chorus of "Your Time Is My Time," and Rudolph took a solo on the trumpet, putting everything he had into it, because Julie was in the room tonight, sitting alone at a table, watching and listening to him. The River Five was the name of Rudolph's band, himself on the trumpet, Kessler on the bass, Westerman on the saxophone, Dailey on the percussion, and Flannery on the clarinet. The River Five was Rudolph's name for the band, because they all lived in Port Philip, on the Hudson, and because Rudolph thought it had an artistic and professional sound to it.

They had a three-week engagement, six nights a week, at a roadhouse outside Port Philip. The place, called Jack and Jill's, was a huge clapboard shack that shook to the beat of the dancers' feet. There was a long bar and a lot of small tables and most of the people just drank beer. The Saturday night standard of dress was relaxed. Boys wore T-shirts and many of the girls came in slacks. Groups of girls came unescorted and waited to be asked to dance or the girls danced with each other. It wasn't like playing the Plaza or 52nd Street in New York, but the money wasn't bad.

As he played, Rudolph was pleased to see Julie shake her head in refusal when a boy in a jacket and tie, obviously a preppie, came over and asked her to dance.

Julie's parents allowed her to stay out late with him on Saturday nights because they trusted Rudolph. He was a born parent-pleaser. With good reason. But if she fell into the clutches of a hard-drinking preppie, smooching around the floor, with his superior Deerfield or Choate line of talk, there was no telling what sort of trouble she might get into. The shake of the head was a promise, a bond between them as solid as an engagement ring.

Rudolph played the three trick bars of the band's signature for the fifteen-minute break, put his horn down, and signaled to Julie to come out with him for a breath of air. All the windows were open in the shack, but it was hot and wet inside, like the bottom of the Congo.

Julie held his hand as they walked out under the trees where the cars were parked. Her hand was dry and warm and soft and dear in his. It was hard to believe that you could have so many complicated sensations all through your body just holding a girl's hand.

"When you played that solo," Julie said, "I just sat there shivering. I curled up inside—like an oyster when you squirt lemon on it."

He chuckled at the comparison. Julie laughed too. She had a whole list of oddball phrases to describe her various states of mind. "I feel like a PT boat," when she raced him in the town swimming pool. "I feel like the dark side of the moon," when she had to stay in and do the dishes at home and missed a date with him.

They went all the way to the end of the parking lot, as far away as possible from the porch outside the shack, where the dancers were coming out for air. There was a car parked there and he opened the door for her to slide in. He got in after her and closed the door behind them. In the darkness, they locked in a kiss. They kissed interminably, clutching each other. Her mouth was a peony, a kitten, a peppermint, the skin of her throat under his hand was a butterfly's wing. They kissed all the time, whenever they could, but never did anything more.

Drowned, he was gliding and diving, through fountains, through smoke, through clouds. He was a trumpet, playing his own song. He was all of one piece, loving, loving . . . He took his mouth away from hers softly and kissed her throat as she put her head back against the seat. "I love you," he said. He was shaken by the joy he had in saying the words for the first time. She pulled his head fiercely against her throat, her swimmer's smooth summer arms wonderfully strong, and smelling of apricots.

Without warning the door opened and a man's voice said, "What the hell are you two doing in here?"

Rudolph sat up, an arm tightening protectively around Julie's shoulder. "We're discussing the atom bomb," he said coolly. "What do you think we're doing?" He would die rather than let Julie see that he was embarrassed.

The man was on his side of the car. It was too dark for him to see who it was. Then, unexpectedly, the man laughed. "Ask a foolish question," he said, "and get a foolish answer." He moved a little and a pale beam from one of the lights strung under the trees hit him. Rudolph recognized him. The yellow tightly combed hair, the thick, double bushes of blond eyebrows.

"Excuse me, Jordache," Boylan said. His voice was amused.

He knows me, Rudolph thought. How does he know me?

"This happens to be my car, but please make yourself at home," Boylan said. "I do not want to interrupt the artist at his moments of leisure. I've always heard that ladies show a preference for trumpet players." Rudolph would have preferred to hear this in other circumstances and from another source. "I didn't want to leave anyway," Boylan said. "I really need another drink. When you've finished, I'd be honored if you and the lady would join me for a nightcap at the bar." He made a little bow and softly closed the door and strolled off through the parking lot.

Julie was sitting at the other side of the car, straight up, ashamed. "He knows us," she said in a small voice.

"Me," Rudolph said.

"Who is he?"

"A man called Boylan," Rudolph said. "From the Holy Family."

"Oh," Julie said.

"That's it," said Rudolph. "Oh. Do you want to leave now? There's a bus in a few minutes." He wanted to protect her to the end, although he didn't know exactly from what.

"No," Julie said. Her tone was defiant. "I've got nothing to hide. Have you?"

"Never."

"One more kiss." She slid toward him and put out her arms.

But the kiss was wary. There was no more gliding through clouds.

They got out of the car and went back into the shack. As they passed through the door, they saw Boylan at the end of the bar, his back to it, leaning on it with his elbows behind him, watching them. He gave a little salute of recognition, touching the tips of his fingers to his forehead.

Rudolph took Julie to her table and ordered another ginger ale for her and then went back on the bandstand and began arranging the music sheets for the next set.

When the band played "Good Night Ladies" at two o'clock and the musicians began packing their instruments as the last dancers drifted off the floor, Boylan was still at the bar. A medium-sized, confident man, in gray-flannel slacks and a crisp linen jacket. Negligently out of place among the T-shirts and enlisted men's suntans and the young workingmen's Saturday night blue suits, he strolled leisurely away from the bar as Rudolph and Julie left the bandstand.

"Do you two children have transportation home?" he asked as they met.

"Well," Rudolph said, not liking the *children,* "one of the fellows has a car. We usually all pile into that." Buddy Westerman's father loaned him the family car when they had a club date and they lashed the bass and the drums onto the top. If any of them had girls along, they dropped the girls off first and all went to the Ace All Night Diner for hamburgers, to wind down.

"You'll be more confortable with me," Boylan said. He took Julie's arm and guided her through the doorway. Buddy Westerman raised his eyebrows questioningly as he saw them leaving. "We've got a hitch into town," Rudolph said to Buddy. "Your bus is overcrowded." The fraction of betrayal.

Julie sat betwen them on the front seat of the Buick as Boylan swung out of the parking lot and onto the road toward Port Philip. Rudolph knew that Boylan's leg was pressing against Julie's. That same flesh had been pressed against his sister's naked body. He felt peculiar about the whole thing, all of them clamped together in the same front seat on which he and Julie had kissed just a couple of hours before, but he was determined to be sophisticated.

He was relieved when Boylan asked for Julie's address and said he'd drop her off first. He wasn't going to have to make a scene about leaving her alone with Boylan. Julie seemed subdued, not like herself, as she sat between the two of them, watching the road rush at them in the Buick's headlights.

Boylan drove fast and well, passing cars in racing-driver spurts, his hands calm on the wheel. Rudolph was disturbed because he had to admire the way the man drove. There was a disloyalty there somewhere.

"That's a nice little combination you boys have there," Boylan said.

"Thanks," Rudolph said. "We could do with some more practice and some new arrangements."

"You manage a smooth beat," Boylan said. *Amateur.* "It made me regret that my dancing days are over."

Rudolph couldn't help but approve of this. He thought people over thirty dancing were ludicrous, obscene. Again he felt guilty about approving of anything about Theodore Boylan. But he was glad that at least Boylan hadn't danced with Gretchen and made fools in public of both of them. Older men dancing with young girls were the worst.

"And you, Miss . . . ?" Boylan waited for one or the other of them to supply the name.

"Julie," she said.

"Julie what?"

"Julie Hornberg," she said defensively. She was sensitive about her name.

"Hornberg?" Boylan said. "Do I know your father?"

"We just moved into town," Julie said.

"Does he work for me?"

"No," Julie said.

Moment of triumph. It would have been degrading if Mr. Hornberg was another vassal. The name was Boylan, but there were some things beyond his reach.

"Are you musical, too, Julie?" Boylan asked.

"No," she said, surprisingly. She was making it as hard as she could for Boylan. He didn't seem to notice it. "You're a lovely girl, Julie," he said. "You make me happy that my kissing days, unlike my dancing days, are not yet over."

Dirty old lecher, Rudolph thought. He fingered his black trumpet case nervously and thought of asking Boylan to stop the car so that he and Julie could get out. But walking back to town, he wouldn't get Julie to her door before four o'clock. He marked a sorrowful point against his character. He was practical at moments that demanded honor.

"Rudolph . . . It is Rudolph, isn't it?"

"Yes." His sister must have run off at the mouth like a faucet.

"Rudolph, do you intend to make a profession of the trumpet?" Kindly old vocational counselor, now.

"No. I'm not good enough," Rudolph said.

"That's wise," Boylan said. "It's a dog's life. And you have to mix with scum."

"I don't know about that," Rudolph said. He couldn't let Boylan get away with *everything*. "I don't think people like Benny Goodman and Paul Whiteman and Louis Armstrong are scum."

"Who knows?" Boylan said.

"They're artists," Julie said tightly.

"One thing does not preclude the other, child." Boylan laughed gently. "Rudolph," he said, dismissing her, "what *do* you plan to do?"

"When? Tonight?" Rudolph knew that Boylan meant as a career, but he didn't intend to let Boylan know too much about himself. He had a vague idea that all intelligence might one day be used against him.

"Tonight I hope you're going to go home and get a good night's sleep, which you eminently deserve after your hard evening's work," Boylan said. Rudolph bridled a little at Boylan's elaborate language. The vocabulary of deceit. Trapped English. "No, I mean, later on, as a career," Boylan said.

"I don't know yet," Rudolph said. "I have to go to college first."

"Oh, you're going to college?" The surprise in Boylan's voice was clear, a pinprick of condescension.

"Why shouldn't he go to college?" Julie said. "He's a straight *A* student. He just made Arista."

"Did he?" Boylan said. "Forgive my ignorance, but just what is Arista?"

"It's a scholastic honor society," Rudolph said, trying to extricate Julie. He didn't want to be defended in the terms of adolescence. "It's nothing much," he said. "If you can just read and write, practically . . ."

"You know it's a lot more than that," Julie said, her mouth bunched in disappointment at his self-deprecation. "The smartest students in the whole school. If *I* was in the Arista, I wouldn't poor-mouth it."

Poor-mouth, Rudolph thought, she must have gone out with a Southern boy in Connecticut. The worm of doubt.

"I'm sure it's a great distinction, Julie," Boylan said soothingly.

"Well it is." She was stubborn.

"Rudolph's just being modest," Boylan said. "It's a commonplace male pretense."

The atmosphere in the car was uncomfortable now, with Julie in the middle angry at both Boylan and Rudolph. Boylan reached over and turned on the radio. It warmed up and a radio announcer's voice swam out of the rushing night, with the news. There had been an earthquake somewhere. They had tuned in too late to hear where. There were hundreds killed, thousands homeless, in the new whistling, 186,000-miles-per-second darkness which was the world of radio land.

"You'd think with the war just over," Julie said, "God would lay off for awhile."

Boylan looked at her in surprise and turned off the radio. "God never lays off," he said.

Old faker, Rudolph thought. Talking about God. After what he's done.

"What college do you intend to go to Rudolph?" Boylan talked across Julie's plump, pointy, little chest.

"I haven't made up my mind yet."

"It's a very grave decision," Boylan said. "The people you meet there are likely to change your whole life. If you need any help, perhaps I can put in a good word at my Alma Mater. With all the heroes coming back, boys of your age are going to have difficulties."

"Thank you." The last thing in the world. "I don't have to apply for months yet. What college did you go to?"

"Virginia," Boylan said.

Virginia, Rudolph thought disdainfully. Anybody can go to Virginia. Why does he talk as though it's Harvard or Princeton, or at least Amherst?

They drew up in front of Julie's house. Automatically, Rudolph looked up at Miss Lenaut's window, in the next building. It was dark.

"Well, here we are, child," Boylan said, as Rudolph opened the door on his side and got out. "It's been delightful talking to you."

"Thank you for the ride," Julie said. She got out and bounced past Rudolph toward her front door. Rudolph went after her. He could kiss her good night, at least, in the shadow of the porch. As she felt in her bag for her key, her head down, her pony tail swinging down over her face, he tried to pick up her chin so he could kiss her, but she pulled away fiercely. "Kowtower," she said. She mimicked him savagely. "It's nothing much. If you can just read and write, practically . . ."

"Julie . . ."

"Suck up to the rich." He had never seen her face looking like that, pale and closed down. "Scaly old man. He bleaches his hair. *And* his eyebrows. Boy, some people'll do anything for a ride in a car, won't they?"

"Julie, you're being unreasonable." If she knew the whole truth about Boylan, he might understand her anger. But just because he was ordinarily polite . . .

"Take your hands off me." She had the key out and was fumbling at the door, still smelling of apricot.

"I'll come by tomorrow about four . . ."

"That's what you think," she said. "Wait until I have a Buick and then come around. That's more your speed." She had the door open now and was through it, a rustle of girl, a fragrant, snapping shadow, and was gone as the door slammed shut.

Rudolph went back to the car slowly. If this was love, the hell with it. He got into the car and closed the door. "That was a quick good night," Boylan said as he started the car. "In my day, we used to linger."

"Her folks like her to get in early."

Boylan drove through the town in the direction of Vanderhoff Street. Of course he knows where I live, Rudolph thought. He doesn't even bother to hide it.

"A charming girl, little Julie," Boylan said.

"Yeah."

"You do anything more than kiss her?"

"That's my business, sir," Rudolph said. Even in his anger at the man, he admired the way the words came out, clipped and cold. Nobody could treat Rudolph Jordache as though Rudolph Jordache was a cad.

"Of course it is," Boylan said. He sighed. "The temptation must be great. When I was your age . . ." He left it unfinished, a suggestion of a procession of virgins, virginal no more.

"By the way," he said in a flat conversational tone, "do you hear from your sister?"

"Sometimes," Rudolph said guardedly. She wrote to him care of Buddy Westerman. She didn't want her mother reading her letters. She was living in a Y.W.C.A. downtown in New York. She had been making the rounds of theatrical offices, looking for a job as an actress but producers weren't falling all over themselves to hire girls who had played Rosalind in high school. She hadn't found any work yet, but she loved New York. In her first letter she had apologized for being so mean to Rudolph the day she left, at the Port Philip House. She had been all churned up and not really responsible for what she was saying. But she still thought it was bad for him to stay on at home. The Jordache family was quicksand, she wrote. Nothing was going to change her opinion about that.

"Is she well?" Boylan asked.

"Okay."

"You know I know her," Boylan said, without emphasis.

"Yes."

"She spoke to you about me?"

"Not that I remember," Rudolph said.

"Ah-hah." It was difficult to know what Boylan meant to convey by this. "Do you have her address? I sometimes go down to New York and I might find the time to buy the child a good dinner."

"No, I don't have her address," Rudolph said. "She's moving."

"I see." Boylan saw through him, of course, but didn't press. "Well, if you do hear from her, let me know. I have something of hers she might like to have."

"Yeah."

Boylan turned into Vanderhoff and stopped in front of the bakery.

"Well, here we are," he said. "The home of honest toil." The sneer was plain. "I bid you good night, young man. It's been a most agreeable evening."

"Good night," Rudolph said. He got out of the car. "Thanks."

"Your sister told me you liked to fish," Boylan said. "We have quite a good stream on the property. It's stocked every year. I don't know why. Nobody goes near it anymore. If you'd like to give it a try, just come any time."

"Thank you," Rudolph said. Bribery. And he knew he would be bribed. The slippery innocence of trout. "I'll be along."

"Good," Boylan said. "I'll have my cook do up the fish for us and we can have dinner together. You're an interesting boy and I enjoy talking to you. Maybe when you come up, you'll have heard from your sister, with her new address."

"Maybe. Thanks again."

Boylan waved and drove off.

Rudolph went in and up to his room through the dark house. He could hear his father snoring. It was Saturday night and his father didn't work on Saturday night. Rudolph walked past his parents' door and up the steps to his room carefully. He didn't want to wake his mother and have to talk to her.

III

"I'm going to sell my body, I do declare," Mary Jane Hackett was saying. She came from Kentucky. "They don't want talent anymore, just bare, fruity flesh. The next call anybody puts out for showgirls I'm going to say, Farewell Stanislavsky, and wiggle my little old Dixie behind for pay."

Gretchen and Mary Jane Hackett were sitting in the cramped, poster-lined anteroom of the Nichols office on West 46th Street, waiting with a collection of other girls and young men to see Bayard Nichols. There were only three chairs behind the railing which divided the aspirants from the desk of Nichols's secretary, who was typing with spiky malice, her fingers stabbing at the keys, as though the English language were her personal enemy, to be dispatched as swiftly as possible.

The third chair in the anteroom was occupied by a character actress who wore a fur stole, even though it was eighty-five degrees in the shade outside.

Without losing a syllable on her machine, the secretary said, "Hello, dear," each time the door opened for another actor or actress. The word was that Nichols was casting a new play, six characters, four men, two women.

Mary Jane Hackett was a tall, slender, bosomless girl, who made her real money modeling. Gretchen was too curvy to model. Mary Jane Hackett had been in two flops on Broadway and had played a half-season of summer stock and already spoke like a veteran. She looked around her at the actors standing along the walls, lounging gracefully against the posters of Bayard Nichols's past productions. "You'd think, with all those hits," Mary Jane Hackett said, "going all the way back to the dark ages,

1935, for God's sake, Nichols could afford something grander than this foul little rat trap. At least air conditioning, for heaven's sake. He must have the first nickel he ever made. I don't know what I'm doing here. He dies if he has to pay more than minimum and even then, he gives you a long lecture about how Franklin D. Roosevelt has ruined this country."

Gretchen looked uneasily over at the secretary. The office was so small, there was no possibility that she hadn't heard Mary Jane. But the secretary typed on, stolidly disloyal, defeating English.

"Look at the size of them." Mary Jane gestured with a toss of her head at the young men. "They don't come up to my shoulder. If they wrote women's parts playing all three acts on their knees, I'd stand a chance of getting a job. The American theater, for God's sake! The men're midgets and if they're over five feet tall they're fairies."

"Naughty, naughty, Mary Jane," a tall boy said.

"When was the last time you kissed a girl?" Mary Jane demanded.

"Nineteen-twenty-eight," the boy said. "To celebrate the election of Herbert Hoover."

Everybody in the office laughed good-naturedly. Except the secretary. She kept on typing.

Even though she still had to get her first job, Gretchen enjoyed this new world into which she had been thrown. Everybody talked to everbody else, everybody called everybody by his first name; Alfred Lunt was Alfred to anyone who had ever been in a play with him, even if it was only for two lines at the beginning of the first act; everybody helped everybody else. If a girl heard of a part that was up for casting, she told all her friends and might even lend a particular dress for the interview. It was like being a member of a generous club, whose entrance requirements were not birth or money, but youth and ambition and belief in one another's talent.

In the basement of Walgreen's drugstore, where they all congregated over endless cups of coffee, to compare notes, to denigrate success, to mimic matinee idols and lament the death of the Group Theatre, Gretchen was now accepted, and talked as freely as anyone about how idiotic critics were, about how Trigorin should be played in *The Sea Gull,* about how nobody acted like Laurette Taylor any more, about how certain producers tried to lay every girl who came into their offices. In two months, in the flood of youthful voices, speaking with the accents of Georgia, Maine, Texas, and Oklahoma, the mean streets of Port Philip had almost disappeared, a dot on the curve of memory's horizon.

She slept till ten in the morning, without feeling guilty. She went to young men's apartments and stayed there till all hours, rehearsing scenes, without worrying what people would think. A Lesbian at the Y.W.C.A., where she was staying until she found a job, had made a pass at her, but they were still good friends and sometimes had dinner and went to the movies together. She worked out in a ballet class three hours a week, to learn how to move gracefully on a stage, and she had changed the way she walked completely, keeping her head so still that she could have balanced a glass of water on it, even when going up and down stairs . . . Primitive serenity, the exballerina who taught the class, called it.

She felt that when people looked at her they were sure she had been born in the city. She believed that she was no longer shy. She went out to dinners with some of the young actors and would-be directors whom she met at Walgreen's and in producers' offices and rehearsal classes and she paid for her own meals. She didn't mind cigarette smoke any more. She had no lovers. She had decided she would wait for that until she had a job. One problem at a time.

She had almost made up her mind to write Teddy Boylan and ask him to send down the red dress he had bought for her. There was no telling when she would be invited to that kind of party.

The door to the inner office opened and Bayard Nichols came out with a short, thin man in the suntan uniform of a captain in the Air Force. " . . . if anything comes up,

Willie," Nichols was saying, "I'll let you know." He had a sad, resigned voice. He remembered only his failures. His eyes made a sweep of the people who were waiting to see him, like the beam of a lighthouse, sightless, casting shadows.

"I'll come by next week sometime and mooch a meal off you," the Captain said. He had a voice in the low tenor range, unexpected in a man who couldn't have weighed more than a hundred and thirty pounds and wasn't more than five feet, six inches, tall. He held himself very erect, as though he were still in Air Cadets' school. But his face was unmilitary, and his hair was chestnut, unruly, long for a soldier, making you disbelieve the uniform. His forehead was high, a little bulgy, an unsettling hint of Beethoven, massive and brooding, and his eyes were Wedgwood blue.

"You're still being paid by Uncle," Nichols was saying to the Captain. "My taxes. I'll mooch the meal off you." He sounded like a man who would not cost much to feed. The theater was an Elizabethan tragedy being played nightly in his digestive tract. Murders stalked the duodenum. Ulcers lurked. He was always going on the wagon next Monday. A psychiatrist or a new wife might help.

"Mr. Nichols . . ." The tall young man who had had the exchange with Mary Jane took a step away from the wall.

"Next week, Bernie," Mr. Nichols said. One more sweep of the beam. "Miss Saunder," he said to the secretary, "can you come inside for a moment, please?" A languid, dyspeptic wave of the hand and he disappeared into his office. The secretary sprayed a last mortal burst out of the typewriter, enfilading the Dramatists' Guild, then stood up and followed him, carrying a shorthand pad. The door closed behind her.

"Ladies and gentlemen," the Captain said to the room at large, "we are all in the wrong business. I suggest Army surplus. The demand for used bazookas will be overwhelming. Hello, Tiny." This was for Mary Jane, who stood up, towering over him, and leaning over, kissed his cheek.

"I'm glad to see you got home alive from that party, Willie," Mary Jane said.

"I confess, it was a little drunk out," the Captain said. "We were washing the somber memories of combat from our souls."

"Drowning, I'd say," Mary Jane said.

"Don't begrudge us our poor little entertainments," the Captain said. "Remember, you were modeling girdles while we were walking on flak in the terrible skies over Berlin."

"Were you ever over Berlin, Willie?" Mary Jane asked.

"Of course not." He grinned at Gretchen, disclaiming valor. "I am standing here patiently, Tiny," he said.

"Oh," she said, "Gretchen Jordache, Willie Abbott."

"I am happy I walked down 46th Street this morning," Abbott said.

"Hello," said Gretchen. She nearly stood up. After all, he *was* a captain.

"I suppose you're an actress," he said.

"Trying."

"Dreadful trade," Abbott said. "To quote Shakespeare on samphire?"

"Don't show off, Willie," Mary Jane said.

"You will make some man a fine wife and mother, Miss Jordache," Abbott said. "Mark my words. Why haven't I seen you before?"

"She just came to town," Mary Jane said, before Gretchen could answer. It was a warning, a go slow sign. Jealousy?

"Oh, the girls who have just come to town," Abbott said. "May I sit in your lap?"

"Willie!" Mary Jane said.

Gretchen laughed and Abbott laughed with her. He had very white, even, small teeth. "I was not mothered sufficiently as a child."

The door to the inner office opened and Miss Saunders came out. "Miss Jordache," she said, "Mr. Nichols can see you now."

Gretchen stood up, surprised that Miss Saunders remembered her name. This was only the third time she had been in the Nichols office. She hadn't talked to Nichols at all, ever. She brushed out the wrinkles in her dress nervously, as Miss Saunders held open the little swinging gate in the partition.

"Ask for a thousand dollars a week and ten percent of the gross," Abbott said.

Gretchen went through the gate and toward Nichols's door. "Everybody else can go home," Miss Saunders said. "Mr. Nichols has an appointment for lunch in fifteen minutes."

"Beast," said the character woman with the stole.

"I just work here," Miss Saunders said.

Confusion of feelings. Pleasure and fright at the prospect of being tested for a job. Guilt because the others had been dismissed and she chosen. Loss, because now Mary Jane would leave with Willie Abbott. Flak above Berlin.

"See you later," Mary Jane said. She didn't say where. Abbott didn't say anything.

Nichols's office was a little larger than the anteroom. The walls were bare and his desk was piled with playscripts in leatherette covers. There were three yellowish wooden armchairs and the windows were coated with dust. It looked like the office of a man whose business was somehow shady and who had trouble meeting the rent on the first of the month.

Nichols stood up as she came into the office and said, "It was good of you to wait, Miss Jordache." He waved to a chair on one side of his desk and waited for her to sit down before he seated himself. He stared at her for a long time, without a word, studying her with the slightly sour expression of a man who is being offered a painting with a doubtful signature. She was so nervous that she was afraid her knees were shaking. "I suppose," she said, "you want to know about my experience. I don't have much to . . ."

"No," he said. "For the moment we can dispense with experience. Miss Jordache, the part I'm considering you for is frankly absurd." He shook his head sorrowfully, pitying himself for the grotesque deeds his profession forced him to perform. "Tell me, do you have any objection to playing in a bathing suit? In three bathing suits to be exact."

"Well . . ." She laughed uncertainly. "I guess it all depends." Idiot. Depends upon what? The size of the bathing suit? The size of the part? The size of her bosom? She thought of her mother. Her mother never went to the theater. Lucky.

"I'm afraid it isn't a speaking role," Nichols said. "The girl just walks across the stage three times, once in each act, in a different suit each time. The whole play takes place at a beach club."

"I see," Gretchen said. She was annoyed with Nichols. Because of him, she had let Mary Jane walk off with Willie Abbott, out into the city. *Captain, Captain* . . . Six million people. Get into an elevator and you are lost forever. For a walk-on. Practically naked.

"The girl is a symbol. Or so the playwright tells me," Nichols said, long hours of struggle with the casuistry of artists tolling like a shipwrecks's bell under the phrase. "Youth. Sensual beauty. The Mystery of Woman. The heartbreaking ephemeralness of the flesh. I am quoting the author. Every man must feel as she walks across the stage, 'My God, why am I married?' Do you have a bathing suit?"

"I . . . I think so." She shook her head, annoyed with herself now. "Of course."

"Could you come to the Belasco at five with your bathing suit? The author and the director will be there."

"At five." She nodded. Farewell, Stanislavsky. She could feel the blush starting. Prig. A job was a job.

"That's most kind of you, Miss Jordache." Nichols stood, mournfully. She stood with him. He escorted her to the door and opened it for her. The anteroom was empty, except for Miss Saunders, blazing away.

"Forgive me," Nichols murmured obscurely. He went back into his office.

"So long," Gretchen said as she passed Miss Saunders.

"Good-bye, dear," Miss Saunders said, without looking up. She smelled of sweat. Ephemeral flesh. I am quoting.

Gretchen went out into the corridor. She didn't ring for the elevator until the blush had subsided.

When the elevator finally came, there was a young man in it carrying a Confederate officer's uniform and a cavalry saber in a scabbard. He was wearing the hat that went with the uniform, a dashing wide-brimmed felt, plumed. Under it his beaked, hard-boiled 1945 New York face looked like a misprint. "Will the wars never end?" he said amiably to Gretchen as she got into the elevator.

It was steamy in the little grilled car and she felt the sweat break out on her forehead. She dabbed at her forehead with a piece of Kleenex.

She went out into the street, geometric blocks of hot, glassy light and concrete shadow. Abbott and Mary Jane were standing in front of the building, waiting for her. She smiled. Six million people in the city. Let there be six million people. They had waited for her.

"What I thought," Willie was saying, "was lunch."

"I'm starving," Gretchen said.

They walked off toward lunch on the shady side of the street, the two tall girls, with the slender, small soldier between them, jaunty, remembering that other warriors had also been short men, Napoleon, Trotsky, Caesar, probably Tamerlane.

Naked, she regarded herself in the dressing-room mirror. She had gone out to Jones Beach with Mary Jane and two boys the Sunday before and the skin of her shoulders and arms and legs was a faint rosy tan. She didn't wear a girdle any more and in the summer heat she dispensed with stockings, so there were no prosaic ridges from clinging elastic on the smooth arch of her hips. She stared at her breasts. *I want to see how it tastes with whiskey on it.* She had had two Bloody Marys at lunch, with Mary Jane and Willie, and they had shared a bottle of white wine. Willie liked to drink. She put on her one-piece, black bathing suit. There were grains of sand in the crotch, from Jones Beach. She walked away from the mirror, then toward it, studying herself critically. The Mystery of Woman. Her walk was too modest. Remember Primitive Serenity. Willie and Mary Jane were waiting for her at the bar of the Algonquin, to find out how it all came out. She walked less modestly. There was a knock on the door. "Miss Jordache," the stage manager said, "we're ready when you are."

She began to blush as she opened the door. Luckily, in the harsh work light of the stage, nobody could tell.

She followed the stage manager. "Just walk across and back a couple of times," he said. There were shadowy figures sitting toward the tenth row of the darkened auditorium. The stage floor was unswept and the bare bricks of the back wall looked like the ruins of Rome. She was sure her blush could be seen all the way out to the street. "Miss Gretchen Jordache," the stage manager called out into the cavernous darkness. A message in a bottle over the night waves of seats. *I am adrift.* She wanted to run away.

She walked across the stage. She felt as though she were stumbling up a mountain. A zombie in a bathing suit.

There was no sound from the auditorium. She walked back. Still no sound. She walked back and forth twice more, worried about splinters in her bare feet.

"Thank you very much, Miss Jordache." Nichols's dejected voice, thin in the empty theater. "That's fine. If you'll stop in the office tomorrow we'll arrange about the contract."

It was as simple as that. Abruptly, she stopped blushing.

Willie was sitting alone at the small bar in the Algonquin, erect on a stool, nursing a whiskey in the greenish, submarine dusk that was the constant atmosphere of the room. He swiveled around to greet her as she came in carrying the little rubberized beach bag with her bathing suit in it. "The beautiful girl looks like a beautiful girl who has just landed herself a job as the Mystery of Woman at the Belasco Theatre," he said. "I am quoting." Over lunch, they had all laughed at Gretchen's account of her interview with Nichols.

She sat down on the stool next to his. "You're right," she said. "Sarah Bernhardt is on her way."

"She never could have handled it," Willie said. "She had a wooden leg. Do we drink champagne?"

"Where's Mary Jane?"

"Gone. She had a date."

"We drink champagne." They both laughed.

When the barman set their glasses in front of them, they drank to Mary Jane. Delicious absence. It was the second time in her life Gretchen had drunk champagne. The hushed, gaudy room in the four-story house on a side street, the one-way mirror, the magnificent whore with the baby face, stretched triumphantly on the wide bed.

"We have many choices," Willie said. "We can stay here and drink wine all night. We can have dinner. We can make love. We can go to a party on Fifty-sixth Street. Are you a party girl?"

"I would like to be," Gretchen said. She ignored the "make love." Obviously it was a joke. Everything was a joke with Willie. She had the feeling that even in the war, at the worst times, he had made fun of the bursting shells, the planes diving in, the flaming wings. Images from newsreels, war movies. *Old Johnny bought it today, chaps. This is my round.* Was it like that? She would ask him later, when she knew him better.

"The party it is," he said. "There's no hurry. It'll go on all night. Now, before we fling ourselves into the mad whirl of pleasure, are there things I should know about you?" Willie poured himself another glass of champagne. His hand was not quite steady and the bottle made a little clinking music against the rim of the glass.

"What kind of things?"

"Begin at the beginning," he said. "Place of residence?"

"The Y.W.C.A. downtown," she said.

"Oh, God." He groaned. "If I dress in drag could I pass as a young Christian woman and rent a room next to yours? I'm petite and I have a light beard. I could borrow a wig. My father always wanted daughters."

"I'm afraid not," Gretchen said. "The old lady at the desk can tell a boy from a girl at a hundred yards."

"Other facts. Fellas?"

"Not at the moment," she said after a slight hesitation. "And you?"

"The Geneva Convention stipulates that when captured, a prisoner of war must only reveal his name, rank, and serial number." He grinned at her and laid his hand on hers. "No," he said. "I'll tell you everything. I shall bare my soul. I shall tell you, in many installments, how I wished too murder my father when I was a babe in a crib and how I was not weaned from my mother's breast until I was three and what us boys used to do behind the barn with the neighbor's daughter in the good old summertime." His face became serious, the forehead prominent, as he brushed back his hair with his hand. "You might as well know now as later," he said. "I'm married."

The champagne burned in her throat. "I liked you better when you were joking," she said.

"Me, too," he said soberly. "Still, there's a brighter side to it. I'm working on a divorce. The lady found other divertissements while daddy was away playing soldier."

"Where is she? Your wife?" The words came out leadenly. Absurd, she thought. I've only known him for a few hours.

"California," he said. "Hollywood. I guess I have a thing for actresses."

A continent away. Burning deserts, impassable peaks, the fruited plain. Beautiful, wide America. "How long have you been married?"

"Five years."

"How old are you anyway?" she asked.

"Will you promise not to discard me if I tell you the truth?"

"Don't be silly. How old?"

"Twenty fucking nine," he said. "Ah, God."

"I'd have said twenty-three at the outside," Gretchen shook her head wonderingly. "What's the secret?"

"Drink and riotous living," Willie said. "My face is my misfortune. I look like an ad for the boys' clothing department of Saks. Women of twenty-two are ashamed to be seen with me in public places. When I made captain the Group Commander said, 'Willie, here's your gold star for being a good boy in school this month.' Maybe I ought to grow a moustache."

"Wee Willie Abbott," Gretchen said. His false youthfulness was reassuring to her. She thought of the gross, dominating maturity of Teddy Boylan. "What did you do before the war?" she asked. She wanted to know everything about him. "How do you know Bayard Nichols?"

"I worked for him on a couple of shows. I'm a flak. I'm in the worst business in the world. I'm a publicity man. Do you want your picture in the paper, little girl?" The disgust was not put on. If he wanted to look older, there was no need to grow a moustache. All he had to do was talk about his profession. "When I went into the Army, I thought I'd finally get away from it. So they looked up my card and put me in public relations. I ought to be arrested for impersonating an officer. Have some more champagne." He poured for them again, the bottle clinking an icy code of distress against the glasses, the nicotined fingers trembling minutely.

"But you were overseas. You did fly," she said. During lunch, he had talked about England.

"A few missions. Just enough to get an Air Medal, so I wouldn't feel naked in London. I was a passenger. I admired other men's wars."

"Still, you could've been killed." His bitterness disturbed her and she would have liked to move him out of it.

"I'm too young to die, Colonel." He grinned. "Finish your bubbly. They're waiting for us all over town."

"When do you get out of the Air Force?"

"I'm on terminal leave now," he said. "I wear the uniform because I can get into shows free with it. I also have to go over to the hospital on Staten Island a couple of times a week for therapy for my back and nobody'd believe I was a Captain if I didn't wear the suit."

"Therapy? Were you wounded?"

"Not really. We made an aggressive landing and bounced. I had a little operation on my spine. Twenty years from now I'll say the scar came from shrapnel. All drunk up, like a good little girl?"

"Yes," Gretchen said. The wounded were everywhere. Arnold Simms, in the maroon bathrobe, sitting on the table and looking down at the foot that no longer was any good for running. Talbot Hughes, with everything torn out of his throat, dying silently in his corner. Her own father, limping from another war.

Willie paid for the drinks and they left the bar. Gretchen wondered how he could walk so erectly with a bad back.

Twilight made a lavender puzzle out of New York as they came out of the bar onto the street. The stone heat of the day had gentled down to a meadowed balminess and they walked against a soft breeze, hand in hand. The air was like a drift of pollen. A three-quarter moon, pale as china in the fading sky, sailed over the towered office buildings.

"You know what I like about you?" Willie said.

"What?"

"You didn't say you wanted to go home and change your dress when I said we were going to a party."

She didn't feel she had to tell him she was wearing her best dress and had nothing to change to. It was cornflower-blue linen, buttoned all the way down the front, with short sleeves and a tight red cloth belt. She had changed into it when she had gone down to the Y.W.C.A. after lunch to get her bathing suit. Six ninety-five at Ohrbach's. The only piece of clothing she had bought since she came to New York. "Will I shame you in front of your fine friends?" she said.

"A dozen of my fine friends will come up to you tonight and ask for your telephone number," he said.

"Shall I give it to them?"

"Upon pain of death," Willie said.

They went slowly up Fifth Avenue, looking in all the windows. Finchley's was displaying tweed sports jackets. "I fancy myself in one of those," Willie said. "Give me bulk. Abbott, the tweedy Squire."

"You're not tweedy," Gretchen said. "I fancy you smooth."

"Smooth I shall be," Willie said.

They stopped a long time in front of Brentano's and looked at the books. There was an arrangment of recent plays in the window. Odets, Hellman, Sherwood, Kaufman and Hart. "The literary life," Willie said. "I have a confession to make. I'm writing a play. Like every other flak."

"It will be in the window," she said.

"Please God, it will be in the window," he said. "Can you act?"

"I'm a one-part actress. The Mystery of Woman."

"I am quoting," he said. They laughed. They knew the laughter was foolish, but it was dear because it was for their own private joke.

When they reached Fifty-fifth Street, they turned off Fifth Avenue. Under the St. Regis canopy, a wedding party was disembarking from taxis. The bride was very young, very slender, a white tulip. The groom was a young infantry lieutenant, no hashmarks, no campaign ribbons, razor-nicked, peach-cheeked, untouched.

"Bless you, my children," Willie said as they passed.

The bride smiled, a whitecap of joy, blew a kiss to them. "Thank you, sir," said the lieutenant, restraining himself from throwing a salute, by the book.

"It's a good night for a wedding," Willie said as they walked on. "Temperature in the low eighties, visibility unlimited, no war on at the moment."

The party was between Park and Lexington. As they crossed Park, at Fifty-fifth Street, a taxi swung around the corner and down toward Lexington. Mary Jane was sitting alone in the taxi. The taxi stopped midway down the street and Mary Jane got out and ran into a five-story building.

"Mary Jane," Willie said. "See her?"

"Uhuh." They were walking more slowly now.

Willie looked across at Gretchen, studying her face. "I have an idea," he said. "Let's have our own party."

"I was hoping you'd say that," Gretchen said.

"Company, about face," he barked out. He made a smart military turn, clicking his heels. They started walking back toward Fifth Avenue. "I don't cotton to the idea of all those guys asking for your telephone number," he said.

She squeezed his hand. She was almost sure now that Willie had slept with Mary Jane, but she squeezed his hand just the same.

They went to the Oak Room Bar of the Plaza and had mint julep in frosted pewter mugs. "For Kentucky's sake," Willie explained. He didn't mind mixing his drinks. Scotch, champagne, bourbon. "I am an exploder of myths," he said.

After the mint juleps they left the Plaza and got onto a Fifth Avenue bus heading downtown. They sat on the top deck, in the open air. Willie took off his overseas cap with the two silver bars and the officer's braid. The wind of the bus's passage tumbled his hair, making him look younger than ever. Gretchen wanted to take his head and put it down on her breast and kiss the top of his head, but there were people all around them so she took his cap and ran her fingers along the braid and the two bars instead.

They got off the bus at Eighth Street and found a table on the sidewalk at the Brevoort and Willie ordered a Martini. "To improve my appetite," he said. "Give notice to the gastric juices. Red Alert."

The Algonquin, the Plaza, the Brevoort, a job, a captain. All in one day. It was a cornucopia of firsts.

They had melon and a small roast chicken for dinner and a bottle of California red wine from the Napa Valley. "Patriotism," Willie said. "And because we won the war." He drank most of the bottle himself. Nothing of what he had drunk seemed to affect him. His eyes were clear, his speech the same.

They weren't talking much any more, just looking at each other across the table. If she couldn't kiss him soon, Gretchen thought, they would carry her off to Bellevue.

Willie ordered brandy for both of them after the coffee. What with paying for lunch and all the eating and drinking of the evening, Gretchen figured that it must have cost Willie at least fifty dollars since noon. "Are you a rich man?" she asked, as he was paying the bill.

"Rich in spirit only," Willie said. He turned his wallet upside down and six bills floated down onto the table. Two were for a hundred apiece, the rest were fives. "The complete Abbott fortune," he said. "Shall I mention you in my will?"

Two hundred and twenty dollars. She was shocked at how little it was. She still had more than that in the bank herself, from Boylan's eight hundred, and she never paid more than ninety-five cents for a meal. Her father's blood? The thought made her uneasy.

She watched Willie gather up the bills and stuff them carelessly into his pocket. "The war taught me the value of money," he said.

"Did you grow up rich?" she asked.

"My father was a customs inspector, on the Canadian border," he said. "And honest. And there were six children. We lived like kings. Meat three times a week."

"I worry about money," she confessed. "I saw what not having any did to my mother."

"Drink hearty," Willie said. "You will not be your mother's daughter. I will turn to my golden typewriter in the very near future."

They finished their brandies. Gretchen was beginning to feel a little lightheaded, but not drunk. Definitely not drunk.

"Is it the opinion of this meeting," Willie said, as they stood up from the table and passed through the boxed hedges of the terrace onto the avenue, "that a drink is in order?"

"I'm not drinking any more tonight," she said.

"Look to women for wisdom," Willie said. "Earth mother. Priestesses of the oracle. Delphic pronouncements, truth cunningly hidden in enigmas. No more drink shall be drunk tonight. Taxi!" he called.

"We can walk to the Y.W.C.A. from here," she said. "It's only about fifteen minutes . . ."

The taxi braked to a halt and Willie opened the door and she got in.

"The Hotel Stanley," Willie said to the driver as he got into the cab. "On Seventh Avenue."

They kissed. Oasis of lips. Champagne, Scotch, Kentucky mint, red wine of Napa Valley in Spanish California, brandy, gift of France. She pushed his head down onto her breast and nuzzled into the thick silkiness of his hair. The hard bone of skull under it. "I've been wanting to do this all day," she said. She held him against her, child soldier. He opened the top two buttons of her dress, his fingers swift, and kissed the cleft between her breasts. Over his cradled head, she could see the driver, his back toward her, busy with red lights, green lights, rash pedestrians, what the passengers do is the passengers' business. His photograph stared at her from the lighted tag. A man of about forty with glaring, defiant eyes and kidney trouble, a man who had seen everything, who knew the whole city. Eli Lefkowitz, his name, prominently displayed by police order. She would remember his name forever. Eli Lefkowitz, unwatching charioteer of love.

There was little traffic at this hour and the cab swept uptown. Airman in the quick sky.

One last kiss for Eli Lefkowitz and she buttoned her dress, proper for the bridal suite.

The facade of the Hotel Stanley was imposing. The architect had been to Italy, or had seen a photograph. The Doges' Palace, plus Walgreen's. The Adriatic coast of Seventh Avenue.

She stood to one side of the lobby while Willie went to the desk for the key. Potted palms, Italianate dark wood chairs, glaring light. Traffic of women with the faces of police matrons and hair the frizzed blonde of cheap dolls. Horse-players in corners, G.I.'s on travel orders, two show girls, high-assed, long-lashed, an old lady in men's work shoes, reading *Seventeen*, somebody's mother, traveling salesmen after a bad day, detectives, alert for Vice.

She drifted toward the elevator shaft, as though she were alone, and did not look at Willie when he came up to her with the key. Deception easily learned. They didn't speak in the elevator.

"Seventh floor," Willie said to the operator.

There was no hint of Italy on the seventh floor. The architect's inspiration had run out on the way up. Narrow corridors, peeling dark-brown metal doors, uncarpeted tile floors that must have once been white. *Sorry, folks, we can't kid you anymore, you might as well know the facts, you're in America.*

They walked down a narrow corridor, her heels making a noise like a pony trotting. Their shadows wavered on the dim walls, uncertain poltergeists left over from the 1925 boom. They stopped at a door like all the other doors. 777. On Seventh Avenue, on the seventh floor. The magic orderliness of numbers.

Willie worked the key and they went into Room 777 of the Stanley Hotel on Seventh Avenue. "You'll be happier if I don't put on a light," Willie said. "It's a hole. But it's the only thing I could get. And even so, they'll only let me stay five days. The town's full up."

But enough light filtered in from electric New York outside the chipped tin blinds, so that she could see what the room was like. A small cell, a slab of a single bed, one upright wooden chair, a basin, no bathroom, a shadowy pile of officer's shirts on the bureau.

Deliberately, he began to undress her. The red cloth belt first, then the top button of her dress and then, going all the way, one button after another. She counted with his movements as he kneeled before her. " . . . seven, eight, nine, ten, eleven . . ." What conferences, what soul searching in the workrooms farther down on Seventh Avenue to come to that supreme decision—not ten buttons, not twelve buttons, ELEVEN!

"It's a full day's work," Willie said. He took the dress from her shoulders and put it neatly over the back of the chair. Officer and gentleman. She turned around so that he could undo her brassiere. Boylan's training. The light coming in through the blinds cut her into a tiger's stripes. Willie fumbled at the hooks on her back. "They must finally invent something better," he said.

She laughed and helped him. The brassiere fell away. She turned to him again and he gently pulled her innocent white cotton panties down to her ankles. She kicked off her shoes. She went over to the bed and with a single movement ripped off the cover and the blanket and top sheet. The linen wasn't fresh. Had Mary Jane slept there? No matter.

She stretched out on the bed, her legs straight, her ankles touching, her hands at her sides. He stood over her. He put his hand between her thighs. Clever fingers. "The Vale of Delight," he said.

"Get undressed," she said.

She watched him rip off his tie and unbutton his shirt. When he took his shirt off, she saw he was wearing a medical corset with hooks and laces. The corset went almost up to his shoulders and down past the web belt of his trousers. That's why he stands so erectly, the young Captain. *We made an aggressive landing and bounced.* The punished flesh of soldiers.

"Did you ever make love to a man with a corset before?" Willie asked, as he started pulling at the laces.

"Not that I remember," she said.

"It's only temporary," he said. He was embarrassed by it. "A couple of months more. Or so they tell me at the hospital." He was struggling with the laces.

"Should I turn the light on?" she asked.

"I couldn't bear it."

The telephone rang.

They looked at each other. Neither of them moved. If they didn't move, perhaps it wouldn't ring again.

The telephone rang again.

"I guess I'd better answer it," he said.

He picked up the phone from the bedtable next to her head. "Yes?"

"Captain Abbott?" Willie held the phone loosely and she could hear clearly. It was a man's voice, aggrieved.

"Yes," Willie said.

"We believe there is a young lady in your room." The royal *We,* from the Mediterranean throne room.

"I believe there is," Willie said. "What of it?"

"You have a single room," the voice said, "for the occupancy of one individual."

"All right," Willie said. "Give me a double room. What's the number?"

"I'm sorry, every room is occupied," the voice said. "We're all booked until November."

"Let's you and I pretend this is a double room, Jack," said Willie. "Put it on my bill."

"I'm afraid I can't do that," the voice said. "Room number 777 is definitely a single room for a single occupancy. I'm afraid the young lady will have to leave."

"The young lady isn't *living* here, Jack," Willie said. "She isn't occupying anything. She's visiting me. Anyway, she's my wife."

"Do you have your marriage certificate, Captain?"

"Dear," Willie said loudly, holding the phone out over Gretchen's head, "have you got our marriage certificate?"

"It's home," Gretchen said, close to the receiver.

"Didn't I tell you never travel without it?" Marital annoyance.

"I'm sorry, dear," Gretchen said meekly.

"She left it home," Willie said into the phone. "We'll show it to you tomorrow. I'll have it sent down by special delivery."

"Captain, young ladies are against the rules of the establishment," the voice said.

"Since when?" Willie was getting angry now. "This dive is famous from here to Bangkok as a haunt of pimps and bookies and hustlers and dope peddlers and receivers of stolen goods. One honest policeman could fill the Tombs from your guest list."

"We are under new management," the voice said. "A well-known chain of respectable hotels. We are creating a different image. If the young lady is not out of there in five minutes, Captain, I'm coming up."

Gretchen was out of bed now and pulling on her panties.

"No," Willie said beseechingly.

She smiled gently at him.

"Fuck you, Jack," Willie said into the phone and slammed it down. He started to do up his corset, pulling fiercely at the laces. "Go fight a war for the bastards," he said. "And you can't find another room at this hour in the goddamn town for love or money."

Gretchen laughed. Willie glared at her for a moment, then he burst into laughter too. "Next time," he said, "remember for Christ's sake to bring your marriage license."

They walked grandly through the lobby, blatantly arm in arm, pretending they were not defeated. Half the people in the lobby looked like house detectives, so there was no way of knowing which one was the voice on the telephone.

They didn't want to leave each other, so they went over to Broadway and had orangeades at a Nedick stand, faint taste of tropics in a Northern latitude, then continued on to 42nd Street and went into an all-night movie and sat among derelicts and insomniacs and perverts and soldiers waiting for a bus and watched Humphrey Bogart playing Duke Mantee in *The Petrified Forest*.

When the picture ended, they still didn't want to leave each other, so they saw *The Petrified Forest* over again.

When they got out of the movie house, they still didn't want to leave each other, so he walked her all the way down to the Y.W.C.A., among silent, empty buildings which looked like fortresses that had fallen, no quarter shown.

Dawn was breaking as they kissed in front of the Y.W.C.A. Willie looked with loathing at the dark bulk of the building, one lamp on at the entrance, lighting proper young ladies out on the town to their proper beds. "Do you think that in the entire, glorious history of this structure," he said, "that anybody got laid here?"

"I doubt it," she said.

"It sends shivers down your spine, doesn't it?" he said gloomily. He shook his head, "Don Juan," he said. "The corseted lover. Call me schmuck."

"Don't take it so hard," she said. "There're other nights."

"Like when?"

"Like tonight," she said.

"Like tonight," he repeated soberly. "I can live through the day. I suppose. I'll spend the hours in good works. Like looking for a hotel room. It may be in Coney Island or Babylon or Pelham Bay, but I'll find a room. For Captain and Mrs. Abbott. Bring along a valise, for Queen Victoria. Fill it with old copies of *Time*, in case we get bored and want something to read."

A last kiss and he strode off, small and defeated in the fresh dawn light. It was a lucky thing he would still be in uniform tonight. In civilian clothes, she doubted that any desk clerk would believe he was old enough to be married.

When he had disappeared, she climbed the steps and went demurely into the Y.W.C.A. The old lady at the desk leered at her knowingly, but Gretchen took her key and said, "Good night," as though the dawn coming in through the windows was merely a clever optical illusion.

CHAPTER 8

I

As CLOTHLIDE WASHED his hair, he sat in Uncle Harold's and Tante Elsa's big bathtub, steaming in the hot water, his eyes closed, drowning, like an animal sunning himself on a rock. Uncle Harold, Tante Elsa, and the two girls were at Saratoga for their annual two-week holiday and Tom and Clothilde had the house to themselves. It was Sunday and the garage was closed. In the distance a church bell was ringing.

The deft fingers massaged his scalp, caressed the back of his neck through foaming, perfumed suds. Clothilde had bought a special soap for him in the drugstore with her own money. Sandalwood. When Uncle Harold came back, he'd have to go back to good old Ivory, five cents a cake. Uncle Harold would suspect something was up if he smelled the sandalwood.

"Now, rinse, Tommy," Clothilde said.

Tom lay back in the water and stayed under as her fingers worked vigorously through his hair, rinsing out the suds. He came up blowing.

"Now your nails," Clothilde said. She kneeled beside the tub and scrubbed with the nail brush at the black grease ground into the skin of his hands and under his nails. Clothilde was naked and her dark hair was down, falling in a cascade over her low, full breasts. Even kneeling humbly, she didn't look like anybody's servant.

His hands were pink, his nails rosy, as Clothilde scrubbed away, her wedding ring glistening in foam. Clothilde put the brush on the rim of the tub, after a last meticulous examination. "Now the rest," she said.

He stood up in the bath. She rose from her knees and began to soap him down. She had wide, firm hips and strong legs. Her skin was dark and with her flattish nose, wide cheek bones, and long straight hair she looked like pictures he had seen in history books of Indian girls greeting the first white settlers in the forest. There was a scar on her right arm, a jagged crescent of white. Her husband had hit her with a piece of kindling. Long ago, she said. In Canada. She didn't want to talk about her husband. When he looked at her something funny happened in his throat and he didn't know whether he wanted to laugh or cry.

Motherly hands touched him lightly, lovingly, doing unmotherly things. Between his buttocks, slipperiness of scented soap, between his thighs, promises. An orchestra in his balls. Woodwinds and flutes. Hearing Tante Elsa's phonograph blaring all the time, he had come to love Wagner. "We are finally civilizing the little fox," Tante Elsa had said, proud of her unexpected cultural influence.

"Now the feet," Clothlide said.

He obediently put a foot up on the rim of the tub, like a horse being shod. Bending, careless of her hair, she soaped between his toes and used a washcloth devotedly, as though she were burnishing church silver. He learned that even his toes could give him pleasure.

She finished with his other foot and he stood there, glistening in the steam. She looked at him, studying him. "A boy's body," she said. "You look like Saint Sebastian. Without the arrows." She wasn't joking. She never joked. It was the first intimation of his life that his body might have a value beyond its functions. He knew that he was strong and quick and that his body was good for games and fighting, but it had never occurred to him that it would delight anybody just to look at it. He was a little ashamed that he had no hair yet on his chest and that it was so sparse down below.

With a quick motion of her hands, she did her hair up in a knot on top of her head. Then she stepped into the bathtub, too. She took the bar of soap and the suds began to glisten on her skin. She soaped herself all over methodically, without coquetry. Then they slid down into the tub together and lay quietly with their arms around each other.

If Uncle Harold and Tante Elsa and the two girls fell sick and died in Saratoga, he would stay in this house in Elysium forever.

When the water began to cool they got out of the tub and Clothilde took one of the big special towels of Tante Elsa and dried him off. While she was scrubbing out the tub, he went into the Jordaches' bedroom and lay down on the freshly made crisp bed.

Bees buzzed outside the screened windows, green shades against the sun made a grotto of the bedroom, the bureau against the wall was a ship on a green sea. He would burn a thousand crosses for one such afternoon.

She came padding in, her hair down now, for another occasion. On her face the soft, distant, darkly concentrated expression he had come to look for, yearn for.

She lay down beside him. Wave of sandalwood. Her hand reached out for him, carefully. The touch of love, cherishing him, an act apart from all other acts, profoundly apart from the giggly high-school lust of the twins and the professional excitement of the woman on McKinley Street back in Port Philip. It was incredible to him that anyone could want to touch him like that.

Sweetly, gently, he took her while the bees foraged in the window boxes. He waited for her, adept now, taught, well and quickly taught, by that wide Indian body, and when it was over, they lay back side by side and he knew that he would do anything for her, anything, any time.

"Stay here." A last kiss under the throat. "I will call you when I am ready."

She slipped out of the bed and he heard her in the bathroom, dressing, then going softly down the stairs toward the kitchen. He lay there, staring up at the ceiling, all gratitude, and all bitterness. He hated being sixteen years old. He could no nothing for her. He could accept her rich offering of herself, he could sneak into her room at night, but he couldn't even take her for a walk in the park or give her a scarf as a gift, because a tongue might wag, or Tante Elsa's sharp eye might search out the new color in the warped bureau drawer in the room behind the kitchen. He couldn't take her away from this grinding house in which she slaved. If only he were twenty . . .

Saint Sebastian.

She came silently into the room. "Come eat," she said.

He spoke from the bed. "When I'm twenty," he said, "I'm coming here and taking you away."

She smiled. "My man," she said. She fingered her wedding ring absently. "Don't take long, The food is hot."

He went into the bathroom and dressed and went on down to the kitchen.

There were flowers on the kitchen table, between the two places laid out there. Phlox. Deep blue. She did the gardening, too. She had a knowing hand with flowers. "She's a pearl, my Clothilde," he had heard Tante Elsa say. "The roses're twice as big this year."

"You should have your own garden," Tom said, as he sat before his place. What he could not give her in reality he offered in intention. He was barefooted and the linoleum felt cool and smooth against his soles. His hair, still damp, was neatly combed, the blond, tight curls glistening darkly. She liked everything neat and shining clean, pots and pans, mahogany, front halls, boys. It was the least he could do for her.

She put a bowl of fish chowder in front of him.

"I said you should have your own garden," he repeated.

"Drink your soup," she said, and sat down at her own place across from him.

A leg of lamb, still tender and rare, came next, served with parsleyed new potatoes, roasted in the same pan with the lamb. There was a heaped bowl of buttered young string beans and a salad of crisp romaine and tomatoes. A plate of fresh, hot biscuits stood to one side, and a big slab of sweet butter, next to a frosted pitcher of milk.

Gravely, she watched him eat, smiled when he offered his plate again. During the family's holiday, she got on the bus every morning to go to the next town to do her shopping, using her own money. The shopkeepers of Elysium would have been sure to report back to Mrs. Jordache about the fine meats and carefully chosen first fruits for the feasts prepared in her kitchen in her absence.

For dessert there was vanilla ice cream that Clothilde had made that morning, and hot chocolate sauce. She knew her lover's appetites. She had announced her love with two bacon and tomato sandwiches. Its consummation demanded richer fare.

"Clothilde," Tom said, "why do you work here?"

"Where should I work?" She was surprised. She spoke in a low voice, always without inflection. There was a hint of French Canada in her speech. She almost said *v* for *w*.

"Anyplace. In a store. In a factory. Not as a servant."

"I like being in a house. Cooking meals," she said. "It is not so bad. Your aunt is proper with me. She appreciates me. It was kind of her to take me in. I came here, two years ago, I didn't know a soul, I didn't have a penny. I like the little girls very much. They are always so clean. What could I do in a store or a factory? I am very slow at adding and subtracting and I'm frightened of machines. I like being in a house."

"Somebody else's house," Tom said. It was intolerable that those two fat slobs could order Clothide around.

"This week," she said, touching his hand on the table, "it is our house."

"We can never go out with each other."

"So?" She shrugged. "What are we missing?"

"We have to sneak around," he cried. He was growing angry with her.

"So?" She shrugged again. "There are many things worth sneaking around for. Not everything good is out in the open. Maybe I like secrets." Her face gleamed with one of her rare soft smiles.

"This afternoon . . . " he said stubbornly, trying to plant the seed of revolt, arouse that placid peasant docility. "After a . . . a *banquet* like this . . . " He waved his hand over the table. "It's not right. We should go out, do something, not just sit around."

"What is there to do?" she asked seriously.

"There's a band concert in the park," he said. "A baseball game."

"I get enough music from Tante Elsa's phonograph," she said. "You go to the baseball game for me and tell me who won. I will be very happy here, cleaning up and waiting for you to come home. As long as you come home, I do not want anything else, Tommy."

"I'm not going anywhere without you today," he said, giving up. He stood up. "I'll wipe the dishes."

"There's no need," she said.

"I'll wipe the dishes," he said, with great authority.

"My man," she said. She smiled again, beyond ambition, confident in her simplicities.

The next evening after work, on his way home from the garage on his wobbly Iver Johnson he was passing the town library. On a sudden impulse, he stopped, leaned the bike against a railing, and went in. He hardly read anything at all, not even the sports pages of the newspapers, and he was not a frequenter of libraries. Perhaps in reaction to his brother and his sister, always with their noses in books, and full of fancy sneering ideas.

The hush of the library and the unwelcoming examination of his grease-stained clothes by the lady librarian made him ill at ease, and he wandered around among the shelves, not knowing which book of all these thousands held the information he was looking for. Finally, he had to go to the desk and ask the lady.

"Excuse me," he said. She was stamping cards, making out prison sentences for books with a little mean snapping motion of her wrist.

"Yes?" She looked up, unfriendly. She could tell a nonbook-lover at a glance.

"I want to find out something about Saint Sebastian, ma'am," he said.

"What do you want to find out about him?"

"Just anything," he said, sorry he had come in now.

"Try the Encyclopaedia Britannica," the lady said. "In the Reference Room. SARS to SORC." She knew her library, the lady.

"Thank you very much, ma'am." He decided that from now on he would change his clothes at the garage and use Coyne's sandsoap to get out the top layer of grease from his skin, at least. Clothilde would like that better, too. No use being treated like a dog when you could avoid it.

It took him ten minutes to find the Encyclopaedia Britannica. He pulled out SARS to SORC and took it over to a table and sat down with the book. SEA-URCHIN-SEA-WOLF, SEA-WRACK-SEBASTIANO DEL PIOMBO. The things some people fooled with!

There it was, "SEBASTIAN, ST., a Christian martyr whose festival is celebrated on Jan. 20." Just one paragraph. He couldn't have been so damned important.

"After the archers had left him for dead," Tom read, "a devout woman, Irene, came by night to take his body away for burial, but finding him still alive, carried him to her house, where his wounds were dressed. No sooner had he wholly recovered than he hastened to confront the emperor, who ordered him to be instantly carried off and beaten to death with rods."

Twice, for Christ's sake, Tom thought. Catholics were nuts. But he still didn't know why Clothilde had said Saint Sebastian when she had looked at him naked in the bathtub.

He read on. "St. Sebastian is specially invoked against the plague. As a young and beautiful soldier, he is a favorite subject of sacred art, being most generally represented undraped, and severly though not mortally wounded with arrows."

Tom closed the book thoughfully. "A young and beautiful soldier, being most generally represented undraped . . . " Now he knew. Clothilde. Wonderful Clothilde. Loving him without words, but saying it with her religion, with her food, her body, everything.

Until today he had thought he was kind of funny looking, a snotty kid with a flat face and a sassy expression. Saint Sebastian. The next time he saw those two beauties, Rudolph and Gretchen, he could look them straight in the eye. I have been compared by an older, experienced woman to Saint Sebastian, a young and beautiful soldier. For the first time since he had left home he was sorry he wasn't going to see his brother and sister that night.

He got up and put the book away. He was about to leave the reference room when it occurred to him that Clothilde was a Saint's name, too. He searched through the volumes and took out CASTIR to COLE.

Practiced now, he found what he was looking for quickly, although it wasn't Clothilde, but "CLOTILDA, ST. (d. 544) daughter of the Burgundian king Chilperic, and wife of Clovis, king of the Franks."

Tom thought of Clothilde sweating over the stove in the Jordache kitchen and washing Uncle Harold's underwear and was saddened. Daughter of the Burgundian king Chilperic, and wife of Clovis, king of the Franks. Poeple didn't think of the future when they named babies.

He read the rest of the paragraph, but Clotilda didn't seem to have done all that much, converting her husband and building churches and stuff like that, and getting into trouble with her family. The book didn't say what entrance requirements she had met to be made a saint.

Tom put the book away, eager to get home to Clothilde. But he stopped at the desk to say, "Thank you, ma'am," to the lady. He was conscious of a sweet smell. There was a bowl of narcissus on the desk, spears of green, with white flowers, set in a bed of multi-colored pebbles. Then, speaking without thinking, he said, "Can I take out a card, please?"

The lady looked at him, surprised. "Have you ever had a card anywhere before?" she asked.

"No, ma'am. I never had the time to read before."

The lady gave him a queer look, but pulled out a blank card and asked him his name, age, and address. She printed the information in a funny backward way on the card, stamped the date, and handed the card to him.

"Can I take out a book right away?" he asked.

"If you want," she said.

He went back to the Encyclopaedia Britannica and took out SARS to SORC. He wanted to have a good look at that paragraph and try to memorize it. But when he stood at the desk to have it stamped, the lady shook her head impatiently. "Put that right back," she said. "That's not supposed to leave the Reference Room."

He returned to the Reference Room and put the volume back. They keep yapping at you to read, he thought resentfully, and then when you finally say okay, I'll read, they throw a rule in your face.

Still, walking out of the library, he patted his back pocket several times, to feel the nice stiffness of the card in there.

There was fried chicken, mashed potatoes, and apple sauce for dinner and blueberry pie for dessert. He and Clothilde ate in the kitchen, not saying much.

When they had finished and Clothilde was clearing off the dishes, he went over to her and held her in his arms and said, "Clotilda, daughter of the Burgundian king Chilperic, and wife of Clovis, king of the Franks."

She looked at him, wide-eyed. "What's that?

"I wanted to find out where your name came from," he said. "I went to the library. You're a king's daughter and a king's wife."

She looked at him a long time, her arms around his waist. Then she kissed him on the forehead, gratefully, as if he had brought home a present for her.

II

There were two fish in the straw creel already, speckled on the bed of wet fern. The stream was well stocked, as Boylan had said. There was a dam at one edge of the property where the stream entered the estate. From there the stream wound around the property to another dam with a wire fence to keep the fish in, at the other edge of the property. From there it fell in a series of cascades down toward the Hudson.

Rudolph wore old corduroys and a pair of fireman's rubber boots, bought second-hand and too big for him, to make his way along the banks, with the thorns and the interlaced branches tearing at him. It was a long walk up the hill from the last stop on the local bus line, but it was worth it. His own private trout stream. He hadn't seen Boylan or anybody else on the property any of the times he had come up there. The stream was never closer at any point to the main house than five hundred yards.

It had rained the night before and there was rain in the gray, late-afternoon air. The brook was a bit muddy and the trout were shy. But just slowly moving upstream, getting the fly lightly, lightly, where he wanted it, with nobody around, and the only sound the water tumbling over the rocks, was happiness enough. School began again in a week and he was making the most of the last days of the holiday.

He was near one of the stream's two ornamental bridges, working the water, when he heard footsteps on gravel. A little path, overgrown with weeds, led to the bridge. He reeled in and waited. Boylan, hatless, dressed in a suede jacket, a paisley scarf, and jodhpur boots, came down the path and stopped on the bridge. "Hello, Mr. Boylan," Rudolph said. He was a little uneasy, seeing the man, worried that perhaps Boylan hadn't remembered inviting him to fish the stream, or had merely said it for politeness' sake, not really meaning it.

"Any luck?" Boylan asked.

"There're two in the basket."

"Not bad for a day like this," Boylan said, examining the muddied water. "With flies."

"Do you fish?" Rudolph moved nearer the bridge, so that they wouldn't have to talk so loud.

"I used to," Boylan said. "Don't let me interfere. I'm just taking a walk. I'll be back this way. If you're still here, perhaps you'll do me the pleasure of joining me in a drink up at the house."

"Thank you," Rudolph said. He didn't say whether he'd wait or not.

With a wave, Boylan continued his walk.

Rudolph changed the fly, taking the new one from where it was stuck in the band of the battered old brown felt hat he used when it rained or when he went fishing. He made the knots precisely, losing no time. Perhaps one day he would be a surgeon, suturing incisions. "I think the patient will live, nurse." How many years? Three in premed, four in medical school, two more as an intern. Who had that much money? Forget it.

On his third cast, the fly was taken. There was a thrash of water, dirty white against the brown current. It felt like a big one. He played it carefully, trying to keep the fish away from the rocks and brushwood anchored in the stream. He didn't know how long it took him. Twice the fish was nearly his and twice it streaked away, taking line with it. The third time, he felt it tiring. He waded out with his net. The water rushed in over the top of his fireman's boots, icy cold. It was only when he had the trout in the net that he was conscious that Boylan had come back and was on the bridge watching him.

"Bravo," Boylan said, as Rudolph stepped back on shore, water squelching up from the top of his boots. "Very well done."

Rudolph killed the trout and Boylan came around and watched him as he laid the fish with the two others in the creel. "I could never do that," Boylan said. "Kill anything with my hands." He was wearing gloves. "They look like miniature sharks," he said, "don't they?"

They looked like trout to Rudolph. "I've never seen a shark," he said. He plucked some more fern and stuffed it in the creel, around the fish. His father would have trout for breakfast. His father liked trout. A return on his investment in the birthday rod and reel.

"Do you ever fish in the Hudson?" Boylan asked.

"Once in awhile. Sometimes, in season, a shad gets up this far."

"When my father was a boy, he caught salmon in the Hudson," Boylan said. "Can you imagine what the Hudson must have been like when the Indians were here? Before the Roosevelts. With bear and lynx on the shores and deer coming down to the banks."

"I see a deer once in awhile," Rudolph said. It had never occurred to him to wonder what the Hudson must have looked like with Iroquois canoes furrowing it.

"Bad for the crops, deer, bad for the crops," Boylan said.

Rudolph would have liked to sit down and take his boots off and get the water out, but he knew his socks were darned, and he didn't cherish the idea of displaying the thick patches of his mother's handiwork to Boylan.

As though reading his mind, Boylan said, "I do believe you ought to empty the water out of those boots. That water must be cold."

"It is." Rudolph pulled off one boot, then another. Boylan didn't seem to notice. He was looking around him at the overgrown woods that had been in his family's possession since just after the Civil War. "You used to be able to see the house from here. There was no underbrush. Ten gardeners used to work this land, winter and summer. Now the only ones who come are the state fisheries people once a year. You can't get anybody anymore. No sense to it, really, anyway." He studied the massed foliage of the shrub oak and blossomless dogwood and alder. "Trash trees," he said. "The forest primeval. Where only Man in vile. Who said that?"

"Longfellow," Rudolph said. His socks were soaking wet, as he put his boots back on.

"You read a lot?" Boylan said.

"We had to learn it in school." Rudolph refused to boast.

"I'm happy to see that our educational system does not neglect our native birds and their native wood-notes wild," Boylan said.

Fancy talk again, Rudolph thought. Who's he impressing? Rudolph didn't much like Longfellow, himself, but who did Boylan think he was to be so superior? What poems have you written, brother?

"By the way, I believe there's an old pair of hip-length waders up at the house. God knows when I bought them. If they fit you, you can have them. Why don't you come up and try them on?"

Rudolph had planned to go right on home. It was a long walk to the bus and he had been invited for dinner at Julie's house. After dinner they were to go to a movie. But waders . . . They cost over twenty dollars new. "Thank you, sir," he said.

"Don't call me sir," Boylan said. "I feel old enough as it is."

They started toward the house, on the overgrown path. "Let me carry the creel," Boylan said.

"It's not heavy," Rudolph said.

"Please," said Boylan. "It will make me feel as though I've done something useful today."

He's sad, Rudolph thought with surprise. Why, he's as sad as my mother. He handed the creel to Boylan, who slung it over his shoulder.

The house sat on the hill, huge, a useless fortress in Gothic stone, with ivy running wild all over it, defensive against knights in armor and dips in the Market.

"Ridiculous, isn't it?" Boylan murmured.

"Yes," Rudolph said.

"You have a nice turn of phrase, my boy." Boylan laughed. "Come on in." He opened the massive oak front doors.

My sister has passed through here, Rudolph thought. I should turn back.

But he didn't.

They went into a large, dark, marble-floored hall, with a big staircase winding up from it. An old man in a gray alpaca jacket and bow tie appeared immediately, as though merely by entering the house Boylan set up waves of pressure that drove servants into his presence.

"Good evening, Perkins," Boylan said. "This is Mr. Jordache, a young friend of the family."

Perkins nodded, the ghost of a bow. He looked English. He had a for King and Country face. He took Rudolph's battered hat and laid it on a table along the wall, a wreath on a royal tomb.

"I wonder if you could be kind enough, Perkins, to go into the Armory," Boylan said, "and hunt around a bit for my old pair of waders. Mr. Jordache is a fisherman." He opened the creel. "As you can see."

Perkins regarded the fish. "Very good size, sir." Caterer to the Crown.

"Aren't they?" The two men played an elaborate game with each other, the rules of which were unknown to Rudolph. "Take them in to Cook," Boylan said to Perkins.

"Ask her if she can't do something with them for dinner. You are staying to dinner, aren't you, Rudolph?"

Rudolph hesitated. He'd miss his date with Julie. But he *was* fishing Boylan's stream, and he *was* getting a pair of waders. "If I could make a telephone call," he said.

"Of course," Boylan said. Then to Perkins. "Tell Cook we'll be two." Axel Jordache would not eat trout for breakfast. "And while you're at it," Boylan said, "bring down a pair of nice, warm socks and a towel for Mr. Jordache. His feet are soaked. He doesn't feel it now, being young, but as he creaks to the fireside forty years from now, he will feel the rheumatism in his joints, even as you and I, and will remember this afternoon."

"Yes, sir," Perkins said and went off to the kitchen or to the Armory, whatever that was.

"I think you'll be more comfortable if you take your boots off here," Boylan said. It was a polite way of hinting to Rudolph that he didn't want him to leave a trail of wet footprints all over the house. Rudolph pulled off the boots. Silent reproach of darned socks.

"We'll go in here," Boylan pushed open two high carved wooden doors leading off the hallway. "I think Perkins has had the goodness to start a fire. This house is chilly on the best of days. At the very best it is always November in here. And on a day like this, when there's rain in the air, one can ice-skate on one's bones."

One. One, Rudolph thought, as, bootless, he went through the door which Boylan held open for him. One can take a flying hump for oneself.

The room was the largest private room Rudolph had ever been in. It didn't seem like November at all. Dark-red velvet curtains were drawn over the high windows, books were ranged on shelves on the walls, there were many paintings, portraits of highly colored ladies in nineteenth-century dresses and solid, oldish men with beards, and big cracked oils. Rudolph recognized the latter as views of the neighboring valley of the Hudson that must have been painted when it was all still farmland and forest. There was a grand piano with a lot of bound music albums strewn on it, and a table against a wall with bottles. There was a huge upholstered couch, some deep leather armchairs, and a library table heaped with magazines. An immense pale Persian carpet that looked hundreds of years old, was shabby and worn to Rudolph's unknowing eye. Perkins had, indeed, started a fire in the wide fireplace. Three logs crackled on heavy andirons and six or seven lamps around the room gave forth a tempered evening light. Instantly, Rudolph decided that one day he would live in a room like this.

"It's a wonderful room," he said sincerely.

"Too big for a single man," Boylan said. "One rattles around in it. I'm making us a whiskey."

"Thank you," Rudolph said. His sister ordering whiskey in the bar in the Port Philip House. She was in New York now, because of this man. Good or bad? She had a job, she had written. Acting. She would let him know when the play opened. She had a new address. She had moved from the Y.W.C.A. Don't tell Ma or Pa. She was being paid sixty dollars a week.

"You wanted to phone," Boylan said, pouring whiskey. "On the table near the window."

Rudolph picked up the phone and waited for the operator. A beautiful blonde woman with an out-of-style hairdo smiled at him from a silver frame on the piano. "Number, please," the operator said.

Rudolph gave her Julie's number. He hoped that Julie wasn't home, so that he could leave a message. Cowardice. Another mark against him in the Book of Himself.

But it was Julie's voice that answered, after two rings.

"Julie . . . " he began.

"Rudy!" Her pleasure at hearing his voice was a rebuke. He wished Boylan were not in the room. "Julie," he said, "about tonight. Something's come up . . . "

"What's come up?" Her voice was stony. It was amazing how a pretty young girl like that, who could sing like a lark, could also make her voice sound like a gate clanging, between one sentence and the next.

"I can't explain at the moment, but . . . "

"Why can't you explain at the moment?"

He looked across at Boylan's back. "I just can't," he said. "Anyway, why can't we make it for tomorrow night? The same picture's playing and . . . "

"Go to hell." She hung up.

He waited for a moment, shaken. How could a girl be so . . . so *decisive?* "That's fine, Julie," he said into the dead phone. "See you tomorrow. 'Bye." It was not a bad performance. He hung up.

"Here's your drink," Boylan called to him across the room. He made no comment on the telephone call.

Rudolph went over to him and took the glass. "Cheers," Boylan said as he drank.

Rudolph couldn't bring himself to say Cheers, but the drink warmed him and even the taste wasn't too bad.

"First one of the day," Boylan said, rattling the ice in his glass. "Thank you for joining me. I'm not a solitary drinker and I needed it. I had a boring afternoon. Please do sit down." He indicated one of the big armchairs near the fire. Rudolph sat in it and Boylan stood to one side of the hearth, leaning against the mantelpiece. There was a Chinese clay horse on the mantelpiece, stocky and warlike-looking. "I had insurance people here all afternoon," Boylan went on. "About that silly fire I had here on VE Day. Night, rather. Did you see the cross burn?"

"I heard about it," Rudolph said.

"Curious that they should have picked my place," Boylan said. "I'm not Catholic and I'm certainly not black or Jewish. The Ku Klux Klan up in these parts must be singularly misinformed. The insurance people keep asking me if I have any particular enemies. Perhaps you've heard something in town?"

"No," Rudolph said carefully.

"I'm sure I have. Enemies, I mean. But they don't advertise," Boylan said. "Too bad the cross wasn't nearer the house. It would be a blessing if this mausoleum burnt down. You're not drinking your drink."

"I'm a slow drinker," Rudolph said.

"My grandfather built for eternity," Boylan said, "and I'm living through it." He laughed. "Forgive me if I talk too much. There's so few opportunities of talking to anybody who has the faintest notion of what you're saying around here."

"Why do you live here, then?" Rudolph asked, youthful logical.

"I am doomed," said Boylan, with mock melodrama. "I am tied to the rock and the bird is eating my liver. Do you know that, too?"

"Prometheus."

"Imagine. Is that school, too?"

"Yes." I know a lot of things, mister, Rudolph wanted to say.

"Beware families," Boylan said. He had finished his drink fast and he left the mantelpiece to pour another for himself. "You pay for their hopes. Are you family-ridden, Rudolph? Are there ancestors you must not disappoint?"

"I have no ancestors," Rudolph said.

"A true American," said Boylan. "Ah, the waders."

Perkins was in the room, carrying a hip-length pair of rubber boots and a towel, and a pair of light-blue wool socks. "Just put everything down, please, Perkins," Boylan said.

"Very good, sir." Perkins put the waders within Rudolph's reach and draped the towel over the edge of the armchair. He put the socks on the end table next to the chair.

Rudolph stripped off his socks. Perkins took them from him, although Rudolph had intended to put them in his pocket. He had no idea what Perkins could do with a pair of soggy patched cotton socks in that house. He dried his feet with the towel. The towel smelled of lavender. Then he drew on the socks. They were of soft wool. He stood up and pulled on the waders. There was a triangular tear at the knee of one of them. Rudolph didn't think it was polite to mention it. "They fit fine," he said. Fifty dollars. At least fifty dollars, he thought. He felt like D'Artagnan in them.

"I think I bought them before the war," Boylan said. "When my wife left me, I thought I'd take up fishing."

Rudolph looked over quickly to see if Boylan was joking, but there was no glint of humor in the man's eyes. "I tried a dog for company. A huge Irish wolfhound. Brutus. A lovely animal. I had him for five years. We were inordinately attached to each other. Then someone poisoned him. My surrogate." Boylan laughed briefly. "Do you know what surrogate means, Rudolph?"

The school-teacher questions were annoying. "Yes," he said.

"Of course," said Boylan. He didn't ask Rudolph to define it. "Yes, I must have enemies. Or perhaps he was just chasing somebody's chickens."

Rudolph took off the boots and held them uncertainly. "Just leave them anywhere," Boylan said. "Perkins will put them in the car when I take you home. Oh, dear." He had seen the rip in the boot. "I'm afraid they're torn."

"It's nothing. I'll have it vulcanized," Rudolph said.

"No. I'll have Perkins attend to it. He loves mending things." Boylan made it sound as though Rudolph would be depriving Perkins of one of his dearest pleasures if he insisted upon mending the boot himself. Boylan was back at the bar table. The drink wasn't strong enough for him and he added whiskey to his glass. "Would you like to see the house, Rudolph?" He kept using the name.

"Yes," Rudolph said. He was curious to find out what an armory was. The only armory he had ever seen was the one in Brooklyn where he had gone for a track meet.

"Good," Bosylan said. "It may help you when you become an ancestor yourself. You will have an idea of what to inflict upon your descendants. Take your drink along with you."

In the hall there was a large bronze statue of a tigress clawing the back of a water buffalo. "Art," Boylan said. "If I had been a patriot I would have had it melted down for cannon." He opened two enormous doors, carved with cupids and garlands. "The ballroom," he said. He pushed at a switch on the wall.

The room was almost as big as the high school gymnasium. A huge crystal chandelier, draped in sheets, hung from the two-story-high ceiling. Only a few of the bulbs in the chandelier were working and the light through the muffling sheets was dusty and feeble. There were dozens of sheet-draped chairs around the painted wooden walls. "My father said his mother once had seven hundred people here. The orchestra played waltzes. Twenty-five pieces. Quite a club date, eh, Rudolph? You still play at the Jack and Jill?"

"No," Rudolph said, "our three weeks are finished."

"Charming girl, that little . . . what's her name?"

"Julie."

"Oh, yes, Julie. She doesn't like me, does she?"

"She didn't say."

"Tell her I think she's charming, will you? For what it's worth."

"I'll tell her.

"Seven hundred people," Boylan said. He put his arms up as though he were holding a partner and made a surprising little swoop waltz step. The whiskey sloshed over from his glass onto his hand. "I was in great demand at debutantes' parties." He took a handkerchief out of his pocket and dabbed at his hand. "Perhaps I'll give a ball myself. On the eve of Waterloo. You know about that, too?"

"Yes," Rudolph said. "Wellington's officers. I saw Becky Sharp." He had read

Byron, too, but he refused to show off for Boylan.

"Have you read *The Charterhouse of Parma?*"

"No."

"Try it, when you're a little older," Boylan said, with a last look around the dim ballroom. "Poor Stendhal, rotting in Civitavecchia, then dying unsung, with his mortgage on posterity."

All right, Rudolph thought, so you've read a book. But he was flattered at the same time. It was a literary conversation.

"Port Philip is my Civitavecchia," Boylan said. They were in the hall again and Boylan switched off the chandelier. He peered into the sheeted darkness. "The haunt of owls," he said. He left the doors open and walked toward the rear of the house. "That's the library," he said. He opened a door briefly. It was an enormous room, lined with books. There was a smell of leather and dust; Boylan closed the door. "Bound sets. All of Voltaire. That sort of thing. Kipling."

He opened another door. "The armory," Boylan said, switching on the lights. "Everybody else would call it a gun room, but my grandfather was a large man."

The room was in polished mahogany, with racks of shotguns and hunting rifles locked in behind glass. Trophies lined the walls, antlers, stuffed pheasants with long brilliant tails. The guns shone with oil. Everything as meticulously dusted. Mahogany cabinets with polished brass knobs made it look like a cabin on a ship.

"Do you shoot, Rudolph?" Boylan asked, sitting astride a leather chair, shaped like a saddle.

"No." Rudolph's hands itched to touch those beautiful guns.

"I'll teach you, if you want," Boylan said. "There's an old skeet trap somewhere on the property. There's nothing much left here, a rabbit or so, and once in a while a deer. During the season I hear the guns popping around the house. Poachers, but there's nothing much to be done about it." He gazed around the room. "Convenient for suicide," he said. "Yes, this was game country. Quail, partridge, doves, deer. I haven't fired a gun in years. Perhaps teaching you will reawaken my interest. A virile sport. Man, the hunter." His tone showed what he thought of this description of himself. "When you're making your way in the world it may help you one day to be known as a good gun. A boy I knew in college married into one of the biggest fortunes in North Carolina because of his keenness of eye and steadiness of hand. Cotton mills. The money, I mean. Reeves, his name was. A poor boy, but he had beautiful manners, and that helped. Would you like to be rich, Rudolph?"

"Yes."

"What do you plan to do after college?"

"I don't know," Rudolph said. "It depends upon what comes along."

"Let me suggest law," Boylan said. "This is a lawyer's country. And it's becoming more so each year. Didn't your sister tell me that you were the captain of the debating team at school?"

"I'm on the debating team." The mention of his sister made him wary.

"Perhaps you and I will drive down to New York some afternoon and visit her," Boylan said.

As they left the gun room, Boylan said, "I'll have Perkins set up the skeet trap this week, and order some pigeons. I'll give you a ring when it's ready."

"We don't have a phone."

"Oh, yes," Boylan said. "I believe I once tried looking it up in the directory. I'll drop you a line. I think I remember the address." He looked vaguely up the marble staircase. "Nothing much up there to interest you," he said. "Bedrooms. Mostly closed off. My mother's upstairs sitting room. Nobody sits there anymore. If you'll excuse me a moment, I'll go up and change for dinner. Make yourself at home. Give yourself another drink." He looked frail going up the sweeping staircase to the other floors, which would be of no interest to his young guest, except, of course, if his young guest were interested in seeing the bed upon which his sister had lost her virginity.

III

Rudolph went back into the living room and watched Perkins laying a table for dinner in front of the fire. Priestly hands on chalices and goblets. Westminster Abbey. Graves on the poets. A bottle of wine poked out of a silver ice bucket. A bottle of red wine, uncorked, was on a sideboard.

"I have made a telephone call, sir," Perkins said. "The boots will be ready by Wednesday next."

"Thank you, Mr. Perkins," Rudolph said.

"Happy to be of service, sir."

Two sirs in twenty seconds, Perkins returned to his sacraments.

Rudolph would have liked to pee, but he couldn't mention anything like that to a man of Perkins' stature. Perkins whispered out of the room, a Rolls-Royce of a man. Rudolph went to the window and parted the curtains a little and looked out. A fog swirled up from the valley in the darkness. He thought of his brother, Tom, at the window, peering in at a naked man with two glasses in his hands.

Rudolph sipped at his drink. Scotch got a grip on you. Maybe one day he would come back and buy this place, Perkins and all. This was America.

Boylan came back into the room. He had merely changed from the suede jacket to a corduroy one. He still was wearing the checked wool shirt and paisley scarf. "I didn't take the time for a bath," Boylan said. "I hope you don't mind." He went over to the bar. He had put some sort of cologne on himself. It gave a tang to the air around him.

"The dining room is chilling," Boylan said, glancing at the table in front of the fire. He poured himself a fresh drink. "President Taft once ate there. A dinner for sixty notables." Boylan walked over to the piano and sat down on the bench, putting his glass beside him. He played some random chords. "Do you play the violin, by any chance, Rudolph?"

"No."

"Any other instrument besides the trumpet?"

"Not really. I can fake a tune on the piano."

"Pity. We could have tried some duets. I don't think I know of any duets for piano and trumpet." Boylan began to play. Rudolph had to admit he played well. "Sometimes one gets tired of canned music," he said. "Do you recognize this, Rudolph?" He continued playing.

"No."

"Chopin, Nocturne in D-flat. Do you know how Schumann described Chopin's music?"

"No." Rudolph wished Boylan would just play and stop talking. He enjoyed the music.

"A cannon smothered in flowers," Boylan said. "Something like that. I think it was Schumann. If you have to describe music, I suppose that's as good a way as any."

Perkins came in and said, "Dinner is served, sir."

Boylan stopped playing and stood up. "Rudolph, do you want to pee or wash your hands or something?"

Finally. "Thank you, yes."

"Perkins," Boylan said, "show Mr. Jordache where it is."

"This way, sir," Perkins said.

As Perkins led him out of the room, Boylan sat down at the piano again and started playing from where he left off.

The bathroom near the front entrance was a large room with a stained-glass window, which gave the place a religious air. The toilet was like a throne. The faucets on the basin looked like gold. The strains of Chopin drifted in as Rudolph peed. He was sorry he had agreed to stay for dinner. He had the feeling that Boylan was trapping him. He was a complicated man, with his piano-playing, his waders and whiskey, his poetry and guns and his burning cross and poisoned dog. Rudolph didn't feel equipped to handle him. He could understand now why Gretchen had felt she had to get away from him.

When he went out into the hall again, he had to fight down the impulse to sneak out through the front door. If he could have gotten his boots without anyone's seeing him, he might have done it. But he couldn't see himself walking down to the bus stop and getting on it in stockinged feet. Boylan's socks.

He went back into the living room, enjoying Chopin. Boylan stopped playing and stood up and touched Rudolph's elbow formally as he led him to the table, where Perkins was pouring the white wine. The trout lay in a deep copper dish, in a kind of broth. Rudolph was disappointed. He liked trout fried.

They sat down facing each other. There were three glasses in front of each place, and a lot of cutlery. Perkins transferred the trout to a silver platter, with small boiled potatoes on it. Perkins stood over Rudolph and Rudolph served himself cautiously, uneasy with all the implements and determined to seem at ease.

"*Truit au bleu,*" Boylan said. Rudolph was pleased to note that he had a bad accent, or at least different from Miss Lenaut's. "Cook does it quite well."

"Blue trout," Rudolph said. "That's the way they cook it in France." He couldn't help showing off on this one subject, after Boylan's phoney accent.

"How do you know?" Boylan looked at him questioningly. "Have you ever been in France?"

"No. In school. We get a little French newspaper for students every week and there was an article about cooking."

Boylan helped himself generously. He had a good appetite. "*Tu parles français?*"

Rudolph made a note of the *tu*. In an old French grammar he had once looked through, the student was instructed that the second-person singular was to be used for servants, children, non-commissioned soldiers, and social inferiors.

"*Un petit peu.*"

"*Moi, j'étais en France quand j'étais jeune,*" Boylan said, the accent rasping. "*Avec mes parents. J'ai veçu mon premier amour à Paris. Quand c'était? Mille neuf cent vingt-huit, vingt-neuf. Comment s'appelait-elle? Anne? Annette? Elle était délicieuse.*"

She might have been delicious, Boylan's first love, Rudolph thought, tasting the profound joys of snobbery, but she sure didn't work on his accent.

"*Tu as l'envie d'y aller? En France?*" Boylan asked, testing him. He had said he could speak a little French and Boylan wasn't going to let him get away with it unchallenged.

"*J'irai, je suis sûr,*" Rudolph said, remembering just how Miss Lenaut would have said it. He was a good mimic. "*Peut-être après l'Université. Quad le pays sera rétabli.*"

"Good God," Boylan said, "you speak like a Frenchman."

"I had a good teacher." Last bouquet for poor Miss Lenaut, French cunt.

"Maybe you ought to try for the Foreign Service," Boylan said. "We could use some bright young men. But be careful to marry a rich wife first. The pay is dreadful." He sipped at the wine. "I thought I wanted to live there. In Paris. My family thought differently. Is my accent rusty?"

"Awful," Rudolph said.

Boylan laughed. "The honesty of youth." He grew more serious. "Or maybe it's a family characteristic. Your sister matches you."

They ate in silence for awhile, Rudolph carefully watching how Boylan used his knife and fork. A good gun, with beautiful manners.

Perkins took away the fish dishes and served some chops and baked potatoes and green peas. Rudolph wished he could send his mother up for some lessons in the kitchen here. Perkins presided over the red wine, rather than poured it. Rudolph wondered what Perkins knew about Gretchen. Everything, probably. Who made the bed in the room upstairs?

"Has she found a job yet?" Boylan asked, as though there had been no interruption in the conversation. "She told me she intended to be an actress?"

"I don't know," Rudolph said, keeping all information to himself. "I haven't heard from her recently."

"Do you think she'll be successful?" Boylan asked. "Have you ever seen her act?"

"Once. Only in a school play." Shakespeare battered and reeling, in homemade costumes. The seven ages of man. The boy who played Jacques nervously pushing at his beard, to make sure it was still pasted on. Gretchen looking strange and beautiful and not at all like a young man in her tights, but saying the words clearly.

"Does she have talent?" Boylan asked.

"I think so. She has *something*. Whenever she came onto the stage everybody stopped coughing."

Boylan laughed. Rudolph realized that he had sounded like a kid. "What I mean . . ." He tried to regain lost ground. "Is, well, you could feel the audience focusing on her, being for her, in a way that they weren't for any of the other actors. I guess that's talent."

"It certainly is." Boylan nodded. "She's an extraordinarily beautiful girl. I don't suppose a brother would notice that."

"Oh, I noticed it," Rudolph said.

"Did you?" Boylan said absently. He no longer seemed interested. He waved for Perkins to take the dishes away and got up and went over to a big phonograph and put on the Brahms Second Piano Concerto, very loud, so that they didn't talk for the rest of the meal. Five kinds of cheese on a wooden platter. Salad. A plum tart. No wonder Boylan had a paunch.

Rudolph looked surreptitiously at his watch. If he could get out of there early enough maybe he could catch Julie. It would be too late for the movies, but maybe he could make up to her, anyway, for standing her up.

After dinner, Boylan had a brandy with the demitasse, and put on a symphony. Rudolph was tired from the long afternoon's fishing. The two glasses of wine he had drunk made him feel blurred and sleepy. The loud music was crushing him. Boylan was polite, but distant. Rudolph had the feeling the man was disappointed in him because he hadn't opened up about Gretchen.

Boylan sat sunk in a deep chair, his eyes almost closed, concentrating on the music, occasionally taking a sip of the brandy. He might just as well have been alone, Rudolph thought resentfully, or with his Irish wolfhound. They porobably had some lively evenings here together, before the neighbors put out the poison. Maybe he's getting ready to offer me a position as his dog.

There was a scratch on the record now and Boylan made an irritated gesture as the clicking recurred. He stood up and turned off the machine. "I'm sorry about that," he said to Rudolph. "The revenge of the machine age on Schumann. Shall I take you on down to town now?"

"Thank you," Rudolph stood up, gratefully.

Boylan looked down at Rudolph's feet. "Oh," he said. "You can't go like that, can you?"

"If you'll give me my boots . . . "

"I'm sure they're still soaking wet inside," Boylan said. "Wait here a minute. I'll find something for you." He went out of the room and up the stairway.

Rudolph took a long look around the room. How good it was to be rich. He wondered if he ever was going to see the room again. Thomas had seen it once, although he had not been invited in. *He came down into the livingroom bare-assed, with his thing hanging down to his knees, he's a regular horse, and made two whiskies and called up the stairs, "Gretchen, do you want your drink up there or do you want to come down for it?"*

Now that he had a chance to listen to Boylan, Rudolph recognized that Tom's caricature of the man's voice had been an accurate one. He had caught the educated flattening out on the "there," and the curious way he had of making questions not sound like questions.

Rudolph shook his head. What could Gretchen have been thinking of? "*I liked it.*" He heard her voice again in the Port Philip House bar. "*I liked it better than anything that had ever happened to me.*"

He walked restlessly around the room. He looked at the album of the symphony that Boylan had cut off. Schumann's Third, the Rhenish Symphony. Well, at least he had learned something today. He would recognize it when he heard it again. He picked up a silver cigarette lighter a foot long and examined it. There was a monogram on it. T.B. Purposely expensive gadgets for doing things that cost nothing to the poor. He flicked it open. It spouted flame. The burning cross. Enemies. He heard Boylan's footsteps on the marble floor in the hall and hurriedly doused the flame and put the lighter down.

Boylan came into the room. He was carrying a little overnight bag and a pair of mahogany-colored moccasins. "Try these on, Rudolph," he said.

The moccasins were old but beautifully polished, with thick soles and leather tassels. They fit Rudolph perfectly. "Ah," Boylan said, "you have narrow feet, too." One aristocrat to another.

"I'll bring them back in a day or two," Rudolph said, as they started out.

"Don't bother," Boylan said. "They're old as the hills. I never wear them."

Rudolph's rod, neatly folded, and the creel and net were on the back seat of the Buick. The fireman's boots, still damp inside, were on the floor behind the front seat. Boylan swung the overnight bag onto the back seat and they got into the car. Rudolph had retrieved the old felt hat from the table in the hallway, but didn't have the courage to put it on with Perkins watching him. Boylan turned on the radio in the car, jazz from New York, so they didn't talk all the way to Vanderhoff Street. When Boylan stopped the Buick in front of the bakery, he turned the radio off.

"Here we are," he said.

"Thank you very much," Rudolph said. "For everything."

"Thank *you*, Rudolph," Boylan said. "It's been a refreshing day." As Rudolph put his hand on the handle of the car door, Boylan reached out and held his arm lightly. "Ah, I wonder if you'd do me a favor."

"Of course."

"In that bag back there . . . " Boylan twisted a little holding onto the wheel to indicate the presence of the leather overnight bag behind him. ". . . there's something I'd particularly like your sister to have. Do you think you could get it to her?"

"Well," Rudolph said, "I don't know when I'll be seeing her."

"There's no hurry," Boylan said. "It's something I know she wants, but it's not pressing."

"Okay," Rudolph said. It wasn't like giving away Gretchen's address, or anything like that. "Sure. When I happen to see her."

"That's very good of you, Rudolph." He looked at his watch. "It's not very late. Would you like to come and have a drink with me someplace? I don't fancy going back to that dreary house alone for the moment."

"I have to get up awfully early in the morning," Rudolph said. He wanted to be by himself now, to sort out his impressions of Boylan, to assess the dangers and the possible advantages in knowing the man. He didn't want to be loaded with any new impressions, Boylan drunk, Boylan with strangers at a bar, Boylan perhaps flirting with a women, or making a pass at a sailor. The idea was sudden. Boylan, the fairy? Making a pass at *him*. The delicate hands on the piano, the gifts, the clothes that were like costumes, the unobtrusive touching.

"What's early?" Boylan asked.

"Five," Rudolph said.

"Good God!" Boylan said. "What in the world does anyone do up at five o'clock in the morning?"

"I deliver rolls on a bicycle for my father," Rudolph said.

"I see," Boylan said. "I suppose *somebody* has to deliver rolls." He laughed. "You just don't *seem* like a roll-deliverer."

"It's not my main function in life," Rudolph said.

"What is your main function in life, Rudolph?" Absently, Boylan switched off the headlights. It was dark in the car because they were directly under a lamppost. There was no light from the cellar. His father hadn't begun his night's work. If his father were asked, would he say that his main function in life was baking rolls?

"I don't know yet," Rudolph said. Then aggressively, "What's yours?"

"I don't know," Boylan said. "Yet. Have you any idea?"

"No." The man was split into a million different parts. Rudolph felt that if he were older he might be able to assemble Boylan into one coherent pattern.

"A pity," Boylan said. "I thought perhaps the clear eyes of youth would see things in me I am incapable of seeing in myself."

"How old are you, anyway?" Rudolph asked. Boylan spoke so much of the past that he seemed to stretch far, far back, to the Indians, to President Taft, to a greener geography. It occurred to Rudolph that Boylan was not old so much as old-fashioned.

"What would you guess, Rudolph?" Boylan asked, his tone light.

"I don't know." Rudolph hesitated. Everybody over thirty-five seemed almost the same age to Rudolph, except for real tottering graybeards, hunching along on canes. He was never surprised when he read in the papers that somebody thirty-five had died. "Fifty?"

Boylan laughed. "Your sister was kinder," he said. "Much kinder."

Everything comes back to Gretchen, Rudolph thought. He just can't stop talking about her. "Well, Rudolph said, "how old *are* you?"

"Forty." Boylan said. "Just turned forty. With all my life still ahead of me, alas," he said ironically.

You have to be damn sure of yourself, Rudolph thought, to use a word like "alas."

"What do you think you'll be like when you're forty, Rudolph?" Boylan asked lightly. "Like me?"

"No," Rudolph said.

"Wise young man. You wouldn't want to be like me, I take it?"

"No." He'd asked for it and he was going to get it.

"Why not? Do you disapprove of me?"

"A little," Rudolph said. "But that's not why."

"What's the reason you don't want to be like me?"

"I'd like to have a room like yours," Rudolph said. "I'd like to have money like you and books like you and a car like you. I'd like to be able to talk like you—some of the time, anyway—and know as much as you and go to Europe like you . . . "

"But . . . "

"You're lonesome," Rudolph said. "You're sad."

"And when you're forty you do not intend to be lonesome and sad?"

"No."

"You will have a loving, beautiful wife," Boylan said, sounding like someone reciting a fairy story for children, "waiting at the station each evening to drive you home after your day's work in the city, and handsome, bright children who will love you and whom you will see off to the next war, and . . . "

"I don't expect to marry," Rudolph said.

"Ah," Boylan said. "You have studied the institution. I was different. I expected to marry. And I married. I expected to fill that echoing castle on the hill with the laughter of little children. As you may have noticed, I am not married and there is very little laughter of any kind in that house. Still, it isn't too late . . ." He took out a cigarette from his gold case and used his lighter. In its light his hair looked gray, his face deeply lined with shadows. "Did your sister tell you I asked her to marry me?"

"Yes."

"Did she tell you why she wouldn't?"

"No."

"Did she tell you she was my mistress?"

The word seemed dirty to Rudolph. If Boylan had said, "Did she tell you that I fucked her?" it would have made him resent Boylan less. It would have made her seem less like another of Theodore Boylan's possessions. "Yes," he said. "She told me."

"Do you disapprove?" Boylan's tone was harsh.

"Yes."

"Why?"

"You're too old for her."

"That's my loss," Boylan said. "Not hers. When you see her, will you tell her the offer still holds?"

"No."

Boylan seemed not to have noticed the no. "Tell her," he said, "that I cannot bear to lie in my bed without her. I'll tell you a secret, Rudolph. I wasn't at Jack and Jill's that night by accident. I never go to places like that, as you can well imagine. I made it a point to find out where you were playing. I followed you out to my car. I was looking for Gretchen. Maybe I had some foolish notion I could find something of the sister in the brother."

"I'd better go to sleep," Rudolph said cruelly. He opened the car door and got out. He reached into the back for his rod and creel and net and the fireman's boots. He put on the ridiculous felt hat. Boylan sat smoking, squinting through the smoke at the straight line of lights of Vanderhoff Street, like a lesson in drawing class in perspective. Parallel to infinity, where lines meet or do not meet, as the case may be.

"Don't forget the bag, please," Boylan said.

Rudolph took the bag. It was very light, as though there were nothing in it. Some new scientific infernal machine.

"Thenk you for your delightful visit," Boylan said. "I'm afraid I got all the best of it. Just for the price of an old pair of torn waders that I was never going to use anymore anyway. I'll let you know when the skeet trap is up. Roll on, young unmarried roll-deliverer. I'll think of you at five A.M." He started the motor of the car and drove off abruptly.

Rudolph watched the red tail lights speeding off toward infinity, twin signals saying Stop! then unlocked the door next to the bakery and lugged all the stuff into the hall. He turned on the light and looked at the bag. The lock was open. The key, on a leather thong, hung from the handle. He opened the bag, hoping that his mother hadn't heard him come in.

There was a bright-red dress lying in a careless heap in the bag. Rudolph picked it up and studied it. It was lacy and cut low in front, he could tell that. He tried to imagine his sister wearing it, showing practically everything.

"Rudolph?" It was his mother's voice, from above, querulous.

"Yes, Ma." He turned the light out hurriedly. "I'll be right back. I forgot to get the evening papers." He picked up the bag and got out of the hallway before his mother could come down. He didn't know whom he was protecting, himself or Gretchen or his mother.

He hurried, over to Buddy Westerman's, on the next block. Luckily, there were still lights on. The Westerman house was big and old. Buddy's mother let the River Five practice in the basement. Rudolph whistled. Buddy's mother was a jolly, easy-going woman who liked boys and served them all milk and cake after the practice sessions, but he didn't want to have to talk to her tonight. He took the key of the bag off the handle and locked the bag and put the key in his pocket.

After awhile, Buddy came out. "Hey," he said, "what's up? This time of night?"

"Listen, Buddy," Rudolph said, "will you hold onto this for me for a couple of days?" He thrust the bag at Buddy. "It's a present for Julie and I don't want my old lady to see it." Inspired lie. Everybody knew what misers the Jordaches were. Buddy also knew that Mrs. Jordache didn't like the idea of Rudolph going around with girls.

"Okay," Buddy said carelessly. He took the bag.

"I'll do as much for you some day," Rudolph said.

"Just don't play flat on 'Stardust.' " Buddy was the best musician in the band and that gave him the right to say things like that. "Any other little thing?"

"No."

"By the way," Buddy said, "I saw Julie tonight. I was passing the movie. She was going in. With a guy I didn't know. An old guy. Twenty-two, at least. I asked her where you were and she said she didn't know and didn't care."

"Pal," Rudolph said.

"No use living your life in total ignorance," Buddy said. "See you tomorrow." He went in, carrying the bag.

Rudolph went down to the Ace Diner to buy the evening paper. He sat at the counter reading the sports page while drinking a glass of milk and eating two doughnuts. The Giants had won that afternoon. Other than that, Rudolph couldn't decide whether it had been a good day or a bad day.

IV

Thomas kissed Clothilde good night. She was lying under the covers, with her hair spread on the pillow. She had turned on the lamp so that he could find his way out without bumping into anything. There was the soft glow of a smile as she touched his cheek. He opened the door without a sound and closed it behind him. The crack of light under the door disappeared as Clothilde switched off the lamp.

He went through the kitchen and out into the hallway and mounted the dark steps carefully, carrying his sweater. There was no sound from Uncle Harold's and Tante Elsa's bedroom. Usually, there was snoring that shook the house. Uncle Harold must be sleeping on his side tonight. Nobody had died in Saratoga. Uncle Harold had lost three pounds, drinking the waters.

Thomas climbed the narrow steps to the attic and opened the door to his room and put on the light. Uncle Harold was sitting there in striped pajamas, on the bed.

Uncle Harold smiled at him peculiarly, blinking in the light. Four of his front upper teeth were missing. He had a bridge that he took out at night.

"Good evening, Tommy," Uncle Harold said. His speech was gappy, without the bridge.

"Hi, Uncle Harold," Thomas said. He was conscious that his hair was mussed and that he smelled of Clothilde. He didn't know what Uncle Harold was doing there. It was the first time he had come to the room. Thomas knew he had to be careful about what he said and how he said it.

"It is quite late, isn't it, Tommy?" Uncle Harold said. He was keeping his voice down.

"Is it?" Thomas said. "I haven't looked at a clock." He stood near the door, away from Uncle Harold. The room was bare. He had few possessions. A book from the library lay on the dresser. *Riders of the Purple Sage.* The lady at the library had said he would like it. Uncle Harold filled the little room in his striped pajamas, making the bed sag in the middle, where he sat on it.

"It is nearly one o'clock," Uncle Harold said. He sprayed because of the missing teeth. "For a growing boy who has to get up early and do a day's work. A growing boy needs his sleep, Tommy."

"I didn't realize how late it was," Thomas said.

"What amusements have you found to keep a young boy out till one o'clock in the morning, Tommy?"

"I was just wandering around town."

"The bright lights," Uncle Harold said. "The bright lights of Elysium, Ohio."

Thomas faked a yawn and stretched. He threw his sweater over the one chair of the room. "I'm sleepy now," he said. "I better get to bed fast."

"Tommy," Uncle Harold said, in that wet whisper, "you have a good home here, hey?"

"Sure."

"You eat good here, just like the family, hey?"

"I eat all right."

"You have a good home, a good roof over your head."

The "roof" came out "woof" through the gap.

"I'm not complaining." Thomas kept his voice low. No sense in waking Tante Elsa and getting her in on the conference.

"You live in a nice clean house," Uncle Harold persisted. "Everybody treats you like a member of the family. You have your own personal bicycle."

"I'm not complaining."

"You have a good job. You are paid a man's wages. You are learning a trade. There will be unemployment now, millions of men coming home, but for the mechanic, there is always a job. Am I mistaken?"

"I can take care of myself," Thomas said.

"You can take care of youself," Uncle Harold said. "I hope so. You are my flesh and blood. I took you in without a question, didn't I, when your father called? You were in trouble, Tommy, in Port Philip, weren't you, and Uncle Harold asked no questions, he and Tante Elsa took you in."

"There was a little fuss back home," Thomas said. "Nothing serious."

"I ask no questions." Magnanimously, Uncle Harold waved away all thought of interrogation. His pajamas opened. There was a view of plump, pink rolls of beer-and-sausage belly over the drawstrings of the pajama pants. "In return for this, what do I ask? Impossibilities? Gratitude? No. A little thing. That a young boy should behave himself properly, that he should be in bed at a resonable hour. His own bed, Tommy."

Oh, that's it, Thomas thought. The sonofabitch knows. He didn't say anything.

"This is a clean house, Tommy," Uncle Harold said. "The family is respected. Your aunt is received in the best homes. You would be surprised if I told you what my credit is at the bank. I have been approached to run for the State Legislature in Columbus on the Republican ticket, even though I have not been born in this country. My two daughters have clothes . . . I challenge any two young ladies to dress better. They are model students. Ask me one day to show you their report cards, what their teachers say about them. They go to Sunday school every Sunday. I drive them myself. Pure young souls, sleeping like angels, right under this very room, Tommy."

"I get the picture," Thomas said. Let the old idiot get it over with.

"You were not wandering around town tonight till one o'clock, Tommy," Uncle Harold said sorrowfully. "I know where you were. I was thirsty. I wanted a bottle of beer from the Frigidaire. I heard noises. Tommy, I am ashamed even to mention it. A boy your age, in the same house with my two daughters."

"So what?" Thomas said sullenly. The idea of Uncle Harold outside Clothilde's door nauseated him.

"So what? Is that all you have to say, Tommy? So what?"

"What do you want me to say?" He would have liked to be able to say that he loved Clothilde, that it was the best thing that had ever happened to him in his whole rotten life, that she loved him, that if he were older he would take her away from Uncle Harold's clean, goddamn house, from his respected family, from his model, pale-blonde daughters. But, of course, he couldn't say it. He couldn't say anything. His tongue strangled him.

"I want you to say that you are sorry for the filthy thing that ignorant, scheming peasant has done to you," Uncle Harold whispered. "I want you to promise you will never touch her again. In this house or anywhere else."

"I'm not promising anything," Thomas said.

"I'm being kind," Uncle Harold said. "I am being delicate. I am speaking quietly, like a reasonable and forgiving man, Tommy. I do not want to make a scandal. I don't want your Aunt Elsa to know her house has been dirtied, that her children have been exposed to . . . *Ach,* I can't find the words, Tommy."

"I'm not promising anything," Thomas said.

"Okay. You are not promising anything," Uncle Harold said. "You don't have to promise anything. When I leave this room, I am going down to the room behind the kitchen. She will promise plenty, I assure you."

"That's what you think." Even to his own ears, it sounded hollow, childish.

"That's what I know, Tommy," Uncle Harold whispered. "She will promise anything. She's in trouble. If I fire her, where will she go? Back to her drunken husband in Canada who's been looking for her for two years so he can beat her to death?"

"There're plenty of jobs. She doesn't have to go to Canada."

"You think so. The authority of International Law," Uncle Harold said. "You think it's as easy as that. You think I won't go to the police."

"What've the police got to do with it?"

"You are a child, Tommy," Uncle Hahrold said. "You put it up in between a married woman's legs like a grown man, but you have the mind of a child. She has corrupted the morals of a minor, Tommy. You are the minor. Sixteen years old. That is a crime, Tommy. A serious crime. This is a civilized country. Children are protected in this country. Even if they didn't put her in jail, they would deport her, an undesirable alien who corrupts the morals of minors. She is not a citizen. Back to Canada she would go. It would be in the papers. Her husband would be waiting for her. Oh, yes," Uncle Harold said. "She will promise." He stood up. "I am sorry for you, Tommy. It is not your fault. It is in your blood. Your father was a whoremaster. I was ashamed to say hello to him in the street. And your mother, for your information, was a bastard. She was raised by the nuns. Ask her some day who her father was. Or even her mother. Get some sleep, Tommy." He patted him comfortingly on the shoulder. "I like you. I would like to see you grow up into a good man. A credit to the family. I am doing what is best for you. Go—get some sleep."

Uncle Harold padded out of the room, barefooted, beery mastodon in the shapeless striped pajamas, all weapons on his side.

Thomas put out the light. He lay face down on the bed. He punched the pillow, once with all his strength.

The next morning, he went down early, to try to talk to Clothilde before breakfast. But Uncle Harold was there, at the dining-room table, reading the newspaper.

"Good morning, Tommy," he said, looking up briefly. His teeth were back in. He sipped noisily at his coffee.

Clothilde came in with Thomas's orange juice. She didn't look at him. Her face was dark and closed. Uncle Harold didn't look at Clothilde. "It is terrible what is happening in Germany," he said. "They are raping women in Berlin. The Russians. They have been waiting for this for a hundred years. People are living in cellars. If I hadn't met your Tante Elsa and come to this country when I was a young man, God knows where I would be now."

Clothilde came in with Thomas's bacon and eggs. He searched her face for a sign. There was no sign.

When he finished breakfast, Thomas stood up. He would have to get back later in the day, when the house was empty. Uncle Harold looked up from his paper. "Tell Coyne, I'll be in at nine-thirty," Uncle Harold said. "I have to go to the bank. And tell him I promised Mr. Duncan's car by noon, washed."

Thomas nodded and went out of the room as the two daughters came down, fat and pale. "My angels," he heard Uncle Harold say as they went into the dining room and kissed him good morning.

He had his chance at four o'clock that afternoon. It was the daughters' dentist day for their braces and Tante Elsa always took them, in the second car. Uncle Harold, he knew, was down at the showroom. Clothilde should be alone.

"I'll be back in a half-hour," he told Coyne. "I got to see somebody."

Coyne wasn't pleased, but screw him.

Clothilde was watering the lawn when he pedaled up. It was a sunny day and rainbows shimmered in the spray from the hose. The lawn wasn't a big one and was shadowed by a linden tree. Clothilde was in a white uniform. Tante Elsa liked her maids to look like nurses. It was an advertisement of cleanliness. You could eat off the floor in my house.

Clothilde looked at Thomas once as he got off his bicycle, then continued watering the lawn.

"Clothilde," Thomas said, "come inside. I have to talk to you."

"I'm watering the lawn." She turned the nozzle and the spray concentrated down to a stream, with which she soaked a bed of petunias along the front of the house.

"Look at me," he said.

"Aren't you supposed to be at work?" She kept turned away from him.

"Did he come down to your room last night?" Thomas said. "My uncle?"

"So?"

"Did you let him in?"

"It's his house," Clothilde said. Her voice was sullen.

"Did you promise him anything?" He knew he sounded shrill, but he couldn't help himself.

"What difference does it make? Go back to work. People will see us."

"Did you promise him anything?"

"I said I wouldn't see you alone anymore," she said flatly.

"You didn't mean it, though," Thomas pleaded.

"I meant it." She fiddled with the nozzle again. The wedding ring on her finger gleamed. "We are over."

"No, we're not!" He wanted to grab her and shake her. "Get the hell out of this house. Get another job. I'll move away and . . ."

"Don't talk nonsense," she said sharply. "He told you about my crime." She mocked the word. "He will have me deported. We are not Romeo and Juliet. We are a schoolboy and a cook. Go back to work."

"Couldn't you say anything to him?" Thomas was desperate. He was afraid he was going to break down and cry, right there on the lawn, right in front of Clothilde.

"There is nothing to say. He is a wild man," Clothilde said. "He is jealous. When a man is jealous you might as well talk to a wall, a tree."

"Jealous?" Thomas said. "What do you mean?"

"He has been trying to get into my bed for two years," Clothilde said calmly. "He comes down at night when his wife is asleep and scratches on the door like a kitten."

"That fat bastard," Thomas said. "I'll be there waiting for him the next time."

"No you won't," Clothilde said. "He is going to come in the next time. You might as well know."

"You're going to let him?"

"I'm a servant," she said. "I lead the life of a servant. I do not want to lose my job or go to jail or go back to Canada. Forget it," she said. "*Alles kaput.* It was nice for two weeks. You're a nice boy. I'm sorry I got you into trouble."

"All right, all right," he shouted. "I'm never going to touch another woman again as long as—"

He was too choked to say anything more and ran over to his bicycle and rode blindly away, leaving Clothilde watering the roses. He didn't turn around. So he didn't see the tears on the dark, despairing face.

St. Sebastian, well supplied with arrows, he headed for the garage. The rods would come later.

CHAPTER 9

I

WHEN SHE CAME out of the Eighth Street subway station she stopped for six bottles of beer and then went into the cleaner's for Willie's suit. It was dusk, the early dusk of November, and the air was nippy. People were wearing coats and moving quickly. A girl in slacks and a trench coat slouched in front of her, her hair covered by a scarf. The girl looked as though she had just gotten out of bed, although it was after five o'clock in the afternoon. In Greenwich Village, people might get out of bed at any time of the day or night. It was one of the charms of the neighborhood, like the fact that most of the population was young. Sometimes, when she walked through the neighborhood, among the young, she thought, "I am in my native country."

The girl in the trench coat went into Corcoran's Bar and Grill. Gretchen knew it well. She was known in a dozen bars of the neighborhood. A good deal of her life was spent in bars now.

She hurried toward Eleventh Street, the beer bottles heavy in the big brown-paper sack and Willie's suit carefully folded over her arm. She hoped Willie was home. You never could know when he'd be there. She had just come from an understudy rehearsal uptown and she had to go back for the eight o'clock call. Nichols and the director had her read for the understudy's job and had told her that she had talent. The play was a moderate success. It would almost certainly last till June. She walked across the stage in a bathing suit three times a night. The audience laughed each time, but the laughter was nervous. The author had been furious the first time he had heard the laughter, at a preview, and had wanted to cut her out of the play, but Nichols and the director had persuaded him that the laughter was good for the play. She received some peculiar letters backstage and telegrams asking her if she wanted to go out to supper and twice there were roses. She never answered anybody. Willie was always there in her dressing room after the show to watch her wash off the body make-up and get into her street clothes. When he wanted to tease her, he said, "Oh, God, why did I ever get married? I am quoting."

His divorce was dragging along, he said.

She went into the hallway of the walkup and looked to see if there was any mail in the box. Abbott-Jordache. She had printed the little card herself.

She opened the downstairs door with her key and ran up the three flights of stairs. She was always in a hurry, once she got into the house. She opened the door of the apartment, a little breathless from the stairs. The door opened directly on the living room. "Willie . . ." she was calling. There were only two small rooms, so there was no real reason to call out. She found excuses to say his name.

Rudolph was sitting on the tattered couch, a glass of beer in his hand.

"Oh," Gretchen said.

Rudolph stood up. "Hello, Gretchen," he said. He put down his glass and kissed her cheek, over the bag full of beer bottles and Willie's suit.

"Rudy," she said, getting rid of the bag and dropping the suit over the back of a chair, "what're you doing here?"

"I rang the bell," Rudolph said, "and your friend let me in."

"Your friend is getting dressed," Willie called from the next room. He often sat around in his bathrobe all day. The apartment was so small that you heard everything that was said in either of the rooms. A little kitchenette was concealed by a screen from the living room. "I'll be right out," Willie said from the bedroom. "I blow you a kiss."

"I'm so glad to see you." Gretchen took off her coat and hugged Rudolph hard. She stepped back to look at him. When she had been seeing him every day she hadn't realized how handsome he was, dark, straight, a button-down blue shirt and the blazer she had given him for his birthday. Those sad, clear, greenish eyes.

"Is it possible you've grown? In just a couple of months?"

"Almost six months," he said. Was there an accusation there?

"Come on," she said. "Sit down." She pulled him down on the couch next to her. There was a little leather overnight bag near the door. It didn't belong to Willie or her, but she had a feeling that she had seen it someplace before.

"Tell me about everything," she said. "What's happening at home? Oh, God, it's good to see you, Rudy." Still, her voice didn't sound completely natural to her. If she had known he was coming she'd have warned him about Willie. After all, he was only seventeen, Rudolph, and just to come barging in innocently and discover that his sister was living with a man . . . Abbott-Jordache.

"Nothing much is happening at home," Rudolph said. If he was embarrassed, he didn't show it. She could take lessons in control from Rudy. He sipped at his beer. "I am bearing the brunt of everybody's love, now that I'm the only one left."

Gretchen laughed. It was silly to worry. She hadn't realized how grown-up he was.

"How's Mom?" Gretchen asked.

"Still reading *Gone With the Wind*," Rudolph said. "She's been sick. She says the doctor says it's phlebitis."

Messages of cheer and comfort from the family hearth, Gretchen thought. "Who takes care of the store?" she asked.

"A Mrs. Cudahy," Rudolph said. "A widow. She costs thirty dollars a week."

"Pa must love that," Gretchen said.

"He isn't too happy."

"How is he?"

"To tell the truth," Rudolph said, "I wouldn't be surprised if he's actually sicker than Ma. He hasn't been out in the yard to hit the bag in months and I don't think he's been out on the river since you left."

"What is it?" Gretchen was surprised to find out that she was really concerned.

"I don't know, Rudolph said. "He just moves that way. You know Pa. He never says anything?"

"Do they talk about me?" Greatchen asked carefully.

"Not a word."

"And Thomas?"

"Gone and forgotten," Rudolph said. "I never did find out what happened. He never writes, of course."

"Our family," Gretchen said. They sat in silence, honoring the clan Jordache for a moment. "Well . . ." Gretchen shook herself. "How do you like our place?" She gestured to indicate the apartment, which she and Willie had rented furnished. The furniture looked as though it had come out of somebody's attic, but Gretchen had bought some plants and tacked some prints and travel posters on the walls. An Indian in a sombrero in front of a pueblo. Visit New Mexico.

"It's very nice," Rudolph said gravely.

"It's awfully tacky," Gretchen said. "But it has one supreme advantage. It's not Port Philip."

"I understand what you mean," Rudolph said. She wished he didn't look so serious. She wondered what had brought him down to see her.

"How's that pretty girl," she asked. Her voice was falsely bright. "Julie?"

"Julie," Rudolph said. "We have our ups and downs."

Willie came into the room combing his hair. He wasn't wearing a jacket. She had seen him only some five hours earlier, but if they had been alone she would have enfolded him as if they were meeting again after an absence of years. Willie kissed Gretchen quickly, leaning over the couch. Rudolph stood up politely. "Sit down, sit down, Rudy," Willie said. "I'm not your superior officer."

Briefly, Gretchen regretted Willie was so short.

"Ah," Willie said, seeing the beer and the pressed suit, "I told her the day I saw her for the first time that she would make some man a good wife and mother. Is it cold?"

"Uhuh."

Willie busied himself opening a bottle. "Rudy?"

"This will do me for awhile," Rudolph said, sitting down again.

Willie poured the beer in a glass that had been used and still had a rim of foam around it. He drank a lot of beer, Willie. "We can speak frankly," Willlie said, grinning. "I have explained everything to Rudy. I have told him that we are only technically living in sin. I've told him I have asked for your hand in marriage and that you've rejected me, although not for long."

This was true. He *had* asked her to marry him again and again. Quite often she was sure that he meant it.

"Did you tell him you were married?" she asked. She was anxious to have Rudy leave with no questions unanswered.

"I did," Willie said. "I hide nothing from brothers of women I love. My marriage was a whim of youth, a passing cloud, no bigger than a man's hand. Rudy is an intelligent young man. He understands. He will go far. He will dance at our wedding. He will support us in our old age."

For once, Wille's jokes made her uneasy. Although she had told him about Rudolph and Thomas and her parents, this was the first time he had had to cope with the actual presence of her family and she was worried that it was setting his nerves on edge.

Rudolph said nothing.

"What're you doing in New York, Rudy?" she said, to cover up for Willie.

"I got a ride down," Rudolph said. Plainly, he had something to say to her and he didn't feel like saying it in front of Willie. "It's a half-holiday at school."

"How's it going at school?" After she had said it she was afraid it sounded condescending, the sort of thing you say to other people's children because you don't know what else to talk about.

"Okay." Rudolph dismissed school.

"Rudy," Willie said, "what would you think of me as a brother-in-law?"

Rudolph looked at him soberly. Considering green eyes. "I don't know you," he said.

"That's it, Rudy, don't give anything away. That's my big trouble. I'm too open. I wear my heart on my tongue." Willie poured himself some more beer. He couldn't stay in one place. By contrast, Rudy seemed settled, sure of himself, judging. "I told Rudy I'd take him to see your show tonight," Willie said. "The toast of New York."

"It's a silly show," Gretchen said. She didn't like the idea of her brother watching her practically nude in front of a thousand people. "Wait till I play Saint Joan."

"I'm busy anyway," Rudolph said.

"I invited him to supper after the show, too," Willie said. "He pleads a prior engagement. See what you can do with him. I like him. I am tied to him by profound bonds."

"Some other night, thank, you," Rudolph said. "Gretchen, there's something for you in that bag." He indicated the little overnight bag. "I was asked to deliver it to you."

"What is it?" Gretchen asked. "Who's it from?"

"Somebody called Boylan," Rudolph said.

"Oh." Gretchen touched Willie's arm. "I think I'd like a beer, too, Willie." She got up and went over to the bag. "A present. Isn't that nice?" She picked the bag up and put it on a table and opened it. When she saw what was in the bag, she knew that she had known all along. She held the dress up against her. "I didn't remember that it was so *red,*" she said calmly.

"Holy man," Willie said.

Rudolph was watching them closely, first one, then the other.

"A memento of my depraved youth," Gretchen said. She patted Rudolph's arm. "That's all right, Rudy," she said. "Willie knows about Mr. Boylan. Everything."

"I will shoot him down like a dog," Willie said. "On sight. I'm sorry I turned in my B-17."

"Should I keep it, Willie?" Gretchen asked doubtfully.

"Of course. Unless it fits Boylan better than it fits you."

Gretchen put the dress down. "How come he got you to deliver it?" she asked Rudolph.

"I happened to meet him," Rudolph said. "I see him from time to time. I didn't give him your address, so he asked me . . ."

"Tell him I'm most grateful," Gretchen said. "Tell him I'll think of him when I wear it."

"You can tell him yourself, if you want," Rudolph said. "He drove me down. He's in a bar on Eighth Street, waiting for me now."

"Why don't we all go and have a drink with the bugger?" Willie said.

"I don't want to have a drink with him," Gretchen said.

"Should I tell him that?" Rudolph asked.

"Yes."

Rudolph stood up. "I'd better go," he said. "I told him I'd be right back."

Gretchen stood, too. "Don't forget the bag," she said.

"He said for you to keep it."

"I don't want it." Gretchen handed the smart little leather bag to her brother. He seemed reluctant to take it. "Rudy," she said curiously, "do you see much of Boylan?"

"A couple of times a week."

"You like him?"

"I'm not sure," Rudy said. "He's teaching me a lot."

"Be careful," she said.

"Don't worry." Rudolph put out his hand to Willie. "Goodbye," he said. "Thanks for the beer."

Willie shook his hand warmly. "Now you know where we are," he said, "come and see us. I mean it."

"I will," Rudolph said.

Gretchen kissed him. "I hate to see you run off like this."

"I'll come down to New York soon," Rudolph said. "I promise."

Gretchen opened the door for him. He seemed to want to say something more, but finally he just waved, a small troubled movement of his hand, and went down the stairs, carrying the bag. Gretchen closed the door slowly.

"He's nice, your brother," Willie said. "I wish I looked like that."

"You look good enough," Gretchen said. She kissed him. "I haven't kissed you for ages."

"Six long hours," Willie said. They kissed again.

"Six long hours," she said, smiling. "Please be home every time I come home."

"I'll make a point of it," Willie said. He picked up the red dress and examined it critically. "You brother's awfully grownup for a kid that age."

"Too, maybe."

"Why do you say that?"

"I don't know." She took a sip of beer. "He figures things out too carefully." She thought of her father's unlikely generosity toward Rudolph, of her mother's standing at night over an ironing board doing Rudolph's shirts. "He collects on his intelligence."

"Good for him," Willie said. "I wish I could collect on mine."

"What did you two talk about before I came?" she asked.

"We praised you."

"Okay, okay, aside from that?"

"He asked me about my work. I guess he wondered what his sister's feller was doing home in the middle of the afternoon while his sister was out earning her daily bread. I hope I put his fears to rest."

Willie had a job on a new magazine that a friend of his hand just started. It was a magazine devoted to radio and a lot of Willie's work consisted of listening to daytime programs and he preferred listening to them at home rather than in the little cramped office of the magazine. He was making ninety dollars a week and with her sixty they got along well enough, although they usually found themselves broke by the end of the week, because Willie liked to eat out in restaurants and stay up late in bars.

"Did you tell him you were a playwright, too?" Gretchen said.

"No. I'll leave him to find that out for himself. Some day."

Willie hadn't shown her his play yet. He only had an act and a half done and he was going to rewrite that completely.

Willie draped the dress against his front and walked like a model, with an exaggerated swing of the hips. "Sometimes I wonder what sort of a girl I would have made. What do you think?"

"No," she said.

"Try it on. Let's see what it looks like." He gave her the dress. She took it and went into the bedroom because there was a full-length mirror there on the back of a closet door. She had made the bed neatly before leaving the house, but the bedcover was mussed. Willie had taken a nap after lunch. They had been living together only a little over two months but she had amassed a private treasury of Willie's habits. His clothes were strewn all over the room. His corset was lying on the floor near the window. Gretchen smiled as she took off her sweater and skirt. She found Willie's childish disorder endearing. She liked picking up after him.

She zipped up the dress with difficulty. She had only put it on twice before, once in the shop and once in Boylan's bedroom, to model it for Boylan. She had never really worn it. She looked at herself critically in the mirror. She had the feeling that the lacy top exposed too much of her bosom. Her reflection in the red dress was that of an older woman, New Yorkish, certain of her attractions, a woman ready to enter any room, disdainful of all competition. She let her hair down so that it flowed darkly over her shoulders. It had been piled up in a practical knot on top of her head for the day's work.

After a last look at herself she went back into the living room. Willie was opening another bottle of beer. He whistled when he saw her. "You scare me," he said.

She pirouetted, making the skirt flare out. "Do you think I dare wear it?" she asked. "Isn't it a little naked?"

"Dee-vine," Willie drawled. "It is the perfectly designed dress. It is designed to make every man want to take you out of it immediately." He came over to her. "Suiting action to the thought," he said, "the gentlemen unzips the lady." He pulled at the zipper and lifted the dress over her head. His hands were cold from the beer bottle and she shivered momentarily. "What are we doing in this room?" he said.

They went into the bedroom and undressed quickly. The one time she had put on the dress for Boylan they had done the same thing. There was no avoiding echoes.

Willie made love to her sweetly and gently, almost as though she were frail and breakable. Once, in the middle of love-making the word *respectfully* had crossed her consciousness and she chuckled. She didn't tell Willie what had caused the chuckle. She was very different with Willie than with Boylan. Boylan had overcome her, obliterated her. It had been an intense and ferocious ceremony of destruction, a tournament, with winners and losers. After Boylan, she had come back into herself like someone returning from a long voyage, resentful of the rape of personality that had taken place. With Willie the act was tender and dear and sinless. It was a part of the flow of their lives together, everyday and natural. There was none of that sense of dislocation, abandonment, that Boylan had inflicted upon her and that she had hungered for so fiercely. Quite often she did not come with Willie but it made no difference.

"Precious," she murmured and they lay still.

After awhile Willie rolled carefully on his back and they lay side by side, not touching, only their hands entwined, childishly, between them.

"I'm so glad you were home," she said.

"I will always be home," he said.

She squeezed his hand.

He reached out with his other hand for the package of cigarettes on the bedside table and she disentangled her fingers, so that he could light up. He lay flat, his head on the thin pillow, smoking. The room was dark except for the light that was coming in through the open door from the living room. He looked like a small boy who would be punished if he were caught smoking. "Now," he said, "that you have finally had your will of me, perhaps we can talk a bit. What sort of day did you have?"

Gretchen hesitated. Later, she thought. "The usual," she said. "Gaspard made a pass at me again." Gaspard was the leading man of the show and during a break in the rehearsal he had asked her to come into his dressing room to run over some lines and had practically thrown her on the couch.

"He knows a good thing when he sees one, old Gaspard," Willie said comfortably.

"Don't you think you ought to talk to him and tell him he'd better leave your girl alone?" Gretchen said. "Or maybe hit him in the nose?"

"He'd kill me," Willie said, without shame. "He's twice my size."

"I'm in love with a coward," Gretchen said, kissing his ear.

"That's what happens to simple young girls in from the country." He puffed contentedly on his cigarette. "Anyway, in this department a girl's on her own. If you're old enough to go out at night in the Big City you're old enough to defend yourself."

"I'd beat up anybody who made a pass at *you*," Gretchen said.

Willie laughed. "I bet you would, too."

"Nichols was at the theater today. After the rehearsal he said he might have a part for me in a new play next year. A big part, he said."

"You will be a star. Your name will be in lights," Willie said. "You will discard me like an old shoe."

Just as well now as any other time, she thought. "I may not be able to take a job next season," she said.

"Why not?" He raised on one elbow and looked at her curiously.

"I went to the doctor this morning," she said. "I'm pregnant."

He looked at her hard, studying her face. He sat up and stubbed out his cigarette. "I'm thirsty," he said. He got out of bed stiffly. She saw the shadow of the long scar low on his spine. He put on an old cotton robe and went into the living room. She heard him pouring his beer. She lay back in the darkness, feeling deserted. I shouldn't have told him, she thought. Everything is ruined. She remembered the night it must have happened. They had been out late, nearly four o'clock, there had been a long loud argument in somebody's house. About Emperor Hirohito, of all things. Everybody had had a lot to drink. She had been fuzzy and hadn't taken any precautions. Usually, they were too tired when they came home to make love. That one goddamn night, they hadn't been too tired. One for the Emperor of Japan. If he says anything, she thought, I'm going to tell him I'll have an abortion. She knew she could never have an abortion, but she'd tell him.

Willie came back into the bedroom. She turned on the bedside lamp. This conversation was going to be adequately lit. What Willie's face told her was going to be more important than what he said. She pulled the sheet over herself. Willie's old cotton robe flapped around his frail figure. It was faded with many washings.

"Listen," Willie said, seating himself on the edge of the bed. "Listen carefully. I am going to get a divorce or I am going to kill the bitch. Then we are going to get married and I am going to take a course in the care and feeding of infants. Do you read me, Miss Jordache?"

She studied his face. It was all right. Better than all right.

"I read you," she said softly.

He leaned over her and kissed her cheek. She clutched the sleeve of his robe. For Christmas, she would buy him a new robe. Silk.

II

Boylan was standing at the bar in his tweed topcoat, staring at his glass, when Rudolph came down the little flight of steps from Eighth Street, carrying the overnight bag. There were only men standing at the bar and most of them were probably fairies.

"I see you have the bag," Boylan said.

"She didn't want it."

"And the dress?"

"She took the dress."

"What are you drinking?"

"A beer, please."

"One beer, please," Boylan said to the bartender. "And I'll continue with whiskey."

Boylan looked at himself in the mirror behind the bar. His eyebrows were blonder than they had been last week. His face was very tan, as though he had been lying on a southern beach for months. Two or three of the fairies at the bar were equally brown. Rudolph knew about the sun lamp by now. "I make it a point to look as healthy and attractive as I can at all times," Boylan had explained to Rudolph. "Even if I don't see anybody for weeks on end. It's a form of self-respect."

Rudolph was so dark, anyway, that he felt he could respect himself without a sun lamp.

The bartender put the drinks down in front of them. Boylan's fingers trembled a little as he picked up his glass. Rudolph wondered how many whiskies he had had.

"Did you tell her I was here?" Boylan asked.

"Yes."

"Is she coming?"

"No. The man she was with wanted to come and meet you, but she didn't." There was no point in not being honest.

"Ah," Boylan said. "The man she was with."

"She's living with somebody."

"I see," Boylan said flatly. "It didn't take long, did it?"

Rudolph drank his beer.

"Your sister is an extravagantly sensual woman," Boylan said. "I fear for where it may lead her."

Rudolph kept drinking his beer.

"They're not married, by any chance?"

"No. He's still married to somebody else."

Boylan looked at himself in the mirror again for a while. A burly young man in a black turtle-neck sweater down the bar caught his eye in the glass and smiled. Boylan turned away slightly, toward Rudolph. "What sort of fellow is he? Did you like him?"

"Young," Rudolph said. "He seemed nice enough. Full of jokes."

"Full of jokes," Boylan repeated. "Why shouldn't he be full of jokes? What sort of place do they have?"

"Two furnished rooms in a walkup."

"Your sister has a romantic disregard of the advantages of money," Boylan said. "She will regret it later. Among the other things she will regret."

"She seemed happy." Rudolph found Boylan's prophecies distasteful. He didn't want Gretchen to regret anything.

"What does her young man do for a living? Did you find out?"

"He writes for some kind of radio magazine."

"Oh," Boylan said. "One of those."

"Teddy," Rudolph said, "if you want my advice I think you ought to forget her."

"Out of the depths of your rich experience," Boylan said, "you think I ought to forget her."

"Okay," Rudolph said, "I haven't had any experience. But I *saw* her. I saw how she looked at the man."

"Did you tell her I still was willing to marry her?"

"No. That's something you'd better tell her yourself," Rudolph said. "Anyway you didn't expect me to say it in front of her fellow, did you?"

"Why not?"

"Teddy, you're drinking too much."

"Am I?" Boylan said. "Probably. You wouldn't want to walk back there with me and go up and pay your sister a visit, would you?"

"You know I can't do that," Rudolph said.

"No you can't," Boylan said. "You're like the rest of your family. You can't do a fucking thing."

"Listen," Rudolph said, "I can get on the train and go home. Right now."

"Sorry, Rudolph." Boylan put out his hand and touched Rudolph's arm. "I was standing here, telling myself she was going to walk through that door with you and she didn't walk through. Disappointment makes for bad manners. It's a good reason never to put yourself in a position in which you can be disappointed. Forgive me. Of course, you're not going home. We're going to take advantage of our freedom to have a night on the town. There's quite a good restaurant a few blocks from here and we'll start with that. Barman, may I have the check, please?"

He put some bills on the bar. The young man in the turtleneck sweater came up to them. "May I invite you gentlemen for a drink?" He kept his eyes on Rudolph, smiling.

"You're a fool," Boylan said, without heat.

"Oh, come off it, dearie," the man said.

Without warning, Boylan punched him, hard, on the nose. The man fell back against the bar, the blood beginning to seep from his nose.

"Let's go, Rudolph," Boylan said calmly.

They were out of the place before the barman or anyone else could make a move.

"I haven't been there since before the war," Boylan said, as they headed toward Sixth Avenue. "The clientele has changed."

If Gretchen had walked through the door, Rudolph thought, there would have been one less nosebleed in New York City that night.

After dinner at a restaurant where the bill, Rudolph noted, was over twelve dollars, they went to a night club in a basement that was called Cafe Society. "You might get some ideas for the River Five," Boylan said. "They have one of the best bands in the city. And there's usually a new colored girl who can sing."

The place was crowded, mostly with young people, many of whom were black, but Boylan got them a little table next to the small dance floor with an accurate tip. The music was deafening and wonderful. If the River Five was to learn anything from the band at Cafe Society it would be to throw their instruments into the river.

Rudolph leaned foward intently, gloriously battered by the music, his eyes glued on the Negro trumpeter. Boylan sat back smoking and drinking whiskies, in a small, private zone of silence. Rudolph had ordered a whiskey, too, because he had to order something, but it stood untouched on the table. With all the drinking Boylan had done that afternoon and evening, he would probably be in no condition to drive and Rudolph knew that he had to remain sober to take the wheel. Boylan had taught him to drive on the back roads around Port Philip.

"Teddy!" A woman in a short evening dress, with bare arms and shoulders, was standing in front of the table. "Teddy Boylan, I thought you were dead."

Boylan stood up. "Hello, Cissy," he said. "I'm not dead."

The woman flung her arms around him and kissed him, on the mouth. Boylan looked annoyed and turned his head. Rudolph stood up uncertainly.

"Where on earth have you been *hiding* yourself?" The woman stepped back a little, but held onto Boylan's sleeve. She was wearing a lot of jewelry that glittered in the reflection of the spotlight on the trumpet. Rudolph couldn't tell whether the jewelry was real or not. She was startlingly made up, with colored eyeshadow and a brilliantly rouged mouth. She kept looking at Rudolph, smiling. Boylan didn't make any move to introduce him and Rudolph didn't know whether he ought to sit down or not. "It's been *centuries*," she went on, not waiting for any answers, continuing to look boldly at Rudolph. "There've been the *wildest* rumors. It's just *sinful,* the way your nearest and dearest drop out of sight these days. Come on over to the table. The whole gang's there. Susie, Jack, Karen . . . They're just *longing* to see you. You're looking absolutely marvelous, darling. Ageless. Imagine finding you in a place like this. Why, it's an absolute *resurrection.*" She still kept smiling widely at Rudolph. "Do come over to the table. Bring your beautiful young friend with you. I don't think I caught the name, darling."

"May I present Mr. Rudolph Jordache," Boylan said stiffly. "Mrs. Alfred Sykes."

"Cissy to my friends," the woman said. "He *is* ravishing. I don't blame you for switching, darling."

"Don't be more idiotic than God originally made you, Cissy," Boylan said.

The woman laughed. "I see you're just as much of a shit as ever, Teddy," she said. "Do come over to the table and say hello to the group." With a fluttery wave of the hand, she turned and made her way through the jungle of tables toward the back of the room.

Boylan sat down and motioned to Rudolph to sit down, too. Rudolph could feel himself blushing. Luckily, it was too dark for anyone to tell.

Boylan drained his whiskey. "Silly woman," he said. "I had an affair with her before the war. She wears badly." Boylan didn't look at Rudolph. "Let's get out of here," he said. "It's too damned noisy. And there are too many of our colored brethren on the premises. It's like a slave ship after a successful mutiny."

He waved to a waiter and got the check and paid it and they redeemed their coats from the hatcheck girl and went out. Mrs. Sykes, Cissy to her friends, was the first person Boylan had ever introduced Rudolph to, not counting Perkins, of course. If that's what Boylan's friends were like, you could understand why Boylan stayed up on his hill, alone. Rudolph was sorry the woman had come over to the table. The blush reminded him painfully that he was young and unworldly. Also, he would have liked to stay in there and listen to that trumpeter all night.

They walked east on Fourth street, toward where the car was parked, past darkened shop fronts and bars which were little bursts of light and music and loud conversation on their way.

"New York is hysterical," Boylan said. "Like an unsatisfied, neurotic woman. It's an aging nymphomaniac of a city. God, the time I've wasted here." The woman's appearance had plainly disturbed him. "I'm sorry about that bitch," he said.

"I didn't mind," Rudolph said. He did mind, but he didn't want Boylan to think it bothered him.

"People're filthy," Boylan said. "The leer is the standard expression on the American face. Next time we come to town, bring your girl along. You're too sensitive a boy to be exposed to rot like that."

"I'll ask her," Rudolph said. He was almost sure Julie wouldn't come. She didn't like his being friendly with Boylan. Beast of prey, she called him, and the Peroxide Man.

"Maybe we'll ask Gretchen and her young man and I'll go through my old address books and see if any of the girls I used to know are still alive and we'll make it a party."

"It ought to be fun," Rudolph said. "Like the sinking of the *Titanic*."

Boylan laughed. "The clear vision of youth," he said. "You're a rewarding boy." His tone was affectionate. "With any luck, you'll be a rewarding man."

They were at the car now. There was a parking ticket under the windshield wiper. Boylan tore it up without looking at it.

"I'll drive, if you like," Rudolph said.

"I'm not drunk," Boylan said curtly and got behind the wheel.

III

Thomas sat in the cracked chair, tilted back against the garage wall, a grass-stalk between his teeth, looking across at the lumberyard. It was a sunny day and the light reflected metallically off the last blaze of autumn leaves on the trees along the highway. There was a car that was supposed to be greased before two o'clock, but Thomas was in no hurry. He had had a fight the night before at a high-school dance and he was sore all over and his hands were puffed. He had kept cutting in on a boy who played tackle for the high-school team because the tackle's girl was giving him the eye all night. The tackle had warned him to lay off, but he'd kept cutting in just the same. He knew it was going to wind up in a fight and he'd felt the old mixture of sensations, pleasure, fear, power, cold excitement, as he saw the tackle's heavy face getting darker and darker while Thomas danced with his girl. Finally the two of them, he and the tackle, had gone outside the gym where the dance was taking place. The tackle was a monster, with big, heavy fists, and fast. That sonofabitch Claude would have pissed in his pants with joy if he had been there. Thomas had put the tackle down in the end, but his ribs felt as though they were caving in. It was his fouth fight in Elysium since the summer.

He had a date with the tackle's girl for tonight.

Uncle Harold came out of the little office behind the filling station. Thomas knew that people had complained to Uncle Harold about his fights, but Uncle Harold hadn't said anything about them. Uncle Harold also knew that there was a car to be greased before two o'clock, but he didn't say anything about that either, although Thomas could tell from the expression on Uncle Harold's face that it pained him to see Thomas lounging like that against the wall, chewing lazily on a stalk of grass. Uncle Harold didn't say anything about anything anymore. Uncle Harold looked bad these days—his plump pink face was now yellowish and sagging and he had the expression on his face of a man waiting for a bomb to go off. The bomb was Thomas. All he had to do was hint to Tante Elsa about what was going on between Uncle Harold and Clothilde and they wouldn't be singing Tristan and Isolde for a long time to come in the Jordache household. Thomas had no intention of telling Tante Elsa, but he didn't let Uncle Harold in on the news. Let him stew.

Thomas had stopped bringing his lunch from home. For three days running he had left the paper bag of sandwiches and fruit that Clothilde prepared for him lying on the kitchen table when he had gone off to work. Clothilde hadn't said anything. After three days she had caught on, and there were no more sandwiches waiting for him. He ate at the diner down the highway. He could afford it. Uncle Harold had raised him ten dollars a week. Slob.

"If anybody wants me," Uncle Harold said, "I'm down at the showroom."

Thomas kept staring out across the highway, chewing on the stalk of grass. Uncle Harold sighed and got into his car and drove off.

From inside the garage there came the sound of Coyne working a lathe. Coyne had seen him in one of his fights on a Sunday down at the lake and now was very polite with him and if Thomas neglected a job, Coyne more often than not would do it himself. Thomas played with the idea of letting Coyne do the two o'clock grease job.

Mrs. Dornfeld drove up in her 1940 Ford, and stopped at a pump. Thomas got up and walked over to the car slowly, not rushing anything.

"Hello, Tommy," Mrs. Dornfeld said.

"Hi."

"Fill her up, please, Tommy," Mrs. Dornfeld said. She was a plump blonde of about thirty with disappointed, childish, blue eyes. Her husband worked as a teller in the bank, which was convenient, as Mrs. Dornfeld always knew where he was during business hours.

Thomas hung up the hose and screwed the cap back on and started washing the windshield.

"It would be nice if you paid me a visit today, Tommy," Mrs. Dornfeld said. That was always what she called it—a visit. She had a prissy way of talking, with little flutterings of her eyelids and lips and hands.

"Maybe I can break loose at two o'clock," Thomas said. Mr. Dornfeld was settled behind the bars of his teller's cage from one-thirty on.

"We can have a nice long visit," Mrs. Dornfeld said.

"If I can break loose." Thomas didn't know how he would feel after lunch.

She gave him a five-dollar bill and clutched at his hand when he gave her change. Every once in awhile after one of his visits she slipped him a ten-dollar bill. Mr. Dornfeld must be giving her nothing, but nothing.

There was always lipstick on his collar when he came from visiting Mrs. Dornfled and he left it on purposely so that when Colthilde collected his clothes for washing she'd be sure to see it. Clothilde never mentioned the lipstick. The shirt would be neatly washed and ironed and left on his bed the next day.

None of it really worked. Not Mrs. Dornfeld, nor Mrs. Berryman, nor the twins, nor any of the others. Pigs, all of them. None of them really helped him get over Clothilde. He was sure Clothilde knew—you couldn't hide anything in this stinking little town—and he hoped it made her feel bad. At least as bad as he felt. But if she did feel bad, she didn't show it.

"Two o'clock is happy time," Mrs. Dornfeld said.

It was enough to make a man throw up.

Mrs. Dornfeld started the motor and fluttered off. He went back and sat down on the chair tilted against the wall. Coyne came out of the garage, wiping his hands. "When I was your age," Coyne said, looking after the Ford disappearing down the highway, "I was sure it would fall off if I did it with a married woman."

"It doesn't fall off," Thomas said.

"So I see," Coyne said. He wasn't a bad guy, Coyne. When Thomas had celebrated his seventeenth birthday Coyne had broken out a pint of bourbon and they'd finished it off together in one afternoon.

Thomas was wiping the gravy of the hamburger off his plate with a piece of bread when Joe Kuntz, the cop, came into the diner. It was ten to two and the diner was almost empty, just a couple of hands from the lumberyard finishing up their lunch, and Elias, the counterman, swabbing off the grill. Thomas hadn't decided yet whether or not he was going to visit Bertha Dornfeld.

Kuntz came up to where Thomas was sitting at the counter and said, "Thomas Jordache?"

"Hi, Joe," Thomas said. Kuntz stopped in at the garage a couple of times a week to shoot the breeze. He was always threatening to leave the force because the pay was so bad.

"You acknowledge that you are Thomas Jordache?" Kuntz said in his cop voice.

"What's going on, Joe?" Thomas asked.

"I asked you a question, son," Kuntz said, bulging out of his uniform.

"You know my name," Thomas said. "What's the joke?"

"You better come with me, son," Kuntz said. "I have a warrant for your arrest." He grabbed Thomas's arm above the elbow. Elias stopped scrubbing the grill and the guys from the lumberyard stopped eating and it was absolutely quiet in the diner.

"I ordered a piece of pie and a cup of coffee," Thomas said. "Take your meathooks off me, Joe."

"What's he owe you, Elias?" Kuntz asked, his fingers tight on Thomas's arm.

"With the coffee and pie or without the coffee and pie?" Elias said.

"Without."

"Seventy-five cents," Elias said.

"Pay up, son, and come along quiet," Kuntz said. He didn't make more than twenty arrests a year and he was getting mileage out of this one.

"Okay, okay," Thomas said. He put down eighty-five cents. "Christ, Joe," he said, "you're breaking my arm."

Kuntz walked him quickly out of the diner. Pete Spinelli, Joe's partner, was sitting at the wheel of the prowl car, with the motor running.

"Pete," Thomas said, "will you tell Joe to let go of me."

"Shut up, kid," Spinelli said.

Kuntz shoved him into the back seat and got in beside him and the prowl car started toward town.

"The charge is statutory rape," Sergeant Horvath said. "There is a sworn complaint. I'll notify your uncle and he can get a lawyer for you. Take him away, boys."

Thomas was standing between Kuntz and Spinelli. They each had an arm now. They hustled him off and put him in the lockup. Thomas looked at his watch. It was twenty past two. Bertha Dornfeld would have to go without her visit today.

There was one other prisoner in the single cell of the jail, a ragged, skinny man of about fifty, with a week's growth of beard on his face. He was in for poaching a deer. This was the twenty-third time he had been booked for poaching deer, he told Thomas.

IV

Harold Jordache paced nervously up and down the platform. Just tonight the train had to be late. He had heartburn and he pushed anxiously at his stomach with his hand. When there was trouble, the trouble went right to his stomach. And ever since two-thirty yesterday afternoon, when Horvath had called him from the jail, it had been nothing but trouble. He hadn't slept a wink, because Elsa had cried all night, in between bouts of telling him that they were disgraced for life, that she could never show her face in town again, and what a fool he had been to take a wild animal like that into the house. She was right, he had to admit it, he had been an idiot, his heart was too big. Family or no family, that afternoon when Axel called him from Port Philip, he should have said no.

He thought of Thomas down in the jail, talking his head off like a lunatic, admitting everything, not showing any shame or remorse, naming names. Who could tell what he would say, once he started talking like that? He knew the little monster hated him. What was to stop him from telling about the black-market ration tickets, the faked-up secondhand cars with gear boxes that wouldn't last for more than a hundred miles, the under-the-counter markups on new cars to get around the Price Control, the valve and piston jobs on cars that had nothing more wrong with them than a clogged fuel line? Even about Clothilde? You let a boy like that into your house and you became his prisoner. The heartburn stabbed at Uncle Harold like a knife. He began to sweat, even though it was cold on the station, with the wind blowing.

He hoped Axel was bringing plenty of money along with him. And the birth certificate. He had sent Axel a telegram asking Axel to call him because Axel didn't have a telephone. In this day and age! He had made the telegram sound as ominous as he could, to make sure Axel would call, but even so he was half-surprised when the phone rang in his house and he heard his brother's voice on the wire.

He heard the train coming around the curve toward the station and stepped back nervously from the edge of the platform. In his state he wouldn't be surprised if he had a heart attack and fell down right where he stood.

The train slowed to a halt and a few people got off and hurried away in the wind. He had a moment of panic. He didn't see Axel. It would be just like Axel to leave him alone with the problem. Axel was an unnatural father; he hadn't written once to either Thomas or himself, all the time that Thomas had been in Elysium. Neither had the mother, that skinny hoity-toity whore's daughter. Or the other two kids. What could you expect from a family like that?

Then he saw a big man in a workman's cap and mackinaw limping slowly toward him on the platform. What a way to dress. Harold was glad it was dark and there were so few people around. He must have been crazy that time in Port Philip when he'd invited Axel to come in with him.

"All right, I'm here," Axel said. He didn't shake hands.

"Hello, Axel," Harold said. "I was beginning to worry you wouldn't come. How much money you bring with you?"

"Five thousand dollars," Axel said.

"I hope it's enough," Harold said.

"It better be enough," Axel said flatly. "There isn't any more." He looked old, Harold thought, and sick. His limp was worse than Harold remembered.

They walked together through the station toward Harold's car.

"If you want to see Tommy," Harold said, "you'll have to wait till tomorrow. They don't let anybody in after six o'clock."

"I don't want to see the sonofabitch," Axel said.

Harold couldn't help feeling that it was wrong to call your own child a sonofabitch, even under the circumstances, but he didn't say anything.

"You have your dinner, Axel?" he asked. "Elsa can find something in the icebox."

"Let's not waste time," Axel said. "Who do I have to pay off?"

"The father, Abraham Chase. He's one of the biggest men in town. Your son had to pick somebody like that," Harold said aggrievedly. "A girl in a factory wasn't good enough for him."

"Is he Jewish?" Axel asked, as they got into the car.

"What?" Harold asked, irritatedly. That would be great, that would help a lot, if Axel turned out to be a Nazi, along with everything else.

"Why should he be Jewish?"

"Abraham."

"No. It's one of the oldest families in town. They own practically everything. You'll be lucky if he takes your money."

"Yeah," Axel said. "Lucky."

Harold backed out of the parking lot and started toward the Chase house. It was in the good section of town, near the Jordache house. "I talked to him on the phone," Harold said. "I told him you were coming. He sounded out of his mind. I don't blame him. It's bad enough to come home and find one daughter pregnant. But *both* of them! And they're twins, besides."

"They can get a wholesale rate on baby clothes." Axel laughed. The laughter sounded like a tin pitcher rattling against a sink. "Twins. He had a busy season, didn't he, Thomas?"

"You don't know the half of it," Harold said. "He's beat up a dozen people since he came here, besides." The stories that had reached Harold's ears had been exaggerated as they passed along the town's chain of gossip. "It's a wonder he hasn't been in jail before this. Everybody's scared of him. It's the most natural thing in the world that something like this comes up, they pin it on him. But who suffers? Me. And Elsa."

Axel ignored his brother's suffering and the suffering of his brother's wife. "How do they know it was my kid?"

"The twins told their father." Harold slowed the car down. He was in no hurry to confront Abraham Chase. "They've done it with every boy in town, the twins, and plenty of the men too, everybody knows that, but when it comes to naming names, naturally the first name anybody'd pick would be your Tommy. They're not going to say it was the nice boy next door or Joe Kuntz, the policeman, or the boy from Harvard whose parents play bridge with the Chases twice a week. They pick the black sheep. Those two little bitches're smart. Big shot. Under eighteen, my lawyer says, you can't be held for statutory rape."

"So what's the fuss?" Axel said. "I have his birth certificate."

"Don't think it's going to be that easy," Harold said. "Mr. Chase swears he can have him locked up until he's twenty-one as a juvenile delinquent. And he can. That's four years. And don't think Tommy is making it any easier for himself telling the cops he knows twenty fellows personally who've been in there with those girls and giving a list of names. It just makes everybody sorer, that's all. It gives the whole town a bad name and they'll make him pay for it. And me and Elsa. That's my shop," he said automatically. They were passing the showroom. "I'll be lucky if they don't put a brick through the window.

"You friendly with Abraham?"

"I do some business with Mr. Chase," Harold said. "I sold him a Lincoln. I can't say we move in the same circles. He's on the waiting list for a new Mercury. I could sell a hundred cars tomorrow if I could get delivery. The goddamn war. You don't know what I've been going through for four years, just to keep my head above water. And now, just when I begin to see a little daylight, this has to come along."

"You don't seem to be doing so bad," Axel said.

"You have to keep up appearances." One thing was sure. If Axel thought for a minute that he was going to borrow any money, he was barking up the wrong tree.

"How do I know Abraham won't take my money and the kid'll go to jail just the same?"

"Mr. Chase is a man of his word," Harold said. He had a sudden horrible fear that Axel was going to call Mr. Chase Abraham in his own house. "He's got this town in his pocket. The cops, the judge, the mayor, the party organization. If he tells you the case'll be dropped, it'll be dropped."

"It better be," Axel said. There was a threat in his voice and Harold remembered what a rough boy his brother had been when they had both been young back home in Germany. Axel had gone off to war and had killed people. He was not a civilized man, with that harsh, sick face and that hatred of everybody and everything, including his own flesh and blood. Harold wondered if maybe he hand't made a mistake calling his brother and telling him to come to Elysium. Maybe it would have been better if he had just tried to handle it himself. But he had known it was going to cost money and he'd panicked. The heartburn gripped him again as they drove up to the white house, with big pillars, where the Chase family lived.

The two men went up the walk to the front door and Harold rang the bell. He took off his hat and held it across his chest, almost as if he were saluting the flag. Axel kept his cap on.

The door opened and a maid stood there. Mr. Chase was expecting them, she said.

V

"They take millions of clean-limbed young boys." The poacher was chewing on a wad of tobacco and spitting into a tin can on the floor beside him, as he talked. "Clean-limbed boys, and send them off to kill and maim each other with inhuman instruments of destruction and they congratulate themselves and hang their chests with medals and parade down the main thoroughfares of the city and they put me in jail and mark me as an enemy of society because every once in awhile I drift out into the woodlands of America and shoot myself a choice buck with an old 1910 Winchester 22." The poacher originally had come from the Ozarks and he spoke like a country preacher.

There were four bunks in the cell, two on one side and two on the other. The poacher, whose name was Dave, was lying in his bunk and Thomas was lying in the lower bunk on the other side of the cell. Dave smelled rather ripe and Thomas preferred to keep some space between them. It was two days now that they had been in the cell together and Thomas knew quite a bit about Dave, who lived alone in a shack near the lake and appreciated a permanent audience. Dave had come down from the Ozarks to work in the automobile industry in Detroit and after fifteen years of it had had enough. "I was in there in the paint department," Dave said, "in the stink of chemicals and the heat of a furnace, devoting my numbered days on this earth to spraying paint on cars for people who didn't mean a fart in hell to me to ride around in and the spring came and the leaves burgeoned and the summer came and the crops were taken in and the autumn came and city folk in funny caps with hunting licenses and fancy guns were out in the woods shooting the deer and I might just as well have been down in the blackest pit, chained to a post, for all the difference the seasons meant to me. I'm a mountain man and I pined away and one day I saw where my path laid straight before me and I took to the woods. A man has to be careful with his numbered days on this earth, son. There is a conspiracy to chain every living child of man to an iron post in a black pit, and you mustn't be fooled because they paint it all the bright colors of the rainbow and pull all sorts of devilish tricks to make you think that it isn't a pit, it isn't an iron post, it isn't a chain. The president of General Motors, up high in his glorious office, was just as much chained, just as deep down in the pit as me coughing up violet in the paint shop."

Dave spat tobacco juice into the tin can on the floor next to his bunk. The gob of juice made a musical sound against the side of the can.

"I don't ask for much," Dave said, "just an occasional buck and the smell of woodsy air in my nostrils. I don't blame nobody for putting me in jail from time to time, that's their profession just like hunting is my profession, and I don't begrudge 'em the coupla months here and there I spend behind bars. Somehow, they always seem to catch me just as the winter months're drawing on, so it's really no hardship. But nothing they say can make me feel like a criminal, no sir. I'm an American out in the American forest livin' off American deer. They want to make all sorts of rules and regulations for those city folk in the gun clubs, that's all right by me. They don't apply, they just don't apply."

He spat again. "There's just one thing that makes me a mite forlorn—and that's hypocrisy. Why, once the very judge that condemned me had eaten venison I shot just the week before and ate it right at the dining-room table in his own house and it was bought with his own money by his own cook. The hypocrisy is the canker in the soul of the American people. Why, just look at your case, son. What did you do? You did what everybody knows he'd do if he got the chance—you were offered a nice bit of juicy tail and you took it. At your age, son, the loins're raging, and all the rules in the book don't make a never-no-mind. I bet that the very judge who is going to put you away for years of your young life, if he got the offer from those two little plump-assed young girls you told me about, if that same judge got the offer and he was certain sure nobody was around to see him, he'd go cavorting with those plump-assed young girls like a crazy goat. Like the judge who ate my venison. Statutory rape." Dave spat in disgust. "Old man's rules. What does a little twitching young tail know about statutory? It's the hypocrisy, son, the hypocrisy, son, the hypocrisy everywhere."

Joe Kuntz appeared at the cell door and opened it. "Come on out, Jordache," Kuntz said. Ever since Thomas had told the lawyer Uncle Harold had got for him that Joe Kuntz had been in there with the twins, too, and Kuntz had heard the news, the policeman had not been markedly friendly. He was married, with three kids.

Axel Jordache was waiting in Horvath's office with Uncle Harold and the lawyer. The laywer was a worried-looking young man with a bad complexion and thick glasses. Thomas had never seen his father looking so bad, not even the day he hit him.

He waited for his father to say hello, but Axel kept quiet, so he kept quiet, too.

"Thomas," the lawyer said, "I am happy to say that everything has been arranged to everybody's satisfaction."

"Yeah," Horvath said behind the desk. He didn't sound terribly satisfied.

"You're a free man, Thomas," the lawyer said.

Thomas looked doubtfully at the five men in the room. There were no signs of celebration on any of the faces. "You mean I can just walk out of this joint?" Thomas asked.

"Exactly," the lawyer said.

"Let's go," Axel Jordache said. "I wasted enough time in this goddamn town as it is." He turned abruptly and limped out.

Thomas had to make himself walk slowly after his father. He wanted to cut and run for it, before anybody changed his mind.

Outside it was sunny late afternoon. There were no windows in the cell and you couldn't tell what the weather was from in there. Uncle Harold walked on one side of Thomas and his father on the other. It was another kind of arrest.

They got into Uncle Harold's car. Axel sat up in front and Thomas had the back seat all to himself. He didn't ask any questions.

"I bought your way out, in case you're curious," his father said. His father didn't turn in the seat, but talked straight ahead, at the windshield. "Five thousand dollars to that Shylock for his pound of flesh. I guess you got the highest-priced lay in history. I hope it was worth it."

Thomas wanted to say he was sorry, that somehow, some day, he'd make it up to his father. But the words wouldn't come out.

"Don't think I did it for you," his father said, "or for Harold here . . ."

"Now, Axel," Harold began.

"You could both die tonight and it wouldn't spoil my appetite," his father said. "I did it for the only member of the family that's worth a damn—your brother Rudolph. I'm not going to have him start out in life with a convict brother hanging around his neck. But this is the last time I ever want to see you or hear from you. I'm taking the train home now and that's the end of you and me. Do you get that?"

"I get it," Thomas said flatly.

"*You're* getting out of town, too," Uncle Harold said to Thomas. His voice was quivering. "That's the condition Mr. Chase made and I couldn't agree with him more. I'll take you home and you pack your things and you don't sleep another night in my house. Do you get that too?"

"Yeah, yeah," Thomas said. They could have the town. Who needed it?

There was no more talking. When Uncle Harold stopped the car at the station, his father got out without a word and limped away, leaving the door of the car open. Uncle Harold had to reach over and slam it shut.

In the bare room under the roof, there was a small, battered valise on his bed. Thomas recognized it. It belonged to Clothilde. The bed was stripped down and the mattress was rolled up, as though Tante Elsa were afraid that he might sneak in a few minutes' sleep on it. Tante Elsa and the girls were not in the house. To avoid contamination, Tante Elsa had taken the girls to the movies for the afternoon.

Thomas threw his things into the bag quickly. There wasn't much. A few shirts and underwear and socks, an extra pair of shoes and a sweater. He took off the garage uniform that he had been arrested in and put on the new gray suit Tante Elsa had bought for him on his birthday.

He looked around the room. The book from the library, the *Riders of the Purple Sage*, was lying on a table. They kept sending postcards saying he was overdue and they were charging him two cents a day. He must owe them a good ten bucks by now. He threw the book into the valise. Remember Elysium, Ohio.

He closed the valise and went downstairs and into the kitchen. He wanted to thank Clothilde for the valise. But she wasn't in the kitchen.

He went out through the hallway. Uncle Harold was eating a big piece of apple pie in the dining room, standing up. His hands were trembling as he picked up the pie. Uncle Harold always ate when he was nervous. "If you're looking for Clothilde," Uncle Hrold said, "save your energy. I sent her to the movies with Tante Elsa and the girls."

Well, Thomas thought, at least she got a movie out of me. One good thing.

"You got any money?" Uncle Harold asked. "I don't want you to be picked up for vagrancy and go through the whole thing again." He wolfed at his apple pie.

"I have money," Thomas said. He had twenty-one dollars and change.

"Good. Give me your key."

Thomas took the key out of his pocket and put it on the table. He had an impulse to push the rest of the pie in Uncle Harold's face, but what good would that do?

They stared at each other. A piece of pie dribbled down Uncle Harold's chin.

"Kiss Clothilde for me," Thomas said, and went out the door, carrying Clothilde's valise.

He walked to the station and bought twenty dollars' worth of transportation away from Elysium, Ohio.

CHAPTER 10

THE CAT STARED at him from its corner, malevolent and unblinking. Its enemies were interchangeable. Whoever came down in the cellar each night, to work in the hammering heat, was regarded by the cat with the same hatred, the same topaz lust for death in his yellow eyes. The cat's night-long cold stare disconcerted Rudolph as he put the rolls in the oven. It made him uneasy when he was not liked, even by an animal. He had tried to win the cat over with an extra bowl of milk, with caresses, with a "Nice, kitty," here and there, but the cat knew it wasn't a nice kitty and lay there, it's tail twisting, contemplating murder.

Axel had been gone for three days now. There had been no word from Elysium and there was no telling how many more nights Rudolph would have to come down into the cellar and face the heat, the flour dust, the arm-numbing lifting and shoving and hauling. He didn't know how his father could stand it. Year in and year out. After only three nights, Rudolph was almost completely worn out, with purplish bruises of fatigue under his eyes and his face haggard. And he still had to take the bicycle and deliver the rolls in the morning. And school after that. There was an important exam in math the next day and he hadn't been able to prepare for it and he never was all that good in math anyway.

Sweating, fighting the greasy, huge trays, the flour smearing chalkily over his bare arms and face, after three nights he was his father's ghost, staggering under the punishment his father had endured six thousand nights. Good son, faithful son. Shit on that. Bitterly, he regretted the fact that he had come down to help his father on holidays, when there was a rush on, and had learned, approximately, his father's profession. Thomas had been wiser. Let the family go to hell. Whatever trouble Thomas was in now (Axel had not told Rudolph what it was when he got the telegram from Elysium). Thomas just had to be better off than the dutiful son in the blazing cellar.

As for Gretchen, just walking across a stage three times a night for sixty dollars a week . . . .

In the last three nights Rudolph had figured out approximately how much the Jordache Bakery earned. About sixty dollars a week, on the average, after rent and expenses, and the thirty dollars for salary for the widow who took care of the shop now that his mother was sick.

He remembered the bill for more than twelve dollars that Boylan had paid in the restaurant in New York, and all the money for drinks that one night.

Boylan had gone down to Hobe Sound, in Florida, for two months. Now that the war was over, life was returning to normal.

He put another tray of rolls into the oven.

He was awakened by the sound of voices. He groaned. Five o'clock so soon? He got out of bed mechanically. He noticed that he was dressed. He shook his head stupidly. How could he be dressed? He looked blearily at his watch. A quarter to six. Then he remembered. It wasn't morning. He had come home from school and thrown himself on the bed to get some rest before the night's work. He heard his father's voice. His father must have come home while he was asleep. His first thought was selfish. I don't have to work tonight.

He lay down again.

The two voices, the one high and excited, the other low and explaining, came up from downstairs. His father and mother were fighting. He was too tired to care. But he couldn't go to sleep, with all that noise downstairs, so he listened.

Mary Pease Jordache was moving out. She wasn't moving far. Just to Gretchen's room across the hall. She stumbled back and forth, her legs hurting from the phlebitis, carrying dresses, underwear, sweaters, shoes, combs, photographs of the children when they were young. Rudolph's scrapbook, a sewing kit, *Gone With the Wind,* a rumpled package of Camels, old handbags. Everything she owned, getting it out of the room she had hated for twenty years and piling everything on Gretchen's unmade bed, raising a small cloud of dust every time she came in with a new load in her arms.

She kept up a surging monologue as she went back and forth. "I'm through with this room. Twenty years too late, but I'm finally through. No one shows any consideration for me, I'm going to go my own way from now on. I am not going to be at the disposal of a fool. A man who travels halfway across the country to give away five thousand dollars to a perfect stranger. The savings of a lifetime. *My* lifetime, I slaved, day in and day out, I denied muself everything, I became an old woman, to save that money. My son was going to go to college, my son was going to be a gentleman. But now he's not going anywhere, he's not going to be anything, my brilliant husband had to show what a great man he was—handing out thousand dollar bills to millionaires in Ohio, so that his precious brother and his fat wife wouldn't be embarrassed when they went to the opera in their Lincoln Continental."

"It wasn't for my brother or his fat wife," Axel Jordache said. He was sitting on the bed, his hands dangling between his knees. "I explained to you. It was for Rudy. What good would it do going to college if one day all of a sudden people found out he had a brother in jail?

"He belongs in jail," Mary Pease Jordache said. "Thomas. It's the natural place for him. If you're going to hand out five thousand dollars each time they want to put him in jail, you'd better get out of the bakery right away and go into the oil business or become a banker. I bet you felt *good* giving that man the money. You felt *proud.* Your son. A chip off the old block. Full of sex. Potent. Right on the target. It isn't enough for him to get one girl pregnant at a time. Oh, no, not Axel Jordache's son. Two at a time, that's the kind of family *he* comes from. Well, if Axel Jordache wants to show what a great big he-man he is in bed from now on he'd better start looking for a couple of twins on his own. It's all finished here. My Calvary is over."

"Oh, Christ," Jordache said. "Calvary."

"Filth, filth!" Mary Jordache screamed. "From one generation to another. Your daughter's a whore, too, I saw the money she took from men for her services, right in this house, eight hundred dollars, I saw it with my own eyes, she hid it in a book. *Eight hundred dollars.* Your children command a good price. Well, I'm going to have a price, too. You want anything from me, you want me to go down into that store, you want to come to my bed, you pay. We give that woman downstairs thirty dollars a week, and she only does half the job, she goes home at night. Thirty dollars a week is my price. I'm giving you a bargain rate. Only I want my back pay first. Thirty dollars a week for twenty years. I figured it out. Thirty thousand dollars on the table. You put thirty thousand dollars on the table and I'll talk to you. Not before."

She had the last bundle of clothes in her arms now and she rushed out of the room. The door to Gretchen's room slammed behind her.

Jordache shook his head, then got up and limped up the stairs to Rudolph's room. Rudolph was lying on he bed, his eyes open.

"You heard, I suppose," Jordache said.

"Yeah," Rudolph said.

"I'm sorry," Jordache said.

"Yeah," said Rudolph.

"Well, I'm going down to the shop, see how things are." Jordache turned away.

"I'll come down and give you a hand tonight," Rudolph said.

"You sleep," Jordache said. "I don't want to see you down there."

He went out of the room.

CHAPTER 11

1946

I

THE LIGHTS WERE down low in the Westerman basement. They had it fixed up as a sort of den and they gave parties there. There was a party on tonight, about twenty boys and girls, some of them dancing, some of them necking a little in the dark corners of the room, some of them just listening to Benny Goodman playing "Paper Doll" on a record.

The River Five didn't practice much anymore there because some guys back from the Army had started a band, too, and were getting most of the dates. Rudolph didn't blame people for hiring the other band. The guys were older and they played a lot better than the River Five.

Alex Dailey was dancing closely with Lila Belkamp in the middle of the room. They told everybody they were going to get married when they got out of school in June. Alex was nineteen and a little slow in school. Lila was all right, a little gushy and silly, but all right. Rudolph wondered if his mother had looked anything like Lila when she was nineteen. Rudolph wished he had a recording of his mother's speech the night his father came home from Elysium, to play to Alex. It should be required listening for all prospective bridegrooms. Maybe there wouldn't be such a rush to the church.

Julie was sitting on Rudolph's lap in a broken-down old easy chair in a corner of the den. There were other girls sitting on boys' laps around the room, but Rudolph wished she wouldn't do it. He didn't like the idea of people seeing him like that and guessing how he was feeling. There were some things that ought to be kept private. He couldn't imagine Teddy Boylan letting any girl sit in his lap in public, at any age. But if he even hinted about it to Julie, she'd blow up.

Julie nuzzled her head around and kissed him. He kissed her back, of course, and enjoyed it, but wished she'd quit.

She had applied to Barnard for the fall and was pretty sure of getting in. She was smart in school. She wanted Rudolph to try to get into Columbia, so they would be right next to each other in New York. Rudolph pretended he was considering Harvard or Yale. He never could get himself to tell Julie that he wasn't going to college.

Julie snuggled closer, her head under his chin. She made a purring sound that at other times made him chuckle. He looked over her head at the other people at the party. He was probably the only virgin among the boys in the room. He was sure about Buddy Westerman and Dailey and Kessler and most of the others, although maybe there were one or two who probably lied when the question came up. That wasn't the only way he was different from the others. He wondered if they'd have invited him if they knew that his father had killed two men, that his brother had been in jail for rape, that his sister was pregnant (she had written him to tell him, so that it wouldn't come as a horrid surprise, she said) and living with a married man, that his mother had demanded thirty thousand dollars from his father if he wanted to go to bed with her.

The Jordaches were special, there was no doubt about that.

Buddy Westerman came over and said, "Listen, kids, there's punch upstairs and sandwiches and cake."

"Thanks, Buddy," Rudolph said. He wished Julie would get the hell off his lap.

Buddy went around passing the word along to the other couples. There was nothing wrong with Buddy. He was going to Cornell, and then to law school, because his father had a solid law practice in town. Buddy had been approached by the new group to play bass for them, but out of loyalty to the River Five had said no, Rudolph gave Buddy's loyalty just about three weeks to wear out. Buddy was a born musician and as he said, "Those guys really make music," and you couldn't expect Buddy to hold out forever, especially as they didn't get more than one date a month any more.

As he looked at the boys in the room, Rudolph realized that almost every one of them knew where he was going. Kessler's father had a pharmacy and Kessler was going to go to pharmaceutical school after college and take over the old man's business. Starrett's father dealt in real estate and Starrett was going to Harvard and to the school of business there, to make sure he could tell his father how to use his money. Lawson's family had an engineering concern and Lawson was going to study engineering. Even Dailey, who probably was too slow to get into college, was going into his father's plumbing supply business.

There was a great opening for Rudolph in the ancestral oven. "I am going into grains." Or perhaps, "I intend to join the German army. My father is an alumnus."

Rudolph felt a sick surge of envy for all his friends. Benny Goodman was playing the clarinet like silver lace on the phonograph and Rudolph envied *him*. Maybe most of all.

On a night like this you could understand why people robbed banks.

He wasn't going to come to any more parties. He didn't belong there, even if he was the only one who knew it.

He wanted to go home. He was tired. He was always tired these days, somehow. Aside from the bicycle route in the morning, he had to tend the store every day from four to seven, after school closed. The widow had decided she couldn't work the whole day, she had children at home to take care of. It had meant giving up the track and the debating teams and his marks were slipping, too, as he never seemed to find the energy to study. He'd been sick, too, with a cold that started after Christmans and seemed to be hanging on all winter.

"Julie," he said, "let's go home."

She sat up straight on his lap, surprised.

"It's early," she said, "it's a nice party."

"I know, I know," he said, sounding more impatient than he intended. "I just want to get out of here."

"We can't do anything in my house," she said. "My folks have people over for bridge. It's Friday."

"I just want to go home," he said.

"You go." She got off his lap and stood over him angrily. "I'll find somebody else to take me home."

He was tempted to spill out everything he had been thinking. Maybe she'd understand then.

"Boy, oh boy," Julie said. There were tears in her eyes. "This is the first party we've been to in months and you want to go home practically before we get here."

"I just feel lousy," he said. He stood up.

"It's peculiar," she said. "Just the nights you're with me you feel lousy. I bet you feel just fine the nights you go out with Teddy Boylan."

"Oh, lay off Boylan, will you, Julie?" Rudolph said, "I haven't seen him for weeks."

"What's the matter—he run out of peroxide?"

"Joke," Rudolph said wearily.

She turned on her heel, her pony tail swinging, and went over to the group around the phonograph. She was the prettiest girl in the room, snub-nosed, scrubbed, smart, slender, dear, and Rudolph wished she would go away someplace for six months, a year, and then come back, after he had gotten over being tired, and had a chance to figure everything out in peace and they could start all over again.

He went upstairs and put on his coat and left the house without saying good night to anyone. Judy Garland was on the phonograph now, singing "The Trolley Song."

It was raining outside, a cold, drifting, February misty river rain, blowing at him in the wind. He coughed inside his coat, with the wet trickling down inside his turned-up collar. He walked slowly toward home, feeling like crying. He hated these spats with Julie, and they were becoming more and more frequent. If they made love to each other, really made love, not that frustrating, foolish necking that made them both ashamed after it, he was sure they wouldn't be scratching at each other all the time. But he couldn't bring himself to do it. It would have to be hidden, they'd have to lie, they'd have to sneak off somewhere like criminals. He had long ago made up his mind. It was going to be perfect or it wasn't going to happen.

The hotel manager threw open the door of the suite. There was a balcony overlooking the Mediterranean. There was a smell of jasmine and thyme in the air. The two bronzed young people looked around the room cooly, glanced at the Mediterranean. Uniformed bellboys brought in many pieces of leather luggage and distributed them around the rooms.

"Ça vous plaît, Monsieur?" the manager asked.

"Ça va," the bronzed young man said.

"Merci, Monsieur." The hotel manager backed out of the room.

The two bronzed young people went out onto the balcony and looked at the sea. They kissed against the blueness. The smell of jasmine and thyme became stronger.

Or . . .

It was only a small log cabin, with the snow piled high against its sides. The mountains reared behind it. The two bronzed young people came in shaking the snow from their clothes, laughing. There was a fire roaring in the fireplace. The snow was so high it covered the windows. They were all alone in the high world. The two bronzed young people sank down to the floor in front of the fire.

Or . . .

The two bronzed young people walked along the red carpet on the platform. The Twentieth Century to Chicago stood on the tracks, gleaming. The two young people went past the porter in his white coat, into the car. The stateroom was full of flowers. There was the smell of roses. The two bronzed young people smiled at each other and strolled through the train to the club car for a drink.

Or . . .

Rudolph coughed miserably in the rain as he turned into Vanderhoff Street. I've seen too goddamn many movies, he thought.

The light from the cellar was coming up through the grating in front of the bakery. The Eternal Flame. Axel Jordache, the Unknown Soldier. If his father died, Rudolph thought, would anyone remember to put out the light?

Rudolph hesitated, the keys to the house in his hand. Ever since the night his mother had made that crazy speech about thirty thousand dollars, he had felt sorry for his father. His father walked around the house slowly and quietly, like a man who has just come out of a hospital after a major operation, a man who had felt the warning tap of death on his shoulder. Axel Jordache had always seemed strong, terrifyingly strong, to Rudolph. His voice had been loud, his movements abrupt and careless. Now his long silences, his hesitant gestures, his slow, apologetic way of spreading a newspaper or fixing himself a pot of coffee, careful not to make any unnecessary noise, was somehow frightening. Suddenly, it seemed to Rudolph that his father was preparing himself for his grave. Standing in the dark hallway with his hand on the banister, for the first time since he was a little boy he asked himself whether he loved his father or not.

He went over to the door leading to the bakery, unlocked it and passed through it to the back room and descended into the cellar.

His father wasn't doing anything, just sitting on his bench, staring ahead of him at the oven, the bottle of whiskey on the floor beside him. The cat lay crouched in the corner.

"Hello, Pa," Rudolph said.

His father turned his head slowly toward him and nodded.

"I just came down to see if there was something I could do."

"No," his father said. He reached down and picked up the bottle and took a small swig. He offered the bottle to Rudolph. "Want some?"

"Thanks." Rudolph didn't want any whiskey, but he felt his father would like it if he took some. The bottle was slippery from his father's sweat. He took a swig. It burned his mouth and throat.

"You're soaking wet," his father said.

"It's raining out."

"Take off your coat. You don't want to sit there in a wet coat."

Rudolph took off his coat and hung it on a hook on the wall. "How're things, Pa?" he asked. It was a question he had never asked his father before.

His father chuckled quietly, but didn't answer. He took another swig of the whiskey.

"What'd you do tonight?" Axel asked.

"I went to a party."

"A party." Axel nodded. "Did you play your horn?"

"No."

"What do people do at a party these days?"

"I don't know. Dance. Listen to music. Kid around."

"Did I ever tell you I went to dancing school when I was a boy?" Axel said. "In Cologne. In white gloves. They taught me how to bow. Cologne was nice in the summertime. Maybe I ought to go back there. They'll be starting everything up from scratch there now, maybe that's the place for me. A ruin for the ruins."

"Come on, Pa," Rudolph said. "Don't talk like that."

Axel took another drink. "I had a visitor today," he said. "Mr. Harrison."

Mr. Harrison was the owner of the building. He came on the third of each month for the rent. He was at least eighty years old, but he never missed collecting. In person. It wasn't the third of the month, so Rudolph knew that the visit must have been an important one. "What'd he want?" Rudolph said.

"They're tearing down the building," Axel said. "They're going to put up a whole block of apartments with stores on the ground floor. Port Philip is expanding, Mr Harrison says, progress is progress. He's eighty years old, but he's progressing. He's investing a lot of money. In Cologne they knock the building down with bombs. In America they do it with money."

"When do we have to get out?"

"Not till October. Mr. Harrison says he's telling me early, so I'll have a chance to find something else. He's a considerate old man, Mr. Harrison."

Rudolph looked around him at the familiar cracked walls, the iron doors of the ovens, the window open to the grating on the sidewalk. It was queer to think of all this, the house he had known all his life, no longer there, vanished. He had always thought he would leave the house. It had never occurred to him that the house would leave him.

"What're you going to do?" he asked his father.

Axel shrugged. "Maybe they need a baker in Cologne. If I happen to find a drunken Englishman some rainy night along the river maybe I could buy passage back to Germany."

"What're you talking about, Pa?" Rudolph asked sharply.

"That's how I came to America," Axel said mildly. "I followed a drunken Englishman who'd been waving his money around in a bar in the Sankt Pauli district of Hamburg and I drew a knife on him. He put up a fight. The English don't give up anything without a fight. I put the knife in him and took his wallet and I dropped him into the canal. I told you I killed a man with a knife that day with your French teacher, didn't I?"

"Yes," Rudolph said.

"I've always meant to tell you the story," Axel said. "Anytime any of your friends says his ancestors came over on the Mayflower, you can say *your* ancestors came over on a wallet full of five-pound notes. It was a foggy night. He must've been crazy, that Englishman, going around a district like Sankt Pauli with all that money. Maybe he thought he was going to screw every whore in the district and he didn't want to be caught short of cash. So that's what I say, maybe if I can find an Englishman down by the river, maybe I'll make the return trip."

Christ, Rudolph thought bitterly, come on down and have a nice cosy little chat with old Dad in his office . . .

"If you ever happened to kill an Englishman," his father went on, "you'd want to tell your son about it, now, wouldn't you?"

"I don't think you ought to go around talking about it," Rudolph said.

"Oh," Axel said, "you planning to turn me over to the police? I forgot you were so high principled."

"Pa, you ought to forget about it. It's no good thinking about it after all these years. What good does it do?"

Axel didn't answer. He drank reflectively from the bottle.

"Oh, I remember a lot of things," he said. "I get a lot of remembering-time down here at night. I remember shitting my pants along the Meuse. I remember the way my leg smelled the second week in the hospital. I remember carrying two-hundred-pound sacks of cocoa on the docks in Hamburg, with my leg opening up and bleeding every day. I remember what the Englishman said before I pushed him into the canal. 'I say there,' he said, 'you can't do that.' I remember the day of my marriage. I could tell you about that, but I think you'd be more interested in your mother's report. I remember the look in the face of a man called Abraham Chase in Ohio when I laid five thousand dollars on the table in front of him to make him feel better for getting his daughters laid." He drank again. "I worked twenty years of my life," he went on, "to keep your brother out of jail. Your mother has let it be known that she thinks I was wrong. Do you think I was wrong?"

"No," Rudolph said.

"You're going to have a rough time from now on, Rudy," Axel said. "I'm sorry. I tried to do my best."

"I'll get by," Rudolph said. He wasn't at all sure he would.

"Go for the money," Axel said. "Don't let anybody fool you. Don't go for anything else. Don't listen to all the crap they write in the papers about Other Values. That's what the rich preach to the poor so that they can keep raking it in, without getting their throats cut. Be Abraham Chase with that look on his face, picking up the bills. How much money you got in the bank?"

"A hundred and sixty dollars," Rudolph said.

"Don't part with it," Axel said. "Not with a penny of it. Not even if I come dragging up to your door starving to death and ask you for the price of a meal. Don't give me a dime."

"Pa, you're getting yourself all worked up. Why don't you go upstairs and go to bed. I'll put in the hours here."

"You stay out of here. Or just come and talk to me, if you want. But stay away from the work. You got better things to do. Learn your lessons. All of them. Step careful. The sins of the fathers. Unto how many generations. My father used to read the Bible after dinner in the living room. I may not be leaving you much, but I sure as hell am leaving you well visited with sins. Two men killed. All my whores. And what I did to your mother. And letting Thomas grow up like wild grass. And who knows what Gretchen is doing. Your mother seems to have some information. You ever see her?"

"Yeah," Rudolph said.

"What's she up to?"

"You'd rather not hear," Rudolph said.

"That figures," his father said. "God watches. I don't go to church, but I know God watches. Keeping the books on Axel Jordache and his generations."

"Don't talk like that," Rudolph said. "God doesn't watch anything." His atheism was firm. "You've had some bad luck. That's all. Everything can change tomorrow."

"Pay up, God says." Rudolph had the feeling his father wasn't talking to him anymore, that he would be saying the same things, in the same dreamlike dead voice if he were alone in the cellar. "Pay up, Sinner, I will afflict you and your sons for your deeds." He took a long drink, shook himself, as though a shiver had run coldly through his body. "Go to bed," he said. "I got work to do."

"Good night, Pa." Rudolph took his coat off the hook on the wall. His father didn't answer, just sat there, staring, holding the bottle.

Rudolph went upstairs. Christ, he thought, and I thought it was Ma who was the crazy one.

II

Axel took another drink from the bottle, then went back to work. He worked steadily all night. He found himself humming as he moved around the cellar. He didn't recognize the tune for a while. It bothered him, not recognizing it. Then he remembered. It was a song his mother used to sing when she was in the kitchen.

He sang the words, low,

Schlaf', Kindlein, schlaf'
Dein Vater hüt' die Schlaf'
Die Mutter hüt die Ziegen,
Wir wollen das Kindlein wiegen?

His native tongue. He had traveled too far. Or not far enough.

He had the last pan of rolls ready to go into the oven. He left it standing on the table and went over to a shelf and took down a can. There was a warning skull-and-bones on the label. He dug into the can and measured out a small spoonful of the powder. He carried it over to the table and picked up one of the raw rolls at random. He kneaded the poison into the roll thoroughly, then reshaped the roll and put it back into the pan. My message to the world, he thought.

The cat watched him. He put the pan of rolls into the oven and went over to the sink and stripped off his shirt and washed his hands and face and arms and torso. He dried himself on flour sacking and redressed. He sat down, facing the oven, and put the bottle, now nearly empty, to his lips.

He hummed the tune his mother had sung in her kitchen when he was a small boy.

When the rolls were baked, he pulled out the pan and left them to cool. All the rolls looked the same.

Then he turned off the gas in the ovens and put on his mackinaw and cap. He went up the steps into the bakery and went out. He let the cat follow him. It was dark and still raining. The wind had freshened. He kicked the cat and the cat ran off.

He limped toward the river.

He opened the rusty padlock of the warehouse and turned on a light. He picked up the shell and carried it to the rickety wharf. The river was rough, with whitecaps, and made a sucking, rushing sound as it swept past. The wharf was protected by a curling jetty and the water there was calm. He put the shell down on the wharf and went back and got the oars and turned out the light and snapped the padlock shut. He carried the oars back to the wharf and lay them down along the edge, then put the shell in the water. He stepped in lightly and put the oars into the outriggers.

He pushed off and guided the shell out toward open water. The current caught him and he began to row steadily out toward the river's center. He went downstream, the waves washing over the sides of the shell, the rain beating in his face. In a little while the shell was low in the water. He continued to row steadily, as the river ran swiftly down toward New York, the bays, the open ocean.

The shell was almost completely awash as he reached the heart of the river.

The shell was found, overturned, the next day, near Bear Mountain. They didn't ever find Axel Jordache.

Part Two

CHAPTER 1

1949

DOMINIC JOSEPH AGOSTINO sat at the little desk in his office behind the gym with the newspaper spread out in front of him to the sports page, reading about himself. He had his Ben Franklin reading glasses on and they gave a mild, studious look to his round, ex-pug's face, with the broken nose and the small, dark eyes under the heavy scar tissue. It was three o'clock, the mid-afternoon lull, and the gym was empty, the best time of day. There wouldn't be anything much doing until five o'clock when he gave a calisthenics class to a group of club members, middle-aged businessmen most of them, fighting their waistlines. After that he might spar a few rounds with some of the more ambitious members, being careful not to damage anybody.

The article about him had come out the night before, in a box on the sports page. It was a slow day. The Red Sox were out of town and weren't going anyplace, anyway, and they had to fill the sports page with something.

Dominic had been born in Boston, and had been introduced in his fighting days as Joe Agos, the Boston Beauty, because he lacked a punch and had to do a lot of dancing around to keep from getting killed. He had fought some good lighweights in the late twenties and thirties and the sportswriter, who was too young ever to have seen him fight, had written stirring accounts of his matches with people like Canzoneri and McLarnin, when Canzoneri and McLarnin were on the way up. The sportswriter had written that he was still in good shape, which wasn't all that true. The sportswriter quoted Dominic as saying jokingly that some of the younger members of the exclusive Revere Club were beginning to get to him in the sparring sessions in the gym and that he was thinking of getting an assistant or putting on a catcher's mask to protect his beauty in the near future. He hadn't said it all that jokingly. The article was friendly, and made Dominic sound like a wise old veteran of the golden days of the sport who had learned to accept life philosophically in his years in the ring. He had lost every cent he'd ever made, so there wasn't much else left but philosophy. He hadn't said anything about that to the writer and it wasn't in the article.

The phone on his desk rang. It was the doorman. There was a kid downstairs who wanted to see him. Dominic told the doorman to send the kid up.

The kid was about nineteen or twenty, wearing a faded blue sweater and sneakers. He was blond and blue-eyed and baby-faced. He reminded Dominic of Jimmy McLarnin, who had nearly torn him apart the time they had fought in New York. The kid had grease-stained hands, even though Dominic could see that he had tried to wash it all out. It was a cinch none of the members of the Revere Club had invited the kid up for a workout or a game of squash.

"What is it?" Dominic asked, looking up over his Ben Franklin glasses.

"I read the paper last night," the kid said.

145

"Yeah?" Dominic was always affable and smiling with the members and he made up for it with non-members.

"About how it's getting a little tough for you, Mr. Agostino, at your age, with the younger members of the club and so on," the kid said.

"Yeah?"

"I was thinking maybe you could take on an assistant, kind of," the kid said.

"You a fighter?"

"Not exactly," the kid said. "Maybe I want to be. I seem to fight an awful lot of the time . . ." He grinned. "I figure I might as well get paid for it."

"Come on." Dominic stood up and took off his glasses. He went out of the office and through the gym to the locker room. The kid followed him. The locker room was empty except for Charley, the attendant, who was dozing, sitting up at the door, his head on a pile of towels.

"You got any things with you?" Dominic asked the kid.

"No."

Dominic gave him an old sweat suit and a pair of shoes. He watched as the kid stripped. Long legs, heavy, sloping shoulders, thick neck. A hundred and fifty pounds, fifty-five, maybe. Good arms. No fat.

Dominic led him out to the corner of the gym where the mats were and threw him a pair of sixteen-ounce gloves. Charley came out to tie the laces for both of them.

"Let's see what you can do, kid," Dominic said. He put up his hands, lightly. Charley watched with interest.

The kid's hands were too low, naturally, and Dominic jabbed him twice with his left. But the kid kept swarming in.

After three minutes, Dominic dropped his hands and said, "Okay, that's enough." He had rapped the kid pretty hard a few times and had tied him up when he came in close, but with all that, the kid was awfully fast and the twice he had connected it had hurt. The kid was some kind of a fighter. Just what kind of fighter Dominic didn't know, but a fighter.

"Now listen, kid," Dominic said, as Charley undid the laces on his gloves, "this isn't a barroom. This is a gentlemen's club. The gentlemen don't come here to get hurt. They come to get some exercise while learning the manly art of self-defense. You come swinging in on them the way you did with me, you wouldn't last one day here."

"Sure," the kid said, "I understand. But I wanted to show you what I could do."

"You can't do much," Dominic said. "Yet. But you're fast and you move okay. Where you working now?"

"I was over in Brookline," the kid said. "In a garage. I'd like to find something where I can keep my hands clean."

"When you figure you could start in here?"

"Now. Today. I quit at the garage last week."

"How much you make there?"

"Fifty a week," the kid said.

"I think I can get you thirty-five here," Dominic said. "But you can rig up a cot in the massage room and sleep here. You'll have to help clean the swimming pool and vacuum the mats and stuff like that and check the equipment."

"Okay," the kid said.

"You got a job," Dominic said. "What's your name?"

"Thomas Jordache," the kid said.

"Just keep out of trouble, Tom," said Dominic.

He kept out of trouble for quite some time. He was quick and respectful and besides the work he had been hired to do, he cheerfully ran errands for Dominic and the members and made a point of smiling agreeably, at all times, with especial attention to the older men. The atmosphere of the club, muted, rich, and friendly, pleased him, and when he wasn't in the gym he liked to pass through the high-ceilinged, dark, wood-paneled reading and gaming rooms, with their deep leather armchairs and smoked-over oil paintings of Boston during the days of sailing ships. The work was undemanding, with long gaps in the day when he just sat around listening to Dominic reminisce about his years in the ring.

Dominic was not curious about Tom's past and Tom didn't bother to tell him about the months on the road, the flophouses in Cincinnati and Cleveland, and Chicago, about the jobs at filling stations, or about the stretch as a bellboy in the hotel in Syracuse. He had been making good money at the hotel steering whores into guests' rooms until he had to take a knife out of a pimp's fist because the pimp objected to the size of the commission his girls were passing on to the nice baby-faced boy they could mother when they weren't otherwise occupied. Thomas didn't tell Dominic, either, about the drunks he had rolled on the Loop or the loose cash he had stolen in various rooms, more for the hell of it than for the money, because he wasn't all that interested in money.

Dominic taught him how to hit the light bag and it was pleasant on a rainy afternoon, when the gym was empty, to tap away, faster and faster, at the bag, making the gym resound with the tattoo of the blows. Once in awhile, when he was feeling ambitious, and there were no members around, Dominic put on the gloves with him and taught him how to put together combinations, how to straighten out his right hand, how to use his head and elbows and slide with the punches, to keep up on the balls of his feet and how to avoid punches by ducking and weaving as he came in instead of falling back. Dominic still didn't allow him to spar with any of the members, because he wasn't sure about Thomas yet and didn't want any incidents. But the squash pro got him down to the courts and in just a few weeks made a fair player of him and when some of the lesser players of the club turned up without a partner for a game, Thomas would go in there with them. He was quick and agile and he didn't mind losing and when he won he learned immediately not to make the win too easy and he found himself collecting twenty to thirty dollars a week extra in tips.

He became friendly with the cook in the club kitchen, mostly by finding a solid connection for buying decent marijuana and doing the cook's shopping for him for the drug, so before long he was getting all his meals free.

He tactfully stayed out of all but the most desultory conversations with the members, who were lawyers, brokers, bankers, and officials of shipping lines and manufacturing companies. He learned to take messages accurately from their wives and mistresses over the telephone and pass them on with no hint that he understood exactly what he was doing.

He didn't like to drink, and the members, as they downed their post-exercise whiskies at the bar, commented favorably on that, too.

There was no plan to his behavior; he wasn't looking for anything; he just knew that it was better to ingratiate himself with the solid citizens who patronized the club than not. He had knocked around too much, a stray in America, getting into trouble and always finishing in brawls that sent him on the road again. Now the peace and security and approval of the club were welcome to him. It wasn't a career, he told himself, but it was a good year. He wasn't ambitious. When Dominic talked vaguely of his signing up for some amateur bouts just to see how good he was, he put the old fighter off.

When he got restless he would go downtown and pick up a whore and spend the night with her, honest money for honest services, and no complications in the morning.

He even liked the city of Boston, or at least as much as he had ever liked any place, although he didn't travel around it much by daylight, as he was pretty sure that there was an assault and battery warrant out for him as a result of the last afternoon at the garage in Brookline, when the foreman had come at him with a monkey wrench. He had gone right back to his rooming house that afternoon and packed and got out in ten minutes, telling his landlady he was heading for Florida. Then he had booked into the

Y.M.C.A. and lain low for a week, until he had seen the article in the newspaper about Dominic.

He had his likes and dislikes among the members, but was careful to be impartially pleasant to all of them. He didn't want to get involved with anybody. He had had enough involvements. He tried not to know too much about any of the members, but of course it was impossible not to form opinions, especially when you saw a man naked, his pot belly swelling, or his back scratched by some dame from his last go in bed, or taking it badly when he was losing a silly game of squash.

Dominic hated all the members equally, but only because they had money and he didn't. Dominic had been born and brought up in Boston and his *a* was as flat as anybody's, but in spirit he was still working by the day in a landlord's field in Sicily, plotting to burn down the landlord's castle and cut the throats of the landlord's family. Naturally, he concealed his dreams of arson and murder behind the most cordial of manners, always telling the members how well they looked when they came back after a vacation, marveling about how much weight they seemed to have lost, and being solicitous about aches and sprains.

"Here comes the biggest crook in Massachusetts," Dominic would whisper to Thomas, as an important-looking, gray-haired gentleman came into the locker room, and then, aloud, to the member, "Why, sir, it's good to see you back. We've missed you. I guess you've been working too hard."

"Ah, work, work," the man would say, shaking his head sadly.

"I know how it is, sir." Dominic would shake his head, too. "Come on down and I'll give you a nice turn on the weights and then you take a steam and a swim and a massage and you'll get all the kinks out and sleep like a babe tonight."

Thomas watched and listened carefully, learning from Dominic, useful dissembler. He liked the stony-hearted ex-pug, committed deep within him, despite all blandishments, to anarchy and loot.

Thomas also liked a man by the name of Reed, a hearty, easy-going president of a textile concern, who played squash with Thomas and insisted upon going onto the courts with him, even when there were other members hanging around waiting for a game. Reed was about forty-five and fairly heavy, but still played well and he and Thomas split their matches most of the time, Reed winning the early games and just losing out when he began to tire. "Young legs, young legs," Reed would say laughing, wiping the sweat off his face with a towel, as they walked together toward the showers after an hour on the courts. They played three times a week, regularly, and Reed always offered Thomas a Coke after they had cooled off and slipped him a five-dollar bill each time. He had one peculiarity. He always carried a hundred-dollar bill neatly folded in the right-hand pocket of his jacket. "A hundred-dollar bill saved my life once," Reed told Thomas. He had been caught in a dreadful fire one night in a night club, in which many people had perished. Reed had been lying under a pile of bodies near the door, hardly able to move, his throat too seared to cry out. He had heard the firemen dragging at the pile of bodies and with his last strength he had dug into his pants pocket, where he kept a hundred-dollar bill. He had managed to drag the bill out and work one arm free. His hand, waving feebly, with the bill clutched in it, had been seen. He had felt the money being taken from his grasp and then a fireman had moved the bodies lying on him and dragged him to safety. He had spent two weeks in the hospital, unable to talk, but he had survived, with a firm faith in the power of a single one-hundred-dollar bill. When possible, he advised Thomas, he should always try to have a hundred-dollar bill in a convenient pocket.

He also told Thomas to save his money and invest in the stock market, because young legs did not remain young forever.

The trouble came when he had been there three months. He sensed that something was wrong when he went to his locker to change after a late game of squash with Brewster Reed. There were no obvious signs, but he somehow knew somebody had been in there going through his clothes, looking for something. His wallet was half out of the back pocket of his trousers, as though it had been taken out and hastily stuffed back. Thomas took the wallet out and opened it. There had been four five-dollar bills in it and they were still there. He put the five-dollar bill Reed had tipped him into the wallet and slipped the wallet back in place. In the side pocket of his trousers there were some three dollars in bills and change, which had also been there before he had gone to the courts. A magazine which he had been reading and which he remembered putting front cover up on the top shelf was now spread open on the shelf.

For a moment Thomas thought of locking up, but then he thought, hell, if there's anybody in this club so poor he has to steal from me, he's welcome. He undressed, put his shoes in the locker, wrapped himself in a towel and went to the shower room, where Brewster Reed was already happily splashing around.

When he came back after the shower, there was a note pinned onto the inside of the locker door. It was in Dominic's handwriting and it read, "I want you in my office after closing time. D. Agostino."

The curtness of the message, the fact of its being written at all when he and Dominic passed each other ten times an afternoon, meant trouble. Something official, planned. Here we go again, he thought and almost was ready to finish dressing and quietly slip away, once and for all. But he decided against it, had his dinner in the kitchen, and afterward chatted unconcernedly with the squash pro and Charley in the locker room. Promptly at ten o'clock, when the club closed, he presented himself at Dominic's office.

Dominic was reading a copy of *Life*, slowly turning the pages on his desk. He looked up, closed the magazine and put it neatly to one side of the desk. He got up and looked out into the hall to make sure it was empty, then closed his office door. "Sit down, kid," he said.

Thomas sat down and waited while Dominic sat down opposite him behind the desk.

"What's up?" Thomas asked.

"Plenty," Dominic said. "The shit is hitting the fan. I've been getting reamed out all day."

"What's it got to do with me?"

"That's what I'm going to find out," Dominic said. "No use beatin' around the bush, kid. Somebody's been lifting dough out of people's wallets. Some smart guy who takes a bill here and there and leaves the rest. These fat bastards here're so rich most of 'em don't even know what they have in their pockets and if they do happen to miss an odd ten or twenty here or there, they think maybe they lost it or they made a mistake the last time they counted. But one guy is sure he don't make no mistakes. That bastard Greening. He says a ten-dollar bill was lifted from his locker while he was working out with me yesterday and he's been on the phone all day today talking to other members and now suddenly everybody's sure he's been robbed blind the last few months."

"Still, what's that got to do with me?" Thomas said, although he knew what it had to do with him.

"Greening figured out that it's only begun since you came to work here."

"That big shit," Thomas said bitterly. Greening was a cold-eyed man of about thirty who worked in a stock broker's office and who boxed with Dominic. He had fought light-heavy for some school out West and kept in shape and took no pity on Dominic, but went after him savagely for three two-minute rounds four times a week. After his sessions with Greening, Dominic, who didn't dare really to counter hard, was often bruised and exhausted.

"He's a shit all right," Dominic said. "He made me search your locker this afternoon. It's a lucky thing you didn't happen to have any ten-dollar bills there. Even so, he wants to call the police and have you booked on suspicion."

"What did you say to that?" Thomas asked.

"I talked him out of it," Dominic said. "I said I'd have a word with you."

"Well, you're having a word with me," Thomas said. "Now what?"

"Did you take the dough?"

"No. Do you believe me?"

Dominic shrugged warily. "I don't know. *Somebody* sure as hell took it."

"A lot of people walk around the locker room all day. Charley, the guy from the pool, the pro, the members, you . . ."

"Cut it out, kid," Dominic said. "I don't want no jokes."

"Why pick on me?" Thomas asked.

"I told you. It only started since you came to work here. Ah Christ, they're talking about putting padlocks on all the lockers. Nobody's ever locked anything here for a hundred years. The way they talk they're in the middle of the biggest crime wave since Jesse James."

"What do you want me to do? Quit?"

"Naah." Dominic shook his head. "Just be careful. Keep in *somebody's* sight all the time." He sighed. "Maybe it'll all blow over. That bastard Greening and his lousy ten bucks . . . Come on out with me." He stood up wearily and stretched. "I'll buy you a beer. What a lousy day."

The locker room was empty when Thomas came through the door. He had been sent out to the post office with a package and he was in his street clothes. There was an interclub squash match on and everybody was upstairs watching it. Everybody but one of the members called Sinclair, who was on the team, but who had not yet played his match. He was dressed, ready to play, and was wearing a white sweater. He was a tall, slender young man who had a law degree from Harvard and whose father was also a member of the club. The family had a lot of money and their name was in the papers often. Young Sinclair worked in his father's law office in the city and Thomas had overheard older men in the club saying that young Sinclair was a brilliant lawyer and would go far.

But right now, as Thomas came down the aisle silently in his tennis shoes, young Sinclair was standing in front of an open locker and he had his hand in the inside pocket of the jacket hanging there and he was deftly taking out a wallet. Thomas wasn't sure whose locker it was, but he knew it wasn't Sinclair's, because Sinclair's locker was only three away from his own on the other side of the room. Sinclair's face, which was usually cheerful and ruddy, was pale and tense and he was sweating.

For a moment, Thomas hesitated, wondering if he could turn and get away before Sinclair saw him. But just as Sinclair got the wallet out, he looked up and saw Thomas. They stared at each other. Then it was too late to back away. Thomas moved quickly toward the man and grabbed his wrist. Sinclair was panting, as though he had been running a great distance.

"You'd better put that back, sir," Thomas whispered.

"All right," Sinclair said. "I'll put it back." He whispered, too.

Thomas did not release his wrist. He was thinking fast. If he denounced Sinclair, on one excuse or another he would lose his job. It would be too uncomfortable for the other members to be subjected daily to the presence of a lowly employee who had disgraced one of their own. If he didn't denounce him . . . Thomas played for time. "You know, sir," he said, "they suspect me."

"I'm sorry." Thomas could feel the man trembling, but Sinclair didn't try to pull away.

"You're going to do three things," Thomas said. "You're going to put the wallet back and you're going to promise to lay off from now on."

"I promise, Tom. I'm very grateful . . ."

"You're going to show just how grateful you are, Mr. Sinclair," Thomas said. "You're going to write out an IOU for five thousand dollars to me right now and you're going to pay me in cash within three days."

"You're out of your mind," Sinclair said, sweat standing out on his forehead.

"All right," Thomas said. "I'll start yelling."

"I bet you would, you little bastard," Sinclair said.

"I'll meet you in the bar of the Hotel Touraine, Thursday night at eleven o'clock," Thomas said. "Pay night."

"I'll be there." Sinclair's voice was so low that Thomas could barely hear it. He dropped the man's hand and watched as Sinclair put the wallet back into the jacket pocket. Then he took out a small notebook in which he kept a record of petty expenses he laid out on errands and opened it to a blank page and handed Sinclair a pencil.

Sinclair looked down at the open notebook thrust under his nose. If he could steady his nerves, Thomas knew, he could just walk away and if Thomas told anybody the story he could laugh it off. But never completely laugh it off. Anyway, his nerves were shot. He took the notebook, scribbled in it.

Thomas glanced at the page, put the notebook in his pocket and took back the pencil. Then he gently closed the locker door and went upstairs to watch the squash.

Fifteen minutes later Sinclair came onto the court and beat his opponent in straight games.

In the locker room later, Thomas congratulated him on his victory.

He got to the bar of the Touraine at five to eleven. He was dressed in a suit with a collar and tie. Tonight he wanted to pass for a gentleman. The bar was dark and only a third full. He carefully sat down at a table in a corner, where he could watch the entrance. When the waiter came over to him, he ordered a bottle of Budweiser. Five thousand dollars, he thought, five thousand . . . They had taken that amount from his father and he was taking it back from them. He wondered if Sinclair had had to go to *his* father to get the money and had to explain why he needed it. Probably not. Probably Sinclair had so much dough in his own name he could lay his hands on five thousand cash in ten minutes. Thomas had nothing against Sinclair. Sinclair was a pleasant young man, with nice, friendly eyes and a soft voice and good manners who from time to time had given him some pointers on how to play drop shots in squash and whose life would be ruined if it became known he was a kleptomaniac. The system had just worked out that way.

He sipped at his beer, watching the door. At three minutes after eleven, the door opened and Sinclair came in. He peered around the dark room and Thomas stood up. Sinclair came over to the table and Thomas said, "Good evening, sir."

"Good evening, Tom," Sinclair said evenly and sat down on the banquette, but without taking off his topcoat.

"What are you drinking?" Thomas asked, as the waiter came over.

"Scotch and water, please," Sinclair said with his polite, Harvard way of talking.

"And another Bud, please," said Thomas.

They sat in silence for a moment, side by side on the banquette. Sinclair drummed his fingers briefly on the table, scanning the room. "Do you come here often?" he asked.

"Once in awhile."

"Do you ever see anybody from the Club here?"

"No."

The waiter came over and put down their drinks. Sinclair took a thirsty gulp from his glass. "Just for your information," Sinclair said, "I don't take the money because I need it."

"I know," Thomas said.

"I'm sick," Sinclair said. "It's a disease. I'm going to a psychiatrist."

"That's smart of you," Thomas said.

"You don't mind doing what you're doing to a sick man?"

"No," Thomas said. "No, sir."

"You're a hard little son of a bitch, aren't you?"

"I hope so, sir," said Thomas.

Sinclair opened his coat and reached inside and brought out a long, full envelope.

He put it down on the banquette between himself and Thomas. "It's all there," he said. "You needn't bother to count it."

"I'm sure it's all there," Thomas said. He slipped the envelope into his side pocket.

"I'm waiting," Sinclair said. Thomas took out the IOU and put it on the table. Sinclair glanced at it, tore it up and stuffed the shreds into an ashtray. He stood up. "Thanks for the drink," he said. He walked toward the door past the bar, a handsome young man, the marks of breeding, gentility, education, and good luck clearly on him.

Thomas watched him go out and slowly finished his beer. He paid for the drinks and went into the lobby and rented a room for the night. Upstairs, with the door locked and the blinds down, he counted the money. It was all in hundred-dollar bills, all new. It occurred to him that they might be marked, but he couldn't tell.

He slept well in the big double bed and in the morning called the Club and told Dominic that he had to go to New York on family business and wouldn't be in until Monday afternoon. He hadn't taken any days off since he'd started working at the Club, so Dominic had to say okay, but no later than Monday.

It was drizzling when the train pulled into the station and the gray, autumnal drip didn't make Port Philip look any better as Thomas went out of the station. He hadn't brought his coat, so he put up the collar of his jacket to try to keep the rain from going down his neck.

The station square didn't look much different. The Port Philip House had been repainted and a big radio and television shop in a new, yellow-brick building was advertising a sale in portable radios. The smell of the river was still the same and Tom remembered it.

He could have taken a taxi, but after the years of absence he preferred to walk. The streets of his native town would slowly prepare him—for just what he was not quite sure.

He walked past the bus station. The last ride with his brother Rudolph. *You smell like a wild animal*.

He walked past Bernstein's Department Store, his sister's rendezvous point with Theodore Boylan. The naked man in the living room, the burning cross. Happy boyhood memories.

He walked past the public school. The returned malarial soldier and the samurai sword and the Jap's head spouting blood.

Nobody said hello. All faces in the mean rain looked hurried, closed, and unfamiliar. Return in Triumph. Welcome, Citizen.

He walked past St. Anselm's, Claude Tinker's uncle's church. *By the Grace of God, he was not observed*.

He turned into Vanderhoff Street. The rain was coming down more strongly. He touched the bulge in the breast of his jacket that concealed the envelope with the money in it. The street had changed. A square prisonlike building had been put up and there was some sort of factory in it. Some of the old shops were boarded up and there were names he didn't recognize on the windows of other shops.

He kept his eyes down to keep the rain from driving into them, so when he looked up finally he was stupidly puzzled because where the bakery had been, where the house in which he was born had stood, there was now a large supermarket, with three stories of apartments above it. He read the signs in the windows. Special Today, Rib Roast. Lamb Shoulder. Women with shopping bags were going in and out of a door which, if the Jordache house had been still there, would have opened onto the front hallway.

Thomas peered through the windows. There were girls making change at the front desks. He didn't know any of them. There was no sense in going in. He was not in the market for rib roasts or lamb shoulders.

Uncertainly, he continued down the street. The garage next door had been rebuilt and the name on it was a different one and he didn't recognize any of the faces there, either. But near the corner he saw that Jardino's Fruits and Vegetables was still where it always had been. He went in and waited while an old woman argued with Mrs. Jardino about string beans.

When the old woman had gone, Mrs. Jardino turned to him. She was a small, shapeless woman with a fierce, beaked nose and a wart on her upper lip from which spraing two long, coarse, black hairs. "Yes," Mrs. Jardino said. "What can I do for you?"

"Mrs. Jardino," Thomas said, putting down his coat collar to look more respectable, "you probably don't remember me, but I used to be a . . . well . . . a kind of neighbor of yours. We used to have the bakery. Jordache?"

Mrs. Jardino peered nearsightedly at him. "Which one were you?"

"The youngest one."

"Oh, yes. The little gangster."

Thomas tried a smile, to compliment Mrs. Jardino on her rough humor. Mrs. Jardino didn't smile back. "So, what do you want?"

"I haven't been here for awhile," Thomas said. "I've come back to pay a family visit. But the bakery isn't there any more."

"It's been gone for years," Mrs. Jardino said impatiently, arranging apples so that the spots wouldn't show. "Didn't your family tell you?"

"We were out of touch for awhile," Thomas said. "Do you know where they are?"

"How should I know where they are? They never talked to dirty Italians." She turned her back squarely on him and fussed with bunches of celery.

"Thank you very much, just the same," Thomas said and started out.

"Wait a minute," Mrs. Jardino said. "When you left, your father was still alive, wasn't he?"

"Yes," Thomas said.

"Well, he's dead," she said. There was a certain satisfaction in her voice. "He drowned. In the river. And then your mother moved away and then they tore the building down and now . . ." bitterly, "there's a supermarket there cutting our throats."

A customer came in and Mrs. Jardino began to weigh five pounds of potatoes and Thomas went out of the shop.

He went and stood in front of the supermarket for awhile, but it didn't tell him anything. He thought of going down to the river, but the river wasn't going to tell him anything, either. He walked back toward the station. He passed a bank and went in and rented a safety deposit box and put forty-nine hundred of the five thousand dollars in the box. He figured he might as well leave his money in Port Philip as anywhere. Or throw it into the river in which his father had drowned.

He supposed he might be able to find his mother and brother by going to the post office, but he decided against the effort. It was his father he had come to see. And pay off.

CHAPTER 2

1950

CAPPED AND GOWNED, Rudolph sat in the June sunlight, among the other graduates in rented black.

"Now, in 1950, at the exact mid-point of the century," the speaker was saying, "we Americans must ask ourselves several questions: What do we have? What do we want? What are our strengths and weaknesses? Where are we going?" The speaker was a cabinet member, up from Washington as a favor for the President of the college, who had been a friend of his at Cornell, a more illustrious place of learning.

Now at the exact mid-point of the century, Rudolph thought, moving restlessly on the camp chair set up on the campus lawn, what do I have, what do I want, what are my strengths and weaknesses, where am I going? I have a B.A., a debt of four thousand dollars, and a dying mother. I want to be rich and free and beloved. My strength—I can run the two twenty in 23:8. My weakness? I am honest. He smiled inwardly, innocently regarding the Great Man from Washington. Where am I going? You tell me, brother.

The man from Washington was a man of peace. "The curve of military power is rising everywhere," he said in solemn tones. "The only hope for peace is the military might of the United States. To prevent war the United States needs a force so big and strong, so capable of counterattack as to serve as a deterrent."

Rudolph looked along the rows of his fellow graduates. Half of them were veterans of World War II, in college on the G.I. Bill of Rights. Many of them were married, their wives sitting with newly set hair in the rows behind them, some of them holding infants in their arms because there was nobody to leave them with in the trailers and cluttered rented rooms which had been their homes while their husbands had struggled for the degrees being awarded today. Rudolph wondered how they felt about the rising curve of military power.

Sitting next to Rudolph was Bradford Knight, a round-faced florid young man from Tulsa, who had been a sergeant in the infantry in Europe. He was Rudolph's best friend on the campus, an energetic, overt boy, cynical and shrewd behind a lazy Oklahoma drawl. He had come to Whitby because his captain had graduated from the school and recommended him to the Dean of Admissions. He and Rudolph had drunk a lot of beer together and had gone fishing together. Brad kept urging Rudolph to come out to Tulsa with him after graduation and go into the oil business with him and his father. "You'll be a millionaire before you're twenty-five, son," Brad had said. "It's overflowin' country out there. You'll trade in your Cadillac every time the ashtrays have to be emptied." Brad's father had been a millionaire before he was twenty-five, but was in a low period now ("Just a little bad run of luck," according to Brad) and couldn't afford the fare East at the moment for his son's graduation.

Teddy Boylan wasn't at the ceremony, either, although Rudolph had sent him an invitation. It was the least he could do for the four thousand dollars. But Boylan had declined. "I'm afraid I can't see myself driving fifty miles on a nice June afternoon to listen to a Democrat make a speech on the campus of an obscure agricultural school." Whitby was not an agricultural school, although it did have an important agricultural department, but Boylan still resented Rudolph's refusal even to apply to an Ivy League university when he had made his offer in 1946 to finance Rudolph's education. "However," the letter had gone on in Boylan's harsh, heavily accented handwriting, "the day shall not go altogether uncelebrated. Come on over to the house when the dreary mumblings are over, and we'll break out a bottle of champagne and talk about your plans.

Rudolph had decided for several reasons to choose Whitby rather than to take a chance on Yale or Harvard. For one, he'd have owed Boylan a good deal more than four thousand dollars at the end, and for another, with his background and his lack of money, he'd have been a four-year outsider among the young lords of American society whose fathers and grandfathers had all cheered at Harvard-Yale games, who whipped back and forth to debutantes' balls, and most of whom had never worked a day in their lives. At Whitby, poverty was normal. The occasional boy who didn't have to work in the summer to help pay for his books and clothes in the autumn was unusual. The only outsiders, except for an occasional stray like Brad, were bookish freaks who shunned their fellow students and a few politically minded young men who circulated petitions in favor of the United Nations and against compulsory military service.

Another reason that Rudolph had chosen Whitby was that it was close enough to Port Philip so that he could get over on Sundays to see his mother, who was more or less confined to her room and who, friendless, suspicious, and half mad, could not be allowed just to founder into absolute neglect. In the summer of his sophomore year, when he got the job after hours and on Saturdays at Calderwood's Department Store, he had found a cheap little two-room apartment with a kitchenette in Whitby and had moved his mother in with him. She was waiting for him there, now. She hadn't felt well enough to come to the graduation, she said, and besides, she would disgrace him, the way she looked. Disgrace was probably too strong a word, Rudolph thought, looking around at the neatly clothed, sober parents of his classmates, but she certainly wouldn't have dazzled anybody in the assemblage with her beauty or her style of dress. It was one thing to be a dutiful son. It was a very different thing not to face facts.

So—Mary Pease Jordache, sitting in a rocking chair at the window of the shabby apartment, cigarette ashes drifting down on her shawl, legs swollen and almost useless, was not there to see her son rewarded with his roll of imitation parchment. Among the other absentees—Gretchen, linked by blood, detained in New York by a crisis with her child; Julie, being graduated herself that day from Barnard; Thomas, more blood, address unknown; Axel Jordache, blood on his hands, sculling through eternity.

He was alone this day and it was just as well.

"The power of the military establishment is appalling," the speaker was saying, his voice magnified over the public address system, "but one great thing on our side is the wish of the ordinary man everywhere for peace."

If Rudolph was an ordinary man, the cabinet member was certainly speaking for him. Now that he had heard some of the stories about the war in bull sessions around the campus he no longer envied the generation before his which had stood on Guadalcanal and the sandy ridges of Tunisia and at the Rapido River.

The fine, intelligent, educated voice sang on in the sunny quadrangle of red-brick Colonial buildings. Inevitably, there was the salute to America, land of opportunity. Half the young men listening had had the opportunity to be killed for America, but the speaker was looking forward this afternoon, not toward the past, and the opportunities he mentioned were those of scientific research, public service, aid to those nations throughout the world who were not as fortunate as we. He was a good man, the cabinet member, and Rudolph was glad that such a man was near the seat of power in Washington, but his view of opportunity in 1950 was a bit lofty, evangelical, Washingtonian, all very well for a Commencement exercise, but not likely to coincide with the down-to-earth views of the three hundred or so poor men's sons who sat before him in black robes waiting to receive their degrees from a small, underfinanced school known, if it was known at all, for its agricultural department, and wondering how they were going to start earning a living the next day.

Up front, in the section reserved for professors, Rudolph saw Professor Denton, the head of the History and Economics departments, squirming in his seat and turning to whisper to Professor Lloyd, of the English Department, sitting on his right. Rudolph smiled, guessing what Professor Denton's comments would be on the cabinet member's ritualistic pronouncements. Denton, a small, fierce, graying man, disappointed because by now he realized he would rise no higher in the academic world, was also a kind of outdated Midwestern Populist, who spent a good deal of his time in the classroom ranting about what he considered the betrayal of the American economic and political system, dating back to the Civil War, by Big Money and Big Business. "The American economy," he had said in class, "is a rigged crap table, with loaded dice. The laws are carefully arranged so that the Rich throw only sevens and everybody else throws only snake-eyes."

At least once a term he made a point of referring to the fact that in 1932, by his own admission before a congressional committee, J. P. Morgan had not paid a cent in income tax. "I want you gentlemen to keep this in mind," Professor Denton would declaim bitterly, "while also keeping in mind that in the same year, on a mere tutor's salary, I paid five hundred and twenty-seven dollars and thirty cents in tax to the Federal Government."

The effect on the class, as far as Rudolph could discern, was not the one Denton sought. Rather than firing the students up with indignation and a burning desire to rally forth to do battle for reform, most of the students, Rudolph included, dreamed of the time when they themselves could reach the heights of wealth and power, so that they, too, like J. P. Morgan, could be exempt from what Denton called the legal enslavement of the electorate body.

And when Denton, pouncing upon some bit of news in *The Wall Street Journal* describing some new wily tax-saving amalgamation or oil jobbing that kept millions of dollars immune from the federal treasury, Rudolph listened carefully, admiring the techniques that Denton lovingly dissected, and putting everything carefully down in his notebooks, against the blessed day when he perhaps might be faced with similar opportunities.

Anxious for good marks, not so much for themselves as for the possible advantages later, Rudolph did not let on that his close attention to Denton's tirades were not those of a disciple, but rather those of a spy in enemy territory. His three courses with Denton had been rewarded with three *A*'s and Denton had offered him a teaching fellowship in the History Department for the next year.

Despite his secret disagreement with what he thought were Denton's naive positions, Denton was the one instructor Rudolph had come to like in all the time he had been in the college, and the one man he considered had taught him anything useful.

He had kept this opinion, as he had kept almost all his other opinions, strictly to himself, and he was highly regarded as a serious student and a well-behaved young man by the faculty members.

The speaker was finishing, with a mention of God in his last sentence. There was applause. Then the graduates were called up to receive their degrees, one by one. The President beamed as he bestowed the rolls of paper bedecked with ribbon. He had scored a coup getting the cabinet member to his ceremony. He had not read Boylan's letter about an agricultural school.

A hymn was sung, a decorous march played. The black robes filed down through the rows of parents and relatives. The robes dispersed under the summer foliage, of oak trees, mixing with the bright colors of women's dresses, making the graduates look like a flock of crows feeding in a field of flowers.

Rudolph limited himself to a few handshakes. He had a busy day and night ahead of him. Denton sought him out, shook his hand, a small, almost hunchbacked man with thick, silver-rimmed glasses. "Jordache," he said, his hand enthusiastic, "you will think it over won't you?"

"Yes, sir," Rudolph said. "It's very kind of you." Respect your elders. The academic life, serene, underpaid. A Master's in a year, a Ph.D. a few years later, a chair perhaps at the age of forty-five. "I am certainly tempted, sir." He was not tempted at all.

He and Brad broke away to turn in their robes and go, as prearranged, to the parking lot. Brad had a pre-war Chevy convertible, and his bags, already packed, were in the trunk. Brad was ready to take off for Oklahoma, that overflowing country.

They were the first ones out of the parking lot. They did not look back. Alma Mater disappeared around a bend in the road. Four years. Be sentimental later. Twenty years from now.

"Let's go by the store for a minute," Rudolph said. "I promised Calderwood I'd look in."

"Yes, sir," Brad said, at the wheel. "Do I sound like an educated man?"

"The ruling class," Rudolph said.

"My time has not been wasted," Brad said. "How much do you think a cabinet member makes a year?"

"Fifteen, sixteen thousand," Rudolph hazarded.

"Chickenfeed," Brad said.

"Plus honor."

"That's another thirty bucks a year at least," Brad said. "Tax free. You think he wrote that speech himself?"

"Probably."

"He's overpaid." Brad began to hum the tune of "Everything's Up-to-Date in Kansas City." "Will there be broads there tonight?"

Gretchen had invited them both to her place for a party to mark the occasion. Julie was to come, too, if she could shake her parents.

"Probably," Rudolph said. "There're usually one or two girls hanging around."

"I read all that stuff in the papers," Brad said querulously, "about how modern youth is going to the dogs and how morality has broken down since the war and all, but I'm not getting any of that little old broken-down morality, that's for sure. The next time I go to college it's going to be coed. You're looking at a pure-bred, sex-starved Bachelor of Arts, and I ain't just talking." He hummed gaily.

They drove through the town. Since the war there had been a lot of new construction, small factories with lawns and flower-beds pretending to be places of recreation and gracious living, shop-fronts redone to look as though they were on eighteenth-century village streets in the English counties, a white clapboard building that had once been the town hall and was now a summer theater. People from New York had begun buying farmhouses in the adjoining countryside and came up for weekends and holidays. Whitby, in the four years that Rudolph had spent there, had grown visibly more prosperous with nine new holes added to the golf course and an optimistic real-estate development called Greenwood Estates, where you had to buy at least two acres of land if you wanted to build a house. There was even a small artists' colony and when the President of the university attempted to lure staff away from other institutions, he always pointed out that Whitby was situated in an up-and-coming town, improving in quality as well as size, and that it had a cultural atmosphere.

Calderwood's was a small department store on the best corner of the main shopping street of the town. It had been there since the 1890's, first as a kind of general store serving the needs of a sleepy college village with a back country of solid farms. As the town had grown and changed its character, the store had grown and changed accordingly. Now it was a long, two-story structure, with a considerable variety of goods displayed behind plateglass windows. Rudolph had started as a stock boy in busy seasons, but had worked so hard and had come up with so many suggestions that Duncan Calderwood, descendant of the original owner, had had to promote him. The store was still small enough so that one man could do many different jobs in it, and by now Rudolph acted as part-time salesman, window dresser, advertising copy writer, adviser on buying, and consultant on the hiring and firing of personnel. When he worked full time in the summer, his salary was fifty dollars a week.

Duncan Calderwood was a spare, laconic Yankee of about fifty, who had married late and had three daughters. Aside from the store, he owned a good deal of real estate in and around the town. Just how much was his own business. He was a closemouthed man who knew the value of a dollar. The day before, he had told Rudolph to drop around after the graduation exercises were over, he might have an interesting proposition to put to him.

Brad stopped the car in front of the entrance to the store.

"I'll just be a minute," Rudolph said, getting out.

"Take your time," Brad said. "I've got my whole life ahead of me." He opened his collar and pulled his tie loose, free at last. The top of the car was down and he lay back and closed his eyes luxuriously in the sunlight.

As Rudolph went into the store, he glanced approvingly at one of the windows, which he had arranged three nights before. The window was devoted to carpentry tools and Rudolph had set them out so that they made a severe abstract pattern, uncluttered and gleaming. From time to time Rudolph went down to New York and studied the windows of the big stores on Fifth Avenue to pick up ideas for Calderwood's.

There was a comfortable, female hum of shopping on the main floor and a slight, typical odor of clothes and new leather and women's scents that Rudolph always enjoyed. The clerks smiled at him and waved hello as he went toward the back of the store, where Calderwood's private office was located. One or two of the clerks said "Congratulations," and he waved at them. He was well liked, especially by the older people. They did not know that he was consulted on hiring and firing.

Calderwood's door was open, as it always was. He liked to keep an eye on what was happening in the store. He was seated at his desk, writing a letter with a fountain pen. He had a secretary, who had an office beside his, but there were some things about his business he didn't want even his secretary to know. He wrote four or five letters a day by hand and stamped them and mailed them himself. The door to the secretary's office was closed.

Rudolph stood in the doorway, waiting. Although he left the door open, Calderwood did not like to be interrupted.

Calderwood finished a sentence, reread it, then looked up. He had a sallow, smooth face with a long blade of a nose and receding black hair. He turned the letter face down on his desk. He had big farmer's hands and he dealt clumsily with frail things like sheets of paper. Rudolph was proud of his own slender, long-fingered hands, which he felt were aristocratic.

"Come in, Rudy," Calderwood said. His voice was dry, uninflected.

"Good afternoon, Mr. Calderwood." Rudolph stepped into the bare room in his good, blue, graduation suit. There was a giveaway Calderwood calendar on the wall, with a colored photograph of the store on it. Aside from the calendar the only other adornment in the room was a photograph of Calderwood's three daughters, taken when they were little girls, on the desk.

Surprisingly, Calderwood stood up and came around the desk and shook Rudolph's hand. "How did it go?" he asked.

"No surprises."

"You glad you did it?"

"You mean go to college?" Rudolph asked.

"Yes. Sit down." Calderwood went back behind his desk and sat on the straight-backed wooden chair. Rudolph seated himself on another wooden chair on the right side of the desk. In the furniture department on the second floor there were dozens of upholstered leather chairs, but they were for customers only.

"I suppose so," Rudolph said. "I suppose I'm glad."

"Most of the men who made the big fortunes in this country, who are making them today," Calderwood said, "never had any real schooling. Did you know that?"

"Yes," Rudolph said.

"They hire schooling," said Calderwood. It was almost a threat. Calderwood himself had not finished high school.

"I'll try not to let my education interfere with my making a fortune," Rudolph said.

Calderwood laughed, dry, economical. "I'll bet you won't Rudy," he said affably. He pulled open a drawer of the desk and took out a jeweler's box, with the name of the store written in gilt script on the velvet cover. "Here," he said, putting the box down on the desk. "Here's something for you."

Rudolph opened the box. In it was a handsome steel Swiss wristwatch, with a black suede band. "It's very good of you, sir," Rudolph said. He tried not to sound surprised.

"You earned it," Calderwood said. He adjusted his narrow tie in the notch of his starched white collar, embarrassed. Generosity did not come easily to him. "You put in a lot of good work in this store, Rudy. You got a good head on your shoulders, you have a gift for merchandising."

"Thank you, Mr. Calderwood." This was the *real* Commencement address, none of that Washington stuff about the rising military curve and aid to our less fortunate brothers.

"I told you I had a proposition for you, didn't I?"

"Yes, sir."

Calderwood hesitated, cleared his throat, stood up, walked toward the calendar on the wall. It was as though before he took a stupendous final plunge, he had to recheck his figures one last time. He was dressed as always in a black suit with vest, and high-topped black shoes. He liked full support for his ankles, he said. "Rudy," he began, "how would you like to work for Calderwood's on a full-time basis?"

"That depends," Rudolph said, carefully. He had expected this and he had decided what terms he would accept.

"Depends on what?" Calderwood asked. He sounded pugnacious.

"Depends on what the job is," Rudolph said.

"The same as you've been doing," Calderwood said. "Only more so. A little bit of everything. You want a title?"

"That depends on the title."

"Depends, depends," Calderwood said. But he laughed. "Who ever made up the idea about the rashness of youth? How about Assistant Manager? Is that a good enought title for you?"

"For openers," Rudolph said.

"Maybe I ought to kick you out of this office," Calderwood said. The pale eyes iced up momentarily.

"I don't want to sound ungrateful," Rudolph said, "But I don't want to get into any dead ends. I have some other offers and . . . "

"I suppose you want to rush down to New York, like all the other young damn fools," Calderwood said. "Take over the city in the first month, get yourself invited to all the parties."

"Not particularly," Rudolph said. Actually he didn't feel ready for New York yet. "I like this town."

"With good reason," Calderwood said. He sat down behind his desk again, with a sound that was almost a sigh. "Listen, Rudy," he said, "I'm not getting any younger; the doctor says I've got to start taking it easier. Delegate responsibility, is the way he puts it, take holidays, prolong my life. The usual doctor's sales talk. I have a high cholesterol count. That's a new gimmick they got to scare you with, cholesterol count. Anyway, it makes sense. I have no sons . . . " He glared at the photograph of the three girl children at his desk, triply betrayed. "I've done the whole thing myself in here since my father died. Somebody's got to help take over. And I don't want any of those high-powered young snots from the business schools, changing everything and asking for a share in the shop after the first two weeks." He lowered his head and looked at Rudolph measuringly from under his thick black eyebrows. "You start at one hundred a week. After a year we'll see. Is that fair or isn't it fair?"

"It's fair," Rudolph said. He had expected seventy-five.

"You'll have an office," Calderwood said. "The old wrapping room on the second floor. Assistant Manager on the door. But I want to see you on the floor during store hours. We shake on it?"

Rudolph put out his hand. Calderwood's handshake was not that of a man with a high cholesterol count.

"I suppose you'll want to take some sort of holiday first," Calderwood said. "I don't blame you. What do you want—two weeks, a month?"

"I'll be here at nine o'clock tomorrow morning." Rudolph stood up.

Calderwood smiled, a flare of unconvincing dentures. "I hope I'm not making a mistake," he said. "I'll see you tomorrow morning."

He was turning over his unfinished letter and picking up his fountain pen with his big, square hand, as Rudolph left the office.

As he went through the store Rudolph walked slowly, looking around at the counters, the clerks, the customers, with a new, appraising, owning eye. At the doorway he stopped, took off his cheap watch and put on the new one.

Brad was dozing at the wheel in the sunlight. He sat up as Rudolph got into the car. "Anything new?" he asked, as he started the engine.

"The old man gave me a present." Rudolph held up his hand to display the watch.

"He's got a soft heart," Brad said, as they pulled away from the curb.

"One hundred and fifteen dollars," Rudolph said, "at the watch counter. Fifty dollars wholesale." He didn't say anything about reporting to work at nine o'clock in the morning. Calderwood's was not overflowing country.

Mary Pease Jordache sat at the window looking down at the street, waiting for Rudolph. He had promised he'd come right home after the Commencement exercises to show her his degree. It would have been nice to arrange some sort of party for him, but she didn't have the energy. Besides, she didn't know any of his friends. It wasn't that he wasn't popular. The phone was always ringing and young voices would say, "This is Charlie," or "This is Brad, is Rudy in?" But somehow he never seemed to bring any of them home. Just as well. It wasn't much of a home. Two dark rooms over a dry-goods store on a treeless, bare side street. She was doomed to live her life out over stores. And there was a Negro family living right smack across the street from them. Black faces at the window staring at her. Pickaninnies and rapists. She had learned all about *them* at the orphanage.

She lit a cigarette, her hand shaking, and brushed inaccurately at the ashes from former cigarettes on her shawl. It was a warm June day, but she felt better with her shawl.

Well, Rudolph had made it, despite everything. A college graduate, holding his head high, any man's match. Thank God for Theodore Boylan. She had never met him, but Rudolph had explained what an intelligent, generous man he was. It was no more than Rudolph deserved, though. With his manners and his wit. People *liked* to help him. Well, he was on his way now. Though when she'd asked him what he was going to do after college he'd been vague. He had plans, though, she was sure. Rudolph was never without plans. As long as he didn't get caught up with some girl and get married. Mary Pease shivered. He was a good boy, you couldn't ask for a more thoughtful son; if it hadn't been for him God knows what would have happened to her since that night Axel disappeared. But once a girl came into the picture, boys became like wild animals, even the best of them, sacrificing everything, home, parents, career, for a pair of soft eyes and the promise under the skirt. Mary Pease Jordache had never met his Julie, but she knew she went to Barnard and she knew about Rudolph's trips to New York on Sundays, all those miles there and back, coming home at all hours, pale and dark under the eyes, restless and short of speech. Still, Julie had lasted over five years and he should be ready for someone else by now. She would have to talk to him, tell him now was the time to enjoy himself, take his time, there would be hundreds of girls who would be more than honored to throw themselves at his head.

She really ought to have done something special for this day. Baked a cake, gone down and bought a bottle of wine. But the effort of descending and climbing the stairs, making herself presentable for the neighbors . . . Rudolph would understand. Anyway, he was going to New York that afternoon to be with his friends. Let the old lady sit alone at the window, she thought with sudden bitterness. Even the best of them.

She saw the car turn the corner into the street, its tires squealing, going too fast. She saw Rudolph, his black hair blowing, young Prince. She saw well at a distance, better than ever, but close-up was another story. She had given up reading because it was too much of a strain, her eyes kept changing, no glasses seemed to help for more than a few weeks at a time, old eyes. She was under fifty, but her eyes were dying before her. She let the tears overflow.

The car stopped below her and Rudolph leaped out. Grace, grace. In a fine blue suit. He had a figure for clothes, slender, with wide shoulders and long legs. She pulled back from the window. He had never said anything, but she knew he didn't like her sitting at the window all day peering out.

She stood up, with an effort, dried her eyes with the edge of her shawl, and hobbled over to a chair near the table which they used for eating. She stubbed out her cigarette as she heard him bounding up the steps.

He opened the door and came in. "Well," he said, "here it is." He opened the roll of paper and spread it on the table in front of her. "It's in Latin," he said.

She could read his name, in Gothic script.

The tears came again. "I wish I knew your father's address," she said. "I'd like him to see this, see what you did without any help from him."

"Ma," Rudolph said gently, "he's dead."

"That's what he likes people to believe," she said. "I know him better than anybody. He's not dead, he escaped."

"Ma . . . " Rudolph said again.

"He's laughing up his sleeve right this minute," she said. "They never found the body, did they?"

"Have it your own way," Rudolph said. "I have to pack a bag. I'm staying in town overnight." He went into his room and started to throw some shaving things and a pair of pajamas and a clean shirt into a bag. "You got everything you need? Supper?"

"I'll open a can," she said. "You going to drive down with that boy in the car?"

"Yes," he said. "Brad."

"He's the one from Oklahoma? The Westerner?"

"Yes."

"I don't like the way he drives. He's reckless. I don't trust Westerners. Why don't you take the train?"

"What's the sense in spending money for the train?"

"What good will your money do if you're killed, trapped under a car?"

"Ma . . . "

"And you'll make plenty of money now. A boy like you. With this." She smoothed the stiff paper with the Latin lettering. "Do you ever think of what would happen to me if anything happened to you?"

"Nothing will happen to me." He clipped the bag shut. He was in a hurry. She saw he was in a hurry. Leave her by the window.

"They will throw me on the barbage heap, like a dog," she said.

"Ma," he said, "this is a day for celebration. Rejoicing."

"I'll have this framed," she said. "Enjoy yourself. You earned it. Don't stay up too late. Where're you staying in New York? Do you have the phone number, in case there's an emergency?"

"There won't be any emergency."

"In case."

"Gretchen's," he said.

"The harlot," she said. They did not talk about Gretchen, although she knew he saw her.

"Oh, Christ," he said. She had gone too far, and she knew it, but she had to make her position clear.

He leaned over and kissed her to say goodbye and to make up for the "Oh, Christ." She held him. She had doused herself with the toilet water he had bought her for her birthday. She was afraid she smelled like an old woman. "You haven't told me what your plans were," she said. "Now your life is really beginning. I thought you would spare me a minute and sit down and tell me what to expect. If you want, I'll make you a cup of tea . . . "

"Tomorrow, Ma. I'll tell you everything tomorrow. Don't worry." He kissed her again and she released him and he was gone, lightfooted, down the stairs. She got up and hobbled over to the window and sat down in her rocking chair, old lady at the window. Let him see her.

The car drove away. He never looked up.

They all leave. Every one of them. Even the best of them.

The Chevy labored up the hill and through the familiar stone gate. The poplar trees that lined the road leading to the house cast a funereal shade, despite the June sunshine. The house quietly decayed behind its unkempt flower borders.

"The Fall of the House of Usher," Brad said as he rounded the curve into the courtyard. Rudolph had been to the house so often that he no longer had an opinion of it. It was Teddy Boylan's house, that was all. "Who lives here—Dracula?"

"A friend," Rudolph said. He had never spoken about Boylan to Brad. Boylan belonged to another compartment of his life. "A friend of the family. He helped me through school."

"Dough?" Brad asked, stopping the car and staring critically at the stone pile of the building.

"Some," Rudolph said. "Enough."

"Can't he afford a gardener?"

"He's not interested. Come on in and meet him. There's some champagne waiting for us." Rudolph got out of the car.

"Should I button my collar?" Brad asked.

"Yes," Rudolph said. He waited while Brad struggled with his collar, and pulled up his tie. He had a thick, short, plebeian neck, Rudolph noticed for the first time.

They crossed the graveled courtyard to the heavy oak front doors. Rudolph rang the bell. He was glad he was not alone. He didn't want to be alone with Teddy Boylan with the news that he had for him. The bell rang in the muffled distance, a question in a tomb, *Are you alive?*

The door opened. Perkins stood there. "Good afternoon, sir," he said. There was the sound of the piano being played. Rudolph recognized a Schubert sonata. Teddy Boylan had taken him to concerts at Carnegie Hall and had played a great deal of music for him on his phonograph, pleased at Rudolph's pleasure in learning about it and his quick ability to tell good playing from bad, mediocre from great. "I was about to give up music before you arrived on the scene," Boylan had told him once. "I don't like to listen to it alone and I hate listening to it with people who are faking an interest in it."

Perkins led the two young men toward the living room. Even in taking five paces, Perkins suggested a procession. Brad straightened out of his usual slouch and walked more erectly, the great dark hall working on him.

Perkins opened the door to the living room. "Mr. Jordache and a friend, sir," he said.

Boylan finished the passage he was playing and stopped. There was a bottle of champagne in a bucket and two fluted glasses beside it.

Boylan stood up and smiled. "Welcome," he said, extending his hand to Rudy. "It's good to see you again." Boylan had been south for two months and he was very brown, his hair and straight eyebrows sun-bleached. There was some slight little difference in his face that Rudolph puzzled over momentarily, as he shook Boylan's hand. "May I present a friend of mine," Rudolph said. "Bradford Knight, Mr. Boylan. He's a classmate of mine."

"How do you do, Mr. Knight." Boylan shook Brad's hand.

"Happy to make your acquaintance, suh," Brad said, sounding more Oklahoman than usual.

"You're to be congratulated today, too, I take it," Boylan said.

"I reckon so. At least, that's the theory." Brad grinned.

"We'll need a third glass, Perkins." Boylan moved toward the champagne bucket.

"Yes, sir." Perkins, leading his lifelong imaginary procession, left the room.

"Was the Democrat edifying?" Boylan asked, twirling the bottle in the ice. "Did he mention malefactors of great wealth?"

"He talked about the bomb," Rudolph said.

"That Democratic invention," Boylan said. "Did he say whom we're going to drop it on next?"

"He didn't seem to want to drop it on anybody," Rudolph said. For some reason, Rudolph felt he had to defend the cabinet member. "Actually, he made a great deal of sense."

"Did he?" Boylan said, twirling the bottle again with the tips of his fingers. "Perhaps he's a secret Republican."

Suddenly Rudolph realized what was different about Boylan's face. There were no more bags under his eyes. He must have got a lot of sleep on his holiday, Rudolph thought.

"You've got yourself quite a fine little old place here, Mr. Boylan," Brad said. He had been staring around him frankly during the conversation.

"Conspicuous consumption," Boylan said carelessly. "My family was devoted to it. You're from the South, aren't you, Mr. Knight?"

"Oklahoma."

"I drove through it once," Boylan said. "I found it depressing. Do you plan to go back there now?"

"Tomorrow," Brad said. "I've been trying to get Rudy to go with me."

"Ah, have you?" Boylan turned to Rudolph. "Are you going?"

Rudolph shook his head.

"No," Boylan said. "I can't quite see you in Oklahoma."

Perkins came in with the third glass and set it down.

"Ah," said Boylan. "Here we are." He undid the wire around the cork, his hands working deftly as the wire came away. He twisted the cork gently and as it came out with a dry popping noise he poured the foam expertly into the glasses. Ordinarily, he allowed Perkins to open bottles. Rudolph realized that Boylan was making a special symbolic effort today.

He handed a glass to Brad and one to Rudolph, then lifted his own. "To the future," he said. "That dangerous tense."

"This sure beats Coca-Cola," Brad said. Rudolph frowned slightly. Brad was being purposely bumpkinish, reacting unfavorably to Boylan's mannered elegance.

"Yes, doesn't it?" Boylan said evenly. He turned to Rudolph. "Why don't we go out into the garden and drink the rest of the bottle in the sunlight? It always seems more festive—drinking wine in the open."

"Well," Rudolph said, "We don't really have much time . . . "

"Oh?" Boylan raised his eyebrowns. "I had thought we could have dinner together at the Farmer's Inn. You're invited, too, of course, Mr. Knight."

"Thank you, suh," Brad said. "But it's up to Rudy."

"There're some people expecting us in New York," said Rudolph.

"I see," Boylan said.

"A party, no doubt. Young people."

"Something like that."

"Only natural," Boylan said. "On a day like this." He poured more champagne for the three of them. "Will you see your sister?"

"It's at her house." Rudolph lied to no man.

"Give her my best," said Boylan. "I must remember to send a gift for her child. What is it again?

"A boy."

Rudolph had told him the day the child was born that it was a boy.

"A small piece of silver," Boylan said, "For it to eat its darling little porridge from. In my family," Boylan explained to Brad, "the custom was to give a newly born boy a block of stock. But that was in the family, of course. It would be presumptuous of me to do anything like that for Rudolph's nephew, although I'm very fond of Rudolph. For that matter, I'm quite attached to his sister, too, although we've allowed ourselves to drift apart in the last few years."

"When I was born my father put an oil well in my name," Brad said. "A dry hole." He laughed heartily.

Boylan smiled politely. "It's the thought that counts."

"Not in Oklahoma," Brad said.

"Rudolph," Boylan said. "I had thought we could discuss various matters quietly over dinner, but since you're busy, and I understand very well you want to be among young people your own age on a night like this, perhaps you could spare a minute or two now . . ."

"If you want," Brad said, "I'll take a little walk."

"You *are* sensitive, Mr. Knight," Boylan said, a knifeflick of mockery in his voice, "but there's nothing that has to be hidden between Rudolph and me. Is there, Rudolph?"

"I don't know," Rudolph said bluntly. He wasn't going to play whatever game Boylan was setting up.

"I'll tell you what I've done," Boylan said, businesslike now. "I've bought you a round-trip ticket on the *Queen Mary*. The sailing is in two weeks, so you'll have plenty of time to see your friends and get your passport and make whatever arrangements are necessary. I've drawn up a little itinerary of places I think you ought to see, London, Paris, Rome, the usual. Round off your education a bit. Education really begins *after* college. Don't you agree, Mr. Knight?

"I can't do that," Rudolph said. He put his glass down.

"Why not?" Boylan looked surprised. "You're always talking about going to Europe.

"When I can afford it," Rudolph said.

"Oh, is that all?" Boylan chuckled tolerantly. "You misunderstand. It's a gift. I think it'll do you good. Rub off the provincial edges a bit, if you don't mind my saying so. I might even come over some time in August and join you in the south of France."

"Thanks, no, Teddy," Rudolph said. "I can't."

"I'm sorry." Boylan shrugged, dismissing the matter. "Wise men know when to accept gifts and when to turn them down. Even dry holes." With a nod for Brad. "Of course, if you have something better to do . . ."

"I have something to do," Rudolph said. Here it comes he thought.

"May I inquire what it is?" Boylan poured himself more champagne, without attending to the other glasses.

"I'm starting work tomorrow at Calderwood's on a full-time basis," Rudolph said.

"Poor boy," Boylan said. "What a dreary summer lies ahead of you. I must say your tastes are curious. Preferring to sell pots and pans to sleazy small-town housewives to going to the south of France. Ah, well, if that's your decision, you must have your reasons. And after the summer—have you decided to go to law school as I suggested, or to make a stab at the Foreign Service examinations?

For more than a year now, Boylan had on many occasions urged Rudolph to opt for one or another profession, with Boylan's preference for the law. "For a young man with no assets but his personality and his wits"—Boylan had written him—"the law is the way to power and preference. This is a lawyer's country. A good one often becomes indispensable to the companies which hire him. Frequently he finds himself in positions of command. We live in an intricate age, which is daily becoming more intricate. The lawyer, the good lawyer, finally is the only trusted guide through the intricacies and he is rewarded accordingly. Even in politics . . . Look at the percentage of lawyers in the Senate. Why shouldn't you crown your career that way? God knows the country could use a man of your intelligence and character instead of some of those dishonest clowns who bumble away on Capitol Hill. Or consider the Foreign Service. Whether we like it or not, we master the world, or should. We should put our best men in positions where they can influence our actions and the actions of our friends and enemies."

Boylan was a patriot. Out of the mainstream himself, through sloth or fastidiousness, he still had strong and virtuous opinions about the conduct of public life. The one man in Washington Rudolph had heard Boylan praise was James Forrestal, Secretary of the Navy. "If you were my own son—Boylan had continued—"I wouldn't give you different advice. In the Foreign Service you wouldn't be highly paid, but you would live the life of a gentleman among gentlemen and you could do us all honor. And there would be nothing to prevent you from marrying well and moving on to an ambassadorship. Whatever help I could give you, I would give gladly. I would be rewarded enough if you invited me to the Embassy for lunch once every few months—and could say to myself that in a little way I made it possible."

Remembering all this, and remembering Calderwood glaring at the photograph of his three daughters that same afternoon, Rudolph thought, feeling oppressed, everybody is looking for a son. A son in some private, particular impossible image.

"Well, Rudolph," Boylan was saying, "you haven't answered me. Which is it going to be?"

"Neither," Rudolph said. "I told Calderwood I'd stay on at the store for a year at least."

"I see," Boyland said flatly. "You don't aim very high, do you?"

"Yes, I do," Rudolph said. "In my own way."

"I'll cancel the booking for Europe," Boylan said. "I won't keep you from your friends any longer. It has been very nice having you here, Mr. Knight. If you ever happen to get away from Oklahoma again, you must come visit me again with Rudolph." He finished his champagne and went out of the room, his tweed jacket impeccably on his shoulders, the silk scarf a flash of color about his neck.

"Well . . . " Brad said. "What was that all about?"

"He once had something to do with my sister," Rudolph said. He started toward the door.

"Chilly bastard, isn't he?"

"No," Rudolph said. "Far from it. Let's get out of here."

As they drove through the gateway, Brad finally spoke. "There's something funny about the feller's eyes. What the hell is it? The skin looks as though—as though—" He puzzled for the exact works he wanted. "As though it's zippered up at the sides. Hey, you know something—I bet that feller just had his face lifted."

Of course, Rudolph thought. That was it. It wasn't that sleep down South. "Maybe," he said. "Anything is possible with Teddy Boylan."

Who are all these people, she thought, looking around her own living room. "Drinks in the kitchen," she said gaily to a new couple who had just come through the open door. She'd have to wait till Willie came back to get the names. He had gone down to the bar on the corner for more ice. There always was enough Scotch, bourbon, gin, and red wine in half gallon jugs, but never enough ice.

There were at least thirty people in the room, about half of whom she knew, and more to come. How many more she never knew. Sometimes she had the feeling Willie just picked people up in the street and invited them. Mary Jane was in the kitchen, acting as barmaid. Mary Jane was getting over her second husband and you had to invite her to everthing. Feeling herself an object of pity, Mary Jane tried to pay her way by helping out with the drinks, rinsing glasses, emptying ashtrays and taking lone stragglers home to bed with her. You needed *somebody* like that at a party.

Gretchen winced as she watched a Brooks Brothers type let ashes drop onto the floor and a moment later grind the stub of his cigarette into the carpet with his heel.

The room looked so pretty when there was nobody in it, pale-rose walls, books in order on the shelves, curtains crisp, the hearth of the fireplace swept, cushions plumped, the wood polished.

She was afraid that Rudolph disapproved of the party, although there was nothing in his manner that showed that he did. As always, when he was in the same room with Johnny Heath, they were off in a corner together, Johnny doing most of the talking and Rudolph most of the listening. Johnny was only about twenty-five, but he was already a partner in a broker's office in Wall Street, and was reputed to have made a fortune on his own in the stock market. He was an engaging, soft-spoken young man, his face modest and conservative, his eyes quick. She knew that from time to time Rudolph came down to the city to have dinner with Johnny or go to a ball game with him. Whenever she happened to overhear what they were talking about, it was always the same thing—stock deals, mergers, new companies, margins, tax-shelters, all supremely boring to Gretchen, but seemingly fascinating to Rudolph, although he certainly wasn't in any position to deal in stock, merge with anybody, or form any kind of company.

Once, when she asked Rudolph why he had picked Johnny, of all the people he had met in her house, to latch onto, Rudolph replied, very seriously, "He's the only friend you have who can educate me."

Who could know her own brother? Still, she hadn't meant to have *this* kind of party for Rudolph's graduation night and Willie had agreed. But somehow, it always turned out to be the same kind of party. The cast changed somewhat, actors, actresses, young directors, magazine writers, models, girls who worked for Time, Inc., radio producers, an occasional man from an advertising agency who could not be insulted; women like Mary Jane who had just been divorced and told everybody that their husbands were fags, instructors at NYU or Columbia who were writing novels, young Wall Street men who looked as though they were slumming, a dazzlingly sensual secretary who would flirt with Willie after the third drink; an ex-pilot from Willie's war who would corner her to talk about London; somebody's discontented husband who would try to make a pass at her late in the evening, and who would probably slip out at the end with Mary Jane.

Even though the cast changed the activity remained almost the same. Arguments about Russia and Alger Hiss and Senator Joe McCarthy, intellectual girls with bangs praising Trotsky . . . (Drinks in the kitchen," she said gaily to a new couple, sunburned, who had obviously been to the beach that day) . . . somebody who had just discovered Kierkegaard or who had met Sartre and had to tell about it, or who had just been to Israel or Tangier and had to tell about it. Once a month would have been fine. Or if they just didn't drop their ashes all over the room, even twice a month. They were by and large handsome and educated young people, all somehow with enough money to dress well and buy each other drinks and take a place in the Hamptons for the best part of the summer. Just the sort of people she had dreamed would be her friends when she was a girl in Port Philip. But she had been surrounded by them for nearly five years now. Drinks in the kitchen. The endless party.

Looking purposeful, she made her way to the staircase and started up toward the room under the roof where Billy slept. After Billy was born, they had moved to the top floor of an old brownstone on West Twelfth Street and had converted the attic into a large room and put in a skylight. Aside from Billy's bed and his toys, there was a big table on which Gretchen worked. There was a typewriter on it and it was piled with books and papers. She liked working in the same room with young Billy and the sound of her typing didn't bother him, but seemed to serve as a kind of clicking lullaby for him. A child for the machine age, soothed by Remington.

When she turned on the table lamp, she saw that he wasn't asleep now, though. He lay in the small bed in his pajamas, a cloth giraffe on the pillow beside him, his hands moving above his head slowly through the air, as though to make patterns in the cigarette smoke that drifted up from below. Gretchen felt guilty about the cigarette smoke but you couldn't ask people not to smoke because a four-year-old boy on another floor might not like it. She went over to the bed and leaned down and kissed Billy's forehead. There was the clean smell of soap from his bath and the sweet aroma of childish skin.

"When I grow up," he said, "I am not going to invite anybody."

Not your father's child, Gretchen thought. Even though he looked exactly like him, blond, serenely dimpled. No Jordache there at all. Yet. Unless her brother Thomas had looked like that as a child. She kissed him again, leaning low over the bed. "Go to sleep, Billy," she said.

She went over to the work table and sat down, grateful to be out of the chatter of the room below. She was sure nobody would miss her, even if she sat up there all night. She picked up a book that was lying on the table. Elementary psychology. She opened it idly. Two pages devoted to the blots of the Rorschach test. Know thyself. Know thine enemy. She was taking extension courses at NYU in the late afternoons and at night. If she stuck at it she would have her degree in two years. She had a nagging sense of inadequacy that made her shy with Willie's educated friends and sometimes with Willie himself. Besides, she liked classrooms, the unhurried sense that she was among people who were not merely interested in money or position or being seen in public.

She had slipped away from the theater after Billy was born. Later, she had told herself, when he's old enough not to need me all the time. By now she knew she would never try to act again. No loss. She had had to look for work that she could do at home and luckily she had found it, by the simplest of means. She had begun by helping Willie write his criticisms of radio and later television programs, whenever he was bored with them or busy doing something else or had a hangover. At first, he kept signing his name to her pieces, but then he was offered an executive job in the office of the magazine at a raise in pay and she had begun signing the pieces herself. The editor had told her privately that she wrote a lot better than Willie, but she had made her own judgment on Willie's writing. She had come across the first act of his play one day, while cleaning out a truck. It was dreadful. What was funny and bright in Willie's speech turned arch on paper. She hadn't told him her opinion of his writing or that she had read his play. But she had encouraged him to take the executive job in the office.

She glanced at the sheet of yellow paper in the typewriter. She had penciled in a tentative title. "The Song of the Salesman." She glanced at random down the page. "The innocent air," she had written, "which theoretically is a national asset, the property of all Americans, has been delivered to merchants, so that they may beguile us or bully us into buying their products, whether the products are benevolent, needful, or dangerous to us. They sell us soup with laughter, breakfast food with violence, automobiles with *Hamlet,* purgatives with drivel . . . "

She frowned. Not good enough. And useless, besides. Who would listen, who would act? The American people were getting what they thought they wanted. Her guests downstairs were most of them in one way or another living off the thing their hostess was denouncing above their heads. The liquor they were drinking was bought with money earned by a man singing the salesman's song. She tore the sheet of paper from the machine and balled it up and threw it in the wastebasket. She would never get it printed, anyway. Willie would see to that.

She went over to the child's bed. He had fallen asleep, grasping the giraffe. He slept, miraculously complete. What are you going to buy, what are you going to sell when you are my age? What errors are ahead of you? How much of love will be wasted?

There was a tread on the stairs and she hurriedly bent over, pretending to be tucking in the child. Willie, provider of ice, opened the door. "I wondered where you were," he said.

"I was restoring my sanity," she said.

"Gretchen," he said reproachfully. He was a little flushed from drink and there were beads of perspiration on his upper lip. He had begun to bald, the forehead more Beethovenesque than ever, but somehow he still looked adolescent. "They're your freinds, as well as mine."

"They're nobody's friends," Gretchen said. "They're drinkers, that's all." She was feeling bitchy. Rereading the lines from her article had crystallized the dissatisfaction that had sent her upstairs in the first place. And, suddenly, she was annoyed that the child resembled Willie so closely. I was there, too, she wanted to say.

"What do you want me to do," Willie said, "send them home?"

"Yes. Send them home."

"You know I can't do that," Willie said. "Come on down, honey. People'll begin to wonder what's wrong with you."

"Tell them I had a sudden wild urge to breast-feed," Gretchen said. "In some tribes they breast-feed children until the age of seven. They know everything down there. See if they know that."

"Honey . . . " He came over and put his arms around her. She could smell the gin. "Give a little. Please. You're getting awfully nervy."

"Oh. You noticed."

"Of course I noticed." He kissed her cheek. A nothing kiss, she thought. He hadn't made love to her in two weeks. "I know what's wrong," he said. "You're doing too much. Taking care of the kid, working, going to school, studying . . . " He was always trying to get her to drop her courses. "What're you proving?" he had asked. "You're the smartest girl in New York as it is.

"I'm not doing half enough," she said. "Maybe I'll go down and pick a likely candidate and go off and have an affair. For my nerves."

Willie dropped his arms from around her waist and stepped back, martinis receding. "Funny. Hah-hah," he said coldly.

"On to the cockpit," she said, putting out the lamp on the table. "Drinks are in the kitchen."

He grabbed her wrist in the dark. "What've I done wrong?" he demanded.

"Nothing," she said. "The perfect hostess and her mate will now rejoin the beauty and chivalry of West Twelfth Street." She pulled her arm away from his grasp and went down the stairs. A moment later Willie came down, too. He had stayed behind to plant a martini'd kiss on his son's forehead.

She saw Rudolph had quit Johnny Heath and was in a corner of the room talking earnestly to Julie, who must have come in while she was upstairs. Rudolph's friend, the boy from Oklahoma, Babbitt material, was laughing too hard over something that one of the executive secretaries had said. Julie had her hair up and was wearing a soft, black-velvet dress. "I am in contant battle," Julie had confided to her, "to suppress the high-school cheerleader in me." This evening she had managed. Too well. She looked too sure of herself for a girl that young. Gretchen was certain that Julie and Rudolph had never slept with each other. After five years ! Inhuman. There was something wrong with the girl, or Rudolph, or both.

She waved to Rudolph but she did not catch his eye and as she went toward him she was stopped by an advertising account executive, too beautifully dressed, and with a haircut that was too becoming. "Mine hostess," the man said, thin as an English actor. His name was Alec Lister. He had started as a page boy at CBS, but that was long behind him. "Let me congratulate you on an absolutely splendid do."

"Are you a likely candidate?" she asked, staring at him.

"What?" Lister transferred his glass uneasily from one hand to another. He was not used to being asked pussling questions.

"Nothing, she said. "Train of thought, I'm glad you like the animals."

"I like them very much." Lister put his imprimatur firmly on the assemblage. "I'll tell you something else I like. Your pieces in the magazine.

"I will be known as the Samuel Taylor Coleridge of radio and television," she said.

Lister was one of the guests who could not be insulted, but she was out after all scalps tonight.

"What was that?" He was puzzled for the second time in thirty seconds and he was beginning to frown. "Oh, yes, I get it." He didn't seem happy to have gotten it. "If I may make a comment, Gretchen," he said, knowing that anywhere between Wall Street and Sixtieth Street he could make whatever comment he pleased, "the pieces are excellent, but just a little bit too—well—biting, I find. There's a tone of hostility in them—it gives them a welcome tang, I have to admit—but there's a general underlying feeling of being against the whole industry . . . "

"Oh," she said calmly, "you caught that."

He stared at her evenly, all cordiality gone, his office face, cool and pitiless, replacing in a fraction of a second his tolerant English actor party face. "Yes, I caught it," he said. "And I'm not the only one. In today's atmosphere, with everybody being investigated, and advertisers being damn careful that they're not giving their good money to people whose motives might not be acceptable . . . "

"Are you warning me?" Gretchen asked.

"You might put it like that," the man said. "Out of friendship."

"It's good of you, dear," she touched his arm lightly, smiling tenderly at him, "but I'm afraid it's too late. I'm a red, raving Communist, in the pay of Moscow, plotting to destroy NBC and MGM and bring Ralston's Cereals crashing to the ground."

"She's putting on everyone tonight, Alec." Willie was standing next to her, his hand tightening on her elbow. "She thinks it's Holloween. Come on into the kitchen, I'll freshen your drink."

"Thanks, Willie," Lister said, "but I'm afraid I have to push on. I have two more parties I said I'd look in on tonight." He kissed Gretchen's cheek, a brush of ether on her skin. "Good night, sweets. I do hope you remember what I told you."

"Chiseled in stone," she said.

Expressionless, flat-eyed, he made his way toward the door, putting his glass down on a bookcase, where it would leave a ring.

"What's the matter?" Willie said in a low voice. "You hate money?"

"I hate *him*," she said. She pulled away from Willie and wove through the guests, smiling brightly, to where Rudolph and Julie were talking in the corner. They were talking in near whispers. There was an air of tenison about them which built an invisible wall around them, cutting them off from all the laughter and conversation in the room. Julie seemed on the verge of tears and Rudolph looked concentrated and stubborn.

"I think it's terrible," Julie was saying. "That's what I think."

"You look beautiful tonight, Julie," Gretchen interrupted. "Very femme-fatalish."

"Well, I don't feel it." Julie's voice quavered.

"What's the matter?" Gretchen asked.

"You tell her," Julie said to Rudolph.

"Some other time," Rudolph said, lips tight. "This is a party."

"He's going to work permanently at Calderwood's," Julie said. "Starting tomorrow morning."

"Nothing is permanent," Rudolph said.

"Stuck away behind a counter for his whole life," Julie rushed on. "In a little one-horse town. What's the sense of going to college, if that's all you're going to do with it?"

"I told you I'm not going to be stuck anywhere all my life," Rudolph said.

"Tell her the rest," Julie said hotly. "I dare you to tell her the rest."

"What's the rest?" Gretchen asked. She, too, was disappointed, Rudolph's choice *was* inglorious. But she was relieved, too. Working at Calderwood's, he would continue to take care of their mother and she would not have to face the problem herself or ask for help from Willie. The sense of relief was ignoble, but there was no denying to herself that it existed.

"I've been offered the summer in Europe," Rudolph said evenly, "as a gift."

"By whom?" Gretchen, asked, although she knew the answer.

"Teddy Boylan."

"I know my parents would let me go, too," Julie said. "We could have the best summer of our whole lives."

"I haven't got time for the best summer of our whole lives," Rudolph said, biting on the words.

"Can't you talk to him, Gretchen?" Julie said.

"Rudy," Gretchen said, "don't you think you owe yourself a little fun, after the way you've been working?"

"Europe won't go away," he said. "I'll go there when I'm ready for it."

"Teddy Boylan must have been pleased when you turned him down," Gretchen said.

"He'll get over it."

"I wish somebody would offer me a trip to Europe," Gretchen said. "I'd be on that boat so fast . . ."

"Gretchen, can you give us a hand?" One of the younger male guests had come over. "We want to play the phonograph and it seems to be kaput."

"I'll talk to you two later," Gretchen said to Rudolph and Julie. "We'll work something out." She went over to the phonograph with the young man. She bent down and fumbled for the plug. The colored maid had been in to clean that day and she always left the plug out after she vacuumed. "I bend enough," she had told Gretchen when Gretchen complained.

The phonograph warmed up with a hollow sound and then it began to play the first record from the album of *South Pacific*. Childish voices, sweet and American, far away on a make-believe warm island, piped the words to "Dites-moi." When Gretchen stood up she saw that Rudolph and Julie had gone. I'm not going to have a party in this place for a whole year, she decided. She went into the kitchen and had Mary Jane pour her a stiff drink of Scotch. Mary Jane had long, red hair these days and a great deal of blue eye shadow and long false eyelashes. From a distance she was a beauty but close up things came apart a little. Still, now, in the third hour of the party, with all the men passing through her domain and flattering her, she was at her peak for the day, flashing-eyed, her bright-red lips half open, avid and provocative. "What glory," she said, whiskey-hoarse. "This party. And that new man, Alec What's-his-name . . ."

"Lister," Gretchen said, drinking, noting that the kitchen was a mess and deciding that she'd do nothing about it till morning. "Alec Lister."

"Isn't he *dazzling*?" Mary Jane said. "Is he attached?"

"Not tonight."

"Blessings on him," Mary Jane said. "the dear fellow. He drowned the kitchen in charm when he was in here. And I've heard the most terrible things about him. He beats his women, Willie told me." She giggled. "Isn't it *exciting*? Did you notice, does he need a new drink? I'll appear at his side, goblet in hand, Mary Jane Hackett, the faithful cup-bearer."

"He left five minutes ago," Gretchen said, meanly pleased at being able to pass on the information to Mary Jane and wondering at the same time what women Willie was intimate enough with to hear from them that they had been beaten by Alec Lister.

"Ah, well," Mary Jane shrugged philosophically, "there are other fish in the sea."

Two men came into the kitchen and Mary Jane swung her red hair and smiled radiantly at them. "Here you are, boys," she said, "the bar never closes."

It was a chinch that Mary Jane had not gone two weeks without making love. What's so wrong with being divorced, Gretchen thought, as she went back into the living room.

Rudolph and Julie walked toward Fifth Avenue in the balmy June evening air. He did not hold her arm. "This is no place to talk seriously," he had said at the party. "Let's get out of here."

But it wasn't any better on the street. Julie strode along, careful not to touch him, the nostrils of her small nose tense, the full lips bitten into a sharp wound. As he walked beside her on the dark street he wondered if it wouldn't just be better to leave her then and there. It would probably come sooner or later anyway and sooner was perhaps to be preferred than later. But then he thought of never seeing her again and despaired. Still, he said nothing. In the battle that was being waged between them, he knew that the advantage would have to go to the one who kept silent longest.

"You have a girl there," she said finally. "That's why you're staying in the awful place."

He laughed.

"Your laughing doesn't fool me." Her voice was bitter, with no memory in it of the times they had sung together or the times she had said, I love you. "You're infatuated with some ribbon clerk or cashier or something. You've been sleeping with somebody there all this time. I know."

He laughed again, strong in his chastity.

"Otherwise you're a freak," she said harshly. "We've been seeing each other for five years and you say you love me and you haven't tried once to make love to me, really make love to me."

"I haven't been invited," he said.

"All right," she said. "I invite you. Now. Tonight. I'm in room 923 at the St. Moritz."

Wary of traps, fearful of helpless surrenders on a tumbled bed. "No," he said.

"Either you're a liar," she said, "or you're a freak."

"I want to marry you," he said. "We can get married next week."

"Where will we spend our honeymoon?" she asked. "In the garden-furniture department of Calderwood's Department Store? I'm offering you my pure-white, virgin body," she said mockingly. "Free and clear. No strings. Who needs a wedding? I'm a free, liberated, lustful, all-American girl. I've just won the Sexual Revolution by a score of ten to nothing."

"No," he said. "And stop talking like my sister."

"Freak," she said. "You want to bury me along with you forever in that dismal little town. And all this time, I've thought you were so smart, that you were going to have such a brilliant future. I'll marry you. I'll marry you next week. If you take the trip to Europe and start law school in the autumn. Or if you don't want to do that, if you just come down here to New York and work here. I don't care what you do here, I'll work, too. I *want* to work. What'll I do in Whitby? Spend my days deciding which apron to wear when you come home at night?"

"I promise you that in five years you can live in New York or anyplace you say."

"You promise," she said. "It's easy to promise. And I'm not going to bury myself for five years either. I can't understand you. What in God's name do you think you're getting out of it?"

"I'm starting two years ahead of anybody in my class," Rudolph said. "I know what I'm doing. Calderwood trusts me. He's got a lot more going for him than just his store. The store's just a beginning, a base. He doesn't know it yet, but I do. When I come down to New York I'm not going to be just another college graduate from a school nobody ever heard of, waiting in everybody's outer office, with his hat in his hand. When I come down, they're going to greet me at the front door. I've been poor a long time, Julie," he said, "and I am going to do what I have to do never to be poor again."

"Boylan's baby," Julie said. "He's ruined you. Money! Does money mean that much to you? Just *money?*"

"Don't sound like Little Miss Rich Bitch," he said.

"Even if it does," she said, "if you went into law . . . ."

"I can't wait," he said. "I've waited long enough. I've been in enough school-rooms. If I need law, I'll hire lawyers." Echo of Duncan Calderwood, that hard-headed man. *They hire schooling.* "If you want to come along with me, fine. If not . . ." But he couldn't say it. "If not," he repeated lamely. "Oh, Julie, I don't know. I don't know. I think I know about everything else, but I don't know about you."

"I lied to my father and mother . . . " She was sobbing now. "So I could be alone with you. But it's not you. It's Boylan's doll. I'm going back to the hotel. I don't want to talk to you anymore." Weeping uncontrollably, she hailed a cab on the Avenue. It squealed to a halt and she opened the door and got in and slammed the door behind her.

He watched the cab roar away without moving. Then he turned and started back toward the party. He had left his bag there and Gretchen was going to make up a bed for him on the living room couch. 923, he remembered, the number of the hotel room.

Alimonied, Mary Jane did well for herself. Rudolph had never been in a wider or softer bed and in the glow of a lamp on the dressing table (Mary Jane insisted on keeping a light on) the large, warmly carpeted room, its walls pearl-gray silk, showed an expensive decorator's touch. Deep-green velvet curtains shut out the sounds of the city. The preliminaries (they had been brief) had taken place in the high-ceilinged living room furnished with gilt Directoire pieces and large, gold-tinted mirrors, in which the embracing couple were caught in a vague and metallic luminosity. "The main event takes place inside," Mary Jane had said, breaking away from a kiss, without any further agreement from Rudolph had led him into the bedroom. "I'll get ready in the bathroom," she said, and kicked off her shoes and walked splendidly and almost steadily into the adjoining bathroom, from which had immediately come the sound of water running and the clink of bottles.

It was a little bit like being in a doctor's office while he prepared for a minor operation, Rudolph thought resentfully, and he had hesitated before getting undressed. When Mary Jane had asked him to take her home from the party, well after midnight, with only four or five guests still sprawled around, he had no idea that anything like this was going to happen. He felt a bit dizzy from all the drinking he had done and he was worried about what his head would feel like when he lay down. For a moment, he had considered stealing quietly out and through the front door, but Mary Jane, her intuition or her experience at work, had called out sunnily, "I'll just be a minute more, darling. Make yourself comfortable."

So Rudolph had undressed, putting his shoes soberly side by side under a chair and folding his clothes neatly on the seat of the chair. The bed was already made up for the night (lace-fringed pillows, he noticed, and pale-blue sheets) and he had slipped under the covers, shivering a little. This was one way of making sure he wouldn't be knocking on a hotel door that night. 923.

As he lay under the blankets, curious, a little fearful, he closed his eyes. It had to happen some day, he thought. What better day than this?

With his eyes closed, the room seemed to be dipping and wheeling around him and the bed under him seemed to move in an uneasy rhythm, like a small boat anchored in a chop. He opened his eyes just as Mary Jane came into the room, tall, naked, and superb, the long body with the small, round breasts and splendid hips and thighs unwearied by matrimony, unscarred by debauch. She stood over him, looking down at him with hooded eyes, veteran of many seasons, sweeper-up of stragglers, her red hair, dark in the glow of the lamp, swinging down toward him.

His erection was swift and sudden and huge, a pylon, a cannon barrel. He was torn between pride and embarrassment and almost asked Mary Jane to put out the light. But before he could say anything, Mary Jane bent and swept back the covers in a single tearing gesture.

She stood beside the bed, inspecting him, smiling softly.

"Little brother," she whispered, "little beautiful brother of the poor." Then, soft-handed, she touched him. He jumped convulsively.

"Lie still," she ordered. Her hands moved like small, expert animals on him, fur on damask. He quivered. "Lie still, I said," she said harshly.

It was over soon, shamefully soon, a fierce, arching jet and he heard himself sobbing. She knelt on the bed, kissed him on the mouth, her hands intolerable now, the smell of her hair, cigarette smoke and perfume smothering him.

"I'm sorry," he said, when she raised her head. "I just couldn't . . . "

She chuckled. "Don't be sorry. I'm flattered. I consider it a tribute." With a long graceful movement, she slid into bed beside him, pulled the covers over them, clamped him to her, her leg silken over his thighs, his semen oiling them both. "Don't worry, about any little thing, little brother," she said. She licked his ear and he was shaken once more by a quiver that started from her tongue and convulsed his body down to the tips of his toes, electrocution by lamp light. "I'm sure that in a very few minutes you'll be as good as new, little brother."

He wished she'd stop calling him little brother. He didn't want to be reminded of Gretchen. Gretchen had given him a peculiar look as he had left with Mary Jane.

Mary Jane's gift of prophecy in her chosen field had not deserted her. In less than a very few minutes her hands had awakened him once more and he did what Mary Jane had brought him to her bed to do. He plunged into her with all the hoarded strength of years of abstinence. "Oh, Christ, please, that's enough," she cried finally, and he let himself go in one great thrust, delivering them both.

Freak, he heard Julie's bitter voice, freak. Let her come to this room and this woman for testimony.

"Your sister said you were still a virgin," Mary Jane was saying.

"Let's not talk about it," he said shortly.

They were lying side by side now, on their backs, Mary Jane's leg, just a leg now, thrown lightly across his knee. She was smoking, inhaling deeply, and smoke drifting slowly up when she let it go from her lungs.

"I must discover me some more virgins," she said. "Is it true?"

"I said let's not talk about it."

"It is true."

"Not anymore, anyway."

"That's not fair," she said. "Why?"

"Why what?"

"A beautiful young man like you," she said. "The girls must be ravenous."

"They manage to restrain themselves. Let's talk about something else."

"How about that cute little girl you go around with?" Room 923. "What's her name?"

"Julie." He did not like saying Julie's name in this place.

"Isn't she after you?"

"We were supposed to get married."

"Were? And now?"

"I don't know," he said.

"She doesn't know what she's missing. It must come in the family," Mary Jane said.

"What do you mean by *that?*"

"Willie says your sister's absolutely delirious in the hay."

"Willie ought to learn to keep his mouth shut." Rudolph was shocked that Willie would say something like that to a woman, any woman, to *anybody* about his wife. He would never quite trust Willie again or completely like him again.

Mary Jane laughed. "We're in the big city now," she said "where they burn the gas. Willie's an old friend of mine. I had an affair with him before he ever met your sister. And occasionally, when he's feeling down or needs a change of scenery, he still comes around."

"Does my sister know?" Rudolph tried to keep the sudden anger out of his voice. Willie, that drifting, frivolous man.

"I don't think so," Mary Jane said lightly. "Willie's awfully good at being vague. And nobody signs any affidavits. Did you ever lay her—Gretchen?"

"She's my sister, for Christ's sake." His voice sounded shrill in his ears.

"Big deal," Mary Jane said. "Sister. From what Willie says, it'd be worth the trouble."

"You're making fun of me." That was it, he told himself, the older, experienced woman amusing herself teasing the simple boy up from the country.

"Hell, no," Mary Jane said calmly. "My brother laid me when I was fifteen. In a beached canoe. Be a doll, honey, and get me a drink. The Scotch is on the table in the kitchen. Plain water. Never mind the ice."

He got out of bed. He would have liked to put on some clothes, a robe, his pants, wrap himself in a towel, anything to keep from parading around before those knowing, measureing, amused eyes. But he knew if he did anything to cover himself she would laugh. Damn it, he thought desperately, how did I ever let myself in for anything like this?

The room suddenly seemed cold to him and he felt the goose flesh prickle all over his body. He tried not to shiver as he walked toward the door and into the living room. Gold and shadowy in the metaled mirrors, he made his way soundlessly over the deep carpets toward the kitchen. He found the light and switched it on. Huge white refrigerator, humming softly, a wall oven, a mixer, a juicer, copper pans arranged on the white walls, steel double sink, a dish-washing machine, the bottle of Scotch in the middle of the red formica table, the domestic American dream in the bright white neon light. He took two glasses down from a cupboard (bone china, flowered cups, coffe pots, huge wooden pepper mills, housewifely accoutrements for the non-housewife in the bed in the other room). He ran the water until it was cold and first rinsed his mouth, spitting into the steel sink, xylophones of the night, then drank two long glasses of water. Into the other glass he poured a big slug of Scotch and half filled the glass with water. There was the ghost of a sound, a faint scratching and scurrying. At the back of the sink black insects, fat and armored, roaches, disappeared into cracks. Slob, he thought.

Leaving the light on in the kitchen, he carried the drink back to the mistress of the household in her well-used bed. We aim to serve.

"There's a doll," Mary Jane said, reaching up for the glass, long, pointed finger-nails glinting a crimson. She raised against the pillows, red hair wanton against the pale blue and lace, and drank thirstily. "Aren't you having one?"

"I've drunk enough." He reached down for his shorts and started to put them on.

"What're you doing?" she asked.

"I'm going home." He put on his shirt, relieved to be covered at last. "I've got to be at work at nine in the morning." He strapped on his new watch. A quarter to four.

"Please," she said, in a small, childish voice. "Please. Don't do that."

"I'm sorry," he said. He wasn't sorry. The thought of being out on the street, dressed, alone, was exhilarating to him.

"I can't stand being alone at night." She was begging now.

"Call up Willie," he said, sitting down and pulling on his socks and slipping into his shoes.

"I can't sleep, I can't sleep," she said.

He tied his shoelaces deliberately.

"Everybody leaves me," she said, "every goddam sonofabitch leaves me. I'll do anything. Stay till six, until daylight, until five please, honey. I'll suck you, please . . . " She was crying now.

Tears all night, the world of women, he thought coldly, as he stood up, buttoned his shirt and did up his tie. The sobs echoed behind him as he stood before the mirror. He saw that his hair was mussed, plastered with sweat. He went into the bathroom. Dozens of bottles of perfume, bath-oil, Alka-seltzer, sleeping pills. He combed his hair carefully, erasing the night. She had stopped crying when he went back into the bedroom. She was sitting up straighter, watching him coldly, her eyes narrowed. She had finished her drink but was still holding her glass.

"Last chance," she said harshly.

He put on his jacket.

"Good night," he said.

She threw the glass at him. He refused to duck. The glass hit him a glancing blow on the forehead, then shattered against the mirror over the mantel piece of the white marble fireplace.

"Little shit," she said.

He went out of the room, crossed to the front hallway and opened the door. He stepped out through the doorway and closed the door silently behind him and rang for the elevator.

The elevator man was old, good only for short trips, late at night. He looked speculatively at Rudolph as they went down the whining shaft. Does he keep count of his passengers, Rudolph thought, does he make a neat record at dawn?

The elevator man opened the elevator door as they came to a halt. "You're bleeding, young man," he said. "Your head."

"Thank you," Rudolph said."

The elevator man said nothing as Rudolph crossed the hall and went out into the dark street. Once on the street and out of sight of the rheumy recording eyes, Rudolph took out his handkerchief and put it up to his forehead. The handkerchief came away bloody. There are wounds in all encounters. He walked, alone, his footsteps echoing on the pavement, toward the lights of Fifth Avenue. At the corner he looked up. The street sign read '63rd Street.' He hesitated. The St. Moritz was on Fifty-ninth Street, along the Park. Room 923. A short stroll in the light morning air. Dabbing at his forehead again with his hankerchief he started toward the hotel.

He didn't know what he was going to do when he got there. Ask for forgiveness, swear, "I will do anything you say," confess, denounce, cleanse himself, cry love, reach out for a memory, forget lust, restore tenderness, sleep, forget . . .

The lobby was empty. The night clerk behind the desk looked at him briefly, incuriously, used to lone men late at night, wandering in from the sleeping city.

"Room 923," he said into the house phone.

He heard the operator ringing the room. After ten rings he hung up. There was a clock in the lobby. 4:35. The last bars in the city had been closed for thirty-five minutes. He walked slowly out of the lobby. He had begun and ended the day alone. Just as well.

He hailed a cruising taxi and got in. That morning, he was going to start earning one hundred dollars a week. He could afford a taxi. He gave Gretchen's address, but then as the taxi started south, he changed his mind. He didn't want to see Gretchen and he certainly didn't want to see Willie. They could send him his bag. "I'm sorry, driver," he said, leaning forward, "I want Grand Central Station."

Although he hadn't slept for twenty-four hours, he was wide-awake when he reported to work at nine o'clock in Duncan Calderwood's office. He did not punch the time clock, although his card was in its slot. He was through punching clocks.

CHAPTER 3

1950

THOMAS TWIRLED THE combination of the padlock and threw open his locker. For many months now, every locker had been equipped with a padlock and members were requested to leave their wallets at the office, where they were put into sealed envelopes and filed in the office safe. The decision had been pushed through by Brewster Reed, whose talismanic hundred-dollar bill had been lifted from his pocket the Saturday afternoon of the weekend Thomas had gone down to Port Philip. Dominic had been pleased to announce this development the Monday afternoon when Thomas reported back to work. "At least," Dominic said, "now they know it isn't you and they can't blame me for hiring a thief, the bastards." Dominic had also pushed through a raise for Thomas of ten dollars and he was now getting forty-five dollars a week.

Thomas undressed and got into a clean sweatsuit and put on a pair of boxing shoes. He was taking over the five o'clock calisthenics class from Dominic and there were usually one or two members who asked him to spar a couple of rounds with them. He had learned from Dominic the trick of looking aggressive without inflicting any punishment whatever and he had learned enough of Dominic's phrases to make the members believe he was teaching them how to fight.

He hadn't touched the forty-nine hundred dollars in the safety deposit box in Port Philip and he still called young Sinclair sir when they met in the locker room.

He enjoyed the calisthenics classes. Unlike Dominic, who just called out the cadences, Thomas did all the exercises with the class, pushups, situps, bicycle riding, straddles, knee bending, touching the floor with the knees straight and the palms of the hand flat, and all the rest. It kept him feeling fit and at the same time it amused him to see all those dignified, self-important men sweating and panting. His voice, too, developed a tone of command that made him seem less boyish than before. For once, he began to wake up in the morning without the feeling that something bad, out of his control, was going to happen to him that day.

When Thomas went into the mat room after the calisthenics, Dominic and Greening were putting on the big gloves. Dominic had a cold and he had drunk too much the night before. His eyes were red and he was moving slowly. He looked shapeless and aging in his baggy sweatsuit and since his hair was mussed, his bald spots shone in the light from the big lamps of the room. Greening, who was tall for his weight, moved around impatiently, shuffling his boxing shoes against the mats with a dry, aggressive sound. His eyes seemed bleached in the strong light and his blond hair, crew-cut, almost platinum. He had been a captain in the Marines during the war and had won a big decoration. He was very handsome in a straight-nosed, hard-jawed, pink-cheeked way and if he hadn't come from a family that was above such things, he probably could have done well as a hero in Western movies. In all of the time since he had told Dominic that he thought Thomas had stolen ten dollars from his locker, he had never addressed a word to Thomas and now, as Thomas came into the mat room to wait for one of the members who had made a date to spar with him, Greening didn't even look Thomas's way.

"Help me with these, kid," Dominic said, extending his gloves. Thomas tied the laces. Dominic had already done Greening's gloves.

Dominic looked up at the big clock over the mat room door to make sure that he wouldn't inadvertently box more than two minutes without resting and put up his gloves and shuffled toward Greening, saying, "Whenever you're ready, sir."

Greening came at him fast. He was a straight-up, conventional, schooled kind of fighter who made use of his longer reach to jab at Dominic's head. His cold and his hangover made Dominic begin to breathe hard immediately. He tried to get inside the jab and put his head out of harm's way under Greening's chin while he punched away without much enthusiasm or power at Greening's stomach. Suddenly, Greening stepped back and brought up his right in an all-out uppercut that caught Dominic flush on the mouth.

The shit, Thomas thought. But he said nothing and the expression on his face didn't change.

Dominic sat on the mat pushing reflectively at his bleeding mouth with the big glove. Greening didn't bother to help him up, but stepped back and looked thoughtfully at him, his hands dangling. Still sitting, Dominic held out his gloves toward Thomas.

"Take 'em off me, kid," Dominic said. His voice was thick. "I've had enough exercise for today."

Nobody said anything as Thomas bent and unlaced the gloves and pulled them off Dominic's hands. He knew the old fighter didn't want to be helped up, so he didn't try. Dominic stood up wearily, wiping his mouth with the wrist band of his sweatsuit. "Sorry, sir," he said to Greening. "I guess I'm under the weather today."

"That wasn't much of a workout," Greening said. "You should have told me you weren't feeling well. I wouldn't have bothered getting undressed. How about you, Jordache?" he asked. "I've seen you in here a couple of times. You want to go a few minutes?"

Jordache, Thomas thought. He knows my name. He looked inquiringly over at Dominic. Greening was another story entirely from the pot-bellied, earnest, physical culture enthusiasts Dominic assigned him usually.

A flame of Sicilian hatred glowed momentarily in Dominic's hooded dark eyes. The time had come to burn down the landlord's mansion. "If Mr. Greening wants to, Tom," Dominic said mildly, spitting blood, "I think you might oblige him."

Thomas put on the gloves and Dominic laced them for him, his head bent, his eyes guarded, saying nothing. Thomas felt the old feeling, fear, pleasure, eagerness, an electric tingling in his arms and legs, his gut pulling in. He made himself smile boyishly over Dominic's bent head at Greening, who was watching him stonily.

Dominic stepped away. "Okay," he said.

Greening came right to Thomas, his long left out, his right hand under his chin. College man, Thomas thought contemptuously, as he picked off the jab and circled away from the right. Greening was taller than he but had only eight or nine pounds on him. But he was faster than Thomas realized and the right caught him, hard, high up on the temple. Thomas hadn't been in a real fight since the time with the foreman at the garage in Brookline and the polite exercises with the pacific gentlemen of the club membership had not prepared him for Greening. Greening feinted, unorthodoxically, with his right, and crashed a left hook to Thomas's head. The sonofabitch isn't fooling, Thomas thought, and went in low, looping a left to Greening's side and following quickly with a right to the man's head. Greening held him and battered at his ribs with his right hand. He was strong, there was no doubt about it, very strong.

Thomas got a glimpse of Dominic and wondered if Dominic was going to give him some sort of signal. Dominic was standing to one side, placidly, giving no signals.

Okay, Thomas thought, deliciously, here it goes. The hell with what happens later.

They fought without stopping for the usual two-minute break. Greening fought controlledly, brutally, using his height and weight, Thomas with the swift malevolence that he had carefully subdued within himself all these months. Here you are, Captain, he was saying to himself as he burrowed in, using everything he knew, stinging, hurting, ducking, here you are Rich-boy, here you are, Policeman, are you getting your ten dollars' worth?

They were both bleeding from the nose and mouth, when Thomas finally got in the one he knew was the beginning of the end. Greening stepped back, smiling foolishly, his hands still up, but feebly pawing the air. Thomas circled him, going for the last big one, when Dominic stepped between them.

"I think that's enough for the time being, gentlemen," Dominic said. "That was a very nice little workout."

Greening recovered quickly. The blank look went out of his eyes and he stared coldly at Thomas. "Take these off me, Dominic," was all he said. He made no move to wipe the blood off hs face. Dominic unlaced the gloves and Greening walked, very straight, out of the mat room.

"There goes my job," Thomas said.

"Probably," Dominic said, unlacing the gloves. "It was worth it. For me." He grinned.

For three days, nothing happened. Nobody but Dominic, Greening, and Thomas had been in the mat room and neither Thomas nor Dominic mentioned the fight to any of the members. There was the possibility that Greening was too embarrassed about being beaten by a twenty-year-old kid a lot smaller than he to make a fuss with the committee.

Each night, when they closed up, Dominic would say, "Nothing yet," and knock on wood.

Then, on the fourth day, Charley, the locker-room man, came looking for him. "Dominic wants to see you in his office," Charley said. "Right away."

Thomas went directly to Dominic's office. Domininc was sitting behind hs desk, counting out ninety dollars in ten-dollar bills. He looked up sadly as Thomas came into the office. "Here's your two weeks' pay, kid," he said. "You're through as of now. There was a committee meeting this afternoon."

Thomas put the money in his pocket. *And I hoped it was going to last at least a year,* he thought.

"You should've let me get that last punch in, Dom," he said.

"Yeah," said Dominic, "I should've."

"Are you going to get into trouble, too?"

"Probably. Take care of yourself," Dominic said. "Just remember one thing—never trust the rich."

They shook hands. Thomas went out of the office to get his things out of the locker and went out of the building without saying good-bye to anyone.

CHAPTER 4

1954

HE WOKE EXACTLY at a quarter to seven. He never set the alarm. There was no need to.

The usual erection. Forget it. He lay quietly in bed for a minute or two. His mother was snoring in the next room. The curtains at the open window were blowing a little and it was cold in the room. A pale winter light came through the curtains, making a long, dark blur of the books on the shelves across from the bed.

This was not going to be an ordinary day. At closing the night before he had gone into Calderwood's office and laid the thick Manila envelope on Calderwood's desk. "I'd like you to read this," he said to the old man, "when you find the time."

Calderwood eyed the envelope suspiciously. "What's in there?" he asked, pushing gingerly at the envelope with one blunt finger.

"It's complicated," Rudolph said. "I'd rather we didn't discuss it until you've read it."

"This another of your crazy ideas?" Calderwood asked. The bulk of the envelope seemed to anger him. "Are you pushing me again?"

"Uhuh," Rudolph said, and smiled.

"Do you know, young man," Calderwood said, "my cholesterol count has gone up appreciably since I hired you? Way up."

"Mrs. Calderwood keeps asking me to try to make you take a vacation."

"Does she, now?" Calderwood snorted. "What she doesn't know is that I wouldn't leave you alone in this store for ten consecutive minutes. Tell her that the next time she tells you to try to make me take a vacation." But he had carried the thick envelope, unopened, home with him, when he left the store the night before. Once he started reading what was in it, Rudolph was sure he wouldn't stop until he had finished.

He lay still under the covers in the cold room, almost deciding not to get up promptly this morning, but lie there and figure out what to say to the old man when he came into his office. Then he thought, the hell with it, play it cool, pretend it's just another morning.

He threw back the covers, crossed the room quickly and closed the window. He tried not to shiver as he took off his pajamas and pulled on his heavy track suit. He put on a pair of woolen socks and thick, gum-soled tennis shoes. He put a plaid mackinaw on over the track suit and went out of the apartment, closing the door softly so as not to wake his mother.

Downstairs, in front of the house, Quentin McGovern was waiting for him. Quentin was also wearing a track suit. Over it he had a bulky sweater. A wool stocking hat was pulled down over his ears. Quentin was fourteen, the oldest son of the Negro family across the street. They ran together every morning.

"Hi, Quent," Rudolph said.

"Hi, Rudy," said Quentin. "Sure is cold. Mornings like this, my mother thinks we're out of our minds."

"She'll sing a different tune when you bring home a gold medal from the Olympics."

"I bet," Quentin said. "I can just hear her now."

They walked quickly around the corner. Rudolph unlocked the door of the garage where he rented space, and went to the motorcycle. Dimly, at the back of his mind, a memory lurked. Another door, another dark space, another machine. The shell in the warehouse, the smell of the river, his father's ropy arms.

Then he was back in Whitby again, with the boy in the track suit, in another place, with no river. He rolled out the motorcycle. He pulled on a pair of old wool-lined gloves and swung onto the machine and started the motor. Quentin got on the pillion and put his arms around him and they sped down the street, the cold wind making their eyes tear.

It was only a few minutes to the university athletic field. Whitby College was Whitby University now. The field was not enclosed but had a group of wooden stands along the side. Rudolph set up the motorcycle beside the stands and threw his mackinaw over the saddle of the machine. "Better take off your sweater," he said. "For later. You don't want to catch cold on the way back."

Quentin looked over the field. A thin, icy mist was ghosting up from the turf. He shivered. "Maybe my mother is right," he said. But he took off his sweater and they began jogging slowly around the cinder track.

While he was going to college, Rudolph had never had time to go out for the track team. It amused him that now, as a busy young executive, he had time to run half an hour a day, six days a week. He did it for the exercise and to keep himself hard, but he also enjoyed the early morning quiet, the smell of turf, the sense of changing seasons, the pounding of his feet on the hard track. He had started doing it alone, but one morning Quentin had been standing outside the house in his track suit and had said, "Mr. Jordache, I see you going off to work out every day. Do you mind if I tag along?" Rudolph had nearly said no to the boy. He liked being alone that early in the morning, surrounded as he was all day by people at the store. But Quentin had said, "I'm on the high-school squad. The four-forty. If I know I got to run seriously every morning, it's just *got* to help my time. You don't have to *tell* me anything, Mr. Jordache, just let me run along with you." He spoke shyly, softly, not asking for secrets, and Rudolph could see that he had had to screw up his courage to make a request like that of a grown-up white man who had only said hello to him once or twice in his life. Also, Quentin's father worked on a delivery truck at the store. Labor relations, Rudolph thought. Keep the working man happy. All democrats together. "Okay," he said. "Come on."

The boy had smiled nervously and swung along down the street beside Rudolph to the garage.

They jogged around the track twice, warming up, then broke into a sprint for a hundred yards, then jogged once more, then went fast for the two twenty, then jogged twice around the track and went the four-forty at almost full speed. Quentin was a lanky boy with long, skinny legs and a nice, smooth motion. It was good to have him along, since he pushed Rudolph to run harder than he would have alone. They finished by jogging twice more around the track, and finally, sweating, threw on their overclothes and drove back through the awakening town to their street.

"See you in the morning, Quent," Rudolph said as he parked the motorcycle along the curb.

"Thanks," Quentin said. "Tomorrow."

Rudolph waved and went into the house, liking the boy. They had conquered normal human sloth together on a cold winter's morning, had tested themselves together against weather, speed, and time. When the summer holidays came, he would find some sort of job for the boy at the store. He was sure Quentin's family could use the money.

His mother was awake when he came into the apartment. "How is it out?" she called.

"Cold," he said. "You won't miss anything if you stay home today." They continued with the fiction that his mother normally went out every day, just like other women.

He went into the bathroom, took a steaming-hot shower, then stood under an ice-cold stream for a minute and came out tingling. He heard his mother squeezing orange juice and making coffee in the kitchen as he toweled himself off, the sound of her movements like somebody dragging a heavy sack across the kitchen floor. He remembered the long-paced sprinting on the frozen track and, thought, if I'm ever like that, I'll ask somebody to knock me off.

He weighed himself on the bathroom scale. One-sixty. Satisfactory. He despised fat people. At the store, without telling Calderwood his real reasons, he had tried to get rid of clerks who were overweight.

He rubbed some deodorant under his armpits before dressing. It was a long day and the store was always too hot in winter. He dressed in gray-flannel slacks, a soft blue shirt with a dark red tie, and put on a brown-tweed sports jacket, with no padding at the shoulders. For the first year as assistant manager he had dressed in sober, dark business suits, but as he became more important in the company's hierarchy he had switched to more informal clothes. He was young for his responsibilities and he had to make sure that he didn't appear pompous. For the same reason he had bought himself a motorcycle. Nobody could say as the assistant manager came roaring up to work, bareheaded, on a motorcycle, in all weathers, that the young man was taking himself too seriously. You had to be careful to keep the envy quotient down as low as possible. He could easily afford a car, but he preferred the motorcycle anyway. It kept his complexion fresh and made him look as though he spent a good deal of his time outdoors. To be tanned, especially in winter, made him feel subtly superior to all the pale, sickly looking people around him. He understood now why Boylan had always used a sun lamp. It was deceitful and cheap, he decided, a form of masculine cosmetics and made you vulnerable to people who knew about sun lamps and saw through the artifice.

He went into the kitchen and kissed his mother good morning. She smiled girlishly. If he forgot to kiss her, there would be a long monologue over the breakfast table about how badly she had slept and how the medicines the doctor prescribed for her were a waste of money. He did not tell his mother how much money he earned or that he could very well afford to move them to a much better apartment. He didn't plan any entertainment at home and he had other uses for his money.

He sat down at the kitchen table and drank his orange juice and coffee and munched some toast. His mother just drank coffee. Her hair was lank and there were shocking, huge rings of purple sag under her eyes. But with all that, she didn't seem any worse to him than she had been for the last three years. She would probably live to the age of ninety. He did not begrudge her her longevity. She kept him out of the draft. Sole support of an invalid mother. Last and dearest maternal gift—she had spared him an icebound foxhole in Korea.

"I had a dream last night," she said. "About your brother, Thomas. He looked the way he looked when he was eight years old. Like a choirboy at Easter. He came into my room and said, Forgive me, forgive me . . ." She drank her coffee moodily. "I haven't dreamt about him in forever. Do you ever hear from him?"

"No," Rudolph said.

"You're not hiding anything from me, are you?" she asked.

"No. Why would I do that?"

"I would like to see him once more before I die," she said. "After all he is my own flesh and blood."

"You're not going to die."

"Maybe not," she said. "I have a feeling when spring comes, I'm going to feel much better. We can go for walks again."

"That's good news," Rudolph said, finishing his coffee and standing. He kissed her good-bye. "I'll fix dinner tonight," he said. "I'll shop on the way home."

"Don't tell me what it's going to be," she said coquettishly, "surprise me."

"Okay," he said, "I'll surprise you."

The night watchman was still on duty at the employees' entrance when Rudolph got to the store, carrying the morning papers, which he had bought on the way over.

"Good morning, Sam," Rudolph said.

"Hi, Rudy," the night watchman said. Rudolph made a point of having all the old employees, who knew him from his first days at the store, call him by his Christian name.

"You sure are an early bird," the night watchman said. "When I was your age you couldn't drag me out of bed on a morning like this."

That's why you're a night watchman at *your* age, Sam, Rudolph thought, but he merely smiled and went on up to his office, through the dimly lit and sleeping store.

His office was neat and bare, with two desks, one for himself and one for Miss Giles, his secretary, a middle-aged, efficient spinster. There were piles of magazines geometrically stacked on wide shelves, *Vogue,* French *Vogue, Seventeen, Glamour, Harper's Bazaar, Esquire, House and Garden,* which he combed for ideas for various departments at the store. The quality of the town was changing rapidly; the new people coming up from the city had money and spent it freely. The natives of the town were more prosperous than they had ever been and were beginning to imitate the tastes of the more sophisticated newer arrivals. Calderwood fought a stubborn rear guard action against the transformation of his store from a solid lower-middle-class establishment to what he called a grab bag of fads and fancy gewgaws, but the balance sheet could not be gainsaid as Rudolph pushed through one innovation after another, and each month it was becoming easier for Rudolph to put his ideas into practice. Calderwood had even agreed, after nearly a year of opposition, to wall off part of what had been an unnecessarily capacious delivery room and turn it into a liquor store, with a line of fine French wines that Rudolph, remembering what Boylan had taught him on the subject through the years, took pleasure in selecting himself.

He hadn't seen Boylan since the day of the Commencement exercises. He had called twice that summer to ask if Boylan was free for dinner and Boylan had said, "No," curtly, each time. Every month, Rudolph sent a hundred-dollar check to Boylan, toward repaying the four-thousand-dollar loan. Boylan never cashed the checks, but Rudolph made sure that if at any time Boylan decided to cash them all at once there would be enough money in the account to honor them. Rudolph didn't think about Boylan often, but when he did, he realized that there was contempt mixed with gratitude he felt for the older man. With all that money, Rudolph thought, all that freedom, Boylan had no right to be as unhappy as he was. It was a symptom of Boylan's fundamental weakness, and Rudolph, fighting any signs of weakness in himself, had no tolerance for it in anybody else. Willie Abbott and Teddy Boylan, Rudolph thought, there's a good team.

Rudolph spread the newspapers on his desk. There was the Whitby *Record,* and the edition of the New York *Times* that came up on the first train of the morning. The front page of the *Times* reported heavy fighting along the 38th parallel and new accusations of treason and infiltration by Senator McCarthy in Washington. The *Record*'s front page reported on a vote for new taxes for the school board (not passed) and on the number of skiers who had made use of the new ski area nearby since the season began. Every city to its own interests.

Rudolph turned to the inside pages of the *Record.* The half-page two-color advertisement for a new line of wool dresses and sweaters was sloppily done, with the colors bleeding out of register, and Rudolph made a note on his desk pad to call the paper that morning about it.

Then he opened to the Stock Exchange figures in the *Times* and studied them for fifteen minutes. When he had saved a thousand dollars he had gone to Johnny Heath and asked him, as a favor, to invest it for him. Johnny, who handled some accounts in the millions of dollars, had gravely consented, and worried over Rudolph's transactions as though Rudolph were one of the most important of his firm's customers. Rudolph's holdings were still small, but they were growing steadily. Looking over the Stock Exchange page, he was pleased to see that he was almost three hundred dollars richer this morning, on paper, than he had been the morning before. He breathed a quiet prayer of thanks to his friend Johnny Heath, and turned to the crossword puzzle and got out his pen and started on it. It was one of the pleasantest moments of the day. If he managed to finish the puzzle before nine o'clock, when the store opened, he started the day's work with a faint sense of triumph.

14 across. *Heep. Uriah,* he printed neatly.

He was almost finished with the puzzle, when the phone rang. He looked at his watch. The switchboard was at work early, he noted approvingly. He picked up the phone with his left hand. "Yes?" he said, printing *ubiquitous* in one of the vertical columns.

"Jordache? That you?"

"Yes. Who's this?"

"Denton, Professor Denton."

"Oh, how are you sir?" Rudolph said. He puzzled over *Sober* in five letters, *a* the third letter.

"I hate to bother you," Denton said. His voice sounded peculiar, as though he were whispering and was afraid of being overheard. "But can I see you sometime today?"

"Of course," Rudolph said. He printed *staid* along the lowest line of the puzzle. He saw Denton quite often, when he wanted to borrow books on business management and economics at the college. "I'm in the store all day."

Denton's voice made a funny, sliding sound in the phone. "I'd prefer it if we could meet somewhere besides the store. Are you free for lunch?"

"I just take forty-five minutes . . ."

"That's all right. We'll make it someplace near you." Denton sounded gaspy and hurried. In class he was slow and sonorous. "How about Ripley's? That's just around the corner from you, isn't it?"

"Yes," Rudolph said, surprised at Denton's choice of a restaurant. Ripley's was more of a saloon than a restaurant and was frequented by workmen with a thirst rather than anybody who was looking for a decent meal. It certainly wasn't the sort of place you'd think an aging professor of history and economics would seek out. "Is twelve-fifteen all right?"

"I'll be there, Jordache. Thank you, thank you. It's most kind of you. Until twelve-fifteen, then," Denton said, speaking very quickly. "I can't tell you how I appreciate . . ." He seemed to hang up in the middle of his last sentence.

Rudolph frowned, wondering what was bothering Denton, then put the phone down. He looked at his watch. Nine o'clock. The doors were open. His secretary came into the office and said, "Good morning, Mr. Jordache."

"Good morning, Miss Giles," he said and tossed the *Times* into the wastebasket, annoyed. Because of Denton he hadn't finished the puzzle before nine o'clock.

He made his first round of the store for the day, walking slowly, smiling at the clerks, not stopping or seeming to notice when his eye caught something amiss. Later in the morning, back in his office, he would dictate polite memos to the appropriate department head that the neckties piled on the counter for a sale were not arranged neatly enough, that Miss Kale, in cosmetics, had on too much eye make-up, that the ventilation in the fountain and tea shop was not sufficient.

He looked with special interest at the departments that had not been there until he had induced Calderwood to put them in—the little boutique, which sold junk jewelry, Italian sweaters, French scarves, and fur hats and did a surprising amount of business; the fountain and tea shop (it was amazing how women never stopped eating all day), which not only showed a solid profit on its own but had become a meeting place for lunch for many of the housewives of the town who then rarely got out of the store without buying something; the ski shop, in a corner of the old sporting goods department, presided over by an athletically built young man named Larsen who dazzled the local girls on the nearby slopes on winter Sundays and who was being criminally underpaid considering how much trade he lured into the shop merely by sliding down a hill once a week. The young man had offered to teach Rudolph how to ski, but Rudolph had declined, with a smile. He couldn't afford to break a leg, he explained.

The record counter was his idea, too, and that brought in the young trade with their weirdly lavish allowances. Calderwood, who hated noise, and who couldn't stand the way most young people behaved (his own three daughters, two of them now young ladies and the third a pallid teen-ager, behaved with cowed Victorian decorum), had fought bitterly against the record counter. "I don't want to run a goddamn honky-tonk," he had said. "Deprave the youth of America with those barbaric noises that passes for music these days. Leave me in peace, Jordache, leave a poor old-fashioned merchant in peace."

But Rudolph had produced statistics on how much teenagers in America spent on records every year and had promised to have soundproof booths put in and Calderwood as usual had capitulated. He often seemed to be irritated with Rudolph, but Rudolph was unfailingly polite and patient with the old man and in most things had learned how to manage him. Privately, Calderwood boasted about his pipsqueak of an assistant manager and how clever he himself had been in picking the boy out of the herd. He had also doubled his salary, with no urging from Rudolph, and had given him a bonus at Christmas of three thousand dollars. "He is not only modernizing the store," Calderwood had been heard to say, although not in Rudolph's presence, "the sonofabitch is modernizing me. Well, when it comes down to it, that's what I hired a young man for."

Once a month, Rudolph was invited to dinner at the Calderwoods' house, grim Puritanical affairs, at which the daughters spoke only when spoken to and nothing stronger than apple juice was served. The oldest daughter, Prudence, who was also the prettiest, had asked Rudolph to escort her to several of the country club dances, and Rudolph had done so. Once away from her father, Prudence did not behave with Victorian decorum, but Rudolph carefully kept his hands off her. He was not going to do anything as banal or as dangerous as marrying the boss's daughter.

He was not marrying anybody. That could come later. Three months ago, he had received an invitation to Julie's wedding. She was marrying a man called Fitzgerald in New York. He had not gone to the wedding and he had felt the tears come to his eyes when he had composed the telegram of congratulations. He had despised himself for the weakness and had thrown himself more completely into his work and almost managed to forget Julie.

He was wary of all other girls. He could tell as he walked through the store that there were girls who looked at him flirtatiously, who would be delighted to go out with him, Miss Sullivan, raven haired, in the Boutique; Miss Brandywine, tall and lithe, in the Youth Shop; Miss Soames, in the Record Shop, small, blonde, and bosomy, jiggling to the music, smiling demurely as he passed; maybe six or seven others. He was tempted, of course, but he fought the temptation down, and behaved with perfect, impersonal courtesy to everybody. There were no parties at Calderwood's, so there was no occasion on which, with the excuse of liquor and celebration, any real approach could be made.

The night with Mary Jane in New York and the forlorn telephone call in the deserted lobby of the St. Moritz Hotel had steeled him against the pull of his own desire.

Of one thing he was certain—the next time he asked a girl to marry him, he was going to be damn sure she would say yes.

As he repassed the record counter, he made a mental note to try to get some older woman in the store tactfully to suggest to Miss Soames that perhaps she ought to wear a brassiere under her sweater.

He was going over the drawings for the March window with Bergson, the young man who prepared the displays, when the phone rang.

"Rudy," it was Calderwood, "can you come down to my office for a minute?" The voice was flat, giving nothing away.

"I'll be right there, Mr. Calderwood," Rudolph said. He hung up. "I'm afraid these'll have to wait a little while," he said to Bergson. Bergson was a find. He had done the sets for the summer theater in Whitby. Rudolph liked them and had approached him about a job as window designer for Calderwood's during the winter. Until Bergson had come on the scene the windows had been done haphazardly, with the different departments fighting for space and then doing their own displays without any reference to what was being shown in any window besides their own. Bergson had changed all that. He was a small, sad young man who couldn't get into the scene designers' union in New York. He was grateful for the winter's work and put all his considerable talent into it. Used to working on the cheap for summer-theater productions, he made use of all sorts of unlikely inexpensive materials and did the art work himself.

The plans laid out on Rudolph's desk were on the theme of spring in the country and Rudolph had already told Bergson that he thought they were going to be the best set of windows Calderwood's had ever had. Glum as Bergson was, Rudolph enjoyed the hours he spent working with him, as compared with the hours he spent with the heads of departments and the head of Costs and Accounting. In an ideal scheme of things, he thought, he would never have to look at a balance sheet or go through a monthly inventory.

Calderwood's door was open and Calderwood saw him immediately and said, "Come in, Rudy, and close the door behind you." The papers that had been in the Manila envelope were spread over Calderwood's desk.

Rudolph sat down across from the old man and waited.

"Rudy," Calderwood said mildly, "you're the most astonishing young man I've ever come across."

Rudolph said nothing.

"Who else has seen all this?" Calderwood waved a hand over the papers on his desk.

"Nobody."

"Who typed them up? Miss Giles?"

"I did. At home."

"You think of everything, don't you?" It was not a reproach, but it wasn't a compliment, either.

Rudolph kept quiet.

"Who told you I owned thirty acres of land out near the lake?" Calderwood asked flatly.

The land was owned by a corporation with a New York address. It had taken all of Johnny Heath's cleverness to find out that the real owner of the corporation was Duncan Calderwood. "I'm afraid I can't say, sir," Rudolph said.

"Can't say, can't say." Calderwood accepted it, with a touch of impatience. "The feller can't say. The Silent Generation like they say in *Time* magazine. Rudy, I haven't caught you in a lie since the first day I set eyes on you and I don't expect you to lie to me now."

"I won't lie to you, sir," Rudolph said.

Calderwood pushed at the papers on his desk. "Is this some sort of a trick to take me over?"

"No, sir," Rudolph said. "It's a suggestion as to how you can take advantage of your position and your various assets. To expand with the community and diversify your interests. To profit from the tax laws and at the same time protect your estate for your wife and children when you die."

"How many pages are there in this?" Calderwood said. "Fifty, sixty?"

"Fifty-three."

"Some suggestion." Calderwood snorted. "Did you think this up all by yourself?"

"Yes." Rudolph didn't feel he had to tell Calderwood that for months he had been methodically picking Johnny Heath's brain and that Johnny was responsible for the more involved sections of the overall plan.

"All right, all right," Calderwood grumbled. "I'll look into it."

"If I may make the suggestion, sir," Rudolph said, "I think you should talk this over with your lawyers in New York and your bankers."

"What do you know about my lawyers in New York?" Calderwood asked suspiciously.

"Mr. Calderwood," Rudolph said, "I've been working for you for a long time."

"Okay. Supposing, after studying this some more, I say Yes and do the whole goddamn thing the way you outline it—go public, float a stock issue, borrow from the banks, build the goddamn shopping center near the lake, with a theater, too, like an idiot, supposing I do all that, what's in it for you?"

"I would expect to be made chairman of the board with you as president of the company, at an appropriate salary," Rudolph said, "and an option to buy a certain amount of stock in the next five years." Good old Johnny Heath. Don't niggle. Think big. "I would bring in an assistant to help take over here when I'm otherwise occupied." He had already written Brad Knight in Oklahoma about the job.

"You've got everything figured out, haven't you, Rudy?" Now Calderwood was frankly hostile.

"I've been working on this plan for more than a year," Rudolph said mildly. "I've tried to face all the problems."

"And if I just say no," Calderwood said, "if I just put all this pile of papers in a file and forget it, then what would you do?"

"I'm afraid I'd have to tell you I'm leaving at the end of the year, Mr. Calderwood," Rudolph said. "I'm afraid I'd have to look for something with more of a future for me."

"I got along without you for a long time," Calderwood said. "I could get along without you now."

"Of course you could," Rudolph said.

Calderwood looked down morosely at his desk, flicked out a sheet of paper from a pile, glared at it with especial distaste.

"A theater," he said angrily. "We already have a theater in town."

"They're tearing it down next year," Rudolph said.

"You sure do your homework, don't you?" Calderwood said. "They're not going to announce it until July."

"Somebody always talks," Rudolph said.

"So it seems. And somebody always listens, don't they, Rudy?"

"Yes, sir." Rudolph smiled.

Finally, Calderwood smiled, too. "What makes Rudy run, eh?" he said.

"That's not my style, at all," Rudolph said evenly. "You know that."

"Yes, I do," Calderwood admitted. "I'm sorry I said it. All right. Get back to work. You'll be hearing from me."

He was staring down at the papers on his desk as Rudolph left his office. Rudolph walked slowly among the counters, looking youthful and smiling benevolently as usual.

The plan that he had submitted to Calderwood was a complicated one and he had argued every point closely. The community was growing in the direction of the lake. What was more, the neighboring town of Cedarton, about ten miles away, was linked with Whitby by a new highway and was also growing in the direction of the lake. Suburban shopping centers were springing up all over America and people were becoming accustomed to doing the greater part of their shopping, for all sorts of things, in them. Calderwood's thirty acres were strategically placed for a market to siphon off trade from both towns and from the upper-middle-class homes that dotted the borders of the lake. If Calderwood didn't make the move himself, somebody or some corporation would undoubtedly seize the opportunity in the next year or two and besides profiting from the new trade would cut drastically into Calderwood's volume of business in the Whitby store. Rather than allow a competitor to undermine him, it was to Calderwood's advantage to compete, even partially, with himself.

In his plans Rudolph had argued for a place for a good restaurant, as well as the theater, to attract trade in the evenings as well. The theater, used for plays during the summer, could be turned into a movie house for the rest of the year. He also proposed building a middle-priced housing development along the lake, and suggested that the marshy and up to now unusuable land at one end of Calderwood's holdings could be used for light industry.

Coached by Johnny Heath, Rudolph had meticulously outlined all the benefits the law allowed on enterprises of this kind.

He was sure that his arguments for making a public company out of the new Calderwood Association were bound to sway the old man. The real assets and the earning power, first of the store and then of the center, would insure a high price of issue for the stock. When Calderwood died, his heirs, his wife and three daughters, would not be faced with the possibility of having to sell the business itself at emergency prices to pay the inheritance taxes, but could sell off blocks of stock while holding onto the controlling interest in the corporation.

In the year that Rudolph had been working on the plan and digging into corporation and tax and realty laws, he had been cynically amused by the manner in which money protected itself legally in the American system. He had no moral feeling about trying to turn the law to his own advantage. The game had rules. You learned the rules and abided by them. If there were another set of rules you would abide by them.

Professor Denton was waiting for him, at the bar, uncomfortable and out of place among other patrons, none of whom looked as though he had ever been near a college.

"Good of you," Denton said, in a low, hurried voice, "good of you to come, Jordache. I'm drinking bourbon. Can I order you something?"

"I don't drink during the day," Rudolph said, then was sorry he said it, because it sounded disapproving of Denton, who was drinking at a quarter past noon.

"Quite right," Denton said, "quite right. Keep the head clear. Ordinarily, I wait until the day's work is over myself, but . . ." He took Rudolph's arm. "Perhaps we can sit down." He waved toward the last booth of the row that lined the wall opposite the bar. "I know you have to get back." He left some change in the bar for his drink, carefully counting it out, and still with his hand holding Rudolph's arm, guided him to the booth. They sat down facing each other. There were two greasy menus on the table and they studied them.

"I'll take the soup and the hamburger," Denton said to the waitress. "And a cup of coffee. How about you, Jordache?"

"The same," Rudolph said.

The waitress wrote the order down laboriously on her pad, illiteracy a family heritage. She was a woman of about sixty, gray haired and shapeless in an incongruously pert, revealing orange uniform with a coquettish, small, lace apron, age paying its iron debt to the ideal of youthful America. Her ankles were swollen and she shuffled flatly as she went back toward the kitchen. Rudolph thought of his mother, of her dream of the neat little candlelit restaurant that had never materialized. Well, she had been spared the orange uniform.

"You're doing well, Jordache," Denton said, hunched over the table, his eyes worried and magnified behind the thick, steel-rimmed glasses. He waved his hand impatiently, to ward off any contradiction. "I hear, I hear," he said. "I get reports from many sources. Mrs. Denton, for one. Faithful customer. She must be in the store three times a week. You must see her from time to time."

"I ran into her only last week," Rudolph said.

"She tells me the store is booming, booming, a new lease on life, she says. Very big-city. All sorts of new things. Well, people like to buy things. And everybody seems to have money these days. Except college professors." Indigence creased Denton's forehead briefly. "No matter. I didn't come here to complain. No doubt about it, Jordache, you did well to turn down the job in the department. The academic world," he said bitterly. "Rife with jealousy, cabals, treachery, ingratitude, a man has to walk as if on eggs. Better the world of business. Give and take. Dog eat dog. Frankly. On the up and up."

"It isn't exactly like that," Rudolph said mildly. "Business."

"No, of course not," Denton said. "Everything is modified by character. It doesn't pay to ride a theory too hard, you lose sight of the reality, the living shape. At any rate, I'm gratified at your success, and I'm sure that there was no compromise of principle involved, none whatsoever."

The waitress appeared with their soup. Denton spooned it in. "Yes," he said, "if I had it to do all over again, I'd avoid the ivy-covered walls like the plague. It has made me what you see today, a narrow man, an embittered man, a failure, a coward . . ."

"I wouldn't call you any of those things," Rudolph said, surprised at Denton's description of himself. Denton had always seemed to Rudolph to be pleased with himself, enjoying acting out his visions of economic villainy before a captive audience of young people.

"I live in fear and trembling," Denton said through the soup. "Fear and trembling."

"If I can help you in any way," Rudolph began. "I'd . . ."

"You're a good soul, Jordache, a good soul," Denton said. "I picked you out immediately. Serious among the frivolous. Compassionate among the pitiless. On the search for knowledge where others were merely searching for advancement. Oh, I've watched you carefully through the years, Jordache. You're going to go far. Mark my words. I have been teaching young men for over twenty years, thousands of young men, they have no secrets from me, their future has no mysteries for me. Mark my words, Jordache."

Denton finished his soup and the waitress came and put down their hamburger steaks and coffee.

"And you won't do it by riding roughshod over your fellow men," Denton went on, darting at his hamburger with his fork. "I know your mind, I know your character, I observed you through the years. You have a code, a sense of honor, a fastidiousness of mind and body. These eyes don't miss much, Jordache, in class or out."

Rudolph ate silently, waiting for the spate of approval to die down, knowing that Denton must have a great favor to ask to be so effusive before making his demand.

"Before the war," Denton went on, chewing, "there were more young men of our mold, clear seeing, dependable, honorable. Most of them are dead now, killed in places whose names we have almost forgotten. This generation—" he shrugged despairingly. "Crafty, careful, looking to get something for nothing, hypocritical. You'd be astounded at the amount of cheating I find in each examination, term papers. Ah, if I had the money, I'd get away from it all, live on an island." He looked nervously at his watch. "Time, ever on the wing," he said. He peered around the dark bar conspiratorially. The booth next to theirs was empty and the four or five men hunched over the bar near the doorway were well out of earshot. "Might as well get to the nub of it." Denton dropped his voice and leaned foward over the table. "I'm in trouble, Jordache."

He's going to ask me for the name of an abortionist, Rudolph thought wildly. *Love on the Campus*. He saw the headlines. *History Professor Makes History by Moonlight with Coed. Doctor in Jail.* Rudolph tried to keep his face noncommittal and went on eating. The hamburger was gray and soggy and the potatoes were oily.

"You heard what I said?" Denton whispered.

"You're in trouble, you said."

"Exactly." There was a professorial tone of approval—the student had been paying attention. "*Bad* trouble." Denton sipped at his coffee, Socrates and hemlock. "They're out to get me."

"Who's out to get you?"

"My enemies." Denton's eyes scanned the bar, searching out enemies, disguised as workmen drinking beer.

"When I was in school," Rudolph said, "you seemed to be well liked everywhere."

"There are currents, currents," Denton said, "eddies and whirlpools that the undergraduate never has an inkling of. In the faculty rooms, in the offices of power. In the office of the President himself. I am too outspoken, it is a failing of mine. I am naive, I have believed in the myth of academic freedom. My enemies have bided their time. The vice-chairman of the department, I should have fired him years ago, a hopeless scholar; I restrained myself only out of pity, lamentable weakness. As I said, the vice-chairman, yearning for my job, has prepared a dossier, scraps of gossip over a drink, lines out of context, insinuations. They are preparing to offer me up as a sacrifice, Jordache."

"I think you'd better tell me specifically what's happening," Rudolph said. "Then perhaps I'd be able to judge if I could help."

"Oh, you could help, all right, no doubt about that." Denton pushed the half-eaten hamburger away from him. "They have found their witch," he said. "Me."

"I don't quite understand . . ."

"The witch hunt," Denton said. "You read the papers like everyone else. Throw the Reds out of our schools."

Rudolph laughed. "You're no Red, Professor, you know that," he said.

"Keep your voice low, boy." Denton looked around worriedly. "One does not broadcast on this subject."

"I'm sure you have nothing to worry about, Professor." Rudolph said. He decided to make it seem like a joke. "I was afraid it was something serious. I thought maybe you'd got a girl pregnant."

"You can laugh," Denton said. "At your age. Nobody laughs in a college or a university anymore. The wildest charges. A five-dollar contribution to an obscure charity in 1938, a reference to Karl Marx in a class, for God's sake, how is a man to teach the economic theories of the nineteenth century without mentioning Karl Marx! An ironic joke about prevalent economic practices, picked up by some stone-age moron in a class in American History and repeated to the moron's father, who is the Commander of the local American Legion Post. Ah, you don't know, boy, you don't know. And Whitby gets a yearly grant from the State. For the School of Agriculture. So some windbag of an upstate legislator makes a speech, forms a committee, demands an investigation, gets his name in the newspaper. Patriot, Defender of the Faith. A special board has been set up within the university, Jordache, don't mention it to a soul, headed by the President, to investigate charges against various members of the faculty. They hope to head off the State, throw them a few bodies, mine chief among them, not imperil the grant from the State. Does the picture grow clearer, Jordache?"

"Oh, Christ," Rudolph said.

"Exactly. Oh, Christ. I don't know what your politics are . . ."

"I don't have any politics," Rudolph said. "I vote independently."

"Excellent, excellent," Denton said. "Although it would have been better if you were a registered Republican. And to think that I voted for Eisenhower." He laughed hollowly. "My son was in Korea and he promised to end the war. But how to prove it. There is much to be said for public balloting."

"What do you want me to do, Professor?" Rudolph asked. "Specifically?"

"Now we come to it," Denton said. He finished his coffee. "The board meets to consider my case one week from today. Tuesday at two P.M. Mark the hour. I have only been allowed to see a general outline of the charges against me; contributions to Communist front organizations in the thirties, atheistic and radical utterances in the classroom, the recommendation of certain books for outside reading of a doubtful character. The usual academic hatchet job, Jordache, all too usual. With the temper of the country what it is, with that man Dulles roaring up and down the world, preaching nuclear destruction, with the most eminent men traduced and dismissed like errand boys in Washington, a poor teacher can be ruined by a whisper, the merest whisper. Luckily, they still have a sense of shame at the university, although I doubt it will last the year, and I am to have a chance to defend myself, bring in witnesses to vouch for me . . ."

"What do you want me to say?"

"Whatever you will, boy," Denton said, his voice broken. "I do not plan to coach you. Say what you think of me. You were in three of my classes, we had many instructive hours outside the courses, you have been to my house. You're a clever young man, you are not to be fooled. You know me as well as any man in this town. Say what you will. Your reputation is high, your record at the university was impeccable, not a blot on it, you are a rising young businessman, untainted, your testimony will be of the utmost value."

"Of course," Rudolph said. *Premonitions of trouble. Attacks. Calderwood's atti-*

ude. Dragging the store into politics on the Communist issue. "Of course I'll testify," he said. This is the wrong day for something like this, he thought annoyedly. He suddenly and for the first time understood the exquisite pleasure that cowards must enjoy.

"I knew you would say that, Jordache." Denton gripped his hand emotionally across the table. "You'd be surprised at the refusals I've had from men who have been my friends for twenty years, the hedging, the pusillanimity. This country is becoming a haunt of whipped dogs, Jordache. Do you wish me to swear to you that I have never been a Communist?"

"Don't be absurd, Professor," Rudolph said. He looked at his watch. "I'm afraid I've got to get back to the store. When the board meets next Tuesday I'll be there." He dug into his pocket for his money clip. "Let me pay my share."

Denton stopped him with a gesture. "I invited you. You're my guest. Go ahead, boy, go ahead. I won't keep you." He stood up, looked around for a last time to see if anybody was making a point of watching him, then, satisfied, put out his hand and shook Rudolph's hand fervently.

Rudolph got his coat and went out of the bar. Through the fogged window he saw Denton stop and order a drink at the bar.

Rudolph walked slowly back toward the store, leaving his coat open, although the wind was keen and the day raw. The street looked as it always looked and the people passing him did not seem like whipped dogs. Poor Denton. He remembered that it was in Denton's class that he had been given the first glimmerings of how to make himself successfully into a capitalist. He laughed to himself. Denton, poor bastard, could not afford to laugh.

He was still hungry after the disastrous meal, and once in the store, he went to the fountain in the basement and ordered a malted milk and drank it among the soprano twitterings of the lady shoppers all around him. Their world was safe. They would buy dresses at fifty dollars that afternoon, and portable radios and television consoles and frying pans and living room suites and creams for the skin and the profits would mount and they were happy over their club sandwiches and ice cream sodas.

He looked over the calm, devouring, rouged, spending, acquiring faces, mothers, brides, virgins, spinsters, mistresses, listened to the voices, breathed in the jumbled bouquet of perfumes, congratulated himself that he was not married and loved no one. He thought, I cannot spend my life serving these worthy women, paid for his malted milk, and went up to his office.

On his desk, there was a letter. It was a short one. "I hope you're coming to New York soon. I'm in a mess and I have to talk to you. Love, Gretchen."

He threw the letter in the wastebasket and said, "Oh, Christ," for the second time in an hour.

It was raining when he left the store at six-fifteen. Calderwood hadn't said a word since their talk in the morning. That's all I needed today, rain, he thought miserably, as he made his way through the streaming traffic on the motorcycle. He was almost home when he remembered that he had promised his mother that he would do the shopping for dinner. He cursed and turned the machine back toward the business section, where the stores remained open until seven. A surprise, he remembered his mother saying. Your loving son may be out on his ass in two weeks, Mother, will that be surprise enough?

He did his shopping hastily, a small chicken, potatoes, a can of peas, half an apple pie for dessert. As he pushed his way through the lines of housewives he remembered the interview with Calderwood and grinned sourly. The boy wonder financier, surrounded by admiring beauties, on his way to one of his usual elegantly prepared repasts at the family mansion, so often photographed for *Life* and *House and Garden*. At the last minute, he bought a bottle of Scotch. This was going to be a night for whiskey.

He went to bed early, a little drunk, thinking, just before he dropped off to sleep. The only satisfactory thing I did all day was run this morning with Quentin McGovern.

The week was routine. When he saw Calderwood at the store, Calderwood made no mention of Rudolph's proposition, but spoke to him of the ordinary business of the store in his usual slightly rasping and irritable tone. There was no hint either in his manner or in what he said of any ultimate decision.

Rudolph had called Gretchen on the phone in New York (from a pay station—Calderwood did not take kindly to private calls on the store's phones) and Gretchen had sounded disappointed when he told her he couldn't get down to the city that week, but would try the following weekend. She had refused to tell him what the trouble was. It could wait, she said. If it could wait, he thought, it couldn't be so bad.

Denton didn't call again. Perhaps he was afraid that if given a chance at further conversation Rudolph would withdraw his offer to speak in his behalf before the board next Tuesday afternoon. Rudolph found himself worrying about his appearance before the board. There was always the chance that some evidence produced against Denton that Denton didn't know about or had hidden that would make Rudolph seem like a confederate or a liar or a dupe. What worried him more, though, was that the board was bound to be hostile, prepared to do away with Denton, and antagonistic to anyone who stood in the way. All his life Rudolph had attempted to get people, especially older people in authority, to like him. The thought of facing a whole room full of disapproving academic faces disturbed him.

Throughout the week he found himself making silent speeches to those imagined, unrelenting faces, speeches in which he defended Denton honorably and well while at the same time charming his judges. None of the speeches he composed seemed, in the end, worthwhile. He would have to go into the board as relaxed as possible, gauge the temper of the room and extemporaneously do the best he could for both Denton and himself. If Calderwood knew what he intended to do . . .

By the weekend he was sleeping badly, his dreams lascivious but unsatisfactory, images of Julie dancing naked before a body of water, Gretchen stretched out in a canoe, Mary Jane opening her legs in bed, then sitting up, her breasts bare, her face contorted, accusing him. A ship pulled away from a pier, a girl, her skirts blowing in the wind, smiled at him as he ran desperately down the pier to catch the ship, he was held back by unseen hands, the ship pulled away, open water . . .

Sunday morning, with church bells ringing, he decided he couldn't stay in the house all day, although he had planned to go over a copy of the papers he had given Calderwood and make some corrections and additions that had occurred to him during the week. But his mother was at her worst on Sundays. The bells made her mournful about her lost religion and she was apt to say that if only Rudolph would go with her, she would attend Mass, confess, take Communion. "The fires of hell are waiting for me," she said over breakfast, "and the church and salvation are only three blocks away."

"Some other Sunday, Mom," Rudolph said. "I'm busy today."

"I may be dead and in hell some other Sunday," she said.

"We'll just have to take that chance," he said, getting up from the table. He left her weeping.

It was a cold, clear day, the sun a bright wafer in the pale winter sky. He dressed warmly, in a fleece-lined surplus Air Force jacket, a knitted wool cap, and goggles, and took the motorcycle out of the garage. He hesitated about which direction to take. There was nobody he wanted to see that day, no destination that seemed promising. Leisure, the burden of modern man.

He got on the motorcycle, started it, hesitated. A car with skis on its roof sped down the street, and he thought, why not, that's as good a place as any, and followed the car. He remembered that Larsen, the young man in the ski department, had told him that there was a barn near the bottom of the tow that could be converted into a shop for renting skis on the weekend. Larsen had said that there was a lot of money to be made there. Rudolph felt better as he followed the car with ski rack. He was no longer aimless.

He was nearly frozen when he got to the slope. The sun, reflected off the snow, dazzled him and he squinted at the brightly colored figures swooping toward him down the hill. Everybody seemed young, vigorous, and having a good time, and the girls, tight pants over trim hips and round buttocks, made lust a healthy outdoor emotion for a Sunday morning.

He watched, enjoying the spectacle for awhile, then became melancholy. He felt lonely and deprived. He was about to turn away and get his machine and go back to town, when Larsen came skimming down off the hill and made a dashing, abrupt stop in front of him, in a cloud of snow.

"Hi, Mr. Jordache," Larsen said. He had two rows of great shining white teeth and he smiled widely. Behind him two girls who had been following him came to a halt.

"Hello, Larsen," Rudolph said. "I came out to see that barn you told me about."

"Sure thing," Larsen said. Supple, in one easy movement, he bent over to free himself from his skis. He was bare headed and his longish, fine, blond hair fell over his eyes as he bent over. Looking at him, in his red sweater, with the two girls behind him, Rudolph was sure that Larsen hadn't dreamt about any boat pulling away from a pier the night before.

"Hello, Mr. Jordache," one of the girls said. "I didn't know you were a skier."

He peered at her and she laughed. She was wearing big green-tinted snow goggles that covered most of her small face. She pushed the goggles up over her red-and-blue woolen hat. "I'm in disguise," she said.

Now Rudolph recognized her. It was Miss Soames, from the Record Department. Jiggling, plump, blonde, fed by music.

"Good morning, good morning," Rudolph said, somehow flustered, noticing how small Miss Soames's waist was, and how well rounded her thighs and hips. "No, I'm not a skier. I'm a voyeur."

Miss Soames laughed. "There's plenty to voyeur about up here, isn't there?"

"Mr. Jordache . . ." Larsen was out of his skis by now, "may I present my fiancée? Miss Packard."

Miss Packard took off her goggles, too, and revealed herself to be as pretty as Miss Soames, and about the same age. "Pleasure," she said. Fiancée. People were still marrying.

"Be back in a half hour or so, girls," Larsen said. "Mr. Jordache and I have some business to transact." He stuck his skis and poles upright in the snow, as the girls, with a wave of their hands, skied off to the bottom of the lift.

"They look like awfully good skiers," Rudolph said as he walked at Larsen's side back toward the road.

"Mediocre," Larsen said carelessly. "But they have other charms." He laughed, showing the magnificent teeth in the brown face. He made sixty-five dollars a week, Rudolph knew. How could he be so happy on a Sunday morning on sixty-five dollars a week?"

The barn was about two hundred yards away, and on the road, a big, solid structure, protected from the weather. "All you'd need," Larsen said, "is a big iron stove and you'd be plenty warm. I bet you could rent a thousand pairs of skis and two to three hundred pairs of boots out of this place a weekend, and then there're the Christmas and Easter vacations and other holidays. And you could get two college boys to run it for beans. It could be a gold mine. If we don't do it, somebody else sure as hell will. This is only the second year for this area, but it's catching on and somebody's bound to see the opportunity."

Rudolph recognized the argument, so much like the one he had used that week on

Calderwood, and smiled. In business you sometimes were the pusher and sometimes the pushee. I'm a Sunday pushee, he thought. If we do it, I'll get Larsen a good hike in salary.

"Who owns this place?" Rudolph asked.

"Dunno," Larsen said. "It's easy enough to find out."

Poor Larsen, Rudolph thought, not made for business. If it had been my idea, I would have had an option to buy it before I said a word to anyone. "There's a job for you, Larsen," Rudolph said. "Find out who owns the barn, whether he'll rent it and for how much, or sell it and for how much. And don't mention the store. Say you're thinking of swinging it yourself."

"I get it, I get it," Larsen said, nodding seriously. "Keep 'em from asking too much."

"We can try," Rudolph said. "Let's get out of here. I'm freezing. Is there a place to get a cup of coffee near here?"

"It's just about time for lunch. There's a place a mile down the road that's not bad. Why don't you join me and the girls for lunch, Mr. Jordache?"

Automatically, Rudolph almost said no. He had never been seen outside the store with any of the employees, except once in awhile with one of the buyers or a head of a department. Then he shivered. He *was* awfully cold. He had to go in someplace. Dancy, dainty Miss Soames. What harm could it do? "Thanks, Larsen," he said. "I'd like that very much."

They walked back toward the ski tow. Larsen had a plowing, direct, uncomplicated kind of walk, in his heavy ski boots with their rubber bottoms. The soles of Rudolph's shoes were of leather and the way was icy and Rudolph had to walk delicately, almost mincingly, to keep from slipping. He hoped the girls weren't watching him.

The girls were waiting, their skis off, and Miss Soames was saying, "We're starving. Who's going to nourish the orphans?" even before Larsen had a chance to say anything.

"Okay, okay, girls," Larsen said commandingly, "we're going to feed you. Stop wailing."

"Oh, Mr. Jordache," Miss Soames said, "are you going to dine with us? What an honor." She dropped her lashes demurely over freckles, the mockery plain.

"I had an early breakfast," Rudolph said. Clumsy, he thought bitterly. "I could stand some food and drink." He turned to Larsen. "I'll follow you on the machine."

"Is that beautiful thing *yours,* Mr. Jordache?" Miss Soames waved toward where the motorcycle was parked.

"Yes," Rudolph said.

"I *yearn* for a ride," Miss Soames said. She had a gushy, cut-up manner of talking, as though confidences were being unwillingly forced from her. "Do you think you could find it in your heart to let me hang on?"

"It's pretty cold," Rudolph said stiffly.

"I have two pairs of long woolen underwear on," Miss Soames said. "I guarantee I'll be toasty. Benny," she said to Larsen, as though the matter were settled, "put my skis on your car, like a pal. I'm going with Mr. Jordache."

There was nothing Rudolph could do about it and he led the way to the machine while Larsen fixed the three pairs of skis on the rack on a brand-new Ford. How does he do it on sixty-five dollars a week? Rudolph thought. For an unworthy moment he wondered if Larsen was honest with his accounts at the ski shop.

Rudolph got onto the motorcycle and Miss Soames swung lightly on behind him, putting her hands around his waist and holding on firmly. Rudolph adjusted his goggles and followed Larsen's Ford out of the parking lot. Larsen drove fast and Rudolph had to put on speed to keep up with him. It was much colder than before, and the wind cut at his face, but Miss Soames, holding on tighter than ever, shouted in his ear, "Isn't this *bliss?*"

The restaurant was large and clean and noisy with skiers. They found a table near a window and Rudolph took off his Air Force jacket while the others stripped themselves of their parkas. Miss Soames was wearing a pale-blue cashmere sweater, delicately shaped over her small, full breasts. Rudolph was wearing a sweater over a wool shirt, and a silk scarf, carefully arranged around his throat. Too fancy, he thought, memories of Teddy Boylan, and took it off, pretending it was warm in the restaurant.

The girls ordered Cokes and Larsen a beer. Rudolph felt he needed something more convincing and ordered an old-fashioned. When the drinks came, Miss Soames raised her glass and made a toast, clinking her glass against Rudolph's. "To Sunday," she said, "without which we'd all just *die.*" She was sitting next to Rudolph on the banquette and he could feel the steady pressure of her knee against his. He pulled his knee away, slowly, so as to make it seem merely a natural movement, but the girl's eyes, clear and cold blue, were amused and knowing over the rim of her glass as she looked at him.

They all ordered steaks. Miss Soames asked for a dime for the juke box and Larsen was faster out of his pocket than Rudolph. She took the dime from him and climbed over Rudolph to go to the machine, getting leverage by putting her hand on his shoulder, and walking across the room, her tight, lush bottom swinging and graceful, despite the clumsy boots on her feet.

The music blared out and Miss Soames came back to the table, doing little, playful dance steps as she crossed the floor. This time, as she climbed over Rudolph to her place, there was no doubt about what she was doing, and when she sat down, she was closer than before and the pressure of her knee was unmistakable against his. If he tried to move away now, everybody would notice, so he remained as he was.

He wanted wine with his steak, but hesitated to order a bottle because he was afraid the others might think he was showing off or being superior. He looked at the menu. On the back were listed a California red and a California white. "Would anybody like some wine?" he asked, putting the decision elsewhere.

"I would," Miss Soames said.

"Honey . . .?" Larsen turned to Miss Packard.

"If everybody else does . . ." she said, being agreeable.

By the time the meal was over they had drunk three bottles of red wine among them. Larsen had drunk the most, but the others had done their fair share.

"What a story I'll have to tell the girls tomorrow at the store," Miss Soames, flushed rosy by now, was saying, her knee and thigh rubbing cosily against Rudolph's. "I have been led astray on a Sunday by the great, unapproachable Mr. Frigidaire himself . . ."

"Oh, come on now, Betsy," Larsen said uneasily, glancing at Rudolph to see how he had taken the Mr. Frigidaire. "Watch what you're saying."

Miss Soames ignored him, sweeping her blonde hair loosely back from her forehead, with a little, plump, cushiony hand. "With his big-city ways and his dirty California wine, the Crown Prince lured me on to drunkenness and loose behavior in public. Oh, he's a sly one, our Mr. Jordache." She put a finger up to the corner of her eye and winked. "When you look at him you'd think he could cool a case of beer with one glance of his eyes. But come Sunday, aha, out comes the real Mr. Jordache. The corks pop, the wine flows, he drinks with the help, he laughs at Ben Larsen's corny old jokes, he plays footsy with the poor little shopgirls from the ground floor. My God, Mr. Jordache, you have bony knees."

Rudolph couldn't help but laughing, and the others laughed with him. "Well, *you* don't, Miss Soames," he said. "I'm prepared to swear to that."

They all laughed again.

"Mr. Jordache, the daredevil motorcycle rider, the Wall of Death, sees all, knows all, feels all," Miss Soames said. "Oh, Christ, I can't keep on calling you Mr. Jordache. Can I call you Young Master? Or will you settle for Rudy?"

"Rudy," he said. If there had been nobody else there, he would have grabbed her, kissed that flushed small tempting face, the glistening, half mocking, half inviting lips.

"Rudy, it is," she said. "Call him Rudy, Sonia."

"Hello, Rudy," Miss Packard said. It didn't mean anything to her. She didn't work at the store.

"Benny," Miss Soames commanded.

Larsen looked beseechingly at Rudolph. "She's loaded," he began. .

"Don't be silly, Benny," Rudolph said.

"Rudy," Larsen said reluctantly.

"Rudy, the mystery man," Miss Soames went on, sipping at her wineglass. "They lock him away at closing time. Nobody sees him except at work, no man, no woman, no child. Especially no woman. There are twenty girls on the ground floor alone who weep into their pillows nightly for him, to say nothing of the ladies in the other departments, and he passes them by with a cold, heartless smile."

"Where the hell did you learn to talk like that?" Rudolph asked, embarrassed, amused, and, at the same time, flattered.

"She's bookish," Miss Packard said. "She reads a book a day."

Miss Soames ignored her. "He is a mystery wrapped in an enigma, as Mr. Churchill said on another occasion. He has been reported running at dawn followed by a young colored boy. What is he running from? What message does the colored boy have for him? He is reported as having been seen in New York, in low neighborhoods. What sins does he commit in the big city? Why doesn't he commit his sins locally?"

"Betsy," Larsen said weakly. "Let's go skiing."

"Tune in on this same station next Sunday and perhaps all these questions will be answered," Miss Soames said. "You may now kiss my hand." She held out her hand, the wrist arched, and Rudolph kissed it, blushing a little.

"I've got to get back to town," he said. The check was on the table and he put down some bills. With tip, it came to fifteen dollars.

When they went outside, a light snow was falling. The mountain was bleak and dangerous looking, its outlines only suggested in the light swirl of snow.

"Thanks for the lunch, Mr. Jordache," Larsen said. One Rudy a week was enough for him. "It was great."

"I really enjoyed it, Mr. Jordache," Miss Packard said, practicing to be Larsen's wife. "I mean I really did."

"Come on, Betsy," Larsen said, "let's hit the slope, work off some of that wine."

"I am returning to town with my good and old friend, Rudy, on his death-defying machine," Miss Soames said. "Aren't I, Rudy?"

"It's an awfully cold ride," Rudolph said. She looked small and crushable in her parka, with her oversized goggles incongruously strapped onto her ski cap. Her head, especially with the goggles, seemed very large, a weighty frame for the small, wicked face.

"I will ski no more today," Miss Soames said grandly. "I am in the mood for other sports." She went over to the motorcycle. "Let us mount," she said.

"You don't have to take her if you don't want to," Larsen said anxiously, responsible.

"Oh, let her come," Rudolph said. "I'll go slow and make sure she doesn't fall off."

"She's a funny girl," Larsen said, still worried. "She doesn't know how to drink. But she doesn't mean any harm."

"She hasn't done any harm, Benny." Rudolph patted Larsen's thick, sweatered shoulder. "Don't worry. And see what you can find out about that barn." Back in the safe world of business.

"Sure thing, Mr. Jordache," Larsen said. He and Miss Packard waved as Rudolph gunned the motorcycle out of the restaurant parking lot, with Miss Soames clinging on behind him, her arms around his waist.

The snow wasn't thick, but it was enough to make him drive carefully. Miss Soames's arms around him were surprisingly strong for a girl so lightly made, and while she had drunk enough wine to make her tongue loose, it hadn't affected her balance and she leaned easily with him as they swept around curves in the road. She sang from time to time, the songs that she heard all day in the record department, but with the wind howling past, Rudolph could only hear little snatches, a phrase of melody in a faraway voice. She sounded like a child singing fitfully to herself in a distant room.

He enjoyed the ride. The whole day, in fact. He was glad his mother's talk about church had driven him out of the house.

At the outskirts of Whitby, as they were passing the university, he slowed down, to ask Miss Soames where she lived. It wasn't far from the campus and he zoomed down the familiar streets. It was still fairly early in the afternoon, but the clouds overhead were black and there were lights to be seen in the windows of the houses they passed. He had to slow down at a stop sign and as he did so, he felt Miss Soames's hand slide down from his waist, where she had been holding on, to his crotch. She stroked him there softly and he could hear her laughing in his ear.

"No disturbing the driver," he said. "State law."

But she only laughed and kept on doing what she had been doing.

They passed an elderly man walking a dog and Rudolph was sure the old man looked startled. He gunned the machine and it had some effect. Miss Soames just held on to the place she had been caressing.

He came to the address she had given him. It was an old, one-family clapboard house set on a yellowed lawn. There were no lights on in the house.

"Home," Miss Soames said. She jumped off the pillion. "That was a nice ride, Rudy. Especially the last two minutes." She took off her goggles and hat and put her head to one side, letting her hair swing loose over her shoulders. "Want to come inside?" she asked. "There's nobody home. My mother and father are out visiting and my brother's at the movies. We can go on to the next chapter."

He hesitated, looked at the house, guessed what it was like inside. Papa and Mama off on a visit but likely to return early. Brother perhaps bored with the movie and coming rattling in an hour earlier than expected. Miss Soames stood before him, one hand on her hip, smiling, swinging her goggles and ski cap in the other.

"Well?" she asked.

"Some other time, perhaps," he said.

"Scaredy-cat," she said, and giggled. Then she ran up the front walk toward the house. At the door she turned and stuck out her tongue at him. The dark building engulfed her.

Thoughtfully, he started the motorcycle and drove slowly toward the center of the town along the darkening streets. He didn't want to go home, so he parked the machine and went into a movie. He hardly saw the movie and would not have been able to tell what it was about when he got out.

He kept thinking about Miss Soames. Silly, cheap little girl, teasing, teasing, making fun of him. He didn't like the idea of seeing her in the store next morning. If it were possible he would have had her fired. But she would go to the union and complain and he would have to explain the grounds on which he had had her fired. *"She called me Mr. Frigidaire, then she called me Rudy and finally she held my cock on a public thoroughfare."*

He gave up the idea of firing Miss Soames. One thing it all proved—he had been right all along in having nothing to do with anybody from the store.

He had dinner alone in a restaurant and drank a whole bottle of wine by himself and nearly hit a lamp post on the way home.

He slept badly and he groaned at a quarter to seven Monday morning, when he knew he had to get up and run with Quentin McGovern. But he got up and he ran.

When he made his morning round of the store he was careful to avoid going near the record counter. He waved to Larsen in the ski shop and Larsen, red sweatered, said, "Good morning, Mr. Jordache," as though they had not shared Sunday together.

Calderwood called him into his office in the afternoon. "All right, Rudy," he said, "I've been thinking about your ideas and I've talked them over with some people down in New York. We're going down there tomorrow, we have a date at my lawyer's office in Wall Street at two o'clock. They want to ask you some questions. We'll take the 11:05 train down. I'm not promising anything, but the first time around, my people seem to think you got something there." Calderwood peered at him. "You don't seem particularly happy, Rudy," he said accusingly.

"Oh, I'm pleased, sir. Very pleased." He managed to smile. Two o'clock Tuesday, he was thinking, I promised Denton I'd go before the board two o'clock Tuesday. "It's very good news, sir." He smiled again, trying to seem boyish and naive. "I guess I just wasn't prepared for it—so soon, I mean."

"We'll have lunch on the train," Calderwood said, dismissing him.

Lunch on the train with the old man. That means no drink, Rudolph thought, as he went out of the office. He preferred to be gloomy about that than gloomy about Professor Denton.

Later in the afternoon, the phone rang in his office and Miss Giles answered. "I'll see if he's in," she said. "Who's calling please?" She put her hand over the mouthpiece and said, "Professor Denton."

Rudolph hesitated, then stretched out his hand for the phone, "Hello, Professor," he said heartily. "How're things?"

"Jordache," Denton said, his voice hoarse, "I'm at Ripley's. Can you come over for a few minutes? I've got to talk to you."

Just as well now as later. "Of course, Professor," he said. "I'll be right there." He got up from his desk. "If anybody wants me," he said to Miss Giles, "say I'll be back in a half hour."

When he came into the bar, he had to search to find Denton. Denton was in the last booth again, with his hat and coat on, hunched over the table, his hands cupped around his glass. He needed a shave and his clothes were rumpled and his spectacles clouded and smeared. It occurred to Rudolph that he looked like an old wino, waiting blearily on a park bench in the winter weather for a cop to come and move him on. The self-confident, loud, ironic man of Rudolph's classrooms, amused and amusing, had vanished.

"Hello, Professor." Rudolph slid into the booth opposite Denton. He hadn't bothered to put on a coat for the short walk from the store. "I'm glad to see you." He smiled, as though to reassure Denton that Denton was the same man he had always known, to be greeted in the usual manner.

Denton looked up dully. He didn't offer to shake hands. His face, ordinarily ruddy, was gray. Even his blood has surrendered, Rudolph thought.

"Have a drink." Denton's voice was thick. He had obviously already had a drink. Or several. "Miss," he called loudly to the lady in the orange uniform, who was leaning, like an old mare in harness, against the end of the bar. "What'll you have?" he asked Rudolph.

"Scotch, please."

"Scotch and soda for my friend, miss," Denton said. "And another bourbon for me."

After that, he sat silently for awhile, staring down at the glass between his hands. On the way over from the store, Rudolph had decided what he had to do. He would have to tell Denton that it was impossible for him to appear before the board the next day, but that he would offer to do so any other day, if the board would postpone. Failing that, he would go to see the President that night and say what he had to say. Or if Denton disapproved of that, he would write out his defense of Denton that night for Denton to read before the board when they considered his case. He dreaded the moment when he would have to make these proposals to Denton, but there was no question of not going down to New York with Calderwood on the 11:05 tomorrow morning. He was grateful that Denton kept silent, even for a moment, and he made a big business of stirring his drink when it came, the noise a little musical barrier against conversation for a few seconds.

"I hate to drag you away from your work like this, Jordache," Denton said, not lifting his eyes, and mumbling now. "Trouble makes a man egotistic. I pass a movie theater and I see people lined up to go in, to laugh at a comedy, and I say, 'Don't they know what's happening to me, how can they go to the movies?'" He laughed sourly. "Absurd," he said. "Fifty million people were being killed in Europe alone between 1939 and 1945, and I went to the movies twice a week." He took a thirsty gulp of his drink, bending low over the table and holding the glass with his two hands. The glass rattled as he put it down.

"Tell me what's happening," Rudolph said, soothingly.

"Nothing." Denton said. "Well, that's not true, either. A lot. It's over."

"What are you talking about?" Rudolph spoke calmly, but it was difficult to keep the excitement out of his voice. So, it was nothing, he thought. A storm in a teacup. People finally couldn't be *that* idiotic. "You mean they've dropped the whole thing?"

"I mean I've dropped the whole thing," Denton said flatly, lifting his head and looking out from under the brim of his battered, brown felt hat at Rudolph. "I resigned today."

"Oh, no," Rudolph said.

"Oh, yes," Denton said. "After twelve years. They offered to accept my resignation and drop the proceedings. I couldn't face tomorrow. After twelve years. I'm too old, too old. Maybe if I were younger. When you're younger, you can face the irrational. Justice seems obtainable. My wife has been crying for a week. She says the disgrace would kill her. A figure of speech, of course, but a woman weeping seven days and seven nights erodes the will. So, it's done. I just wanted to thank you and tell you you don't have to be there tomorrow at two P.M."

Rudolph swallowed. Carefully, he tried to keep the relief out of his voice. "I would have been happy to speak up," he said. He would not have been happy, but one way or another he had been prepared to do it, and a more exact description of his feelings would do no good at the moment. "What are you going to do now?" he asked.

"I have been thrown a lifeline," Denton said dully. "A friend of mine is on the faculty of the International School at Geneva, I've been offered a place. Less money, but a place. They are not as maniacal, it seems, in Geneva. They tell me the city is pretty."

"But it's just a high school," Rudolph protested. "You've taught in colleges all your life."

"It's in Geneva," Denton said. "I want to get out of this goddamn country."

Rudolph had never heard anybody say this goddamn country about America and he was shocked at Denton's bitterness. As a boy in school he had sung "God shed his Grace on Thee" about his native land, along with the forty other boys and girls in the classroom, and now, he realized that what he had sung as a child he still believed as a grown man. "It's not as bad as you think," he said.

"Worse," Denton said.

"It'll blow over. You'll be asked back."

"Never," Denton said. "I wouldn't come back if they begged me on their knees."

"The Man Without a Country," Rudolph remembered from grade school, the poor exile being transferred from ship to ship, never to see the shores of the land where he was born, never to see the flag without tears. Geneva, that flagless vessel. He looked at Denton, exiled already in the back booth of Ripley's Bar, and felt a confused mixture of emotions, pity, contempt. "Is there anything I can do?" he asked. "Money?"

Denton shook his head. "We're all right. For the time being. We're selling the house. Real estate values have gone up since I bought it. The country is booming." He laughed drily. He stood up abruptly. "I have to go home now," he said. "I'm giving my wife French lessons every afternoon."

He allowed Rudolph to pay for the drinks. Outside on the street, he put his collar up, looking more like an old wino than ever, and shook Rudolph's hand slackly. "I'll write you from Geneva," he said. "Noncommittal letters. God knows who opens mail these days."

He shuffled off, a bent, scholarly figure among the citizens of his goddamn country. Rudolph watched him for a moment, then walked back to the store. He breathed deeply, feeling young, lucky, lucky.

He was in the line waiting to laugh, while the sufferers shuffled past. Fifty million dead, but the movies were always open.

He felt sorry for Denton, but overriding that, he felt joyous for himself. Everything from now on was going to be all right, everything was going to go his way. The sign had been made clear that afternoon, the omens were plain.

He was on the 11:05 the next morning with Calderwood, composed and optimistic. When they went into the dining car for lunch, he didn't mind not being able to order a drink.

CHAPTER 5

1955

"WHY DO YOU have to come and wait for me?" Billy was complaining, as they walked toward home. "As though I'm a baby."

"You'll go around by yourself soon enough," she said, automatically taking his hand as they crossed a street.

"When?"

"Soon enough."

"When?"

"When you're ten."

"Oh, Christ."

"You know you mustn't say things like that."

"Daddy does."

"You're not Daddy."

"So do you sometimes."

"You're not me. And I shouldn't say it, either."

"Then why do you say it?"

"Because I get angry."

"I'm angry now. All the other kids don't have their mothers waiting for them outside the gate like babies. They go home by themselves."

Gretchen knew this was true and that she was being a nervous parent, not faithful to Spock, and that she or Billy or both of them would have to pay for it later, but she couldn't bear the thought of the child wandering by himself around the doubtful traffic of Greenwich Village. Several times she had suggested to Willie that they move to the suburbs for their son's sake, but Willie had vetoed the idea. "I'm not the Scarsdale type," he said.

She didn't know what the Scarsdale type was. She knew a lot of people who lived in Scarsdale or in places very much like Scarsdale, and they seemed as various as people living anywhere else—drunks, wife-swappers, churchgoers, politicians, patriots, scholars, suicides, whatever.

"When?" Billy asked again, stubbornly, pulling away from her hand.

"When you're ten," she repeated.

"That's a whole year," he wailed.

"You'll be surprised how fast it goes," she said. "Now, button your coat. You'll catch cold." He had been playing basketball in the schoolyard and he was still sweating. The late-afternoon October air was nippy and there was a wind off the Hudson.

"A whole year," Billy said. "That's inhuman."

She laughed and bent and kissed the top of his head, but he pulled away. "Don't kiss me in public," he said.

A big dog came trotting toward them and she had to restrain herself from telling Billy not to pat him. "Old boy," Billy said, "old boy," and patted the dog's head and pulled his ears, at home in the animal kingdom. He thinks nothing living wishes him harm, Gretchen thought. Except his mother.

The dog wagged his tail, went on.

They were on their own street now, and safe. Gretchen allowed Billy to dawdle behind her, balancing on cracks in the pavement. As she came up to the front door of the brownstone in which she lived, she saw Rudolph and Johnny Heath standing in front of the building, leaning against the stoop. They each were holding a paper bag with a bottle in it. She had just put on a scarf over her head and an old coat and she hadn't bothered to change from the slacks she was wearing around the house when she had gone to fetch Billy. She felt dowdy as she approached Rudolph and Johnny, who were dressed like sober young businessmen and were even wearing hats.

She was used to seeing Rudolph in New York often. For the past six months or so, he had come to the city two or three times a week, in his young businessman's suits. There was some sort of deal being arranged, with Calderwood and Johnny Heath's brokerage house, although when she asked Rudolph about it, and he tried to explain, she never could quite grasp the details. It had something to do with setting up an involved corporation called Dee Cee Enterprises, after Duncan Calderwood's initials. Eventually, it was supposed to make Rudolph a wealthy man and get him out of the store, and for half the year, at least, out of Whitby. He had asked her to be on the lookout for a small furnished apartment for him.

Both Rudolph and Johnny looked somehow high, as though they had already done some drinking. She could see by the gilt paper sticking out of the brown paper bags that the bottles they were carrying contained champagne. "Hi boys," she said. "Why didn't you let me know you were coming?"

"We didn't know we were coming," Rudolph said. "This is an impromptu celebration." He kissed her cheek. He had not been drinking.

"Hi, Billy," he said to the little boy.

"Hi," Billy said perfunctorily. The relationship between uncle and nephew was tenuous. Billy called his uncle Rudy. From time to time Gretchen tried to get the boy to be more polite and say Uncle Rudolph, but Willie backed up his son, saying, "Old forms, old forms. Don't bring up the kid to be a hypocrite."

"Come on upstairs," Gretchen said, "and we'll open these bottles."

The living room was a mess. She worked there now, having surrendered the upstairs room completely to Billy, and there were bits and pieces of two articles she had promised for the first of the month. Books, notes, and scraps of paper were scattered all over the desk and tables. Not even the sofa was immune. She was not a methodical worker, and her occasional attempts at order soon foundered into even greater chaos than before. She had taken to chain-smoking when she worked and ash trays full of stubs were everywhere. Willie, who was far from neat himself, complained from time to time. "This isn't a home," he said, "it's the goddamn city room of a small-time newspaper."

She noticed Rudolph's quick glance of disapproval around the room. Was he judging her now against the fastidious girl she had been at nineteen? She had an unreasonable flash of anger against her impeccable, well-pressed brother. I'm running a family, I'm earning a living, don't forget any of that, brother.

"Billy," she said, as she hung up her coat and scarf, with elaborate precision, to make up for the state of the room, "go upstairs and do your homework."

"Aah . . . " Billy said, more for form's sake than out of any desire to remain below with the gronwups.

"Go ahead, Billy."

He went upstairs happily, pretending to be unhappy.

Gretchen got out three glasses. "What's the occasion?" she asked Rudolph, who was working on opening the bottle of champange.

"We did it," Rudolph said. "Today we had the final signing. We can drink champagne morning, noon, and night for the rest of our lives." He got the cork out and let the foam splash over his hand as he poured.

"That's wonderful," Gretchen said mechanically. It was difficult for her to understand Rudolph's single-minded immersion in business.

They touched glasses.

"To Dee Cee Enterprises and the Chairman of the Board," Johnny said. "The Newest Tycoon of them all."

Both men laughed, nerves still taut. They gave Gretchen the curious impression of being survivors of an accident, almost hysterically congratulating themselve on their escape. What goes on in those offices downtown, Gretchen wondered.

Rudolph couldn't sit still. He prowled around the room, glass in hand, opening books, glancing at the confusion of her desk, ruffling the pages of a newspaper. He looked trained down and nervy, with very bright eyes and hollows showing in his cheeks.

By contrast, Johnny looked chubby, soft, smooth, unedged, and now that he had a glass in his hand, composed, almost sleepy. He was more familiar with money and its uses than Rudolph and was prepared for sudden strokes of fortune and misfortune.

Rudolph turned on the radio and the middle of the first movement of the *Emperor* Concerto blared out. Rudolph grinned. "They're playing Our Song," he said to Johnny. "Music to million by."

"Cut it out," Gretchen said. "You fellows are making me feel like a pauper."

"If Willie has any sense," Johnny said, "he'll beg, borrow, or steal to scrape up some dough and come in on the ground floor of Dee Cee Enterprises. I mean it. There's no limit to how high this stuff can go."

"Willie," Gretchen said, "is too proud to beg, too well known to borrow, and too cowardly to steal."

"You're talking about my friend," Johnny said, pretending to be shocked.

"He was once a friend of mine, too," Gretchen said.

"Have some more champagne," Johnny said, and poured.

Rudolph picked up a sheet of paper from her desk.

"'The Age of Midgets,'" he read. "What sort of title is that?"

"It started out to be an article about the new television programs this season," Gretchen said, "and somehow I branched out. Last year's plays, this year's plays, a bunch of novels, Eisenhower's cabinet, architecture, public morality, education . . . I'm aghast at how Billy's being educated and maybe that really started me off."

Rudolph read the first paragraph. "You're pretty rough," he said.

"I'm paid to be a common scold," Gretchen said. "That's my racket."

"Do you really feel as black as you sound?" Rudolph asked.

"Yes," she said. She held out her glass toward Johnny.

The telephone rang. "Probably Willie saying he can't come home for dinner," Gretchen said. She got up and went to the telephone on the desk. "Hello," she said, her voice aggrieved in advance. She listened, puzzled. "One moment, please," she said, and handed the phone to Rudolph. "It's for you," she said.

"Me?" Rudolph shrugged. "Nobody knows I'm here."

"The man said Mr. Jordache."

"Yes?" Rudolph said into the phone.

"Jordache?" The voice was husky, secretive.

"Yes."

"This is Al. I put down five hundred for you for tonight. A good price. Seven to Five."

"Wait a minute," Rudolph said, but the phone went dead. Rudolph stared at the instrument in his hand. "That was the queerest thing. It was a man called Al. He said he put down five hundred for me for tonight at seven to five. Gretchen, do you gamble secretly?"

"I don't know any Al," she said, "and I don't have five hundred dollars and besides, he asked for Mr. Jordache, not Miss Jordache." She wrote under her maiden name and was listed as G. Jordache in the Manhattan directory.

"That's the damnedest thing," Rudolph said. "Did I tell anyone I'd be at this number?" he asked Johnny.

"Not to my knowledge," Johnny said.

"He must have gotten the numbers mixed up," Gretchen said.

"That doesn't sound reasonable," Rudolph said. "How many Jordaches can there be in New York? Did you ever come across any others?"

Gretchen shook her head.

"Where's the Manhattan book?"

Gretchen pointed and Rudolph picked it up and opened it to the J's. "T. Jordache," he read, "West Ninety-third Street." He closed the book slowly and put it down. "T. Jordache," he said to Gretchen. "Do you think it's possible?"

"I hope not," Gretchen said.

"What's all this about?" Johnny asked.

"We have a brother named Thomas," Rudolph said.

"The baby of the family," Grechen said. "Some baby."

"We haven't seen him or heard of him in ten years," Rudolph said.

"The Jordaches are an extraordinarily close-knit family," Gretchen said. After the work of the day, the champagne was beginning to take effect, and she lolled back on the couch. She remembered that she hadn't eaten any lunch.

"What does he do?" Johnny said. "Your brother?"

"I haven't the faintest idea," Rudolph said.

"If he's living up to his early promise," Gretchen said, "he is dodging the police."

"I'm going to find out." Rudolph opened the book again and looked up the number of T. Jordache on West Ninety-third Street. He dialed. The phone was answered by a woman, young from the sound of her voice.

"Good evening, madam," Rudolph said, impersonal, institutional. "May I speak to Mr. Thomas Jordache, please?"

"No, you can't," the woman said. She had a high, thin soprano voice. "Who's this?" Now she sounded suspicious.

"A friend of his," Rudolph said. "Is Mr. Jordache there?"

"He's sleeping," the woman said angrily. "He's got to fight tonight. He hasn't got time to talk to anybody."

There was the sound of the receiver slamming down.

Rudolph had been holding the receiver away from his ear and the woman had talked loudly, so both Gretchen and Johnny had heard every word of the conversation.

"Fighting tonight on the old camp grounds," Gretchen said. "Sounds like our Tommy."

Rudolph picked up the copy of the New York *Times* that was lying on a char beside the desk and turned to the sports section. "Here it is," he said. "Main bout. Tommy Jordache versus Virgil Walters, middleweights, ten rounds. At the Sunnyside Gardens."

"It sounds bucolic," Gretchen said.

"I'm going," Rudolph said.

"Why?" Gretchen asked.

"He's my brother, after all."

"I've gotten along for ten years without him," Gretchen said. "I'm going to try for twenty."

"Johnny?" Rudolph turned to Heath.

"Sorry," Johnny said. "I'm invited to a dinner. Tell me how it works out."

The telephone rang again. Rudolph picked it up eagerly, but it was only Willie. "Hi, Rudy," Willie said. There were barroom noises behind him. "No, I don't have to speak to her," Willie said. "Just tell her I'm sorry, but I've got a business dinner tonight and I can't make it home until late. Tell her not to wait up."

Gretchen smiled, lying on the couch. "Don't tell me what he said."

"He's not coming home to dinner."

"And I'm not to wait up."

"Something along those lines."

"Johnny," Gretchen said, "don't you think it's time to open the second bottle?"

By the time they had finished the second bottle, Gretchen had called for a baby sitter and they had found out where Sunnyside Gardens was. She went in and took a shower, did her hair, and put on a dark-wool dress, wondering if it was *comme il faut* for prizefights. She had grown thinner and the dress was a little loose on her, but she caught the quick glances of approval of the two men at her appearance and was gratified by it. I must not let myself fall into slobhood, she thought. Ever.

When the baby sitter came, Gretchen gave her instructions and left the apartment with Rudolph and Johnny. They went to a nearby steak house. Johnny had a drink with them at the bar and was saying, "Thanks for the drink," and was preparing to leave when Rudolph said, "I only have five dollars." He laughed. "Johnny, be my banker for tonight, will you?"

Johnny took out his wallet and put down five ten-dollar bills. "Enough?" he said.

"Thanks." Rudolph put the bills carelessly in his pocket. He laughed again.

"What's so funny?" Gretchen asked.

"I never though I'd like to see the day," Rudolph said. "when I didn't know exactly how much money I had in my pocket."

"You have taken on the wholesome and mind-freeing habits of the rich," Johnny said gravely. "Congratulations. I'll see you tomorrow at the office, Rudy. And I hope your brother wins."

"I hope he gets his head knocked off," Gretchen said.

A preliminary bout was under way as an usher led them to their seats three rows from ringside. Gretchen noted that there were few women present and that none of them was wearing a black-wool dress. She had never been to a prizefight before and she tuned out the television set whenever one was being shown. The idea of men beating each other senseless for pay seemed brutish to her and the faces of the men around her were just the sort of faces that one would expect at such an entertainment. She was sure she had never seen so many ugly people collected in one place.

The men in the ring did not appear to be doing much harm to each other and she watched with passive disgust as they clinched, wrestled, and ducked away from blows. The crowd, in its fog of tobacco smoke, was apathetic and only once in awhile, when there was the thud of a heavy punch, a sort of sharp, grunting, animal noise filled the arena.

Rudolph, she knew, went to prizefights from time to time and she had heard him discussing particular boxers like Ray Robinson enthusiastically with Willie. She looked surreptitiously over at her brother. He seemed interested by the spectacle in the ring. Now that she was actually seeing a fight, with the smell of sweat in her nostrils and the red blotches on pale skin where blows had landed, Rudolph's whole character, the subtle, deprecating air of educated superiority, the well-mannered lack of aggressiveness, seemed suddenly suspect to her. He was linked with the brutes in the ring, with the brutes in the rows around her.

In the next fight, one man was cut over the eye and the wound spurted blood all over him and his opponent. The roar of the crowd when they saw the blood sickened her and she wondered if she could sit there and wait for a brother to climb through the ropes to face similar butchery.

By the time the main bout came on, she was pale and sick and it was through a haze of tears and smoke that she saw a large man in a red bathrobe climb agilely through the ropes and recognized Thomas.

When Thomas's handlers took off his robe and threw it over his shoulders to put the gloves on over the bandaged hands, the first thing Rudolph noticed, with a touch of jealousy, was that Thomas had almost no hair on his body. Rudolph was getting quite hairy, with thick, tight, black curls on his chest and sprouting on his shoulders. His legs, too, were covered with dark hair, and it did not fit with the image he had of himself. When he went swimming in the summer, his hairiness embarrassed him and he felt that people were snickering at him. For that reason he rarely sunbathed and put on a shirt as soon as he got out of the water.

Thomas, except for the ferocious, muscular, overtrained body, looked surprisingly the same. His face was unmarked and the expression was still boyish and ingratiating. Thomas kept smiling during the formalities before the beginning of the bout, but Rudolph could see him flicking the corner of his mouth nervously with his tongue. A muscle in his leg twitched under his shiny silk, purple trunks while the referee was giving the final instructions to the two men in the center of the ring. Except for the moment when he had been introduced (*In this corner, Tommy Jordache, weight one fifty-nine and a half*), and had raised his gloved hand and looked quickly up at the crowd, Thomas had kept his eyes down. If he had seen Rudolph and Gretchen, he made no sign.

His opponent was a rangy Negro, considerably taller than Tommy, and with much longer arms, shuffling dangerously in his corner in a little dance, nodding as he listened to the advice being whispered into his ear by his handler.

Gretchen watched with a rigid, painful grimace on her face, squinting through the smoke at her brother's powerful, destructive, bare figure. She did not like the hairless male body—Willie was covered with a comfortable redish fuzz—and the ridged professional muscles made her shudder in primitive distaste. *Siblings, out of the same womb*. The thought dismayed her. Behind Thomas's boyish smile she recognized the sly malevolence, the desire to hurt, the pleasure in dealing pain, that had alienated her when they lived in the same house. The thought that it was her own flesh and blood exposed there under the bright lights in this dreadful ceremony was almost unbearable to her. Of course, she thought, I should have known; this is where he had to end. Fighting for his life.

The men were evenly matched, equally fast, the Negro less aggressive, but better able to defend himself with his long arms. Thomas kept burrowing in, taking two punches to get in one, slugging away at the Negro's body, making the Negro give ground and occasionally punishing him terribly when he got him in a corner against the ropes.
· "Kill the nigger," a voice from the back of the arena cried out each time Thomas threw a volley of punches. Gretchen winced, ashamed to be there, ashamed for every man and woman in the place. Oh, Arnold Simms, limping, in the maroon bathrobe,

saying, "You got pretty feet, Miss Jordache," dreaming of Cornwall, oh, Arnold Simms, forgive me for tonight.

It lasted eight of the ten rounds. Thomas was bleeding from the nose and from a cut above the eye, but never retreating, always shuffling in, with a kind of hideous, heedless, mechanical energy, slowly wearing his man down. In the eighth round, the Negro could hardly lift his hands and Thomas sent him to the canvas with a long, looping right hand that caught the Negro high on the forehead. The Negro got up at the count of eight, staggering, barely able to get his guard up, and Thomas, his face a bloody smear, but smiling, leapt after him mercilessly and hit him what seemed to Gretchen at least fifty times in the space of seconds. The Negro collapsed onto his face as the crowd yelled ear-splittingly around her. The Negro tried to get up, almost reached one knee. In a neutral corner, Thomas crouched alertly, bloody, tireless. He seemed to want his man to get up, to continue the fight, and Gretchen was sure there was a swift look of disappointment that flitted across his battered face as the Negro sank helplessly to the canvas and was counted out.

She wanted to vomit, but she merely retched drily, holding her handkerchief to her face, surprised at the smell of the perfume on it, among the rank odors of the arena. She sat huddled over in her seat, looking down, unable to watch any more, afraid she was going to faint and by that act announce to all the world her fatal connection to the victorious animal in the ring.

Rudolph had sat through the whole bout without uttering a sound, his lips twisted a little in disapproval at the clumsy bloodthirstiness, without style or grace, of the fight.

The fighters left the ring, the Negro, swathed in towels and robe, was helped through the ropes by his handlers, Thomas grinning, waving triumphantly, as people clapped him on the back. He left the ring on the far side, so that there was no chance of seeing his brother and sister as he made his way to the locker room.

The crowd began to drift out, but Gretchen and Rudolph sat side by side, without saying a word to each other, fearful of communicating after what they had seen. Finally Gretchen said, thickly, her eyes still lowered, "Let's get out of here."

"We have to go back," Rudolph said.

"What do you mean?" Gretchen looked up in surprise to her brother.

"We came," Rudolph said. "We watched. We have to see him."

"He's got nothing to do with us." As she said this, she knew she was lying.

"Come on." Rudolph stood up and took her elbow, making her stand. He met all challenges, Rudolph, the cold, veray parfit gentil knight at Sunnyside Gardens.

"I won't, I won't . . . " Even as she was babbling this, she knew, Rudolph would lead her inexorably to face Thomas, bloody, victorious, brutal, rancorous.

There were some men standing at the door of the dressing room, but nobody stopped Rudolph as he pushed the door open. Gretchen hung back. "I'd better wait outside," she said. "He may not be dressed."

Rudolph paid no attention to what she had said, but held her wrist and pulled her into the room after him. Thomas was sitting on a stained rubbing table with a towel around his middle and a doctor was sewing up the cut over his eye.

"It's nothing," the doctor was saying. "One more stitch and it's done."

Thomas had his eyes closed, to make it easier for the doctor to work. There was an orange stain of antiseptic above the eyebrow that gave him a clownish, lopsided air. He had obviously already taken his shower, as his hair was dark with water and plastered to his head, making him look like a print of an old-time bare-knuckle pugilist. Grouped around the table were several men, whom Rudolph recognized as having been in or near Thomas's corner during the fight. A curvy young woman in a tight dress kept making little sighing sounds each time the doctor's needle went into flesh. She had startling black hair and wore black nylon stockings over outlandishly shapely legs. Her eyebrows, plucked into a thin pencil line, high up, gave her a look of doll-like surprise. The room stank of old sweat, liniment, cigar smoke, and urine from the toilet visible through an open door leading off the dressing room. A bloodstained towel lay on the greasy floor, in a heap with the sweat-soaked purple tights and supporter and socks and shoes that Thomas had worn during the fight. It was sickeningly hot in the room.

What am I doing in a place like this, Gretchen thought. How did I get here?

"There we are," the doctor said, stepping back, his head cocked to one side, admiring his work. He put on a pad of gauze and a strip of adhesive tape over the wound. "You'll be able to fight again in ten days."

"Thanks, Doc," Thomas said and opened his eyes. He saw Rudolph and Gretchen. "Good Christ," he said. He smiled crookedly. "What the hell are you two doing here?"

"I have a message for you," Rudolph said. "A man called Al phoned me this afternoon and told me he'd put five hundred at seven to five for tonight."

"Good old Al," Thomas said. But he looked worriedly over at the curvy young woman with the black hair, as though he had wanted to keep this information from her.

"Congratulations on the fight," Rudolph said. He took a step forward and put out his hand. Thomas hesitated for a fraction of a second, then smiled again, and put out his swollen, reddened hand.

Gretchen couldn't get herself to congratulate her brother. "I'm glad you won, Tom," she said.

"Yeah. Thanks." He looked at her amusedly. "Let me introduce everybody to everybody," he said. "My brother, Rudolph; my sister, Gretchen. My wife, Teresa, my manager, Mr. Schultz, my trainer, Paddy, everybody . . . " He waved his hand vaguely at the men he hadn't bothered to introduce.

"Pleased to make your acquaintance," Teresa said. It was the suspicious voice of the telephone that afternoon.

"I didn't know you had family," Mr. Schultz said. He, too, seemed suspicious, as though having family was somehow perilous or actionable at law.

"I wasn't sure myself," Thomas said. "We have gone our separate ways, like they say. Hey, Schultzy, I must be getting to be one helluva draw at the gate if I even get my brother and sister to buy tickets."

"After tonight," Mr. Schultz said, "I can get you the Garden. It was a nice win." He was a small man with a basketball pouch under a greenish sweater. "Well, you people must have a lot to talk about, catch up with the news, as it were, we'll leave you alone. I'll drop in tomorrow sometime, Tommy, see how the eye's doing." He put on a jacket, just barely managing to button it over his paunch. The trainer gathered up the gear from the floor and put it into a bag. "Nice going, Tommy," he said, as he left with the doctor, the manager, and the others.

"Well, here we are," Thomas said. "A nice family reunion. I guess we ought to celebrate, huh, Teresa?"

"You never told me anything about a brother and sister," Teresa said aggrievedly, in her high voice.

"They slipped my mind for a few years," Thomas said. He jumped down off the rubbing table. "Now, if the ladies will retire, I'll put on some clothes."

Gretchen went out into the hall with her brother's wife. The hall was empty now and she was relieved to get away from the stink and heat of the dressing room. Teresa was putting on a shaggy red fox coat with angry little movements of her shoulders and arms. "If the ladies will retire," she said. "As though I never saw him naked before." She looked at Gretchen with open hostility, taking in the black-wool dress, the low-heeled shoes, the plain, belted polo coat, considering it, Gretchen could see, an affront of her style of living, her dyed hair, her tight dress, her over-voluptuous legs, her marriage. "I didn't know Tommy came from such a high-toned family," she said.

"We're not so high-toned," Gretchen said. "Never fear."

"You never bothered to see him fight before tonight," Teresa said aggressively, "did you?"

"I didn't know he was a fighter before today," said Gretchen. "Do you mind if I sit down? I'm feeling very tired." There was a chair across the hall and she moved away from the woman and sat down, hoping to put an end to conversation. Teresa ruffled her shoulders irritably under the red fox, then began to walk peckishly up and down, her high stiletto heels making a brittle, impatient sound on the concrete floor of the hallway.

Inside the dressing room Thomas was dressing slowly, turning away modestly when he put on his shorts, occasionally wiping at his face with a towel, because the shower had not completely broken the sweat. From time to time he looked across at Rudolph and smiled and shook his head and said, "Goddamn."

"How do you feel, Tommy?" Rudolph asked.

"Okay. But I'll piss blood tomorrow," Thomas said calmly. "He got in a couple of good licks to the kidney, the sonofabitch. It was a pretty good fight, though, wasn't it?"

"Yes," Rudolph said. He didn't have the heart to say that in his eyes it had been a routine, ungraceful, second rate brawl.

"I knew I could take him," Thomas said. "Even though I was the underdog in the betting. Seven to five. That's a hot one. I made seven hundred bucks on that bet." He sounded like a small boy boasting. "Though it's too bad you had to say anything about it in front of Teresa. Now she knows I have the dough and she'll be after it like a hound dog."

"How long have you been married?" Rudolph asked.

"Two years. Legally. I knocked her up and I thought what the hell." Thomas shrugged. "She's okay, Teresa, a little dumb, but okay. The kid's worth it, though. A boy." He glanced maliciously over at Rudolph. "Maybe I'll send him to his Uncle Rudy, to teach him how to be a gentleman and not grow up to be a poor stupid pug, like his old man."

"I'd like to see him some day," Rudolph said stiffly.

"Any time. Come up to the house." Thomas put on a black turtle-neck sweater and his voice was muffled for a moment as he stuck his head into the wool. "You married yet?"

"No."

"Still the smart one of the family," Thomas said. "How about Gretchen?"

"A long time. She's got a son aged nine."

Thomas nodded. "She was bound not to hang around long. God, what a hot-looking dame. She looks better than ever, doesn't she?"

"Yes."

"Is she still as much of a shit as she used to be?"

"Don't talk like that, Tom," Rudolph said. "She was an awfully nice girl and she's grown into a very good woman."

"I guess I'll have to take your word for it, Rudy," Thomas said cheerfully. He was combing his hair carefully before a cracked mirror on the wall. "I wouldn't know, being on the outside the way I was."

"You weren't on the outside."

"Who you kidding, brother?" Thomas said flatly. He put the comb in his pocket, took a last critical look at his scarred, puffed face, with the diagonal white slash of adhesive tape above his eye. "I sure am a beauty tonight," he said. "If I'd known you were coming, I'd've shaved." He turned and put a bright-tweed jacket over the turtle-neck sweater. "You look as though you're doing all right, Rudy," he said. "You look like a goddamn vice-president of a bank."

"I'm not complaining," Rudolph said, not pleased with the vice-president.

"You know," Thomas said, "I went up to Port Philip a few years ago. For Auld

Lang Syne. I heard Pop is dead."

"He killed himself," Rudolph said.

"Yeah, that's what the fruit-lady said." Thomas patted his breast pocket to make sure his wallet was in place. "The old house was gone. No light in the cellar window for the prodigal son," he said mockingly. "Only a supermarket. I still remember they had a special that day. Lamb shoulders. Mom alive?"

"Yes. She lives with me."

"Lucky you." Thomas grinned. "Still in Port Philip?"

"Whitby."

"You don't travel much, do you?"

"There's plenty of time." Rudolph had the uncomfortable feeling that his brother was using the conversation to tease him, undermine him, make him feel guilty. He was accustomed to controlling conversations himself by now and it took an effort not to let his irritation show. As he had watched his brother dress, watched him move that magnificent and fearsome body slowly and bruisedly, he had felt a huge sense of pity, love, a confused desire somehow to save that lumbering, brave, vengeful almost-boy from other evenings like the one he had just been through; from the impossible wife, from the bawling crowd, from the cheerful, stitching doctors, from the casual men who attended him and lived off him. He didn't want that feeling to be eroded by Thomas's mockery, by that hangover of ancient jealously and hostility which by now should have long since subsided.

"Myself," Thomas was saying. "I been in quite a few places. Chicago, Cleveland, Boston, New Orleans, Philadelphia, San Francisco, Hollywood, Tia Juana. Name it and I've been there. I'm a man broadened by travel."

The door burst open and Teresa charged in, scowling under her pancake makeup. "You fellows going to talk in here all night?" she demanded.

"Okay, okay, honey," Thomas said. "We were just coming out. Do you want to come and have something to eat with us, you and Gretchen?" he asked Rudolph.

"We're going to eat Chinese," Teresa said. "I'm dying to eat Chinese."

"I'm afraid not tonight, Tom," Rudolph said. "Gretchen has to get home. She has to relieve the baby sitter." He caught the quick flicker of Thomas's eyes from him to his wife and then back again and he was sure Thomas was thinking, he doesn't want to be seen in public with my wife.

But Thomas shrugged and said amiably, "Well, some other time. Now we know we're all alive." He stopped abruptly in the doorway, as though he had suddenly thought of something, "Say," he said, "you going to be in town tomorrow around five?"

"Tommy," his wife said loudly, "are we going to eat or ain't we going to eat?"

"Shut up," Thomas said to her. "Rudy?"

"Yes." He had to spend the whole day in town, with architects and lawyers.

"Where can I see you?" Thomas asked.

"I'll be at my hotel. The Hotel Warwick on . . . "

"I know where it is," Thomas said. "I'll be there."

Gretchen joined them in the hallway. Her face was strained and pale, and for a moment Rudolph was sorry he had brought her along. But only for a moment. She's a big girl now, he thought, she can't duck *everything*. It's enough that she has so gracefully managed to duck her mother for ten years.

As they passed the door to another dressing room, Thomas stopped again. "I just have to look in here for a minute," he said, "say hello to Virgil. Come on in with me, Rudy, tell him you're my brother, tell him what a good fight he put up, it'll make him feel better."

"We'll never get out of this goddamn place tonight," Teresa said.

Thomas ignored her and pushed open the door and motioned for Rudolph to go first. The Negro fighter was still undressed. He was sitting, droop-shouldered, on the rubbing table, his hands hanging listlessly between his legs. A pretty young colored girl, probably his wife or sister, was sitting quietly on a camp chair at the foot of the table and a white handler was gently applying an icebag to a huge swelling on the fighter's forehead. Under the swelling the eye was shut tight. In a corner of the room an older, light-colored Negro with gray hair, who might have been the fighter's father, was carefully packing away a silk robe and trunks and shoes. The fighter looked up slowly with his one good eye as Thomas and Rudolph came into the room.

Thomas put his arm gently around his opponent's shoulders. "How you feeling, Virgil?" he asked.

"I felt better," the fighter said. Now Rudolph could see that he couldn't have been more than twenty years old.

"Meet my brother, Rudy, Virgil," Thomas said. "He wants to tell you what a good fight you put up."

Rudolph shook hands with the fighter, who said, "Glad to meet you, sir."

"It was an awfully good fight," Rudolph said, although what he would have liked to say was, Poor young man, please never put on another pair of gloves again.

"Yeah," the fighter said. "He awful strong, your brother."

"I was lucky," Thomas said. "Real lucky. I got five stitches over my eye."

"It wasn't a butt, Tommy," Virgil said. "I swear it wasn't a butt."

"Of course not, Virgil," Thomas said. "Nobody said it was. Well, I just wanted to say hello, make sure you're all right." He hugged the boy's shoulders again.

"Thanks for comin' by," Virgil said. "It's nice of you."

"Good luck, kid," Thomas said. Then he and Rudolph shook hands gravely with all the other people in the room and left.

"It's about time," Teresa said as they appeared in the hall.

I give the marriage six months, Rudolph thought as they went toward the exit.

"They rushed that boy," Thomas said to Rudolph as they walked side by side. "He had a string of easy wins and they gave him a main bout. I watched him a couple of times and I knew I could take him downstairs. Lousy managers. You notice, the bastard wasn't even there. He didn't even wait to see if Virgil ought to go home or to the hospital. It's a shitty profession." He glanced back to see if Gretchen objected to the word, but Gretchen seemed to be moving in a private trance of her own, unseeing and unhearing.

Outside, they hailed a taxi and Gretchen insisted upon sitting up front with the driver. Teresa sat in the middle on the back seat, between Thomas and Rudolph. She was overpoweringly perfumed, but when Rudolph put the window down she said, "For God's sake, the wind is ruining my hair," and he said, "I'm sorry," and wound the window up again.

They drove back to Manhattan in silence, with Teresa holding Thomas's hand and occasionally bringing it up to her lips and kissing it, marking out her possessions.

When they came off the bridge, Rudolph said. "We'll get out here, Tom."

"You're sure you don't want to come with us?" Thomas said.

"It's the best Chinese food in town," Teresa said. The ride had been neutral, she no longer felt in danger of being attacked, she could afford to be hospitable, perhaps in the future there was an advantage there for her. "You don't know what you're missing."

"I have to get home," Gretchen said. Her voice was quivering, on the point of hysteria. "I just must get home."

If it hadn't been for Gretchen, Rudolph would have stayed with Thomas. After the noise of the evening, the public triumph, the battering, it seemed sad and lonely to leave Thomas merely to go off to supper with his twittering wife, anonymous in the night, unsaluted, uncheered. He would have to make it up to Thomas another time.

The driver stopped the car and Gretchen and Rudolph got out. "Good-bye for now, in-laws," Teresa said, and laughed.

"Five o'clock tomorrow, Rudy," Thomas said and Rudolph nodded.

"Good night," Gretchen whispered. "Take care of yourself, please."

The taxi moved off and Gretchen gripped Rudolph's arm, as though to steady herself. Rudolph stopped a cruising cab and gave the driver Gretchen's address. Once in the darkness of the cab, Gretchen broke down. She threw herself into Rudolph's arms and wept uncontrollably, her body racked by great sobs. The tears came to Rudolph's eyes, too, and he held his sister tightly, stroking her hair. In the back of the dark cab, with the lights of the city streaking past the windows, erratically illuminating, in bursts of colored neon, the contorted, lovely, tear-stained face, he felt closer to Gretchen, bound in stricter love, than ever before.

The tears finally stopped. Gretchen sat up, dabbed at her eyes with a handkerchief. "I'm sorry," she said. "I'm such a hateful snob. That poor boy, that poor, poor boy . . ."

The baby sitter was asleep on the couch in the living room when they came into the apartment. Willie hadn't come home yet. There had been no calls, the baby sitter said. Billy had read himself to sleep quietly and she had gone up and turned off his light without awakening him. She was a girl of about seventeen, a high-school student, bobby-soxed, pretty, in a snub-nosed, shy way, and embarrassed at being caught asleep. Gretchen poured two Scotches and soda. The baby sitter had straightened out the room and the newspapers, which had been strewn around, were now in a neat pile on the window sill and the cushions were plumped out.

There was only one lamp lit and they sat in shadow, Gretchen with her feet curled up under her on the couch, Rudolph in a large easy char. They drank slowly, exhausted, blessing the silence. They finished their drinks and silently Rudolph rose from his chair and refilled the glasses, sat down again.

An ambulance siren wailed in the distance, somebody else's accident.

"He *enjoyed* it," Gretchen said finally. "When that boy was practically helpless and he hit him so many times. I always thought—when I thought anything about it—that it was just a man earning a living—in a peculiar way—but just that. It wasn't like that at all tonight, was it?"

"It's a curious profession," Rudolph said. "It's hard to know what really must be going on in a man's head up there."

"Weren't you *ashamed?*"

"Put it this way," Rudolph said. "I wasn't happy. There must be at least ten thousand boxers in the United States. They have to come from *somebody's* family."

"I don't think like you," Gretchen said coldly.

"No, you don't."

"Those sleazy purple trunks," she said, as though by finding an object on which she could fix her revulsion, she could exorcise the complex horror of the entire night. She shook her head against memory. "Somehow I feel it's our fault, yours, mine, our parents', that Tom was up there in that vile place."

Rudolph sipped at his drink in silence. *I wouldn't know,* Tom had said in the dressing room, *being on the outside the way I was.* Excluded, he had reacted as a boy in the most simple, brutal way, with his fists. Older, he had merely continued. They all had their father's blood in them, and Axel Jordache had killed two men. As far as Rudolph knew, Tom at least hadn't killed anybody. Perhaps the strain was ameliorating.

"Ah, what a mess," Gretchen said. "All of us. Yes, you, too. Do you enjoy *anything,* Rudy?"

"I don't think of things in those terms," he said.

"The commercial monk," Gretchen said harshly. "Except that instead of the vow of poverty, you've taken the vow of wealth. Which is better in the long run?"

"Don't talk like a fool, Gretchen." Now he was sorry he had come upstairs with her.

"And the two others," she continued. "Chastity and obedience. Chaste for our

Virgin Mother's sake—is that it? Obedience to Duncan Calderwood, the Pope of Whitby's Chamber of Commerce?"

"That's all going to change now," Rudolph said, but he was unwilling to defend himself further.

"You're going to go over the wall, Father Rudolph? You're going to marry, you're going to wallow in the fleshpots, you're going to tell Duncan Calderwood to go fuck himself?"

Rudolph stood up and went over and poured some more soda into his glass, biting back his anger. "It's silly, Gretchen," he said, as calmly as possible, "to take tonight out on me."

"I'm sorry," she said, but her voice was still hard. "Ah—I'm the worst of the lot. I live with a man I despise, I do work that's mean-spirited and piddling and useless, I'm New York's easiest lay . . . Do I shock you, brother?" she said mockingly.

"I think you're giving yourself a title you haven't earned," Rudolph said.

"Joke," Gretchen said. "Do you want a list? Beginning with Johnny Heath? Do you think he's been so good to you because of your shining bright eyes?"

"What does Willie think about all this?" Rudolph asked, ignoring the jibe. No matter how it had started and for whatever reasons, Johnny Heath was now his friend.

"Willie doesn't think about anything but infesting bars and occasionally screwing some drunken broad and getting by in this world with as little work and as little honor as possible. If he somehow was given the original stone tablets of the Ten Commandments, his first thought would be which sponsor he could sell it to at the highest price to advertise vacation tours to Mount Sinai."

Rudolph laughed and despite herself Gretchen had to laugh, too. "There's nothing like a failing marriage," she said, "to bring out flights of rhetoric."

Rudolph's laughter was part relief. Gretchen had switched targets and he no longer was under attack.

"Does Willie know what your opinion is of him?" he asked.

"Yes," Gretchen said. "He agrees with it. That's the worst thing about him. He says there's not a man or a woman or a *thing* in this world that he admires, especially himself. He'd be deeply dissatisfied with himself, he told me, if he was anything but a failure. Beware romantic men."

"Why do you live with him?" Rudolph asked bluntly.

"Do you remember the note I sent you saying I was in a mess and I wanted to see you?"

"Yes." Rudolph remembered it very well, remembered that whole day very well. When he had come down to New York the next week and asked Gretchen what the trouble was she had said, "Nothing. It's blown over."

"I'd more or less decided I wanted to ask Willie for a divorce," Gretchen said, "and I wanted your advice."

"What changed your mind?"

Gretchen shrugged. "Billy got sick. Nothing. For a day the doctor thought it was appendicitis, but it wasn't. But Willie and I stayed up with him all night and as I looked at him lying all white faced and in pain on the bed and Willie hovering over him, so obviously loving him, I couldn't bear the thought of making him another one of those poor forlorn statistics—child of a broken marriage, permanently homesick, preparing for the psychiatrist's couch. Well . . . " her voice hardened, "that charming fit of maternal sentimentality has passed on. If our parents had divorced when I was nine, I'd be a better woman that I am today."

"You mean you want a divorce now?"

"If I get custody of Billy," she said. "And that's one thing he won't give me."

Rudolph hesitated, took a long drink of his whiskey. "Do you want me to see what I can do with him?" He would't have offered to interfere if it hadn't been for the tears in the taxicab.

"If it'll do any good," Gretchen said. "I want to sleep with one man, not ten, I want to be honest, do something useful, finally. God, I sound like *The Three Sisters*. Divorce is my Moscow. Give me one more drink, please." She held out her glass.

Rudolph went over to the bar and filled both their glasses. "You're running low on Scotch," he said.

"I wish that were true," she said.

There was the sound of an ambulance siren again, wailing, diminishing, a warning as it approached, a lament as it departed. The Doppler phenomenon. Was it the same accident, completing the round trip? Or one of an endless series, limitless blood on the avenues of the city?

Rudolph handed her her drink and she sat curled up on the couch, staring at it. A clock chimed somewhere. One o'clock.

"Well," Gretchen said, "I guess they're finished eating Chinese by now, Tommy and that lady. Is it possible that he has the only happy marriage in the history of the Jordaches? Do they love, honor and cherish each other as they eat Chinese and warm the bosomy marriage bed?"

There was the sound of a key in the front door lock. "Ah," Gretchen said, "the veteran is returning home, wearing his medals."

Willie came into the room, walking straight. "Hi, darling," he said, and went over and kissed Gretchen's cheek. As always, when he hadn't seen Willie for some time, Rudolph was surprised at how short he was. Perhaps that was his real flaw—his size. He waved at Rudolph. "How's the merchant prince tonight?" he said.

"Congratulate him," Gretchen said. "He signed that deal today."

"Congratulations," Willie said. He squinted around the room. "God, it's dark in here. What've you two been talking about—death, tombs, foul deeds done by night?" He went over to the bar and poured the last of the whiskey. "Darling," he said, "we need a fresh bottle."

Automatically, Gretchen stood up and went into the kitchen.

Willie looked after her anxiously. "Rudy," he whispered, "is she sore at me for not coming home to dinner?"

"No, I don't think so."

"I'm glad you're here," Willie said. "Otherwise, I'd be getting Lecture Number 725. Thanks, darling," he said as Gretchen came into the room carrying a bottle. He took the bottle from her, opened it, and strengthened his drink. "What'd you kids do tonight?" he asked.

"We had a faimly reunion," Gretchen said, from her place on the couch. "We went to a prize fight."

"What?" Willie said puzzledly. "What is she talking about, Rudy?"

"She can tell you about it later." Rudolph stood up, leaving most of his last whiskey undrunk. "I've got to be moving along. I have to get up at the crack of dawn." He felt uncomfortable sitting there with Willie, pretending that this night was no different from others, pretending he had not heard what Gretchen had said about him and about herself. He bent over and kissed Gretchen and Willie accompanied him to the door.

"Thanks for coming by and keeping the old girl company," Willie said. "It makes me feel like less of a shit, leaving her alone. But it was unavoidable."

It wasn't a butt, Tommy, Rudolph remembered. *I swear it wasn't a butt.* "You don't have to make any excuses to me, Willie," he said.

"Say," Willie said, "she was joking, wasn't she? That stuff about the prize fight? What is it—a kind of riddle, or something?"

"No. We went to a fight."

"I'll never understand that woman," Willie said. "When I want to watch a fight on television, I have to go to somebody else's house. Ah, well, I suppose she'll tell me about it." He pressed Rudolph's hand warmly and Rudolph went out the door. He heard Willie locking it securely behind him and fixing the anti-burglar chain. The danger is inside, Willie, Rudolph wanted to say. You are locking it in with you. He went down the stairs slowly. He wondered where he would be tonight, what evasions he would be offering, what cuckoldry and dissatisfaction would have been in the air, if that night in 1950, room 923 in the St. Moritz Hotel had answered?

If I were a religious man, he thought, going out into the night, I would believe that God was watching over me.

He remembered his promise to try to do what he could to get Gretchen a divorce, on her terms. There was the logical first step to be taken and he was a logical man. He wondered where he could find a reliable private detective. Johnny Heath would know. Johnny Heath was made for New York City. Rudolph sighed, hating the moment ahead of him when he would enter the detective's office, hating the detective himself, still unknown to him, preparing, all in the week's work, to spy on the breakdown and end of love.

Rudolph turned and took a last look at the building he had just left and against which he was sworn to conspire. He knew he'd never be able to mount those steps again, shake that small, desperate man's hand again. Duplicity, too, must have its limits.

CHAPTER 6

I

HE HAD PISSED blood in the morning, but not very much and he wasn't hurting. The reflection of his face in the train window when they went through a tunnel was a little sinister, because of the slash of bandage over his eye, but otherwise, he told himself, he looked like anybody else cn the way to the bank. The Hudson was cold blue in the October sun and as the train passed Sing Sing he thought of the prisoners peering out at the broad river running free to the sea, and he said, "Poor bastards," aloud.

He patted the bulge of his wallet under his jacket. He had collected the seven hundred dollars from the bookie on the way downtown. Maybe he could get away with giving Teresa just two hundred of it, two fifty if she made a stink.

He pulled the wallet out. He had been paid off in hundreds. He took out a bill and studied it. Founding father, Benjamin Franklin, stared out at him, looking like somebody's old mother. Lightning on a kite, he remembered dimly; at night all cats are gray. He must have been a tougher man than he looked to get his picture on a bill that size. Did he once say, Gentlemen we must hang together or we will hang separately? I should have at least finished high school, Thomas thought, vague in the presence of one hundred dollars' worth of history. *This note is legal tender for all debts, public and private and is redeemable in lawful money at the United States Treasury or at any Federal Reserve Bank.* If this wasn't lawful money, what the hell was? It was signed in fancy script by somebody called Ivy Baker Priest, Treasurer of the United States. It took a someone with a name like that to give out with double talk about debts and money and get away with it.

Thomas folded the bill neatly and slipped it by itself in a side pocket, to be put with the other hundred-dollar bills, reposing in the dark vault for just such a day as this.

The man on the seat in front of him was reading a newspaper, turned to the sports page. Thomas could see that he was reading about last night's fight. He wondered what the man would say if he tapped him on the shoulder and said, "Mister, I was there, how would you like an account of the battle right from the middle of the ring?" Actually, the reports of the fight in the papers had been pretty good and there had been a picture on the back page of the *News* of Virgil trying to get up the last time and himself in a neutral corner. One newspaperman had even said the fight had raised him into the ranks of the contenders for the title and Schultzy had called him all excited, right before he left the house, to say that a promoter over from England had seen the fight and was offering them a bout in London in six weeks. "We're going international," Schultzy had said excitedly. "We can fight all over the Continent. And you'll knock 'em dead. They ain't got anybody half as good even as Virgil Walters in England at your weight. And the guy said he'd give us some of the purse under the table and we won't have to declare it to the goddamn income tax."

So, all in all, he should have been feeling pretty good, sitting there in the train, with the prison falling away behind him, full of a lot of guys who probably were a damn sight smarter than he was and maybe less guilty of one thing and another, too. But he wasn't feeling good. Teresa had given him a load of grief about not telling her about the bet and about his la-di-da family, as she called them. She was sore because he'd never said anything about them, as though he was hiding some fucking treasure or something.

"That sister of yours looked at me like I was dirt," Teresa had said. "And your fancy brother opened the window as though I smelled like horseshit and he pulled away to his side of the cab like if he happened to touch me for a second he'd catch the clap. And after not seeing their brother for ten years they were just too fine even to come and have a cup of coffee with him, for God's sake. And you, the big fighter, you never said a word, you just took it all."

This had been in bed, after the restaurant, where she had eaten in sullen silence. He had wanted to make love to her, as he always did after a fight, because he didn't touch her for weeks before a fight and his thing was so hard you could knock out fungoes to the outfield with it, but she had closed down like a stone and wouldn't let him near her. For Christ's sake, he thought, I didn't marry her for her conversation. And it wasn't as though even in her best moments Teresa was so marvelous in bed. If you mussed her hair while you were going at it hammer and tongs, she'd complain bloody murder, and she was always finding excuses to put it off till tomorrow or next week or next year and when she finally opened her legs it was like a tollgate being fed a counterfeit coin. She came from a religious family, she said, as though the Angel Michael with his sword was standing guard over all Catholic cunts. He'd bet his next purse his sister Gretchen, with her straight hair and her no make-up and her black dress and that ladylike don't-you-dare-touch-the-hem-of-my-garment look would give a man a better time in one bang than Teresa in twenty ten-minute rounds.

So he'd slept badly, his wife's words ringing in his ears. The worst of it was that what she said was true. Here he was a big grown man, and all his brother and sister had to do was come into the room and he felt just the way they had made him feel when he was a kid—slimy, stupid, useless, suspect.

Go win fights, have your picture in the papers, piss blood, go have people cheer you and clap you on the back and ask you to appear in London; two snots you thought you'd never see or hear from again show up and say hello, just hello, and everything you are is nothing. Well, his goddamn brother, momma's pet, poppa's pet, blowing his golden horn, opening taxi windows, was going to be in for a shock from his nothing pug brother today.

For a crazy moment he though maybe he wouldn't get off the train, he'd go on to Albany and make the change and arrive in Elysium, Ohio, and go to the one person in the whole world who had touched him with love, who had made him feel like a whole man, when he was just a kid of sixteen. Clothilde, servant to his uncle's bed. St. Sebastian, in the bathtub.

But when the train pulled into Port Philip, he got off and went to the bank, just as he had planned.

II

She tried not to show her impatience as Billy played with his lunch. Superstitiously (children sensed things that transcended the years) she had not dressed yet for the afternoon ahead of her, but was sitting with him in her work clothes, slacks and a sweater. She picked at her food, without appetite, trying not to scold the boy as he pushed bits of lamb chop and lettuce around his plate.

"Why do I have to go to the Museum of Natural History?" Billy demanded.

"It's a treat," she said, "a special treat."

"Not for me. Why do I have to go?"

"The whole class is going."

"They're dopes. Except for Conrad Franklin they're all dopes." Billy had had the same morsel of lamb chop in his mouth for what seemed like five minutes. Occasionally, he would move it symbolically from one side of his mouth to the other. Gretchen wondered if, finally, she should hit him. The clock in the kitchen suddenly ticked louder and louder and she tried not to look at it, but couldn't resist. Twenty to one. She was due uptown at a quarter to two. And she had to take Billy to school, hurry back, bathe and dress, carefully, carefully, and then make sure not to arrive panting as though she had just run a marathon.

"Finish your lunch," Gretchen said, marveling at the motherly calmness of her voice, on this afternoon when she felt anything but motherly. "There's Jello for dessert."

"I don't like Jello."

"Since when?"

"Since today. And what's the sense in going to see a lot of old stuffed animals? At least if they want us to look at animals we could go see some live ones."

"On Sunday," Gretchen said, "I'll take you to the zoo."

"I told Conrad Franklin I'd go over to his house on Sunday," Billy said. He reached into his mouth and took out the piece of lamb chop and put it on his plate.

"That's not a polite thing to do," Gretchen said, as the clock ticked.

"It's tough."

"All right," Gretchen said, reaching for his plate. "If you're through, you're through."

Billy held onto the plate. "I haven't finished my salad." Deliberately, he cut a lettuce leaf into geometric forms with his fork.

He is asserting his personality, Gretchen made herself think, to keep from hitting him. It bodes well for his future.

Unable to bear watching his measured game with the lettuce, she got up and took a cup of Jello out of the refrigerator.

"Why're you so nervous today?" Billy asked. "Jumping around."

Children and their goddamn intuition, Gretchen thought. Not in utter nakedness, but trailing clouds of radar do we come. She put the Jello down on the table. "Eat your dessert," she said, "it's getting late."

Billy folded his arms and leaned back. "I told you I don't like Jello."

She was tempted to say that he'd eat his Jello or he'd sit there all day. Then she had the dark suspicion that that was exactly what Billy wanted her to say. Was it possible that in that mysterious pool of emotion, love, hate, sensuality, greed, that lay within a child, somehow he knew what her errand uptown was going to be and that in his own instinctive way he was defending himself, defending his father, guarding the unity of the home in which he felt himself, with casual childish arrogance, the center?

"Okay," she said. "No Jello. Let's go."

Billy was a good winner. No smile of triumph lit his face. Instead, he said, "Why do I have to go see a lot of old dead stuffed animals?"

She was hot and panting as she unlocked the door. She had practically run all the way from the school gates, after depositing Billy. The phone was ringing, but she let it ring as she hurried into the bathroom, stripping off her clothes. She took a warm shower, looked briefly and critically at her body in the long mirror as she stood there, glistening wetly, before she toweled herself off. I could have gone either way, she thought, plump or thin. Thank God I went thin. But not too. My body, the luring, damp house of my soul. She laughed and went naked into the bedroom and took out the diaphragm which she kept hidden under a pile of scarves. *Oh, well-used device.* She put it in carefully, sinning. One day they have to invent something better than a piece of machinery.

As she touched herself, she remembered the curious flush of desire that had come over her the night before when she had finally gone to bed. The images of the fighters, white and black, that had sickened her while she was in the arena, suddenly became the inspirers of desire, the magnificent, harsh bodies tumbled around her. Sex for a woman was in a demonstrable way an intrusion, a profound invasion of privacy, as was a blow given by one man to another. In the uneasy, early-morning bed, after the disturbing night, the lines crossed, blows became caresses, caresses blows, and she turned, aroused, under the covers. If Willie had come into her bed she would have welcomed him ardently. But Willie was sleeping, on his back, snoring softly from time to time.

She had gotten up and taken a pill to sleep.

During the morning, she had put it all from her mind, the shame of the night covered with the innocent mask of daylight.

She shook her head, opened a drawer full of panties and brassieres.. When she thought about it, "panties" seemed a hypocritically innocuous word, falsely childish, to cover such desperate territory. Girdle was a better word, though it was from more melodious periods of language, and she didn't wear girdles. Boylan's teaching.

The phone rang again, persistently, but she ignored it as she dressed. She stared for a moment at the clothes hanging in the closet, then chose a simple, severe blue suit. *No advertising the mission.* The emergent rosy body better appreciated later for having been concealed before. She brushed her dark hair, straight and long to her shoulders, the broad, low forehead clear, serene, unwrinkled, concealing all betrayals, all doubts.

She couldn't find a taxi so she took the Eighth Avenue subway uptown, remembering to get on the Queens train that crossed over to the East Side on Fifty-third Street. Persephone, coming from the underground in the flowertime of love.

She got out at the Fifth Avenue exit and walked in the windy autumn sunshine, her demure navy-blue figure reflected in the glitter of shop windows. She wondered how many of the other women she passed were, like her, briefly parading the avenue, drifting cunningly through Saks, diaphragms in place.

She turned east on Fifty-fifth Street, past the entrance of the St. Regis, remembered a wedding party on a summer evening, a white veil, a young lieutenant. There were only a certain number of streets in the city. One could not avoid them all. The echoes of urban geography.

She looked at her watch. Twenty to two. Five full minutes, in which to walk slowly, to arrive cool, controlled.

Colin Burke lived on Fifty-sixth between Madison and Park. Another echo. On that street there had once been a party from which she had turned away. When renting an apartment, a man could not be blamed for not picking through his future lover's memories before putting down the first month's rent.

She went into the familiar white vestibule, rang the bell. How many times, on how many afternoons, had she rung that bell? Twenty? Thirty? Sixty? Some day she would make the count.

The buzzer hummed at the doorlatch and she went in and took the small elevator up to the fourth floor.

He was standing at the door, in pajamas and a robe, his feet bare. They kissed briefly, no rush, no rush.

There were breakfast things on the coffee table in the big, disordered living room, and a half-finished cup of coffee, among piles of leatherette-bound scripts. He was a director in the theater and he kept theatrical hours, rarely going to bed before five in the morning.

"Can I give you a cup of coffee?" he asked.

"No, thanks," she said. "I've just had lunch."

"Ah, the orderly life," he said. "So to be envied." The irony was gentle.

"Tomorrow," she said, "you can come down and feed Billy a lamb chop. Envy me later."

Burke had never seen Billy, had never met her husband, or been to their home. She had met him at a luncheon with one of the editors of a magazine for which she did occasional pieces. The idea was that she was to do an article on him, because she had praised a play he had directed. At the luncheon she hadn't liked him, had thought him cocky, theory ridden, too confident of himself. She hadn't written the article, but three months later, after several scattered meetings, she had gone to bed with him, out of lust, revenge, boredom, hysteria, indifference, accident . . . She no longer probed her reasons.

He sipped at his coffee, standing up, watching her over the cup, his dark-gray eyes tender under thunderous black eyebrows. He was thirty-five years old, a short man, shorter than she (*Am I doomed all my life to small men?*) but there was a thin intensity about his face, dark-stubbled with beard now, a strained intellectual rigor, an impression of directness and strength, that made one forget his size. In his profession he was used to ordering complex and difficult people about and the look of command was on him. He was moody and sometimes sharply spoken, even to her, tortured by failures in excellence in himself and others, easily scornful, given sometimes to disappearing without a word for weeks at a time. He was divorced and was reputed to be a ladies' man and in the beginning, last year, she felt that he was using her for the simplest and most obvious of reasons, but now, standing across the room from him, watching the slim, barefooted, small man in the soft, navy-blue bathrobe (happy matching of afternoon colors) she was sure she loved him and that she wanted none else but him and would make great sacrifices to remain at his side for her entire life.

She was talking about Burke when she had said last night to her brother that she wanted to sleep with one man, not ten. And in fact, since the beginning of their affair she had made love with no one else but him, except for the infrequent times when Willie had come to her bed, in nostalgic moments of tenderness; unhappy, fleeting reconciliations; the almost forgotten habits of marriage.

Burke had asked if she still slept with her husband and she had told him the truth. She had also confessed that it gave her pleasure. She had no need to lie to him and he was the one man she had ever known to whom she could say anything that came to her mind. He had told her that since their first meeting he had not slept with another woman and she was sure that this was so.

"Beautiful Gretchen," he said, taking the cup from his lips, "bounteous Gretchen, glorious G. Oh, to have you come in every morning with the breakfast tray."

"My," she said, "you're in a good mood today."

"Not really," he said. He put down the cup and came over and they slipped their arms around each other. "I have a disastrous afternoon ahead of me. My agent called me an hour ago and I have to go to the Columbia office at two-thirty. They want me to go out West and do a movie. I called you a couple of times, but there was no answer."

The phone had rung as she had entered the apartment, again as she had dressed. Love me tomorrow, not today, courtesy of American Tel and Tel. But tomorrow, there was no trip to the museum for Billy's class, freeing her until five o'clock. She would have to be at the school gate at three. Passion by children's hours.

"I heard the phone ring," she said, moving away from him, "but I didn't answer it." Abstractedly, she lit a cigarette. "I thought you had a play to do this year," she said.

"Throw away that cigarette," Burke said. "Whenever a bad director wants to show unspoken tension between two characters, he has them lighting a cigarette."

She laughed, stubbing it out.

"The play isn't ready," Burke said, "and the way the rewrite's going it won't be ready for another year. And everything else that I've been offered is junk. Don't look so sad."

"I'm not sad," she said. "I'm horny and unlaid and disappointed."

It was his turn to laugh. "The vocabulary of Gretchen," he said. "Always to be trusted. Can't you make it this evening?"

"Evenings're out. You know that. That would be flaunting it. And I'm not a flaunter." There was no telling with Willie. He might come home for dinner, whistling cheerfully, two weeks in a row. "Is it a good picture?"

"It can be." He shrugged, rubbing the blue-black stubble of his beard. "The whore's cry," he said. "It can be. Frankly, I need the money."

"You had a hit last year," she said, knowing she shouldn't push him, but pushing him nevertheless.

"Between Uncle Sam and the alimony, my bank is howling." He grimaced. "Lincoln freed the slaves in 1863, but he overlooked the married men."

Love, like almost everything else these days, was a function of the Internal Revenue Service. We embrace between tax forms. "I ought to introduce you," she said, "to Johnny Heath and my brother. They swim like fish among the deductions."

"Businessmen," he said. "They know the magic. When my tax man sees my records he puts his head in his hands and weeps. No use crying over spilt money. On to Hollywood. Actually, I look forward to it. There's no reason these days why a director shouldn't do movies as well as plays. That old idea that there's something holy about the theater and eternally grubby about film is just snobbism and it's as dead as David Belasco. If you asked me who was the greatest dramatic artist alive today I'd say Federico Fellini. And there hasn't been anything better on the stage in my time than *Citizen Kane* and that was pure Hollywood. Who knows—I may be the Orson Welles of the fifties."

Burke was walking back and forth as he spoke and Gretchen could tell that he meant what he was saying, or at least most of it, and was eager to take up the new challenge in his career. "Sure, there're whores in Hollywood, but nobody would seriously claim that Shubert Alley is a cloister. It's true I need money and I'm not averse to the sight of the dollar, but I'm not hunting it. Yet. And I hope never. I've been negotiating with Columbia for more than a month now and they're giving me an absolute free hand—the story I want, the writer I want, no supervision, the whole thing shot on location, final cut, everything, as long as I stay within the budget. And the budget's a fair one. If it's not as good as anything I've done on Broadway, the fault'll be mine and nobody else's. Come to the opening night. I will expect you to cheer."

She smiled, but it was a dutiful smile. "You didn't tell me you were so far along. More than a month . . ."

"I'm a secretive bastard," he said. "And I didn't want to say anything until it was definite."

She lit a cigarette, to give her something to do with her hands and her face. The hell with directors' clichés of tension. "What about me? Back here?" she asked, through smoke, knowing again she shouldn't ask it.

"What about you?" He looked at her thoughtfully. "There are always planes."

"In which direction?"

"In both directions?"

"How long do you think we'd last?"

"Two weeks." He flipped his finger against a glass on the coffee table and it tinkled faintly, a small chime marking a dubious hour. "Forever."

"If I were to come out West," she said evenly, "with Billy, could we live with you?"

He came over to her and kissed her forehead, holding her head with his two hands. She had to bend a little for the kiss. His beard scraped minutely against her skin. "Ah,

God," he said softly, then pulled back. "I have to shave and shower and dress," he said. "I'm late as it is."

She watched him shave, shower and dress, then drove with him in a taxi to the office on Fifth Avenue where he had the appointment. He hadn't answered her question, but he asked her to call him later so that he could tell her what the people at Columbia had said.

She got out of the taxi with him and spent the afternoon shopping, idly, buying a dress and a sweater, both of which she knew she would return later in the week.

At five o'clock, dressed once more in slacks, and wearing her old tweed coat, she was at the gates of Billy's school, undiaphragmed, waiting for the class to come back from the Museum of Natural History.

III

By the end of the afternoon he was tired. There had been lawyers all morning and lawyers, he had discovered, were the most fatiguing group of people in the world. At least for him. Even the ones who were working for him. The constant struggle for advantage, the ambiguous, tricky, indigestible language, the search for loopholes, levers, profitable compromises, the unashamed pursuit of money, was abhorrent to him, even while he was profiting from it all. There was one good thing about dealing with lawyers—it reassured him a hundred times over that he had acted correctly in refusing Teddy Boylan's offer to finance him through law school.

Then there had been the architects in the afternoon, and they had been trying, too. He was working on the plans for the center and his hotel room was littered with drawings. On Johnny Heath's advice, he had chosen a firm of young architects who had already won some important prizes, but were still hungry. They were eager and talented, there was no doubt about that, but they had worked almost exclusively in cities and their ideas ran to glass and steel or poured cement, and Rudolph, knowing that they considered him hopelessly square, insisted upon traditional forms and traditional materials. It was not exactly his own taste, but he felt it would be the taste best appreciated by the people who would come to the center. And it certainly would be the only thing that Calderwood might approve of. "I want it to look like a street in an old New England village," Rudolph kept saying, while the architects groaned. "White clapboard and a tower over the theater so that you can mistake it for a church. It's a conservative rural area and we're going to be catering to conservative people in a country atomosphere and they will spend their money more easily in an ambience that they feel happy and at home in."

Again and again the architects had almost quit, but he had said, "Do it this way this time, boys, and the next time it'll be more your way. This is only the first of a chain and we'll get bolder as we go along."

The plans they had sketched for him were still a long way from what he wanted, but as he looked at the last rough drawings they had shown him that day, he knew they would finally surrender.

His eyes ached and he wondered if he needed glasses as he made some notes on the plans. There was a bottle of whiskey on the bureau and he poured himself a drink, topping it off with water from the tap in the bathroom. He sipped at the drink as he spread the sheets of stiff paper out on the desk. He winced at the drawing of a huge sign, CALDERWOOD'S, that the architects had sketched in at the entrance to the center. It was to be outlined in flashing neon at night. In his old age, Calderwood sought renown, immortality in flickering multicolored glass tubing, and all Rudolph's tactful intimations about keeping a single modest style for the center had fallen on deaf ears.

The telephone rang, and Rudolph looked at his watch. Tom had said he would come by at five and it was almost that now. He picked up the phone, but it wasn't Tom. He recognized the voice of Johnny Heath's secretary on the phone. "Mr. Jordache? Mr. Heath calling."

He waited, annoyed for Johnny to get on the phone. In his organization, he decided, when anybody made a call, whoever was making it would have to be ready to speak when the phone was answered. How many slightly angered clients and customers there must be each day in America, hung up on a secretary's warning trill, how many deals lost, how many invitations refused, how many ladies who, in that short delay, had decided to say, No.

When Johnny Heath finally said, "Hello, Rudy," Rudolph concealed his irritation.

"I have the information you asked me for," Johnny said. "Have you got a pencil and piece of paper?"

"Yes."

Johnny gave him the name and address of a detective agency. "I hear they're very dependable," Johnny said. He didn't inquire why Rudolph needed a private detective, although there must have been some guessing going on in his mind.

"Thanks, Johnny," Rudolph said, after he had written down the name and address. "Thanks for your trouble."

"It was nothing," Johnny said. "You free for dinner tonight?"

"Sorry," Rudolph said. He had nothing on for the evening and if Johnny's secretary had not kept him waiting he would have said yes.

After he hung up, he felt more tired than ever and decided to postpone calling the detective agency until the next day. He was surprised that he felt tired. He didn't remember ever feeling tired at five o'clock in the afternoon.

But he was tired now, no doubt about it. Age? He laughed. He was twenty-seven years old. He looked at his face in the mirror. No gray hairs in the even, smooth blackness. No bags under the eyes. No signs of debauchery or hidden illness in the clear, olive skin. If he had been overworking, it did not show in that youthful, contained, unwrinkled face.

Still, he was tired. He lay, fully clothed, on the bed, hoping for a few minutes of sleep before Tom arrived. But he could not sleep. His sister's contemptuous words of the night before kept running through his mind, as they had been all day, even when he was struggling with lawyers and architects. "Do you enjoy *anything?*" He hadn't defended himself, but he could have pointed out that he enjoyed working, that he enjoyed going to concerts, that he read enormously, that he went to the theater, prizefights, art galleries, that he enjoyed running in the morning, riding a motorcycle, he enjoyed, yes, seeing his mother sitting across from him at the table, unlovely, unlovable, but alive, and *there,* by his efforts, not in a grave, or a pauper's hospital bed.

Gretchen was sick with the sickness of the age. Everything was based on sex. The pursuit of the sacred orgasm. She would say love, he supposed, but sex would do as a description as far as he was concerned. From what he had seen, what happiness lay there was bought at too high a price, tainting all other happiness. Having a sleazy woman clutch you at four in the morning, trying to claim you, hurling a glass at you with murderous hatred because you'd had enough of her in two hours, even though that had been the implicit bargain to begin with. Having a silly little girl taunt you in front of her friends, making you feel like some sort of frozen eunuch, then grabbing your cock disdainfully in broad daylight. If it was sex or even anything like love that had brought his mother and father together originally, they had wound up like two crazed animals in a cage in the zoo, destroying each other. Then the marriages of the second generation. Beginning with Tom. What future faced him, captured by that whining, avaricious, brainless, absurd doll of a woman? And Gretchen, herself, superior and scathing in her helpless sensuality, hating herself for the beds she fell into, adrift from a worthless and betrayed husband. Who was immersing himself in the ignominy of detectives, keyholepeeping, lawyers, divorce—he or she?

Screw them all, he thought. Then laughed to himself. The word was ill chosen. The telephone rang. "Your brother is in the lobby, Mr. Jordache," the clerk said. "Will you send him up, please?" Rudolph swung off the bed, straightened out the covers. For some reason, he didn't want Tom to see that he had been lying down, with its implication of luxury and sloth. Hurriedly, he stuffed all the architects' drawings into a closet. He wanted the room to look bare, without clues. He did not want to seem important, engrossed in large affairs, when his brother appeared.

There was a knock on the door and Rudolph opened it. At least he's wearing a tie, Rudolph thought meanly, for the opinion of the clerks and bellboys in the lobby. He shook Thomas's hand and said, "Come on in. Sit down. Want a drink? I have a bottle of Scotch, but I can ring down if you'd like something else."

"Scotch'll do." Thomas sat stiffly in an armchair, his already-gnarled hands hanging down, his suit bunched up around his great shoulders.

"Water?" Rudolph said. "I can call down for soda if you . . ."

"Water's fine."

I sound like a nervous hostess, Rudolph thought, as he went into the bathroom and poured water out of the tap into Thomas's drink.

Rudolph raised his glass. "Skoal."

"Yeah," Thomas said. He drank thirstily.

"There were some good write-ups this morning," Rudolph said.

"Yeah," Thomas said. "I read the papers. Look, there's no sense in wasting any time, Rudy." He dug into his pocket and brought out a fat envelope. He stood up and went over to the bed and opened the envelope flap and turned it upside down. Bills showered over the bedspread.

"What the hell are you doing, Tom?" Rudolph asked. He did not deal in cash—he rarely had more than fifty dollars in his pocket—and the scattering of bills on the hotel bed was vaguely disquieting to him, illicit, like the division of loot in a gangster movie.

"They're hundred-dollar bills." Thomas crumpled the empty envelope and tossed it accurately into the wastebasket. "Five thousand dollars' worth. They're yours."

"I don't know what you're talking about," Rudolph said. "You don't owe me anything."

"There's your goddamn college education that I did you out of," Thomas said. "Paying off those crooks in Ohio. I tried to give it to Pa, but he happened to be dead that day. Now it's yours."

"You work too hard for your money," Rudolph said, remembering the blood of the night before, "to throw it away like this."

"I didn't work for this money," Thomas said. "I got it easy—the way Pa lost his—by blackmail. A long time ago. It's been in a vault for years, waiting. Feel free, brother. I didn't take any punishment for it."

"It's a stupid gesture," Rudolph said.

"I'm a stupid man," Thomas said. "I make stupid gestures. Take it. Now I'm rid of you." He turned away from the bed and finished his drink in one gulp. "I'll be going now."

"Wait a minute. Sit down." Rudolph pushed at his brother's arms, feeling, even at that hurried touch, the ferocious power in them. "I don't need it. I'm doing great. I just made a deal that's going to make me a rich man, I . . ."

"I'm happy to hear it, but it's beside the point." Stonily, Thomas remained standing. "I want to pay off our fucking family and this does it."

"I won't take it, Tom. Put it in the bank for your kid, at least."

"I'll take care of my kid my own way, don't you worry about that." Now he sounded dangerous.

"It's not mine," Rudolph said helplessly. "What the hell am I going to do with it?"

"Piss on it. Blow it on dames. Give it to your favorite charity," Thomas said. "I'm not walking out of this room with it."

"Sit down, for Christ's sake." This time Rudolph pushed hard at his brother, edging him toward the armchair, risking the blow that could come at any moment. "I have to talk to you."

Rudolph refilled Thomas's glass and his own and sat across from his brother on a straight wooden chair. The window was open a little and the city wind entered in little gusts. The bills on the bed fluttered a little, like a small, complicated animal, shuddering. Both Thomas and Rudolph sat as far away from the bed as possible, as though the first one inadvertently to touch a bill would have to claim them all.

"Listen, Tom," Rudolph began, "we're not kids anymore, sleeping in the same bed, getting on each other's nerves, competing with each other, whether we knew it or not. We're two grown men and we're brothers."

"Where were you for ten years, Brother, you and Princess Gretchen?" Thomas said. "Did you ever send a postcard?"

"Forgive me," Rudolph said. "And if you talk to Gretchen, she'll ask you to forgive her, too."

"If I see her first," Thomas said, "she'll never get a chance to get close enough to me to say hello."

"Last night, watching you fight, made us realize," Rudolph persisted. "We're a family, we owe each other something . . ."

"I owed the family five thousand bucks. There it is, on the bed. Nobody owes anybody anything." Thomas kept his head down, his chin almost on his chest.

"Whatever you say, whatever you think about the way I behaved all this time," Rudolph said, "I want to help you now."

"I don't need any help." Thomas drank most of his whiskey.

"Yes, you do. Look, Tom," Rudolph said, "I'm no expert, but I've seen enough fights to have an idea of what to expect from a fighter. You're going to get hurt. Badly. You're a club fighter. It's one thing to be the champ of the neighborhood, but when you go up against trained, talented, ambitious men—and they're going to get better each time now for you—because you're still on the way up—you're going to get chopped to pieces. Aside from the injuries—concussions, cuts, kidneys—"

"I only have half hearing in one ear," Thomas volunteered, surprisingly. The professional talk had drawn him out of his shell. "For more than a year now. What the hell, I'm not a musician."

"Aside from the injuries, Tom," Rudolph went on, "there's going to come the day when you've lost more than you've won, or you're suddenly all worn out and some kid will drop you. You've seen it dozens of times. And that'll be the end. You won't get a bout. How much money will you have then? How will you earn your living then, starting all over at thirty, thirty-five, even?"

"Don't hex me, you sonofabitch," Thomas said.

"I'm being realistic." Rudolph got up and filled Thomas's glass again, to keep him in the room.

"Same old Rudy," Thomas said mockingly. "Always with a happy, realistic word for his kid brother." But he accepted the drink.

"I'm at the head of a large organization now," Rudolph said, "I'm going to have a lot of jobs to fill. I could find a place in it for you, a permanent place . . ."

"Doing what? Driving a truck at fifty bucks a week?"

"Better than that," Rudolph said. "You're no fool. You could wind up as a manager of a branch or a department," Rudolph said, wondering if he was lying. "All it takes is some common sense and a willingness to learn."

"I have no common sense and I'm not willing to learn anything," Thomas said. "Don't you know that?" He stood up. "I've got to get going now. I have a family waiting for me."

Rudolph shrugged, looked across at the bills fluttering gently on the bedspread. He stood up, too.

"Have it your own way," he said. "For the time being."

"There ain't no time being." Thomas moved toward the door.

"I'll come and visit you and see your kid," Rudolph said. "Tonight? I'll take you and your wife to dinner tonight. What do you say to that?"

"I say balls to that." Thomas opened the door, stood there. "Come and see me fight sometime. Bring Gretchen. I can use fans. But don't bother to come back to the dressing room."

"Think everything over. You know where you can reach me," Rudolph said wearily. He was unused to failure and it exhausted him. "Anyway, you might come up to Whitby and say hello to your mother. She asks about you."

"What does she ask—have they hung him yet?" Thomas grinned crookedly.

"She says she wants to see you at least once more before she dies."

"Maestro," Thomas said, "the violins, please."

Rudolph wrote down the Whitby address and the telephone number. "Here's where we live, in case you change your mind."

Thomas hesitated, then took the slip of paper and jammed it carelessly into his pocket. "See you in ten years, brother," he said. "Maybe." He went out and closed the door behind him. The room seemed much larger without his presence.

Rudolph stared at the door. How long can hatred last? In a family, forever, he supposed. Tragedy in the House of Jordache, now a supermarket. He went over to the bed and gathered up the bills and put them carefully into an envelope and sealed it. It was too late in the afternoon to put the money in the bank. He'd have to lock it in the hotel safe overnight.

One thing was certain. He was not going to use it for himself. Tomorrow he'd invest it in Dee Cee stock in his brother's name. The time would come, he was sure, when Thomas could use it. And it would be a lot more than five thousand dollars by then. Money did not negotiate forgiveness, but it could be depended upon, finally, to salve old wounds.

He was bone tired, but sleep was out of the question. He got out the architect's drawings again, grandiose imaginings, paper dreams, the hopes of years, imperfectly realized. He stared at the pencil lines that would be transformed within six months into the neon of the name of Calderwood, against the northern night. He grimaced unhappily.

The phone rang. It was Willie, buoyant but sober. "Merchant Prince," Willie said, "how would you like to come down here and have dinner with the old lady and me? We'll go to a joint in the neighborhood."

"I'm sorry, Willie," Rudolph said. "I'm busy tonight. I have a date."

"Put it in once for me, Prince," Willie said lightly. "See you soon."

Rudolph hung up slowly. He would not see Willie soon, at least not for dinner. Look behind you, Willie, as you pass through doors.

CHAPTER 7

I

"MY DEAR SON," he read, in the round schoolgirlish handwriting, "your brother Rudolph was good enough to provide me with your address in New York City and I am taking the opportunity to get in touch with my lost boy after all these years."

Oh, Christ, he thought, another county heard from. He had just come in and had found the letter waiting for him on the table in the hallway. He heard Teresa clanging pots in the kitchen and the kid making gobbling sounds.

"I'm home," he called and went into the living room and sat down on the couch, pushing a toy fire engine out of the way. He sat there, on the orange-satin couch Teresa had insisted upon buying, holding the letter dangling from his hand, trying to decide whether or not to throw it away then and there.

Teresa came in, in an apron, a little sweat glistening on her make-up, the kid crawling after her.

"You got a letter," she said. She was not very friendly these days, ever since she had heard about his going to England and leaving her behind.

"Yeah."

"It's a woman's handwriting."

"It's from my mother, for Christ's sake."

"You expect me to believe that?"

"Look." He shoved the letter under her nose.

She squinted to read. She was very nearsighted but refused to wear glasses. "It's awful young handwriting for a mother," she said, retreating reluctantly. "A mother, now. Your family is growing in leaps and bounds."

She went back to the kitchen, picking up the kid, who was squalling that he wanted to stay where he was.

To spite Teresa, Thomas decided to read the letter and see what the old bitch had to say.

"Rudolph described the circumstances of your meeting"—he read—"and I must say I was more than a little shocked at your choice of a profession. Although I shouldn't be surprised, considering your father's nature and the example he set you with that dreadful punching bag hanging out in the back yard all the time. Still, it's an honest living, I suppose, and your brother says you seem to have settled down with a wife and a child and I hope you are happy.

"Rudolph did not describe your wife to me, but I hope that your family life is happier than your father's and mine. I don't know whether Rudolph mentioned it to you but your father just vanished one fine night, with the cat.

"I am not well and I have the feeling my days are numbered. I would like to come to New York City and see my son and my new grandson, but traveling is very difficult for me. If Rudolph saw fit to buy an automobile instead of the motorcycle he charges around town on perhaps I could manage the trip. He might even be able to drive me to church one Sunday, so I could begin to make up for the years of paganism your father forced me to endure. But I guess I shouldn't complain. Rudolph has been very kind and takes good care of me and has got me a television set which makes the long days bearable. He seems to be so busy on his own projects that he barely comes home to sleep.From what I can tell, especially from the way he dresses, he is doing quite well. But he was always a good dresser and always managed to have money in his pocket.

"I cannot honestly say that I would like to see the entire family reunited, as I have crossed your sister from my heart, for good and sufficient reason, but seeing my two sons together again would bring tears of joy to my eyes.

"I was always too tired and overworked and struggling to meet your father's drunken demands to show the love I felt for you, but maybe now, in my last days, we can have peace between us.

"I gathered from Rudolph's tone that you were not very friendly with him. Perhaps you have your reasons. He has turned into a cold man although a thoughtful one. If you do not wish to see him, I could let you know when he is out of the house, which happens more and more often, for days on end, and you and I could visit with each other undisturbed. Kiss my grandson for me. Your loving Mother."

Holy God, he thought, voices from the tomb.

He sat there, holding the letter, staring into space, not hearing his wife scolding the kid in the kitchen, thinking of the years over the bakery, years when he had been more thoroughly exiled although he lived in the same house than when he had been sent away and told never to show his face again. Maybe he would go to visit the old lady, listen to the complaints, so late in coming, about her beloved Rudolph, her fair-haired boy.

He would borrow a car from Schultzy and ride her over to church, that's what he would do. Let the whole goddamn family see how wrong they were about him.

II

Mr. McKenna went out of the hotel room, aldermanic, benign, ex-cop on pension now pursuing private crime, having taken the report from a neat, black-seal briefcase and laid it on Rudolph's desk. "I am quite certain this will provide all the information you need about the individual in question," Mr. McKenna had said, kindly, plump, rubbing his bald head, his sober, gray-felt hat, neatly rimmed, on the desk beside him. "Actually, the investigation was comparatively simple, and unusually short for such complete results." There had been a note of regret in Mr. McKenna's voice at Willie's artless simplicity, which had required so little time, so little professional guile to investigate. "I think the wife will find that any competent lawyer can get her a divorce with no difficulty under the laws of the State of New York dealing with adultery. She is very clearly the injured party, very clearly indeed."

Rudolph looked at the neatly typed report with distaste. Tapping telephone wires, it seemed, was as easy as buying a loaf of bread. For five dollars, hotel clerks would allow you to attach a microphone to a wall. Secretaries would fish out torn love letters from waste baskets and piece them together carefully for the price of a dinner. Old girls, now rejected, would quote chapter and verse. Police files were open, secret testimony before committees was available, nothing was unpleasant enough to be disbelieved. Communication, despite what poets were saying at the moment, was rife.

He picked up the phone and asked for Gretchen's number. He listened as the operator dialed. The busy signal, that snarling sound, came over the wire. He hung up and went over to the window and parted the curtains and looked out. The afternoon was cold and gray. Down below pedestrians leaned against the wind, hurrying for shelter, collars up. It was an ex-policeman's kind of day.

He went back to the phone, asked for Gretchen's number again. Once more, he heard the busy signal. He slammed down the instrument, annoyed. He wanted to get this miserable business over with as quickly as possible. He had spoken to a lawyer friend, without mentioning names, and the lawyer friend had advised him that the injured party should move out of the communal habitation with the child before bringing any action, unless there was some way of keeping the husband out of the apartment completely from that moment on. Under no conditions should the injured party sleep one night more under the same roof with the defendant-to-be.

Before he called Willie and confronted him with the detective's report, he had to tell Gretchen this and tell her also that he intended to speak to Willie immediately.

But again the phone rang busy. The injured party was having a chatty afternoon. With whom she was talking—Johnny Heath, quiet, bland lover, constant guest, or one of the other ten men she had said she no longer wanted to sleep with? The easiest lay in New York. Sister mine.

He looked at his watch. Five minutes to four. Willie would undoubtedly be back in his office by now, happily dozing off the pre-lunch martinis.

Rudolph picked up the phone and called Willie's number. Two secretaries in Willie's office wafted him along, disembodied sweet voices, electric with public relations charm. "Hi, Merchant Prince," Willie said, when he came on the line. "To what do I owe the honor?" It was a three-martini voice this afternoon.

"Willie," Rudolph said, "You have to come over here to my hotel right away."

"Listen, kid, I'm sort of tied up here and . . . "

"Willie, I warn you, you'd better come over here this minute."

"Okay," Willie said, his voice subdued. "Order me a drink."

Drinkless, Willie sat in the chair the ex-policeman had used earlier, and carefully read the report. Rudolph stood at the window, looking out. He heard the rustle of paper as Willie put the report down.

"Well," Willie said, "it seems I've been a very busy little boy. What are you going to do with this now?" He tapped the report.

Rudolph reached over and picked up the clipped-together sheets of paper and tore them into small pieces and dropped the pieces into the wastebasket.

"What does that mean?" Willie asked.

"It means that I can't go through with it," Rudolph said. "Nobody's going to see it and nobody's going to know about it. If your wife wants a divorce, she'll have to figure out another way to get it."

"Oh," Willie said. "It was Gretchen's idea?"

"Not exactly. She said she wanted to get away from you, but she wanted to keep the kid, and I offered to help."

"Blood is thicker than marriage. Is that it?"

"Something like that. Only not *my* blood. This time."

"You came awfully close to being a shit, Merchant Prince," Willie said, "didn't you?"

"So I did."

"Does my beloved wife know you have this on me?"

"No. And she's not going to."

"In days to come," Willie said, "I shall sing the praises of my shining brother-in-law. Look, I shall tell my son, look closely at your noble uncle and you will be able to discern the shimmer of his halo. Christ, there must be one drink somewhere in this hotel."

Rudolph brought out the bottle. With all his jokes, if ever a man looked as though he needed a drink, it was Willie at this moment. He drank off half the glass. "Who's picking up the tab for the research?" he asked.

"I am."

"What does it come to?"

"Five hundred and fifty dollars."

"You should've come to me," Willie said. "I'd've given you the information for half the price. Do you want me to pay you back?"

"Forget it," Rudolph said. "I never gave you a wedding present. Consider this my wedding present."

"Better than a silver platter. I thank you, brother-in-law. Is there more in that bottle?"

Rudolph poured. "You'd better keep sober," he said. "You're going to have some serious conversation ahead of you."

"Yeah." Willie nodded. "It was a sorrowful day for everybody when I bought your sister a bottle of champagne at the Algonquin bar." He smiled wanly. "I loved her that afternoon and I love her now and there I am in the trash basket." He gestured to where the shreds of the detective's report lay scattered in the tin bucket, decorated with a hunting print, riders with bright-red coats. "Do you know what love is?"

"No."

"Neither do I." Willie stood up. "Well, I'll leave you. Thanks for an interesting half hour."

He went out without offering to shake hands.

III

He was incredulous when he came to the house. He looked again at the piece of paper Rudolph had given him to make sure that he was at the right address. Still over a store. And in a neighborhood that was hardly any better than the old one in Port Philip. Seeing Rudolph in that fancy room at the Hotel Warwick and hearing him talk you'd think that he was just rolling in dough. Well, if he was, he wasn't wasting any of it on rent.

Maybe he just kept the old lady in this joint and had a rich pad for himself in some other part of town. He wouldn't put it past the bastard.

Thomas went into the dingy vestibule, saw the name Jordache printed next to a bell, rang. He waited, but the buzzer remained silent. He had called and told his mother he was coming to visit today, and she said she'd be home. He couldn't make it on a Sunday, becuse when he suggested it to Teresa, she'd started to cry. Sunday was her day, she wept, and she wasn't going to be done out of it by an old hag who hadn't even bothered to send a card when her grandson was born. So they'd left the kid with a sister of Teresa's up in the Bronx and they'd gone to a movie on Broadway and had dinner at Toots Shor's, where a sportswriter recognized Thomas, which made Teresa's day for her and maybe it was worth the twenty bucks the dinner had cost.

Thomas pushed the bell again. Still, there was no response. Probably, Thomas thought bitterly, at the last minute Rudolph called and said he wanted his mother to come down to New York and shine his shoes or something, and she'd rushed off, falling all over herself with joy.

He started to turn away, half relieved that he didn't have to face her. It hadn't been such a hot idea to begin with. Let sleeping mothers lie. He was just about out of the door when he heard the buzzer. He went back, opened the door and went up the steps.

The door opened at the first floor landing and there she was, looking a hundred years old. She took a couple of steps toward him and he understood why he had had to wait for the buzzer. The way she walked it must take her five minutes to cross the room. She was crying already and had her arms outstretched to embrace him.

"My son, my son," she cried, as her arms, thin sticks, went around him. "I thought I'd never see your face again."

There was a strong smell of toilet water. He kissed her wet cheek gently, wondering what he felt.

Clinging to his arm, she led him into the apartment. The living room was tiny and dark and he recognized the furniture from the apartment on Vanderhoff Street. It had been old and worn-out then. Now it was practically in ruins. Through an open door he could look into an adjoining room and see a desk, a single bed, books everywhere.

If he can afford to buy all those books, Thomas thought, he sure can afford to buy some new furniture.

"Sit down, sit down," she said excitedly, guiding him to the one threadbare easy chair. "What a wonderful day." Her voice was thin, made reedy by years of complaint. Her legs were swollen, shapeless, and she wore wide, soft, invalid's shoes, like a cripple. She moved as though she had been broken a long time ago in an accident. "You look splendid. Absolutely splendid." He remembered those words she used, out of *Gone With the Wind*. "I was afraid my little boy's face would be all battered, but you've turned out handsomely. You resemble my side of the family, that's plain to see, Irish. Not like the other two." She moved in a slow awkward flutter before him as he sat stiffly in the chair. She was wearing a flowered dress that blew loosely about her thin body. Her thick legs stuck out below her skirt like an error in engineering, another woman's limbs. "That's a lovely gray suit," she said, touching his sleeve. "A gentleman's suit, I was afraid you'd still be in a sweater." She laughed gaily, his childhood already a romance. "Ah, I knew Fate couldn't be so unkind," she said, "not letting me see my child's face before I die. Now let me see my grandson's face. You must have a picture. I'm sure you carry one in your wallet, like all proud fathers."

Thomas took out a picture of his child.

"What's his name?" his mother asked.

"Wesley," Thomas said.

"Wesley Pease," his mother said. "It's a fine name."

Thomas didn't bother to remind her that the boy's name was Wesley Jordache, nor did he tell her that he had fought Teresa for a week to try to get her to settle for a less fancy name. But Teresa had wept and carried on and he'd given in.

His mother stared at the photograph, her eyes dampening. She kissed the snapshot.

"Dear little beautiful thing," she said.

Thomas didn't remember her ever kissing *him* as a child.

"You must take me to see him," she said.

"Sure."

"Soon."

"When I come back from England," he said.

"England! We've just found each other again and you're leaving for the other side of the earth!"

"It's only for a couple of weeks."

"You must be doing very well," she said, "to be able to afford vacations like that."

"I have a job to do there," he said. He was reluctant to use the word fight. "They pay my way." He didn't want her to get the idea that he was rich, which he wasn't, by a long shot. In the Jordache family, it was safer to cry poverty. One woman grabbing at every cent that came into the house was enough for one family.

"I hope you're saving your money," she said. "In your profession . . . "

"Sure," he said. "Don't worry about me." He looked around him. "It's a cinch Rudy's saving his money."

"Oh," she said. "The apartment. It's not very grand, is it? But I can't complain. Rudy pays for a woman to come in and clean every day and do the shopping for me the days I can't make the stairs. And he says he's looking for a bigger place. On the ground floor somewhere, so it'll be easier for me, without steps. He doesn't talk to me much about his work, but there was an article last month in the paper all about how he was one of the up-and-coming young businessmen in town, so I suppose he's doing well enough. But he's right to be thrifty. Money was the tragedy of the family. It made an old woman of me before my time." She sighed, self-pitying. "Your father was demented on the subject. I couldn't get ten dollars from him for the barest necessities of life without a pitched battle every time. When you're in England you might make some confidential inquiries, find out if anyone has seen him there. He's liable to be *anyplace,* that man. After all, he was European, and it would be the most natural thing in the world for him to go back there to hide out."

Off her rocker, he thought. Poor old lady. Rudy hadn't prepared him for this. But he said, "I'll ask around when I get over there."

"You're a good boy," she said. "I always knew deep down that you were essentially a good boy, but swayed by bad companions. If I had had the time to be a proper mother to my family, I could have saved you from so much trouble. You must be strict with your son. Loving, but strict. Is your wife a good mother to him?"

"She's okay," he said. He preferred not to talk about Teresa. He looked at his watch. The conversation and the dark apartment were depressing him. "Look," he said, "it's nearly one o'clock. Why don't I take you out to lunch? I have a car downstairs."

"Lunch? In a restaurant. Oh, wouldn't that be lovely," she said, girlishly. "My big strong son taking his old mother out to lunch."

"We'll go to the best place in town," he said.

On his way home, driving Schultzy's car down toward New York late in the afternoon, he thought about the day, wondering if he would ever make the trip again.

The image of his mother formed in adolescence, that of a scolding, perpetually disapproving hard woman, fanatically devoted to one son, to the detriment of another, was now replaced by that of a harmless and pitiful old lady, pathetically lonely, pleased by the slightest attention, and anxious to be loved.

At lunch he had offered her a cocktail and she had grown a little tipsy, had giggled and said, "Oh, I do feel naughty." After lunch he had driven her around town and was surprised to see that most of it was entirely unknown to her. She had lived there for years, but had seen practically nothing of it, not even the university from which her son had been graduated. "I had no idea it was such a beautiful place," she kept saying over and over again, as they passed through neighborhoods where comfortable, large houses were set among trees and wintry lawns. And when they passed Calderwood's, she said, "I had no idea it was so big. You know, I've never been in there. And to think that Rudy practically runs it!"

He had parked the car and had walked slowly with her along the ground floor and insisted upon buying her a suede handbag for fifteen dollars. She had had the salesgirl wrap up her old bag and carried the new one proudly over her arm as they left the store.

She had talked a great deal in the course of the afternoon, telling him for the first time about her life in the orphanage ("I was the brightest girl in the class. They gave me a prize when I left."), about working as a waitress, being ashamed of being illegitimate, about going to night school in Buffalo to improve herself, about not ever letting a man even kiss her until she married Axel Jordache, about only weighing ninety-two pounds on the day of her wedding, about how beautiful Port Philip was the day she and Axel came down to inspect the bakery, about the white excursion boat going by up the river, with the band playing waltzes on the deck, about how nice the neighborhood was when they first came there and her dream of starting a cosy little restaurant, about her hopes for her family. . . .

When he took her back to the apartment she asked him if she could have the photograph of his son to frame and put on the table in her bedroom and when he gave it to her, she hobbled into her room and came back with a photograph of herself, yellowed with age, taken when she was nineteen, in a long, white dress, slender, grave, beautiful. "Here," she said, "I want you to have this."

She watched silently as he put it carefully in his wallet in the same place that he had kept his son's picture.

"You know," she said, "I feel closer to you somehow than to anybody in the whole world. We're the same kind of people. We're simple. Not like your sister and your brother. I love Rudy, I suppose, and I should, but I don't understand him. And sometimes I'm just afraid of him. While you . . . " She laughed. "Such a big, strong young man, a man who makes his living with his fists. . . . But I feel so at home with you, almost as though we were the same age, almost as though I had a brother. And today . . . today was so wonderful. I'm a prisoner who has just come out from behind the walls."

He kissed her and held her and she clutched at him briefly.

"Do you know," she said, "I haven't smoked a single cigarette since you arrived."

He drove down slowly through the dusk, thinking about the afternoon. He came to a roadhouse and went in and sat at the empty bar and had a whiskey. He took out his wallet and stared at the young girl who had turned into his mother. He was glad he had come to see her. Perhaps her favor wasn't worth much, but in the long race for the meager trophy he had finally won. Alone in the quiet bar he enjoyed an unaccustomed tranquillity. For an hour, at least, he was at peace. Today, there was one less person in the world that he had to hate.

Part Three

CHAPTER 1

1960

THE MORNING WAS a pleasant one, except for the smog that lay cupped, a thin, metallic soup, in the Los Angeles basin. Barefooted, in her nightgown, Gretchen went through the open French windows, sliding between the still curtains, out onto the terrace, and looked down from her mountain top at the stained but sunlit city and the distant flat sea below her. She breathed deeply of the September morning air, smelling of wet grass and opening flowers. No sound came from the city and the early silence was broken only by the calls of a covey of quail crossing the lawn.

Better than New York, she thought for the hundredth time, much better than New York.

She would have liked a cup of coffee, but it was too early for Doris, the maid, to be up, and if she went into the kitchen to make the coffe herself, Doris would be awakened by the sound of running water and clinking metal and would come fussing out, apologizing but aggrieved at being deprived of rightful sleep. It was too early to awake Billy, too, especially with the day he had ahead of him, and she knew better than to rouse Colin, whom she had left sleeping in the big bed, flat on his back, frowning, his arms crossed tightly, as though in his dreams he was watching a performance of which he could not possibly approve.

She smiled, thinking of Colin, sleeping, as she sometimes told him, in his important position. His other positions, and she had told him about them in detail, were amused, vulnerable, pornographic, and horrified. She had been awakened by a thin shaft of sunlight coming through a rift in the curtains and had been tempted to reach for him and unfold those clenched arms. But Colin never made love in the morning. Mornings were for murder, he said. Used to New York theatrical hours, he was, as he freely admitted, a savage before noon.

She went around to the front of the house, padding happily through the dewy grass with her bare feet, her transparent cotton nightgown blowing around her body as she walked. They had no neighbors and the chance of any cars passing by at this hour was almost nil. Anyway, in California, nobody cared how you dressed. She often sunbathed naked in the garden and her body was a deep brown after the summer. Back East she had always been careful to stay out of the sun, but if you weren't brown in California people assumed that you were either ill or too poor to take a holiday.

The newspaper was lying in the front driveway, folded and bound by a rubber band. She opened it up and glanced at the headlines as she walked slowly back around the house. Nixon and Kennedy had their pictures on the front page and they were promising everybody everything. She mourned briefly for Adlai Stevenson and wondered if it was morally right for somebody as young and as good looking as John Fitzgerald Kennedy to run for the Presidency. "Charm boy," Colin called him, but

Colin had charm thrown at him every day by actors and its effect on him was almost invariably negative.

She reminded herself to make sure to apply for absentee ballots for herself and Colin, because they were going to be in New York in November and every vote against Nixon was going to be precious. Although now that she no longer wrote for magazines she didn't get too worked up about politics. The McCarthy period had disillusioned her with the value of private righteousness and alarmed public utterance. Her love for Colin, whose politics were, to say the least, capricious, had led her to abandon old attitudes along with old friends. Colin described himself at various times as a socialist without hope, a nihilist, a single-taxer, and a monarchist, depending upon whom he was arguing with at the moment, although he usually wound up voting for Democrats. Neither he nor Gretchen was involved in the passionate political activities of the movie colony, the feting of candidates, the signing of advertisements, the fund-raising cocktail parties. In fact, they hardly went to any parties at all. Colin didn't like to drink much and he found the boozy, aimless conversation of the usual Hollywood gatherings intolerable. He never flirted, so the presence of battalions of pretty ladies available at the functions of the rich and famous had no attraction for him. After the loose, gregarious years with Willie, Gretchen welcomed the domestic days and quiet nights with her second husband.

Colin's refusal to "go public," as he phrased it, had not damaged his career. As he said, "Only people without talent have to play the Hollywood game." He had asserted his talent with his first picture, confirmed it with his second, and now, with his third picture in five years in the final cutting and mixing stage, was established as one of the most gifted directors of his generation. His only failure had come when he had gone back to New York, after completing his first picture, to put on a play that closed after only eight performances. He had disappeared for three weeks after that. When he returned he was morose and silent and it had been months before he felt he was ready to go to work again. He was not a man designed for failure and he had made Gretchen suffer along with him. It had not helped, either, that Gretchen had told him in advance that she didn't think the play was ready for production. Still, he always asked for her opinions on every aspect of his work and demanded absolute frankness, which she gave him. Right now she was troubled by a sequence in his new film, which they had seen together in rough cut at the studio the night before. Only Colin, she, and Sam Corey, the cutter, had seen it. She had felt there was something wrong, but couldn't give coherent reasons why. She hadn't said anything after the running, but she knew he would question her at breakfast. As she went back into the bedroom, where Colin was still sleeping in his important position, she tried to remember the sequence of the film, frame by frame, so that she could make sense when she spoke about it.

She looked at the bedside clock and saw that it was still too early to wake Colin. She put on a robe and went into the living room. The desk in the corner of the room was strewn with books and manuscripts and reviews of novels torn out of the *Sunday Times Book Review* section and *Publisher's Weekly* and the London newspapers. The house was not a large one and there was no other place for the never-diminishing pile of print that they both attacked methodically, searching for possible ideas for films.

Gretchen took a pair of glasses off the desk and sat down to finish the newspaper. They were Colin's glasses, but they fitted her well enough so that she didn't bother to go back into the bedroom to get her own. Matched imperfections.

On the theater page there was a review from New York of a new play that had just opened, with a rave for a young actor whom nobody had ever heard of before and she made a note to get tickets for the play for herself and Colin as soon as she got into the city. In the listing of movies for Beverly Hills she saw that Colin's first picture was being revived over the weekend and she neatly tore out the listing to show it to him. It would make him less savage at breakfast.

She turned to the sports section to see what horses were running at Hollywood Park that afternoon. Colin loved the races and was a not inconsiderable gambler and they went as often as they could. The last time they had gone he had won enough to buy her a lovey spray brooch. There didn't seem to be any jewelry on today's card and she was about to put the paper down when she saw a photograph of two boxers sparring in training. Oh, God, she thought, there he is again. She read the caption under the photograph. "Henry Quayles with Sparmate Tommy Jordache at Las Vegas in workout for middleweight fight next week."

She hadn't seen or heard from her brother since that one night in New York and she knew almost nothing about boxing, but she knew enough to understand that if he was working as somebody's sparring partner Thomas had gone downhill since the winning bout in Queens. She folded the paper neatly, hoping that Colin would overlook the photograph. She had told him about Thomas, as she told him about everything, but she didn't want Colin's curiosity to be aroused and perhaps insisting on meeting Thomas and seeing him fight.

There were sounds from the kitchen now and she went into Billy's room to wake him. He was sitting cross-legged in his pajamas on the bed, silently fingering chords on his guitar. Pure blond hair, grave, thoughtful eyes, fuzzed pink cheeks, nose too big for the undeveloped face, skinny, young boy's neck, long, coltish legs, concentrated, unsmiling, dear.

His valise, with the lid up, was on the chair, packed. Neatly packed. Somehow Billy, despite his parents, or perhaps because of his parents, had grown up with a passion for order.

She kissed the top of his head. No reaction. No hostility, but no love. He fingered a final chord.

"You all ready?" she asked.

"Uhuh." He uncurled the long legs, slid off the bed. His pajama top was open. Skinny, long torso, ribs countable, close to the skin, skin California summer color, days on the beach, body-surfing, girls and boys together on the hot sand, salt and guitars. As far as she knew he was still a virgin. Nothing had been said.

"You all ready?" he asked.

"Bags all packed," she said. "All I have to do is lock them." Billy had an almost pathological fear of being late for anything, school, trains, planes, parties. She had learned to be well in advance for anything she had to do with him.

"What do you want for breakfast?" she asked, prepared to feast him.

"Orange juice."

"That all?"

"I better not eat. I puke on planes."

"Remember to take your Dramamine."

"Yeah." He stripped off the top of his pajamas and went into the bathroom to brush his teeth. After she had moved in with Colin, Billy had suddenly refused to be seen naked in front of her. Two theories about that. She knew that Billy admired Colin, but she also knew that the boy admired her less for having lived with Colin before they were married. The strict, painful conventions of childhood.

She went to wake Colin. He was talking in his sleep and moving uneasily on the bed. "All that blood," he said.

War? Celluloid? It was impossible to tell with a movie director.

She woke him with a kiss under his ear. He lay still, staring blackly up at the ceiling. "Christ," he said, "it's the middle of the night."

She kissed him again. "Okay," he said, "morning," He rumpled her hair. She was sorry she had gone in to see Billy. One morning, on a national or religious holiday perhaps, Colin would finally make love to her. This might have been the morning. Non-coordinated rhythms of desire.

With a groan he tried to life himself from the bed, fell back. He extended his hand. "Give a poor old man a lift," he said. "Out of the depths."

She grasped his hand and pulled. He sat on the edge of the bed rubbing his eye with the back of his hand, regretting daylight.

"Say," Colin stopped rubbing his eye and looked at her alertly, "last night, at the running, in the next to the last reel, there was something you thought was lousy . . . "

He didn't even wait for breakfast, she thought. 'I didn't say anything," she said.

"You don't have to *say* anything. All you have to do is *breathe*."

"Don't be sure a naked nerve," she said, stalling for time. "Especially before you've had your coffee."

"Come on."

"All right," she said. "There was something I didn't like, but I didn't figure out why I didn't like it."

"And now?"

"I think I know."

"What is it?"

"Well, the sequence after he gets the news and he believes it's his fault . . . "

"Yes," Colin said impatiently. "It's one of the key scenes in the picture."

"You have him going around the house, looking at himself in one mirror after another, in the bathroom, in the full-length mirror on the closet wall, in the dark mirror in the living room, in the magnifying shaving mirror, at his own reflection in the puddle on the front porch . . . "

"The idea's simple enough," Colin said irritably, defensively. "He's examining himself—okay, let's be corny—he's looking into his soul in various lights, from different angles, to discover . . . Okay, what do you think is wrong about it?"

"Two things," she said calmly. Now she realized she had been gnawing at the problem subconsciously ever since she had come out of the projection room—in bed before falling asleep, on the terrace looking out over the smoggy city, while going through the newspaper in the living room. "Two things. First, the tempo. Everything in the whole picture has moved fast up to then, it's the style of the whole work, and then, suddenly, as though to show the audience that a Big Moment has arrived, you slow it down to a drag. It's too obvious."

"That's me," he said, biting his words. "Obvious."

"If you're going to get angry I'll shut up."

"I'm already angry and don't shut up. You said two things. What's the other thing?"

"You have all those big close-ups of him, going on forever and I'm supposed to be seeing that he's tortured, doubtful, confused."

"Well, at least you got that, for Christ's sake . . . "

"Do you want me to go on or should we go in and have breakfast?"

"The next dame I marry," he said, "is not going to be so goddamn smart. Go on."

"Well, you may think that he's showing that he's tortured and doubtful and confused," she said, "and *he* may think he's showing that he's tortured and doubtful and confused, but all I get out of it is a handsome young man admiring himself in a mirror and wondering if the lighting is doing all it can for his eyes."

"Shit," he said, "you are a bitch. We worked four days on that sequence."

"I'd cut it if I were you," she said.

"The next picture," he said, "you go on the set and I'll stay home and do the cooking."

"You asked me," she said.

"I'll never learn." He jumped up off the bed. "I'll be ready for breakfast in five minutes." He stumped off toward the bathroom. He slept without the tops of his pajamas and the sheets had made pink ridges on the skin of his neatly muscled, lean back, small welts after the night's faint flogging. At the door, he turned. "Every other dame I ever knew thought everything I did was glorious," he said, "and I had to go and marry you."

"They didn't think" she said sweetly. "They *said*."

She went over to him and he kissed her. "I'm going to miss you," he whispered. "Hideously." He pushed her away roughly. "Now, go see that the coffee's *black*."

He was humming as he went in to shave, an unusually merry thing for him to be doing at that time of day. She knew that he had been worried by the sequence, too, and was relieved now that he believed he knew what was wrong with it and that in the cutting room that morning he was going to have the exquisite pleasure of throwing away four days' hard work, representing forty thousand dollars of the studio's money.

They reached the airport early and the lines of worry on Billy's forehead vanished as he saw his and his mother's bags disappear across the counter. He was dressed in a gray-tweed suit and buttoned-down pink shirt, with a blue tie, for traveling, and his hair was neatly brushed and there were no adolescent pimples on his chin. Gretchen thought he looked very grown-up and handsome, much more than his fourteen years. He was already as tall as she, taller than Colin, who had driven them to the airport and was making an admirable effort to hide his impatience to get to the studio and back to work. Gretchen had had to control herself on the trip to the airport, because Colin's driving made her nervous. It was the one thing she thought he did badly, sometimes mooning along slowly, thinking about other things, then suddenly becoming fiercely competitive and cursing out other drivers as he spurted ahead of them or tried to prevent them from passing him. When she couldn't resist from warning him about near-misses, he would snarl at her, "Don't be the All-American wife." He was convinced he drove superbly. As he pointed out to her, he had never had an accident, although he had been caught several times for speeding, incidents that had been discreetly kept off his record by the studio fixers, those valuable, doubtful gentlemen.

As other passengers came up to the counter with their bags, Colin said, "We've got lots of time. Let's go get a cup of coffee."

Gretchen knew that Billy would have preferred to go stand at the gate so that he could be the first to board the plane. "Look, Colin," she said, "you don't have to wait. Good-byes're such a bore anyway . . . "

"Let's get a cup of coffee," Colin said. "I'm still not awake yet."

They walked across the hall toward the restaurant, Gretchen between her husband and her son, conscious of their beauty and her own, and happy about it as she caught people staring at the three of them. Pride, she thought, that delicious sin.

In the restaurant, she and Colin had coffee and Billy had a Coca-Cola, with which he washed down his dose of Dramamine.

"I used to puke on buses until I was eighteen," Colin said, watching the boy swallow the pills. "Then I had my first girl and I stopped puking."

There was a quick, judging flick of Billy's eyes. Colin spoke in front of Billy as he did to any grown-up. Sometimes Gretchen wondered if it was altogether wise. She didn't know whether the boy loved his stepfather, merely endured him, or hated him. Billy was not one to volunteer information about his emotions. Colin did not seem to make any extra effort to win the boy over. He was sometimes brusque with him, sometimes deeply interested and helpful with his work at school, sometimes playful and charming, sometimes distant. Colin made no concessions to his audience, but what was admirable in his work, Gretchen thought, was not necessarily healthy in the case of a withdrawn only child living with a mother who had left his father for a temperamental and difficult lover. She and Colin had had their fights, but never on the subject of Billy, and Colin was paying for the boy's education because Willie Abbott had fallen upon hard times and could not afford to. Colin had forbidden Gretchen to tell the boy where the money was coming from, but Gretchen was sure Billy guessed.

"When I was just your age," Colin was saying, "I was sent off to school. I cried the first week. The first year I hated school. The second year I endured it. The third year I edited the school newspaper and I had my first taste of the pleasures of power and although I didn't admit it to anybody, even to myself, I liked it. My last year I wept because I had to leave."

"I don't mind going," Billy said.

"Good," Colin said. "It's a good school, if any school these days can be said to be good, and at the very worst you'll come out of it knowing how to write a simple declarative sentence in the English language. Here." He produced an envelope and gave it to the boy. "Take this and never tell your mother what's in it."

"Thank you," Billy said. He put the envelope in the inside pocket of his jacket. He looked at his watch. "Don't you think we'd better be going?"

They walked three abreast toward the gate, Billy carrying his guitar. Briefly, Gretchen worried about how the school, which was old New England Presbyterian Respectable, would react to the guitar. Probably no reaction at all. By this time they must be prepared for anything from fourteen-year-old boys.

The plane was just beginning to load when they reached the gate. "Go ahead on board, Billy," Gretchen said. "I want to say good-bye to Colin."

Colin shook Billy's hand and said. "If there's anything you need, call me. Collect."

Gretchen searched his face as he spoke to her son. The tenderness and caring were real on the sharp, thin features, and the dangerous eyes under the heavy black brows were gentle and loving. I didn't make a mistake, she thought, I didn't.

Billy smiled gravely, en route from father to father, disturbing journey, and went aboard, guitar held like an infantryman's gun on patrol.

"He'll be all right," Colin said as the boy went through the gate and out onto the tarmac where the big jet waited.

"I hope so," Gretchen said. "There was money in that envelope, wasn't there?"

"A few bucks," Colin said carelessly. "Buffer money. Ease the pain. There are moments when a boy can't survive education without an extra milkshake or the latest issue of *Playboy*. Willie meeting you at Idlewild?"

"Yes."

"You taking the kid up to the school together?"

"Yes."

"I suppose you're right," Colin said flatly. "Parents should be present in twos at the ceremonies of adolescents." He looked away from her, staring at the passengers going through the gate. "Every time I see one of those ads for airlines with pictures of people smiling broadly as they climb the steps getting onto a plane, I realize what a lying society we inhabit. Nobody's happy getting onto a plane. Are you going to sleep with ex-husband Willie tonight?"

"Colin!"

"Ladies have been known to. Divorce, the final aphrodisiac."

"Goddamn you," she said. She started toward the gate.

He put out his hand and held her back, gripping her arm.

"Forgive me," he said. "I am a dark, self-destructive, happiness-doubting, unforgivable man." He smiled, sadly, pleadingly. "Just one thing—don't talk to Willie about me."

"I won't." She had already forgiven him and was facing him, close to him. He kissed her lightly. The public address system was announcing the last call for the flight.

"See you in New York in two weeks," Colin said. "Don't enjoy the city until I get there."

"Not to worry," she said. She brushed his cheek with her lips and he turned abruptly and strode away, walking, as always, in a way that made her smile secretly to herself, as though he were on his way to a dangerous encounter from which he was determined to emerge the victor.

She watched him for a moment, then went through the gate.

Despite the Dramamine, Billy threw up as they were approaching Idlewild for the landing. He did it neatly and apologetically into the bag provided for the purpose, but the sweat stood out on his forehead and his shoulders heaved uncontrollably. Gretchen stroked the back of Billy's neck, helplessly, knowing that it wasn't serious, but racked, just the same, by her inability at such a moment to stand between her son and pain. The irrationality of mothering.

When he had finished retching, Billy neatly closed the bag and went down the aisle to the toilet to dispose of the bag and rinse out his mouth. He was still white when he came back. He had wiped the sweat off his face and seemed composed, but as he seated himself next to Gretchen, he said, bitterly, "Goddamn, I'm such a *baby*."

Willie was wearing sunglasses as he stood in the small crowd that awaited the passengers from Los Angeles. The day was gray and humid and even before she was close enough to say hello to him, Gretchen knew that he had been drinking the night before and that the sunglasses were meant to hide the evidence of bloodshot eyes from her and his son. At least one night, just before he greets a son he hasn't seen for months, she thought, he might have kept sober. She fought down her annoyance. Friendliness and serenity between divorced parents in the presence of offspring. The necessary hypocrisy of divided love.

Billy saw his father and hurried through the lines of debarking passengers toward him. He put his arms around his father and kissed his cheek. Gretchen purposely walked more slowly, not to interfere. Together, father and son were plainly linked. Although Billy was taller than his father and better looking than Willie ever could have been, their blood connection was absolutely clear. Once again, Gretchen felt her old irritation that her contribution to the genetic make-up of the child was nowhere in evidence.

Willie was smiling widely (fatuously?) at his son's demonstration of affection, as Gretchen finally approached him. He kept his arm around Billy's shoulder and said, "Hello, dear," to Gretchen and leaned forward to kiss her cheek. Two similar kisses, on the same day, on two sides of the continent, departing and arriving. Willie had been wonderful about the divorce and about Billy, and she couldn't deny him the "dear" or the rueful kiss. She didn't say anything about the dark glasses or the unmistakable aroma of alcohol on Willie's breath. He was dressed neatly, soberly proper, just the costume for taking a son to introduce him to the headmaster of a good New England school. Somehow, she would keep him from drinking when they drove up to the school the next day.

She sat alone in the small living room of the hotel suite, the lights of evening New York outside the windows, the growl of the city, familiar and exciting, rising from the avenues. Foolishly, she had expected Billy to stay with her that night, but in the rented car driving into the city from Idlewild, Willie had said to Billy, "I hope you don't mind sleeping on the couch. I've only got one room, but there's a couch. A couple of springs're busted, but at your age I imagine you'll sleep all right."

"That's great," Billy said, and there was no mistaking his tone. He hadn't even turned around to look questioningly at his mother. Even if he had appealed to her, what could she have said?

When Willie had asked her where she was staying, and she had told him, "The Algonquin," he had raised his eyebrows sardonically.

"Colin likes it," she said defensively. "It's near the theater district and it saves him a lot of time being able to walk to rehearsals and to the office."

When Willie stopped the car in front of the Algonquin to let her out, he said, not looking either at her or at Billy, "I once bought a girl a bottle of champagne in this hotel."

"Call me in the morning, please," Gretchen said. "As soon as you wake up. We ought to get to the school before lunch."

Billy was on the far side of the front seat as she got out on the sidewalk and the porter took her bags, so she didn't get to kiss him good-bye and it was just with a little wave of her hand that she had sent him off to dinner with his father and the broken couch for the night in his father's single room.

There had been a message waiting for her at the desk when she registered. She had wired Rudolph that she was arriving in New York and had asked him to have dinner with her. The message had been from Rudolph, saying that he couldn't meet her that night, but would call her in the morning.

She went up to the suite, unpacked, took a bath, and then hesitated about what to wear. Finally she just threw on a robe, because she didn't know what she was going to do with the evening. All the people she knew in New York were Willie's friends, or her ex-lovers, or people she had met briefly with Colin when she had been in the city three years ago for the play that was a disaster, and she wasn't going to call any of them. She wanted a drink badly, but she couldn't go down to the bar and sit there by herself and get drunk. That miserable Rudolph, she thought, as she stood at the window, looking down at the traffic on Forty-fourth Street below her, can't even spare one night from his gainful activities for his sister. Rudolph had come out to Los Angeles twice during the years on business and she had shepherded him around every free minute. Wait till he gets out there again, she promised herself. There'll be a hot message waiting for *him* at his hotel when he arrives.

She almost picked up the telephone to call Willie. She could pretend that she wanted to find out if Billy was feeling all right after his sickness on the plane and perhaps Willie would ask her to have dinner with them. She even went over to the phone, but with her hand reaching out to pick it up, she halted herself. Keep female tricks to an absolute minimum. Her son deserved at least one complete, unemotional evening with his father, unwatched by mother's jealous eye.

She prowled back and forth in the small, old-fashioned room. How happy she had been once to arrive in New York, how wide open and inviting the city had seemed to her. When she was young, poor, and alone, it had welcomed her, and she had moved about its streets freely and without fear. Now, wiser, older, richer, she felt a prisoner in the room. A husband three thousand miles away, a son a few blocks away, put invisible restrictions on her behavior. Well, at least she could go downstairs and have dinner in the hotel's dining room. Another lonely lady, with her half-bottle of wine, sitting at a small table, trying not to hear the conversation of other diners, growing slightly tipsy, talking too much and too brightly to the headwaiter. Christ, what a bore it was sometimes to be a woman.

She went into the bedroom and pulled out her plainest dress, a black concoction that had cost too much and that she knew Colin didn't like, and started to dress. She was careless with her make-up and hardly bothered to brush her hair and was just going out the door when the telephone rang.

She almost ran back into the room. If it's Willie, she thought, no matter what, I'll have dinner with them.

But it wasn't Willie. It was Johnny Heath. "Hi," Johnny said. "Rudolph said you'd be here and I was just passing by and I thought I'd take a chance . . . "

Liar, she thought, nobody just is passing by the Algonquin at a quarter to nine in the evening. But she said, happily, "Johnny! What a nice surprise."

"I'm downstairs," Johnny said, echoes of other years in his voice, "and if you haven't eaten yet . . . "

"Well," she said, sounding reluctant, and despising herself for the ruse, "I'm not dressed and I was just about to order dinner up here. I'm exhausted from the flight and I have to get up early tomorrow and . . . "

"I'll be in the bar," Johnny said, and hung up.

Smooth, confident Wall Street sonofabitch, she thought. Then she went in and changed her dress. But she made him wait twenty full minutes before she went down to the bar.

"Rudolph was heartbroken that he couldn't come down and see you tonight," Johnny Heath was saying, across the table from her.

"I bet," Gretchen said.

"He was. Honestly. I could tell over the phone that he was really upset. He made a special point of calling me to ask me to fill in for him and explain why . . . "

"May I have some more wine, please," Gretchen said.

Johnny signaled to the waiter, who refilled the glass. They were eating in a small French restaurant in the fifties. It was almost empty. Discreet, Gretchen thought. The sort of place you were not likely to meet anyone you knew. Good for dining out with married ladies you were having an affair with. Johnny probably had a long list of similar places. The Quiet Philanderer's Guide for Dining in New York. Put it between covers and you'd probably have a big best-seller. The headwaiter had smiled warmly when they had come in and had placed them at a table in a corner, where nobody could overhear what they were saying . . .

"If he possibly could have made it," Johnny persisted, excellent go-between in times of stress for friends, enemies, lovers, blood relations, "he'd have come. He's deeply attached to you," said Johnny, who had never been deeply attached to anyone. "He admires you more than any woman he's ever met. He told me so."

"Don't you boys have anything better to chat about on the long winter nights?" Gretchen took a sip from her glass. At least she was getting a good bottle of wine out of the evening. Maybe she would get drunk tonight. Make sure she'd get some sleep before tomorrow's ordeal. She wondered if Willie and her son were also dining in a discreet restaurant. Do you hide a son, too, with whom you had once lived?

"In fact," Johnny said, "I think it's a lot your fault that Rudy's never been married. He admires you and he hasn't found anybody yet who lives up to his idea of you and . . . "

"He admires me so much," Gretchen said, "that after not seeing me for nearly a year he can't take a night off to come and see me."

"He's opening a new center at Port Philip next week," Johnny Heath said. 'One of the biggest so far. Didn't he write you?"

"Yes," she admitted. "I guess I didn't pay attention to the date."

"There's a million last-minute things he has to do. He's working twenty hours a day. It was just physically impossible. You know how he is when it comes to work."

"I know," Gretchen said. "Work now, live later. He's demented."

"What about your husband? Burke?" Johnny demanded. "Doesn't he work? I imagine he admires you, too, but I don't notice that he took time off to come to New York with you."

"He's arriving in two weeks. Anyway, it's a different kind of work."

"I see," Johnny said. "Making movies is a sacred enterprise and a woman is ennobled when she's sacrificed to it. While running a big business is sordid and crass and a man ought to be delighted to get away from all that filth and run down to New York to meet his lonely, innocent, purifying sister at the plane and buy her dinner."

"You're not defending Rudolph," Gretchen said. "You're defending yourself."

"Both," Johnny said. "Both of us. And I don't feel I have to defend anybody. If an artist wants to feel that he's the only worthwhile creature spewed up by modern civilization, that's his business. But to expect poor, money-soiled slobs like myself to agree with him is idiotic. It's a great line with the girls and it gets a lot of half-baked painters and would-be Tolstoys into some pretty fair beds, but it doesn't wash with me. I bet that if I worked in a garret in Greenwich Village instead of in an air-conditioned office in Wall Street, you'd have married me long before you ever met Colin Burke."

"Guess again, brother," Gretchen said. "I'd like some more wine." She extended her glass.

Johnny poured the wine, almost filling her glass, then signaled to the waiter, who was out of earshot, for another bottle. He sat in silence, immobile, brooding. Gretchen was surprised at his outburst. It wasn't like Johnny at all. Even when they had been making love, he had seemed cool, detached, as technically expert at that as he was at everything he undertook. By now, the last roughnesses, physical and mental, seemed to have been planed away from the man. He was like a highly polished, enormous, rounded stone, an elegant weapon, siege ammunition.

"I was a fool," he said, finally, his voice low, without timbre. "I should have asked you to marry me."

"I was married at the time. Remember?"

"You were married at the time you met Colin Burke, too. Remember?"

Gretchen shrugged. "It was in a different year," she said. "And he was a different man."

"I've seen some of his pictures," Johnny said. "They're pretty good."

"They're a lot more than that."

"The eyes of love," Johnny said, pretending to smile.

"What're you trying to do, Johnny?"

"Nothing," he said. "Ah, hell. I guess what I'm doing is being bitchy because I made such poor use of my time. Unmanly fellow. I now brighten up and ask polite questions of my guest, ex-wife of one of my best friends. I suppose you're happy."

"Very."

"Good answer." Johnny nodded approvingly. "Very good answer. Lady found fulfillment, long denied, in fulfilling second marrige to short but active artist of the silver screen."

"You're still being bitchy. If you want, I'll get up and leave."

"There's dessert coming." He put out his hand and touched hers. Smooth, fleshed, round fingers, soft palm. "Don't leave. I have other questions. A girl like you, so *New York*, so busy with a life of your own—what the hell do you do with yourself day after day in that goddamn place?"

"Most of the time," she said, "I spend thanking God I'm no longer in New York."

"And the rest of the time? Don't tell me you like just sitting there and being a housewife, waiting for Daddy to come home from the studio and tell you what Sam Goldwyn said at lunch."

"If you must know," she said, stung, "I do very little just sitting around, as you put it. I'm part of the life of a man I admire and can help, and it's a lot better than what I had here, being important and snotty, secretly screwing, and getting my name in magazines and living with a man who had to be dragged up from the bottom of a bottle three times a week."

"Ah—the new female revolution—" Johnny said. "Church, children, kitchen. Jesus, you were the last woman in the world I'd've thought . . . "

"Leave out the church," Gretchen said, "and you've got a perfect description of my life, okay?" She stood up. "And I'll skip dessert. Those short, active artists of the silver screen like their women skinny."

"Gretchen," he called after her, as she strode out of the restaurant. His voice had the ring of innocent surprise. Something had just happened to him that had never happened before, that was unimaginable within the rules of the nicely regulated games he played. Gretchen didn't look back, and she went out the door before any of the flunkeys in the restaurant had time to push it open for her.

She walked quickly toward Fifth Avenue, then slackened her pace as her anger cooled. She was silly to have become so upset, she decided. Why should she care what Johnny Heath thought about what she was doing with her life? He pretended he liked what he considered free women because that meant he could be free with them. He had been turned away from the banquet and he was trying to make her pay for it. What could he know of what it was like for her to wake up in the morning and see Colin lying beside her? She wasn't free of her husband and he wasn't free of her and they were both better and more joyous human beings because of it. What crap people believed freedom to be.

She hurried to the hotel and went up to her room and picked up the phone and asked the operator for her own number in Beverly Hills. It was eight o'clock in California and Colin ought to be home by now. She had to hear his voice, even though he detested talking on the phone and was most often sour and brusque on it, even with her, when she called him. But there was no answer and when she called the studio and asked them to ring the cutting room, she was told that Mr. Burke had left for the night.

She hung up slowly, paced the room. Then she sat down at the desk and drew out a sheet of paper and began to write: "Dear Colin, I called and you weren't home and you weren't at the studio and I am sad and a man who once was my lover said some untrue things that bothered me and New York is too warm and Billy loves his father more than he does me and I am very unhappy without you and you should have been home and I am thinking unworthy thoughts about you and I am going down to the bar to have a drink or two drinks or three drinks and if anybody tries to pick me up I am going to call for the police and I don't know how I'm going to live the two weeks before I see you again and I hope I didn't sound like a conceited know-it-all about the mirror sequence and if I did forgive me and I promise not to change or reform or keep my mouth shut on the condition that you promise not to change or reform or keep your mouth shut and your collar was frayed when you took us to the airport and I am a terrible housewife, but I am a houswife, housewife, housewife, a wife in your house, the best profession in the whole world and if you're not home the next time I call you God knows what revenge I shall prepare for you. Love, G."

She put the letter into an airmail envelope without rereading it and went down into the lobby and had it stamped and put it into the slot, connected by paper and ink and night-flying planes to the center of her life three thousand miles away across the dark great continent.

Then she went into the bar and nobody tried to pick her up and she drank two whiskies without talking to the bartender. She went up and undressed and got into bed.

When she woke the next morning, it was the phone ringing that awoke her and Willie was speaking, saying, "We'll be over to pick you up in a half hour. We've already had breakfast."

Ex-husband, ex-airman Willie drove swiftly and well. The first leaves were turning toward autumn on the small lovely hills of New England as they approached the school. Willie was wearing his dark glasses again, but today against the glare of the sun on the road, and not because of drink. His hands were steady on the wheel and there was none of the tell-tale shiftiness in his voice that came after a bad night. They had to stop twice because Billy got carsick, but aside from that the trip was a pleasant one, a handsome, youngish American family, comfortably off, driving in a shining new car through some of the greenest scenery in America on a sunny September day.

The school was mostly red-brick Colonial, with white pillars here and there and a few old wooden mansions scattered around the campus as dormitories. The buildings were set among old trees and widespread playing fields. As they drove up to the main building, Willie said, "You're enrolling in a country club, Billy."

They parked the car and went up the steps to the big hall of the main building in a bustle of parents and other schoolboys. A smiling middle-aged lady was behind the desk, set up for signing in the new students. She shook their hands, said she was glad to see them, wasn't it a beautiful day, gave Billy a colored tag to put through his lapel, and called out, "David Crawford," toward a group of older boys with different-colored tags in their lapels. A tall, bespectacled boy of eighteen came briskly over to the desk. The middle-aged lady made introductions all around and said, "William, this is David, he'll settle you in. If you have any problems today or any time during the school year, you go right to David and pester him with them."

"That's right, William," Crawford said. Deep, responsible Sixth Former voice. "I am at your service. Where's your gear? I'll show you to the room." He led the way out of the building, the middle-aged lady already smiling behind him at another family trio at the desk.

"William," Gretchen whispered as she walked behind the two boys with Willie.

"For a minute I didn't know whom she was talking to."

"It's a good sign," Willie said. "When I went to school everybody called everybody by their last names. They were preparing us for the Army."

Crawford insisted upon carrying Billy's bag and they crossed the campus to a three-story red-brick building that was obviously newer than most of the other structures surrounding it.

"Sillitoe Hall," Crawford said, as they went in. "You're on the third floor, William."

There was a plaque just inside the doorway announcing that the dormitory was the gift of Robert Sillitoe, father of Lieutenant Robert Sillitoe, Jr., Class of 1938, fallen in the service of his country, August 6th, 1944.

Gretchen was sorry she had seen the plaque, but took heart from the sound of young male voices singing from other rooms and the pounding of jazz groups from phonographs, all very much alive, as she climbed the stairs behind Crawford and Billy.

The room assigned to Billy wasn't large, but it was furnished with two cots, two small desks, and two wardrobes. The small trunk they had sent ahead with Billy's belongings was under one of the cots and there was another trunk tagged Fournier next to the window.

"Your roommate's already here," Crawford said. "have you met him yet?"

"No," Billy said. He seemed very subdued, even for him, and Gretchen hoped that Fournier, whoever he was, would not turn out to be a bully or a pederast or a marijuana smoker. She felt suddenly helpless—a life was out of her hands.

"You'll see him at lunch," Crawford said. "You'll hear the bell any minute now." He smiled his sober responsible smile at Willie and Gretchen. "Of course, all parents are invited. Mrs. Abbott."

She caught the agonized glance from Billy, saying plainly, Not now, *please!* and she checked the correction before it crossed her lips. Time enough for Billy to explain that his father was Mr. Abbott but his mother was called Mrs. Burke. Not the first day. "Thank you, David," she said, her voice unsteady in her own ears. She looked at Willie. He was shaking his head. "It's very kind of the school to invite us," she said.

Crawford gestured at the bare, unmade cot. "I advise you to get three blankets, William," he said. "The nights up here get beastly cold and they're Spartan about heat. They think freezing is good for our unfolding characters."

"I'll send you the blankets from New York today," Gretchen said. She turned toward Willie. "Now about lunch . . ."

"You're not hungry, are you, dear?" Willie's voice was pleading, and Gretchen knew that the last thing Willie wanted was to eat lunch in a school dining room, without a drink in sight.

"Not really," Gretchen said, pitying him.

"Anyway, I have to get back to town by four o'clock," Willie said. "I have an appointment that's very . . . " His voice trailed off unconvincingly.

There was a booming of bells and Crawford said, "There it is. The dining room is just behind the desk where you signed in, William. Now if you'll excuse me, I have to wash up. And remember—anything you need." Upright and gentlemanly in his blazer and scuffed white shoes, a credit to the three years of schooling behind him, he went into the corridor, still resounding with the clashing melodies from three different phonographs, Elvis Presley's wail, frantic and forlorn, dominating.

"Well," Gretchen said, "he does seem like an awfully nice boy, doesn't he?"

"I'll wait and see what he's like when you're not around," Billy said, "and tell you."

"I guess you'd better get over for your lunch," Willie said. Gretchen could tell he was panting for the first drink of the day. He had been very good about not suggesting stopping at any of the roadhouses they had passed on the way up and he had been a proper father all morning. He had earned his martini.

"We'll walk you over to the dining room," Gretchen said. She wanted to cry, but of course she couldn't, in front of Billy. She looked erratically around the room. "When you and your roommate do a little decorating here," she said, "this place ought to be very cosy. And you do have a pretty view." Abruptly, she led the way into the hall.

They crossed the campus, along with other small groups converging on the main building. Gretchen stopped some distance from the steps. The moment had come to say good-bye and she didn't want to have to do it in the middle of the herd of boys and parents at the foot of the steps.

"Well, she said, "we might as well do it here."

Billy put his arms around her and kissed her brusquely. She managed a smile. Billy shook his father's hand. "Thanks for driving me up," he said evenly, to both of them. Then, dry-eyed, he turned and walked, not hurrying, toward the steps joining in the stream of students, lost, gone, a thin, gangling, childish figure departed irrevocably for that budding company of men where mothers' voices which had comforted and lullabyed and admonished were now and forever heard only from afar.

Through a haze of tears she watched him vanish through the white pillars, the open doors, out of sunlight into shadow. Willie put his arm around her and, grateful for the touch of each other's body, they walked toward the car. They drove down the winding drive, along a treeshaded street that bordered the school's playing fields, deserted now of athletes, goals undefended, base paths clear of runners.

She sat in the seat beside Willie staring straight ahead. She heard a curious sound from Willie's side of the car and he stopped the car under a tree. Willie was sobbing uncontrollably and now she couldn't hold it back any more and she clutched him and, their arms around each other, they wept and wept, for Billy, and the life ahead of him, for Robert Sillitoe, Jr., for themselves, for love, for Mrs. Abbott, for Mrs. Burke, for all the whiskey, for all their mistakes, for the flawed life behind them.

"Just don't pay any attention to me," the girl with the cameras was saying to Rudolph as Gretchen and Johnny Heath got out of the car and walked across the parking lot to where Rudolph was standing under the huge sign that traced the name of Calderwood against the blue September sky. It was the opening day of the new shopping center on the northern outskirts of Port Philip, a neighborhood that Gretchen knew well, because it was on the road that led, a few miles farther on, to the Boylan estate.

Gretchen and Johnny had missed the opening ceremony because Johnny couldn't break loose from his office until lunchtime. Johnny had been apologetic about that, as he had been apologetic about his conversation at dinner two nights before, and the drive up had been a friendly one. Johnny had done most of the talking, but not about himself or Gretchen. He had spent the time explaining, admiringly, the mechanics of Rudolph's rise as an entrepreneur and manager. According to Johnny, Rudolph understood the complexities of modern business better than any man his age Johnny had ever come across. When Johnny tried to explain what a brilliant coup Rudolph had pulled off last year in getting Calderwood to agree to buy a firm that had shown a two-million-dollar loss in the last three years, she had to admit to him that he had finally taken her beyond her intellectual depth, but that she would accept his opinion of the deal on faith.

When Gretchen came to where Rudolph was standing, making notes on a pad on a clipboard he was carrying, the photographer was crouched a few feet in front of him, shooting upward, to get the Calderwood sign in behind him. Rudolph smiled widely when he saw her and Johnny and moved toward them to greet them. Dealer in millions, juggler with stock options, disposer of risk capital, he merely looked like her brother to Gretchen, a well-tanned, handsome young man in a nicely tailored, unremarkable suit. She was struck once again by the difference between her brother and her husband. From what Johnny had told her she knew that Rudolph was many times wealthier than Colin and wielded infinitely more real power over a much greater number of people, but nobody, not even his own mother, would ever accuse Colin of being modest. In any group, Colin stood out, arrogant and commanding, ready to make enemies. Rudolph blended into groups, affable and pliant, certain to make friends.

"That's good," the crouching girl said, taking one picture after another. "That's very good."

"Let me introduce you," Rudolph said. "My sister, Mrs. Burke, my associate, Mr. Heath. Miss . . . uh . . . Miss . . . I'm terribly sorry."

"Prescott," the girl said. "Jean will do. Please don't pay any attention to me." She stood up and smiled, rather shyly. She was a small girl, with straight, long, brown hair, caught in a bow at the nape of her neck. She was freckled and unmade-up and she moved easily, even with the three cameras hanging from her, and the heavy film case slung from her shoulder.

"Come on," Rudolph said, "I'll show you around. If you see old man Calderwood, make admiring noises."

Wherever they went, Rudolph was stopped by men and women who shook his hand and said what a wonderful thing he had done for the town. While Miss Prescott clicked away, Rudolph smiled his modest smile, said he was glad they were enjoying themselves, remembered an amazing number of names.

Among the well-wishers, Gretchen didn't recognize any of the girls she had gone to school with or had worked with at Boylan's. But all of Rudolph's schoolmates seemed to have turned out to see for themselves what their old friend had done and to congratulate him, some sincerely, some with all too obvious envy. By a curious trick of time, the men who came up to Rudolph with their wives and children, and said, "Remember me? We graduated in the same class?" seemed older, grosser, slower, than her unmarried, unimpeded brother. Success had put him in another generation, a slimmer, quicker, more elegant generation. Colin, too, she realized, seemed much younger than he was. The youth of winners.

"You seem to have the whole town here today," Gretchen said.

"Just about," Rudolph said. "I even heard that Teddy Boylan put in an appearance. We'll probably bump into him." Rudolph looked over at her carefully.

"Teddy Boylan," she said flatly. "Is he still alive?"

"So the rumor goes," Rudolph said. "I haven't seen him for a long time, either."

They walked on, a small, momentary chill between them. "Wait a minute for me here," Rudolph said. "I want to talk to the band leader. They're not playing enough of the old standards."

"He sure likes to keep everything under control, doesn't he?" Gretchen said to Johnny, as she watched Rudolph hurry toward the bandstand, followed, as ever, by Miss Prescott.

When Rudolph came back to them, the band was playing "Happy Days are Here Again," and he had a couple in tow, a slender, very pretty blonde girl in a crisp, white-linen dress, and a balding, sweating man somewhat older than Rudolph, wearing a wrinkled seersucker suit. Gretchen was sure she had seen the man somewhere before, but for the moment she couldn't place him.

"This is Virginia Calderwood, Gretchen," Rudolph said. "The boss's youngest. I've told her all about you."

Miss Calderwood smiled shyly. "He has, indeed, Mrs. Burke."

"And you remember Bradford Knight, don't you?" Rudolph asked.

"I drank you dry the night of the graduation party in New York," Bradford said.

She remember then, the ex-sergeant with the Oklahoma accent, hunting girls in the apartment in the Village. The accent seemed to have been toned down somewhat and it was too bad he was losing his hair. She remembered now that Rudolph had coaxed him to come back to Whitby a few years ago and was grooming him to be an assistant manager. Rudolph liked him, she knew, although looking at the man she couldn't tell just why. Rudolph had told her he was shrewd, behind his Rotarian front, and was wonderful at getting along with people while carrying out instructions to the letter.

"Of course, I remember you, Brad," Gretchen said. "I hear you're invaluable."

"I blush, ma'am," Knight said.

"We're all invaluable," Rudolph said.

"No," the girl said. She spoke seriously, keeping her eyes fixed, in a way that Gretchen recognized, on Rudolph.

They all laughed. Except for the girl. Poor thing, Gretchen thought. Better learn to look at another man that way.

"Where is your father?" Rudolph asked. "I want to introduce my sister to him."

"He went home," the girl said. "He got angry at something the Mayor said, because the Mayor kept talking about you and not about him."

"I was born here," Rudolph said lightly, "and the Mayor wants to take credit for it."

"And he didn't like her taking pictures of you all the time." She gestured at Miss Prescott, who was focusing on the group from a few feet away.

"Hazards of the trade," Johnny Heath said. "He'll get over it."

"You don't know my father," the girl said. "You'd better give him a ring later," she said to Rudolph, "and calm him down."

"I'll give him a ring later," Rudolph said, carelessly. "If I have the time. Say, we're all going to have a drink in about an hour. Why don't you two join us?"

"I can't be seen in bars," Virginia said. "You know that."

"Okay," Rudolph said. "We'll have dinner instead. Brad, just wander around and break up anything that looks as if it's getting rough. And later on, the kids're bound to start dancing. Make them keep it clean, in a polite way."

"I'll insist on minuets," Knight said. "Come on, Virginia, I'll treat you to a free orange pop, courtesy of your father."

Reluctantly, the girl allowed herself to be pulled away by Knight.

"He is not the man of her dreams," Gretchen said, as they started walking again. "That's plain."

"Don't tell Brad that," Rudolph said. "He has visions of marrying into the family and starting an empire."

"She's nice," Gretchen said.

"Nice enough," said Rudolph. "Especially for a boss's daughter."

A heavy-set woman, rouged and eye-shadowed, wearing a turbanlike hat that made her look like something from a movie of the 1920's, stopped Rudolph, winking and working her mouth coquettishly. "*Eh bien, mon cher Rudolph,*" she said, her voice high with a desperate attempt at girlishness, "*tu parles français toujours bien?*"

Rudolph bowed gravely, taking his cue from the turban. "*Bonjour, Mlle. Lenaut,*" he said, "*je suis très content de vous voir.* May I present my sister, Mrs. Burke. And my friend, Mr. Heath."

"Rudolph was the brightest pupil I ever taught," Miss Lenaut said, rolling her eyes. "I was certain that he would rise in the world. It was plain in everything he did."

"You are too kind," Rudolph said, and they walked on. He grinned. "I used to write love letters to her when I was in her class. I never sent them. Pop once called her a French cunt and slapped her face."

"I never heard that story," Gretchen said.

"There're a lot of stories you never heard."

"Some evening," she said, "you've got to sit down and tell me the history of the Jordaches."

"Some evening," Rudolph said.

"It must give you an awful lot of satisfaction," Johnny said, "coming back to your old town on a day like this."

Rudolph reflected for an instant. "It's just another town," he said offhandedly. "Let's go look at the merchandise."

He led them on a tour of the shops. Gretchen's acquisitive instinct was, as Colin had once told her, subnormal, and the gigantic assembly of things to buy, that insensate flood of objects which streamed inexorably from the factories of America saddened her.

Everything, or almost everythng that most depressed Gretchen about the age in which she lived, was crammed into this artfully rustic conglomeration of white buildings, and it was her brother, whom she loved, and who softly and modestly surveyed this concrete, material proof of his cunning, who had put it all together. When he told her the history of the Jordaches, she would reserve one chapter for herself.

After the shops, Rudolph showed them around the theater. A touring company from New York was to open that night in a comedy and a lighting rehearsal was in progress when they went into the auditorium. Here old man Calderwood's taste had not been the deciding factor. Dull-pink walls and deep-red plush on the chairs softened the clean severity of the interior lines of the building and Gretchen could tell, from the ease with which the director was getting complicated lighting cues, that no expense had been spared on the board backstage. For the first time in years she felt a pang of regret that she had given up the theater.

"It's lovely, Rudy," she said.

"I had to show you one thing of which you could approve," he said quietly.

She reached out and touched his hand, begging forgiveness with the gesture for her unspoken criticism of the rest of his accomplishment.

"Finally," he said. "We're going to have six theaters like this around the country and we're going to put on our own plays and run them at least two weeks in each place. That way each play will be guaranteed a run of three months at a minimum and we won't have to depend upon anybody else. If Colin ever wants to put on a play for me . . ."

"I'm sure he'd love to work in a place like this," Gretchen said. "He's always grumbling about the old barns on Broadway. When he gets to New York I'll bring him up to see it. Though maybe it's not such a good idea . . ."

"Why not?" Rudolph askcd.

"He sometimes gets into terrible fights with the people he works with."

"He won't fight with me," Rudolph said confidently. He and Burkc had likcd each other from their first meeting. "I am deferential and respectful in the presence of artists. Now for that drink."

Gretchen looked at her watch. "I'm afraid I'll have to skip it. Colin's calling me at the hotel at eight o'clock and he fumes if I'm not there when the phone rings. Johnny, do you mind if we leave now?"

"At your service, ma'am," Johnny said.

Gretchen kissed Rudolph good-bye and left him in the theater, his face glowing in the light reflected from the stage, with Miss Prescott changing lenses and clicking away, pretty, agile, busy.

Johnny and Gretchen passed the bar going toward the car and she was glad they hadn't gone in because she was sure that the man she glimpsed, in the dark interior, bent over a drink, was Teddy Boylan, and even after fifteen years she knew he had the power to disturb her. She didn't want to be disturbed.

The phone was ringing when she opened the door to her room. The call was from California, but it wasn't Colin. It was the head of the studio and he was calling to say that Colin had been killed in an automobile accident at one o'clock that day. He had been dead all afternoon and she hadn't known it.

She thanked the man on the phone calmly for his muted words of sympathy and hung up and for a long while sat alone in the hotel room without turning on the light.

CHAPTER 2

THE BELL RANG for the last round of the sparring session and Schultzy called, "See if you can crowd him more, Tommy." The boxer Quayles was going to meet in five days was a crowder and Thomas was supposed to imitate his style. But Quayles was a hard man to crowd, a dancer and jabber, quick and slippery on his feet and with fast hands. He never hurt anybody much, but he had come a long way with his cleverness. The bout was going to be nationally televised and Quayles was getting twenty thousand dollars for his end. Thomas, on the supporting card, was going to get six hundred. It would have been less if Schultzy, who handled both fighters, at least for the record, hadn't held out for the money with the promoters. There was Mafia money behind the fight and those boys didn't go in for charity.

The training ring was set up in a theater and the people who came to watch the sessions sat in the orchestra seats in their fancy Las Vegas shirts and canary-yellow pants. Thomas felt more like an actor than a fighter up there on the stage.

He shuffled toward Quayles, who had a mean flat face and dead-cold pale eyes under the leather headguard. When Quayles sparred with Thomas, there was always a little derisive smile on his lips, as though it was absurd for Thomas to be in the same ring with him. He made a point of never talking to Thomas, not as much as a good morning, even though they were both in the same stable. The only satisfaction Thomas got out of Quayles was that he was screwing Quayles's wife and one day he was going to let Quayles know it.

Quayles danced in and out, tapping Thomas sharply, slipping Thomas's hooks easily, showing off for the crowd, letting Thomas swing at him in a corner and just bobbing his head, untouched, as the crowd yelled.

Sparring partners were not supposed to damage maineventers, but this was the last round of the training schedule and Thomas attacked doggedly, ignoring punishment, to get just one good one in, sit the bastard down on the seat of his fancy pants. Quayles realized what Thomas was trying to do and the smile on his face became loftier than ever as he flicked away, danced in and out, picked off punches in mid-air. He wasn't even sweating at the end of the round and there wasn't a mark on his body, although Thomas had been hacking away trying to reach him there, for a solid two minutes.

When the bell rang, Quayles said, "You ought to pay me for a boxing lesson, you bum."

"I hope you get killed Friday, you cheap ham," Thomas said, then climbed down and went into the showers, while Quayles did some rope skipping and calisthenics and worked on the light bag. He never got tired, the bastard, and he was a glutton for work, and would probably wind up middleweight champion, with a million bucks in the bank.

When Thomas came back out after his shower, his skin reddened under the eyes by Quayles's jabs, Quayles was still at it, showing off, shadow boxing, with the hicks in the crowd in their circus clothes oh-ing and ah-ing.

Schultzy gave him the envelope with the fifty bucks in it for his two rounds and he walked quickly through the crowd and out into the glare of the searing Las Vegas afternoon. After the air-conditioned theater the heat seemed artificial and malevolent, as though the entire town were being cooked by some diabolical scientist who wanted to destroy it in the most painful way possible.

He was thirsty after the workout and went across the blazing street to one of the big hotels. The lobby was dark and cold. The expensive hookers were on patrol and the old ladies were playing the slot machines. The crap and roulette tables were in action as he passed them on his way to the bar. Everybody in the whole stinking town was loaded with money. Except him. He had lost over five hundred dollars, almost all the money he had earned, at the crap tables in the last two weeks.

He felt the envelope with Schultzy's fifty in his pocket and fought back the urge to try the dice. He ordered a beer from the barman. His weight was okay and Schultzy wasn't there to bawl him out. Anyway, Schultzy didn't much care what he did any more, now that he had a contender in the stable. He wondered how much of Schultzy's end of the purse he had to give to the gunslingers.

He drank a second beer, paid the barman, started out, stopped for a moment to watch the crap game. A guy who looked like a small-town undertaker had a pile of chips about a foot high in front of him. The dice were hot. Thomas took out the envelope and bought chips. In ten minutes he was down to ten dollars and he had sense enough to hold onto that.

He got the doorman to beg a ride for him from a guest to his hotel downtown, so he wouldn't have to pay taxi fare. His hotel was a grubby one, with a few slot machines and one crap table. Quayles was staying at the Sands, with all the movie stars. And his wife. Who lay around the pool all day getting stoned on Planter's Punches when she wasn't sneaking down to Thomas's hotel for a quick one. She had a loving nature, she said, and Quayles slept alone, in a separate room, being a serious fighter with an important bout coming up. Thomas wasn't a serious fighter any more and there were no more important bouts for him so it didn't make much difference what he did. The lady was active in bed and some of the afternoons were really worth the trouble.

There was a letter at the desk for him. From Teresa. He didn't even bother to open it. He knew what was in it. Another demand for money. She was working now and making more money than he did, but that didn't stop her. She had gone to work as a hatcheck and cigarette girl in a nightclub, wiggling her ass and showing her legs as high up as the law allowed and raking in the tips. She said she was bored just hanging around the house with the kid, with him away so much of the time and she wanted to have a career. She thought being a hatcheck girl was some sort of show business. The kid was stashed away with her sister in the Bronx and even when Thomas was in town Teresa came in at all hours, five, six in the morning, with her purse stuffed with twenty-dollar bills. God knows what she did. He didn't care any more.

He went up to his room and lay down on his bed. That was one way to save money. He had to figure how to get from today to Friday on ten bucks. The skin under his eyes smarted where Quayles had peppered him. The air conditioning in the room was almost useless and the desert heat made him sweat.

He closed his eyes and slept uneasily, dreaming. He dreamt of France. It had been the best time of his life and he often dreamt about the moment on the shore of the Mediterranean, although it had been almost five years ago now, and the dreams were losing their intensity.

He woke, remembering the dream, sighed as the sea and the white buildings disappeared and he was surrounded once more by the cracked Las Vegas walls.

He had gone down to the Côte d'Azur after winning the fight in London. It had been an easy victory and Schultzy had gotten him another bout in Paris a month later, so there was no sense in going back to New York. Instead he had picked up one of those wild London girls. She had said she knew a great little hotel in Cannes and since Thomas was rolling in money for once and it looked as though he could beat everybody in Europe with one hand tied behind him, he had taken off for the weekend. The weekend had stretched into ten days, with frantic cables from Schultzy. Thomas had lain on the beach and eaten two great, heavy meals a day, developed a taste for vin rosé, and had put on fifteen pounds. When he finally got to Paris, he had just managed to make the weight the morning of the fight and the Frenchman had nearly killed him. For the first time in his life he had been knocked out and suddenly there were no more bouts in Europe. He had blown most of his money on the English girl, who happened to like jewelry, aside from her other attractions, and Schultzy hadn't talked to him all the way back to New York.

The Frenchman had taken something out of him and nobody was writing that he should be considered for a shot at the title anymore. The time between bouts became greater and greater and the purses smaller and smaller. Twice he had to take a dive for walking-around money and Teresa closed him off entirely and if it hadn't been for the kid he'd have just gotten up and left.

Lying in the heat on the wrinkled bed, he thought of all these things and remembered what his brother had told him that day at the Hotel Warwick. He wondered if Rudolph had followed his career and was saying, to his snooty sister, "I told him it would happen."

Screw his brother.

Well, maybe on Friday night, there'd be some of the old juice in him and he'd score spectacularly. People could start hanging around him again and he'd made a comeback. Plenty of fighters—older than he—had made comebacks. Look at Jimmy Braddock, down to being a day laborer and then beating Max Baer for the heavyweight championship of the world. Schultzy just had to pick his opponents for him more carefully—keep him away from the dancers, give him somebody who came to fight. He'd have to have a talk with Schultzy. And not only about that. He had to get some money in advance, before Friday, to keep alive in this lousy town.

Two, three good wins and he could forget all this. Two, three good wins and they'd be asking for him in Paris again and he'd be down on the Côte sitting at a sidewalk café, drinking vin rosé and looking out at the masts of the boats anchored in the harbor. With real luck he might even get to rent one of them, sail around, out of reach of everybody. Maybe only two, three fights a year just to keep the bank balance comfortable.

Just thinking about it made him cheerful again and he was just about to go downstairs and put his ten bucks on the come at the crap table when the phone rang.

It was Cora, Quayles's wife and she sounded demented, screaming and crying into the phone. "He's found out, he's found out," she kept saying. "Some lousy bellboy got to him. He nearly killed me just now. I think he broke my nose, I'm going to be a cripple the rest of my life . . ."

"Go easy now," Thomas said. "What has he found out?"

"You know what he found out. He's on his way right now to . . ."

"Wait a minute. What did you tell him?"

"What the hell do you think I told him?" she screamed. "I told him no. Then he clouted me across the face. I'm blood all over. He doesn't believe me. That lousy bellboy in your hotel must've had a telescope or something. You'd better get out of town. This minute. He's on his way over to see you, I tell you. Christ knows what he'll do to you. And later on, to me. Only I'm not waiting. I'm going to the airport right now. I'm not even packing a bag. And I advise you to do the same. Only stay away from me. You don't know him. He's a murderer. Just get on something and get out of town. Fast."

Thomas hung up on the terrified, high-pitched babble. He looked at his one valise in a corner of the room, then stood up and went to the window and peered out through the Venetian blinds. The street was empty in the four o'clock afternoon desert glare. Thomas went over to the door and made sure it was unlocked. Then he moved the one chair to a corner. He didn't want to get charged and sent backward over the chair in the first rush.

He sat on the bed, smiling a little. He had never run away from a fight and he wasn't going to run away from this one. And this one might be the most enjoyable fight of his entire career. The small hotel room was no place for jabbers and dancers.

He got up and went over to the closet and took out a leather windjacket and put it on, zipping it up high and turning the collar up to protect his throat. Then he sat on the edge of the bed again, waiting placidly, hunched over a little, his hands hanging loose between his legs. He heard a car screech to a halt in front of the hotel, but he didn't move. One minute later there were steps outside in the hall and then the door was flung open and Quayles came into the room, stopping just inside the doorway.

"Hi," Thomas said. He stood up slowly.

Quayles closed the door behind him and turned the key in the lock.

"I know all about it, Jordache," Quayles said.

"About what?" Thomas asked mildly, keeping his eyes on Quayles's feet for the first hint of movement.

"About you and my wife."

"Oh, yes," Thomas said. "I've been screwing her. Did I forget to mention it?"

He was ready for the leap and almost laughed when he saw Quayles, that dandy and stylist of the ring, lead with a blind long right, a sucker's punch if ever there was one. Because he was ready, Thomas went inside it easily, tied Quayles up, held onto him, with no referee to part them, and clubbed at Quayles's body, with delicious, pent-up ferocity. Then, old street fighter with all the tricks, he rushed Quayles to the wall, ignoring the man's attempt to writhe out of his grasp, stepped back just far enough to savage Quayles with an uppercut, then closed, wrestled, hit, held, used his elbows, his knee, butted Quayles's forehead with his head, wouldn't let him drop, but kept him up against the wall with his left hand around Quayles's throat, and pounded at his face with one brutal right hand after another. When he stepped back, Quayles crumpled onto the blood-stained rug and lay there on his face, out cold.

There was a frantic knocking on the door and he heard Schultzy's voice in the hall. He unlocked the door and let Schultzy in.

Schultzy took the whole thing in with one glance.

"You stupid bastard," he said, "I saw that bird-brained wife of his and she told me. I thought I'd get here in time. You're a great indoor fighter, aren't you, Tommy? You can't beat your grandmother for dough, but when it comes to fighting for nothing you're the all-time beauty." He knelt beside Quayles, motionless on the rug. Schultzy turned him over, examined the cut on Quayles's forehead, ran his hand alongside Quayles's jaw. "I think you broke his jaw. Idiots. He won't be able to fight this Friday or a month of Fridays. The boys're going to like that. They're going to like it a lot. They've got a big investment tied up in this horse's ass—" He prodded the inert Quayles fiercely. "They're going to be just overjoyed you took him apart. If I was you I'd start going right now, before I get this—this *husband* out of the room and into a hospital. And I'd keep on going until I got to an ocean and then I'd cross the ocean and if I wanted to stay alive I wouldn't come back for ten years. And don't go by plane. By the time the plane comes down anywhere, they'll be waiting for you and they won't be waiting for you with roses in their hands."

"What do you want me to do," Thomas asked, "walk? I got ten bucks to my name."

Schultzy looked worriedly down at Quayles, who was beginning to stir. He stood up. "Come on out into the hall." He took the key out of the lock and when they were both outside, he locked the door.

"It would serve you right if they filled you full of holes," Schultzy said. "But you've been with me a long time . . ." He looked nervously up and down the hallway. "Here," he said, taking some bills out of his wallet. "All I got. A hundred and fifty. And take my car. It's downstairs, with the key in the ignition. Leave it in Reno in the airport parking lot and bus East from there. I'll tell 'em you stole the car. Don't get in touch with your wife, whatever you do. They'll be after her. I'll get in touch with her and tell her you're running and not to expect to hear from you. Don't go in a straight line anywhere. And I'm not kidding when I tell you to get out of this country. Your life isn't worth two cents anywhere in the United States." He wrinkled his seamy brow, concentrating. "The safest thing is getting a job on a ship. When you get to New York go to a hotel called the Aegean. It's on West Eighteenth Street. It's full of Greek sailors, Ask for the manager. He's got a long Greek name, but everybody calls him Pappy. He handles jobs for freighters that don't fly the American flag. Tell him I sent you and I want you out of the country fast. He won't ask questions. He owes me a favor from when I was in the Merchant Marine during the war. And don't be a wise guy. Don't think you can pick up a few bucks fighting anywhere, even in Europe or Japan, under another name. As of this minute you're a sailor and nothing else. Do you hear that?"

"Yes, Schultzy," Thomas said.

"And I never want to hear from you again. Got that?"

"Yes." Thomas made a move toward the door of his room.

Schultzy stopped him. "Where do you think you're going?"

"My passport's in there. I'll be needing it."

"Where is it?"

"In the top dresser drawer."

"Wait here," Schultzy said. "I'll get it for you." He turned the key in the lock and went into the room. A moment later he was back in the hall with the passport. "Here." He slapped the booklet into Thomas's hand. "And from now on try to think with your head instead of your cock. Now breeze. I got to start putting that bum together again."

Thomas went down the steps, into the lobby, past the crap game. He didn't say anything to the clerk, who looked at him curiously, because there was blood on his windjacket. He went out to the street. Schultzy's car was parked right behind Quayles's Cadillac. Thomas got in, started the motor and slowly drove toward the main highway. He didn't want to be picked up this afternoon for a traffic violation in Las Vegas. He could wash the windjacket later.

CHAPTER 3

THE DATE WAS for eleven o'clock, but Jean had phoned to say that she would be a few minutes late and Rudolph had said that was all right, he had a few calls to make, anyway. It was Saturday morning. He had been too busy to telephone his sister all week and he felt guilty about it. Since he had flown back from the funeral, he had usually managed at least two or three calls a week. He had suggested to Gretchen that she come East and stay with him in his apartment, which would mean that she would have the place to herself more often than not. Old man Calderwood refused to move the central office down to the city, so Rudolph couldn't count on more than ten days a month in New York. But Gretchen had decided she wanted to stay in California, at least for awhile. Burke had neglected to leave a will, or at least one that anyone could find, and the lawyers were squabbling and Burke's ex-wife was suing for the best part of the estate and trying to evict Gretchen from the house, among other unpleasant legal maneuvers.

It was eight o'clock in the morning in California, but Rudolph knew that Gretchen was an early riser and that the ringing of the phone wouldn't awaken her. He placed the call with the operator and sat down at the desk in the small living room and tried to finish a corner of the *Times* crossword puzzle that had stumped him when he had tried it at breakfast.

The apartment had come furnished. It was decorated with garish solid colors and spiky metal chairs, but Rudolph had only taken it as a temporary measure and it did have a good small kitchen with a refrigerator that produced a lot of ice. He often liked to cook and eat by himself, reading at the table. That morning he had made the toast, orange juice, and coffee for himself early. Sometimes Jean would come in and fix breakfast for both of them, but she had been busy this morning. She refused to stay overnight, although she had never explained why.

The phone rang and Rudolph picked it up, but it wasn't Gretchen. It was Calderwood's voice, flat and twangy and old. Saturdays and Sundays didn't mean much to Calderwood, except for the two hours on Sunday morning he spent in church.

"Rudy," Calderwood said, as usual without any polite preliminaries, "you going to be up here this evening?"

"I hadn't planned to, Mr. Calderwood, I have some things to do here over the weekend and there's a meeting scheduled downtown for Monday and . . . "

"I'd like to see you as soon as can be, Rudy." Calderwood sounded testy. As he had grown older he had become impatient and bad tempered. He seemed to resent his increasing wealth and the men who had made it possible, as he resented the necessity of depending more and more upon dealing with financial and legal people in New York for important decisions.

"I'll be in the office on Tuesday morning, Mr. Calderwood," Rudolph said. "Can't it wait until then?

"No, it can't wait until then. And I don't want to see you in the office. I want you to come to the house." The voice on the telephone was grating and tense. "I'll wait until tomorrow night after supper, Rudy."

"Of course, Mr. Calderwood," Rudy said.

The phone clicked, as Calderwood hung up, without saying good-bye.

Rudolph frowned at the phone as he put it down. He had tickets for the Giant game at the Stadium for himself and Jean Sunday afternoon and Calderwood's summons meant he'd have to miss it. Jean had had a boy friend on the team when she went to Michigan and she knew a surprising amount about football so it was always fun to go to a game with her. Why didn't the old man just lie down and die?

The phone rang again and this time it was Gretchen. Ever since Burke's death, something had gone out of her voice, a sharpness, an eagerness, a quick music that had been special to her ever since she was a young girl. She sounded pleased to hear Rudolph, but dully pleased, like an invalid responding to a visit in her hospital bed. She said she was all right, that she was being kept busy going through Colin's papers and sorting them and answering letters of condolence that still came drifting in and conferring with lawyers about the estate. She thanked him for the check he had mailed her the week before, saying that when the estate was finally settled she would pay back all the money he had sent her.

"Don't worry about that," Rudolph said. "Please. You don't have to pay back anything."

She ignored that. "I'm glad you called," she said. "I was going to call you myself and ask for another favor.,"

"What is it?" he asked, then said, "Hold on a second," because the bell was ringing on the intercom from downstairs. He hurried over to the box and pushed the button.

"There's a Miss Prescott in the lobby, Mr. Jordache." It was the doorman, protecting him.

"Send her up, please," Rudolph said, and went back to the phone. "I'm sorry, Gretchen," he said, "what were you saying?"

"I got a letter from Billy from school yesterday," she said, "and I don't like the way it sounds. There's nothing that you can grasp in it, but that's the way he is, he never really tells you what's bothering him, but somehow I have the feeling he's in despair. Do you think you could find the time to go and visit him and see what's wrong?"

Rudolph hesitated. He doubted that the boy liked him enough to confide in him and he was afraid he might do more harm than good by going to the school. "Of course I"ll go," he said, "if you want. But don't you think it might be better if his father went?"

"No," Gretchen said. "He's a bungler. If there's a wrong word to be said, he'll say it."

The front door was ringing now. "Hold on again, Gretchen," Rudolph said. "There's somebody at the door." He hurried over to the door and threw it open. "I'm on the phone," he said to Jean and trotted back into the room. "Back again, Gretchen," he said, using his sister's name to show Jean he wasn't talking to another lady. "I tell you what I"ll do—I'll drive up to the school tomorrow morning and take him to lunch and see what's up."

"I hate to bother you," Gretchen said. "But the letter was so—so *dark.*"

"It's probably nothing. He came in second in a race or he flunked an algebra exam or something like that. You know how kids are."

"Not Billy. I tell you, he's in despair." She sounded unlike herself, near tears.

"I'll call you tomorrow night, after I see him," Rudolph said. "Will you be home?"

"I'll be home," she said.

He put down the phone slowly, thinking of his sister alone, waiting for a telephone call, in the isolated house on the mountain crest, overlooking the city and the sea, going over her dead husband's papers. He shook his head. He would worry about her tomorrow. He smiled across the room at Jean, sitting neatly on a straight-backed wooden chair, wearing red-woolen stockings and moccasins, her hair brushed and bright and pulled together low on the nape of her neck in a black-velvet bow, and falling down her back freely below the bow. Her face, as always, looked scrubbed and schoolgirlish. The slender, beloved body was lost in a floppy camel's-hair polo coat. She was twenty-four years old, but at moments like this she seemed no more than sixteen. She had been out on a job and she had her camera equipment with her, which she had dumped carelessly on the floor next to the front door.

"You look as though I ought to offer you a glass of milk and a cookie," he said.

"You can offer me a drink," she said. "I've been on the streets since seven this morning. Not too much water."

He went over to her and kissed her forehead. She smiled, rewarding him. Young girls, he thought, as he went into the kitchen and got a pitcher of water.

While she drank the bourbon, she checked the list of art galleries in last Sunday's *Times*. When he was free on Saturdays they usually made the rounds of galleries. She worked as a free-lance photographer and many of her assignments were for art magazines and catalogue publishers.

"Put on comfortable shoes," she said. "We're in for a long afternoon." She had a surprisingly low voice, with husky overtones, for such a small girl.

"Where you walk," he said, "I shall follow."

They were just going out the door when the phone rang again. "Let it ring," he said. "Let's get out of here."

She stopped in the doorway. "Do you mean to say you can hear a telephone ring and not answer it?"

"I certainly can."

'I never could. It might be something absolutely wonderful."

"Nothing wonderful has ever happened to me over the phone. Let's get out of here."

"Answer it. It'll bother you all day if you don't.

"No, it won.t"

"It'll bother me. *I'll* answer it." She started back into the room.

"All right, all right." He pushed past her and picked up the phone.

It was his mother, calling from Whitby. From the tone in which she said, "Rudolph," he knew the conversation was not going to be wonderful.

"Rudolph," she said, "I don't want to interfere with your holiday—" It was his mother's fixed conviction that he left Whitby for New York only for unseemly, secret pleasures. "But the heating's gone off and I'm freezing in this drafty old place—" Rudolph had bought a fine old low-ceilinged eighteenth-century farmhouse on the outskirts of town three years before, but his mother referred to it at all times as this crumbling dark hole or this drafty old place.

"Can't Martha do anything about it?" Rudolph asked. Martha was the live-in maid who kept the house, cooked, and took care of his mother, a job for which Rudolph felt she was grossly underpaid.

"Martha!" his mother snorted. "I'm tempted to fire her on the spot."

"Mom . . . "

"When I told her to go down to look at the furnace, she flatly refused." His mother's voice rose a half octave. "She's afraid of cellars. She said for me to put on a sweater. If you weren't so lenient with her, she wouldn't be so free with her advice about putting on sweaters, I guarantee. She's so fat, swilling down our food, she wouldn't feel cold at the North Pole. When you get back home, if you ever do deign to come back home, I implore you to have a word with that woman."

"I'll be home tomorrow afternoon and I'll talk to her," Rudolph said. He was aware of Jean smiling maliciously at him. Her parents lived somewhere in the Midwest and she hadn't seen them for two years. "In the meanwhile, Mom, call the office. Get Brad Knight. He's on today. Tell him I told you to ask him to send one of our engineers."

"He'll think I'm an old crank."

"He won't think anything. Do as I say, please."

"You have no idea how cold it is up here. The wind just howls under the windows. I don't know why we can't live in a decent new house like everybody else."

This was an old song and Rudolph ignored it. When his mother had finally realized that Rudolph was making a good deal of money she had suddenly developed a glutonous taste for luxury. Her charge account at the store made Rudolph wince every month when the bills came in.

"Tell Martha to build a fire in the living room," Rudolph said, "and close the door and you'll be warm in no time."

"Tell Martha to build a fire," his mother said. "If she'll condescend. Will you be home in time for dinner tomorrow night?"

"I'm afraid not," he said. "I have to see Mr. Calderwood." It wasn't quite a lie. He wasn't going to dine with Calderwood, but he *was* going to see him. In any case, he didn't want to have dinner with his mother.

"Calderwood, Calderwood," his mother said. "Sometimes I think I'll scream if I ever hear that name again."

"I have to go now, Mom. Somebody's waiting for me."

He heard his mother begin to cry as he hung up. "Why can't old ladies just lie down and die?" he said to Jean. "The Eskimos do it better. They expose them. Come on, let's get out of here before anybody else calls."

As they went out the door he was glad to see that Jean was leaving her camera equipment in the flat. That meant she'd have to come back with him that afternoon to pick it up. She was unpredictable in that department. Sometimes she'd come in with him when they'd been out together as though it were inconceivable that she could do anything else. Other times, without any explanation, she'd insist on getting into a taxi and going downtown alone to the apartment she shared with another girl. Then, on several occasions, she had merely appeared at his door, on the off chance that he'd be home.

She went her own way, Jean, and pleased her own appetites. He had never even seen the place she lived. She always met him at his apartment or in a bar uptown. She didn't explain this, either. Young as she was, she seemed self-reliant, confident. Her work, as Rudolph had seen when she came up to Whitby with the proofs after the opening of the Port Philip center, was highly professional, surprisingly bold for a girl who had seemed so young and shy when he had first met her. She wasn't shy in bed, either, and however she behaved and for whatever reasons, she was never coy. She never complained that because of his work in Whitby there were long periods when he couldn't see her, two weeks at a time. It was Rudolph who complained of their separations, and he found himself plotting all sorts of stratagems, unnecessary appointments in the city, merely for an evening with Jean.

She was not one of those girls who lavished a full autobiography on her lover. He learned little about her. She came from the Midwest. She was on bad terms with her family. She had an older brother who was in the family firm, something to do with drugs. She had finished college at the age of twenty. She had majored in sociology. She had been interested in photography ever since she was a child. To get anywhere,

you had to start in New York, so she had come to New York. She liked the work of
Cartier-Bresson, Penn, Capa, Duncan, Klein. There was room among those names
for a woman's name. Perhaps, eventually, it would be hers.

She went out with other men. Not described. In the summer she sailed. Names of
craft unmentioned. She had been to Europe. A Yugoslavian island to which she
would like to return. She was surprised that he had never been out of the United
States.

She dressed youthfully, with a fresh eye for colors that at first glance seemed to
clash, but then, after a moment, subtly complemented each other. Her clothes,
Rudolph could see, were not expensive and after the first three times he had gone out
with her, he was fairly certain he was familiar with her entire wardrobe.

She did the Sunday New York *Times* crossword puzzle faster than he did. Her
handwriting was without frills, like a man's. She liked new painters whose work
Rudolph couldn't appreciate or understand. "Keep looking," she said, "and then one
day, a door will open, you will suddenly cross the barrier."

She never went to church. She never cried at sad movies. She never introduced him
to any of her friends. She was unimpressed by Johnny Heath. She didn't mind getting
her hair wet in the rain. She never complained about the weather or traffic jams. She
never said, "I love you."

"I love you," he said. They were lying close together in bed, his hand on her breast,
the covers pulled up under their chins. It was seven o'clock in the evening and the
room was dark. They had strolled through twenty galleries. He had crossed no
barriers. They had had lunch in a small Italian retaurant, where the proprietors had no
objection to girls with red-wool stockings. He had told her at lunch that he couldn't
take her to the game tomorrow and told her why. She wasn't disturbed. He had given
her the tickets. She said she would take a man she knew who had once played tackle
for Columbia. She ate heartily.

They had been cold when they came in from their wanderings around the city,
because the December afternoon had turned bitter early, and he had made them both
hot tea spiked with rum.

"It would be nice if we had a fire," she said, curled up on the sofa, her moccasins
kicked off on the floor.

"The next apartment I rent," he said.

When they kissed they both tasted of rum, perfumed with lemon.

They had made love unhurriedly, completely.

"This is what a Saturday afternoon in New York in the winter should be like," she
said, when they had finished and were lying together quietly. "Art, spaghetti, rum,
and lust."

He laughed, pressed her closer. He regretted his years of abstinence. Then he
wasn't so sure. Perhaps it was because of the abstinence that he was ready for her, free
for her.

"I love you," he said. "I want to marry you."

She lay still for a moment, then moved away, threw the covers back, started to
dress in silence.

I have ruined everything, he thought. "What's the matter?"

"It's a subject I never discuss naked," she said gravely.

He laughed again, but was not happy. How many times had this beautiful, assured
girl, with her own mysterious rules of behavior, discussed marriage, and with how
many men? He had never been jealous before. Unprofitable emotion.

He watched the slender shadow move around the dark room, heard the rustle of
cloth over skin. She went into the living room. Bad sign? Good sign? Would it be
better just to lie here as he was, not go after her? He hadn't planned on saying either "I
love you" or "I want to marry you."

He got out of bed and dressed quickly. She was sitting in the living room, other people's furniture, fiddling with the radio. Announcers' voices, honeyed and smooth, voices you would never believe if they said, "I love you."

"I want a drink," she said, without turning around, still fiddling with the dials.

He poured them both some bourbon and water. She drank like a man. What previous lover had taught her that?

"Well?" he said. He stood before her, feeling at a disadvantage, pleading. He hadn't put on his shoes or his jacket and tie. Barefooted and in his shirtsleeves he felt he wasn't properly dressed for the occasion.

"Your hair is mussed," she said: "You look much better with your hair mussed."

"Maybe my language is mussed," he said. "Maybe you didn't understand what I said in the bedroom."

"I understood." She turned the radio off, sat down in an easy chair, holding the glass of bourbon in her two hands. "You want to marry me."

"Exactly."

"Let's go to the movies," she said. "There's a picture I want to see just around the corner . . . "

"Don't be flip."

"It's only on till tomorrow night and you won't be here tomorrow night."

"I asked you a question."

"Am I supposed to be flattered?"

"No."

"Well, I *am* flattered. Now let's go to the movies . . . " But she didn't make any move to get up from the chair. Sitting there, half in shadow, because the one lamp that was lit threw its light obliquely from the side, she was fragile, vulnerable. Looking at her he knew that he had been right to say what he had in bed, that he hadn't spoken just from a flicker of tenderness on a cold afternoon, but from a deep and abiding need.

"I will be broken," he said, "if you say no."

"Do you believe that?" She was looking down into her glass, swirling the drink around now with a finger. He could see only the top of her head, her loose hair gleaming in the lamplight.

"Yes."

"Tell the truth."

"Partially," he said. "I partially believe it. Partially broken."

It was her turn to laugh. "At least you'll make somebody an honest husband," she said.

"Well," he demanded. He stood above her and put his hand under her chin and made her look up at him. Her eyes seemed doubtful, frightened, the small face pale.

"The next time you come to town, give me a ring," she said.

"That's no answer."

"In a way, it is," she said. "The answer is I want time to think."

"Why?"

"Because I've done something I'm not particularly proud of," she said, "and I want to figure out how I can be proud of myself again."

"What've you done?" He didn't know whether he wanted to know or not.

"I've overlapped," Jean said. "It's a female disease. I was having an affair with a boy when I started with you and I haven't broken it off. I'm doing something I thought I'd never do in my whole life. I'm sleeping with two men at once. And he wants to marry me, too."

"Lucky girl," Rudolph said bitterly. "Is he the girl roommate you share you apartment with?"

"No. The girl is an authentic girl. I'll produce her for you if you want."

"Is that why you never let me come to your place? He's there?"

"No, he's not there."

"But he *has* been there." With surprise, Rudolph realized that he had been wounded, deeply wounded, and worse yet, that he himself was intent on turning the knife in the wound.

"One of the most attractive things about you," Jean said, "was that you were too sure of yourself to ask questions. If love is going to make you unattractive, forget love."

"What a goddamn afternoon," Rudolph said.

"I guess that wraps it up." Jean stood up, put her glass down carefully. "No movies tonight."

He watched her put on her coat. If she walks out now, like this, he thought, I'll never see her again. He went over to her and put his arms around her and kissed her.

"You're all wrong," he said. "There'll be movies tonight."

She smiled at him, but tremulously, as though it cost her an effort. "You'd better finish getting dressed," she said. "I hate to miss the beginning of a picture."

He went into the bedroom, combed his hair, put on a tie and got into his shoes. He looked briefly at the tumbled bed, now a confused battlefield, as he put on his jacket.

When he came out into the living room again, he saw that she had slung her camera equipment around her. He tried to argue but she insisted upon taking the stuff with her.

"I've been in this place enough," she said, "for one Saturday."

As he drove along the rain-drenched highway the next morning on the way to Billy's school, through sparse early traffic, he was thinking about Jean, not about Billy. They had gone to the movie, which was disappointing, had eaten supper afterward in a joint on Third Avenue, had talked about things that hardly mattered to either of them, the movie they had seen, other movies, plays they had seen, books and magazine articles they had read, rumors from Washington. The conversation of strangers. They had avoided mentioning marriage or overlapping lovers. They were both unaccountably weary, as though a great physical effort had drained them earlier. They drank more than they usually did. If this had been the first time they had gone out together, they would have thought each other dull. When they had finished their steaks, in the emptying restaurant, and had a cognac apiece, he was relieved to be able to put her into a taxi, walk home alone and turn the key behind him in the silent apartment, although the raw colors of the décor and the arty spikiness of the furniture made it look like an abandoned float from last year's Mardi Gras. The bed now was just messy, the neglected tangle of a slatternly housewife, not the warm abode of love. He slept heavily and when he awoke in the morning and remembered the night before and his errand for the day, the sooty December rain outside his window seemed the appropriate weather for the weekend.

He had called the school and left a message for Billy that he would be there around twelve-thirty to take him to lunch, but he arrived earlier than he expected, a little after noon. Even though the rain had stopped and a faint cold sun was filtering through the clouds in the south, there was no one to be seen on the campus, coming or going into any of the buildings. From what Gretchen had told him about the school, in fine weather and a more clement season it was a place of beauty, but under the wet sky, seemingly abandoned, there was something forbiddingly prisonlike about the cluster of buildings and the muddy lawns. He drove up to what was obviously the main building and got out uncertainly, not knowing where to find Billy. Then, from the chapel a hundred yards away he heard young voices singing strongly, "Onward Christian Soldiers."

Sunday. Compulsory services, he thought. They still do that in schools. Christ. When he was a boy Billy's age, all he had to do was salute the flag every morning and pledge allegiance to the United States of America. The advantages of public education. Separation of Church and State.

A Lincoln Continental drove up to the steps and stopped. It was a richly endowed school. Future rulers of America. He himself drove a Chevrolet. He wondered what would have been said at faculty teas if he had arrived on his motorcycle, which he still owned, though he now seldom used it. An important-looking man in a smart raincoat got out of the Lincoln, leaving a lady in the car. Parents. Occasional faint weekend communication with a future ruler of America. From his manners, the man had to be at least the president of a company, ruddy and brisk, well exercised. By now Rudolph could spot the type.

"Good morning, sir," Rudolph said, in his automatic speaking-to-company-presidents' voice. "I wonder if you could tell me where Sillitoe Hall is?"

The man smiled widely, showing five thousand dollars' worth of exquisite dental work. "Good morning, good morning. Yes, of course. My boy was there last year. In some ways the best house on the campus. It's just over there." He pointed. The building was four hundred yards away. "You can drive there if you want. Just down this driveway and around."

"Thank you," Rudolph said.

The hymn rang out from the chapel. The parent cocked an ear. "They're still praising God," he said. "All in favor of it. We could stand more of it."

Rudolph got into his Chevrolet and drove to Sillitoe Hall. He looked at the plaque commemorating Lieutenant Sillitoe as he went into the silent building. A girl of about four, in blue overalls, was pedaling a three-wheeler around the cluttered common room on the ground floor. A large setter in the room barked at him. Rudolph was a little disconcerted. He hadn't expected four-year-old girls in a boys' school.

A door opened and a chubby, pleasant-faced young woman in slacks came into the room and said, "Shut up, Boney," to the dog. She smiled at Rudolph. "He's harmless," she said.

Rudolph didn't know what she was doing there, either.

"Are you a father?" the woman asked, grabbing the dog by the collar and half strangling him, while he wagged his tail madly, full of love.

"Not exactly," Rudolph said. "I'm Billy Abbott's uncle. I called this morning."

A curious little expression—concern? suspicion? relief?—shadowed the pleasant, chubby, young face. "Oh, yes," the woman said. "He expects you. I'm Mollie Fairweather. I'm the housemaster's wife."

That explained the child, the dog, herself. Whatever was wrong with Billy, Rudolph decided instantly, it wasn't the fault of this healthy, agreeable woman.

"The boys'll be back from chapel any minute now," the woman said. "Don't you want to come into our place and have a drink, perhaps, while you're waiting?"

"I don't want to put you to any trouble," Rudolph said, but didn't protest further, as Mrs. Fairweather waved him in.

The room was large, comfortable, the furniture well worn, the books many. "My husband's at chapel, too," Mrs. Fairweather explained. "But I do think we have some sherry." A child cried from another room. "My youngest," Mrs. Fairweather said, "making an announcement." She poured the sherry hurriedly and said, "Excuse me," and went off to see what announcement her child was making. The cries stopped immediately. She came back, smoothing her hair, poured herself a sherry, too. "Do sit down, please."

There was an awkward pause. It occurred to Rudolph as he sat down that this woman, who had only met Billy a few months ago, must know him much better than himself, who was on a mission, unbriefed and flying blind, to rescue the boy. He should have asked Gretchen to read the letter that disturbed her so to him over the phone.

"He's a very nice boy," Mrs. Fairweather said, "Billy. So handsome and well behaved. We do get some wild ones, Mr. . . . " she hesitated.

"Jordache," Rudolph said.

"So we appreciate the ones who know their manners." She sipped at her sherry. Looking at her, Rudolph decided that Mr. Fairweather was a lucky man.

"His mother is worried about him," Rudolph said.

"Is she?" The response was too quick. Gretchen wasn't the only one who had noticed something.

"She got a letter from him this week. She said—well, of course, mothers are prone to exaggeration—but she said it sounded as though Billy is in despair." There was no sense in not revealing to this obviousy level-headed and well-meaning woman what his errand was. "The word seems a little strong to me," he said, "but I've come to see what can be done. His mother's in California. And . . . " He was a little embarrassed now. "She remarried."

"That's not so uncommon around here," Mrs. Fairweather said. She laughed. "I don't mean about parents living in California. I mean the remarried."

"Her husband died several months ago," Rudolph said.

"Oh," Mrs. Fairweather said. "I'm so sorry. Perhaps that's why Billy—" She left the sentence unfinished.

"Have you observed anything in particular?" Rudolph asked.

The woman pushed at her short hair uncomfortably. "I'd prefer it if you talked to my husband. It's really his department."

"I'm certain you wouldn't say anything that your husband wouldn't agree to," Rudolph said. Without meeting the husband, he was sure that the wife would be less guarded, less defensive about the school, if indeed the school was at fault.

"Your glass is empty," Mrs. Fairweather said. She took it from him and refilled it.

"Is it his marks?" Rudolph asked. "Are any of the boys bullying him for some reason?"

"No." Mrs. Fairweather handed him the tiny glass of sherry. "His marks are fine and we don't allow any bullying here." She shrugged. "He's a puzzling boy. I've talked it over several times with my husband and we've tried to sound him out. Without success. He—he's remote. He doesn't seem to connect with anybody. Not with any of the other boys. Or any of his teachers. His roommate has asked to be transferred to another house . . . "

"Do they fight?"

She shook her head. "No. The roommate says Billy just doesn't talk to him. Ever. About anything. He does his share of housekeeping neatly, he studies at the proper hours, he doesn't complain, but he barely answers yes or no when he's spoken to. Physically he's a strong boy, but he doesn't join in any of the games. He doesn't even throw a football around and during this season there're always dozens of boys playing pickup touch tackle games or just passing the ball back and forth in front of the house. And on Saturdays when we play other schools and the whole school is in the stands, he stays in his room and reads." As she spoke, her voice sounded just as troubled as Gretchen's when she had spoken over the phone about Billy.

"If he were a grown man, Mr. Jordache," Mrs. Fairweather said, "I'd be inclined to say he was suffering from melancholy. I know that's not very helpful . . . " She smiled apologetically. "It's a description, not a diagnosis. But it's the best my husband and I have been able to come up with. If you can find out anything specific, anything the school can do, we'll be most grateful."

The bells of the chapel were ringing far away across the campus and Rudolph could see the first boys crossing from the chapel porch.

"I wonder if you could tell me where Billy's room is," Rudolph said. "I'll wait for him there." Perhaps there would be some clues there that would prepare him for his meeting with the boy.

"It's on the third floor," Mrs. Fairweather said. "All the way down the corridor, the last door to the left."

Rudolph thanked her and left her with the two children and the setter. What a nice woman, he thought as he mounted the steps. There certainly had been nobody as good as that connected with his education. If she was worried about Billy, there was something to be worried about.

The door, like most of the doors along the corridor, was open. The room seemed to be divided by an invisible curtain. On one side the bed was rumpled and strewn with phonograph records. Books were piled on the floor beside the bed and there were pennants and pictures of girls and athletes torn from magazines pinned to the wall. On the other side, the bed was tightly made and there were no decorations on the wall. The only photographs on that side were on the neatly ordered small desk. They were separate ones of Gretchen and Burke. Gretchen was sitting in a deck chair in the garden of the house in California. The portrait of Burke was one that had been published in a magazine. There was no picture of Willie Abbott.

One book, open and face down, lay on the bed. Rudolph leaned over to see what it was. *The Plague,* by Camus. Peculiar reading for a fourteen-year-old boy and hardly designed to rescue him from melancholy.

If excessive neatness was a symptom of adolescent neurosis, Billy was neurotic. But Rudolph remembered how neat he had been at the same age and no one had considered him abnormal.

Somehow, though, the room oppressed him, and he didn't want to have to meet Billy's roommate, so he went downstairs and waited in front of the door. The sun was stronger now, and with the groups of boys, all shined up for chapel, advancing across the campus, the place no longer seemed prisonlike. Most of the boys were tall, much taller than the boys Rudolph had gone to school with. Increasing America. Everybody took it for granted that it was a good thing. But was it? The better to look down upon you, my dear.

He saw Billy at a distance. He was the only boy walking alone. He walked slowly, naturally, with his head up, nothing hangdog about him. Rudolph remembered how he had practiced walking himself at that age, keeping his shoulders still, trying to glide, making himself seem older, more graceful than his comrades. He still walked that way, but out of habit, not thinking about it.

"Hello, Rudy," Billy said, without smiling, as he came up to the front of the building. "Thanks for coming to visit me."

They shook hands. Billy had a strong, quick grasp. He still didn't have to shave, but his face was not babyish and his voice had already changed.

"I have to be up in Whitby this evening," Rudolph said, "and since I was going to be on the road anyway, I thought I'd drop in and have lunch with you. It's only a couple of hours out of the way. Not even that."

Billy eyed him levelly and Rudolph was sure that the boy knew that the visit wasn't as off-hand as all that.

"Is there a good restaurant around here?" Rudolph asked, quickly. "I'm starving."

"My father took me to lunch at a place that wasn't too bad," Billy said, "when he was up here the last time."

"When was that?"

"A month ago. He was going to come up last week, but he wrote that the man who was going to lend him the car had to go out of town at the last minute."

Rudolph wondered if originally Willie Abbott's picture had been on the neat desk, next to the photographs of Gretchen and Colin Burke and had been put away after that last letter.

"Do you have to do anything in your room or tell anybody you're going out to lunch with your uncle?"

"I have nothing to do," Billy said. "And I don't have to tell anybody anything."

Rudolph suddenly became conscious as they stood there, with boys passing them in a steady stream, laughing and fooling around and talking loudly, that Billy hadn't said hello to a single one of them and that no one had come up to him. It's as bad as Gretchen feared, he thought. Or worse.

He put his arm briefly around Billy's shoulder. There was no reaction. "Let's be off," he said. "You show me the road."

As he drove through the lovely school grounds, with the somber boy beside him, past the handsome buildings and playing fields, so intelligently and expensively designed to prepare young men for useful and happy lives, so carefully staffed with devoted men and women of the caliber of Mrs. Fairweather, Rudolph wondered how anyone dared to try to educate anybody.

"I know why the man didn't lend my father the car last week," Billy was saying as he went at his steak. "He backed into a tree getting out of the parking lot here when we had lunch together and crushed the fender. He had three martinis before lunch and a bottle of wine and two glasses of brandy after lunch."

The censorious young. Rudolph was glad he wasn't drinking anything but water. "Maybe he was unhappy about something," he said. He was not there to destroy the possibility of love between father and son.

"I guess so. He's unhappy a lot of the time." Billy went on eating. Whatever he was suffering from had not impaired his appetite. The food was hearty American, steaks, lobster, clams, roast beef, hot biscuits, served by pretty waitresses in modest uniforms. The room was large and rambling, the tables were covered with red-checkered cloths and there were many groups from the school, five or six boys at a table with the parents of one of the students, who had invited his friends to take advantage of the parental visit. Rudolph wondered if one day he would claim a son of his own from a school and take him and his friends out for a similar lunch. If Jean said yes and married him, perhaps in fifteen years. What would he be like in fifteen years, what would she be like, what would his son be like? Withdrawn, taciturn, troubled, like Billy? Or open and gay, as the boys at the other tables seemed to be? Would schools like this still exist, meals like this still be served, fathers still drunkenly ram into trees at two o'clock in the afternoon? What risks the gentle women and comfortable fathers sitting proudly at table with their sons had run fifteen years ago, with the war just over and the atomic cloud still drifting across the skies of the planet.

Maybe, he thought, I will tell Jean I have reconsidered.

"How's the food at school?" he asked, just to break the long silence.

"Okay," Billy said.

"How're the boys?"

"Okay, Ah—not so okay. There's an awful lot of talk about what bigshots their fathers are, how they have lunch with the President and tell him how to run the country, how they go to Newport for the summertime, how they have horses at home, and how their sisters have debutante parties that cost twenty-five thousand dollars."

"What do you say when they talk like that?"

"I keep quiet." Billy's glance was hostile. "What am I supposed to say? My father lives in one room and he's been fired from three jobs in two years? Or should I tell them what a great driver he is after lunch?" Billy said all this in an even, uninflected conversational tone, alarmingly mature.

"What about your stepfather?"

"What about him? He's dead. And even before he died, there weren't six boys in the school who ever heard of him. They think people who do plays and make movies are some kind of freak."

"What about the teachers?" Rudolph asked, desperate to find one thing at least that the boy approved of.

"I don't have anything to do with them," Billy said, putting more butter on his baked potato. "I do my work and that's all."

"What's wrong, Billy?" It was time now to be direct. He did not know the boy well enough to be indirect.

"My mother asked you to come here, didn't she?" Billy looked at him shrewdly, challengingly.

"If you must know—yes."

"I'm sorry if I worried her," Billy said. "I shouldn't have sent that letter."

"Of course, you should have sent the letter. What is it, Billy?"

"I don't know." The boy had stopped eating by now and Rudolph could see that he was fighting to control his voice. "Everything. I feel like I am going to die if I have to stay here."

"Of course you won't die," Rudolph said sharply.

"No, I guess not. I just *feel* as though I am." Billy was petulant, juvenile, for a moment. "That's a whole different thing, isn't it? But feeling is real, too, isn't it?"

"Yes, it is," Rudolph admitted. "Come on. Talk."

"This is no place for me," Billy said. "I don't want to be trained to grow up into what all these fellows are going to grow up into. I see their fathers. A lot of them went to this same school twenty-five years ago. They're like their kids, only older, telling the President what to do, not knowing that Colin Burke was a great man, not evening knowing he's dead. I don't belong here, Rudy. My father doesn't belong here. Colin Burke wouldn't have belonged here. If they keep me here, by the end of four years they'll make me belong here and I don't want that. I don't know . . . " He shook his head despondently, his fair hair swinging over the high forehead he had inherited from his father. "I guess you think I'm just not making any sense. I guess you think I'm just another homesick kid griping because he wasn't elected captain of the team or something . . . "

"I don't think that at all, Billy. I don't know whether you're right or not, but you certainly have figured out your reasons." Homesick, he thought. The word had reared up from the sentence. Which home?

"Compulsory chapel," Billy said, "Making believe I'm a Christian seven times a week. I'm no Christian, Mom isn't a Christian, my father's not a Christian, Colin wasn't a Christian, why do I have to take the rap for the whole family, listen to all those sermons? Be upright, have clean thoughts, don't think about sex. Our Lord Jesus died to cleanse our sins. How would you like to sit through crap like that seven times a week?"

"Not much." The boy certainly had a point there. Atheists did have a religious responsibility toward their children.

"And money," Billy said, his voice low but intense, as a waitress passed nearby. "Where's the money going to come for my big fat education now that Colin's dead?"

"Don't worry about that," Rudolph said. 'I've told your mother I'd take care of it."

Billy looked at him malevolently, as though Rudolph had just confessed that he had been plotting against him. "I don't like you enough, Uncle Rudy," he said, "to take that from you."

Rudolph was shaken, but he managed to speak calmly. After all, Billy was only fourteen, only a child. "Why don't you like me well enough?"

"Because you belong here," Billy said. "Send your own son here."

"I won't comment on that."

"I'm sorry I said it. But I meant it." There was a pressure of tears in the long-lashed, blue, Abbott eyes.

"I admire you for saying it," Rudolph said. "By the time boys reach your age they usually have learned to dissemble for rich uncles."

"What am I doing here, on the other side of the country, when my mother is sitting alone, all by herself, night after night, crying?" Billy went on, in a rush. "A man like Colin is killed and what am I supposed to be doing—cheering at a silly football game or listening to some Boy Scout in a black suit telling us Jesus saves. I'll tell you something—" The tears were rolling down his cheeks now and he was mopping them with a handkerchief, but speaking fiercely at the same time. "If you don't get me out of here, I'm going to run away. And, somehow, I'm going to turn up in that house where my mother is, and anyway I can help her I'm going to help her."

"All right," Rudolph said. "We can stop talking about it. I don't know what I can do, but I promise you I'll do something. Fair enough?"

Billy nodded miserably, mopped some more, put the handkerchief away.

"Now let's finish our lunch" Rudolph said. He didn't eat much more, but watched

Billy clean his plate, then order apple pie à la mode and clean that plate. Fourteen was an all-absorbing age. Tears, death, pity, apple pie, and ice cream mingled without shame.

After lunch, in the car driving over to the school, Rudolph said, "Go up to your room. Pack a bag. Then come down and wait for me in the car."

He watched the boy go into the building, neat in his Sunday go-to-chapel suit, then got out of the car and followed. Behind him, a touch-tackle game was in progress on the drying lawn, boys crying, "Throw it to me, throw it to me," in one of the hundreds of games of their youth that Billy never joined.

The Common Room off the hallway was full of boys playing Ping-Pong, sitting over chess boards, reading magazines, listening to the Giant game on a transistor radio. From upstairs came the roar of a folk-singing group from another radio. Politely, the boys around the Ping-Pong table made way for him, older man, as he walked across the room, toward the doorway of the Fairweathers' apartment. They seemed like fine boys, good looking, healthy, well mannered, content, the hope of America. If he were a father he would have been happy to see his own son in this company this Sunday afternoon. But among them, his nephew, misfitted, felt that he was going to die. The Constitutional right to be a misfit.

He rang the bell to the Fairweather apartment and the door was opened by a tall, slightly stooping man, with a lock of hair hanging over his forehead, a healthy complexion, a ready and welcoming smile. What nerves a man must have to be able to live in a house full of boys like this.

"Mr. Fairweather?" Rudolph said.

"Yes?" Amiable, easy.

"I hate to disturb you, but I'd like to talk to you for a moment. I'm Billy Abbott's uncle. I was . . . "

"Oh, yes," Fairweather said. He extended his hand. "My wife told me you paid her a visit before lunch. Won't you please come in?" He led the way down a book-lined hallway into the book-lined living room, the noise from the Common Room miraculously extinguished with the closing of the door. Sanctuary from youth. Insulation from the young by books. Rudolph wondered if perhaps when Denton had offered him the post at the college, the book-lined life, he had made the wrong choice.

Mrs. Fairweather was sitting on the couch, drinking a cup of coffee, her child sitting on the floor leaning against her knee, turning the pages of a picture book, the setter sprawled, asleep, against her. Mrs. Fairweather smiled at him, raised her cup in greeting.

They can't be *that* happy, Rudolph thought, conscious of jealousy.

"Please sit down," Fairweather said. "Would you like some coffee?"

"No, thank you, I've just had some. And I can only stay a minute." Rudolph sat, stiffly, feeling awkward because he was an uncle, not a father.

Fairweather sat comfortably next to his wife. He was wearing green-stained tennis shoes and a wool shirt, making the most of Sunday afternoon. "Did you have a good talk with Billy?" he asked. There was a little pleasant holdover of the South in his voice, gentlemanly Tidewater Virginia.

"I had a talk," Rudolph said. "I don't know how good it was. Mr. Fairweather, I want to take Billy away with me. For a few days at least. I think it's absolutely necessary."

The Fairweathers exchanged glances.

"It's as bad as that, is it?" the man said.

"Pretty bad."

"We've done everything we can," Fairweather said, but without apology.

"I realize that," Rudolph said. "It's just that Billy's a certain kind of boy, certain things have happened to him—in the past, recently . . . " He wondered if the Fairweathers had ever heard of Colin Burke, mourned the vanished talent. "There's no need to go into it. A boy's reasons can be fantasy, but his feelings can be horribly real."

"So you want to take Billy away?" Mr. Fairweather said.

"Yes."

"When?"

"In ten minutes."

"Oh, dear," Mrs. Fairweather said.

"For how long?" Fairweather asked calmly.

"I don't know. A few days. A month. Perhaps permanently."

There was an uncomfortable silence. From outside the window, thinly, came the sound of a boy calling signals in the touch-tackle game, 22, 45, 38, *Hut!* Fairweather stood up and went over to the table where the coffee pot was standing and poured himself a cup. "You're sure you don't want some, Mr. Jordache?"

Rudolph shook his head.

"The Christmas holidays come in just two and a half weeks," Fairweather said. "And the term-end examinations begin in a few days. Don't you think it would be wiser to wait until then?"

"I don't think it would be wise for me to leave here this afternoon without Billy," Rudolph said.

"Have you spoken to the headmaster?" Fairweather asked.

"No."

"I think it would be advisable to consult with him," Fairweather said. "I don't really have the authority to . . . "

"The less fuss we make, the fewer the people who talk to Billy," Rudolph said, "the better it will be for the boy. Believe me."

Again the Fairweathers exchanged glances.

"Charles," Mrs. Fairweather said to her husband, "I think we could explain to the headmaster."

Fairweather sipped thoughtfully at his coffee, still standing at the table. A ray of pale sunlight came through the windows, outlining him against the bookshelves behind him. Healthy, pondering man, head of family, doctor of young souls.

"I suppose we could," he said. "I suppose we could explain. You *will* call me in the next day or two and tell me what's been decided, won't you?"

"Of course."

Fairweather sighed. "There're so many defeats in this quiet profession, Mr. Jordache," he said. "Tell Billy he's welcome to come back any time he wishes. He's bright enough to make up any time he's lost."

"I'll tell him," Rudolph said. "Thank you. Thank you both for everything."

Fairweather escorted him back along the hallway, opened the door into the turmoil of boys, didn't smile as he shook Rudolphs hand and closed the door behind him.

As Rudolph drove away from the school, Billy, in the front seat beside him, said, "I never want to see this place again." He didn't ask where they were going.

It was half-past five when they got to Whitby and the street lights were on in the wintry darkness. Billy had slept a good deal of the way. Rudolph dreaded the moment when he would have to introduce his mother to her grandson. "Spawn of the harlot," might not be beyond the powers of his mother's rhetoric. But he had the appointment with Calderwood after the Calderwood Sunday supper, which would be over by seven, and it would have been impossible to take Billy back to New York and then arrive in Whitby on time. And even if he had had the time to drive the boy down to the city, to whom could he have turned him over? Willie Abbott? Gretchen had asked him to bypass Willie in the matter and he had done so and there was no having it both ways. And after what Billy had said about his father at lunch, being put in Willie's alcoholic care could hardly have seemed like much of an improvement over staying in school.

Briefly, Rudolph had considered putting Billy in a hotel, but had discarded the idea as too cold-blooded. This was no night for the boy to spend alone in a hotel. Also, it would have been cowardly. He would have to face the old lady down.

Still, when he awakened the boy as he stopped the car in front of the house, and led him through the door, he was relieved to see that his mother was not in the living room. He looked down the hallway and saw that her door was closed. That meant she had probably had a fight with Martha and was sulking. He could confront her alone and prepare her for her first meeting with her grandson.

He went into the kitchen with Billy. Martha was sitting at the table reading a newspaper and there was a smell of something cooking coming from the oven. Martha was not fat, as his mother spitefully described her, but in fact was an angular, virginal, gaunt woman of fifty, sure of the world's displeasure, anxious to give back as good as she got.

"Martha," he said, "this is my nephew, Billy. He's going to stay with us for a few days. He's tired and he needs a bath and some hot food. Do you think you can give him a hand? He'll sleep in the guest room, next to mine."

Martha smoothed out the newspaper on the kitchen table. "Your mother said you weren't going to be in for dinner."

"I'm not. I'm going out again."

"Then there'll be enough for him," Martha said. "She"— with a savage gesture of the head toward the part of the house inhabited by his mother—"she didn't say nothing about no nephews."

"She doesn't know yet," Rudolph said, trying to make his voice sound cheery, for Billy's sake.

"That'll make her day," Martha said. "Finding out about nephews."

Billy stood quietly to one side, testing the atmosphere, not liking it.

Martha stood up, her face no more disapproving, really, than usual, but how could Billy know that. "Come on, young man," Martha said. "I guess we can make room for a skinny little thing like you."

Rudolph was surprised at what was, in Martha's vocabulary, practically a tender invitation.

"Go ahead, Billy," he said. "I'll be up to see you in a little while."

Billy followed Martha out of the kitchen, hesitantly. Attached now to his uncle, any separation was full of risk.

Rudolph heard their footsteps going up the stairs. His mother would be alerted that someone strange was in the house. She recognized his tread and invariably called out to him when he was on his way to his room.

He got some ice out of the refrigerator. He needed a drink after the almost teetotaling day and before the meeting with his mother. He carried the ice out into the living room and was pleased to find that the living room was warm. Brad must have sent over an engineer yesterday for the furnace. His mother's tongue would at least not be honed by cold.

He made himself a bourbon and water, with plenty of ice, sank into a chair, put his feet up, and sipped at his drink, enjoying it. He was pleased with the room, not too heavily furnished, with modern, leather chairs, globular glass lamps, Danish wood tables and simple, neutral-colored curtains, all of it making a carefully thought-out contrast with the low-beamed ceiling and the small eighteenth-century, square-paned windows. His mother complained that it looked like a dentist's waiting room.

He finished his drink slowly, in no hurry for the scene ahead of him. Finally, he pushed himself up out of the chair, went down the hallway, and knocked on the door. His mother's bedroom was on the ground floor so that she wouldn't have to manage the stairs. Although, now, since the two operations, one for phlebitis, the second for cataracts, she got around fairly well. Complainingly, but well.

"Who is it?" The voice was sharp behind the closed door.

"It's me, Mom," Rudolph said. "You asleep?"

"Not any more," she said.

He pushed the door open.

"Not with people tramping up and down like elephants all over the house," she said from the bed. She was propped up against lacy pillows, wearing a pink bed jacket that was trimmed with what seemed to be some kind of pinkish fur. She was wearing the thick glasses that the doctor had prescribed for her after the operation. They permitted her to read, watch television, and go to the movies, but they gave a wild, blank, soulless stare to her hugely magnified eyes.

Doctors had done wonders for her since they had moved to the new house. Before that, when they were still living over the store, although Rudolph had pleaded with his mother to undergo the various operations he was sure she needed, she had adamantly refused. "I will be nobody's charity patient," she had said, "being experimented on by interns who shouldn't be allowed to put a knife to a dog." Rudolph's protestations had fallen then on deaf ears. While they lived in the poor apartment nothing could convince her that she was not poor and doomed to suffer the fate of the poor once confided to the cold care of an institution. But once they made the move and Martha read the write-ups in the newspapers about Rudy's successes to her and she had ridden in the new car that Rudy had bought, she went boldly into surgery, after ascertaining that the men who treated her were the best and most expensive available.

She had been literally rejuvenated, resuscitated, brought back from the lip of the grave, by her belief in money. Rudy had thought that decent medical care would make his mother's last years a little more comfortable. Instead, they had almost made her young. With Martha glooming at the wheel, she now went out in Rudy's car whenever it was free; she frequented beauty parlors (her hair was almost blue and waved); patronized the town's movie houses; called for taxis; attended Mass; played bridge with newly found church acquaintances twice a week; fed priests on nights when Rudy was not at home; had bought a new copy of *Gone With the Wind,* as well as all the novels of Frances Parkinson Keyes.

A wide variety of clothes and hats for all occasions were stored in the wardrobe in her room, which was as full of furiture as a small antique shop, gilt desks, a chaise longue, a dressing table with ten different flasks of French perfume on it. For the first time in her life her lips were heavily rouged. She looked ghastly, Rudolph thought, with her painted face and gaudy dresses, but she was infinitely more alive than before. If this was the way she was making up for the dreadful years of her childhood and the long agony of her marriage, it was not up to him to deprive her of her toys.

He had played with the idea of moving her to an apartment of her own in town, with Martha to tend her, but he could not bear the thought of the expression on her face at the moment when he would take her through the door of the house for the last time, stricken by the ingratitude of a son whom she had loved above all things in her life, a son whose shirts she had ironed at midnight after twelve hours on her feet in the store, a son for whom she had sacrificed youth, husband, friends, her other two children.

So she stayed on. Rudolph was not one to miss payment on his debts.

"Who is it upstairs? You've brought a woman into the house," she said accusingly.

"I've never brought a woman into the house, as you put it, Mom," Rudolph said, "although if I wanted to, I don't see why I shouldn't."

"Your father's blood," his mother said. Dreadful charge.

"It's your grandson. I brought him home from school."

"That was no six-year-old boy going up the staircase," she said. "I have ears."

"It isn't Thomas's son," Rudolph said. "It's Gretchen's son."

"I will not hear that name," she said. She put her hands to her ears. Television-watching had left its mark on her gestures.

Rudolph sat on the edge of his mother's bed and gently took her hands down, holding them. I have been lax, he thought. This conversation should have been held years ago.

"Now listen to me, Mom," he said. "He's a very good boy and he's in trouble and . . ."

"I won't have that whore's brat in my house," she said.

"Gretchen is not a whore," Rudolph said. "Her son is not a brat. And this is not your house."

"I was waiting for the day you would finally say those words," she said.

Rudolph ignored the invitation to melodrama. "He's going to stay only a few days," he said, "and he needs kindness and attention and I'm going to give it to him and Martha's going to give it to him and you're going to give it to him."

"What will I ever tell Father McDonnell?" His mother looked, eyes magnified and blank, up toward Heaven, before whose gates stood, theoretically, Father McDonnell.

"You're going to tell Father McDonnell that you have finally learned the virtue of Christian charity," Rudolph said.

"Ah," she said, "you're a fine one to talk about Christian charity. Have you ever seen the inside of a church?"

"I haven't got time to argue," Rudolph said. "Calderwood is expecting me any minute now. I'm telling you how you're going to behave with the boy."

"I will not allow him in my presence," she said, quoting from some portion of her favorite reading. "I will close my door and Martha will serve my meals on a tray."

"You can do that if you want, Mom," Rudolph said quietly. "But if you do, I'm cutting you off. No more car, no more bridge parties, no more charge accounts, no more beauty parlors, no more dinners for Father McDonnell. Think about it." He stood up. "I've got to go now. Martha's prepared to give Billy dinner. I suggest you join them."

Tears as he closed his mother's bedroom door. What a cheap way to threaten an old lady, he thought. Why didn't she just die? Gracefully, unwaved, unrinsed, unrouged.

There was a grandfather's clock in the hallway and he saw that he had time to phone Gretchen if he made an immediate connection to California. He put in the call and made himself another drink while waiting for the call to come through. Calderwood might smell the liquor on his breath and disapprove, but he was past that, too. As he sipped his drink he thought of what he had been doing the day before at just this hour. Entwined in twilit warmth in the soft bed, the red-wool stockings strewn on the floor, the sweet warm breath mingled with his, rum and lemon. Had his mother once lain sweetly in a lover's arms on a cold December afternoon, clothes carelessly discarded in lover's haste? The image refused to materialize. Would Jean, old, one day lie in a fussed-up bed, eyes staring behind thick glasses, old lips rouged in scorn and avarice? Better not to think about it.

The phone rang and it was Gretchen. He explained the afternoon as quickly as he could and said that Billy was safely with him and that if she thought best he would put Billy on a plane to Los Angeles in two or three days, unless, of course, she wanted to come East.

"No," she said. "Put him on a plane."

A tricky little sense of pleasure. An excuse to get to New York on Tuesday or Wednesday. Jean.

"I don't have to tell you how grateful I am, Rudy," Gretchen said.

"Nonsense," he said. "When I have a son I will expect you to take care of him. I'll let you know what plane he's on. And maybe one day soon, I'll come out and visit you."

The lives of others.

Calderwood himself answered the door when Rudolph rang. He was dressed for Sunday, even though his Sabbath duties were behind him, dark suit with vest, white shirt, somber tie, his high, black shoes. There never was enough light in the frugal Calderwood house and it was too dark for Rudolph to see what sort of expression Calderwood had on his face as he said, neutrally, "Come in, Rudy. You're a little late."

"Sorry, Mr. Calderwood," Rudolph said. He followed the old man, who walked heavily now, a certain measured number of steps between him and the grave, to be economized, doled out.

Calderwood led him into the somber oak-paneled room he called his study, with a big mahogany desk and cracked oak and leather easy chairs. The glassed bookcases were filled with files, records of bills paid, twenty-year-old transactions that Calderwood still didn't trust putting in the modest basement vaults where the ordinary business files were kept, open to any clerk's prying eye.

"Sit down." Calderwood gestured toward one of the leather and oak easy chairs. "You've been drinking, Rudy," he said mournfully. "My sons-in-law, I regret to say, are also drinkers." Calderwood's two older daughters had married some time before, one a man from Chicago, another a man from Arizona. Rudolph had the feeling that the girls had picked their mates not out of love, but geography, to get away from their father.

"That isn't what I brought you here to talk about though," Calderwood said. "I wanted to speak to you man-to-man, when Mrs. Calderwood and Virginia were not on the premises. They have gone to the movie show and we can speak freely." It was not like the old man to indulge in elaborate preliminaries. He seemed ill at ease, which also was not like him.

Rudolph waited, conscious that Calderwood was fiddling with objects on his desk, a paper opener, an old-fashioned inkstand.

"Rudolph . . . " Calderwood cleared his throat portentously. "I'm surprised at your behavior."

"My behavior?" For a wild instant Rudolph thought that Calderwood had somehow found out about himself and Jean.

"Yes. It's not like you at all, Rudy." The tone was sorrowful now. "You've been like a son to me. Better than a son. Truthful. Open. Trustworthy."

The old Eagle Scout, covered with merit badges, Rudolph thought, waiting, wary.

"Suddenly something has come over you, Rudy," Calderwood continued. "You have been operating behind my back. With no apparent reason. You know you could have come to the door of my house and rung my bell and I would have been glad to welcome you."

"Mr. Calderwood," Rudolph said, thinking, old age here, too. "I don't know what you're talking about."

"I am talking about the affections of my daughter Virginia, Rudy. Don't deny."

"Mr. Calderwood . . . "

"You have been tampering with her affections. Gratuitously. You have stolen where you could have demanded." There was anger in the voice now.

"I assure you, Mr. Calderwood, that I haven't . . . "

"It's not like you to lie, Rudy."

"I'm not lying. I don't know . . .

"What if I told you the girl has confessed everything?" Calderwood boomed.

"There's nothing to confess." Rudolph felt helpless, and at the same time like laughing.

"Your story differs from my daughter's. She has told her mother that she is in love with you and that she intends to go to New York City to learn to be a secretary to be free to see you."

"Holy God!" Rudolph said.

"We do not use the name of God in vain in this house, Rudy."

"Mr. Calderwood, the most I've ever done with Virginia," Rudolph said, "is buy her a lunch or an ice cream soda when I've bumped into her at the store."

"You've bewitched her," Calderwood said. "She's in tears five times a week about you. A pure young girl doesn't indulge in antics like that unless she's been led on artfully by a man."

The Puritan inheritance has finally exploded, Rudolph thought. Land on Plymouth Rock, hang around for a couple of centuries in the bracing air of New England, prosper, and go crackers. It was all too much for one day—Billy, the school, his mother, now this.

"I want to know what you intend to do about it, young man." When Calderwood said young man, he was apt to be dangerous. Instanteously, Rudolph's mind flashed over the possibilities—he was well entrenched, but the final power in the business lay with Calderwood. There could be a fight, but in the long run Calderwood could get him out. That silly bitch Virginia.

"I don't know what you want me to do, sir." He was stalling for time.

"It's very simple," Calderwood said. Obviously he had been thinking about the problem ever since Mrs. Calderwood had come to him with the happy news about their daughter's shame. "Marry Virginia. But you must promise not to move down to New York." He was demented about New York City, Rudolph decided. Haunt of evil. "I will make you a full partner with me. Upon my death, after I make adequate provisons for my daughters and Mrs. Calderwood, you will get the bulk of my shares. You will have voting control. I shall never bring up this conversation again and there will be no reproaches. In fact, I shall put it out of my mind forever. Rudy, I couldn't be happier than to have a boy like you in the family. It has been my fondest wish for years and both Mrs. Calderwood and I were disappointed when we invited you to partake of the hospitality of our home that you seemed to take no interest in any of our daughters, although they are all pretty in their way, and well brought up, and if I may say so, independently wealthy. I have no idea why you thought you couldn't approach me directly when you had made your choice."

"I haven't made any choice," Rudolph said distractedly. "Virginia's a charming girl, and she'll make the best of wives, I'm sure. I had no inkling she had any interest in me whatever . . . "

"Rudy," Calderwood said sternly. "I've known you a long time. You're one of the smartest men I've ever met. And you have the nerve to sit there and tell me . . . "

"Yes, I do." The hell with the business. "I'll tell you what I'll do. I'll sit right here with you and wait until Mrs. Calderwood and Virginia come home and I'll ask her point-blank in front of both of you whether I've ever made any advances to her, if I've ever as much as tried to kiss her." It was all pure farce but he had to go on with it. "If she says yes, she's lying, but I don't care. I'll walk out right now and you can do whatever you want with your goddamn business and your goddamn stocks and your goddamn daughter."

"Rudy!" Calderwood's voice was shocked, but Rudolph could see that he had suddenly become uncertain of his ground.

"If she'd had the sense to tell me long ago that she loved me," Rudolph went on swiftly pressing his advantage, reckless now, "maybe something would have come of it. I *do* like her. But it's too late now. Yesterday evening, if you must know, in New York City, I asked another girl to marry me."

"New York City," Calderwood said, resentfully. "Always New York City."

"Well, do you want me to sit here and wait until the ladies come home?" Rudolph crossed his arms menacingly.

"This could cost you a lot of money, Rudy," Calderwood said.

"Okay, it could cost me a lot of money." Rudolph said it firmly, but he could feel the sick quiver inside his stomach.

"And this—this lady in New York," Claderwood said, sounding plaintive. "Has she accepted you?"

"No."

"Love, by God!" The insanity of the tender emotion, the cross-purposes of desire, the sheer anarchy of sex, was too much for Calderwood's piety. "In two months you'll forget her and then maybe you and Virginia . . . "

"She said no for yesterday," Rudolph said. "But she's thinking it over. Well, should I wait for Mrs. Calderwood and Virginia?" He still had his arms crossed. It kept his hands from trembling.

Calderwood pushed the inkstand irritably back to the edge of the desk. "Obviously you're telling the truth, Rudy," Calderwood said. "I don't know what possessed my foolish daughter. Ah—I know what my wife will say—I brought her up all wrong. I made her shy. I overprotected her. If I were to tell you some of the arguments I've had with that woman in this house. It was different when I was a boy, I'll tell you that. Girls didn't go around telling their mothers they were in love with people who never even looked at them. The damned movies. They rot women's brains. No, you don't have to wait. I'll handle it alone. Go ahead. I have to compose myself."

Rudolph stood up and Calderwood with him. "Do you want some advice?" Rudolph asked.

"You're always giving me advice," Calderwood said petulantly. "When I dream it's always about you whispering in my ear. For years. Sometimes I wish you'd never showed up that summer at the store. What advice?"

"Let Virginia go down to New York and learn to be a secretary and leave her alone for a year or two."

"Great," Calderwood said bitterly. "You can say that. You have no daughters. I'll see you to the door."

At the door, he put his hand on Rudolph's arm. "Rudy," he said, pleading, "if the lady in New York says no, you'll think about Virginia, won't you? Maybe she's an idiot, but I can't stand to see her unhappy."

"Don't worry, Mr. Calderwood," Rudolph said ambiguously, and went down to his car.

Mr. Calderwood was still standing in the open doorway, lit by the frugal hall light, as Rudolph drove away.

He was hungry, but decided to wait before going to a restaurant for dinner. He wanted to return to the house and see how Billy was doing. He also wanted to tell him that he had talked to Gretchen and that he would be going out to California in two or three days. The boy would sleep better after hearing that news, the specter of the school no longer hanging over him.

When he opened the front door with his key he heard voices in the kitchen. He went silently through the living and dining rooms and listened outside the kitchen door. "There's one thing I like to see in a growing boy—" Rudolph recognized his mother's voice—"And that's a good appetite. I'm happy to see you appreciate food, Billy. Martha, give him another slice of meat and some more salad. No back talk, Billy, about not eating salad. In my house, all children eat salad."

Holy God! Rudolph thought.

"There's another thing I like to see in a boy, Billy," his mother went on. "Old as I am, and I should be beyond such feminine weaknesses—and that's good looks combined with good manners." The voice was coquettish, cooing. "And you know whom you remind me of—and I never said so to his face for fear of spoiling him—there's nothing worse than a vain child—you remind me of your Uncle Rudolph and he was by common agreement the handsomest boy in town and he grew up into the handsomest young man."

"Everybody says I look like my father," Billy said, with the bluntness of his fourteen years, but not aggressively. From his tone he was obviously feeling at home.

"I have not had the good fortune ever to meet your father," the mother said, a slight chill in her speech. "No doubt there must be a certain resemblance here and there, but fundamentally you resemble my branch of the family, especially Rudolph. Doesn't he, Martha?"

"I can see some signs," Martha said. She was not out to give the mother a perfect Sunday night supper.

"Around the eyes," the mother said. "And the intelligent mouth. In spite of the difference in the hair. I never think hair makes too much difference. There's not much character in hair."

Rudolph pushed the door and went into the kitchen. Billy was seated at one end of the table, flanked by the two women. Hair flattened down wet after his bath, Billy looked shining clean and smiling as he packed into his food. The mother had put on a sober-brown dress and was consciously playing grandmother. Martha looked less grumpy than usual, her mouth less thin, welcoming a bit of youth into the household.

"Everything all right?" Rudolph asked. "They giving you enough to eat?"

"The food's great," Billy said. There was no trace of the agony of the afternoon in his face.

"I do hope you like chocolate pudding for dessert, Billy," the mother said, hardly looking up for a moment at Rudolph, standing at the door. "Martha makes the most delicious chocolate pudding."

"Yeah," Billy said. "I really like it."

"It was Rudolph's favorite dessert, too. Wasn't it, Rudolph?"

"Uhuh," he said. He didn't remember ever getting it more than once a year and he certainly didn't remember ever remarking on it, but this was not the night to halt the flights of his mother's fancy. She had even refrained from putting on rouge, the better to play the role of grandmother and she deserved some marks for that, too.

"Billy," Rudolph said, "I spoke to your mother."

Billy looked at him gravely, fearing a blow. "What did she say?"

"She's waiting for you. I'm going to put you on a plane Tuesday or Wednesday. As soon as I can break away from the office here and take you down to New York."

The boy's lips trembled, but there was no fear that he was going to cry. "How did she sound?" he asked.

"Delighted that you're coming out," Rudolph said.

"That poor girl," his mother said. "The life she's led. The blows of fortune."

Rudolph didn't allow himself to look at her.

"Though it's a shame, Billy," she continued, "that now that we've found each other you can't spend a little time with your old grandmother. Still, now that the ice has been broken, perhaps I can come out and visit you. Wouldn't that be a nice idea, Rudolph?"

"Very nice."

"California," she said. "I've always wanted to see it. The climate is kind to old bones. And from what I hear, it's a virtual paradise. Before I die . . . Martha, I think Billy is ready for the chocolate pudding."

"Yes, ma'am," Martha said, rising from the table.

"Rudolph," the mother said, "don't you want a bite? Join the happy family circle?"

"No, thanks." The last thing he wanted was to join the happy family circle. "I'm not hungry."

"Well, I'm off to bed," she said. She stod up heavily. "Must get my beauty sleep at my age, you know. But before you go upstairs to sleep you'll come in and give your grandmother a great big good-night kiss, won't you Billy?"

"Yes, ma'am," Billy said.

"Grandma."

"Grandma," Billy said obediently.

She swept out of the room. One last triumphant glare at Rudolph. Lady Macbeth, the blood behind her, undetected, now splendidly running a nursery for precocious children in a warmer country than Scotland.

Mothers should not be exposed, Rudolph thought, as he said, "Good night, Mom, sleep well." They should be shot out of hand.

He left the house, ate dinner at a restaurant, tried to call Jean in New York to find out what night she could see him, Tuesday or Wednesday. There was no answer at her apartment.

CHAPTER 4

DRAW THE CURTAINS at sunset. Do not sit in the evenings and look out at the lights of the city spread below you. Colin did so, with you at his side, because he said it was the view he liked most in the world, America at its best at night.

Do not wear black. Mourning is a private matter.

Do not write emotional letters in answer to letters of condolence from friends or from strangers using words like genius or unforgettable or generous or strength of character. Answer promptly and politely. No more.

Do not weep in front of your son.

Do not accept invitations to dinner from friends or colleagues of Colin who do not wish you to suffer alone.

When a problem comes up do not reach for the phone to call Colin's office. The office is closed.

Resist the temptation to tell the people who are now in charge of finishing Colin's last picture how Colin wanted it to be done.

Give no interviews, write no articles. Do not be a source of anecdote. Do not be a great man's widow. Do not speculate on what he would have done had he lived.

Commemorate no birthdays or anniversaries.

Discourage restrospective showings, festivals, laudatory meetings to which you have been invited.

Attend no previews or opening nights.

When planes fly low overhead, leaving the airport, do not remember voyages you have taken together.

Do not drink alone or in company, whatever the temptation. Avoid sleeping pills. Bear in unassuaged silence.

Clear the desk in the living room of its pile of books and scripts. They are now a lie.

Refuse, politely, the folios of clippings, reviews of plays and films your husband has directed, which the studio has kindly had made up in tooled-leather covers. Do not read the eulogies of critics.

Leave only one hasty snapshot of husband on view in house. Pack all other photographs in a box and put them away in the cellar.

Do not, when thinking about preparing dinner, arrange a menu that would please husband. (Stone crabs, chili, piccata of veal pizzaiola.)

When dressing, do not look at the clothes hanging in the closet and say, "He likes me in that one."

Be calm and ordinary with your son. Do not overreact when he gets into trouble at school, when he is robbed by a group of hoodlums or comes home with a bloody nose. Do not cling to him or allow him to cling to you. When he is invited with friends to go swimming or to a ball game or to a movie, tell him, "Of course. I have an awful lot of things to do about the house and I'll get them done faster if I'm alone."

Do not be a father. The things your son must do with men let him do with men. Do not try to entertain him, because you fear it must be dull for him living alone with a grieving woman on top of a hill far away from the centers where boys amuse themselves.

Do not think about sex. Do not be surprised that you do think about it.

Be incredulous when ex-husband calls and emotionally suggests that he would like to remarry you. If the marriage that was founded on love could not last, the marriage based on death would be a disaster.

Neither avoid nor seek out places where you have been happy together.

Garden, sunbathe, wash dishes, keep a neat house, help son with homework, do not show that you expect more of him than other parents expect of other sons. Be prompt to take him to the corner where he picks up the school bus, be prompt to meet the bus when it returns. Refrain from kissing him excessively.

Be understanding about your own mother, whom son now says he wishes to visit during the summer vacation. Say, "Summer is a long time off."

Be careful about being caught alone with men whom you have admired or Colin has admired and who admire you and have been known to admire many other women in this town of excess women, and whose sympathy will skillfully turn into something else in three or four sessions and who will then try to lay you and will probably succeed. Be careful about being caught alone with men who have admired Colin or Colin had admired and whose sympathy is genuinely only that but who will eventually want to lay you, too. They, too, will probably succeed.

Do not build your life on your son. It is the most certain way to lose him.

Keep busy. But at what?

"Are you sure you've looked everywhere, Mrs. Burke?" Mr. Greenfield asked. He was the lawyer Colin's agent had sent her to. Or rather, one of a huge battery of lawyers, all of whose names were on the door of the suite of offices in the elegant building in Beverly Hills. All of the names on the door seemed equally concerned with her problem, equally intelligent, equally well dressed, equally urbane, smiling, and sympathetic, equally costly, and equally helpless.

"I've turned the house upside down, Mr. Greenfield," Gretchen said. "I've found hundreds of scripts, hundreds of bills, some of them unpaid, but no will."

Mr. Greenfield almost sighed, but refrained. He was a youngish man in a button-down collar, to show that he had gone to law school in the East, and a bright bow tie, to show that he now lived in California. "Do you have any knowledge of any safety deposit boxes that your husband might have had?"

"No," she said. "And I don't believe he had any. He was careless about things like that."

"I'm afraid he was careless about quite a few things," Mr. Greenfield said. "Not leaving a will . . ."

"How did he know he was going to die?" she demanded. "He never had a sick day in his life."

"It makes it easier if one thinks about all the possibilities," Mr. Greenfield said. Gretchen was sure he had been drawing up wills for himself since he was twenty-one. Mr. Greenfield finally permitted himself the withheld sigh. "For our part, we've explored every avenue. Incredibly enough, your husband never employed *any* lawyer. He allowed his agent to draw up his contracts and from what his agent said, most of the time he hardly bothered to read them. And when he allowed the ex-Mrs. Burke to divorce him, he permitted *her* lawyer to write the divorce settlement."

Gretchen had never met the ex-Mrs. Burke, but now, after Colin's death, she was beginning to get to know her very well. She had been an airline hostess and a model. She had an abiding fondness for money and believed that to work for it was unfeminine and repugnant. She had been getting twenty thousand dollars a year as alimony and at the time of Colin's death had been starting proceedings to get it raised to forty thousand dollars a year because Colin's income had risen steeply since he had come to Hollywood. She was living with a young man, in places like New York, Palm Beach, and Sun Valley, when she wasn't traveling abroad, but sensibly refused to marry the young man, since one of the clauses that Colin *had* managed to insert in the divorce settlement would cut off the alimony on her remarriage. She or her lawyers seemed to have a wide knowledge of the law, both State and Federal, and immediately after the funeral, which she had not attended, she had had Colin's bank deposits impounded and had secured an injunction against the estate to prevent

Gretchen from selling the house.

Since Gretchen had had no separate bank account and had merely asked Colin for money when she needed it and allowed his secretary at the office to pay the bills, she found herself without any cash and had to depend upon Rudolph to keep her going. Colin had left no insurance because he thought insurance companies were the biggest thieves in America, so there was no money there, either. As the accident had been his fault alone, with no one else involved (he had hit a tree and the County of Los Angeles was preparing to sue the estate for damage to the tree), there was nobody against whom Gretchen could press claims for compensation.

"I have to get out of that house, Mr. Greenfield," Gretchen said. The evenings were the worst. Whispers in shadowy corners of rooms. Half expecting the door to open at any moment and Colin to come in, cursing an actor or a cameraman.

"I quite understand," Mr. Greenfield said. He really was a decent man. "But if you don't remain in possession, physical possession, Mr. Burke's ex-wife might very possibly find legal grounds for moving in. Her lawyers are very good, very good indeed—" The professional admiration was ungrudging, all the names on one door of an elegant building paying sincere tribute to all the names on the door of another elegant building just a block away. "If there's a loophole, they'll find it. And in law, if one looks long enough, there is almost always a loophole."

"Except for me," Gretchen said despairingly.

"It's a question of time, my dear Mrs. Burke." Just the gentlest of rebukes at a layman's impatience. "There's nothing clear-cut about this case, I regret to say. The house was in your husband's name, there is a mortgage on it, payments to be made. The size of the estate is undetermined and may remain undetermined for many years. Mr. Burke had a percentage, quite a large percentage of the three films he directed and a continuing interest in stock and foreign royalties and possible movie sales of quite a number of the plays he was connected with." The enumeration of these spendid difficulties that remained to be dealt with before the file of Colin Burke could be marked "Closed" obviously brought Mr. Greenfield an elegiac pleasure. If the law were not as complicated as it was he would have sought another and more exigent profession. "There will have to be expert opinions, the testimony of studio officials, a certain amount of give and take between parties. To say nothing of the possibility of other claims against the estate. Relatives of the deceased, for example, who have a habit of cropping up in cases like this."

"He only has one brother," Gretchen said. "And he told me he didn't want anything." The brother had come to the cremation. He was a taut young colonel in the Air Force who had been a fighter pilot in Korea and who had crisply taken charge of everything, even putting Rudolph on the sidelines. It was he who had made sure there were no religious services and who had told her that when Colin and he had spoken about death, they had each promised the other unceremonious burning. The day after the cremation, Colin's brother had hired a private plane, had flown out to sea and strewn Colin's ashes over the Pacific Ocean. He had told Gretchen if there was anything she needed to call on him. But short of strafing the ex-Mrs. Burke or bombing her lawyer's offices, what could a straightforward colonel in the Air Force do to help his brother's widow, enmeshed in the law?

Gretchen stood up. "Thank you for everything, Mr. Greenfield," she said. "I'm sorry I've taken so much of your time."

"Not at all." Mr. Greenfield stood, legally courteous. "I'll keep you informed, naturally, of all developments."

He escorted her to the door of his office. Although his face showed nothing, she was sure he disapproved of the dress she was wearing, which was pale blue.

She went down a long aisle flanked by rows of desks at which secretaries typed rapidly, without looking up, deeds, wills, complaints, summonses, contracts, bankruptcy petitions, transfers, mortgages, briefs, enjoinders, writs of replevin.

They are typing away the memory of Colin Burke, she thought. Day after day after day.

CHAPTER 5

IT WAS COLD up in the bow of the ship, but Thomas liked it up there alone, staring out at the long, gray swells of the Atlantic. Even when it wasn't his watch, he often went up forward and stood for hours, in all weathers, not saying anything to the man whose watch it happened to be, just standing there silently, watching the bow plunge and come up in a curl of white water, at peace with himself, not thinking consciously of anything, not wanting or needing to think about anything.

The ship flew the Liberian flag, but in two voyages he hadn't come close to Liberia. The man called Pappy, the manager of the Aegean Hotel, had been as helpful as Schultzy had said he would be. He had fitted him out with the clothes and seabag of an old Norwegian seaman who had died in the hotel and had gotten him the berth on the *Elga Andersen,* Greek ownership, taking on cargo at Hoboken for Rotterdam, Algeciras, Genoa, Piraeus. Thomas had stayed in his room in the Aegean all the time he was in New York, eight days, and Pappy had brought him his meals personally, because Thomas had said he didn't want any of the help to see him and start asking questions. The night before the *Elga Andersen* was due to sail Pappy had driven him over to the pier in Hoboken himself and watched while he signed on. The favor that Pappy owed Schultzy from Schultzy's days in the Merchant Marine during the war must have been a big one.

The *Elga Andersen* had sailed at dawn the next day and anybody who was looking for Tommy Jordache was going to have a hard time finding him.

The *Elga Andersen* was a Liberty ship, ten thousand tons. It had been built in 1943 and had seen better days. It had gone from owner to owner, for quick profits, and nobody had done more to maintain it than was absolutely necessary to keep it afloat and moving. Its hull was barnacled, its engines wheezed, it hadn't been painted in years, there was rust everywhere, the food was miserable, the captain an old religious maniac who knelt on the bridge during storms and who had been beached during the war for Nazi sympathies. The officers had papers from ten different countries and had been dismissed from other berths for drunkenness or incompetence or theft. The men in the crew were from almost every country with a coast on the Atlantic or the Mediterranean, Greeks, Yugoslavs, Norwegians, Italians, Moroccans, Mexicans, Americans, most of them with papers that could not stand inspection. There were fights almost every day in the mess room, where a poker game was always in progress, but the officers carefully refrained from interfering.

Thomas kept out of the poker game and the fights and spoke only when necessary and answered no questions and was at peace. He felt that he had found his place on the planet, plowing the wide waters of the world. No women, no worrying about weight, no pissing blood in the morning, no scrambling for money at the end of every month. Someday, he'd pay Schultzy back the one fifty he had given him in Las Vegas. With interest.

He heard steps behind him, but didn't turn around.

"We're in for a rough night," said the man who had joined him in the bow. "We're going right into a storm."

Thomas grunted. He recognized the voice. A young guy named Dwyer, a kid from the Middle West who somehow managed to sound like a fag. He was rabbit-toothed and was nicknamed Bunny.

"It's the skipper," Dwyer went on. "Praying on the bridge. You know the saying— you have a minister on board, watch out for lousy weather."

Thomas didn't say anything.

"I just hope it's not a big one," Dwyer said. "Plenty of these Liberty ships have just broke in half in heavy seas. And the way we're loaded. Did you notice the list to port we got?"

"No."

"Well, we got it. This your first voyage?"

"Second."

Dwyer had signed on in Savannah, where the *Elga Andersen* had put in after Thomas's first return voyage on her.

"It's a hell hole," Dwyer said. "I'm only on it for the opportunity."

Thomas knew Dwyer wanted him to ask what opportunity but just stood there staring out at the darkening horizon.

"You see," Dwyer went on, when he realized Thomas wasn't going to talk, "I've got my third mate's papers. On American ships I might have to wait years before I move up top. But on a tub like this, with the kind of scum we got as officers, one of them's likely to fall overboard drunk or get picked up by the police in port and then it'd be my opportunity, see?"

Thomas grunted. He had nothing against Dwyer, but he had nothing for him, either.

"You planning to try for mate's papers, too?" Dwyer asked.

"Hadn't thought about it." Spray was coming over the bow now as the weather worsened and he huddled into his pea jacket. Under the jacket he had a heavy turtle-neck blue sweater. The old Norwegian who had died in the Hotel Aegean must have been a big man, because his clothes fit Thomas comfortably.

"The only thing to do," Dwyer said. "I saw that the first day I set foot on the deck of my first ship. The ordinary seaman or even the A.B. winds up with nothing. Lives like a dog and winds up a broken old man at fifty. Even on American ships, with the union and everything and fresh fruit. Big deal. Fresh fruit. The thing is to plan ahead. Get some braid on you. The next time I'm back I'm going up to Boston and I'm going to take a shot at second mate's papers."

Thomas looked at him curiously. Dwyer was wearing a gob's white hat, pulled down all around a yellow sou'wester and solid new rubber-soled, high, working shoes. He was a small man and he looked like a boy dressed up for a costume party, with the new, natty, sea-going clothes. The wind had reddened his face but not like an outdoor man's face, rather like a girl's who is not used to the cold and has suddenly been exposed to it. He had long, dark eyelashes over soft, black eyes and he seemed to be begging for something. His mouth was too large and too full and too busy. He kept moving his hands in and out of his pockets restlessly.

Christ, Thomas thought, is that why he's come up here to talk to me and he always smiles at me when he passes me? I better put the bastard straight right now. "If you're such an educated hotshot," he said roughly, "with mate's papers and all, what're you doing down here with all of us poor folks? Why aren't you dancing with some heiress on a cruise ship in your nice white officer's suit?"

"I'm not trying to be superior, Jordache," Dwyer said. "Honest I'm not. I like to talk to somebody once in awhile and you're about my age and you're American and you got dignity, I saw that right away, dignity. Everybody else on this ship—they're animals. They're always making fun of me, I'm not one of them, I've got ambition, I won't play in their crooked poker games. You must've noticed."

"I haven't noticed anything," Thomas said.

"They think I'm a fag or something," Dwyer said. "You didn't notice that?"

"No, I didn't." Except for meals, Thomas stayed out of the mess room.

"It's my curse," Dwyer said. "That's what happens when I apply for third mate anywhere. They look at my papers, my recommendations, then they talk to me for awhile and look me over in that queer way and they tell me there's no openings. Boy, I can see that look coming from a mile off. I'm no fag. I swear to God, Jordache."

"You don't have to swear anything for me," Thomas said. The conversation made him uncomfortable. He didn't want to be let in on anybody's secrets or troubles. He wanted to do his job and go from one port to another and sail the seas in solitude.

"I'm engaged to be married, for Christ's sake," Dwyer cried. He dug into the back pocket of his pants and brought forth a wallet and took out a photograph. "Here, look at this." He thrust the snapshot in front of Thomas's nose. "That's my girl and me. Last summer on Narragansett Beach." A very pretty, full-bodied young girl, with curly blonde hair, in a bathing suit, and beside her, Dwyer, small but trim and well muscled, like a bantamweight, in a tightly fitting pair of swimming trunks. He looked in good enough shape to go into the ring, but of course that meant nothing. "Does that look like a fag?" Dwyer demanded. "Does that girl look as though she was the type to marry a fag?"

"No," Thomas admitted.

The spray coming over the bow sprinkled the photograph. "You better put the picture away," he said. "The water'll ruin it."

Dwyer took out a handkerchief and dried the snapshot and put it back in his wallet. "I just wanted you to know," he said, "that if I like to talk to you from time to time it's nothing like that."

"Okay," Thomas said. "Now I know it."

"As long as we have matters on a firm basis," Dwyer said, almost belligerently. "That's all." Abruptly, he turned away and made his way along the temporary wooden cat track built over the oil drums stowed as deck cargo forward.

Thomas shook his head, feeling the sting of spray on his face. Everybody has his troubles. A boatload of troubles. If everybody on the whole goddamn ship came up and told you what was bothering him, you'd want to jump overboard there and then.

He crouched in the bow, to escape the direct blows of spray, only occasionally lifting his head to do his job, which was to see what was ahead of the *Elga Andersen* on his watch.

Mate's papers, he thought. If you were going to make your living out of the sea, why not? He'd ask Dwyer, offhandedly, later, how you went about getting them. Fag or no fag.

They were in the Mediterranean, passing Gibraltar, but the weather, if anything, was worse. The captain no doubt was still praying to God and Adolf Hitler on the bridge. None of the officers had gotten drunk and fallen overboard and Dwyer still hadn't moved up top. He and Thomas were in the old naval gun crew's quarters at the stern, seated at the steel table riveted to the deck in the common room. The anti-aircraft guns had long since been dismounted, but nobody had bothered to dismantle the crew's quarters. There were at least ten urinals in the head. The kids of the gun crew must have pissed like mad, Thomas thought, every time they heard a plane overhead.

The sea was so rough that on every plunge the screw came out of the water and the entire stern shuddered and roared and Dwyer and Thomas had to grab for the papers and books and charts spread on the table to keep them from sliding off. But the gun crew's quarters was the only place they could get off alone and work together. They got in at least a couple of hours a day and Thomas, who had never paid any attention at school, was surprised to see how quickly he learned from Dwyer about navigation, sextant reading, star charts, loading, all the subjects he would have to have at his fingertips when he took the examination for third mate's papers. He was also surprised how much he enjoyed the sessions. Thinking about it in his bunk, when he was off watch, listening to the other two men in the cabin with him snore away, he felt he knew why the change had come about. It wasn't only age. He still didn't read anything else, not even the newspapers, not even the sporting pages. The charts, the pamphlets, the drawings of engines, the formulas, were a way out. Finally, a way out.

Dwyer had worked in the engine rooms of ships, as well as on deck, and he had a rough but adequate grasp of engineering problems and Thomas's experience around garages made it easier to understand what Dwyer was talking about.

Dwyer had grown up on the shores of Lake Superior and had sailed small boats ever since he was a kid and as soon as he had finished high school he had hitchhiked to New York, gone down to the Battery to see the ships passing in and out of port, and had got himself signed on a coastal oil tanker as a deckhand. Nothing that had happened to him since that day had diminished his enthusiasm for the sea.

He didn't ask any questions about Thomas's past and Thomas didn't volunteer any information. Out of gratitude for what Dwyer was teaching him, Thomas was almost beginning to like the little man.

"Some day," Dwyer said, grabbing for a chart that was sliding forward, "you and I will both have our own ships. Captain Jordache, Captain Dwyer presents his compliments and asks if you will honor him and come aboard."

"Yeah," Thomas said. "I can just see it."

"Especially if there's a war," Dwyer said. "I don't mean a great big one, like World War II, where if you could sail a rowboat across Central Park Lake, you could get to be skipper of *some* kind of ship. I mean even a little one like Korea. You have no idea how much money guys come home with, with combat zone pay, stuff like that. And how many guys who didn't know their ass from starboard came out masters of their own ships. Hell, the United States has got to be fighting somewhere soon and if we're ready, there's no telling how high we can go."

"Save your dreams for the sack," Thomas said. "Let's get back to work."

They bent over the chart.

It was in Marseilles that the idea hit Thomas. It was nearly midnight and he and Dwyer had had dinner together at a seafood place on the Vieux Port. Thomas remembered that this was the south coast of France and they had drunk three bottles of vin rosé between them because they were on the south coast of France, even though Marseilles hardly could be considered a tourist resort. The *Elga Andersen* was due to lift anchor at 5 A.M. and as long as they got back on board before that, they were okay.

After dinner they had walked around, stopping in several bars and now they were at what was going to be their last stop, a small dark bar off the Canebiere. A juke box was playing and a few fat whores at the bar were waiting to be asked if they wanted a drink. Thomas wouldn't have minded having a girl, but the whores were sleazy and probably had the clap and didn't go with his idea of the kind of lady you ought to have on the south coast of France.

Drinking, a little blearily, at a table along the wall, looking at the girls, fat legs showing under loud, imitation silk dresses, Thomas remembered ten of the best days in his life, the time in Cannes with the wild English girl who liked jewelry.

"Say," he said to Dwyer, sitting across from him, drinking beer, "I got an idea."

"What's that?" Dwyer was keeping a wary eye on the girls, fearful that one of them would come over and sit down next to him and put her hand on his knee. He had offered earlier in the evening to pick up a prostitute to prove, once and for all, to Thomas that he wasn't a fag, but Thomas had said it wasn't necessary, he didn't care whether he was a fag or not and anyway it wouldn't prove anything because he knew plenty of fags who also screwed.

"What's what?" Thomas asked.

"You said you had an idea."

"An idea. Yeah. An idea. Let's skip the fucking ship."

"You're crazy," Dwyer said. "What the hell'll we do in Marseilles without a ship? They'll put us in jail."

"Nobody'll put us in jail," Thomas said. "I didn't say for good. Where's the next port she pulls into? Genoa. Am I right?"

"Okay. Genoa," Dwyer said reluctantly.

"We pick her up in Genoa," Thomas said. "We say we got drunk and we didn't wake up until she was out of the harbor. Then we pick her up in Genoa. What can they do to us? Dock us a few days' pay, that's all. They're shorthanded as it is. After Genoa, the ship goes straight back to Hoboken, right?"

"Yeah."

"So we don't lose any shore time, them keeping us on board in a port. I don't want to sail on that lousy tub any more, anyway. We can always pick up something better in New York."

"But what'll we do between now and Genoa?" Dwyer asked worriedly.

"We tour. We make the grand tour," Thomas said. "We get on the train and we go to Cannes. Haunt of millionaires, like they say in the papers. I been there. Time of my life. We lay on the beach, we find ourselves some dames. We got our pay in our pocket . . ."

"I'm saving my money," Dwyer said.

"Live a little, live a little," Thomas said impatiently. By now it was inconceivable to him that he could go back to the gloom of the ship, stand watches, chip paint, eat the garbage they handed out, with Cannes so close by, available, waiting.

"I don't even have my toothbrush on me," Dwyer said.

"I'll buy you a toothbrush," Thomas said. "Say, you're always telling me what a great sailor you are, how you sailed a dory all over Lake Superior when you were a kid . . ."

"What's Lake Superior got to do with Cannes?"

"Sailor boy . . ." It was one of the whores from the bar, in a spangled dress showing most of her bosom. "Sailor boy, want to buy nize lady nize little drink, have good time, wiz ozzer lady later?" She smiled, showing gold teeth.

"Get outa here," Thomas said.

"*Salaud,*" the woman said amiably, and spangled over to the juke box.

"What's Lake Superior got to do with Cannes?" Thomas said. "I'll tell you what Lake Superior's got to do with Cannes. You're a hot small boat sailor on Lake Superior . . ."

"Well, I . . ."

"Are you or aren't you?"

"For Christ's sake, Tommy," Dwyer said, "I never said I was Christopher Columbus or anybody like that. I said I sailed a dory and some small power boats when I was a kid and . . ."

"You know how to handle boats. Am I right in supposing that or ain't I right?"

"Sure, I can handle small boats," Dwyer admitted. "I still don't see . . ."

"On the beach at Cannes," Thomas said, "they got sailboats you can rent by the hour. I want to see with my own eyes how you rate. You're big on theory, with charts and books. All right, I want to see you actually get a boat in and out of some place. Or do I have to take that on faith, too, like your not being a fag?"

"Tommy!" Dwyer said, hurt.

"You can teach me," Thomas said. "I want to learn from an expert. Ah—the hell with it—if you're too yellow to come with me, I'll do it myself. Go on back to the boat, like a nice little boy."

"Okay," Dwyer said. "I never did anything like this before. But I'll do it. The hell with the ship." He drained his beer.

"The grand tour," Thomas said.

It wasn't as good as he'd remembered it, because he had Dwyer with him, not that wild English girl. But it was good enough. And it certainly was a lot better than standing watches on the *Elga Andersen* and eating that slop and sleeping in the same stinking hole with two snoring Moroccans.

They found a cheap little hotel that wasn't too bad behind the rue d'Antibes and went swimming off the beach, although it was only springtime and the water was so cold you could only stay in a little while. But the white buildings were the same, the pink wine was the same, the blue sky was the same, the great yachts lying in the harbor were the same. And he didn't have to worry about his weight or fighting some murderous Frenchman when the holiday was over.

They rented a little sailboat by the hour and Dwyer hadn't been lying, he really knew how to handle small boats. In two days he had taught Thomas a great deal and Thomas could slip a mooring and come up to it dead, with the sail rattling down, nine times out of ten.

But most of the time they spent around the harbor, walking slowly around the quays, silently admiring the sloops, the schooners, the big yachts, the motor cruisers, all still in the harbor and being sanded down and varnished and polished up for the season ahead.

"Christ," Thomas said, "would you believe there's so much money in the world and we don't have any of it."

They found a bar on the Quai St. Pierre frequented by the sailors and captains working on pleasure craft. Some of them were English and many of the others could speak a little and they got into conversations with them whenever they could. None of the men seemed to work very hard and the bar was almost always at least half full at all hours of the day. They learned to drink pastis because that was what everybody else drank and because it was cheap. They hadn't found any girls and the ones who accosted them from cars on the Croisette or back behind the port asked too much money. But for once in his life Thomas didn't mind going without a woman. The harbor was enough for him, the vision of the life based on it, of grown men living year in and year out on beautiful ships was enough for him. No boss to bother about nine months of the year, and then in the summer being a big shot at the wheel of a hundred-thousand-dollar craft, going to places like St. Tropez and Monte Carlo and Capri, coming into harbor with girls in bathing suits draped all over the decks. And they all seemed to have money. What they didn't earn in salary they got in kickbacks from ship chandlers and boatyards and rigged expense accounts. They ate and drank like kings and some of the older ones weren't sober from one day to the next.

"These guys," Thomas said, after they had been in town for four days, "have solved the problems of the universe."

He even thought of skipping the *Elga Andersen* for good and trying to get a job on one of the yachts for the summer, but it turned out that unless you were a skipper you most likely only got hired for three or four months, at lousy pay, and you were let go for the rest of the year. Much as he liked Cannes, he couldn't see himself starving eight months a year just to be there.

Dwyer was just as dazzled as he was. Maybe even more so. He hadn't even been in Cannes before but had admired and had been around boats all his life. What was an adult discovery for Thomas was a reminder for Dwyer of the deepest pleasures of his boyhood.

There was one Englishman in the bar, a dark-brown colored little man with white hair, named Jennings, who had been in the British navy during the war and who owned, actually *owned*, his boat, a sixty-footer with five cabins. It was old and cranky, the Englishman told them, but he knew it like his own mother, and he coaxed her all around the Med, Malta, Greece, Sicily, everywhere, as a charter captain during the summer. He had an agent in Cannes who booked his charters for him, for ten per cent. He had been lucky, he said. The man who had owned the boat and for whom he had worked, had hated his wife. When he died, out of spite, he had left the boat to Jennings. Well, you couldn't bank on things like that.

Jennings sipped complacently at his pastis. His motor yacht, the Gertrude II, stubby, but clean and comfortable looking, was moored for the winter across the street, just in front of the bar, and as he drank Jennings could look fondly at it, all good things close at hand. "It's a lovely life," he said. "I fair have to admit it, Yanks. Instead of fighting for a couple of bob a day, hauling cargo on the docks of Liverpool or sweating blood oiling engines in some tub in the North Sea in a winter's gale. To say nothing of the climate and taxes." He waved largely toward the view of the harbor outside the bar where the mild sun tipped the gently bobbing masts of the boats moored side by side at the quay. "Rich man's weather," Jennings said. "Rich man's weather."

"Let me ask you a question, Jennings," Thomas said. He was paying for the Englishman's drinks and he was entitled to a few questions. "How much would it cost to get a fair-sized boat, say one like yours, and get into business?"

Jennings lit a pipe and pulled at it reflectively. He never did anything quickly, Jennings. He was no longer in the British navy, or on the docks, there was no foreman or mate to snarl at him, he had time for everything. "Ah, that's a hard question to answer, Yank," he said. "Ships are like women—some come high and some come cheap, but the price you pay has little to do with the satisfaction you get from them." He laughed appreciatively at his own worldliness.

"The minimum," Thomas persisted. "The absolute minimum?"

Jennings scratched his head, finished his pastis. Thomas ordered another round.

"It's a matter of luck," Jennings said. "I know men put down a hundred thousand pounds, cash on the barrelhead, ships designed by the fanciest naval architects, built in the best shipyards in Holland or Britain, steel hulls, teak decks, every last little doodad on board, radar, electric toilets, air conditioning, automatic pilot, and they cursed the day the bloody thing was put in the water and they would have been glad to get rid of it for the price of a case of whiskey, and no takers."

"We don't have any hundred thousand pounds," Thomas said shortly.

"We?" Dwyer said bewilderedly. "What do you mean, *we?*"

"Shut up," Thomas said. "*Your* boat never cost any hundred thousand pounds," he said to Jennings.

"No," Jennings said. "I don't pretend it ever did."

"I mean something *reasonable,*" Thomas said.

"Reasonable aren't a word you use about boats," Jennings said. He was beginning to get on Thomas's nerves. "What's reasonable for one man is pure lunacy for another, if you get my meaning. It's a matter of luck, like I was saying. For example, a man has a nice snug little ship, cost him maybe twenty, thirty thousand pounds, but maybe his wife gets seasick all the time, or he's had a bad year in business and his creditors are panting on his traces and it's been a stormy season for cruising and maybe the market's been down and it looks as though the Communists're going to take over in Italy or France or there's going to be a war or the tax people're after him for some hanky-panky, maybe he didn't tell them he paid for the ship with money he had stowed away quiet-like in some bank in Switzerland, so he's pressed, he's got to get out and get out fast and suddenly nobody wants to buy boats that week . . . You get my drift, Yank?"

"Yeah," Thomas said. "You don't have to draw a map."

"So he's desperate," Jennings went on. "Maybe he needs five thousand guineas before Monday or the house falls in on his head. If you're there and you have the five thousand guineas . . ."

"What's a guinea?" Dwyer asked.

"Five thousand guineas is fifteen thousand bucks," Thomas said. "Isn't it?"

"Give or take a few bob," Jennings said. "Or you hear about a naval vessel that's up for auction or a vessel that's been confiscated by the Customs for smuggling. Of course, it needs refitting, but if you're clever with your hands and don't pay these pirates in the shipyards around here to do your work for you—never trust a Frenchman on the Côte, especially along the waterfront, he'll steal the eyes right out of your head—why, maybe, playing everything close and counting your money every night, maybe with luck, and getting some people to trust you till the end of the season for gear and provisions, you're in the water and ready for your first charter for as little as eight, ten thousand pounds."

"Eight, ten thousand pounds," Dwyer said. "It might as well be eight, ten million dollars."

"Shut up," Thomas said. "There're ways of making money."

"Yeah?" Dwyer said. "How?"

"There're ways. I once made three thousand bucks in one night."

Dwyer took in a deep breath. "How?"

It was the first time Thomas had given anybody a clue to his past since he had left the Hotel Aegean, and he was sorry he had spoken. "Never mind how," he said sharply. He turned to Jennings. "Will you do me a favor?"

"Anything within my power," Jennings said. "As long as it don't cost me no money." He chuckled softly, boat owner, sitting on top of the system, canny graduate of the Royal Navy, survivor of war and poverty, pastis drinker, wise old salt, nobody's fool.

"If you hear of anything," Thomas said. "Something good, but cheap, get in touch with us, will you."

"Happy to oblige, Yank," Jennings said. "Just write the address down."

Thomas hesitated. The only address he had was the Hotel Aegean and the only person he had given it to was his mother. Before the fight with Quayles, he had visited her fairly regularly, when he was sure he wouldn't run into his brother Rudolph. Since then he had written her from the ports he had touched at, sending her folders of postcards and pretending he was doing better than he was doing. When he had come back from his first voyage there had been a bundle of letters from her waiting for him at the Aegean. The only trouble with her letters was that she kept asking to see her grandson and he didn't dare get in touch with Teresa even to see the boy. It was the one thing he missed about America.

"Just write the address down, lad," Jennings repeated.

"Give him your address," Thomas said to Dwyer. Dwyer got his mail at the headquarters of the National Maritime Union in New York. Nobody was looking for *him*.

"Why don't you stop dreaming?" Dwyer said.

"Do like I say."

Dwyer shrugged, wrote out his address, and gave it to Jennings. His handwriting was clear and straight. He would keep a neat log, Third Mate Dwyer. If he ever got the chance.

The old man put the slip of paper into an old, cracked, leather wallet. "I'll keep my eyes peeled and my ears open," he promised.

Thomas paid the bill and he and Dwyer started along the quay, examining all the boats tied up there, as usual. They walked slowly and silently. Thomas could feel Dwyer glancing at him uneasily from time to time.

"How much money you got?" Thomas asked, as they reached the foot of the harbor, where the fishing boats, with their acetylene lamps, were tied up, with the nets laid out along the pavement, drying.

"How much money I got?" Dwyer said querulously. "Not even a hundred bucks. Just enough to buy one-millionth of an ocean liner."

"I don't mean how much money you got *on* you. I mean altogether. You keep telling me you save your dough."

"If you think I've got enough for a crazy scheme like . . ."

"I asked you how much money you got. In the bank?"

"Twenty-two hundred dollars," Dwyer said reluctantly. "In the bank. Listen, Tommy, stop jerking off, we'll never . . ."

"Between us," Thomas said, "you and me, one day, we're going to have our own boat. Right here. In this port. Rich man's weather, like the Englishman said. We'll get the money somehow."

"I'm not going to do anything criminal." Dwyer sounded scared. "I never committed a crime in my life and I'm not going to start now."

"Who said anything about committing a crime?" Thomas said. Although the thought had crossed his mind. There had been plenty of what Dwyer would call criminals hanging around during his years in the ring, in two-hundred-dollar suits and big cars, with fancy broads hanging on their arms, and everybody being polite and glad to see them, cops, politicans, businessmen, movie stars. They were just about like everybody else. There was nothing so special about them. Crime was just another way of earning a buck. Maybe an easier way. But he didn't want to scare Dwyer off. Not yet. If it ever came off, he'd need Dwyer to handle the boat. He couldn't do it alone. Yet. He wasn't that much of an idiot.

Somehow, he told himself, as they passed the old men playing boules on the quay-side, with the harbor behind them, the protected sheet of water crowded with millions of dollars worth of pleasure craft, shining in the sun. The one time he had been here before, he had sworn he'd come back. Well, he had come back. And he was going to come back again. SOMEHOW.

The next morning, early, they caught the train on the way to Genoa. They gave themselves an extra day, because they wanted to stop off and see Monte Carlo. Maybe they'd have some luck at the Casino.

If he had been at the other end of the platform he'd have seen his brother Rudolph getting out of one of the sleeping cars from Paris, with a slender, pretty, young girl and a lot of new luggage.

CHAPTER 6

WHEN THEY WALKED through the exit gate of the station, they saw the Hertz sign and Rudolph said, "There's the man with our car." The concierge at the hotel in Paris had taken care of everything. As Jean had said, after the concierge had arranged for tickets to the theater, for a limousine to tour the chateaux of the Loire, for tables at ten restaurants, for places at the Opera and Longchamps, "Every marriage should have its own private Paris concierge."

The porter trundled their luggage over to the car, said *merci* for the tip and smiled, although they were plainly American. According to the newspapers back home Frenchmen were not smiling at Americans this year. The man from the Hertz agency started to talk in English but Rudolph showed off with his French, mostly to amuse Jean, and the remaining formalities for renting the Peugeot convertible were concluded in the language of Racine. Rudolph had bought a Michelin map of the Alpes-Maritimes in Paris, and after consulting it, with the car top down, and the soft Mediterranean morning sun shining on their bare heads, they drove through the white town and then along the edge of the sea, through Golfe Juan, where Napoleon had landed, through Juan-les-Pins, it big hotels still in their pre-season sleep, to the Hotel du Cap, shapely, cream colored and splendid on its gentle hill among the pines.

As the manager showed them up to their suite, with a balcony overlooking the calm, blue sea below the hotel park, Rudolph said, coolly, "It's very nice, thank you." But it was only with the greatest difficulty that he kept from grinning idiotically at how perfectly the manager, himself, and Jean were playing their roles in his ancient dream. Only it was better than the dream. The suite was larger and more luxuriously furnished; the air was sweeter; the manager was more of a manager than anyone could imagine; he himself was richer and cooler and better dressed than he had been in his poor-boy reverie; Jean, in her slim Paris suit, was more beautiful than the imaginary girl who had walked out onto the balcony overlooking the sea and kissed him in his fantasy.

The manager bowed himself out, the porters finished placing the bags on folding stools around the gigantic bedroom. Solid, real, with a solid, real wife, he said, "Let's go out on the balcony."

They went out on the balcony and kissed in the sunlight.

They nearly hadn't married at all. Jean had hesitated and hesitated, refusing to say yes or no and for awhile he was on the brink of delivering an ultimatum to her every time he saw her, which was tantalizingly seldom. He was kept in Whitby and Port Philip a great deal of the time by work and then, when he did get to New York it was often only to find a message with his answering service from Jean telling him that she was out of town on a job. One night, he had seen her in a restaurant after the theater with a small, beady-eyed young man with matted long hair and a week-old growth of dark stubble on his jaws. The next time he saw her he asked her who the young man was and she admitted it still was the same one, the one she was overlapping with. When he asked her if she was still sleeping with him, she answered that it was none of his business.

He had felt humiliated that he was in competition with anyone that unsavory looking and it didn't make him feel any better to be told by Jean that the man was one of the most famous fashion photographers in the country. He had walked out on her that time and waited for her to get in touch with him, but she never called him and finally he couldn't bear it any longer and called her, swearing to himself that he would screw her but he'd be damned if he ever would marry her.

His whole conception of himself was damaged by her treatment of him and it was only in bed, where she delighted him and seemed to be delighted by him that he found any relief from his brooding feeling that he was being debased by the entire affair. All the men he knew assured him that all the girls *they* knew did nothing but plot constantly to get married. What sensational lack was there in his character or his lovemaking or general desirability that had made the only two girls he had asked to marry reject him?

Virginia Calderwood hadn't helped matters either. Old man Calderwood had followed Rudolph's advice about allowing his daughter to come down to New York and live alone and take a secretarial course. But if she was learning typing and stenography, Virginia must have done it at very odd hours indeed, because almost every time Rudolph went to his New York apartment, he would spot her, lurking in a doorway across the street or pretending just to be walking by. She would telephone in the middle of the night, sometimes three or four times, to say, "Rudy, I love you, I love you. I want you to fuck me."

To avoid her, he took to staying in different hotels when he came to New York, but for some prudish reason, Jean refused to visit him in a hotel and even the pleasures of the bed were denied him. Jean still wouldn't let him call for her at her apartment and he had never seen the place where she lived or met her roommate.

Virginia sent him long letters, horrifyingly explicit about her sensual longings for him, the language straight out of Henry Miller, whom Virginia must have studied assiduously. The letters were sent to his home at Whitby, to his apartment, to the main office at the store, and all it would take would be for one careless secretary to open any one of them and he doubted if old man Calderwood would ever talk to him again.

When he told Jean about Virginia, she just laughed and said, "Oh, you poor attractive man." Mischievously, one night, when they came back late to his apartment and he spotted Virginia in the shadows across the street, Jean wanted to go over and invite the girl up for a drink.

His work suffered and he found that he had to read simple reports over three and four times before they registered on his brain. He slept restlessly and awoke weary. For the first time in his life he had a rash of pimples on his chin.

At a party in New York he met a bosomy blonde lady who seemed to have three men around her at all times during the evening, but who made it plain to him that she

wanted to go home with him. He took her to her apartment in the East Eighties, off
Fifth Avenue, learned that she was rich, that she was divorced, that she was lonely,
that she was tired of the men who pursued her around New York, that she found him
ravishingly sexy (he wished she had found another style of expressing herself). They
went to bed together after one drink and he was impotent and he left on a volley of
coarse laughter from the useless bed.

"The unluckiest day of my life," he told Jean, "was the day you came up to Port
Philip to take those pictures."

Nothing that happened made him stop loving her or wanting to marry her and live
with her for the rest of his life. He had called her all day, ten times, a dozen times, but
there never was any answer. One more time, he decided, sitting disconsolately in the
living room of his apartment, I'll try one more goddamn time and if she's not home I
will go out and get roaring drunk and pick up girls and fight in bars and if Virginia
Calderwood is outside the door when I come home I will bring her up here and screw
her and then call the men with the straitjacket and tell them to come and take us both
away.

The phone rang and he was just about to put it down when it was picked up and Jean
said, "Hello," in the hushed, childish little way she had.

"Has your phone been out of order?" he asked.

"I don't know," she said. "I've been out all day."

"Are you going to be out all night?"

There was a pause. "No," she said.

"Do we meet?" He was ready to slam the phone down if she said no. He had once
told her that he only had two alternating emotions about her—rage and ecstasy.

"Do you want to meet?"

"Eight o'clock?" he said. "I'll give you a drink here." He had looked out the
window and had not spotted Virginia Calderwood.

"I have to take a bath," she said, "and I don't feel like hurrying. Why don't you
come down here and I'll give *you* a drink."

"I hear the sound of cymbals and trumpets," he said.

"Stop trying to sound educated," she said, but she chuckled.

"What floor?"

"Fourth," she said. "No elevator. Be careful of your heart." She hung up.

He went in and showered and shaved. His hand wasn't steady and he cut himself
badly on the chin. The cut wouldn't stop bleeding for a long time and he didn't ring
the bell of her apartment on East Fortieth Street until five minutes past eight.

The door was opened by a girl in blue jeans and a sweater whom he had never seen
before, who said, "Hi, I'm Florence," and then called, "Jeanny, the man's here."

"Come in, Rudy." Jean's voice floated out of an open door leading off the foyer.
"I'm making up."

"Thanks, Florence," Rudolph said and went into Jean's room. She was seated
naked at a table in front of a small mirror putting mascara on her eyelashes. He hadn't
realized before that she used mascara. But he didn't say anything about the mascara.
Or her being naked. He was too busy looking around the room. Almost every inch of
wall space was taken up with photographs of himself, smiling, frowning, squinting,
writing on the clip board. Some of the photographs were small, others were immense
blowups. All of them were flattering. It's over, he thought gratefully, it's all over.
She's decided.

"I know that man from somewhere," he said.

"I thought you'd recognize him," Jean said. Pink, firm, and dainty, she went on
putting on mascara.

Over dinner, they talked about the wedding. By the time dessert came, they nearly
called it off.

"What I like," Rudolph said bitterly, "is a girl who knows her own mind."

"Well, I know mine," Jean said. She had grown sullen as Rudolph had argued with her. "I think I know what I'm going to do with my weekend," she said. "I'm going to stay home and tear down every one of those photographs and whitewash the walls."

To begin with, she was grimly devoted to secrecy. He wanted to let everybody know immediately, but she shook her head. "No announcements," she said.

"I have a sister and a mother," Rudolph said. "Actually, I have a brother, too."

"That's the whole idea. I've got a father and a brother. And I can't stand either of them. If they find out that you told your family and I didn't tell them, there'll be thunder from the West for ten years. And after we're married I don't want to have anything to do with your family and I don't want you to have anything to do with mine. Families're out. Thanksgiving dinners at the old homestead. Christ!"

Rudolph had given in on that without too much of a fight. His wedding couldn't be a gloriously happy occasion for Gretchen, with Colin dead just a few months. And the thought of his mother blubbering away in some horrible concoction of a church-going dress was not an appealing one. He could also easily do without the scene Virginia Calderwood would make upon hearing the news. But not telling Johnny Heath or Calderwood or Brad Knight would lead to complications around the office, especially if he wanted to leave immediately after the wedding on the honeymoon. The points that Jean and he *had* agreed upon were that there was to be no party, that they would get out of New York promptly, that they would not be married in church, and that they would go to Europe on the honeymoon.

They had not agreed upon what they would do when they returned from Europe. Jean refused to stop working and she refused to live in Whitby.

"Damn it," Rudolph said, "here we're not even married yet and you've got me down as a part-time husband."

"I'm not domestic," Jean had said stubbornly. "I don't like small towns. I'm on my way up in this city. I'm not going to give it all up just because a man wants to marry me."

"Jean . . ." Rudolph said warningly.

"All right," she said. "Just because I want to marry a man."

"That's better," he said.

"You've said yourself, the office rightly ought to be in New York."

"Only it's not in New York," he said.

"You'll like me better if you don't see me all the time."

"No, I won't.

"Well, I'll like *you* better."

He had given in on that, too. But without grace. "That's my last surrender," he said.

"Yes, dear," she said, mock demurely, fluttering her eyelashes. She stroked his hand exaggeratedly on the table. "I do admire a man who knows how to assert himself."

Then they had both laughed and everything was all right and Rudolph said, "There's one sonofabitch that's going to get an announcement and that's that slimy photographer and if he wants to come to the wedding tell him he's welcome, but he's got to shave."

"Fair enough," Jean said, "if I can send an announcement to Virginia Calderwood."

Cruel and happy, hand in hand, they left the restaurant and went into bar after bar on Third Avenue secretly and lovingly and finally, drunkenly, to toast the years ahead of them.

The next day he bought a diamond engagement ring at Tiffany's, but she made him take it back. "I hate the trappings of wealth," she said. "Just make sure to show up at City Hall on the day with a nice simple gold band."

It was impossible, finally, not to tell Calderwood and Brad and Johnny Heath that he was going to be away for at least a month and why. Jean conceded the point, but on condition that he swear them to secrecy, which he did.

Calderwood was mournful. Rudolph couldn't tell whether it was because of his daughter or because he didn't like the idea of Rudolph being away from the business for a month. "I hope you're not being rash," Calderwood said. "I remember the girl. She seemed like a poor little thing to me. I'll bet she doesn't have a dime."

"She works," Rudolph said defensively.

"I don't approve of wives working," Calderwood said. He shook his head. "Ah, Rudy—and you could have had everything."

Everything, Rudolph thought. Including crazy Virginia Calderwood and her pornographic letters.

Neither Brad nor Johnny Heath was wildly enthusiastic, but he wasn't marrying to please them. Enthusiastic or not, they both came to the wedding at City Hall and drove out to the airport with the bride and groom and Florence.

Rudolph's first husbandly moment came when they checked in and Jean's luggage was nearly a hundred pounds overweight. "Good Lord," he said, "what have you got in there?"

"A change of clothes," Jean said. "You don't want your wife to walk around naked in front of all those Frenchmen, do you?"

"For a girl who doesn't like the trappings of luxury," he said, as he wrote out the check for the overweight, "you sure carry around a lot of supplies." He tried to make it sound light, but he had a moment of foreboding. The long years of having to pinch pennies had made him fitfully careful about money. Extravagant wives had ruined men many times wealthier than he. Unworthy fear. I'll handle her, if necessary, he thought. Today he felt he could handle anything. He took her hand and led the way toward the bar.

They had time for two bottles of champagne before they took off and Johnny Heath promised to call Gretchen and Rudolph's mother and tell them the news once the plane was off the ground. The days grew warmer. They lazed in the sun. They became dark brown and Jean's hair turned almost blond, bleached by the sun and salt water. She gave him tennis lessons on the courts of the hotel and said that he had talent for the game. She was very serious about the lessons and spoke sharply to him when he didn't hit out correctly. She taught him how to water ski. She kept amazing him with the number of things she could do well.

They had lunch brought to them at their cabana overlooking the speed-boat mooring. They ate cold langouste and drank white wine and after lunch they went up to their rooms to make love, with the windows shuttered against the afternoon sun.

He didn't look at any of the girls lying almost naked around the hotel pool and on the rocks next to the diving board, although two or three of the girls well deserved to be looked at.

"You're unnatural," Jean said to him.

"Why am I unnatural?"

"Because you don't ogle."

"I ogle you."

"Keep it up," she said.

They found new restaurants and ate bouillabaisse on the *terrasse* of Chez Feliz, where you could look through the arch of the rampart at the boats in the harbor of Antibes. When they made love later they both smelled of garlic and wine, but they didn't mind.

They took excursions to the hill towns and visited the Matisse chapel and the pottery works at Vallauris and ate lunch on the terrace of the Colombe d'Or at St.-Paul-de-Vence, in the white flutter of doves' wings. They learned with regret that the flock was kept white because the white doves drove off pigeons of any other color. When occasionally the doves did tolerate their impure fellows, the proprietor killed them off himself.

Wherever they went, Jean took her cameras along, and took innumerable pictures of him against backgrounds of masts, ramparts, palms, waves. "I am going to make you into the wallpaper for our bedroom in New York," she said.

He no longer bothered to put on a shirt when he came out of the water. Jean said she liked the hair on his chest and the fuzz on his shoulders.

They planned a trip to Italy when they got tired of the Cap d'Antibes. They got out a map and circled the towns of Menton, San Remo, Milano for the Last Supper, Rappallo, Santa Margherita, Firenze, for Michelangelo and the Botticellis, Bologna, Siena, Assisi, Rome. The names were like little bells chiming in sunshine. Jean had been everywhere. Other summers. It would be a long time before he learned everything about her.

They didn't get tired of the Cap d'Antibes.

One day, he took a set from her in tennis. She fought off set point three times, but he finally won. She was furious. For two minutes.

They sent a cable to Calderwood to say that they weren't coming back for awhile.

They didn't speak to anyone at the hotel except an Italian movie actress who was so beautiful that you had to speak to her. Jean spent a morning taking photographs of the Italian movie actress and sent them to *Vogue* in New York. *Vogue* cabled back that they were going to run a set in their September issue.

Nothing could go wrong that month.

Although they still were not tired of the Cap d'Antibes, they got into the car and started driving south to visit the towns they had circled on the map. They were disappointed nowhere.

They sat in the cobbled square of Portofino and ate chocolate ice cream, the best chocolate ice cream in the world. They watched the women selling postcards and lace and embroidered tablecloths from their stands to tourists and they eyed the yachts moored in the harbor.

There was one slender, white yacht, about fifty feet long, with racy, clean Italian lines and Rudolph said, "That's what machinery is all about. When it comes out like that."

"Would you like to own it?" Jean asked, scooping up her chocolate ice cream.

"Who wouldn't like to own it?" he said.

"I'll buy it for you," she said.

"Thanks," he said. "And how about a Ferrari and a mink-lined overcoat and a forty-room house on the Cap d'Antibes, too, while you're at it?"

"No," she said, still eating her ice cream. "I really mean it. If you really want it."

He examined her closely. She was calm and serious. "Wait a minute," he said. "*Vogue* isn't paying you *that* much for those pictures."

"I don't depend on *Vogue*," she said. "I'm *awfully* rich. When my mother died she left me an obscene amount of stocks and bonds. Her father owned one of the biggest drug companies in the United States."

"What's the name of the company?" Rudolph asked suspiciously.

Jean told him the name of the company.

Rudolph whistled softly and put down his spoon.

"It's all in a trust fund that my father and brother control until I'm twenty-five," Jean said, "but even now my income is at least three times the size of yours. I hope I haven't spoiled your day."

Rudolph burst into a roar of laughter. "Christ," he said. "What a honeymoon!"

She didn't buy him a yacht that afternoon, but as a compromise, she bought him a shocking-pink shirt in a faggy shop alongside the harbor.

Later on, when he asked why she hadn't told him before, she was evasive. "I hate talking about money," she said. "That's all they ever talked about in my family. By the time I was fifteen I came to the belief that money degrades the soul if you think about it all the time. I never went home a single summer after the age of fifteen. Since I got out of college I never used a cent of the money my mother left me. I let my father and brother put it back into the business. They want me to let them keep using the income when the trust expires, but they're in for a big surprise. They'll cheat me if they can and I'm not out to be cheated. Especially not by them."

"Well, what *are* you going to do with it?"

"You're going to handle it for me," she said. "I'm sorry. For *us*. Do whatever you think best. Just don't talk to me about it. And don't use it to make us lead soggy, fancy, useless lives."

"We've been leading pretty fancy lives these past few weeks," Rudolph said.

"We've been spending your money and you worked for it," Jean said. "Anyway, this is a honeymoon. It isn't for real."

When they got to the hotel in Rome there was a cable waiting for Rudolph. It was from Bradford Knight and it read, "Your mother in hospital Stop Doctor fears end is near Stop Believe you should return soonest."

Rudolph handed the cable to Jean. They were still in the lobby and had just handed over their passports to the clerk at the desk. Jean read the cable silently, gave it back to him. "I suppose we ought to see if there's a plane out tonight," she said. It had been nearly five o'clock in the afternoon when they drove up to the hotel.

"Let's go upstairs," Rudolph said. He didn't want to have to think about what to do about his mother's dying in a crowded Roman hotel lobby.

They went up in the elevator and watched while the clerk who had accompanied them opened the shutters and let in the late sunlight and the roar of Rome.

"I hope you enjoy your stay," the clerk said, and left.

They watched the porters come in and arrange their luggage. The porters went and they stared at the unopened bags. They had planned to stay in Rome at least two weeks.

"No," Rudolph said. "We're not going to see if there's a plane tonight. The old lady is not going to do me out of Rome completely. We'll leave tomorrow. I'll take one day for you and me. She'll be alive when I get there. She wouldn't do herself out of the pleasure of dying before my eyes for anything in the world. Unpack."

CHAPTER 7

I

As soon as he got back on board the *Elga Andersen* in Genoa, he knew he was in for trouble with Falconetti. Falconetti was the bully of the ship, a huge, ham-handed man, with a small turnip-shaped head, who had been in jail for armed robbery. He cheated at cards, but the one time he had been called on it by an oiler from the engine room he had nearly strangled the oiler before he was pulled away from the man's throat by the rest of the men in the mess room. He was free and dangerous with his fists. At the beginning of each voyage he made a point of picking fights with four or five men and beating them up brutally, so that there would be no doubt about his position below decks. When he was in the mess room, no one else dared touch the radio there and everybody listened to the programs of Falconetti's choice, whether they liked it or not. There was one Negro on board by the name of Renway, and when Falconetti came into the mess room he slipped away. "I don't sit in any room with a nigger," Falconetti had announced the first time he saw the man in the mess room. Renway hadn't said anything, but he hadn't moved, either.

"Nigger," Falconetti said, "I guess you didn't hear me." He strode over to where the man was sitting at the table, grabbed him under the armpits, carried him to the door and hurled him against the bulkhead. Nobody said or did anything. You took care of yourself on the *Elga Andersen,* and the next man took care of himself.

Falconetti owed money to half the crew. Theoretically they were loans, but nobody expected to see his money again. If you didn't lend Falconetti a five- or ten-dollar bill when he asked for it, he wouldn't do anything about it at the time, but two or three days later, he would pick a fight with you and there would be black eyes and broken noses and teeth to spit out.

Falconetti hadn't tried anything with Thomas, although he was much larger than Thomas. Thomas was not looking for trouble and stayed out of Falconetti's way, but even though he was taciturn and pacific and kept to himself, there was something about Thomas's manner that made Falconetti pick on easier targets.

But the first night out of Genoa, Falconetti, who was dealing a poker hand in the mess room, said, when Thomas and Dwyer came in together, "Ah, here come the lovebirds," and made a wet, kissing noise. The men at the table laughed, because it was dangerous not to laugh at Falconetti's jokes. Dwyer turned red, but Thomas calmly poured himself a cup of coffee and picked up a copy of the Rome *Daily American* that was lying there, and began to read it.

"I'll tell you what, Dwyer," Falconetti said, "I'll be your agent. It's a long way home and the boys could use a nice piece of ass to while away the lonely hours. Couldn't you, boys?"

There were little embarrassed murmurs of assent from the men around the table.

Thomas read his paper and sipped his coffee. He knew that Dwyer was trying to catch his eye, pleading, but until it got much worse he wasn't going to get into a brawl.

"What's the sense in giving it away free like you do, Dwyer," Falconetti said, "when you could make a fortune and distribute happiness at the same time just by setting yourself up in business with my help. What we have to do is fix a scale—say five bucks for buggering, ten bucks for sucking. I'll just take my ten per cent, like a regular Hollywood agent. What do you say, Dwyer?"

Dwyer jumped up and fled. The men at the table laughed. Thomas read his paper, although his hands were trembling. He had to control himself. If he beat up on a big thug like Falconetti, who had terrorized whole shiploads of men for years, somebody would begin to wonder who the hell he was and what made him so tough and it wouldn't take too long for somebody to recognize his name or remember that he had seen him fight somewhere. And there were mob members of hangers-on everywhere along the waterfront, just waiting to rush to some higher up with the news that he'd been spotted.

Read your goddamn newspaper, Thomas said to himself, and keep your mouth shut.

"Hey, lover." Falconetti made the wet kissing noise again. "You going to let your boy friend cry himself to sleep all by his little itsy-bitsy self?"

Methodically, Thomas folded the paper, put it down. He walked slowly across the room, carrying his coffee cup. Falconetti looked at him from across the table, grinning. Thomas threw the coffee into Falconetti's face. Falconetti didn't move. There was dead silence at the table.

"If you make that noise once more," Thomas said, "I'll slug you every time I pass you on this ship from here to Hoboken."

Falconetti stood up. "You're for me, lover," he said. He made the kissing noise again.

"I'll be waiting for you on deck," Thomas said. "And come alone."

"I don't need no help," Falconetti said.

Thomas wheeled and went out onto the stern deck. There would be room to move around there. He didn't want to have to tangle with a man Falconetti's size in close quarters.

The sea was calm, the night balmy, the stars bright. Thomas groaned. My goddamn fists, he thought, always my goddamn fists.

He wasn't worried about Falconetti. That big fat gut hanging over his belt wasn't made for punishment.

He saw the door open onto the deck, Falconetti's shadow thrown on the deck by the light in the gangway. Falconetti stepped on deck. He was alone.

Maybe I'm going to get away with it, Thomas thought. Nobody's going to see me take him.

"I'm over here, you fat slob," Thomas called. He wanted Falconetti to rush him, not take the chance of going in on him and perhaps being grappled by those huge arms and wrestled down. It was a cinch Falconetti wasn't going to fight under Boxing Commission rules. "Come on, Fatso," Thomas called. "I haven't got all night."

"You asked for it, Jordache," Falconetti said and rushed at him, flailing his fists, big round house swings. Thomas stepped to one side and put all his strength into the one right hand to the gut. Falconetti sounded as though he was strangling, teetered back. Thomas stepped in and hit him again in the gut. Falconetti went down and lay writhing on the deck, a gurgling noise bubbling up from his throat. He wasn't knocked out and his eyes were glaring up at Thomas as Thomas stood over him, but he couldn't say anything.

It had been neat and quick, Thomas thought with satisfaction, and there wasn't a mark on the man and if he didn't say anything none of the crew would ever know what happened out on the deck. It was a cinch Thomas wasn't going to do any talking. Falconetti had learned his lesson and it wouldn't do *his* reputation any good to pass the news around.

"All right, slob," Thomas said. "Now you know what it's all about. Now you'll keep that toilet of a mouth of yours shut."

Falconetti made a sudden move and Thomas felt the big hand gripping at his ankle, bringing him down. There was a gleam in Falconetti's other hand and Thomas saw the knife there. He gave suddenly and dropped onto Falconetti's face with his knees, hard, grabbing at the hand with the knife, twisting. Falconetti was still fighting for his breath and the fingers holding the knife handle weakened quickly. Thomas, now with his knees pinning Falconetti's arms to the deck, reached the knife, pushed it away. Then he methodically chopped at Falconetti's face for two minutes.

Finally, he stood up. Falconetti lay inert on the deck, the blood black on the starlit deck around his head. Thomas picked up the knife and threw it overboard.

With a last look at Falconetti, he went in. He was breathing hard, but it wasn't from the exertion of the fight. It was exultation. Goddamn it, he thought, I enjoyed it. I'm going to wind up a crazy old man fighting orderlies in the Old Folks' Home.

He went into the mess room. The poker game had stopped, but there were more men in there than before, as the players who had seen the clash between Thomas and Falconetti had gone to tell their bunkmates and bring them back to the mess room to get the dope on the action. The room had been alive with talk, but when Thomas came in, calmly, breathing normally now, no one said a word.

Thomas went over to the coffee pot and poured himself a cup. "I wasted half the last cup," he said to the men in the mess room.

He sat down and unfolded the paper and continued reading.

He walked down the gangplank with his pay in his pocket and the dead Norwegian's seabag over his shoulder. Dwyer followed him. Nobody had said good-bye. Ever since Falconetti had jumped overboard at night, in the middle of the storm, they had given him the silent treatment on the ship. The hell with them. Falconetti had it coming to him. He had stayed away from Thomas, but when his face had healed, he'd begun to take it out on Dwyer when Thomas wasn't around. Dwyer reported that

Falconetti made the kissing sound every time he saw him and then one night, just as he was coming off his watch, Thomas heard screams from Dwyer's cabin. The door was unlocked and when Thomas went in, Dwyer was on the floor and Falconetti was pulling his pants off. Thomas slugged Falconetti across the nose and kicked him in the ass as he went through the door "I warned you," he said. "You better stay out of sight. Because you're going to get more of the same every time I lay eyes on you on this ship."

"Jesus, Tommy," Dwyer said, his eyes wet, as he struggled back into his pants, "I'll never forget what you've done for me. Not in a million years, Tommy."

"Stop bawling," Thomas said. "He won't bother you any more."

Falconetti didn't bother anyone any more. He did his best to avoid Thomas, but at least once a day, they'd run across each other. And each time, Thomas would say, "Come over here, slob," and Falconetti would shamble over, his whole face twitching, and Thomas would punch him hard in the gut. Thomas made a point of doing it when there were other crewmen around, although never in front of an officer. He had nothing to hide any more; after one look at what Thomas had done to Falconetti's face that night on the deck, the men in the crew had caught on. In fact, a deckhand by the name of Spinelli had said to Thomas, "been puzzling ever since I set eyes on you where I seen you before."

"You never saw me before," Thomas said, but he knew it was no use.

"Yeah, yeah," Spinelli said. "I saw you knock out a nigger five, six years ago, one night in Queens."

"I never been in Queens in my whole life," Thomas said.

"Have it your own way." Spinelli spread his hands pacifically. "It ain't none of my business."

Thomas knew that Spinelli would spread the news around that he was a pro and that you could look up his record in *Ring Magazine*, but while they were still at sea, there was nothing anybody could do about it. When they landed, he'd have to be careful. But meanwhile he had the pleasure of grinding Falconetti down to nothing. The curious thing, though, was that the men on the crew whom Falconetti had terrorized, and whom the crew now treated with contempt, hated Thomas for what he was doing. Somehow, it made them all seem ignoble in their own eyes, for having submitted to a big bag of wind who had been deflated in ten minutes by a man who was smaller than many of them and who hadn't even raised his voice on two voyages.

Falconetti tried to stay out of the mess room when he knew Thomas would be there. The one time he got caught there, Thomas didn't hit him but said, "Stay there, slob. I got company for you. "

He went down the gangway to Renway's cabin. The Negro was sitting alone, on the edge of his bunk. "Renway," Thomas said, "come on with me."

Frightened, Renway had followed him back to the mess room. He had tried to pull back when he saw Falconetti sitting there, but Thomas pushed him into the room. "We're just going to sit down like gentlemen," Thomas said, "next to this gentleman here, and enjoy the music." The radio was playing.

Thomas sat down on one side of Falconetti and Renway on the other. Falconetti didn't move. He just sat with his eyes lowered, his big hands flat on the table in front of him.

When Thomas said, "Okay, that's enough for tonight. You can go now, slob," Falconetti had stood up, not looking at any of the men in the room who were watching him, and had gone out on deck and thrown himself overboard. The second mate, who was on deck at the time, had seen him, but was too far away to stop him. The ship had swung around and they had made a halfhearted search, but the seas were mountainous, the night black, and there wasn't a chance.

The captain had ordered an inquiry, but not one of the crew had volunteered information. Suicide, causes unknown, the captain had put down in his report to the owners.

*   *   *   *   *   *   *   *   *   *   *   *   *   *   *   *   *   *   *

Thomas and Dwyer found a taxi near the pier and Thomas said, "Broadway and Ninety-sixth Street," to the driver. He had said the first thing that came to his mind, but as they drove toward the tunnel, he realized that Broadway and Ninety-sixth Street was near where he had lived with Teresa and the kid. He didn't care if he never saw Teresa again in his whole life, but the ache in him to see his son had subconsciously made him direct the driver to the old neighborhood, just on the chance.

As they drove up Broadway, Thomas remembered that Dwyer was going to stay at the Y.M.C.A. on Sixty-second Street, and to wait there for word from Thomas. Thomas had not told Dwyer about the Hotel Aegean.

The driver stopped the cab at Sixty-second Street and Thomas said to Dwyer, "Okay, you get out here."

"I'll be hearing from you soon, won't I, Tommy?" Dwyer said anxiously, as he descended from the cab.

"That depends." Thomas closed the cab door. He didn't want to be bothered with Dwyer and his slobbering gratitude.

When they reached Ninety-sixth Street, Thomas asked the driver to wait. He got out of the cab to discover there were other children at Broadway and Ninety-sixth Street but no Wesley. Back in the cab, he ordered the driver to go to Ninety-sixth Street and Park.

At Ninety-sixth and Park, he got out of the cab, made sure the man drove off, then hailed another cab and told the driver, "Eighteenth Street and Fourth Avenue." When they got there, he walked west one block, turned the corner and came back and walked to the Aegean Hotel.

Pappy was behind the desk, but didn't say anything, just gave him a key. There were three seamen arguing in the lobby next to the one potted palm that was the sole adornment in what was really just a narrow hall, with a bulge in it for the desk. The seamen were talking in a language Thomas couldn't understand. Thomas didn't wait for them to get a good look at him. He walked quickly past them and up the two floors to the room whose number was on the key. He went in, threw the bag down, and lay down on the lumpy bed, with a mustard-colored spread, and stared up at the cracks of the ceiling. The shade had been down when he came into the room and he didn't bother to pull it up.

Ten minutes later, there was a knock on the door. Pappy's knock. Thomas got off the bed and let him in.

"You hear anything?" Thomas demanded.

Pappy shrugged. You couldn't tell what his expression was behind the dark glasses he wore night and day. "Somebody knows you're here," he said. "Or at least that when you're in New York you're here."

They were closing in. His throat felt dry. "What're you talking about Pappy?" he said.

"A guy was in the hotel seven, eight days ago," Pappy said, "wanting to know if you were registered."

"What'd you say?"

"I said I never heard of you."

"What'd he say?"

"He said he knew you came here. He said he was your brother."

"What did he look like?"

"Taller than you, slim, maybe one-fifty-five, one-sixty, black hair cut short, greenish eyes, darkish complexion, sunburned, good suit, college-boy talk, manicured nails . . ."

"That's my fucking brother," Thomas said. "My mother must've given him the address. I made her swear not to tell anybody. Not anybody. I'm lucky it's not all over town. What'd my brother want?"

"He wanted to talk to you. I said if anybody by your name happened in here, I'd pass on the message. He left a telephone number. In a place called Whitby."

"That's him. I'll call him when I'm good and ready. I got other matters on my mind. I never heard any good news from him yet. There're some things I want you to do for me, Pappy."

Pappy nodded. At his prices he was happy to be of service.

"First—get me a bottle," Thomas said. "Second—get me a gun. Third—get hold of Schultzy for me and find out if the heat is still on. And if he thinks I can take a chance seeing my kid. Fourth—get me a girl. In that order."

"One hundred dollars," Pappy said.

Thomas took out his wallet and gave Pappy two fifties, from his pay. Then he gave him the wallet. "Put it in the safe." He didn't want to have a pocket full of cash with him drunk and some strange broad in the room, going through his clothes.

Pappy took the wallet and went out of the room. He didn't talk more than was necessary. He did all right, not talking. He had two diamond rings on his fingers and he wore alligator shoes. Thomas locked the door behind him and didn't get up until Pappy came back with the bottle and three cans of beer, a plate of ham sandwiches, and a Smith and Wesson British army revolver, with the serial number filed off. "I happened to have it in the house," Pappy said as he gave Thomas the gun. He had a lot of things in the house. "Don't use it on the premises, that's all."

"I won't use it on the premises." Thomas opened the bottle of bourbon and offered it to Pappy. Pappy shook his head. "I don't drink. I got a delicate stomach."

"Me, too," Thomas said and took a long gulp from the bottle.

"I bet," Pappy said, as he went out.

What did Pappy know? What did anyone know?

The bourbon didn't help, although he kept swigging at the bottle. He kept remembering the silent men standing along the rail watching him and Dwyer go down the gangplank, hating him. Maybe he didn't blame them. Putting a loud-mouth ex-con in his place was one thing. Putting the boots to him so hard that he killed himself was another. Somewhere, Thomas realized, a man who considered himself a human being should know where to stop, leave another man a place to live in. Sure, Falconetti was a pig and deserved a lesson, but the lesson should have ended somewhere else than in the middle of the Atlantic.

He drank some more whiskey to try to help him forget the look on Falconetti's face when Thomas said, "You can go now, slob," and Falconetti had got up from the table and walked out of the mess room with everybody watching him.

The whiskey didn't help.

He had been bitter when Rudolph had called him a wild animal when they were kids, but would he have the right now to be bitter if somebody said it to him today? He really believed that if people would leave him alone he would leave them alone. He yearned for peace. He had felt that the sea had finally relieved him of his burden of violence; the future he and Dwyer hoped for for themselves was harmless and unobjectionable, on a mild sea, among mild men. And here he was, with a death on his conscience, hiding away with a gun in a crumbling hotel room, exiled in his own country. Christ, he wished he could cry.

Half the bottle was empty when Pappy knocked on the door again.

"I talked to Schultzy," Pappy said. "The heat's still on. You better ship out again as soon as you can."

"Sure," Thomas nodded, maudlin, bottle in hand. The heat was still on. The heat had been on all his life. There had to be people like that. If only for the sake of variety. "Did Schultzy say there was any chance of sneaking a look at my kid?"

"He advised against it," Pappy said. "This trip."

"He advised against it. Good old Schultzy. It's not his kid. You hear anything else about me?"

"There's a Greek from the *Elga Andersen* just checked in," Pappy said. "He's talking in the lobby. About how you killed a certain individual called Falconetti."

"When they have it in for you," Thomas said, "they don't lose any time, do they?"

"He knows you fought as a pro. You better stick close to this room until I get you a berth."

"I'm not going anywhere," Thomas said. "Where's that dame I asked for?"

"She'll be here in an hour," Pappy said. "I told her your name was Bernard and she won't ask any questions."

"Why Bernard?" Thomas asked irritably.

"I had a friend once by that name." Pappy left lightly, on his wary alligator feet.

Bernard, Thomas thought, what a name!

He hadn't been out of the room all week. Pappy had brought him six bottles of whiskey. No more girls. He had lost his taste for whores. He had started to grow a moustache. The trouble was it came out red. With his blond hair it looked more like a disguise than a false moustache. He practiced loading and unloading the revolver. He tried not to think about the look on Falconettie's face. He paced up and down all day like a prisoner. Dwyer had lent him one of his books on navigation and he managed a couple of hours a day on that. He felt he could plot a course from Boston to Johannesburg. But he didn't dare go downstairs and buy himself a newspaper. He made his bed and cleaned his room himself, to keep out the chambermaid. He was paying Pappy ten bucks a day, everything included, except the booze, of course, and his money was running low. He yelled at Pappy because Pappy didn't come up with a berth, but Pappy only shrugged and said it was a slack time and to have patience. Pappy came and went, a free man. It was easy for him to have patience.

It was three o'clock in the afternoon when he heard Pappy's knock. It was a strange hour for him to come up. Usually, he only came in three times a day, with the meals.

Thomas unlocked the door. Pappy came in, light on his feet, expressionless behind his dark glasses.

"You got something for me?" Thomas asked.

"Your brother was at the desk a few minutes ago," Pappy said.

"What'd you tell him?"

"I said maybe I knew a place where I could get hold of you. He's coming back in a half hour. You want to see him?"

Thomas thought for a moment. "Why not?" he said. "If it'll make the sonofabitch happy."

Pappy nodded. "I'll bring him up when he comes," he said.

Thomas locked the door behind him. He felt the stubble of his moustache, decided to shave. He looked at his face in the peeling mirror in the grimy little bathroom. The moustache was ridiculous. His eyes were bloodshot. He lathered up, shaved. He needed a haircut. He was balding on the top of his head, but his hair hung halfway down over his ears and over the collar of his shirt in back. Pappy was useful in many ways but he didn't give haircuts.

The half hour took a long time passing.

The knock on the door was not Pappy's. "Who's there?" Thomas whispered. He was uncertain about the tone of his voice after not talking to anyone but Pappy for a week. And you didn't hold long conversations with Pappy.

"It's me Rudy."

Thomas unlocked the door. Rudolph came into the room and Thomas locked the door before they shook hands. Thomas didn't ask him to sit down. Rudolph didn't need a haircut, he wasn't going bald and he was wearing a pressed seersucker country-gentleman kind of suit because the weather had turned warm. He must have a laundry bill a yard long, Thomas thought.

Rudolph smiled tentatively. "That man downstairs is pretty mysterious about you," he said.

"He knows what he's doing."

"I was here about two weeks ago."

"I know," Thomas said.

"You didn't call."

"No."

Rudolph looked curiously around the room. The expression on his face was peculiar, as though he didn't quite believe what he saw. "I suppose you're hiding from somebody," he said.

"No comment," Thomas said. "Like they say in the newspapers."

"Can I help you?"

"No." What could he say to his brother? Go look for a man called Falconetti, longitude 26.24, latitude 38.31, depth ten thousand feet? Go tell some gangster in Las Vegas with a sawed-off shotgun in the trunk of his car he was sorry he'd beaten up Gary Quayles, he wouldn't do it again?

"I'm glad to see you, Tom," Rudolph said, "although this isn't exactly a social visit."

"I gathered that."

"Mom is dying," Rudolph said. "She wants to see you."

"Where is she?"

"In the hospital at Whitby. I'm on my way there now and if you . . . "

"What do you mean dying? Dying today or dying next week or dying in a couple of years?"

"Dying any minute," Rudolph said. "She's had two heart attacks."

"Oh, Christ." It had never occurred to Thomas that his mother could die. He even had a scarf that he'd bought for her in Cannes, in his sea bag. The scarf had an old map of the Mediterranean on it, in three colors. People you were bringing presents to didn't die.

"I know you've seen her from time to time," Rudolph said, "and that you've written her letters. She turned religious, you know, and she wants to make her peace with everybody before she goes. She asked for Gretchen, too."

"She doesn't have to make her peace with me," Thomas said. "I got nothing against the old lady. It wasn't her fault. I gave her a rough time. And what with our goddamn father . . . "

"Well," Rudolph said, "do you want to come with me? I have the car downstairs in front of the door."

Thomas nodded.

"You'd better pack some things in a bag," Rudolph said. "Nobody knows exactly how long . . . "

"Give me ten minutes," Thomas said. "And don't wait in front of the door. Drive around for awhile. Then in ten minutes come up Fourth Avenue going north. I'll be walking that way, near the curb. If you don't see me, go back two blocks below here and drive up Fourth Avenue again. Make sure the door on the right side isn't locked. Go slow. What kind of car you got?

"A Chevrolet, 1960. Green."

Thomas unlocked the door. "Don't talk to anybody on the way out."

When he'd locked the door again, he threw some things into his shaving kit. He didn't have a valise, so he stuffed two shirts and some underwear and socks and the scarf, wrapped in tissue paper, into the bag in which Pappy had brought the last bottle of bourbon. He took a gulp of bourbon to steady his nerves. He decided that he might need the whiskey on the trip, so he put the half-empty bottle in another bag.

He put on a tie and the blue suit which he had bought in Marseilles. If your mother was dying you had to be dressed for the occasion. He took the Smith and Wesson out of the dresser drawer, checked the safety, stuck it in his belt, under his jacket, and unlocked the door. He peeked out. There was nobody in the hallway. He went out, locked the door and dropped the key into his pocket.

Pappy was behind the desk but didn't say anything when he saw Thomas going through the lobby carrying the shaving kit under his left arm and the paper bags in hs left hand. Thomas blinked as the sun hit him outside the hotel. He walked quickly, but not as though he was trying to get away from anything, toward Fourth Avenue.

He had only walked a block and a half up the Avenue when the Chevy drew up alongside. He took one last look around and jumped inside.

Once they got out of the city he began to enjoy the trip. The breeze was cool, the countryside light green. Your mother was dying and you were sorry about that, but your body didn't know anything about mothers dying, it just knew it liked to be cool and moving and out of prison and breathing country air. He took the bottle out of the bag and offered it to Rudolph, but Rudolph shook his head. They hadn't talked much. Rudolph had told him that Gretchen had remarried and that her husband had been killed not long ago. He also told Thomas that he had just gotten married. The Jordaches never learn, Thomas thought.

Rudolph drove fast and he concentrated on the road. Thomas took a swig from the bottle from time to time, not enough to start getting drunk, just enough to keep him feeling good.

They were going seventy when they heard the siren behind them. "Damn it," Rudolph said, as he pulled over to the side.

The State trooper came up to them and said, "Good afternoon, sir." Rudolph was the sort of man cops said, "Good afternoon, sir," to. "Your license, please," the trooper said, but he didn't examine the license until he'd taken a good look at the bottle on the front seat between Rudolph and Thomas. "You were going seventy in a fifty-mile zone," he said staring coldly at Thomas, with his wind-beaten face, busted nose, and his Marseilles blue suit.

"I'm afraid I was, officer," Rudolph said.

"You fellas've been drinking," the trooper said. It was not a question.

"I haven't touched a drop," Rudolph said, "and I'm driving."

"Who's he?" The trooper pointed with the hand holding Rudolph's license at Thomas.

"He's my brohter," Rudolph said.

"You got any identification?" The trooper's voice was hard and suspicious as he spoke to Thomas.

Thomas dug into his pocket and produced his passport. The trooper opened it as though it were loaded. "What're you doing carrying your passport around?"

"I'm a seaman."

The trooper gave Rudolph his license, but put Thomas's passport in his pocket. "I'll hold onto this. And I'll take that." He gestured toward the bottle and Rudolph gave it to him. "Now turn around and follow me."

"Officer," Rudolph said, "why don't you just give me the ticket for speeding and let us go on our way. It's absolutely imperative for us to . . . "

"I said turn around and follow me," the trooper said. He strode back to his car, where another trooper was sitting at the wheel.

They had to drive back more than ten miles the way they had come, to the State Troopers' barracks. Thomas managed to get the pistol out from under his belt and slide it under the seat without Rudolph's noticing it. If the cops searched the car, it would be six months to a year, at least. Concealed weapon. No permit. The trooper who arrested them explained to a sergeant that they had been speeding and that they had committed a further violation by having an opened bottle of liquor in a moving vehicle and that he wanted a sobriety test run on them. The Sergeant was impressed by Rudolph and was apologetic, but he smelled both their breaths and made them take a breathing test and he made Thomas piss in a bottle.

It was dark by the time they got out of the building without the whiskey, but with a ticket for speeding. The Sergeant had decided neither of them was drunk, but Thomas saw that the trooper who had arrested them took, a long hard look at his passport before he gave it back to him. Thomas was unhappy about it, because there were plenty of cops who traded with the gangs, but there was nothing he could do about it.

"You should've known better than to offer me a ride," Thomas said when they were back on the road. "I get arrested for breathing."

"Forget it," Rudolph said shortly and stepped on the gas.

Thomas felt under the seat. The gun was still there. The car hadn't been searched. Maybe his luck was changing.

They got to the hospital a little after nine but the nurse at the entrance stopped Rudolph and whispered to him for awhile. Rudolph said, "Thank you," in a funny voice, then came over to Thomas and said, "Mom died an hour ago."

II

"The last thing she said," Gretchen was saying, "was, 'You tell your father, wherever he is, that I forgave him.' Then she went into a coma and never came out of it."

"She was nutty on the subject," Thomas said. "She asked me to be on the lookout for him in Europe."

It was late that night and the three of them were sitting in the living room of the house that Rudolph shared with his mother for the last few years. Billy was asleep upstairs and Martha was weeping in the kitchen for the woman who had been her daily opponent and tormentor. Billy had begged to be allowed to come East to see his grandmother for one last time and Gretchen had decided that death was a part of a child's education, too, and brought him along. Her mother had forgiven Gretchen, too, before they had put her in the oxygen tent for the last time.

Rudolph had already made the arrangements for the funeral. He had spoken to Father McDonnell and consented to the whole rigamarole, as he had told Jean when he had called her in New York. Eulogy, Mass, the whole thing. But he stopped at having the windows of the house closed and the blinds drawn. He was only going to coddle his mother up to a certain point. Jean had said morosely she'd come up if he wanted but he had said there was no sense in that.

The cable in Rome had had an unsettling effect on her. "Families," she said. "Always goddamn families." She had drunk a great deal that night and all the way back on the plane. If he hadn't held her he was sure she would have fallen going down the steps from the plane. When he left her in New York she was in bed, looking frail and worn out. Now, facing his brother and sister in the hushed house he had shared with the dead woman, Rudolph was thankful his wife was not with him.

"After all this time," Thomas said, "when your mother dies you're pissing in a bottle for a cop." Thomas was the only one drinking, but he was sober.

Gretchen had kissed him at the hospital, and held him close and in her grief she wasn't the snooty, superior woman, looking down her nose at him, that he had remembered, but warm, loving, familiar. Thomas felt there was a chance they would forget the past and be reconciled finally. He had enough enemies in the world as it was, without keeping up a running battle with his family.

"I dread the funeral," Rudolph said. "All those old ladies she used to play bridge with. And what the hell will that idiot McDonnell have to say?"

"She was broken in spirit by poverty and lack of love and she was devoted to God," Gretchen said.

"If I can keep him to that," Rudolph said.

"Excuse me," Thomas said. He went out of the room and to the guest bedroom he was sharing with Billy. Gretchen was in the second extra room. Nobody had gone into their mother's room yet.

"He seems different, doesn't he?" Gretchen said, when she and Rudolph were alone.

"Yeah."

"Subdued. Beaten, somehow."

"Whatever it is," Rudolph said, "it's an improvement."

They heard Thomas's footsteps coming down the stairs and they broke off the conversation. Thomas came into the room, carrying something soft wrapped in tissue paper. "Here," he said, handing it to Gretchen, "Here's something for you."

Gretchen unwrapped the gift, spread out the scarf with the old map of the Mediterranean on it in three colors. "Thank you," she said. "It's lovely." She got up and kissed him. For some reason the kiss unnerved him. He felt he might do something crazy, like breaking down and crying or smashing furniture or going up and getting the Smith and Wesson and shooting out the window at the moon. "I bought it in Cannes," Thomas said, "for Mom."

"Cannes?" Rudolph said. "When were you in Cannes?"

Thomas told him and they figured out that they must have been there at the same time, at least one day. "That's terrible," Rudolph said. "Brothers just passing each other by like that. From now on, Tom, we've got to keep in touch with each other."

"Yeah," Thomas said. He knew he wanted to keep seeing Gretchen, but Rudolph was another matter. He had suffered too much at Rudolph's hands. "Yeah," Thomas said. "I'll have my secretary send you a copy of my itinerary in the future." He stood up. "I'm going to bed. I've had a long day."

He went up the stairs. He wasn't all that tired. He just didn't want to be in the same room with Rudolph. If he'd known where the funeral home was, he'd have slipped out of the house and gone there and sat up all night with the body of his mother.

He didn't want to wake Gretchen's kid, asleep in blue pajamas in the other bed, so he didn't turn on the light as he undressed, but just left the door open a little so that enough light came in from the hallway to see what he was doing. He didn't have any pajamas and he wondered if the kid would comment on his sleeping in his shorts when he woke in the morning. Probably not. The kid seemed like a nice boy and he wouldn't know automatically that he was supposed to have a low opinion of his uncle. The kid smelled clean, soapy. He had tried to comfort Gretchen at the hospital, hugging her, both of them crying. He didn't remember ever having hugged his mother.

Looking at the kid made him think about Wesley. He had to see him. He had to do something about him. He couldn't let him be brought up all his life by a tramp like Teresa.

He closed the door and got into the soft, clean bed. Rudolph slept in a bed like this every night of his life.

III

Teddy Boylan was at the funeral. So were a great many other people. The newspapers in Whitby and Port Philip had considered the news of the death of the mother of that leading citizen Rudolph Jordache important enough to display the obituary prominently. There wasn't much to say about Mary Jordache, but the newspapers made up for it with descriptions of Rudolph's honors and accomplishments, Chairman of the Board of Dee Cee Enterprises, President Junior Chamber of Commerce of Whitby, graduate *cum laude*, Whitby University, Member of the Board of Trustees, Whitby University, Member Town Planning Committee of both Whitby *and* Port Philip, bold and forward-looking merchant and real-estate developer. There was even a mention of the fact that Rudolph had run the two twenty for the Port Philip track team and that he had played the trumpet in a jazz combination called the River Five in the middle 1940's.

Poor Mom, Rudolph thought, as he surveyed the crowded church, she would have enjoyed seeing so many people come out for a ceremony in her honor.

Father McDonnell was worse and longer than Rudolph feared and he tried not to listen to the lies spoken above the flower-banked coffin. He hoped Gretchen wasn't taking it too hard, remembering the other coffin in the crematorium in California. He glanced at her. There was no sign on her face that she was remembering anything.

The birds were singing in the cemetery trees, pleased with the onset of summer. At the grave, as the coffin was being lowered, to the sobs of the bridge ladies, Rudolph and Thomas and Gretchen stood side by side, Gretchen holding Billy by the hand.

Boylan caught up with them as they walked away from the grave toward the line of waiting black limousines. "I don't want to intrude," he said, as they halted, "Gretchen, Rudolph—I just wanted to say how sorry I was. Such a young woman."

For a moment, Rudolph was confused. His mother had looked ancient to him, *was* ancient. She had been old at thirty, had started dying before that. For the first time her real age made a conscious impression on him. Fifty-six. Just about Boylan's age. No wonder Boylan said, "Such a young woman."

"Thank you, Teddy," Rudolph said. He shook hands with Boylan. Boylan didn't look ready for the grave. His hair was the same color as always, his face was tanned and unlined, his carriage was as erect, his shoes were as well shined as ever.

"How've you been, Gretchen?" Boylan asked. The mourners had stopped behind the group, not wishing to push past them on the narrow graveled walk between the gravestones. As usual, Boylan accepted without thinking about it the fact that others waited on his pleasure.

"Very well, thank you, Teddy," Gretchen answered.

"I take it this is your son." Boylan smiled at Billy, who stared at him soberly.

"Billy, this is Mr. Boylan," Gretchen said. "He's an old friend."

"How do you do, Billy." Boylan shook the boy's hand. "I hope we meet again on a happier occasion."

Billy said nothing. Thomas was regarding Boylan through narrowed eyes, hiding, Rudolph thought, what could only have been a desire to laugh under the lowered lids. Was Thomas remembering the night he had seen Boylan parading naked around the house on the hill, preparing a drink to take to Gretchen, in bed upstairs? Graveyard thoughts.

"My brother, Thomas," Rudolph said.

"Oh, yes," Boylan said. He didn't offer to shake hands. He spoke to Rudolph. "If you have the time, Rudy," he said, "with all your multifarious activities, perhaps you could give me a ring and we could get together for dinner sometime. I want to confess that I was wrong and you were right about your choice of career. And bring Gretchen along, if she's available. Please."

"I'm leaving for California," Gretchen said.

"What a pity. Well, I won't keep you any longer." He made a little bow and stepped back, a slender, expensively maintained figure, brilliantly out of place, even in his dark suit, in the drab march of small-town mourners.

As the walked toward the first limousine, from which Rudolph had steadfastly barred Father McDonnell, Gretchen realized, with a little shock, how much alike Rudolph and Boylan were, not in looks, of course, but she hoped not in character, but in attitudes, turns of speech, gestures, choice of clothes, manner of moving. She wondered if Rudolph knew how much he owed to the man and whether he would be pleased if she pointed it out to him.

She thought about Boylan on the trip back to Rudolph's house. She supposed she ought to think about her mother, whose grave was being filled with earth at that moment in the sunny cemetery, full of the summery sound of birds. But she thought about Boylan. There was no sense of loving or desire, but no feeling, either of distaste or hatred or wish for revenge. It was like taking an old girlhood toy, a special doll, out of a forgotten trunk and holding it curiously, trying to remember how you felt when it meant something to you and not succeeding and deciding to throw it away or give it to some later child down the block. First love. Be my Valentine.

When they got to the house they all decided they needed a drink. Billy, who looked pale and drawn, complained that he had a headache and went upstairs and lay down. Martha, despite her unceasing flow of tears, went into the kitchen to prepare a cold lunch.

Rudolph made martinis for Gretchen and himself and gave some bourbon over ice to Thomas, who had taken off his coat, which was uncomfortably tight across his massive shoulders. He had unbuttoned his collar, too, and was sitting hunched forward on a straight-backed wooden chair, his elbows resting on his thighs, his hands hanging between his legs. He makes every place he sits look like a stool in the corner of a ring, Rudolph thought, as he gave him the drink.

They raised their glasses, although they did not mention their mother.

They had decided to leave for New York all together after lunch, because they didn't want to be in the house for the calls of condolence. Great heaps of flowers had been delivered, but Rudolph had instructed Martha to send all but one bunch to the hospital where his mother had died. The flowers he had kept, daffodils, made a little yellow explosion on the coffee table in front of the couch. The windows were open and the sun streamed in, a smell of warm grass came in from the lawn. The low beamed eighteenth-century room was handsome, subdued and orderly, not quaint or cluttered, not aggressively modern, Rudolph's taste.

"What are you going to do with the house?" Gretchen asked. "Now?"

Rudolph shrugged. "Keep it, I suppose. I still have to be up here a good part of the time. Although, it's a lot too big for me now. Would you like to come and live here?"

Gretchen shook her head. The debates with the lawyers went on and on. "I'm committed to California."

"What about you?" Rudolph asked Thomas.

"Me?" Thomas said, surprised. "What the hell would I do here?"

"You'd find something." Rudolph was careful not to say, "I'll find you something." He sipped at the martini, grateful for it. "You must admit it's an improvement on where you stay in New York."

"I don't plan to stay there long. Anyway, this is no place for me. The people here look at me as though I'm an animal in the zoo."

"You're exaggerating," Rudolph said.

"Your friend Boylan wouldn't shake my hand at the cemetery. If you don't shake a man's hand in a cemetery, where the hell would you shake his hand?"

"He's a special case."

"He sure is." Thomas began to laugh. The laughter wasn't loud, but it was somehow alarming in the atmosphere.

"What're you laughing about?" Rudolph asked as Gretchen looked at Thomas puzzledly.

"The next time you see him," Thomas said, "tell him he was right not to shake my hand."

"What're you talking about, Tom?"

"Ask him if he remembers the night of VE Day. The night they burned a cross on his property and there was the fire."

"What're you saying?" Rudolph asked sharply. "That you did it?"

"Me and a friend." Thomas stood up and went over to the sideboard and refilled his glass.

"Why did you do it?" Gretchen asked.

"Boyish high spirits," Thomas said, as he put in some more ice. "We just won the war."

"But why did you pick on *him?*" Gretchen asked.

Thomas fiddled with his drink, pushing the ice down, his back to Gretchen, "He happened to be involved with a lady I knew at the time," he said. "I didn't approve of the involvement. Should I mention the lady's name?"

"There's no need," Gretchen said quietly.

"Who was the friend?" Rudolph asked.

"What difference does it make?"

"It was that Claude, Claude What's-his-name that you used to hang around with, wasn't it?"

Thomas smiled, but didn't answer. He drank standing up, leaning against the sideboard.

"He disappeared right after that," Rudolph said. "I remember now."

"He sure did," said Thomas. "And I disappeared right after him, if you remember *that.*"

"Somebody knew you boys had done it," Rudolph said.

"Somebody." Thomas nodded ironically.

"You're lucky you didn't go to jail," Gretchen said.

"That's what Pa was intimating," said Thomas. "When he kicked me out of town. Well, there's nothing like a funeral to get people to remembering the good old days, is there?"

"Tom," Gretchen said, "you're not like that *any more,* are you?"

Thomas crossed over to where Gretchen was sitting on the couch and bent over and kissed her forehead gently. "I hope I'm not," he said. Then he straightened up and said, "I'll go up and see how the kid's doing. I like him. He'll probably feel better if he's not alone."

He took his drink with him as he went upstairs.

Rudolph mixed two more martinis for himself and Gretchen. He was glad to have something to do with his hands. His brother was not a comfortable man to be with. Even after he went out of a room, he left an air of tension, of anguish.

"God," Gretchen said finally, "it doesn't seem possible that we all have the same genes, does it?"

"The runt of the litter," Rudolph said. "Who is it—you, me—him?"

"We were awful, Rudy, you and I," Gretchen said.

Rudolph shrugged. "Our mother was awful. Our father was awful. You knew why they were awful, or at least you thought you knew why—but that didn't change matters. I *try* not to be awful."

"You're saved by your luck," Gretchen said.

"I worked pretty hard," Rudolph said defensively.

"So did Colin. The difference is, you'll never run into a tree."

"I'm terribly sorry, Gretchen, that I'm not dead." He couldn't hide the hurt in his voice.

"Don't take it the wrong way, please. I'm *glad* that there's somebody in the family who'll never run into a tree. It's certainly not Tom. And I know it isn't me. I'm the worst, maybe. I carried the luck of the whole family. If I hadn't been on a certain road at lunchtime near Port Philip one Saturday afternoon, all our lives would've been completely different. Did you know that?"

"What're you talking about?"

"Teddy Boylan," she said matter-of-factly. "He picked me up. I am what I am today largely because of him. I've slept with the men I've slept with because of Teddy Boylan. I ran away to New York because of Teddy Boylan. I met Willie Abbott because of Teddy Boylan and despised him finally because he wasn't different enough from Teddy Boylan and I loved Colin because he was the opposite of Teddy Boylan. All those scolding articles I wrote that everybody thought were so smart, were digs at America because it produced men like Teddy Boylan and made life easy for men like Teddy Boylan."

"That's maniacal. . . . The luck of the family! Why don't you go consult the gypsies and wear an amulet and be done with it?"

"I don't need any gypsies," Gretchen went on. "If I hadn't met Teddy Boylan and laid him, do you think Tom would have burned a cross on his hill? Do you think he'd have been sent away like a criminal if there'd never been a Teddy Boylan? Do you think he'd be just what he is today if he'd stayed in Port Philip with his family around him?"

"Maybe not," Rudolph admitted. "But there would've been something else."

"Only there wasn't anything else. There was Teddy Boylan, screwing his sister. As for you—"

"I know all I have to know about me," Rudolph said.

"You do? You think you'd have gone to college without Teddy Boylan's money? You think you'd dress the way you do or be so interested in success and money and how to get there the fastest way possible without Teddy Boylan? Do you think somebody else would have sought you out and taken you to concerts and art galleries and pampered you through school, and given you all that lordly confidence in yourself, if it hadn't been Teddy Boylan?" She finished her second martini.

"Okay," Rudolph said, "I'll build a monument in his honor."

"Maybe you should. You certainly can afford it now, with your wife's money."

"That's below the belt," Rudolph said angrily. "You know I didn't have the faintest idea . . ."

"That's what I was talking about," Gretchen said. "Your Jordache awfulness is turned into something else by your luck."

"How about *your* Jordache awfulness?"

Gretchen's entire tone changed. The sharpness went out of her voice, her face became sad, soft, younger. "When I was with Colin I wasn't awful," she said.

"No."

"I don't think I'm ever going to find a Colin again."

Rudolph reached out and touched her hand, his anger blunted by his sister's continuing sorrow. "You wouldn't believe me," Rudolph said, "if I told you I think you will."

"No," she said.

"What're you going to do? Just sit and mourn forever?"

"No."

"What're you going to do?"

"I'm going back to school."

"School?" Rudolph said incredulously. "At your age?"

"Postgraduate school," Gretchen said. "At UCLA. That way I can live at home and take care of Billy, all at the same time. I've been to see them and they've agreed to take me."

"To study what?"

"You'll laugh."

"I'm not laughing at anything today," Rudolph said.

"I got the idea from the father of a boy in Billy's class," Gretchen said. "He's a psychiatrist."

"Oh, Christ," Rudolph said.

"That's more of your luck," Gretchen said. "To be able to say, Oh, Christ, when you hear the word psychiatrist."

"Sorry."

"He works part time at a clinic. With lay analysts. They're people who aren't M.D.'s, but who've studied analysis, who've been analyzed, and are licensed to treat cases that don't call for deep analysis. Group therapy, intelligent children who refuse to learn how to read or write or are wilfully destructive, kids from broken homes who have retreated into themselves, girls who have been made frigid by their religion or by some early sexual trauma, and who are breaking up with their husbands, Negro and Mexican children who start school far behind the others and never catch up and lose their sense of identity . . . "

"So," Rudolph said. He had been listening impatiently. "So, you're going to go out and solve the Negro problem and the Mexican problem and the religious problem all on your own, armed with a piece of paper from UCLA, and . . . "

"I will try to solve one problem," Gretchen said. "Or maybe two problems, or maybe a hundred problems. And I'll be solving my own problems at the same time. I'll be busy and I'll be doing something useful."

"Not something useless like your brother," Rudolph said, stung. "Is that what you're trying to say?"

"Not at all," Gretchen said. "You're being useful in your own way. Let me be useful in mine, that's all."

"How long is all this going to take?"

"Two years, minimum, for the degree," Gretchen said. "Then finishing the analysis . . . "

"You'll never finish," he said. "You'll find a man and . . . "

"Maybe," Gretchen said. "I doubt it, but maybe . . . "

Martha came in, red eyed, and said that lunch was ready on the dining-room table. Gretchen went upstairs to get Billy and Thomas and when they came down the entire family went into the dining room and had lunch, everybody being polite to everybody else, saying, "Please pass the mustard," and "Thanks," and "No, I think that's enough for me right now."

After lunch, they got into the car and drove out of Whitby for New York, leaving their dead behind them.

They reached the Hotel Algonquin at a little after seven. Gretchen and Billy were staying there, because there was no room for them in Rudolph's one-bedroom apartment, where Jean was waiting for him. Rudolph asked Gretchen if she and Billy wanted to have dinner with him and Jean, but Gretchen said this was no day to meet a new sister-in-law. Rudolph invited Thomas, too, but Thomas, who was sitting low in the front seat, said, "I have a date."

When Billy got out of the car, Thomas got out too, and put his arm around the boy's shoulders. "I have a son, too, Billy," Thomas said. "A lot younger than you. If he grows up anything like you, I'll be a proud father."

For the first time in three days, Billy smiled.

"Tom," Gretchen said, standing under the hotel's canopy, "am I ever going to see you again?"

"Sure," Thomas said. "I know where to reach you. I'll call you."

Gretchen and her son went into the hotel, a porter carrying the two bags.

"I'll get a cab from here, Rudy," Thomas said. "You must be anxious to get home to your wife."

"I'd like a drink," Rudolph said. "Let's go in the bar here and . . . "

"Thanks. I'm pressed for time," Thomas said. "I got to be on my way." He kept peering over Rudolph's shoulder at the traffic on Sixth Avenue.

"Tom," Rudolph insisted, "I have to talk to you."

"I thought we were all talked out," Thomas said. He tried to hail a cab, but the driver was off duty. "You got nothing more to say to me."

"No?" Rudolph said savagely. "Don't I? What if I told you you're worth about sixty thousand dollars as of the close of the market today? Would that make you change your mind?"

"You're a great little old joker, aren't you, Rudy?" Thomas said.

"Come on in to the bar. I'm not joking."

Thomas followed Rudolph into the bar.

The waiter brought them their whiskies and then Thomas said, "Let's hear."

"That goddam five thousand dollars you gave me," Rudolph said. "You remember that?"

"Blood money," Thomas said. "Sure I remember."

"You said to do anything I wanted with it," Rudolph said. "I think I recall your exact works, 'Piss on it, blow it on dames, give it to your favorite charity . . .'"

"That sounds like me." Thomas grinned.

"Well, what I wanted to do with it was invest it," Rudolph said.

"Always a head for business," Thomas said. "Even as a kid."

"I invested it in your name, Tom," Rudolph said deliberately. "In my own company. There haven't been much in the way of dividends so far, but what there've been I've plowed back. But the stock has been divided four times and it's gone up and up. I tell you, you have about sixty thousand dollars in shares that you own outright."

Thomas gulped down his drink. He closed his eyes and pushed at his eyeballs with his fingers.

"I tried to get hold of you time and time again in the past two years," Rudolph said. "But the phone company said your phone was disconnected and when I sent letters to your old address, they always came back with a stamp on them saying 'Unknown at this address.' And Ma never told me she was in touch with you until she went to the hospital. I read the sports pages, but you seemed to have dropped out of sight."

"I was campaigning in the West," Thomas said, opening his eyes. The room looked blurry now.

"Actually, I was just as glad I couldn't find you," Rudolph said, "because I knew the stock would keep going up and I didn't want you to be tempted to sell prematurely. In fact, I don't think you ought to sell now."

"You mean I can go somewhere tomorrow," Thomas asked, "and just say I got some stock I want to sell and somebody'll give me sixty thousand dollars, *cash?*"

"I told you I don't advise you to . . ."

"Rudy," Thomas said, "you're a great guy and all that and maybe I take back a lot of what I've been thinking about you all these years, but right now I ain't listening to any advice. All I want is for you to go give me the address of the place where that man is waiting to give me that sixty thousand dollars cash."

Rudolph gave up. He wrote out Johnny Heath's office address, and gave it to Thomas. "Go to this place tomorrow," he said, "I'll call Heath and he'll be expecting you. Please, Tom, be careful."

"Don't worry about me, Rudy. From now on I'll be so careful, you won't even recognize me." Thomas ordered another round of drinks. When he lifted his arm to call the waiter, his jacket slipped back and Rudolph saw the pistol stuck in the belt. But he didn't say anything. He had done what he could for his brother. He could do no more.

"Wait a minute for me here, will you?" Thomas said. "I have to make a phone call."

He went into the lobby and found a booth and looked up the number of TWA. He dialed the number and asked about flights the next day to Paris. The girl at TWA told him there was a flight at eight P.M. and asked him if he wished to make a reservation. He said, "No thank you," and hung up, then called the Y.M.C.A. and asked for Dwyer. It was a long time before Dwyer came to the phone and Thomas was just about ready to hang up the phone and forget him.

"Hello," Dwyer said, "who's this?"

"Tom. Now listen to . . ."

"Tom!" Dwyer said excitedly. "I've been hanging around and hanging around waiting to hear from you. Jesus, I was worried. I thought maybe you were dead . . ."

"Will you stop running off at the mouth?" Thomas said. "Listen to me. There's a TWA plane leaving Idlewild for Paris tomorrow night at eight o'clock. You be there at the Reservations Counter at six-thirty. All packed."

"You meant you got reservations? On a *plane?*"

"I don't have them yet," Thomas said, wishing Dwyer wasn't so excitable. "We'll get them there. I don't want my name on any lists all day."

"Oh, sure, sure, Tom, I understand."

"Just be there. On time."

"I'll be there. Don't worry."

Thomas hung up.

He went back to the bar and insisted on paying for the drinks.

Outside, on the sidewalk, just before he got into the cab, that drew up next to the curb, he shook hands with his brother.

"Listen, Tom," Rudolph said, "let's have dinner this week. I want you to meet my wife."

"Great idea," Thomas said. "I'll call you Friday."

He got into the cab and told the driver, "Fourth Avenue and Eighteenth Street."

He settled back in the cab luxuriously, holding on to the paper bag with his belongings. When you had sixty thousand dollars everybody invited you to dinner. Even your brother.

Part Four

CHAPTER 1

1963

IT WAS RAINING when she drove up to the house, the torrential, tropical rain of California that flattened flowers, bounced off the tiles of roofs, like ricocheting silvery bullets and sent bulldozed hillsides sliding down into neighbors' gardens and swimming pools. Colin had died two years ago but she still automatically looked into the open garage to see if his car was there.

She left her books in the 1959 Ford and hurried to the front door, her hair soaking, even though it was only a few yards. Once inside she took off her coat and shook her wet hair. It was only four-thirty in the afternoon, but the house was dark and she turned on the front hall light. Billy had gone off on a camping trip to the Sierras with friends for the weekend and she hoped that the weather was better up in the mountains than down on the coast.

She reached into the mailbox. There were some bills, some circulars, a letter from Venice, in Rudolph's handwriting.

She went into the living room, turning on lights as she went. She kicked off her wet shoes, made herself a Scotch and soda, and seated herself on the couch, her legs curled up under her, pleased with the warmly lit room. There were no whispers in the shadows anymore. She had won the battle with Colin's ex-wife and she was going to stay in the house. The judge had awarded her a temporary allowance from the estate, against a final settlement, and she didn't have to depend upon Rudolph anymore.

She opened Rudolph's letter. It was a long one. When he was in America, he preferred to phone, but now that he was wandering around Europe, he used the mails. He must have had a lot of time on his hands, because he wrote often. She had had letters from him from London, Dublin, Edinburgh, Paris, St.-Jean-de-Luz, Amsterdam, Copenhagen, Geneva, Florence, Rome, Ischia, Athens, and from little inns in towns that she had never heard of where he and Jean stopped en route for the night.

"Dear Gretchen"—she read—"It's raining in Venice and Jean is out in it taking pictures. She says it's the best time to get the quality of Venice, water on water. I'm snug in my hotel, undriven by art. Jean also likes to take pictures of people for the series she's doing under the worst possible circumstances. Hardship and age, she tells me, preferably the two together, tell more about the character of a people and a country than anything else. I do not attempt to argue with her. I prefer handsome young people in sunshine, myself, but I am only her Philistine husband.

"I am enjoying to the utmost the glorious fruits of sloth. Within me, after all the years of hustle and toil, I have discovered a happy, lazy man, content to look at two masterpieces a day, to lose myself in a foreign city, to sit for hours at a cafe table like any Frenchman or Italian, to pretend I know something about art and haggle in galleries for paintings by new men whom nobody ever heard about and whose works will probably make my living room in Whitby a chamber of horrors when I eventually get back there.

"Curiously enough, with all our traveling, and despite the fact that Pa came from Germany and probably had as much German in him as American, I have no desire to visit the country. Jean has been there, but isn't anxious to go back. She says it's too much like America, in all essential ways. I'll have to take her opinion on the subject.

"She is the dearest woman alive and I am terribly uxorous and find myself carting her cameras around so as not to miss a moment with her. Except when it rains, of course. She has the sharpest of eyes and I have seen and understood more about Europe in six months with her than I would in sixty years alone. She has absolutely no literary sense and never reads a newspaper and the theater bores her, so I fill in that section of our communal life. She also drives our little Volkswagen very well, so I get a chance to moon and sightsee and enjoy things like the Alps and the valley of the Rhone without worrying about falling off the road. We have a pact. She drives in the morning and drinks a bottle of wine at lunch and I drive in the afternoon, sober.

"We don't stay in the fancy places, as we did on our honeymoon, because as Jean says, now it's for real. We do not suffer. She talks freely to everybody and with my French and her Italian and everybody's English, we find ourselves striking up friendships with the widest variety of people—a wine-grower from Burgundy, a masseur on the beach at Biarritz, a rugby player from Lourdes, a nonobjective painter, priests galore, fishermen, a bit-part actor in the French movies, old English ladies on bus tours, excommandos in the British army, GI's based in Europe, a representative in the Paris Chamber of Deputies who says the only hope for the world is John Fitzgerald Kennedy. If you happen to bump into John Fitzgerald Kennedy, pass the word on to him.

"The people it is almost impossible not to love are the English. Except for other English. The English are dazed, although it doesn't do to tell them so. Somehow, all the wheels of power went wrong, and after winning the war with their last ounce of blood and courage, they gave the whole thing away to the Germans. I don't want the Germans, or anybody, to starve, but the English had a right to expect that they could live in a world at least approximately as comfortable as the old enemy once the guns fell silent. Chalk one up against us, I'm afraid.

"Whatever you do, you must make sure that Billy gets a good dose of Europe before he's twenty, while it's still Europe and before it becomes Park Avenue and the University of Southern California and Scarsdale and Harlem and the Pentagon. All those things, or at least some of them, may be good for us, but it would be sad to see it happen to places like Rome and Paris and Athens.

"I have been to the Louvre, to the Rijks-museum in Amsterdam, to the Prado, and I have seen the lions at Delos and the gold mask in the museum in Athens, and if I had seen nothing else and had been deaf and mute and unloved, these things alone would have been worth much more than the six months of my life I have been away."

The phone rang and Gretchen put the letter down and got up and answered. It was Sam Corey, the old cutter who had worked with Colon on the three pictures he had made. Sam called faithfully, at least three times a week, and occasionally she would go with him to the showing of a new film at the studio that he thought would interest her. He was fifty-five years old, solidly married, and was comfortable to be with. He was the only one of the people who had been around Colin that she had kept up with.

"Gretchen," Sam said, "we're running one of the *Nouvelle Vague* pictures that just came in from Paris tonight. I'll take you to dinner after."

"Sorry, Sam," Gretchen said. "Somebody, one of the people from my classes, is coming over to work with me."

"School days, school days," Sam croaked, "dear old golden rule days." He had left school in the ninth grade and was not impressed with higher education.

"We'll do it some other night, eh, Sam?"

"Sure thing," he said. "Your house wash down the hill yet?"

"Just about."

"California," Sam said.

"It's raining in Venice, too," Gretchen said.

"How do you get top-secret information like that?"

"I'm reading a letter from my brother Rudolph. He's in Venice. And it's raining."

Sam had met Rudolph when Rudolph and Jean had come out to stay with her for a week. After they had left Sam had said Rudolph was okay, but he was crazy about his wife.

"When you write him back," said Sam, "ask him if he wants to put five-million dollars in a little low-budget picture I would like to direct."

Sam, who had been around enormously wealthy people for so long in Hollywood, believed that the sole reason for the existence of a man who had more than a hundred thousand dollars in the bank was to be fleeced. Unless, of course, he had talent. And the only talents Sam recognized were those involved in making films.

"I'm sure he'll be delighted to," Gretchen said.

"Keep dry, Baby," Sam said, and hung up.

Sam was the calmest man she knew. In the storms of temperament that he had been through in the years in the studios, he had survived serenely, knowing what he knew, running a hundred thousand miles of film through his hands, catching mistakes, patching up other men's blunders, never flattering, doing the utmost with the material he was handed, walking off pictures when the people making them became insufferable, going through one style after another with imperturbable efficiency, something of an artist, something of a handyman, loyal to the few directors, who, despite failures, were always what Sam considered pro's, committed to their craft, painstaking, perfectionist. Sam had seen Colin's plays and when Colin had come to Hollywood had sought Colin out and said he wanted to work with him, modest, but secure enough in what he did to know that the new director would be grateful for his experience and that their collaboration would be fruitful.

After Colin died, Sam had a long talk with Gretchen and had warned her that if she just was going to hang around Hollywood, doing nothing, just being a widow, she would be miserable. He had seen her with Colin enough in the course of the three films Colin had made, with Sam as the cutter, to understand that Colin had depended upon her, and with reason. He had offered to take her in with him, teach her what he knew about the business. "For a lone woman in this town," he had said, "the cutting room is the best place. She isn't on her own, she isn't flinging her sex around, she isn't challenging anybody's ego, she has something methodical and practical to do, like baking a cake, every day."

Gretchen had said, "Thank you, no," at the time, because she didn't want to profit, even by that much, on Colin's reputation, and had opted for the graduate course. But every time she talked to Sam she wondered if she hadn't said no too quickly. The people around her in school were too young, moved too fast, were interested in things that seemed useless to her, learned and discarded huge gobs of information in hours while she still was painfully struggling with the same material for weeks and weeks.

She went back to the couch and picked up Rudolph's letter again. Venice, she remembered, Venice. With a beautiful young wife who, just by chance, happened to turn out to be rich. Rudolph's luck.

"There are murmurs of unrest from Whitby,"—she read.—"Old man Calderwood is taking very unkindly to my prolonged version of the Grand Tour and even Johnny, who has a Puritan conscience under the egg-smooth debauchee face, hints delicately to me that I have vacationed long enough. In fact, I don't even see it as a vacation, although I have never enjoyed anything more. It is the continuation of my education, the continuation that I was too poor to pay for when I got out of college and went to work full time in the store.

"I have many things to solve when I get back, which I am slowly turning over in my mind even as I look at a Titian in the Doges' Palace or drink an espresso at a table in the Piazza San Marco. At the risk of sounding grandiose, what I have to decide is what to do with my life. I am thirty-five years old and I have enough money, both capital and yearly income, so that I can live extremely well for the rest of my life. Even if my tastes were wildly extravagant, which they're not, and even if Jean were poor, which she isn't, this would still be true. Once you are rich in America, it takes genius or overpowering greed to fall back into poverty. The idea of spending the rest of my life buying and selling, using my days to increase my wealth, which is already more than sufficient, is distasteful to me. My acquisitive instinct has been deadened by acquisition. The satisfaction I might get by opening new shopping centers throughout the country, under the Calderwood sign, and gaining control of still more companies, is minimum. A commercial empire, the prospects of which enchant men like Johnny Heath and Bradford Knight, has small charms for me and running one seems to me to be the drabbest kind of drudgery. I like travel and would be desolate if I were told that I could not come here ever again, but I cannot be like the characters in Henry James, who, in the words of E. M. Forster, land in Europe and look at works of art and at each other and that is all. As you can tell, I've used my new-found leisure to do some reading.

"Of course, I could set myself up as a philanthropist and dole out sums to the deserving poor or deserving artists or deserving scientists and scholars, but although I give, I hope generously, to many causes, I can't see putting myself into the position of arbiter in such matters. It certainly is not a full-time vocation, at least not for me.

"It must seem funny to you, as it does to me, for anyone in the Jordache family to be worrying so because he has money, but the swings and turns of American life are so weird that here I am doing just that.

"Another complication. I love the house in Whitby and I love Whitby itself. I do not, really, want to live anywhere else. Jean, too, sometime ago, confessed that she liked it there, and said that if we ever had children she would prefer bringing them up there than in the city. Well, I shall see to it that she'll have children, or at least a child, to bring up. We can always keep a small apartment in New York for when we want a bit of worldly excitement or when she has work to do in the city. But there is nobody in Whitby who just does nothing. I would be immediately branded as a freak by my neighbors, which wouldn't make the town as attractive to me as it now is. I don't want to turn into a Teddy Boylan.

"Maybe when I get back to America, I'll buy a copy of the *Times* and look through the want-ads.

"Jean has just come in, soaked and happy and a little drunk. The rain drove her into a cafe and two Venetian gentlemen plied her with wine. She sends her love.

"This has been a long egotistical letter. I expect one of equal length, equally egotistical, from you. Send it to the American Express in Paris. I don't know just when we'll be in Paris, but we'll be there sometime in the next couple of weeks and they'll hold the letter for me. Love to you and Billy, Rudolph. P.S. Have you heard from Tom? I haven't had a word from him since the day of Mom's funeral."

Gretchen put down the flimsy sheets of air-mail stationery, covered densely with her brother's firm, clearly formed handwriting. She finished her drink and decided against another one. She got up and went to the window and looked out. The rain was pouring down. The city below her was erased by water.

She mused over Rudolph's letter. They were friendlier through the mails than when they saw each other. In writing, Rudolph showed a hesitant side, a lack of pride and confidence, that was endearing and that he somehow hid at other times. When they were together, at one moment or another, the urge to wound him swept over her. His letters showed a largeness of spirit, a willingness to forgive that was the sweeter because it was tacit and he never showed any signs that he knew that there was anything that needed forgiving. Billy had told her about his assault on Rudolph at the school and Rudolph had never even mentioned it to her and had been warm and thoughtful with the boy every time he saw him. And the letters were always signed "Love to you and Billy."

I must learn generosity, she thought, staring out at the rain.

She didn't know what to do about Tom. Tom didn't write her often, but he kept her abreast of what he was doing. But as he had done with his mother, he made her promise to say nothing of his whereabouts to Rudolph. Right now, right this day, Tom was in Italy, too. On the other side of the peninsula, it was true, and farther south, but in Italy. She had received a letter from him just a few days before, from a place called Porto Santo Stefano, on the Mediterranean, above Rome. Tom and a friend of his called Dwyer had finally found the boat they were looking for at a price they could manage and had been working on it in a shipyard there all autumn and winter, to get it ready for service by June first. "We do everything ourselves,"—Tom had written in his large, boyish handwriting, on ruled paper.—"We took the Diesels apart piece by piece and we put them together again, piece by piece and they're as good as new. We've rewired the entire boat, calked and scraped the hull, trued the propellers, repaired the generator, put in a new galley, painted the hull, painted the cabins, bought a lot of second hand furniture and painted that. Dwyer turns out to be quite an interior decorator and I'd love you to see what he's done with the saloon and the cabins. We've been putting in a fourteen-hour day seven days a week, but it's worth it. We live on board, even though the boat is up on blocks on dry land, and save our money. Neither Dwyer or me can cook worth a damn, but we don't starve. When we go out on charter we'll have to find somebody who can cook to crew with us. I figure we can make do with three in crew. If Billy would like to come over for the summer we have room for him on board and plenty of work. When I saw him he looked as though a summer's hard work out in the open might do him a lot of good.

"We plan to put the boat in the water in ten days. We haven't decided on a name yet. When we bought it it was called the *Penelope II,* but that's a little too fancy for an ex-pug like me. Talking about that—nobody hits anybody here. They argue a lot, or at least they talk loud, but everybody keeps his hands to himself. It's restful to go into a bar and be sure you won't have to fight your way out. They tell me it's different south of Naples, but I wouldn't know.

"The man who runs the shipyard here is a good guy and from what I gather, asking around, he is giving us a very good deal on everything. He even found us two charters already. One in June and one in July and he says more will be coming up. I had some run-ins with certain Italians in the U.S., but these Italians are altogether different. Nice people. I am learning a few words in Italian, but don't ask me to make a speech.

"When we get into the water, my friend Dwyer will be the skipper, even though it was my money that bought the boat. He's got third mate's papers and he knows how to handle a boat. But he's teaching me. The day I can get into a harbor on my own without busting into anything, I am going to be the skipper. After expenses, we're splitting on everything, because he's a pal and I couldn't have done it without him.

"Again, I got to remind you of your promise not to tell Rudy anything. If he hears I did something crazy like buying a leaky old boat on the Mediterranean with the money he made for me, he'll split a gut. His idea of money is something you hide in the bank. Well, everybody to his own pleasure. When I have the business on a good, solid, paying basis, I'll write and tell him and invite him to come on a cruise with us, with his wife. Free. Then he can see for himself just how dumb his brother is.

"You don't write much, but in your letters I get the impression things aren't so hot with you. I'm sorry. Maybe you ought to change whatever it is you're doing and do something else. If my friend Dwyer wasn't so close to being a fag as to make no difference, I'd ask you to marry him, so you could be the cook. Joke.

"If you have any rich friends who like the idea of a Mediterranean cruise this coming summer, mention my name. No joke.

"Maybe it seems gaga to you and Rudy, your brother's being a yacht captain but I figure it must be in the blood. After all Pa sailed the Hudson in his own boat. One time too many. Not such a joke.

"The boat is painted white, with blue trim. It looks like a million dollars. The shipyard owner says we could sell it like it is right now and make 10,000 dollars profit. But we're not selling.

"If you happen to go East you could do me a favor. See if you can find out where my wife is and what she's doing and how the kid is. I don't miss the flag and I don't miss the bright lights, but I sure miss him.

"I am writing such a long letter because it is raining like crazy here and we can't finish the second coat of the deck house (blue). Don't believe anybody who tells you it doesn't rain on the Mediterranean.

"Dwyer is cooking and he is calling me to come eat. You have no idea how awful it smells. Love and kisses, Tom."

Rain in Porto Santo Stefano, rain in Venice, rain in California. The Jordaches weren't having much luck with the weather. But two of them, at least, were having luck with everything else, if only for one season. "Five o'clock in the afternoon is a lousy time of day," Gretchen said aloud. To stave off self-pity, she drew the curtains and made herself another drink.

It was still raining at seven o'clock, when she got into the car and went down to Wilshire Boulevard to pick up Kosi Krumah. She drove slowly and carefully down the hill, with the water, six inches deep, racing ahead of her, gurgling at the tires. Beverly Hills, city of a thousand rivers.

Kosi was taking his master's in sociology and was in two of her courses and they sometimes studied together, before examinations. He had been at Oxford and was older than the other students and more intelligent, she thought. He was from Ghana and had a scholarship. The scholarship, she knew, was not a lavish one, so when they worked together, she tried to arrange to give him dinner first at the house. She was sure he wasn't getting quite enough to eat, although he never talked about it. She never dared to go into restaurants too far off campus with him, as you never knew how headwaiters would behave if a white woman came in with a black man, no matter how properly dressed he was and regardless of the fact that he spoke English with a pure Oxford accent. In class there never was any trouble and two or three of the professors seemed even unduly to defer to him when he spoke. With her, he was polite but invariably distant, almost like a teacher with a student. He had never seen any of Colin's movies. He didn't have the time to go to movies, he said. Gretchen suspected he didn't have the money. She never saw him with girls and he didn't seem to have made any friends except for herself. If she was his friend.

Her practice was to pick him up at the corner of Rodeo and Wilshire in Beverly Hills. He didn't have a car, but he could take the bus along Wilshire from Westwood, where he lived, near the university campus. As she came along Wilshire, peering through the spattered windshield, the rain so dense that the wipers couldn't work fast enough to clear the glass, she saw him standing on the corner, with no raincoat, with not even the collar of his jacket turned up for protection. His head was up and he was looking out at the stream of traffic through his blurred glasses as though he were watching a parade.

She stopped and opened the door for him and he got in leisurely, water dripping from his clothes and forming an immediate pool on the floor around his shoes.

"Kosi!" Gretchen said. "You're drowning. Why didn't you wait in a doorway, at least?"

"In my tribe, my dear," he said, "the men do not run from a little water."

She was furious with him. "In my tribe," she mimicked him, "in my tribe of white weaklings, the men have sense enough to come in out of the rain. You . . . you . . ." She racked her brain for an epithet. "You *Israeli!*"

There was a moment of stunned silence. Then he laughed, uproariously. She had to laugh with him. "And while you're at it," she said, "you might as well wipe your glasses, tribesman."

Obediently, he dried off his glasses.

When they got home, she made him take off his shirt and jacket and gave him one of Colin's sweaters to wear. He was a small man, just about Colin's size, and the sweater fit him. She hadn't known what to do with Colin's things, so they just lay in the drawers and hung in the closets, where he had left them. Every once in a while she told herself that she should give them to the Red Cross or some other organization, but she never got around to it.

They ate in the kitchen, fried chicken, peas, salad, cheese, ice cream, and coffee. She opened a bottle of wine. Kosi had once told her he had gotten used to drinking wine with his meals at Oxford.

He always protested that he wasn't hungry and that she needn't have bothered, but she noticed that he ate every morsel she put before him, even though she wasn't much of a cook and the food was just passable. The only difference in their eating habits was that he used his fork with the left hand. Another thing he had learned in Oxford. He had gone through Oxford on a scholarship, too. His father kept a small cotton-goods shop in Accra, and without the scholarship there never would have been enough money to educate the brilliant son. He hadn't been home in six years, but planned to go back and settle in Accra and work for the government as soon as he had written his thesis.

He asked where Billy was. Usually, they all ate together. When Gretchen said that Billy was away for the weekend, he said, "Too bad. I miss the little man."

Actually, Billy was taller than he, but Gretchen had become accustomed to Kosi's speech, with its "my dears" and its "little men."

The rain drummed on the flagstones of the patio outside the window. They dawdled over dinner and Gretchen opened another bottle of wine.

"To tell you the truth," she said, "I don't feel like working tonight."

"None of that, now," he said reprovingly. "I didn't make that fearful journey in a flood just to eat."

They finished the wine as they did the dishes, Gretchen washing and Kosi wiping. The dishwasher had been broken for six months, but there wasn't much need for it, as there were never more than three people for any one meal and fiddling with the machine was more trouble than it was worth for so few dishes.

She carried the pot of coffee into the living room with her and they each had two cups as they went over the week's work. He had a quick, agile mind, by now severely trained, and he was impatient with her slowness.

"My dear," he said, "you're just not concentrating. Stop being a dilettante."

She slammed the book shut. It was the third or fourth time he had reprimanded her since they had sat down at the desk together. Like a—like a governess, she thought, a big black mammy governess. They were working on a course on statistics and statistics bored her to stupefaction. "Not everyone can be as goddamn clever as you," she said. "I was never the brightest student in Accra, I never won a scholarship to . . ."

"My dear Gretchen," he said quietly, but obviously hurt, "I never claimed to be the brightest student anywhere . . ."

"Never claimed, never claimed," she said, thinking, hopelessly, I'm being shrill. "You don't have to claim. You just sit there being superior. Or stand out in the rain like some idiotic tribal god, looking down on the poor, cowardly white folk slinking past in their decadent Cadillacs."

Kosi stood up, stepped back. He took off his glasses and put them in his pocket "I'm sorry," he said. "This relationship doesn't seem to be working out . . ."

"This relationship," she taunted him. "Where did you learn to talk like that?"

"Good night, Gretchen," he said. He stood there, his mouth tight, his body taut. "If you'll just give me the time to change back into my shirt and jacket . . . I won't be a minute."

He went into the bathroom. She heard him moving around in there. She drank what was left in her cup. The coffee was cold and the sugar at the bottom of the cup made it too sweet. She put her head in her hands, her elbows on the desk, above the scattered books, ashamed of herself. I did it because of Rudolph's letter this afternoon, she thought. I did it because of Colin's sweater. Because of nothing to do with that poor young man with his Oxford accent.

When he came back, wearing his shirt and jacket, still shapeless and damp, she was standing, waiting for him. Without his glasses his close-cropped head was beautiful, the forehead wide, the eyelids heavy, the nose sharply cut, the lips rounded, the ears small and flat against the head. All done in flawless, dark stone, and all somehow pitiful and defeated.

"I shall be leaving you now, my dear," he said.

"I'll take you in the car," she said, in a small voice.

"I'll walk, thank you."

"It's still pouring," she said.

"We Israelis," he said somberly, "do not pay attention to the rain."

She essayed a laugh, but there was no answering glint of humor.

He turned toward the door. She reached out and seized his sleeve. "Kosi," she said. "Please don't go like that."

He stopped and turned back toward her. "Please," she said. She put her arms loosely around him, kissed his cheek. His hands came up slowly and held her head between them. He kissed her gently. Then not so gently. She felt his hands sliding over her body. Why not? she thought, why not, and pressed him to her. He tried to pull away and move her toward the bedroom, but she dropped onto the couch. Not in the bed in which she and Colin had lain together.

He stood over her. "Undress," he said.

"Put out the lights."

He went over to the switch on the wall and the room was in darkness. She heard him undressing as she took off her clothes. She was shivering when he came to her. She wanted to say, "I have made a mistake, please go home," but she was ashamed to say it.

She was dry and unready but he plunged into her at once, hurting her. She moaned, but the moan was not one of pleasure. She felt as though she were being torn apart. He was rough and powerful and she lay absolutely still, absorbing the pain.

It was over quickly, without a word. He got up and she heard him feeling his way across the room toward the light switch. She jumped up and ran into the bathroom and locked the door. She washed her face repeatedly in cold water and stared at her reflection in the mirror above the basin. She wiped off what was left of her lipstick which had smeared around her mouth. She would have liked to take a hot shower, but she didn't want him to hear her doing it. She put on a robe and waited as long as she dared, hoping he would be gone when she went out. But he was still there, standing in the middle of the living room, dressed, impassive. She tried to smile. She had no idea of how it came out.

"Don't you ever do anything like that again to anybody, my dear," he said evenly. "And certainly not to me. I will not be tolerated. I will not be condescended to. I will not be part of anybody's program of racial integration."

She stood with her head lowered, unable to speak.

"When you get your degree," he went on in the same flat, malevolent tone, "you can play Lady Bountiful with the poor bastards in the charity clinics, the beautiful, rich white lady proving to all the niggers and all the little greasers how democratic and generous this wonderful country is and how loving and Christian educated beautiful white ladies who don't happen to have husbands can be. I won't be here to see it. I'll be back in Africa, praying that the grateful little niggers and the grateful little greasers are getting ready to slit your throat."

He went out silently. There was only the smallest sound as the front door closed.

After a while, she cleared the desk they had been working on. She put the cups and saucers and the coffee pot in the sink in the kitchen and piled the books on one side of the desk. I'm too old for school books, she thought. I can't cope. Then, walking painfully, she went around and locked up. Arnold Simms, in your maroon bathrobe, she thought as she switched off the lights, rest easy. I have paid for you.

In the morning, she didn't attend her two Saturday clases, but called Sam Corey at the studio and asked if she could come over and talk to him.

CHAPTER 2

1964

EVEN PREGNANT AS she was, Jean insisted upon coming down and having breakfast with him every day. "At the end of the day," she said, "I want to be as tired as you. I don't want to be one of those American women who lie around all day and then when their husbands come home, drag the poor beasts out every evening, because they're bursting with unused vigor. The energy gap has ruined more marriages by half than adultery."

She was nearly at term and even under the loosely flowing nightgown and robe she was wearing, the bulge was huge and clumsy. Rudolph had a pang of guilt when he watched her. She had had such a neat delicate way of walking and now she was forced to balance herself painfully, belly protruding, pace careful, as she went from room to room. Nature has provided women with a kind of necessary lunacy, he thought, for them to desire to bring children into the world.

They sat in the dining room, with the pale April sun streaming through the windows, while Martha brought them fresh coffee. Martha had changed miraculously since his mother's death. Although she ate no more than before, she had filled out and was now matronly and comfortable. The sharp lines of her face had disappeared and the everlasting downward twitch of her mouth had been replaced by something that might even have been a smile. Death has its uses, Rudolph thought, watching her gently place the coffee pot in front of Jean. In the old days she would have banged it down on the table, her daily accusation against Fate.

Pregnancy had rounded Jean's face and she no longer looked like a schoolgirl fiercely determined to get the best marks in the class. Placid and womanly, her face glowed softly in the sunlight.

"This morning," Rudolph said, "you look saintly."

"You'd look saintly, too," Jean said, "if you hadn't had any sex for two months."

"I hope the kid turns out to be worth all this," Rudolph said.

"He'd better."

"How is it this morning?"

"Okay. He's marching up and down wearing paratroop boots, but otherwise okay."

"What if it's a girl?" Rudolph asked.

"I'll teach her not to overlap," Jean said. They both laughed.

"What have you got to do this morning?" he asked.

"There's a nurse coming to be interviewed, and the furniture's coming for the nursery and Martha and I have to put it in place and I have to take my vitamins and I have to weigh myself," Jean said. "A big morning. How about you?"

"I have to go to the university," Rudolph said. "There's a board of trustees' meeting. Then I ought to look in at the office . . . "

"You're not going to let that old monster Calderwood nag at you again, are you?"

Ever since Rudolph had told Calderwood he intended to retire from the business in June, Calderwood had argued with him almost every time he saw him. "Who retires at the age of thirty-six, for the Lord's sake?" Calderwood kept repeating.

"I do," Rudolph had once replied, but Calderwood had refused to believe him. Suspicious, as always, Calderwood felt that Rudolph was really manuevering for more control and had hinted that if Rudolph would stay he would give it to him. Calderwood had even offered to move the main office down to New York, but Rudolph said he no longer wanted to live in New York. Jean now shared his attachment to the old farmhouse in Whitby and was pouring over plans with an architect to enlarge it.

"Don't worry about Calderwood," Rudolph said, standing. "I'll be home for lunch."

"That's what I like," Jean said. "A husband who comes home for lunch. I'll make love to you after lunch."

"You'll do nothing of the kind." He leaned over to kiss the dear, smiling face.

It was early and he drove slowly, enjoying the town. Small children in bright-colored parkas were riding tricycles on the sidewalks or played on the drying lawns, burgeoning with the first frail green of spring. A young woman in slacks pushed a baby carriage in the sunshine. An old dog dozed on the warm steps of a big gingerbread house, painted white. Hawkins, the mailman, waved at him and he waved back. Slattery, standing beside his prowl car and talking to somebody's gardener, saluted him with a smile; two professors from the biology department, walking toward the university deep in conversation, looked up long enough to indicate a mild hello. This part of town, with its trees and large wooden houses and quiet streets, had an innocent nineteenth-century neighborly air, before the wars, before booms and depressions. Rudolph wondered how he ever had been anxious to get away from the town, where he was known and greeted at every turn, for the anonymous uncertainties and stony hostility of New York.

He had to pass the athletic field on the way to the Administration Building and he saw Quentin McGovern in a gray suit, jogging along the track. He stopped the car and got out and Quentin came over to him, a tall, serious young man, his skin gleaming with the sweat of his exercise. They shook hands. "I don't have my first class till eleven," Quentin said. "And it was a nice day for running, after being indoors on the boards all winter."

They didn't run in the morning anymore. Since his marriage, Rudolph had taken up tennis, for Jean's sake. Anyway, it was too Spartan a deed to make himself get up every morning at seven o'clock in all weathers from the bed of his bride to pound around a track for three-quarters of an hour, trying to keep pace with a young ahtlete at the top pitch of his form. Besides, it made him feel old. There was time enough for that bit.

"How's it going, Quentin?" Rudolph asked.

"Not bad. I'm twenty-two eight for the two twenty and the Coach says he's going to run me in the four forty and the relay as well."

"What does your mother say now?"

Quentin smiled, remembering the cold winter mornings. "She says for me not to get too swell-headed. Mothers don't change."

"How about your work in school?"

"They must have made a mistake at the office," Quentin said. "They put me on the Dean's List."

"What does your mother say about *that?*"

"She says it's because I'm colored and they want to show how liberal they are." Quentin smiled faintly.

"If you have any further trouble with your mother," Rudolph said, "tell her to call me."

"I'll do that, Mr. Jordache."

"Well, I've got to be going. Give my regards to your father."

"My father's dead, Mr. Jordache," Quentin said quietly.

"I'm sorry." Rudolph got back into his car. Christ, he thought. Quentin's father must have worked at least twenty-five years at Calderwood's. You'd think somebody would have had the sense to pass the word around.

The morning was no longer as pure and pleasurable as it had been before his conversation with Quentin.

All the parking places were taken in front of the Administration Building and Rudolph had to leave his car almost five hundred yards away. Everything is turning into a parking lot, he thought irritably, as he locked the car. The radio had been stolen out of it some time before, in New York, and Rudolph now locked the car wherever he left it, even if he was only going to be five minutes. He had had a mild argument with Jean on the subject, because she refused to lock the car at any time and even left the front door of the house open when she was home alone. You could love your neighbor, he had told her, but it was foolish to ignore the larceny in his heart.

As he was testing the door, he heard his name called. "Hey, Jordache!" It was Leon Harrison, who was also on the board of trustees and was on his way to the meeting. Harrison was a tall portly man of about sixty, with senatorial white hair and a misleading heartiness of manner. He was the publisher of the local newspaper, which he had inherited from his father, along with a great deal of real estate in and around Whitby. The newspaper was not doing very well, Rudolph knew. He wasn't sorry about it. It was badly run by a small, underpaid, drunken, brokendown staff of men who had been thrown off other papers all across the country. Rudolph made a point in not believing anything he read in Harrison's paper, even reports on the weather.

"How are you, boy," Harrison said, putting his arm around Rudolph's shoulder as they walked toward the Administration Building. "All prepared to put a fire under us old fogies again this morning?" He laughed loudly, to show his lack of malice. Rudolph had had many dealings with Harrison, not all of them agreeable, about the Calderwood advertising in his paper. Harrison had started out calling him, boy, then Rudy, then Jordache, and by now was back to boy, Rudolph noted.

"Just the same routine suggestions," Rudolph said. "Like burning down the Science Building to get rid of Professor Fredericks." Fredericks was the head of the department and Rudolph was sure that it was safe to say that the science courses were the worst in any university the size of Whitby north of the Mason-Dixon Line. Fredericks and Harrison were cronies and Fredericks often wrote scientific articles for Harrison's paper, articles that made Rudolph blush with shame for the university. At least three times a year Fredericks would write an article acclaiming a new cure for cancer that would appear on the editorial page of the Whitby *Sentinel*.

"You businessmen," Harrison said largely, "you never can appreciate the role of pure science. You want to see a return on your investment every six months. You expect to see the simoleons come pouring out of every test tube."

When it suited his convenience, Harrison, with his acres of choice downtown property and his interest in a bank, was very much the hard-headed businessman. At other times, publisher that he was, immersed in printer's ink, he was a literary figure, decrying the elimination of Latin as a required subject for graduation or inveighing against a new English syllabus because it did not include enough of the works of Charles Dickens.

He tipped his hat grandly to a woman instructor in the psychology department who crossed their path. He had old-fashioned manners and up-to-date hatreds, Harrison. "I hear there're some interesting things going on down at Dee Cee," he said.

"There are always interesting things going on at Dee Cee," Rudolph said.

"More interesting than usual," said Harrison. "There's a rumor that you're going to step down."

"I never step down," Rudolph said and then was sorry he said it. The man brought out the worst in him.

"If you *do* happen to step down," Harrison persisted, "who's the next in line? Knight?"

"The matter hasn't come up," Rudolph said. Actually, the matter had come up, between him and Calderwood, but no decision had been reached. He didn't like to lie, but if you didn't lie to a man like Harrison you would deserve canonization.

"Dee Cee means a lot to this town," Harrison said, "largely thanks to you, and you know I'm not a man who indulges in flattery, and my readers have a right to know what's going on behind the scenes." The words were banal and innocuous, but there was a threat there, and both Harrison and Rudolph understood it.

"If anything happens," Rudolph said, "your readers will be the first to know."

As he went up the steps of the Administration Building, with Harrison at his side, Rudolph couldn't help but feel that the morning was deteriorating rapidly.

The President of the university was a new, youngish, brisk man from Harvard, by the name of Dorlacker, who stood for no nonsense from his board. He and Rudolph were friendly and he came over to the house quite often with his wife and talked freely, mostly about getting rid of the majority of the board of trustees. He detested Harrison.

The meeting ran along familiar lines. The finance committee chairman reported that although endowments were going up, costs were going up even faster and advised raising the price of tuition and putting a freeze on the number of scholarships. The motion was tabled for further study.

The board was reminded that the new wing for the library would be ready for the fall term and had not yet been given a name. It was recalled from the last meeting that Mr. Jordache had suggested that it be called the Kennedy Wing, or even better, have the whole building, now merely called the Memorial Library, be renamed the Kennedy Library.

Harrison protested that the late President had been a controversial figure, and had represented only half the country and that a unversity campus was no place to introduce divisive politics. On a vote, it was decided to call the new wing the Kennedy Wing, leaving the entire building under its old title, the Memorial Library. The President drily appointed Mr. Harrison to find out for the board what or whom the library was in memory of.

Another member of the board, who also had had to park at some distance from the Administration Building, said that he thought there ought to be a strict rule that no students be allowed to own automobiles. Impossible to enforce, Dorlacker said, therefore unwise. Perhaps a new parking lot could be built.

Harrison was disturbed by an editorial in the student newspaper, calling for a ban-the-bomb demonstration. The editor should be disciplined for introducing politics to the campus and for disrespect for the government of the United States. Dorlacker explained that it was his opinion that a university was not the place to put down freedom of speech in America. On a vote, it was decided not to discipline the editor.

"This board," Harrison growled, "is running away from its responsibilities."

Rudolph was the youngest member of the board and he spoke softly and deferentially. But because of his alliance with Dorlacker and his ability to dig up endowments from alumni and foundations (he had even got Calderwood to donate fifty thousand dollars toward the new library wing) and his close knowledge of the town and its inter-relation with the university, he was the most influential member of the board and he knew it. What had started as almost a hobby and a mild boost to his ego had become a ruling interest in his life. It was with pleasure that he dominated the board and pushed one project after another down the throats of the die-hards like Harrison on the board. The new wing on the library, the expanded courses in sociology and foreign affairs, the introduction of a resident artist and the expansion of the Art School, the donation for two weeks a year of the theater at the Shopping Center to the Drama Department had all been his ideas. Remembering Boylan's sneer, Rudolph was resolved that before he got through, nobody, not even a man like Boylan, could call Whitby an agricultural school.

As an added satisfaction, he could at the end of each year deduct a good part of his travel expenses, both in the United States and abroad, from his income tax, as he made it a point to visit schools and universities wherever he went, as part of his duties as a trustee of the university. The training he had received at the hands of Johnny Heath had made this almost automatic. "The amusements of the rich," Johnny called the game with the Internal Revenue Service.

"As you know," Dorlacker was saying, "at this meeting we are to consider new appointments to the faculty for the next school year. There is one department post that will be open—the head of the department of economics. We have inspected the field and conferred with the members of the department and we would like to offer for your approval the name of an ex-head of what used to be the combined departments of history and economics here, a man who has been gaining valuable experience in Europe for the past few years, Professor Lawrence Denton." As he spoke the name, Dorlacker casually turned toward Rudolph. There was the barest hint of a wink. Rudolph had exchanged letters with his old teacher and knew that Denton wanted to come back to America. He was not made to be a man without a country, Denton had written, and his wife had never gotten over being homesick. Rudolph had told Dorlacker all about Denton and Dorlacker had been sympathetic. Denton had helped his own case by using the time in Europe to write a book about the rebirth of the German economy, which had gotten respectful reviews.

Denton's resurrection was only poetic justice, Rudolph thought. He had not testified in his old friend's behalf at a time when it might have helped. But if he *had* testified the chances were that he never would have been elected to the board of trustees and been able to politick for Denton's reinstatement. There was something pleasingly ironic about the situation that made Rudolph smile to himself as Dorlacker spoke. He knew that between them Dorlacker and he had canvassed enough votes to put Denton across. He sat back comfortably, in silence, allowing Dorlacker to make the necessary moves.

"Denton," Harrison said. "I remember the name. He got kicked out for being a Red."

"I've looked into the record thoroughly, Mr. Harrison," Dorlacker said, "and I've found that there never was any kind of accusation against Professor Denton or any formal investigation. Professor Denton resigned to work in Europe."

"He was a Red of some kind," Harrison said doggedly. "We have enough wild men as it is on this campus without importing any new ones."

"At the time," Dorlacker said gently, "the country was under the McCarthy cloud and a great number of estimable people were made to suffer groundlessly. Fortunately, that is far behind us, and we can judge a man by his abilities alone. I, for one, am happy to be able to demonstrate that Whitby is guided only by strict scholastic standards."

"If you put that man in here," Harrison said, "my paper will have something to say about it."

"I consider your remark unseemly, Mr. Harrison," Dorlacker said, without heat, "and I'm certain that upon reflection you will think better of it. Unless somebody else has more to add, I believe it is time to put the appointment to a vote."

"Jordache," Harrison said, "I don't suppose you had anything to do with this?"

"Actually, I did," Rudolph said. "Professor Denton was the most interesting teacher I had when I was an undergraduate here. I also found his recent book most illuminating."

"Vote, vote," Harrison said. "I don't know why I bother to come to these meetings."

His was the only vote against Denton and Rudolph planned to send a cable to the exile in Geneva as soon as the meeting was over.

There was a knock on the door and Dorlacker said, "Come in."

His secretary entered. "I'm sorry to disturb you, sir," she said to Dorlacker, "but there's a call for Mr. Jordache. I said that he was in a meeting, but . . . "

Rudolph was out of his chair and walking toward the secretary's phone in the anteroom.

"Rudy," Jean said. "I think you'd better come here. Quick. The pains are starting." She sounded happy and unworried.

"I'll be right there," he said. "Make my excuses to President Dorlacker and the members of the board, please," he said to the secretary. "I have to take my wife to the hospital. And will you please call the hospital and tell them to get in touch with Dr. Levine and say that Mrs. Jordache will be there in about a half hour."

He ran out of the office and all the way to where his car was parked. He fumbled with the lock, cursing whoever had stolen the radio in New York City, and for a wild moment looked in the car parked next to his to see if by chance the keys were in the ignition. They weren't. He went back to his own car. This time the locked turned and he jumped in and sped through the campus and down the quiet streets toward home.

Waiting all through the long day, holding Jean's hand, Rudolph didn't know how she could stand it. Dr. Levine was calm. It was normal, he said, for a first birth. Dr. Levine's calmness made Rudolph nervy. Dr. Levine just dropped in casually from time to time during the day, as though it were just a routine social call. When he suggested that Rudolph go down to the hospital cafeteria to have some dinner, Rudolph had been shocked that the doctor could think he could leave his suffering wife and gorge himself, abandoning her to her agony. "I'm a father," he said, "not an obstetrician."

Dr. Levine had laughed. "Fathers have been known to eat, also," he had said. "They have to keep their strength up."

Materialistic, casual bastard. If ever they were crazy enough to have another baby, they'd hire somebody who wasn't a machine.

The child was born just before midnight. A girl. When Dr. Levine came out of the delivery room for a minute to tell Rudolph the news that mother and child were fine, Rudolph wanted to tell Dr. Levine that he loved him.

He walked beside the rolling bed on which Jean was being taken back to her room. She looked flushed and small and exhausted and when she tried to smile up at him the effort was too much for her.

"She's going to sleep now," Dr. Levine said. "You might as well go home."

But before he went out of the room, she said, in a surprisingly strong voice, "Bring my Leica tomorrow, Rudy, please. I want to have a record of her first day."

Dr. Levine took him to the nursery to see his daughter, asleep with five other infants, behind glass. Dr. Levine pointed her out. "There she is."

All six infants looked alike. Six in one day. The endless flood. Obstetricians must be the most cynical men in the world.

The night was cold outside the hospital. It had been warm that morning when he left the house and he hadn't taken a coat. He shivered as he walked toward his car. This time he had neglected to lock the doors, but the new radio was still there.

He knew he was too excited to sleep and he would have liked to call someone and have a drink in celebration of fatherhood, but it was past one o'clock now and he couldn't awaken anybody.

He turned the heater on in the car and was warm by the time he stopped the car in his driveway. Martha had left the lights on to guide him home. He was crossing the front lawn when he saw the figure move in the shadow of the porch.

"Who's there?" he called sharply.

The figure came slowly into the light. It was Virginia Calderwood, a scarf over her head, in a fur-trimmed gray coat.

"Oh, Christ Virginia," he said, "what are you doing here?"

"I know all about it." She came up and stood close to him, staring at him, her eyes large and dark in her pale, thin, pretty face. "I kept calling the hospital for news. I said I was your sister. I know everything. She's had the child. *My* child."

"Virginia, you'd better go home." Rudolph stepped back a little, so that she couldn't touch him. "If your father finds out that you've been hanging around here like this, he'll . . . "

"I don't care what anyone finds out," Virginia said. "I'm not ashamed."

"Let me drive you home," Rudolph said. Let her own family cope with her madness, not him. And not on a night like this. "What you need is a good night's sleep and you'll . . . "

"I have no home," Virginia said. "I belong in your arms. My father doesn't even know I'm in town. I'm here, with you, where I belong."

"You don't belong here, Virginia," Rudolph said despairingly. Devoted to sanity himself, he was helpless in the face of aberration. "I live here with my wife."

"She lured you away from me," Virginia said. "She came between one true love and another. I prayed for her to die in the hospital today."

"Virginia!" He had not been really shocked by anything she had said or done before. He had been annoyed or amused or pitying, but this was beyond annoyance or amusement or pity. For the first time it occurred to him that she might be dangerous. He would call the hospital as soon as he got into the house and warn them to keep Virginia Calderwood away from the nursery or his wife's room. "I'll tell you what," he said soothingly, "get in my car and I'll take you home."

"Don't try to treat me like a child," she said. "I'm no child. And I have my own car parked down the block. I don't need anyone to drive me anyplace."

"Virginia," he said, "I'm awfully tired and I really have to get some sleep. If there's anything you really have to talk to me about, call me in the morning."

"I want you to make love to me," she said, standing there, staring at him, her hands sunk in the pockets of her coat, looking normal, everyday, neatly dressed. "I want you to make love to me tonight. I know you want to do it. I've seen it in your eyes from the beginning." She spoke in a rushed, flat whisper. "It's just that you haven't dared. Like everybody else, you're afraid of my father. Come on. I'm worth trying. You keep thinking of me as a little girl, like when you first saw me in my father's house. Well, I'm nobody's little girl, don't worry about that. I've been around. Maybe not as much as your precious wife with her photographer friend—oh, you're surprised I know about that—I made it my business to know, I tell you, and I could tell you plenty more if you want to hear."

But by this time, he had opened the door and slammed and locked it behind him, leaving her raving there on the porch and beating with her fists on the door. He went to all the doors of the house and the windows on the ground floor and made sure they were locked. When he came back to the front door the hammering of small, mad, feminine fists had stopped. Luckily, Martha had slept through it all. He turned the light out on the porch, from inside. After he had called the hospital, he climbed wearily to the bedroom he shared with Jean.

Happy birthday, daughter, in this quiet, respectable town, he thought, just before he fell asleep.

It was Saturday afternoon in the country club bar, but early, and the bar was empty because most of the members were still on the golf course and on the tennis courts. Rudolph had the bar to himself, as he drank his beer. Jean was still in the women's locker room getting dressed. She had only been out of the hospital five weeks, but she had beaten him in two straight sets. Rudolph smiled as he remembered how gleeful she had been as she came off the court, victorious.

The clubhouse was a low, nondescript, rambling clapboard structure. The club was always on the point of going into bankruptcy and accepted anyone who paid the low initiation fees and had summer memberships for the people who came up only for the season. The bar was adorned with the faded photographs of people in long, flannel pants who had won club tournaments thirty years ago and a fly-specked photograph of Bill Tilden and Vincent Richards, who had once played an exhibition match on the club courts.

While waiting for Jean, Rudolph picked up the weekend edition of the Whitby *Sentinel* and was immediately sorry he had done so. On the front page there was an article about the hiring of Professor Denton by the college, with all the old insinuations and made-up quotes from unidentified sources which expressed concern that the impressionable youth of the college were going to be exposed to such a doubtful influence. "That sonofabitch Harrison," Rudolph said.

"You want something, Mr. Jordache?" asked the bartender, who was reading a magazine at the other end of the bar.

"Another beer, please, Hank," Rudolph said. He tossed the paper aside. At that moment, he decided that if he could swing it, he was going to buy Harrison's paper. It would be the best thing he could do for the town. And it shouldn't be too difficult to do. Harrison hadn't shown a profit on it for at least three years and if he didn't know that it was Rudolph who was after it, he probably would be willing to let it go at a fair price. Rudolph resolved to talk to Johnny Heath about procedure on Monday.

He was sipping his beer, trying to forget about Harrison until Monday, when Brad Knight came in from the golf course with the other three men in his foursome. Rudolph winced at the orange pants that Brad was wearing. "You entered in the Ladies' Handicap Cup?" he asked Brad as the men came up to the bar and Brad slapped him on the back.

Brad laughed. "Male plumage, Rudy," he said. "In nature always more brilliant than the female's. On weekends, I'm the natural man. This round is on me, Hank, I'm the big winner."

The men ordered and went over their cards. Brad and his partner had won close to three hundred dollars. Brad was one of the best golfers in the club and played a hustler's game, often starting badly and then getting his opponents to double bets. Well, that was his business. If people could lose nearly a hundred and fifty dollars apiece on a Saturday afternoon, Rudolph supposed they could afford it. But it made him uneasy to listen to men taking that much of a loss so lightly. He was not a born gambler.

"I saw Jean on the court with you," Brad said. "She looks just great."

"She comes from tough stock," Rudolph said. "Oh, by the way, thanks for the present for Enid." Jean's mother's maiden name had been Enid Cunningham and as soon as Jean had been strong enough to talk lucidly, she had asked Rudolph if he minded naming the child after her mother. "We're rising in the world, we Jordaches," Rudolph had said. "We are moving into three-name, ancestral territory." There had been no christening ceremony and there would be none. Jean shared his atheism, or as he himself preferred to think of it, his agnosticism. He had merely written the name in on the birth certificate, thinking as he did so that Enid Cunningham Jordache was a lot of letters for a seven-pound child to start life with. Brad had sent a sterling silver porringer with matching saucer and pusher for the baby. They now had eight sterling silver porringers in the house. Brad was not terribly original. But he had also started a savings account for the child with a deposit of five hundred dollars. "You never know," Brad had said when Rudolph had protested at the size of the gift, "when a girl has to pay for an abortion, fast."

One of the men Brad had been playing with was the chairman of the greens committee, Eric Sunderlin, and he was talking about his pet project, lengthening and improving the course. There was a large parcel of abandoned farm and timber land adjoining the course and Sunderlin was circulating a petition among the club members to float a loan and buy it. "It would put us in the big time," Sunderlin was saying. "We could even have a stab at a PGA tournament. We'd double our membership."

Everything in America, Rudolph thought resentfully, has a built-in tendency to double itself and move into the big time. He himself didn't play golf. Still, he was grateful that they were talking about golf at the bar and not about the article in the *Sentinel*.

"What about you, Rudy?" Sunderlin asked, finishing his Tom Collins. "Are you going to sign up with the rest of us?"

"I haven't given it much thought," Rudolph said. "Give me a couple of weeks to think it over."

"What's there to think over?" Sunderlin asked aggressively.

"Good old Rudy," Brad said. "No snap decisions. He thinks it over for two weeks if he has to have a haircut."

"It would help if a man of your stature was behind us," Sunderlin said. "I'll be after you."

"I'm sure you will, Eric," Rudy said. Sunderlin laughed at this tribute to him and he and the two other men went off to the showers, their spiked golf shoes clattering on the bare wooden floor. It was a club rule that spikes were not to be worn in the bar or restaurant or card room, but nobody paid any attention to it. If we ever move into the big time, Rudolph thought, you will have to take off your shoes.

Brad remained at the bar and ordered another drink. He always had a high flush on his face, but it was impossible to tell whether it was from the sun or from drink.

"A man of your stature," Brad said. "Everybody in this town always talks about you as though you're ten feet tall."

"That's why I stick to this town," Rudolph said.

"You going to stay here when you quit?" Brad didn't look at Rudolph while he spoke, but nodded at Hank as Hank put his glass in front of him on the bar.

"Who said anything about quitting?" Rudolph had not talked to Brad about his plans.

"Things get around."

"Who told you?"

"You *are* going to quit, aren't you?"

"Who told you?"

"Virginia Calderwood," Brad said.

"Oh."

"She overheard her father talking to her mother."

Spy, information gatherer, demented night-lurker, on quiet feet, Virginia Calderwood, listening in and out of shadows.

"I've been seeing her the last couple of months," Brad said. "She's a nice girl."

Student of character, Bradford Knight, originally from Oklahoma, open Western plains, where things were what they seemed to be.

"Uhuh," Rudolph said.

"Have you and the old man discussed who's going to take your place?"

"Yes, we've discussed it."

"Who's it going to be?"

"We haven't decided yet."

"Well," Bradford said, smiling, but more flushed than ever, "give an old college chum at least ten minutes notice before it's announced, will you?"

"Yes. What else has Miss Calderwood told you?"

"Nothing much," Brad said offhandedly. "That she loves me. Stuff like that. Have you seen her recently?"

"No." Rudolph hadn't seen her since the night Enid was born. Six weeks wasn't recently.

"We've had some laughs together," Brad said. "Her appearance is deceptive. She's a fun girl."

New aspects of the lady's character. Given to laughter. A fun girl. Merriment on porches at midnight.

"Actually," Brad said, "I'm considering marrying her."

"Why?" Rudolph asked. Although he could guess why.

"I'm tired of whoring around," Brad said. "I'm getting on toward forty and it's becoming wearing." Not the whole answer, friend, Rudolph thought. Nowhere nearly the whole answer.

"Maybe I'm impressed with your example," Brad said. "If marriage is good enough for a man of your stature—" He grinned, burly and red. "It ought to be good enough for a man of mine. Conjugal bliss."

"You didn't have much conjugal bliss the last time."

"That's for sure," Brad said. His first marriage, to the daughter of an oil man, had lasted six months. "But I was younger then. And I wasn't married to a decent girl like Virginia. And maybe my luck's changed."

Rudolph took a deep breath. "Your luck hasn't changed, Brad," he said quietly. Then he told Brad about Virginia Calderwood, about the letters, the phone calls, the ambushes in front of his apartment, the last crazy scene just six weeks ago. Brad listened in silence. All he said, at the end, was, "It must be plain glorious to be as wildly desirable as you, kid."

Jean came up then, shining from her shower, her hair tied back in a velvet bow, her brown legs bare in moccasins. "Hi, Mom," Brad said, getting off his bar stool and kissing her. "Let me buy everybody a drink."

They talked about the baby and golf and tennis and the new play that was going into the Whitby Theater, which was opening for the season next week. Virginia Calderwood's name wasn't mentioned, and after he had finished his drink, Brad said, "Well, me for a shower," and signed for the drinks and ambled off, a thickening, aging man in orange pants, his expensive golf shoes making a pecking noise with their spikes on the scarred wooden floor.

Two weeks later, the invitation to the wedding of Miss Virginia Calderwood to Mr. Bradford Knight was in the morning mail.

The organ struck up the wedding march and Virginia came down the aisle on her father's arm. She looked pretty, delicate, fragile, and composed, in her bridal white. She did not look at Rudolph as she passed him, although he was standing in a front pew, with Jean beside him. Bradford Knight, bridegroom, sweating a little and flushed in the June heat, was waiting at the altar, with Johnny Heath, best man, both of them in striped pants and Prince Alberts. People had been surprised that Rudolph hadn't been chosen as best man, but Rudolph had not been surprised.

It's my doing, Rudolph thought, as he half listened to the service. I brought him here from Oklahoma, I took him into the business, I refused the bride. It's my doing, am I responsible?

The wedding lunch was held at the Country Club. The buffet was laid on a long table under an awning and tables were set all around the lawn, under brightly colored umbrellas. A band played on the terrace, where the bride and bridegroom, now dressed for traveling, had led the first dance, a waltz. Rudolph had been surprised at how well Brad, who did not seem like a graceful man, had danced.

Rudolph had kissed the bride dutifully. Virginia had smiled at him with exactly the same smile she had given everybody else. Maybe, Rudolph thought, it's all over, she's going to be all right.

Jean had insisted upon dancing with him, although he had protested, "How can you dance in the middle of the day?"

"I love weddings," Jean said, holding him close. "Other people's." Then, maliciously, "Shouldn't you get up and make a toast to the bride? You might mention what a loyal friend she is—waiting outside your door night after night to make sure you got home safely and calling you at all hours to see if you were afraid in the dark and offering to keep you company in your poor lonely bed?"

"Ssh," Rudolph said, looking around apprehensively. He hadn't told her about the night of the hospital.

"She does look beautiful," Jean said. "Are you sorry about your choice?"

"In despair," he said. "Now, dance."

The boys in the band were a combination from the college and Rudolph was saddened by how well they played. He remembered his days with the trumpet when he was about their age. The young did everything so much better these days. The boys on the Port Philip track team were running the two twenty, his old distance, at least two seconds faster than he had ever run it. "Let's get off this damned floor," he said. "I feel crowded."

They went over and had a glass of champagne and talked to Brad's father, who had come from Tulsa for the occasion, wearing a wide-brimmed Stetson hat. He was weatherbeaten and thin and had deep sun-creases in the back of his neck. He didn't look like a man who had won and lost fortunes, but rather like a small-part player in the movies, hired to play the sheriff in a Western.

"Brad sure has talked enough about you, sir," old man Knight said to Rudolph. "And about your beautiful young bride." He raised his glass gallantly to Jean, who had taken off her hat and who now looked not bridal, but coeducational. "Yes, sir, Mister Jordache," old man Knight went on, "my son Brad is eternally in your debt, and don't think he don't know it. He was turning on his own tail out there in Oklahoma, hardly knowing where his next square meal was coming from when he got the call from you to come East. And I was in mighty poor straits myself at the time, I don't mind telling you, and I couldn't raise the price of a broken-down oil rig to help my boy. I'm proud to say I'm back on my own two feet again, now, but for awhile there it really looked like poor old Pete Knight was finally ready to be put to rest. Me and Brad were living in one room and eating chili three times a day for sustenance when like a bolt from the blue, the call came from his friend Rudy. I told him when he came home from the service, now you see here, Brad, you take the offer of the United States Government, and you get yourself to a college with that old GI Bill of Rights, from now on a man ain't going to be worth spit in this country if he ain't been to college. He's a good boy, Brad, and he had the sense to listen to his pa, and now look at him." He beamed across the dance floor to where his son and Virginia and Johnny Heath were drinking champagne among a group of the younger guests. "All dressed up, drinking champagne, with all the future in the world, married to a beautiful young heiress. And if ever he says he doesn't owe it all to his friend Rudy, his pa'll be the first to call him a liar."

Brad and Virginia came over with Johnny to pay their respects to Knight and the old man took Virginia onto the floor to dance with her, while Brad danced with Jean.

"You're not celebrating much today, are you, Rudy?" Johnny asked. Nothing escaped those sleepy eyes in that smooth round face.

"The bride is pretty, the champagne plentiful, the sun is shining, my friend thinks he's got it made for life," Rudolph said. "Why shouldn't I be celebrating?"

"As I said," Johnny said.

"My glass is empty," said Rudolph. "Let's get some more wine." He started toward the end of the buffet table under the awning, where the bar had been set up.

"We're going to have an answer on Monday from Harrison," Johnny said. "I think he's going to go for the deal. You'll have your toy."

Rudolph nodded. Although it annoyed him when Johnny, who didn't see how any real money could ever be made out of the *Sentinel,* called it a toy. Whatever his feelings were, Johnny, as usual, had come through. He had found a man called Hamlin, who was putting together a chain of small-town newspapers, to act as the buyer of record. He was contracted to sell out his interest to Rudolph three months later. Hamlin was a hard dealer and he had demanded three percent of the purchase price for his services, but he had beaten down Harrison's first demands so far that it was worthwhile to meet his conditions.

At the bar, Rudolph was clapped on the back by Sid Grossett, who had been Mayor of Whitby until the last election, and who was sent every four years as a delegate to the Republican convention. He was a hardy, friendly man, a lawyer by profession, who had successfully squashed rumors that he had taken bribes while he was in office, but had chosen not to run at the last election. Wisely, people said. The present mayor of the town, a Democrat, was at the other end of the bar, equally drinking Calderwood's champagne. Everybody had turned out for the wedding.

"Hi, young man," Grosset said. "I've been hearing about you."

"Good or bad?" Rudolph asked.

"Nobody ever hears anything bad about Rudolph Jordache," Grosset said. He wasn't a politician for nothing.

"Hear, hear," Johnny Heath said.

"Hi, Johnny." A handshake for everybody. There was always another election. "I got it from the horse's mouth," Grossett said. "You're quitting Dee Cee at the end of the month."

"Who's the horse this time?"

"Mr. Duncan Calderwood."

"The emotions of the day must have gone to the poor old man's head," Rudolph said. He didn't want to talk about his business to Grossett, or answer questions about what he was giong to do next. There was plenty of time for that later.

"The day any emotions go to Duncan Calderwood's head," Grosset said, "you call me. I'll come running. He tells me he doesn't know what your future plans are. In fact, he said, he didn't know if you *had* any plans. But just in case you're open to suggestions—" He swiveled around, sniffing the air for possible Democrats. "Maybe we could talk in a day or two. Maybe you could come around to my office some afternoon next week."

"I'm going to be in New York next week."

"Well, there's no sense beating about the bush," Grossett said. "Have you ever thought you'd like to go into politics?"

"When I was twenty," Rudolph said. "Now that I'm old and wise . . . "

"Don't give me that," Grossett said roughly. "Everybody thinks about going into politics. Especially somebody like you. Rich, popular, with a big success behind you, a beautiful wife, looking for new worlds to conquer."

"Don't tell me you want to run me for President, now that Kennedy's dead," Rudolph said.

"I know that's a joke," Grossett said earnestly. "But who knows if it'll still be a joke ten years, twelve years from now? No. You got to start politics on a local level, Rudy, and right here in this town you're everybody's fair-haired boy. Am I right Johnny." He turned, pleadingly, to the best man.

"Everybody's fair-haired boy." Johnny nodded.

"Up from poverty, went to college right here, handsome, educated, public-spirited."

"I've always felt I was actually private spirited," Rudolph said, to cut off the praise.

"Okay, be smart. But just look at all the goddamn committees you're on. And you haven't got an enemy in the world."

"Don't insult me, Sid." Rudolph was enjoying baiting the insistent little man, but he was listening more closely than he seemed to be.

"I know what I'm talking about."

"You don't even know whether I'm a Democrat or a Republican," Rudolph said. "Ask Leon Harrison and he'll tell you I'm a Communist."

"Leon Harrison is an old fart," Grossett said. "If I had my way I'd take up a collection to buy his paper away from him."

Rudolph couldn't refrain from winking at Johnny Heath.

"I know what you are," Grossett went plugging on. "You're a Kennedy-type

Republican. It's a winning model. Just what the old Party needs."

"Now that you've got the pin in me, Sid," Rudolph said, "mount me and put me in a glass case." He disliked being categorized, no matter what the category.

"The place I want to put you is in the Whitby Town Hall," Grossett said. "As Mayor. And I bet I can do it. How do you like that? And from then on, up the ladder. I suppose you wouldn't like to be a Senator, the Senator from New York, I suppose that rubs you the wrong way, doesn't it?"

"Sid," Rudolph said gently, "I've been teasing you. I'm flattered, really I am. I'll be in next week to see you, I promise. Now, let's remember this is a wedding; not a smoke-filled room. I'm off to dance with the bride."

He set down his glass and gave Grossett's shoulder a friendly pat, then went looking for Virginia. He hadn't danced with her yet and if he didn't go around the floor at least once with her, there would undoubtedly be talk. It was a small town and there were sharp eyes and tongues everywhere.

Good Republican, potential Senator, he approached the bride where she stood, demure and gay, under an awning, her hand light and loving on her new husband's arm. "May I have the honor?" Rudolph asked.

"Anything I have is yours," Brad said. "You know that."

Rudolph swung Virginia onto the floor. She danced bridally, her hand cool in his, her touch on his back feathery, her head thrown back proudly, conscious of being watched by girls who wished they were in her place today, by men who wished they were in her husband's.

"All happiness," Rudolph said. "Many, many years of happiness."

She laughed softly. "I'll be happy," she said, her thighs touching his. "Never fear. I'll have Brad for a husband and you for a lover."

"Oh, Christ," Rudolph said.

With the tip of a finger she touched his lips to silence him, and they finished the dance. As he walked her back to where Brad was standing, he knew that he had been too optimistic. Things were not going to work out all right. Never in a million years.

He did not throw rice along with the other guests as the newlyweds drove off in Brad's car to begin their honeymoon. He was on the front steps of the club, next to Calderwood. Calderwood didn't throw any rice either. The old man was frowning, but it was hard to tell whether it was because of something he was thinking or because the sun was in his eyes. As the guests drifted back for one last glass of champagne, Calderwood remained on the steps looking into the shimmering summer afternoon distance in which his last daughter had disappeared with her husband. Earlier, Calderwood had said to Rudolph that he wanted to talk to him so Rudolph gave a sign to Jean that he would meet her later and she left the two men alone.

"What do you think?" Calderwood said finally.

"It was a beautiful wedding."

"Not about that."

Rudolph shrugged. "Who knows how a marriage is going to turn out?"

"He expects he's going to get your job now."

"That's normal," Rudolph said.

"I wish to God it was you riding off down to New York with her this afternoon."

"Life doesn't work out that neatly most of the time," Rudolph said.

"It certainly doesn't." Calderwood shook his head. "I don't trust him completely," he said. "I hate to say that about any man who's worked loyally for me the way he has and who's married my daughter, but I can't hide it from myself."

"He's never made a wrong move since he came here," Rudolph said. Except one, he thought. Not believing what I told him about Virginia. Or worse, believing it and marrying her anyway. But he couldn't tell Calderwood that.

"I know he's your friend," Calderwood said, "and he's smart as a fox and you've known him a long time and you had enough confidence in him to bring him here and give him a big load of responsibility, but there's something about him—" Calderwood shook his big, sallow, death-marked head again. "He drinks, he's a whoremon-ger—don't contradict me, Rudy, I know what I know—he gambles, he comes from Oklahoma . . . "

Rudolph chuckled.

"I know," Calderwood said. "I'm an old man and I have my prejudices. But there they are. I guess I've been spoiled by you, Rudy. I never dealt with a man in my whole life I knew I could trust the way I trust you. Even when you talked me into acting against my better judgment—and you'd be surprised how many times that's happened—I knew you'd never do anything that you thought was against my interests or was underhanded or would reflect against my reputation."

"Thank you, Mr. Calderwood," Rudolph said.

"Mr. Calderwood, Mr. Calderwood," the old man said peevishly. "Are you still going to be calling me Mr. Calderwood on my death bed?"

"Thank you, Duncan." It was an effort to say Duncan.

"To turn the whole damn shebang over to that man." There was a cranky, aged complaint in Calderwood's voice. "Even if it's after I die. I don't feel like doing it. But if you say so . . . " He trailed off unhappily.

Rudolph sighed. There is always someone to betray, he thought. "I don't say so," he said quietly. "There's a young lawyer in our legal department by the name of Mathers . . . "

"I know him," Calderwood said. "Light-complected fellow with glasses and two kids. From Philadelphia."

"He has a degree from the Wharton School of Business that he took before he went to Harvard Law. He's been with us more than four years. He knows every department. He asks all the right questions. He's been in and out of my office. He could earn a lot more than he does here in any one of a dozen law firms in New York, but he likes living here."

"Okay," Calderwood said. "Tell him tomorrow."

"I would prefer it if you told him, Duncan." Second Duncan in his life.

"As usual," Calderwood said. "I don't like to do what you're telling me to do, and I know you're right. I'll tell him. Now let's go back and drink some more of that champagne. I paid enough for it, God knows, I might as well drink it."

The new appointment was announced the day before the newlyweds were due back from the honeymoon.

Brad took it calmly, like a gentleman, and never queried Rudolph about who had made the decision. But three months later he quit his job and he and Virginia went out to Tulsa, where Brad's father had made a place for him in his oil business. On Enid's first birthday, he sent a check for five hundred dollars to the bank to be deposited in Enid's savings account.

Brad wrote regularly, jovial, breezy, friendly letters. He was doing very well, he wrote, and was making more money than he ever had before. He liked Tulsa, where the golf bets were on a generous Western scale and on three successful Saturdays he had won more than a thousand dollars a round. Virginia was liked by everyone and had made dozens of friends. She had taken up golf. Brad invited Rudolph to invest with him—"It's like picking money off a tree," was the way he put it. He said he wanted somehow to pay back all that Rudolph had done for him, and this was one way of doing it.

Out of a sense of guilt—he could not forget the moment on the steps of the Country Club with Duncan Calderwood—Rudolph started taking shares in wells that Brad prospected, drilled, and managed. Besides, as Johnny Heath pointed out, for a man in his income bracket, considering the twenty-seven-per-cent depletion tax allowance that the oil industry enjoyed, it was more than worth the gamble. Johnny checked on the credit rating of Peter Knight and son, found it was A one, then matched Rudolph's investments dollar for dollar.

CHAPTER 3

1965

THOMAS SQUATTED ON the forward deck, whistling tunelessly, polishing the bronze spool of the anchor winch. Although it was only early June, it was already warm and he worked barefooted and stripped to the waist. His torso was dark brown from the sun, as dark as the skin of the swarthiest Greeks or Italians on any of the ships in the harbor of Antibes. His body wasn't as hard as it had been when he was fighting. The muscles didn't stand out in ridges as they had then, but were smoother, not as heavy. When he was wearing something to cover his small bald spot, as he was now, he looked younger than he had two years ago. He tilted the white American gob's hat, which he wore with the rim turned down all around, over his eyes, to protect him from the glare of the sun off the water.

From the engine room below there was the sound of hammering. Pinky Kimball was down there with Dwyer, working on a pump. The first charter of the year began tomorrow and the port engine had overheated on a trial run. Pinky, who was the engineer on the *Vega,* the biggest ship in the harbor, had volunteered to come over and take a look at it. Dwyer and Thomas could handle simple repairs themselves, but when it came to anything really complicated they had to ask for help. Luckily, Thomas had struck up a friendship with Kimball during the winter and Kimball had given them a hand on various things as they got the *Clothilde* into shape for the summer. Thomas had not explained to Dwyer why he had decided to call the ship the *Clothilde* when they changed it from the *Penelope* at Porto Santo Stefano. To himself, he had said, a ship had to be called by a woman's name, why not Clothilde? He certainly wasn't going to call it Teresa.

He was happy on the *Clothilde*, although even in his own eyes it wasn't one of the smartest craft on the Mediterranean. He knew its superstructure was a little topheavy and presented too much surface to the wind and its top speed was only twelve knots, cruising speed ten knots, and it rolled alarmingly in certain seas. But everytning that two determined men, working month after month, could do to make a craft snug and seaworthy had been done to the peeling hulk they had bought at Porto Santo Stefano two and a half years before. They had had two good seasons, and while neither of them had gotten rich off the boat, they both had some money in the bank, in case of trouble. The season coming up looked as though it was going to be even better than the first two and Thomas felt a calm pleasure as he burnished the bronze spool and saw it reflect the sun from its surface. Before taking to sea he would never have thought that a simple, brainless act like polishing a piece of metal could give him pleasure.

It was the same with everything on the ship. He loved to stroll from bow to stern and back again, touching the hand rails, pleased to see the lines curled into perfect spiral patterns on the calked, pale, teak deck, admiring the polished brass handles on the old-fashioned wheel in the deck house and the perfectly arranged charts in their slots and the signal flags tightly rolled in their pigeonholes. He, who had never washed a dish in his life, spent long hours in the galley scrubbing pans until they shone and making sure that the icebox was immaculate and fresh smelling, the range and oven scrubbed. When there was a charter on board he and Dwyer and whoever they signed on as a cook dressed in tan drill shorts and immaculate white cotton T-shirts with *Clothilde* printed across the chest in blue. In the evenings, or in cold weather, they wore identical heavy navy-blue sailor's sweaters.

He had learned to mix all sorts of drinks and serve them frosty and cold in good glasses, and there was one party, Americans, who swore they only took the ship for his Bloody Marys. A pleasure craft on the Mediterranean, going between one country and another, could be a cheap holiday for a drunkard, because you could take on case after case of duty-free liquor and you could buy gin and whiskey for about a dollar and a half a bottle. He rarely drank anything himself, except for a little pastis and an occasional beer. When charters came aboard he wore a peaked captain's cap, with the gilt anchor and chain. It made his clients' holidays more seagoing, he felt.

He had learned a few words of French and Italian and Spanish, enough to go through harbor-master formalities and do the shopping, but too little to get into arguments. Dwyer picked up the languages quickly and could rattle away with anybody.

Thomas had sent a photograph of the *Clothilde,* spraying through a wave, to Gretchen and Gretchen had written back that she kept it on the mantelpiece of her living room. One day, she wrote, she would come over and take a trip with him. She was busy, she wrote, doing some sort of job at a movie studio. She said that she had kept her promise and had not told Rudolph where he was or what he was doing. Gretchen was his one link with America and the times when he felt lonely or missed the kid, he wrote to her. He had asked Dwyer to write his girl in Boston, whom Dwyer still said he was going to marry, to try to go down to the Aegean Hotel when she had the time and talk to Pappy, but the girl hadn't replied yet.

Some year, soon, no matter what, he was going to go to New York and try to find his kid.

He hadn't had a single fight since Falconetti. He still dreamed about Falconetti. He wasn't sentimental about him, but he was sorry Falconetti was dead and the passage of time hadn't persuaded him that it wasn't his fault that the man had thrown himself overboard.

He finished with the winch and stood up. The deck was promisingly warm under his bare feet. As he went aft, running his hands along the newly varnished mahogany-colored rails, the hammering below stopped and Kimball's flaming red hair appeared, as he came out of the saloon and onto the deck. To get to the engine room, you had to pick up sections of the floor from the saloon. Dwyer appeared after Kimball. They were both wearing oil-stained green overalls, because there was no keeping clean in the confined space of the engine room. Kimball was wiping his hands on a piece of waste, which he threw overboard. "That ought to do it, mate," Kimball said. "Why don't we give it a spin?"

Thomas went into the pilot house and started the engines while Dwyer and Pinky cast off from the dock and clambered forward to bring up the hook, Dwyer working the winch and cleaning off the harbor muck from the chain with the hose before it dropped into the well. They had a lot of chain out, for stability, and the *Clothilde* was almost in the middle of the harbor before Pinky gave the sign that they were clear and helped Dwyer bring the hook on board with the gaff.

By now Thomas was skilled at handling the ship and only when he was coming into a very crowded harbor, with a bad wind blowing, did he hand over the wheel to Dwyer. Today, he turned the bow toward the harbor entrance and, keeping the speed down until they were outside, chugged beyond the fishermen with their rods at the end of the rampart and around the buoy before he increased speed, turning toward the Cap d'Antibes, leaving the fortress of the Vieux Carré on its hill, behind them. He watched the gauges of both engines and was relieved to see that the port engine wasn't heating up. Good old Pinky. Through the winter he must have saved them at least a thousand dollars. The ship he was on, the *Vega,* was so new and so pampered that there was almost nothing for him to do when they were in port. He was bored on it and delighted to be able to putter about in the *Clothilde's* cluttered, hot engine room.

Kimball was a knotty Englishman whose freckled face never got tan, but remained a painful hot pink all summer. He had a problem with the drink, as he put it. When he drank he became pugnacious and challenged people in bars. He quarreled with his owners and rarely stayed on one ship more than a year, but he was so good at his job that he never had any trouble finding other berths quickly. He only worked on the very big yachts, because his skill would be wasted on smaller craft. He had been raised in Plymouth and had been on the water all his life. He was amazed that somebody like Thomas had wound up the owner-skipper of a ship like the *Clothilde* in Antibes harbor, and was making a go of it. "Yanks," Kimball said, shaking his head. "They're fucking well capable of anything. No wonder you own the world."

He and Thomas had been friendly from the beginning, greeting each other as they passed on the quay or buying each other beers in the little bar at the entrance to the port. Kimball had guessed that Thomas had been in the ring and Thomas had told him about some of his fights and what it was like and about the win in London and the later two dives he had had to take and even about the last fight in the hotel room with Quayles in Las Vegas, which had especially delighted Kimball's belligerent heart. Thomas had not told him about Falconetti and Dwyer knew enough to keep quiet on that subject.

"By God, Tommy," Kimball said, "if I knew I could fight like that I would clean out every bar from Gib to Piraeus."

"And get a knife between your ribs in the process," Thomas said.

"No doubt you're right," Kimball agreed. "But man, the pleasure before!"

When he got very drunk and saw Thomas he would pound the bar and shout, "See that man? If he wasn't a friend of mine, I'd drive him into the deck." Then loop an affectionate tattooed arm around Thomas's neck.

Their friendship had been cemented one night in a bar in Nice. They hadn't gone to Nice together, but Dwyer and Thomas had wandered into the bar, near the port, by accident. There was a cleared space around the bar and Kimball was holding forth, loudly, to a group that included some French seamen and three or four flashily dressed but dangerous-looking young men of a type that Thomas had learned to recognize and avoid—small-time hoodlums and racketeers, doing odd jobs along the Côte for the chiefs of the *milieu* with headquarters in Marseilles. His instinct told him that they were probably armed, if not with guns, certainly with knives.

Pinky Kimball spoke a kind of French and Thomas couldn't understand him, but he could tell from the tone of Kimball's voice and the grim looks on the faces of the other patrons of the bar that Kimball was insulting them. Kimball had a low opinion of the French when he was drunk. When he was drunk in Italy, he had a low opinion of Italians. When he was drunk in Spain, he had a low opinion of the Spanish. Also, when he was drunk, he seemed to forget how to count and the fact that he was alone and outnumbered at least five to one only spurred him on to greater feats of scornful oratory.

"He's going to get himself killed here tonight," Dwyer whispered, understanding most of what Kimball was shouting. "And us, too, if they find out we're his friends."

Thomas grasped Dwyer's arm firmly and took him with him to Kimball's side at the bar.

"Hi, Pinky, he said cheerfully.

Pinky swung around, ready for new enemies. "Ah," he said. "I'm glad you're here. I'm telling these *maquereaux* a few home truths for their own good."

"Knock it off, Pinky," Thomas said. Then, to Dwyer. "I'm going to say a few words to these gentlemen. I want you to translate. Clearly and politely." He smiled cordially at the other men in the bar, arranged now in an ominous semicircle. "As you see, gentlemen," he said, "this Englishman is my friend." He waited while Dwyer nervously translated. There was no change in the expression of the faces lined up around him. "He is also drunk," Thomas said. "Naturally, a man does not like to see a friend damaged, drunk or sober. I will try to prevent him from making any more speeches here, but no matter what he says or has said, there will be no trouble here tonight. I am the policeman tonight in this bar and I am keeping the peace. Please translate," he said to Dwyer.

As Dwyer was translating, haltingly, Pinky said, disgustedly, "Shit, mate, you're lowering the flag."

"What is further," Thomas went on, "the next round of drinks is on me. Barman." He was smiling as he spoke, but he could feel the muscles tightening in his arms and he was ready to spring on the biggest one of the lot, a heavy-jawed Corsican in a black leather jacket.

The men looked at each other uncertainly. But they hadn't come into the bar to fight and while they grumbled a little among themselves they each came up to the bar and accepted the drinks that Thomas had bought for them.

"Some fighter," Pinky sneered. "Every day is Armistice day with you, Yank." But he allowed himself to be led safely out of the bar ten minutes later. When he came over to the *Clothilde* the next day, he brought a bottle of pastis with him and said, "Thanks, Tommy. They'd have kicked in my skull in the next two minutes if you hadn't come along. I don't know what it is comes over me when I have a few. And it's not as though I ever *win*. I've got scars from head to toe in tribute to my courage." He laughed.

"If you've got to fight," Thomas said, remembering the days when he felt he had to fight, no matter whom and for no matter what reason, "fight sober. And pick on one man at a time. And don't take me along. I've given all that up."

"What would you have done, Tommy, boy," Pinky said, "if they'd jumped me?"

"I'd have created a diversion," Thomas said, "just long enough for Dwyer to get you out of the saloon, and then I'd have run for my life."

"A diversion," Pinky said. "I'd pay a couple of bob to have seen that diversion."

Thomas didn't know what it was in Pinky Kimball's life that changed him from a friendly, amiable, if profane man, into a suicidal, fighting animal when he got a few drinks in him. Sometime, perhaps, he'd have it out with him.

Pinky came into the pilot house, looked at the gauges, listened critically to the throb of the Diesels. "You're ready for the summer, lad," he said. "On your own craft. And I envy you."

"Not quite ready," Thomas said. "We're missing one in crew."

"What?" Pinky asked. "Where's that Spaniard you hired last week?"

The Spaniard had come well recommended as a cook and steward and he hadn't asked for too much money. But one night, when he was leaving the ship to go ashore, Thomas had seen him putting a knife into his shoe, alongside his ankle, hidden by his pants.

"What's that for?" Thomas had asked.

"To make respect," the Spaniard said.

Thomas had fired him the next day. He didn't want anybody aboard who had to keep a knife in his shoe to make respect. Now he was short-handed.

"I put him ashore," Thomas said to Pinky, as they crossed outside the bay of La Garoupe. He explained why. "I still need a cook-steward. It doesn't make much difference the next two weeks. My charter just wants the boat during the day and they bring their own food aboard. But I'll need somebody for the summer."

"Have you ever thought about hiring a woman?" Pinky asked.

Thomas grimaced. "There's a lot of heavy work beside the cooking and stuff like that," he said.

"A *strong* woman," Pinky said.

"Most of the trouble in my life," Thomas said, "came because of women. Weak and strong."

"How many days a summer do you lose," Pinky asked, "with your charters grousing that they're wasting their valuable time, waiting in some godforsaken port just to get their washing and ironing done?"

"It *is* a nuisance," Thomas agreed. "You got somebody in mind?"

"Righto," Pinky said. "She works as a stewardess on the *Vega* and she's pissed off with her job. She's crazy about the sea and all she sees all summer long is the inside of the laundry."

'Okay," Thomas said, reluctantly. "I'll talk to her. And tell her to leave her knives at home."

He didn't need a woman aboard as a *woman*. There were plenty of girls to be picked up around the ports. You had your fun with them, spent a few bucks on them for a dinner and maybe a night club and a couple of drinks and then you moved on to the next port, without complications. He didn't know what Dwyer did for sex and thought it better not to ask.

He turned the *Clothilde* around, to go back to the harbor. She was ready. There was no sense in using up fuel. He was paying for his own fuel until tomorrow, when the first charter began.

At six o'clock he saw Pinky coming down the quay with a woman. The woman was short and a little thick in the body and wore her hair in two plaits on either side of her head. She had on a pair of denim pants, a blue sweater, and espadrilles. She kicked off her espadrilles before she came up the gangplank in the stern of the ship. In the Mediterranean harbors most of the time you tied up stern to the quay, unless there was room to come alongside, which there rarely was.

"This is Kate," Pinky said. "I told her about you."

"Hello, Kate." Thomas put out his hand and she shook it. She had soft hands for a girl who worked in the laundry room and could do heavy work on deck. She was English, too, and came from Southampton and looked about twenty-five. She spoke in a low voice when she talked about herself. She could cook, as well as do laundry, she said, and she could make herself useful on deck, and she spoke French and Italian, "not mightily," she said, with a smile, but she could understand the météo on the radio in both languages and could follow a charted course and stand watches, and drive a car if ever that was necessary. She would work for the same salary as the Spaniard with the knife. She wasn't really pretty, but healthy and buxom in a small, brown way, with a direct manner of looking at the person she was talking to. In the winter, if she was laid off, she went back to London and got a job as a waitress. She wasn't married, and she wasn't engaged and she wanted to be treated like any member of the crew, no better and no worse.

"She's a wild English rose," Pinky said. "Aren't you, Kate?"

"None of your jokes, Pinky," the girl said. "I want this job. I'm tired of going from one end of the Med to the other all dressed up in a starched uniform with white cotton stockings, like a nurse, and being called Miss or Mademoiselle. I've been taking a glance at your ship, Tom, from time to time, as I've passed by, and it's pleased me. Not so big to be hoity-toity and British Royal Yacht Club. It's nice and clean and friendly looking. And it's a dead sure thing there won't be many ladies coming aboard that need to have their ballgowns pressed all one hot steaming afternoon in Monte Carlo harbor for a ball at the Palace that night."

"Well," Thomas said, defending the elegance of his clientele, "we don't exactly cater to paupers."

"You know what I mean," the girl said. "I'll tell you what. I don't want you to take a pig in a poke. Have you had your dinner yet?"

"No." Dwyer was down in the galley messing around desolately with some fish he'd bought that morning, but Thomas could tell by the sounds coming from the galley that nothing of any importance had as yet been done.

"I'll cook you a dinner," the girl said. "Right now. If you like it, you take me on, I'll go back to the *Vega* and clear out my things tonight and come aboard. If you don't like it, what have you lost? If you're hungry the restaurants in town keep open late. And Pinky, you can stay and eat with us."

"Okay," Thomas said. He went down to the galley and told Dwyer to get out of there, they had a cook from the Cordon Bleu, at least for a night. The girl looked around the galley, nodded approvingly, opened the ice box, opening drawers and cupboards to see where everything was, looked at the fish that Dwyer had bought and said he didn't know how to buy fish, but that they'd do in a pinch. Then she told them both to get out of there, she'd call them when dinner was ready. All she wanted was to have somebody go into Antibes to get some fresh bread and two ripe Camembert cheeses.

They ate on the after deck, behind the pilot house, instead of in the little dining alcove forward of the saloon that they would have used if there had been clients aboard. Kate had set the table and somehow it looked better than when Dwyer did it. She had put two bottles of wine in an icebucket, uncorked them, and put the bucket on a chair.

She had made a stew of the fish, with potatoes, garlic, onions, tomatoes, thyme, a lot of rock salt and pepper, and a little white wine and diced bacon. It was still light when they sat down at the table, with the sun setting in the cloudless, greenish-blue sky. The three men had washed, shaved, and put on fresh clothes and had had two pastis apiece while sitting on deck, sniffing the aromas coming from the galley. The harbor itself was quiet, with just the sound of little ripples lapping at hulls to be heard.

Kate brought up a big tureen with the stew in it. Bread and butter were already on the table, next to a big bowl of salad. After she served them all, she sat down with them, unhurried and calm. Thomas, as captain, poured the wine.

Thomas took a first bite, chewed it thoughtfully. Kate, her head down, also began to eat. "Pinky," Thomas said, "you're a true friend. You're plotting to make me a fat man. Kate, you're hired."

She looked up and smiled. They raised their glasses to the new member of the crew. Even the coffee tasted like coffee.

After dinner, while Kate was doing the dishes, the three men sat out in the silent evening, smoking cigars that Pinky had produced, watching the moon rise over the mauve hills of the alpes Maritimes.

"Bunny," Thomas said, leaning back in his chair and spreading his legs in front of him, "this is what it's all about."

Dwyer did not contradict him.

Later, Thomas went with Kate and Pinky to where the *Vega* was berthed. It was late and the ship was almost dark, with very few lights showing, but Thomas waited some distance away while Kate went on board to collect her things. He didn't want to get into an argument with the skipper, if he happened to be awake and angry about losing a hand on five minutes' notice.

A quarter of an hour later Thomas saw Kate coming noiselessly down the gangplank, carrying a valise. They walked together, along the fortress wall, past the boats moored one next to another to where the *Clothilde* was tied up. Kate stopped for a moment, looked gravely at the white-and-blue boat, groaning a little with the pull of the water against the two lines that made it fast to the quay. "I'm going to remember this evening," she said, then kicked off her espadrilles and, holding them in her hand, went barefooted up the gangplank.

Dwyer was waiting up for them. He had made up the extra bunk in Thomas's cabin for himself and put clean sheets for Kate on the bunk in the other cabin that he had been living in alone. Thomas snored, because of his broken nose, but Dwyer was going to have to get used to it. At least for awhile.

A week later, Dwyer moved back to his own cabin, because Kate moved into Thomas's. She said she didn't mind Thomas's snoring.

The Goodharts were an old couple who stayed at the Hotel du Cap every June. He owned cotton mills in North Carolina, but had handed over the business to a son. He was a tall, erect, slow-moving heavy man with a shock of iron-gray hair and looked like a retired colonel in the Regular Army. Mrs. Goodhart was a little younger than her husband, with soft white hair. Her figure was good enough so that she could get away with wearing slacks. The Goodharts had chartered the *Clothilde* for two weeks the year before and had liked it so much that they had arranged a similar charter with Thomas for this year by mail early in the winter.

They were the least demanding of clients. Each morning at ten, Thomas anchored as close inshore as he could manage opposite the row of the hotel's cabanas and the Goodharts came out in a speedboat. They came with full hampers of food, prepared in the hotel kitchen, and baskets of wine bottles wrapped in napkins. They were both over sixty and if the water was at all rough the transfer could be tricky. On those days, their chauffeur would drive them down to the *Clothilde* in Antibes harbor. Sometimes there would be other couples, always old, with them, or they would tell Thomas that they were to pick up some friends in Cannes. Then they'd chug out to the straits between the Isles de Lérins, lying about four thousand yards off the coast, and anchor there for the day. It was almost always calm there and the water was only about twelve feet deep and brilliantly clear so that you could see the seagrass waving on the bottom. The Goodharts would put on bathing suits and lie on mattresses in the sun, reading or dozing, and occasionally dive in for a swim.

Mr. Goodhart said that he felt safer about Mrs. Goodhart's swimming when Thomas or Dwyer swam beside her. Mrs. Goodhart, who was a robust woman with full shoulders and young, strong legs, swam perfectly well, but Thomas knew that it was Mr. Goodhart's way of telling him that he wanted Thomas and anybody else on the boat to feel free to enjoy the clear, cool water between the islands whenever they felt like taking a dip.

Sometimes, if they had guests, Thomas would spread a blanket for them on the after deck and they would play a few rubbers of bridge. Both Mr. and Mrs. Goodhart were soft-spoken and enormously polite with each other and everybody else.

Promptly at one-thirty every day, they were ready for the first drink, invariably a Bloody Mary, which Thomas made for them. After that, Dwyer unrolled the awning, and in its shade they ate the food they had brought with them from the hotel. On the table there would be cold langouste, cold roast beef, fish salad or cold loup de mer with a green sauce, melon with prosciutto, cheese, and fruit. They always brought along so much food, even when they had friends with them, that there was plenty left over for the crew, not only for lunch, but for dinner, too. With their meal they each had a bottle of white wine apiece.

The only thing Thonas had to worry about was the coffee and now with Kate aboard that was no problem. The first day of the charter she came up from the galley with the coffee pot, dressed in white shorts and white T-shirt with the legend *Clothilde* stretched tightly across her plump bosom and when Thomas introduced her, Mr. Goodhart nodded approvingly and said, "Captain, this ship is improving every year."

After lunch, Mr. and Mrs. Goodhart went below for their siesta. Quite often, Thomas heard muffled sounds that could only come from lovemaking. Mr. and Mrs. Goodhard had told Thomas they had been married more than thirty-five years and Thomas marveled that they still did it and still so obviously enjoyed it. The Goodharts shook his entire conception of marriage.

Around about four o'clock the Goodharts would reappear on deck, grave and ceremonious, as usual, in their bathing suits, and would swim for another half hour, with either Dwyer or Thomas accompanying them. Dwyer swam poorly and there were one or two times when Mrs. Goodhart was more than a hundred yards away from the *Clothilde* that Thomas thought there was a good chance she'd have to tow Dwyer back to the boat.

At five o'clock promptly, showered, combed, and dressed in cotton slacks, white shirt, and a blue blazer, Goodhart would come up on deck from below and say,

"Don't you think it's time for a drink, Captain?" and, if there were no guests aboard, "I'd be honored if you'd join me."

Thomas would prepare two Scotch and sodas and give the signal to Dwyer, who would start the engines and take the wheel. With Kate handling the anchor up forward, they would start back toward the Hotel du Cap. Seated on the aft deck Mr. Goodhart and Thomas would sip at their drinks as they pulled out of the straits and went around the island, with the pink-and-white towers of Cannes across the water on their port side.

On one such afternoon, Mr. Goodhart said, "Captain, are there many Jordaches in this part of the world?"

"Not that I know of," Thomas said. "Why?"

"I happened to mention your name to the assistant manager of the hotel yesterday," Mr. Goodhart said, "and he said that a Mr. and Mrs. Rudolph Jordache were sometimes guests at the hotel."

Thomas sipped at his whiskey. "That's my brother," he said. He could feel Mr. Goodhart glancing at him curiously, and could guess what he was thinking. "We've gone our different way," he said shortly. "He was the smart one of the family."

"I don't know." Mr. Goodhart waved his glass to take in the boat, the sunlight, the water churning away from the bows, the green and ochre hills of the coast. "Maybe you were the smart one. I worked all my life and it was only when I became an old man and retired that I had the time to do something like this two weeks a year." He chuckled ruefully. "And I was considered the smart one of *my* family."

Mrs. Goodhart came up then, youthful in slacks and a loose sweater and Thomas finished his drink and went and got a whiskey for her. She matched her husband drink for drink, day in and day out.

Mr. Goodhart paid two hundred and fifty dollars a day for the charter, plus fuel, and twelve hundred old francs a day for food for each of the crew. After the charter the year before he had given Thomas five hundred dollars as a bonus. Thomas and Dwyer had tried to figure out how rich a man had to be to afford two weeks at that price, while still paying for a suite at what was probably one of the most expensive hotels in the world. They had given up trying. "Rich, that's all, rich," Dwyer had said. "Christ, can you imagine how many hours thousands of poor bastards in those mills of his in North Carolina have to put in at the machines, coughing their lungs out, so that he can have a swim every day?" Dwyer's attitude toward capitalists had been formed young by a Socialist father who worked in a factory. All workers, in Dwyer's view of labor, coughed their lungs out.

Until the Goodharts, Thomas's feeling about people with a great deal of money, while not quite as formally rigid as Dwyer's, had been composed of a mixture of envy, distrust, and the suspicion that whenever possible a rich man would do whatever harm he could to anyone within his power. His uneasiness with his brother, which had begun when they were boys, for other reasons, had been compounded by Rudolph's rise to wealth. But the Goodharts had shaken old tenets of faith. They had not only made him reflect anew on the subject of marriage, but about old people as well, and the rich, and even about Americans in general. It was too bad that the Goodharts came so early in the season, because after them, it was likely to be downhill until October. Some of the other charter parties they took on more than justified Dwyer's darkest strictures on the ruling classes.

On the last day of the charter, they started back toward the hotel earlier than usual because the wind had sprung up and the sea beyond the island was full of whitecaps. Even between the islands the *Clothilde* was rolling and pulling at her chain. Mr. Goodhart had drunk more than usual, too, and neither he nor his wife had gone below for their siesta. When Dwyer upped anchor they were still in their bathing suits, with sweaters, against the spray. But they stayed out on deck, like children at a party that was soon to end, hungry for the last drop of joy from the declining festival. Mr. Goodhart was even a little curt with Thomas when Thomas didn't automatically produce the afternoon whiskeys.

Once they were out of the lee of the islands it was too rough to use the deck chairs and the Goodharts and Thomas had to hold onto the after rail while they drank their Scotch and sodas.

"I think it's going to be impossible to get the dinghy into the hotel landing," Thomas said. "I'd better tell Dwyer to go around the point and into Antibes."

Mr. Goodhart put out his hand and held Thomas's arm as Thomas started toward the pilot house. "Let's just take a look," Mr. Goodhart said. His eyes were a little bloodshot. "I like a little rough weather from time to time."

"Whatever you say, sir," Thomas said. "I'll go tell Dwyer."

In the pilot house, Dwyer was already fighting the wheel. Kate was seated on the bench that ran along the rear of the structure, munching a roast beef sandwich. She had a hearty appetitie and was a good sailor in all seas.

"We're in for a blow," Dwyer said. "I'm going around the point."

"Go to the hotel," Thomas said.

Kate looked over her sandwich at him in surprise.

"Are you crazy?" Dwyer said. "All the speedboats must have gone back to the harbor hours ago, with this wind. And we'll never get the dinghy in."

"I know," Thomas said. "But they want to take a look."

"It's a pure waste of time," Dwyer grumbled. They had a new charter beginning the next morning at St. Tropez and they had planned to start immediately after discharging the Goodharts. Even with a calm sea and no wind, it would have been a long day, and they would have had to prepare the ship for the new clients en route. The wind was from the north, the mistral, and they would have to hug the coast for protection, which made the voyage much longer. They would also have to reduce speed to keep the hull from pounding too badly. And there would be no question, in this weather, of doing any work below while they were moving.

"It's only a few more minutes," Thomas said soothingly. "They'll see it's impossible and we'll make for Antibes."

"You're the captain," Dwyer said. He pulled viciously at the wheel as a wave quartered against their port side and the *Clothilde* yawed.

Thomas stayed in the pilot house, keeping dry. The Goodharts remained out on deck, soaked by spray, but seeming to enjoy it. There were no clouds and the high afternoon sun shone brightly and when the spray swept over the deck, the two old people shimmered in brief rainbows.

As they passed Golfe Juan, far off to port, with the boats at anchor in the little harbor already bobbing, Mr. Goodhart signaled to Thomas that he and Mrs. Goodhart wanted another drink.

When they got within five hundred yards of the palisade on which the cabanas stood, they saw that the waves were breaking over the little concrete dock to which the speedboats were usually tied. The speedboats, as Dwyer had predicted, were all gone. At the regular swimming place farther along the cliff, the red flag was up and the chain was across the swimming ladder below the restaurant of Eden Roc. The waves went crashing in high over the steps, then pulled back, frothing and green-white, leaving the ladder uncovered down to the last rung before the next wave roared in.

Thomas left the shelter of the pilot house and went out on deck. "I'm afraid I was right, sir," he said to Mr. Goodhart. "There's no getting a boat in with this sea. We'll have to go into port."

"You go into port," Mr. Goodhart said calmly. "My wife and I have decided we'll swim in. Just get the ship in as close as you can without endangering her."

"The red flag's up," Thomas said. "Nobody's in the water."

"The French," Mr. Goodhart said. "My wife and I have swum in surf twice as bad as this at Newport, haven't we, dear?"

"This isn't Newport, sir," Thomas said, making one last attempt. "It's not a sandy beach. You'll get thrown against the rocks if you . . ."

"Like everything in France," Mr. Goodhart said, "it looks worse than it is. Just pull in as close to shore as you think is wise and we'll do the rest. We both feel like a swim."

"Yes, sir," Thomas said. He went back into the pilot house, where Dwyer was spinning the wheel, first revving up one engine, then another, to make tight circles that brought the ship at its closest about three hundred yards from the ladder. "Bring her in another hundred yards," Thomas said. "They're going to swim for it."

"What do they want to do," Dwyer asked, "commit suicide?"

"It's their bones," Thomas said. Then, to Kate, "Put on your bathing suit." He himself was wearing swimming trunks and a sweater.

Without a word, Kate went below for her bathing suit.

"As soon as we're off," Thomas said to Dwyer, "pull away. Get well off the rocks. When you see we've made it, head for port. We'll get a ride in a car and join you. One trip in this stuff is enough. I don't want to swim back."

Kate came up in two minutes, in an old, bleached, blue suit. She was a strong swimmer. Thomas took off his sweater and they both went out on deck. The Goodharts had taken off their sweaters and were waiting for them. In his long, flowered swimming trunks, Mr. Goodhart was massive and tanned by his holiday. His muscles were old muscles, but he must have been powerful in his prime. The little wrinkles of age showed in the skin of Mrs. Goodhart's still shapely legs.

The swimming raft, anchored midway between the *Clothilde* and the steps, was dancing in the waves. When a particularly large one hit it it would go up on end and stand almost perpendicularly for a moment.

"I suggest we make for the raft first," Thomas said, "so we can take a breather before we go in the rest of the way."

"We?" Mr. Goodhart said. "What do you mean, we?" He was definitely drunk. And so was Mrs. Goodhart.

"Kate and I decided we'd like a swim this afternoon, too," Thomas said.

"As you wish, Captain," Mr. Goodhart said. He climbed over the rail and dove in. Mrs. Goodhart followed. Their heads, gray and white, bobbed up and down in the dark green, frothing water.

"You stick with her," Thomas said to Kate. "I'll go with the old man."

He dove overboard and heard Kate splash in just after him.

Getting to the raft wasn't too difficult. Mr. Goodhart swam an old-fashioned trudgeon stroke and kept his head out of the water most of the time. Mrs. Goodhart swam an orthodox crawl and when Thomas turned to look at her she seemed to be swallowing water and breathing hard. But Kate was close beside her at all times. Mr. Goodhart and Thomas climbed onto the raft, but it was too rough to stand up on and they stayed on their knees as they helped pull Mrs. Goodhart up. She was gasping a little and she looked as though she was going to be sick.

"I think we ought to stay here for awhile," Mrs. Goodhart said, trying to keep her balance on the wet cord surface of the heaving raft. "Until it calms down a little."

"It's going to get worse, Mrs. Goodhart," Thomas said. "In a few minutes you won't have a chance of getting in."

Dwyer, worried about being too close to shore, had gone out another five hundred yards and was circling there. Anyway, there was no chance of getting Mrs. Goodhart up on the rolling boat in that sea without hurting her badly.

"You'll just have to come in with us right now," Thomas said to Mrs. Goodhart.

Mr. Goodhart didn't say anything. He was sober now.

"Nathaniel," Mrs. Goodhart said to her husband, "will you tell him I'm going to stay here until the sea calms a bit."

"You heard what he said," Mr. Goodhart said. "You wanted to swim in. Swim in." He toppled into the water.

By now there were at least twenty people clustered on the rocks, safely out of reach of the spume, watching the group on the raft.

Thomas took Mrs. Goodhart's hand and said, "In we go. Together." He stood up shakily and brought her to her feet and they jumped in, holding hands. Once in the sea, Mrs. Goodhart was less frightened and they swam side by side toward the ladder. As they came closer to the rocks, they felt themselves being swept forward by a wave, then sucked back as it broke against the rocks and receded. Thomas trod water and shouted, to be heard above the noise of the sea. "I'll go in first. Then Mrs. Goodhart. Watch how I do it. I'll go in on a wave and catch onto the railing and hold on. Then, I'll give you the signal when to start. Swim as hard as you can. I'll grab you when you get to the ladder. Just hold onto me. You'll be all right." He wasn't sure that anybody would be all right, but he had to say something.

He waited, looking over his shoulder at the oncoming waves. He saw a big one, thrashed hard with his arms, rode it in, smashed against the steel of the ladder, grabbed the railing, hung on against the pull away. Then he stood up, faced seaward. "Now!" he shouted at Mrs. Goodhart, and she came in fast, high above him for an instant, then breaking down. He grabbed her, held her tight, just managing to keep her from sliding back. Hurriedly, he pushed her up the ladder. She stumbled, but got to the safety of the rock platform before the next wave crashed in.

Mr. Goodhart, when he came in, was so heavy that, for a moment, Thomas lost his grip and he thought they were both going to be washed back. But the old man was strong. He swung in the water and grabbed the other pipe, holding onto Thomas at the same time. He didn't need any help up the ladder, but climbed it decorously, looking coldly at the silent group of spectators above him, as though he had caught them prying into some intensely private affair of his own.

Kate came in lightly and she and Thomas climbed the ladder together.

They got towels from the locker room attendant and dried themselves off, although there was nothing to do about their wet suits.

Mr. Goodhart called the hotel for his car and chauffeur and merely said, "That was very well done, Captain," when the car came down for Thomas and Kate. He had borrowed terrycloth robes for himself and Mrs. Goodhart and had ordered them all drinks at the bar while Kate and Thomas were drying themselves off. As he stood there, in the long robe, like a toga, you'd never think that he had been drinking all afternoon and had nearly got them all drowned just fifteen minutes before.

He held the door of the car open for Kate and Thomas. As Thomas got in, Mr. Goodhart said, "We have to settle up, Captain. Will you be in the harbor after dinner?"

Thomas had planned to set out for St. Tropez before sunset, but he said, "Yes, sir. We'll be there all evening."

"Very good, Captain. We'll have a farewell drink aboard." Mr. Goodhart closed the car door and they drove up the driveway, with the pines along its borders thrashing their branches about in the increasing wind.

When Thomas and Kate got out of the car on the quay they left two wet spots on the upholstery where they had been sitting in their bathing suits. The *Clothilde* hadn't come into the harbor yet and they sat with towels wrapped around their shoulders on an overturned dinghy on the quay and shivered.

Fifteen minutes later the *Clothilde* came into port. They grabbed the lines from Dwyer, made her fast, jumped on board, and rushed to put on dry clothes. Kate made a pot of coffee and as they drank it in the pilot house, with the wind whistling through the rigging, Dwyer said, "The rich. They always find a way of making you pay." Then he got out the hose, attached it to a water line on the quay and they all three of them began to scrub down the ship. There was salt crusted everywhere.

*   *   *   *   *   *   *   *   *   *   *   *   *   *   *   *   *   *

After dinner, which Kate prepared from the food left over from the Goodhart's lunch, she and Dwyer went into Antibes with the week's sheets, pillowcases, and towels. Kate did all the personal laundry, but the heavy items had to be done ashore. The wind had died down as suddenly as it had risen, and while the sea was still thundering at the harbor walls outside, the port itself was calm and the *Clothilde*'s buffers were merely nudging gently at the boats on either side from time to time.

It was a clear, warm night, and Thomas sat on the afterdeck, smoking a pipe, admiring the stars, waiting for Mr. Goodhart. He had made up the bill and it was in an envelope in the pilot house. It didn't amount to very much—just fuel, laundry, a few bottles of whiskey and vodka, ice and the twelve hundred francs a day for food for himself and the two others. Mr. Goodhart had given him a check for the charter itself the first day he had come aboard. Before going ashore, Kate had packed the Goodharts' belongings, extra bathing suits, clothes, shoes, and books, in two of the hotel baskets. The baskets were on deck, near the after rail.

Thomas saw the lights of Mr. Goodhart's car coming up to the quay. He stood up as the car stopped and Mr. Goodhart got out and came up the gangplank. He was dressed for the evening, in a gray suit and white shirt and dark silk tie. Somehow he looked older and frailer in his city clothes.

"May I offer you something to drink?" Thomas asked.

"A whiskey would be nice, Captain," Mr. Goodhart said. He was absolutely sober now. "If you'll join me." He sat down in one of the folding canvas-and-wood chairs while Thomas went to the saloon for the drinks. On his way up, he went into the pilot house and got the envelope with the bill.

"Mrs. Goodhart has a slight chill," Mr. Goodhart said, as Thomas gave him the glass. "She's gone to bed for the night. She especially commanded me to tell you how much she enjoyed these two weeks."

"That's very kind of her," Thomas said. "It was a pleasure having her with us." If Mr. Goodhart wasn't going to mention the afternoon's adventure, he wasn't going to say a word about it, either. "I made up the bill, sir," he said. He gave the envelope to Mr. Goodhart. "If you want to go over it and . . ."

Mr. Goodhart waved the envelope negligently. "I'm sure it's in order," he said. He took the bill out, squinted at it briefly in the light of the quay lamp post. He had a checkbook with him and he wrote out a check and handed it to Thomas. "There's a little something extra there for you and the crew, Captain." he said.

Thomas glanced at the check. Five-hundred-dollar bonus. Like last year. "It's most generous of you, sir." Oh, for summers of Goodharts!

Mr. Goodhart waved off gratitude. "Next year," he said, "perhaps we can make it a full month. There's no law that says that we have to spend the whole summer in the house in Newport, is there?" He had explained that ever since he was a boy he had spent July and August in the family house in Newport and now his married son and two daughters and their children spent their holidays there with Mrs. Goodhart and himself. "We could give the house over to the younger generation," Mr. Goodhart went on, as though trying to convince himself. "They could have orgies or whatever the younger generation has these days when we're not around. Maybe we could steal a grandchild or two and go on a real cruise with you." He settled comfortably back in his chair, sipping at his drink, playing with this new idea. "If we had a month, where could we go?"

"Well," Thomas said, "the party we're picking up tomorrow at St. Tropez, two French couples, are only taking the boat for three weeks and with any break in the weather, we can go down the coast of Spain, the Costa Brave, Cadaques, Rosas, Barcelona, then across to the Balearics. And after them, we come back here and there's an English family who want to go south—that's another three week cruise— the Ligurian coast, Portofino, Porto Venere, Elba, Porto Ercole, Corsica, Sardinia, Ischia, Capri . . ."

Mr. Goodhart chuckled. "You're making Newport sound like Coney Island, Captain. Have you been to all those places?"

"Uhuh."

"And people pay you for it?"

"A lot of them make you earn your money, and more," Thomas said. "Not everybody's like you and Mrs. Goodhart."

"Old age has sweetened us, perhaps," Mr. Goodhart said slowly. "In some ways. Do you think I might have another drink, Captain?"

"If you don't plan to do any more swimming tonight," Thomas said, rising and taking Mr. Goodhart's glass.

Mr. Goodhart chuckled. "That was a horse's ass thing to do today, wasn't it?"

"Yes, sir, it was." Thomas was surprised at Mr. Goodhart's using an expression like that. He went below and mixed two more drinks. When he came back on deck, Mr. Goodhart was stretched out in his chair, his long legs crossed at the ankles, his head back, looking up at the stars. He took the glass from Thomas's hand without changing his position.

"Captain," he said, "I've decided to pamper myself. And my wife. I'll make a firm commitment with you right now. Starting June first next year we'll take the *Clothilde* for six weeks and go south to all those pretty names you were reeling off. I'll give you a deposit tonight. And when you say no swimming, nobody will swim. How does that strike you?"

"It would be fine for me, but . . ." Thomas hesitated.

"But what?"

"The *Clothilde*'s all right for you using it during the day the way you do, going to the islands . . . but for six weeks, living aboard . . . I don't know. For some people it's fine, but for others, who are used to luxury . . ."

"You mean for spoiled old crocks like my wife and myself," Mr. Goodhart said, "it's not grand enough, is that it?"

"Well," Thomas said uncomfortably, "I wouldn't like you not to enjoy yourselves. The *Clothilde* rolls quite a bit in rough weather and it's pretty stuffy down below when we're under way, because we have to close all the portholes, and there's no proper bath, just showers, and . . ."

"It'll do us good. We've had it too easy all our lives. Oh, it's ridiculous, Captain." Mr. Goodhart sat up. "You make me ashamed of myself. To have you feel as though going around the Mediterranean on a boat as nice as this one is roughing it for me and my wife. God, it sends cold shivers down my spine to think of the opinion people must have of us."

"People get used to living in different ways," Thomas said.

"You've lived yours the hard way, haven't you?" Mr. Goodhart said.

"No worse than a lot of others."

"You don't seem any the worse for it," Mr. Goodhart said. "In fact, if I may say so, if my son had turned out like you, I'd be more pleased with him than I am now. Considerably more pleased."

"It's hard to know," Thomas said neutrally. If he knew about Port Philip, he thought, burning the cross on VE day, and hitting my father, and taking money for screwing married ladies in Elysium, Ohio, if he knew about blackmailing Sinclair in Boston, and throwing fights, and about Quayles and Quayles's wife in Las Vegas, and about Pappy and Teresa and Falconetti, maybe he wouldn't be sitting there being friendly, with a glass in his hand, wishing his son was more like me. "There's a lot of things I've done I'm not so goddamn proud of," he said.

"That doesn't make you any different from the rest of us, Captain," Goodhart said quietly. "And while we're on the subject—forgive me for this afternoon. I was drunk and I had had two weeks of watching three splendid young people happily working together, moving around like graceful animals, and I felt old and I didn't want to feel old and I wanted to prove that I wasn't all that old and I risked all our lives. Knowingly, Captain, knowingly. Because I was sure you weren't going to let us make that swim alone."

"It's better not to talk about it, sir," Thomas said. "Anyway, no harm was done."

"Old age is an aberration, Tom," Mr. Goodhart said bitterly. "A terrible, perverted aberration." He stood up and put his glass down carefully. "I'd better be getting back to the hotel and see how my wife is doing," he said. He extended his hand and Thomas shook it. "Until next June first," he said and strode off the ship, carrying the two baskets with him.

When Kate and Dwyer came back, with the freshly laundered linen, all Thomas said was that Mr. Goodhart had been and gone and that they had their first charter, six weeks, for the following year.

Dwyer had a letter from his girl. She had been down to the Aegean Hotel, but she had no information for Tom, she said, because Pappy was dead. He had been found, knifed and with a gag in his mouth, in his room, the new man at the desk had told her. Three months ago.

Thomas listened to the news without surprise. That was the kind of business Pappy had run and he had finally paid his dues.

There was something else in the letter that was obviously bothering Dwyer, but he didn't tell the others what it was, although Thomas could guess. Dwyer's girl didn't want to wait any more and she wouldn't leave Boston and if Dwyer wanted to marry her he'd have to go back to America. He hadn't asked Thomas's advice yet, but if he had, Thomas would have told him that no dame was worth it.

They went to bed early, because they were going to set out for St. Tropez at four in the morning, before the wind sprang up.

Kate had made up the big bed in the master cabin for herself and Thomas for the night, because there were no clients on board. It was the first time they had a chance to make love in comfort and Kate said she wasn't going to miss it. In the cabin they shared forward, they had two narrow bunks, one above the other.

Kate's stocky, solid, full-breasted body was not made for showing off clothes, but her skin was wonderfully soft and she made love with gentle avidity and as Thomas lay later, with her in his arms in the big bed, he was grateful that he was not old, that his girl was not in Boston, that he had allowed himself to be persuaded by Pinky to have a woman on board.

Before she went to sleep, Kate said, "Dwyer told me tonight that when you bought the boat you changed the name. Who was Clothilde?"

"She was a queen of France," Thomas said. He pulled her closer to him. "She was somebody I knew as a boy. And she smelled like you."

The cruise to Spain wasn't bad, although they hit some weather off Cap Cruz and had to stay in port for five days at a stretch. The French couples consisted of two paunchy Parisian businessmen and two young women who were definitely not their wives. There was some trading going on between the couples in the after cabins, but Thomas hadn't come to the Mediterranean to teach French businessmen how to behave. As long as they paid their bills and kept the two ladies from walking around in high heels and poking holes in the deck, he wasn't going to interfere with their fun. The ladies also lay on deck with the tops of their bikinis off. Kate took a poor view of that, but one of the ladies had really sensational tits and it didn't interfere with the navigation too much, although if there had been any reefs on the course while Dwyer was at the wheel, Dwyer would have most likely run them aground. That particular lady also made it clear to Thomas that she wouldn't mind sneaking up on deck in the middle of the night to have a go with him while her Jules was snoring away below. But Thomas told her he didn't come with the charter. You got into enough complications with clients without any of that.

Because of the delay caused by the storm, the two French couples got off at

Marseilles, to catch the train up to Paris. The two businessmen had to meet their wives in Paris to go to Deauville for the rest of the summer. When they paid Thomas off at the dock in front of the Mairie in the Vieux Port, the two Frenchmen gave Thomas fifty thousand francs as a tip, which wasn't bad, considering they were Frenchmen. After they had gone, Thomas took Kate and Dwyer to the same restaurant that Dwyer and Thomas had eaten at when they first came to Marseilles on the *Elga Andersen*. It was too bad that the *Elga Andersen* wasn't in port. It would have been satisfying to sail across her rusty bows in the shining white-and-blue *Clothilde* and dip the flag in salute to the old Nazi captain.

They had three days before picking up the next charter in Antibes, and again Kate made up the big bed in the aster cabin for herself and Thomas. She had had the portholes and the doors wide open all evening to get out the smell of perfume.

"That *poule*," Kate said as they lay in the darkness. "Parading around naked. You had a hard on for three weeks running."

Thomas laughed. There were times when Kate talked like any sailor.

"I don't like the way you laugh," Kate said. "Let me warn you—if I ever catch you grabbing any of that stuff, I'm going to go out and jump into the kip with the first man I see as I walk off the boat."

"There's one sure way," Thomas said, "that you can keep me honest."

Kate then made sure that he was going to be honest. That night, anyway. As she lay in his arms he whispered, "Kate, every time I make love to you I forget one more bad thing in my life." A moment later he could feel her tears on his shoulders.

Luxuriously, they slept late the next morning and when they sailed out of the harbor in the sunlight, they even took time off to do a little sight-seeing. They went out to the Château d'If and walked around the fortress and saw the dungeon where the Count of Monte Cristo was supposed to have been chained. Kate had read the book and Thomas had seen the movie. Kate translated the signs that told how many Protestants had been imprisoned in the place before being sent to the galleys.

"There's always somebody sitting on somebody else's back," Dwyer said. "If it's not the Protestants sitting on the Catholics, it's the Catholics sitting on the Protestants."

"Shut up, you Communist," Thomas said.

"Are you a Protestant?" he asked Kate.

"Yes."

"I'm going to imprison you in my galley," he said.

By the time they got back into the *Clothilde* and started East, the last whiff of perfume had vanished from the main cabin.

They sailed without stopping, with Dwyer taking eight full hours at night at the wheel so that Thomas and Kate could sleep. They reached Antibes before noon. There were two letters waiting for Thomas, one from his brother, and one in a handwriting he didn't recognize. He opened the letter from Rudolph first.

"Dear Tom,"—he read,—"I finally got news of you after all this time and I must say it sounds as if you're doing all right for yourself. A few days ago I received a call at my office from a Mr. Goodhart, who told me he had been on your boat, or ship, as I believe you fellows like to call it. It turns out that we have done some business with his firm, and I guess he was curious to see what your brother looked like. He invited Jean and myself over for a drink and he and his wife turned out to be charming old people, as you must know. They were most enthusiastic about you and about your ship and the life you lead. Maybe you've made the best investment of the century with the money you made on Dee Cee. If I weren't so busy (it looks as though I'm going to allow myself to be talked into running for mayor of Whitby this fall!), I'd take a plane with Jean immediately and come over to sail the deep blue sea with you. Maybe next year. In the meantime, I've taken the liberty of suggesting renting the *Clothilde* (as you see the Goodharts were most explicit about everything) to a friend of mine who is getting married and would like to spend his honeymoon on the Mediterranean. Perhaps you remember him—Johnny Heath. If he bothers you, put him adrift in a raft.

"But seriously, I am very happy for you and I'd like to hear from you and if there's anything I can do for you, please don't hesitate to let me know what it is. Love, Rudolph."

Thomas scowled as he read the letter. He didn't like to be reminded that it was because of Rudolph that he now owned the *Clothilde*. Still, the letter was so friendly, the weather was so fine, and the summer was going so well, it was silly to spoil things by remembering old grudges. He folded the letter carefully and put it in his pocket. The other letter was from Rudolph's friend and asked if he could charter the *Clothilde* from September fifteenth to the thirtieth. It was the end of the season, and they had nothing on the books, and it would be found money. Heath said he only wanted to sail up and down the coast between Monte Carlo and St. Tropez, and with only two people on board and very little mileage to cover, it would be a lazy way to end the season.

Thomas sat down and wrote a letter to Heath, telling him he'd meet him either at the Nice airport or the Antibes station on the fifteenth.

He told Kate about the new charter and how it was his brother who had arranged it, and she made him write a letter of thanks to Rudolph. He had signed it and was just going to seal the envelope, when he remembered that Rudolph had written him that if there was anything he could do for him not to hesitate to let him know what it was. Well, why not, he thought. It couldn't do any harm. In a P.S. he wrote, "There's one thing you can do for me. For various reasons I haven't been able to come back to New York so far but maybe those reasons don't hold any more. I haven't had any news of my kid for years and I don't know where he is or whether I'm still married or not. I'd like to come over and see him and if possible take him back here with me for awhile. Maybe you remember the night you and Gretchen came back after my fight in Queens, there was my manager, a man I introduced you to called Schultzy. Actually his name is Herman Schultz. The last address I had for him is the Bristol Hotel on Eighth Avenue, but maybe he doesn't live there any more. But if you ask somebody in the Garden office if they know where you can lay your hands on Schultzy they're bound to know if he's still alive and in town. He's likely to have some news about Teresa and the kid. Just don't tell him where I am for the time being. But ask him if the heat's still on. He will understand. Let me know if you find him and what he says. This will be a real good turn and I will be really grateful."

He air-mailed the two letters at the Antibes post office and then went back to the ship to get it ready for the English party.

CHAPTER 4

I

NOBODY HAD REMEMBERED Herman Schultz at the Bristol Hotel, but somebody in the publicity department at Madison Square Garden had finally come up with the address of a rooming house on West Fifty-third Street. Rudolph was getting to know Fifty-third Street very well. He had been there three times in the last four weeks, on every trip he had made to New York in the month of August. Yes, the man at the rooming house said, Mr. Schultz stayed there when he was in New York, but he was out of town. He didn't know where out of town. Rudolph left his telephone number with him, but Schultz never called him. Rudolph had to suppress a quiver of distaste every time he rang the bell. It was a decaying building in a dying neighborhood, inhabited, you felt, only by doomed old men and derelict young men.

A shuffling, bent old man with a twisted hair piece opened the peeling door, the color of dried blood. From the gloom of the hallway he peered nearsightedly at Rudolph standing on the stoop in the hot September sun. Even with the distance between them, Rudolph could smell him, mildew and urine.

"Is Mr. Schultz at home?" Rudolph asked.

"Fourth floor back," the old man said. He stepped aside to allow Rudolph to enter.

As he climbed the steps, Rudolph realized that it wasn't only the old man who smelled like that, it was the entire house. A radio was playing Spanish music, a fat man, naked to the waist, was sitting at the head of the second flight of steps, his head in his hands. He didn't look up as Rudolph squeezed past him.

The door to the fourth floor back was open. It was stifling hot, under the roof. Rudolph recognized the man he had been introduced to as Schultzy in Queens. Schultzy was sitting on the edge of an unmade bed, grayish sheets, staring at the wall of the room, three feet across from him. Rudolph knocked on the framework of the doorway. Schultzy turned his head slowly, painfully.

"What do you want?" Schultz said. His voice was reedy and hostile.

Rudolph went in. "I'm Tom Jordache's brother." He extended his hand.

Schultz put his right hand behind his back. He was wearing a sweat-stained skivvy shirt. He still had the basketball of a stomach. He moved his mouth uneasily, as though he was wearing plates that fit badly. He was pasty and totally bald. "I don't shake hands," Schultz said. "It's the arthritis." He didn't ask Rudolph to sit down. There was no place to sit down except on the bed, anyway.

"That sonofabitch," Schultz said. "I don't want to hear him name."

Rudolph took out his wallet and extracted two twenty-dollar bills. "He asked me to give you this."

"Put it on the bed." Schultz's expression, snakelike and livid, did not change. "He owes me one fifty."

"I'll have him send the rest over tomorrow," Rudolph said.

"It's about fucking well time," Schultz said. "What does he want now? Did he put the boots to somebody else again?"

"No," Rudolph said, "he's not in trouble."

"I'm sorry to hear it," Schultz said.

"He asked me to ask you if the heat's still on." The words sounded strange to him as they came off his tongue.

Schultz's face became sly, secretive, and he looked sideways at Rudolph. "You sure he's going to give me the rest of the money tomorrow?"

"Positive," Rudolph said.

"Nah," Schultz said. "There's no more heat. There's no more anything. That bum Quayles never had a good night again after your shitty brother got through with him. The one chance I ever had to make a real buck. Not that they left me much of a share, the dagoes. And I was the one who discovered Quayles and brought him along. No, there's no heat. Everybody's dead or in jail. Nobody remembers your goddamn brother's name. He can walk down Fifth Avenue at the head of the Columbus Day Parade and nobody'd raise a finger. Tell him that. Tell him that's worth a lot more than one fifty."

"I will, Mr. Schultz," Rudolph said, trying to sound as though he knew what the old man was talking about. "And then there's another question . . ."

"He wants a lot of anwers for his money, don't he?"

"He wants to know about his wife."

Schultz cackled. "That whore," he said, pronouncing the word in two syllables.

"She got her picture in the papers. In the *Daily News*. Twice. She got picked up twice for soliciting in bars. She said her name was Theresa Laval in the papers. French. But I recognized the bitch. Some French. They're all whores, every last one of them. I could tell you stories, mister . . ."

"Do you know where she lives?" Rudolph didn't relish the thought of spending the afternoon in the sweltering, evil-smelling room listening to Schultz's opinions of the female sex. "And where the boy is?"

Schultz shook his head. "Who keeps track? I don't even know where *I* live. Theresa Laval. French." He cackled again. "Some French."

"Thank you very much, Mr. Schultz," Rudolph said. "I won't trouble you any more."

"Ain't no trouble. Glad for a little conversation. You for sure going to send over that money tomorrow?"

"I guarantee."

"You're wearing a good suit," Schultz said. "But that ain't no guarantee."

Rudolph left him sitting on the bed, his head nodding in the heat. He went down the steps quickly. Even West Fifty-third Street looked good to him when he put the rooming house behind him.

II

He had Rudolph's cable in his pocket when he got off the plane at Kennedy and went with hundreds of other passengers through the Health and Immigration formalities. The last time he had been at the airport it had been called Idlewild. Taking a bullet through your head was an expensive way of getting an airport named after you.

The big Irishman with the Immigration badge looked at him as though he didn't like the idea of letting him back into the country. And he thumbed through a big, black book, full of names, hunting for Jordache, and seemed disappointed that he couldn't find it.

He went into the Customs hall to wait for his bag. The whole population of America seemed to be coming back from a holiday in Europe. Where did all the money come from?

He looked up at the glass-enclosed balcony where people were lined up two and three deep waving at relatives down below that they had come to meet. He had cabled Rudolph his flight number and time of arrival, but he couldn't pick him out in the crowd behind the glass window. He had a moment of irritation. He didn't want to go wandering around New York hunting for his brother.

The cable had been waiting for him for a week when he came back to Antibes after the charter with Heath and his wife. "Dear Tom," the cable read, "Everything OK for you here Stop Believe will have sons address soonest Love Rudolph."

He finally saw his bag in the bin and grabbed it and went and stood in line to go through the Customs counter. Some idiot from Syracuse was sweating and telling a long story to the inspector about where he had gotten two embroidered dirndls and whom they were for. When it was his turn, the inspector made him open his bag and went through everything. He had no gifts for anyone in America, and the inspector passed him through.

He said no to a porter who wanted to carry his bag and carried it through the exit doors himself. Standing bareheaded among the crowd, looking cooler than anybody else in a pair of slacks and a lightweight jacket, Rudolph waved at him. They shook hands and Rudolph tried to take the bag from him, but Thomas wouldn't let him.

"Have a good trip?" Rudolph asked him as they walked out of the building.

"Okay."

"I've got my car parked near here," Rudolph said. "Wait here. I'll just be a minute."

As he went for the car, Thomas noted that Rudolph still walked in that peculiar gliding way, not moving his shoulders.

He opened his collar and pulled his tie down. Although it was the beginning of October, it was stinking hot, wet smoggy heat, smelling of burned kerosene. He had forgotten the climate of New York. How did anyone live here?

Five minutes later Rudolph drove up in a blue Buick coupe. Thomas threw his bag in the back and got in. The car was air-conditioned, which was a relief. Rudolph drove at just the legal speed and Thomas remembered being picked up by the state troopers with the bottle of bourbon and the Smith and Wesson in the car on the way to his mother's deathbed. Times had changed. For the better.

"Well?" Thomas said.

"I found Schultz." Rudolph said. "That's when I sent you the wire. He said the heat's off. Everybody's dead or in jail, he said. I didn't inquire what that meant."

"What about Teresa and the kid?"

Rudolph fiddled with the air-conditioning levers, frowning. "Well, it's a little hard to begin."

"Come on. I'm a big, strong fella."

"Schultz didn't know where either of them was. But he said he saw your wife's picture in the newspapers. Twice."

"What the hell for?" For a moment, Thomas was rattled. Maybe the crazy dame had finally made it on the stage or in a nightclub.

"She was arrested for soliciting in a bar. Twice," Rudolph said. "I hate to be the one who has to tell you this, Tom."

"Forget it," Thomas said roughly. "It figured."

"Schultz said she was using another name, but he recognized her," Rudolph said. "I checked. It was her. The police gave me her address."

"If I can afford her prices," Thomas said, "maybe I'll go around and give her a screw. Maybe she's learned how to do it by now." He saw the pained expression on Rudolph's face, but he hadn't crossed the ocean to be polite. "How about the kid?"

"He's up at a military school near Poughkeepsie," Rudolph said. "I just found out two days ago."

"Military school," Thomas said. "Christ. Do the officers get to bang his mother on maneuvers?"

Rudolph drove without speaking, allowing Thomas to get his bitterness out.

"That's just what I want my kid to be," Thomas said. "A soldier. How did you get all this good news?"

"A private detective."

"Did he talk to the bitch?"

"No."

"So nobody knows I'm here?"

"Nobody," Rudolph said. "Except me. I did one other thing. I hope you won't mind."

"What's that?"

"I talked to a lawyer friend of mine. Without mentioning any names. You can get a divorce and custody without any trouble. Because of the two convictions."

"I hope they put her in jail and throw away the key."

"Just overnight each time. And a fine."

"They got some great lawyers in this city, don't they?" He remembered his days in the jail in Elysium. Two out of three in the family.

"Look," Rudolph said, "I have to get back to Whitby tonight. You can come with me if you want. Or you can stay in the apartment. It's empty. There's a maid comes in every morning to clean up."

"Thanks. I'll take you up on the apartment. I want to see that lawyer you talked to first thing in the morning. Can you fix it?"

"Yes."

"You got her address and the name of the school and all that?"

Rudolph nodded.

"That's all I need," Thomas said.

"How long do you plan to stay in New York?"

"Just long enough to make sure of the divorce and go up and get the kid and take him back to Antibes with me."

Rudolph didn't say anything for awhile and Thomas looked out the window to his right at the boats moored in Flushing Bay. He was glad the *Clothilde* was in Antibes harbor and not in Flushing Bay.

"Johnny Heath wrote me that he had a wonderful trip with you," Rudolph said. "He said his bride loved it."

"I don't know when she had the time to love anything," Thomas said. "She was going up and down the ladder changing her clothes every five minutes. She must have had thirty bags with her. It was lucky there were only two of them. We filled two empty cabins with her luggage."

Rudolph smiled. "She comes from a very rich family."

"It sticks out all over her. He's okay, though. Your friend. Didn't mind rough weather and asked so many questions by the end of the two weeks he could have sailed the *Clothilde* by himself right to Tunis. He said he was going to ask you and your wife to come with him on a cruise next summer."

"If I have the time," Rudolph said quickly.

"What's this about your running for mayor of that little one-horse town?" Thomas asked.

"It's far from a one-horse town," Rudolph said. "Don't you think it's a good idea?"

"I wouldn't wipe my feet on the best politician in the country," Thomas said.

"Maybe I'll make you change your mind," Rudolph said.

"They had one good man," Thomas said, "so naturally they shot him."

"They can't shoot all of them."

"They can try," Thomas said. He leaned over and turned on the radio. The roar of a crowd filled the car and then an excited announcer's voice, saying, ". . . a clean line drive into center field, the runner is rounding second, it's going to be close, close, he goes into his slide. Safe! Safe!" Thomas turned the radio off.

"The World Series," Rudolph said.

"I know. I get the Paris *Herald Tribune.*"

"Tom," Rudolph said, "don't you ever miss America?"

"What's America done for me?" Thomas said. "I don't care if I never see it again after this time."

"I hate to hear you talk like that."

"One patriot in the family is enough," Thomas said.

"What about your son?"

"What about him?"

"How long are you figuring you'll keep him in Europe?"

"Forever," Thomas said. "Maybe when you get elected President and straighten out the whole country and put all the crooks and generals and policemen and judges and congressmen and high-priced lawyers in jail and if they don't shoot you maybe I'll send him over on a visit."

"What about his education?" Rudolph persisted.

"There're schools in Antibes. Better than a crappy military academy."

"But he's an American."

"Why?" Thomas asked.

"Well, he's not a Frenchman."

"He won't be a Frenchman either," Thomas said. "He'll be Wesley Jordache."

"He won't know where he belongs."

"Where do you think *I* belong? Here?" Thomas laughed. "My son'll belong on a boat in the Mediterranean, sailing from one country where they make wine and olive oil to another country where they make wine and olive oil."

Rudolph quit then. They drove the rest of the way in silence to the building on Park Avenue where Rudolph had an apartment. The doorman double-parked the car for him when he said he'd only be a few minutes. The doorman gave a queer look at Thomas, with his collar open and his tie loose and his blue, wide-trousered suit and green fedora hat with the brown band that he had bought in Genoa.

"Your doorman doesn't approve of my clothes," Thomas said as they went up in the elevator. "Tell him I buy my clothes in Marseilles and everybody knows Marseilles is the greatest center of *haute couture* for men in Europe."

"Don't worry about the doorman," Rudolph said as he led Thomas into the apartment.

"Not a bad little place you have here," Thomas said, standing in the middle of the large living room, with its fireplace and long, straw-colored corduroy couch, with two winged easy chairs on each side of it. There were fresh flowers in vases on the tables, a pale-beige wall-to-wall carpet, and bright, non-objective paintings on the dark-green walls. The room faced west and the afternoon sun streamed in through the curtained windows. The air-conditioning was on, humming softly, and the room was comfortably cool.

"We don't get down to the city as much as we'd like," Rudolph said. "Jean's pregnant again and she's having a bad couple of months just now." He opened a cupboard "Here's the bar," he said. "There's ice in the refrigerator. If you want to eat here, just tell the maid when she gets in in the morning. She's a pretty good cook." He led Thomas into the spare room, which Jean had made over to look exactly like the guest room in the farmhouse in Whitby, countrified and delicate. Rudolph couldn't help but notice how out of place his brother looked in the neat, feminine room, with its four-poster twin beds and patchwork quilts.

Thomas threw his battered valise and his jacket and hat on one of the beds and Rudolph tried not to wince. On his boat, Johnny Heath had written, Tom was a stickler for neatness. Obviously, he did not carry his seagoing habits with him when he went ashore.

Back in the living room Rudolph poured a whiskey and soda for Thomas and himself and while they drank, got out the papers he had collected from the Police Department and the report from the private detective and gave them to Thomas. He called the lawyer's office and made an appointment for Thomas for the next morning at ten.

"Now," he said, as they finished their drinks, "is there anything else you need? Do you want me to go with you when you go up to the school?"

"I'll handle the school on my own," Thomas said. "Don't worry."

"How are you fixed for money?"

"I'm rolling," Thomas said. "Thanks."

"If anything comes up," Rudolph said, "call me."

"Okay, mayor," Thomas said.

They shook hands and Rudolph left his brother standing next to the table on which lay the reports from the Police Department and the detective. Thomas was picking them up to read as Rudolph went out the front door.

Teresa Jordache, Thomas read from the police file, alias Theresa Laval. Thomas grinned. He was tempted to call her up and ask her to come over. He'd disguise his voice. "Apartment 14B, Miss Laval. It's on Park Avenue between Fifty-seventh and Fifty-eighth street." Even the most suspicious whore wouldn't think there'd by any trouble at an address like that. He would love to see her face when she rang the bell and he opened the door. He nearly went to the phone to dial the last number the detective had ferreted out, then stopped. It would be almost impossible not to give her the beating she deserved and that wasn't what he had come to America for.

*   *   *   *   *   *   *   *.   *   *   *   *   *   *   *   *   *

He shaved and showered, using the perfumed soap in the bathroom, and had another drink and put on a clean shirt and the blue Marseilles suit, then went down in the elevator and walked over to Fifth Avenue in the dusk. On a side street he saw a steak place and went in and had a steak with half a bottle of wine and apple pie à la mode, to salute his native country. Then he strolled over to Broadway. Broadway was worse than ever, with noise coming out of the music shops and bigger and uglier signs than he remembered and the people pushing and sick looking, but he enjoyed it. He could walk anywhere, go to any bar, any movie.

Everybody was dead or in jail. Music.

The Hilltop Military Academy was on top of a hill and it was military. A high, gray, stone wall enclosed it, like a prison, and when Thomas drove through the front gate in the car he had rented, he could see boys in blue-gray uniforms doing close-order drill on a dusty field. The weather had turned cooler and some of the trees on the grounds had begun to change color. The driveway passed close to the parade grounds and Thomas stopped the car and watched. There were four separate groups wheeling and marching on different parts of the field. The group of boys nearest to him, perhaps thirty of them, were between twelve and fourteen, just about Wesley's age. Thomas stared at them as they passed him, but if Wesley was among them he didn't recognize him.

He started the car again and went up the driveway to a stone building that looked like a small castle. The grounds were well kept, with flower beds and closely mown lawns and the other buildings were large and solidly built, of the same stone as the little castle.

Teresa must get a fancy price for her services, Thomas thought, to afford a place like this for the kid.

He got out of the car and went into the building. The granite hallway was dark and chilly. It was lined with flags, sabers, crossed rifles, and marble lists of the names of graduates who had been killed in the Spanish-American War, the Mexican Expedition, the First World War, the Second World War, and the war in Korea. It was like the head office of a company, with a display advertising their product. A boy with close-cropped hair and a lot of fancy chevrons on his arm was coming down the steps, and Thomas asked him, "Son, where's the main office here?"

The boy came to attention, as though Thomas were General MacArthur, and said, "This way, sir." They obviously taught respect to the older generation at Hilltop Military Academy. Maybe that was why Teresa had sent the kid here. She could use all the respect going.

The boy opened the door to a big office. Two women were working at desks behind a small fence. "Here you are, sir," the boy said, and clicked his heels before turning smartly back into the hallway. Thomas went over toward the nearest desk behind the fence. The woman there looked up from papers she was making checks on and said, "May I help you, sir?" She was not in uniform and she didn't click her heels.

"I have a son in the school," Thomas said. "My name is Jordache. I'd like to speak to whoever is in charge here."

The woman gave him a peculiar look, as though the name meant something not particularly pleasant to her. She stood up and said, "I'll tell Colonel Bainbridge you're here, sir. Won't you please take a seat." She indicated a bench along the wall and waddled off to a door on the other side of the office. She was fat and about fifty and her stocking were crooked. They were not tempting the young soldiers with much sex at the Hilltop Military Academy.

After a little while she came out of the door and opened a gate in the little fence and said, "Colonel Bainbridge will see you now, sir. Thank you for waiting." She led Thomas to the rear of the room and closed the door after him as he went into Colonel Bainbridge's office. There were more flags there and photographs of General Patton and General Eisenhower and of Colonel Bainbridge looking fierce in a combat jacket and pistol and helmet, with binoculars hanging around his neck, taken during World War Two. Colonel Bainbridge himself, in a regular U.S. Army uniform, was standing behind his desk to greet Thomas. He was thinner than in the photograph, with almost no hair, and he was wearing silver-rimmed glasses and no weapons or binoculars and he looked like an actor in a war play.

"Welcome to Hilltop, Mr. Jordache," Colonel Bainbridge said. He was not standing at attention but he gave the impression that he was. "Won't you sit down?" His expression was peculiar, too, a little like the doorman's at Rudolph's building.

If I stay in America much longer, Thomas thought as he sat down, I guess I'll have to change my tailor.

"I don't want to take up much of your time, Colonel," Thomas said. "I just came up here to see my son, Wesley."

"Yes, of course, I understand," Bainbridge said. He was stumbling a little over his words. "There's a games period shortly and we'll have him sent for." He cleared his throat embarrassedly. "It's a pleasure to have a member of the young man's family finally visit the school. I am correct in assuming that you *are* his father, am I not?"

"That's what I told the lady outside," Thomas said.

"I hope you'll forgive me for the question, Mr. . . . . Mr. Jordache," Bainbridge said, looking distractedly at General Eisenhower on the wall, "but in Wesley's application it was clearly stated that his father was dead."

The bitch, Thomas thought, oh, the stinking, miserable bitch. "Well," he said, "I'm not dead."

"I can see that," Bainbridge said nervously. "Of course I can see that. It must be a clerical error of some kind, although it's hard to understand how . . ."

"I've been away a few years," Thomas said. "My wife and I are not on friendly terms."

"Even so." Bainbridge's hand fluttered over a small model brass cannon on his desk. "Of course, one doesn't meddle in intimate family matters . . . I've never had the honor of meeting Mrs. Jordache. Our communication was entirely by mail. It *is* the same Mrs. Jordache, isn't it?" Bainbridge said desperately. "In the antique business in New York?"

"She may handle some antiques," Thomas said. "I wouldn't know. Now, I want to see my son."

"They'll be finished with drill in five minutes," Bainbridge said. "I'm sure he'll be happy to see you. Very happy. Seeing his father may just be what he needs at this particular moment . . ."

"Why? What's the matter with him?"

"He's a difficult boy, Mr. Jordache, very difficult. We have our problems with him."

"What problems?"

"He's extraordinarily . . . uh . . . pugnacious." Bainbridge seemed happy to have found the word. "He's constantly getting into fights. With everyone. No matter what age or size. On one occasion last term he even hit one of the instructors. General science. The instructor missed a whole week of classes. He's very . . . adept . . . shall we say, with his fists, young Wesley. Of course, we like a boy to show a normal amount of aggressiveness in a school of this nature, but Wesley . . ." Bainbridge sighed. "His disagreements are not ordinary schoolboy fights. We've had to hospitalize boys, upperclassmen . . . To be absolutely frank with you, there's a kind of, well, the only word is adult, adult *viciousness* about the boy that we on the staff consider very dangerous."

Jordache blood, Thomas thought bitterly, fucking Jordache blood.

"I'm afraid I have to tell you, Mr. Jordache, that Wesley is on probation this term, with no privileges," Bainbridge said.

"Well, Colonel," Thomas said, "I have some good news for you. I'm going to do something about Wesley and his problems."

"I'm glad to hear that you propose to take the matter in hand, Mr. Jordache," Bainbridge said. "We've written innumerable letters to his mother but she seems to be too busy even to reply."

"I propose to take him out of school this afternoon," Thomas said. "You can stop worrying."

Bainbridge's hand trembled on the brass cannon on his desk. "I wasn't suggesting anything as drastic as that, sir," he said. His voice quavered a little. The battlefields of Normandy and the Rhine basin were far behind him and he was an old man, dressed up like a soldier.

"Well, *I'm* suggesting it, Colonel."

Bainbridge stood up too, behind his desk. "I'm afraid it's most . . . most irregular," he said. "We would have to have his mother's written permission. After all, all our dealings have been with her. She has paid the tuition for the entire school year. We would have to authenticate your relationship with the boy."

Thomas took out his wallet and drew his passport from it and put it on the desk in front of Bainbridge. "Who does this look like?" he asked.

Bainbridge opened the little green book. "Of course," he said, "your name is Jordache. But otherwise . . . Really, sir, I must get in touch with the boy's mother . . ."

"I don't want to waste any more of your time, Colonel," Thomas said. He dug into his inside pocket once more and brought out the Police Department report on Teresa Jordache, alias Theresa Laval. "Read this, please," he said, handing the paper to the Colonel.

Bainbridge glanced at the report, then took off his glasses and rubbed his eyes wearily. "Oh dear," he said. He handed the paper back to Thomas, as though he were afraid that if it lay around his office one moment more it would go permanently into the files of the school.

"Do you still want to keep the kid?" Thomas asked brutally.

"Of course, this alters things," Bainbridge said. "Considerably."

A half hour later, they drove out the gate of the Hilltop Military Academy. Wesley's footlocker was on the back seat and Wesley, still in uniform, was up front beside Thomas. He was big for his age, sallow skinned and pimpled, and around his sullen eyes and wide, set mouth, he resembled, as a son does his father, Axel Jordache. He had not been effusive when he was brought in to see Thomas and had seemed neither glad nor sorry when he was told he was being taken from the school and he hadn't asked where Thomas was taking him.

"Tomorrow," Thomas said, as the school disappeared behind them, "you're going to get some decent clothes. And you've had your last fight."

The boy was silent.

"Did you hear me?"

"Yes, sir."

"Don't call me sir. I'm your father," Thomas said.

CHAPTER 5

1966

FOR A FEW minutes at a time, while she was working, Gretchen forgot that it was her fortieth birthday. She sat on the high steel stool in front of the moviola, pushing the levers, gazing intently into the glass screen. She ran film and sound track together, her hands in dirty white-cotton gloves, emulsion stained. The spoor of film. She made swift marks in soft red pencil, giving the strips to her assistant to splice and file. From adjacent cutting rooms on the floor in the building on Broadway, where other companies rented rooms, came scraps of voices, screeches, explosions, orchestral passages, and the shrill gabble as track was run backward at high speed. Engrossed in her own labor she hardly noticed the noise. It was part of the furniture of a cutting room, with the clacking machines, the distorted sounds, the round tins of film stacked on the shelves.

This was her third picture as a head cutter. Sam Corey had taught her well as his assistant and then, after praising her highly to directors and producers, had sent her off on her own, to get her first independent job. Skilled and imaginative, with no ambition to become a director herself that would arouse jealousy, she was in great demand and could pick and choose among the jobs offered her.

The picture she was working on now was being shot in New York and she found the city's impersonal variety exhilarating after the inbred, ambiguously jovial, big-family atmosphere of Hollywood, where everybody lived in everyone else's pocket. In her free hours she tried to continue with the political activities that had taken up a great deal of her time in Los Angeles since Colin's death. With her assistant, Ida Cohen, she went to meetings where people made speeches about the war in Viet Nam and school busing. She signed dozens of petitions and tried to get the important people in the movie business to sign them, too. All this helped her assuage her sense of guilt about having given up her studies in California. Also, Billy was now of a draftable age, and the thought of her one son being killed in Viet Nam was intolerable to her. Ida had no sons but was even more intense about the meetings, demonstrations, and petitions than Gretchen. They both wore Ban the Bomb buttons on their blouses and on their coats.

When she wasn't going to meetings in the evenings, Gretchen went as often as she could to the theater, with a renewed appetite for it, after the years of being away. Sometimes she went with Ida, a small, dowdy, shrewd woman of about her own age, with whom she had developed a steady friendship, sometimes she went with Evans Kinsella, the director of the picture, with whom she was having an affair, sometimes with Rudolph and Jean, when they were in town, or with one or another of the actors she met when she visited the locations on which they were shooting.

The images passed before her on the glass screen and she grimaced. The way Kinsella had done the shooting made it difficult to get the tone that she felt the sequence needed. If she couldn't somehow correct it by more ingenious cutting, or if Kinsella himself couldn't come up with some ideas on it, she knew that eventually the whole scene would have to be reshot.

She stopped for a cigarette. The film tins she and Ida used for ash trays were always brimming with butts. Here and there stood empty coffee containers, lipstick stained.

Forty years old, she thought inhaling.

Nobody today had as yet congratulated her. With good reason. Although she had looked for a telegram, at least, in her box at the hotel, from Billy. There had been no telegram. She hadn't told Ida, now rewinding long strips of film on spools out of a big canvas basket. Ida was past forty herself, why drive in another spike? And she certainly hadn't told Evans. He was thirty-two. A forty-year-old woman did not remind a thirty-two-year-old lover of her birthday.

She thought of her dead mother, forty years ago today. First born, a girl, to a girl scarcely more than twenty herself. If Mary Pease Jordache had known that day what words were going to pass between herself and the new infant in her arms, what tears would she have shed? And Billy . . . ?

The door opened and Evans Kinsella came in. He was wearing a white, belted raincoat over his corduroy slacks and red polo shirt and cashmere sweater. He made no sartorial concessions to New York. His raincoat was wet. She hadn't looked out the window for hours and didn't know it was raining.

"Hi, girls," Evans said. He was a tall thin man with tousled black hair and a blue-black beard that made him look as if he needed a shave at all times. His enemies said he looked like a wolf. Gretchen varied between thinking he was alertly handsome and Jewishly ugly, although he was not a Jew. Kinsella was his real name. He had been in analysis for three years. He had already made six pictures, three of which had been very successful. He was a lounger. As soon as he entered a room he leaned against something or sat on a desk, or if there were a couch handy lay down and put his feet up. He was wearing suede desert boots.

He kissed Ida on the cheek, then Gretchen. He had made one picture in Paris and had learned to kiss everybody there. The picture had been disastrous. "A foul day," he said. He swung himself up on one of the high, metal cutting benches. He made a point of seeming at home wherever he was. "We got in two set-ups this morning and then the rains came. Just as well. Hazen was drunk by noon." Richard Hazen was the male star of the picture. He was always drunk by noon. "How's it going here?" Evans asked. "We ready to run?"

"Just about," Gretchen said. She was sorry she hadn't realized how late it was. She would have done something about her hair and put on fresh make-up to be ready for Evans. "Ida," she said, "will you take the last sequence with you and tell Freddy to run it after the rushes?"

They went down the hall to the small projection room at the end of the corridor. Evans pinched her arm secretly. "Gretchen," he said, "beautiful toiler in the vineyards."

They sat in the darkened projection room and watched the rushes of the day before, the same scene, from different angles, done over and over again, that would one day, they hoped, be arranged into one harmonious flowing entity and be shown on huge screens in theaters throughout the world. As she watched, Gretchen thought again how Evans' talent, kinky and oblique, showed in every foot of film he shot. She made mental notes of how she would make the first cut of the material. Richard Hazen had been drunk before noon yesterday, too, she saw. In two years nobody would give him a job.

"What do you think?" Evans asked, when the lights went up.

"You might as well quit every morning by one," Gretchen said, "if Hazen's working."

"It shows, eh?" Evans was sitting slouched low in his chair, his legs over the back of the chair in front of him.

"It shows," Gretchen said.

"I'll talk to his agent."

"Try talking to his bartender," Gretchen said.

"Drink," Evans said, "Kinsella's curse. When drunk by others."

The room went dark again and they watched the sequence Gretchen had been working on all day. Projected that way, it seemed even worse to Gretchen than it had been on the moviola. But when it was over and the lights went up again, Evans said, "Fine. I like it."

Gretchen had know Evans for two years and had already done a picture with him before this one and she had come to recognize that he was too easily pleased with his own work. Somewhere in his analysis he had come to the conclusion that arrogance was good for his ego and it was dangerous to criticize him openly. "I'm not so sure," Gretchen said. "I'd like to fiddle with it some more."

"A waste of time," Evans said. "I tell you it's okay."

Unlike most directors he was impatient in the cutting room and careless about details.

"I don't know," Gretchen said. "It seems to me to drag."

"That's just what I want right there," Evans said. "I *want* it to drag." He argued like a stubborn child.

"All those people going in and out of doors," Gretchen persisted, "with those ominous shadows with nothing ominous happening . . . "

"Stop trying to make me into Colin Burke." Evans stood up abruptly. "My name is Evans Kinsella, in case it slipped your mind, and Evans Kinsella it will remain. Please remember that."

"Oh, stop being an infant," Gretchen snapped at him. Sometimes the two functions she served for Evans became confused.

"Where's my coat? Where did I leave my goddamn coat?" he said loudly.

"You left it in the cutting room."

They went back to the cutting room together, Evans allowing her to carry the cans of film they had just run and which she picked up from the projectionist. Evans put on his coat, roughly. Ida was making out the sheet for the film they had handled that day. Evans started out of the door, then stopped and came back to Gretchen. "I had intended to ask you to have dinner with me and take in a movie," he said. "Can you make it?" He smiled placatingly. He dreaded the thought of being disliked, even for a moment.

"I'm sorry," Gretchen said. "My brother's coming to pick me up. I'm going up to his place for the weekend."

Evans looked forlorn. He was capable of sixty moods a minute. "I'm free as a bird this weekend. I'd hoped we could . . . " He looked over at Ida, as though he wished she were out of the room. Ida continued working stolidly on her sheets.

"I'll be back Sunday night in time for dinner," Gretchen said.

"Okay," Evans said. "I suppose I'll have to settle for that. Give my regards to your brother. And congratulate him for me."

"For what?"

"Didn't you see his picture in *Look?* He's famous all over America. This week."

"Oh, that," Gretchen said. The magazine had run a piece under the title "Ten Political Hopefuls Under Forty," and there had been two photographs of Rudolph, one with Jean in the living room of their house, one at his desk in the town hall. Rising fast in Republican councils, the article had said about handsome young Mayor with beautiful, rich young wife. Moderate liberal thinker, energetic administrator. Was not just another theoretical politician; had met a payroll all his life. Had streamlined town government, integrated housing, cracked down on industrial pollution, jailed former police chief and three patrolmen for accepting bribes, raised a bond issue for new schools; as influential trustee of Whitby University had been instrumental in making it a co-educational institution; far-seeing town-planner, had experimented with closing off center of town to traffic on Saturday afternoons and evenings so that people could stroll about in a neighborly fashion while they did their shopping; had used the Whitby *Sentinel,* of which he was the publisher, as a platform for hardhitting articles on honest government, both local and national, and had won awards for newspapers in cities of under fifty thousand population; had made a forceful speech at a convention of mayors in Atlantic City and had been enthusiastically applauded; had been invited to the White House for thirty minutes with a select committee of other mayors.

"Reading that piece," Gretchen said, "you'd think he's done everything but raise the dead in Whitby. It must have been written by a lady journalist who's wildly in love with him. He knows how to turn on the charm, my brother."

Evans laughed. "You don't let emotional attachments cloud your opinions of your near and dear ones, do you?"

"I just hope my near and dear ones don't believe all the gush people write about them."

"The barb has found its mark, sweetie," Evans said. "I now am going home to burn all my scrapbooks." He kissed Ida good-bye first, then Gretchen, and said, "I'll pick you up at your hotel at seven Sunday night."

"I'll be there," Gretchen said.

"Out into the lonely night," Evans said, as he left, pulling the belt of his white raincoat tight around his slim waist, young double agent playing his dangerous game in a low-budget movie.

Gretchen had an idea of just how lonely the night and the weekend were likely to be. He had two other mistresses in New York. That she knew of.

"I can never make up my mind," Ida said, "whether he's a jerk or a genius."

"Neither," Gretchen said and began putting the sequence that displeased her on the moviola again, to see if there was anything she could do with it.

Rudolph came into the cutting room at six-thirty, looking politically hopeful in a dark-blue raincoat and a beige cotton rain hat. Next door a train was going over a trestle on the sound track and farther down the hall an augmented orchestra was playing the 1812 Overture. Gretchen was rewinding the sequence she was working on and the dialogue was coming out in whistling, loud, incomprehensible gibberish.

"Holy man," Rudolph said. "How can you stand it?"

"The sounds of honest labor," Gretchen said. She finished rewinding and gave the spool to Ida. "Go home immediately," she said to her. If you didn't watch her, and if she didn't have a meeting to go to, Ida would stay every night until ten or eleven o'clock, working. She dreaded leisure, Ida.

Rudolph didn't say Happy Birthday when they went down in the elevator and out onto Broadway. Gretchen didn't remind him. Rudolph carried the small valise Gretchen had packed in the morning for the weekend. It was still raining and there wasn't a cab to be had, so they started walking in the direction of Park Avenue. It hadn't been raining when she had come to work and she didn't have an umbrella. She was soaked by the time they reached Sixth Avenue.

"This town," Rudolph said, "Needs ten thousand more taxis. It's insane, what people will put up with to live in a city."

"Energetic administrator," Gretchen said. "Moderate liberal thinker, far-seeing town-planner."

Rudolph laughed. "Oh, you read that article. What crap." But she thought he sounded pleased.

They were on Fifty-second Street and the rain was coming down harder than ever. In front of Twenty-One he stopped her and said, "Let's duck in here and have a drink. The doorman'll get us a taxi later."

Gretchen's hair was lank with the rain and the backs of her stockings were splattered and she didn't relish the idea of going into a place like Twenty-One looking bedraggled and wearing a Ban the Bomb button on her coat, but Rudolph was already pulling her to the door.

Inside, four or five different door guarders, hatcheck girls, managers, and head waiters said, "Good evening, Mr. Jordache," and there was considerable handshaking. There was nothing much that Gretchen could do to repair the ruin of her hair and stockings, so she didn't bother to go to the ladies' room, but went into the bar with Rudolph. Because they weren't having dinner, they didn't ask for a table, but went to the far corner of the bar, which was empty. Near the entrance there were people grouped three deep, men with booming advertising and oil voices who almost certainly did not want to ban the bomb, and women who had obviously just come from Elizabeth Arden and who always found taxis. The lighting was low and artful and was designed to make it worthwhile for women to spend the afternoon getting their hair done and their faces massaged at Elizabeth Arden.

"This'll destroy your reputation in this place," Gretchen said. "Coming in with someone who looks the way I look tonight."

"They've seen worse," Rudolph said. "Much worse."

"Thanks, brother."

"I didn't mean it the way it sounded," Rudolph said. "Actually, you're beautiful."

She didn't feel beautiful. She felt wet and shabby and old and tired and lonely and wounded. "This is my night for self-pity," she said. "Pay no heed."

"How's Jean?" Gretchen asked. Jean had had a miscarriage with her second child and had taken it hard and the times Gretchen had seen her she had seemed remote and subdued, dropping suddenly out of conversations or getting up in the middle of a sentence and walking off into another room. She had quit her photography and when Gretchen had asked her once when she was going back to it she had merely shaken her head.

"Jean?" Rudolph said shortly. "She's improving."

A barman came up and Rudolph ordered a Scotch and Gretchen a martini.

Rudolph lifted his glass to her. "Happy birthday," he said.

He had remembered. "Don't be nice to me," she said, " or I'll cry."

He took an oblong jeweler's box from his pocket and put it on the bar in front of her. "Try it on for size," he said.

She opened the box, which had Cartier inscribed on it. Inside was a beautiful gold watch. She took off the heavy steel watch she was wearing and clipped on the slim gold band. Time, jeweled and fleeing, exquisitely. The day's one gift. She kissed Rudolph's cheek, managed not to cry. I must make myself think better of him, she thought. She ordered another martini.

"What other loot did you get today?" Rudolph asked.

"Nothing."

"Did Billy call?" He said it too casually.

"No."

"I ran into him two days ago on the campus and reminded him," Rudolph said.

"He's awfully busy," Gretchen said defensively.

"Maybe he resented my telling him about it and suggesting he call you," Rudolph said. "He's not too fond of his Uncle Rudolph."

"He's not too fond of anybody," Gretchen said.

Billy had matriculated at Whitby because when he finished high school in California he said he wanted to go East to college. Gretchen had hoped he would go to UCLA or the University of Southern California, so that he could still live at home, but Billy had made it clear that he didn't want to live at home any more. Although he was very intelligent, he didn't work, and his marks weren't good enough to get him into any of the prestige schools in the East. Gretchen had asked Rudolph to use his influence to have him accepted at Whitby. Billy's letters were rare—sometimes she wouldn't hear from him for two months at a time. And when they did come they were short and consisted mostly of lists of courses he was taking and projects for the summer holidays, always in the East. She had been working more than a month now in New York, just a few hours from Whitby, but he hadn't come down once. Until this weekend she had been too proud to go up to see him but finally couldn't bear it any longer.

"What is it with that kid?" Rudolph said.

"He's making me suffer," Gretchen said.

"What for?"

"For Evans. I tried to be as discreet as possible—Evans never stayed overnight at the house and I always came home to sleep, myself, and I never went on weekends with him, but, of course, Billy caught on right away and the freeze was on. Maybe women ought to have fits of melancholy when they *have* babies, not when they lose them."

"He'll get over it," Rudolph said. "It's a kid's jealousy. That's all."

"I hope so. He despises Evans. He calls him a phoney."

"Is he?"

Gretchen shrugged. "I don't think so. He doesn't measure up to Colin, but then, neither did I."

"Don't run yourself down," Rudolph said gently.

"What better occupation could a lady find on her fortieth birthday?"

"You look thirty," Rudolph said. "A beautiful, desirable thirty."

"Dear brother."

"Is Evans going to marry you?"

"In Hollywood," Gretchen said, "successful directors of thirty-two don't marry widows of forty, unless they're famous or rich or both. And I'm neither."

"Does he love you?"

"Who knows?"

"Do you love him?"

"Same answer. Who knows? I like to sleep with him, I like to work for him, I like to be attached to him. He fulfills me. I have to be attached to a man and feel useful to him and somehow Evans turned out to be the lucky man. If he asked me to marry him, I'd do it like a shot. But he won't ask."

"Happy days," Rudolph said thoughtfully. "Finish your drink. We'd better be getting on. Jean's waiting for us in the apartment."

Gretchen looked at her watch. "It's now exactly eighteen minutes past seven, according to Mr. Cartier."

It was still raining outside, but a taxi drove up and a couple got out and the doorman protected Gretchen with a big umbrella as she ran for the cab. Outside Twenty-One, you'd never guess that the city needed ten thousand more taxis.

When Rudolph let them into the apartment, they heard the violent sound of metal on metal. Rudolph ran into the living room with Gretchen on his heels. Jean sat on the floor, in the middle of the room, with her legs spread apart, like a child playing with blocks. She had a hammer in her hand and she was methodically destroying a pile of cameras and lenses and camera equipment that lay between her knees. She was wearing a pair of slacks and a dirty sweater and her unwashed hair hung down, masking her face, as she bent over her work.

"Jean," Rudolph said, "what the hell are you doing?"

Jean looked up, peering slyly through her hair. "His Honor the Mayor wants to know what his beautiful, rich young wife is doing. I'll tell his Honor the Mayor what his beautiful, rich young wife is doing. She is making a junk pile." Her speech was thick and she was drunk. Jean smashed the hammer down on a big wide-angle lens and splintered it.

Rudolph grabbed the hammer from her. She did not struggle. "His Honor the Mayor now has taken the hammer from his beautiful rich young wife's hand," Jean said. "Don't worry, little junk pile. There are other hammers. You'll grow up and one day you'll be one of the biggest most beautiful junk piles in the world and his Honor the Mayor will claim it as a public park for the citizens of Whitby."

Still holding the hammer, Rudolph glanced over at Gretchen. There was a shamed, frightened look in his eyes. "Christ, Jean," he said to his wife, "there's at least five thousand dollars' worth of stuff there."

"Her Honor the Mayor's wife doesn't need cameras," Jean said. "Let people take pictures of *me*. Let poor people take pictures. Talented People. Hoopla!" She made a spreading, gay ballet gesture with her arms. "Bring on the hammers. Rudy, darling, don't you think you ought to give your beautiful rich young wife a drink?"

"You've had enough to drink."

"Rudolph," Gretchen said, "I'd better be off. We're not going to Whitby tonight."

"Beautiful Whitby," Jean said. "Where the beautiful rich young wife of his Honor the Mayor smiles at Democrats and Republicans alike, where she opens charity bazaars and appears faithfully at her husband's side at banquets and political meetings, where she is to be seen at Commencements and Fourth of July celebrations and the home games of the Whitby University football team and the dedication of new science laboratories and the ground-breaking ceremonies for housing projects with real toilets for colored folk."

"Cut it out, Jean!" Rudolph said harshly.

"Really, I think I'd better go," Gretchen said. "I'll call you in . . . "

"Sister of his Honor the Mayor, what's your rush to leave?" Jean said. "Who knows, one day he may need your vote. Stay and we'll have a nice cosy little family drink. Maybe if you play your cards right, he may even marry you. Stay and listen. It may be in . . . instructive." She stumbled on the word. "How to be an appendage, in a hundred easy lessons. I'm having visiting cards printed up. Mrs. Rudolph Jordache, ex-career girl, now in the appendage business. One of the ten most hopeful appendages in the United States. Parasitism and hypocrisy a specialty. Courses given in appendaging." She giggled. "Any true-blue American girl guaranteed a diploma."

Rudolph didn't try to stop Gretchen as she went out of the room and into the hallway, leaving him standing in his raincoat, the hammer in his hand, staring down at his drunken wife.

The elevator door opened directly into the apartment and Gretchen had to wait in the hallway and she heard Jean say, in a childish, aggrieved voice, "People are always taking away my hammers," before the elevator door opened and she could flee.

When she got back to the Algonquin she called Evans's hotel, but there was no answer from his apartment. She left a message with the operator that Mrs. Burke had not left for the weekend and could be reached all night at her hotel. Then she took a hot bath and changed her clothes and went down to the hotel dining room and had dinner.

Rudolph called at nine the next morning. She was alone. Evans hadn't called. Rudolph said that Jean had gone to sleep after Gretchen had left and had been contrite and ashamed when she woke up and was all right now and they were going to Whitby after all and they'd wait for Gretchen in the apartment.

"You're sure you don't think it's wiser to spend the day alone with her?" Gretchen asked.

"It's better when we're not alone," Rudolph said. "You left your bag here, in case you think you've lost it."

"I remember," Gretchen said. "I'll be up at your place by ten."

As she dressed she puzzled over the scene the night before and remembered Jean's less violent, but almost equally strange behavior at other times. Now it all added up. She had managed to hide it from Gretchen until now, because Gretchen hadn't seen her all that often. But it was plain now—Jean was an alcoholic. Gretchen wondered if Rudolph realized it, and what he was going to do about it.

By a quarter to ten Evans hadn't called, and Gretchen went down in the elevator and into the sun of Forty-fourth Street, a slender, tall woman, with fine legs, her hair soft and black, her skin unblemished and pale, her tweed suit and jersey blouse exactly right for a gracious country weekend. Only the Ban the Bomb button, worn like a brooch on the well-tailored lapel, might indicate to the passerby that not everything was as it seemed on that sunny American spring morning of 1966.

The debris of the cameras had been cleared away from the living room. Rudolph and Jean were listening to a Mozart piano concerto on the radio when Gretchen came in.

Rudolph seemed unruffled and although Jean was pale and a little shaky when she stood up to kiss Gretchen hello, she, too, seemed to have recovered from the night before. She gave Gretchen a quick glance, that perhaps asked for pity and understanding, but after that, in her normal, quick, low-timbred voice, with a hint of gaiety that didn't seem forced, she said, "Gretchen, don't you look smashing in that suit. And tell me where I can get one of those buttons. The color goes with my eyes."

"Yes," Rudolph said. "I'm sure it'll make a big hit the next time we have to go down to Washington." But his voice was tender and he laughed, relaxed.

Jean held his hand, like a child on an outing with a father, as they went downstairs and waited for the man from the garage to bring the car. Her hair was washed and shone chestnut brown, and she had it tied in back with a bow and she was wearing a very short skirt. Her legs, without stockings, were lovely, slender, straight, and already tanned. As usual, she looked no more than eighteen.

While they were waiting for the car, Rudolph said to Gretchen, "I called my secretary and told her to get in touch with Billy and tell him we were expecting him for lunch at our place."

"Thank you, Rudy," Gretchen said. She hadn't seen Billy in so long that for their first meeting it would be much better if there were others around.

When the car came, the two women sat in front with Rudolph. He turned on the radio. Mozart, unworried and spring-like, accompanied them as far as the Bronx.

They drove through dogwood and tulips and skirted fields where men and boys were playing baseball. Mozart gave way to Loesser on the radio, and Ray Bolger sang, irresistibly, "Once in love with Amy, Always in love with Amy," and Jean sang along with the radio, in a low, true, sweet voice. They all remembered Bolger in the show and how much pleasure he had given them. By the time they reached the farmhouse in Whitby, where the first twilight-colored lilacs were budding in the garden, the night before was almost as if it had never happened. Almost.

Enid, now two, blond and round, was waiting for them. She leaped at her mother and they embraced and kissed each other again and again. Rudolph carried Gretchen's bag as he and Gretchen went up the stairs to the guest room. The room was crisp and sparkling, full of flowers.

Rudolph put her bag down and said, "I think you have everything you need."

"Rudy," Gretchen said, keeping her voice low, "We ought to skip drinks today."

"Why?" He sounded surprised.

"You mustn't tempt her. Jean. Even if she doesn't take any herself—seeing others drink . . . "

"Oh," Rudolph said negligently, "I wouldn't worry about that. She was just a little upset last night . . . "

"She's an alcoholic, Rudy," Gretchen said gently.

Rudolph made a dismissive, light gesture. "You're being melodramatic," he said. "It's not like you. Every once in a while she goes on a little bender, that's all. Even as you and I."

"Not even as you and I," Gretchen said. "She shouldn't touch one drop. Not even a sip of beer. And as much as possible, she should be kept away from people who drink. Rudy, I know. Hollywood is full of women like her. In the beginning stages, like her, and in later stages, horrible stages, the way she's liable to be. You've got to protect her."

"Nobody can say I don't protect her." There was a thin edge of anger in his voice.

"Rudy, lock up every bottle of liquor in this house." Gretchen said.

"Calm yourself," Rudolph said. "This isn't Hollywood."

The phone was ringing and then Jean called up and said, "Gretchen, it's Billy, for you. Down here."

"Please listen to me," Gretchen said.

"Go talk to your son," Rudolph said coldly.

On the phone, Billy's voice was very grown-up. "Hello, Mother. It's wonderful that you could come up. He had begun calling her Mother when Evans had appeared on the scene. Before that it had been Mummy. She had thought it childish for a boy as big and as old as he, but now, on the phone, she longed for the Mummy. "Say, I'm awfully sorry," Billy said. "Will you make my excuses to Rudolph? He invited me to come to lunch, but there's a softball game on here at one o'clock and I'm pitching, so I'm afraid I'll have to ask for a raincheck."

"Yes," Gretchen said. "I'll make your excuses. When will I see you?"

"Well, it's a little difficult to say." Billy sounded honestly perplexed. "There's a kind of giant beer-fest after the game at one of the houses and . . . "

"Where're you playing?" Gretchen said. "I'll come down and watch you. We can visit between the innings."

"Now you sound sore."

"I'm not sore, as you put it. Where're you playing?"

"There's a whole bunch of fields on the east side of the campus," Billy said. "You can't miss it."

"Good-bye, Billy," Gretchen said, and hung up. She went out of the hall where the phone was and into the living room. Jean was on the couch, cradling Enid and rocking her back and forth. Enid was making small cooing noises. Rudolph was shaking up Daiquiris.

"My son sends his regrets," Gretchen said. "He has weighty affairs that will detain him all afternoon. He cannot lunch."

"That's too bad," Rudolph said. But his mouth hardened for a moment. He poured the cocktails for himself and Gretchen. Jean, occupied with her child, said she was not drinking.

After lunch, Gretchen borrowed the car and drove to the Whitby University campus. She had been there before but now she was struck afresh by the quiet, countrified beauty of the place, with its homely old buildings spread out haphazardly on acres of green, its wandering graveled walks, the tall oaks and elms. Because it was Saturday afternoon there were few students about and the campus dozed in a peaceful sunny trance. It was a place to look back upon, she thought, an image for later nostalgia. If a university was a place that prepared young people for life, these peaceful lawns, these unpretentious welcoming halls and classrooms might be found wanting. The life Whitby's graduates would have to face in the last third of the twentieth century was almost certainly not going to be anything like this.

There were three desultory baseball games in progress on the playing fields. The most desultory, in which almost half the players were girls, was the one in which Billy was playing. The girl who was in field had a book with her. She sat on the grass reading it and only looked up and ran after a ball when her teammates shouted at her. The game must have been going on for some time, because as Gretchen came up behind the first-base line there was a mild argument between the first-baseman and some of the members of the opposing team who were sprawled on the grass awaiting their turn at bat, about whether the score was nineteen to sixteen or eighteen to fifteen. It could hardly have made any difference to anyone whether or not Billy had played.

Dressed in fringed blue jeans stained with bleach, and a gray T-shirt, Billy was pitching, just lobbing it up to the girls, but throwing the ball hard to the boys when they came to bat. Billy didn't see Gretchen immediately and she watched him, tall and moving lazily and gracefully, his hair too long over the face that was a beautiful, improved version, sensual, strong, dissatisfied, of Willie Abbott's face, the forehead as broad and high, the eyes deeper set and darker, the nose longer, with tense, wide nostrils, a single asymmetrical dimple in the right cheek when he smiled, his teeth pure, youthful white.

If only he will live up to his face, Gretchen thought, as her son tossed the ball up to a pretty, chubby girl, who swung and missed and cried, in mock despair. "I'm *hopeless!*"

It was the third out of the inning and Billy saw Gretchen standing behind first base and came over to her and said, "Hi, Mother," and kissed her. There was a little crinkle of amusement around his eyes as he glanced at the Ban the Bomb button. "I told you you'd find us without trouble."

"I hope I'm not interfering," she said. The wrong tone, she knew. Love me, I'm your mother.

"No, of course not," he said. "Say, kids," he called, "Somebody bat for me. I have a visitor. I'll see you all later at the house." He didn't introduce her to anyone. "Why don't we take a little walk? I'll show you around."

"Rudolph and Jean were disappointed you couldn't come for lunch," Gretchen said, as they walked away from the game. Wrong tone again.

"Were they?" Billy said evenly. "I'm sorry."

"Rudolph says he's invited you over again and again and you never come."

Billy shrugged. "You know how it is," he said. "Something's always coming up."

"I'd feel better if you went there once in awhile," Gretchen said.

"I'll go. Sometime. We can discuss the generation gap. Or how everybody on the campus smokes pot. His newspaper's great on those subjects."

"Do *you* smoke pot?"

"Mother, darling, come into the twentieth century."

"Don't condescend to me," she said sharply.

"It's a nice day," he said. "I haven't seen you for a long time. Let's not argue. That building over there is the dormitory where I lived when I was a freshman."

"Was your girl there in that game?" He had written her that he was interested in a girl in one of his classes.

"No. Her mother and father are here for the weekend and she has to pretend I don't exist. Her father can't stand me and I can't stand him. I'm an immoral, depraving influence, her father says. He's Neanderthal."

"Have you got a good word to say for anybody?"

"Sure. Albert Camus. But he's dead. That reminds me. How's that other poet, Evans Kinsella?"

"He's alive," Gretchen said.

"That's great news," said Billy. "That's really sensational news."

If Colin hadn't died he wouldn't be like this, Gretchen thought. He would be completely different. An absent-minded, busy man gets behind the wheel of a car and hits a tree and the impact spreads and spreads, never stopping, through the generations.

"Do you ever come down to New York?" she asked.

"Once in awhile."

"If you'll let me know, the next time you're coming," she said. "I'll get tickets for a show. Bring your girl, if you want. I'd like to meet her."

"She's not much," Billy said.

"Anyway, let me know."

"Sure."

"How are you doing in your work?" she asked.

Billy made a face.

"Rudolph says you're not doing very well. He says there's a chance that you'll be dropped from school."

"Being Mayor of this burg must be an easy job," Billy said, "if he has time to check up on how many classes I cut a semester."

"If you get kicked out, you'll be drafted. Do you want that?"

"Who cares?" Billy said. "The Army can't be more boring than most of the courses around here."

"Do you ever think about me?" Immensely wrong. Classically wrong. But she had said it. "How do you think I'd feel if you were sent to Viet Nam?"

"Men fight and women weep," Billy said. "Why should you and I be different?"

"Do you do anything about trying to change things? About stopping the war, for example? A lot of students all over the country are working day and night to . . . "

"Kooks," Billy said. "Wasting their time. The war's too good a racket for too many big shots. What do they care what a few spastic kids do? If you want, I'll take your button and wear it. Big deal. The Pentagon will quake when they hear that Billy Abbott is protesting against the bomb."

"Billy," Gretchen stopped walking and faced him, "are you interested in *anything?*"

"Not really," he said calmly. "Is there something wrong with that?"

"All I hope," Gretchen said, "is that it's a pose. A silly, adolescent pose."

"It's not a pose," he said. "And I'm not an adolescent, in case you haven't noticed. I'm a big, grown man and I think everything stinks. If I were you, I'd forget about me for awhile. If it's any hardship to you to send me the money to keep me in school, don't send it. If you don't like the way I am and you're blaming yourself for the way I turned out, maybe you're right, maybe you're not. I'm sorry to have to talk this way, but there's one thing I know I don't want to be and that's a hypocrite. I think you'll be happier if you don't have to worry about me, so you go back to my dear Uncle Rudolph and to your dear Evans Kinsella and I'll go back to my ball game." He turned and strode away, along the path toward the playing fields.

Gretchen watched him until he was just a small blue-and-gray figure in the distance, then walked slowly, heavily, toward where she had parked Rudolph's car.

There was no sense in staying for the whole weekend anymore. She had a quiet dinner with Rudolph and Jean and took the morning train down to New York.

When she got back to her hotel, there was a message from Evans saying that he couldn't have dinner with her that night.

CHAPTER 6

1967

ON THE PLANE to Dallas, Johnny Heath, sitting next to him, was going through a briefcase full of papers, Rudolph was going through his own briefcase full of papers. He had to submit the budget for the next year to the town council and he frowned as he went over the thick booklet which contained the Comptroller's estimates. The price of everything was going up, the police and fire departments, the public school staffs, and the clerical employees were all due for a rise in salary; there was an alarming increase in the number of welfare recipients, especially in the Negro section of town; a new sewage-disposal plant was on the books; everybody was fighting tax increases; state and federal aid were being kept at their old levels. Here I am, he thought, at thirty thousand feet, worrying about money again.

Johnny Heath was worrying about money in the seat next to his, too, but at least it was his own money, and Rudolph's. Brad Knight had moved his office from Tulsa to Dallas after his father had died, and the purpose of their trip was to confer with Brad about their investments in the Peter Knight and Son Oil Company. Suddenly, Brad had seemed to have lost his touch, and they had found themselves investing in one dry hole after another. Even the wells that had come in had suffered from a series of disasters, salt water, collapsing scale, unpredictable, expensive formations to drill through. Johnny Heath had made some quiet investigations and was sure Brad had been rigging his report and was stealing from them and had been doing so for some time. The figures Johnny had come up with looked conclusive, but Rudolph refused to move against Brad until they had had it out in person. It seemed impossible to him that a man he had known so long and so well could turn like that. Despite Virginia Calderwood.

When the plane landed, Brad wasn't at the airport to greet them. Instead, he had sent an assistant, a burly, tall man in a brown straw hat, a string tie, and a madras jacket, who made Mr. Knight's excuses (he was tied up in a metting, the assistant said) and drove with them in an air-conditioned Cadillac along a road that throbbed in heat mirages, to the hotel in the center of Dallas where Brad had rented a suite with a salon and two bedrooms for Johnny and Rudolph.

The hotel was brand new and the rooms were decorated in what the decorator must have thought was a Lone Star improvement of Second Empire. On a long table against the wall were ranged six bottles of bourbon, six of Scotch, six of gin and vodka, plus a bottle of vermouth, a filled ice bucket, dozens of bottles of Coke and soda water, a basket of lemons, a huge bowl of ovrsized fruit, and an array of glasses of all sizes.

"You'll find beer and champagne in the refrigerator in the closet," the assistant said. "If that's you're pleasure. You're the guests of Mr. Knight."

"We're only staying overnight," Rudolph said.

"Mr. Knight told me to make you gentlemen comfortable," the assistant said. "You're in Texas now."

"If they had all this stuff at the Alamo," Rudolph said, "they'd still be holding out."

The assistant laughed politely and said that Mr. Knight was almost sure to be free by five P.M. It was a little past three now. "Remember," he said, as he left, "if you gentlemen need anything, you call me at the office, hear?"

"Window dressing," Johnny said, with a gesture for the suite and the table loaded with drink.

Rudolph felt a twinge of irritation with Johnny and his automatic reflex of suspicion in all situations.

"I have some calls to make," Rudolph said. "Let me know when Brad arrives." He went into his own room and closed the door.

He called his home first. He tried to call Jean at least three times each day. He had finally taken Gretchen's advice and there was no liquor in the house, but Whitby was full of liquor stores and bars. No worry today. Jean was cheerful and bright. It was raining in Whitby. Two months before, she had had an accident while driving drunk with Enid in the rear seat. The car had been demolished but aside from a few scratches neither of them had been hurt.

"What's it like in Dallas?" she asked.

"All right for Texans, I suppose," Rudolph said. "Intolerable for the rest of the human race."

"When will you be back?"

"As soon as possible."

"Hurry," she said. He hadn't told her why he and Johnny had had to come to Texas. Sober, she was depressed by duplicity.

He then called his office at the Town Hall and got his secretary on the phone. His secretary was a young man, a little effeminate, but usually serene. He wasn't serene this afternoon. There had been a demonstration of students that morning in front of the offices of the *Sentinel* because of an editorial in favor of the continued existence of the ROTC at the university. Rudolph had approved the editorial himself, as it was moderate and had not advocated compulsory military training but said it should be open to those students who felt that they wanted a career in the armed forces or even those students who felt that in case of need they would like to be ready to defend their country. The sweet voice of reason had not helped to mollify the demonstrators. A rock had been thrown through a plate-glass window and the police had had to be called. President Dorlacker, of the university, had phoned, in a black mood, the secretary said, and had said, quote, If he's the Mayor, why isn't he at his desk?

Unquote. Rudolph had not deigned to tell the secretary the nature of his business. Police Chief Ottman had been into the office, looking harassed. Something very, *very* important, Ottman had said. The Mayor was to get back to him soonest. Albany had telephoned twice. A Black delegation had presented a petition about something to do with a swimming pool.

"That's enough, Walter," Rudolph said, wearily. He hung up the phone and lay back on the baby-blue, slippery silk bedspread. He got ten thousand dollars a year for being Mayor of Whitby. And he donated the entire amount to charity. Public service.

He got up from the bed, maliciously pleased to see that his shoes had left a stain on the silk, and went into the living room. Johnny was sitting at a huge desk, going over his papers in his shirt sleeves. "There's no doubt about it, Rudy," Johnny said, "the sonofabitch has taken us for a ride."

"Later, please," Rudolph said. "I'm busy being a devoted and self-sacrificing public servant at the moment." He poured a Coke over some ice and went to the window and looked out at Dallas. Dallas glittered in the baking sun, rising from its desolate plain like a senseless eruption of metal and glass, the result of a cosmic accident, inorganic and arbitrary.

Rudolph went back into his bedroom, and gave the number of the office of the Chief of Police in Whitby to the telephone operator. While waiting for the call to come through he looked at himself in the mirror. He looked like a man who needed a vacation. He wondered when he was going to have his first heart attack. Although in America only businessmen were supposed to have heart attacks, and theoretically he had abandoned all that. Professors lived forever, he had read somewhere, and most generals.

When he got Ottman on the phone, Ottman sounded mournful. But he always sounded mournful. His *métier,* which was crime, offended him. Bailey, the former Chief of Police, whom Rudolph had put in jail, had been a hearty and happy man. Rudolph often regretted him. The melancholy of integrity.

"We've opened up a can of worms, Mr. Mayor," Ottman said. "Officer Slattery picked up a Whitby freshman at eight-thirty this morning in a diner, smoking a marijuana cigarette. At eight-thirty in the morning!" Ottman was a family man who kept regular hours, and the mornings were precious to him. "The boy had one and one-third ounces of the drug on him. Before we booked him he talked and talked. He says in his dormitory there are at least fifty kids who smoke hash and marijuana. He says if we go there we'll find a pound of the stuff, at least. He's got a lawyer and he'll be out on bail by this evening, but by now the lawyer must have told a few people and what am I supposed to do? President Dorlacker called me a little while ago and told me to stay away from the campus, but it's bound to be all over town and if I stay away from the campus what does that make me look like? Whitby University isn't Havana or Buenos Aires, for Christ's sake, it's within the city limits and the law's the law, for Christ's sake."

I picked a great day to come to Dallas, Rudolph thought. "Let me think for a minute, Chief," he said.

"If I can't go in there, Mr. Mayor," Ottman said, "you can have my resignation as of this minute."

Oh, God, Rudolph thought, honest men! Some day he was going to try marijuana himself and see what all the fuss was about. Maybe it would be just the thing for Jean.

"The lawyer for the kid is Leon Harrison's lawyer, too," Ottman said. "Harrison's already been in here and asked what I intend to do. He's talking about calling a special meeting of the board of trustees."

"All right, Chief," Rudolph said. "Call Dorlacker and tell him you've spoken to me and that I've ordered a search for eight o'clock tonight. Get a warrant from Judge Satterlee and tell your men to leave their clubs at home. I don't want anybody hurt. The news'll get around and maybe the kids'll have the sense to get rid of the stuff before you hit the dormitory."

"You don't know kids these days, Mr. Mayor," Ottman said sorrowfully. "They ain't got the sense to wipe their ass."

Rudolph gave him the number of the hotel in Dallas and told him to get back to him after the raid that evening. He hung up and finished his Coke. The lunch on the plane coming down had been dreadful and he had heartburn. He had foolishly drunk the two Manhattans the stewardess had plunked down on his tray. For some reason he drank Manhattans when he was in the air. Never on the ground. What significance there?

The phone rang. He waited for Johnny to pick it up in the other room, but it wasn't ringing in the other room. "Hello," he said.

"Rudy?" It was Gretchen's voice.

"Yes." There had been a coolness between them since she had told him that Jean was an alcoholic. Gretchen had been right, but that only made the coolness more pronounced.

"I called Jean at your house," Gretchen said, "and she told me where you are. I hope I'm not disturbing you." She sounded disturbed herself.

"No, no," Rudolph lied. "I'm just dawdling idly in that well-known holiday spot, Dallas Les Bains. Where are you anyway?"

"Los Angeles. I wouldn't have called you, but I'm out of my mind."

Depend upon families to pick the right time and place to be out of their minds. "What is it?" Rudolph asked.

"It's Billy. Did you know he dropped out of school a month ago?"

"No," Rudolph said. "He hardly ever whispered his secrets to me, you know."

"He's down in New York, living with some girl . . . "

"Gretchen, darling," Rudolph said, "there are probably half a million boys Billy's age in New York right this minute living with some girl. Be thankful he isn't living with some boy."

"Of course it isn't that," Gretchen said. "He's being drafted, now that he's not a student anymore."

"Well, it might do him some good," Rudolph said. "A couple of years in the Army might make a man of him."

"You have a baby daughter," Gretchen said bitterly. "You can talk like that. I have one son. I don't think a bullet through his head is going to make a man of my son."

"Now, Gretchen," Rudolph said, "don't make it so automatic. Induct the boy and two months later send the corpse home to mother. There are an awful lot of boys who serve their time and come home without a scratch."

"That's why I'm calling you," Gretchen said. "I want you to make sure that he comes home without a scratch."

"What can I do?"

"You know a lot of people in Washington."

"Nobody can keep a kid out of the draft if he's goofed school and he's in good health, Gretchen. Not even in Washington."

"I'm not so sure about that, either," Gretchen said, "from some of the things I've heard and read. But I'm not asking you to try to keep Billy out of the Army."

"Then what *are* you trying to get me to do?"

"Use your connections to make sure that once Billy is in, he doesn't ever get sent to Viet Nam."

Rudolph sighed. The truth was that he did know some people in Washington who could most probably do it and who would most probably do it if he asked them. But it was just the sort of petty, privileged, inside politicking that he despised the most. It offended his sense of rectitude and cast a shadow on his entire reason for going into public life. In the world of business it was perfectly normal for a man to come to you and ask you to place a nephew or a cousin in some favored position. Depending upon how much you owed the man or how much you expected to get from him in the future, or even how much you liked him, you helped the nephew or cousin, if you could, without thinking twice about it. But to use the power you had gained by the votes of people to whom you had promised impeccable representation and the sternest respect for the law to deliver your sister's son from the threat of death while actively or tacitly approving of sending thousands of other boys the same age to their destruction was another thing.

"Gretchen," he said over the slight buzz of wire between Dallas and Los Angeles, "I wish you could figure out some other way . . . "

"The only other person I know who might be able to do something," Gretchen said, her voice rising, "is Colin Burke's brother. He's a general in the Air Force. He's in Viet Nam right now. I bet he'd just fall all over himself with eagerness to keep Billy from hearing a shot fired."

"Not so loud, Gretchen," Rudolph said, holding the phone away from his ear. "I hear you perfectly well."

"I'm going to tell you something." She was shouting hysterically now. "If you don't help, I'm coming to New York and I'm taking Billy with me to Canada or Sweden. And I'm going to make one hell of a loud noise about why I'm doing it."

"Christ, Gretchen," Rudolph said, "what's wrong with you—are you approaching the menopause or what?"

He heard the phone slam at the other end. He got up slowly and went over to the window and looked out at Dallas. It didn't look any better from the bedroom than it had from the salon.

Family, he thought. Without reasoning it out, he had always been the one to try to protect his family. He was the one who helped his father at the ovens and made the deliveries for the bakery; he was the one who had kept his mother alive. He was the one who had had the shabby dealings with detectives and the painful scene with Willie Abbott and had helped Gretchen with her divorce and befriended her second husband. He was the one who had made the money for Tom, so that he could escape the savage life he had fallen into. He was the one who had gone to Colin Burke's funeral on the other edge of the continent to comfort his sister at the worst moments of her sorrow. He was the one who had taken the responsibilty of taking Billy, ungrateful and derisive as he was, out of his school when Billy was suffering there; he was the one who had gotten Billy into Whitby, when the boy's marks were hardly good enough to get him into a trade school. He was the one who had hunted down Tom at the Aegean Hotel, for his mother's sake, and had learned all about West Fifty-third Street and put up the money for Schultz and made the arrangement with the lawyer for Tom's reunion with his son and his divorcee from a prostitute . . .

He had not asked for gratitude and, he thought wryly, he had gotten damn little for it. Well, he hadn't done it for gratitude. He was honest with himself. He was conscious of the duties owed to himself and others and wouldn't have been able to live comfortably with himself if he hadn't fulfilled them.

Duties never end. It is their essential characteristic.

He went over to the phone and asked for Gretchen's number in California. When she answered, he said, "All right, Gretchen. I'll stop over in Washington on the way North and see what I can do. I think you can stop worrying."

"Thank you, Rudy," Gretchen said in a small voice. "I knew you'd come through."

Brad arrived at the suite at five-thirty. Texas sun and Texas liquor had made him ruddier than ever. Also heavier and more expansive. He was wearing a dark, summer-weight, striped suit and a ruffled blue shirt with huge pearl cufflinks. "Sorry I couldn't meet you at the airport, but I hope my boy treated you all right." He poured himself a slug of bourbon over ice and beamed at his friends. "Well, it's about time you fellas came down and paid me a visit and took a look for yourselves at where your money's coming from. We're bringing in a new well and maybe tomorrow I'll hire a plane and we'll fly over and take a look at how it's doing. And I've got tickets on the fifty-yard line for Saturday. The big game of the season. Texas against Okalhoma. This town's got to be seen to be believed on that weekend. Thirty thousand happy drunks. I'm sorry Virginia's not here to welcome you. She'll be heartbroken when she hears you've been and gone. But she's up North visiting her Pappy. I hear he's not too well. I hope it's nothing serious. I'm real fond of the old critter."

It was too painful, the Western heartiness, the lush hospitality, and desperate rush of Southern blarney. "Cut it out, please, Brad," Rudolph said. "For one thing, we know why Virginia's not here. And it isn't to visit her Pappy, as you describe him." Two weeks ago Calderwood had come to Rudolph's office and had told him that Virginia had left Brad for good because Brad had taken up with some movie actress in Hollywood three times a week and was having money troubles. It was after Calderwood's visit that Rudolph had begun to suspect something and had called Johnny.

"Pardner," Brad said, drinking, "I don't know what all you're talking about. I just talked to my wife and she said she expected to be coming home any day now and . . ."

"You didn't just talk to your wife and she's not coming home, Brad," Rudolph said. "And you know it."

"And you know a lot of other things, too," Johnny said. He was standing between Brad and the door, almost as if he expected Brad to make a sudden run for it. "And so do we."

"By God," Brad said, "if you fellas weren't my lifelong buddies, I'd swear you sounded hostile." He was sweating, despite the air-conditioning and his blue shirt was darkly stained. He filled his glass again. His stubby, manicured fingers were shaking as he fumbled with the ice.

"Come clean, Brad," Johnny said.

"Well . . ." Brad laughed, or tried to laugh. "Maybe I've been stepping out a little on my wife, here and there. You know how I am, Rudy, I don't have the strength of character you have, I can't resist a little bit of soft, cuddly poontang when it's waved in my face. But Virginia's taking it too big, she . . ."

"We're not interested in you and Virginia," Johnny said. "We're interested in where our money's gone to."

"You get a statement every month," Brad said.

"We sure do," Johnny said.

"We've run into a little hard luck recently." Brad wiped his face with a large, monogrammed, linen handkerchief. "Like my Pappy, bless his soul, used to say about the oil business, if you don't like the waves, don't go in the water."

"We've been doing some checking," Johnny said, "and we figure that in the last year you've stolen roughly seventy thousand dollars apiece from me and Rudy."

"You fellas must be kidding," Brad said. His face was almost purple now and his smile was fixed, as though it were permanently ironed on the florid, stretched skin over the damp collar. "You *are* kidding, aren't you? This is some kind of practical joke. Jesus, a hundred and forty thousand dollars!"

"Brad . . ." Rudolph said warningly.

"Okay," Brad said. "I guess you're not kidding." He sank down heavily on the flowered couch, a thick, round-shouldered weary man against the gay colors of the best piece of furniture in the best suite of the best hotel in Dallas, Texas. "I'll tell you how it happened."

The way it happened was that Brad had met a starlet by the name of Sandra Dilson a year before when he had gone out to Hollywood to scout around for more investors. "A sweet, innocent young thing," were Brad's words for Miss Dilson. He'd gone ape for her, he said, but it was a long time before she'd let him touch her. To impress her he'd started buying her jewelry. "You have no idea what they charge for stones out there in that town," Brad said. "It's as though they printed their own money." And to impress her further, he'd bet heavily when they went to the races. "If you want to know the truth," Brad said, "that girl is walking around with about four hundred thousand dollars' worth of jewelry on her back that I paid for. And there were times in bed with her," he said defiantly, "that I felt it was worth it, every cent of it. I love her and I lost my head over her and in a way I'm proud of it and I'm willing to take the consequences."

To find the money, Brad had started to falsify the monthly statements. He had reported prospecting and drilling for oil in holes that had been abandoned as dry or worthless years before and had hiked up the cost of equipment ten or even fifteen times what the actual price would have been. There was a bookkeeper in his office who was in on it, but whom he paid to keep quiet and to work with him. There had been some ominous inquiries from other people who invested with him, but up to now he had been able to fend them off.

"How many investors have you got backing you at this moment?" Johnny asked.

"Fifty-two."

"Fifty-two idiots," Johnny said bitterly.

"I never did anything like this before," Brad said ingenuously. "My reputation in Oklahoma and Texas is as clean as a hound's tooth. You ask anyone. People trusted me. And they had a right to."

"You're going to go to jail, Brad," Rudolph said.

"You wouldn't do that to me, to your old friend, Brad, who sat next to you the day you graduated from college, would you, Rudy?"

"I certainly would," Rudolph said.

"Wait a minute, wait a minute," Johnny said, "before we start talking about jail. I'm more interested in seeing if we can get our money back than in sending this moron to jail."

"That's it," Brad said eagerly, "that's the way to talk. Sensibly."

"What have you got in the way of assets?" Johnny asked. "Right now?"

"That's it," repeated Brad. "Now we're talking business. It's not as though I'm wiped out. I still have credit."

"When you walk out of this room, Brad," Rudolph said, "you won't be able to borrow ten cents from any bank in the country. I'll see to that." He found it hard not to show his disgust.

"Johnny . . . " Brad appealed to Heath. "He's vindictive. Talk to him. I can understand he's a little sore, but to be vindictive like that . . . "

"I asked you about assets," Johnny said.

"Well," Brad said, "on the books, it's not so . . . so optimistic." He grinned, hopefully. "But from time to time, I've been able to accumulate a little cash. For a rainy day, you might say. I've got it in safety-deposit boxes here and there. It's not enough to pay off everybody, of course, but I could go pretty far toward paying you fellas back."

"Is it Virginia's money?" Rudolph asked.

"Virginia's money!" Brad snorted. "Her old man tied up the money he gave her so tight, I couldn't buy a hot dog with any of it if I was dying of hunger in a ballpark."

"He was a lot smarter than we were," Rudolph said.

"Jesus, Rudolph," Brad complained, "you don't have to keep rubbing it in. I feel bad enough as it is."

"How much is there in cash?" Johnny asked.

"You understand, Johnny," Brad said, "it's not on the company's books anywhere or anything like that."

"I understand," Johnny said. "How much?"

"Close to a hundred thousand. I could give each of you nearly fifty thousand dollars on account. And I'd personally guarantee to pay the rest back later."

"How?" Rudolph asked brutally.

"Well, there's still some wells being dug . . . " Rudolph could tell he was lying. "And then I could go to Sandra and explain how I'm in a little hole for the time being and ask her to give me back the jewelry, and . . . "

Rudolph shook his head, wonderingly. "You really believe she'd do that?"

"She's a fine little girl, Rudy. I have to introduce her to you sometime."

"Oh, grow up, for Christ's sake," Rudolph said.

"You wait here," Johnny said to Brad. "I want to talk to Rudy alone." He ostentatiously took the papers he had been working on with him as he went toward Rudolph's bedroom door.

"You fellas don't mind if I mix myself a little drink while I'm waiting, do you?" Brad said.

Johnny closed the door behind them when he and Rudolph were in the bedroom. "We have a decision to make," he said. "If as he says he's got close to a hundred thousand cash, we can take it and cut our losses. That is, about twenty thousand give or take a few dollars in one way or another. If we don't take it, we have to report it and ask for a creditors' meeting and probably put him through bankruptcy. If we don't start criminal proceedings. All his creditors would have an equal shot at the money, or at least pro rata, according to the size of their investments and the amount he actually owes them."

"Does he have the right to pay us off like that, preferentially?"

"Well, he isn't in bankruptcy yet," Johnny said. "I think it would stand up in a court of law."

"Nothing doing," Rudolph said. "Let him throw it into the pot. And let's get the safety-deposit box keys from him tonight, so he can't lift the money before we can stop him."

Johnny sighed. "I was afraid you'd say that," he said. "When knighthood was in flower."

"Just because he's a crook," Rudolph said, "doesn't mean that I'm going to be a crook to cut my losses, as you say."

"I said I thought it would probably stand up in a court of law," Johnny said.

"Not good enough," Rudolph said. "Not good enough for me."

Johnny looked speculatively at Rudolph. "What would you do if I went to him and said, okay, I'll take my half, and drop out of the rest of it?"

"I'd report it at the creditors' meeting," Rudolph said evenly, "and make a motion to sue you for recovery."

"I surrender, dear," Johnny said. "Who can stand up to an honest politician?"

They went back into the living room. Brad was standing at the window, a full glass in hand, tickets at the fifty yard line for the big game of the season in his wallet, gazing out at the rich, friendly city of Dallas. Johnny explained what they had decided. Brad nodded, numbly, not quite understanding.

"And we want you back here tomorrow morning at nine o'clock," Rudolph said. "Before the banks open. We'll go around with you to those safety-deposit boxes you spoke about and we'll take care of the money for you. We'll give you a receipt for your files. If you're not here by one minute before nine, I'll call the police and make out a complaint for fraud."

"Rudy . . . " Brad said plaintively.

"And if you want to hold onto those fancy, pearl cufflinks," Rudolph said, "you'd better hide them someplace, because by the end of the month the sheriff is going to come around to seize your property, every bit of property you own, including that pretty, frilled shirt you're wearing, to satisfy your debts."

"You guys," Brad said brokenly. "You guys . . . you don't know what it's like. You're rich, you've got wives with millions, you've got everything you want. You don't know what it's like to be somebody like me."

"Don't break our hearts," Rudolph said roughly. He had never been as angry with anyone in his whole life. He had to restrain himself from jumping on the man and trying to strangle him. "Just be here at nine o'clock."

"Okay. I'll be here." Brad said. "I don't suppose you want to have dinner with me . . . ?"

"Get out of here before I kill you," Rudolph said.

Brad went to the door. "Well," he said, "have a good time in Dallas. It's a great city. And remember . . . " He gestured for the suite, the liquor. "All this on my bill."

Then he went out.

Rudolph didn't have time to call home the next morning. Brad came over at nine o'clock, as ordered, red eyed and looking as though he hadn't slept all night, with a collection of keys for safety-deposit boxes in various Dallas banks. Ottman hadn't called the night before, although Rudolph and Johnny had dined in the hotel to be ready for his call. Rudolph took it as a sign that all had gone smoothly on the Whitby campus and that Ottman's fears had been exaggerated.

Rudolph and Johnny, with Brad in tow, went to the office of a lawyer whom Johnny knew. There, the lawyer drew up a power of attorney, for Johnny to act as Rudolph's representative. Johnny was going to stay in Dallas to sort out the mess. Then, with a clerk from the lawyer's office as a witness, they went from bank to bank and watched as Brad, not wearing his pearl cufflinks, opened the boxes and took out neat packages of cash. All four men counted the bills methodically, before the clerk made out a receipt, which Rudolph and Johnny signed, acknowledging that they had received the sum from Bradford Knight, and the date. The lawyer's clerk would then duly witness the slip of paper, after which they would all go up to the main floor from the bank's vault and deposit the money in a joint account in Rudolph's and Johnny's names, all withdrawals to be made on presentation of *both* signatures. Rudolph and Johnny had planned the procedure the night before, knowing that from now on anything to do with Bradford Knight would have to stand up to scrutiny.

After the last box had been emptied, the final figure stood at ninety-three thousand dollars. Brad had been almost accurate in his estimate of what he had hidden away for what he called a rainy day. Neither Johnny nor Rudolph asked him where the money had come from. That would be somebody else's job.

The visit to the lawyer's office and the round of the banks had taken up most of the morning and Rudolph had to hurry to catch his plane, which was to leave Dallas for Washington at noon. As he rushed out of the suite, carrying his bag and small briefcase, he saw that the only bottles of the array in the salon that had been opened had been the one Coke he had taken himself and the fifth of bourbon that Brad had drunk from.

Brad had offered him the use of his car to take him to the airport. "This morning, anyway," he had said, trying to smile, "I still got my Cadillac. Might as well enjoy it." But Rudolph had refused and called for a taxi. As he climbed into the taxi he asked Johnny to telephone his office in Whitby and tell his secretary that he couldn't get home tonight, but would be staying over at the Mayflower Hotel in Washington.

On the plane he did not eat the lunch nor drink the two Manhattans. He got the Comptroller's estimates out of his briefcase and tried to work, but he couldn't concentrate on the figures before him. He kept thinking about Brad, doomed, branded, bankrupt, with a jail sentence hanging over his head. Ruined for what? For a money-digging Hollywood tart. It was sickening. He loved her, Brad had said, it had been worth it. Love, the Fifth Horseman of the Apocalypse. At least in Texas. It was almost impossible to associate Brad with the emotion. He was a man born, Rudolph saw now, for saloons and brothels. Maybe he had known it all the time and had refused to acknowledge it. Still, it was always difficult to believe in the existence of the love of others. Perhaps his refusal to accept the fact that Brad actually was capable of love was condescension on his part. He himself loved Jean, he thought, but would he face ruin for her? The answer had to be no. Was he then more superficial than the blubbering, sweating man in the ruffled shirt? And was he responsible in some way for the hideous day his friend was passing through now and the even more hideous days to come? When he had killed Brad's chances with Calderwood on the steps of the Country Club, the afternoon of the wedding, had he subconsciously prepared Brad's fate for him? When he had invested in Brad's business, out of guilt, hadn't he really known that one day Brad would revenge himself, and in the only way possible to Brad, by cheating? And had he not, in fact, wanted it to happen to rid himself finally of Brad because Brad had not believed him about Virginia? And even more disturbingly, if he had succumbed to Virginia Calderwood's proposals and slept with her, would she have married Brad, and in marrying him, carried her husband out of the area of his friend's protection? For there was no doubt about it—he had protected

Brad through the years, first in calling him East for a job that dozens of other men could initially have done better, then in training him carefully (and overpaying him in the process) so that in Brad's mind at least the idea of being awarded the top post in the firm was a reasonable one. At what point was it moral to stop protecting a friend? Never?

It would have been easier to allow Johnny Heath to go down to Dallas and handle the matter alone. Johnny had been Brad's friend, too, and the best man at his wedding, but it had never been the same thing as between Rudolph and Brad. Somehow, it had been more hurtful to Brad to have to answer to Rudolph, face to face. God knows, it would have been easy for Rudolph to have pleaded pressure of work in Whitby and sent Johnny off on his own. He had considered it, but rejected it as cowardly. He had made the trip to maintain his own self-esteem. Self-esteem might be another way of saying vanity. Had his continued success dulled his sensibilities, led him into complacency and self-righteousness?

When the bankruptcy was finally settled, he decided, he would somehow pension Brad off. Five thousand dollars a year, paid secretly, so that neither Brad's creditors nor the government could touch it? Would the money, which Brad would so desperately need and have to accept, pay for the sting of having to accept it from a man who had turned his back on him?

The seat-belt sign went on. They were making the approach for the landing. Rudolph put the papers back into his briefcase, sighed, and hooked up his belt.

When he got to the Mayflower there was a message waiting for him from his secretary. It was urgent, the message read, for him to call his office as soon as possible.

He went up to his room, where nobody had bothered to supply any liquor, and called his office. Twice, the line was busy, and he nearly decided to abandon the attempt to reach his office and get in touch with the Senator who was most likely to help him in keeping Billy Abbott out of harm's way in the United States army. It was not something that could be arranged over the phone and he hoped to make an appointment for lunch the next day and then take an afternoon plane for New York.

On the third try, he got his secretary. "I'm terribly sorry, Mr. Mayor," Walter said, sounding exhausted, "but I'm afraid you'd better get up here right away. After the office closed last night and I'd gone home, all hell broke lose, I just found out about it this morning or I'd have tried to get through to you sooner."

"What is it? What is it?" Rudolph asked impatiently.

"It's all terribly confused and I'm not sure that I have the sequence of events all straight," Walter said. "But when Ottman tried to go into the dormitory last night, they had it barricaded, the students, I mean, and they wouldn't let the police in. President Dorlacker tried to get Ottman to call the police off, but Ottman refused. Then when they tried to get in again, the students began to throw things. Ottman got hit in the eye with a stone, nothing serious, they say, but he's in the hospital, and the police gave up, at least for last night. Then other students organized a mass march and I'm afraid they demonstrated in front of your house. I went out to your house just awhile ago and the lawn is in frightful condition. Mrs. Jordache is under sedation and . . ."

"You can tell me the rest of the story when I get there," Rudolph said. "I'm getting the first plane out of Washington."

"I thought that's what you would do," Walter said, "and I took the liberty of sending Scanlon down with your car. He'll be waiting at La Guardia."

Rudolph picked up his bags and hurried down to the lobby and checked out. Billy Abbott's military career would have to hang in abeyance for awhile.

Scanlon was a fat man who wheezed when he talked. He was on the police force, but was nearly sixty years old and was scheduled for retirement. He suffered from rheumatism and it was almost as an act of mercy that he had been assigned as chauffeur to Rudolph. As an object lesson in civic economy Rudolph had sold the former mayor's car, which had been owned by the town, and used his own car.

"If I had it to do all over again," Scanlon said breathily, "I swear to God I'd never sign on any police force in a town where there was college students or niggers."

"Scanlon, please," Rudolph said. He had been trying to correct Scanlon's vocabulary since the first day, with little success. He was sitting up front with the old patrolman, who drove at a maddeningly slow pace. But he would have been offended if Rudolph took the wheel.

"I mean it, sir," Scanlon said. "They're just wild animals. With no more respect for the law than a pack of hyenas. As for the police—they just laugh at us. I don't like to tell you your business, Mr. Mayor, but if I was you, I'd go right to the Governor and ask for the Guard."

"There's time enough for that," Rudolph said.

"Mark my words," said Scanlon. "It'll come to it. Look what they've done down in New York and out in California."

"We're not in New York or California," Rudolph said.

"We got students and niggers," Scanlon said stubbornly. He drove silently for awhile. Then he said, "You shoulda been at your house last night, Mr. Mayor, then maybe you'd know what I was talking about."

"I heard about it," Rudolph said. "They trampled the garden."

"They did a lot more than that," Scanlon said. "I wasn't there myself, but Ruberti was there, and he told me." Ruberti was another policeman. "It was sinful what they did, Ruberti told me, sinful. They kept calling for you and singing dirty-minded songs, young girls, using the dirtiest language anybody ever heard, and they pulled up every plant in your garden and then when Mrs. Jordache opened the door . . . "

"She opened the door?" Rudolph was aghast. "What did she do that for?"

"Well, they started throwing things at the house. Clods of dirt, beer cans, and yelling, 'Tell that motherfucker to come out.' They meant you, Mr. Mayor, I'm ashamed to say. There was only Ruberti and Zimmermann there, the whole rest of the force was up at the college, and what could just two of them do against those howling wild Indians, maybe three hundred of them. So like I said, Mrs. Jordache opened the door and yelled at them."

"Oh, Jesus," Rudolph said.

"You might as well hear it now from me as later from somebody else," Scanlon said. "When Mrs. Jordache opened the door, she was drunk. And she was stark naked."

Rudolph made himself stare straight ahead at the tail lights of the cars ahead of him and into the blinding beams of light of the cars going the other way.

"There was a kid photographer there, from the school paper," Scanlon went on, "and he took some flashlight pictures. Ruberti went for him, but the other kids made a kind of pocket and he got away. I don't know what use they think they're going to make of the pictures, but they got them."

Rudolph ordered Scanlon to drive directly to the university. The main administration building was brilliantly floodlit and there were students at every window, throwing out thousands of pieces of paper from the files and shouting at the line of policemen, alarmingly few, but armed with their clubs now, who cordoned off the buildling. As he drove up to where Ottman's car was parked under a tree, Rudolph saw what use had been made of the photograph of his wife taken naked the night before. It had been enormously blown up and it was hanging from a first-story window. In the glare of the floodlights, the image of Jean's body, slender and perfect, her breasts full, her fists clenched and threatening, her face demented, hung, a mocking banner, over the entrance of the building, just above the words carved in the stone, "Know the truth and the truth shall make ye free."

When Rudolph got out of the car, some of the students at the windows recognized him and greeted him with a wild, triumphant howl. Somebody leaned out the window and shook Jean's picture, so that it looked as though she were doing an obscene dance.

Ottman was standing beside his car, a big bandage over one eye, making his cap sit on the back of his head. Only six of the policemen had helmets. Rudolph remembered vetoing a request from Ottman for two dozen more helmets six months before, because it had seemed an unnecessary expense.

"Your secretary told us you were on your way," Ottman said, without any preliminaries, "so we held off on any action until you got here. They have Dorlacker and two professors locked in there with them. They only took the building at six o'clock tonight."

Rudolph nodded, studying the building. At a window on the ground floor he saw Quentin McGovern. Quentin was a graduate student now and had a job as an assistant in the chemistry department. Quentin was grinning down at the scene. Rudolph was sure that Quentin saw him and he felt that the grin was directed, personally, at him.

"Whatever else happens tonight, Ottman," Rudolph said, "I want you to arrest that black man there, the third window from the left on the ground floor. His name is McGovern and if you don't get him here get him at his home."

Ottman nodded. "They want to talk to you, sir. They want you to go in there and discuss the situation with them."

Rudolph shook his head. "There's no situation to be discussed." He wasn't going to talk to anybody under the photograph of his naked wife. "Go in and clear the building."

"It's easier said than done," Ottman said. "I've already called on them three times to come out. They just laugh."

"I said clear the buildling." Rudolph was raging, but cold. He knew what he was doing.

"How?" Ottman asked.

"You've got weapons."

"You don't mean you want us to use guns?" Ottman said incredulously. "As far as we know, none of them is armed."

Rudolph hesitated. "No," he said. "No guns. But you've got clubs and you've got tear gas."

"You sure you don't want us just to sit tight and wait till they get tired?" Ottman said. He sounded more tired himself than any of the students in the building would ever be. "And if things don't improve, ask for the Guard, maybe?"

"No, I don't want to sit and wait." Rudolph didn't say it, but he knew that Ottman knew he wanted that picture down immediately. "Tell your men to start with the grenades."

"Mr. Mayor," Ottman said slowly, "you'll have to put that in writing for me. Signed."

"Give me your pad," Rudolph said.

Ottman gave him the pad, and Rudolph used the fender of Ottman's car to steady it and wrote out the order, making sure that his handwriting was clear and legible. He signed his name and gave the pad back to Ottman, who tore off the top sheet on which Rudolph had written and carefully folded the piece of paper and put it in the pocket of his blouse. He buttoned the pocket of the blouse and then went along the line of police, some thirty strong, the town's entire force, to give his orders. As he passed them, the men began to put on their gas masks.

The line of police moved slowly across the lawn toward the building, their shadows, in the blaze of the floodlights, intense on the brilliant green grass. They did not keep a straight line, but wavered uncertainly, and they looked like a long, wounded animal, searching not to do harm, but to find a place to hide from its tormentors. Then the first grenade was shot off through one of the lower windows and there was a shout from within. Then more grenades were sent through other windows and the faces that had been there disappeared and one by one the policemen, helping each other, began to climb through the windows into the building.

There hadn't been enough police to send around to the back of the building, and most of the students escaped that way. The acrid smell of the gas drifted out toward where Rudolph was standing, looking up toward where Jean's picture was still hanging. A policeman appeared at the window above and ripped it away, taking it in with him.

It was all over quickly. There were only about twenty arrests. Three students were bleeding from scalp wounds and one boy was carried out with his hands up to his eyes. A policeman said he was blinded but that he hoped it was only temporary. Quentin McGovern was not among the group arrested.

Dorlacker came out with his two professors, their eyes tearing. Rudolph went over to him. "Are you all right?" he asked.

Dorlacker squinted to see who was addressing him. "I'm not talking to you, Jordache," he said. "I'm making a statement to the press tomorrow and you can find out what I think of you if you'll buy your own paper tomorrow night." He got into somebody's car and was driven away.

"Come on," Rudolph said to Scanlon. "Drive me home."

As they drove away from the campus, ambulances passed them, their sirens going. A school bus, for the students who had been arrested, lumbered past them.

"Scanlon," Rudolph said, "as of tonight, I'm no longer Mayor of this town, am I?"

Scanlon didn't answer for a long time. He scowled as he watched the road and he wheezed like an old man when he had to turn a corner. "No, Mr. Jordache," he finally said, "I wouldn't think you were."

CHAPTER 7

1968

I

THIS TIME, WHEN he got off the plane at Kennedy, there was nobody there to greet him. He was wearing dark glasses and he moved uncertainly. He hadn't written Rudolph that he was coming because he knew from Gretchen's letters that Rudolph had enough to think about without bothering with a half-blind brother. While he was working on the boat in the Antibes harbor during the winter, a line had snapped and whipped across his face and the next day he had started having dizzy spells and suffering from double vision. He had pretended nothing was wrong, because he didn't want Kate and Wesley to worry about him. He had written Mr. Goodhart for the name of an eye specialist in New York and when he received Goodhart's answer had announced to Kate that he was going to New York to arrange finally about his divorce. Kate had been after him to marry her and he didn't blame her. She was pregnant and was due to have the child in October and it was the middle of April already.

She had made him buy a new suit and he was ready to face any lawyer or doorman now. He was wearing the dead Norwegian's pea jacket because it was still in good condition and there was no sense in throwing money away.

A planeload of people who had been on a ski holiday had landed just before him and the baggage hall was full of skis and tanned, healthy-looking, fancily dressed men and women, many of them loud and more or less drunk. He tried not to be anti-American as he searched for his bag.

He took a cab, although it was expensive, because he felt he couldn't cope with getting on and off the airport bus and fiddling with his bag again and struggling to find a taxi in New York.

"The Paramount Hotel," he said to the taxi driver and settled back wearily on the seat, closing his eyes.

When he had checked in and gone up to his room, which was small and dark, he called the doctor. He would have liked to go over right away, but the nurse said that the doctor couldn't see him before eleven o'clock the next day. He undressed and got into bed. It was only six o'clock New York time, but it was eleven o'clock Nice time and he had taken the plane at Nice. His body felt as though he hadn't slept for forty-eight hours.

"The retina is partially detached," the doctor said. The examination had been slow and thorough and painful. "I'm afraid I'll have to turn you over to a surgeon."

Thomas nodded. Another wound. "How much is it going to cost?" he asked. "I'm a working man and I can't pay Park Avenue prices."

"I understand," the doctor said. "I'll explain to Dr. Halliwell. The nurse has your telephone number, hasn't she?"

"Yes."

"She'll call you and tell you when to report to the hospital. You'll be in good hands." He miled reassuringly. His own eyes were large and clear, unscarred, without lesions.

Three weeks later he was out of the hospital. His face was drained and pale and the doctor had warned him that he was to avoid any sudden movements or strenuous exertion for a long time. He had lost about fifteen pounds and his collar swam around his neck and his clothes hung loosely from his shoulders. But he wasn't seeing double any more and he wasn't attacked by dizzy spells when he turned his head.

The whole thing had cost him a little over twelve hundred dollars, but it was worth it.

He checked in again at the Paramount Hotel and called the number of Rudolph's apartment. Rudolph answered himself.

"Rudy," Thomas said, "how are you?"

"Who is this?"

"Tom."

"Tom! Where are you?"

"Right here. In New York. At the Hotel Paramount. Can I see you sometime soon?"

"You certainly can." Rudolph sounded genuinely pleased. "Come on right over. You know where it is."

When he arrived at Rudolph's building, he was stopped by the doorman, new suit or no new suit. He gave his name and the doorman pressed a button and said, "Mr. Jordache, there's a Mr. Jordache to see you."

Thomas heard his brother say, "Please tell him to come up," and crossed the marbled lobby to the elevator, thinking, With all that protection, he still got hurt.

Rudolph was standing in the hallway when the elevator door opened. "Lord, Tom," he said, as they shook hands, "I was surprised to hear your voice." Then he stepped back and regarded Thomas critically. "What's happened to you?" he asked. "You look as though you've been sick."

Thomas could have said that he didn't think that Rudolph looked so hot, himself, but he didn't say it. "I'll tell you all about it," he said, "if you give me a drink." The doctor had said to go easy on the drink, too.

Rudolph let him into the living room. It looked just about the same as it had the last time Thomas had been there, comfortable, spacious, a place for comfortable small events, not decorated for failure.

"Whiskey?" Rudolph asked, and when Thomas nodded, poured one for Thomas and one for himself. He was fully dressed, with collar and tie, as though he were in an office. Thomas watched him as he picked up the bottles from the sideboard and hit the ice in the bucket with a small silver hammer. He looked much older than when Thomas had seen him last, with lines deep around his eyes and in his forehead. His movements were hesitant, tentative. Finding the tool to open the soda water bottle was a problem. He didn't seem to be certain about how much soda water he should put in each glass. "Sit down, sit down," he said. "Tell me what brings you here. How long have you been in New York?"

"About three weeks." He took the glass of whiskey and sat down on a wooden chair.

"Why didn't you call me?" He sounded hurt by the delay.

"I had to go to the hospital for an operation," Thomas said. "On my eyes. When I'm sick I like to be alone."

"I know," Rudolph said, sitting across from him in an easy chair. "I'm the same way myself."

"I'm okay now," Thomas said. "I have to take it easy for a little while, that's all. Cheers." He raised his glass. Between Pinky Kimball and Kate he had learned to say cheers before drinking.

"Cheers," Rudolph said. He stared soberly at Thomas. "You don't look like a fighter, any more, Tom," he said.

"You don't look like a mayor any more," Thomas said, and regretted having said it, immediately.

But Rudolph laughed. "Gretchen told me she wrote you all about it," he said. "I had a little bad luck."

"She wrote me you sold the house in Whitby," Thomas said.

"There wasn't much sense in trying to hang on." Rudolph swished the ice in his drink around the glass thoughtfully. "This place is enough for us now. Enid's out in the park with her nurse. She'll be back in a few minutes. You can say hello to her. How's your boy?"

"Fine," Thomas said. "You ought to hear him talk French. And he handles the boat better than I do. And nobody's making him do close-order drill in the afternoons."

"I'm glad it turned out well," Rudolph said. He sounded as if he meant it. "Gretchen's boy—Billy—is in the Army in Brussels, at NATO."

"I know. She wrote me that, too. And she wrote me you arranged it."

"One of my last official acts," Rudolph said. "Or maybe I should say, semiofficial acts." He had a hushed, quiet way of talking now, as though he didn't want to make any statements too positively.

"I'm sorry the way things happened, Rudy," Thomas said. For the first time in his life he pitied his brother.

Rudolph shrugged. "It could have been worse," he said. "That kid could have been killed instead of just blinded."

"What're you going to do now?"

"Oh, I keep myself busy, one way and another," Rudolph said. "New York's a great place to be a gentleman of leisure in. When Jean gets back maybe we'll do a bit of traveling. Maybe even visit you."

"Where is she?"

"In a home upstate," Rudolph said, making noise with the ice in his glass. "Not a home, really—more of a clinic—a drying-out place. They have a remarkable record of cures. This is the second time she's been there. After the first time, she didn't touch a drop for nearly six months. I'm not supposed to go up there and visit her—some goddamn doctor's theory—but I hear from the man who runs the place and he says she's doing very well. . . ." He swallowed some whiskey the wrong way and coughed a little. "Maybe I can use a little cure myself," he said, smiling, when the coughing fit had passed. "Now," he said, brightly, "now that the eye is all right, what are your plans?"

"I've got to get a divorce, Rudy," Thomas said. "And I thought maybe you could help me."

"That lawyer I sent you to said there wouldn't be any problem. You should've done it then."

"I didn't have the time," Thomas said. "I wanted to get Wesley out of the country as quick as possible. And in New York, I'd have to come out with the reason. I don't want Wesley to find out I got a divorce from his mother because she's a whore. And even if I did get the divorce in New York, it would take too long. I'd have to hang around here and I'd miss a good part of my season and I can't afford that. And I have to be divorced by October at the latest."

"Why?"

"Well . . . I'm living with a woman. An English girl. A wonderful girl. And she's going to have a baby in October."

"I see," Rudolph said. "Congratulations. The increasing tribe of Jordaches. Maybe the line can stand some English blood. What do you want me to do?"

"I don't want to have to talk to Teresa," Thomas said. "If I see her, I'm afraid of what I'll do to her. Even now. If you or somebody could talk to her and get her to go out to Reno or a place like that . . ."

Rudolph put his glass down neatly. "Sure," he said. "I'll be glad to help." There was a noise at the door. "Ah, here's Enid." He called, "Come here, baby." Enid came bouncing in, dressed in a red coat. She stopped short when she saw the strange man in the room with her father. Rudolph picked her up, kissed her. "Say hello to your Uncle Thomas," he said. "He lives on a boat."

Three mornings later, Rudolph called Thomas and made a date for lunch with him at P. J. Moriarty's, on Third Avenue. The atmosphere there was male and plain and not likely to make Thomas feel ill at ease or give him the idea that Rudolph was showing off.

Thomas was waiting for him at the bar when he came in, a drink in front of him. "Well," Rudolph said, as he sat down on the stool next to his brother's, "the lady's on her way to Nevada."

"You're kidding," Thomas said.

"I drove her to the airport myself," Rudolph said, "and watched the plane take off."

"Christ, Rudy," Thomas said, "you're a miracle worker."

"Actually, it wasn't so hard," Rudolph said. He ordered a martini, to get over the effects of a whole morning with Teresa Jordache. "She's thinking of remarrying, too, she says." This was a lie, but Rudolph said it convincingly. "And she saw the wisdom of not dragging her good name, as she calls it, through the courts in New York."

"Did she hit you for dough?" Thomas asked. He knew his wife.

"No," Rudolph lied again. "She says she makes good money and she can afford the trip."

"It doesn't sound like her," Thomas said doubtfully.

"Maybe life has mellowed her." The martini was sustaining. He had argued with the woman for two whole days and had finally agreed to pay for her round-trip fare, first class, her hotel bill in Reno for six weeks, plus five hundred dollars a week, for what Teresa had described as loss of trade. He had paid her half in advance and would pay her the rest when she came back and gave him the papers that formally ended her marriage.

They had a good, solid lunch, with two bottles of wine, and Thomas became a little maudlin and kept telling Rudy how grateful he was and how stupid he had been all these years not to realize what a great guy he had for a brother. Over cognacs, he said, "Look, the other day you said you were going to do some traveling when your wife got out of the clinic. The first two weeks in July I haven't got a charter. I'll keep it open and you and your wife can come on board, as my guests, and we'll do a little cruising. And if Gretchen can come, bring her along, too. You've got to meet Kate. Christ, the divorce'll be final by then and you can come to my wedding. Come on, Rudy, I won't take no for an answer."

"It depends upon Jean," Rudolph said. "How she feels . . ."

"It'll be the best thing in the world for her," Thomas said. "There won't be a bottle of liquor on board. Rudy, you just got to do it."

"Okay," Rudy said. "The first of July. Maybe it'll do us both good to get out of this country for awhile."

Thomas insisted upon paying for the lunch. "It's the least I can do," he said. "I got a lot to celebrate. I got back an eye and got rid of a wife all in the same month."

II

The Mayor was wearing a sash, the bride was dressed in cornflower blue and did not look pregnant. Enid was wearing white gloves and was holding her mother's hand and was frowning a little at the mysterious games the grown-ups were playing in a language she did not understand. Thomas was brown and healthy again. He had put back the weight he had lost and his muscular neck bulged at the collar of the white shirt he was wearing. Wesley stood just behind his father, a tall, graceful boy of fifteen in a suit whose sleeves were too short for him, his face deeply tanned, and his blond hair bleached by the Mediterranean sun. They were all tanned because they had been cruising for a week and had only come back to Antibes for the ceremony. Gretchen, Rudolph thought, looked superb, her dark hair with just a little animal sheen of gray in it, severely drawn around the bony, wide-eyed, magnificent face. Queenlike, Rudolph thought, nobly tragic. Rhetoric went with weddings. Rudolph knew that the single week on the sea had made him look years younger than when he had stepped off the plane at Nice. He listened, amused, to the Mayor, who was describing, in a rich Midi accent, full of rolling hard *g*'s, the duties expected of the bride. Jean understood French, too, and they exchanged little smiles as the Mayor went on. Jean hadn't had a drink since she had come down from the clinic and she looked clear and beautifully fragile in the room full of Thomas's friends from the harbor, with their weather-worn, strong, dark faces, above unaccustomed neckties and jackets. There was an aura of voyages in the sunny, flower-bedecked Mayor's office, Rudolph thought, a tang of salt, the flavors of a thousand ports.

Only Dwyer seemed sad, touching the white carnation in his button-hole. Thomas had told Rudolph Dwyer's story and Rudolph thought perhaps the sight of his friend's happiness made Dwyer regret the girl in Boston he had foresworn for the *Clothilde*.

The Mayor was robust and obviously liked this part of his job. He was as sun-darkened as the seamen around him. When I was the mayor of another town, Rudolph thought, I didn't spend much time in the sun. He wondered if the Mayor was worried about kids smoking pot in dormitories and whether or not to order the police to use tear gas. Whitby, too, at certain seasons, looked idyllic.

When he had first met Kate, Rudolph had been disappointed in his brother's choice. He was partial to pretty women and Kate, with her flat, dark, humble face, and her stubby body, was certainly not pretty in any conventional terms. She reminded him of some of the native women in Gauguin's Tahitian paintings. *Vogue* and *Harper's Bazaar*, he thought, have much to answer for. With all those long, slender beauties, they have tuned us out from simpler and more primitive appeals.

Kate's speech, shy, uneducated, and Liverpudlian, had jarred on his ears in the beginning, too. It was curious, Rudolph thought, how Americans, with their ideas of the English formed by visiting actors and lecturers, were more snobbish about British accents than those of their own countrymen.

But after a day or two of watching Kate with Tom and Wesley, uncomplainingly doing all sorts of chores on board the ship, handling the man and the boy with the most transparent, undemonstrative love and trust, he had felt ashamed of his first reactions to the woman. Tom was a lucky man, and he told him so and Tom had soberly agreed.

The Mayor came to the end of his speech, rings were exchanged, bride and groom kissed each other. The Mayor kissed the bride, beaming, as though he had brilliantly performed some extraordinarily delicate bureaucratic function.

The last wedding Rudolph had attended had been that of Brad Knight and Virginia Calderwood. He preferred this one.

Rudolph and Gretchen signed the register, after the newlyweds. Rudolph hesitantly kissed the bride. There were finger-mangling handshakes all around, and the entire party trooped out into the sunlight of the town that had been founded more than two thousand years ago by men who must have looked very much like the men who accompanied his brother in the wedding procession.

There was champagne waiting for them at Chez Felix au Port and melon and bouillabaisse for lunch. An accordionist played, the Mayor toasted the bride, Pinky Kimball toasted the bridegroom in Southampton French, Rudolph toasted the couple in French that made the guests gaze at him with wonder and got him a great round of applause when he finished. Jean had brought along a camera and took roll after roll of photographs to commemorate the occasion. It was the first time since the night she had broken her cameras that she had taken any pictures. And Rudolph hadn't suggested it. She had suggested it herself.

The lunch broke up at four o'clock and all the guests, some of them weaving now, paraded the bridal couple back to where the *Clothilde* lay at the quay. On the after deck there was a big crate tied up in red ribbon. It was Rudolph's wedding gift and he had arranged for it to be put aboard during the festivities. He had had it shipped over from New York to Thomas's agent, with instructions to hold it until the wedding day.

Thomas read the card. "What the hell is this?" he asked Rudolph.

"Open it and find out."

Dwyer went to get a hammer and chisel and the bridegroom stripped down to the waist and with all the guests crowding around, broke open the crate. Inside it was a beautiful Bendix radar set and scanner. Before leaving New York, Rudolph had spoken to Mr. Goodhart and asked him what Thomas would like best for the *Clothilde* and Mr. Goodhart had suggested the radar.

Thomas held the set up triumphantly, and the guests applauded Rudolph again, as though he personally had invented and manufactured the machine with his own hands.

There were tears in Thomas's eyes, a little drunken, to be sure, as he thanked Rudolph. "Radar," he said. "I've been wanting this for years."

"I thought it made a fitting wedding present," Rudolph said. "Mark the horizon, recognize obstacles, avoid wrecks."

Kate, sea-going wife, kept touching the machine as though it were a delightful young puppy.

"I tell you," Thomas said, "this is the greatest goddamn wedding anybody ever had."

The plan was to set sail that afternoon for Portofino. They would stay along the coast past Monte Carlo, Menton, and San Remo, then cross the Gulf of Genoa during the night and make a landfall on the Italian mainland some time the next morning. The *météo* was good and the entire voyage, according to Thomas, shouldn't take more than fifteen hours.

Dwyer and Wesley wouldn't allow Thomas or Kate to touch a line, but made them sit enthroned on the afterdeck while they got the *Clothilde* under way. As the anchor finally came up and the ship turned its nose seaward, from various boats in the harbor there came the sound of horns, in salute, and a fishing boat full of flowers accompanied them to the buoy, with two men strewing the flowers in their wake.

As they hit the gentle swell of open water they could see the white towers of Nice far off across the Baie des Anges.

"What a place to live," Rudolph said. "France."

"Especially," Thomas said, "if you're not a Frenchman."

III

Gretchen and Rudolph sat in deck chairs near the stern of the *Clothilde,* watching the sun begin to set behind them. They were just opposite the Nice airport and could watch the jets swoop in, one every few minutes. Coming in, their wings gleamed in the level sunlight and nearly touched the silvery sea as they landed. Taking off, they climbed above the escarpment of Monaco, still brightly sunlit to the east. How pleasant it was to be moving at ten knots, Rudolph thought, and watch everybody else going at five hundred.

Jean was below putting Enid to bed. When she was on deck Enid wore a small orange life-jacket and she was attached by a line around her waist to a metal loop on the pilot house to make sure she wasn't lost overboard. The bridegroom was forward sleeping off his champagne. Dwyer was with Kate in the galley preparing dinner. Rudolph had protested about this and had invited them all to dinner in Nice or Monte Carlo, but Kate had insisted. "I couldn't think of a better thing to do on my wedding night," Kate had said. Wesley, in a blue turtle-neck sweater, because it was getting cool, was at the wheel. He moved around the boat, barefooted and sure handed, as though he had been born at sea.

Gretchen and Rudolph were wearing sweaters, too. "What a luxury it is," Rudolph said, "to be cold in July."

"You're glad you came, aren't you?" Gretchen asked.

"Very glad," Rudolph said.

"The family restored," Gretchen said. "No, not even that. *Assembled,* for the first time. And by Tom, of all people."

"He's learned something we never quite learned," Rudolph said.

"He certainly has. Have you noticed—wherever he goes, he moves in an atmosphere of love. His wife, Dwyer, all those friends at the wedding. Even his own son." She laughed shortly.

She had talked to Rudolph about her visit with Billy in Brussels before she had come down to Antibes to join them, so Rudolph knew what was behind the laugh. Billy, safe in an Army office as a typist and clerk, was, she had told Rudolph, cynical, ambitionless, sweating out his time, mocking of everything and everybody, including his mother, incurious about the wealth of the Old World around him, shacking up with silly girls in Brussels and Paris, one after the other, smoking marijuana, if he wasn't going in for stronger stuff, risking jail with the same lack of interest that he had risked getting kicked out of college, unwavering in his icy attitude toward his mother. At their last dinner in Brussels, Gretchen had reported, when the subject of Evans Kinsella had finally come up, Billy had been savage. "I know all about people your age," he had said. "Big phoney ideals, going into raptures about books and plays and politicians that just make people my age horse laugh, out saving the world and going from one crap-talking artist to another to pretend you're still young and the Nazis have just been licked and the brave new world is just around the corner or at the next bar or in the next bed."

"In a way," Gretchen had told Rudolph, "maybe he's right. Hateful but right. When he says the word phoney. You know better than anyone about me. When the time came I didn't tell him, 'Go to prison,' or 'Desert.' I just called my influential brother and saved my son's miserable skin and let other mothers persuade their sons to go to prison or desert or march on the Pentagon, or go die in the jungle someplace. Anyway, I've signed my last petition."

There was nothing much Rudolph could say to that. He had been the necessary accomplice. They were both guilty as charged.

But the week on the sea had been so healing, the wedding so gay and optimistic, that he had consciously put it all from his mind. He was sorry that the sight of Wesley at the wheel, brown and agile, had made them both, inevitably, think about Billy.

"Look at him," Gretchen was saying, staring at Wesley. "Brought up by a whore. With a father who never got past the second year in high school, who hasn't opened a book since then and who's been beaten and hunted and knocked down and lived ever since he was sixteen with the scum of the earth. And no questions asked. When Tom decided the time was right he got his kid and took him to another country and made him learn another language and threw him in with a whole group of ruffians who can barely read and write. And he's made him go to work at an age when Billy was still asking for two dollars on Saturday night to go to the movies. As for the amenities of family life." She laughed. "That boy sure has his share of elegant privacy, living in the next room to a little English peasant girl who's his father's mistress, with his father's illegitimate child in her belly. And what's the result? He's healthy and useful and polite. And he's so devoted to his father. Tom doesn't ever have to raise his voice to him. All he has to do is *indicate* what he wants the boy to do and the boy does it. Christ," she said, "we'd better start rewriting all those books on child care. And one thing that boy is sure of. No draft board is going to send *him* to Viet Nam. His father will see to that. I'll tell you something—if I were you, as soon as Enid is big enough to walk around this boat without falling overboard, I'd send her over here to let Tom bring her up for you. Lord, I could use a drink. Tom must have one bottle of something stashed away on this Woman's Christian Temperance Union vessel."

"I imagine he has," Rudolph said. "I'll ask." He got up from his chair and went forward. It was getting dark and Wesley was putting the running lights on. Wesley smiled at him as he passed him. "I guess the excitement was too much for the old man," he said. "He hasn't even been up to check whether I'm heading into the Alps or not."

"Weddings don't happen every day," Rudolph said.

"They sure don't," Wesley said. "It's a lucky thing for Pa they don't. His constitution couldn't stand it."

Rudolph went through the saloon to the galley. Dwyer was washing lettuce in the sink and Kate, no longer dressed for celebration, was basting a roast in the oven. "Kate," Rudolph said, "has Tom got a bottle hidden away down here somewhere?"

Kate closed the oven door and stood up and looked troubledly at Dwyer. "I thought he promised you we'd be bone dry all the time you were on board," she said.

"That's all right, Kate," Rudolph said. "Jean's in the cabin with the kid. It's for Gretchen and me. We're up on deck and it's getting nippy."

"Bunny," Kate said to Dwyer, "go get it."

Dwyer went up forward to his cabin and came back with a bottle of gin. Rudolph poured the gin into two glasses and put some tonic in with it.

When he returned to Gretchen and gave her her glass, she made a face. "Gin and tonic. I hate it."

"If Jean happens to come up on deck, we can pretend it's just plain tonic. It disguises the smell of the gin."

"You hope," Gretchen said.

They drank. "It's Evans's favorite drink," Gretchen said. "Among our many points of difference."

"How's it going?"

"The same," she said carelessly. "A little worse each year, but the same. I suppose I ought to quit him, but he needs me. He doesn't want me so damned much, but he needs me. Maybe needing is better than wanting at my age."

Jean came on deck, in tight, low-waisted pink denim pants and a pale-blue cashmere sweater. She glanced at the glasses in their hands but didn't say anything.

"How's Enid?" Rudolph asked.

"Sleeping the sleep of the just. She asked if Kate and Uncle Thomas got to keep the rings they gave each other." She shivered. "I'm cold," she said and snuggled up against Rudolph's shoulder. He kissed her cheek.

"Fee-fie-fo-fum," Jean said. "I smell the blood of an Englishman."

The tonic hadn't fooled her. Not for an instant.

"One drop," she said.

Rudolph hesitated. If he had been alone, he would have held onto his glass. But Gretchen was there, watching them. He couldn't humiliate his wife in front of his sister. He gave Jean the glass. She took a tiny sip, then handed the glass back to him.

Dwyer came out on deck and began to set the table for dinnr, putting out little weighted brass hurricane lamps with candles in them. The table was always tastefully set on board, with the candles at night and straw place mats and a little bowl of flowers and a wooden salad bowl. Somehow, Rudolph thought, watching Dwyer work, neat in his pressed chino pants and blue sweater, somehow among the three of them they have developed a sense of style. The candles winked in their glasses, like captured fireflies, making small, warm pools of light in the center of the big, scrubbed table.

Suddenly, there was a dull, thudding noise against the hull and a chattering under the stern. The boat throbbed unevenly and there was a clanking below decks before Wesley could cut the engines. Dwyer ran to the after rail and peered at the wake, pale in the dark sea.

"Damn it," he said, pointing, "we hit a log. See it?"

Rudolph could see a dim shadow floating behind him, just a bare two or three inches protruding from the water. Thomas came running out, barefooted and bare chested, but clutching a sweater. Kate was on his heels.

"We hit a log," Dwyer said to him. "One or maybe both of the screws."

"Are we going to sink?" Jean asked. She sounded frightened. "Should I get Enid?"

"Leave her alone, Jean," Thomas said calmly. "We're not going to sink." He pulled on his sweater and went into the pilot house and took the wheel. The ship had lost way and was swinging a little in the light wind, bobbing against the swell. Thomas started the port engine. It ran normally and the propeller turned smoothly. But when he started the starboard engine there was a metallic clanking below and the *Clothilde* throbbed irregularly. Thomas cut the starboard engine and they moved forward slowly. "It's the starboard propeller. And maybe the shaft, too," he said.

Wesley was near tears. "Pa," he said, "I'm sorry. I just didn't see it."

Thomas patted the boy's shoulder. "It's not your fault, Wes," he said. "Really not. Look into the engine room and see if we're taking any water in the bilge." He cut the port engine and in a moment they were drifting again. "A wedding present from the Med," he said, but without bitterness. He filled a pipe and lighted it and put his arm around his wife and waited for Wesley to come up on deck.

"Dry," Wesley said.

"She's solid," Thomas said. "The old *Clothilde*." Then he noticed the glasses in Rudolph's and Gretchen's hands. "We continuing the celebration?" he asked.

"Just one drink," Rudolph said.

Thomas nodded. "Wesley," he said, "take the wheel. We're going back to Antibes. On the port engine. Keep the revs low and watch the oil and water gauges. If the pressure drops or it begins to heat up, cut it right away."

Rudolph could sense that Thomas would have preferred to take the wheel himself, but he wanted to make sure that Wesley didn't feel guilty about the accident.

"Well, folks," Thomas said as Wesley started the engine and slowly swung the *Clothilde*'s bow around, "I'm afraid there goes Portofino."

"Don't worry about us," Rudolph said. "Worry about the boat."

"There's nothing we can do tonight," Thomas said. "Tomorrow morning, we'll put on the masks and go down and take a look. If it's what I think it is, it'll mean waiting for a new screw and maybe a new shaft and putting her up on land to fit them. I could go on to Villefranche, but I get a better deal from the yard in Antibes."

"That's all right," Jean said. "We all love Antibes."

"You're a nice girl," Thomas said to Jean. "Now, why don't we all sit down and have our dinner?"

They could only do four knots on the one engine and Antibes harbor was silent and dark as they entered it. No horns greeted their arrival and no flowers were strewn in their wake.

IV

There was a small, insistent tapping sound in his dream and as he swam up from sleep Thomas thought, Pappy is at the door. He opened his eyes, saw that he was in his bunk with Kate sleeping beside him. He had rigged up another section to the lower bunk so that he and Kate could sleep comfortably together. The new section could be folded back during the day, to give them room to walk around the small cabin.

The tapping continued. "Who's there?" he whispered. He didn't want to wake Kate.

"It's me," came the answering whisper. "Pinky Kimball."

"In a minute," Thomas said. He didn't turn on the light, but dressed in the dark. Kate slept deeply, worn out by the day's activities.

Barefoot, in sweater and pants, Thomas cautiously opened the cabin door and went out into the gangway, where Pinky was waiting for him. There was a huge smell of drink coming from Pinky, but it was too dark in the gangway for Thomas to tell just how drunk he was. He led the way up to the pilot house, past the cabin where Dwyer and Wesley slept. He looked at his watch. Two-fifteen on the phosphorescent dial. Pinky stumbled a little going up the ladder. "What the hell is it, Pinky?" Thomas asked irritably.

"I just came from Cannes," Pinky said thickly.

"So what? Do you always wake up people when you come from Cannes?"

"You got to listen to me, mate," Pinky said. "I saw your sister-in-law in Cannes."

"You're drunk, Pinky," Thomas said disgustedly. "Go to sleep."

"In pink pants. Listen, why would I say a thing like that if I didn't glom her? I saw her all day, didn't I? I'm not that drunk. I can recognize a woman I see all day, can't I? I was surprised and went up to her and I said I thought you were on the way to Portofino and she said I am not on my way to Portofino, we had an accident and we're bloody well in Antibes harbor."

"She didn't say bloody well," Thomas said, not wishing to believe that Jean was anyplace else but on the *Clothilde,* asleep.

"A turn of phrase," Pinky said. "But I saw her."

"Where in Cannes?" He had to remember to keep his voice down, so as not to awaken the others.

"In a strip-tease joint. La Porte Rose. It's on the rue Bivouac Napoléon. At the bar with a big Yugoslav or something in a gabardine suit. I've seen him around. He's a pimp. He's done time."

"Oh, Christ. Was she drunk?"

"Looping," Pinky said. "I offered to take her back to Antibes with me but she said, This gentleman here will drive me home when we are ready."

"Wait here," Thomas said. He went down into the saloon and along the aft gangway, passing the cabins where Gretchen and Enid slept. There was no sound from either cabin. He opened the door to the master cabin in the stern. There was a light on in the gangway all night, in case Enid wanted to go to the bathroom. When Thomas opened the main cabin door, just enough to look in, he saw Rudolph sleeping in pajamas, in the big bed. Alone.

Thomas closed the door gently and went back up to Pinky. "You saw her," he said.

"What're you going to do?" Pinky asked.

"Go and get her," Thomas said.

"Do you want me to come with you? It's a rough crowd."

Thomas shook his head. Pinky sober was no help. Drunk he'd be worthless. "Thanks. You go to sleep. I'll see you in the morning." Pinky started to remonstrate, but Thomas said, "Go ahead, go ahead," and pushed him gently toward the gangplank. He watched Pinky walk unsteadily along the quay, going in and out of shadow, toward where the *Vega* was berthed. He felt his pockets. He had some loose change in his wallet. Then he went down to his own cabin, stepping carefully past the cabin that Dwyer and Wesley shared. He woke up Kate with a slight tap on her shoulder.

"Keep it low," he said. "I don't want to wake up the whole ship." Then he told her Pinky's news. "I've got to go get her," he said.

"Alone?"

"The fewer the better," he said. "I'll bring her back and put her in her husband's bed and tomorrow he can say his wife has a headache and is staying in bed for a day or so and nobody'll catch on to anything. I don't want Wesley or Bunny to see the lady drunk." He also didn't want Wesley or Dwyer to be around if there was going to be any trouble.

"I'll go with you," Kate said. She started to get up. He pushed her down.

"I don't want her to know that you've seen her drunk with a pimp either. We've got to live the rest of our lives as friends."

"You'll be careful, won't you?"

"Of course, I'll be careful," he said. He kissed her, "Sleep well, darling."

Any other woman would have made a fuss, he thought as he went up on deck. Not Kate. He put on the espadrilles he always left at the gangplank and went down to the quay. He was lucky. Just as he was going through the archway a taxi drove up and let off a couple in evening clothes. He got into the taxi and said, "La rue Bivouac Napoléon, Cannes."

She wasn't at the bar when he went into La Porte Rose. And there was no Yugoslav in a gabardine suit, either. There were two or three men standing at the bar, watching the show, and a couple of hookers. There were some single men at tables and three men whose looks he didn't like, sitting with one of the performers at a table near the entrance. Two elderly American couples sat at a table on the edge of the dance floor. An act was just beginning. The band was playing loudly and a red-headed girl in an evening dress was swaying around the floor in the spotlight, slowly taking off a long glove that went up nearly to her shoulder.

Thomas ordered a Scotch and soda. When the barman brought the drink and placed it in front of him, he said, in English, "I'm looking for an American lady who was in here awhile ago. Brown hair. Wearing pink pants. With a monsieur in a gabardine suit."

"Have not zee no American lady," the barman said.

Thomas put a hundred-franc note on the bar.

"Maybe I begin to remembair," the barman said.

Thomas put down another hundred-franc note. The barman looked around him quickly. The two notes disappeared. He took up a glass and began to polish it assiduously. He spoke without looking at Thomas. With all the noise from the band there was no danger of his being overheard.

"Be-ind *les toilettes*," the barman said, speaking rapidly, "is found *un escalier*, staircase, to ze cave. Ze *plongeur*, ze dishwasher, he sleep there after work. Per'aps you find what you look for in cave. The name of fellow is Danovic. *Sal* type. Be careful. He has friends."

Thomas watched while the strip-teaser took off one stocking and waved it and began to work on the garter of the other stocking. Then, still seeming to be interested in the act, he strolled slowly toward the illuminated sign in the rear that said Toilettes, Telephone. Everybody in the room seemed to be watching the girl in the spotlight and he was fairly sure that no one noticed him as he went through the archway under the sign. He passed the stink of the toilets and saw the steps going to the cellar. He went down them quickly. There was a thin, veneered wooden door at the bottom of the steps, with patched strips showing in the dim light of the small bulb that lit the stairway. Over the noise of the band, he could hear a woman's voice from behind the door, pleading hysterically, then being cut off, as though by a hand across the mouth. He tried the door, but it was locked. He backed off a little and lunged at the door. The rotten wood and the flimsy lock gave at the same time and he plunged through the doorway. Jean was there, struggling to sit up, on the dishwasher's cot. Her hair was streaming wildly about her face and her sweater was half torn from one shoulder. The man in the gabardine suit, Danovic, was standing beside her, facing the door. In the light of the one bulb strung on a wire from the ceiling. Thomas could see stacks of empty wine bottles, a work bench, some carpentry tools spread about.

"Tom!" Jean said. "Get me out of here." She had been frightened out of her drunkenness or she hadn't been as drunk as Pinky had imagined. She tried to stand up, but the man pushed her back roughly, still facing Thomas.

"What do you want?" Danovic said. He spoke English, but thickly. He was about the same size as Thomas, with heavy shoulders. He had a knife or razor scar down one side of his face.

"I came to take the lady home," Thomas said.

"I'll take the lady home when I'm good and ready," Danovic said. "*Fout-moi le camp*, Sammy." He pushed heavily at Jean's face, as she struggled again to get up.

Overhead, the noise of the band increased as another garment came off.

Thomas took a step nearer the cot. "Don't make any trouble," he said to the man quietly. "The lady's coming with me."

"If you want her, you will have to take her from me, Sammy," Danovic said. He reached back suddenly and grabbed a ball-peen hammer from the workbench and held it up in his fist.

Oh, Christ, Thomas thought, Falconettis everywhere.

"Please, please, Tom," Jean was sobbing.

"I give you five seconds to leave," Danovic said. He moved toward Thomas, the hammer ready, at the level of Thomas's face.

Somehow, Thomas knew, no matter what happened, he had to keep the hammer away from his head. If it hit him even a glancing blow, that would be the end of it. "Okay, okay," he said, retreating a little and putting up his hands placatingly. "I'm not looking for a fight." Then he dove at Danovic's legs as the hammer swung. He got his head into the crotch, butting as hard as he could. The hammer hit his shoulder and he felt the shoulder going numb. The man was reeling backward, off balance, and Thomas wrapped his arms around his knees and toppled him. His head must have hit something, because for a fraction of a second he didn't struggle. Thomas took the chance and pulled his head up. Danovic swung the hammer and hit the elbow that Thomas threw up to protect himself. He went for the hand with the hammer again, clawing at the man's eyes with his other hand. He missed the hammer and felt a stab of pain in his knee as the hammer came down again. This time he got hold of the hammer. He ignored the blows of the other hand and twisted hard. The hammer slid a little way on the cement floor and Thomas leapt for it, using his knees to keep the man away from him. They both were on their feet agan, but Thomas could hardly move because of his knee and he had to switch the hammer to his left hand because his right shoulder was numb.

Over the noise of the band and his own gasping he could hear Jean screaming, but faintly, as though she were far away.

Danovic knew Thomas was hurt and tried to circle him. Thomas made himself swing around, making the leg work for him. Danovic lunged at him and Thomas hit him above the elbow. The arm dropped, but Danovic still swung the good arm. Thomas saw the opening and hit the man on the temple, not squarely, but it was enough. Danovic staggered, fell on his back. Thomas dropped on him, straddling his chest. He lifted the hammer above Danovic's head. The man was gasping, protecting his face with his arm. Thomas brought the hammer down three times on the arm, on the shoulder, the wrist and the elbow, and it was all over. Danovic's two arms lay useless alongside his body. Thomas lifted the hammer to finish him off. The man's eyes were opaque with fear as he stared up, the blood streaming down from the temple, a dark river in the delta of his face.

"Please," he cried, "please, don't kill me. *Please*." His voice rose to a shriek.

Thomas rested on Danovic's chest, getting his breath back, the hammer still raised in his left hand. If ever a man deserved to get killed, this was the man. But Falconetti had deserved to get killed, too. Let somebody else do the job. Thomas reversed the hammer and jammed the handle hard into Danovic's gaping, twitching mouth. He could feel the front teeth breaking off. He no longer was able to kill the man, but he didn't mind hurting him.

"Help me up," he said to Jean. She was sitting on the cot, holding her arms up in front of her breasts. She was panting loudly, as though she had fought, too. She stood up slowly, unsteadily, and came over and put her hands under his armpits and pulled. He rose to his feet and nearly fell as he stepped away from the shivering body beneath him. He was dizzy and the room seemed to be whirling around him, but he was thinking clearly. He saw a white-linen coat that he knew belonged to Jean thrown over the back of the room's single chair, and he said, "Put on your coat." They couldn't walk through the nightclub with Jean's sweater torn from her shoulder. Maybe he couldn't walk through the nightclub at all. He had to use his two hands to pull his bad leg up, one step after another, on the staircase. They left Danovic lying on the cement floor, the hammer sticking up from his broken mouth, bubbling blood.

As they went through the archway under the Toilettes, Telephone sign, a new strip-tease was starting. The entertainment was nonstop at La Porte Rose. Luckily, it was dark outside the glare of the spotlight on the *artiste,* who was dressed in a black, skirted riding habit, with derby and boots and whip. Leaning heavily on Jean's arm, Thomas managed not to limp too nticeably and they were almost out of the door before one of the three men sitting near the entrance with the girl spotted them. The man stood up and called, "*Allô! Vous là. Les Americains. Arrêtez. Pas si vive.*"

But they were out of the door and somehow they managed to keep walking and a taxi was passing by and Thomas hailed it. Jean struggled to push him in and then tumbled in after him and the taxi was on its way to Antibes by the time the man who had called out to them came out on the sidewalk looking for them.

In the cab, Thomas leaned back, exhausted, against the seat. Jean huddled in her white coat in a corner, away from him. He couldn't stand his own smell, mingled with the smell of Danovic and blood and the dank cellar, and he didn't blame Jean for keeping as far away from him as possible. He passed out, or fell asleep, he couldn't tell which. When he opened his eyes again they were going down the street toward the harbor of Antibes. Jean was weeping uncontrollably in her corner, but he couldn't worry any more about her tonight.

He chuckled as they came up to where the *Clothilde* was tied up.

The chuckle must have startled Jean. She stopped crying abruptly. "What're you laughing about, Tom?" she asked.

"I'm laughing about the doctor in New York," he said. "He told me to avoid any sudden movements or strenuous exertion for a long time. I'd have loved to see his face if he'd been there tonight."

He forced himself to get out of the cab unaided and paid the driver off and limped up the gangplank after Jean. He had a dizzy spell again and nearly fell sideways off the gangplank into the water.

"Should I help you to your cabin?" Jean asked, when he finally made it to the deck.

He waved her away. "You go down and tell your husband you're home," he said. "And tell him any story you want about tonight."

She leaned over and kissed him on the lips. "I swear I'll never touch another drop of liquor again as long as I live," she said.

"Well, then," he said, "we've had a successful evening, after all, haven't we?" But he patted her smooth, childish cheek, to take the sting out of his words. He watched as she went down through the saloon and to the main cabin. Then he painfully went below and opened the door to his own cabin. Kate was awake and the light was on. She made a hushed, choked sound when she saw what he looked like.

"Sssh," he said.

"What happened?" she whispered.

"Something great," he said. "I just avoided killing a man," He dropped onto the bunk. "Now get dressed and go get a doctor."

He closed his eyes, but he heard her dressing swiftly. By the time she was out of the room he was asleep.

He was up early, awakened by the sound of hissing water, as Dwyer and Wesley hosed off the deck. They had come into port too late the night before to do it then. He had a big bandage around his knee and every time he moved his right shoulder he winced with pain. But he could have been worse. The doctor said there were no broken bones, but that the knee had been badly mauled and perhaps some cartilage had been torn away. Kate was already in the galley preparing breakfast and he lay alone in the bunk, his body remembering all the other times in his life he had awakened bruised and aching. His memory bank.

He pushed himself out of the bunk with his good arm and stood in front of the little cabinet mirror on his good leg. His face was a mess. He hadn't felt it at the time, but when he had toppled Danovic his face had crashed against the rough concrete floor and his nose was swollen and his lip puffed out and there were gashes on his forehead and cheekbones. The doctor had cleaned out the cuts with alcohol and compared to the rest of him his face felt in good shape, but he hoped Enid wouldn't go screaming to her mother when she got a glimpse of him.

He was naked and there were black-and-blue welts blooming all over his chest and arms. Schultzy should see me now, he thought, as he pulled on a pair of pants. It took him five minutes to get the pants on and he couldn't manage a shirt at all. He took the shirt with him and clumped, hopping mostly, into the galley. The coffee was on and Kate was squeezing oranges. Once the doctor had assured her that nothing serious was wrong, she had become calm and businesslike. Before he had gone to sleep, after the doctor had left, he had told her the whole story.

"You want to kiss the bridegroom's beautiful face?" he said.

She kissed him gently, smiling, and helped him on with his shirt. He didn't tell her how much it hurt when he moved his shoulder.

"Does anybody know anything yet?" he asked.

"I haven't told Wesley or Bunny," she said. "And none of the others have come up yet."

"As far as anybody is concerned, I was in a fight with a drunk outside Le Cameo," Thomas said. "That will be an object lesson to anybody who goes out drinking on his wedding night."

Kate nodded. "Wesley's been down with the mask already," she said. "There's a big chunk out of the port screw and as far as he can tell the shaft is twisted, too."

"If we get out of here in a week," Thomas said, "we'll be lucky. Well, I might as well go up on deck and start lying."

He followed Kate as she went up the ladder carrying the orange juice and the coffee pot on a tray. When Wesley and Dwyer saw him, Dwyer said, "For Christ's sake what did you do to yourself?" and Wesley said, "Pa!"

"I'll tell everybody about it when we're all together," Thomas said. "I'm only going to tell the story once."

Rudolph came up with Enid and Thomas could tell from the look on his face that Jean had probably told him the true story or most of the true story. All Enid said was, "Uncle Thomas, you look funny this morning."

"I bet I do, darling," Thomas said.

Rudolph didn't say anything, except that Jean had a headache and was staying in bed and that he'd take her some orange juice after they'd all had their breakfast. They had just sat down around the table when Gretchen came up. "Good God, Tom," she said, "what in the world happened to you?"

"I was waiting for someone to ask that question," Thomas said. Then he told the story about the fight with the drunk in front of Le Cameo. Only, he said, laughing, the drunk hadn't been as drunk as he had been.

"Oh, Tom," Gretchen said, distractedly, "I thought you'd given up fighting."

"I thought so, too," Thomas said. "Only that drunk didn't."

"Were you there, Kate?" Gretchen asked accusingly.

"I was in bed asleep," Kate said placidly. "He sneaked out. You know how men are."

"I think it's disgraceful," Gretchen said. "Big, grown men fighting."

"So do I," Thomas said. "Especially when you lose. Now let's eat breakfast."

V

Later that morning Thomas and Rudolph were up in the bow alone. Kate and Gretchen had gone to do the marketing, taking Enid along with them, and Wesley and Dwyer were down looking at the screws again with the masks.

"Jean told me the whole story," Rudolph said. "I don't know how to thank you, Tom."

"Forget it. It wasn't all that much. It probably looked a lot worse than it was to a nicely brought up girl like Jean."

"All that drinking going on all day," Rudolph said bitterly, "and then the final straw—Gretchen and me drinking here on board before dinner. She just couldn't stand it. And alcoholics can be so sly. How she could have gotten out of bed and dressed and off the ship without my waking up . . ." He shook his head. "She's behaved so well, I guess I thought there was nothing to worry about. And when she has a couple, she's not responsible. She's not the same girl at all. You don't think that when she's sober she goes around picking men up in bars in the middle of the night?"

"Of course not, Rudy."

"She told me, she told me," Rudolph said. "This polite-looking, well-spoken young man came up to her and said he had a car outside and he knew a very nice bar in Cannes that stayed open until dawn and would she like to come with him, he'd bring her back whenever she wanted . . ."

"Polite-looking, well-spoken young man," Thomas said, thinking of Danovic lying on the floor of the cellar with the handle of the ball-peen hammer sticking up from his broken teeth. He chuckled. "He's not so polite looking or well spoken this morning. I can tell you that."

"And then when they got to that bar, a strip-tease joint—God, I can't even *imagine* Jean in a place like that—" he said it was too noisy for him at the bar, there was a little cosy club downstairs . . ." Rudolph shook his head despairingly. "Well, you know the rest."

"Don't think about it, Rudy, please," Thomas said.

"Why didn't you wake me up and take me along with you?" Rudolph's voice was harsh.

"You're not the sort of man for a trip like that, Rudy."

"I'm her husband, for Christ's sake."

"That was another reason for not waking you up," said Thomas.

"He could have killed you."

"For a little while there," Thomas admitted, "the chances looked pretty good."

"And you could have killed him."

"That's the one good thing about the night," Thoma said. "I found out I couldn't. Now, let's go back and see what the divers're up to." He hobbled down the deck from the bow, leaving his brother and his brother's guilts and gratitudes behind him.

VI

He was sitting alone on the deck, enjoying the calm late evening air. Kate was down below and the others had all gone on a two-day automobile trip to the hill towns and into Italy. It had been five days since the *Clothilde* had come back into the harbor and they were still waiting for the new propeller and shaft to be delivered from Holland. Rudolph had said that a little sightseeing was in order. Jean had been dangerously quiet since her night of drunkenness and Rudolph kept doing his best to distract her. He had asked Kate and Thomas to come along with them, but Thomas had said the newlyweds wanted to be alone. He had even privately told Rudolph to invite Dwyer along with the party. Dwyer had been pestering him to point out the drunk who had beaten him up outside Le Cameo and he was sure Dwyer was thinking of cooking up some crazy scheme of retaliation with Wesley. Also, Jean kept following him around without saying anything, but with a peculiar, haunted look in her eyes. Lying for five days had been something of a strain and it was a relief to have the ship to himself and Kate for a little while.

The harbor was silent, the lights out in most of the ships. He yawned, stretched, stood up. His body had gotten over feeling bruised and while he still limped, his leg had stopped feeling as though it was broken in half somewhere along the middle when he walked. He hadn't made love to his wife since the fight and he as thinking that this might be a good night to start in again, when he saw the car without lights driving swiftly along the quay. The car stopped. It was a black DS 19. The two doors on his side opened and two men got out, then two more. The last man was Danovic, one arm in a sling.

If Kate hadn't been aboard, he would have dived over the side and let them try to get him. But there was nothing for him to do but stand there. There was nobody on the boats on either side of him. Danovic remained on the quay, as the other three men came aboard.

"Well, gentlemen," Thomas said. "what can I do for you?"

Then something hit him.

He came out of the coma only once. Wesley and Kate were in the hospital room with him. "No more . . ." he said, and then slipped back into the coma again.

Rudolph had called a brain specialist in New York and the specialist was on his way to Nice when Thomas died. The skull had been fractured, the surgeon had explained to Rudolph and there had been catastrophic bleeding.

Rudolph had moved Gretchen and Jean and Enid to a hotel. Gretchen had strict orders not to leave Jean alone for a minute.

Rudolph had told the police what he knew and they had talked to Jean, who had broken down hysterically after a half hour's questioning. She had told them about La Porte Rose and they had picked up Danovic, but there had been no witnesses to the beating and Danovic had an alibi for the entire night that couldn't be shaken.

VII

The morning after the cremation Rudolph and Gretchen went by taxi to the place and got the metal box with their brother's ashes. Then they drove toward Antibes harbor, where Kate and Wesley and Dwyer were expecting them. Jean was at the hotel with Enid. It would have been too much for Kate to bear, Rudolph thought, to have to stand by Jean's side today. And if Jean got drunk, Rudolph thought, she would finally have good reason to do so.

Gretchen now knew the true story of the wedding night, as did the others.

"Tom," Gretchen said in the taxi, as they drove through the bustle of holiday traffic, "the one of us who finally made a life."

"Dead for the one of us who didn't," Rudolph said.

"The only thing you did wrong," Gretchen said, "was not waking up one night."

"The only thing," Rudolph said.

After that they didn't speak until they reached the *Clothilde*. Kate and Wesley and Dwyer, dressed in their working clothes, were waiting for them on the deck. Dwyer and Wesley were red eyed from crying, but Kate, although grave faced, showed no signs of tears. Rudolph came on board carrying the box and Gretchen followed him. Rudolph put the box in the pilot house and Dwyer took the wheel and started the one engine. Wesley pulled up the gangplank and then jumped ashore to throw off the two stern lines, which Kate reeled in. Wesley leaped across open water, landed catlike on the stern, and swung himself aboard, then ran forward to help Kate with the anchor.

It was all so routine, so much like every other time they had set out from a port, that Rudolph, on the after deck, had the feeling that at any moment Tom would come rolling out of the shadow of the pilot house, smoking his pipe.

The immaculate white-and-blue little ship chugged past the harbor mouth in the morning sunlight, only the two figures standing in incongruous black on the open deck making it seem any different from any other pleasure craft sailing out for a day's sport.

Nobody spoke. They had decided what they were to do the day before. They sailed for an hour, due south, away from the mainland. Because they were only on one engine they did not go far and the coast line was clear behind them.

After exactly one hour, Dwyer turned the boat around and cut the engine. There were no other craft within sight and the sea was calm, so there wasn't even the small sound of waves. Rudolph went into the pilot house, took out the box and opened it. Kate came up from below with a large bunch of white and red gladioli. They all stood in a line on the stern, facing the open, empty sea. Wesley took the box from Rudolph's hands and, after a moment's hesitation, his eyes dry now, started to strew his father's ashes into the sea. It only took a minute. The ashes floated away, a faint sprinkling of dust on the blue glint of the Mediterranean.

The body of their father, Rudolph thought, also rolled in deep waters.

Kate threw the flowers in with a slow, housewifely gesture of her round, tanned arms.

Wesley tossed the metal box and its cover over the side, both face down. They sank immediately. Then Wesley went to the pilot house and started the engine. They were pointed toward the coast now and he held a straight course for the mouth of the harbor.

Kate went below and Dwyer went forward to stand in the prow, leaving Gretchen and Rudolph, death colored, together on the after deck.

Up in the bow, Dwyer stood in the little breeze of their passage, watching the coast line, white mansions, old walls, green pines, grow nearer in the brilliant light of the morning sun.

Rich man's weather, Dwyer remembered.

Beggarman, Thief

TO JIM AND GLORIA

AUTHOR'S NOTE

ORDINARILY THERE IS no need for a preface for a novel, but because of the television presentation of "Rich Man, Poor Man" (Part I and Part II), I believe the readers of *Beggarman, Thief* should know that the new book is a sequel to the *printed* version of *Rich Man, Poor Man,* not the televised one, and any similarities to the Part II television offering are purely coincidental.

I hope this note helps clear up any confusion in the mind of the reader of this book who has also viewed either or both of the two television series.

Part One

CHAPTER 1

1968

From Billy Abbott's notebook—

I am worthless, Monika says. She says it only half-seriously. Monika, on the other hand, is not demonstrably worthless. Being in love with her undoubtedly clouds my vision of her. More about that later.

She asked me once what I write in this notebook. I told her that the Colonel keeps saying we here in NATO are on the firing line of civilization. It is important for future generations, I told her, to know what it was like to be on the firing line of civilization in Brussels in the second half of the twentieth century. Maybe some dusty, irradiated scholar will dig around in the ruins of the city and come upon this notebook, charred a little around the edges and perhaps stiff with the rusty stains of my blood, and be grateful to Wm. Abbott, Junior, for his forethought in jotting down his observations of how the simple American soldier lived while defending civilization on the edge of Europe. What the price of oysters was, the shape and dimensions of his beloved's breasts, his simple pleasures, like fucking and stealing gasoline from the army, things like that.

Monika said, Did I always have to be frivolous? And I said, what else is there to be? Don't you believe in anything? She asked me.

I believe in not bucking the tide, I told her. If there's a parade going down the street I fall in line and keep step, waving to the populace, friend and foe alike.

Go back to your scribbling, she said. Write down that you're not a true representative of your generation.

Scribbling perhaps is the word for what I'm doing. I come from a literary family. Both my mother and father are—or were—writers. Of a sort. My father was a public relations man, a member of a profession not held in particularly high esteem in the halls of Academe or in publishers' offices. Still whatever the merits or failures that can be put to his account, he achieved them at a typewriter. He lives in Chicago now and writes me often, especially when he is drunk. I reply dutifully. We are great friends when we are four thousand miles apart.

My mother used to write criticism for nasty little magazines. Our communications are minimal. She does something for the movies now. I grew up to the music of typewriters and it seems normal for me to put my thoughts, such as they are, on paper. The amusements are limited here, although it's better than Nam, as the Colonel keeps saying.

I play tennis with the Colonel and praise his feeble backhand, which is one way of getting ahead in the army.

If the preemptive Russian strike doesn't hit NATO, as the Colonel warns it will, I'll keep scribbling. It gives me something to do when things get slow at the motor pool, where I am called the Truckmaster.

I wonder what the guy in charge of the motor pool at the headquarters of the Warsaw Pact Forces is doing tonight as I write this.

ALEXANDER HUBBELL WAS a newspaperman. Or at least he worked for *Time* Magazine in Paris. He was not supposed to be a newspaperman this week because he was on holiday with his wife. His wife was taking a siesta in the hotel at the base of the cape and Alexander Hubbell was approaching the *préfecture* of police in Antibes. He had been puzzling over a name that he had read in *Nice-Matin* three days ago, Jordache. An American named Jordache had been murdered in the port of Antibes just five days after his wedding. The murderer or murderers were being sought. For the time being no motive for the crime had been found. The victim who had been the owner of a yacht called the *Clothilde,* berthed in the harbor of Antibes, had been clubbed to death on the deck of his own ship.

Hubbell prided himself on his newspaperman's memory and it had annoyed him that a name he felt he should have recognized and classified played only at the edges of his consciousness. He was relieved when he remembered. When he was still working in New York, there had been an issue of *Life* Magazine with the photographs of ten promising young politicians throughout the United States and one of the pictures had been of somebody called Jordache, he couldn't recall the Christian name, who was the mayor of a small town about a hundred miles from New York City called Whitby. Then he remembered more. After the piece in *Life* there had been a scandal at the college in Whitby when rioting students had demonstrated in front of the mayor's home and the mayor's wife had appeared at the doorway drunk and naked. Somebody had taken a photograph and the print had gone around the office.

Still, a man whose wife had exposed herself bare-assed in front of a howling mob of students might well have gotten rid of her and married somebody with less flamboyant habits.

Of course, it might be somebody entirely different with the same name, Hubbell thought, as he waited for a light to change. A yacht in Antibes was a long way from Whitby, New York. Anyway, it was worth looking into. If it turned out to be the same promising young politician it would make a useful little story, vacation or no vacation. He had been on holiday five days already and was beginning to get bored.

The single policeman in the paint-flaked empty anteroom was dozing behind his desk, but brightened, glad for company, when Hubbell told him, in his good French, that he was a newspaperman and that he had come to make inquiries about the murder. The policeman went into another room and came out a moment later to tell him that the *chef* could see him now. Crime, it seemed, was not rife in Antibes that afternoon.

The *chef* was a sleepy-eyed, small, dark man in a blue T-shirt and rumpled cotton pants. A gold front tooth gleamed when he spoke: "What can I do for you, *monsieur?*"

Hubbell explained that the details of the murder of an American in France, especially if this was the Jordache he thought it was, a man of considerable importance back home, would be of interest to the American public. He and his editors would be most grateful to the *chef* for any light he could shed on the affair.

The *chef* was used to French newspapermen, who had treated the murder as a routine settling of waterfront accounts. This shrewd-looking American, representative of a prestigious magazine, investigating the death of a fellow countryman in a holiday resort that attracted many Americans, was a different matter. The *chef* would have been happier if the arrest had already been made and the culprit behind bars, but there was no help for that at the moment.

"Are there any clues," the man was saying, "as to who might have done it or what the motives were?"

"We are working on the case with diligence," the *chef* said. "Twenty-four hours a day."

"Do you have any leads?"

The *chef* hesitated for a moment. In the movies reporters were always finding clues the police overlooked. The American seemed like an intelligent man and there was the possibility that he might come up with something useful. "On the night of his wedding," the *chef* said, "*Moniseur* Jordache was involved in an argument—a brutal argument, I have been told by his sister-in-law—in a bar in Cannes called La Porte Rose—with a man who is known to the police. A foreigner. Yugoslav. By name Danovic. We have interrogated him. He has a perfect alibi, but we would like to question him again. Unfortunately, he seems to have disappeared. We are at the moment looking for him."

"A brutal argument," Hubbell said. "You mean a fight."

The *chef* nodded. "Of extreme brutality, I have been told by the sister-in-law."

"Do you know what it was about?"

"The sister-in-law claims that the foreigner was about to commit rape on her when *Monsieur* Jordache intervened."

"I see," Hubbell said. "Was Jordache in the habit of getting into fights in bars?"

"Not to my knowledge," the *chef* said. "I knew *Monsieur* Jordache. In fact, we occasionally had a glass together. It was with great sorrow that I learned of his death. I knew him as a peaceful man. He was very well liked. He had no known enemies. However—I cannot believe that he was a man of some importance in America, as you have said."

"*Nice-Matin* says he owned a yacht," Hubbell said. He laughed lightly. "That's pretty important."

"He worked the yacht," the *chef* said. "He was a charter captain. It was his means of livelihood."

"I see," Hubbell said. He couldn't imagine one of the ten most promising young politicians in America making his living out of ferrying boating parties around the Mediterranean, no matter how many times his wife had displayed herself naked back home. The story was becoming less interesting. "Perhaps the murder was political?" he asked hopefully.

"I don't believe so. He was not a political man at all. We tend to accumulate information on political people."

"Smuggling?"

"I hardly think so. In that field, too, we have our information. Or at least suspicions."

"How would you describe him, then?" Hubbell persisted, out of force of habit.

The *chef* shrugged. "A decent workingman. A good type." *Brave type* in French. Measured praise, slightly patronizing from a French cop. "Honest, as far as anyone knew," the *chef* went on. "We were not really intimate. He spoke very little French. Not like you, *monsieur*." Hubbell nodded recognition of the compliment. "And my English, I regret to say, is most rudimentary." The *chef* smiled at his disability. "We did not discuss our private philosophies."

"What did he do before he came here? Do you know?"

"He was a merchant seaman." The *chef* hesitated. Jordache had told him over a glass of wine, after the *chef* had commented on the broken nose, the scar tissue, that he had been a boxer. But he had asked the *chef* to keep quiet about it. In waterfront cafés boxers were likely targets for large men made belligerent by drink. "I didn't come to France to fight," Jordache had said. "It isn't my lucky country for fighting. I had one bout in Paris and got my brains knocked out." He'd laughed as he said it. From the look of the body the fight he'd been in before he died hadn't been a lucky one, either.

Well, the *chef* thought, why not tell the newspaperman? It couldn't do any harm anymore to Jordache, who wasn't going to be doing much drinking in waterfront cafés from now on. "It appears," said the *chef*, "that he was a professional pugilist. He even fought in Paris. Once. In the main event. He was knocked out."

"A fighter?" Hubbell's interest was aroused once more. The sports section might run a couple of hundred words. If the man had fought a main event in Paris he must have had some sort of reputation. People would be curious about an American fighter being killed in France. He would telex into the office as much of the story as he could dig up here and tell it to get the background dope out of the morgue. They rewrote all of his stories in New York anyway. "Jordache?" Hubbell said. "I don't remember any fighter by that name."

"He fought under an assumed name," the *chef* said, making a mental note for himself to look into that part of Jordache's history. Professional boxing was a business that gangsters were always mixed up in. There might be a lead there—a promise broken, a deal gone sour. He should have thought of it sooner. "He fought under the name of Tommy Jordan."

"Ah," the newspaperman said. "That helps. Certainly. I remember some stories in the papers about him. That he was promising."

"I know nothing about that," the *chef* said. "Just the fight in Paris. I looked it up in *l'Equipe*. He was a great disappointment, *l'Equipe* said." Now he wanted to call a promoter in Marseilles who had connections with the *milieu*. He stood up. "I'm afraid I have to go back to work now," he said. "If you want more information perhaps you could speak to the members of his family. His wife, his brother, his son."

"His brother? He's here?"

"The entire family," the *chef* said. "They had been on a cruise together."

"Would you happen to know the brother's first name?"

"Rudolph. The family was originally German."

Rudolph, Hubbell thought, remembering, Rudolph Jordache, that was the name in *Life*. "So," he said, "he wasn't the one who was married here?"

"No," the *chef* said impatiently.

"And his wife is here, too?"

"Yes, and under the circumstances she, the sister-in-law, might be able to help you more than I can . . ."

"The sister-in-law?" Hubbell said, standing too. "The one in the bar?"

"Yes. I suggest you ask her," the *chef* said. "If you find out anything that might assist me I would be grateful if you visited me again. Now, I'm afraid I . . ."

"Where can I find her?"

"She is at the Hôtel du Cap at present." He had ordered Jean Jordache to remain in Antibes for the time being, and had taken her passport. He would need Jean Jordache for help in the case when he found Danovic. *If* he ever found him again. He had interviewed the woman, but she had been hysterical and drunk and he had gotten only a confused and disjointed story from her. And now the idiot of a doctor had put her under sedation. The doctor had said she was unstable, a confirmed alcoholic, and that he wouldn't be responsible for her sanity if the *chef* kept after her with questions. "The others," the *chef* said, "I believe can be found on the *Clothilde* in the harbor. Thank you for your interest, *monsieur*. I trust I haven't wasted your time." He put out his hand.

Hubbell said, "*Merci bien, monsieur.*" He had gotten all the information he was going to get, and left.

The *chef* sat down at his desk and picked up the phone to dial Marseilles.

The small white ship moved slowly in the afternoon sunlight across the Mediterranean swell. On the far-off coast, the buildings along the shore and back in the hills made a pink and white pattern against the green background of pine and olive and palm. Dwyer stood in the bow, the name of the ship, *Clothilde*, printed on his clean white jersey. He was a short, tight-muscled man and he had been crying. Because of his protruding long front teeth he had always been called Bunny, as far back as he could remember. Despite his muscles and his workingman's clothes, there was something ineradicably girlish about him. "I'm not a fag," he had said the first time he had had any kind of conversation with the dead man, whose ashes had just been strewn over the sea. He stared at the pretty coast through tear-blurred, soft black eyes. *Rich man's weather,* the murdered man had said.

You could say that again, Dwyer thought. *Not his weather, nor mine either. We fooled ourselves. We came to the wrong place.*

Alone in the pilothouse, dressed like Dwyer in chinos and white jersey, his hand on a spoke of the polished oak and brass wheel, stood Wesley Jordache, his eyes fixed on the point of land on which stood the citadel of Antibes. He was tall for his age, a lanky, powerful, raw-boned boy, tanned, his blond hair bleached in streaks by sun and salt. Like Dwyer, he was thinking of the man whose ashes he had consigned to the sea, the man who had been his father. "Poor, stupid, crazy son of a bitch," the boy said aloud, bitterly. He remembered the day his father, whom he hadn't seen for years, had come to take him out of the military school on the Hudson, where he had fought half the students, all ages, all classes, all sizes, in blind, incomprehensible, meaningless fury.

"You've had your last fight," his father had said.

Then the silence. And the rough man saying, "Did you hear me?"

"Yes, sir."

"Don't call me sir," the man had said. "I'm your father."

His father had laid down the rules for the wrong member of the family, the boy thought, his eyes on the citadel where, he had been told, Napoleon had been imprisoned one night on his return from Elba.

At the rail aft, dressed in incongruous black, stood the boy's uncle, Rudolph Jordache, and his aunt, Gretchen Burke, brother and sister of the murdered man. City people, unaccustomed to the sea, accustomed to tragedy; stiff figures of death against the sunny horizon. They did not touch or speak or look at each other. What was left unsaid on this azure summer afternoon would not have to be explained or mourned or apologized for later.

The woman was in her early forties, tall, slender and straight, her black hair blowing a little in the offshore breeze, framing a luminously pale face, the signs of age just omens now, hints of things to come. She had been beautiful as a girl and was beautiful in a different way now, her face stern, marked by sorrow and a troubled sensuality that was not temporary or fleeting but a permanent habit. Her eyes, squinting against the glare, were a deep blue that in some lights shaded down to violet. There was no damage of tears.

It had to happen, she thought. *Of course. We should have known. He probably knew. Maybe not consciously, but known just the same. All that violence could not have a nonviolent end. True son of his father, the blond stranger in the family, alien to the dark brother and the dark girl, although all from the same bed.*

The man was slim, too, a well-cared-for, aristocratic Yankee slimness, inherited from no parent, acquired by an act of will now accentuated by the neatly cut, almost ambassadorial dark American suit. He was younger by two years than his sister and looked younger than that, a false, gentle echo of youth in the face and bearing of a man whose speech and movements were always deliberate and considered, a man who had known great authority, had struggled all his life, had won and lost, had taken on responsibility in all situations, had come up from penury and want to amass a considerable fortune, who had been ruthless when necessary, cunning when it was useful to be cunning, harsh with himself and others, generous, by his lights, when it was possible to be generous. The resignation that had been forced upon him was there in the thin, controlled mouth, the watchful eyes, was there to be discovered or guessed at. It was a face that could have been that of a youthful air force general whose command had been taken away from him for a failure in the ranks below him that might or might not have been his fault.

He went alone, Rudolph Jordache was thinking; *he came into the cabin where I was sleeping and closed the door softly and left alone. Left for what was to become his death, disdaining my help, disdaining me, disdaining my manhood or what he would think of it, if he ever thought, as my lack of manhood, in a situation that required a man.*

Down below, Kate Jordache was packing her bag. It didn't take long. On top of her other things she first put the white jersey with the ship's name on it that had made Thomas laugh when he saw what her full bosom had done to the lettering, then the bright dress he had bought her for their wedding just eight days ago.

She had nagged Thomas into marrying her. That was the word—nagged. They had been perfectly happy before, but then when she knew she was pregnant—Proper, bloody little well-brought-up, lower-class, obedient, English working girl . . . Here comes the bride. If there had been no wedding, that awful, twittery, smart-talking woman, that fancy wife of Rudolph's, would never have had an excuse to get drunk, would not have gone off with a Yugoslav pimp, would have kept her expensive pink pants on her, would not have needed rescuing or a man fighting for her, and a man a lot better than her husband would be alive today.

Enough of that, Kate thought. *Enough. Enough.*

She closed the bag with a snap and sat down on the edge of the bunk, her solid brown body just beginning to show the swell of the child within her, her capable, quick hands folded quietly in her lap as she looked around her, for the last time, she had decided, at the cramped cabin with the familiar noise of the sea swishing past the open porthole.

Thomas, she thought, *Thomas, Thomas.*

"Who was Clothilde?" she had asked once.

"She was a queen of France. She was somebody I knew as a boy. She smelled like you."

Absent from the small company of mourners on the vessel heading for the coast of France was Jean, Rudolph Jordache's wife. She sat on a bench in the park of the hotel watching her daughter playing with the young girl Rudolph had hired to take care of the child until, as Rudolph had put it, she was in condition to handle Enid again herself. How long would that be? Jean had asked herself. Two days, ten years, never?

She was dressed in slacks and a sweater. She had not brought along clothes suitable for a funeral. Rudolph had been relieved when she said she wouldn't go. She could not bear the thought of stepping aboard the *Clothilde* again, of facing the silent, accusing stares of the wife, the son, the beloved friend.

When she had looked at herself in the mirror in the morning she was shocked at what the last days had done to the small, pretty, girlish face.

The skin of her face, her entire body, seemed to be stretched unbearably on some invisible rack. She felt as though at any moment her body would explode and her nerves erupt through the skin, snapping and crackling like wild lines of wire, crackling under fatal electrical charges.

The doctor had given her some Valium, but she was past Valium. If it weren't for the child, she thought, she would go down to the sea and throw herself off the rocks into it.

As she sat there in the shadow of a tree, in the spicy fragrance of pine and sun-warmed lavender, she said to herself, *Everything I touch I destroy.*

Hubbell sat over a coffee on the *terrasse* of a café in the main square, thinking over what the policeman had told him. The policeman obviously knew more than he was telling, but you had to expect that from the police, especially with an embarrassing unsolved murder on their hands. The sister-in-law might be able to help you more than I can, the cop had said. The sister-in-law. The naked lady, the wife of the promising young mayor. Definitely worth a couple of hundred words. The harbor could wait.

He paid for his coffee and walked over to a parked taxi and got in and said, "The Hôtel du Cap."

Madame Jordache was not in her room, the concierge said, but he had seen her go out into the park with her child and the child's nurse. Hubbell asked the concierge if there was a telex in the hotel and was told that there was one. He asked if he might use it that evening and after a moment's hesitation the concierge said he thought that could be arranged. The hesitation Hubbell rightly interpreted to mean that a tip would be involved. No matter. *Time* Magazine could afford it. He thanked the concierge and went out to the terrace and the steps leading to the long avenue through the noble park down to the bathing pavilion and restaurant and the sea. He suffered a moment of envy as he thought of the small room in the noisy little hotel on the highway in which his wife was taking her siesta. *Time* Magazine paid well, but not well enough for the Hôtel du Cap.

He went down the steps and into the fragrant park. A minute later he saw a little girl in a white bathing suit throwing a beach ball back and forth with a young girl. Seated on a bench nearby was a woman in slacks and a sweater. It was not the sort of scene that you would associate with a murder.

He approached the group slowly, stopping for a moment as if to admire a bed of flowers, then smiling at the child as he neared the group. *"Bonjour,"* he said. "Good afternoon."

The girl said, *"Bonjour,"* but the woman on the bench said nothing. Hubbell noticed that she was very pretty, with a trim, athletic figure, that her face was drained and pale, with dark circles under the eyes. "Mrs. Jordache?" he said.

"Yes?" Her voice was flat and toneless. She looked up at him dully.

"I'm from *Time* Magazine." He was an honorable man and would not pretend to be a friend of her husband's or of the murdered man or an American tourist who had heard about her trouble and wished, in his frank American way, to offer his sympathy. Leave the tricks for the young fellows fighting for by-lines. "I've been sent down to do a story on your brother-in-law." A white lie, but permissible within his code. If people thought you were assigned to do a job, they often felt some small obligation to help.

Still the woman said nothing, just stared at him with those lifeless eyes.

"The chief of police said you might be able to give me some information about the affair. Background information." The "background" had an innocuous ring to it, with its assumption that what would be said would not actually be published, but merely used as a guide for a responsible journalist who wanted to avoid errors in writing his story.

"Have you talked to my husband?" Jean asked.

"I haven't met him yet."

"Haven't met him yet," Jean repeated. "I wish I hadn't. And I bet *he* wishes I hadn't."

Hubbell was taken aback, as much by the intensity with which the woman had spoken as by what she had said.

"Did the policeman tell you why I could give you information?" the woman demanded, her voice harsh and rasping now.

"No," Hubbell lied.

Jean stood up abruptly. "Ask my husband," she said, "ask the whole goddamn family. Just leave me alone."

"Just one question, Mrs. Jordache, if I may," Hubbell said, his throat constricted.

"Would you be prepared to lay criminal charges against the man who attacked you?"

"What difference would it make?" she said dully. She sat heavily on the bench, stared at her child, running after the beach ball in the sunshine. "Go away. Go away. Please."

Hubbell got out of the taxi and walked along the port. Not a fitting place to die, he thought as he went toward the port captain's shack to find out where the *Clothilde* was berthed. The port captain was a weathered old man, sitting outside his shack, smoking a pipe, his chair tilted against the wall as he took the afternoon sun.

The port captain gestured with his pipe toward the mouth of the port, where a white boat was slowly coming in. "There she is. They'll be here for a while," the old man said. "They chewed up their starboard propeller and shaft. You American?"

"I am."

"It's a shame what happened, isn't it?"

"Terrible," Hubbell said.

"They just buried his ashes in the sea," the old man volunteered. "As good a place to be buried as anywhere else for a sailor. I wouldn't mind it myself." Even in midseason, the port captain had plenty of time for conversation.

Hubbell thanked the man and walked around the port and sat down on an upturned dory near the place on the quay into which the *Clothilde* was being maneuvered. He saw the two figures in black at the stern, with the American flag rippling in the breeze behind them. He saw a short, tight-muscled man working on the chain forward and a tall blond boy spinning the wheel in the pilothouse as the ship slowly came in, stern first, with the engine now off and the blond boy running aft to throw a line to a sailor on the quay, as the man ran to the stern and jumped nimbly to the quay to catch a second line that the boy threw to him. When the two lines were secure, the man leaped back onto the deck and he and the boy manhandled the gangplank into place, practiced and skillful, no word between them. The two people in black had moved from the stern, out of the way, superfluous.

Hubbell got up from where he was sitting on the dory, feeling clumsy and heavy after the display of seagoing agility, and started up the gangplank. The boy looked at him sullenly.

"I'm looking for Mr. Jordache," Hubbell said.

"My name is Jordache," the boy said. He had a deep, non-adolescent voice.

"I believe I mean that gentleman over there," Hubbell said, gesturing toward Rudolph.

"Yes?" Rudolph came over to the head of the gangplank.

"Mr. Rudolph Jordache?"

"Yes." The tone was short.

"I'm from *Time* Magazine . . ." Hubbell saw the man's face set. "I'm very sorry about what happened . . ."

"Yes?" Impatiently, questioning.

"I don't like to intrude on you at a moment like this . . ." Hubbell felt foolish, talking at a distance, blocked off by the invisible wall of the boy's hostility, and now the man's. "But I wonder if I could ask you a few questons about . . ."

"Talk to the chief of police. It's his business now."

"I have talked to him."

"Then you know as much as I do, sir," Rudolph said and turned away. There was a cold, small smile on the boy's face.

Hubbell stood there another moment, feeling that perhaps he had been wrong in his choice of a profession, then said, "I'm sorry," to nobody in particular because he couldn't think of anything else to say or do and turned around and walked toward the entrance to the port.

When he got back to his hotel, his wife was sitting on the small balcony outside their room in a bikini, working on her tan. He loved her deeply, but he couldn't help noticing that she looked absurd in a bikini. "Where've you been all afternoon?" she asked.

"Working on a story," he said.

"I thought this was going to be a vacation," she said.

"So did I," he said.

He got out his portable typewriter, took off his jacket and began to work.

CHAPTER 2

1968

From Billy Abbott's notebook—

The telegram from my mother came to my APO number. Your Uncle Tom has been murdered, the telegram read. Suggest you try to come to Antibes for funeral. Your Uncle Rudolph and I are at the Hotel du Cap Antibes. Love, Mother.

I had seen my Uncle Tom once, the time I had flown from California to Whitby for my grandmother's funeral when I was a boy. Funerals are great occasions for families to get to know each other again. I was sorry my Uncle Tom was dead. I had liked him the night we had spent together in my Uncle Rudolph's guest room. I was impressed by the fact that he carried a gun. He thought I was sleeping when he took the gun out of his pocket and put it away in a drawer. It gave me something to think about during the funeral the next day.

If an uncle had to be murdered, I would have preferred it to be Rudolph. We were never friendly and as I grew older he showed me, very politely, that he disapproved of me and my views on society. My views have not changed radically. Jelled, my uncle would probably say, if he took the trouble to examine them. But he is rich and there might have been some mention of me in his will, if not out of any fondness for me then out of brotherly love for my mother. Thomas Jordache was not the type of man to leave a fortune behind him.

I showed the telegram to the Colonel and he gave me ten days compassionate leave to go to Antibes. I didn't go to Antibes, but I sent a telegram of condolence to the hotel and said that the army wouldn't let me off for the funeral.

Monika got time off her job, too, and we went to Paris. We had a marvelous time. Monika is exactly the sort of girl you want to have with you in Paris.

"I'M AFRAID THE time has come," Rudolph said, "to discuss a few things we've avoided up to now. We have to talk about what we're going to do next. The legacy. Painful as it is, we're going to have to talk about money."

They were all in the saloon of the *Clothilde*, Kate in a dark dress that was obviously old and now too tight for her, with her scuffed, imitation-leather suitcase on the floor next to her chair. The saloon was painted white, with blue trim and blue curtains at the portholes and on the bulkhead old prints of sailing ships that Thomas had picked up in Venice. Everybody kept looking at Kate's suitcase, although no one had said anything about it yet.

"Kate, Bunny," Rudolph went on, "do you know if Tom left a will?"

"He never said anything to me about a will," Kate said.

"Me, neither," said Dwyer.

"Wesley?"

Wesley shook his head.

Rudolph sighed. Same old Tom, he thought, consistent to the end. Married, with a son and a pregnant wife, and never took an afternoon off to write a will. He himself had drawn up his first will in a lawyer's office when he was twenty-one years old and five or six later ones since then, the last one when his daughter Enid was born. And now that Jean was spending more and more time in drying-out clinics he was working on a new one. "How about a safe-deposit box?" he asked.

"Not that I know of," Kate said.

"Bunny?"

"I'm pretty sure not," Dwyer said.

"Did he have any securities?"

Kate and Dwyer looked at each other, puzzled. "Securities?" Dwyer asked. "What's that?"

"Stocks, bonds." Where have these people been all their lives? Rudolph wondered.

"Oh, that," Dwyer said. "He used to say that was just another way they'd figured out to screw the workingman." He had also said, "Leave stuff like that to my goddamn brother," but that was before the final reconciliation between the two men and Dwyer didn't think this was the time for that particular quotation.

"Okay, no securities," Rudolph said. "Then what did he do with his money?" He tried not to sound irritated.

"He had two accounts," Kate said. "A checking account in francs at the Crédit Lyonnais here in Antibes and a dollar savings account in Crédit Suisse in Geneva. He preferred being paid in dollars. That account is illegal, because we're French residents, but I wouldn't worry about that. Nobody ever asked."

Rudolph nodded. At least his brother hadn't been *totally* devoid of financial sense.

"The bankbook and the last statements from the Crédit Lyonnais and the checkbook are in the drawer under the bunk in the cabin," Kate said. "Wesley, if you'll go in there . . . "

Wesley went forward toward the captain's cabin.

"If I may ask, Bunny," Rudolph said, "how did Thomas pay you?"

"He didn't," Dwyer said. "We were partners. At the end of the year, we split up what was left over."

"Did you have any kind of papers—a contract, some kind of formal agreement?"

"Christ, no," Dwyer said. "What would we need a contract for?"

"Is the boat in his name or in your joint names, Bunny? Or perhaps in his and Kate's name?"

"We were only married five days, Rudy," Kate said. "We didn't have any time for anything like that. The *Clothilde* is in his name. The papers are in the drawer with the bankbooks. With the insurance policy for the ship and the other papers."

Rudolph sighed again. "I've been to a lawyer . . . "

Of course, Gretchen thought. She had been standing at the doorway, looking aft. She had been brooding over Billy's telegram. It had been a brief message from a polite stranger, with no feeling of grief or attempt at consolation. She didn't know the army all that well, but she knew that soldiers got leave, if they wanted it, to attend funerals. She had written Billy, too, about coming to the wedding, but he had written back saying he was too busy dispatching half-tons and command cars through the streets and roads that led through Belgium to Armageddon to dance at half-forgotten relatives' weddings. She, too, she thought bitterly, was included among the half-forgotten relatives. Let him wallow in Brussels. Worthy son of his father. She focused her attention on her brother, patiently trying to disentangle tangled lives. Of course, Rudy would have gone immediately to a lawyer. Death, after all, was a legal matter.

"A French lawyer," Rudolph went on, "who luckily speaks good English; the manager of the hotel gave me his name. He seems like a reliable man. He told me that although you're all French residents, since you live on the boat and have no home on land and by French law the boat is technically American territory, it would be best to ignore the French and accept the jurisdiction of the American consul in Nice. Do either of you have any objection to that?"

"Whatever you say, Rudolph," Kate said. "Whatever you think best."

"If you can get away with it, okay with me," Dwyer said. He sounded bored, like a small boy in school during an arithmetic lesson, wishing he was outside playing baseball.

"I'll try to talk to the consul this afternoon," Rudolph said, "and see what he advises."

Wesley came in with the Crédit Suisse passbook and the Crédit Lyonnais checkbook and the last three monthly bank statements.

"Do you mind if I look at these?" Rudolph asked Kate.

"He was your brother."

As usual, thought Gretchen, at the door, her back to the saloon, nobody lets Rudy off any hook.

Rudolph took the books and papers from Wesley. He looked at the last statement from the Crédit Lyonnais. There was a balance of a little over ten thousand francs. About two thousand dollars Rudolph calculated as he read the figure aloud. Then he opened the passbook. Eleven thousand, six hundred and twenty-two dollars," he said. He was surprised that Thomas had saved that much.

"If you ask me," Kate said, "that's the whole thing. The whole kit and caboodle."

"Of course, there's the ship," said Rudolph. "What's to be done with it?"

For a moment there was silence in the cabin.

"I know what *I'm* going to do with the ship," Kate said mildly, without emotion, standing up. "I'm going to leave it. Right now." The outdated, too-tight dress pulled up over her plump, dimpled, brown knees.

"Kate," Rudolph protested, "something has to be decided."

"Whatever you decide is all right with me," Kate said. "I'm not going to stay aboard another night."

Dear, normal, down-to-earth woman, Gretchen thought, waiting to say a last good-bye to her man and then leaving, not looking for profit or advantage from the object that had been her home, her livelihood, the source of her happiness.

"Where are you going?" Rudolph asked Kate.

"For the time being to a hotel in town," Kate said. "After that, I'll see. Wesley, will you carry my bag for me to a taxi?"

Silently, Wesley picked up the bag in his big hand.

"I'll call you at your hotel when I feel I can talk, Rudy," Kate said. "Thank you for everything. You're a good man." She kissed him on the cheek, the kiss a benediction, a tacit gesture of exoneration, and followed Wesley past Gretchen out the saloon door to the deck.

Rudolph sank into the chair she had been sitting on and rubbed his eyes wearily. Gretchen came over to him and touched his shoulder affectionately. Affection, she had learned, could be mixed with criticism, even with scorn. "Take it easy, Brother," she said. "You can't settle everybody's lives in one afternoon."

"I've been talking to Wesley," Dwyer said. "He knew Kate was leaving. He wants to stay on the *Clothilde* with me. At least for a while. At least until the screw and the shaft're fixed. Don't worry about him. I'll take care of him."

"Yes," Rudolph said. He stood up, hunched over a little, his shoulders burdened. "It's getting late. I'd better try to get to Nice before the consulate closes. Gretchen, do you want me to drive you to the hotel?"

"Thanks, no," Gretchen said. "I think I'll stay on here a few minutes and have a drink with Bunny. Maybe two drinks." This was no afternoon to leave Dwyer alone.

"As you say," Rudolph said. He put the bankbooks and the statements he had been holding in his hand on the table. "If you see Jean, tell her I won't be back for dinner."

"I'll do that," Gretchen said.

It was no afternoon, she thought, to be forced to speak to Jean Jordache, either.

****

"I think it might be nicer on deck," Gretchen said to Dwyer after Rudolph had gone. The saloon, which had until now seemed like a welcoming, cosy room, had been darkened for her into a sinister countinghouse, where lives were entered in ledgers, became symbols, credits and debits, not flesh and blood.

She had gone through it before. When her husband had been killed in the automobile accident there hadn't been a will, either. Perhaps Colin Burke, who had never hit a man in his life, who had lived surrounded by books, play scripts, screenplays, who had dealt gently and diplomatically with the writers and actors whom he had directed, and often enough hated, had more in common than was apparent on the surface with her barely literate, ruffian brother.

Without a will, there had been confusion about the disposal of Colin's property. There was an ex-wife who lived on alimony, a mortgaged house, royalties. The lawyers had moved in, the estate tied up for more than a year. Rudy had handled everything then, as he was doing now, as he always did.

"I'll bring the drinks," Dwyer was saying. "It's nice of you to visit with me. The hardest part is being alone. After everything we been through, Tom and me. And now Kate's gone. Most women would have made trouble aboard. Between two men been friends and partners for so long. Not Kate." Dwyer's mouth was quivering, almost imperceptibly. "She's all right, old Kate, isn't she?"

"A lot better than all right," Gretchen said. "Make it a stiff one, Bunny."

"Whiskey, isn't it?"

"Plenty of ice, please." She went forward where the saloon cabin and wheelhouse would hide them from passersby on the quay. She had had enough of friends of Tom and Dwyer and Kate from the other boats in the harbor coming on board with doleful faces to mumble their condolences. Their grief was plain. She was not as sure of her own.

In the bow, with the neat coiled spirals of lines and the polished brass and the bleached, immaculate teak deck, she looked out at the now familiar scene of the crowded harbor which had enchanted her when she saw it the first day: the bobbing masts, the men working slowly and carefully at the million small tasks that seemed to make up the daily routine of those who took their living from the sea. Even now, after all that had happened, she could not help but be affected by its quiet beauty.

Dwyer came up behind her, barefooted, the ice tinkling in the glasses in his hands. He gave her her glass. She raised it to him, smiling ruefully. She hadn't had anything to eat or drink all day and the first mouthful tingled on her tongue. "I don't usually drink hard stuff," Dwyer said, "but maybe I ought to learn." He drank in small sips, thoughtfully savoring the taste and affect. "I tell you," he said, "your brother Rudy is one hell of a man. A take-hold guy."

"Yes," Gretchen said. That was one way of describing him.

"We'd've been in a stink of a mess without him. . . . "

Or no mess at all, Gretchen thought, if he'd kept his wife at home and stayed on the other continent.

"We'd've been stolen blind without him," Dwyer said.

"By whom?"

"Lawyers," Dwyer said vaguely. "Ships' brokers, the law. Everybody."

Here was a man, Gretchen thought, who had been caught at sea in hurricanes, had done his job at the extremity of physical endurance, when a failure would have sent him and those who depended upon him to the bottom, who had survived the company of violent and brutal men, but who felt reduced to helplessness by a slip of paper, a mention of land-based authority. Another race, thought Gretchen, who all her adult life had been surrounded by men who moved among paper, in and out of offices, as surefooted and confident as an Indian in the forest. Her dead brother had belonged to another race, perhaps from birth.

"The one I'm worried about," Dwyer said, "is Wesley."

Worried, not for himself, she thought, who saw no need for contracts, who just split up what was left over at the end of the year, who had no legal right, even, at this moment, to be standing on the scrubbed deck of the pretty boat on which he had earned his living for years. "Wesley will be all right," she said. "Rudy'll take care of him."

"He won't want that," Dwyer said, drinking. "Wesley. He wanted to be like his father. Sometimes it was funny, watching him, trying to move like his father, talk like his father, live up to his father." He took a gulp of his drink, made a little grimace, looked thoughtfully at the glass in his hand as if trying to decide whether it contained a friend or an enemy. He sighed, uncertain, then went on. "They used to stand up in the pilothouse all hours of the night; at sea or in port, you could hear them talking below, Wesley asking a question, Tom taking his time answering, long answers. I asked Tom once what the hell they had to talk about so much. Tom laughed. 'The kid asks me questions about my life and I tell him. I guess he wants to know what his old man is all about. I was the same about my father, only he didn't give me any answers, he gave me a kick in the ass.' From what Tom let drop," Dwyer said, careful, understated, "I guess there wasn't no love lost between them, was there?"

"No," Gretchen said, "he wasn't a lovable man, our father. There wasn't much love in him. If there was, he reserved it for Rudolph."

Dwyer sighed. "Families," he said.

"Families," Gretchen repeated.

"I asked Tom what sort of questions Wesley asked him about him," Dwyer went on. "'The usual,' Tom told me. 'What I was like when I was a kid in school, what my brother and sister'—that's you and Rudy—'were like. How come I became a fighter, then a merchant seaman. When I had my first girl. What the other women I'd had were like, his goddamn mother. . . .' I asked Tom if he told the kid the truth. 'Nothing but,' Tom said. 'I'm a modern father. Tell the kids where babies come from, everything.' He had his own kind of sense of humor, Tom."

"Those must have been some conversations," Gretchen said.

"'Spare the truth and spoil the child,' Tom said to me once. Every once in a while he sounded as though he'd picked up a little education here and there. Though he wasn't big on education. Tom had a deep suspicion of education. Maybe I shouldn't be saying this to you," Dwyer said earnestly, swishing the last of the ice around in his glass, "but he used your brother Rudy as an example. He'd say, 'Look at Rudy, he had all the education a man's brain could stand and look where he wound up, dry as an old raisin, a laughingstock after what his drunk wife did in his hometown, out on his ass, sitting there wondering what he was going to do with the rest of his life.'"

"I believe I could use another drink, Bunny," Gretchen said.

"Me, too," Dwyer said. "I'm beginning to like the taste." He took her glass and went aft and into the saloon.

Gretchen reflected on what Dwyer had said. It told more about Dwyer than it told about either Tom or Wesley. Tom had been the center of Dwyer's life, she realized; he probably could reproduce word for word everything that Tom had said to him from beginning to end. If Dwyer were a woman, you'd say he'd been in love with Tom. Even as a man . . . That girlish mouth, that little peculiarity in the way he used his hands. . . . Poor Dwyer, she thought, maybe he's finally going to be the one who's going to suffer most. She had no real fix on Wesley. He had seemed like a mannerly, healthy boy when they had first come aboard. After his father's death, he had fallen silent, his face giving nothing away, avoiding them all. Rudy would take care of him, she had told Dwyer. She wondered if Rudy or anybody else would be capable of it.

Dwyer came back with the whiskey. The first drink was beginning to take effect. She felt dreamy, remote, all problems misty, removed. It was a better way to feel than the way she had been feeling recently. Maybe Jean, with her hidden bottles, knew something useful to know. Gratefully, she took a sip from the new glass.

Dwyer looked different, somehow troubled as he stood there, leaning against the rail, in his clean white jersey and chino pants, the comical protruding teeth that had burdened him with his nickname, chewing on his lip. It was as though he had decided something, something difficult, while he was alone in the saloon pouring the drinks. "Maybe I oughtn't to say this, Mrs. Burke . . . "

"Gretchen."

"Thank you, ma'am. But I feel like I can talk to you. Rudy's a fine man. I admire him, you couldn't ask for a better man to have on your side in the kind of situation we're in now—but he's not the sort of a man a guy like myself can talk to, I mean *really* talk to—you understand what I mean?"

"Yes," she said, "I understand."

"He's a fine man, like I said," Dwyer went on, uncomfortable, his mouth fidgeting, "but he's not like Tom.

"No, he's not," Gretchen said.

"Wesley's talked to me. He don't want to have nothing to do with Rudy. Or with his wife. That's just natural human nature, wouldn't you say, considering what's happened?"

"I'd say," Gretchen said. "Considering what's happened."

"If Rudy moves in on the kid—with the best intentions in the world, which I'm sure Rudy has—there's going to be trouble. Awful trouble. There's no telling what the kid will do."

"I agree with you," Gretchen said. She hadn't thought about it before but the moment the words had passed Dwyer's lips she had seen the truth of it. "But what's to be done? Kate's not his mother and she has her own problems. You?"

Dwyer laughed sadly. "Me? I don't know where I'll be twenty-four hours from now. The only thing I know is ships. Next week I may be sailing to Singapore. A month later to Valparaiso. Anyway, I ain't made to be anybody's father."

"So?"

"I been watching you real careful," Dwyer said. "Even though you didn't take no more notice of me than a piece of furniture . . ."

"Oh, come on now, Bunny," Gretchen said, guilty because almost the same thought had passed through her mind just a few minutes ago.

"I'm not sore about it and I'm not making any judgments, ma'am . . . "

"Gretchen," she said automatically.

"Gretchen," he repeated dutifully. "But since it happened—and now, staying here with me and letting me gab on—I see a real human being. I'm not saying Rudy ain't a human being," Dwyer added hastily, "only he's not Wesley's kind of human being. And his wife—" Dwyer stopped.

"Let's not talk about his wife."

"If *you* went up to Wesley and said, fair and square, right out in the open, 'You come along with me . . . ' he'd recognize it. He'd see you're the kind of woman he could take as a mother."

A new idea in the process of natural conception, Gretchen thought, sons choosing mothers. Would evolution never cease? "I'm not what you might call a model mother," she said dryly. The thought of being responsible in any way for the lanky, sullen-faced, silent boy with Tom's wild genes in him frightened her. "No, Bunny, I'm afraid it wouldn't work out."

"I thought I'd give it a try," Dwyer said listlessly. "I just don't want to see Wesley left on his own. He's not old enough to be left on his own, no matter what he thinks. There's an awful lot of commotion ahead for Wesley Jordache."

She couldn't help smiling a little at the word "commotion."

"Pinky Kimball, that's the engineer on the *Vega*," Bunny went on, "he's the one who saw Mrs. Jordache in the nightclub with the Yugoslav, he tells me Wesley's been pestering him. He wants Pinky to help find the guy, point him out to him. . . . I may be wrong, but what I believe, what Pinky thinks, too, is that Wesley wants to get revenge for his father."

"Oh, God," Gretchen said.

"You look around you here"—Dwyer made a gesture to take in the quiet harbor, the green hills, the useless fort and the picturesque, obsolete military walls—"and you think, what a nice, peaceful place this is. But the truth is, from Nice to Marseilles you got just about as many thugs as anyplace in the world. What with whores and drugs and smuggling and gambling there's an awful lot of gun and knife toting in this neighborhood and plenty of guys who'd kill their mother for ten thousand francs, or for nothing, if it came to that. And from what Pinky Kimball's told me, the fella Tom had the fight with is right in with them. If Wesley goes looking for the fella and finds him there's no telling what'll happen to him. At that military school Wesley was at, they had to tear him off other kids in fights, it wasn't just sparring in a gym, he would've killed them if there'd been nobody else around. If he wants Pinky Kimball to point out somebody it's because there's a good chance he wants to kill him."

"Oh, Christ," Gretchen said. "What're you trying to say, Bunny?"

"I'm trying to say that no matter what happens you got to get the kid out of here, out of the country. And Rudolph Jordache ain't the man to do it. Now," he said, "I'm drunk. I wouldn't've talked like this if I wasn't drunk. But I mean it. Drunk or sober. I mean every word of it."

"Bunny," Gretchen said, "thank you for telling me all this." But she was sorry she had decided to stay on with him when the others had gone. The problem was not hers, she thought resentfully, and the solution was beyond her grasp. "I'll talk to my brother," she said; "see what we can figure out. Do you think it would be a good idea if I waited until Wesley came back and we all three had dinner together?"

"You want me to be honest?"

"Of course."

"I believe Wesley likes you. In fact I know he does, he's told me as much," Dwyer said. "But tonight I don't think he wants to see any Jordache for dinner. I'll take him out myself. We got some things to talk about together, private, him and me."

"Thanks for the drinks," Gretchen said.

"On the house."

"Drop me a postcard. From Singapore or Valparaiso or wherever."

"Sure." Dwyer laughed, a dry little laugh.

She nursed her drink. She had the feeling that if she left Dwyer alone, he would break down, sit on the deck and weep. She didn't want Wesley to find him like that when he got back. "I'll just finish my drink and . . . "

"You want another one? I'll go get you one."

"This'll do, thanks."

"I've become a whiskey drinker," Dwyer said. "What do you know about that?" He shook his head. "Do you believe in dreams?" he asked abruptly.

"Sometimes." She wondered if Dwyer had ever heard of Freud.

"I had a dream last night," Dwyer said. "I dreamed Tom was laying on a floor—I don't know where it was—he was just laying on the floor looking dead. I picked him up and I knew I had to carry him someplace. I wasn't big enough in the dream to carry him in my arms so I laid him across my back. He's a lot taller than me, so his legs were dragging on the floor, and I put his arms around my neck so I could get a strong hold on him and I began to walk, I don't know where, someplace I just knew I had to take him. You know how it is in a dream, I was sweating, he was heavy, he was a deadweight around my neck, on my back. Then, all of a sudden, I felt he was getting a hard-on against my ass. I kept on walking. I wanted to say something to him, but I didn't know what to say to a dead man with a hard-on. The hard-on kept getting bigger and bigger. And I felt warm all over. And even in my dream I was ashamed. You know why I was ashamed? Because I *wanted* it." He shook his head. He had been talking dreamily, compulsively. He shook his head angrily. "I had to tell someone," he said harshly. "Excuse me."

"That's all right, Bunny," Gretchen said softly. "We're not responsible for our dreams."

"*You* can say that, Mrs. Burke," he said.

This time she did not correct him and tell him to call her Gretchen. She could not bear to look at Dwyer, because she was afraid she could not control what her face would tell him. The best she might manage would be pity and she feared what her pity might do to the man.

She reached out and touched his hand. He gripped it hard, in his tough seaman's fingers, then in a swift, instinctive movement, brought her hand to his lips and kissed it. He let her hand go and turned away from her. "I'm sorry," he said brokenly. "It was just . . . I don't know . . . I . . . "

"You don't have to say anything, Bunny," she said gently. Silence now would heal wounds, staunch blood. She felt confused, helpless. What if she said, Take me down to your cabin, make love to me? Womanly thought, the central act. Would her body be a consolation or a rebuke? What would it mean to her? An act of charity, a confirmation of continuing life or a last, unworthy cry of despair? She looked at the neat, muscular back of the small man who had kissed her hand and turned away from her. She almost took a step toward him, then pulled back, a psychic retreat rather than a physical one.

The hand with which she still held the whiskey glass was cold from the melting ice. She put the glass down. "I've got to be getting on," she said. "There are so many things to decide. Tell Wesley to call me if he needs anything."

"I'll tell him," Dwyer said. He wasn't looking at her, was staring, his mouth quivering, toward the entrance to the port. "Do you want me to go to the café and call a taxi?"

"No, thank you. I think I'll walk; I could stand a little walk."

She left him there in the bow of the *Clothilde,* barefooted and neat in his white jersey, with the two empty glasses.

She walked slowly away from the ships, into the town, up the narrow street, the night looming threatening ahead of her. She looked into the window of an antique shop. There was a brass ship's lamp there that attracted her. She would have liked to buy it, take it home with her; it would brighten the corner of a room. Then she remembered she had no real home, had come from an apartment rented for six months in New York; there was no room of hers for a lamp to brighten.

She went deeper into the town, thronged with people buying and selling, reading newspapers at café tables, scolding children, offering them ice-cream sandwiches, no one concerned with death. She saw the advertisement for a movie house, saw that an American picture, dubbed into French, was playing that night, resolved to have dinner in town alone and see it.

She passed in front of the cathedral, stopped for a moment to look at it, almost went in. If she had, she would have found Wesley on a bench, far back in the empty nave, his lips moving in a prayer he had never learned.

CHAPTER 3

1968

From Billy Abbott's notebook—

My father was in Paris once, when they let him out of the hospital just after the war. He had not yet met my mother. He said he was too drunk for the three days he was there to remember anything about it. He said he wouldn't know the difference between Paris and Dayton, Ohio. He didn't talk much about the war, which made him a lot better company than some of the other veterans I've been exposed to. But on some of the weekends that I spent with him under the terms of the divorce, when he had had enough to drink, which usually was early on, he'd make fun of what he did as a soldier. I was mostly concerned with Red Cross girls and my personal safety, he'd say; I was in the air force and flew a tight desk, tapping out stories for hometown newspapers about the brave boys who flew the missions.

Still, he did enlist, he did get wounded, or any way hurt, on the way back from a mission. I wonder if I would have done as much. The army, as I see it from here and from what I read in the papers about Vietnam, is a macabre practical joke. Of course, as everyone says, that was a different war. With the Colonel I assume an extreme military pose, but if war in Europe did break out, I'd probably desert the first time I heard a shot fired.

NATO is full of Germans, all very palsy and comrades-in-arms, and they're not much different from the other animals. Monika, who is German, is another story.

IT WAS ALMOST dark when Rudolph left the consulate. The consul had been an agreeable man, had listened thoughtfully, made notes, called in an aide, promised he would do everything he could to help, but it would take time, he would have to call Paris, get legal advice, he was not convinced that the lawyer in Antibes had been on sure ground when he had told Rudolph to ignore the French, there would have to be a determination from higher authorities as to what documents would be needed to transfer the ownership of the *Clothilde* and free the bank accounts. The death of an American in a foreign country always presented knotty problems, the consul had said, his tone hinting that it bordered on treason to commit an act of such importance on alien soil. That day, Rudolph thought, hundreds of Americans had died in Vietnam, which might be considered a foreign country, but the deaths had not produced knotty problems for consuls anywhere.

The demise of Thomas Jordache was going to be even more complicated than usual, the consul warned; it could not be solved overnight. Rudolph had gone out into the gathering dusk feeling hopeless, trapped in a dark web of legalisms which would entangle him ever more tightly with every move he made to free himself. Trapped once more, he thought, self-pityingly, in other people's necessities.

What did they do, Rudolph wondered as he left the consulate behind him, in the old days in the American wilderness when the leader of the tribe was killed in battle? Who got the wampum, the wives, custody of the children, the tepee, the warbonnets, the eagle feathers, the lances and arrowheads? What clever nonwarrior, what shaman or medicine man, took the role of administrator and justifier?

He had left his car along the shore, in front of the Hôtel Negresco on the Promenade des Anglais because he hadn't wanted to risk getting lost in the streets of the unfamiliar city and had taken a taxi to the consulate. On foot now, not knowing exactly where he was going, not caring, he went in the general direction of the Negresco, not paying attention to the people around him hurrying home to dinner. Suddenly he stopped. His cheeks were wet. He put his hand to his eyes. He was crying. He had been crying without knowing it as he walked blindly toward the sea. Oh God, he thought, I had to come all the way from the Hudson River to Nice to cry for the first time since I was a boy. None of the passersby seemed to notice his tears; there were no curious stares. It could be that the French were used to seeing grown men walking weeping through their streets; maybe it was a national custom. Perhaps, he thought, after what their country had gone through since Louis the Sixteenth, there was plenty to cry about.

When he reached his car it was already dark. He had wandered through back streets, changed direction aimlessly. *Bella Nizza*, he remembered. The Italians had taken it back in the Second World War. Briefly. In the Italian equivalent of the Pentagon there probably was a plan for recapturing it at some belligerent future date. Good neighbors. They were growing jasmine and roses for the moment on all battlefields, waiting for the next war to come along. Poor, hopeful, doomed Italian generals. Not worth the trouble, not worth the bones of a single Calabrian peasant. It wasn't *Bella Nizza* anymore, it was a modern, junked-up commercial city, a peeling jumble of tenements, with rock music blaring from the loudspeakers of music shops, promoting its past loveliness in fake tourist brochures. All things became worse.

The lamps of the Promenade des Anglais were lit, reflecting off the roofs of the endless stream of cars, twinkling in the polluted sea murmuring against the meager strip of gravelly beach. In his conversation with the consul the man had said that Nice was a good post in the Foreign Service. The consul must know something about Nice that was not evident to the naked eye. Or perhaps he had been stationed in the Congo or Washington and even Nice would look good after that. Rudolph wondered if he had passed his brother's murderer somewhere between the consulate and the sea. Entirely possible. Murderers were constantly being arrested by the police in Nice. He speculated about what he would do if a man sat down next to him in a café and recognized him and said, calmly, "*Bonjour, monsieur*, you may be interested to know that I am the one who did it."

He opened the door to his car, then stood there, not getting in, thinking of the night ahead of him, going back to the hotel in Antibes, having to explain to Jean that they would have to plan on staying on in the place that had become a horror for them, having to explain to Kate and Wesley and Dwyer that nothing was settled, that everything was in abeyance, that they were tied indefinitely to death, that there was no way of knowing when they could get on with the business of living.

He closed the door of the car. He could not face what was ahead of him in Antibes. As unattractive as Nice was it was better this evening than Antibes. At least he had stopped crying.

Careful in the traffic, his nostrils assailed by the fumes the scientists of his country had assured him were deadly to the human race, he crossed to the other side of the Promenade des Anglais, bright with illuminated storefronts and the lights of cafés. He went into a café, seated himself at a table on the *terrasse*, ordered a whiskey and soda. Time-hallowed cure, palliative, nepenthe, transient unraveler of knotty problems. When the whiskey came, he drank slowly, glad that Jean was not with him, since he could not drink in her presence. Sometimes he felt he could not breathe in her presence—a condition to be dealt with at another time. He took another sip of his drink.

Suddenly, he was ravenously hungry. He hadn't eaten since breakfast and then only a croissant and coffee. The body had its own rhythms, made its own uncomplicated, imperative claims. His hunger drove all other thoughts from his mind. He sat back in his chair sipping his whiskey, luxuriously composing the menu for the evening meal. Melon with a dash of port to begin with, then fish soup, he decided, specialty of the region, with garlicked croutons and a sprinkling of grated cheese, steak and salad, slab of Brie, strawberries for dessert. A half bottle of *blanc de blancs* with the soup and a half bottle of heavy red wine of Provence with the steak and cheese. The evening stretched out ahead of him in gluttonous splendor. He never had to worry about getting fat, but he knew that he would have been ashamed to order so self-indulgent a meal at a time like this if he were not alone. But he knew nobody in Nice. The mourners were in another town. He paid for his whiskey and went along the promenade to the Negresco and asked the concierge for the name of the best restaurant in Nice. He walked to the address he was given, striding out briskly, his eyes dry.

The best restaurant in Nice was lit by candles, decorated with glowing bouquets of pink roses, with just the right faint aroma of good cooking from the kitchen. There were not many diners, but they looked prosperous and well-fed. The room was quiet, the atmosphere fittingly serious, the headwaiter a smiling Italian gentleman with brilliant teeth who spoke English. Perhaps, Rudolph thought, he is a spy for the

Italian Army, goes home every night to draw up plans of the harbor to be microfilmed by an accomplice. *Bella Nizza.*

Seated at a table with a gleaming white tablecloth, breaking a crisp roll and spreading butter over it, Rudolph felt that perhaps he had been wrong in thinking that the town was not worth the bones of a single Calabrian peasant. He knew no one in Calabria.

To put an even keener edge to his appetite he ordered a martini. The martini came to the table, pale and icy cold. He fished out the olive and nibbled at it. It tasted of juniper and Mediterranean sunlight. He waved away the menu that the headwaiter offered him. "I know what I want," he said.

The meal, when it came, did justice to the concierge's estimate of the restaurant's cuisine. Rudolph ate and drank slowly, feeling newly restored with every bite of the food, every drop of the wines. Sometimes, he thought, the best of holidays can be fitted into only two hours of your life.

When he had finished with the strawberries he asked for the check. He wanted to take a stroll, replete, nameless, unencumbered, sit at a café table and watch the evening traffic on the promenade while having his coffee and a brandy. He tipped the maitre d'hôtel and the waiters grandly and sauntered out into the balmy night air. He walked the few minutes to the beach. Oldest sea. Ulysses had survived it. Strapped to the mast, his sailors' ears stopped by wax against the songs. Many brave men asleep in the deep. Tom now among them. Rudolph stood on the stony strand a few yards from where the gentle waves slid into France in a small lace of foam. It was a moonless night, but the stars were brilliant, and along the curve of the dark coast thousands of pinpoints of light made jeweled strings against the hills.

He breathed deeply of the salt air. Even though there was the mumble of traffic behind his back he felt beautifully alone, the beach deserted except for him, with nothing before him but the dark expanse of water. Tomorrow, he knew, would be a day of guilt and turmoil, but that was tomorrow. He leaned down and picked up a smooth round stone and threw it, skipping, along the surface of the sea. It skipped three times. He chuckled. If he had been a younger man, a boy, he would have sprinted like a halfback down the beach, along the water's edge, dodging the irregular ebb and flow of the waves. But at his age, in his black suit, it did not seem advisable, even in his mellow after-dinner state, to draw attention to himself from the strollers on the walk above the beach.

He went back to the promenade and entered a brightly lit café, seating himself so that he could watch the crowded pavement, the sauntering men and women, their day's work done or their tourists' duties performed, now just enjoying the climate, the momentary exchange of glances, the opportunity to walk, unhurried in the soft night, arm in arm with a loved one.

The café was not crowded. At a table, just one removed from his, a woman was reading a magazine, her head bent so that he could not see her face. She had looked up when he came in, then quickly gone back to her magazine. She had a half-full glass of white wine on the table in front of her. She had dark hair, nice legs, he noticed, was wearing a light blue dress.

He was conscious of another, unspecific hunger.

Don't spoil the evening, he warned himself.

He ordered a brandy and coffee from the waiter, in English. The woman, he noted, looked up again when he spoke. He detected, or thought he detected, a momentary glimmer of a smile on her face. She was not young, in her late thirties, he would have said, somewhere around his age, carefully made up, eye shadow. A little old for a prostitute, but attractive just the same.

The waiter put down his coffee and brandy and the little stamped check and went back toward the bar inside. Rudolph took a sip of the coffee, strong and black. Then he lifted the small glass of brandy and sniffed it. Just as he was about to drink, the woman raised her glass of wine to him. This time there was no doubt about it. She was smiling. She had a full red mouth, dark gray eyes, black hair. Politely, Rudolph raised his glass a little higher in salute, drank a little.

"You're American, aren't you?" She had only a slight accent.

"Yes."

"I knew as soon as you came in," she said. "The clothes. Are you here on a pleasure trip?"

"In a way," he said. He didn't know whether he wanted to continue the conversation or not. He was not easy with strangers, especially strange women. She didn't look like the prostitutes he had seen prowling the streets of New York, but he was in a foreign country and he wasn't sure how French prostitutes dressed and spoke. He was not used to being accosted by women. There was something forbidding about him, his friend and lawyer Johnny Heath had said, austere. Johnny Heath was accosted wherever he went, on the street, in bars, at parties. There was nothing austere about Johnny Heath.

From adolescence Rudolph had developed an aloof, cool manner, believing that it gave him the air of belonging to another class than that of the boys and men he had grown up among, with their easy comradeship, their loud, plebeian conviviality. Perhaps, he thought, looking at the woman at the other table, I have overdone the act.

"Are you enjoying yourself?" the woman asked. Her voice was husky, with a certain harshness in it that was not displeasing.

"Moderately," he said.

"Are you in a hotel here in Nice?"

"No," he said. He supposed that there was a certain set routine ladies such as this one went through. He guessed that she was one of the higher paid members of her profession, who did not get to the point immediately but flattered a man by pretending that she was interested in him, putting the eventual transaction on a level that was not merely physical and commercial. "I'm just passing through," he said. He was beginning to think, Why not? Once in my life, he thought, why not see what it's like? Besides, he had been continent for a long time. Too long. He had not slept in the same room with Jean since she had had her miscarriage. More than a year. Sometimes, he thought, you must remember you are a man. Bare, forked animal. Even he. He smiled at the woman. It felt good to smile. "May I offer you a drink?"

He had never offered a drink to a stranger before, man or woman. About time to begin. What have I been saving myself for, what have I been proving? In the one city of Nice itself, at this moment, there were probably thousands of men tumbling with women in joyous beds, regretting nothing, grasping the pleasure their bodies were conceived for, forgetting the day's labors, the day's fears. What put him above common humanity? "I'm alone," he said daringly. "I don't really speak French. I would enjoy some company. Somebody who speaks English." Always the saving, modifying hypocritical clause, he thought.

The woman looked at her watch, pretended at decision. "Well," she said, "that would be very nice." She smiled at him. She was pretty when she smiled, he thought, even white teeth and nice little wrinkles around the dark gray eyes. She folded her magazine and picked up her handbag and stood up and took the three steps to his table. He stood up and held the chair for her and she said, "Thank you," as she sat down. "I like to talk to Americans whenever I get a chance. I was in Washington for three years and I learned to like Americans."

Gambit, Rudolph thought, but keeping his face agreeable. If I were Swedish or Greek, she'd say she liked Swedes and Greeks. He speculated on how she had spent her three years in Washington. Entertaining lobbyists, subverting congressmen in the bedrooms of motels for pay?

"I like some Americans myself," he said.

She chuckled, a small, ladylike chuckle. She was definitely not a sister to the prowling, gaudy savages of the streets of New York, regardless of the bond of their profession. He had heard that there were well-mannered whores in America, too, who charged a hundred dollars or more for an hour's visit, and who could only be ordered by telephone, out-of-work actresses and models, elegant housewives working on a mink coat, but he had never met any of them. In fact, he had never spoken more than three words to any prostitute: "Thank you, no."

"And the French," the woman was saying. "Do you like them?"

"Moderately," he said. "Do you?"

"Some of them." She chuckled again.

The waiter appeared, his face stolid, accustomed to movements from table to table. *"La même chose? Un vin blanc?"* Rudolph asked the woman.

"Ah," she said, "you speak French."

"Un petit peu," Rudolph said. He felt playful, tipsy. It was a night for games, masks, pretty French toys. Whatever happened that night, the lady was going to see that she didn't have just another ordinary American tourist on her hands. *"Je l'ai étudié à l'école.* High school. What's that in French?"

"Collège? Lycée."

"Lycée," he said, with a sense of triumph.

The waiter shuffled his feet, a small reminder that he didn't have all night to stand around listening to an American trying to remember his high-school French to impress a lady who had just picked him up. *"Monsieur?"* the waiter said. *"Encore un cognac?"*

"S'il vous plaît," Rudolph said with dignity.

After that, they spoke in a mixture of the two languages, both of them laughing at the kind of French Rudolph managed to dredge up from his memory, as he told her about the bosomy French teacher he had had as a teenaged boy at home, about how he had believed he was in love with her, had written her ardent letters in French, had once drawn a picture of her, naked, which she had confiscated. For her part, the woman had seemed to be pleased to listen to him, to correct his mistakes in her language, to praise him when he got out more than three words in a row. If this was what French whores were like, Rudolph thought drunkenly, after a bottle of champagne, he understood why prostitution was such a respected fixture of French civilization.

Then, the woman—he had asked her name, which was Jeanne—had looked at her watch and become serious. "It's getting late," she said in English, gathering in her bag and magazine, "I must be getting on."

"I'm sorry if I've wasted your time," he said. His voice was thick and he was having difficulty getting the words out.

She stood up. "I've enjoyed it very much, Jimmy," she said. He had told her that was his name. One more mask. He would not be traced. "But I expect an important call . . ."

He stood up to say good-bye, half relieved, half sorry that he wasn't going to make love to her. His chair fell back and he teetered a little as he rose. "It's been sharm—charming," he said.

She frowned at him. "Where is your hotel?" she asked.

Where was his hotel? For a moment the map of France was blotted from his consciousness. "Where's my—my hotel . . ." he said, his voice blurred. "Oh. Antibes."

"Do you have a car?"

"Yes."

She thought for a moment. "You are in no condition to drive, you know."

He hung his head, abashed. Americans, he felt she was saying, scornfully, arrived in France in no condition to drive. In no condition to do anything. "I'm not really a drinking man," he said, making it sound like an excuse. "I've had a bad day."

"The roads are dangerous, especially at night," she said.

"Especially at night," he agreed.

"Would you like to come with me?" she asked.

At last, he thought. It would not be a sin now, merely a safety measure. As a businessman, he really should ask her what it would cost, but after the drinks together and the friendly conversation it would sound crass. Later would do just as well. Whatever the price turned out to be, he certainly could afford one night in Europe with a courtesan. He was proud of himself for thinking of the word—courtesan. Suddenly he felt his head clearing. "*Volontiers*," he said, using her language to show her he wasn't as far gone as she thought. He called loudly for the waiter: "*Garçon*," and got out his wallet. He covered his wallet with his hands so that she couldn't see how many bills he had in it. In situations like this, even though he was not used to them, he knew one had to be careful.

The waiter came over and told him, in French, how much he owed. He couldn't understand the man and turned helplessly, ashamed, to the woman. "What did he say?"

"Two hundred and fifteen francs," she said.

He took three hundred-franc bills out of his wallet and waved away the waiter's fumbling effort to make change.

"You shouldn't have tipped him that much," she whispered as she took his arm and guided him out of the restaurant.

"Americans," he said. "A noble and generous race."

She laughed, held his arm more tightly.

They found a taxi and he admired the grace with which she raised her arm to hail the driver, the shapeliness of her legs, the warm curve of her bosom.

She held his hand in the taxi, no more. It was a short ride. The taxi now smelled of perfume, musky, just the hint of flowers in its past. The taxi stopped in front of a small apartment house on a dark street. She paid the driver, then took his arm again and led him into the house. He followed her up one flight of stairs, admiring her from below now. She opened the door with a key, guided him along a dark hallway and through a doorway and switched on a lamp. He was surprised at how large the room was and how tastefully furnished, although he couldn't make out too many details in the shaded light of the single lamp. She must have a generous clientele, he thought, Arabs, Italian industrialists, German steel barons.

"Now . . ." she began to say, when the telephone rang.

She wasn't lying, he thought, she *was* expecting a call. She hesitated, as though she didn't want to pick up the phone. "Would you mind . . .?" she said. She gestured toward another doorway. "I think it would be better if I was alone for this."

"Of course." He went into the next room and switched on a light. It was a small bedroom, with a double bed, already made up. He heard her voice through the door that he had closed behind him. He got the impression that she was angry with whomever she was talking to, although he couldn't make out what she was saying. He looked thoughtfully at the big bed. Last chance to leave. The hell with it, he thought and undressed, dropping his clothes carelessly on a chair and switching his wallet to a different pocket from the one he had been carrying it in. He got into bed and pulled the covers over him.

He must have fallen asleep because the next thing he knew a warm perfumed body was in bed beside him, the room was dark, there was a satiny, firm leg thrown across him, a soft, exploring hand on his belly, a mouth against his ear, murmuring words he could not understand.

He did not know what time it was when, all nerves quiescent, his body glowingly at rest, he finally lay still, his fingertips just touching the now familiar body that had given him so much pleasure. Fragrant, accidental humanity lying in the bed beside him. All praise to the animal hidden in the black suit. Disregarded, gloriously disregarded the deprived Puritan. He raised his head, leaned on one elbow over the woman, kissed her gently on the cheek. "It must be late," he whispered. "I have to go now."

"Drive carefully, *chéri*," the woman said, dreamy, replete. His doing.

"I'm all right now," he said. "I'm not drunk anymore."

The woman twisted and reached out and lit a lamp on the bedside table. He got out of bed, proud of his nakedness. Adolescent vainglory, he admitted wryly to himself, and dressed. The woman rose, too, strong, supple body, breasts full, haunches muscled, and covered herself in a gown, sat in a chair watching him with a little smile as he put on his clothes. He wished she hadn't put on the light, had not wakened. Then he could have left a hundred francs, maybe a thousand francs, on the mantelpiece, darkness and sleep concealing his provincial American ignorance of such matters; he could have slipped out of the apartment and out of the house, all connections broken. But the light was on, the woman was watching him, smiling. Waiting?

There was no avoiding the moment. He took out his wallet. "Is a thousand francs enough?" he asked, stumbling a little over the "enough."

She looked at him curiously, the smile vanishing. Then she began to laugh. The laugh was low at first, then became raucous. She bent over, put her head in her hands, her thick, gleaming hair falling in a dark cascade, hiding her face, the laugh continuing. He watched her, feeling his nerves twitching, regretting that he had been in her bed, that he had offered her a drink, that he was in Nice, regretting that he had ever set foot in France.

"I'm sorry," he said inanely. "It's just that I'm not accustomed . . ."

She raised her head, her face still distorted by laughter. She stood up and came over to him and kissed his cheek. "Poor dear," she said, the laughter still there, at the back of her throat. "I didn't know I was worth that much."

"If you want more . . ." he said stiffly.

"Much more," she said. "I want nothing. The most exorbitant price. Dear man. Thinking all this time that I was professional. And being so polite and gentle, too. If all customers were like you, I think we'd all become whores. I liked Americans before, but I like them even better now."

"Christ, Jeanne," he said. It was the first time he had spoken her name. "It never occurred to me that anybody would pick me out, take me home with her and . . . I don't know what to say."

"Don't say anything. You're too modest, my charming American, too modest by half."

"Well," he said, "it never happened to me before." He was afraid she was going to start laughing again.

She shook her head wonderingly. "What's wrong with American women?" she said. She moved over to the bed and sat on the edge. She patted it. "Come, sit down, please," she said.

He sat down next to her. She took his hand, sisterly now. "If it will make you feel any better, *chéri*," she said, "it never happened to me before, either. But I have been so lonely—starved—Couldn't you tell?"

"No," he admitted. "I'm not really a ladies' man."

"Not a ladies' man," she said, gently mocking. "Not a drinking man. Just the sort of man I needed tonight. Let me tell you a little about myself. I'm married. To a major in the army. He was an aide to the military attaché in Washington."

That's where the English came from, he thought, no lobbyists, no congressmen, no motels.

"Now he is stationed temporarily in Paris. At the Ecole Militaire," she said. "Temporarily." She laughed shortly, harshly. "He's been there three months now. I have two children in school here in Nice. They are visiting their grandmother tonight."

"You weren't wearing a wedding ring," he said. "I looked."

"Not tonight." Her face grew grim. "I didn't want to be married tonight. When I got my husband's telegram this afternoon telling me he was going to call, I knew what I was going to say. He was going to say that once again he would be too busy with his work to come to Nice. He has been too busy for three months. They must be preparing a terrible war at the Ecole Militaire when a poor little major can't get off for even one day to fly to Nice to see his wife once in three months. I have a very good idea of what kind of war my major is preparing in Paris. You heard me on the telephone . . .?"

"Yes," Rudolph said. "I couldn't hear what you were saying. . . . You sounded angry."

"It wasn't a friendly conversation," Jeanne said. "No, not friendly at all. So now you are beginning to have some idea of why I was sitting at a café table, not wearing a wedding ring?"

"More or less," Rudolph said.

"I was on the point of quitting and going home when you came into the café and sat down," she said quietly. "Two men had approached me before. Posing, stuffy men, experts, connoisseurs of—what's the American phrase—one-night . . .?"

"One-night stands," Rudolph said.

"That's it."

"At least they didn't think you were a whore," he said ruefully. "Forgive me."

She patted his hand. "There's nothing to forgive," she said. "It added just the right note of comedy to the evening. When you came in and sat down, with your decent, bony, respectable American face, I decided not to go home." She smiled. "Not just then. It turns out I didn't make a mistake. You must never be modest again." Another sisterly pat of the hand. "Now, it's late. You said you had to go. . . . Do you want my telephone number? Can I see you again?"

"I suppose I ought to tell you about myself, too," Rudolph said. "First of all, my name isn't Jimmy. I don't know why I . . ." He shrugged. "I guess I was ashamed of what I was doing." He smiled. "What I *thought* I was doing. Maybe I half believed if it wasn't my own name it wasn't me who was really doing it. More likely, if we ever met and I was with somebody else and you said hello, Jimmy, I could say, I'm sorry, madam, you must be thinking of somebody else."

"I wish I could dare keep a diary," Jeanne said. "I would write down all that happened tonight in detail. In great detail. It would give my children something to laugh at when they discovered it after my death. What do you know, dear, old, sensible *Maman*?"

"My name is Rudolph," he said. "I was never fond of the name. When I was a boy I thought it sounded un-American, though it's hard to tell what sounds American anymore and what doesn't. And why anybody should care. But when you're a boy in his teens, your head full of books, with heroes with names like Huckleberry Finn, Daniel Boone, Studs Lonigan . . . Well, it seemed to me that Rudolph sounded like . . . like heavy German cooking. Especially during the war." He had never told anyone how he felt about his Christian name, had never formulated it clearly for himself even, and now found that it was with a sense of relief, mixed with wry amusement, that he could speak about it openly to this handsome stranger, or almost stranger. Also, sitting in the muted lamplight on the bed which had been the furniture of exquisite pleasure, he wanted to make a further offering of himself to the woman, find reasons for delaying leave-taking, join her in the pretense that the dawn was not near, departure inevitable.

"Rudolph," Jeanne said. "Neither good nor bad. Think of it as Rodolfo. That has a better sound, doesn't it?"

"Much better."

"Good," she said teasingly. "From now on I will call you Rodolfo."

"Rodolfo Jordache," he said. It gave him a new, more dashing view of himself. "Jordache. That's my family name. I'm at the Hôtel du Cap." All defenses down now. Names and addresses. Each at the other's mercy. "One more thing. I'm married."

"I expected as much," Jeanne said. "Your affair. Just as my marriage is my affair."

"My wife is with me in Antibes." He didn't feel he had to tell her that they were not on the best of terms, either. "Give me your telephone number."

She got up and went over to a little desk where there was a pen and some paper and wrote down her telephone number. She gave him the slip of paper and he folded it carefully and put it in his pocket.

"Other times," she said, "you will have to rent a hotel room. The children will be here."

Other times. . . .

"Now," she said, "I'll call you a taxi." They went into the salon and she dialed a number, spoke quickly for a moment, waited a little while, said, "*Très bien*," hung up. "The taxi will be here in five minutes," she said. Before she opened the front door for him they kissed, a long, grateful, healing kiss. "Good night, Rodolfo," she said. She smiled, a smile he knew he would remember for a long time.

The taxi was waiting for him when he got down to the street, its diesel motor making it sound like a launch waiting to put out to sea. Voyages.

"*L'hôtel Negresco*," Rudolph said as he got in. When the taxi started, he looked back at the house. It was imperative for him to be able to find it again, to recognize it in his dreams. When they got to the Negresco he made sure he was not run down as he crossed to where his car was parked. Then, at the wheel of his rented car, he drove slowly and very carefully on the deserted road along the sea to Antibes.

When he reached the port he slowed down even more, then abruptly swung the car into the parking lot and got out and walked along the quay to where the *Clothilde* was berthed in the silent harbor. There were no lights to be seen on the *Clothilde*. He didn't want to wake Wesley or Bunny. He took off his shoes and climbed down from the deck into the dory lying alongside, slipped the line, sat amidships and noiselessly put the oars through the locks. He rowed almost soundlessly away from the ship toward the middle of the harbor, then, pulling more strongly, toward the harbor entrance, the tarry smell of the water strong in his nostrils, mixed with the flowery fragrance from shore.

He had acted almost automatically, not asking himself why he was doing this. The pull of the oars against his shoulders and arms gave him a sober pleasure, and the sigh of the small bow wave against the sides of the dory seemed a fitting music with which to end the night.

The city of Antibes, looming shadows, with a light here and there, receded slowly as he headed toward the red and green lights that marked the channel into the sea. The rhythm of his body as he bent forward, then leaned back, satisfied him. How many times had these same oars moved in the hands of his brother. His own hands were soft against the smooth wood, polished by the strong hands of his brother. The thought that perhaps in the morning his palms would be blistered pleased him.

Being alone on the dark surface of the water was a benediction to him and the blinking lights of the harbor entrance comforted him, with their promise of safe anchorages. Grief was possible here, but also hope. "Thomas, Thomas," he said softly as he went out into the sea and felt its gentle swell lift the dory. He remembered, as he rowed, all the times they had failed each other, and the end, when they had forgotten the failures or at least forgiven them.

He felt tireless and serene, alone in the dark night, but then he heard the coughing of a small fishing boat putting out to sea behind him, one small acetylene lamp at its bow. The fishing boat passed near him and he could see two men in it staring curiously at him. He was conscious of how strange it must look to them, a man in a dark business suit, alone, headed out to sea at that hour. He kept on rowing until they were out of sight, then let the oars dangle and stared up at the starlit sky.

He thought of his father, that enraged and pitiful old man, who had also rowed in darkness, who had picked a night of storm for his last voyage. Suicide had been possible for his father, who had found the peace in death he had never achieved in life.

It was not possible for him. He was a different man, with different claims upon him. He took one long, deep breath, then turned the dory around and rowed back to the *Clothilde*, his hands burning.

Quietly, he tied up to the *Clothilde's* stern, climbed the ladder and went ashore. He put on his shoes, a rite observed, a ceremony celebrated, and got into his car and started the engine.

It was past three in the morning when he got to the hotel. The lobby was deserted, the night concierge yawning behind the desk. He asked for his key and was turning toward the elevator when the concierge called after him. "Oh, Mr. Jordache, Mrs. Burke left a message for you. You are to call her whenever you get in. She said it was urgent."

"Thank you," Rudolph said wearily. Whatever it was, Gretchen would have to wait until morning.

"Mrs. Burke told me to call her when you got in. No matter what time." She had guessed he would try to avoid her, had taken steps to make sure he couldn't.

"I see," said Rudolph. He sighed. "Call her, please. Tell her I'll come to her room as soon as I look in on my wife." He should have stayed the night in Nice. Or rowed till dawn. Faced everything in daylight.

"One more thing," said the concierge. "There was a gentlemen here asking for you. A Mr. Hubbell. He said he was from *Time* Magazine. He used the telex."

"If he comes here and asks for me again, tell him I'm not in."

"I understand. *Bonne nuit, monsieur.*"

Rudolph rang for the elevator. He had planned to telephone Jeanne, say good night to her, try to tell her what she had done for him, listen to the husky voice, with its rough, sensual shading, fall off to sleep with the memory of the night to take the weight from his dreams. He could forget that now. He shuffled into the elevator, feeling old, got off at his floor, opened the door to the suite as silently as he could. The lights were on, both in the salon and in the bedroom in which Jean slept. Since the murder she refused to sleep in the dark. As he approached her doorway she called out, "Rudolph?"

"Yes, dear." He sighed. He had hoped she was asleep. He went into her room. She was sitting up in bed, staring at him. Automatically he looked for a glass or a bottle. There was no glass or bottle and he could tell from her face she hadn't been drinking. She looks old, he thought, old. The drawn face, the dull eyes over the lacy nightgown made her look like a malicious sketch of the woman she would be forty years from now.

"What time is it?" she asked harshly.

"After three. You'd better go to sleep."

"After three. The consulate in Nice keeps odd hours, doesn't it?"

"I took the night off," he said.

"From what?"

"From everything," he said.

"From me," she said bitterly. "That's become quite a habit, hasn't it? A way of life with you, wouldn't you say?"

"Let's discuss it in the morning, shall we?" he said.

She sniffed. "You stink of perfume," she said. "Shall we discuss that in the morning, too?"

"If you wish," he said. "Good night."

He started out of the room. "Leave the door open," she called. "I have to keep all avenues of escape open."

He left the door open. He wished he could pity her.

He went into his bedroom through the salon, closing his own door behind him. Then he unlocked the door that led from his room into the corridor and went out. He didn't want to have to explain to Jean that he had to see Gretchen about something that his sister thought was urgent.

Gretchen's room was down the corridor. He went past the pairs of shoes left out by the guests to be shined while they slept. Europe was on the brink of Communism, he thought, but shoes were still shined by future commissars, budding Trotskies, between midnight and six each morning.

He knocked on Gretchen's door. She opened it immediately, as though she had been standing there, alerted by the concierge's call, as though she couldn't bear to wait the extra second or two it would have taken her to cross the room and confront her brother. She was in a terry cloth bathrobe, light blue, the blue almost identical with the blue of the dress Jeanne had been wearing in the café. With her small pale face, dark hair and strong, graceful body, she bore a striking resemblance to Jeanne, he thought. Echoes everywhere. The idea hadn't occurred to him before.

"Come in," she said. "I've been so worried. God, where've you been?"

"It's a long story," he said. "Can't it wait till morning?"

"It can't wait until morning," she said, closing the door. She sniffed. "You smell heavenly, Brother," she said sarcastically. "And you look as though you've just been laid."

"I'm a gentleman," Rudolph said, trying to make light of the accusation. "Gentlemen don't discuss matters like that."

"Ladies do," she said. She had her vulgar side, Gretchen.

"Let's drop it, please," he said. "I need some sleep. What's so damned urgent?"

Gretchen fell back into a big armchair, sprawling, as though she were too tired to stand anymore. "Bunny Dwyer called an hour ago," she said flatly. "Wesley's in jail."

"What?"

"Wesley's in jail in Cannes. He got into a fight in a bar and nearly killed a man with a beer bottle. He hit a cop and the police had to subdue him. Is that urgent enough for you, Brother?"

CHAPTER 4

1968

From Billy Abbott's notebook—

There've been riots in Brussels today and bombs exploded. It's all about whether kids from Flemish-speaking families should be taught in their own language or in French and having the street signs in both languages. And the blacks in the units here are talking about mutiny if they aren't allowed to have Afros. People are ready to tear each other apart about anything. Which, sad to relate, is why I'm in uniform although I haven't the faintest desire to do the least bit of harm to anybody and as far as I'm concerned anybody who wants to can speak Flemish or Basque or Serbo-Croat or Sanskrit and all I'd do would be to say, It sounds great to me.

Is there something lacking in my character?

I suppose so. If you're strong you want to dominate everything and everybody around you. It's hard to dominate people if they don't speak your language and being strong you react angrily, like American tourists in restaurants in Europe who begin to shout when a waiter can't understand what it is they're ordering. In political terms this is translated into riot police and tear gas.

Monika speaks German, English, French, Flemish and Spanish and she says she can read Gaelic. As far as I can tell she is as pacific as myself but because of her job as translator for NATO she gets to hurl the most awesome threats, composed by belligerent old men, at other belligerent old men in the opposite wing of the great lunatic asylum we all inhabit.

I spent the day in bed with her.

We do that occasionally.

DWYER WAS WAITING outside the Cannes *préfecture* when Rudolph's taxi drove up to it. The taxi, Rudolph had decided, was a wiser choice than his own car. He didn't want to go charging into a French police station to demand his nephew's freedom, only to be forced to take a breathalator test. Even in his heavy, dark blue seaman's sweater, Dwyer was shivering as he leaned against the wall and his face was pale, greenish, in the watery light from the *préfecture*'s lamps. Rudolph looked at his watch as he got out of the taxi. Past 4:00 A.M. The streets of Cannes were deserted, all errands but his completed for the night or postponed until morning.

"God," Dwyer said, "I'm glad to see you. What a night! Shit, what a night."

"Where is he?" Rudolph asked, trying to keep his voice calm to take the edge off the hysteria that was showing in Dwyer's face, in the way he was rubbing the knuckles of one hand against his other palm.

"Inside somewhere. In a cell, I guess. They wouldn't let me see him. I can't go in there. They said they'd throw me into the can, too, if I showed my face in there once more. French police," he said bitterly. "You might as well talk to Hitler."

"How is he?" Rudolph asked. Looking at Dwyer, hunched against the cold night air, he felt small shivers run down his spine, too. He was dressed for the day's warmth, had neglected to grab a coat at the hotel.

"I don't know how he is *now*," Dwyer said. "He wasn't too bad when they dragged him in. But he hit a cop and God knows what they've done to him since they got him in there."

Rudolph wished that there was a café open, a lighted place with at least the semblance of warmth. But the street stretched away on both sides, narrow and dark except for the weak glow of lampposts. "All right, Bunny," he said soothingly. "I'm here, I'll see what I can do. But you have to fill me in. What happened?"

"I took him out to dinner in Antibes," Bunny said. He said it defensively, as though Rudolph was accusing him, as though his innocence had to be claimed and confirmed before anything else was said or done. "I couldn't leave the kid alone on a night like this, could I?"

"Of course not."

"We drank some wine. Wesley drank wine with all of us, in front of his father, his father would pour it out of the bottle for him as though he was a grown-up, you forget that he's just a kid . . . You know, in France . . . " His voice trailed off, as though the shared bottle of wine between the boy and himself in the restaurant in Antibes was another unjust charge against him.

"I know," Rudolph said, trying not to sound impatient. "Then what?"

"Then the kid wanted a brandy. Two brandies. I thought, why not? After all, the day you bury your father . . . Even if he got drunk, we were right near the port, I could get him back to the ship with no trouble. Only he wouldn't go back to the ship. All of a sudden he got up from the table and he said, 'I'm going to Cannes.' 'What the hell do you want to go to Cannes for, this time of night?' I said. 'I'm going to visit a nightclub,' he said. His exact words. Visit. 'I'm going to visit the Porte Rose.' God knows what the brandy, the day, everything, was doing to that kid's head. I tried to reason with him, I swear to God I did. 'Fuck you, Bunny,' he said. He never swore at me before. He had a funny dead look on his face. You couldn't budge him with a bulldozer. 'Nobody's asking you to come with me,' he said. 'Go get your beauty sleep.' He was half out of the restaurant before I could get to him, grab his arm, at least. I couldn't let him go to that goddamn place alone, could I?"

"No," Rudolph said wearily. "You did the right thing." He wondered if he would have done better or worse in Dwyer's place. Worse, he thought.

"So we got a taxi and we went to the Porte Rose," Dwyer rattled on, made garrulous by grief or fear or impotence. "He never said a word in the taxi. Not word one. Just sat there looking out of the window, like a tourist. Who the hell knew what he had in his mind? I'm not a psychologist, I never had kids, who knows what crazy things they think of?" The tone of innocence, not expecting the innocence to be believed or recognized was in the voice again. "So," Dwyer went on, "I thought, Okay, he's disturbed. Who isn't today, a day like this one, he has some crazy notion maybe that he owes it to his old man to go and see the place where it all began. He saw the end, with the ashes floating out to sea, maybe he had to see the beginning, too."

The beginning, Rudolph thought, thinking of the ferocious brother he had slept with in the same bed over the bakery store, the beginning was not in a nightclub in Cannes. You'd have to go back further than that. A lot further.

"Maybe even it was a good idea, I thought," Dwyer said. "Anyway, one sure thing, the Yugoslav Tom had the fight with wasn't going to be there—the police've been hunting for him ever since they talked to him the day after the murder and they ain't found any trace of him yet. And I never saw the guy, anyway, and neither did Wesley, we wouldn't know him from Adam, even if he was standing along the bar right next to us with a spotlight on him. It wouldn't be a pleasant experience for me, but what's the harm, a couple of drinks and then home to bed and a hangover tomorrow and that's it?"

"I understand, Bunny," Rudolph said, shivering. "You couldn't do anything else, given the circumstances."

Dwyer nodded vigorously. "Given the circumstances," he said.

"How did the fight start?" Rudolph asked. Dwyer's excuses for himself could wait until another day. It was four in the morning and he was cold and Wesley was inside the police station and maybe the cops were working him over. "Was it Wesley's fault?"

"Fault? Who ever knows whose fault it is when something like that happens?" Dwyer's mouth quivered. "We were standing at the bar, not saying anything to each other, maybe after two, maybe three whiskeys, we were on Scotch now, Wesley wanted Scotch—he didn't seem drunk—that kid must have a head like iron—and there was a big Englishman next to him, and he was drinking beer and talking loud. He was off some ship in the harbor, you could tell he was a seaman, he was saying something about Americans in English to the girl, I guess it wasn't very complimentary because all of a sudden Wesley turned to him and said, quiet-like, 'Shut your big trap about Americans, limey.'"

Oh God, Rudolph thought, what a time and place for patriotism.

"It was something about how the Americans let the English fight their war for them—Wesley wasn't even *born* then, what the hell did he care? Christ, his own father would never've had a fight in a bar if *ten* Englishmen said Americans were all yellow pimps and whoremongers. But Wesley was spoiling for a fight. I never saw him fight before—but Tom told me about him and I could see the signs and I grabbed his arm and said, 'Come on, kid, time to go.' But the Englishman, Christ, he must've weighed two hundred pounds, thirty, thirty-two years old, drinking all that beer, he said, 'Would you repeat that, please, sonny?' So, nice and calm, Wesley said, 'Shut your big trap about Americans, limey.'

"Even then, it could've been avoided, because the girl kept tugging at the Englishman's sleeve and saying, 'Let's go home, Arnold.' But he shook her off and said to Wesley, 'What ship you off, mate?' and I could see him reaching, slow, toward the beer bottle on the bar. 'The *Clothilde,*' Wesley said, and I could feel all his muscles tensing up in his arm. The Englishman laughed. 'You better be looking for another berth, sonny,' he said. I don't believe the *Clothilde* is going to be a popular ship from now on.' It was the laugh that got Wesley, I think. He reached out sudden and grabbed the beer bottle first and cracked it across the man's face. The Englishman went down, blood all over him and everybody screaming all around and Wesley started stomping him, with the craziest expression you ever saw on a boy's face. Where he ever learned to fight like that nobody'll ever know. Stomping, for Christ's sake. And laughing, crazy as a bedbug, with me hanging on him to pull him back and making no more impression on him than if I was a mosquito buzzing around his neck.

"It didn't take long. There were two cops in plainclothes at a table and they jumped him, but he got one good punch in on one of the cops and the cop went down to his knees. But the other cop got out a billy and clouted him on the neck and that was the end of the match right there. They hauled Wesley away and into a police car outside and they wouldn't let me come with them, so I just ran to the police station and an ambulance went by full speed with the lights full on and the siren going and god knows what sort of shape that Englishman is in right now." Dwyer sighed. "That's about it," he said breathlessly. "Just about it. Now you know what it's all about, why I called your hotel."

Rudolph sighed, too. "I'm glad you called," he said. "Wait here. I'll see what I can do."

"I'd go in with you," Dwyer said, "but they hate the sight of my face."

Rudolph settled his shoulders into the jacket of his suit and went into the police station, the sudden light glaring in his eyes, but the warmth, even on this errand, welcome. He was conscious that he needed a shave, that his clothes were rumpled. He would have felt more confident if, in Gretchen's words, he didn't look as if he had just been laid. He was still conscious, too, of the musky fragrance of perfume that still clung to him. You are not dressed or properly deodorized for the occasion, he told himself as he went toward the high desk behind which sat a fat policeman with blue jaws, scowling at him.

Travel, he thought, as he smiled, or hoped he smiled, at the policeman, travel broadens one's horizons; one visits cathedrals, the beds of the wives of continental military men, one sails over the hulks of ships sunk in many wars, one becomes familiar with foreign customs, strange foods, police stations, crematories . . .

"My name," he said to the policeman behind the desk, in slow French, "is Jordache. I am American . . . " Did the policeman know of Lafayette, the Marshall Plan, D day? Take a chance on gratitude. A long chance. "I believe you have my nephew Wesley Jordache here."

The policeman said something rapidly in French which Rudolph couldn't understand.

"Speak slowly, please," he said. "I am not good in French."

"Come back at eight o'clock in the morning," the policeman said slowly enough so that Rudolph could understand him.

"I would like to see him now," Rudolph said.

"You heard what I said." The policeman spoke with exaggerated slowness and held up his two hands, with eight fingers extended.

Rudolph decided that the policeman had not heard of Lafayette or D day. "He may need medical attention," he said.

Again, with mocking slowness, the policeman said, "He is getting excellent medical attention. Eight o'clock in the morning. French time." He laughed.

"Does anybody here speak English?"

"This is a police station, *monsieur,*" the policeman said. "You are not at the Sorbonne."

Rudolph would have liked to ask about bail but he didn't know the word for bail. There must be fifty thousand American and English tourists each year in Cannes, you'd think at least one of the bastards could take the trouble to learn English. "I'd like to talk to your superior officer," he said stubbornly.

"He is not here at the present time."

"Somebody."

"I am somebody." Again the policeman laughed. Then he scowled. The scowl was more natural to him than laughter. "You are invited to leave, *monsieur*," he said harshly. "This room must be kept clear."

For a moment, Rudolph thought of offering a bribe. But he had made the mistake once that night of offering money in the wrong place. Here it would be considerably more dangerous.

"Get out, get out, *monsieur*." The policeman waved a thick hand impatiently. "I have work to do."

Beaten, Rudolph left the room. Dwyer was still hitting the knuckles of one hand against the palm of his other hand outside. "Well?" Dwyer asked.

"Nothing doing," Rudolph said flatly. "Not until eight o'clock in the morning. We might as well go to a hotel here. There's no sense in going back to Antibes for just a couple of hours."

"I don't like to leave the *Clothilde* alone," Dwyer said. "There's no telling, what with the way things are . . . " He left the thought unfinished. "I'll be back in the morning."

"Whatever you say," Rudolph said. He felt as though he had run for hours. In the morning, early, he would call the lawyer in Antibes. He remembered old Teddy Boylan, whose family owned the brickworks in Port Philip, where Rudolph was born, and who had befriended him, if that was the word, and had, in a way, educated him. Teddy Boylan, who had advised him to go to law school. "Lawyers run the world," Boylan had said. Good advice perhaps for men who wanted to run the world. He had once been one of them. No longer was. If he had taken the advice, been admitted to the bar, would the blue-jowled policeman inside have laughed at him and kicked him out? Would Wesley be behind bars now, at the mercy of a cop he had knocked down in a brawl? Would Tom be alive or at least have had a neater death? Four-o'clock-in-the-morning thoughts.

He trudged through the empty streets, cleared now of whores and gamblers and ambulances, toward the Hotel Carlton, where he could get a room for a few hours' sleep and Dwyer could find a taxi to take him back to the *Clothilde*.

This is the way my father must have felt a hundred times in his life, beat up and aching, not wanting much to move, Wesley thought as he lay on the bare board that pulled down from the wall of the cell into which he had been thrown. The thought somehow comforted him, made him feel closer to his father, as the prayer the afternoon before had not. He felt quiet now, relaxed, not caring about anything, at least not just yet. He was glad they'd pulled him off the Englishman and he hoped he hadn't killed the son of a bitch.

If the son of a bitch didn't die, his Uncle Rudy would get him off. Little old Mr. fixit, Rudy Jordache. He had to smile, even though it hurt to smile, when he thought this.

The smile didn't last long. He hadn't known his father long enough. He didn't know how long was enough, but he knew that the time he'd had wasn't it. There wouldn't be any more of those long conversations in the darkened wheelhouse. Makeup time, his father used to call it, filling in the blanks, making up for the years when his mother had run away with him, had shuffled him off to one miserable school after another, telling him his father had deserted him, had run off with a cheap tart, was probably dead, the life he led, drinking, whoring, gambling, fighting, throwing his money away, everybody's enemy. His mother had a lot to answer for.

For that matter, he had a lot to answer for himself. If he had been a little more alert, had seen or sensed the sunken log they'd hit, and they hadn't had to come back to Antibes for repairs, they'd all be along the coast of Italy now, Portofino, Elba, Sicily, his father talking in that low, rough voice with everybody sleeping below, telling him about Clothilde Devereaux, the woman the boat was named for, the servant in Tom's fat, German Uncle Harold's house, scrubbing him down naked in the bathtub, feeding him gigantic meals, making love to him. His first real love, his father had said sadly, there for a while and then gone.

Or if he hadn't been sleeping like a baby, he'd have heard the footsteps on the deck, the way his father always did, no matter how tired he was or how deep in sleep, and come up to see his father on the way to rescue Jean Jordache, alone. He could have gone with him, maybe had the sense to make him call the police, at least be with him so that the Yugoslav would have realized there was no sense in fighting.

Who'm I kidding? Wesley thought. One night it would have happened in Portofino or Elba or Sicily. There was no stopping Jean Jordache from getting into trouble and dragging everybody along with her. He hadn't liked her from the beginning and he'd told his father so. His father had said, "I admit she has her problems. *I* wouldn't've married her, but Rudy is a different kind of man. She's rich, she was pretty and smart . . ." Tom had shrugged. "Maybe you got to pay for rich, pretty and smart." Only it was his father who'd paid. Too brave for his own good, too sure of himself. "I've had plenty of woman troubles myself." He'd smiled a little sadly in the dark as he'd said that, and told his son about the twins they said he'd knocked up in Elysium, Ohio, when they jailed him on the charge of statutory rape. "Looking back," Tom had said philosophically, "maybe it was worth it, though I didn't think so at the time. I suppose I could tell you to be careful, but I don't suppose it'd do any good, would it, Wesley?"

"I'm half careful," Wesley had said. He'd screwed two married ladies on two different voyages, taking chances, with their husbands on board, and he knew his father knew about it.

"I noticed you like the stuff," Tom said dryly.

"About like average, I guess," Wesley said. "I wouldn't know."

"I did, too," Tom said. "There was a wild English girl by the name of . . . let me see if I can remember her name . . . Betty, Betty Something—Betty Johns—that nearly got me killed in Paris because I spent two weeks with her down in Cannes, squandering my money and blowing up on wine and fancy meals before a fight. By the time the fight was over in Paris, with that Frenchman hitting me with everything but the water bucket, I was ready to take orders and become a monk." He chuckled.

There were other names that came up in his reminiscences of his past for his son's benefit, names he did not chuckle over: the boy with whom he had set fire to the cross on Boylan's lawn and who had turned him in; Schultzy, his manager; the man he had blackmailed at the Revere Club for five thousand dollars; Falconetti, whom he had shamed before twenty-seven other members of a ship's crew and caused to commit suicide. It was as though he felt the boy, starved for a father, now that he had finally found one, might get a false, noble impression of him that Tom could not live up to and had to correct to save the boy from inevitable and bitter disillusionment.

What advice he gave was practical. "You like the sea. Follow it. It's a good life, at least if you get lucky, like me. It's a nice mixture of laziness and work and variety and you're out in the open air. In the end, you'll have the *Clothilde* or maybe a better boat. Know what it's all about. Give it loving care, like Dwyer and me. And I'd advise not screwing the lady guests." He grinned. Father or no father, he couldn't be holy about a young man's overpowering interest in sex. "Be your own boss, because working for anybody else is the big trap. Learn everything. Above deck and below deck. You got a good chance with me and Bunny and Kate here to watch. Don't skimp on equipment. If you don't like anybody you hire on, for whatever reason, put him off at the next port. If you catch a guest with drugs, throw the drugs overboard without any conversation about it. If possible, don't booze with them. You'll be able to afford your own booze. Don't be greedy. The word gets around. Fast. If you don't like the looks of the sea, make for port, regardless of what some fat cat on board tells you about having to get to Rome or Cannes or Athens for an important business conference or to pick up a girlfriend. Don't volunteer for any wars. Don't back down, but don't pick fights. . . ."

He should've put that on tape, Wesley thought, remembering, and played it before he went to sleep every night.

"Keep a gun on board. Just in case. Locked up. It can come in handy." His father's legacy—Don't skimp on the equipment and keep a gun handy.

Wesley didn't know where the gun on the *Clothilde* was locked away. Probably Bunny knew, but he was sure Bunny wouldn't tell. It hadn't been handy when it was needed.

His father talked on in the barred darkness, the voice calm, slightly amused, but the words incomprehensible.

The ache in the back of his head throbbed, the memory of his father's voice dwindled away, like the sound of a buoy left to stern in a fog, and he slept.

CHAPTER 5

1968

From Billy Abbott's notebook—

I have a weakness for my father, who is a weak man. I forgave him. I have no weakness for my mother, who is a strong woman, and whom I do not forgive. Let the scholar who sifts through the ruins of Brussels in the next century figure this out. We are all haunted by our parents, one way or another. I am haunted by two fathers. William Abbott, who sired me, was, and I suppose still is, small and delightful, charming and useless.

Colin Burke, second husband of my mother, was a glittering, selfish, talented man, who could make actors perform like angels and the screen light up like a bonfire. I loved him and admired him and wished I could grow up to be like him. I did not. I grew up, I'm afraid, like Willie Abbott, although without some of his essential attractive qualities. I loved him, too.

I have put him to bed, drunk, fifty times.

I played five sets of tennis today for side bets, and won them all.

HE HAD BEEN to the consulate in Nice again, to the jail in Grasse, to which Wesley had been moved, twice during the week and three times to the lawyer's office. The consul had been vague and apologetic about being vague, the lawyer had been helpful, up to a point, Wesley not helpful, just silent, unrepentant, physically no worse for wear and less interested in his own fate than that of the men imprisoned along with him, among them a jewel thief, a passer of stolen checks and an art forger. He hadn't shaved since his arrest and the blondish thick stubble gave him an unkempt and wolfish look, at home among criminals. When he came into the small room in which Rudolph was permitted to speak to him, there was a rank, feral smell, a hunting beast caged in an unsanitary zoo. The smell transported Rudolph uncomfortably back to the room above the family bakery, the bed he shared with his brother Tom when they were in their teens, when Tom would come back late at night after a night of brawling in the town. He took out his handkerchief and pretended to be blowing his nose as Wesley sat down, grinning a little, opposite him across the small, unpainted, scarred table, guaranteed Provençal antique, provided by courtesy of the police of the floral city of Grasse.

Rudolph put on a solemn face, to indicate that this was no laughing matter. The police, through the lawyer, had let Rudolph know that the case was grave—a beer bottle might be construed to be a dangerous weapon—and that Wesley was not going to be let out of jail for some weeks, if then.

Rudolph had also spoken several times to his lawyer, Johnny Heath, in New York, who had told him that if he could extricate himself from the French, in all probability the estate would have to be settled in New York, as the last known residence in the United States of the murdered man, and that it would take time.

We will all be drowned in paper, Rudolph thought. He could see the *Clothilde* going down with all aboard in a sea of writs, court orders and legal foolscap, as he listened to Johnny Heath saying he guessed that the judge would almost certainly appoint Kate Jordache, the wife, even though she was a British subject, as executrix of the estate, which would probably be divided one-third to her and two-thirds to the son, although the child she was bearing was a complicating factor. The son, being a minor, would have to have a guardian until he reached the age of eighteen, and he didn't see any reason why Rudolph, as the oldest and nearest male relative, couldn't have the job. The estate would most probably have to be liquidated and taxes paid, which would mean selling the *Clothilde* within the year. But, Heath warned, he could not say definitely as yet—he would have to get other opinions.

He said nothing to Wesley of the problems that Heath had discussed. He merely asked if he were being treated well, if there was anything he wanted. Carelessly, the boy said that he was being treated like everybody else, wanted nothing. Baffling, unrewarding young man, Rudolph thought resentfully, immutably hostile. He cut the visits as short as possible.

When he returned wearily to the hotel, it was no better. Worse, in fact. The scenes with Jean were becoming more violent. She wanted to go home, get out of her prison, as she called it, probably the only time in its history that the Hôtel du Cap had been so described. Somehow, she had gotten it into her head that it was Rudolph's fault that she couldn't leave and his telling her that it was the policeman who was holding her passport and not himself could not stem the flood of her hysteria. "God damn it," she had said, during their latest argument, "your idiotic brother should have minded his own business. So I'd've been fucked. Big deal. It wouldn't've been the first time an American lady got fucked in France and I'd've been on my way home by now."

As the shrill voice battered at his ears, he had a quick vision of Jean as she had been when they had first married, a quick, lovely girl, passionate in the warm, afternoon lovemaking in the room overlooking the sea (was it the same room in which she slept now?—he couldn't remember), offering to buy him a yacht on that surprising afternoon when she confessed that she, who he had believed before their marriage was a poor working girl, was wealthier by far than he was. Better not think of those days. . . .

The fact that Wesley had nearly killed a man Jean took as proof that it was the Jordaches' inherent lust for violence, not her drunkenness or emotional instability, that had been at the root of the tragedy. "One way or another," she had screamed at her husband, "with or without me, with their characters, those two men, that man and that boy, were doomed from the beginning. It's in the blood." Gretchen, he remembered, had said much the same thing and he damned her for it. He had seen Wesley in jail. It was not only Jordache blood in Wesley's veins. He remembered the pouting, hard-eyed, curvaceous mother—Teresa. Who knew what Sicilian bandits had contributed to that rank smell, that wolfish grin? Guilt, if it *was* guilt, had to be fairly apportioned.

"I know about your crazy father," Jean ranted on, accusing him, his crime-stained German ancestors. "I don't know how you and your holy sister escaped it this long. And look at your sister—how did her husband die? Killed, killed, killed . . . ."

"In an automobile accident." Rudolph tried to break through her high-pitched, intoning chant. "Fifty thousand people a year . . . ."

"Killed," Jean repeated stubbornly. "I'm frightened to think of what kind of life our child is going to have with you as the father. . . ."

Rudolph felt helpless before her attacks. He felt confident of himself, able to solve rational problems, but irrationality frightened him, confused him, left him unarmed. When he left the room Jean had thrown herself facedown on a couch, beating her hands against the pillows like a child, sobbing, "I want to go home, I want to go home. . . ."

Gretchen, too, although she didn't say anything, was growing restive. She had work to go back to, a man kept telephoning her from New York, the attractions of the Côte d'Azur had long since lost their charm for her, and Rudolph realized that she was only staying on out of loyalty to him. Another debt.

Once, during the week, when they were alone together, she asked quietly, "Rudy, has it ever occurred to you to just pull out?"

"What do you mean?"

"I mean quit. It isn't your mess after all. Just pick up and leave. One way or another, they'll all survive."

"No," he said shortly, "it's never occurred to me."

"I admire you, Brother," Gretchen said, although there was no admiration in the manner in which she said it. "I admire you and I wonder at you."

"*You* don't have to stay, you know."

"I know," she said. "And I don't intend to stay forever. I suppose you will, if necessary."

"If necessary." He had no job to go back to, nobody was calling him from New York.

"Add pity to what I just said, Brother." Gretchen said. "I am now going to go down to the sea and bask in the sunshine."

Kate had not yet called from her hotel and he was thankful to her for that. But he dreaded the moment when he would have to go to her and tell her what had to be done and what it would mean for her.

Poor Bunny Dwyer, he thought, as he walked slowly once again through the narrow streets of the old city toward the lawyer's office—old companion, old partner, unprovided for by law or custom, friendship and the work of years not bearing the weight of a feather in any legal balance.

The only thing that had kept him sane was the two afternoons in a hotel in Nice with Jeanne. No complications, no iron cables of love or duty to consider, only the unthinking satisfactions of the flesh to make forgetfulness possible for an hour or two in a darkened room rented in a strange town.

Was that really the reason he was willing to stay, for those precious afternoons in Nice? For the selfish sport of double adultery? Was he being admired and pitied for a lie?

His steps were heavy as he approached the lawyer's office and the bright sunlight made him sweat uncomfortably.

The lawyer had his office in his own house along the ramparts, in two of the old humble stone buildings now turned into a single exquisite mansion, where once the fishermen who sailed out of Antibes had lived, but which, converted and modernized, now were owned by people who had never cast a net, had never pulled an oar or survived a squall. Contrary to established economic doctrine, Rudolph thought, the rich follow the poor, not the other way around. At least to the good spots the poor have accidentally found, where they in times past had been the first citizens of the town exposed to pirates, enemy fire and the erosion of storms.

The lawyer's office was impressive, the walls lined with calf-bound legal books, the furniture elegant, dark, eighteenth-century pieces, gleaming with wax, the wide window opening on a view of the sea that lapped at the rampart walls. The lawyer was an old man, but straight and as impressive as his surroundings, beautifully dressed, with large, well-kept hands, sprinkled with liver spots. He had a shining bald pate over a large-nosed, sharp face, and sad eyes. Why shouldn't he be sad, Rudolph thought, as he shook the old man's hand, think of what he must have been through to arrive in this room.

"I have considerable news for you," the lawyer said when Rudolph had seated himself across the great polished desk from him. He spoke English slowly but with care. He had let Rudolph know from the beginning that he had spent the war years in England. His voice was juicy. "First, about your wife. I have her passport here." He opened a drawer, bent a little, produced the passport and pushed it gently across the desk toward Rudolph. "The police have found Danovic, the man they wished to question further. They assure me their interrogation was—er—vigorous. Unfortunately, while he has a police record of previous arrests for various crimes, he has been discharged each time without going to trial. Besides, his alibi has stood up. He was in Lyon all day, having his teeth fixed. The dentist's records are irrefutable."

"That means what?"

The lawyer shrugged. "That means that unless the police can prove that the dentist lied or that Danovic had accomplices whom he directed or ordered or conspired with to commit the murder they cannot arrest him. So far, there is no evidence that he knew anything about it. The police would like to continue to question him, of course, but there is no way at the present time that they can hold him. Unless . . . " He paused.

"Unless what?"

"Unless your wife wishes to place a charge of attempted rape against him."

Rudolph groaned. He knew that it would be impossible to get Jean to do anything of the kind. "All my wife wants," he said, "is to go home."

The lawyer nodded. "I quite understand that. And of course, there are no witnesses."

"The only witness was my brother," Rudolph said, "and he's dead."

"In that case, I think the best thing your wife could do would be to leave for home as soon as possible. I can imagine the ordeal . . ."

No, you can't, old man, Rudolph thought, not for a minute. He was thinking of himself more than of his wife.

"In any case, rape cases are most difficult to sustain," the old man said. "Especially in France."

"They're not so easy in America, either," Rudolph said.

"It's a crime in which the law finds itself in an uncomfortable position," the lawyer said. He smiled, aged and used to injustice.

"She'll be on the plane tomorrow," Rudolph said.

"Now—" The lawyer smoothed the shining surface of his desk with a loving gesture, his white hand reflecting palely off the wood, one problem neatly disposed of. "About your nephew." He looked obliquely, pale eyes in yellowing pouches of wrinkled skin, at Rudolph. "He is not a communicative boy. At least to me. Or to the police, either, for that matter. Under questioning, he refuses to divulge his motive for attacking the man in the bar. Perhaps he has said something to you?" Again the oblique, old, shrewd glance.

"Not to me," Rudolph said. "I have some notions, but . . . " He shrugged. "Of course they wouldn't mean anything in a court of law."

"So—there is no defense. No extenuating circumstances. Physical attacks are regarded seriously under French law." The lawyer breathed heavily. A touch of asthma, Rudolph thought, or a sign of approval, an unspoken pride in the civilized nature of France where hitting a man with a beer bottle was considered a matter of utmost gravity, as compared with the frontier attitude of America, where everybody struck everybody else with unpunishable lightness of heart. "Luckily," the lawyer went on, regaining his breath, "the Englishman is well out of danger. He will be discharged in a few days from the hospital. He, himself, has had several brushes with the local police regulations and is not disposed to bring charges. Also, the *juge d'instruction* has taken into consideration the age of the boy and the loss he has recently suffered and in a spirit of mercy has merely indicated that the boy will be taken to the nearest border or to the airport in the next eight days. Forgive me—that is one week in French." He smiled again, doting on his native language. "Don't ask me why." He smoothed the desk again, making a small, papery noise. "If the boy wishes to come back to France, to continue his education, perhaps—" With a little genteel snuffle into a handkerchief, the old man implied, with perfect politeness, that education was a rare commodity in America. "I am sure that after a year or so, when it has all been forgotten, I could arrange for him to be allowed back."

"I'm glad to hear that," Rudolph said. "From what his father and Mr. Dwyer have told me, he likes it here and has done very well in school."

"He should continue in the *lycée,* at least until he gets his *baccalauréat.* If he ever wants to get anyplace in the world that, I would say, in our day and age, is the minimum requirement."

"I'll think about it. And, of course, talk it over with the boy."

"Good," the old man said. "I trust, my dear friend, that you consider that I have served you well and faithfully and, if I may say so, have used what small influence I have in this—this"— for once he hesitated over the English word —"in this *pays—* this section of the coast—to good effect."

"I thank you very much, *Maître,*" Rudolph said. At least he had learned how to address a lawyer in France. "How will it all be arranged?" he asked. "I mean—taken to the nearest border?" He frowned. "I mean, nobody I've ever known has been taken to the nearest border before."

"Oh, that," the old man said airily. It was an old, commonplace story for him. "If you will be at the Nice airport with a ticket for the boy one week from today, he will arrive accompanied by a detective who will make certain that he boards a plane for some other country. The United States, if you wish. Since the man will not be in uniform, it will arouse no curiosity: he will seem like an uncle, a friend of the family, wishing the boy *bon voyage.*"

"Has the boy been told?" Rudolph asked.

"I informed him myself this morning," the lawyer said.

"What did he say?"

"As usual, nothing."

"Did he seem happy, sad?" Rudolph persisted.

"He seemed neither happy nor sad."

"I see."

"I took the liberty of looking at the schedules of the American airlines that serve Nice. The most convenient would be the plane that will leave at eleven-thirty in the morning."

"I'll be there," Rudolph said. He reached out for Jean's passport and put it in his pocket.

"I must compliment you, *Monsieur* Jordache," the old man said, "on the calm, the gentlemanly equilibrium with which you have endured this painful episode."

"Thank you." The moment I leave this beautiful office, Rudolph thought, I will not be calm or demonstrate equilibrium of any kind, gentlemanly or otherwise. As he started to get up, he felt dizzy, almost as if he were going to faint, and had to steady himself by putting a hand against the desk. The old man looked at him quizzically. "A bit too much lunch?" he asked.

"No lunch at all." He had skipped lunch for seven days.

"It is important to guard one's health," the old man said, "especially when one is in a foreign country."

"Would you like my address in the United States," Rudolph asked, "so that you can mail me your bill?"

"That will not be necessary, *monsieur,*" the old man said smoothly. "My clerk has it prepared for you in the outer office. You do not have to bother with francs. A check in dollars will do, if you will be kind enough to send it to the bank in Geneva whose address you will find on the bill."

Impressive, able, surrounded by gleaming eighteenth-century furniture, with a view of the blue sea and an untaxed account in Switzerland, the old man stood up, slowly, careful of his advanced years, and shook Rudolph's hand, then accompanied him to the door, saying, "*Enfin,* I must extend my sympathies to you and your family and I hope that what has happened will not prevent you from visiting this lovely part of the world in the future."

First things first, he thought as he walked away from the lawyer's house along the ramparts toward the port, past the Musée Grimaldi, with all the Picassos in it. The bad news to begin with. That meant Dwyer and Kate. He would have to tell them of his conversation with Heath yesterday. Together, preferably, so that there would be no misunderstanding, no suspicion of secret dealing. After that, the good news for Jean and Gretchen, that they were free now to go back home. He relished the thought of neither meeting. Then there would have to be the jail again, some decision made about where and how and with whom Wesley would stay in America. Maybe that would be the worst conversation of all. He hoped the boy had shaved by now. And taken a shower.

He stopped and looked out to sea, across the Baie des Anges toward Nice. The Bay of Angels. The French didn't care what they named things. Antibes, for example. Antipolis, the Greek settlers had called it—Opposite the City. What city? Athens, a thousand miles away by oared galley? Homesick Greeks? He himself was homesick for no place. Lucky Greeks. What were the laws then, what had those exemplary politicians judged a fair punishment for a boy who had hit someone in a tavern with a beer bottle? What civic spirit or lust for fame or profit had driven the lawmakers among the statutes and the measured rhetoric to leave their academies and festivals to seek election, take on the burden of ruling that intelligent and warlike race? He himself had made speeches on the hustings, had cajoled, promised, heard the cheers of crowds, won and accepted office. Why? He couldn't remember now.

There was a bustle of traffic around him, even on the narrow stone road along the top of the ramparts. Antibes had once been a sleepy, forgotten town, but it was crowded now by the beneficiaries or the victims of the twentieth century, leaving winter behind them in the rush to the climate of the south, to work and live there, not only to play. Flowers and light industry. He himself was a northern man but he could use a few years of the south himself. If what had happened here had not happened, he might have settled cosily here, anonymous, unknown, retired gratefully, as some men did, in his thirties. He had the rudiments of French—think of Jeanne—he could have worked at it, learned to read Victor Hugo, Gide, Cocteau, whatever new men were worth reading, visited Paris for the theater. Dreams. Impossible now.

He breathed deeply of the salt balmy air off the sea. Almost every place was open for him, but not this particular, haunted, beautiful place.

He started walking again, down from the ramparts toward the port. He would get Dwyer to find Kate and they could have their discussion in a café, because Kate had said she never wanted to see the *Clothilde* again. She might have changed her mind by now, with the first shock over, she was not a sentimental woman, but he was not the one who was going to force her.

Just at the entrance to the port there was a small seamen's café. At a tiny table in front of it Dwyer was sitting with a woman, her back to Rudolph. When he called out to Dwyer the woman turned and he saw that it was Kate. She was thinner now, or was it the black dress she wore that made her look so? The nut brown of her complexion had faded and her hair was careless around her face. He felt a twinge of anger or something akin to anger. Knowing everything that he was trying to do for her, she had not even bothered to call to tell him where she was staying, and here she was sitting with Dwyer, the two of them looking like an old married couple, sharing secrets in the sunshine. She stood up to say hello to him and he was embarrassed.

"May I join you for a moment?" he asked. There were moments and moments.

Without a word, Dwyer drew up a chair from the next table. He was dressed as usual, tanned, muscular, his bantamweight arms ridged below the short sleeves of the white jersey with the printing on it. What mourning he carried was not on public display. "What will you have to drink?" Dwyer asked.

"What are you two drinking?"

"Pastis."

"Not for me, thanks," Rudolph said. He didn't like its sweet, licorice taste. It reminded him of the long, black, pliant sticks of candy, like miniature snakes, that his father had bought for him when he was a boy. He was in no mood to be reminded of his father. "If I could have a brandy?"

Dwyer went into the café to fetch the brandy. Rudolph looked across the table at Kate. She was sitting there stolidly, no emotion showing on her face. She could be a Mexican peasant woman, Rudolph thought, all work done for the moment, sitting in front of an adobe wall in the sunlight, waiting for her husband to come home from the fields. She lowered her eyes, refusing to look at him, a baked mud wall around her primitive thoughts. He sensed hostility. Had the parting kiss when she left the *Clothilde* been a sardonic salute? Or had it been real, meant then and later regretted?

"How is Wesley?" she said, her eyes still averted. "Bunny told me all about it."

"He's all right. They're letting him leave France a week from today. Most probably for the States."

She nodded. "I thought they might," she said. Her voice was low and flat. "It's better that way. He shouldn't hang around this part of the world."

"That was a foolish thing he did," Rudolph said, "getting into a fight like that. I don't know what could've come over him."

"Maybe," Kate said, "he was saying good-bye to his father."

Rudolph was silent for a moment, ashamed of what he had said. He felt the way he had the day he had left the consulate for the first time, weeping in the streets. He wondered if his cheeks were wet with tears now. "You know him better than I do," he said. He had to change the subject. "And how are you, Kate?" he said, trying to sound tender.

She made a curious, deprecating, blowing sound. "As well as might be expected," she said. "Bunny's been company."

Maybe they ought to get married, Rudolph thought. Two of a breed. From the same graduating class, from the same hard school. Keep each other company, as she put it. "I had hoped you would call," he said, lying.

She raised her eyes, looking at him. "I knew where I could find you," she said levelly, "if I had piss-all to say to you."

Bunny came back with the brandy and two fresh glasses of pastis. Rudolph watched as they poured the water into the glasses and the pastis turned milky yellow. Rudolph raised his glass mechanically. "To . . ." He stopped, laughed uncertainly. "To nothing, I guess."

Dwyer raised his glass, but Kate just slowly twirled her glass on the table.

The brandy was raw and Rudolph gasped a little as it struck his throat. "There have been certain developments that I think you ought to know about . . ." I must stop sounding as though I'm addressing a board meeting, he thought. "I'm glad I found you both together . . ." Then, as clearly as he knew how, he explained the meaning of what Heath had told him about the estate. They listened politely, but without interest. Don't you care what happenes to your lives? he wanted to shout at them.

"I don't want to be, what's the word . . . ?" Kate said slowly.

"Executrix." Heath had told him that was probably what the judge would do.

"Executrix. I don't know tuppence about executrix," Kate said. "Anyway, I plan to go back to England. Bath. My ma's there and I can go on the National Health for the baby and my ma can watch after it when I go out to work."

"What sort of work?" Rudolph asked.

"I was a waitress in a restaurant," Kate said, "before I listened to the call of the sea." She laughed sardonically. "A waitress can always find work."

There'll be some money left," Rudolph said, "when the estate's settled. You won't have to work."

"What'll I do all day, sit around and look at the telly?" Kate said. "I'm not an idler, you know." Her tone was challenging, the implication clear that he and his women were idlers all. "Whatever money there is, and I don't imagine there'll be much after the lawyers and them others, I'll put aside for the kid's education. Educated, if it's a girl, maybe she won't have to wait on table and iron ladies' dresses in a steaming ship's laundry, like her ma."

There was no arguing with her. "If you ever need anything—money, anything," he said, without hope, "please let me know."

"There won't be any need," she said, lowering her eyes again, still twirling her glass on the table.

"Just in case," Rudolph said. "Maybe, for example, one day you'd like to visit America."

"America's no attraction for me," she said. "They'd laugh at me in America."

"Wouldn't you want to see Wesley again?"

"Wouldn't mind," she said. "If he wants to see me, there're planes every day from America to London."

"In the meantime," Rudolph went on, trying to keep the note of pleading out of his voice, "while the estate's being held up, you'll need some money."

"Not me," she said. "I have my savings. And I made Tom pay me my wages, just like before, even when we were sleeping in the same bed and fixing to marry. Love is one thing, I told him," she said, a proud declaration of categories, "and work is another." She finally lifted her glass and sipped some of the pastis.

"I give up." Rudolph couldn't help sounding exasperated. "You sound as if I'm your enemy."

She stared at him, blank pueblo eyes. "I don't rightly remember saying anything that could be construed like enemy. Did I, Bunny?"

"I wasn't really paying much heed," Dwyer said uneasily, "I couldn't pass judgment."

"How about you?" Rudolph turned to Dwyer. "Don't *you* need money?"

"I've always been a saving type of man," Dwyer said. "Tom used to tease me, saying I was mean and miserly. I'm well set, thank you."

Defeated, Rudolph finished his brandy. "At least," he said, "leave me your addresses. Both of you. So I can keep in touch."

"Leave Wesley's address with the shipyard here," Kate said. "I'll drop them a line from time to time and they'll pass on a card. I'd like to let him know whether he's got a sister or brother when the time comes."

"I'm not sure where Wesley will be," Rudolph said. He was beginning to feel hoarse, his throat rasped by the brandy and the effort of talking to these two evasive, stubborn human beings. "If you write to him care of me, I'll make sure he gets the letter."

Kate stared at him for a long moment, then lifted the glass to her lips again. She drank. "I wouldn't want your wife to be reading any mail of mine," she said, putting down her glass.

"My wife doesn't open my mail," Rudolph said. He couldn't help sounding angry now.

"I'm glad to see she's a woman of some character," Kate said. There was just the hint of a malicious glint in her eye, or was he imagining it?

"I'm only trying to be of help," Rudolph said wearily. "I feel an obligation . . ." He stopped, but it was too late.

"I thank you for your intentions," Kate said, "but you're under no obligation to me."

"I say we just would do better not to talk about it, Mr. . . . . Rudy," Dwyer said.

"All right, let's not talk about it. I'm going to be in Antibes for at least a week. When do you plan to leave for England, Kate?"

Kate smoothed the wrinkles in the lap of her dress with her two hands. "As soon as I get my things together."

Rudolph remembered the single, scuffed, imitation-leather suitcase Wesley had carried off the *Clothilde* for her. It probably couldn't take her more than fifteen minutes to get her things together. "How long do you think that will take?" Rudolph asked patiently.

"Hard to tell," Kate said. "A week. A fortnight. I have some good-byes to make."

"I'll have to have your address here, at least," Rudolph said. "Something may come up, may have to be signed in front of a notary . . ."

"Bunny knows where I am," she said.

"Kate," Rudolph said slowly, "I want to be your friend."

She nodded slowly. "Give it a little time, mate," she said harshly. The kiss of parting in the saloon of the *Clothilde* had been one of numbness. A week's reflection had embittered her. Rudolph couldn't blame her. He turned to Dwyer. "How about you," he asked, "How long do you expect to stay?"

"You'll know that better than I do, Rudy," Dwyer said. "I mean to stay until they throw me off. They'll be arriving any day now with the new shaft and the new screw and that'll mean hauling her up on dock for at least three days, that is if the insurance comes in. . . . You *could* do me a favor—get after the insurance. They're slow as shit if you don't get after them. And you'd know how to talk to them better than me. So if . . ."

"Goddamn the insurance," Rudolph said, letting go. "You handle the insurance yourself."

"No need to yell at poor old Bunny," Kate said placidly. "He's just trying to keep the ship in shape so that when you sell it you won't have a rotten hulk on your hands."

"I'm sorry," Rudolph said. "I've been going through a lot . . ."

"To be sure, you have," Kate said. If it was ironic, there was no telling it from her tone.

Rudolph stood up. "I have to go back to the hotel now. What do I owe here?"

"The drinks're on me," Dwyer said. "My pleasure."

"I'll keep you posted about what's going on," Rudolph said.

"That's kind of you," said Dwyer. "I'd like to see Wesley before he leaves for America."

"You'll have to see him at the airport," Rudolph said. "He's going right there from the jail. With a policeman."

"French cops," Dwyer said. "It don't pay to let them get their hands on you, does it? Tell Wesley I'll be at the airport."

"Take care of yourselves," Rudolph said. "Both of you."

They didn't answer, but sat there in silence with their glasses in front of them, in shadow now, because the sun was going down and the building across the street was blocking it out. Rudolph made a little gesture and walked back toward the Agence de Voyages near the square where he could buy the three plane tickets for tomorrow's flight.

Husband and wife, he thought bitterly, as he passed the antique shops and the cheese shops and the shops that sold newspapers, they'd make a good pair. What's wrong with me? What makes me so goddamn sure I can take care of anybody? Everybody? I'm like those idiotic dogs at the greyhound races. Show me a responsibility, mine, not mine, anybody's, and I'm off after it, like the dogs after the mechanical rabbit, even if they never catch it, *know* they never can catch it. What disease infected me when I was young? Vanity? Fear of not being liked? A substitute for denied religion? It's a lucky thing I never had to fight a war—I'd be dead the first day, shot by my own men, stopping a retreat or volunteering to go for the ammunition for a lost and surrounded gun. My project for the next year, he told himself, is to learn how to say, Fuck you, to one and all.

CHAPTER 6

1968

From Billy Abbott's notebook—

Monika disturbed me tonight. She was working on the printed proofs of a speech she had translated from the French into English, when she looked up and said, I've just noticed something. In both languages—and in most others, too—the verbs—to have, to be, to go, and to die—are all irregular. In English—I have, he has, I had—not too much of a variation, but there all the same. More striking in French. J' ai, tu as, il a, nous avons. To be wanders much more. I am, you are, he is, we were, you are being, they had been, I shall, he will. In French, je suis, tu es, nous sommes, vous etes, il sera. Then sois et soyons and je fus and il fut in other tenses. Think of I go, I went, I have been gone. And aller—je vais, nous allons, ils vont. Dying is a bit more in a straight line, but it gives you pause. I die. I am dead. In French, mourir in the infinitive, but je meurs, nous mourions, nous sommes morts. What does that all mean—that actions—existing, owning, moving from place to place, dying? That we seek to disown or disguise or flee from our most basic activities? The verb to kill, however, is straightforward as could be, I kill, you kill, he kills. I killed, you killed. He killed. Nothing to hide there or cope with uneasily. The same with fuck. Is there judgment there?

I am glad I am not a translator, I told her. But it set me thinking and I was up half the night worrying about myself and my connection to language.

GRETCHEN WAS IN the bar when Rudolph got back to the hotel. She was drinking a champagne cocktail and talking to a young man in tennis clothes. She had been doing quite a bit of drinking the last few days, which was not like her, and had been talking to any men who happened to be around, which, he thought, maliciously, was very much like her. Had he heard footsteps softly passing his door last night, past the paired shoes, in the direction of her room? Remembering Nice, he could hardly complain. And whatever diversions she found to amuse herself with in the limbo in which she found herself were at the very least excusable. "May I introduce my brother, Rudolph Jordache," she said as Rudolph came over to the table at which they were sitting. "Basil—I forget your second name, dear."

She must have had at least three champagne cocktails, Rudolph thought, to say dear to a man whose name she'd forgotten.

The young man stood up. He was tall and slender, actorish, dyed hair, frivolously good-looking, Rudolph decided.

"Berling," the young man said, bowing a little. "Your sister's been telling me about you."

Berling, Basil Berling, Rudolph thought, as he nodded acknowledgment of the bow. Who has a name like Basil Berling? British, from his accent.

"Won't you sit down and join us?" Basil Berling said.

"Just for a moment," Rudolph said, without grace. "I have some things I have to discuss with my sister."

"My brother is a great discusser," Gretchen said. "Beware his discussions."

Four cocktails, not three, Rudolph thought.

"What will it be, sir?" Basil Berling asked, polite British member of Actors Equity, working hard on his speech, conscious that he came from a mediocre school, as the waiter came up.

"The same," Rudolph said.

"Three of the same," Basil Berling said to the waiter.

"He's been plying me with drinks," Gretchen said.

"So I see."

Gretchen made a face. "Rudolph is the sober one in the family," she explained to Basil Berling.

"Somebody has to be."

"Oh, dear, I fear the discussion to follow," Gretchen said. "Basil—what is the name again, dear . . .?"

She's pretending to be further gone than she really is, Rudolph thought. To annoy me. Today I'm everybody's target.

"Berling," the man said, always pleasant.

"Mr. Berling is an actor," Gretchen said. "Isn't it a coincidence," she asked, her tone girlish and drunk at the same time, "here we are at the very end of the world and we meet by sheerest jolly happenstance in a low bar and we're both in the flicks?" She was mocking him now with a fake English accent, but the young man seemed beyond offense.

"Are you?" The Englishman sounded surprised. "I mean in films? I say—I should have guessed."

"Isn't that gallant?" Gretchen touched Rudolph's arm flirtatiously, brother or no. "I have to admit the fearful truth. I'm in the unglamorous part." She sipped at her new drink, smiling over the rim at Basil Berling.

"Hard to believe," Berling said heavily.

Must get rid of him forthwith, Rudolph thought, before I ask the manager to throw him out.

"Oh, yes," Gretchen said. "Behind the scenes. I'm one of those ladies with the black fingernails. Up to my ass in acetate. Film editor. There, now, the secret's out. Just a plain, humble cutter."

"You do honor to the profession," Basil Berling said.

God save me from the mating rites of others, Rudolph thought, as Gretchen said, "Sweet," and patted the back of Berling's hand. For a moment Rudolph was curious about how his sister *really* was in bed, how many men were in her past, her present. She'd tell him if he asked.

"Gretchen," Rudolph said, as Gretchen tilted her head with too much charm at the actor, "I have to go up and tell Jean she has to pack. I have her passport and she'll want to be leaving tomorrow. I'd like a word with you first, please."

Gretchen made a pretty grimace. Rudolph would have liked to slap her. The day's events had worn his nerves thin. "Drink up, dear," Gretchen said to Berling. "My brother is a busy man, the conscientious bee going from flower to flower."

"Of course." The actor stood up. "I better get out of these clothes, anyway. I played three sets of singles and I'll come down with a monstrous cold if I sit around wet much longer."

"Thanks for the wine," Gretchen said.

"My pleasure."

Dwyer had said, "My pleasure," too, Rudolph remembered. Everybody was enjoying himself this afternoon, he thought sourly. Except him.

"Will I see you later, Gretchen? For dinner?" Berling said, tall, but with skinny, stringy legs, Rudolph noticed. I'd look better in tennis shorts, he thought meanly.

"I daresay," Gretchen said.

"A pleasure to have met you, sir," Berling said to Rudolph.

Rudolph grunted. If the man was going to call him sir, as though he were on the edge of the grave, he'd be crusty, as befitted his age.

Brother and sister watched the actor stride out, springy and virile, treading the boards.

"God, Gretchen," Rudolph said, when the actor had gone, "you certainly know how to pick them, don't you?"

"There's very little choice at this season," Gretchen said. "A girl has to take what comes along. Now, what unpleasant thing are you in such a hurry to tell me?" She wasn't drunk at all, he saw.

"It's about Enid," he said. "I'd like you to get on the plane with Jean and Enid tomorrow and keep an eye on her. On both of them."

"Oh, God," Gretchen said.

"I don't trust my daughter with Jean," Rudolph went on doggedly.

"What about you? Aren't you coming along?"

"I can't. There's too much still to attend to here. And when you get to New York I want you to stay with them in my apartment. Mrs. Johnson's off on a holiday in St. Louis for another week."

"Come on now, Rudy," Gretchen said. "I'm too old to take up baby-sitting."

"Damn it, Gretchen," Rudolph said, "after all I've done for you . . ."

Gretchen put her head back and closed her eyes as though by that physical act she was holding back an angry reply. Still in the same position, and with her eyes still closed, she said, "I don't have to be reminded every day of what you've done for me."

"Every day?" Rudolph bit off the words. "When was the last time?"

"Not in so many words, my dear brother." She opened her eyes and leaned forward again. "Let's not argue about it." She stood up. "You've got yourself a baby-sitter. Anyway, it will be nice to be back again in a place where murders happen in the newspapers, not in the bosom of your own family. What time does the plane leave?"

"Eleven-thirty. I have your ticket."

"Think of everything, don't you?"

"Yes. Everything."

"I wouldn't know what to do without you, Brother," Gretchen said. "I'd better start packing myself." She smiled at him, but he noticed the effort. "Truce?"

"Truce," he said.

On the way to the elevator he stopped at the desk to get his key. "While you were out, Mr. Jordache," the concierge said, "a lady came by and left a letter for you." He took an envelope out of the box and gave it to Rudolph with his key. The envelope had only his name on it, in a woman's handwriting that he felt he had seen someplace before. In the elevator he tore open the envelope and picked the single piece of paper out of it.

It was from Jeanne.

Dear American,

This is just to tell you to please not call me. You can guess the reason why. I'll call you when I can. It may not be for a week or two. It may be that they have called off the war in Paris permanently. I hope you are having a good time in Antibes and are prolonging your stay. The afternoons are dreary without you. If you wish to write me, do it through Poste Restante, Central Post Office, Nice. I hope I have spelled everything correctly.

Drive carefully,
Jeanne

He crumpled the letter and put it in his pocket, got out of the elevator, went over to the door of the suite, arranged his face, put the key in the lock and went in.

Jean was standing at the window, staring out to sea. She didn't turn around when he came in. Against the fading light which came through the open window, her silhouette was slender and young in a linen summer dress. She reminded him of the girls he had gone to college with, girls who wore their boyfriends' fraternity pins on their bosoms and went to the Saturday-afternoon football games in bulky fur coats and bright woolen stockings and to the proms at which he had played the trumpet in the band, to help pay his way through school. Standing at the door, looking at the illusion of vulnerable youthfulness which his wife created, he felt a pang of pity for her, unsought, unprofitable.

"Good evening, Jean," he said, advancing toward her. Jean, Jeanne, he thought. What's in a name?

She turned slowly. He saw that she had had her soft, shoulder-length hair done that day and that she had put on makeup. The old woman she would one day be had gone from her face.

"Good evening," she said gravely. Her voice, too, had returned to normal, if normal for her meant not rasping with drink or fury or self-laceration.

"Here's your passport," he said, giving it to her. "The lawyer got it back today."

"Thank you," she said.

"I have your ticket for the plane tomorrow. You can go back home now."

"Thank you," she said again. "And you?"

"I'll have to stay at least a week more."

She nodded, opened her passport, glanced at her photograph, shook her head sadly, threw the passport on the table.

My passport photo doesn't flatter me either, Rudolph would have liked to say.

"At least a week . . ." Jean said. "You must be exhausted."

"I'm all right." He sank into an easy chair. Until she had said he must be exhausted he hadn't realized how tired he really was. He had been sleeping badly, waking often in the middle of the night, with uneasy dreams. Last night he had had the most curious, disturbing dream. He had awakened with a start. The bed had seemed to be shaking and the first thought he had was that there was an earthquake. In his dream, he had remembered, he seemed to have been pinched all over his legs by invisible, mischievous fingers. Poltergeists, he remembered thinking in his dream. Awake, he had thought, Now where did that word come from? He had read it, of course, but he had never spoken it or written it.

"How is Enid?" he asked.

"Fine," Jean said. "I took her to Juan-les-Pins this afternoon and bought her a miniature striped sailor's jersey. She looks charming in it and she's been posing in front of the mirror in it ever since. She's having her supper now with the nurse."

"I'll look in and say good night to her," he said. "In a while." He loosened his collar and tie. Unyoked for the day, he would put on an open-necked sports shirt for dinner. "Gretchen will be on the plane with you and Enid," he said.

"She needn't bother," Jean said, but with no hint of resentment. "Perhaps she'd like to stay on. The weather's glorious now and I saw her walking up from the sea with a handsome young man."

"She's anxious to get back to New York," he said. "I've asked her to stay with you and Enid until Mrs. Johnson gets back from St. Louis."

"That will be dull for her," Jean said. "I can take care of Enid myself. I have nothing else to do." But again calmly, without resentment or the tone of argument.

"I think it would be better if Gretchen was there to help out," he said carefully.

"Whatever you say. Although I can stay sober for a week, you know."

"I know," he said. "Just to be on the safe side."

"I've been thinking, Rudy," Jean said, standing with her hands clasped in front of her, her fingers interlaced, as though she were on a platform giving a prepared speech. "About what we've been through."

"Why don't you forget what we've been through?" Rudolph said. He was in no mood for prepared speeches.

"I've been thinking about us," she said evenly, without hostility. "For your sake and for Enid's, I think we ought to get a divorce."

Finally, he thought. At least I wasn't the one to say the word. "Why don't we wait awhile to talk about things like that?" he said gently.

"If you want. But I'm no good for you. Or for her. You don't want me any-more. . . ." Jean put up her hand, although he hadn't begun to say anything. "You haven't come near me in over a year. And you've found somebody down here, I'm sure. Please don't deny it."

"I won't deny it," he said.

"I don't blame you, dear," she said. "I've been poison for you for a long time. Another man would have left me long ago. And the crowd would have cheered." She smiled crookedly.

"I wish you'd wait until we were both home in America . . ." he started to say, although he felt that a great weight was being lifted from his shoulders.

"I feel like talking this evening," she said, without insistence. "I've been thinking about us all day and I haven't had a drink in more than a week and I'm as sane and sensible as I'm ever going to be for the rest of my life. Don't you want to hear what I've been thinking about?"

"I don't want you to say anything that you're going to regret later."

"Regret." She made a little awkward movement, as though she were jerking away from a wasp. "I regret everything I say. And just about everything I've done. Listen carefully, my dear. I am a drunk. I am disappointed with myself and I am a drunk. I will be disappointed with myself and remain a drunk all my life. And I won't get over it."

"We haven't tried hard enough up to now," he said. "The places you've gone to weren't thorough enough. There are other clinics that . . ."

"You can send me to every clinic in America," she said. "Every psychiatrist in America can poke among my dreams. They can give me antabuse and I can vomit my guts out. And I will still be a drunk. And I will scream at you like a shrew and disgrace you. . . . Remember, I did it before and not only once . . . and I can ask forgiveness and I can do it again and I can risk my child's life driving her around drunkenly in a car and I can forget everything and go looking for a bottle over and over again until the day I die and I wish it was going to be soon only I don't have the courage to kill myself, which is another disappointment. . . ."

"Please don't talk like that, Jean," he said. He stood up and went toward her, but she pulled away, as though she feared his touch.

"I'm sober now," she said, "and I've dried out for more than a week and let's take advantage of this lovely, unexpected moment and look things in the face and make sober, world-shaking decisions. I will retire to myself somewhere, out of sight—is Mexico far enough away? Spain? I speak Spanish, did you know that? Switzerland? The clinics are excellent there, I am told, and for two or three months at a time you can expect great results."

"Okay," he said, "let's live two or three months at a time then. Divorce or no divorce."

"There's no use pretending I can hold down a job anymore." Nothing could stop the chanting, obsessed voice. "But thanks to my dear, dead father I can live more than comfortably—extravagantly. You must help me draw up a trust fund for Enid because when I'm drunk there's a chance I'll meet some scheming, dazzling young Italian who will conspire to rob me of my fortune and I wouldn't like that. I've even figured out a way of making you not feel guilty for neglecting me and letting me wander unprotected around this dark and dangerous world. I'll hire a nice, strong young woman, probably a lesbian, who will keep me company and make sure I come to no harm when I am steeped in drink . . . and if necessary will supply me with innocent and undangerous sex. . . ."

"You must stop," he cried. "Enough, enough."

"Don't sound so shocked, my dear Puritan Rudolph," she said. "I've done it before and haven't disliked it and I'm sure I can do it again, especially after a bottle or two, and not dislike it again. The truth is, darling, I can't struggle anymore. Even the Confederate Army finally surrendered. I've had enough dead. I'm out of room to maneuver. I have come to Appomattox. You see, my education has not been wasted on me. You can return my sword, General Grant. No, that sounds mocking. I don't mean to mock. I'm in despair. I can't fight anymore. I can't fight you or the drink or guilt or marriage, whatever *that* word means to you and me at this time. Occasionally, when I'm in a calm period, I'll appear, with my Lesbian companion, I'll make sure she's not too obvious, I'll have her dressed girlishly, as will I, and visit Enid. You need not be present. Don't say anything tonight, please, but remember what I've offered in the morning when you put me on the plane, and admire me for my renunciation. Take it before I change my mind and hang for the rest of my life around your neck like a corpse."

"Look," he said, "when you get away from here, away from this morbid atmosphere, you'll . . ."

"Between us, we've made shit out of your life, too," she intoned. "And you're not getting any younger, you can't just sit in a corner staring at the fire for another fifty years, you've got to do *something*. Be thankful for today. Grab the offer. Who knows how long the merchandise is going to be on the market? And now, I know you've had a long hard day, and want to shave and take a nice hot shower and put on fresh clothes and have a martini and go to dinner. While you're in the shower, I'll order you the drink. Never fear, I won't touch a drop between now and New York—I have spurts of superhuman willpower. And then, if you'll be so kind, you'll take me to dinner, just you and I alone—and we'll talk of other things—like the rest of your life and what schools Enid should go to and what kind of woman you might finally consider marrying and whom you've been screwing on the Côte d'Azur and then when it's late and we're both tired, we'll come back here to our lovely, insanely expensive hotel suite and you'll let me sleep in your bed with you because tomorrow I'm taking a plane to America and you're staying on for the rest of the summer weather to tie up all the loose ends that I have loosened."

He stood up and went over and put his arms around her. She was trembling violently. Her face was flushed and she felt feverishly hot to his touch.

"I'm sorry," she whispered, trembling in his arms, her head against his chest, her arms gripping him. "I suppose I should have made this speech long ago—before we were married, maybe, except I don't think I was like this before I was married."

"Sssh, sssh," he said, helplessly. "When you get home things will look different."

"When I get home," she said, "the only difference will be that I'll be one day older." She pulled away, smiled wanly at him. "It's hard to think of that as any great improvement. Now go take your shower. I'll be less eloquent when you come out and there'll be a martini here for you to remind you that all is not lost. I'll join you for the cocktail hour. With another Coca-Cola."

In the shower he allowed himself to weep. Somewhere along the years there must have been a moment when she could have been saved. He had been too busy, too preoccupied, to recognize the moment, make the necessary gesture toward her, before all avenues of escape finally closed to her.

He couldn't seem to regulate the temperature of the water. It seemed to come out too hot and burn his skin like a thousand needles or when he turned the knob it spurted out icy cold, freezing him, making him shiver, as though he were standing naked in a sleet storm.

He got out, dried himself with a big rough towel, looking at himself in the long mirror, ashamed of his trim adulterous body, the muscles all neat, strong, useless in the life he lived, his sex an impediment to charity. *Chair,* he thought. Flesh, in French. Close enough at least in spelling, to charity. Save that, he thought bitterly, for the afternoons in Nice.

He dressed slowly, the expensive, well-fitting clothing agreeable against his skin. The body's small, restorative pleasures. He put on a light wool shirt, soft cashmere socks, pressed flannel trousers, snug polished moccasins (the Communists in the corridors at night), a crisp seersucker jacket. Gretchen would not say tonight that he looked as though he had just been laid.

The martini was on the table near the couch when he went back into the salon, and Jean was standing in front of the window staring out at the fragrant darkness pierced by bright points of color as the lights of the coast that swept away west from the peninsula of Antibes went on. Jean had lit a single lamp and had a glass of Coca-Cola in her hand. She turned when she heard him come in. "Gretchen called while you were in the shower," she said. "I told her we were having dinner alone. Is that all right with you?"

"Of course."

"She's having dinner in Golfe Juan with a friend, anyway, she said."

"I met him," Rudolph said.

"I often wonder how she gets along with men. She doesn't confide in me."

"She confides in me too much," Rudolph said.

"As does all the world," Jean said lightly. "Poor Rudolph."

She wandered aimlessly around the room, touching the back of a chair absently, opening a drawer in the desk. "Tell me, Rudy—I don't quite remember," she said. "Is this the room we had when we came here just after we were married?"

"I don't remember, either," he said, and picked up the martini.

"Well," she said, lifting her glass, "here's to . . . to what?" She smiled. She looked beautiful and young in the shadowed room. "To divorce, say?" She sipped at her Coca-Cola.

Rudolph put his glass down. "I'll have my drink later," he said. "I want to go in and say good night to Enid."

"Go ahead," Jean said. "I believe you ought to give the French girl a nice little bonus. She's been very good with Enid. Very gentle and patient. She's almost a child herself, but somehow she always seems to have been able to invent games to amuse Enid. It's a talent I don't have."

"Nor do I," Rudolph said. "Don't you want to come with me?"

"Not tonight," Jean said. "Anyway, I have to make some repairs on my face."

"I won't be long."

"No hurry," she said. "We have the whole night ahead of us."

Enid was just finishing her supper, dressed in the striped seaman's jersey. She was laughing when Rudolph came into the room. Somehow, although the nurse couldn't speak English, the two of them seemed to understand each other perfectly. Education, Rudolph thought, with a pang, will wipe out that particular shared gift. He kissed the top of Enid's head, said, *"Bon soir"* to the girl. The girl said in French, "I'm sorry about the shirt. She has had her bath all right, but she wouldn't put on pajamas; she insists she wants to sleep tonight in the shirt. I hope you don't mind? I didn't think it was worth a struggle. . . ."

"Of course not." Sensible, flexible Frenchwoman. "She'll sleep all the better for it." Then he told her to please have the child's things packed in the morning, as they were leaving for New York. By the time I'm through here, he thought, I'll be able to speak enough French even to talk to a Corsican policeman. One for the plus side.

The girl said, *"Bien, monsieur."*

Rudolph took a long look at his daughter. She looked healthy and happy, with a light bloom on her cheeks from the sun. Well, he though, another plus; at least *someone's* getting some good out of this trip. Seeing her sitting there, contentedly playing with her food, and suddenly reaching out to hold the girl's hand, he thought, when I get back to New York I'm going to fire Mrs. Johnson. Mrs. Johnson was in her fifties, efficient and quiet, but she wasn't one for games.

He kissed the top of Enid's head again and bent down farther as she said, "Good night, Daddy," and planted a wet, oatmeally kiss inaccurately on his cheek. She smelled of soap and talcum powder and if the girl hadn't been there he would have picked her up from the chair on which she was sitting, propped up on pillows, and hugged her, hard.

But he merely said, "Good night, little sailor, sleep well," and went out of the room.

The dinner was excellent, the moon shone over the sea, the restaurant was uncrowded and the waiters buzzed devotedly around their table. Jean insisted that he order a bottle of wine for himself and he allowed himself to be persuaded. They found they had a great deal to say to each other, none of it important or troubling, and there were no uncomfortable lapses in the conversation. We are all made out of rubber, Rudolph thought, admiring Jean's soft hair as she bent slightly over her food; we stretch all out of shape and then, at least to all appearances, snap back again, back to the original form, or almost back to the original form.

They lingered a long time over coffee, looking, he was sure, content with themselves, with each other, in front of the big window that gave on the dark sea, with its silver path of moonlight shimmering away toward the distant islands.

They walked slowly up to the hotel and when they came into the suite, Jean said, "Get into bed, darling. I'll be in in a little while."

Naked, he lay in the bed in the dark room, waiting. The door opened softly; there was a rustling as Jean took off her robe and then she was in bed with him. He put his arm around her, her body not trembling, warm, but without the blaze of fever. They didn't move and in a little while they both were asleep. This night he didn't dream that the hotel was rocking in an earthquake or that he was visited by poltergeists.

Farther down the hall, Gretchen slept uneasily, alone. The dinner had been delicious, the wine had flowed freely, the young man had been almost the handsomest man in the room and had been attentive, then importunate: she had nearly said yes. But finally, she was sleeping alone. Before she dropped off, she thought, If only my goddamn brother hadn't said, "You certainly know how to pick them, don't you?" she wouldn't have been sleeping alone that night.

CHAPTER 7

1968

From Billy Abbott's notebook—

Happened to pick up a copy of the international issue of the week's Time *magazine. Lo and behold, under CRIME there was the saga of the Jordaches, with nude photograph and whole unpleasant history of the family. Failure, murder and disgrace in several hundred well-chosen words.*

I am clipping out the story and putting it with my other notes. It will give my descendants, if there are any, a useful rundown on their family tree.

About the last place you'd expect to find the three children of a Hudson River town, German-immigrant suicide baker would be a yacht on the Riviera. But after the recent Antibes waterfront killing of Thomas Jordache, better known years ago as middleweight **Tommy Jordan,** a number of names from the past bubbled to the surface of a French police murder dossier. Among them: **Rudolph**

Jordache, 40, Tom's brother, millionaire, ex-mayor of Whitby, N.Y.; Jordan's teenage son, **Wesley; Jean Prescott Jordache,** Rudolph's wife and heiress to the Midwestern Prescott drug empire; and **Gretchen Burke,** sister to both Jordaches and widow of stage and screen director, **Colin Burke.**

Sources in Antibes say that Jordan was bludgeoned to death only days after his wedding and after he'd extricated his tipsy sister-in-law from the clutches of a harbor ruffian in a seedy Cannes nightspot.

Staying in the plush Hôtel du Cap while police continued their investigation, Jean Jordache says she was accosted while having a solitary, quayside nightcap. Jordan, appearing on the scene, savagely beat the man who had accosted her. Later, Jordan was found murdered on his yacht.

French police will only confirm that they have a list of suspects.

Luckily, it doesn't mention me. It would have to be an outside chance for anyone to connect me with Mrs. Burke, once married to eminent director, now dead, earlier to an obscure flack named Abbott. Monika would, of course, because I've talked to her a lot about my mother, but fortunately Monika doesn't read Time. *Information for entertainment, she calls it, not information for the sake of truth.*

I sometimes wonder if I shouldn't try to be a newspaperman. I am inquisitive and mischievous, two important qualities in the trade.

Monika not home. Note on table. Will be gone a few days. She believes in the double standard all right—but in reverse.

I miss her already.

THE LIMOUSINE THAT the concierge had ordered for them was packed. Gretchen, Jean and Enid were already on the back seat, Enid a little tearful because the French girl was being left behind. Rudolph had checked for the third time that he had all their plane tickets, and the chauffeur was holding the front door open for him to get in, when a car drove up to the courtyard in front of the hotel and stopped. A small, plump, plainly dressed woman with graying hair got out of the car and a small plump man in a business suit emerged from behind the wheel.

"Rudolph Jordache, if you please," the woman called, coming toward him.

"Yes?" The woman looked vaguely familiar.

"I suppose you don't remember me," the woman said. She turned to the small plump man. "I told you he wouldn't remember me."

"Yes, you told me," the man said.

"I remember you, though," the woman said to Rudolph. "Very well. I'm Tom's wife, Wesley's mother. I came to get my son." She dug into the big handbag she was carrying and pulled out a copy of *Time* Magazine and waved it at Rudolph.

"Oh, Lord," Rudolph said. He had forgotten about the newspaperman and the telex. But the newspaperman obviously hadn't forgotten about him. Poor Wesley, he thought, his name known for a week in millions of homes, the stares of the curious to be dealt with for years to come, the strangers approaching him wherever he went, saying, "Excuse me, aren't you the one . . . ?"

"May I see what the story's like?" Rudolph reached out for the magazine. The journalist had been down to the boat before Wesley had been jailed, but he might have followed up on the story. He winced, thinking of what *Time* might have done with the account of Wesley's fight in the nightclub and the Englishman in the hospital with a concussion.

Teresa drew back, put the magazine behind her. "You can go out and buy your own magazine," she said. "According to what it says, you can damn well afford it. You and your fancy naked wife."

Oh, God, Rudolph thought, they've dug up that old picture. What a blessing it would be for the entire world if the files in the office of every newspaper on the face of the globe suddenly went up in smoke in a single day.

"It's all in the magazine," Teresa said malevolently. "This time your money didn't bail my great ex-husband out, did it? He finally got what he was looking for, didn't he?"

"I'm sorry, Teresa," Rudolph said. Tom must have been dead drunk or drugged when he married her. The last time Rudolph had seen her, three years ago in Heath's office, when he had paid her off to go to Reno for a divorce, her hair had been dyed platinum blond and she must have been twenty pounds lighter. Looking no better and no worse than she looked now.

"Forgive me for not recognizing you. You've changed a bit."

"I didn't make much of an impression on you, did I?" Now the malevolence was more pronounced. "I'd like you to meet my husband, Mr. Kraler."

"How do you do, Mr. Kraler?"

The man grunted.

"Where's my son?" Teresa said harshly.

"Rudy," Gretchen called from the car, "we don't want to miss the plane." She hadn't heard any of the exchange.

Rudolph began to sweat, although it was a cool morning. "You'll have to excuse me, Mrs. Kraler," he said, "but we have to go to the airport . . . "

"You don't get off that easy, Mr. Jordache," Teresa said, waving the rolled-up magazine at him. "I didn't come all the way here from America to let you fly off just like that."

"I'm not flying off anywhere," Rudolph said, his voice rising, to match the woman's tone. "I have to put my family on the plane and I'm coming back here. I'll see you in two hours."

"I want to know where my son is," Teresa said, grabbing his sleeve and holding on as he started to get into the car.

"He's in jail, if you must know."

"In jail!" Teresa shrieked. She put her hand to her throat in a tragic gesture. Her reaction reassured Rudolph. At least that part of the story hadn't been in the magazine.

"Don't carry on so," Rudolph said sharply. Her shriek had been the loudest noise he had heard at the hotel since he had come there. "It's not that serious."

"Did you hear that, Eddie?" she screamed. "My son is behind bars and he says it's not serious."

"I heard him say it," Mr. Kraler said.

"That's the sort of family it is. Put a child in their hands," as loudly as before, "and before you know it he has a police record. It's a blessing his father got murdered or else I'd never have known where he was and God knows what these people would have made out of him. You know who belongs in jail—" She released Rudolph's sleeve and stepped back a pace to point a shaking, accusatory finger at him, her arm outstretched operatically. "You! With your tricks and your bribes and your crooked money."

"When you calm down," Rudolph said, moving to get into the front seat of the limousine, "I'll explain everything to you." Then to the chauffeur, "*Allons-y.*"

She lunged at him and gripped his arm again. "No, you don't," she said. "You're not getting off that easy, mister."

"Let go of me, you silly woman," Rudolph said. "I haven't time to talk to you now. The plane won't wait, no matter how loudly you scream."

"Eddie," Teresa shrieked at her husband, "are you going to let him get away with this?"

"See here, Mr. Jordache . . . " the man began.

"I don't know you, sir," Rudolph said. "Keep out of this. If you want to talk to me, be here when I get back." Roughly, he shook the woman's hand off his sleeve, and the concierge, who had come out to say good-bye, moved, quietly threatening, toward her.

Rudolph got into the car quickly and slammed and locked the door behind him. The chauffeur hurried around to the wheel and started the engine. Teresa was standing, waving the magazine angrily at the car, as they drove out of the gate.

"What was that all about?" Gretchen asked. "I couldn't hear what she was saying."

"It's not important," Rudolph said shortly. "She's Wesley's mother."

"She certainly has changed," Gretchen said. "Not for the better."

"What does she want?"

"If she's running true to form," he said, "she wants money." He would have to get Gretchen aside and tell her to make sure Jean didn't get hold of a copy of *Time* Magazine.

From the terrace of the airport building Rudolph watched the plane take off. The good-byes had been quiet. He had promised to get back to New York as soon as possible. He had tried not to think of the comparison between today's subdued farewell and the holiday gaiety with which they had arrived at this same airport, with Tom waiting for them with his bride-to-be and the *Clothilde* in port ready to take them all out to the channel between the islands off Cannes for a swim and a reunion lunch.

When the plane was out of sight, Rudolph sighed, went through the building, fighting down the temptation to buy a copy of *Time* Magazine at the newsstand. Whatever the story was like, it certainly could not bring him joy. He wondered how people who were constantly being written about, politicians, cabinet ministers, actors, people like that, could ever bring themselves to open a morning newspaper.

He thought of the plump, graying woman and her round little husband waiting for him back at the hotel, and sighed again. How had that dreadful woman ever managed to find a husband? And a second husband, at that. Perhaps, he thought, if the man from *Time* were still in Antibes, he should ask him to dig up the newspaper photograph of Teresa, with her old fake name, being taken away by the police after the raid on the brothel. One photograph deserved another. Poor Wesley.

Delaying, he asked the chauffeur to drive into Nice, directed him to the street on which Jeanne lived. He didn't know what he would do if by chance he saw her coming out of the house with her children or her martial husband. Nothing, most likely. But she did not appear. The street was like any other street.

"Back to the hotel, please," he said. "Go the long way, along the sea."

When they got to Antibes, they skirted the port. He saw the *Clothilde,* in the distance, with Dwyer, a tiny figure, moving on the deck. He did not ask the chauffeur to stop.

"I know my rights," Teresa was saying. The three of them were sitting on the chairs in a little glade in the park of the hotel, where there was no one to hear their conversation. The couple had been sitting stiffly in two chairs facing each other in the hotel lobby when Rudolph had come in. Their expressions were grim and disapproving, their presence a silent rebuke to the idle, pleasure-seeking guests, dressed for sport, who passed them on their way to tennis or to the swimming pool. They had listened sullenly as Rudolph led them into the park, explaining quickly, keeping his voice calm and neutral, how Wesley had fallen into the hands of the police and about his departure for America.

"We've been to a lawyer in Indianapolis, where we live, Mr. Kraler and myself, and I know my rights as a mother." Teresa's voice grated on his ears like chalk on a blackboard. "Wesley is a minor and with his father dead, the lawyer said I am his legal guardian. Isn't that what the lawyer said, Eddie?"

"That's what the lawyer said," Mr. Kraler said. "Exactly."

"When I get him out of jail," Teresa went on, "I'm going to take him back to a proper home where he can get a decent Christian upbringing."

"Don't you think it would be wiser to leave religion out of this?" Rudolph said.

"After all, the life you've lead . . . "

"You don't have to beat about the bush about the life I've led. Mr. Kraler knows all about it. Don't you, Eddie?"

"All about it." Eddie nodded, little pudgy sacks of flesh under his chin shaking rhythmically.

"I was a whore, and no bones about it," Teresa said, almost with pride. "But I've seen the light. The strayed lamb is dearer in the eyes of the Lord . . . " She hesitated. "You know the rest, I'm sure, even if you and your whole family are lost heathens."

"Actually," Rudolph said, with false innocence, "I don't know the rest."

"It makes no difference," she said quickly. "Mr. Kraler is a Mormon and by his efforts I have been converted and accepted into the fold. For your information, I don't dye my hair any longer, as you may have noticed, if you ever stoop to notice anything about me, and I don't drink alcohol or even coffee or tea."

"That may be most admirable, Teresa," Rudolph said. He had read somewhere that Mormonism was the fastest-growing Christian religion in the modern world, but with Teresa in the fold the believers must feel that they had cast their net too wide. He could imagine the shudder in the Tabernacle in Salt Lake City when the elders of the Church of Jesus Christ of Latter-day Saints had to accept Teresa Jordache into their blessed company. "But I don't really see what that's got to do with Wesley."

"One thing that it's got to do with him is that he'll stop being a jailbird. I know your family, I know the Jordaches, don't think I don't. Fornicators and mockers, all of you."

Teresa's vocabulary, Rudolph noted, had expanded considerably with her conversion. He was not sure it was an improvement. "I don't really think that Wesley's being in jail for a few days because he had a fight in a bar is because I happen to be an atheist," he said. "And for your information," he couldn't help adding, "fornication and mocking are not my principal occupations."

"I'm not accusing anyone," Teresa said, although there was accusation in every syllable she spoke and every gesture she made. "But it can't be denied that he was in your charge, you being his uncle and head of the family when he nearly killed a man. . . . "

"All right, all right," Rudolph said wearily. He wanted her to leave, disappear, with her pudgy, purse-lipped, righteous husband, but the thought of Wesley being at the mercy of the couple back in Indianapolis appalled him. He didn't know what he could do to prevent it, but he had to try to do what he could. "What do you want?" He had explained that Wesley was to be put on a plane to America in six days, but he hadn't told her of his own hardly formed notion of putting Wesley into a good boarding school in America for a year and then sending him back to France to continue his education there, or his own plan (selfish? generously avuncular?) to come back to France himself to keep an eye on the boy.

"What do I want?" Teresa repeated. "I want to make him a decent citizen, not a wild animal in the jungle, like his father."

"You realize, of course," Rudolph said, "that in a little more than two years, he'll be eligible for the draft if he stays in the United States, and may be sent to get killed in Vietnam."

"If that is God's will, that is God's will," Teresa said. "Do you agree with me, Eddie?"

"God's will," Mr. Kraler said. "My son is in the Army and I'm proud of it. The boy has to take his chances, just like everybody else."

"I don't want any favors for any son of mine," Teresa said.

"Don't you think you ought to ask Wesley what he wants to do?"

"He's my son," Teresa said. "I don't have to ask him anything. And I'm here to make sure he's not going to get gypped of his just share in his father's big fat estate." Ah, Rudolph thought, now we come to the heart of the matter. "When that fancy yacht they wrote about in the magazine is sold," Teresa said shrilly, "you can bet your boots that I'm going to be looking over everybody's shoulder to make sure my son isn't left out in the cold. And our lawyer is going to go over every slip of paper with a fine-tooth comb, don't make any mistake about that either, Mr. Jordache."

Rudolph stood up. "In that case," he said, "I don't think there's any need to continue this conversation any longer. Wesley's stepmother, who will probably be appointed as executrix for the estate, will hire a lawyer and the two lawyers can work everything out between them. I have other things to do. Good-bye."

"Wait a minute," Teresa said. "You can't keep running off like that."

"I have to take a nap," Rudolph said, "I've been up since dawn."

"Don't you want to know where we're staying here?" she cried, victory slipping from her grasp, the argument won so easily that she was sure that it was a ruse on her opponent's part. "Our address in America? Mr. Kraler is a higly respected merchant in Indianapolis. He's a bottler. He has three hundred people working for him. Soft drinks. Give him your card, Eddie."

"Never mind, Mr. Kraler," Rudolph said. "I don't want to have your address here or in Indianapolis. Bottle away," he added crazily.

"I want to see my boy in jail," Teresa cried. "I want to see what they've done to my poor son."

"Naturally," Rudolph said. "By all means, do so." Her maternal instincts had been less evident in Heath's office when he had paid her off and she had signed away custody of her son at the sight of a check made out in her name.

"I intend to adopt him legally," Mr. Kraler said. "Mrs. Kraler wants him to forget he was ever called Jordache."

"That will have to be settled between him and his mother," Rudolph said. "Although when I visit him in jail I'll mention the idea to him."

"When're you going to the jail?" Teresa asked. "I don't want you talking to him alone, filling his ear with poison. . . . I'm going with you."

"No, you're not going anyplace with me," Rudolph said. "I always make a point of visiting jails unaccompanied."

"But I don't speak French," she wailed. "I don't even know where the jail is. How will I convince the cops I'm his mother."

"I'm afraid you'll have to figure all that out yourself, Mrs. Kraler," Rudolph said. "Now I don't want to see either of you two people ever again. Tell your lawyer that the law firm he will have to get into contact with is Heath, Burrows and Gordon. The address is in Wall Street. I believe you were there once before, Mrs. Kraler."

"You bastard," Teresa said, un-Mormon-like.

Rudolph smiled. "Have a pleasant afternoon," he said. He nodded and left the two plump, little angry people sitting silently on the bench in the shade of the pine trees. He was trembling with rage and frustration and despair for the poor boy in the jail in Grasse, but for the moment there was nothing he could do about it. It would take a rescue mission of enormous proportions to tear Wesley out of the grasp of his mother, and today he was not up to thinking even about the first step to be taken. Christian or not, when there was the scent of money in the air, Mrs. Teresa Kraler remembered the habits of her ancient profession. He dreaded having to tell Kate what was in store for her.

He packed quickly. The concierge had gotten him a reservation at the Colombe d'Or in Saint-Paul-de-Vence. A hotel in Grasse would have been closer to the jail he visited almost daily. Saint-Paul-de-Vence was closer to Jeanne. He had chosen Saint-Paul-de-Vence. There was no reason for his remaining any longer at the Hôtel du Cap and many reasons for leaving it. He had told the concierge to forward his mail, but under no circumstances to tell anyone where he was staying. He wrote to Jeanne, telling her where he was going to be, and sealed the note in an envelope addressed to her, care of Poste Restante, Nice.

When he went down to the desk, to pay his bill while his bags were being put in his car, he was relieved to see that the Kralers had gone. He was shocked at the size of his bill. You pay a lot for agony, he thought, on the Côte d'Azur. It was one of the best hotels in the world, but he knew he would never come back to it again. And not because of the cost.

He drove first to the port. Dwyer and Kate had to know where to find him. Dwyer was polishing one of the small brass bitts up forward when he came aboard. He stood up when he saw Rudolph and they shook hands.

"How're things?" Rudolph asked.

Dwyer shrugged. "It ain't no holiday," he said. "They ain't delivered the shaft and the propeller yet. They have to come from Italy and the Italians ain't going to send it across the border until they get paid. I been on the phone to the insurance every day, but they're in no hurry. They never are. They keep sending me new forms to fill out," he said aggrievedly. "And they keep asking for Tom's signature. Maybe the Italians don't think anybody dies in France. And I have to keep getting everything translated. There's a waitress in town who's a friend of mine, she got the language, only she don't know fuck-all about boats and she had to keep asking for the names of things like equipment, running lights, fathoms, flotsam, things like that. It's driving me up the wall."

"All right, Bunny," Rudolph said, suppressing a sigh. "Send all the papers to me. I'll have them attended to."

"That'll be a relief," Dwyer said. "Thanks."

"I'm moving to the Colombe d'Or in Saint-Paul-de-Vence," Rudolph said. "You can reach me there."

"I don't blame you, moving out of that hotel. It must have cost you a pile."

"It wasn't cheap."

"You look around you," Dwyer said, "all those big boats, all these expensive hotels, and you wonder where the money comes from. At least *I* do."

"Bunny," Rudolph said, absurdly feeling on the defensive, "when I was young I was poorer than practically anyone you ever knew."

"Yeah, Tom told me. You worked like a dog. I got no beef against people who came up the way you did. I admire it. I would say you're entitled to anything you can get."

"There're a lot of things I can get," Rudolph said, "that I'd gladly give away."

"I know what you mean," Dwyer said.

There was a short, uncomfortable silence between them.

"I had hoped Kate would be here with you," Rudolph said. "Something's come up that she has to know about. How is she?"

Dwyer looked at him consideringly, as though trying to decide whether or not he should tell him anything about Kate. "She's gone," he said. "She left for England this morning."

"You have her address?"

"I do. Yeah," Dwyer said carefully.

"I need it," Rudolph said. As quickly as possible, he told Dwyer about the Kralers' visit, about the legal problems that Kate would have to deal with, or at least would have to be handled in Kate's name.

Dwyer nodded slowly. "Tom told me about that wife of his. A real ball-breaker, isn't she?"

"That's the least of her virtues," Rudolph said. He saw that Dwyer was hesitant about giving him Kate's address. "Bunny," he said, "I want to ask you something. Don't you believe that I'm trying to do the best for Kate? And for Wesley? And for you, too, for that matter?"

"Nobody has to worry about me," Dwyer said. "About Kate—" He made his curious, almost feminine gesture with his hands, as if explaining the situation in words was beyond him. "I know she sounded . . . well . . . snappish the other day. It's not that she's sore at you or anything like that. I'd say, what it is—" Again the little gesture. "It's that she's—" He searched for the word. "She's *bruised*. She's a sensible woman; she'll get over it. Especially now that she's back home in England. You got a pencil and a piece of paper?"

Rudolph took a notebook and pen out of his pocket. Bunny gave him the address and Rudolph wrote it down. "She doesn't have a telephone," Bunny said. "I gather her folks ain't rolling in money."

"I'll write her," Rudolph said, "when anything develops." He looked around him at the scrubbed deck, the polished rails and brasswork. "The ship looks fine," he said.

"There's always something to be done," Dwyer said. "I made a date to have it hauled up in the yard two weeks from today. The goddamn stuff ought to be here from Italy by then."

"Bunny," Rudolph asked, "how much do you think the *Clothilde* is worth? What it would sell for?"

"What it's worth and what it would sell for are two different things," Dwyer said. "If you figure what it cost originally and all the work and improvements Tom and me put into it and the new radar you gave him as a wedding present—that'll have to be installed, too—I'd say it would come to almost a hundred thousand dollars. That's what it's *worth*. But if you have to sell it fast, like you said when you were telling us about settling the estate—and in this month, with the season more than half gone— nobody likes to pay for the upkeep of a boat for a whole winter—if people're going to buy, they're most likely to buy in the late spring—if you have to sell it fast in the off months and people know you *have* to sell, why then, naturally, they'll try to cut your throat and maybe you'd be lucky if you got fifty thousand dollars for it. Anyway, I'm not the one to talk about this. You ought to go around, talk to some of the yacht brokers here and in Cannes, Saint-Tropez, you see what I mean, maybe they have somebody on their books'd be interested for a fair price. . . . "

"Has anybody approached you so far?" Rudolph asked.

Dwyer shook his head. "I really don't think anybody who knows Antibes'd make a bid. After the murder and all. I think you'd do better to change the name and sail her to another harbor. Maybe another country. Italy, Spain, somewhere like that. Maybe even in Piraeus, that's in Greece. . . . People're superstitious about ships."

"Bunny," Rudolph said, "I don't want you to get angry at what I'm going to say, but I have to talk to you about it. Somebody's got to stay with the boat until it's sold. . . . "

"I would think so."

"And he'd have to be paid, wouldn't he?"

"Yeah," Dwyer said uncomfortably.

"What would the usual salary be?"

"That depends," Dwyer said evasively, "how much work you expected him to do, if he was an engineer or not, things like that."

"You, for example. If you were on another ship?"

"Well, if I'd been hired on earlier—I mean people've got their crews fixed by now—I guess about five hundred dollars a month."

"Good," Rudolph said. "You're going to get five hundred dollars a month."

"I didn't ask for it," Dwyer said harshly.

"I know you didn't. But you're going to get it."

"Just remember I didn't ask for it." Dwyer put out his hand and Rudolph shook it. "I just wish," Dwyer said, "there was some way of Tom knowing all you're doing for me, for Kate and the kid, for the *Clothilde*."

Rudolph smiled. "I didn't ask for it," he said, "but I got it."

Dwyer chuckled. "I think there's still some whiskey left on board," he said.

"I wouldn't mind a drink," Rudolph said.

As they went aft, Dwyer said, "Your sister, Mrs. Burke—Gretchen—made me into a whiskey drinker. Did she tell you?"

"No. She kept your romance secret."

He saw that Dwyer didn't smile and said nothing more about Gretchen.

They had the whiskey in the wheelhouse, warm. Dwyer apologized for not having any ice. He didn't want to have the generator that supplied the electricity running, wasting fuel.

"It's a funny thing," Dwyer said, relaxed now, with the glass in his hand. "You and Gretchen and Tom all in the same family." He took a big gulp of his drink. "Fire and ice," he said obscurely.

Rudolph didn't ask him to explain what he meant by that.

As he left, Rudolph said, "If I don't see you before then, I'll see you at the airport when Wesley leaves. You remember the date?"

"I have it written down," Dwyer said. "I'll pack his things for him and bring them along with me." He hesitated, coughed a little. "He's got a whole folder full of photos up forward. You know—pictures of the ship, ports we put into, him and his father, me and Kate. . . . That sort of thing. Should I pack them in?" He lifted his glass and closed his eyes as he drank, as though the matter were of no great importance.

"Pack them in," Rudolph said. Memory hurt, but it was necessary baggage.

"I got a whole bunch of pictures from the wedding. All of us . . . you know— drinking toasts, dancing, stuff like that, all of us. . . . "

"I think it would be a good idea to leave them out," Rudolph said. Too much was too much.

Dwyer nodded. "Kate didn't want them either. And I don't think I have room to keep them. I'll be traveling finally, you know. . . . "

"Send them to me," Rudolph said. "I'll keep them in a safe place. Maybe after a while Wesley would like to see them." He remembered the pictures that Jean had taken that day. He would put the other ones with them.

Dwyer nodded again. "Another drink?"

"No, thanks," Rudolph said. "I haven't eaten lunch yet. Would you like to join me?"

Dwyer shook his head. "Kind of you, Rudy," he said, "but I already ate." Dwyer had a quota, Rudolph saw. One favor accepted a day. No more.

They put their glasses down, Dwyer carefully wiping away with a cloth the damp the glasses left.

He was going forward to finish polishing the bitts as Rudolph left the *Clothilde*.

After he had checked in at the new hotel Rudolph had lunch on the terrace overlooking the valley that looked as though it had been designed from a painting by Renoir. When he had finished lunch, he made a call to the old lawyer in Antibes. He explained that the *Clothilde* was for sale and that he would like the lawyer to act as agent for the estate in the transaction. "If the best offer you can get," he said, "is not at least one hundred thousand dollars, let me know. I'll buy it."

"That's most gentlemanly of you," the lawyer said, his voice thin over the faulty telephone wires.

"It's a simple business matter."

"I see," the lawyer said. They both knew he was lying. No matter.

After that Rudolph called Johnny Heath in New York and talked at length. "Oh, what a mess," Heath said. "I'll do my best. I await the letter from Mr. and Mrs. Kraler's lawyer with impatience."

Then Rudolph put on his swimming trunks and did forty laps in the pool, his mind empty in the swish of water, his body used and healthily tired by the time he had finished.

After the swim he sat drying off by the side of the pool, sipping at a cold beer.

He felt guilty for feeling so well. He wondered, displeased with himself for the thought, how he would act if the telephone rang and the call was for him and a voice announced that the plane with his family aboard had gone down into the sea.

Fire and ice, Dwyer had said.

CHAPTER 8

1968

From Billy Abbott's notebook—

Families. There's a subject.

Love and destroy. Not necessarily. But often enough to show up well in the averages. For Freud the stage for Greek tragedy—incest, patricide, other intimate delights. Dreadful to imagine what the good doctor's family life in Vienna had been like.

Was Jung more lenient? Must ask Monika, fountain of wisdom. Come to think of it, she never talks about her family. Skeletons in every closet.

Have never met Wesley Jordache. Poor little bastard. Lost in the shuffle. Will the murder of his father turn out to be an enlarging experience for his soul? My grandfather died when Rudolph and my mother were comparatively young and their souls do not seem noticeably enlarged.

I liked my grandmother because she doted on me. She did not dote on my mother and even on the day of her funeral my mother had no use for her. Will my mother have any use for me on the day of my funeral? I have a premonition I will die young. My mother is made of steel, will last forever, outwearing man after man.

Does her sexuality offend me? Yes.

Does my sexuality, that of Monika, offend me? No. Injustice is the coin that is exchanged between the generations.

My mother is a promiscuous woman. My father, when younger and could manage it, was, by his own accounts, a promiscuous man. I am not. Like the drunkard's child, I stay away from the vice I see in the parent.

Sons revolt. Daughters run off. I did neither. I hid. The army has made it easier. It would be interesting to meet with Cousin Wesley, so far unknown to me, compare notes, the same blood running in our veins.

The flower children rearranged the idea of family. I could not live in a commune. Unhygienic entanglements. Desperate experiments, doomed to failure. We are too far past the tribe. I do not want someone else's child to disturb me while I am reading or shaving or taking my wife to bed.

Will I live in a suburb ten years from now and play bridge and watch football games on the television all weekend long? Commute? Swap wives? Vote for that year's Nixon?

It is late. I miss Monika.

WESLEY WAS SITTING, cleanly shaved, neatly dressed in a suit that Rudolph had brought him from the *Clothilde,* waiting for the *agent* who was to take him to the airport. The suit had been bought for him by his father more than a year ago and was now very much too short in the arms and too tight across the chest. As he had expected, his Uncle Rudolph had somehow fixed it for him. Although having to leave France wasn't such a great arrangement. He had never been happy in America—and he had been happy in France, at least until the day his father died.

It hadn't been so bad in the prison in Grasse. The cop he had hit in the bar was stationed in Cannes and hadn't been around to bug him, and among the guards and with the *juge d'instruction* who had examined him he had enjoyed a certain celebrity because of what had happened to his father and because he spoke French and had knocked out the Englishman, who had a moderate reputation as a barroom fighter with the local police. Also he had been polite and had caused nobody any trouble. The occasional bill his uncle had slipped to the guards and a call from the American consulate, which his uncle had prompted, hadn't hurt, either.

One good thing about Uncle Rudy, he never even hinted that Wesley ought to show some gratitude for what he'd done for him. Wesley would have liked to show gratitude but he didn't know how. Eventually, he thought, he'd have to work on that. As it was, there was nothing much he could think of saying to his uncle, who seemed embarrassed to see Wesley behind bars, as though it was somehow his fault.

One of the guards had even smuggled in a photograph from the police files of the man called Danovic his father had had the fight with in the Porte Rose. Wesley would remember the face when it was necessary to recognize it.

He said nothing of this to anyone. He had never been an open boy—even with his father it had been difficult for him to talk about himself, although his father had told him almost everything he wanted to hear about his own life. Now, he kept what he was feeling to himself. He felt threatened, although he wasn't certain what was threatening him. Whatever it was, silence was the first line of defense. He had learned that a long time ago, when his mother had put him in that damned military school.

His mother was another ball game. She had screamed and cried and scolded and slobbered all over him and promised him he would lead a different life when she got him back with her new husband in Indianapolis. He didn't want to lead a different life. He had asked his uncle if he had to go to Indianapolis and Rudolph had looked sad and said, "At least while you're still a minor." It had something to do with money, he didn't understand just what. No matter. He could take a look at the scene and blow if he didn't like it.

He had learned about flight.

Meanwhile, he missed not being able to go to school when the year began. They were starting the basketball season in September. He had been the star of the team last year and he knew they had been depending upon him this year. He hoped they had a lousy season, so they would know how much they needed him. It seemed a piddling thing to be worrying about when your father had just been murdered, but school was a big part of his life and he couldn't just turn it off because it would be unimportant to grown-ups at this time. He felt his father would have understood, even if nobody else did.

Some of the boys had made fun of him in school because he was American and spoke funny. He had never hit them, as he had wanted to, because his father would have beat the shit out of him if he had found out Wesley was fighting. It would be different now, he thought grimly. With the sorrow, there was a new sense of freedom. I make my own mistakes now, he told himself, and people can just lump them or leave them. The mistake his father had made would take a lot of getting over. He had prayed for his father, but he'd be damned if he forgave him. One night, one crazy grandstand act, and his father had left him in the shit. Shit, he thought, sitting in his clean clothes, shit.

The *agent* who was going to take him to the airport unlocked the door and came in. He was dressed in slacks and a sports jacket but he could be dressed like a ballet dancer and anybody would know he was a cop, right off.

The air smelled wonderful outside. He had forgotten how good air could smell.

They got into an unmarked car, Wesley sitting in front beside the *agent*. The *agent* had a big belly and let out a little poof through his broken nose as he squeezed in under the wheel. Wesley would have liked to ask if he had ever been hit with a beer bottle or shot a man, but decided it would be better to keep the conversation on other things.

The *agent* drove slowly down the winding mountain road, with all the windows open. "The weather is beautiful," he said, "we might as well profit from it." It was an easy morning's work for him and he was making the most of it. He already smelled from wine. "So," he said, "no more France for you. Pity. Next time you will learn to hit people where there are no witnesses." He laughed at his lawman's joke. "What are you going to do in America?"

"Keep away from the police," Wesley said.

The *agent* laughed again. "That's a smart young man. My wife keeps after me. We ought to visit America, she says." He wagged his head. "On a policeman's salary, you can imagine." He looked sidelong at Wesley. "Your uncle is a man of important wealth, isn't he?" he asked.

"One of the richest."

"It shows." The policeman sighed, looked down at his rumpled jacket. "I admire his clothes. He is a man of great authority. That is evident. No wonder you're on the way home."

Home was not the word to describe where he was going, Wesley thought.

"You will come back here eventually—as a tourist—and spend a great deal of money, I suppose," the *agent* said.

"If you don't turn Communist first," Wesley said. In the prison there had been two men who said they were Communists and the day was near.

"Don't say things like that," the *agent* said darkly. "Especially in America. They will turn their backs on us." On the subject now of the bad opinion Americans had of the French, he said, "You are not going back and tell the newspapers how you were tortured by the police to make you confess?"

"I had nothing to confess," Wesley said. "Everybody saw me hit the *salaud*. I might say something about how one of your friends beat me up in the car on the way to the *préfecture*, though," he added mischievously. He was enjoying the ride through the ripe, flowery countryside after the weeks indoors. And just talking idly away with the man, who was friendly enough, postponed having to think what was waiting for him at the airport and in Indianapolis.

"Ah, what would you expect?" the *agent* said aggrievedly. "To be knocked down with one blow by a child in full view of the entire world and not get a little bit of your own back in a dark car? We are all human, you know."

"All right," Wesley said magnanimously, "I won't say anything."

"You're a good boy," the *agent* said. "You made a good reputation for yourself in Grasse. I have seen the man your father had the *fracas* with. He looked as though he had been run over by a locomotive." He nodded, an expert in these matters. "Your father did an excellent job. Excellent." He looked sidelong again at Wesley, his face serious now. "The fellow is known to the police. Unfavorably," he said. "So far he has been able to escape the punishment he richly deserves. He associates with dangerous men. It is as much for your sake as for the sake of France that you are being sent on your way."

"It just seems queer," Wesley said, "that a man that everybody knows is responsible for a murder can get away with it."

"You just forget about what people know, my friend," the *agent* said censoriously. "You just forget everything and go home and be a nice young American."

"Yes, sir," Wesley said, remembering every detail in the photograph, the slit eyes, the high, sharp cheekbones, the thin mouth and dark curly hair. *You* forget the man who killed my father, he wanted to say, but didn't. You just try and forget. "I wonder if you could do me a favor."

"What is it?" The *agent*'s voice was professionally suspicious.

"Could you drive along the port? I'd like to take a look at the boat."

The *agent* glanced at his watch. "It's early yet," he said. "We have time. Why not?"

"That's very kind of you, sir," Wesley said. "*C'est très gentil de votre part, monsieur*," in French. It was one of the first things his father had taught him when he had brought him to Antibes. Although his father knew almost no French, he had said, "They're two expressions the Frogs pay a lot of attention to. First—*S'il vous plaît*, that means please. And *C'est très gentil de votre part*. Got it? Repeat them."

Wesley had not forgotten the lesson.

"I have a son about your age," the *agent* said. "He's crazy about boats, too. He's always hanging around the ports, whenever he gets a chance. I told him I'd disown him if he ever became a sailor. If it wasn't for all the boats down here, the police would be put out of work. The people it attracts," he said gloomily, "Algerians, Yugoslavs, Greeks, Corsicans, Sicilians, nudists, English kids in trouble with the law back home, girls who've run away from home, rich playboys with giant dope habits . . ." He shook his head as he went over the list of seaborne malefactors. . . . "And now every stinking town with a view of the Mediterranean is building a new port. It will take the entire *gendarmerie* of France to control it. Witness your case." He shook his finger angrily at Wesley, reminded by his outburst that he was conducting a criminal to exile. "Do you think what happened to you would have happened if you inhabited Clermont-Ferrand, for example?"

"My case was an accident," Wesley said, sorry he had asked to see the port.

"That's what they all say. And who has to clean up the mess? The police."

"What would you like your son to be?" Wesley thought it was time to change the subject.

"A lawyer. That's where the money is, my boy. Take my advice, go back to America and be a lawyer. How many lawyers do you know who have ever been in jail?"

"I was considering it," Wesley said, hoping to get the cop back into his earlier expansive mood.

"Consider it seriously."

"I intend to," Wesley said, sage and appreciative and wishing that the cop would shut up.

"And don't ever carry a weapon. Do you hear me?"

"Yes, sir."

"Listen to the advice of an older man who is interested in the next generation and who has seen the world."

Now Wesley knew why they had picked this particular cop for the errand this morning. Anything to get him out of the *préfecture* and avoid having to listen to his lectures.

The cop grumbled, wordlessly, and lit a cigarette, the car swaying dangerously as he took his hands momentarily off the wheel. The smoke came Wesley's way and he coughed. Neither his father nor Bunny had smoked.

"And don't ever smoke, either," the cop said. "I despise myself for the habit." He lapsed into silence.

When they came to the port, Wesley saw the *Clothilde*, its decks deserted. Unreasonably, he half expected to see his father come out of the wheelhouse and pull at a line. His father had always been nervous that a sudden storm might arise and the lines would give way. Stop it, Wesley thought, stop it, he's not going to come on deck ever again. For a moment he wondered what would happen if he suddenly opened the door of the car and jumped out and ran. He could lose the fat cop in a minute, hide out, slip onto the *Clothilde* at night and handle her out of the port into the open sea, make for Italy. That was the nearest border, actually. Would the cop use his gun? It bulged in a shoulder holster under his sports jacket. Too risky. Crazy. Today, at least, he had to be sane. He would come back to Antibes another day.

"Boats," the cop said contemptuously and stepped on the accelerator.

Wesley closed his eyes. He didn't want to look at the *Clothilde* anymore.

Rudolph and Dwyer were waiting for him at the check-in counter at the airport. Dwyer had Wesley's canvas and leatherette bag with him and was carrying a big manila envelope.

"Your mother and her husband," Rudolph said, "have gone through passport control already. They'll look for you inside. They're on the same plane with you."

Wesley nodded. He couldn't trust himself to speak.

"All is in order, *Monsieur* Jordache," the *agent* said respectfully. "I'll go through with him and put him on the plane."

"*Merci,*" Rudolph said.

"Here's your things," Dwyer said, indicating the bag. "You'll have to have it weighed." Dwyer had put on a suit for the occasion. Wesley didn't remember having seen Dwyer in a whole suit before, not even at the wedding. He seemed smaller than Wesley remembered, and a lot older, with tiny, fine wrinkles in his forehead and around his mouth. "And this," Dwyer said, giving him the envelope, "has some of the photos you kept up forward. I thought you might like to look at them sometime." His voice sounded wandery, vague.

"Thanks, Bunny," Wesley said, taking the envelope.

Rudolph gave him a slip of paper. "There are two addresses on that, Wesley," he said. "My home address and my friend Johnny Heath's office, in case I'm off someplace. If you ever need anything . . ." He, too, sounded unsure of himself.

He's not used to seeing members of his family being seen off from one country to another by a cop, Wesley thought as he took the slip of paper and put it in his pocket.

"Take care of yourself," Dwyer said, as Rudolph gave Wesley's ticket to the girl behind the counter and watched while the bag was being weighed.

"Don't you worry about me, old shipmate," Wesley said, trying to sound hearty.

"Never." Dwyer smiled, but it didn't look like much of a smile. "See you around, eh?"

"Sure." He didn't even try to smile.

"Well," the cop said in French, "time to go."

Wesley shook hands with his uncle, who looked as though he would be seeing Wesley in an hour or two and Dwyer, who looked as though he would never see him again.

Wesley didn't glance backward as he went through passport control with the *agent,* who showed his identification card as he came up to the desk and winked at the officer there.

His mother and her husband, whom he had never seen before, were standing in the departure lounge just as he passed through the control, as if to make sure he wasn't going to escape. "You look pale," his mother said. Her hair was all over her face. She looked as though she had been caught in a force ten gale.

"I feel fine," he said. "This is my friend." He touched the *agent*'s arm. "He's a policeman. He doesn't speak English."

The *agent* bowed a little. The affair had passed off without incident and he could afford to be gallant. "Explain to them that I have to see you safely aboard," he said in French.

Wesley explained. His mother drew back as though the policeman had an infectious disease. "Meet your new father," his mother said. "Mr. Kraler."

"Welcome," Mr. Kraler said, like a master of ceremonies on television greeting a famous guest. He extended his hand.

"Keep your hands off me," Wesley said calmly.

"Don't worry about him, Eddie," his mother said. "He's disturbed today. That's natural. He'll learn. Do you want a drink, baby? A Coca-Cola, an orange juice?"

"A whiskey," Wesley said.

"Now see here, young man . . ." Mr. Kraler began.

"He's joking," his mother said hastily. "Aren't you joking, Wesley?"

"No."

A woman's voice was announcing the departure of the plane over the loudspeaker system. The *agent* took his arm. "I'll accompany you aboard," he said in French. "Those're my orders."

Maybe, Wesley thought as he walked toward the gate, I should have taken my chances when we were down at the port. His mother and her husband followed them closely.

Rudolph drove Dwyer toward Antibes. Neither of them said a word on the entire trip. When they reached the entrance to the port, Dwyer said, "I'll get off here. I have to see someone." Both he and Rudolph knew that he was going to stop at the little café and get drunk and that he wanted to be alone. "You going to be around for a while?"

"A week or so," Rudolph said. "Until I get it all cleared up."

"See you," Dwyer said, and went into the café, unbuttoning the collar of his shirt and tearing off his tie and stuffing it carelessly into his pocket.

Rudolph started the car again. In his pocket he had a letter from Jeanne. She would meet him for lunch at the Colombe d'Or and could see him every afternoon that week. The war in Paris was on again, she had written.

When the seat belt sign went off in the cabin of the plane as it turned west in the sky above Monte Carlo, Wesley was looking at the photographs that had been in the envelope that Dwyer had given him. He didn't notice his mother cross the aisle to stand over him. She looked down at the photographs in his hand. Suddenly, she reached over and grabbed them all. "You won't need these anymore," she said. "You poor baby, you have a lot to forget."

He didn't want to make a scene, not this soon anyway, so he didn't say anything. He watched as she stood there in the aisle, tearing the photographs one by one and dropping the pieces in the aisle. She didn't have any objections to making scenes, he thought. Boy, it was going to be great in Indianapolis.

He looked out the window and saw the peninsula of Antibes, green and beloved, sliding away into the blue sea below him.

Part Two

CHAPTER 1

1969

From Billy Abbott's notebook—

There is a lot of talk at NATO about displaced populations, the Germans kicked out of Poland, the East Germans, refugees in West Germany, the Palestinians, the Armenians, the Jews kicked out of the Arab countries, the Italians out of Tunisia and Libya, the French colons from Algeria. More undoubtedly to come. Natural conversation among military men, on the lookout for occasions for war.

It has occurred to me that I am a displaced population all by myself, far from home, with sentimental and no doubt distorted memories of a happier life and better time in another country, feeling no allegiance to the society (the U.S. Army) in which I spend my exile, even though it feeds, clothes, and pays me more generously than I, with my meager talents and complete lack of ambition, could ever hope to feed, clothe and pay myself in my native land.

I have no allegiances, which is the same as saying that I could become a desperate man. My allegiance, such as it is, to Monika, is temporary at best. A casual transfer of posts, the Colonel appointed to an outfit in Greece or Guam and not being sure he could find a useful tennis partner there, a shift in command ordered by someone in Washington who does not know or care if I am alive, an offer of a better job for Monika in another country, and it would be destroyed.

It might not even be anything as accidental as that. Lately Monika has become edgy. I find her watching me more and more often with a speculative look in her eye that bodes no good. It would be the height of blind egotism in me if I believed that the speculation included sorrow at the thought of losing me.

If Monika leaves me I will screw the Colonel's wife.

BILLY ABBOTT, IN civilian clothes, feeling at peace with the world, after an excellent meal at the restaurant that overlooked La Grande Place of the city of Brussels, came out into the cool night air, holding on to Monika's arm. The meal had been expensive, as the restaurant was overpraised in all the guidebooks, but it had been worth it. Besides, he had won sixty dollars that afternoon playing tennis with the Colonel as his partner. The Colonel was a tennis nut and tried to play at least an hour a day, and as befitted a true graduate of West Point, liked to win.

The Colonel had seen Billy play when Billy was only a corporal and had liked Billy's style, which was cool and tricky, so that he could beat players who hit the ball twice as hard as he did. Billy was also very quick and could cover three-quarters of the court in doubles. Since the Colonel was forty-seven years old, he needed a partner who could cover three-quarters of the court. So now Billy was no longer a corporal, but a master sergeant in command of the motor pool, a job that meant considerable extra money beyond his sergeant's pay, what with an occasional grateful tip from officers who had motorized business to conduct that was not officially Army business, and the not so occasional opportunity to sell Army gasoline clandestinely at prices cannily just below the prices in the city. The Colonel also invited Billy to dinner. He liked to know what the enlisted men were thinking, as he often said, and the Colonel's wife thought Billy was a charming young man and behaved like an officer, especially in civilian clothes. The Colonel's wife liked to play tennis, too, and lived in hope of the day when the Colonel would be sent off on an assignment for a month or two, leaving Billy behind.

It was not the Old Army, the Colonel sometimes said, but you had to keep up with the times. While the Colonel was his commanding officer there was no danger that Billy would be sent to Vietnam.

Billy knew that it was through his Uncle Rudolph's good offices in Washington that he had been spared the unpleasant sound of hostile fire and one day he would show his gratitude. Right now, he had in his pocket a letter from his uncle which contained a check for one thousand dollars. Billy's mother had run dry as a source of funds, and Monika, to whom Billy had spoken about his rich uncle, had pushed him into writing for money. She had been mysterious about why she needed it, but Billy had long ago resigned himself to the fact that she was a mysterious girl. She never told him anything about her family in Munich or why she had taken it into her head at the age of eighteen to take a degree at Trinity College in Dublin. She was always going off on secret appointments, but except for that, most of the time was extremely agreeable to live with. That had been the condition on which she had moved into his cosy little flat off the Place. He was to ask no questions when she said she had to be away for an evening or sometimes a week. There were some delicate meetings among the delegates to NATO that could not be talked about. He was not a curious young man when it came to matters that did not concern him.

Monika was not really pretty, with her black, tangled hair and low-heeled shoes and sensible stockings, but she had large blue eyes that lit up her face when she smiled and a lovely small figure. The small was important. Billy was only five feet six inches tall and slightly built, and he didn't like the feeling of inferiority taller women gave him.

If he had been asked on this evening what profession he intended to follow he would most probably have said that he was going to reenlist. Every once in a while, Monika would get angry with him and denounce him for his lack of ambition. With his engaging youthful athlete's smile, he would agree with her that he had no ambition. The melancholy darkness of his eyes, fringed by heavy black lashes, gave his smile an extra value, as though he had made a special sad effort at gaiety for its recipient. Billy knew enough about himself not to turn the smile on too often.

Tonight was one of the times Monika had a mysterious appointment. "Don't wait up for me," she said as they gazed at the spotlit gilt magnificence of the Place's walls and windows. "I may be late. Maybe all night."

"You're ruining my sex life," he said.

"I bet," she said. Trinity College, plus the troops of NATO, had given her an easy command of both the English and American languages.

He kissed her lightly and watched her get into a cab. She sprang into it as if she were doing the running broad jump at a track meet. He admired her energy. He couldn't hear the address that she gave the driver. It occurred to him that every time he put her in a cab, he never heard where she was going.

He shrugged and strolled toward a café. It was too early to go home and there was nobody else he especially wanted to see that night.

In the café he ordered a beer and took out the envelope with the check and his uncle's letter in it. There had been an exchange of letters, quite cordial, since Billy had seen the item in *Time* Magazine about Tom Jordache's death and the awful photograph of Rudolph's wife naked that they'd dug up somewhere. He hadn't mentioned the photograph in the letter to Rudolph and had been sincere, or as sincere as he could be, with his condolences. Uncle Rudolph had been chatty in his letters, with all the family news. He sounded like a lonely man who didn't know quite what to do with himself, and he had written sadly, if reticently, of his divorce and the claiming of Cousin Wesley by the lady from Indianapolis. He had not mentioned the police record of Wesley's mother as a common prostitute, but Billy's own mother had not been sparing in details. His mother's letters tended to be stern and admonitory. She had never forgiven him for his refusal to keep away from the army—she would have enjoyed playing the honored martyr, he felt resentfully, if he had gone to jail instead. Everyone to his or her principles. For himself, he preferred playing tennis with a forty-seven-year-old colonel and living in comparative luxury with a bright, shapely, multilingual, and—admit it—a beloved *fräulein* in the civilized city of Brussels.

His letter to his uncle asking for a loan had been graceful and rueful rather than importunate. There had been some unlucky poker games, he had hinted, an expensive automobile breakdown, the necessity to buy a new car . . . Rudolph's letter, which had arrived that morning, had been understanding, although he had made it clear that he expected to be repaid.

Monika wanted the cash the next morning and he would have to go to the bank. He wondered what she might need it for. What the hell, he thought, dismissing the subject, it's only money and it's not even mine. He ordered a second beer.

In the morning he discovered what she wanted the money for. She woke him up when she came in at dawn, made him a cup of coffee, sat him down and told him the thousand dollars was to be used to bribe a sergeant at the Army arms depot, so that the people she was working with, whom she wouldn't name or describe, could go in with a U.S. Army truck, which he, Billy, was expected to supply from the motor pool, and lift an unspecified number of guns, grenades and rounds of ammunition. He himself was not to be involved in the deal. Only to the extent of driving the truck out of the pool one night, with authentic orders, and delivering it half a mile down the road to a man who would be dressed as a U.S. Army MP lieutenant. The truck would be back before dawn. She said all this calmly, while he sat in silence, sipping his coffee, wondering if she had been on drugs all night. In the course of her explanation, given in the same even tones she might have used back in Trinity at a seminar on an obscure Irish poet, she also explained that he had been picked as her lover because of his job at the motor pool, although she admitted that she had become fond of him, very fond, since then.

He tried to control his voice when he finally spoke. "What the hell is all this stuff going to be used for?"

"I can't tell you, darling," she said, stroking his hand across the kitchen table. "And you'll be better off never knowing."

"You're a terrorist," he said.

"That's a word like any other," she said, shrugging. "I might prefer the word idealist, or a phrase like seeker after justice or an enemy of torture or just plain lover of the ordinary, traumatized, brainwashed common man. Take your pick."

"What if I just went to NATO and told them about you? About this crazy scheme?" He felt silly sitting there shivering in a small, cold, bourgeois kitchen, dressed only in an old bathrobe that was half open, with his balls hanging out, talking about blowing people up.

"I wouldn't try that, darling," she said. "First of all they would never believe you. I'd say that I had told you I'd leave you and this was your weird way of getting revenge. And some of the boys I know can be very nasty customers indeed. . . . "

"You're threatening me," he said.

"I guess you could call it that."

By the look in her eye he knew that she was deadly serious. Serious was exactly the word. And deadly. He felt cold and frightened. He had never posed as a hero. He had never even had a fistfight in his life. "If I do this, this once," he said, trying to keep his voice from quavering, "I never want to see you again."

"That's for you to decide," she said evenly.

"I'll tell you at noon," he said, his mind racing, searching for a way he could get out of the whole thing, fly to America, hide out in Paris, London, escape the whole insane, surrealist plot in six hours.

"That will be time enough," Monika said. "The banks are open in the afternoon. But I must tell you, for your own sake—you will be watched."

"What the hell kind of woman are you?" he shouted, his voice out of control.

"If you weren't so superficial and frivolous and self-satisfied," she said, without raising her voice, "you'd know by now, after living with me as long as you've done."

"I don't know what's so frivolous and self-satisfied about not wanting to kill people," he said, stung by her description of him. "Don't be so goddamned smug."

"Every day," she said, "you put on a uniform. In the same uniform, thousands of young men your age go out every day to kill hundreds of thousands of people who never did them any harm, I consider *that* frivolous." As she talked, her eyes finally were darkening with anger.

"And *you're* going to stop that?" he said loudly. "You and five or six other murderous thugs?"

"We can try. Among other things that we will try. At least we'll have the satisfaction of knowing that we tried. And what satisfaction will you have?" She sneered at him, her mouth an ugly grimace. "That you played tennis while it all was happening? That there isn't a single human being alive who has any respect for you? That you sat idly by while the men whose boots you lick morning, noon and night are plotting to blow up the world? When everything goes up in the final explosion, are you going to be proud of yourself as you die because you ate well and drank well and fucked well while it all was being prepared? Wake up! Wake up! There's no law that says you have to be a worm."

"Rhetoric," he said. "So what'll you do—hijack an Israeli plane, break some windows in an embassy, shoot a policeman while he's directing traffic? Is that your idea of saving the world?"

"First of all, this has nothing to do with the Israelis. We—my group and I—have varying opinions on that subject, so don't worry about your Jewish friends—my Jewish friends, for that matter."

"Thank you," he said sardonically, "for your German forbearance of the Jews."

"You bastard." She tried to slap him across the table, but he was too fast for her and caught her hand.

"None of that," he said. "You may be wonderful with a machine gun, but you're not a boxer, lady. Nobody's going to get away with hitting me. You've yelled at me and yelled at me and threatened me and asked me to do something that might get me killed or land me in prison for life and you haven't explained anything yet." Recklessly, he went on, raving now. "If I'm going to help you, it's not going to be because you're scaring me into it or bribing me or anything like that. I'll make a deal with you. You're right—there's no law that says I have to be a worm. You convince me and I'm with you. You sit down and keep your goddamn hands and your goddamn threats to yourself and calmly explain. Otherwise, no soap. You understand that?"

"Let go of my hand," she said sullenly.

He dropped her hand. She stared at him furiously. Then she began to chuckle. "Hey, Billy boy, there's something there after all. Who would have guessed that? I think we need some fresh coffee. And you're cold. Go in and get dressed and put on a sweater and we'll have a nice little talk over the breakfast table about the wonder of being alive in the twentieth century."

In the bedroom, while he was getting dressed, he started shivering again. But even while he was shivering, he felt crazily exhilarated. For once he hadn't backed down or slid away or evaded. And it could be a matter of life and death, he was sure of that. There was no sense in underestimating Monika's toughness or passion. The papers were full of stories of hijackings, bombings, political murders, theatrical massacres, and they were plotted and carried out by people who sat at the next desk from yours, who stood by your side in a bus, who went to bed with you, ate dinner with you. It was his tough luck that Monika was one of them. As she had said, he should have guessed *something*. Her insults had wounded him; it was one thing to know that you were worthless, it was another to be told by a woman whom you admired, more than that—much more—loved, who acted as though she loved you, that you had no value.

The chuckle in the cold, dawn-lit kitchen had been a gift of respect and he accepted it gratefully. In Monika's eyes now he was a worthy opponent and had to be treated accordingly. Until now he had let the world go its own way and had been satisfied to find a snug, government-issue corner for himself. Well, the world had caught up with him and he had to deal with it. He was involved, whether he liked it or not. From one moment to another, almost instinctively, he had put a new price on his existence.

The hell with her, he thought, as he put on a sweater. Loss is the risk of breathing. The hell with all of them.

Monika was heating a fresh pot of coffee when he went back into the kitchen. She had taken off her shoes and was padding around in her stockinged feet, her hair a dark mess, like any housewife newly risen from the marital bed to make breakfast for her husband on the way to the office. Terror in the kitchen, bloodshed over a hot stove, victims designated among the clatter of pots and pans. He sat down at the scarred wooden table, rescued from some Belgian farmhouse, and Monika poured the coffee into his cup. Efficient German *hausfrau*. She made good coffee. He tasted it with relish. She poured some coffee for herself, smiled at him gently. The woman who had told him that he had been selected as her lover because he happened to run a motor pool from which trucks could be obtained for deadly errands had disappeared. For the time being. For ten minutes on a cold morning, he thought, as he drank the scalding coffee.

"Well," he said, "where do we begin?" He looked at his watch. "It can't take too long. I have to be at work soon."

"We begin at the beginning," she said. "The state of the world. The world's in a mess. The Fascists are everywhere. . . ."

"In America . . .?" he said. "Come on, Monika."

"In America it's still disguised," she said impatiently. "They can still afford to disguise it. But who gives them the arms, the money, the smoke screens, finally, the real support? The fat cats in Washington, New York, Texas. If you're going to insist on being naive, I won't bother talking to you."

"You sound as though it all comes out of a book."

"Why not?" she said. "What's wrong with learning from a book? It wouldn't do you any harm to read a few books, either. If you're so worried about your beloved native land, you'll be relieved to hear that we're not operating in America now, not the people I'm with anyway, although I'm not saying there aren't some who do. There're bombs going off in America, too, and there'll be more, I promise you. America's at the base of the pyramid and in the end it will be the prime target. And you're going to be surprised how easily it will crumble in the end. Because the pyramid is shaky, it's based on lies, immoral privileges, stolen wealth, subjugated populations; it's based on sand that's hollow beneath the surface."

"You sound more like a book than ever," he said. "Why don't you just get it out of the library and I'll read it myself."

Monika ignored his gibe. "What we have to do," she went on, "is show that it's vulnerable as well as evil."

"How do you plan to do that with a few crazy gangsters?"

"Don't use that word," she said warningly.

"Whatever you want to call them. Gunmen. Assassins. Whatever."

"Castro did it in Cuba with eighteen men."

"America's not Cuba," he said. "And neither is Europe."

"They're near enough. Both of them. The attacks will multiply. The men in power will get uneasy, uncertain, finally frightened. They'll act out of fear, make one mistake after another, each one worse than the last. They'll apply pressure. They'll make disastrous concessions which will only make people realize that they were close to defeat and only inspire more incidents, more cracks in the walls."

"Oh," he said, "turn off the record, will you?"

"A bank president will be assassinated," she chanted, rapt in her vision, "an ambassador kidnapped, a strike paralyze a country, money lose its value. They won't know where the next blow is coming from, just that there will be a next blow. The pressure will build up, until the whole thing explodes. It won't take armies. . . . Just a few dedicated people . . ."

"Like you?" he said.

"Like me," she said defiantly.

"And if you succeed, then what?" he said. "Russia takes the whole pot. Is that what you want?"

"Russia's time will come," she said. "Don't think I'm fool enough to want *that*."

"What *do* you want, then?"

"I want the world to stop being poisoned, stop being headed to extinction, one way or another. I want to stop the warriors we have now, the spies, the nuclear bombers, the bribed politicians, the killing for profit. . . people are suffering and I want them to know who's making them suffer and what they're getting out of it."

"All right," he said, "that's all very admirable. But let's speak practically. Suppose I get you the truck, supposing you put your hands on a few grenades, plastic, guns. Just what, specifically, are you going to do with them?"

"Specifically," she said, "we are planning to blow in the windows of a bank here in Brussels, get some explosive inside the Spanish embassy, wipe out a judge in Germany who's the biggest pig on the Continent. I can't tell you more than that. For your own sake."

"You're ready to do a lot of things for my sake, aren't you?" he said. He bowed sardonically. "I thank you, my mother thanks you, my colonel thanks you."

"Don't be flip," she said coldly. "Don't ever be flip with me again."

"You sound as though you're ready to shoot me right now, dear little gunlady," he said, mocking her, pushing himself to courage, although he was shivering again, sweater and all.

"I've never shot anybody," she said. "And don't propose to. That is not my job. And if your scruples are so delicate, perhaps you'd like to hear that we plan to operate in such a way here in Belgium that nobody will get killed. What we do is merely unsettle, warn, symbolize."

"That's Belgium," he said. "What about other places?"

"That doesn't concern you," she said. "You don't have to know anything about it. Later on, if you are convinced and you want to take a more active part, you will be trained, you will be in on the discussions. Right now, all you are to do is go to the bank and cash your uncle's check and make a truck available for a few hours one night. Christ," she said fiercely, "it's nothing new to you, with your bribes—don't think I don't know how you live so high on a sergeant's pay—with your black market gasoline. . . ."

"My God, Monika," he said, "do you mean to say you can't tell the difference between a little petty larceny and what you're asking me to do?"

"Yes," she said. "One is cheap and distasteful and the other is noble. You've been leading your life in a trance. You don't *like* what you are, you despise everybody around you, I've heard you talk about your family, your mother, your father, your uncle, the animals you work with . . . Don't deny it." She put up her hand to stop him as he tried to speak. "You've kept everything narrow, inside yourself. Nobody's challenged you to face yourself, open up, to see what it all means. Well, I'm challenging you now."

"And hinting that something very nasty will happen to me if I don't do as you want," he said.

"That's the way it goes, laddy," she said. "Think over what I've just said as you work this morning."

"I'll do just that." He stood up. "I've got to get to the office."

"I'll be waiting for you at lunchtime," she said.

"I bet you will," he said, as he went out the door.

The morning in the office passed for him in a blur. As he checked out orders, requests, manifests, operation reports, he made dozens of decisions, each one over and over again, each one discarded, the next one reached and discarded in turn. Three times he picked up the phone to call the Colonel, spill everything, ask him for advice, help, then put the phone down. He looked up the schedule of the planes flying out of Brussels to New York, decided to go to the bank, cash his uncle's check and get on a plane that morning. He could go to the CIA in Washington, explain his predicament, get Monika put behind bars, be something of a secret hero in those secret corridors. Or would he? Would those men, deft in murder and complicated underground maneuvers and the overthrow of governments, congratulate him and secretly, in their own style, scorn him for his cowardice? Or even worse, turn him into a double agent, order him back to join whatever band Monika belonged to, tell him to report weekly on their doings? Did he want Monika behind bars? Even that morning, he could not honestly tell himself that he didn't love her. Love? There was a word. Most women bored him. Usually he made an excuse, after copulation, to jump out of bed and go home. With Monika the night's entwining could never be called copulation. It was absolute delight. To put it coarsely, he told himself, I can come five times a night with her and look forward eagerly to seeing her naked and rosy in bed at lunchtime.

He didn't want to be killed. He knew that, just as he knew he didn't want to give up Monika. But there was something titillating, deeply exciting, about the thought that he was daring enough to make love to a woman, make her gasp in pleasure and pain, at six in the morning and know that she was ready to order his execution at noon.

What would it be like to say to her, "I'm with you"? To slide in and out of shadows? To hear an explosion somewhere nearby while he was playing tennis at the immaculate club with the Colonel and know that he had scheduled it? To pass a bank on whose board his Uncle Rudolph sat and stealthily deposit a bomb that would explode before the bank opened its doors in the morning? To meet fanatics, who flitted from one country to another, who would be heroes in the history books, perhaps, a century from now, who killed with poison, with their bare hands, who could teach him their mysteries, who could make him forget he was only five feet six inches tall?

In the end, he did not call the Colonel, he did not cash the check, he made no arrangements at the motor pool, he did not go out to the airport.

What he did was drift, dazed, through the morning and when the Colonel called and said there was a game on at five-thirty that afternoon, he said, "Yes, sir, I'll be there," although he felt that there was a good chance he'd be dead by then.

She was waiting for him when he came out of the office. He was relieved that she had combed her hair, because the other men streaming past to go to lunch all looked at them speculatively, leers suppressed, mostly because of his rank, and he didn't like the idea of their thinking he consorted with a slob.

"Well?" she said.

"Let's have lunch," he said.

He took her to a good restaurant, where he knew the other men who wanted a change from the food in the Army mess were not likely to go. He wanted the reassurance of crisp tablecloths, flowers on the tables, attentive waiters, a place where there was no suggestion of the world tottering, desperate plotters, crumbling pyramids. He ordered for both of them. She pretended not to be interested in what she ate and couldn't bother with the menu. Meanly, knowing at least that much about her, he understood why she tossed the menu aside. She had to put on thick glasses to read and was vain enough not to wish to be seen in public with them on. But when the food came she ate heartily, more than he did. He wondered how she kept her figure.

They ate quietly, talking politely about the weather, a conference that was to start tomorrow at which she was to act as translator, about his date for tennis with the Colonel at five-thirty, about a play that was coming to Brussels that she wanted to see. There was no reference to what had passed between them that morning until the coffee came. Then she said, "Well, what have you decided?"

"Nothing," he said. Even in the overheated, cosy restaurant he felt cold again. "I sent the check back to my uncle this morning."

She smiled coldly. "That's a decision, isn't it?"

"Partially," he said. He was lying. The check was still in his wallet. He hadn't known he was going to say it. It had come out mechanically, as though something had pushed a lever in his brain. But even as he said it, he knew he *was* going to mail the check back, with thanks, explaining to his uncle that his finances had taken a turn for the better and there was no need at the moment for help. It would prove useful later on when he really needed something from Uncle Rudolph.

"All right," she said calmly, "if you were afraid that the money could be traced, I understand." She shrugged. "It's not too important. We'll find the money someplace else. But how about the truck?"

"I haven't done anything about it."

"You have all afternoon."

"No, I haven't made up my mind yet."

"We can handle that, too, I suppose," she said. "All you have to do is look the other way."

"I'm not going to do that, either," he said. "I have a lot of thinking to do before I decide one way or another. If your friends want to kill me," he said harshly, but keeping his voice low, because he saw their waiter approaching with more coffee, "tell them that I'll be armed." He had had one morning's practice with a .45, could take it apart and reassemble it, but had had a very low score when he had fired at a target for the record. Gunfight at the Brussels OK Corral, he thought. Who was it—John Wayne? What would John Wayne have done today? He giggled.

"What're you laughing about?" she asked sharply.

"I happened to think of a movie I once saw," he said.

"Yes, please," she said in French to the waiter who was standing over her with the silver coffeepot. The waiter filled both their cups.

After the waiter had left, she smiled at him strangely. "You don't have to pack a gun. Nobody's going to shoot you. You're not worth a bullet."

"That's nice to hear," he said.

"Does *anything* ever make an impression on you, touch you?"

"I'll make a list," he said, "and give it to you the next time we meet. If we meet."

"We'll meet," she said.

"When are you moving out of the apartment?" he asked.

She looked at him in surprise. He couldn't tell whether the surprise was real or feigned. "I hadn't intended to move out. Do you want me to move out?"

"I don't know," he said. "But after today . . ."

"For the time being," she said, "let's forget today. I like living with you. I've found that politics has nothing to do with sex. Maybe with other people, but not with me. I adore going to bed with you. I haven't had much luck in bed with other men. The orgasms are few and far between on the New Left—at least for me—and in this day and age ladies have been taught that orgasms are a lady's God-given right. You're the answer to a maiden's prayer for that, darling, if you don't mind my being a little vulgar. At least for this particular maiden. And I like good dinners, which you are obliging enough to supply. So—" She lit a cigarette. She smoked incessantly and the ashtrays in the apartment were always piled with butts. It irritated him, as he did not smoke and took seriously the warnings of the magazine articles about mortality rates for smokers. But, he supposed, you couldn't expect a terrorist who was constantly on the lookout for the police or execution squads to worry about dying from cancer of the lungs at the age of sixty. "So—" she said, exhaling smoke through her nostrils. "I'll divide my life, while it lasts, into compartments. You for sex and lobster and pâté de foie gras, and others for less serious occupations, like shooting German judges. Aren't you glad I'm such a sensible girl?"

She's cutting me to pieces, he thought, little jagged pieces. "I'm not glad about anything," he said.

"Don't look so mournful, laddy," she said. "Everything to his or her own talents. And now, I have most of the afternoon off. Can you sneak away for an hour or two?"

"Yes." He had long ago perfected a system of checking in and out of the office without being noticed.

"Good." She patted his hand. "Let's go home and get into bed and have a perfectly delicious afternoon fuck."

Furious with himself for not being able to stand up, throw a bill on the table for the check and stalk out of the restaurant, he said, "I have to go back to the office for ten minutes. I'll meet you home."

"I can't wait." She smiled at him, her large blue eyes lighting up her Bavarian-Trinity face.

CHAPTER 2

1969

From Billy Abbott's notebook—

This will be the last entry in this notebook for some time.
   I had better not write anything about Monika anymore.
   There are snoops, and authorized burglars everywhere. Brussels abounds in them.
   Monika edgier than ever.
   I love her. She refuses to believe me.

SIDNEY ALTSCHELER WAS standing at the window of his office high up in the Time and Life Building, staring gloomily out at the lights of the buildings around the tower in which he worked. He was gloomy because he was thinking of all the editorial work ahead of him over the weekend.

There was a discreet knock on the door and his secretary came in. "There's somebody called Jordache here who wants to see you."

Altscheler frowned. "Jordache?" he said. "I don't know anybody named Jordache. Tell him I'm busy, let him write me a letter."

The secretary had turned to go when he remembered. "Wait a minute," he said. "We ran a story five, six months ago. About a murder. The man's name was Jordache. Tell him to come up. I've got fifteen minutes free before Thatcher comes in with his rewrite. Maybe there's a follow-up on the Jordache story we can use." He went back to the window and continued being gloomy about the weekend as he stared out at the lights in the surrounding offices, which would be dark tomorrow because it was Saturday and the vice-presidents, the clerks, the bookkeepers, the mailboys, everybody, would be enjoying their holiday.

He was still at the window when there was a rap at the door and the secretary came in with a boy in a suit that was too small for him. "Come in, come in," he said, and seated himself behind his desk. There was a chair next to the desk. He indicated it to the boy.

"Will you need me?" the secretary asked.

"If I do, I'll call you." He looked at the boy. Sixteen, seventeen, he guessed, big for his age. Thin, handsome face, with disturbing intense eyes. Trained down like an athlete.

"Now, Mr. Jordache," he said briskly, "what can I do for you?"

The boy took out a page torn from *Time*. "You did this story about my father." He had a deep, resounding voice.

"Yes, I remember." Altscheler hesitated. "Which one was your father? The mayor?"

"No," the boy said, "the one who was murdered."

"I see," Altscheler said. He made his tone more kindly. "What's your first name, young man?"

"Wesley."

"Have they found the murderer yet?"

"No." Wesley hesitated. Then he said, "That is—technically no."

"I didn't think so. I haven't seen any follow-up."

"I really wanted to see whoever wrote the article," Wesley said. "I told them that downstairs at the desk, but they telephoned around and found it was by a man named Hubbell and said he was still in France. So I bought a copy of *Time* and I saw your name up in front."

"I see," Altscheler said. "What did you want to see Mr. Hubbell for? Did you think the article was unfair or mistaken?"

"No. Nothing like that."

"Is there any new development you think we ought to know about?"

"No. I wanted to talk to Mr. Hubbell about my father and my father's family. There was a lot about all that in the article."

"Yes. But Mr. Hubbell couldn't help you. That was done here; the material came from one of our researchers."

"I didn't know my father well," Wesley said. "I didn't see him from the time I was little until just a couple of years ago. I'd like to know more about him."

"I can understand that, Wesley," Altscheler said kindly.

"In the article you seemed to know a lot more than I ever did. I have a list of people who my father had something to do with at different times in his life and I put *Time* on the list, that's all."

"I understand," Altscheler rang for his secretary. She came in immediately. "Miss Prentice," he said, "will you find out who did the research on the Jordache article? If I remember correctly it was Miss Larkin; take the young man to her office. Tell her to do anything she can for Mr. Jordache." He stood up. "I'm afraid I have to go back to work now," he said. "Thank you for coming to see me, Wesley. And good luck."

"Thank you, sir." Wesley stood, too, and followed the secretary out of the office.

Altscheler went back to the window and stared out. Polite, sad boy. He wondered what he would have done if his father had been murdered and he himself had been sure he knew who had done it. They did not consider these questions at Yale, where he had earned his B.A.

The researcher had a little office without windows, lit by neon tubes. She was a small young woman with glasses, carelessly dressed, but pretty. She kept nodding and looking timidly at Wesley as Miss Prentice explained what he was there for. "Just wait a minute right here, Mr. Jordache," she said, "and I'll go into the files. You can read everything I dug up." She flushed a little as she heard herself using the phrase. "Dug up" was not the sort of thing to say when you were talking to a boy whose father had been murdered. She wondered if she ought to censor the files before she let the boy see them. She remembered very well working on the story—mostly because it was so different from anything she herself had experienced in her own life. She had never been on the Riviera, in fact had never been out of America, but she had been a hungry reader in the literature courses she had taken in college and the south of France was firmly fixed in her imagination as a place of romance and tragedy—Scott Fitzgerald driving to a party or from a party on the Grand Corniche, Dick Diver, desperate and gay on the blazing beaches, with all the trouble ahead of them all when everything collapsed. She had kept her notes, which she didn't usually do, out of a vague feeling of being connected to a literary geography that she would one day explore. She looked at the boy—who had been there, had suffered there, now standing in her office in his clumsy suit—and would have liked to question him, discover if he knew anything of all that. "Would you like a cup of coffee while you wait?" she asked.

"No, thank you, ma'am," he said.

"Would you like a copy of this week's magazine to look through?"

"I bought a copy downstairs, thank you."

"I'll just be a minute," she said brightly. Poor little boy, she thought as she went out of the office. So handsome, too. Even in the ridiculous suit. She was a romantic girl who had read a great deal of poetry, too. She could imagine him, dressed in flowing black, twin to the young Yeats in the early photographs.

When she came back with the file the boy was sitting hunched over on the straight chair, his arms resting on his thighs, his hands hanging between his knees, like a football player on the bench.

"Here's everything," she said brightly. She had debated with herself about whether or not to take out the photograph of Jean Jordache naked, but had decided against it. The picture had been in the magazine, after all, and he must have seen it.

"Now, you just take your time," she said. "I have some work to do." She gestured toward the pile of clippings on her desk. "But you won't bother me." She was pleased to have him in the office. It broke the routine.

Wesley looked down for a long time at the file without opening it, as Miss Larkin busied herself at her desk, using scissors and making notes, occasionally looking at the boy, until he caught her at it, which flustered her. Still, she thought, excusing herself, he'd better get used to girls looking at him. They're going to be doing it in droves.

The first thing she saw him take out of the files was a photograph of his father in boxing trunks, with his fists cocked. He looked fierce and young. To Wesley, he hardly looked older than he himself was now. Every muscle stood out in his arms and torso. He must have scared the wits out of the guys he was going to fight.

Miss Larkin had looked at the picture, too, when she took it out of the files. She thought the fighter looked like a handsome ruffian, somebody it would be wise to stay away from. She preferred men who looked like intellectuals. She studied the boy frankly now, since he was paying attention only to the photograph in his hand. He looked surprisingly like his father, but there was nothing ruffianly about him. He must be at least nineteen, she thought; maybe it would be nice to invite him downstairs for a drink. These days, she thought, nineteen can be very mature for a boy. She was only twenty-four herself; you couldn't call it an impossible gap.

The photograph had been cut out from *Ring* Magazine and there was a little article about Tom Jordan pasted to the bottom of the picture. "Tom Jordan, promising middleweight, undefeated in fourteen bouts, 8 k.o.'s, on his way to London to fight Sammy Wales, contender for British middleweight championship, at Albert Hall. Arthur Schultz, Jordan's manager, predicts that with another four or five matches under his belt, Tommy will be ready for anybody in his division."

Clipped to the photograph, there was another sheet of paper with typing on it. Wesley started reading again. "Won fight in London by knockout. Fought René Badaud three weeks later in Paris. Knocked out in seventh round. From then on, record spotty, slipped down in class. Hired as sparring partner Freddy Quayles, Las Vegas, Nevada (date). Quayles leading challenger middleweight title. Incident between Quayles and Jordan. L.V. stringer reports rumor fight in hotel room over Quayles' wife, later small-part actress Hollywood. Witness claims to have seen Quayles in hospital, badly battered. Quayles never regained form, quit ring, now works as salesman sporting goods store, Denver, Col. T. Jordan disappeared from Las Vegas, warrant out for his arrest, auto theft. Has not surfaced since."

And that was it. A whole life in a few lines, all summed up in four words—"Has not surfaced since." He surfaced all right in Antibes, Wesley thought bitterly. He took out his pen and a piece of paper and wrote, Arthur Schultz, Freddy Quayles.

Then he stared once more at the photograph of his father, the left hand out, the right hand up under the chin, the shoulders bunched, the fierce, confident young face, ready, according to authority, after four or five more matches, for anybody in his division. Not surfaced since.

Wesley looked up at Miss Larkin. "I don't think I'd recognize him if he came through the door right now looking like this." He laughed a little. "I'm glad he didn't believe in hitting kids, with those shoulders."

Miss Larkin saw that Wesley was proud of the hard body, the confident pugnacity of his father when he was just a bit older than the boy was now.

"If you want this picture," she said, "I'll put it in a big envelope for you so you won't crease it."

"You mean that?" Wesley said. "I can really have it?"

"Of course."

"That's really great," Wesley said, "having the picture, I mean. I don't have any picture of him. I had some, but they were all taken later. . . . He didn't look like this. He looked okay," he said hastily, as though he didn't want Miss Larkin to think that he was running his father down or that he had turned into a fat, bald, old man or anything like that. "He just looked different. The expression on his face, I guess. I don't suppose you can go through life always looking about twenty years old."

"No, you can't," Miss Larkin said. She searched for wrinkles around her eyes every morning.

Wesley dug in the file and brought out a biographical note that Miss Larkin had prepared on the members of the family.

Wesley went through the notes quickly. There was very little in them that he didn't already know, his uncle's early success and the scandal at the college, his aunt's two marriages, the outlines of his father's career. One line he read twice. "Rudolph Jordache, when he retired in his mid-thirties, was reputed to be a millionaire many times over." Many times over. How many times would his father have had to fight, how many seasons on the Mediterranean would he have had to serve even to be a millionaire just one time over?

He looked curiously at the pretty girl with glasses working at her desk. Just by accident she had been chosen to learn so much about his family. He wondered what she would say if he asked what she really thought about the Jordaches. In her notes she had written that Rudolph's was the standard American success story, poor boy makes good in a big way. Would she say of his father, poor boy makes bad in standard American way?

He made a funny little noise, almost a laugh. Miss Larkin looked over at him. "That's about all there is," she said. "I'm afraid it isn't very much."

"It's okay," Wesley said. "It's fine." He didn't want the nice young lady to think he wasn't grateful. He gave her back the file and stood up. "Thank you very much. I better be pushing along now."

Miss Larkin stood up, too. She looked at him strangely, as though she was making up her mind about something. "I'm just about finished here for the day," she said. "I was wondering if you'd like to go downstairs with me and have a drink?" She sounded as though she was appealing to him, but he couldn't tell for what. "I have a date later . . ." Even he could tell she was lying. "And I have an hour to kill . . ."

"They won't serve me a drink at the bar," Wesley said. "I'm not eighteen yet."

"Oh, I see." She flushed. "Well, thanks for the visit. If you ever come by again, now you know where my office is. If I can help in any way . . ."

"Yes, ma'am," he said.

She watched him go out of the office, the big shoulders bulging in the tight jacket. Not yet eighteen, she thought. Boy, am I dumb.

She sat staring at the papers on her desk for several minutes. She had a peculiar feeling that something strange was happening to her or was going to happen to her. She reread everything in the file. Murder, a rich brother, an intellectual sister, a brawling prizefighter done to death, the mystery unsolved. A beautiful son, still little more than a child, with strange, tragic eyes, looking for what—revenge?

The novel she was going to write was about a girl very much like herself, growing up in a broken family, lonely, imaginative, her crushes on teachers, her first love, her first disillusionment with men, her coming to New York from a small town. She thought of it now with disdain. Written a thousand times.

Why wasn't the boy's story a novel? After all, Dreiser had started *An American Tragedy* after reading an article in a newspaper. Nobody in Dreiser's family had been murdered, he hadn't *known* anybody who'd been murdered, but he'd written a great novel, just the same. Sitting in the same room with her just a few minutes ago was a handsome, complex boy, carrying the burden of remorse and sorrow on his shoulders almost visibly, nerving himself, she thought, shuddering deliciously, for the inevitable act. Hamlet as an American child. Why not? Revenge was among the oldest of literary traditions. Turn the other cheek, the Bible said, but also an eye for an eye. *Her* father, who was a rabid Irishman, cursed whenever he read what the English were still doing in Ireland, and there was a portrait of Parnell in the living room when she was a child.

Revenge was as much a part of all of us, she thought, as our bones and blood. We liked to pretend we were too civilized for it in the twentieth century, but the man in Vienna who spent his life tracking down Nazis who had killed Jews was honored all over the world. Her father said he was the last hero of World War Two.

She wished she had had the sense to ask the boy where he could be found. She would have to find him, study him, bring him to life on the page, with all his anger, his doubts, his youthfulness. It was cold-blooded, she told herself, but you either were a writer or you weren't. If he ever came into the office again, she would make sure that she'd find out all about him.

Feeling elated, as though she had come upon treasure, creative juices flowing, she carefully put all the papers back in the file and went out to where the master files were kept and put it back into place.

She could hardly wait to get back to her apartment and throw the sixty pages she had written on her novel into the fire.

CHAPTER 3

RUDOLPH WAS SITTING at the little upright piano, trying to pick out the melody of "On a Clear Day," when he heard the bell ring and Mrs. Burton came out of the kitchen to answer it. He saw her pass in the hall on the way to the front door. She had her hat and coat on. She only came in during the day as she had to go home each evening to feed her own family in Harlem. From the kitchen he heard the laughter of Enid, who was having her supper with her nurse there. Rudolph wasn't expecting anyone and he kept working on the melody. Getting the piano had turned out to be a good idea. He had originally bought it because the new nurse he had hired had a sweet voice and he had overheard her singing softly to Enid. She said she could play the piano a bit and he thought it would be useful for Enid to listen to someone actually making music in her own home. If it turned out that Enid had any talent it would be better for her than just hearing it from a box, as though Bach and Beethoven were as commonplace as an electric light, to be turned on or off by pushing a switch. But when the piano had been in the house for a few days he had found himself sitting down at it himself and fooling around with chords, then melodies. He had a good ear and he could pass hours amusing himself and not thinking of anything but the music at his fingertips. Whatever distracted him, even for a few minutes at a time, was so much profit. He had almost decided to take formal lessons.

He heard Mrs. Burton come into the living room. "There's a young man at the door, Mr. Jordache," Mrs. Burton said, "who says he's your nephew. Should I let him in?" Since Rudolph had moved to the two top floors of a brownstone, without a doorman, Mrs. Burton had been nervous about burglars and muggers and always kept the door chained. The neighbors, she complained, were careless about the front door and left it unlocked, so anyone could prowl the staircase.

Rudolph stood up. "I'll go see who it is," he said. In the letter from Brussels the week before from Billy, Billy hadn't said anything about coming to America. From the letters Billy had been writing him he seemed to have grown up into a nice, intelligent young man and on an impulse Rudolph had sent the thousand dollars Billy had asked for. Now he wondered if Billy had gotten into trouble with the army and deserted. That would explain the request for money. As for Wesley, there had been no word from him since Nice, and that was almost nine months ago.

Mrs. Burton followed him down the hallway. Outside the partially opened door, across the chain, Wesley was standing in the dim light of the ceiling bulb.

"It's all right, Mrs. Burton," Rudolph said. He slipped the chain free and opened the door. "Come in, Wesley." He put out his hand. After the slightest of pauses Wesley shook it.

"Will you be needing me any more tonight?" Mrs. Burton asked.

"No, thanks."

"Then I'll be moving along home. Have a nice weekend, Mr. Jordache."

"Thanks, Mrs. Burton." He closed the door behind her when she had left. Wesley merely stood there, his face thin, pale and expressionless, the ghost of his father as a boy, hostile and alert. He was in the same suit he had worn when he had left the jail in Grasse and it was smaller on him now than it had been then. He seemed to have grown and broadened considerably since their last meeting. His hair, Rudolph was happy to see, was not too long, but cropped at the neck.

"I'm glad to see you," Rudolph said as they went into the living room. "Can I get you something to drink?"

"A beer would be nice," Wesley said.

"Make yourself comfortable." Rudolph went into the kitchen where Enid was eating with the nurse. The nurse was a solid woman of about forty, with a marvelously gentle way of making Enid behave.

"Your Cousin Wesley is here, Enid," Rudolph said as he got a bottle of beer out of the refrigerator. He was about to tell her to come into the living room and say hello to Wesley after she had eaten, but thought better of it. He didn't know what Wesley had come for. If it was because of some emotional problem or dramatic adolescent disaster, it would only complicate matters to have Enid in the room. He kissed the top of her head and went into the living room with the beer and a glass. Wesley was standing awkwardly in the middle of the room just where Rudolph had left him. Rudolph poured the beer for him.

"Thank you," Wesley said. "Aren't you having anything to drink?"

"I'll have some wine with dinner. Sit down, sit down." Wesley waited for Rudolph and then sat in a chair facing him. He drank thirstily.

"Well," Rudolph said, "how're things? What brings you to New York?"

"I went to the wrong address," Wesley said. Rudolph noted that the boy didn't answer his question. "The doorman didn't want to tell me where you'd moved to. He wouldn't believe I was your nephew. I had to show him my library card." He sounded resentful, as though Rudolph had moved four blocks farther north just to avoid him.

"Didn't you get the letter I sent you?" Rudolph said. "I wrote you my new address the day I rented this apartment."

"I didn't get any letters." Wesley shook his head. "No, sir, no letters."

"Not even the one about how the estate would probably be finally settled and how much your share will be?"

"Nothing." Wesley drank again.

"What happens to your mail?" Rudolph tried to keep the irritation out of his voice.

"Maybe my mother doesn't approve of my getting mail. Anyway, that's my guess."

"Did you eat dinner yet?"

"No."

"I'll tell you over dinner what was in the letter I sent you."

"I didn't hitchhike all the way from Indianapolis to talk about money, Uncle Rudy," Wesley said softly. "It's a—well, I guess you might say it's a social visit."

"Does your mother know you're here?"

Wesley shook his head. "We're not on very good speaking terms, my mother and me."

"You didn't run away from home, did you?"

"No. It's the Easter vacation. I left a note saying I'd be back in time for school."

"That's a relief," Rudolph said dryly. "How're you doing in school?"

"Okay. I'm a hotshot in the French class." He grinned boyishly. "I teach my friends all the dirty words."

"They can come in handy," Rudolph said, smiling. "At times." Then more seriously, "Why did you have to hitchhike?"

"Money," Wesley said.

"Your mother gets quite a nice sum each month for your support for the time being," Rudolph said. "There's certainly enough for bus fare once a year to New York."

"Not a red cent," Wesley said. "I'm not complaining. I work after school. I get along."

"Do you?" Rudolph said skeptically. "Is that the only suit you have?"

"Like a whole suit—yeah. I got some sweaters and jeans and stuff like that for school and work. And there's an old mackinaw I wore in the winter that belongs to Mr. Kraler's son, he's a soldier, he's in Vietnam, so I don't freeze."

"I think I'll have to write your mother a letter," Rudolph said. "She's not allowed to use your money for herself."

"Don't make waves, please, Uncle Rudy," Wesley said carefully, putting his glass down on the floor beside him. "There's enough crap going on in that house without that. She says she'll give me every cent of the money she's supposed to if I go to church with her and Mr. Kraler, like a decent Christian."

"Oh," Rudolph said, "I'm beginning to get the picture."

"Some picture, eh?" Wesley grinned boyishly again. "The Spanish Inquisition in Indianapolis."

"I think I'll have a drink after all," Rudolph said. He got up and went over to the sideboard and mixed himself a martini. "You want another beer, Wesley?"

"That'd be nice." Wesley picked up the glass from the floor, stood up and handed it to Rudolph.

"Enid's in the kitchen. Would you like to say hello to her?" He saw Wesley hesitate. "Her mother's not in there with her. I wrote you we were divorced." He shook his head annoyedly. "I don't suppose you got that letter, either."

"Nope."

"Damn it. From now on I'll write you care of General Delivery. Didn't you ever think it was queer that nobody wrote you?"

"I guess I never thought much about it."

"Didn't you write Bunny or Kate?"

"Once or twice," Wesley said. "They didn't answer, so I gave up. Do you hear from them?"

"Of course," Rudolph said. Dwyer sent him a monthly report, with the bills from the *Clothilde*. Dwyer had had to be told that Rudolph had bought the ship. The court-ordered official appraisal of the value of the boat had been a hundred thousand—Dwyer had been correct about that—but no other buyers had offered anything near that price and Dwyer had taken the ship for the winter to Saint-Tropez, where it was berthed now. "They're fine. Kate's had a baby. A boy. You've got a brother. A half brother, anyway."

"Poor little bastard," Wesley said, but the news seemed to cheer him. The blood survives, Rudolph thought. "When you write to Kate," Wesley said, "tell her I'll drop in on her in England someday. Kids. That makes my old man the only one in the family with more than one kid. He told me one night that he'd like to have five. He was great with kids. A couple would come on board with the worst little spoiled brat you ever saw and in a week my old man'd have him saying sir to everybody, standing up when grown-ups came on board, hosing down the decks in port, minding his language—everything." He fiddled with his beer, uncomfortably. "I don't like to boast, Uncle Rudy, but look what he did for me. I may not be much, even now, but you should have seen me when he grabbed me out of school—I was spastic."

"Well, you're not spastic now."

"Anyway," Wesley said, "I don't *feel* spastic. That's something."

"It certainly is."

"Talking about kids—you think it would be all right if I went in and said hello to Enid?"

"Of course," Rudolph said, pleased.

"She still talk a blue streak?"

"Yes," Rudolph said as he led the way into the kitchen, "more than ever."

For once, Enid was shy when they entered the kitchen and Wesley said, "Hello, Enid, I'm your cousin, Wesley. Remember?"

Enid looked up at him soberly, then turned her head away. "It's late," the nurse said defensively. "She gets a little temperamental this time of day."

"I'll come around in the morning sometime," Wesley said. In the small kitchen, his deep, mature voice sounded brassy and harsh and Enid put her hands over her ears.

"Manners, miss," the nurse said.

"I guess I talk too loud," Wesley said apologetically, as he followed Rudolph out of the kitchen. "You get in the habit on a boat, with the wind and the noise of the water and all."

In the living room, Rudolph poured the martini out of the shaker into a glass and twisted a piece of lemon peel over the top of the drink. He raised his glass to Wesley, suddenly glad that the boy had come to see him, had asked to see Enid. Maybe, he thought, in some dim, distant future we will be something like a family again. He had little left, he thought, self-pityingly; a family was something to cling to. Even the letter he had received from Billy, with its rather timid, offhand request for money, had been cordial in tone. With no sons of his own, he knew that if the boys permitted it, he would be their friend, more than a friend. Lonely, no longer married, Jeanne an almost forgotten incident in the past, with his own child in the hands of a highly competent woman and still at an age at which he thought of her as no more than a kind of charming toy, he knew that once he began communicating with his nephews he would soon need them more than they would ever need him. He hoped that day would come—and soon.

"Whatever reason brought you to New York," he said, moved, as he raised his glass, "I'm very happy to see you."

Wesley raised his glass, too, self-consciously. "Thanks."

"No more fights in bars, I hope," Rudolph said.

"Don't worry," Wesley said soberly. "My fighting days're over. Though sometimes it's pretty tough to hold back. There're a lot of blacks in the school and the whites pick on them and they pick on the white boys. I guess I have the reputation of being chicken. But, what the hell, I can live with it. I learned my lesson. Anyway, I promised my father, the day he took me out of military school. I forgot only once. It wasn't what you would call a normal occasion." He stared down into his glass, grim, looking older than his years. "Just the once. Well, every dog is entitled to one bite, like they say. I guess I owe it to my father to keep my promise. It's the least I . . . " He stopped. His mouth tightened. Rudolph was afraid the boy was going to cry.

"I guess you do," he said quickly. "Where're you staying in New York?"

"The YMCA. Not too bad."

"Look," said Rudolph, "I'm taking Enid down to Montauk to her mother's tomorrow morning for a week, but I'll be coming back myself on Sunday. Why don't you ride down with me, get a breath of sea air . . . ?" He stopped as he saw Wesley eyeing him warily.

"Thanks," Wesley said. "That would be nice. But some other time. I have to be getting back to Indianapolis."

"You won't have to hitchhike. I'll give you the air fare back." When will I ever stop offering people money, he thought despairingly, instead of what they've really come for?

"I'd rather not," Wesley said. "Actually, I like to hitch rides. You get to talk to a lot of different kinds of people."

"Whatever you say," Rudolph said, rebuffed, but not blaming the boy for not wanting to run the risk of having to see Jean again, being reminded all over again. "Still," he said, "if you'd rather stay here for the night, I can fix you up on the sofa. . . . I don't have a guest room, but you'd be comfortable." Hospitality, family solidarity, not dollar bills.

"That's nice of you," Wesley said carefully, "but I'm fixed at the Y."

"The next time you come to New York let me know in advance. There're some nice hotels in the neighborhood and it would be convenient. We could take in a couple of shows, things like that. . . . " He stopped short. He didn't want the boy to think that he was attempting to bribe him.

"Sure," Wesley said unconvincingly. "Next time. This time, Uncle Rudy, I want to talk to you about my father." He stared soberly at Rudolph. "I didn't have the chance to know my father well enough. I was just a kid, maybe I'm still just a kid, but I want to know what he was like, what he was *worth*. . . . Do you understand what I mean?"

"I think so."

"I keep making up lists, names of people who knew my father at different times in his life—and you and Aunt Gretchen are first on that list. That's natural, isn't it?"

"I suppose so. Yes. That's natural." He was afraid of the questions he was going to be asked, the answers that he would be forced to give the tall, solemn, overgrown boy.

"When I got to know him—" Wesley went on, "just the short time we had together—I thought he was some kind of hero, a saint, almost, the way he treated me and Kate and Dwyer, how he got everybody to do what he wanted without ever even raising his voice, how, no matter what came up, he could handle it. But I know he wasn't always like that, I know my opinion of him was a kid's opinion. I've got to get a real fix on my father. For my own sake. Because that'll help me to get a fix on myself. On what kind of man I want to be, what I want to do with my life. . . . It sounds kind of mixed up, doesn't it . . . ?" He moved his bulky shoulders, as though he was irritated with himself.

"It's not so mixed up, Wesley," Rudolph said gently. "I'll tell you anything you want to know, anything I can remember. But first, I think, we ought to go out and have dinner." Postpone the past—the first rule of civilization.

"I could use a good meal," Wesley said, standing up. "I just ate junk food on the road. And the stuff I eat at home—" He made a face. "My mother is a health food nut. Fine for squirrels. Uncle Rudy," he smiled, "everybody keeps telling me how rich you are. Can you afford a steak?"

"I guess I'm rich enough for that," Rudolph said. "Anyway, a few times a year. Just wait here for me while I go up and say good night to the baby and get a jacket."

He was taking the jacket out of the closet when the phone rang. "Hello," he said, as he picked up the phone.

"Rudy . . . " It was Gretchen's voice. "What are you doing for dinner?" She was always most brusque and direct when she was slightly embarrassed. He hadn't spoken to her in weeks and it was a strange time for her to call, at a quarter past seven on a Friday evening.

"Well . . . " He hesitated. "I've had an unexpected visitor. Wesley. He hitchhiked in from Indianapolis. I'm taking him to dinner. Would you like to join us?"

"Is there anything special he wants to talk to you about?" She sounded disappointed.

"Not that I know of. Not anything he wouldn't want to say in front of you, as far as I know."

"I wouldn't like to interfere . . . "

"Don't be silly, Gretchen. Is there anything special *you* want to talk to me about?" The last time they had had a meal together she had seemed distracted and had let drop enough hints for him to guess that she was having trouble with the Hollywood director with whom she was working and having an on-again, off-again affair. What was his name? Kinsella. Evans Kinsella. Arrogant Hollywood sonofabitch. Gretchen had had luck once in her life with a man and that man had run a car into a tree. Rudolph supposed that Kinsella had something to do with her call, but she could bring that up if she wished after he had packed Wesley off to the YMCA.

"I just called," Gretchen said, "because I'm at something of a loose end for the evening. My boyfriend stood me up. For a change." She laughed mirthlessly. "So I thought about family. Weekends are a good time for loose ends and family." But she still didn't say whether she would come to dinner. Instead she said, "How's Wesley?"

"Getting along," Rudolph said. "Bigger than ever. As serious as ever. More so."

"In trouble?" she asked.

"No more than you and I," he said lightly.

"Do you think he'd object to seeing me?"

"Absolutely not. In fact he said we were at the top of the list of people he wanted to see."

"What did he mean by that?" She sounded worried.

"I'll fill you in after dinner. He wants a steak." He told her the name of the restaurant.

He hung up and put on his jacket and went downstairs. Wesley was standing in the middle of the living room staring about him. "You know something," Wesley said and grinned as he said it. "This is my idea of a real Christian home."

As they went down Third Avenue toward the restaurant, Rudolph noted how much like his brother Tom Wesley walked—the same almost-slouch, with a warning swinging of the shoulders. When he and Tom were young, Rudolph had thought it was a conscious pose, an advertisement that here was a predatory and dangerous male on the loose, to be avoided. Later as a grown man, Rudolph saw his brother's manner of walking as a way of avoiding pain, a signal that he wanted the world to leave him alone.

Rudolph's own gliding, slow walk, with shoulders stiff, was a manufactured gait, which he had developed as a youth because he thought it was gentlemanly, Ivy League. He no longer cared about seeming gentlemanly and he had met enough Ivy Leaguers in business not to be anxious to be taken as one of them. But his way of walking was now a part of him. To change it now would be an affectation.

When he had told Wesley that Gretchen was dining with them, Wesley's face had brightened and he'd said, "That's great. She's swell, a real lady. What a difference between her and some of the dames we had to put up with on the boat." He wagged his head humorously. "Money coming out of their ears, their tits showing day and night, and treating everybody like dirt." The two beers had loosened his vocabulary. "You know, I sometimes wonder how it happens some women who never lifted a finger in their lives can act like they own the whole goddamn world."

"They practice in front of a mirror," Rudolph said.

"Practice in front of a mirror." Wesley laughed. "I got to remember that. Aunt Gretchen works, doesn't she?"

"Very hard," Rudolph said.

"I guess that's what does it. If you don't work, you're just shit. You don't mind the way I talk, do you?" he asked anxiously.

"Not at all."

"My father was kind of free talking," Wesley said. "He said he didn't like people who talked as though they had an anchor up their ass. He said there was a difference between talking dirty and talking ugly."

"Your father had a point there." Rudolph, who had never gotten over his boyhood aversion to swearing and carefully censored his speech at all times, suddenly wondered if his brother had included him among the people who spoke as though they had an anchor up their ass.

"You know," Wesley went on, "Bunny thought your sister was something special, too. He told me *you* should have married somebody like her."

"That would have been a little awkward," Rudolph said, "seeing that we were sister and brother and I wasn't the pharaoh of Egypt."

"What's that?" Wesley said.

"I'm sorry," Rudolph said. His embarrassment—jealousy?—at Wesley's open admiration for his sister had made him pedantic in self-defense. "It was the custom in ancient Egypt in the families of the pharaohs."

"I get it," Wesley said. "I guess I'm not what you might call well educated."

"You're young yet."

"Yeah," Wesley said, brooding over his youth.

The boy had good stuff in him, Rudolph was sure, and it was criminal that by law the Kralers were given the right to warp or destroy it. He was going to see Johnny Heath in the morning when Johnny and his wife came to drive down to Montauk with him and Enid. He'd ask Johnny once more if there weren't some legal way to get the boy out of his mother's clutches.

"What about education?" Rudolph said. "Are you going on to college?"

The boy shrugged. "My mother says it'd be a waste of money on me. I read a lot, but not what they tell me to read in school. I've been studying up some on the Mormons. I guess I wanted to find out if Mr. Kraler and my mother were like they are because they're Mormons or because they're my mother and Mr. Kraler." He grinned. "The way I figure it now, they started out as awful people, and their religion brought out the worst in them. But," he said seriously, "it's a queer religion. They sure were brave, the Mormons, fighting off the whole United States and all, and going in wagons halfway across America and settling in the desert and making it bloom, the way they say. But all those wives! I look at my mother and I swear, it makes you wonder why anybody would ever want to get married. You listen for ten minutes to my mother and one wife is one wife too many. Marriage in general . . . " He scowled. "Our family, for instance. You got divorced, Aunt Gretchen got divorced, my father got divorced . . . What's it all about? I ask myself."

"You're not the first man to ask himself that question," Rudolph said. "Maybe it's the times we live in. We're adjusting to new stances in each other, as the sociologists would put it, and perhaps we're not ready for it."

"There's a girl in school," Wesley said, scowling again, "pretty as a ripe red apple and older than me. I . . . well . . . I fooled around with her in the back of a car, in her own house, when her parents were out—a couple of times—and she started talking about marriage. I couldn't get her off the subject. I just stopped seeing her. You going to get married again?" He peered fiercely at Rudolph, suspecting wedding bells.

"It's hard to say," Rudolph said. "At the moment I have no plans."

"Religion is a funny thing," Wesley said abruptly, as though the exchange about marriage had embarrassed him and he wanted to get away from it as quickly as possible. "I want to believe in God," Wesley said earnestly. "After all, there *had* to be something that started the whole shebang going, wasn't there? I mean how we got here, what we're doing here, how everything works, like how we have air to breathe, water to drink, food to eat. I read the whole Bible through the last few months. There're no answers there, I tell you—at least not for me."

Oh, dear nephew, Rudolph wanted to say, when your uncle was sixteen he was there before you. And found no answers.

"What are you supposed to believe?" Wesley asked. "Do you believe in those copper plates the Mormons say Joseph Smith found in upstate New York and never showed to anybody? How do they expect people to believe stuff like that?"

"Well, Moses came down off Mount Sinai with the Ten Commandments carved in stone by God," Rudolph said, relieved that Wesley had not asked him about his own beclouded lack of religion. "A lot of people have believed *that* story for thousands of years."

"Do you? I mean do *you* believe it?"

"No."

"In school, too, they tell you a lot of things that just want to make you laugh out loud. They spend hours trying to tell you that black and white are the same thing and all you have to do is go out the door and walk one block and you see it just ain't so. It was different in France. Or maybe *I* was different in France. I was doing fine in France, even with the language problem—but in Indianapolis . . . " He shrugged. "Most of the teachers seem full of shit to me. They spend most of the time trying to keep the kids from yelling in classroom and throwing spitballs, if they're not knifing each other. If college is anything like that, I'd say, Fuck it." He looked inquiringly at Rudolph. "What's your opinion about college? I mean, for me?"

"It's all according to what you want to do with your life," Rudolph said carefully. He was touched by the boy's naive garrulousness, his trust that his uncle would not betray him to the adult world.

"Who the hell knows?" Wesley said. "I have some notions. I'm not ready to tell anybody about them yet." His tone was suddenly cold.

"For example," Rudolph said, ignoring the change in Wesley's attitude, "you know something about the sea. You like it, don't you?"

"I did," Wesley said bitterly.

"You might want to go into the merchant marine."

"It's a dog's life, Bunny says."

"Not necessarily. It wasn't a dog's life for Bunny on the *Clothilde*, was it?"

"No."

"It isn't a dog's life if you're an officer on a decent ship, if you get to be a captain . . . "

"I guess not."

"There's a merchant marine academy right here in New York. When you get out of it you're an officer right off."

"Ah," Wesley said reflectively. "Maybe I ought to look into that."

"I'll ask around," Rudolph said, "and write you what I find out. Just remember to ask for your mail at General Delivery."

While they were waiting for Gretchen to arrive before ordering, Rudolph had a martini. It was as good a time as any to explain about the estate. "All told," Rudolph said, "after taxes and expenses for lawyers there should be a little over a hundred thousand dollars to be divided." He didn't intend to let either Wesley or Kate ever know that it was the amount he had paid for the *Clothilde* so that the estate could be liquidated. "One-third to Kate," he went on, "one-third in trust for her child, with Kate as the executrix—" He didn't tell the boy about the endless hours spent in legal wrangling to reach *that* compromise. The Kralers had fought tenaciously to have Teresa, as Wesley's mother, appointed as the administrator of the whole estate. They had some legal backing for their claim, as Kate was not an American citizen and was domiciled in England. Heath had had to threaten to bring up Teresa's two convictions as a prostitute and start proceedings to have her declared unfit on moral grounds to be Wesley's guardian, even though she was the boy's natural mother. Rudolph knew that for Wesley's sake he would never have allowed Johnny to go through with the action, but the threat had worked and the Kralers had finally given in and allowed Rudolph to be appointed administrator of the estate, which meant that he had to answer a long list of vengeful questions each month about the disposition of every penny that went through his hands. In addition, they were constantly threatening to sue him for faulty or criminal behavior in protecting Wesley's interest. What evil angel, Rudolph thought again and again, had touched his brother Tom's shoulder the day he asked the woman to marry him?

"That leaves approximately one-third to . . . " He stopped. "Wesley, are you listening?"

"Sure," the boy said. A waiter had gone by with a huge porterhouse steak crackling on a platter and Wesley had followed its passage across the room hungrily with his eyes. Whatever you could say about him, Rudolph thought, you could never fault him for being spoiled about money.

"As I was saying," Rudolph continued, "there's about thirty-three thousand dollars that will be put in a trust fund for you. That should bring in roughly about nineteen hundred dollars a year, which your mother is supposed to use for your support. At the age of eighteen you get the whole thing to use as you see fit. I advise you leave it in the trust fund. The income won't be very much but it could help you pay for college if that's what you want. Are you following me, Wesley?"

Again he had lost the boy's attention. Wesley was gazing with open admiration at a flashy blond lady in a mink coat who had come in with two paunchy men with gray hair and white ties. The restaurant, Rudolph knew, was a favorite of the more successful members of the Mafia and the girls who came in on their arms made for stern competition with the food.

"Wesley," Rudolph said plaintively. "I'm talking about money."

"I know," Wesley said apologetically. "But, holy man, that is something, isn't it?"

"It comes with money, Wesley," Rudolph said. As an uncle he felt he had to instill a true sense of value in the boy. "Nineteen hundred dollars a year may not mean much to you," he said, "but when I was your age . . . " Now he knew he would sound pompous if he finished the sentence. "The hell with it. I'll write it all down in my letter."

Just then he saw Gretchen come in and he waved to her. Both of the men stood up as she approached the table. She kissed Rudolph on the cheek, then threw her arms around Wesley and kissed him, hard. "Oh, I'm so glad to see you," she said. Her voice, to Rudolph's surprise, was trembling. He felt a twinge of pity for her as he watched the two of them, Gretchen staring hard into the boy's face, fighting with an emotion he could not identify. Perhaps she was thinking of her own son, lost to her, rejecting her, making excuses to her as to why she should not come to Brussels whenever she wrote him that she would like to visit him. "You look wonderful," Gretchen said, still holding onto the boy. "Although you could use a new suit."

They both laughed.

"If you'll stay over until Monday," Gretchen said, finally releasing Wesley and sitting down, "I'll take you to Saks and see if they have anything there to fit you."

"I'm sorry," Wesley said as he and Rudolph seated themselves. "I've got to be on my way tomorrow."

"You just came here for one day?" Gretchen said incredulously.

"He's a busy man," Rudolph said. He didn't want to listen to Gretchen's predictable explosion of wrath if she heard about Mr. and Mrs. Kraler's Christian concept of money for the young. "Now, let's order. I'm starved."

Over the meal, Wesley began to ask the questions about his father. "I told Uncle Rudy, back in his house," Wesley said as he wolfed down his steak, "why I want to know—why I *have* to know, what my old man was like. Really like, I mean. He told me a lot before he died, and Bunny told me even more—but so far it hasn't added up. I mean, my father's just bits and pieces for me. There's all those stories about what a terror he was as a kid and as a young man, how much trouble he got into . . . how people hated him. How he hated people. You and Uncle Rudy, too. . . ." He looked gravely first at Gretchen and then at Rudolph. "But then when I saw him with you, he didn't hate you. He—well—I suppose I got to say it—he loved you. He was unhappy most of his life, he told me—and then—well, he said it himself—he learned to lose enemies—to be happy. Well, I want to learn to be happy, myself." Now the boy was frankly crying, while at the same time eating large chunks of the rare steak, as though he hadn't eaten in weeks.

"The crux of the matter," Gretchen said, putting down her knife and fork and speaking slowly, "is Rudy. Do you mind if I say that, Rudy?"

"Say whatever you want. If I think you're wrong, I'll correct you." Some other time he might tell the boy how and when his father had learned to be happy. The day he found out that Rudolph, unknown to him, had invested the five thousand dollars Tom had laid his hands on by blackmailing a kleptomaniac lawyer in Boston. The return of the blood money, Tom had called it, the same amount their father had to pay to get Tom out of the jail where he was facing a charge of rape. Tom had thrown the hundred-dollar bills on the hotel bed, saying, "I want to pay off our fucking family and this does it. Piss on it. Blow it on dames. Give it to your favorite charity. I'm not walking out of this room with it." Five thousand dollars which by careful babying along had grown to sixty thousand through the years when Rudolph hadn't known where Tom was, whether he was alive or dead, and which had finally enabled Tom to buy a ship and rename it the *Clothilde*. "Your father," he might say at that future date, "became happy through crime, luck and money, and was smart enough to use all three things for the one act that could save him." He didn't believe that saying it would help Wesley much. Wesley did not seem inclined to crime, his luck so far had been all bad and his devotion to money nonexistent.

"Rudy," Gretchen was saying, "was the white-haired boy of the family. If there was any love my parents had to spare, it was for him. I'm not saying he didn't deserve it—he was the one who helped out in the store, he was the one who got the highest marks in school, he was the one who was the star of the track team, he was the one who was expected to go to college. He was the one who got presents, birthday celebrations, he was the only one who had a freshly ironed shirt to go out in, an expensive trumpet, so he could play in a band. All the hope in the family was invested in him. As for me and Tom . . . " She shrugged. "We were outcasts. No college for me—when I finished high school I was sent out to work and had to pay almost all of my salary into the family kitty. When Rudolph went out with a girl, my mother would make sure he had pocket money to entertain her. When I had an affair, she called me a whore. As for Tom—I've heard our parents predict a hundred times that he'd wind up in jail. When they talked to him, which was as little as possible, they snarled at him. I think he said to himself, Well, if that's the way you think I am, that's what I'm going to be. Frankly, I was terrified of him. He had a streak of violence in him that was frightening. I avoided him. When I was walking down the street with any of my friends I'd pretend I didn't see him, so I wouldn't have to introduce him. When he left town and dropped out of sight, I was glad. For years I didn't even think about him. Now I realize I was wrong. At least we two should have made some sort of combination, a common front against the rest of the family. I was too young then to realize it, but I was afraid he'd drag me down to his level. I was a snob, although never as much a snob as Rudy, and I thought of Tom as a dangerous peasant. When I went to New York and for a while became an actress, then started writing for magazines, I cringed in fear that he'd look me up and make me lose all my friends. When I finally did see him—Rudy took me to see him fight once—I was horrified, both by him and your mother. They seemed to come from another world. An awful world. I snubbed them and fled. I was ashamed that I was connected to them in any way. All this may be too painful for you, Wesley . . . "

Wesley nodded. "It's painful," he said, "but I asked you. I don't want any fairy tales."

Gretchen turned to Rudolph. "I hope I haven't been too rough on you, Rudy, with my little history of the happy childhood we spent together."

"No," Rudolph said. "'Beauty is truth, truth beauty'—you know the rest. I was a prig, Wesley," he said, tearing at old scars, "and I imagine you guessed that. In fact, I wouldn't hold it against you if you thought so now. I don't suppose your father would have used that word. What he would have said, if he had thought it out, was that everything I did was fake—not for myself, but for its effects on other people, mostly older people, people in authority. The way I look back on it now, I used the word prig. But back then the way I acted was an escape hatch from the world my mother and father were caught in." He laughed ruefully. "The injustice of it is in that it worked. I *did* escape."

"You ride yourself too hard, Uncle Rudy," Wesley said quietly. "Why don't you give yourself a break once in a while? My father said that you saved his life."

"Did he?" Rudolph said, surprised. "He never told me that."

"He didn't hold with praising people to their face," Wesley said. "He didn't praise me much, I can tell you that. . . . " He grinned. He had even white teeth and a sweet smile that changed the entire look of his sharp brooding face, made it seem boyish and open. Rudolph wished he would smile more. "And he didn't go overboard praising Bunny or even Kate, except for her cooking, and that was more of a joke than anything else, because she was English. Even when I first got to know him, when he was off by himself and didn't think anybody was watching him, there was something sad about him, as though there were a lot of bad things that had happened to him that he couldn't forget. But he did say you saved his life."

"I only gave him some money that was coming to him," Rudolph said. "I guess you realize by now that Gretchen was trying to show you how and why your father became what he was as a young man. . . . That the family made him that way."

"Yeah," Wesley said, "I see that."

"It's true," Rudolph said, "and again, it's not true. There are some excuses, as there always are. It's not my fault that I was the oldest son, that my father was an ignorant and violent man with a hideous past that had been no fault of his own. It wasn't my fault that my mother was a frigid, hysterical woman with idiotically genteel pretensions. It wasn't my fault that Gretchen was a sentimental and selfish little fool. . . . Forgive me," he said to Gretchen. "I'm not going through all this for your sake or mine. It's for Wesley."

"I understand," Gretchen said, bent over her food, half hiding her face.

"After all," Rudolph said, "the three of us had the same genes, the same influences. Maybe that's why Gretchen said just now that your father was frightening. What she was afraid of was that what she saw in him she saw in herself, and recoiled from it. What I saw in him was a reflection of our father, a ferocious man chained to an impossible job, pathologically afraid of ending his life a pauper—so much so that he finally committed suicide rather than face up to the prospect. I recoiled in my own way. Toward money, respectability . . . "

Wesley nodded soberly. "Maybe it's lucky Kraler's kid is in Vietnam. Who knows what he'd do for me if I had to eat dinner every night with him?"

"There have been second sons before your father," Rudolph said, "in worse families, and they didn't go around trying to destroy everything they touched. I don't like to say this, Wesley, but until the day of our mother's funeral, I believed that your father was born with an *affinity* for destruction, an affinity that gave him great pleasure. Destruction of all kinds. Including self-destruction."

"It sure turned out that way," Wesley said bitterly, "didn't it?"

"What he did that night in Cannes," Rudolph said, "was admirable. By his lights. And to tell the truth, by my lights, too. You mustn't forget that."

"I'll try not to forget it," Wesley said. "But it's not easy. Waste, that's what I think it really was. Crazy *macho* waste."

Rudolph sighed. "I think we've told you everything we could for now, as honestly as we could. We'll save the anecdotes for another time. You must be tired. I'll send you a list of names of people you might want to talk to who'll perhaps be more helpful than we've been. Finish your dinner and then I'll ride you over to the YMCA."

"No need," Wesley said shortly. "I can walk through the park."

"Nobody walks through the park in New York at night alone," Gretchen said.

Wesley stared at her coldly. "*I* do," he said.

Christ, Rudolph thought, as he watched the boy finish the last bit of his steak, he looks and sounds just like his father. God help him.

CHAPTER 4

RUDOLPH STOOD ON the sidewalk in the morning sunlight with Enid and her nurse, waiting for Johnny Heath and his wife to come by in their Lincoln Continental and pick Enid and himself up for the trip to Montauk. The nurse had a suitcase with her. She was off for her family in New Jersey for the week. Somehow, Rudolph thought idly, children's nurses never seemed to have families who lived in the same state in which they worked. Enid was carrying some schoolbooks and her homework to do over the holiday. The nurse had packed a bag for her. He had a small overnight bag with his shaving kit, pajamas and a clean shirt.

The night before, after they had said good-bye to Wesley, Rudolph had walked Gretchen to her apartment. He had invited her to come with him and the Heaths to Montauk. She had looked at him strangely and he remembered that she had once had an affair with Heath. "You want a lot of witnesses present when you see your ex-wife, don't you?" she had said.

He hadn't really thought about this, but as she said it, he recognized the truth of what she had said. Jean had visited him once, with the burly masseuse she had hired as her companion in Reno, and the meeting had been an uncomfortable one, although Jean had been sober, reasonable, subdued, even when she had played with Enid. She was leading the quiet life, she said, in a small house she had bought for herself at Montauk. Mexico had not worked out. It was a drinking man's climate, she had

decided, too raw for her nerves. She was completely dried out, she had said, with a
tiny smile, and had even begun to take photographs again. She hadn't tried to place
them in any magazines. She was just doing it for herself, proud of the fact that her
hands were steady again. Once more, except for the heavy presence of the masseuse,
she was so much the woman he had married and loved for so long—shining of hair,
her delicate, pink-tinted complexion healthy and youthful—that he started wondering
uncomfortably all over again if he had done the right thing in consenting to the
divorce. Pity was mixed in his feeling, but pity for himself, too. When she had called
a few days ago to ask if she could have Enid for a week, he could not say no.

He had no fears for Enid, but feared for himself, if he and Jean had to spend any
time alone in what she described as a cosy small house filled with the sound of an
uncosy large ocean. She had invited him to stay in the guest room, but he had made a
reservation at a nearby motel. As an afterthought, he had invited the Heaths. He
didn't want to be tempted by an evening in front of a blazing fire in a silent house,
lulled by the sound of the sea, to go back to domesticity. Let the past belong to the
past. Hence the Heaths. Hence Gretchen's sharp question.

"I don't need any witnesses," he said. "Johnny and I have a lot of things to talk
about and I hate to have to go to his office."

"I see," Gretchen had said, unconvincingly, and had changed the subject. "What's
your opinion about the boy, Wesley?"

"He's a thoughtful young man," Rudolph said. "Maybe too—well—interior. How
he turns out all depends on if he can survive his mother and her husband until he's
eighteen."

"He's a beautiful young man," Gretchen said. "Don't you think so?"

"I hadn't thought about it."

"It's a marvelous face for the movies," Gretchen said. "The tough bones, the sweet
smile, the moral weight, to be fancy about it, the tenderness in the eyes."

"Maybe you're more perceptive than I am," was all that Rudolph had answered.

"Or more vulnerable." She smiled.

"You sounded on the phone as though there was something you wanted to talk to
me about," he said. "Are you in trouble?"

"No more than usual." She smiled again. "I'll tell you about it when you get back to
town."

He had kissed her good night in front of her apartment house and watched her go
into the lighted lobby, guarded by a doorman. She looked trim, capable, desirable,
able to take care of herself. Occasionally, he thought. Only occasionally.

The Lincoln Continental drove up, Johnny Heath at the wheel, his wife Elaine
beside him. The nurse kissed Enid good-bye. "You're going to be a good little girl,
aren't you, miss?" the nurse said.

"No," said Enid, "I'm going to be a horrid little girl." She chortled.

Rudolph laughed and the nurse looked at him reprovingly. "Sorry, Anna," he said,
straightening his face.

Elaine Heath got out of the front of the car and helped establish Enid in the rear with
her. She was a tall, exquisitely groomed woman, with hard, intelligent eyes, fitting
wife to a man who was a partner in one of the most successful firms on Wall Street.
The Heaths had no children.

He got in beside Johnny. Enid waved at the nurse standing with her bag on the
sidewalk and they drove off. "Hi, ho," Johnny said, at the wheel, "on to the orgies of
Montauk, to the lobsters and the nude clambakes on the white beaches." His face was
soft and round, his eyes deceptively mild, his hands on the wheel pale, with only the
smallest suggestion of fat, his paunch just a tiny hint of things to come under his
checked sports jacket. He drove aggressively and well. Other drivers were forced to
respect Johnny Heath's right of way, as other lawyers had to respect his tenacity and
purpose in a boardroom or before the bench. Rudolph did not see Johnny often; after

the Heaths' marriage they had drifted apart somewhat, and each time Rudolph saw his old friend after a lapse of months, he thought, with no regret, I might have looked like that, too.

Behind him he heard the child prattling happily. He heard Elaine whispering into her ear, making Enid laugh. To look at her, one would think that Elaine would dread embracing a child, fear that her handsome tweed suit would be wrinkled or dirtied. When Rudolph turned around he saw that Enid was mussing Elaine's perfectly set hair and that Elaine was smiling happily. You never could tell about anybody, Rudolph thought as he turned back and watched the road. They were crossing the Triborough Bridge and New York stretched alongside the river, towers, glass, smoke, the old, enormous, impossible engine glittering in the morning springtime sun. Only at certain moments, moments like this one, when he saw the city as a great, challenging entity, its harsh, imperial beauty falling into a cohesive pattern, did he feel any of the thrill, the satisfaction of belonging, that had moved him daily when he was younger.

Down below, on the swiftly moving river, a small yacht chugged bravely against the current. Perhaps, he thought, this summer I will board the *Clothilde* and set sail for Italy. Might as well get some use out of the boat. They had been on course once for Portofino but had never reached it. Dispel ghosts. Get Jeanne somehow to escape her husband and children for two weeks and make love at twelve knots and in a softer climate, drink cold local wine out of a carafe at cafés along the Ligurian shore. I must not allow myself just to become a used-up old man. *Fantasia Italiana.*

He shook himself out of his reverie. "Johnny," he said, "you told me over the phone that you wanted to talk to me. What about?"

"I have a client," Johnny said; "actually it's a dead client, whose estate has to be settled." Johnny, Rudolph thought maliciously, makes more money out of the dead than a cityful of undertakers. Lawyers. "The heirs are squabbling," Johnny said, "as heirs will. You know all about that."

"It has become my specialty," Rudolph said.

"To avoid litigation," Johnny went on, "there's a part of the estate that's up for sale at a very decent, low price. It's a big ranch out in Nevada. The usual income tax benefits. I don't have to tell you about *that.*"

"No," Rudolph said.

"You're not doing anything in New York," Johnny said. "You don't look good, you certainly don't seem happy. I don't know what the hell you do with yourself day after day."

"I play the piano," Rudolph said.

"I haven't seen your name recently on the posters outside Carnegie Hall."

"Keep looking," Rudolph said.

"You're just sinking into decay here," Johnny said. "You're not in action anymore. Christ, nobody even sees you at any of the parties these days."

"How're the parties in Nevada?"

"Jamborees," Johnny said defensively. "It's one of the fastest-growing states in the union. People're becoming millionaires by the dozen. Just to show you I'm not kidding, if you say yes, I'll go in half with you—arrange the mortgages, help you find people to run it. I'm not just being altruistic, old buddy, I could use a place to hide from time to time myself. And I could also use a little tax shelter in the golden West. I haven't seen the place myself, but I've seen the books. It's viable. With some smart additional investment, a lot more than viable. There's a great big house there that with a little fixing up would be a dream. And there's no better place to bring up kids—no pollution, no drugs, a hundred miles away from the nearest city. And politics are nicely controlled there; it's a sweet, tight operation—you could move into it like a fish in water. And they never heard of Whitby, New York. Anyway, that's all forgotten by now, even in Whitby, even with that goddamn article in *Time.* In ten years you could wind up being senator. Are you listening to me, Rudy?"

"Of course." Actually, he hadn't been listening too closely for the last few seconds. What Johnny had said about its being a place to bring up kids had intrigued him. He had Enid to think of, of course, but there were also Wesley and Billy. Flesh and blood. He worried for them. Billy was a drifter—even as a boy in school he had been cynical, without ambition, a sardonic dropout from society. Wesley, as far as Rudolph could tell, had no particular talents, and whatever education he might receive was unlikely to improve his chances for an honorable life. On a modern ranch, with its eternal problems of drought, flood and fertility and the newer necessity for shrewd handling of machinery, employees, the marketplace, there would be plenty of work for the two of them to keep them out of trouble. And eventually they'd have families of their own. And there was always the possibility that he'd marry again—why not?—and have more children. "The dream of the patriarch," he said aloud.

"What was that?" Johnny asked, puzzled.

"Nothing, I was talking to myelf. Seeing myself surrounded by my flocks and my progeny."

"It isn't as though you'd be stuck in the wilderness," Johnny said, mistaking the intention of what Rudolph had said, believing it to be ironic. "There's a landing strip on the property. You could have your own plane."

"The American dream," Rudolph said. "A landing strip on the property."

"Well, what's wrong with the American dream?" Johnny demanded. "Mobility isn't a venal sin. You could be in Reno or San Francisco in an hour whenever you wanted. What do you think? It's not like retiring, though it has a lot of its advantages. It's getting into action again—a new kind of action. . . ."

"I'll think about it," Rudolph said.

"Why don't you plan—why don't we *both* plan—to fly out there next week and take a look?" Johnny said. "That can't do any harm, can it? And it'd give me a good excuse to get away from the damned office. Hell, even if it turned out to be worthless, it'd be a vacation. You can bring your piano along."

Heavy irony, Rudolph thought. He knew that Johnny considered his having retired a kind of whimsical aberration, a vastly premature symptom of the male menopause. When Johnny retired it would be to the cemetery. They had come up together, they had made a great deal of money together, they had never cheated each other, they understood each other, and Rudolph knew that Johnny felt that as an act and seal of their friendship he had to get Rudolph moving again.

"Well," Rudolph said, "I've always dreamed of riding across the desert on a horse."

"It's not desert," Johnny said testily. "It's ranchland. And it's at the foot of the mountains. There's a trout stream on the property."

"I can take a couple of days off this week," Rudolph said, "while Enid's with Jean. Can you get away?"

"I'll buy the tickets," Johnny said.

While they drove swiftly past the endless graveyards of Long Island, where the generations of New Yorkers have hidden their dead, Rudolph closed his eyes and dreamed of the mesas and mountains of the silver state of Nevada.

Usually, Gretchen liked to work on Saturdays, just she and her assistant, Ida Cohen, alone in the cutting room in the deserted, silent building. But today Ida could tell Gretchen wasn't enjoying herself at all as she shuttled the moviola back and forth, running the film irritably through her white-gloved hands, pushing the slicing lever down with sharp little snaps and whistling mournfully, when she wasn't sighing in despair. Ida knew why Gretchen was in a bad mood this morning. The director, Evans Kinsella, was up to his old tricks, shooting lazily, incoherently, fighting a hangover, letting the actors get away with murder, trusting that somehow Gretchen would make sense out of the wasteful miles of film he was throwing at her. And Ida had been in the room the day before when Kinsella had phoned to say that he couldn't take Gretchen to dinner as he had promised.

By now, Ida, whose loyalty to the woman she worked with was absolute, loathed Kinsella with an intensity of feeling that she otherwise reserved for the cause of Women's Liberation, a movement whose meetings she attended religiously and at which she made passionate and somewhat demented speeches. Fat and short, she had even gone so far as to renounce wearing a brassiere, until Gretchen had scowled at her and said, "Christ, Ida, with udders like yours, you're putting the movement back a century."

Ida, forty-five years old and plain, with no man in her private life to bully her, believed that Gretchen, beautiful and talented, allowed herself to be taken advantage of by men. She had persuaded Gretchen to accompany her to two of the meetings, but Gretchen had been bored and annoyed by the shrillness of some of the orators and had left early, saying, "When you go to the barricades you can count on me. Not before."

"But we need women just like you," Ida had pleaded.

"Maybe," Gretchen had said, "but I don't need *them*."

Ida had sighed hopelessly at what she told Gretchen was sinful political abdication.

Gretchen had more to bother her that morning than the quality of the film she was working on. During the week, Kinsella had tossed a screenplay at her and asked her to read it. It was by a young writer, unknown to either of them, but whose agent had been insistent that Kinsella look at it.

Gretchen had read it and thought it was brilliant, and when Kinsella had called the afternoon before to break their date for dinner had told him so. "Brilliant?" he had said over the phone. "I think it's a load of shit. Give it to my secretary and tell her to send it back." He had hung up before she could argue with him. Instead, she had stayed up until two in the morning re-reading it. Although it was written by a young man, the central role was that of a strong-minded, young, working-class woman, sunk in the drabness and hopelessness of the people around her, a girl who, of all her generation in the small, dreary town in which she lived, had the wit and courage to break out, live up to her dream of herself.

It could be a bracing corrective, Gretchen believed, to the recent spate of films which, overcorrecting for the happy-ending fairy tales that Hollywood had been sending out for so long, now had all their characters aimlessly drifting, reacting with a poor little flicker of revolt against their fates, and then sinking hopelessly back into apathy, leaving the viewer with a taste of mud in his mouth. If the old Hollywood pictures, with their manufactured sugar-candy optimism were false, Gretchen thought, these new listless dirges were equally false. Heroes emerged daily. If it was true that they did not rise with their class, it wasn't true that they all *sank* with their class.

When she had finished reading, she was more convinced than ever that her first impression had been correct and that if Kinsella could be pulled up again to the level of his earlier work, he would finish with a dazzling movie. She had even called his hotel at two-thirty in the morning to tell him so, but his phone hadn't answered. All this was going through her mind, like a looped piece of film in which the action of a scene is repeated over and over again, as she worked on the shoddy results of Kinsella's last week of shooting.

Suddenly, she turned the machine off. "Ida," she said, "I have something I want you to do for me."

"Yes?" Ida looked up from her filing and registration of film clips.

Gretchen had the script with her in the big shoulder bag she always wore to work. She went over to where it was hanging and took it out. "I'm going to a museum for an hour or so," she said. "Meanwhile I want you to drop that trash you're fiddling with and read this for me." She handed the script to Ida. "When I get back, we'll go out to a girly lunch, just you and me, and I'd like to discuss it with you."

Ida looked at her doubtfully as she took the script. It wasn't like Gretchen to break off in the middle of work for anything more than a container of coffee. "Of course," she said. She adjusted her glasses and looked down at the script in her hands as though afraid it might contain an explosive device.

Gretchen put on her coat and went downstairs and into the bustle of Seventh Avenue, where the building was located. She walked swiftly crosstown and went into the Museum of Modern Art, to soothe her nerves, she told herself, wrongly, with honest works of art. When she came out, she was no more soothed than when she went in. She couldn't bear the thought of going back to the moviola after more than an hour of Picasso and Renoir and Henry Moore, so she telephoned the cutting room and asked Ida to meet her at a restaurant nearby. "And put some makeup on and straighten your stockings," she told Ida cruelly. "The restaurant is French and fancy, but fancy-fancy. I'm treating—because I'm in trouble."

Waiting for Ida in the restaurant, she had a Scotch at the bar. She never drank during the day, but, she told herself defiantly, there's no law against it. It's Saturday.

When Ida came in and saw Gretchen at the bar, she asked, suspiciously, "What're you drinking?"

"Scotch."

"You *are* in trouble." Philosophically in the vanguard of modern thought, as she believed she was, in her daily life Ida was grimly puritanical.

"Two Scotches, please," Gretchen said to the bartender.

"I can't work after I've had anything to drink," Ida said plaintively. "You know that."

"You're not going to work this afternoon," Gretchen said. "Nobody's going to work this afternoon. I thought you were against sweated female labor. Especially on Saturdays. Aren't you always telling me that what this country needs is the twenty-hour week?"

"That's just the theory," Ida said defensively, eyeing the glass that the bartender set down in front of her with repugnance. "Personally I *choose* to work."

"Not today," Gretchen said firmly. She waved to the maitre d'hôtel. "A table for two, please. And send over the drinks." She left two dollars, grandly, as a tip for the bartender.

"That's an awfully big tip for just three drinks," Ida whispered as they followed the maitre d'hôtel toward the rear of the restaurant.

"One of the things that will make us women equal to men," Gretchen said, "is the size of our tips."

The maitre d'hôtel pulled out the two chairs at one of the tables just next to the kitchen.

"You see—" Ida glared around her. "The restaurant's almost empty and he puts us next to the kitchen. Just because there isn't a man along."

"Drink your whiskey," Gretchen said. "We'll get our revenge in heaven."

Ida sipped at her drink and made a face. "While you were at it," she said, "you might have ordered something sweet."

"On to the barricades, where there are no sweet drinks," Gretchen said. "And now tell me what you think of the script."

Ida's face lit up. A well-done scene in a movie, a passage she admired in a book, could make her euphoric.

"It's wonderful," she said. "God, what a picture it's going to make."

"Except it looks as though no one is going to make it," Gretchen said. "I think it's been around and our beloved Evans Kinsella was the agent's last gasp."

"Has he read it yet—Evans?"

"Yes," Gretchen said. "He thinks it's a load of shit. His words. He told me to give the script to his secretary to send back."

"Vulgarian," Ida said hotly. "And to think what a big shot he is. How much is the picture we're on going to cost?"

"Three and a half million."

"There's something goddamn wrong with the business, with the world, for that matter," Ida said, "if they give a fool like that three and a half million dollars to play around with."

"He's had two big hits in the last three years," Gretchen said.

"Luck," Ida said, "that's all—luck."

"I'm not so sure it's only that," Gretchen said. "He has his moments."

"Not three and a half million dollars' worth," Ida said stubbornly. "And I don't know why you stick up for him. The way he treats you. And I'm not talking about only in the office, either."

"Oh," Gretchen said with a lightness that she didn't feel, "a little touch of masochism never hurt a girl."

"Sometimes, Gretchen," Ida said primly, "you drive me crazy, you really do."

The waiter was standing over them now, his pad and pencil ready.

"Time to order," Gretchen said. She looked at the menu. "They have roast duck with olives. That's for two. Do you want to share it with me?"

"All right," Ida said. "I don't like olives. You can have them all."

Gretchen ordered the duck and a bottle of Pouilly Fumé.

"Not a whole bottle," Ida said. "Please. I won't drink more than half a glass."

"A whole bottle," Gretchen said to the waiter, ignoring her.

"You'll be drunk," Ida warned her.

"Good," said Gretchen, "I have some big decisions to make and maybe I won't make them dead sober."

"You have a funny look in your eye today," Ida said.

"You bet your liberated brassiere I have," said Gretchen. She finished her second whiskey in one long gulp.

"What are you planning on doing?" Ida said. "Now don't be reckless. You're angry and you've got all that alcohol in you . . ."

"I'm angry," Gretchen said, "and I have a wee bit of whiskey in me and part of what I'm planning to do is drink most of the bottle of wine all by my little self, if you won't help me. And after that . . ." She stopped.

"After that, what?"

"After that," Gretchen said, "I'm not quite sure." She laughed. The laughter sounded so strange that Ida was convinced that Gretchen was in the first stages of descending alcoholism. "After that I'm going to have a little talk with Evans Kinsella. If I can find him, which I doubt."

"What are you going to say to him?" Ida asked anxiously.

"Some impolite home truths," Gretchen said. "For starters."

"Be sensible," Ida said, worriedly. "After all, no matter what else he is to you, he's still your boss."

"Ida," Gretchen said, "has anyone ever told you that you have a sick respect for authority?"

"I wouldn't say sick." Ida was hurt.

"What would you say then? Exorbitant, slavish, adoring?"

"I'd say normal, if you must know. Anyway, let's get off me for a while. Just what are you going to tell him?"

"I'm going to tell him that the picture we're working on stinks. That'll be the overture," Gretchen said.

"Oh, please, Gretchen . . ." Ida put her hands up as though to stop her physically.

"Somebody ought to buy you some rings," Gretchen said. "You have pretty hands and rings would set them off nicely. Maybe we'll spend the afternoon looking for rings for you if we can't find that bastard Kinsella."

Ida looked around worriedly. The restaurant had filled by now and there were two men sitting near them. "People can hear you."

"Let them hear," Gretchen said. "I want to spread the good word around."

The waiter was at the table and expertly carving their duck. The wine was in a cooler. "No olives for me, please," Ida said. "Give them all to the lady."

Gretchen watched admiringly as the waiter deftly sectioned the duck. "I bet *he* doesn't drink during working hours," she said. Kinsella had been known to do that, too, from time to time.

"Ssh," Ida said. She smiled at the waiter, apologizing for her eccentric friend.

"Do you?" Gretchen asked the waiter.

"No, ma'am," he said. He grinned. "But I would if it was offered."

"I'll send around a bottle the first thing in the morning," Gretchen said.

"Gretchen," said Ida, "I've never seen you like this before. What's come over you?"

"Fury," Gretchen said. "Just plain old healthy fury." She tasted the duck, "Mmm," she said and drank heartily of the wine.

"If I were you," Ida said, nibbling at her food, "I'd wait until after the weekend before you did anything."

"Never postpone fury. That's an old family motto in my family," Gretchen said. "Especially over the weekend. It's hard to be furious on Monday morning. It takes a whole week to get into the proper frame of mind for fury."

"Kinsella will never forgive you if you go on at him like this," Ida said.

"After the overture," Gretchen said, disregarding Ida's interruption, "we go into the full performance. About how I only consented to work on the piece of junk he's making because I wanted to continue to enjoy the favors of his pure white body."

"Gretchen," Ida said reproachfully, "you once told me you loved him." In her spinster heart romance held a prominent place.

"Once," Gretchen said.

"You'll infuriate him."

"That's exactly my intention," said Gretchen. "To continue—I will tell him that I've read the script he told me to send back to the agent and I find it original, witty and too good for the likes of him. However, since he's the only director I happen to be half living with at the moment, and certainly the only director I'm intimate with who can raise money for a picture on the strength of his name, I will tell him that if he has the brains he was born with he'll buy it tomorrow, even if he's doing it only because I'm asking him to."

"You know he'll say no," Ida said.

"Probably."

"Then what will you do? Burst into tears and ask for his forgiveness?"

Gretchen looked at her in surprise. Ida was not ordinarily given to sarcasm. Gretchen could see that the whole conversation was disturbing her. "Ida, darling," she said gently, "you mustn't let it worry you so. After all, I'm the one who's going to do the fighting."

"I hate to see you get into trouble," Ida said.

"There're times when it can't be avoided, and this is one of the times. You asked me what I will do if he says no."

"*When* he says no," Ida said.

"I'll tell him that I'm walking off the picture as of that moment. . . ."

"You have a contract. . . ." Ida cried.

"Let him sue me. He can also go to law to get me back into his bed."

"You know that if you quit, I'll quit, too," Ida said, her voice quivering at the immensity of what she was saying.

"In a war," Gretchen said harshly, "sometimes you have to sacrifice the troops."

"This isn't a war," Ida protested. "It's just a moving picture like a thousand other moving pictures."

"That's exactly the point," Gretchen said, "I don't want to spend my life working on pictures that are just like a thousand others." She saw that Ida was near tears, her soft dark eyes getting puddly. "You don't have to pay for my peculiar notions, Ida," she said. "There's no reason you have to quit if I do."

"I won't talk about it," Ida said.

"Okay," Gretchen said. "The matter's closed. Now finish your duck. You've barely eaten a bite. Don't you like it?"

"I . . . I . . . love it," Ida blubbered.

They ate in silence for more than a minute, Gretchen helping herself to more wine. She could see Ida making an effort to compose her soft, gentle face that could have been that of a chubby child, and for a moment was sorry that she had given Ida the script to read, burdened her with her own problems. Still, with her experience of Ida's stony integrity and purity of taste, she had had to have confirmation of the value of the script. Without it, she would never have been sure enough to confront Kinsella. Evans Kinsella, she thought grimly to herself, is in for a rough afternoon, if he's home, Ida Cohen or no Ida Cohen. If he's home.

Finally, Ida spoke. "I've been thinking," she said, her voice almost timid. "There's another way of going about it. You don't have to do everything head-on, do you?"

"I suppose not. I'm not good at doing things slanty-wise, though."

Ida chuckled. "No, you're not. However—maybe this one time you'll listen to me. You know and I know he'll never say yes. Especially if you argue with him."

"How do you know him so well?" Gretchen asked with mock suspicion. "Have you been having a nasty little affair with him behind my back?"

Ida laughed aloud, her spirits restored. "How could I?" she asked. "He's not even Jewish."

They both laughed together. Then Ida's face became grave. "My idea is this— finish cutting the picture—"

"Oh, God," Gretchen said.

"Hush. Listen to me for a minute. I listened to *you*, didn't I?"

"You certainly did," Gretchen admitted.

"Don't even mention the script to him again. Pretend you've forgotten all about it."

"But I haven't forgotten about it. It's haunting me already. Even now I can see shot after shot . . ."

"I said *pretend*," Ida said crossly. "Get someone to put up option money and buy it yourself."

"Even if I could get the money," Gretchen said, thinking immediately of poor Rudy, "then what?"

"Then," Ida said trimphantly, "direct it yourself."

Gretchen leaned back in her chair. Whatever had been in Ida's head, she hadn't expected this.

"My heavens," she said, "what an idea."

"Why not?" Ida said eagerly, forgetting once more to eat. "In the old days most directors came out of the cutting rooms."

"The old days," Gretchen said. "And they were all men."

"You know I don't like talk like that," Ida said reprovingly.

"Forgive me. For the moment I forgot. But just for fun, Ida, give me the names of twenty-five women directors."

"In the old days there weren't twenty-five women in the army, either." The meetings she attended gave a solid base to Ida's arguments and she was making the most of it. "You won't go to meetings, you won't even read the pamphlets we put out—but you could do us a lot more good by coming along with a beautiful movie than if you went to a million meetings. And if you have any doubts about whether you could pull it off or not, let me tell you, you know more about movies than Evans Kinsella ever did or ever will."

"It's an idea," Gretchen said thoughtfully, "now that the first shock is over, it's an idea."

"It's not an expensive picture to make," Ida went on quickly. "A small town, mostly location and easy indoor shots, a small cast, kids mostly; you couldn't find name actors for the parts even if you had the money to spend. I know some people who put money into pictures. I could go to them. You could go to your brother . . ."

Poor Rudy, Gretchen thought again.

"How much did Evans Kinsella's first picture cost?" Ida asked.

"One hundred and twenty-five thousand," Gretchen said promptly. Kinsella was constantly boasting that his first picture, which had had a huge commercial success, had been brought in for peanuts and he always announced the exact sum.

"A hundred and twenty-five thousand," Ida said. "And now they give him three and a half million."

"That's show business," Gretchen said.

"Times have changed," Ida said, "and a hundred and twenty-five is impossible these days. But I bet we could do this one for no more than seven hundred and fifty thousand. Most of the actors'd work for scale, and with parts like these the leads would defer their salaries and take percentages. All the money would be on the screen, no place else."

"Dear Ida," Gretchen said, "you're already beginning to talk like a movie mogul."

"Just promise me one thing," Ida said.

"What's that?" Gretchen asked suspiciously.

"Don't call Kinsella today or tomorrow. Think everything over at least until Monday."

Gretchen hesitated. "Okay," she said, "but you're depriving me of a lovely fight."

"Just think of what Kinsella's face will look like when the movie comes out, and you won't mind giving up the satisfaction of telling him what a jerk he is."

"All right, I promise," Gretchen said. "Now let's order a gorgeous, gooey French dessert and then we'll indulge ourselves to the full the rest of the afternoon. Tell me—how many times have you seen Bergman's *Wild Strawberries?*"

"Five times."

"All right, I promise," Gretchen said. "Now let's play hooky this afternoon and make it an even half-dozen."

Driving home through the Sunday-afternoon traffic, in the rear of the Continental, with Johnny Heath at the wheel and Elaine in front beside him, Rudolph reflected upon the weekend. It had been a success, he thought. Jean's house had been cosy, as she had promised, and the view of the ocean glorious. The masseuse did not seem to be a lesbian and turned out to be a very good cook indeed. There had been no orgies, no nude clambakes on the beach, despite Johnny's prediction, but there had been long walks on the hard sand left by the ebbing tide, all of them together, with Enid holding her mother's hand. The two of them had been delighted with each other, and without saying anything about it, Rudolph had thought that it might be a good idea for Enid to stay with her mother and go to a small country school rather than face the perils of the streets of New York. He could always see the child on weekends and school holidays. Of course, if he was to take Johnny's wild idea about Nevada seriously there would be complications. Anyway, it wouldn't be tomorrow or next week, probably not even next year.

Jean had looked healthy and fit. She and the masseuse did Spartan exercises each morning and Jean wandered for miles each day along the shore looking for subjects to photograph. She seemed happy, in a dreamy, reticent way, like a child who had just wakened after a pleasant dream. She had been pleased to see the Heaths and content to spend the short weekend in a group. Neither she nor the masseuse, whose name was Lorraine, had attempted to get him off for a private conversation. If Jean had any friends in the neighborhood, they did not appear either on Saturday or Sunday. When Rudolph had asked to see her photographs, she had said, "I'm not ready yet. In a month or so, maybe."

Sitting in the back of the comfortable car, speeding toward the city, he realized, not without a touch of sorrow, that Jean had seemed happier that weekend than at almost any time since their marriage.

There had been wine on the table, but no hard liquor. Jean had not reached for the bottle and Rudolph had caught no warning looks to her from Lorraine.

She has come to terms with herself, Rudolph thought. He could not say as much for himself.

Coming into New York over the bridge, he saw the buildings rearing like battlements against the melodrama of the sun sinking in the west. Lights were being turned on in windows, small, winking pinpoints like candles in archers' loopholes in a stronghold at twilight. It was a view and a time of day that he loved—the empty Sunday streets through which they passed looked clean and welcoming. If only it were always Sunday in New York, he thought, nobody would ever leave it.

When the car stopped in front of his brownstone, he asked the Heaths if they wanted to come in for a drink, but Johnny said they had a cocktail party to go to and were late. Rudy thanked Johnny for the ride, leaned over and kissed Elaine on the cheek. The weekend had made him fonder of her than before.

"Are you going to be all alone tonight?" Elaine asked.

"Yes."

"Why don't you get back into the car and have the evening with us?" she said. "We're going to Gino's for dinner after the party."

He was tempted, but he had a lot of thinking to do and he felt it would be better to be alone. He did not tell her that he felt uncomfortable these days with a lot of people around. It was just a passing phase, he was sure, but it had to be reckoned with. "Thanks," he said, "but I have a pile of letters to answer. Let's do it during the week. Just the three of us."

"I'll call you tomorrow," Johnny said, "when I get the Nevada pilgrimage arranged."

"I'll be in all day," Rudolph said. As he watched the car drive away, he was sorry he had said it. He was afraid that in the car, one or the other of the Heaths was saying, "He'll be in all day because he doesn't know what to do with himself."

Carrying his bag, he went up the steps. He didn't have to use the key to open the front door. The people downstairs again. He would have to talk to them. As he went into the darkened hallway a man's voice said, "Don't move and don't make a sound. I've got a gun on you."

He heard the front door slam behind him.

"Which apartment is yours, mister?" the voice said.

He hesitated. If Enid had been upstairs, he wouldn't have answered. He thanked God she was safely with her mother, more than a hundred miles away. And the nurse was in New Jersey. There was nobody upstairs. He felt what might have been a gun jabbing him roughly in the ribs. "We asked you a question, mister," the voice said. He was conscious of a second man, standing next to him.

"Second floor," he said.

"Climb!" the voice commanded. He started up the steps. There was no light coming through the crack at the bottom of the door of the downstairs apartment. Nobody home. Sunday evening, he thought, as he went mechanically up the stairs, with the sound of two pairs of footsteps heavy behind him.

His hands trembled as he got out his keys again and unlocked the door and went in. "Turn on a light," the same voice said.

He fumbled for the switch, found it, pushed at it. The lamp in the hallway went on and he turned to see the two men who had been lying in wait in the vestibule downstairs. They were young, black, one tall, one medium-sized, both neatly dressed. Their faces were lean and tense and full of hatred. Hopheads, he thought. The tall man was holding a gun, pointing at him, blue-black, gleaming dully in the light of the lamp.

"Into the living room," he said.

They followed him into the living room and the second man found the light switch. All the lamps went on. The room looked comfortable and clean, the drapes drawn across the windows. The nurse had tidied up before they left the morning before. The clock on the mantelpiece ticked loudly. He saw that it was five-thirty. "Let's have your wallet," the tall man said, "and no funny business."

Rudolph dug into his jacket and took out his wallet. The man with the gun grabbed it roughly and tossed it to the other man. "See what's in it," he said.

The second man rifled the wallet. "Thirty dollars," he said, holding the bills in his hand.

"Shit," said the man with the gun. "What've you got in your pants?"

Rudolph took out his money clip and two quarters. The second man put his hand out and grabbed the clip and the change. "You can say shit again, brother," he said. "There's only eight bucks here." He let the two quarters drop to the rug.

"You got the nerve to drive up here in a Lincoln Continental and only have thirty-eight bucks on you?" the man with the gun said. "Smart, aren't you? Afraid of being mugged, aren't you, Mr. Rockefeller?"

"I'm sorry," Rudolph said. "That's all I have. And those credit cards." The credit cards were strewn on the floor now.

"This institution don't accept credit cards, does it, Elroy?" the man said.

"It sure don't," Elroy said. They both laughed hoarsely.

Rudolph felt remote, as though it weren't happening to him but to a tiny, numb figure far off in the distance.

"Where do you keep the money in the house?" the man with the gun demanded. "Where's the safe?"

"I don't keep any money in the house," Rudolph said. "And there's no safe."

"Smarter and smarter, ain't you?" the man said. With his free hand he slapped Rudolph, hard, across the eyes. Rudolph was blinded momentarily by tears and he stumbled back. "That's just to truthen you up a little, mister," the man with the gun said.

"Look for yourself," Rudolph said blindly.

"You got one last chance to show us where it is, mister," the man said.

"I'm sorry. There's nothing I can do about it."

The man with the gun was breathing heavily, irregularly, and his eyes were flicking about, reflecting the light from the various lamps fitfully. "What do you say, Elroy?" he asked.

"Teach the cocksucker a lesson," Elroy said.

The man with the gun palmed it in a sudden gesture and swung against Rudolph's temple. As he crumpled to the floor it seemed to Rudolph that he was falling slowly and not unpleasantly through space and the floor seemed like a beautiful soft bed when he reached it. After a while a voice somewhere far off said, "That's enough, Elroy, you don't want to kill the bastard, do you?"

He was dreaming. Even while he dreamed he knew it was a dream. He was searching for Enid on a beach. There was the roar of breakers. Somehow, there were buses parked on the beach, in an irregular pattern, and people kept running in and out of them, people he didn't know or recognize, who paid no attention to him, who sometimes blocked him, sometimes dissolved into shadows, as he pushed through them, shouting, "Enid! Enid!" He knew it was a dream but he was tortured just the same because he knew he would never find her. The sense of loss was intolerable.

Then he awoke. The lights were still on. Now they were a glare that stabbed his eyes. He was lying on the floor, and everything hurt, his head, his groin. It was torture to move. His face was wet. When he put up his hand it came away streaming with blood.

Around him the room was demolished. All the upholstered chairs and the sofa had been slashed with knives and the stuffing lay like heaps of snow on the floor. The clock was lying, shattered, on the brick apron of the fireplace. Every drawer in the desk and chests and sideboard had been pulled out, their contents thrown around the room. The mirror above the fireplace was splintered into jagged pieces. The wooden chairs and the coffee table and small sideboard had been fractured with the poker from the set of fireplace utensils and the poker itself was bent at a crazy angle. All the bottles from the sideboard had been hurled against the wall and there was broken glass everywhere and a pervading smell of whiskey. The front panel of the piano was leaning against the sofa and the exposed, torn strings hung, broken and loose, over the keyboard, like an animal's intestines. He tried to look at his watch to see how long he had been lying unconscious, but the watch had been cut away from his wrist and there was an ugly seeping wound there.

With a gigantic effort, groaning, he crawled to the telephone. He took the instrument off its cradle, listened. It was working. Thank God. It took him what seemed like many minutes to remember Gretchen's number. Painfully, he dialed. It rang and rang. He lay on the floor with the phone next to his cheek. Finally he heard the phone being picked up at the other end.

"Hello." It was Gretchen's voice.

"Gretchen," he said.

"Where've you been?" she said. She sounded cross. "I phoned you at five; you said you'd be back by . . ."

"Gretchen," he said hoarsely, "come over here. Right away. If the door is locked, get a policeman to break it open for you. I . . ." Then he felt he was falling again. He couldn't talk anymore. He lay there on the floor with Gretchen's voice in his ear, crying. "Rudy! Rudy! Rudy, do you hear me . . .?" Then silence.

He let himself go all the way and fainted again.

He was in the hospital for two weeks and he never did get to Nevada with Johnny Heath.

Part Three

CHAPTER 1

HE HAD DELIVERED seventeen dollars' worth of groceries to Mrs. Wertham from the supermarket and Mrs. Wertham had invited him to have a cup of coffee. Mr. Wertham worked in Mr. Kraler's bottling plant and that, Wesley thought, bridged the social and sexual gap in Mrs. Wertham's mind between a comfortably well-off housewife and a sixteen-year-old delivery boy. He had accepted the coffee. It was the last call of the day and he never was served coffee at the Kralers'.

After the coffee, Mrs. Wertham, coyly, with a certain amount of giggling, told him he was a very handsome young man and invited him into her bed. Coffee was not the only thing he wasn't being served at the Kralers' and Mrs. Wertham was a generously built, dyed-blond lady. He accepted that invitation, too.

The coffee had been good, but the sex better. He had to perform quickly, because the store bike, with the delivery box between the two front wheels, was parked outside, and it was a neighborhood with a lot of kids who could be counted upon to steal anything they could lay their hands on, even a bike with U.M. Supermarket painted in big letters on the box.

That had been just a month ago. He had made ten deliveries to Mrs. Wertham since then. The order for groceries in the Wertham household depended upon the fluctuations in Mrs. Wertham's libido.

This time, as he was getting dressed, Mrs. Wertham put on a housecoat and sat smiling at him as though she had just had a big, creamy dessert. "You sure are a strong-built young man," she said admiringly. "You could lift up my husband with one hand."

"Thanks, ma'am," Wesley said, getting into his sweater. He had no desire to lift Mr. Wertham with one hand.

"I don't usually do things like this," Mrs. Wertham said, perhaps forgetting that Wesley knew how to count, "but . . . " She sighed. "It makes a nice break in the day, doesn't it?"

"Yes, ma'am," Wesley said.

"It would be a sweet gesture on your part," Mrs. Wertham said, "if the next time you have to make a delivery here, you just kind of slipped a little present into the package. Half a ham, something like that. I'm always home between three and five."

"Yes, ma'am," Wesley said ambiguously. That was the last time Mrs. Wertham was going to get him into her bed. "I have to go now. My bike's outside. . . . "

"I understand," Mrs. Wertham said. "You'll remember about the ham, won't you?"

"Yes, ma'am," Wesley said.

The bike was still downstairs. He swung on it and pedaled, disgusted with himself, toward the post office. Half a ham. She thought he came at bargain prices. It was degrading. He felt he had reached a turning point in his life. From now on he wasn't going to accept anything just because it was offered. America was full of wonderful girls. The nice, shy one in the *Time* office in New York, for example, old as she was. He wasn't going to settle for trash anymore. Outside of Indianapolis there must be a girl somewhere whom he could talk to, admire, laugh with, explain about his father and himself, a girl he could love and feel proud of, a girl who wouldn't make him feel like a pig after he left her bed. Meanwhile, he decided, he could just wait.

At the post office there were two letters for him at General Delivery, one from Bunny, the other from Uncle Rudolph. Since he had used Uncle Rudolph's idea and picked up his mail at General Delivery he had received letters from Bunny and Kate regularly. They made life in Indianapolis almost bearable. He stuffed the letters in his pocket, unread, because Mr. Citron, the manager of the U.M., always looked at him sharply if Wesley took even five minutes more than Mr. Citron thought was absolutely necessary, and Mrs. Wertham had already put him slightly behind schedule. Mr. Citron, Wesley thought, smiling innocently at the manager when he got back to the store, must have a time clock in his head. Try always to be your own boss, his father had said, it's the only way of beating the bastards.

In the stockroom behind the market he took the letters out of his pocket. He opened Bunny's letter first. His strong, clear handwriting looked as though it were written by a man who weighed over two hundred pounds.

> Dear Wesley,
>
> The news is that the *Clothilde*'s been sold for a hundred and ten thousand dollars. More dough for you and Kate and Kate's kid. Congratulations. Now I can finally tell you that the real owner wasn't Johnny Heath, as it says in the ship's papers, but your Uncle Rudolph. He had his reasons for hiding it, I suppose. I was beginning to think that we'd never sell it. I tried to talk your uncle into letting me change the name, but he wouldn't hear of it. He's got principles. Maybe too many principles. The new owners are German, very nice people; they knew about what happened, but it didn't seem to bother them. I guess Germans aren't superstitious. They fell in love with the *Clothilde* at first sight, the lady told me. They wanted me to stay on as captain, but I decided against it. There're a lot of reasons and I don't think I have to tell you what they are.
>
> I got to know an American couple with two boys aged around 11 and 9 hanging around St. Tropez who have a 43-foot Chris-Craft and they asked me to work it. I'm the only one in crew, but the kids can help clean up and the wife says she don't mind doing the cooking. The father says he can read a chart and handle the wheel. We'll see. So I'm still on the good old Mediterranean. It should be ok. It's nice having two kids on board.
>
> Heard from Kate. She's got a job as barmaid in a pub not far from where she lives, so she gets to see a lot of her kid. I guess you know she named him Thomas Jordache.
>
> Sorry you fell into a pile of shit in Indianapolis. According to your uncle when you're eighteen you can split. It's not so far off and time goes fast, so sweat it out and don't do anything crazy.
>
> The name of my new ship is the *Dolores*—that's the lady's first name and her home port is St. Tropez, so you can keep writing me here care of the Captain of the Port.
>
> Well, that's the news, friend. If you find yourself along the coast, drop in and see me.
>
>> Au revoir,
>> *Bunny*

Wesley folded the letter carefully and put it back in the envelope. He'd written Bunny twice asking him if he'd heard anything about Danovic, but Bunny never mentioned him. Times goes fast, Bunny had written. Maybe on the Mediterranean.

Not in Indianapolis. There were few things he liked in Indianapolis. One was the big old market building, with its high ceiling and stalls heaped with fruit and vegetables and the smell of baked bread over everything. He went there as often as he could, because it reminded him of the market near the port in Antibes.

When he opened his uncle's letter two twenty-dollar bills fell out. He picked them up and put them in his pocket. He hadn't asked for money—ever—but he was grateful when it came. His uncle had a habit of coming through at odd times for everybody. It was nice, if you could afford it. And Uncle Rudolph obviously could. Don't rap it. The letter began,

> Dear Wesley,
>   Note the address on top of the page. I finally moved out of New York. Since the robbery, the city has lost much of its charm for me and I began to worry, exaggeratedly, I'm sure, for Enid's safety. I've rented this house here in Bridgehampton out on Long Island for a year for a trial run. It's a quiet, charming community, except in the summer months, when it's enlivened by artistic and literary folk, and my house is near the beach and just about fifteen minutes' drive from my ex-wife's house. Enid stays with her during the school week and visits me on the weekends and with that arrange-ment no longer needs a nurse to look after her. She is happy in the country and even if it were only for her sake the move would be a good one.
>   I've fully recovered from the two operations on my face, and although I snort like an old warhorse when I jog along the beach, due to certain rearrangements made on my nasal passages after my accident, I feel fine. The doctors wanted to operate on my nose once more for cosmetic reasons, but I said enough is enough. Gretchen says I look more like your father now, with my flattened nose.
>   Gretchen, incidentally, is off on a new career. She finishes with the movie she is cutting with Mr. Kinsella this next week and is launching out as a director, having bought a screenplay that she likes and that I've read and liked very much myself. In fact, not knowing just what to do with my money, I am investing in it and counseling Gretchen as tactfully as possible on the business end of the venture. Be careful the next time you see her. She thinks you would have a great success in one of the roles in the movie. We have had almost everything in the family by now, but never a movie star and I'm not sure how that would reflect on the family name.
>   I'm afraid that in the to-do after I got beaten up I forgot to keep my promise about sending you the names of some of the people you wanted to know about who might give you information about your father. There's Johnny Heath, of course, who chartered the *Clothilde* with his wife. I don't remember if you were already on board at that time or not. Then there're Mr. and Mrs. Goodhart, who also chartered the ship in different seasons. I'm writing the addresses on the enclosed sheet of paper. If you want to go as far back as when your father was the age that you are now, there was a boy—now a man, of course—called Claude Tinker, in Port Philip, who was a partner of your father in some of his escapades. The Tinker family, I have heard, is still in Port Philip. Then there's a man named Theodore Boylan, who must be quite old by now, but who had intimate ties with our family.
>   I only saw your father fight professionally once—against a

colored boy named Virgil Walters, and perhaps he would have something to remember. Your father had a manager called Schultz and I found him once through *Ring* Magazine when I wanted to get in touch with your father.

If other names occur to me I'll send them along to you. I'm sorry you couldn't come to visit me this summer and hope you can manage it another time.

I'm enclosing a little gift to start the new school year with. If by any chance you need more, don't hesitate to let me know.

Fondly,
Rudolph

Wesley folded the letter and put it back into the envelope, as he had with Bunny's letter. He *writes* with an anchor up his ass, Wesley thought. He *isn't* like that, there's just a wall between what he is and what he sounds like. Wesley wished he could like Uncle Rudolph more than he did.

He gave two letters to Jimmy when Jimmy came in to help sweep up. Jimmy was the other delivery boy. He was a black, the same age as Wesley. Jimmy kept the photograph of his father in boxing trunks that the lady from *Time* had given him and whatever letters Wesley got, because Wesley's mother went through everything in his room at least twice a week looking for signs of sin and whatever else she could find. Letters from his uncle and Kate and Bunny would be incriminating evidence of a giant conspiracy by everybody to rob her of her son's love, an emotion she spoke about often. Her occasional outbursts of affection were hard to bear. She insisted upon kissing him and hugging him and calling him her sweet baby boy and telling him that if he only got a haircut he would be a beautiful young man and if he would accept the joys of religion he would make his mother blissfully happy and there wasn't anything she and Mr. Kraler wouldn't do for him. It wasn't an act and Wesley knew his mother *did* love him and want him to be happy—but in her way, not his. Her demonstrativeness left him uneasy and embarrassed. He thought of Kate with longing.

He never spoke about his mother or Mr. Kraler to Jimmy, although Jimmy was the only friend Wesley had in town. He had avoided all other overtures, except that of Mrs. Wertham, and that didn't really count. He didn't want to feel sorry at leaving anything behind when he departed from Indianapolis.

He didn't feel like going home for dinner, first of all because he knew the meal would be lousy and second because the house, which had been bad enough before, had been as gloomy as the grave since Mr. Kraler had gotten the telegram saying his son Max had been killed in Vietnam. They were expecting the body home for burial any day now and the time of waiting for it had been like one long funeral.

He invited Jimmy to have dinner with him. "I can splurge tonight," he told Jimmy. "My rich uncle came through again."

They ate in a little restaurant near the supermarket where you could get a steak dinner for one fifty and where the owner didn't ask for proof you were of age when you ordered a beer.

Jimmy wanted to be a rock musician and sometimes he took Wesley over to his house and played his clarinet for him with one of his sisters who played the piano, while his other sister brought in the beers. Jimmy's sisters treated Jimmy as though he were a precious object, and anybody Jimmy liked they couldn't do enough for. There was no question of anybody's robbing them of Jimmy's love or theirs for him. Jimmy's crowded warm house, filled with the presence of the two pretty, laughing girls, was another place in Indianapolis that Wesley liked. Indianapolis, with its factories and pale tides of workmen morning and night and its flat expanses of identical houses and its littered streets, made Antibes seem like a suburb of a city in heaven.

Wesley didn't tell his mother about Jimmy. She was polite with blacks, but she believed in their keeping their distance, she said. It had something to do with being a Mormon.

After dinner, he remembered to tell Jimmy that from now on he'd appreciate it if Jimmy would make the deliveries to Mrs. Wertham's house. He didn't say why and Jimmy didn't ask him. That was another good thing about Jimmy—he didn't ask foolish questions.

He walked home slowly. There was an unspoken rule that if he got home by nine o'clock there wouldn't be any hysterical scenes about his tomcatting around town, disgracing his family, like his father. The usual routine was bad enough, but the scenes, especially late at night, tore at his nerves and made it almost impossible for him to get to sleep after them. He had thought again and again of just taking off, but he wanted to give his mother every chance possible. There had to be *something* there. Once, his father had loved her.

When he got home, Mr. Kraler was sobbing in the living room and holding his son's framed photograph. The picture had been taken with Max Kraler in a private's uniform. He was a thin-faced, sad-eyed boy, who looked as though he knew he was going to be killed before he was twenty-one. Wesley's mother took him into the hallway and whispered that Mr. Kraler had received notice that Max's body was going to arrive in two days and had spent the afternoon making funeral arrangements. "Be nice to him, please," she said. "He loved his boy. He wants you to get a haircut tomorrow and go with me to buy a new dark suit for the funeral."

"My hair's okay, Ma," Wesley said. "I'm not going to cut it."

"At a time like this," his mother said, still whispering. "You might just this once—to show respect for the dead."

"I can show as much respect for the dead with my hair the way it is."

"You won't even do a little thing like this to please your mother?" She began to cry, too.

"I like the way my hair is," Wesley said. "Nobody but you and him . . . " he gestured toward the living room, "ever bothers me about it."

"You're a stubborn, hard boy," she said, letting the tears course down her cheeks. "You never give an inch, do you?"

"I do when it makes sense," he said.

"Mr. Kraler won't let me buy you a new suit with that hair."

"So I'll go to the funeral in my old suit," Wesley said. "Max won't care."

"That's a sick joke," she wept.

"I didn't mean it as a joke."

"That old suit and that wild-Indian hair will make us all ashamed in church."

"Okay. I won't go to church. And I won't go to the cemetery. I never even *met* Max. What difference does it make?"

"Mother," Mr. Kraler called from the living room, "can you come in here for a minute?"

"Coming dear," Teresa called. She glared harshly at Wesley, then slapped him, hard.

Wesley didn't react, but merely stood there in the hallway. His mother went into the living room and he went upstairs to his room.

They left it at that. When Max Kraler was buried, Wesley was delivering groceries.

Corporal Healey, who had also served in Vietnam but had not known Mr. Kraler's son, accompanied the body of the boy to Indianapolis. Mr. Kraler, who was a veteran of the Korean War, invited the corporal as a comrade in arms to stay in the house instead of going to a hotel. The night after the funeral Wesley had to share his bed with Healey, because of Mr. Kraler's married daughter, Doris, who lived in Chicago, was using the guest room across the hall. Doris was a small, mousy young woman who looked, Wesley thought, like Mr. Kraler.

Healey was a short, likable man, about twenty-three, who had a Purple Heart with two clusters on his blouse. Mr. Kraler, who had been a clerk in the quartermaster's in Tokyo during the Korean War, had talked Healey's ear off all day about *his* experiences as a soldier, and Healey had been polite, but had signaled to Wesley that he would like to break away. In a pause in Mr. Kraler's conversation Healey had stood up and said he'd like to take a little walk and asked if they'd mind letting Wesley go with him so he wouldn't get lost. Mr. Kraler, one soldier to another, said, "Of course, Corporal," and Teresa had nodded. She hadn't said a word to Wesley since the scene in the hallway and Wesley was grateful to Healey for getting him out of the house.

"Phew!" Healey said as they walked down the street, "that's heavy duty in there. What's the sister like, that Doris?"

"I don't know," Wesley said. "I met her for the first time yesterday."

"She keeps giving me the eye," Healey said. "Do you think she means it?"

"I wouldn't know."

"Sometimes those plain-looking little dolls are power-houses when it comes to putting out," Healey said. "You wouldn't object if I gave it a try, would you?"

"Why should I?" Wesley asked. "Just be careful. My mother patrols the house like a watchdog."

"We'll see how the situation develops," Healey said. He was from Virginia and his speech was soft and drawled. "That Mr. Kraler is something. The way he talks it was hand-to-hand combat every day in Tokyo. And he kept eating up all the gory details about how I was wounded. One thing for sure, I'm not joining the American Legion. I had my war and I don't want to hear word one about that war or anybody else's war. Where can we get a couple of beers?"

"It's not far from here," Wesley said. "I guessed you could use a drink."

"You'd think that if a fella came along with the body," Healey complained, "there'd be a little nip of something to cheer everybody up a bit. Not even a cup of coffee, for Christ's sake."

"They're Mormons."

"That must be some sorrowful religion," Healey said. "I go to Mass every Sunday I can, but I don't spit in the face of Creation. After all, God made whiskey, beer, wine—Christ, he even made coffee and tea. What do they think He made them for?"

"Ask Mr. Kraler."

"Yeah," Healey said mournfully.

They sat in a booth at the restaurant where Wesley had eaten dinner with Jimmy and drank beer. Wesley had explained to Healey that was the one place he was sure he wouldn't be called on being under eighteen.

"You're a big kid," Healey said. "It must be a nice feeling, being big, nobody picks on you much. I tell you something, a guy my size sure gets his share of shit."

"There're a lot of ways of getting picked on," Wesley said, "that got nothing to do with size."

"Yeah," Healey said. "I noticed Mr. Kraler and your mother aren't all warm loving-kindness with you."

Wesley shrugged. "I grin and bear it."

"How old are you, anyway?"

"Sixteen."

"You could pass for twenty-one."

"If necessary," Wesley said.

"What're you going to do about the draft when you're eighteen?"

"I haven't decided yet," Wesley said.

"You want some advice from someone who's been there and almost didn't make it back?" Healey said. "No matter what you do, don't give 'em your name and let them give you a number. It ain't fun, Wesley, it ain't fun at all."

"What can you do?"

"Anything. You just don't want to let them get you in the army. You never saw such a lot of hopeless, disgusted men in your life, getting shot at, getting blown up on mines, coming down with every kind of disease and jungle rot you can think of, and nobody knowing what he's doing there. . . . Believe it or not, Wesley, I enlisted. *Enlisted,* for God's sake!"

"My father told me once," Wesley said, "don't ever volunteer for any wars."

"Your father knew what he was talking about," Healey said. "The army sure knows how to take the patriotism out of a man and it wasn't enemy action that did it for me, either, boy. The final cherry on the whipped cream was when a pal of mine and myself got off the plane in San Francisco, all gussied up in parade dress, with our ribbons and all. There were two pretty chicks walking in front of us at the airport and we hurried a little and caught up with them and I said, 'What're you girls doing tonight?' They stopped and looked at me as though I was a snake. They didn't say nary a word, but the girl nearest me spit at me, right in the face, just as calm as could be. Imagine that. Spit! Then they turned around and walked away from us." Healey shook his head. "We were home from the wars just ten minutes, with our Purple Hearts, and that was the welcome we got. Hail the conquering hero!" He laughed sourly. "You don't want to put your ass on the line for people like that, Wesley. Just keep on the move, float around, so they can't put their hands on you. The best place to get lost, the guys say, is Europe. Paris is the number one spot. Even if you have to register at the embassy, they don't take the trouble to smoke you out."

Talk around the campfire, Wesley thought. Old battles and loving thoughts of home. "I've been in Europe," he said. "I can speak French pretty good."

"I wouldn't wait too long if I was you, Wesley. You just make sure you're in gay Paree on your eighteenth birthday, pal," Healey said and waved for two more beers. The coffin he had accompanied to Indianapolis had been draped with the flag at the church and at the graveside. Mr. Kraler had the flag and had said at dinner that he was going to hang it in Max's room, which was Wesley's now.

The house was dark when they reached it, so there was something to be thankful for. If his mother had been up and smelled the beer on them, there would have been tears and a scene.

They went upstairs quietly and were just starting to get undressed when there was a little knock on the door and the door opened and Doris came in. She was barefooted and was wearing a nightgown that you could see through. She smiled at them and put her finger to her lips as she carefully closed the door behind her. "I heard you boys come in and I thought it might be nice to have a little gabfest. To get better acquainted, so to speak," she said. "Do either of you have a cigarette by any chance?" She talked in a mincing, self-conscious way, as though she had used baby talk until she was through with high school. She had droopy breasts, Wesley saw, though he tried not to keep looking, and a fat, low-slung ass. If I looked like that, he thought, I wouldn't go around dressed like that, except in total darkness. But Healey was smiling widely and there was a new gleam in his eye. He had already taken his shirt off and was naked from his waist up. He didn't have much of a build, either, Wesley noted.

"Here you are, dear lady," Healey said, courtly Virginia gentleman, "I have a pack right here in the pocket." He crossed the room to where his shirt was hanging over the back of a chair. He took out the cigarettes and matches, then started to take the shirt off the chair.

"You don't need to get dressed for Doris," Doris said. She wiggled her thin shoulders and smiled girlishly at Healey. "I'm a married woman. I know what men look like."

She *did* mean it, Wesley thought, when she gave Healey the signal during the day.

Healey gallantly lit Doris's cigarette. He offered one to Wesley. Wesley didn't like cigarettes but he took one because he was in Mr. Kraler's house.

"God," Doris said as she puffed at her cigarette and blew smoke rings, "I'm back in the land of the living. Poor Max. He wasn't much when he was alive, and he turned up dead for his one moment of glory. Boy, the bishop had a hard time making poor Max sound like something in his speech." She shook her head commiseratingly, then looked hard at Wesley. "Are you as bad as *they* say you are?"

"Evil," Wesley said.

"I bet," Doris said. "With your looks. *They* say you're a terror with married women."

"What?" Wesley asked, surprised.

"Just for your information," Doris said, "and because I think you're a nice boy, you better tell a certain Mrs. W. that she'd better get to the mailbox every morning before her husband."

"What the hell are you talking about?" Wesley asked, although he could guess. Some neighborhood gossip must have notice the U.M. bike parked in front of Mrs. Wertham's house more than once and blabbed to his mother.

"While you were out you were the subject of discussion," Doris said. "First of all that you were so different from Max and not different better, I can tell you that."

"I can guess," Wesley said.

"Your mother did not have many kind words for your father, either," Doris said. "He must have been something, if half of what she said was true. And you're following in his footsteps, she said, arrested and all in France for nearly killing a man in a drunken brawl."

"Hey," Healey said, "good for you, pal."

"And," Doris went on, "a virtual sex maniac like the old man. What with that disgusting Mrs. W., who's old enough to be your mother, and God knows how many other houses you go to and deliver more than the groceries." She giggled, her droopy breasts quivering under the transparent nightgown.

"Hey, I have a good idea," Wesley said. He felt he was being choked in the small room, with the loops of cigarette smoke and the coquetting, almost-naked mailicious girl and the leering soldier. "You two obviously have a lot to talk to each other about . . . "

"You can say that again, Wesley," said Healey.

"I'm not sleepy," Wesley said, "and I could use another breath of air. I'll probably be an hour or so," he said warningly. He didn't want to come back to the room and find the two of them in his bed.

"I may just stay for another cigarette," Doris said. "I'm not sleepy yet either."

"That makes three of us," said Healey.

Wesley started to stub out his cigarette, when the door was flung open. His mother was standing there, her eyes stony. Nobody said anything for a moment as Teresa stared first at him, then at Healey, then, for what seemed minutes, at Doris. Doris giggled.

"Wesley," his mother said, "I'm not responsible for the conduct of Mr. Healey or Mr. Kraler's daughter, who is a married woman. But I am responsible for *your* conduct." She spoke in a harsh whisper. "I don't want to wake up Mr. Kraler, so I'd appreciate it if whatever you do or say you do it quietly. And, Wesley, would you be good enough to come downstairs with me?"

When she was formal, as she was now, she was worse than when she was hysterical. He followed her downstairs through the darkened house to the living room. The flag from the coffin was folded on a table.

She turned on him, her face working. "Let me tell you something, Wesley," she said in that harsh whisper, "I've just seen the worst thing in my whole life. That little whore. Who got her in there—you? Who was going to lay her first, you or the soldier?" In her passion her vocabulary lost its pious euphemisms. "To do that on the very night that a son of the family was laid to rest after giving his life for his country. . . . If I told Mr. Kraler what's been going on in his house, he'd take a baseball bat to you."

"I'm not going to explain anything, Ma," Wesley said. "But you can tell Mr. Kraler that if he as much as tries to lift a finger to me, I'll kill him."

She fell back as though he had hit her. "I heard what you said. You said kill, didn't you?"

"I sure did," Wesley said.

"You've got the soul of a murderer. I should have let you rot in that French jail. That's where you belong."

"Get your facts straight," Wesley said roughly. "You had nothing to do with getting me out of jail. My uncle did it."

"Let your uncle take the consequences." She leaned forward, her face contorted. "I've done my best and I've failed." Suddenly she bent over and grabbed his penis through his trousers and pulled savagely at it. "I'd like to cut it off," she said.

He seized her wrist and roughly pulled her arm away. "You're crazy, Ma," he said. "You know that?"

"From this moment on," she said, "I want you to get out of this house. For good."

"That's a good idea," he said. "It's about time."

"And I warn you," she said, "my lawyer will do everything possible to make sure you don't get a penny of your father's dirty money. With your record it won't be too hard to convince a judge that it doesn't make any sense to put a fortune into the hands of a desperate murderer. Go, get out of here, go to your whores and hoodlums. Your father will be proud of you."

"Stuff the money," Wesley said.

"Is that your final word to your mother?" she said melodramatically.

"Yeah. My final word." He left her in the middle of the living room, breathing raucously, as though she were on the verge of a heart attack. He went into his room without knocking. Doris was gone, but Healey was lying propped up on the bed, smoking, still bare from the waist up, but with his pants on.

"Holy shit," Healey said, "that lady sure barged in at the wrong moment, didn't she?"

"Yeah." Wesley began throwing things into a small bag.

Healey watched him curiously. "Where you going, pal?"

"Out of here. Somewhere," Wesley said. He looked into his wallet to make sure he had the list of names he had been adding to ever since he got out of jail. He never left his wallet anywhere that his mother could find it.

"In the middle of the night?" Healey said.

"This minute."

"I guess I don't blame you," Healey said. "Breakfast is going to be a happy meal here." He laughed. "The next time the army sends me out with a coffin I'm going to tell them they got to give me a complete rundown on the family. If you ever get to Alexandria, look me up."

"Yeah," Wesley said. He looked around him to see if he had forgotten anything important in the room. Nothing. "So long, Healey," he said.

"So long, pal." Healey flicked ashes on the floor. "Remember what I said about Paris."

"I'll remember." Silently, his old windbreaker zipped up against the night's cold, he went out of the room, down the dark stairs and out of the house.

He remembered, too, as he walked along the windy dark street, carrying the small bag, that his father had told him that it had been one of the best days of his life when he realized he didn't hate his mother anymore. It had taken time, his father had said.

It would take time for the son, too, Wesley thought.

A day later he was in Chicago. He had gone into an all-night diner on the outskirts of Indianapolis when a truck driver came in who told the girl behind the counter that he was on the way to Chicago. Chicago, Wesley thought, was just as good a place to start whatever he was going to do as anyplace else and he asked the driver if he could come along. The driver said he'd be glad for the company and the trip had been comfortable and friendly and aside from having to listen to the driver talk about the troubles he was having with his seventeen-year-old daughter back in New Jersey, he had enjoyed it.

The driver had dropped him off near Wrigley Field and he'd looked at his list of addresses and seen William Abbott's address. Might as well start somewhere, he'd thought, and had gone to the address. It was about noon, but Abbott was still in pajamas and a rumpled bathrobe, in a beat-up, one-room studio littered with bottles, newspapers and coffee containers and crumpled pieces of paper near the typewriter.

He had not been favorably impressed with William Abbott, who pretended to know a lot more about Thomas Jordache than he really knew, and Wesley left as soon as he could.

The next two days he tried to get a job at two or three supermarkets, but they weren't hiring people at supermarkets that week in Chicago and people kept asking him for his union card. He was low in funds and he decided Chicago was not for him. He called his Uncle Rudolph in Bridgehampton, collect, to warn him he was coming there, because he didn't know where else to go.

Rudolph sounded funny on the phone, uneasy, as though he were afraid somebody who shouldn't be listening in was listening in.

"What's the matter?" Wesley said. "If you don't want me out there, I don't have to come."

"It's not that," Rudolph said, his voice troubled over the wire. "It's just that your mother called two days ago to find out if you were with me. She has a warrant out for your arrest."

"*What?*"

"For your arrest," Rudolph repeated. "She thinks I'm hiding you someplace."

"Arrest? What for?"

"She said you stole a hundred and fifty dollars from her household money, the money she kept in a pitcher over the stove in the kitchen, the night you left. She says she's going to teach you a lesson. *Did* you take the money?"

"I wish I had," Wesley said bitterly. That goddamn Healey, he thought. The army had taught him how to live off the land. Or even more likely, that cheese-faced Doris.

"I'll straighten it out," Rudolph said soothingly, "somehow. But for the time being I don't think it would be wise to come here. Do you need money? Let me know where you are and I'll send you a money order."

"I'm okay," Wesley said. "If I get to New York I'll call you." He hung up before Rudolph could say anything else.

That's all I need, he thought, the jug in Indianapolis.

Then he decided he'd go to New York. Rudolph wasn't the only person he knew in New York. He remembered the nice girl at *Time* saying that if he needed help to come to her. Nobody would think of looking for him at *Time* Magazine.

He was on the road the next morning.

CHAPTER 2

HE DID NOT talk to his uncle for almost two months after the telephone call from Chicago.

When he got to New York he went directly to Alice Larkin's office. He must have looked pretty awful after his days on the road, because she gasped as though someone had thrown a bucket of cold water over her when he came into her cubicle. He had had almost nothing to eat in days and had done his sleeping in truck cabs; he needed a shave, his collar was frayed, his pants were stained with grease from helping a driver change a tire on the big semitrailer outside Pittsburgh; and he had forty-five cents in his pocket.

But after the first shock, Miss Larkin seemed happy to see him and insisted on buying him lunch downstairs even before he could tell her what he was there for.

After he had eaten and was feeling like a human being again he had told her just about everything. He tried to make it sound unimportant, and joke about it, because he didn't want the nice girl to think he was an overgrown crybaby. She was easy to talk to, looking across the table at him intently through her glasses, her small, pink-cheeked face alert, as he explained why he had left Indianapolis and about the warrant for his arrest and the division of the estate, everything.

She didn't interrupt him as he poured it all out, just sighed or shook her head every once in a while in sympathy and indignation.

"Now," she said, when he had finished, "what're you going to do?"

"Well, I told you, the other time I was here," he said, "I sort of have the feeling that I'd like to look up the people who knew my father and get an idea of what he seemed like to them—you know—different people, different times of his life. I knew him less than three years." He was speaking earnestly now, not trying to sound ironic or grown up. "I feel as though there's a great big hole in my head—where my father ought to be—and I want to fill it as much as I can. I guess it sounds kind of foolish to you . . ."

"No, it doesn't," she said, "not at all."

"I told you I had a list of people . . ." He took his wallet out of his pocket and put the worn, creased sheet of paper with the names written on it onto the table. "The magazine seems to be able to find just about anybody they want to," he said, "and I thought, if it wasn't too much trouble for you, maybe in your spare time . . ."

"Of course," Miss Larkin said, "we're not as omniscient as you might . . ." She stopped when she saw the puzzled look on his face. "I mean as all-knowing as you might think, but we're pretty good at hunting down people." She looked at the list. "This is bound to take some time and there's no guaranteeing I can turn them *all* up, but . . ." She looked at him curiously. "Will you be staying in New York?"

"I suppose so."

"Where?"

He moved uncomfortably in his chair. "I haven't decided on any place yet. I came right here."

"Wesley," Miss Larkin said, "tell me the truth—how much money have you?"

"What's the difference?" he said defensively.

"You look like a scarecrow," she said. "You ate as though it was your first meal in a week. How much money have you got on you?"

He grinned weakly. "Forty-five cents," he said. "The heir to the Jordache fortune. Of course," he said hastily, "I could always call my uncle and he'd stake me, but for the time being I'd rather not."

"Do you mind if I take this list with me?" Miss Larkin said. "You'll have to tell me just who they are and where you think they might be found, of course . . ."

"Of course."

"It might take weeks."

"I'm in no hurry."

"And you expect to live for weeks on forty-five cents?" She sounded accusing, as though she were angry with him.

"Something'll turn up," he said vaguely. "Something always does."

"Would you be offended if I told you that something *has* turned up?" Unaccountably, she blushed.

"What?"

"Me," she said, louder than she realized. "*I've* turned up. Now listen carefully. I've got two rooms and a kitchenette. There's a perfectly comfortable sofa on which you can sleep. I'm not much of a cook, but you won't starve. . . ."

"I can't do that," Wesley protested.

"Why not?"

He grinned weakly again. "I don't know why not."

"Do you have any other clothes?"

"I have a clean shirt and a pair of socks and some underwear. I left them downstairs at the desk in your building."

She nodded primly. "A clean shirt," she said. "As far as I can tell, these people on the list are scattered all over the country. . . ."

"I guess so. My father moved around some."

"And you expect to travel all over the United States and go into people's homes and ask them the most intimate questions with one clean shirt to your name?"

"I hadn't thought about it much," he said defensively.

"You'd be lucky to get past the dogs, looking like that," she said. "It's a wonder they let you come up to my office."

"I guess I haven't looked in a mirror the last few days," he said.

"I'm going to tell you what I'm going to do with you," she said, sounding more certain of herself than she actually felt. "I'm going to have you stay with me and I'm going to lend you some money to buy some clothes and . . ."

"I can't let you do that."

"Of course you can," she said crisply. "You heard me say 'lend,' didn't you?"

"God knows when I'll ever get my money."

"I can wait," she said.

He sighed deeply. She could see how relieved he was. "I don't know why you want to be so nice to me," he said. "You hardly know me. . . ."

"I know enough about you to want to be nice to you," she said. Then she sighed, in her turn. "I have to be honest with you and tell you something. I'm not doing this out of random charity. I have an ulterior purpose. You know what ulterior means?"

"I've read a book, Miss Larkin," he said, a little hurt.

"Alice."

"I'm not as stupid as I look is what I meant to say."

"I don't believe you're stupid at all. Whatever," she said, taking a deep breath. "I have my own private, selfish reasons for doing what I'm doing and you might as well know them now as later. I just hope you won't be hurt."

"How can I be hurt if somebody wants to give me a place to live and dress me up like a decent human being?"

"I'll tell you how," she said. "When you left my office last time—No. Let me go back further than that. Like just about everybody else on the magazine I want to be a writer. I think of myself as a novelist. I had sixty pages of a novel done when I met you. When you left I went home and burned them."

"Why'd you do that?" he asked. "What's that got to do with me?"

"It's got everything to do with you. After doing the research and then hearing your story I decided what I was writing was junk—flat, worn-out, repetitive junk. I decided I wanted to write a story about a young boy whose father had been murdered. . . ."

"Oh," Wesley said softly. Now he eyed her cautiously.

"The young boy," she went on, avoiding his glance, looking down at the table, "wants to find out several things—who did it, why it was done, what his father's life was like— He didn't know his father, his parents had been divorced when he was a small boy, and his father had wandered off. If it worries you, let me tell you that the murder doesn't take place in Europe—I don't know anything about Europe, I've never been there. But the plan, in general, isn't so different from what you're doing. . . ."

"I see."

"So you can see what my ulterior purpose is."

"Yes."

"I'll have you right under my nose, I'll be able to study you, I'll be helping you to find all kinds of people. In a way, it could be considered a fair exchange. Would that bother you?"

Wesley shrugged. "Not necessarily," he said. "I don't quite see myself as a character in a book, though."

"It doesn't work like that," Miss Larkin said. "You'll be a character in my head and I'll take what I need and what I can use and hope for the best."

"What if you find out I'm not worth the trouble?"

"That's the chance I take."

"How does the book turn out?" Wesley asked curiously. "Does he find the murderer?"

"Eventually, yes."

"Then what does he do?"

"He takes his revenge."

Wesley chuckled sourly. "Pretty easy in a book, isn't it?"

"I don't intend to make it easy," she said.

"And what happens to the kid?"

She took another deep breath. "He gets killed," she said.

Wesley drummed absently on the tabletop, without looking at her. "That sounds logical," he said.

"It will be fiction, of course," she said.

"Some fiction," he said.

"If you get mixed up with writers," she said seriously, "or even somebody like me who *thinks* she's a writer, that's the chance you take. They'll try to steal a part of your soul."

"I didn't know I had one," Wesley said.

"Let me be the judge of that," Alice said. "Look—if the whole thing seems awful to you—or absurd—you don't have to go along with it."

"Will you write the book anyway?"

"Yes, I'll try."

"What the hell." He grinned. "If I do have a soul I guess I have enough to spare for a few pages in a book."

"Good," she said briskly, although her hands were trembling. She dug in her pocketbook. "I have to go back to work. But here's my charge account card at Bloomingdale's. It's on Fifty-ninth Street and Lexington Avenue." As she spoke she scribbled on a sheet of *Time* stationery. "You take this note along with my card so they'll know I authorized you to use it. You go into there this afternoon and buy yourself a couple of shirts and some flannel pants. Have them sent here, so they know it's my order. You can't go around looking like this. Then come back here about six o'clock and I'll take you home. Oh, and you'll need some money for bus fares and stuff like that." She dug in her bag again and gave him five dollars in singles and change.

"Thanks," he said. "Remember—whatever you give me is only a loan. I'm due to get about thirty thousand bucks when I'm eighteen."

"I'll remember," she said impatiently.

"Write it down," he insisted. "Five dollars and the date."

She made a face. "If you want." She took out a pen and her notebook and wrote in it. She pushed it across the table at him. "Satisfied?"

He looked at the page of the notebook gravely. "Okay," he said.

She put the notebook back in her bag.

"Now that I'm a character in a book," he said, "do I have to behave in any particular way? Do I have to watch my language or save maidens in distress or anything fancy like that?"

"You just behave any way you want," she said. Then she saw that he was grinning and that he had been making fun of her. She laughed. "Just don't be wise beyond your years, boy," she said.

*   *   *   *   *   *   *   *   *   *   *   *   *   *   *

He was on his way to Port Philip. Might as well start at the place where it all began, he had said, when Alice had found out that Theodore Boylan was still alive and still living there. Wesley's father had told him something about Boylan's connection with the family and it was just a couple of hours by train from the city.

He was neatly dressed now in flannel slacks and a sports jacket and good brown shoes from Bloomingdale's and Alice had insisted on trimming his hair, not too short, but neat. She seemed glad to have him around the small apartment on the West Side, near the park, She said she was beginning to feel melancholy living alone and that she looked forward to seeing him there when she got back after work. When young men called to take her out she introduced him as her cousin from the Midwest who was staying with her for a few weeks.

While waiting for Alice to come up with the information he had asked her for, he enjoyed wandering around the city. He went to a lot of movies and investigated things like the Radio City Music Hall and the United Nations building and the garish carnival of Broadway. At night, sometimes, Alice took him to the theater, which opened up a whole new world for him, since he had never seen a live show before.

When they were alone together in the apartment he tried to keep out of her way while she tapped away at the typewriter in her room. She never offered to let him read anything that she was writing and he didn't ask her any questions about it. Sometimes, he felt strange, sitting reading a magazine in the living room and listening to the typewriter and knowing that someone was in there writing about him or inventing somebody who might conceivably be him. Occasionally, she would come out and stare at him silently, a long time, as though she were studying him trying to get inside his head, then go back into her room and start at the machine again.

Whenever she took him to the theater or bought him a meal he made her put the amount of the tickets or the dinner in her notebook.

The train rattled north along the Hudson River. It was a clear sunny day and the river looked bright and clean and he thought how nice it would be to have a small boat and sail up its broad beaches, past the green cliffs, the small drowsy towns, and tie up at night and see what the life was like in them.

He saw the big, forbidding pile of Sing Sing at Ossining and felt a pang of kinship with the men pent up there, with the great free river just below their barred windows, counting off the years. Never, he thought, never for me. Whatever else happens.

When he got to Port Philip, he got into a taxi at the station and said, "The Boylan mansion." The driver looked at him curiously through the rearview mirror as he started the motor. "I don't reckon I've had a fare there for more than ten years," the driver said. "You going to work there?"

"No," Wesley said. "It's a social visit."

The driver made a sound. It was hard to figure out whether it was a cough or a laugh.

Wesley stared out the window as they drove through the town. It was shabby, the streets unkempt, as though the people who lived there, long ago, in the certainty of defeat, had given up the last attempt at civic beautification. In a funny way it reminded Wesley of bums lying on park benches, who, when aroused, spoke in good, college-educated accents.

The gates at the entrance to the Boylan grounds were broken and off their hinges, the gravel road leading up the hill toward the house was full of potholes and the lawns were overgrown, the wild hedges untrimmed. The house itself looked like a smaller version of Sing Sing.

"Wait a minute," he told the driver as he got out of the cab and paid him. "I want to see if they let me in." He pushed at the bell at the front door. He didn't hear any sound inside and he waited, then pushed again. He looked around as he waited. The weeds were almost waist high on the lawns and there were wild vines crawling over the garden walls.

A couple of minutes went by and he was about to turn back to the taxi and return to town when the door opened. A bent old man in a striped butler's vest stood there, peering at him. "Yes?" The man said.

"I'd like to talk to Mr. Boylan, please," Wesley said.

"Who should I say is calling?"

"Mr. Jordache," Wesley said.

The old man peered at him sharply, leaning forward to get a better look. "I will see if Mr. Boylan is in," he said and closed the door again.

The taxi driver honked his horn impatiently.

"Wait just a minute, will you?" Wesley called.

Thirty seconds later, the door opened again. "Mr. Boylan will see you now," the old man said.

Wesley waved to the driver to go and the taxi spurted around the potholed circle in front of the house and sped down the hill.

The old man led Wesley down a long dark hall and opened a door. "If you please, sir," the old man said, holding the door open for him.

Wesley went into a big room, which was dark, too, because of the heavy drapes, although it was sunny outside. A man was sitting in a winged leather chair, reading a book. At a table near one of the tall windows that let out onto the terrace, where there was some sunlight, two young women were sitting across from each other playing cards. They looked at him curiously as he came into the room. Although it was the middle of the afternoon, they were dressed in nightgowns, with frilly robes over them.

The man in the leather chair slowly stood up, carefully putting the book he had been reading facedown on the wing of the chair. "Ah," he said. "Mr. Jordache?" His voice was thin and dry.

"Yes, sir," Wesley said.

"Jordache," the man said. "I know the name." He chuckled thinly. "I'm Theodore Boylan. Sit down." He indicated an identical winged chair facing the one he had been sitting in. He didn't offer to shake hands. He had bright blond hair that had to be dyed, over that lined, quivering old face, the nose sharp, the eyes milky.

Wesley sat, feeling stiff and uncomfortable, wishing the two women weren't there, conscious of their staring at him.

"Whose pup are you?" Boylan asked, seating himself again. "The merchant prince's or the thug's?"

"Thomas," Wesley said. "Thomas Jordache was my father."

"Dead now." Boylan nodded, as if with approval. "Not long for this world. In the cards. Murdered." He addressed the women at the window. "In a pretty part of the world." He squinted maliciously at Wesley. "What do you want?"

"Well," Wesley said, "I know you knew my family . . ."

"Intimately," Boylan said. "All too intimately." Again he spoke to the women at the window. "The young man's aunt was a virgin when I met her. She was not a virgin when she left me. Believe it or not, at one moment I asked her to marry me. She refused." He turned on Wesley. "Has she told you that?"

"No," Wesley said.

"There are many things, I'm sure, they haven't told you. Your aunt and uncle used to take great pleasure in coming to this house. It was in better condition then. As was I." He chuckled again, a raucous little noise. "I taught them many things when they were young and hungry. They learned valuable lessons in this house. They have not been back to visit the old man for lo, these many years. Still, as you see, young man, I am not without company. . . ." He waved carelessly at the two women, who had gone back to playing cards. "Youthful beauties," he said ironically. "The advantages of wealth. You can buy youth. They come and go. Two, three months at a time, selected for me by a discreet madam who is an old and valued acquaintance of mine in the great city of New York and who is constantly surprised at what she hears from their ruby lips about the indomitable appetite of the old man."

"Oh, come off it, Teddy," one of the women said, shuffling the cards.

"My dears," Boylan said, "I would appreciate it if you would leave the men to their conversation for a while."

The woman who had spoken sighed and stood up. "Come on, Elly," she said, "he's in one of his goddamn moods."

The other woman stood up and they both went out, swinging their hips, their high-heeled mules making a clacking noise on the polished floor.

"There is one great advantage to paying for labor," Boylan said when the women had left the room, closing the big door behind them. "The employees are obedient. When one gets old one values obedience above all other virtues. So—young man—you are curious about the noble roots of your family. . . ."

"Actually," Wesley said, "it's my father mostly that I . . ."

"I was only acquainted with him by his deeds," Boylan said, "but Gretchen and Rudolph I knew all too well. Your Uncle Rudolph, I'm afraid, suffered, from an early age, from a prevalent American disease—he was interested only in money. I attempted to guide him, I showed him the way to eminence, an appreciation of the finer things of life, but the almighty dollar was raging in his veins. I warned him he was laying waste to himself, but he suffered from the Jew's deformation . . ." Boylan rubbed his middle finger against his thumb. "The clink of coin was heavenly music in his ears. Not content with the fortune he could amass himself, he married great money and in the end it did him in. He was foredoomed and I warned him, but he was deafened by the harps of gold." He laughed gleefully. Then he spoke more soberly. "He was a man who lacked the essential virtue of gratitude. Well, he's paid his price and I, for one, do not mourn for him."

"Really, Mr. Boylan," Wesley said stiffly, "what I came for was . . ."

"As for Gretchen," Boylan went on as though Wesley had not spoken, "prettiest girl in town. Ripe as a peony, blooming on a slag heap. Demure, she was, eyes downcast and modest. In the beginning. Not later. She could have had a life of ease and respect, travel; I was ready to offer her anything. I once bought her a bright red dress. When she came into a room shimmering in red, every man in the place felt anguish clutching at his throat." He shrugged. "What I offered she spurned. She wanted cheap young men, quick with false words, into bed, out of bed. She destroyed herself with her unbridled sensuality. If you see her, please remember my words and repeat them carefully to her."

Gaga, Wesley thought, absolutely gaga, with a crazy gift of gab. He tried not to think of his Aunt Gretchen walking into a room in a red dress bought for her by this loony old man. "What I'm trying to get at," he said doggedly, "is what my father . . ."

"Your father," Boylan said contemptuously, "was a criminal and an arsonist and belonged behind bars. He came here to spy on his sister and he burned a cross on the hill outside because on one of his marauding raids he discovered that his sister was upstairs in my bed and he saw me naked in this very room fixing her a drink. A burning cross. Symbol of bigotry and ignorance." Boylan spat out the words, still outraged after all the years by the flaming insult on his doorstep. "All this came out many years later, of course—the boy who was his accomplice—Claude Tinker by name, now a respectable citizen in this very town—confessed everything to me over a splendid dinner in my own dining room. Your father." Boylan wrinkled his long, thin, old man's reddened nose. "Good riddance, I'd say. I followed his career. As was to be expected, he failed at everything, even at keeping alive."

Wesley stood up. "Thank you very much, Mr. Boylan," he said, hating the man. "I believe I've heard enough. I'll be going now."

"As you wish," Boylan said carelessly. "You know the way to the door. I thought you might be interested in the truth—at your age the truth is often a useful guide for your own conduct. I'm too old to lie or cosset random young scum because once I was kind to a relative or two." He picked up his book from the wing of the chair and started reading.

As he went out of the room and walked quickly toward the front door, Wesley thought, My old man shouldn't have just burned a cross, he should have set fire to the whole goddamn place. With that sonofabitch in it.

He walked the few miles down the hill and to the station and was lucky because a train was just pulling into the station as he reached it.

When he got to the apartment Alice had dinner waiting for him. She saw that his lips were tight, his jaw tense, and they ate in silence. She didn't ask him how it had gone in Port Philip.

Dominic Joseph Agostino, who in his fighting days in the twenties and thirties had been known as Joe Agos, the Boston Beauty, and who had been in charge of the gym at the Revere Club when Thomas Jordache had worked there, was still alive, Alice told Wesley, and still working at the Revere Club. Tom Jordache had told Wesley that Agostino had been good to him, had saved his job once when he was suspected of rifling the members' lockers and had even persuaded him that he was good enough to start in the amateurs. All things considered, Thomas had told Wesley, he was glad he had had his fling at the fight game, even if in the end he had wound up as a bum. "What the hell," Thomas had said, "I enjoyed fighting. Getting paid for it was so much gravy. For a while, anyway." There was one wonderful thing about Agostino, Thomas had said, he had been as polite as a lady's maid with the members of the club with whom he sparred and full of compliments about how good they were and how they were improving in what he called The Art, but had managed never to let on for a minute that what he really would have liked to do was blow up every one of them, along with the building itself, with its fancy rooms and oil portraits of the old aristocracy of Boston on the walls.

"He was a model of deportment," Thomas had said admiringly, "and he taught me a lot."

Wesley took the shuttle to Boston from LaGuardia—thirty-six dollars round trip, as he wrote in the notebook he now kept for himself, to make sure that Alice wasn't slyly cheating herself about the money she advanced him. The trip would have been enjoyable, except for the ex-paratrooper who sat next to him, who started sweating as soon as the plane began taxiing and digging his nails into the palms of his hands and kept saying, once they were in the air, "Listen to the sound of that port engine. I don't like the sound of that port engine, we're going to crash, for Christ's sake and those guys up front don't give a damn."

The more you knew about anything, Wesley thought, the less you liked it.

The plane didn't crash and once they were on the ground the ex-paratrooper stopped sweating and looked like any other passenger as they got off the plane.

At the Revere Club, the old man at the front desk looked at him queerly when he asked if he could speak to Mr. Agostino.

"I'm Mr. Agostino," the man said. He had a husky, whispery, hoarse voice and he was small and skinny, with his uniform hanging loosely around his bones and his big Adam's apple moving up and down in his stringy neck.

"I mean the one who used to work in the gym," Wesley said.

"That's me." The man eyed him suspiciously. "I ain't worked in the gym for fifteen years. Too fucking old. Besides the arthritis. They made me the doorman. Out of the goodness of their hearts. What'd you want to see Agostino about?"

Wesley introduced himself. "Tommy Jordan's son," Agostino said flatly. "What do you know? I remember him. He got killed, didn't he? I read it somewhere." There was no emotion in the whispering, hoarse voice, with the flat South Boston accent. If the name stirred any pleasant memories in the balding head, decorated by a few wispy gray hairs, he kept them to himself. "You looking for a job?" His tone was accusing.

He eyed Wesley professionally. "You got a good built on you. You planning to go into the ring or anything like that?"

"I'm not a fighter," Wesley said.

"Just as well," Agostino said. "They don't box anymore at this club. They decided it wasn't a sport for gentlemen. All those niggers and all. Now, when they have to settle a difference of opinion, they sue each other." He laughed, his breath whistling through the gaps in his teeth.

"I just wanted to talk to you about my father for a few minutes," Wesley said, "if you have the time."

"Your father. Umm. He could punch, your father, with his right. You might as well have tied his left hand behind him, all the good it did. I saw him fight pro once. I saw him knock the bum out. But after the fight I told him, 'You'll never go to the top,' I told him, 'until you get yourself a left hand.' I guess he never did. Though the way things are now, he might of got himself a couple good paydays, being white and all. He wasn't a bad kid, your old man. Had a streak of larceny in him, I suspected; not that I blamed him, with the wall in this joint practically papered with dollar bills. There were all sorts of stories after he left. Somehow the word got around that he blackmailed one of the members, a lawyer, for God's sake, for five thousand bucks. The guy's father got wind of it and let it be known that his poor little son was sick, he was a kleptomaniac. Money kept disappearing all over the place, and I guess your old man caught the guy at it once and made him pay to keep quiet. Your father ever tell you any of this?"

"Yes," Wesley said. "He said it was his lucky day."

"That's a nice chunk of dough," Agostino said, "five big ones. What did he do with it?"

"He invested it," Wesley said. "Or rather his brother did it for him. He finished with a yacht."

"I read that, too, in the magazine," Agostino said. "A yacht. Shit. I wish I had a brother like that. A young punk like that winding up with a yacht!" He shook his head. "I got along with him okay, bought him a couple of beers from time to time. I wasn't too surprised he got killed. Yeah, I'll talk to you, if that's *all* you want. . . ." Now he sounded suspicious. "I'm not going to contribute to any Tom Jordan Memorial Fund or anything like that, if that's what you're after."

"All I want to do is talk awhile," Wesley said.

Agostino nodded. "Okay. I get a fifteen-minute break in a few minutes. The headwaiter from the dining room takes the desk for me. There's a saloon about five doors down. I'll meet you there. This time you can pay for the beers."

A portly gentleman in a black coat with a velvet collar came up to the desk and said, "Good afternoon, Joe. Any mail for me?"

"Good afternoon, Mr. Saunders," Agostino said, bowing a little. "It's nice to see you in the old place again. You out of the hospital for good now?"

"Until the next time," the portly gentleman said and laughed. Agostino laughed with him, wheezing.

"Age, you know, Joe," the man said.

"Isn't it the sad truth?" Agostino said. He turned and was reaching into the pigeon hole with S printed over it as Wesley went out of the club.

"The thing I remember best about him," Agostino was saying over the beers at the end of the dark bar, "was the day I was sparring with one of the members, big guy he was, young, twenty-five, twenty-six, old fucking Boston family"— the hatred was plain in his voice, in the still-fierce, coal-black, Sicilian eyes —"won some sort of crappy intercollegiate championship, pretty boy by the name of Greening, I remember the name to this day, Greening, thought he was hot shit with the gloves, light heavyweight, me I was still one thirty-six, one thirty-eight at the time, he never changed that cold, superior look on his face, the sonofabitch caught me one on the chin, an uppercut, all his weight behind it, I thought he'd broke my goddamn jaw. I had a bad cold that day, I couldn't breathe, sparring in the gym, for Christ's sake, you didn't dare tap one of the members any harder than you'd stroke a pussy, you'd be out on your ass before you could say boo if you drew two drops of blood from their beautiful Beacon Hill noses and this sonofabitch knocked me down, my teeth loose and my mouth all bloody, not being able to breathe, something to laugh about at the bar later with the other fancy pisspots, sucking the blood of the poor, the bastards." Agostino shook his head, the wisps of hair floating on the bald pate, his hand up to the bony jaw, as though he were still feeling to see if it was broken, the grating, furious old voice quiet for a moment. Looking at him, Wesley found it almost impossible to imagine him young, moving lightly around a ring, giving and receiving blows. One thing I'm sure of, he thought, watching Agostino noisily slurping his beer, I don't ever want to get that old.

"After that," Agostino went on, "it was pure pleasure. Greening was miffed, he hadn't gotten his day's exercise, he said it didn't hardly pay him to have undressed and he asked your father if he wanted to go a round or two. I gave your old man the sign and he put on the gloves. Well, boy, it was a treat to the eyes. That good, old, intercollegiate, straight-up stance didn't mean balls to your father, though he took a couple of real hard ones to the head before he caught on the shit meant business with *him,* too. Then he just massacred the guy, they didn't stop for rounds or anything polite like that, they just tore into each other. For a minute there I felt that boy there was making up to me, personally, for my whole lousy life. Finally your father caught him a beauty and the old Boston family went glassy-eyed and started moving in circles like a drunk comedian and Tom was ready to put the crusher on him, but I stepped in and stopped it. I wasn't worried about Tom, he knew what he was doing, but I had my job to consider. Mr. Greening, sir, came back to the land of the living, blood smeared all over his fucking Harvard Quadrangle face and just walked off with never a thank you. Your old man didn't have any doubts. 'There goes my job,' he said. 'Probably,' I said. 'It was worth it. For me.'" Agostino cackled merrily at the memory of the far-off golden moment. "Four days later I was told I had to fire him. I remember the last thing I told him—'Never trust the rich,' I told him." He looked at the clock above the bar. "I better be gettin' back. Nice of you to come and visit, son. Thanks for the beers." He picked up the visored uniform cap he had placed on the bar and put it on his head, very straight. It was too large for him and under it his pale, bony face looked like a starved child's. He started to leave, then turned and came back. "Tell you something, son, there're a lot of people I'd have like to see killed before your old man."

Then he shuffled, bent and arthritic, out the door to take up his post at the front desk of the club, where he would hand out the mail and laugh obsequiously, full of Sicilian dreams of vengeance and destruction, at the jokes of the members until the end of his days.

When he got back to New York that evening Alice could see that he was in a different mood from when he had returned from the visit to Boylan in Port Philip. "That fellow Agostino," he told her as he helped her prepare dinner in the kitchen, which consisted mostly of putting out plates and cutlery, "is a marvelous, weird old man. He sure was worth the trip." Then he told her as well as he could remember everything that the old boxer had said. She asked him to repeat sentences . . . "in the man's own words, if possible, Wesley," over and over again, as though she was trying to memorize them and get the exact tone of the man's voice, the rhythms of his speech and a picture of what he actually looked like.

"Back home in Sicily," she said, "he probably would have been burning crops and kidnapping *principessas*. Poor man, stuck in Boston, handing out mail. Oh," she said, "I got some news for you today in the office. I wrote a letter to an old newspaperman in Elysium, Ohio, who occasionally strings for us when there's anything of interest happening in that part of the world, and I think he's found your father's Clothilde for you."

"How the hell did he do that?" Wesley asked, although after Alice had discovered the whereabouts of Dominic Joseph Agostino he had begun to believe that nobody could avoid being pinpointed by *Time* Magazine if it were looking for him.

"It seems that there was a juicy divorce in Elysium quite a few years ago," Alice said, "a respected burgher named Harold Jordache—the name's familiar to you, I imagine . . .?" She smiled at him over the platter of cold cuts.

"Oh, come on," he said.

"His wife sued him for divorce because she found him in bed with the maid. It was big news in Elysium, Ohio, and our stringer, his name is Farrell, you might look him up if you have time, covered it for the local sheet. Farrell said the wife walked away with a bundle, the house, half the business, alimony, a woman publicly scorned and all that in a small, God-fearing town. Anyway, can you guess the name of the lady taken *in flagrante delicto?*"

"You tell me," Wesley said, although he could guess the name and even guess what *flagrante delicto* meant.

"Clothilde," Alice said triumphantly. "Clothilde Devereaux. She runs a Laundromat just down the street from Farrell's paper. I have the address in my pocketbook. How does that grab you?"

"I'll leave for Ohio tomorrow," Wesley said.

He stood in front of the Laundromat on the sleepy street. From the bus station he had called the Jordache Garage and Ford Dealer, with the idea of seeing his Great-Uncle Harold for a few minutes before looking up Clothilde Devereaux. Might as well get the ugly part over first. When Harold Jordache finally came to the phone and Wesley told him who he was, the man started to yell at him over the phone. "I don't want to have anything to do with you. Or anybody in your family." He spoke curiously, the traces of the German accent in his speech accentuated because of the high pitch of his voice. "I've had enough trouble from the goddamn Jordaches to last me a lifetime, if I live to be ninety. Don't you come snooping around here or my house or I'll have the police on you. I don't want anything to do with the son of the man who defiled my home. The only good thing I have to say about your father is that he's dead. Do you hear me?"

"I hear you," Wesley said and hung up the phone. He left the booth, shaking his head. He had been impressed by the neatness and beauty of the town as he came in on the bus, the trimmed lawns, the whitepainted, New England-style houses, the wooden churches with their narrow steeples, and he wondered how anybody could remain angry as long as his Great-Uncle Harold obviously had managed to in a pleasant town like this. Divorce had plainly not improved his great-uncle's temper. Idly, as he walked toward the address Alice had given him for the Laundromat, he speculated on how Great-Uncle Harold and his own mother would get along.

The Laundromat belonged to a chain and was like any other establishment of the kind—a big plate-glass window through which he could see rows of machines with chairs opposite them on which some women were sitting talking, waiting for their wash to be done.

He hesitated before going in. The way his father had spoken about Clothilde, with such a melancholy note of longing and regret for her beauty and goodness of character, made it seem almost silly for him to go past the swishing machines and the gossiping women to a counter behind which stood a thickset, short woman handling other people's laundry and making change, to say, "I am my father's son. He told me he loved you very much when he was about my age."

Still, he hadn't come all the way from New York to Ohio just to stare at a Laundromat window. He squared his shoulders and went in and ignored the curious stares of the women who had fallen silent to examine him as he passed them.

The woman had her back turned to him; she was putting paper-wrapped bundles of clean laundry into the racks as he came up to the counter. Her arms were bare and he noticed that they were strong and full, the skin dark. Her hair was pitch black and she had it tied carelessly on top of her head so that he could see the powerful muscles in her neck work as she tossed the bundles into place. She was wearing a loose print dress that made her back and shoulders seem even broader than they were. He waited at the counter until she had finished with the bundles and turned around. "Yes?" she said pleasantly. Her face was broad, with high cheekbones, and almost coppery complexion, and the whole effect, he thought, with the coal-black hair and the deep black eyes, was that of an Indian squaw. He remembered his father telling him that he thought that she had Indian blood in her, some tribe in the wilderness of Canada. To him, she looked very old.

"I'm looking for Mrs. Devereaux, Mrs. Clothilde Devereaux," he said.

She stared at him, unsmiling, studying him, frowning a little, as though she was trying to remember something. "I know you," she said. "You're Tom Jordache's son, aren't you?"

"Yes," he said.

"Good God Almighty," she said. "I thought I was seeing ghosts." She smiled. "The haunted Laundromat." She chuckled. She had a deep, throaty chuckle. He liked her after the chuckle, but, being honest with himself, he couldn't see any of the beauty his father had found in this aging, wide lady. "Lean over the counter, please," she said.

He leaned over and she took his face in her hands, the palms soft and firm, and stared at him, hard, for a moment, close up, then kissed him on the forehead. Behind him he heard one of the women opposite the washing machines giggle.

She released him and he stood erect again, still feeling the touch of soft lips on his forehead. Clothilde smiled, a little, almost dreamy, sad smile. "My Lord," Clothilde said softly, "Tom's son in this town." She began to undo the strings of the apron she wore over the print dress. "We'll get out of this place," she said. "We can't talk here. Sarah!" she called to the back of the store, behind the laundry racks, "will you come here, please?"

A blond young woman with straggly hair shuffled out and Clothilde said, "Sarah, I'm taking off the rest of the afternoon. It's only an hour before closing, anyway, and I have an important date. Take over here for me and lock up like a good girl, will you?"

"Yes, ma'am," the woman said.

Clothilde hung up her apron and did something with her hair, so that it fell straight to her shoulders. It made her look more Indian than ever. She pushed up a hinged portion of the counter and came out. She had wide hips, a generous bosom and thick, strong, unstockinged legs, and suddenly she reminded him almost unbearably of Kate.

She took his arm as they passed the sitting women, who were now staring frankly at the couple, nasty little smiles curling the corners of their mouths. When they were outside, Clothilde said, "Ever since the court case, the ladies of the town keep looking at me as though I'm the Whore of Babylon." She was still holding his arm and they started walking down the street. She breathed deeply. "My," she said, "it's good to get out in the air after smelling dirty laundry all day long." She looked obliquely at him. "You've heard about the case?"

"Yes," he said. "That's how I found out where you were."

"It's an ill wind," she said. "I know your father is dead." She said it flatly, as though whatever emotion she had suffered when she heard the news had been long ago put under control. "I saw in the article that he married twice. Was he happy?"

"The second time."

She nodded her head. "I was afraid he'd never be happy again. They all kept hounding him so. . . ."

"He owned a boat. A yacht," Wesley said. "On the Mediterranean. He loved the sea."

"Imagine that," she said wonderingly. "Tom on the Mediterranean. I always meant to travel, but . . ." She left the sentence unfinished.

"He named the boat the *Clothilde*."

"Oh, God," she said, still walking briskly, holding his arm. "The *Clothilde*." Then he saw that she was crying, the tears falling unheeded from the dark eyes, glistening on the thick black lashes.

"When people asked him how he happened to pick the name *Clothilde* for his ship, he used to say it was the name of an old queen of France. But he told me the real reason."

"After all those years," she said, wonderingly, her voice choked. "After what happened." Now her voice turned harsh. "Did he tell you about that, too?"

"Enough," Wesley said. "That his uncle found you and him—well—together, and threatened to have you deported back to Canada for corrupting the morals of a minor. . . ."

"Did he tell you the rest of it?" Her voice was even harsher than before.

"Enough. About you and his uncle. The stuff that came out in the trial and the papers," Wesley said uncomfortably.

"That ugly, slobbering man," Clothilde said fiercely. "I was a servant in his house. I couldn't run the risk of going back to Canada, my husband would have killed me. I tried to make Tom understand. He refused to understand. He wanted me to run away with him. A sixteen-year-old boy . . ." She laughed, the sound sad on the sunny, tree-lined street.

"He understood in the end," Wesley said. "He told me so. The name of the boat proves that, doesn't it?"

"I suppose so." She walked in silence, drying her tears roughly with the back of her hand. "Did he tell you I put in a note with his sandwiches one day when he went to work?"

"I don't think so."

"I wrote, 'I love you,'" she said. "That's how it all started." She laughed abruptly. "My God, he had an appetite. I never knew anybody, man or boy, who could eat like that. The meals I cooked for him! The roasts, the garden vegetables, the best of everything, when his uncle and the terrible family were away in Saratoga and we had the house to ourselves. I used to sing over the stove in the afternoons, waiting for him to come home. Those two weeks I'll remember all the days of my life." She stopped walking, as though pulled up by an invisible leash, and turned him around and held him by both arms as she stared into Wesley's eyes. "Why've you come here? Do you need anything from me?"

"No," he said. "I came just for what you're doing—talking about him."

After a moment of silence, in which the dark eyes searched his face, she kissed his forehead again.

"It's uncanny," she said, "how much you look like him. He was a beautiful young man—I told him he looked like Saint Sebastian—he looked it up in the encyclopedia in the library—that's where he found out where my name came from, too. It was hard to imagine him, the sort of wild boy he was, looking up anything in the encyclopedia." Her face softened as she spoke, and Wesley imagined that she must have had very much the same expression on her face when his father had come back from the library and told her what he had learned there.

"Are you disappointed?" she asked.

"In what?"

"After what your father must have told you about me, naming a boat after me and all, queen of France . . ." She laughed briefly. "And then you see a fat old lady behind the counter of a Laundromat."

"No," Wesley said, "I'm not disappointed." He wasn't quite sure he was telling the truth. She must have been a lot different when she was younger, he thought.

"You're a decent boy," she said, as they started walking again. "I hope you're having a better time than your father did."

"I'm okay," Wesley said.

"After we—well—after we broke up, in a manner of speaking, although we still lived in the same house and I saw him every day and served him his meals with the family in the dining room, but we never said another word to each other, except for good-bye, he turned ferocious, as though he was tormented. He'd come home bloody from fights night after night, people began to treat him as though he was a stray, dangerous dog, he screwed every little tart in town. I heard about it, of course, I guess it was a kind of revenge, I didn't begrudge him it, although I knew it would one day catch up with him, in this nasty, hypocritical town. They put him in jail for rape—rape, mind you, when every girl and woman in town with hot pants was after him like kids after a fire engine. Did he tell you about that?"

"Yes."

"And the twins he was supposed to have knocked up and the father made the complaint?"

"Yes, he told me."

"He must have loved you very much," Clothilde said, "to tell you things like that."

"I guess he did. He liked to talk to me." Nights on deck, under the stars, or in the dark pilothouse.

"Naturally they would pick on him, his reputation here and all, everybody was glad to believe the worst about him," Clothilde said bitterly. "Those twins had a choice of fifty fathers! Including the cop who arrested Tom. I see them—the twins—they're still in town, grown women. I advise you not to look *them* up. One of the kids looks as though he was your brother." Clothilde chuckled merrily. "Finally, there's some decent blood running through a few veins in this town. Ah . . ." she said softly, "sometimes late at night, I take to wondering what it would have been like, how it all would have turned out if I'd listened to his crazy begging and run off with him, a twenty-five-year-old servant and a sixteen-year-old boy, without a penny between us. . . . I couldn't do it to him, could I?" she asked, pleading.

"No, I guess not," Wesley said.

"Ah, I keep on talking. About myself. About ancient history." Clothilde shook her head impatiently. "What about you? Are you all right?"

"Not too bad," Wesley said.

"You having a good time?"

"I wouldn't go as far as to say that."

"Still," she said, "you look as though you're being taken care of—nice clothes and all, like a young gentleman."

"I've been lucky," Wesley said. "In a way. Somebody is taking care of me. Sort of."

"You can tell me all about yourself, over dinner. You're in no hurry to leave town, are you?"

"Not really," Wesley said. "I figured tomorrow."

"I'll make you a roast loin of pork, with mashed potatoes and applesauce and red cabbage. It was one of your father's favorite meals." She hesitated. "I have to tell you something, Wesley," she said. "I'm not alone. I'm living with a nice man, he's the foreman at the furniture factory. We're not married. He's got a wife and two kids and they're Catholics. . . . He'll be at dinner. You don't mind?" she asked anxiously.

"It's got nothing to do with me," Wesley said, "or my father."

"People're funny," Clothilde said. "You never know how they're going to react." She sighed. "A woman can't live alone. At least not me. Ah, you live two days— every day, with the man coming home and sitting down at night to read his paper and drink his beer and not say anything much to you, and in your memory, the wonderful days you had when you were younger, with a wild boy. Wesley, I have to tell you, your father was the gentlest and tenderest man a woman could ever hope to find in her travels on this earth. And he had the softest skin, like silk, over all those young muscles, that I've ever felt. You don't mind my talking like this, do you?"

"I want to hear it," Wesley said, feeling the tears come to his eyes now, not for himself or even for his dead father, but for this wide-shouldered, Indian-dark, aging woman, marked by a lifetime of work and disappointment, walking by his side.

"Do you like wine with your dinner?" Clothilde asked.

"I wouldn't mind a glass," Wesley said. "I was in France for quite a long time."

"We'll stop in at the liquor store," Clothilde said gaily, "and buy a delicious bottle of red wine to celebrate the visit of my love's beautiful son to an old lady. Frank— that's my man, the foreman at the furniture factory, can give up his beer for the occasion."

Schultz, his father's old manager, was, Alice told him, in the Hebrew Home for the Aged in the Bronx.

"He's that fat old man sitting in the hall with his hat and coat on as though he's going out," the attendant told Wesley. "Only he never goes out. He sits like that all day, every day, never saying anything. I don't know if he'll talk to you. He don't talk to anyone else."

Wesley walked down the bare hall to where an enormously fat man, bloating out of his suit and overcoat, a derby hat squarely on his head, his features little squiggles in the immense expanse of his face, sat on a straight wooden chair, staring at the opposite wall, the eyes half closed, the breath coming in snorts.

"Mr. Schultz," Wesley said, "can I talk to you for a minute?"

The fat man's wrinkled eyelids lifted heavily and the eyes slowly turned in Wesley's direction, although the head, with its derby, remained rigid.

"What's it to you if I'm Schultz or I'm not Schultz?" the fat man said. His voice was guttural and there was a clacking of dentures as he spoke.

"My name is Wesley Jordache," Wesley said. "A long time ago you managed my father. Tom Jordan."

The eyes slowly went back to their original position, staring at the peeling paint of the wall of the corridor. "Tom Jordan," the fat man said. "I don't allow that name to be used in my presence. I hear tell he got himself killed. Son or no son, don't think you're going to hear old Schultzy say he's sorry. He had it in him to go someplace and he screwed it away. Two weeks with an English whore, eating and drinking like a pig, after all I did to bring him along. And then, when he was down on his ass I got him a salary in Las Vegas. He got fifty bucks a day sparring with Freddy Quayles—there was a boy, my one chance in my whole miserable life to handle a champion—and what does he do, he shacks up with Quayles' wife, and then when Quayles goes to his room to object to his conduct, he near murders him. And Quayles couldn't beat my mother after that. If I hadn't taken pity on your stupid old man and loaned him my car to get out of Vegas, the mob would've cut him to little pieces with steak knives. Your old man wasn't anything to be proud of, boy, and that's for certain, but he sure was dynamite in a hotel room. Only, for money, you have to fight in a ring twenty-four by twenty-four feet, with a referee on the premises. If they let your old man fight in a closet and charged admission he'd still be the champion of the world, the sonofabitch. My one chance, Freddy Quayles, moved like a dancer, wrecked for cunt. You want to hear about your old man—I'll tell you about your old man—he let his cock destroy him."

"But you were with him before that," Wesley said, "there were other things . . . ."

"Destroyed by his cock," the fat man said, with the clacking of dentures, as he stared straight ahead of him. "I said my say. Get the fuck out of here, I'm a busy man."

Wesley started to say something else, then realized it was hopeless. He shrugged and went out, leaving the fat man in his overcoat and derby hat staring at the wall across from him.

Dutifully, not knowing whether to laugh or cry as he spoke, Wesley made his report of the visit with Schultz to Alice. When he finished, he said, "I don't know whether I want to talk to anyone else who knew him, at least on this side of the Atlantic. Maybe there are some things a son shouldn't hear about his father. A lot of things, maybe. What's the sense in my listening to people smear him all over the country? He must have been a different man while he was in America. There's no connection between the man I knew and the man these people're talking about. If I hear one more person tell me how rotten my father was and how glad they are he's dead, maybe I'll go back to Indianapolis and let my mother cut my hair and take me to church and forget about my father once and for all. . . ." He stopped when he saw the disapproval on Alice's face.

"That's quitting," she said.

"Maybe that's the name of the game," Wesley said. "At least my game."

"Clothilde didn't talk like that about your father," Alice said, her eyes angry behind her glasses.

"A fat lady in a Laundromat," Wesley said cruelly.

"Say you're sorry you said that," Alice said, sounding schoolteacherly.

"All right," he said listlessly, "I'm sorry. But, I have a feeling I'm just wasting time and money. My time," he said, with a wry smile, "and your money,"

"Don't you worry about my money," she said.

"I suppose," Wesley said, "the character in your book is a fine, upstanding young man who never gets down in the dumps and he finds out that his father was one of nature's noblemen, who went around while he was alive doing good deeds and helping the poor and being nice to old ladies and never screwing a friend's wife. . . ."

"Shut up, Wesley," Alice said. "That's enough of that. Don't you tell me what I'm writing. When the book comes out, if it ever comes out, you can buy it and then tell me what the characters are like. Not before."

They were in the living room, Alice seated in an easy chair and Wesley standing at the window looking out at the dark street. Alice was dressed to go out because she had a date to go to a party and was waiting for the man who was going to escort her.

"I hate this goddamn city," Wesley said, staring down at the empty street, "I wish I was a thousand miles out to sea. Oh, hell!" He moved away from the window and threw himself full length on the sofa. "Christ, if I could only be back in France, just one night, with people I love and who I know love me . . ."

"Take your shoes off the sofa," Alice said sharply. "You're not in a stable."

"Sorry," he said, moving his legs so that his feet were on the floor. "I was brought up uncouth, or so people keep telling me."

Then he heard her sobbing. He lay still for a moment, closing his eyes, wishing the dry, uneven sound would go away. But it didn't go away and he jumped up and went over to the chair in which she was sitting with her head in her hands, her shoulders moving convulsively. He knelt in front of her and put his arms around her. She felt small and fragile and soft in her pretty black party dress.

"I'm sorry," he said gently. "Honest, I didn't mean what I said, honest, I'm just sore at myself and that's how it came out. Don't think I don't appreciate everything you've done for me. I don't want to let you down, only sometimes, like tonight . . ."

She raised her head, her face tearstained. "Forgive me for crying," she said. "I hate women who cry. I had an awful day, too, people were yelling at me all day. You can put your shoes on the sofa anytime you want." She laughed, through her tears.

"Never again," he said, still holding her, glad that she had laughed, wanting to protect her against disappointment and people yelling at her all day and the city and his own black character.

They looked at each other in silence, her clear wet eyes magnified by her glasses.

She smiled tremulously at him. He pulled her gently toward him and kissed her. She put her arm around him and held him. Her lips were as soft as anything he had ever imagined, the very essence of softness. Finally, she pulled away from him. All tears were gone. "So, that's what a girl has to do to get a kiss around here," she said, laughing.

The doorbell rang from downstairs. She jumped out of the chair and he stood up. "There's my date," she said. "Entertain him while I fix my face. His field is archaeology."

She fled into the bathroom.

There was a knock on the door and Wesley opened it. A tall, skinny young man with a domed forehead and steel-rimmed glasses was standing there. "Hello," the man said. "Is Alice in?"

"She'll be out in a minute," Wesley said, closing the door as the man came in. "I'm to entertain you until she's ready. My name is Jordache. I'm her cousin."

"Robinson," the man said. They shook hands.

Wesley wondered how he was expected to entertain him. "You want to listen to the radio?" he asked.

"Not especially," the man said. "May I sit down?"

"Of course."

Robinson sat down in the easy chair and crossed his long legs and took out a package of cigarettes. "Smoke?" he said, offering the package to Wesley.

"No, thanks." He watched Robinson light his cigarette. How did you talk to a man whose field is archaeology? "I saw some ruins in France when I was there," he offered hopefully. "The arena in Nîmes, Arles, stuff like that," he said lamely.

"Is that so?" Robinson said, blowing smoke. "Interesting."

Wesley wondered if Robinson would be so offhand if he was told that just before he rang the bell, Wesley had kissed Alice Larkin, Robinson's date for the night, in the very chair he was sitting in and that before that he had made her cry. He felt condescendingly superior to the lanky man in his baggy slacks and five-colored, nubbly tweed jacket with leather patches on the elbows, although maybe that was the way all archaeologists dressed, maybe it was a uniform that commanded respect in those circles. "Where did you dig?" he said abruptly.

"What's that?" Robinson stopped his cigarette in midair, on the way to his mouth.

"I said, where did you dig?" Wesley said. "Alice told me you were in the field. Isn't that what archaeologists do—dig?"

"Oh, I see what you mean. Syria mostly. A little bit in Turkey."

"What did you find?" Alice had asked him to entertain the man and he was doing his best.

"Shards, mostly."

"I see," Wesley said, resolving to look up the word. "Shards."

"You interested in archaeology?"

"Moderately," Wesley said.

There was a silence and Wesley had the impression Robinson wasn't being entertained. "What's Syria like?" he asked.

"Grim," Robinson said. "Grim and beautiful. You ought to go there some day."

"I plan to," Wesley said.

"What college you go to?" Robinson asked.

"I haven't made up my mind yet," Wesley said.

"I would go to Stanford," said Robinson. "If you could get in. Marvelous people out there."

"I'll remember that."

Robinson peered at him nearsightedly through the steel-rimmed glasses. "You said you were Alice's cousin?"

"Yes."

"I didn't know she had a cousin," Robinson said. "Where you from?"

"Indianapolis," Wesley said promptly.

"Dreadful place. What're you doing in New York?"

"Visiting Alice."

"Oh, I see. Where do you stay in New York?"

"Here," Wesley said, feeling as though the man were excavating him.

"Oh." Robinson looked around at the small room gloomily. "A little cramped, I'd say."

"We make do."

"It's a convenient location. Near Lincoln Center and all . . ." Robinson seemed depressed. "Where do you sleep?"

"On the sofa."

Robinson stubbed out his cigarette and lit another. "Well," he said, sounding more depressed than ever, "I suppose . . . cousins . . ."

Alice came in, bright as a rosebud, with her party contacts in place, so she wouldn't look like a secretarial mouse, as she had explained to Wesley other times she had gone out on dates.

"Well," she said gaily, "have you two gentlemen had a nice chat?"

"Fascinating," Robinson said gloomily as he heaved himself to his feet. "We'd better be going. It's late." Alice must be pretty hard up, Wesley thought, if Robinson was the best she could do, a man who spent his life digging up shards. He wished, despairingly, that he was twenty-seven years old. He was glad he wasn't going to be around when Alice had to explain to the archaeologist just what sort of cousins they were.

"Wesley," Alice said, "there're two roast beef sandwiches and some beer in the icebox if you get hungry. Oh—I nearly forgot—I found the address and telephone number of the man you were looking for—Mr. Renway, who was a shipmate of your father's. I called him today and he said he's looking forward to seeing you. I got his address through the National Maritime Union. It's right near here, in the West Nineties. He lives with his brother when he's not at sea. He sounded awfully nice on the telephone. You going to see him? He said he'd be in all day tomorrow."

"I'll see how I feel tomorrow," Wesley said ungraciously and Alice gave him a reproachful look.

Robinson helped Alice on with her coat, and said as they went out the door, "Remember Stanford."

"I will," Wesley said, thinking, the reason he's so keen on Stanford is it's three thousand miles away from Alice Larkin.

He had no idea what time it was when he was awakened, as he slept under the blanket on the sofa, by the sound of murmured conversation on the other side of the front door. Then there was the click of the key in the lock and he heard Alice come in, softly, alone. She came over silently to the sofa and he felt her staring down at him, but he kept his eyes closed, pretending to be asleep. He heard her sigh, then move away. A moment later he heard her door shut and then the sound of her typewriter.

I wonder what she expected me to do? he thought, just before he fell back to sleep.

Calvin Renway reminded Wesley of Bunny Dwyer. His skin was coffee-colored, almost the same as Bunny's when Bunny had been out in the sun all summer, and he was small and delicate-boned and the muscles of his arms showed sharply in his short-sleeved flowered shirt and his voice was gentle, with an underlying permanent tone of politeness, as he welcomed Wesley at the door of his brother's home, saying, "Well, this is a nice day, the son of Tom Jordache come to visit. Come in, boy, come in. The nice lady on the phone said you'd be coming up, come in."

He led Wesley into the living room and pushed the biggest chair a couple of inches toward him and said, "Make yourself comfortable, boy. Can I get you a beer? It's past noon, time for a beer."

"No, thank you, Mr. Renway," Wesley said.

"The name's Calvin, Wesley," Renway said. "I sure was surprised when that nice lady called and said you'd be looking for me—I haven't seen your father for all these years—you ship out with a man and he means something special to you that you carry with you all your days, and then he goes his way and you go yours—ships that pass in the night, as you might say—and then a big young man rings your doorbell—by God the time does pass, doesn't it?—I never got married, never had any son, to my sorrow, a seaman's life, one port after another, no time to court a woman and the ones who want to enter into wedlock"—he laughed heartily, gleaming white teeth in the wide, kindly mouth —"not the sort you'd want as the mother of your kids, if you ever could be sure, if you know what I mean. But there's no mistaking about you, boy, the moment you appeared at the door, there was no mistake, there was Tom Jordache's kid, yes, sir, I bet he's proud of you, a big strong boy, with Tom Jordache printed all over your face. . . ."

"Mr. Renway—Calvin, I mean—" Wesley said uneasily, "didn't the lady tell you over the phone?"

Renway looked puzzled. "Tell me what?" he said. "All the lady said to me was, Are you the Mr. Renway was once on the same cargo vessel with Tom Jordache? and when I said, Yes, ma'am, the same, she said, Tom Jordache's boy is in town and he'd like to talk to you for a few minutes, that's all she said and asked if my address was the same she got from the Maritime Union."

"Calvin," Wesley said, "my father's dead. He got murdered in Antibes."

"Oh, Lord," Renway whispered. He said nothing more, but turned his face away to the wall, silently, for a long minute, hiding pain, as though somehow it was a breach of manners to show unbearable sorrow publicly. His long dark hands clenched and unclenched in an unconscious spasm, as though his hands were the only part of him that hadn't learned the lesson that it was useless to let the world know when he was hurting.

Finally, he turned back to Wesley. "Murdered," he said flatly. "They sure do away with the good ones, don't they? Don't tell me the story, boy. Some other time. It can wait, I'm in no hurry for any details. It's kind of you to come and tell me what happened—I could've gone on for years without knowing and I might be in a bar in Marseilles or New Orleans or someplace, drinking a couple of beers and talking about the old days when we crewed together on the *Elga Anderson,* maybe the nastiest vessel on the Atlantic or any other ocean, when he saved my life, in a manner of speaking, and somebody would say, 'Tom Jordache, why he died ages ago.' It's better this way and I thank you. I suppose you want to talk about him, boy—that's why you're here, I take it . . . ?"

"If you don't mind," Wesley said.

"Times were different then," Renway said. "On ships, anyway. They didn't call us blacks those days or mister, we were niggers and never forget it. I'm not saying your father was a special friend or a preacher or anything like that, but when he passed me in the morning, it was always, Hi, bud, how're they treating you, nothing special, just a normal human greeting, which was like a band playing those days on that nasty ship, the way just about everybody else was treating me. Your pa ever mention the name Falconetti to you?"

"I know something about him."

"The nastiest man I ever had the misfortune to come across, black or white," Renway said. "Big bull of a man, terrorized the crew, he beat up on men just for the animal pleasure of it and out of meanness of spirit and he said he wouldn't let no niggers sit down in the same messroom with him and I was the only black on board and that meant whenever he came into the room, even if I was in the middle of supper, I'd have to get up and go out. Then your pa took him on, the only one out of a crew of twenty-eight who had the guts to do it—he didn't do it for me, Falconetti'd been bugging Bunny Dwyer too—and your pa gave him the licking of his life, maybe he went too far, like the other men said, he shamed him every day, whenever they happened to pass each other, your pa'd say, come over here, slob, and punch him hard in the stomach, so that that big bull of a man would be left standing there, with people watching, bent over, with tears in his eyes.

"One night, it was dark and stormy, waves thirty feet high, in the messroom Falconetti quiet as a lamb, your pa came and got me and took me back to the messroom, the radio was on, and he said, 'We're just going to sit down like gentlemen next to this gentleman here and enjoy the music.' I sat myself down next to Falconetti—my heart was beating, I can assure you, I was still scared—but nobody said as much as boo and finally, after a while, your pa said to the man, 'You can go now, slob,' and Falconetti got up and looked around at the men in the room, none of them looking at him, and he went out and up to the deck and jumped over the side.

"It didn't make your pa popular with the other men; they said it's one thing to beat up on a man, but it's another to send him to his death like that. I'm not a vengeful man, Wesley, but I didn't go along with that talk—I kept remembering how I felt sitting down next to that nasty man, with the music playing, and him not saying a single word. I tell you it was one of the greatest, most satisfactory moments of my life and I remember it to this day with pleasure and I owe it to your pa and I'll never forget it."

Renway had been talking in a kind of singsong chant, with his eyes almost closed, as though seeing the whole thing over again, as though he was not in the neat little living room in the West Nineties in New York City, but back in the hushed messroom among the silent, uncomfortable men, tasting once more the moment of exquisite pleasure, safe, protected by the courage of the father of the boy sitting across from him.

He opened his eyes and looked thoughtfully at Wesley. "I tell you, boy," he said, "if you turn out to be half the man your father was, you should bless God every day for your luck. Wait here a minute." He stood up and went into a bedroom that gave off the living room. Wesley could hear a drawer opening, then closing a few seconds later. Renway came back into the living room carrying something wrapped in tissue paper. He took off the tissue paper and Wesley saw that he was holding a small leather box, inlaid with gold. "I bought this box in Italy," Renway said, "in the town of Florence, they make them there, it's a specialty of the town. Here." He thrust it toward Wesley. "Take it."

Wesley held back. "It's your box, Calvin," he said. "It must have cost an awful lot of dough. What do you want to give it to me for, you didn't even know I was alive until yesterday afternoon?"

"Take it," Renway said harshly. "I want the son of the man who did what he did for me to have something I cherish." Gently, he placed the box in Wesley's hand.

"It's a beautiful box," Wesley said. "Thanks."

"Save your thanks for a time they're needed," Renway said. "Now I'm going to put on my coat and I'm going to take you to One Hundred and Twenty-Fifth Street and I'm going to feed you the best lunch money can buy in Harlem in the city of New York."

The lunch was enormous, fried chicken and sweet potatoes, and they drank a lot of beer with it and Renway put sorrow aside for a time and told Wesley stories about Glasgow and Rio de Janeiro and Piraeus and the Trieste and said his brother kept after him to quit the sea but whenever he thought of living on land and never seeing a new town rising up from the sea as they made port, he knew that he could never bring himself to stop wandering on good ships and bad ships across the length and breadth of the oceans.

When they said good-bye, he made Wesley swear that whenever he heard he was in town he would come and have a meal with him again.

Going downtown in the subway, with the gold-inlaid, hard leather box in his pocket, Wesley decided he was going to throw away his list. I'm going to quit while I'm ahead, he told himself, feeling a weight lifting from his heart.

CHAPTER 3

RUDOLPH WAS SITTING on the deck in front of the house he had rented, looking out over the high dune at the stretch of white beach and the rollers of the open Atlantic. It was a mild, mid-September morning and the sun was pleasantly warm, reflecting off the script of Gretchen's screenplay he was rereading. Next to him, stretched out on an air mattress in a bathing suit, lay Helen Morison, who had a house farther down the beach, but who spent several nights a week with him. She was a divorcée, who had come over to him at a neighbor's cocktail party and introduced herself because she recognized him. She was a friend of Gretchen's. They had become acquainted at one of Ida Cohen's Women's Liberation meetings, where, according to Gretchen, Helen Morison's ironic, efficient manner of presenting facts and programs was in marked contrast to Ida's wild lunges at the perfidy of the male sex, Helen had no enmity toward the male sex, Rudolph had noted. "Quite the contrary," he had told her and she had laughed and agreed. The fact that she was living on Mr. Morison's alimony and sending her thirteen-year-old son to an exclusive, all-boys' Episcopal school, also at Mr. Morison's expense, did not seem to trouble her. Rudolph, who knew how often his own actions hardly reflected his principles, never pressed the point with her.

She was a tall, slender woman, with a profile that could be stern in response. She did not need a brassiere and she wore her dark, reddish brown hair long and often put it up in the evenings when he came to take her to dinner. In a rigorously Republican community, she was at the forefront of the Democratic Party affairs and had lost friends in the process. She was one of those women who could be depended upon more than most men to act courageously in a disaster.

She had been for her daily swim that morning, even though the sea was growing colder every night and the air was cool. She did not neglect her body. She made no secret of the fact that they were lovers.

He was very fond of her. Perhaps more than that. But he was not the man to rush to expose his emotions or make declarations that would haunt him later, when all the facts were in, the emotions added up.

For the moment he was engrossed in Gretchen's movie project. In rereading the screenplay he liked it more than ever. It was called *Restoration Comedy,* a play on words, since the plot involved the young heroine in bullying, cajoling, begging and arguing an entire dying mill town in Pennsylvania, a fictitious community called Laundston, into restoring five streets of fine old town houses that had fallen into neglect when the mill had shut down. The script was full of the energy of the girl who, with guile, good looks, coquetry and a wild sense of humor, combined with a pragmatic, womanly attitude toward occasional dishonesty, captured cynical bankers, crooked politicians, starving young architects, lonely secretaries, stultified bureaucrats, failing contractors, dragooned college students into doing day-laborers' work, in the process of creating an esthetically satisfactory, financially sound, middle-income suburb, which now, because of the new highways, was easily accessible to commuters from Philadelphia and Camden. The interesting part of it, to Rudolph, was that even though it was a complete work of fiction and no such place existed, it seemed to him, as a hardheaded businessman, like an eminently practical idea.

He was not sure of two things, though: the title, which he thought smacked a little of a course in English literature, and Gretchen's ability to bring it off. Still, it wasn't only brotherly indulgence that had made him back Gretchen to the tune of a third of the film's budget and spend countless hours with Johnny Heath wrangling over contracts in Gretchen's behalf. Ida Cohen and Gretchen herself had found backers for the rest of the cost of the picture and given enough time could have got all the financing without him.

It amused him, and he didn't mind driving into New York twice a week for it, and now he didn't have to say to friends that they could call at any time, he'd be at home all day.

It had taken months and months to get this far and Rudolph had learned a great deal about the movie business, not all of it agreeable, but Gretchen had called to ask him to come to New York the next day, not in his capacity as an angel, but as an "idea man," as she put it, because, when they were talking together about where to find a suitable location, he had suggested, half jokingly, their old hometown, Port Philip, where a whole quarter of great old houses had lain derelict for more than twenty years. Gretchen had gone up there with architects and the scene designer and they had all told Rudolph that the place was perfect and Gretchen was well on her way toward making a deal with the mayor and the town board to get all the help necessary for shooting the picture there. Rudolph was not sure he was ever going to visit the company on location. In the end, Port Philip and the neighboring town of Whitby did not have the most pleasant associations for him.

He finished reading the script with a last little chuckle.

"You still like it?" Helen asked.

"More than ever." He knew that Helen thought the script wasn't openly partisan enough in its politics. She also said the same thing about *his* politics. "You have been numbered by the Cold War," she said, "and the corruption in Washington and Vietnam and general hardening of the arteries. When was the last time you voted?"

"I don't remember," he said, although he did—for Johnson in 1964. After that, the process had seemed footless.

"Shame," Helen said. She voted ferociously, whenever she got the opportunity. There was no hardening of the arteries for Helen Morison. "Don't you think Gretchen needs a political adviser? I'd do it for free."

"I would think that's the last thing she needs," Rudolph said. "For free or no."

"I will finally convert you," Helen said.

"To what?"

"Jeffersonian democracy," she said. "Whatever *that* means."

"Please," Rudolph said, "spare me Jeffersonian democracy. Whatever it means."

Helen chuckled. She had a nice, open chuckle. "Now," she said, "this is the sort of place to talk about politics. On the beach in the sunshine after a nice brisk swim. There'd never be a war."

He leaned over and kissed her. Her skin was salty from the ocean. He wondered why he had gone so long without a woman since Jeanne. With Helen just a little way down the dunes from him there was no need to cross the sea. In recent years doctors had been publicly advocating regular sexual activity as a deterrent to heart disease. Think of Helen as a health measure, he thought with an inward smile, because he knew how furious she would be if he said it aloud. "In your own way," he said lightly, "you are glorious."

"Have you ever paid a woman a compliment," she asked, "without adding a modifying clause?"

"I don't remember," he said. "Actually, I don't remember any other women."

She laughed, mockingly. "Should I wear my scarlet letter into New York tomorrow?"

"Don't forget your wimple, either," he said.

"If we made love right out here, with me all salty and sandy and you thinking about money and contracts," she said, "would the neighbors be shocked?"

"No," he said, "but I would."

"You've got a long way to go, brother," she said.

"You bet. And I won't go there."

"After lunch? I'm cooking."

"What're you cooking?"

"Something light, nourishing and aphrodisiacal," she said. "Like clam chowder. See how you feel at two P.M. The phone's ringing inside." She had a remarkably acute sense of hearing and he was always amused when she repeated, word for word, whispered conversations, usually malicious ones about herself, that she had somehow overheard across a noisy room while she was holding forth to two or three captive listeners on some pet subject of hers. "Should I answer it? I'll say I'm the butler and that you're upstairs doing your yoga and can't be disturbed."

"I'll take it," he said. It still made him a little uneasy whenver she answered the phone and made it plain that she was very much at home in his house. "Just be here when I get back."

"Never fear," she said. "This sun is sleepy-making."

He stood up and went into the house. The maid only came three times a week and this was not one of her days. As always, he was pleased with the way the house looked as he went through the big glass doors facing the sea and saw the pale wood and comfortable corduroy couches and the wide old polished planks of the floor of the living room.

"Rudolph," Gretchen said, "I've got a problem. Are you busy?"

He repressed a sigh. Gretchen had at least one problem a week that she called him about. If she had had a husband, he thought, her telephone bill would be decreased by half. Last week the problem had been Ida Cohen's uncle, who had been a movie producer in Hollywood and had retired after a stroke. He was a shrewd old man who knew the business and when Ida had shown him the script he had volunteered to work for them, sitting in the little office in New York and wrangling with actors' agents and coming up with ideas on casting and distribution and doing the daily dirty work of signing actors' and technicians' contracts and politely letting down candidates for jobs. But he had been sick for three days and Gretchen was afraid he'd had another stroke and she wanted to know what Rudolph thought she ought to do about Ida Cohen's uncle. Rudolph had said talk to his doctor and Gretchen had found out that it was merely a head cold.

Then there was the problem of Billy Abbott, which Gretchen had called Rudolph about in the middle of the night, her voice full of emotion. Billy's father had telephoned from Chicago. "This time sober," Gretchen had said, to underline the gravity of the situation. "Billy's written his father," Gretchen had said, "telling him he's going to reenlist. Willie's just as against it as I am. A professional noncom! That's just what he and I wanted our son to be! Willie wants us both to go over to Brussels together to talk him out of it, but I can't leave New York for a minute at this time, you know that. Then Willie suggested that I offer Billy a job on the picture—third assistant director, anything. But Billy doesn't know the first thing about movies—I don't think he's seen three in his life—he's not normal for this day and age—and he's lazy and disloyal—and if he took the job it would be the same kind of nepotism that sent the old Hollywood studios into oblivion. Even if it didn't mean much money, it would just be stealing from our backers, including you. I told Willie I couldn't give him a job and I couldn't go to Brussels and why didn't *he* go himself and see what he could do and he said he didn't have the money and would I advance the fare? Advance! Hah! Anyway, every cent I have I've got tied up in *Restoration Comedy,* and he said why didn't I get it from you and I said I absolutely forbade him to approach you." As the date for the actual shooting neared, Gretchen's sentences had become more and more rushed and her voice had risen in tense crescendo. It was a bad sign, Rudolph felt, and would give rise to nervous explosions later.

"How about you?" Gretchen had said, hesitant now. "You don't have to be going over to Europe for anything, do you?"

"No," Rudolph had said. "I've finished with Europe for the time being. Anyway, what's so terrible about having a son in the army?"

"You know as well as I do," Gretchen said, "that sooner or later there's going to be another war."

"There's nothing much either you or I can do about it," Rudolph said. "Is there?"

"*You* can say that," she'd said. "You have a daughter." And had hung up.

Then there was the call about the problem of casting the role of the heroine's young brother, the part Gretchen had thought she wanted to test Wesley for. He was supposed to be beautiful and sad and cynical, constantly throwing cold water on his sister's enthusiasm, given to repeating the line, "You can't beat the numbers, man!" In the script, although he was supposed to be intellectually advanced far beyond his years and full of a variety of talents, he deliberately wasted himself, scornfully taking a job as a serviceman at the local airport and playing semiprofessional football on Sundays and consorting with the lowest and idlest and least salvageable of the ruffians of the town. Gretchen was sure, she said, that Wesley would be wonderful for it, just by the way he looked, with a minimum of acting, and none of the other boys she had tested had satisfied her and she had written to Wesley time and time again, but the letters had all been returned unclaimed, with no forwarding address, from General Delivery in Indianapolis. She wanted to know if Rudolph knew where to find Wesley, but Rudolph told her that he hadn't heard from Wesley since the telephone call from Chicago. He had never told Gretchen about the warrant for Wesley's arrest in Indianapolis. He was sure that Wesley would turn up eventually, but that wouldn't help Gretchen with her casting now. He also doubted that Wesley could be useful as an actor. If Wesley had a single outstanding characteristic it was that he kept his emotions to himself, not the highest recommendation for a film career. Added to that there was Rudolph's own unstated but ingrained snobbishness toward the profession of acting. Overpaid, narcissistic grown men at play, he would have said if pressed.

From where he was standing at the phone in the living room he saw Helen rise from the air mattress and begin to do slow and difficult exercises, stretching, bending, like a ballet dancer, outlined in salt against the glittering sea. Gretchen's voice in the receiver grated on his ears.

"What's the problem now?"

"This one's serious," Gretchen said. She said the same thing about each of her problems, but he didn't remind her of that. "Evans Kinsella called me this morning," Gretchen said. "He just got in from California last night. He's changed his mind. He wants to do *Restoration Comedy* himself now. He says he's got two million to do it and major distribution and two stars. He's ready to pay everybody off, with a profit of ten percent for all the backers."

"He's a sonofabitch," Rudolph said. "What did you tell him?"

"I told him I had to think it over," Gretchen said. "We have a date to meet at his hotel in a half hour."

"Talk to him," Rudolph said, "and call me back. Say no, if you want to, but don't say yes until you've talked to me." He hung up the phone. Ten percent on his investment in only two months, he thought. Not a bad return. Still, the idea of it gave him no pleasure. Outside, on the deck, Helen was still doing her exercises. After Gretchen's call he could use the aphrodisiacal lunch this afternoon.

Gretchen carefully put on her makeup, fluffed up her hair, chose her smartest suit and dabbed herself with Femme, a perfume that Evans had once said he liked on her. Ida Cohen would not have approved, she thought, heightening her femininity, making herself the alluring female animal for what, being realistic, was merely a business appointment, and one with unsavory overtones at that. At my age, it gets harder and harder, Gretchen thought, looking in the full-length mirror, to make myself into an alluring female animal. Getting to sleep these nights was difficult, and she had been taking pills and it showed. Damn Evans Kinsella. She put on an extra dab of perfume.

Evans was freshly shaved and was wearing a jacket and tie when she went up to his apartment in the Regency Hotel on Park Avenue. He usually met her in his shirt-sleeves or in a robe when he summoned her to his place. He had decided on charm for this meeting. She felt a tingling all over her body as he kissed her first on one cheek then on the other, a salutation he had brought back with him when he had made a picture in Paris. She resented her body for the tingle.

In the ornate salon with him was Richard Sanford, the young author of *Restoration Comedy,* dressed, as usual, in an open-necked wool shirt, a windbreaker, jeans and high, unpolished boots. Careless, unconventional poverty was the public expression of his background and his beliefs. Gretchen wondered what he would dress like in Hollywood after his third picture. He was a pleasant young man, with a wide, slow smile and respectful manner, and had always been most friendly with Gretchen in all their dealings. Although she had been seeing him almost every day, he had never mentioned that he even knew Kinsella. Conspiracy was the word that crossed her mind.

Today, she saw, Richard Stanford was not going to be friendly, not friendly at all. He would go a long way in California, would Richard Sanford.

Beware young men, Gretchen thought, looking at the two young men. Although at the age of thirty-three, Evans Kinsella, with what he had learned, copied and stolen, could hardly be considered a young man. She should have brought Ida Cohen with her to balance the company, but it would have been like bringing along a small volcano just waiting to erupt. She had not yet told Ida about Kinsella's call. Time enough for that.

"Would you like a wee drop?" Kinsella gestured toward the table on which the bottles were neatly placed, with glasses and ice. There must be a single waiter in hotels like this one, Gretchen thought, expert in his field, who rushes from room to room, distributing bottles in strict formal arrangement as soon as the telex comes announcing the impending arrival of the nabobs of the new aristocracy—the abundance and quality of the arrangement depending upon the current importance of the particular nabob in the manager's files. Gretchen saw, with some malice, that the display on Kinsella's bar was merely medium. His last picture had been a flop and the hotel manager's private *Almanach de Gotha* reflected it. "Our young genius and I have been regaling ourselves," Kinsella said. "In a modest fashion. To get into the proper festive mood for your arrival. What's the lady's pleasure?"

"I'll skip it, thank you," Gretchen said. "It's a little early for a working girl." She was going to keep the tone light and calm, even if it meant bursting a blood vessel. "Young genius," she said, smiling blandly at the boy. "Evans must have changed his mind about you, Richard."

"I happened to reread the script," Kinsella said hastily. "I must have read it the first time on a bad morning."

"As I remember," Gretchen said, her voice honeyed, "you told me it was a load of shit." One assassination deserved another. She saw with pleasure that Sanford flushed as he put his glass down and stared at Kinsella.

"Artists make mistakes all the time, Dick," Kinsella said. Gretchen noted the familiar diminutive. "There're always a thousand people pulling you every which way. Atonement is possible." He turned his attention, smiling with difficulty at Gretchen. "Among other reasons for this little conference," he said, "is that Dick and I have talked the script over and we've agreed on some changes that would be helpful. Rather drastic changes. Haven't we, Dick?"

"Yes," Sanford said. He was still flushed.

"Two days ago," Gretchen said to the young man, "you told me it was ready to go, you didn't want a word changed."

"Evans pointed out a few things to me that I'd missed," Sanford said. He sounded like a little boy who was being stubborn and knew he was going to be punished for it. The conspiracy went back weeks, perhaps months.

"Let's be honest, Gretchen," Kinsella said. "With two million in the pot, Sanford is going to get a guarantee about three times what you've offered him. He's not a rich man, as you know. He has a wife and a young child to support . . . "

"Maestro," Gretchen said, "will you play the violin, tremolo, with that line?"

Kinsella scowled. "You've forgotten what it's like to be poor and struggling for each month's rent, my dear. With your rich brother you've always had a big fat cushion to fall back on. Well, Dick hasn't any cushion."

"What I'd like you to forget, Evans," Gretchen said, "is that I have a brother. Fat or skinny or any shape whatever. And what I'd like you *not* to forget, Richard . . . " She emphasized his name. " . . . is that you have a contract with me."

"I was coming to that," Kinsella said. He was speaking smoothly again now. "I in no way want to shut you or your little friend Ida Cohen, the Jewish Joan of Arc, out of the project. It was always my intention to ask you to come on as associate producer with full perks, of course. And promote Ida to head cutter. There—" He beamed. "What could be fairer than that?"

"I suppose, Richard," Gretchen said, "you agree with Evans in all this? I'd like to hear it in your own words. You also are pleased, no doubt, to hear Ida Cohen, who has slaved to get your script on the screen, described as a Jewish Joan of Arc?"

Sanford flushed again. "I don't go along with that part of it, no. But I do go along with the idea that you can make a better picture with two million dollars than with seven hundred and fifty thousand dollars. And before you called me up, I'll be honest with you, it never occurred to me that a woman could do this picture. . . . "

"And now?"

"Well . . . " The boy flustered. "I know you're smart and I know you've had a lot of experience—but never as a director. It's my first picture, Gretchen, and I'd just feel better if a man like Evans Kinsella, with all his hits and his reputation . . . "

"His reputation stinks," Gretchen said flatly. "Where it counts. Like with me. If he does one more picture like the last, he won't be able to rent a Brownie in California."

"See, Dick," Kinsella said, "I told you she'd turn female and vindictive. She was married to a director who she thought was Stanislavski come again, although I've seen his pictures and I could have lived without them, to say the least. Since he died, she wants to get even on something, anything, everybody, every director, and she's become the great deballer of the twentieth century. And old Polish Ida, the flower of the ghetto, who couldn't get a man to touch her with a ten-foot pole, has puffed her up to think that she's been elected to lead womankind into an Academy Award."

"You awful, conspiring, despicable man," Gretchen said. "It would serve you both right if I gave you the picture and let you turn it into the load of shit you said it was in the first place."

"When I hired her," Kinsella went on, all constraint lost, "a friend told me, never hire the rich. Especially a rich woman. And don't screw her. She'll never forgive you the first time you look at another girl. Get out of here, you bitch." He was screaming shrilly. "I'll come to your opening and have a good laugh."

"Gretchen . . . " Sanford said piteously. He looked appalled and sorry he had ever touched a typewriter. "Please . . . "

"Richard," Gretchen said calmly, feeling wonderfully cleansed and dizzily free, "when we start shooting you're most welcome to come or not come, as you please. Good day, gentlemen," she said and swept grandly out of the beflowered, bebottled, becursed salon.

In the elevator she smiled and she wept, without worrying about the other passengers. Wait till I tell Ida about this morning, she thought.

But on the street she made a resolution: no more younger men. No matter how bright their eye, how white their teeth, how brimming their vitality, how promising their promise, how clear their skin, how sweet their smell. From now on, if she chose any man he would be older than she and grateful for her and not expect her to be grateful for him. She didn't know how that fit in with Ida Cohen's philosophy and she didn't care.

They were in the middle of lunch, the clam chowder and hot biscuits that Helen had prepared, and Helen had just said, "I love cooking for a man who doesn't have to watch his weight," when the doorbell rang.

Helen said, "Damn."

The lunch had been interrupted once before by a telephone call from Gretchen. Gretchen had taken fifteen minutes to tell Rudolph what had happened between Kinsella and herself that morning and had said that she was sure Rudolph would have approved. He was not as sure as she thought he would be.

Now it was the doorbell. Rudolph got up from the table and went to the door and opened it. Wesley was standing there, in the oceanic September sunshine, neatly dressed in slacks, and a sports jacket, looking a bit gaunt, his cheekbones prominent, his hair cut and neatly combed, neither long nor short, his eyes, as always, old and veiled.

"Hello, Wesley," Rudolph said. "I knew you'd turn up sooner or later. You're just in time for lunch. Come in."

CHAPTER 4

BILLY WATCHED WITH interest as George, which Billy knew was not the man's real name, carefully worked at the table on the timing device. Monika, whom George addressed as Heidi, stood on the other side of the table, her face in shadow, above the sharp vee of light the work lamp cut over the table. "Are you following this closely, John?" George said in his Spanish-accented English, looking up at Billy. John was the name assigned to Billy in the group. Monika called him John, too, when members of the group were around. It reminded him of the hocus-pocus of secret societies he had started in the yard of the progressive school in Greenwich Village when he was a small boy. Only George wasn't a small boy and neither was Monika. One laugh, he thought, and they'd kill me.

There were only two other associates of George and Monika-Heidi whom Billy had met, but they were not present this afternoon in the small room in the slum section of Brussels where George was working on the bomb. Billy had never seen George in the same room twice. He knew from various references in George's conversation that there were cells like the one he had joined in other cities of Europe, but so far he had no notion of where they were or what exactly they did. Although for his own safety he was not particularly anxious to know any more than he was told, he could not help resenting the fact that he was still treated as an untested and scarcely trusted outsider by the others, even though he had twice supplied them with a half-ton from the motor pool and had driven the car in Amsterdam the night George had bombed the Spanish tourist office there. He didn't know what other bombings George and Monika had been in on, but he had read about explosions in a branch of an American bank in Brussels and outside the office of Olympic Airways. If Monika and the man he knew as George had been responsible for one or all of them, Monika was keeping her promise—no one had been hurt either in Amsterdam or Brussels.

"Do you think you could put this together yourself, if necessary?" George was saying.

"I think so."

"Good," George said. He always spoke quietly and moved deliberately. He was dark and small, with gentle sad eyes and looked totally undangerous. Regarding himself in the mirror, Billy couldn't believe that anyone could imagine that *he* was dangerous, either.

Monika was a different story, with her tangled hair and her eyes that blazed when she was angry. But he lived with Monika, was frightened of her, and loved her more than ever. It was Monika who had said he must reenlist. When he said that he couldn't face any more time in the army, she had turned furiously on him and had told him it was an order, not a suggestion, and that she would move out if he didn't do as she said.

"Next time we meet," George said, "I'll let you put together a dummy, just for practice."

George turned back to his work, his fine, small hands moving delicately over the wires. Neither he nor Monika had told Billy where the bomb was going to be used or when or for what purpose, and by now he knew that it would be useless to ask any questions.

"There we are," George said, straightening up. "All done." The small plastic charge with the clockwork attachment and detonator lay innocently on the table under the harsh light. "Lesson over for the day. You leave now, John. Heidi will remain with me for a while. Walk to the bus. Take it in the direction *away* from your apartment for eight blocks. Then get off, walk for three more blocks and get a taxi. Give the driver the address of the Hotel Amigo. Go into the hotel. Have a drink at the bar. Then leave the hotel and walk home."

"Yes, George," Billy said. That was about all he ever said to the man. "Will I be seeing you for dinner tonight?" he asked Monika.

"That depends on George," she said.

"George?" Billy said.

"Don't forget," George said. "At least ten minutes in the Hotel Amigo."

"Yes, George," Billy said.

Sitting in the bus going in the opposite direction from the house where he lived, surrounded by women going home after a day's shopping to prepare the family dinner, by children on the way home from school, by old men reading the evening newspaper, he chuckled inwardly. If only they could guess what the small, mild-looking young American in the neat business suit had just been doing on one of the back streets of their city. . . . Although he hadn't shown it in front of George and Monika, while he was watching the bomb being assembled he had felt his pulse race with excitement. Coldly, now, in the everyday light of the rumbling bus, he could call it by another name—pleasure. He had felt the same weird emotion racing away from the tourist office in Amsterdam, hearing the faint explosion six blocks behind him in the dark city.

He didn't believe, as Monika did, that the system was tottering and that a random bomb here and there was going to topple it, but at least he himself was no longer just an insignificant, replaceable cog in the whole lousy inhuman machine. His acts were being studied, important men were trying to figure out who he was and what he meant and where he might strike next. The disdain of his comrades in arms for him as Colonel's pet was now an ironic joke, made juicier by the fact that they had no notion of what he was really like. And Monika had had to admit that she had been wrong when she had said he was worthless. Finally, he thought, they would put a weapon in his hand and order him to kill. And he would do it. He would read the papers the next day and would report meekly to work, filled with secret joy. He didn't believe that Monika and George and their shadowy accomplices would ever achieve their shadowy purposes. No matter. He himself was no longer adrift, at the mercy of the small daily accidents of the enlisted man who had to say, "Yes, sir," "Of course, sir," to earn his daily bread. Now *he* was the accident, waiting to happen, the burning fuse that could not finally be ignored.

He counted the blocks as the bus trundled on. At the eighth block he got off. He walked briskly through a light drizzle the three blocks that George had told him to cover, smiling gently at the passersby. There was a taxi at the corner of the third block, standing there as though it had been ordered expressly for him. He settled back in it comfortably and enjoyed the ride to the Hotel Amigo.

He was just finishing his beer at the dark bar at the Amigo, the small room empty except for two blond men at a corner table who were talking to each other in what he took to be Hebrew when Monika walked in.

She swung up on a stool next to him. "I'll have a vodka on ice," she said to the barman.

"Did George order you to come?" he asked.

"I'm having a social period," she said.

"Is it Monika or Heidi?"

"Shut up."

"You said social," he said. "But it isn't. You were sent here to see if I followed instructions."

"Everybody understands English," she whispered. "Talk about the weather."

"The weather," he said. "It was rather warm this afternoon, wasn't it?"

"Rather," she said. She smiled at the barman as he put her drink in front of her.

He nursed the last bit of his beer at the bottom of the glass. "What would you do," he asked, "if I were sent back to America?"

Monika looked at him sharply. "Are you being shifted? Have you been keeping something from me?"

"No," he said. "But the Colonel's been getting restless. He's been here a long time. Anyway, in the army, you never can tell . . . "

"Pull wires," she said. "Arrange for someplace in Germany."

"It's not as easy as all that," he said.

"It can be done," she said crisply. "You know that as well as I do."

"Still," he said, "you haven't answered my question. What would you do?"

She shrugged. "That would depend," she said.

"On what?"

"On a lot of things. Where you were sent. What kind of job you got. Where I was needed."

"On love, perhaps?"

"Never."

He laughed. "Ask a silly question," he said, "and you get a silly answer."

"Priorities, John," she said, accenting "John" ironically. "We must never forget priorities, must we?"

"Never," he said. He ordered another beer. "There's a chance I'll be going to Paris next week."

Again she looked at him sharply. "A chance?" she asked. "Or definitely?"

"Almost definitely. The Colonel thinks he has to go and he'll put me on orders to accompany him if he does go."

"You must learn not to spring things like this suddenly on me," she said.

"I just heard about it this morning," he said defensively.

"As soon as you know for sure, you let me know. Is that clear?"

"Oh, Christ," he said, "stop sounding like a company commander."

She ignored this. "I'm not talking idly," she said. "There's a package that has to be delivered to Paris next week. How would you go? Civilian plane?"

"No. Army transport. There's an honor guard going for some sort of ceremony at Versailles."

"Oh, good," she said.

"What will be in the package?"

"You'll know when you have to know," she said.

He sighed and drank half the fresh beer. "I've always been partial to nice, uncomplicated, innocent girls."

"I'll see if I can find one for you," she said, "in five or six years."

He nodded dourly. In the corner the two blond men were talking more loudly, as though they were arguing.

"Are those two men speaking Hebrew?" he asked.

She listened for a moment. "Finnish," she said.

"Are they close? Hebrew and Finnish, I mean?"

"No." She laughed and kissed his cheek. She had decided to be Monika now, he saw, not Heidi.

"So," he said, "business hours are over."

"For the day."

"For the day," he said and finished his beer. "You know what I would like to do?"

"What?"

"I'd like to go home with you and fuck."

"Oh, dear," she said with mock gentility, "soldier talk."

"The afternoon's activities have made me horny," he said.

She laughed. "Me, too," she whispered. "Pay the nice man and let's get out of here."

It was dark by the time they got to the street where they lived. They stopped on the corner to see if they were being followed. As far as they could tell they were not. They walked slowly on the opposite side of the street from his house. There was a man standing, smoking a cigarette, in front of the building. It was still drizzling and the man had his hat jammed down low over his forehead. There wasn't enough light for them to see whether they had ever seen the man before.

"Keep walking," Monika said in a low voice.

They went past the house and turned a corner and went into a café. He would have liked another beer but Monika ordered two coffees.

When they came back fifteen minutes later, they saw, from the opposite side of the street, that the man was still there, still smoking.

"You keep walking," Monika said. "I'll go past him and upstairs. Come back in five minutes. If it looks all right, I'll turn on the light in the front room and you can come up."

Billy nodded, kissed her cheek as though they were saying good-bye and went on toward the corner. At the corner he looked back. Hazard of the trade, he thought. Eternal suspicion. The man was still there but Monika had disappeared. Billy turned the corner, went into the café and had the beer that Monika had vetoed. When he left the café he walked quickly around the corner. He saw that the front room light was on. He kept on walking, his head down, over to the side of the street where the man was waiting in front of the house and started up the steps, taking his keys out.

"Hello, Billy," the man said.

"Holy God! Dad!" Billy said. In his surprise he dropped his keys and he and William Abbott almost bumped heads as they both bent over to pick them up. They laughed. His father handed Billy the keys and they embraced. Billy noticed that the smell of gin, which he had associated with his father since early childhood, was absent.

"Come on in," Billy said. "How long have you been waiting?"

"A couple of hours."

"You must be soaked."

"No matter," Abbott said. "Time for reflection."

"Come on upstairs," Billy said, opening the door. "Uh—Dad—we won't be alone. There'll be a lady there," he said as he led the way upstairs.

"I'll watch my language," Abbott said.

Billy unlocked the door and they both went into the little foyer and Billy helped his father off with his wet raincoat. When Abbott took off his hat, Billy saw that his father's hair was iron gray and his face puffy and yellowish. He remembered a photograph of his father in his captain's uniform. He had been a handsome young man, dark, smiling at a private joke, with black hair and humorous eyes. He was no longer a handsome man. The body, which had been erect and slender, was now saggy under the worn suit, a little round paunch at the belt line. I will refuse to look like that when I am his age, Billy thought as he led his father into the living room.

Monika was in the small, cluttered living room. Monika did not waste her time on housework. She was sitting in the one easy chair, reading, and stood up when they came into the room.

"Monika," Billy said, "this is my father."

Monika smiled, her eyes giving a welcoming glow to her face. She has sixty moods to the hour, Billy thought as Monika shook hands with Abbott and said, "Welcome, sir."

"I saw you come in," Abbott said. "You gave me a most peculiar look."

"Monika always looks at men peculiarly," Billy said. "Sit down, sit down. Can I give you a drink?"

Abbott rubbed his hands together and shivered. "That would repair a great deal of damage," he said.

"I'll get the glasses and ice," Monika said. She went into the kitchen.

Abbott looked around him approvingly. "Cosy. You've found a home in the army, haven't you, Billy?"

"You might say that."

"Transient or permanent?" Abbott gestured with his head toward the kitchen.

"Transiently permanent," Billy said.

Abbott laughed. His laugh was younger than his iron-gray hair and puffy face. "The history of the Abbotts," he said.

"What brings you to Brussels, Dad?"

Abbott looked at Billy reflectively. "An exploratory operation," he said. "We can talk about it later, I suppose."

"Of course."

"What does the young lady do?"

"She's a translator at NATO," Billy said. He did not feel called upon to tell his father that Monika also was plotting the destruction of the capitalist system and had almost certainly contributed to the recent assassination of a judge in Hamburg.

Monika came back with three glasses, ice and a bottle of Scotch. Billy saw his father eyeing the bottle hungrily. "Just a small one for me, please," Abbott said. "What with the plane trip and all and walking around Brussels the whole, livelong day, I feel as though I've been awake for weeks."

Billy saw that his father's hand shook minutely as he took the glass from Monika. He felt a twinge of pity for the small man, reduced in size and assurance from the father he remembered.

Abbott raised his glass. "To fathers and sons," he said. He grinned crookedly. He made the ice twirl in his glass, but didn't put it to his lips. "How many years is it since we've seen each other?"

"Six, seven . . . " Billy said.

"So long, eh?" Abbott said. "I'll spare you both the cliché." He sipped at his drink, took a deep, grateful breath. "You've weathered well, Billy. You look in good shape."

"I play a lot of tennis."

"Excellent. Sad to relate. I have neglected my tennis recently." He drank again. "A mistake. One makes mistakes in six or seven years. Of varying degrees of horror." He peered at Billy, squinting like a man who has lost his glasses. "You've changed.

Naturally. Matured, I suppose is the word. Lines of strength in the face and all that. Most attractive, wouldn't you say, Monika?"

"Moderately attractive," Monika said, laughing.

"He was a nice-looking child," Abbott said. "But unnaturally solemn. I should have brought along baby pictures. When we get to know each other better, I'll take you to one side and ask you what he says about his father. Out of curiosity. A man always worries that his son misjudges him. The sting of siredom, you might call it."

"Billy always speaks of you lovingly," Monika said.

"Loyal girl," said Abbott. "As I said, the opportunities for misjudgment are infinite." He sipped at his drink again. "I take it, Monika, that you are fond of my son."

"I would say so," Monika said, her voice cautious. Billy could see that she was unfavorably impressed by his father.

"He's told you, no doubt, that he intends to reenlist." Abbott twirled his glass again.

"He has."

Ah, Billy thought, that's what brought him to Brussels.

"The American Army is a noble and necessary institution," Abbott said. "I served in it once, myself, if my memory is correct. Do you approve of his joining up again in that necessary and noble institution?"

"That's his business," Monika said smoothly. "I'm sure he has his reasons."

"If I may be inquisitive, Monika," Abbott said, "I mean—using the prerogative of a father who is interested in his son's choice of companions—I hope you aren't offended . . ."

"Of course not, Mr. Abbott," Monika said. "Billy knows all about me, don't you, Billy?"

"Too much," Billy said, laughing, uneasy at the tenor of the conversation.

"As I was saying," Abbott said, "if I may be inquisitive—I seem to detect the faintest of accents in your speech—could you tell me where you come from? I mean originally."

"Germany," she said. "Originally, Munich."

"Ah—Munich." Abbott nodded. "I was in a plane once that bombed Munich. I am happy to see that you are too young to have been in that fair city for the occasion. It was early in nineteen forty-five."

"I was born in nineteen forty-four," Monika said.

"My apologies," Abbott said.

"I remember nothing," Monika said shortly.

"What a marvelous thing to be able to say," Abbott said. "I remember nothing."

"Dad," Billy said, "the war's over."

"That's what everybody says." Abbott took another sip, slowly. "It must be true."

"Billy," Monika said, putting down her half-finished glass, "I hope you and your charming father will excuse me. I have to go out. There are some people I have to see. . . ."

Abbott rose gallantly, just a little stiffly, like a rheumatic old man getting out of bed in the morning. "I hope we will have the pleasure of your company at dinner, my dear."

"I'm afraid not, Mr. Abbott. I have a date for dinner."

"Another evening . . ."

"Of course," Monika said.

Billy went into the foyer with her and helped her into her raincoat. He watched as she wrapped a scarf around her tangled hair. "Will I see you later?" he whispered.

"Probably not," she said. "And don't let your father talk you out of anything. You know why he's here, I'm sure."

"I suppose so. Don't worry," he whispered. "And come back tonight. No matter what time. I promise still to be horny."

She chuckled, kissed his cheek and went out the door. He sighed, inaudibly, fixed a smile on his face and went back into the living room. His father was pouring himself another drink, not a small one this time.

"Interesting girl," Abbott said. His hand was no longer shaking as he poured the soda into his glass. "Does she ever comb her hair?"

"She's not concerned with things like that," Billy said.

"So I gathered," Abbott said as he sat down again in the easy chair. "I don't trust her."

"Oh come on now, Dad," Billy said. "After ten minutes. Why? Because she's German?"

"Not at all. I know many good Germans," Abbott said. "I say that, although it isn't true, because it is the expected thing to say. The truth is I don't know *any* Germans and have no special feeling about them one way or another. Although I do have special feelings about ladies, a race I know better than I know Germans. As I said, she gave me a most peculiar look when she passed me coming into the house. It disturbed me."

"Well," Billy says, "she doesn't give *me* any peculiar looks."

"I suppose not." Abbott looked judgingly at Billy. "You're small—too bad you took after me and not your mother in that respect—but with your pretty eyes and manner, I imagine you arouse a considerable amount of female affection."

"Most of the ladies manage to contain themselves in my presence," Billy said.

"I admire your modesty." Abbott laughed. "I was less modest when I was your age. Have you heard from your mother?"

"Yes," Billy said. "She wrote me after you told her I was going to reenlist. I didn't know you kept in such close touch with her."

"You're her son," Abbott said, his face grave, "and you're my son. Neither of us forgets that, although we manage to forget many other things." He took a long gulp of his whiskey.

"Don't get drunk tonight, please, Dad."

Abbott looked thoughtfully at the glass in his hand, then, with a sudden movement, threw it against the small brick fireplace. The glass shattered and the whiskey made a dark stain on the hearth. The two men sat in silence for a moment. Billy heard his father's loud, uneven breathing.

"I'm sorry, Billy," Abbot said. "I'm not angry at what you said. On the contrary. Quite the contrary. You have spoken like a dutiful and proper son. I'm touched by your interest in my health. What I'm angry about is myself." His voice was bitter. "My son is on the verge of making what I consider a huge and perhaps irrecoverable mistake. I borrowed the money for the voyage from Chicago to Brussels from the last man in the world who can occasionally be prevailed upon to lend me a dollar. I came here to try to persuade you to . . . well . . . to reconsider. I walked around this town all day in the rain marshaling arguments to get you to change your mind. I managed not to order even one drink on the plane across the ocean, because I wanted to be at my best"— he smiled wryly —"which is not a very handsome best at best—for my meeting with you. I have antagonized you about your girl, whom I don't know, as you pointed out, because of a peculiar look on a doorstep, and I have begun the proceedings by pouring a double Scotch, which is bound to remind you of painful weekends with your father when your mother lent you to me for paternal Sabbath guidance. Willie Abbott rides again." He stood up abruptly. "Let us go to dinner. I promise not to touch another drop tonight until you deposit me at my hotel. After that I promise to drink myself into oblivion. I will not be in glorious shape tomorrow, but I promise to be sober. Where's the john? I've been standing in the rain for hours and my bladder is bursting. For the sake of you and the United States Army I didn't want to be caught pissing on the good burghers of Brussels."

"Through the bedroom," Billy said. "I'm afraid there's a lot of stuff lying around. Monika and I have to get to work early in the morning and most of the time we don't get back until dinner." He didn't want his father to think that Monika was a slob, although he occasionally complained to her about the mess they lived in. "There's nothing in Marx or Mao or Ché Guevara," he had said recently to her, "about good revolutionaries having to leave their underwear on the floor." "We clean up on the weekends," he said to his father.

"I will make no remarks, Billy," Abbott said, "about the life-style of you and your lady. I am not the neatest man in the world, but paradoxically consider neatness in a woman a useful virtue. No matter. We make do with what comes along." He looked searchingly at Billy. "You're not in uniform, soldier. How is it if you're in the noble and necessary army of the United States Army you're not in uniform?"

"Off duty," Billy said,"we can wear civilian clothes."

"It was different in my day," Abbott said. "I didn't wear civilian clothes for four years. Ah, well, wars change." He walked steadily out into the hall on his way to the bathroom. As he went out, Billy thought, That suit must be at least ten years old. I wonder if he'd let me buy him a new one.

His father said a lot of things over dinner, on a variety of subjects. He insisted upon Billy ordering wine for himself but turned his own glass over when the waiter poured. He said the food was first-rate, but just picked at it. By turns, he was expansive, apologetic, regretful, cynical, optimistic, aggressive, self-denigrating and boastful.

"I'm not through yet," was one of the things he said, "no matter what it looks like. I have a million ideas: I could eat up the field of public relations like a dish of whipped cream if I stayed off the booze. Ten of the top men in the field in Chicago have told me as much—I've been offered jobs in six figures if I joined Alcoholics Anonymous—but I can't see myself making public confessions to a group of professional breast-beaters. If you'd forget this crazy idea of sticking with the army—I can't get over that, I really can't, a smart young man like you, with your education, not even an officer—what the hell do you do all day, just check out cars like a girl in a radio taxi office? Why, if you came out to Chicago with me, we could set up an agency— William Abbott and Son. I've read your letters—I keep them with me at all times— the first thing I pack when I move from one place to another is the box I keep them in—I've read them and I tell you you can write, you really can turn a phrase with the best of them. If I had had your talent, I tell you I just wouldn't have a pile of unfinished plays in my desk drawer, no sir, not by a long shot. We could dazzle the folks, just dazzle them—I know the business from A to Z, you could leave that end of it to me, we'd have the advertisers knocking the door down to beg us to take their accounts. And don't think that Chicago is small time. Advertising *started* there, for God's sake.

"All right, I have a pretty good idea of what you think of the advertising business— the whore of the consumer society, all that crap. But like it or not, it's the only society we have and the rule of the jungle is consume or be consumed. Trade a couple of years of your life and you can do whatever you damn well please after it. Write a book—write a play. When I get back to Chicago I'll have your letters Xeroxed and send them to you, you'll be amazed at yourself reading them all at once like that. Listen, your mother made a living, a damn good living, writing for the magazines, and just the things you dash off to me in a few minutes have more—what's the word I'm looking for?—more *tone,* more spirit, more sense of what writing is about than she had in her best days. And she was highly thought of, let me tell you, by a lot of intelligent people—the editors were always after her for more—I don't know why she quit. Her writing was good enough for the editors, for the public, but not for her. She has some insane idea of perfectionism—be careful of that—it can finally lead to molecular immobility—there's a phrase, my boy—and she quit. Christ, *somebody* in the family ought to finally make it. She complains to me you almost never write her. I'm pleased, of course, you write me as often as you do, but after all, she's your mother, it wouldn't kill you to drop her a line from time to time. I know I was shitty to her, I disappointed her, I was a lousy husband. The truth is, she was too much for me—in every department—physically, intellectually, morally. She swamped me, but that doesn't prevent me so many years later from appreciating her quality. There's no telling how far she could have gone, with another man, with better luck. . . . Colin Burke being killed.

"That family—the Jordaches—the old man a suicide, the brother murdered, and sainted Rudolph just about beaten to death in his own apartment. That would have been something for your mother, if he'd have knocked it off. Three for three. Two brothers and a husband. What a percentage! And the kid—Wesley—did I write you he came to Chicago and looked me up? He wanted me to tell him what I knew about his father—he's haunted by his father—the ramparts of Elsinore, for Christ's sake—I guess you can't blame him for that—but he looks like a zombie, his eyes are scary—God knows how *he's* going to end up. I never even met his father, but I tried to pretend that I'd heard he was a fine fellow and I laid it on thick and the kid just stood up in the middle of a sentence and said, 'Thank you, sir. I'm afraid we're wasting each other's time.'

"You're half Jordache—maybe more than half—if ever a lady had dominant genes it was Gretchen Jordache—so you be careful, don't you ever trust to inherited luck, because you don't have it, on either side of the family tree. . . .

"I'll tell you what—you get through with the goddamn army and you come out to Chicago to work with me and I'll swear never to touch a drop of liquor again in my whole life. I know you love me—we're grown men, we can use the proper words—and you can save your father's life. You don't have to say anything now, but when I get back to Chicago I want to see a letter from you waiting for me telling me when you're arriving in town. I'll be there in a week or so. I have to leave for Strasbourg tomorrow. There's a man there I have to see. Delicate negotiations for an old account of mine. A chemical company. I have to sound out this Frenchman to see if he'll take a fee, an honorarium—not to mince words, a bribe, for swinging my client's business to his company. I won't tell you how much money is involved, but you'd gasp if I did tell you. And I get my cut if I deliver. It's not the jolliest way to earn a living, but it was the only way I could borrow enough money to come over here to see you. Remember what I said about the consumer society.

"And now it's late and your girl is undoubtedly waiting for you and I'm deadbeat tired. If you give one little goddamn for the rest of your father's life, that letter will be waiting for me in Chicago when I get there. And that's blackmail and don't think I don't know it. One last thing. The dinner's on me."

When he got back home after putting his father in a taxi and walking slowly through the wet streets of Brussels, with little aureoles of foggy light around the lampposts, he sat down at his desk and stared at his typewriter.

Hopeless, hopeless, he thought. Poor, hopeless, seedy, fantasizing, beloved man. And I never did get the chance to tell him I'd like to buy him a new suit.

When he finally went to bed, it was alone.

Monika didn't come in that night.

She came home before he went to work in the morning, with the package he was to deliver to an address on the rue du Gros-Caillou in the 7th arrondissement in Paris when he went to the capital of France with his colonel. The package was comparatively harmless—just ten thousand French francs in old bills and an American Army, .45-caliber automatic pistol, equipped with a silencer.

The .45 and the extra clips of ammunition were in his tennis bag as he got out of the taxi at the corner of the Avenue Bosquet and the rue St. Dominique at twenty minutes past three in the afternoon. He had looked at the map of Paris and seen that the rue du Gros-Caillou was a short street that ran between rue St. Dominique and rue de

Grenelle, not far from the Ecole Militaire. The ten thousand francs were folded in an envelope in the inner pocket of his jacket.

He was early. Monika had told him he would be expected at three-thirty. Under his breath he repeated the address she had made him memorize. He strolled, peering in at the shop windows, looking, he hoped, like an idle American tourist with a few minutes to spare before meeting his partners for their tennis game. He was still about thirty yards from the arched gate that led into the street, when a police car, its siren wailing, passed him, going in the wrong direction, up the rue St. Dominique and stopped, blocking the rue du Gros-Caillou. Five policemen jumped out, pistols in their hands, and ran into the rue du Gros-Caillou. Billy quickened his pace, passed the opening of the street. He looked through the arch and saw the policemen running toward a building in front of which there were three other policemen who had come from the other end of the street. He heard shouting and saw the first three policemen plunge through the doorway. A moment later there was the sound of shots.

He turned and went back, making himself walk slowly, toward the Avenue Bosquet. It was not a cold day, but he was shivering and sweating at the same time.

There was a bank on the corner and he went into it. Anything to get off the street. There was a girl sitting at a desk at the entrance and he went up to her and said he wanted to rent a safe-deposit box. He had difficulty getting out the French words, "*Coffre-fort.*" The girl stood up and led him to a counter, where a clerk asked him for his identification. He showed his passport and the clerk filled out some forms. When the clerk asked him for his address he thought for a moment, then gave the name of the hotel he and Monika had stayed at when they were in Paris together. He was staying at another hotel this time. He signed two cards. His signature looked strange to him. He paid a year's fee in advance. Then the clerk led him down into the vault, where he gave the key to the box to the guardian at the desk. The guardian led him to a row of boxes in the rear of the vault, opened one of the locks with Billy's key and the second lock with his own master key, then went back to his desk, leaving Billy alone. Billy opened the tennis bag and put the automatic, the extra clips and the envelope with the ten thousand francs in it into the box. He closed the door of the box and called for the guardian. The guardian came back and turned the two keys and gave Billy his.

Billy went out of the vault and upstairs. Nobody seemed to be paying any attention to him and he went out onto the avenue. He heard no more shots, saw no more police. His father, it had turned out, had been needlessly pessimistic when he had warned him not to trust in inherited luck. He had just had ten minutes of the greatest luck of his or anybody's life.

He hailed a cruising taxi and gave the driver the address of his hotel off the Champs Elysées.

When he got to the hotel, he asked if there were any messages for him. There were none. He went up to his room and picked up the phone and gave the girl at the switchboard the number of his apartment in Brussels. After a few minutes his telephone rang and the girl at the switchboard said there was no answer.

The Colonel had given him the afternoon and evening off and he stayed in his room, calling the number in Brussels every half hour until midnight, when the switchboard closed down. But the number never answered.

He tried to sleep, but every time he dozed off, he woke with a start, sweating.

At six in the morning, he tried the number in Brussels again, but there still was no answer.

He went out and got the morning papers, *Le Figaro* and the *Herald Tribune*. Over coffee and a croissant at a café on the Champs Elysées, he read the stories. They were not prominently featured in either of the papers. A suspected trafficker in drugs had been shot and killed while resisting arrest in the 7th arrondissement. The police were still trying to establish his identity.

They are playing it cosy, Billy thought, as he read the stories—they're not giving away what they know.

When he went back to the hotel, he tried the apartment in Brussels again. There was no answer.

He got back to Brussels two days later. The apartment was empty and everything that had belonged to Monika was gone. There was no note anywhere.

When the Colonel asked him some weeks later if he was going to reenlist, he said, "No, sir, I've decided against it."

CHAPTER 5

COMING IN OUT of the bright seashore sunlight Wesley squinted in the shadow of the hallway as he followed his uncle into the house. A woman was sitting at a table laid for two in front of a big plate-glass window that overlooked the dunes and the Atlantic Ocean. Her face was still a blur against the brilliance of the window, and for a moment he was sure it was his uncle's ex-wife and he was sorry he had come. He hadn't seen her since the day of his father's death and he had spent a good deal of his time since then in trying to forget her. But then his eyes became accustomed to the light and he saw it was not Jean Jordache, but a tall woman with long, reddish-brown hair. Rudolph introduced her.

The woman smiled at him pleasantly and got up and went into the kitchen and came in with a tray with a glass and some plates and some silver on it and set a place for him. The smell from the big crockery pot on the table, mixed with the warm aroma of newly baked biscuits, was tantalizing. He had been on the road, hitchhiking, since seven o'clock in the morning and had walked the mile or two from the main road to the beach and had not had lunch. He had to swallow to hide the fact that his mouth was watering.

The woman was in a bathing suit and was deeply tanned and did not remind him of Mrs. Wertham. The clam chowder was delicious and he tried not to eat too fast. Alice fed him adequately, but she was so busy at the *Time* office that her meals were made up of odds and ends she picked up as she rushed home from work. The satisfactory memory of the feasts Kate used to prepare on the *Clothilde* was being engulfed in floods of tuna salad and cold roast beef sandwiches. He was grateful to Alice for her hospitality and he knew she worked hard both at the office and at her apartment, where she tapped away at her typewriter till all hours of the night, but her interests were not in the kitchen, and he couldn't help thinking that she had better succeed with her writing as she would never earn any honors as a cook.

When he finished the chowder, accompanied by four biscuits, dripping with butter, Mrs. Morison insisted upon filling his bowl again and getting some hot biscuits out of the oven.

"I guess I came at the right time," Wesley said, grinning, as he finished the second bowl.

His uncle didn't ask him any important questions over lunch, just how he had come out to Bridgehampton and how he had found the house. Wesley did not volunteer any information. He would answer questions when they were alone.

"We hadn't planned on any dessert," Mrs. Morison said, "but I think we can rustle up something from the icebox for a young member of the family. I have a son myself and I know about youthful appetites. I believe there's some blueberry pie left over from last night and I know there's some ice cream in the freezer."

Wesley decided that he liked the woman and wondered if his uncle would have been a different man if he had met her and married her long ago, before the other one.

After lunch the woman said she had to be going and put on a beach robe. Rudolph walked out with her to her car, leaving Wesley alone in the house.

"God, he's a handsome boy," Helen said as she got into her car.

"Gretchen says he looks like a young prince in a Florentine painting," Rudolph said. "She wants to try him out for a part in her movie."

"What does he say?"

"I haven't asked him yet," Rudolph said. "That's all we need in our family—a movie actor."

"He did come at the wrong time, though," Helen said.

"You're right. The lunch was aphrodisiacal, as promised."

Helen laughed. "There's always tomorrow," she said.

"What's wrong with tonight?"

"Busy," she said. "Undermining the Rupublican Party. Anyway, I imagine the boy wants to have a long talk with his uncle. He didn't come all the way out here just for lunch." She leaned over and kissed him and then started her car. He watched thoughtfully as she drove off, a woman with a purpose. He wondered if he ever again would have a purpose, sighed and went back into the house.

Wesley was standing in front of the big window, staring out to sea. "If ever I settle down," Wesley said, "I would like it to be in a place like this—with a whole ocean in front of me."

"I was lucky to find this place," Rudolph said.

"Yeah," Wesley said. "Lucky. Boy, that was some meal. She's a nice lady, isn't she?"

"Very nice," Rudolph said. The description of his relations with Helen Morison and an appraisal of her qualities could wait until later. "Would you like to go for a swim? People keep leaving bathing trunks around and I guess I could find a pair that would fit you." He knew he was looking for ways to postpone whatever problem Wesley had brought along to present to him. "The water's pretty cold, but you'll have the whole ocean to yourself."

"That'd be great," Wesley said. "A swim."

They went out onto the deck and down the steps under it to the cubicle where four or five pairs of trunks were hanging. Rudolph left Wesley to undress and went out onto the beach.

When Wesley came out in the swimming trunks, with a towel slung around his neck, Rudolph walked with him to the edge of the water. Wesley dropped the towel to the sand and hesitated a moment before going in. He had sloping powerful shoulders, an athlete's flat belly and long muscled legs. His face, Rudolph thought, was a refined version of his father's face, but the body, although a little taller, was his father's body. Maybe, Rudolph thought, as the boy suddenly started running toward the breakers, the water foaming around him, maybe Gretchen is right about him. He watched the boy plunge into a wave, then begin swimming easily through the waves and into the swell. Enid was still afraid of the ocean and only paddled cautiously near the shore. He had not tried to force her to be more enterprising. He was not going to be one of those fathers who, disappointed in not having a son, tried to make a daughter into one. He had known one or two of those overmuscled ladies and he knew that whatever they said about their fathers, they cursed them in their hearts.

Wesley kept going farther and farther out, until his head was just a small dot in the glittering blue distance. Rudolph began to worry. Was it possible that the boy had come out to see him for the sole purpose of drowning himself in his presence? His old uneasiness with his nephew, the feeling that at any moment the boy was likely to do or say something unpredictable, dangerous or at least embarrassing came back to him. If he only could have more than a few hours at a time with the boy, perhaps he could get over the feeling that the boy was constantly judging him, measuring him against some private, impossible scale of values. He had to restrain himself from waving and calling to the boy to come in. Abruptly, he turned and went back into the house.

Five hundred yards out, Wesley floated on his back, enjoying the sensual feeling of going gently up and down with the swells. He daydreamed, looking up at the unclouded blue sky, that Alice was there with him, that they sank under the surface, kissing, their bodies weightless and laced in the rolling water, to rise again to stare at each other's faces, wet with the ocean's tingle, their love announced on land and sea. The truth was that since the one kiss when he made her cry, they had not touched each other, and a new tension, a shy drawing back on both their parts, had changed their relationship, and not for the better.

But now, rising and falling in the gentle sea, he thought of Alice with a longing he wouldn't dare confess to her—or to anybody else.

His father had told him that once when he was a young man he had made love to a girl while they were taking a bath together and that it had been an amazing experience. If it was amazing in a bathtub, what would it be like in the Atlantic Ocean?

If it had been his father on the beach he wouldn't have dared go out so far because his father would have bawled the bejesus out of him for showing off and taking a chance like that, all alone, no matter how good a swimmer he was. "Take chances," his father had said to him, "only when they mean something. Don't do anything just for show or to prove to yourself how all around marvelous you are."

He began to feel cold and turned and began swimming to shore. The tide was running out and he had to swim as hard as he could to get to where the waves were breaking. He rode in on a wave, tumbling in the curl of foam. He pulled himself to his feet on the smooth sand and got up to the beach. He stood there, drying his face and torso with the towel, looking out at the ocean going off to the horizon, with not a ship in sight. Whatever I finally do, he thought, I am going to end up with the sea.

Dry and dressed, after a shower in the cubicle, he went up to the deck and into the house, carrying his jacket over his shoulder. His uncle was talking on the phone in the living room. ". . .if he hasn't swum all the way to Portugal by now," he heard his uncle saying. His uncle smiled at him. "Wait a minute," Rudolph said into the phone. "He's just walked in. Looking a little waterlogged." He extended the phone toward Wesley. "It's your Aunt Gretchen," he said. "She'd like to say hello."

Wesley took the phone. "How are you?" he said.

"Busy," said Gretchen. "I'm glad you finally turned up. I've been trying to reach you for months. Where've you been?"

"Here and there," Wesley said.

"Listen, Wesley," Gretchen said, "Rudolph's driving into town early tomorrow and meeting me. Can you come with him? I'm dying to see you. He'll explain why."

"Well . . ." Wesley said. "He hasn't asked me to stay all night."

"Consider yourself asked," Rudolph said.

"Okay," Wesley said. "I'll try to make it."

"Don't just try," Gretchen said. "Make it. You won't be sorry."

"Do you want to talk to Rudolph again?"

"No time," Gretchen said. "Good-bye, honey."

Wesley put down the phone. "You sure I'm not fouling up your evening?" he asked Rudolph.

"On the contrary," Rudolph said. "I'm looking forward to it."

"She said you'd explain something to me," Wesley said. "Is there anything wrong?"

"No. Sit down. Let's make ourselves comfortable."

They sat across from each other at the table in front of the window. In the strong light the changes in Rudolph's face were most noticeable. The broken nose and the scar above one eye made him less frosty and distant. His uncle's face, Wesley thought, looked *used* now, more human. For the first time, he thought, his uncle looked unmistakably like his father. Until now he had never seen the resemblance between the brothers. "They must have given you quite a going over," he said, "those two guys."

"It's not too bad, is it?" Rudolph said.

"No," Wesley said. "I kind of like it. I guess I'm used to busted noses. It's more homelike." The reference to his father was easy and natural and they both laughed.

"Gretchen was after me to have it operated on," Rudolph said, "but I told her I thought it gave me character. I'm glad to hear that you agree."

"What's that about explaining . . .? On the phone . . .?"

"Oh, I wrote you she was trying to put together a movie, didn't I?"

"Yeah."

"Well, she finally got everything squared away. She starts shooting in about a month. For some reason," Rudolph said lightly, "she thinks you're a beautiful young man. . . ."

"Oh, come on," Wesley said uneasily.

"Whatever. There's no accounting for tastes," Rudolph said. "Anyway, she thinks you might be just what she needs for a certain part and she'd like to try you out."

"Me?" Wesley said incredulously. "In the movies?"

"I'm no judge," Rudolph said, "but Gretchen knows a great deal about pictures. If she thinks so . . ."

Wesley shook his head. "I'd like to see Gretchen again," he said, "but I won't do anything like that. I have a lot of things I have to do and I don't want to waste my time. I also don't want people walking up to me in the street and saying I recognize your face, Mr. Jordache."

"Those would be my sentiments, too," Rudolph said, "but I think it would be more polite to listen to Gretchen first before you say no. Anyway, they wouldn't say Mr. Jordache. In the movies they change everybody's name, especially if it's one like Jordache. They'd tell you nobody would know how to pronounce it."

"That mightn't be such a bad idea," Wesley said. "Changing my name, I mean. And not just for the movies."

Rudolph stared soberly at his nephew. It was a strange thing for the boy to say. He half understood it, but it troubled him, he wasn't sure quite why. Time to change the subject, he thought. "Tell me," he said, "what have you been doing?"

"I left home," Wesley said.

"You told me on the phone."

"By invitation," Wesley said. "I didn't tell you that."

"No."

"My mother." Wesley said. "I guess you could say we just didn't get along. I don't blame her. We don't belong in the same house together. In the same world, maybe . . . Has she been bugging you about me—about the warrant and all that?"

"That's all been arranged," Rudolph said.

"I suppose by you." Wesley sounded almost accusing.

"The less said about it the better," Rudolph said lightly. "Incidentally, where *have* you been all this time?"

"A lot of places," Wesley said, evasively. "In and out of New York a few times . . ."

"You didn't let me know." Rudolph tried not to sound aggrieved.

"You have troubles enough of your own."

"I might have helped."

Wesley grinned. "Maybe I was saving you for when I really needed help." Then he became grave. "I was lucky. I found a friend. A good friend."

"You look well," Rudolph said. "Almost prosperous. That's a nice suit you're wearing. . . ." It suddenly occurred to him that perhaps Wesley had been taken in by somebody who was using him for some shady undertaking, picking up poor girls at the bus terminal and turning them over to pimps or acting as a courier for a drug dealer. Since his beating, New York had taken on a new and sinister aura for him, a hunting ground where all were victims and no one safe. And a young, inexperienced boy wandering penniless around New York . . . "I hope you're not into something illegal."

Wesley laughed. "No," he said. "At least not yet. It's somebody up at *Time* Magazine. A lady. She helped me when I came to New York looking up the dope on my father. I thought maybe she could help me with finding some other people who knew him. Addresses, things like that. They seem to know everything about everybody up there. I guess she was sorry for me. Anyway, my hunch was right. She put me on a lot of trails."

"Did she buy you that suit?"

"She loaned me the money," Wesley said defensively. "And she picked out the suit—a couple of other things."

"How old is she?" Rudolph had a vision of an ancient spinster, preying on country youth, and was disturbed by the thought.

"A couple of years more than me."

Rudolph smiled. "I guess anything under thirty is okay," he said.

"She's got a long way to go to thirty."

"Are you having an affair with her?" Rudolph asked. "Excuse me for being blunt."

Wesley didn't seem hurt by the question. "No," he said. "I sleep on her couch. She calls me Cousin."

"I'd like to meet the young lady."

"You'll like her. She's awfully nice," Wesley said. "She really did some digging around for me."

"Whom did you talk to?" Rudolph asked curiously.

"Four or five people, here and there," Wesley said. "Some good, some bad. I'd rather keep it all to myself, if you don't mind. I still have some thinking to do about it—see if I can figure out what it all means."

"Do you think you know your father any better now?"

"Not really," Wesley said soberly. "I knew in general he got into an awful lot of trouble when he was young. I just picked up a few facts about the *kinds* of trouble. Maybe I admire him more for turning out the way he did after a start like that—I don't know. What I do know is that I *remember* him better. I was afraid I would start to forget him and I didn't want that. This way," he said earnestly, "he's with me all the time. Inside my head, sort of, almost as if he's there talking to me, if you know what I mean."

"I think I do," Rudolph said. "Now—what did you really come for—?" With a little laugh, "Aside from lunch."

Wesley hesitated. "I came to ask you a favor," he said, staring down at the table. "Two favors, actually."

"What are they?"

"I want to go back to Europe. I want to see Kate and her kid. And Bunny. And Billy Abbott. I'd like to see how the other son in the family survived. And a couple of other people around Antibes. I'm not at home in America, somehow. I haven't had a good day since I came here." His voice was too passionate to make it sound like a complaint. "Maybe that'll pass, but it hasn't yet. You once told me that the lawyer in Antibes said he thought in a year or so he could arrange for me to be let back into France. I was wondering if you could write him and . . . well, see what he can do."

Rudolph stood up and paced slowly toward the fireplace. "I'm going to be blunt again, Wesley," he said. "Have you told me your real reasons for wanting to go to Europe or—" He stopped.

"Or what?" Wesley asked.

"Or are you thinking of looking up the man your father had the fight with?"

Wesley didn't answer immediately. Then he said, "The thought may have crossed my mind."

"That would be foolish, Wesley," Rudolph said. "Very foolish. And very dangerous."

"I promise to be careful," Wesley said.

"I hope I don't have the occasion to remind you of your promise," Rudolph said. "Now, what's the other favor?"

"This is harder," Wesley said. Now he stared out to sea, "It's about money. I won't be eighteen for another year, when I get my share of the inheritance. I thought if it didn't press you too hard, you'd lend me say a thousand dollars and I'd pay you back on my eighteenth birthday. . . ."

"It's not the money," Rudolph said, although he couldn't help thinking that somehow money was involved in almost every decision he had ever made—in paying Wesley's mother off to get a divorce, in helping Gretchen start in her new profession, in achieving his own reconciliation with Wesley's father, in his move to where he was living now, on the shores of the Atlantic, because of the few dollars and change in his pocket when he was ambushed by the two men in the hallway of his house in New York. Even in getting Wesley out of jail because the wily old lawyer in Antibes could be paid his handsome fee in the numbered account in Switzerland. "No, it's not the money," he repeated. "It's your future I'm thinking about."

"I'm thinking about my future, too," Wesley said bitterly. "I want to be in France on my eighteenth birthday, when I have to register for the draft. I don't want my future to be a grave in Vietnam."

"That could be arranged, too, without leaving America," Rudolph said, going over to the boy and standing at his side and looking out with him at the sea. "I wrote you about the Merchant Marine Academy . . ."

"I remember," Wesley said. "It sounded like a good deal."

"How are you in mathematics? That's important for getting accepted."

"Pretty good," Wesley said. "It comes easy to me."

"That's fine," Rudolph said. "But you have to be a high-school graduate. And be recommended by a congressman. I'm sure I could manage *that*. And . . ." He was struck by a sudden idea. "You could come here and live with me—it's not a bad place to live, is it?"

"No. It's great."

"Frankly, I'd like it very much. I think you'd be able to say that you finally had some good days in America. You could finish high school here. That is, if your aunt doesn't make a movie star out of you. . . ."

"Don't worry about that."

"By the time you got out of the academy, the war is bound to be over. It has to end sometime."

"Who says?" Wesley said.

"History," said Rudolph.

"I haven't read that particular book," Wesley said sardonically.

"I'll find it for you. You don't have to make up your mind right away. Meanwhile I'll write the lawyer. Is that fair enough?"

"Fair enough," Wesley said.

CHAPTER 6

As BILLY WAS packing his bags to leave Brussels, he looked at the piece of paper. Honorable Discharge, he read. He smiled wryly as he slipped the document into a stiff envelope. Don't believe everything you see in print.

The next piece of paper he put into the envelope was a letter from his father. His father was happy that he had decided wisely about the army and unhappy that he had decided not to come to Chicago, although he understood the attractions of Europe for a young man. Chicago could wait for a year or two. There was news about his mother, too. She was directing a picture. His father believed Billy should write and congratulate her. Of all things, his father added, one of the leading actors in the movie was Billy's cousin, Wesley. A sullen boy, Wesley, at least in William Abbott's opinion. The Jordaches took care of the Jordaches, his father wrote. A pity he, Billy, was not on better terms with his mother.

The next thing Billy put in his bag was a Spanish-English dictionary. A Belgian businessman with whom he had played tennis and who was involved in building a complex of bungalows and condominiums at a place called El Faro near Marbella, in Spain, with six tennis courts, had offered him a contract for a year as a tennis pro. The idea of Spain was attractive after Brussels and it was no contest against Chicago, and after all, the only thing he did well was play tennis and it was a clean and well-paying job, in the open air, so he had said yes. He could stand some sunshine. Beware the *señoritas,* his father had warned him.

The last piece of paper was undated and signed Heidi. It had been in an unstamped envelope that he had found in his mailbox the night before. "Had to depart suddenly because of the death of a friend. Understand you are not re-enlisting. Leave forwarding address, although I am sure I can find you. We have unfinished business to attend to."

He did not smile as he read the letter and tore it into small pieces and flushed it down the toilet. He did not leave a forwarding address.

He took the train to Paris. He had sold his car. Monika knew it too well, make, year, license number. Who knew how many people had its description and might be looking for it on the roads of Europe?

He could buy a new car in France. He could afford it. There was a modest but sufficient legacy waiting for him in the vault in the bank on the corner of the Avenue Bosquet in the 7th arrondissement in Paris.

"Cut," Gretchen said, and the day's shooting was over and the hum of conversation suddenly started from the actors and crew members on the set. The scene had been shot in front of a dilapidated mansion that now had a false facade and a fake lawn leading to the street. In the scene Wesley and the girl who played his sister had a violent argument about the way Wesley was leading his life. It had taken all day to shoot. His Uncle Rudolph, who had come up for the day, was on the set, and although he had merely waved at Wesley, his presence had made Wesley a little more self-conscious than usual. But since he played the part of a boy who was supposed to be taciturn and unresponsive and the girl had to do most of the work, it had not mattered too much.

After the first few days, during which Wesley had been stiff and trying to hide his shyness about playacting in front of so many people, he had caught on to what was wanted from him—his Aunt Gretchen had taken him aside and told him not to try to act—and had begun to enjoy the whole affair. Gretchen had told him he was doing very well, although she had said it in private, with nobody else around to hear her. But he had learned she was not a lady who lied.

He liked the atmosphere of the company. Most of the people were young and friendly, constantly joking, and anxious to be helpful. He had never had many friends who were near his own age, and it was relaxing not to be always on your best behavior just because you were with people who were a lot older than you.

Gretchen allowed him to use the name Wesley Jordan. After all, his father had used the name Jordan professionally before him, so he had half a claim to the title. Originally, he had allowed himself to be cajoled into taking the job mostly because he was getting three thousand dollars for a month's work, which would mean he could pay Alice back what he owed her and wouldn't have to depend on his uncle to get to Europe, but now he found himself eager to get on the set each morning, even when he wasn't due for any scenes himself. The entire business fascinated him, the expertness of the camera, lighting and soundmen, the devotion of the actors, the calm but firm way in which his aunt ran everything. In her manner of handling people she reminded him of his father. According to Frances Miller, the girl who played his sister and who was only about twenty-two but had been in show business since the age of fourteen, not all movie sets were like that by a long shot. Hysteria and temper were more often than not the order of the day, and she'd told Wesley that she'd take Gretchen as a director any time over most of the men she had worked with.

Frances was a beautiful girl in a funny, wild way, freckled, her eyes wide and deep in her sharply angled, moody, youthful face, her body petite and deliciously rounded, her skin an invitation to the most extreme dreams. She was outspoken and occasionally foul-mouthed. Ocasionally, too, she liked to drink. More often she also liked to make love to him, which she had started early on in Port Philip, when she had come to his room in their hotel to run over the lines for the next day's shooting and stayed the night. Wesley was dazzled by her beauty and by the idea that she had chosen him. He would never have dared make the first move himself. It had not yet occurred to him that he was an extraordinarily handsome young man. When strange young women stared at him he had the uneasy feeling that somehow he was doing something wrong or that they were disapproving of the way he was dressed. For a while, he had felt guilty, because he had thought that he was in love with Alice Larkin. But Alice Larkin still called him Cousin and he still slept on her couch in the living room when he was in New York. Besides, Frances made love with such happy abandon it was hard to feel guilty about anything in her presence.

Frances was married to a young actor who was in California where she ordinarily lived. Wesley tried to forget about the husband. As far as Wesley knew, nobody in the company had any inkling of what was going on between him and the leading lady. When they were in public she treated him as though he were in fact what he was in the movie—a younger brother.

His Aunt Gretchen had caught on, of course. He had discovered that she caught on to everything. She had had dinner alone with him one night and warned him that when the shooting was over Frances would go back to California and then on to a new picture and would almost certainly sleep with another young man in the new company who caught her fancy, because she was known to do things like that, and that he was not to take it too seriously. "I want this whole thing to be a wonderful experience for you," Gretchen said. "I don't want you to hate me for getting you into something you can't handle."

"I can handle it," he said, although he wasn't sure he could.

"Remember what I said about that girl," Gretchen said. "She's messed up the lives of older men than you before this." What she didn't say was that she knew Frances Miller had had an affair for six months with Evans Kinsella and that he had asked her to get a divorce and marry him. And that the day after the picture Frances was doing with him was finished, she stopped answering his calls. She also didn't say that she,

Gretchen, was still jealous of Frances and regretted that she was the girl she had thought would be wonderful in the part. You couldn't cast or not cast a picture out of bedrooms, although many people had done so, to their sorrow. "Just remember," Gretchen said.

"I'll remember," said Wesley.

"You're dear and vulnerable, Old Toughie," Gretchen said. She leaned over and kissed his cheek. "Defend yourself. You're in a much rougher racket than you know."

That night he had made love to Frances almost the whole night long, brutally, until he had had to smother her face in a pillow so that the entire hotel wouldn't be awakened by her screams. She was a girl who made no secret about whether she was enjoying herself.

As they both lay side by side, exhausted, he had thought, triumphantly, She's not going back to anyone after tonight.

At dinner he and the other actors ate together as usual in the hotel dining room. Gretchen and Ida Cohen and Ida Cohen's uncle, along with the scene designer and Uncle Rudolph, ate upstairs in the living room of Gretchen's suite. After dinner, Wesley and Frances decided to go for a walk. It was a cool autumn night with a moon that was almost full and they walked arm in arm, like any young couple out on a date.

The main street was almost empty, neon-lit from forlorn store windows. Port Philip watched television and went to bed early. Frances looked idly at the displays in the windows as they passed. "There's nothing here I'd ever buy," she said. "Imagine living in a place like this. Ugh."

"My family comes from here," Wesley said.

"Oh, my God," Frances said. "You poor boy."

"I never lived here. My father, my grandfather . . ." He stopped himself before he said, my Aunt Gretchen. He hadn't told Frances or any of the company that Gretchen was his aunt, and Gretchen was careful to treat him like any other novice actor in the company.

"Do you see any of them—" Frances asked. "I mean, your family, while you're here?"

"There're none left. They all moved away."

"I can understand why," Frances said. "This town must have gone downhill from the first day they put up the post office."

"My grandmother told my father that when she first came here as a young girl, it was a beautiful place," Wesley said. He was walking the streets of the town in which his father was born and which had formed him and he didn't like the idea of its being thought of as a dreary backwater by a girl from California. Somewhere in the town, he thought, his father must have left a mark, a sign that he had been and gone. He had burned a cross here. Theodore Boylan, at least, remembered. He wondered what his father would have thought of his son walking the old same streets arm in arm with a beautiful, almost famous movie actress. And, more than that, making three thousand dollars for four weeks' work, which was more play than any work his father had ever known. "There were trees everywhere, my grandmother told my father," Wesley said, "and all those big houses were painted and clean and had big gardens. My father used to swim in the Hudson River—it was clean then—and the riverboats used to stop by and there was great fishing . . ." He stopped before telling the girl that aside from the boats and the fishing, his grandfather had used the river in which to drown himself.

"Things get worse, don't they?" Frances said. "I'll bet there was a lot of screwing in those big gardens then. Nothing else to do in the evening and no motels."

"I suppose everybody got his share."

"And her share," Frances said, laughing. "Like now. It's too bad you're on this picture."

"Why?" Wesley asked, hurt.

"If you weren't," she said, "I'd have gone through *War and Peace* by now, these long nights."

"Sorry?"

"*War and Peace* can wait," she said. She hugged his arm. "By the way, I've been meaning to ask you—what drama school did you go to?"

"Me?" He hesitated. "None."

"You act as though you've had years," she said. "Incidentally, how old are you?"

"Twenty-one," he said, without hesitation. He had made the mistake of telling Alice how old he was and she treated him as a child. He wasn't about to make that mistake again.

"How is it you're not in the army?"

"Football knee," he said promptly. Since he had come back to America he had learned how to lie at a moment's notice.

"I see." She sounded suspicious. "Where've you acted before?"

"Me?" he said again, foolishly. "Well . . . noplace." Frances was too knowing about things like that to take a chance on lying.

"Not even summer stock?"

"Not even summer stock."

"How'd you get this job then?"

"Mrs. Burke . . ." It sounded funny in his ears to talk about his aunt as Mrs. Burke. "She saw me at a friend's house and asked me if I wanted to test. What're you asking all these questions for?"

"It's natural for a girl to want to know a few facts about the man she's having an affair with, isn't it?"

"I suppose so." He was pleased with the word "affair." It gave him a new sense of maturity. Teenagers had dates or girlfriends, not affairs.

"There's one thing about me," Frances said, very definitely. "I can't go to bed with a man whom I don't respect." It embarrassed Wesley when Frances spoke in that offhand, plural way about other men she had known. But, he told himself, she had been an actress since she was fourteen, what could he expect? Still, some day soon, he promised himself, he would tell her to keep her reflections on that particular subject to herself.

"You came as a surprise, I must admit," she said cheerfully. "I took one look at the list of the cast and said this is going to be chastity-belt time for me."

"What changed your mind?"

"You." She laughed. "I knew just about all the others, but Wesley Jordan was a new name for me. I didn't know you'd be the prize of the litter. By the way, is that your real name?"

"No," Wesley said, after a pause.

"What is it?"

"It's long and complicated," he said evasively. "It would never look good over the title."

She laughed again. "This is your first picture, but you're learning fast."

He grinned. "I'm a quick study." He was enjoying being in the movies more and more and his vocabulary reflected it.

"What're you going to do after this picture?"

"Don't know." He shrugged. "Go to Europe if I can."

"You're awfully good," she said. "That isn't only my opinion. Freddie Kahn, the cameraman, has seen all the rushes and he's raving about you. You going to try Hollywood?"

"Maybe," he said cautiously.

"Come on out," she said. "I promise you a warm welcome."

Wesley took in a big gulp of air. "I understand you're married," he said.

"Who told you that?" she asked sharply.

"I don't remember. Someone. It just came up in the conversation."

"I wish people would keep their goddamn mouths shut. That's my business. Does that make any difference to you?"

"What would you say if I said it did?"

"I'd say you're a fool."

"Then I won't say it."

"That's better," she said. "Are you in love with me?"

"Why do you ask that question?"

"Because I like it more when people are in love with me," she said. "That's why I'm an actress."

"All right," he said, "I'm in love with you."

"Let's drink to that," she said. "There's a bar on the next block."

"I'm on the wagon," he said. He didn't want to be asked in front of Frances for proof of his age by the bartender.

"I like to drink," she said, "and I like men who don't drink. Come on, I'll buy you a Coke."

When they went into the bar they saw Rudolph and the set designer, a red-bearded young man by the name of Donnelly, sitting at a booth, absorbed in conversation.

"What ho," Frances whispered, "the brass."

Everybody in the cast knew that Rudolph was on the financial end of the undertaking and had been instrumental with the authorities in Port Philip when difficulties had arisen about permits, shooting at night and the use of the town police to block off streets. The cast didn't know, however, that he was Wesley's uncle; on the few occasions that Wesley had spoken to Rudolph in public he had addressed him as Mr. Jordache, and Rudolph had replied, gravely and courteously, by addressing his nephew as Mr. Jordan.

Frances and Wesley had to pass the booth in which the two men sat. Rudolph looked up and smiled at them and stood up and said, "Good evening, ladies and gentlemen."

Wesley mumbled a greeting, but Frances smiled her most winsome smile and said, "What new plot are you two gentlemen concocting against us poor actors in this noisome den now?"

Wesley winced at the false, girlish smile, the fancy language. Suddenly he realized that Frances had too many different ways of addressing different people.

"We were sitting here praising the performance of you two young people," Rudolph said.

Frances giggled. "Aren't you the polite man," she said. "What a delightful lie."

Donnelly grunted.

"Do sit down," Frances said. "In Hollywood nobody ever stands up for the help."

Again Wesley winced. At certain moments, aside from using her abundant charm, Frances managed to remind people whom she considered important of the bright career she had already put behind her.

The two men sat down, Donnelly staring morosely at the glass in front of him. No one had as yet seen him smile during the course of the shooting.

"Mr. Donnelly," Frances said, her voice still girlish, "I haven't dared to tell you this before, but now that the picture's almost over, I'd like to say that it's just wonderful what you've been doing with the sets. I haven't seen any of the film yet"— she made a small grimace—"us poor actors aren't let in on the decisions on who lives and who dies in the projection room, so I don't know how they look on film, but I do have to tell you that as far as I'm concerned I've never been as comfortable moving around in front of the camera as I have in the acting space you've designed for us to work in." She laughed, as though she were a little embarrassed at speaking so boldly.

Donnolly grunted again.

Wesley could see Frances's jaw set then. "I won't disturb you any longer while you two gentlemen arrange our fates," she said. "Young Wesley and I"— now she made it sound as though Wesley were ten years old—"have some problems in our scene tomorrow that we thought we'd do a little homework on."

Wesley tugged at her arm, and with a last dazzling smile, she moved off with him. She made a move to sit in the next booth, but Wesley guided her firmly to the last booth in the rear of the bar, well out of earshot of Donnelly and his uncle.

"What a goddamn performance," he said as they sat down.

"Honey catches more flies than vinegar, darling," Frances said sweetly. "Who knows when those two nice men will do another picture and have the final say about who's going to be in it and who's going to be out on his or her ass?"

"You put on so many acts," Wesley said, "I bet sometimes you have to call up your mother to find out who you really are."

"That's the art, dear," Frances said coolly. "You'd better learn it if you want to get anyplace."

"I don't want to get anyplace at that price," Wesley said.

"That's what I used to say," she said. "When I was fourteen years old. By the time I was fifteen, I changed my mind. You're just a little retarded, dear."

"Thank God for that," Wesley said.

The waiter was standing over them now and Frances ordered for both of them, a gin and tonic for her and a Coke for him.

When the waiter had gone over to the bar Wesley said, "I wish you wouldn't drink gin."

"Why not?"

"Because I don't like the way your breath smells when you drink gin."

"There's no need to worry tonight, dear," Frances said coldly. "I'm due for an early call with the hairdresser tomorrow and I'm not up to any gymnastics tonight."

Wesley sat in glum silence until the waiter brought the drinks.

"Anyway, even if you're so horrendously critical of a few little harmless, girlish tricks," Frances said, sipping at her gin and tonic, "there are others who find them entrancing. That cute Mr. Jordache, with all that money, for example. His eyes light up like a billboard sign whenever he sees me."

"I hadn't noticed," Wesley said, honestly shocked that anyone could call his uncle that cute Mr. Jordache.

"I have," Frances said firmly. "I bet he'd be something. That icy Yankee exterior with a volcano underneath. I know the type."

"He's old enough to be your father, for God's sake."

"Not unless he started awfully young," Frances said. "And I bet he did."

Wesley stood up. "I'm not going to sit here and listen to crap like that. I'm going home. See how you get on with that cute Mr. Jordache with all that money."

"Dear, dear," Frances said, without moving, "aren't we the touchy young man this evening."

"Good night," Wesley said.

"Good night," Frances said calmly. "Don't bother with the check."

Wesley strode past the booth where his uncle was sitting. Neither of the two men looked up as he passed. He went out into the street, feeling childish, hurt and foolishly emotional.

Five minutes later Frances got up and walked toward the door. She stopped and spoke for a moment to the two men, but they didn't ask her to join them. When she went back to the hotel she didn't go down the corridor and open Wesley's door as she did on all other nights, but continued on to her own room and stared at herself in the mirror over the dressing table for a long time.

Back at the bar, the two men were not talking about making movies. Donnelly was an architect who had drifted into scene designing when he discovered that he was offered only unprofitable commissions for mediocre small buildings which he considered beneath his talent. In the course of the preparations for *Restoration Comedy* he and Rudolph had become friendly, and at first timidly, then more enthusiastically, he had spoken about an ambitious project that he was involved in but so far had not been able to get financing for. Now he was giving Rudolph the details. "We live in the age of what the British call redundancy," he was saying, "not only because of new machines or shifts in population, but redundancy because of age. Men retire from business because they're bored and can afford it, or because they can't stand the strain or because younger men are called in to fill their jobs. Their children have grown up and moved away. Their houses are suddenly too big for them, the city in which they live frightens them or has exhausted its attraction for them. Their pensions or savings don't permit them to keep the servants they once had, the neighborhoods where they can afford to find small apartments are crowded with young couples with small children who treat them as invaders from another century, they are separated from friends of their own age who have similar problems but have looked for other solutions in other places— They want to keep their independence but they're frightened of loneliness. What they need is a new habitat, a new atmosphere that fits their condition—where they're surrounded by people approximately their own age, with approximately the same problems and needs, people who can be depended upon in an emergency, just as it gives them a sense of their own humanity to know that they're ready to come to a neighbor's aid when *he* needs help." Donnelly spoke with great urgency, as though he were a general, outlining plans for the relief of a besieged garrison. "It has to be a real community," he continued, gesturing eloquently with his large hands, as if already he was molding brick, mortar and cement into livable, populated shapes, "shops, movies, a small hotel where they can entertain visitors, a golf course, swimming pools, tennis courts, lecture rooms. . . . I'm not talking about the poor. I don't know how they can be taken care of except by the state and I'm not vain enough to think I can rearrange American society. I'm talking about the middle-income group, the ones whose way of life is most drastically affected when the breadwinner stops working." His voice dropped to bitterness. "I know all about this in the case of my own mother and father. They have a little money and I help some, myself, but from being a hearty, outgoing couple, they're now a depressed, fretful pair of people, fiddling the last years of their lives away in useless boredom. My idea isn't so new. It's been tried and found successful all over the country, but so far I haven't been able to get any money men interested in it, because there isn't much profit to be made, if any. What it needs to begin with is to buy a huge piece of land in some pleasant country spot—not too isolated—so that when people want a little city life it's easily available to them—and build a small, but complete village of modest, well-designed, but cheaply built attached homes, say in groups of four or five, scattered in a parklike landscape, houses that can be handled easily by two aging people. With bus service, doctors and nurses on hand, a congenial but unobtrusive management. It wouldn't be an old folks' home, with all the despair that entails— there'd be a constant flow of young people—sons and daughters and grandchildren, hopeful and lively, a view on the future. Your sister has told me that you're a public-spirited man and that you have access to money and you're looking for something to occupy your time. From what I've seen so far, I don't think getting mixed up in movies is exactly your idea of public service. . . ."

Rudolph laughed. "No," he said, "not exactly."

"She also said that you're a born builder," Donnelly went on, "that when you were young you bulled through the idea of a shopping center in what was then practically a wilderness and made almost a whole small town of it. I went out to look at it the other day, the Calderwood complex near here, and I was deeply impressed—it was way ahead of its time and it showed real imagination—"

"When I was young," Rudolph said reflectively. He hadn't shown anything of what he thought as he listened to Donnelly's speech, but he felt an excitement that was both new and old to him as Donnelly spoke. He had been waiting for something, he hadn't known what. Perhaps this was what he was waiting for.

"I've got whole sets of drawings," Donnelly said, "models of the sort of houses I want to put up, schedules of approximate costs . . . everything. . . ."

"I'd like to take a look at them," Rudolph said.

"Can you be in New York tomorrow?"

"No reason why not."

"Good. I'll show them to you."

"Of course," Rudolph said, "the whole thing would depend on just what piece of land you could get, what its suitability was, what the cost would be—all that."

Donnelly looked around him at the empty bar, as though searching out spies. "I've even picked out the spot," he said, lowering his voice. "It's a beauty. It's abandoned, overgrown farmland now and cheap. It's in Connecticut, rolling hill country, and it's no more than an hour from New Haven, maybe two from New York. It's made for something like this."

"Could you show it to me?"

Donnelly glared at him, as though suddenly suspecting him of some dark purpose. "Are you *really* interested?"

"I'm really interested."

"Good," Donnelly said. "You know something—" His voice was solemn now. "I think it was fate that made me say yes to your sister when she asked me to work on this movie. I'll drive you out there and you can see for yourself."

Rudolph left a bill on the table to pay for the drinks. "It's getting late," he said as he stood up. "Shall we go back to the hotel?"

"If you don't mind," Donnelly said, "I'd rather stay here and get drunk."

"Take two aspirin before going to bed," Rudolph said. Donnelly was ordering another whiskey as he went out of the bar, offering a libation to fate, which had brought him and Rudolph Jordache together.

Rudolph walked slowly, alone, down the familiar streets. They had aged since he had pedaled along them, delivering rolls for the family bakery at dawn every morning, but he had the incongruous feeling this night that he was a young man again, with grandiose plans in his head, achievement in his future. Once again, as he had felt on the gravelly strand in Nice, he was tempted to sprint in the darkness, renewing the elation of his youth when he was the best 220 high hurdler in the high school. He even took a few tentative, loping steps, but saw a car's headlights approaching and relapsed into his usual dignified walk.

He passed the big building which housed the Calderwood Department Store and looked into the windows and remembered the nights he had put in arranging the displays. If his fortune had started at any one place, it had started there. The windows were shabby now, he thought, an old lady putting makeup carelessly on her face, the lipstick awry, the eye shadow sloppy, the simulation of youth weary and unconvincing. Old man Calderwood would have bellowed. A dead man's life's work. Useful? Useless?

He remembered, too, marching, playing the trumpet at the head of a column of students on the evening of the day the war had ended, the future a triumphant panorama ahead of him. Yesterday, he had read in the town newspaper, there had been another parade of students, this time to protest the war in Vietnam, the youths chanting obscene slogans, defacing the flag, taunting the police. Eleven students had wound up in jail. Truman then, Nixon now. Decay. He sighed. Better not to remember anything.

When he had suggested to Gretchen that Port Philip would be a good place to shoot her movie—a neglected town, withdrawn from the prosperous and honorable past on the banks of the great river—he had resolved not to have anything to do with the actual machinery of the production or even visit the town. But problems had arisen and Gretchen had called for help and he had reluctantly made the trip, talked to the officials, fearing that they would recall his downfall when the students had turned against *him* and driven him away.

How beautiful Jean had been in those days.

But the officials had been respectful, eager to accommodate him. Scandals passed. New men arrived. Memories faded.

Donnelly reminded him of himself when he was young—passionate, hopeful, driving, self-centered, sure of his purposes. He wondered what Donnelly would feel ten years from now, many accomplishments behind him, the streets of his native town, wherever it was, changed, everything changed. He liked Donnelly. He knew Gretchen liked him, too. He wondered if there was anything between them. He wondered, too, if Donnelly's idea was practical, workable. Was Donnelly too young, too ambitious? He cautioned himself to move slowly, check everything, as he thought he himself had checked everything when he was that age.

He would talk it over with Helen Morison. She was a hard-headed woman. She could be depended on. But she was in Washington now. She had been offered a job there on the staff of a congressman whom she admired and she had moved on. He would have to catch up with her somehow.

He thought of Jeanne. There had been a few letters, with less and less to say in each succeeding one, the emotion of the week on the Côte fading. Perhaps when Wesley finally went to France, he would take it as an excuse to visit her. The lawyer in Antibes had finally written that it had been arranged that Wesley could come back, but he hadn't told Wesley that. He was waiting until the movie was finished. He didn't want Wesley suddenly to take it into his head to quit the picture and fly across the ocean. Wesley was not a flighty boy, but he was driven, driven by his own ghosts, unpredictable.

He himself had been driven by the ghost of his own father, despairing, a failure, a suicide, drunk on poverty and destroyed hopes, so he could half understand his nephew. Weird, that that subterranean, hidden boy could turn out to be such a touching actor.

There had never been anybody with that kind of talent in the family before, although Gretchen had been briefly on the stage, without success. You never could tell where it comes from, Gretchen had told him after a session in the projection room in which they had watched and marveled at what the boy could do. And it wasn't only that particular talent. It was every kind of talent. In America especially, no maps to tell where anybody had set out from or what ports they would sail to. No dependable genealogical trees anywhere.

He went into the sleeping hotel and up to his room and undressed and got into the cold bed. He found it difficult to sleep, thought of the pretty, coquettish girl in the bar, her jeans tight across her hips, her professionally inviting smile. What would it be like, he wondered, that perfect young body, open to invitation? Ask my nephew, he thought enviously, he's probably in bed with her now. A different generation. He had been a virgin, himself, at Wesley's age. He was ashamed of his envy, although he was sure the boy would suffer later. Was suffering now—he'd left the bar alone. Not used to the tricks. Well, neither was he. You suffered according to your capacity to suffer and there was something about the boy that made you feel his capacity was dangerously great.

He hovered between sleeping and waking, missing the body in the bed beside him. Whose body? Jean's, Helen's, Jeanne's, someone he had never met but who would finally lie beside him? He had not found any answer by the time he fell into a deep slumber.

He was awakened by the sound of drunken singing in the street. He recognized Donnelly's voice, harsh and tuneless, singing "Boola, Boola." Donnelly had gone to Yale. Not a typical graduate, Rudolph thought dreamily. The singing stopped. He turned over and went back to sleep.

* * * * * * * * * * * * * * * *

In her room, Gretchen was alone, going over the setups she wanted for the next day's shooting. When she was on the set she made herself seem calm and certain of herself, even at times she wanted to scream in anger or anguish. But when she was alone like this, working by herself, she could sometimes feel her hands shaking in fear and indecision. So many people depended on her and every decision was so final. She had seen the same division of conduct in Colin Burke when he was directing a movie or a play and had wondered how he could manage it. Now she wondered how any human being could survive a whole month at a time, or longer, being cut in half like that. Private faces in public places, in Auden's phrase, had no part in the business of making movies.

Then she heard Donnelly singing "Boola, Boola" outside the hotel. Sadly, she shook her head at the relation between talent and liquor in the arts in America. There again she thought of Colin Burke, whom she had never seen drunk and who rarely even took a drink. An exception. An exception in many ways. She thought of him often these days, while she worked, trying to imagine how he would set up the camera, what he would say to a balky actor, how he'd direct a complicated scene. If you couldn't plagiarize a dead husband, she thought defensively, whom could you plagiarize?

The singing outside stopped and she hoped that Donnelly wouldn't feel too shaken in the morning. For his sake, not for hers—she didn't need him for the next day's shooting—but he always looked so shamefaced when he came onto the set after the night before.

She smiled, thinking of the artful, dour, complicated man, who, she thought, looked like a young Confederate cavalry colonel, with his jutting beard and fierce, unsatisfied eyes. She liked him and she could tell he was attracted to her and, despite her vow never to let a younger man touch her again, if she wasn't so obsessed with the picture, she might . . .

There was a knock on her door.

"Come in," she said. She never locked her door.

The door opened and Donnelly came in, walking almost straight.

"Good evening," she said.

"I have just spent a momentous hour," he said solemnly, "with your brother. I love your brother. I thought you had to be told."

She smiled. "I love my brother, too."

"We are going to engage in grand—grandiloquent undertakings together," Donnelly said. "We are of the same tribe."

"Possibly," Gretchen said good-naturedly; "our mother possibly was Irish, or at least that was what she claimed. Our father was German, though."

"I respect both the Irish and the Germans," Donnelly said, leaning against the doorpost for support, "but that is not what I meant. I am talking of the tribe of the spirit. Do I interrupt you?"

"I'd just about finished," Gretchen said. "If you want to talk don't you think it would be a good idea to shut the door?"

Slowly, with dignity, Donnelly closed the door behind him and leaned against it.

"Would you like some coffee?" Gretchen indicated the thermos pitcher on her desk. She drank twenty cups a day to keep going.

"People are always offering me coffee," Donnelly said pettishly. "I find it degrading. I despise coffee."

"I'm afraid I have nothing harder to drink," Gretchen said, although there was a bottle of Scotch, she knew, in the cupboard.

"I have no need of the drink, madam," Donnelly said. "I come merely as a messenger."

"From whom?"

"From David P. Donnelly," Donnelly said, "himself."

Gretchen laughed.

"Deliver the message," she said, "and then I advise bed."

"I have delivered half the message," Donnelly said. "I love your brother. The other half is more difficult. I love his sister."

"You're drunk."

"Correct," he said. "Drunk I love his sister and sober I love his sister."

"Thank you for the message," Gretchen said, still seated, although she wanted to stand up and kiss the man.

"You will remember what I have said?" He glowered at her over his beard.

"I'll remember."

"In that case," he said oratorically, "I shall retire for the night. Good night, madam."

"Good night," she said. "Sleep well."

"I promise to toss and turn. Ah, me."

Gretchen chuckled. "Ah, you."

If he had stayed another ten seconds she would have sprung from her chair and embraced him. But he waved his arm grandly in salute and went out, almost straight.

She heard him singing "Boola, Boola" as he went down the hallway.

She sat staring at the door, thinking, Why not, why the hell not? She shook her head. Later, later, when the work is over. Perhaps.

She went back to marking her script in the quiet room, which now smelled from whiskey.

On the floor below, Wesley tried to sleep. He had kept listening for the soft turning of the door handle and the rustle of cloth as Frances came into the darkened room. But the door handle didn't turn, there was no sound except the complaint of the bed-springs as he turned restlessly under the covers.

He had said he loved her. True, she had more or less forced it out of him, but when he had said it he had meant it. When you loved someone, though, did you notice when she was faking, putting on an act, did you let her know that she was behaving foolishly? People talked about love as though it was all one piece, as though once you said you were in love nothing else mattered. In the movie he was doing the young politician who fell in love with Frances never criticized her for her behavior, which he adored, but only for some of the wilder schemes she concocted to sway the other characters in the script to see things her way. Love is blind, the saying went. Well, he certainly hadn't been blind that evening. He had felt that the performance Frances had put on in the bar was phony and disgusting and he had told her so. Maybe he had better learn to keep his opinions to himself. If he had, he wouldn't be in bed alone at two o'clock in the morning.

He ached for the touch of her hand, the softness of her breast as he kissed it. If that wasn't love, what was it? When she was in bed with him he couldn't believe she would go back to her husband, be attracted to another man, despite what his aunt had told him. He had enjoyed the women on the *Clothilde,* while their husbands had slept below or been off at the casino, he had liked what he did with Mrs. Wertham, but he had known, with certainty, that what he was feeling then wasn't love. You didn't have to be an experienced man of the world to know the difference between what he had felt then and what he felt with Frances.

He remembered the times when Frances was in his arms in the narrow bed, their bodies entwined in the dark, and Frances had whispered, "I love you." What had she meant those times? He groaned softly.

He had told Frances to call her mother to find out who she really was. Whom could he call to find out who *he* really was? His own mother? She would probably say that like his father he was a defiler of decent Christian homes. His uncle? To his uncle he most likely seemed like an inherited nuisance, with no sense of gratitude, who only showed up when he needed something. His Aunt Gretchen? A freak, who by some mysterious trick of nature was gifted with a talent he was too stupid or unambitious to want to use. Alice? A clumsy, unsophisticated boy who needed pity and mothering. Bunny? A good deckhand who would never be anywhere near the man his father was. Kate? Half brother to her son, a painful, living memory of her dead husband. How to put all this together and make one whole person out of the parts?

Was it only because he was so young that he felt so split up, so uncertain of himself? Retarded, Frances had said that evening. But other people around his age didn't seem to suffer, they put themselves together all right. Jimmy, the other delivery boy at the supermarket, with his music and the firm knowledge that his sisters and his mother had a single, uncomplicated opinion of him, and that opinion based on love. His own mother said she loved him but that kind of love was a whole lot worse than hate.

He thought of Healey, the wounded soldier who had come back with Kraler's son's body. Healey lived on one certainty, that he was a man who always got a raw deal from the world and that nothing would ever change for him and that the world could go fuck itself.

There was only one thing he was certain of, Wesley thought, *he* was going to change. Only he had no inkling, as he lay there alone in the dark room, in what direction. He wondered, if by some miracle he could get a glimpse of himself at the age of twenty-one, twenty-five, thirty, what he would think of himself.

Maybe, after he was finished with Frances, he would finally do what his aunt wanted him to do and become an actor. Learn to live with all the different parts of himself and make full use of them, act not only in front of a camera, but like Frances, every minute of the day. Maybe she had it figured out—that's what the world wanted and that's what she gave it.

In the morning, he knew, on the set, he would be expected to seem like a savage, irresponsible ruffian. It was an easy role for him to play. Maybe he would try it for a year or two. It was as good a starting point as anyplace else.

When he finally slept he dreamed that he was in Alice's living room eating a roast beef sandwich and drinking a beer, only it wasn't Alice across the table from him, but Frances Miller.

CHAPTER 7

1971

From Billy Abbott's notebook—

Back at the typewriter again. Bad habits die hard. Besides, everyone takes a siesta here after lunch and I've never gotten into the habit of sleeping during the day and since there's nobody else to talk to, I might as well talk to myself. Anyway, there's no reason to believe that Franco's police would be interested in the ramblings of an American tennis pro in this enclave of the rich on the edge of the blue sea. It was different in Belgium. Is it possible that privacy is easier to achieve under Fascism than under democracy? Must study the question.

After Brussels, the climate of southern Spain is the weather of heaven and it makes you wonder, how, if people had any choice in the matter, they would continue to live north of the Loire.

Drove down in the neat little secondhand open Peugeot with French transit TTX plates that I got at a good price in Paris. As soon as I crossed the Pyrenees, between the green mountains and the ocean, I felt a peculiar pleasure, as though I recognized the villages and the fields and rivers from another life, as though I were returning home from a long journey, and this was the country for me.

Until I open my mouth I can pass as a Spaniard. Is it possible that the coloring of the Abbott family is the result of a slipup at the time of the Spanish Armada? Shipwrecked, potent Andalusians on the coast of England and Scotland?

The hotel I live in is brand new and good at least a dozen years before it succumbs to wind and tide. But it's solid enough now and I have a comfortable, airy room with a view of a golf course and the sea. Aside from the lessons I have to give to beginners and dubs, there are enough good players around for two hours of fast tennis almost everyday. A simple man, myself, with simple tastes.

The Spaniards here are handsome and agreeable and schooled in courtesy, a change after the American Army. The others are on holiday and on their best behavior. Up to now I have not been insulted or challenged to a duel, forced to see a bullfight or requested to help bring down the system.

Careful to be most correct with the ladies, accent or no. They're likely to have husbands or escorts in the background who have a tendency to be suspicious of a young American professional athlete who spends at least an hour a day, scantily dressed, with their partners. They suddenly appear on the sidelines during lessons, brooding darkly. I have no desire to be ridden out of town in disgrace, charged with dishonoring some Spanish gentleman's wife or mistress. For a year at least it is my intention to stay out of trouble.

After Monika the joys of celibacy are to be recommended. Turmoil, in and out of bed, is not my specialty.

I'm brown from the sun and in better shape than ever before and have taken to admiring myself naked in a mirror.

The pay is good, the tips generous. I find myself actually saving quite a bit of money, something new and strange in my life.

The parties are numerous here and I'm invited to most of them. New boy in town, I suppose. I make sure not to drink too much or speak to any one lady for more than fifteen minutes at a time. By now I know enough Spanish to understand most of the fierce political arguments that erupt here late at night. The participants are likely to bring up such subjects as the menace of bloodshed, expropriation, Communism, and what will happen to the country when the old man dies. I keep silent at such times, thanking my stars that I have settled, even if only for a short period, in a beautiful country which suits my temperament so well, without having to express any opinion more inflammatory than how to grip the handle of a racket when serving.

Once more I have to doubt my father's warning that I come from an unlucky family.

My mother has written me several letters. As usual, she got my address from my father, whom I write on the vain presumption that my letters are the only thing that keeps him from jumping into Lake Michigan. My mother's letters have mellowed in tone. She takes it that my decision not to re-enlist has something to do with her protests and represents a new and welcome maturity in me. She now finishes her letters with "Love, Mother." For years it was just "Mother," a trick of signing off that I understood, I think correctly, as a sign of her complete disgust with me. I have returned the compliment and signed my one letter to her, "Love, Billy."

She tells me that she is enjoying her new career as a director, which comes as no surprise to me, considering her penchant for bossing people around. She writes with great enthusiasm of the ability of my Cousin Wesley as an actor. It's a trade I should have considered, since I can be as false or sincere as any man, but it's too late now. Wesley wants to visit me, my mother writes. How should I greet him? Welcome, Brother Sufferer.

Holy God! Two days after I wrote the above, Monika appeared, accompanied by a middle-aged German tycoon who sells frozen foods. She is in a prosperous period, all decked out in sleek, expensive-looking clothes, with her hair combed. So far she has pretended not to know me, but it may be the lull before the storm. Thoughts of flight haunt me.

I lost in straight sets to a man I have beaten on six consecutive days.

FREDDIE KAHN, THE cameraman, led the singing of "For she's a jolly good fellow," holding Gretchen's hand aloft like a winning prizefighter's, at the traditional party on the set in the studio in New York at the finish of the last day's shooting. The singing of the cast, the technical men, and the grips and the friends invited was loud and hearty. Gretchen was somewhere between tears and laughter as the singing rang out on the set strewn with cables, the cameras hooded, the liquor and sandwiches on improvised, flower-decorated tables set on trestles. Ida Cohen was frankly crying and had her hair done for the occasion. Kahn presented a wristwatch to Gretchen as a gift from the cast, to which Wesley had contributed fifty dollars, and called on Gretchen to make a speech.

"Thank you, thank you everybody," Gretchen said, her voice trembling a little. "You've all been wonderful and I want to congratulate one and all for making my first stab at being a director such a happy one. Although, as the saying goes in Hollywood, Show me a happy company and I'll show you a stinker of a movie."

There was a wave of laughter and a few shouts of, "No, not this time."

Gretchen raised her hand for silence. "For all of you, the job is over and I hope you go on to bigger and better things and that your flops will be forgotten and your hits remembered forever—or at least until the next Academy Award night. But for some of us, the cutters, the people who do the dubbing, the composer and musicians, and for Mr. Cohen, who will have the unenviable job of selling the picture for distribution without all of us being stolen blind, the job is just really beginning. Wish us well, because there're months of work ahead of us, and what we do from now on can mean the difference between success and failure."

She spoke modestly, but Wesley, who was standing near her, could see the light of triumph in her eyes. "Ida," she said, "do stop crying. This isn't a funeral—yet."

Ida sobbed.

Somebody put a glass of whiskey into Gretchen's hand and she raised it in a toast. "To us all—from the oldest here—" She turned to Wesley. "And to the youngest."

Wesley, who had a glass of whiskey in his hand, which he had not yet touched, raised his glass with the others. He was not smiling or looking exuberant, like most of the company, because he had just seen Frances Miller, who was standing to one side with her husband, clink glasses with him and exchange a kiss. Wesley and Frances had made up after the night in the bar in Port Philip and she had again come to his room in the hotel and had let him stay with her for the night several times in her apartment in New York when they resumed shooting interiors there. That was until three days ago, when her husband had arrived from California. Wesley had not yet met her husband, a handsome blond man built like a football player, who, Wesley had to admit to himself, looked nice enough, in a standard Hollywood way. But the familiar manner in which Frances and her husband looked at each other as they raised their glasses, and the tenderness of their kiss, made him wish there had been some way of avoiding the party.

Alice was there, too, although for the moment he could not see her in the shadows of the set. As always, she made herself as unobtrusive as possible. She had behaved peculiarly after the nights he had not come to the apartment to sleep on the sofa, aloof and efficiently nurselike. When he had told her about the party, she had said she'd love to come, she had never been to a party on a movie set before. He had tried to seem gracious about inviting her, but it had been an effort. When you get older, he thought, trying not to look in the direction of Frances and her husband, maybe you can learn how to handle things like this.

He took a big gulp of his whiskey and soda, remembering that the last time he had drunk hard liquor was the night in the Porte Rose in Cannes. The whiskey tasted fine and he took another gulp.

Gretchen walked around the set, shaking hands or kissing people on the cheek and some of the other women were teary-eyed, too. Everybody seemed reluctant to leave, as though they wished to prolong as much as possible the ties they had formed with each other in their common labor over the months. Wesley overheard a middle-aged character woman say to Gretchen, "Bless you, dear; from here on, it's got to get worse."

Wesley wondered how the simple act of just making a movie, which must have become a routine experience to all these professional people, could arouse so much emotion. He himself had enjoyed making the movie, but aside from Frances and Gretchen, he wouldn't care if he never saw any one of them again. Maybe, no matter what Gretchen told him, deep down he was not really cut out to be an actor.

When Gretchen came up to him and kissed him on the cheek and said, "Wesley Jordan, I'm going to miss you," he could see that she meant it.

"That was a nice little speech," he said. "You sure know how to decorate an occasion."

"Thank you, honey," she said. But she kept looking over her shoulder as though she was searching for someone. "Wesley," she said, "did Rudolph say anything to you about not coming here or being late?"

"No." All his Uncle Rudolph had said to him in the last few days of shooting was that the lawyer in Antibes had written that it was okay to come back to France. He had not yet bought his ticket. Without admitting it to himself, he had the feeling that he was not ready to leave America just yet, that there were too many things left unsettled.

"He had to go up to Connecticut again today with Mr. Donnelly," Gretchen said, still searching over the heads of the people who surrounded them, "but he promised to be back by five o'clock. It's past seven now. It's not like Rudolph to be late. I can't leave the party just yet, so will you be a dear and telephone his hotel to see if he left a message?"

"Of course," Wesley said and searched for coins as he went off the stage to the telephone outside to call the Hotel Algonquin, where his uncle kept a room for the nights he had to stay over in the city.

He had to wait to make the call because Frances was there, talking and giggling. He moved away because he didn't want to overhear what she was saying. She took a long time over her conversation and kept feeding dimes into the machine. He had carried his glass with him and by the time she had finished, he had drained it. He could feel his muscles tense as he waited, listening to the tone of the voice without hearing the words, and he was uncomfortably conscious of a spasmodic tingle in the nerves around his groin and in his balls. Never again, never again, he told himself, although he knew he was lying.

With a last soft giggle, Frances hung up and came toward the door to the stage, outside which he was standing. Her hair was hanging long over her shoulders and she swung it back with a womanly gesture of her hand. "Ah," she said, and she giggled again, "the boy wonder, lying in wait."

"I have a call to make," he said, "but first I want to do something." Suddenly, he grabbed her and kissed her on the mouth.

"Well, now," she said, giggling, "you've finally taken acting lessons. How to be passionate in the presence of husbands." Her voice was a little thick from drink.

"When am I going to see you again?" Wesley gripped her arms, as though by the strength in his hands he could keep her from slipping away.

"Who knows?" Frances said. She giggled. "Maybe never. Maybe when you grow up."

"You don't mean that," he said, his voice tortured.

"Who knows what I mean," she said. "Least of all me. I have some good advice for you. We had our fun and it's over. Now forget it."

The door from the stage swung open and Frances' husband bulked against the light from the set.

"Let go of her," the man said.

Wesley dropped his hands and stepped back a little.

"I know what you two have been up to all this time," the man said, "don't think I don't. Slut."

"Oh, cool it, Jack, please," Frances said carefully.

The man slapped her face. The sound was flat and ugly. "As for you, you little bastard," he said to Wesley, "if I ever catch you hanging around my wife again I'll break you in half."

"Oh, the great big he-man," Frances said mockingly. She hadn't put her hand to her face, it was as though her husband hadn't touched her. "Everywhere but in bed."

The man took a deep breath that was more of a gasp, like a rush of air from a suddenly opened door. Then he slapped Frances again, much harder this time.

Still, Frances didn't put her hand to her face. "Pig," she said to her husband. "You and your spies."

The man grabbed her arm. "Now you're marching back in there," he said, "and you're smiling because your husband, who was detained on business on the Coast, has managed to come to New York to spend the weekend with you."

"Whatever you say, pig," Frances said. She took his arm and without looking at Wesley went through the door with her husband onto the set, where there was the sound of music now, a piano and a trumpet and a set of drums, and couples dancing.

Wesley stood immobile in the dimly lit hall, only the muscles in his face working. Then he crushed the empty plastic cup in his hand and threw it against the wall. He took two minutes, until he was sure he wouldn't rush through the door, past the dancing couples, and throw himself at the man's throat.

When he felt he could trust his voice, he called the hotel, where the operator told him that Mr. Jordache had left no messages. He stood beside the phone on the wall for another moment, then went onto the set and found his aunt and repeated what the operator had said. After that he went to the bar and ordered a whiskey, which he drank straight off, then ordered another.

While he was finishing the drink, he felt a tap on his arm. He turned to see Alice standing there, that aloof, nurselike look on her face that he had begun to fear. "I think maybe it would be a good idea," Alice said calmly, "if you repaired your face. You've got lipstick all over it."

"Thank you," he said woodenly, taking out his handkerchief and dabbing at his lips and cheeks. "That better?"

"Much better," she said. "Now I think I'll be going. I've found out movie parties aren't as dazzling as people would lead a girl to believe."

"Good night," Wesley said. He wanted to ask her forgiveness, change that distant, cold expression in her eyes, but he didn't know how to say it or just what she could forgive him for. "I'll see you later."

"Perhaps," she said.

Christ, he thought, as he watched the small girl with the straight, honest walk disappear among the dancers, Christ, am I a mess, I've got to get out of this town. Then he turned back to the bar and asked for another drink. He was taking it from the bartender when Rudolph came up to him. "Having a good time, Mr. Jordan?" Rudolph said.

"Marvelous," Wesley said. "Gretchen is looking for you. She's worried. I called your hotel for her."

"I was delayed," Rudolph said. "I'll go find her. I'd like to talk to you later. Where'll you be?"

"Right here," Wesley said.

Rudolph frowned. "Take it easy, lad," he said. "I'm sure you'll be able to find another bottle of whiskey somewhere in New York tomorrow if you look hard enough." He gave Wesley's arm a friendly small pat, then went looking for Gretchen.

Gretchen was talking to Richard Sanford, the author of *Restoration Comedy,* when Rudolph saw her on the other side of the space where people were dancing. Sanford had made no concessions in his dress, Rudolph saw, for the celebration of the finishing day of shooting for his first opus. He was wearing his usual uniform of open-necked wool shirt and windbreaker.

"What I'm worried about," Sanford was saying earnestly, "is that there aren't enough close-ups of the girl in what I've seen so far. Somehow, I don't get enough emotion in the medium shots and in the . . ."

"Dear Richard," Gretchen said, "I'm afraid that like so many other authors, you are smitten with an actress's charms to the detriment of her talent . . ."

"Oh, come on now," Sanford said, flushing, "I've barely spoken to the girl."

"She's spoken to you," Gretchen said. "That's more than enough with a young lady like that. I regret for your sake that she was otherwise occupied."

"You underestimate me," Sanford said angrily.

"That's been the problem of artists for five thousand years," Gretchen said. "You'll learn to live with it, sonny."

"We're not friends, you and I," Sanford said. "You resent my—my maleness. I've known that from the beginning."

"That's beside the point," Gretchen said. "Aside from being pure bullshit. And if you haven't known it before, let me tell it to you now, young man—art is not created out of friendship."

"You're a bitter, aging woman." Months of resentment grated in his voice. "What you need is a good fuck. Which nobody is polite enough to give you."

Gretchen rubbed her eyes before replying. "You're a talented, unpleasant young man. You will be less unpleasant, and I'm afraid, less talented as you grow older."

"You don't have to insult me, Gretchen," he said.

"In our profession," Gretchen said, "insults are beside the point. You weary me. And I suppose I weary you, too. Also beside the point. But, my dear Richard"— she touched his cheek lightly, half a caress, half a threat of manicured long nails— "I promise to serve you well. Don't ask for more. I promise you all the close-ups you can use and all the emotion anybody can stand. The problem with that girl is not too little, it's too much."

"You've always got an answer to everything," Sanford said. "I never win an argument with you. Kinsella warned me . . ."

"How is dear Evans?" Gretchen asked.

"He's okay." Sanford shifted his feet uneasily. "He's asked me to do his next picture."

"And you're on your way to Hollywood."

"Actually . . . yes."

"Goody for you," Gretchen said. "And goody for him. I know you'll be happy together. And now, if you'll excuse me, I see my brother waiting to talk to me."

As Gretchen walked toward Rudolph, he saw Sanford shake his head despairingly. Rudolph was chuckling as Gretchen came up to him.

"What're you laughing about?" she asked.

"The expression on that young man's face when you left him," he said.

Gretchen grimaced. "We were engaging in that most creative of occupations— wounding each other. One picture and he thinks he's the editor of *Cahiers du Cinéma.* A lost soul. No great tragedy. America is full of one-shot talents. I was worried about you. Where've you been all this time?"

Rudolph shook his head. "We've run into a holy mess in Connecticut. Donnelly's ready to slit his throat. The whole project looks as though it's going to come apart."

"Why?" Gretchen asked. "What's happened?"

"Some damned society for the preservation of the environment or something like that is suing us for an injunction to stop us from building," Rudolph said. "We spent the whole day with lawyers."

"I thought it was all set," Gretchen said.

"So did I," said Rudolph. "Until yesterday. We thought we had bought a tract of abandoned farmland. Now it turns out we have bought a precious piece of Connecticut wilderness, full of rare birds, herds of darling deer, lovely snakes. Three lynx have also been sighted there in recent years. Instead of being semiphilanthropic benefactors of aging humanity, it seems we are grasping city slickers out to pollute the pure air of the sovereign state of Connecticut, besides being the enemy of the lynx." He shook his head again, half-humorously.

"What do the lawyers say?"

"It will take years, even if we finally win. Donnelly almost wept with remorse when he realized how long our money was going to be tied up."

"Where is he?" Gretchen asked. "Donnelly?"

"I put him to bed. Dead drunk. He'll feel even worse tomorrow."

"I'm so sorry," Gretchen said.

"The roll of the dice," said Rudolpoh. "Don't let it spoil your big night. Another thing, I got a call from California yesterday. From a man I know, an agent called Bowen."

"I know him, too," Gretchen said. "He's got a good office."

Rudolph nodded. "He says the word has gotten around about Wesley. He says he can get him a fat contract. If Wesley's going to continue as an actor he'll need an agent and Bowen's as honest as any of them. I have to talk to the young man."

"He was holding up the bar the last I saw of him," Gretchen said, "smeared with lipstick."

"I saw him. I'll give him some sage, avuncular advice." Rudolph leaned over and kissed Gretchen on the cheek. "Congratulations for everything. You've done a wonderful job. And it isn't only your brother who thinks so."

"Things went smoothly. I was afraid it was going to be amateur night from beginning to end."

"Don't be so modest, Sister," Rudolph said and squeezed her hand. "You're in the major leagues now."

"We'll see. Let's keep our fingers crossed," Gretchen said, but she couldn't keep back a pleased smile.

"Now for the young man," Rudolph said. "Save me a dance for when I've finished with him."

"I haven't danced in years."

"Neither have I," Rudolph said. "I'll ask the boys to play a waltz."

Then he went back to the bar, but Wesley was no longer there. The bartender said that he had left five minutes ago.

Alice was sitting reading in the living room when Wesley got to the apartment. He had stopped at two bars on the way home. The bars had been too dark for anyone to ask him for proof of his age. Walking on the city streets had proved something of a problem, as the sidewalks seemed to be sliding away from him at different angles and he had stumbled twice at the curbs at corners.

"Good evening," he said gravely to Alice.

"Good evening," she said. She did not look up from her book. He noticed that the sofa was not made up as usual with sheets and blankets. He had the curious feeling that it was not Alice he was seeing, but a reflection of her in rippling water.

He misjudged the distance when he tried to sit down and just barely made the edge of the chair. He stared intently at Alice, who was still rippling.

"I'm no good," he said. "You're wasting your time worrying about me."

"You're drunk," she said. "And I'm not worrying about you."

"Tomorrow," he said, his voice sounding strange and faraway in his ears, "I will pay you every cent I owe you and I will de—de—depart."

"None too soon," Alice said, still looking down at her book. "I'm sure you'll be able to find another place to sleep. And don't talk about money to me. You don't owe me a cent. What I've done for you I didn't do for money."

He looked at her, focusing with difficulty. "Do you mind if I say thanks?" he said.

"I mind everything you say," she said fiercely. "Hollywood bum."

"I've never been to Hollywood. Not even to California," he said foolishly.

"You and your tarts." She threw the book to the floor. "What am I reading this damned book for? It's a terrible book."

"I thought you were my . . . well . . . " He spoke confusedly. "Well—my sister."

"I'm not your sister."

He groped for what he wanted to say, feeling his brain and tongue misted over. "You say I die," he said. "In your book. You want me to be noble and die. You're asking for too much . . ."

"Oh, my God," she said. She rose from her chair and came over to him and took his head into her hands and pressed him to her body. "I'm so sorry. I don't want you to die, Wesley. You've got to believe that."

"Everybody wants something from me I can't give," Wesley said, his mouth muffled against the stuff of her dress. "I don't know where I am. Tomorrow ask for me in the Lost and Found Department."

"Please, Wesley," she whispered, "don't say things like that."

"You said once you were stealing a piece of my soul . . ." He moaned as he spoke. "I hear you typing at night and I say to myself, There goes another bit of my soul."

"Please, please, Sweet . . ." She held his head tighter to her as though to keep him from saying another word. "You're killing me."

"Everybody shames me." He pulled his head sidewise, so he could speak. "What I went through tonight . . . Now you . . . I haven't lived up to you, I know that, but . . ."

"Sssh, sssh, baby," she crooned.

"I love you," he said.

She pulled him, hard, against herself. Then, amazingly, she laughed. "Why the hell did it take you so long to say that?" She dropped to her knees and kissed him, briefly. Then she moved her head back so that she could look at him. "Say it again," she said.

"I love you," he said.

"You look awful," she said.

"I *feel* awful. This is the second time in my life I've been drunk. Excuse me, please, I have to puke." He stood up, unsteadily, and reeled into the bathroom and there all the whiskey of the night came up. He felt no healthier, still weak and wobbly. He undressed carefully, brushed his teeth for two whole minutes, then took a cold shower. He felt a little better as he dried himself, although when he turned his head he had to do it with great care and his stomach felt as though he had swallowed nails. He put on a robe that Alice had picked out for him and went back, his hair wet, steadying himself with his hand against the wall, into the living room.

The living room was empty and the sofa was still not made up for sleeping.

From the bedroom, he heard Alice's voice. "I'm in here. You don't have to find any other place to sleep tonight."

Still weak and with his head feeling as though a carousel were going around in it, with the calliope playing, he stumbled into the bedroom. There was only one small lamp on and the bedroom was dim, but he saw Alice, still rippling, under the covers of the big bed.

"Come here," she said. "Get in."

He started to climb into the bed with his robe still on.

"Take that damned thing off," she said.

"Turn out the light." The idea of Alice Larkin, that shy and most ladylike girl, seeing him naked was shocking to him.

She chuckled as she turned the lamp off. He stumbled as he dropped the robe on the floor as he felt his way to the bed. She was small and her skin soft and fragrant as he put his arms around her, but he still felt terrible.

"I can't do anything," he whispered. "I love you and I can't do anything. You should have told me earlier tonight, before I drank all that booze."

"I didn't know earlier," she said. "No matter." She kissed his ear as she pulled closer to him. "You'll be all right in the morning."

And he was.

CHAPTER 8

1971

From Billy Abbott's notebook—

She is still here.

She hasn't made a sign that she knows me. She and her frozen-food manufacturer from Dusseldorf, speak, as far as I can tell, to no one. I never see them with anyone else. He plays golf every day. They are not at any of the parties to which I am invited. I have found out that she is registered at the hotel as Senorita Monika Hitzman, which was not her name when I knew her before. When we pass each other by accident, whether she is alone or with her friend, we pass as strangers, although I feel a glacial current of air, very much like the chill you might feel sailing past an iceberg.

Occasionally, sometimes alone, sometimes with her friend, she passes by the tennis courts. More often than not she stops for a moment or two to watch the sport, as do many other of the guests.

My game is deteriorating daily.

There is another complication. I am being wooed, if that is the word, by a young Spanish girl, by name Carmen (is there no escaping that melodic echo?) from Barcelona, who plays a fierce, tireless game of tennis, and whose father, I have learned, was in a high position in the Franco government in Barcelona. He is sometimes with her and sometimes not, an erect, gray-haired gentleman, with an unforgiving face.

His daugher is twenty years old, with dangerous dark eyes, blond hair and a tigerish manner of moving, off the court and on, as though she feels it incumbent upon her to live up to the libretto of the opera. She extends me in singles. She also finds opportunities to offer me a drink when we have finished playing or at other moments, and entrusts me with confidences that I do not wish to hear. She has been to school in England and speaks the language well, although with a strong accent. With her I retreat into my stupid athlete role, although she says she sees through me, which I'm afraid she does. Among the things she has told me is that her father, although Catalan, fought in Franco's armies, and has the outlook on life of the captains of Ferdinand and Isabella who drove the Moors and the Jews from Spain. She infuriates her father by speaking Catalan to him and she loves him profoundly. She will not be happy, she says, until the Catalonian flag flies over Barcelona and the poets of what she calls her country write in that language. She and Monika, who also sets store on the linguistic division of Europe, would have a great deal to say to each other, although I doubt that Carmen has as yet thrown her first bomb. She distributes pamphlets that may or may not be against the law. She has a marvelous, lithe body and I do not know how long I can continue to resist her, although I fear her father, who when he looks at me, which is seldom, does so with the coldest suspicion.

Carmen tells me he looks at all foreigners, especially Americans, with the same suspicion, but I cannot help but feel that there is a repugnance there that is not purely chauvinistic.

She looks like the kind of young woman you see standing at the barrera *in Spanish newspaper photographs as matadors dedicate bulls to them. She does not look like the sort of girl one meets in America who distributes pamphlets.*

She is like Monika in at least one respect. She will never make any man a good wife.

THE NEXT DAY was a bad one for Billy Abbott. Monika came down to the courts with her friend and signed up for a week of instruction, every day at 11:00 A.M.

Billy gave her her first lesson. She was hopeless. He couldn't say anything to her, as her friend sat watching during the entire forty-five minutes. She addressed Billy as Mr. Abbott and he addressed her as Señorita Hitzman. As he tossed balls at her, which more often than not she missed, he thought, I must get her aside somehow and ask her just what she is up to; it can't be coincidence that brought her to El Faro.

In the afternoon he was very nearly beaten by Carmen. She was in a cranky mood and played ferociously.

Later, in the bar of the hotel, where they were alone, he asked her what was the matter.

"Did you read the paper this morning?"

"No."

"On the front page there was a picture of one of your admirals being decorated by Franco."

He shrugged. "That's what admirals are for," he said. "Actually, I don't mind his getting a medal. What I mind is his being here, him and his ships and our air force with its planes. I was in the army a long time and I'm skeptical about how useful we would be if it came to the crunch."

Carmen glared at him. "What would you like to see happen—the Russians overrun Europe?"

"If they had wanted to overrun Europe," he said, "they'd have done it by now. We're in Europe in just enough numbers to annoy the Russians and not in enough to do much about them. If it came to a war, the missiles would do the fighting, not the men on the ground. They'd just be sacrificed on the first day. I was a man on the ground and I wasn't too happy about it."

"I certainly am glad," Carmen said sacastically, "that I have my own private American military expert to explain the facts of life to me."

"It's all for show," Billy said. He didn't know why he was arguing with her. Probably because the last set had gone to eight-six. Maybe because he was tired of being lectured on politics by attractive young women. "A base here and there just gives the military boys a chance to flex their muscles and squeeze more money out of Congress so that they can ride around in big cars and live five times better here than they ever could at home." Then, more to tease her than because he meant what he was saying, he said, "If we took every American soldier out of uniform and sent him home to do some useful work it would be better for everyone concerned—including the Spaniards."

"The weak and lazy always find excuses for their weakness and laziness," Carmen said. "Thank God, all Americans aren't like you." Her politics were complicated. She hated Franco and hated the Communists and now, it seemed, she hated him, as well as the American admiral. "Being here is moral," she said. "Letting a man like Franco pin a medal on your chest if you're an American is immoral. It's one thing to be ready to defend a country in your own interest, after all; it's another to help prop up the reputation of a disgusting regime. If I were an American I'd write to Congress, to the State Department, to the president, to the newspapers, protesting. There—you want to do something useful—at least write a letter to the *Herald Tribune*.

"How long do you think I'd last here if that letter was ever published?"

"Twenty-four hours," Carmen said. "It would be worth it."

"A boy has to eat, too."

"Money," Carmen said disdainfully. "Everything is a question of money for people like you."

"May I remind you," Billy said, "that I don't have a rich father, like some folks I know."

"That's a disgraceful thing to say. At least that's one thing you can say about Spaniards—they don't measure out their lives in dollars and cents."

"I see some pretty rich Spaniards around here," Billy said, "who spend their time making more and more money. Buying up olive groves down here, for example, and turning them into tourist traps. All those big yachts in the harbor aren't owned by people who've taken the vow of poverty."

"Scum," Carmen said. "A fraction of the population. Without soul. Doing what ever Franco and his criminals tell them to do just so they can hold on to their *fincas,* their yachts, their mistresses, while the rest of the country starves. I hate Communism but when I see what the ordinary man or woman has to do to feed a family here, I can understand why they're attracted to it. Out of despair."

"What do you want to see—another civil war?" Billy said. "Another million dead? Blood running in the streets?"

"If it comes to that," Carmen said, "it will be your friends, the yacht owners, who will bring it about. Of course I don't want to see it. What I want to see is decent, orderly change. If you can do it in America, why can't it be done here?"

"I'm not a student of the Spanish character," Billy said, "but somewhere I've heard that your fellow citizens, when aroused, are likely to be bloodthirsty and cruel and violent."

"Oh, I'm so tired of talk like that," Carmen cried. "As though Spain was all bullfights and flagellants and people taking revenge for the honor of their families. How is it that nobody says how cruel and violent the Germans are as a race—after what they did to Europe? Or the French, after Napoleon? And I won't say anything about what the Americans have done in their time, you poor, useless tennis player." They were sitting at the hotel bar during this conversation and Carmen contemptuously signed the chit for their drinks. "There. You've saved the price of four gin and tonics. Aren't you glad you came to cruel and violent Spain and became the lackey of the rich here?"

"Maybe," Billy said, stung, "we ought not to see each other anymore. Find somebody else to play tennis with."

"You will play tennis with me," Carmen said, "because you are paid to play tennis with me. Same time tomorrow." She strode out of the bar, leaving him sitting alone in the big, empty room. God, he thought, and I believed she was wooing me! First Monika with her bombs and now this.

The next morning Monika came to the courts alone. Billy had to admit that she *looked* like a tennis player, small and trim, with good legs, and dressed in a becoming short tennis dress, with a band around her head to keep her neatly set hair in place.

As they walked out onto the court together, Billy said in a low voice, "Monika, what sort of game are you up to?"

"My name is *Señorita* Hitzman," she said coldly, "Mr. Abbott."

"If you want the money I took to Paris—and the other—the other part of the package," Billy said, "I can get it for you. It would take some time, but I could do it . . ."

"I don't know what you're talking about, Mr. Abbott."

"Oh, come on, now," he said, irritated. "Mr. Abbott. You didn't call me Mr. Abbott when we were fucking all afternoon in Brussels."

"If you go on like this, Mr. Abbott," she said, "I'll have to report you to the management for wasting valuable time in conversation instead of doing what you're supposed to do—which is to teach me how to play tennis."

"You'll never learn to play tennis."

"In that case," she said calmly, "that will be another failure for you to remember when you grow old. Now, if you please, I would like to start the lesson."

He sighed, then went to the other side of the court and started lobbing balls onto her racket. She was no better at returning them than she had been the morning before.

When the lesson was over, she said, "Thank you, Mr. Abbott," and walked off the court.

That afternoon he beat Carmen six-love, six-three, maliciously mixing his game with lobs and dropshots to make her run until she was red in the face. She too walked off the court with one curt phrase: "You played like a eunuch." She did not invite him to have a drink with her.

Spain, he thought, as he watched her stride toward the hotel, her blond hair flying, is becoming much less agreeable than it used to be.

Wesley took the train from London to Bath, enjoying looking out the window at the neat green countryside of rural England. After the tensions and uncertainties of America, it had been soothing to walk around London, where he knew no one and no one expected anything of him. He had been having lunch standing up at the bar of a pub when the voice of the barmaid had reminded him of the way Kate spoke. Suddenly he realized how much he had missed her. He finished his sandwich and went to the railroad station and took the first train to Bath. She would be surprised to see him. Pleasantly surprised, he hoped.

When he got to Bath, he gave the address to a taxi driver and sat back and stared curiously at the neat streets and graceful buildings of the town, thinking, This sure has Indianapolis beat.

The taxi stopped in front of a narrow small house, painted white, one of a whole row of similar small houses. He paid the taxi driver and rang the doorbell. A moment later the door opened and a short woman with gray hair, wearing an apron, said, "Good afternoon."

"Good afternoon, ma'am," Wesley said. "Is Kate home?"

"Who are you, please?"

"Wesley Jordache, ma'am."

"Well, Good Lord." The woman smiled widely. She put out her hand and he shook it. It was a callused workingwoman's hand. "I've heard all about you. Come in, come in, boy. I'm Kate's mother."

"How do you do, Mrs. Bailey," Wesley said.

The door opened directly on the small living room. On the floor a baby crawled around in a playpen, cooing to itself. "That's your brother, Wesley," Mrs. Bailey said. "Leastwise, your half brother. Tom's his name."

"I know," Wesley said. He eyed the baby with interest. "He seems like a nice, healthy kid, doesn't he?"

"He's a love," Mrs. Bailey said. "Happy all the day long. Can I fix you a cup of tea?"

"No, thank you. I'd like to see Kate if she's home."

"She's at work," Mrs. Bailey said. "You can find her there. It's the King's Arms Pub. It's just a few blocks away. Lord, she'll be glad to see you. Will you be staying for supper?"

"I'll see how things work out with Kate. Hey, Tommy," he said, going over to the playpen, "how're you doing?"

The baby smiled up at him and made a gurgling sound. Wesley leaned over and put his hand out to the baby, one finger outstretched. The baby sat up, then grabbed the finger and stood up, wobbling, as Wesley gently raised his hand. The baby laughed triumphantly. Wesley was surprised at how strong the little hand felt around his finger. "Tommy," he said, "you've got one powerful grip."

The baby laughed again, then let go and flopped back on his behind. Wesley looked down at him, a peculiar emotion, one he had never felt before, seizing him, tender and at the same time obscurely anxious. The baby was happy now. Maybe he himself had been happy at that age, too. He wondered how long it would last for his brother. With Kate as his mother, maybe forever.

"Now," he said to Mrs. Bailey, "if you'll tell me how to find the pub . . . "

"Left as you go out of the house," Mrs. Bailey said, "for three blocks and you'll see it on the corner." She opened the front door for him. She stood next to him, barely coming up to his shoulder, her face sweet and plain. "I must tell you, Wesley," she said soberly, "the time my daugher was with your father was the loveliest. She'll never forget it. And now would it be too much to ask if I said I'd like one big hug?"

Wesley put his arms around her and hugged her and kissed the top of her head. When she stepped back, he saw her eyes were wet, although she was smiling. "You mustn't be a stranger," she said.

"I'll be back," Wesley said. "Somebody'll have to teach him how to play baseball instead of cricket and it might as well be me."

Mrs. Bailey laughed. "You're a good boy," she said. "You're just as Kate said you were."

She stood at the open door watching him as he turned down the sunny street.

The King's Arms was a small pub, paneled in dark wood, with small casks for sherry and port high up behind the bar. It was almost three o'clock, closing time, and there was only one old man seated at a small round table dozing over a pint of bitter. Kate was rinsing glasses and a man in an apron was putting bottles of beer onto shelves as Wesley came in.

He stood at the bar, not saying anything, waiting for Kate to look up from her work. When she did, she said, "What would you like, sir?"

Wesley grinned at her.

"Wesley!" she cried. "How long have you been standing there?"

"Fifteen minutes," he said. "Dying of thirst."

"Would you really like a beer?"

"No. I just want to look at you."

"I'm a mess," she said.

"No, you're not." She looked very much as he had remembered her, not as brown perhaps, and a little fuller in the face and bosom. "You look beautiful."

She looked at him solemnly. "It's not true," she said, "but it's nice to hear."

The clock over the bar struck three and she called, "Time, gentlemen, please." The old man at the table shook himself awake, drained his glass, stood up and went out.

Kate came out from behind the bar and stopped a few feet from Wesley to examine him. "You've become a man," she said.

"Not exactly," Wesley said.

Then she kissed him and held him for a moment. "I'm so glad to see you again. How did you know where to find me?"

"I went to your house. Your mother told me."

"Did you see the baby?"

"Yes," he said. "Stupendous."

"He's not stupendous, but he'll do." Wesley could see she was pleased. "Let me throw on a coat and we'll go for a nice long walk and you'll tell me everything that's happened to you."

As they went out the door she called to the man behind the bar, "See you at six, Ally."

The man grunted.

"This is a pretty town," Wesley said, as they strolled in the mild sunshine, her hand lightly on his arm. "It looks like a nice place to live."

"Bath." She shrugged. "It's seen better days. The quality used to come here for the season and take the waters and marry off their daughters and gamble. Now it's mostly tourists. It's a little like living in a museum. I don't know where the quality goes these days. Or if there's any quality left."

"Do you miss the Mediterranean?"

She dropped her hand from his arm and stared reflectively ahead of her as she walked. "Some things about the Med, yes. . . . " she said. "Other things not at all. Let's not talk about it, please. Now, tell me what you've been up to."

By the time he had told her about what he'd been doing in America, they had walked over a good part of the small city. She shook her head sadly when he told her about Indianapolis and became pensive when he told her about the people he had talked to about his father and stared at him with a kind of respectful awe when he described his part in Gretchen's movie.

"An actor," she said. "Who would have ever thought? You going to keep it up?"

"Maybe later on," he said. "I have some things I have to attend to in Europe."

"What parts of Europe?" She stared at him suspiciously. "Cannes, for instance?"

"If you must know," he said, "yes. Cannes."

She nodded. "Bunny was afraid that finally you'd come to that."

"Finally," Wesley said.

"I'd like to take revenge on the whole fucking world," she said. "But I serve drinks in a bar. Revenge has to stop somewhere, Wesley."

"Revenge has to *start* somewhere, too," he said.

"And if you get yourself killed, who'll revenge *you?*" Her voice was bitter and harsh.

"Somebody else will have to figure that out."

"I'm not going to argue with you. You're too much like your father. I never could argue him out of anything. If nothing will stop you, I wish you well. Do it smart, at least. And supposing you do it and suppose you get away with it, which is a lot of supposing, what'll you do then?"

"I've been thinking about that, too," Wesley said. "With the money I get from the inheritance and the money I may be able to make in the movies, in a couple of years I might have enough to buy a boat, something like the *Clothilde,* anyway, and charter. . . . "

Kate shook her head impatiently. "You can be your father's son," she said, "but you can't *be* your father. Lead your own life, Wesley."

"It'll be my own life," he said. "I even thought that with the money you're getting from the estate, maybe you'd like to come in with me as a partner and crew the ship with me. By the time we can buy a ship, the kid, Tommy . . . " He stumbled over the name. "He'd be old enough to be safe on board and . . . "

"Dreams," she said. "Old dreams."

They walked in silence for half a block.

"I have to tell you something, Wesley," she said. "My money's gone. I don't have it anymore."

"Gone?" he said incredulously. "The way you live . . . "

"I know the way I live," she said bitterly. "I live like a fool. There's a man who says he wants to marry me. He's in business for himself, he owns a small trucking business in Bath. He said he needed what I had to keep from going into bankruptcy."

"And you gave him the dough?"

She nodded. "I thought I was in love with him. You've got to understand something about me. I'm not a woman that can live without a man. I see him just about every afternoon when the pub closes. I was supposed to go to his place this afternoon and he'll be mortal mad when he comes around this evening and I tell him I spent the afternoon with Tom's son. He won't even *look* at the baby when he comes home to take me out."

"And you want to marry a man like that?"

"He wasn't like that until after he lost the money," she said. "He was plain wonderful until then. With me, the baby, my mother . . ." She sighed. "You're young, you think things are black and white. . . . Well, I've got news for you. For a woman my age, my family, working at lousy jobs all my life, not pretty, nothing is easy." She looked at her watch. "It's nearly five o'clock. I make a point of having at least an hour with Tommy before I have to go back to work."

They walked back to her mother's house in silence. There was a car parked in front of the house, with a man at the wheel. "That's him," Kate said. "Waiting and fuming."

The man got out of the car as Kate and Wesley came up to the house. He was a big, heavy man, red-faced and smelling from drink. "Where the fuck you been?" he said loudly. "I been waiting since three o'clock."

"I took a little walk with this young gentleman," Kate said calmly. "Harry, this is Wesley Jordache, he came to visit me. Harry Dawson."

"Took a little walk did you?" Dawson ignored the introduction. He slapped her, hard. It happened so suddenly that Wesley had no time to react.

"I'll teach you to take little walks," Dawson shouted and raised his hand again.

"Wait a minute, pal," Wesley said and grabbed the man's arm and pushed him away from Kate, who was standing, bent over, her two hands up to protect her face.

"Let go of me, you fucking Yank," Dawson said, trying to pull his arm free.

"You've done all the hitting you're going to do today, mister." Wesley pushed Dawson farther back with his shoulder. Dawson wrenched his hand free and punched Wesley high on the forehead. Wesley nearly went down from the force of the blow, then grunted and swung. He hit Dawson square in the mouth and Dawson grappled with him and they both fell, tangled, to the pavement. Wesley took two more punches to the head before he could knee the man in the groin and use his hands on the man's face. Dawson went limp and Wesley stood up, over him. He kicked Dawson viciously in the head, twice.

Kate, who had been standing, bent over, without making a sound as the men fought, now ran at him and put her arms around him, pulling him away from the man on the ground. "That's enough now," she cried. "You don't want to kill him, do you?"

"That's just what I want to do," Wesley said, trembling with rage. But he allowed Kate to lead him away.

"Are you hurt?" she asked, still with her arms around him.

"Nah," he said, although his head felt as though he had been hit with a brick. "Nothing much. You can let go of me now. I won't touch your goddamn friend."

"Wesley," Kate said, speaking swiftly, "you have to get out of here. Go on right back to London. When he gets up . . ."

"He won't do any more harm," Wesley said. "He learned his lesson."

"He'll come back at you," Kate said. "And not alone. And he'll bring some of the men from his yard with him. And they won't come bare-handed. Go, please go right now. . . ."

"How about you?"

"Don't worry about me," she said. "I'll be all right. Just go."

"I hate to leave you with that miserable, thieving bastard." He looked down at Dawson, who was beginning to move, although his eyes were still closed.

"He won't come near me again," Kate said. "I'm finished with him."

"You just saying that to get me out of here?" Wesley said.

"I swear it's the truth. If he ever tries to come near me again, I'll have the police on him." She kissed Wesley on the mouth. "Good-bye, Tommy."

"Tommy?" Wesley laughed.

Kate laughed, too, putting her hand to her face distractedly. "Too much has happened today. Take care of yourself, Wesley. I'm so sorry you had to get mixed up in this. Now go."

Wesley looked at Dawson, who was trying to sit up and was fumbling blearily at his bloody lips. Wesley knelt on one knee beside Dawson and grabbed him roughly by his necktie. "Listen, you ape," he said, his face close to Dawson's puffed ear, "if I ever hear you touched her again, I'll be back for you. And what you got today will seem like a picnic compared to what you get. Do you understand?"

Dawson blubbered something unintelligible through his cut lips.

Still holding the man's tie, Wesley slapped his face, the noise sharp and loud. He heard Kate gasp as he stood up.

"End of chapter," Wesley said. He kissed Kate on the cheek, then walked down the street without looking back. His head still hurt, but he strode lightly along, feeling better and better, the memory of the fight making him feel wonderfully at peace with the world. He felt wonderful on the train, too, all the way to London.

Billy was playing with Carmen, this time without malice, when a young man in blue jeans, with streaked blond hair, a backpack on his shoulders, appeared at the court, stood watching the game for a while, then took off the backpack and sat down on the grass outside the court to watch in comfort. Travelers with backpacks were not a usual sight at El Faro and Billy found himself glancing over at the young man with curiosity. The expression on the young man's face was grave and interested, although he showed no signs of either approval or disapproval when Carmen or Billy made particularly good shots or committed errors.

Carmen, Billy noticed, seemed equally curious and also kept glancing frequently at the spectator sitting on the grass. "Do you know who that boy is?" she asked, as they were changing courts between games.

"Never saw him before," Billy said, as he used the towel to dry off his forehead.

"He's an improvement on that Hitzman woman," Carmen said. Monika had taken to appearing a little after four o'clock, which was the hour at which they started every day, and watching Carmen and Billy play. "There's something peculiar about that woman, as though she's not interested in the tennis, but somehow in *us*. And not in a nice way."

"I give her a lesson every morning," Billy said, remembering that his father had also said there was something peculiar about Monika when he had seen her in Brussels. "Maybe she's decided to become a student of the game."

They started playing once more and Billy ran out the set, using orthodox, non-eunuch shots.

"Thank you," Carmen said, as she put on a sweater. "That was more like it." She didn't ask him to go up to the hotel with her for a drink and smiled at the young man on the grass as she passed him. He didn't smile back, Billy noticed. Billy didn't have any more lessons that afternoon, so he put on his sweater and started off the court. The young man stood up and said, "Mr. Abbott?"

"Yes." He was surprised that the young man knew his name. He certainly didn't look as though he could afford tennis lessons at El Faro.

"I'm your cousin," the young man said, "Wesley Jordache."

"Well, now," Billy said. "I've heard a lot about you." They shook hands. Billy noted that his cousin's hand was a workingman's hand, hard and powerful.

"I've heard considerable about you, too," Wesley said.

"Anything favorable?"

"Not particularly." Wesley grinned. "You play a pretty hot game of tennis."

"Rosewall isn't worried," Billy said, although he was pleased at the compliment.

"That girl, too," Wesley said. "She really can run, can't she?"

"She's in good shape," Billy said.

"In more ways than one," Wesley said. "She sure is beautiful."

"Skin deep," Billy said. Carmen's treatment of him since their argument about the admiral still rankled.

"Deep enough," Wesley said. "That's not a bad job you have, if all the people you get paid to play with look like that."

"They don't. Where're you staying?"

"Noplace. I'm on the road," Wesley said.

"What brings you here?"

"You," Wesley said soberly.

"Oh."

"I thought it would be a good idea finally to see what the other male half of this generation of Jordaches was like."

"What do you think so far?"

"You've got a good service and you're a demon at the net." They both laughed.

"So far, so good," Billy said. "Listen, I'm dying for a beer. Will you join me?"

"You're my man," Wesley said, shouldering his pack.

As they walked toward the hotel, Billy decided he liked the boy, even though he envied him his size and the obvious strength with which he swung his pack onto his shoulders.

"My—*our* Uncle Rudolph told me you knew my father," Wesley said, as they walked in the direction of the hotel.

"I met him only once," Billy said, "when I was a kid. We slept in the same room for a night in our grandmother's house."

"What did you think of him?" Wesley's tone was carefully noncommittal.

"I liked him. He made everybody else I'd known seem soft. He'd lived the sort of life I thought I would like to have—fighting, going to sea, seeing all kinds of faraway places. Then—" Billy smiled. "He didn't sleep in pajamas. Everybody else I ever knew always slept in pajamas. I suppose that became some crazy kind of symbol for me of a freer way of life."

Wesley laughed. "You must have been a weird kid," he said.

"Not weird enough," Billy said as they went into the bar and ordered two beers.

Carmen was there, sitting with her father at a table. She looked up curiously at them, but made no sign of welcome or recognition.

"The way it turned out," Billy said, as they drank their beers, "I never had a fight, I never wandered around, and I always sleep in pajamas." He shrugged. "One other thing impressed me about your father," he said. "He carried a gun. Boy, oh, boy, I thought when I saw it, there's at least one person in the family who has guts. I don't know what he ever did with it."

"Nothing," Wesley said. "It wasn't within reach when he needed it."

They sat in silence for a moment.

"I'm awfully sorry, Wesley," Billy said gently, "about what happened, I mean."

"Yeah," Wesley said.

"What're your plans?" Billy asked. "I mean from here on in."

"I don't have any real plans just yet," Wesley said. "See what comes up."

Billy had the impression that Wesley knew what he wanted to do, but was evading the question. "My mother," Billy said, "writes she thinks you could have a great future as a movie actor."

"I'm open to offers," Wesley said, "but not just yet. I'll wait and see how the picture turns out."

"My mother writes that it's being considered for the festival in Cannes this year."

"That's news to me," Wesley said. "I'm glad for her sake. She's really something, your mother. If you don't mind my butting in, I think it's about time you were nice to her. I know if she was my mother, I'd do everything I could for her. Maybe it would be a good idea, if they are going to show the picture in Cannes, to visit her there."

"That's a thought," Billy said reflectively. "Would you be going?"

"Yes. I have some other busines in Cannes, too."

"Maybe we could drive up together," Billy said. "When is it?"

"In May. Toward the end of the month."

"That'd be about six weeks from now. It's a good season for traveling."

"Can you get away from here?"

Billy grinned. "You ever heard of tennis elbow?"

"Yes."

"I feel a bad case of tennis elbow coming on. A crippling case, which would take at least two weeks of absolute rest to cure. What'd you be doing until then?"

Wesley shrugged. "Don't know. Hang around here for a while, if it's all the same to you. Maybe take some tennis lessons from you. Maybe get a few weeks' work down at the harbor."

"Do you need dough?"

"I'm not down to the bone yet," Wesley said, "but a little dough would come in handy."

"The guy who works at the pool here—cleaning it up, putting out the mats, stuff like that, with a little lifeguarding on the side—quit two days ago. Can you swim?"

"Well enough."

"Want me to ask if the job's still open?"

"That might be fun," Wesley said.

"I have two beds in my room," Billy said. "You could camp in with me."

"Don't you have a girl?"

"Not at the moment," Billy said. "And nothing, as far as I can tell, on the horizon."

"I don't want to be a nuisance."

"That's what cousins are for," Billy said. "To be nuisances to each other."

The next day, Wesley started working at the pool. At night, under the lights, Billy began teaching him how to play tennis. Wesley was very fast and a natural athlete, and soon he was hitting the ball harder than anybody on the courts. He played with abandon, his face intent, his eyes narrowed, and slugged the ball as though he was disposing of enemies. Although Billy was proud of Wesley's constant improvement under his tutelage, the sober ferocity with which Wesley played made him uneasy and at times he wanted to say, "Remember, it's only a game." He had the disturbing impression that nothing in his young cousin's life was ever a game.

Billy enjoyed having Wesley around and soon discovered that he was an ideal roommate, keeping everything neat and shipshape, which, after Monika's messy housekeeping, was refreshing. The manager of the hotel was pleased with Wesley's work and congratulated Billy for having found him. After Billy had introduced Wesley to Carmen, her attitude changed, too, and she soon was inviting them both to dinner at one of the small restaurants on the port when her father wasn't with her at the hotel. Wesley's manner with Carmen was grave and courteous, and Billy found that Carmen, who had until then not been addicted to swimming, was spending the best part of the hot mornings at the pool. After Billy had told her that his mother had directed Wesley in a movie, Carmen even began to show a moderate respect for Billy and his opinions, and when a movie that she wanted to see was playing in town took them both with her to see it. She was partial to gory films, with sad endings, and liked to come out of the theater with her cheeks streaked with tears.

Best of all, after the second week of her lessons, Monika told him she was discontinuing her daily hours, as she was leaving the next morning. But, she said coldly, as she gave him a generous tip, she would be coming back, although she didn't tell him when. "We look forward to seeing you again," she said, although she didn't tell him who the "we" were.

"Don't you want to hear what happened on the rue du Gros-Caillou?" Billy asked her, as she gathered up her things.

"I know what happened on the rue du Gros-Caillou," she said. "The wrong man got killed. Among several others."

"I tried to call you," he said.

"You didn't leave a forwarding address," she said. "Don't make that mistake again. Do you intend to be a small-time tennis pro in this miserable country all your life?"

"I don't know what I intend," he said.

"How did you meet that boy at the pool?"

"He just wanted in one day," Billy lied. He had told no one that Wesley was his cousin and he didn't want him to get mixed up with a woman like Monika.

"I don't believe you," Monika said calmly.

"I can't help that."

"He has a good face," Monika said. "Strong and passionate. Someday I must have a long talk with him."

"Keep your hands off him."

"I don't take instructions from you," Monika said. "Remember that."

"I remember a lot of things about you," he said. "Some of them delicious. How is your memory these days?"

"Bad," she said, "very bad. Thank you for being so patient with me on the tennis court, even though it wasn't much help, was it?"

"No," he said. "You're hopeless."

"I hope you have more success with your other pupils. That blond Spanish bitch, for example. How much does she pay you to be her gigolo? Do you have to have a union card for that profession in Spain?"

"I don't have to listen to crap like that from anybody," he said angrily.

"You may have to get used to it, laddy," she said, "after a few years at the game. *Adiós!* Johnny."

He watched her walk away. His hands were shaking as he pocketed the tip Monika had given him and picked up his racket to start the next lesson. With it all, he couldn't help hoping she would turn around and come back and give him the number of her room and ask him to come up after midnight.

Wesley was writing a letter at the desk in their room as Billy dressed for a party two weeks later. It was to be a flamenco party with a group of gypsies hired for the occasion, and the guests had been asked to dress in Spanish clothes. Billy had bought a frilled shirt and borrowed some tight black pants, a bolero jacket and high-heeled boots from one of the musicians in the band. Wesley had been invited, too, but had said he'd rather write some letters. Besides, he said, he'd feel like a fool in a getup like Billy's.

He had received a letter from Gretchen that morning, in which she had written that *Restoration Comedy* had been chosen for a showing at the Cannes Festival and asking him to come there and take a bow and share in the kudos. Rudolph was coming over with her and David Donnelly. Frances Miller, as the star of the picture, was going to try to come for at least three days. It promised to be an interesting two weeks. She was pleased, Gretchen wrote, that he had finally met Billy and that they liked each other and she wondered if he could influence Billy to come to Cannes, too.

"Billy," Wesley said as Billy was struggling into the musician's boots, "I'm writing to your mother. She would like us both to come to Cannes. What should I tell her?"

"Tell her . . . " Billy hesitated, one boot on, the other still off, "tell her . . . Okay, why not?"

"She'll be pleased," Wesley said.

"What the hell," Billy said, getting into the second boot and standing up, "I suppose once every ten years a man can do something to please his mother. How do I look?"

"Ridiculous," Wesley said.

"That's what I thought," Billy said agreeably. "Well, I'm off to the gypsies, tra-la, tra-la." He did a little stamping step and they both laughed.

"Have a good time," Wesley said.

"If I'm not back by morning, you'll know I've been kidnapped. You know how those gypsies are.' Don't pay more than thirteen dollars and fifty cents in ransom."

He went out, whistling the toreador song from Carmen.

The gypsies were fine, the guitar and castanets blood-tingling, the music and singing sorrowful, full of wailing passion, the dancing proud and fierce, the wine plentiful. Again, as he had felt when he first crossed the border into Spain, Billy had the feeling he had come to the right country for him.

Why deny it, he thought, as the music boomed around him and the girls with roses in their hair flounced their skirts and advanced erotically toward their partners only to repel them, with a clatter of thick heels, at the last moment, why deny it, the pleasures of the rich are real pleasures. Carmen sat next to him most of the evening, resplendent in a dark dress that showed off her lovely shoulders and full bosom and he could see her eyes gleaming with excitement. It was a long way from the proms at the college in Whitby and Billy was happy that he had put all that distance behind him.

One of the male dancers came over to Carmen and pulled her up from where she was sitting to join him. She danced joyously and very well; as well, Billy thought, as any of the professional dancers, her long bright hair flying, her face set in traditional proud disdain. Whatever else she felt about Spain, Billy saw, its music struck some deep, responsive, racial core in her. The dance finished and the guests applauded loudly, Billy among them. Instead of sitting down again, Carmen came over to him and pulled him up. To general laughter and handclapping, Billy began to dance with her, mimicking the movements of the male dancers. He was a good dancer and he managed to move almost like the gypsies, while at the same moment slyly making fun of his own performance. Carmen caught on to what he was doing and laughed in the middle of one of her wildest passages. When the dance was over she kissed him, although the sweat was streaming down his face.

"I need some air," he said. "Let's go outside for a minute."

Unobtrusively, they left the room and went out onto the terrace. The sky was turbulent and dark, with black, scattered clouds moving across the face of the moon.

"You were wonderful," Carmen said.

He took her in his arms and kissed her. "Later," he whispered, "I want to come to your room."

She stood still in his arms for a moment, then pushed him away from her. "I will dance with you," she said coldly, "and play tennis with you and argue with you. But I wouldn't dream of making love to you in a thousand years."

"But the way you looked at me . . . "

"That was part of the fun," she said, wiping her mouth contemptuously. "*All* of the fun. No more. If I were going to make love to anyone in this corrupt place it would be with the young man at the pool."

"I see." His voice was hoarse with anger and disappointment. "Do you want me to tell him that?"

"Yes," she said. As baldly as that.

"I'll do just that," he said. "As always, at your service, ma'am."

"My room number is 301. Can you remember that?"

"Till my dying day."

She laughed. The laugh was not pleasant. "I must go back," she said. "People noticed we left together. This is a backward country, as you know, and we put great store on appearances. Are you coming in with me?"

"No," he said. "I have a message to deliver. And then I'm going to sleep."

"Pleasant dreams," she said and turned and went back toward the music.

He walked slowly toward his room, the sweat getting suddenly cold on his body in the night wind and making him shiver. Beware the *señoritas,* his father had written.

Good old Dad knew what he was talking about.

Wesley was asleep when he got to the room. He slept restlessly, moving around in sudden jerks, making a tangle of the covers and moaning from time to time, as though at night some ineradicable anguish that he avoided or disguised during the day took hold of him. Billy stood next to the bed, looking down at his new cousin, not knowing whether he pitied him or loved him or hated him.

He nearly started to undress and get into the other bed, leaving Wesley to his sorrowful dreams, but finally he thought, What the hell, it's all in the family, and shook the boy awake.

Wesley sat up with a start. "What is it?" he asked.

"I just came from the party," Billy said, "and I have some news for you. If you go to room 301 you will find a lady waiting for you. Her name is Carmen. She asked me to tell you personally."

Wesley was completely awake now. "You're kidding," he said.

"I was never more serious in my life."

"What in blazes made her say something like that?"

"In your place, I wouldn't ask any questions," Billy said. "You've told me how beautiful she is. If it were me, I'd grab while the grabbing is good."

"I don't love her," Wesley said. He sounded petulant and unhappy, like a small boy being asked to perform a distasteful chore for the first time, making Billy conscious of the seven-year difference in their ages.

"You're playing with the grown-ups now," Billy said. "Love is not always a prime consideration in matters like this. Are you going?"

Wesley swung out of bed and sat on the edge, hunched over. He slept only in pajama bottoms, and the muscles of his torso gleamed in the light of the lamp Billy had turned on when he came into the room. He looks like a beaten fighter, Billy thought, who knows he's going to be knocked out in the next round.

"I don't want to sound like a fool," Wesley said, "but I can't do it. I'm in love with someone else. A great girl. Back in New York. She's going to try to come over to Europe to see me in a few weeks. I don't care what that lady will think of me," he said defiantly, "I'm waiting for my girl."

"You may regret this later," Billy warned him.

"Never. You think she's beautiful, too, you know her a lot better than I do—why don't *you* go?"

"The lady has made it clear," Billy said, "that she would not be pleased to see me in room 301."

"Christ," Wesley said, "who would have thought a lady like that would pick on me?"

"Maybe she likes movie stars."

"This is nothing to joke about," Wesley said severely. "I'm no movie star and she knows it."

"I was just being shitty," Billy said. "Well, I've done my duty. Now I'm going to bed."

"So am I." Wesley looked down at the tangled bedclothes. "What a mess," he said. "Every time I wake up in the morning the bed looks as though I've gone twenty rounds during the night." He straightened the covers a little and laid down under them, his arms raised and his hands under his head. "Someday," he said, as Billy undressed, "maybe I'll figure out just what to do about sex and love and other little things like that."

"Don't count on it," Billy said as he put on his pajamas and got into his bed. "Sleep well, Wesley. You've had a big night and you need your rest."

"Yeah," Wesley said sourly. "Turn off the goddamn light."

Billy reached over and put out the light. He didn't try to close his eyes for a long time, but kept staring up at the dark ceiling. After five minutes he heard Wesley's steady breathing as he slept and an occasional low moan, as his dreams took over once more. Billy lay awake till the light of the dawn filtered into the room. In the distance the throb of the music could still be heard. Spanish hours, he thought, Spanish fucking hours.

The next day, promptly at four, Carmen appeared at the court looking rested and serene. They were playing doubles that afternoon and the other players were already there and Carmen greeted them and Billy with the same radiant smile. Although the others were men, they were weaker players than Carmen, so she and Billy were on opposing teams. She played better than Billy had ever seen her play before, agile and accurate, poaching at the net and making Billy and his partner work hard for every point. The score was four all when, after a long rally, she lobbed over Billy's head. He got a glimpse of her ironic smile as he backpedaled at full speed and by leaping into the air, just managed to reach the ball. He hit the overhead viciously, trying to put it at Carmen's feet, but she had charged the net and the ball whistled toward her head. She stumbled a little, and the smash hit her in the eye and bounced crazily off the court as she dropped her racket and bent over with a cry and put her hands to the eye.

Oh, God, Billy thought, as he jumped over the net to her side, that's all I needed.

The doctor was grave. The eye was in danger, he said. Carmen had to go to Barcelona immediately to see a specialist. An operation might be necessary.

"I'm terribly sorry," Billy said as he drove her back from the doctor's office to the hotel.

"Nothing to be sorry about," Carmen said crisply, although he could see she was in great pain. "It wasn't your fault. I had no business being at the net. I was trying to psych you into missing the shot. Don't let anybody make you believe it was your fault."

He leaned over and kissed her cheek. This time she didn't push him away.

But no matter what she or anybody would say, he knew that it was his fault, that if the night before hadn't happened, he would never have hit the ball at her so hard and at such a short distance.

The next afternoon, the manager of the hotel called him into his office. "Young man," he said, "I'm afraid you're in very deep. The father has just called me. The eye will probably be all right, he said; the specialist doesn't think he will have to operate, but the father is furious. As for me, I did not pay you to brutalize the guests. The father insists that I dismiss you, and although the daughter called me, too, and said she would never forgive me if I did, I'm afraid I have to bow to the father's wishes. You'd better pack your bags and leave. The sooner the better for you." The manager took an envelope out of the drawer of his desk and handed it to Billy. "Here's your month's pay. I have deducted nothing."

"Thank you," Billy said numbly.

The manager shook his hand. "I'm sorry to see you go. You were well liked here."

As Billy walked toward the pool to tell Wesley what had happened, he remembered what his father had said about the luck of the Jordaches. It made no difference that his name wasn't Jordache, but Abbott.

That same afternoon they were on the road for France, driving in the sunshine in the open Peugeot. Billy had tried to persuade Wesley that it was foolish for him to leave his job, but Wesley had insisted and Billy hadn't pressed too hard. He had grown fond of the boy and the prospect of driving through the springtime countryside of Spain and France with him was a tempting one. They went at a leisurely pace, sight-seeing and having picnic lunches of sausage and rough bread with a bottle of wine on the side of the road, shaded by olive trees or on the edge of vineyards. They had their tennis gear with them and usually were able to find a court in the towns through which they passed and play a few sets almost every day. "If you keep at it," Billy said, "you'll be able to beat me in two years."

As they traveled north Billy realized that he was glad they had quit El Faro, although he would always feel guilty for the way it had come about. He regretted leaving Spain but he didn't regret having to wonder every day if Monika would arrive to chill him with her hopeless tennis and oblique threatening hints of future complications.

Wesley spoke more openly about what he had been doing than he had at El Faro and told him of the people in his father's life he had searched out. He told Billy a little about his visit to Bath, just mentioning Kate and not saying anything about Dawson and the fight, but describing his half-brother lovingly. "Pretty little kid," he said. "Strong as a young bull. I think he's going to turn out like his father—our father. He's a real happy little boy."

"*You* don't seem happy," Billy said. "You're young and strong and good-looking and from what my mother writes with a big career ahead of you if you want it, but you don't act like a happy boy."

"I'm happy enough," Wesley said evasively.

"Not when you sleep you aren't. Do you know that you moan practically all night?"

"Dreams. They don't mean anything."

"That isn't what the psychiatrists say."

"What do *you* say?" Wesley's voice was suddenly harsh.

"I'd say that something is bugging you. Something bad. If you want to talk about it, maybe it would help."

"Maybe I will," said Wesley. "Some other time. Now let's drop the subject."

When they crossed into France, they spent the first night in a small hotel overlooking the sea just across the border in Port Vendres. "I have a great idea," Billy said. "We're not due in Cannes for another two weeks—why don't we tool up to Paris and give ourselves a holiday there?"

Wesley shook his head. "No," he said, "I've got to get to Cannes. I've been avoiding it and now it's time to go."

"Why?"

Wesley looked at Billy strangely. "I've got to see Bunny, he was on the *Clothilde* with me. Actually he's in Saint-Tropez. He may have some information for me. Important information. You drive up to Paris. I'll hitchhike east."

"What sort of information?" Billy asked.

Again Wesley looked at him strangely. "I'm looking for someone and Bunny may know where I can find him. That's all."

"Can't whoever it is wait a couple of weeks?"

"He's waited too long.

"Who is it?"

"It's the man who's responsible for the way I sleep. I dream about him every night. I dream that I keep stabbing him with a knife, over and over again, and that he doesn't fall, he just stands there laughing at me. . . . When I wake up I can still hear him laughing."

"Do you recognize him?" Billy asked. "I mean in the dream?"

Wesley nodded slowly. "He's the man who had my father killed."

Billy felt a cold tingle at the base of his neck at the tone of Wesley's voice. "What are you going to do when you find him?"

Wesley took a deep breath. "I finally have to tell someone," he said, "and it might as well be you. I'm going to kill him."

"Oh, Christ," Billy said.

They sat in silence, looking out at the sea.

"How do you plan to do it?" Billy said finally.

"I don't know," Wesley shrugged. "I'll figure it out when the time comes. A knife, maybe."

"Have you got a gun?"

"No."

"Is *he* likely to have one?"

"Probably."

"You'll get yourself killed."

"I'll try to avoid that," Wesley said grimly.

"And if you do manage to knock him off," Billy said, "you'll be the first one the cops would come looking for, don't you know that?"

"I suppose I do," Wesley admitted.

"You'd be lucky to get off with twenty years in jail. Do you want that?"

"No."

"And still you want to go to Cannes and do it?"

"Yes."

"Listen, Wesley," Billy said, "I can't let you go charging ahead to your doom. You've got to let me help you."

"How?"

"I have a gun with a silencer stashed away in Paris, for openers."

Wesley nodded gravely. "That would be useful."

"I could help you plan it. The . . . the murder." Billy stumbled over the word. "After all, I was trained as a soldier. I speak French a lot better than you do. I know how to handle guns. I'm going to tell you something that you've got to keep absolutely to yourself—while I was in the army I joined a cell of terrorists in Brussels. . . . "

"You?" Wesley said incredulously.

"Yes, me. I was in on a job in Amsterdam on the Spanish tourist office. I know how to put together a bomb. Sonny, you couldn't have found a better partner for the job. I'll tell you what I'll do," he went on. "While you head for Saint-Tropez, I'll go up to Paris and get the gun and I'll meet you in either Saint-Tropez or Cannes, whichever you say. Fair enough?"

Wesley looked at Billy consideringly. "Are you hustling me?"

"Oh, come on now, Wesley," Billy said, sounding aggrieved. "I wouldn't do anything like that. What have you got to lose? I'll be back down south in a few days. With the gun. And enough ammunition so that you can practice using it. Does that sound like a hustle?"

"I guess not," Wesley said, but he sounded reluctant to say it. "Okay. You let me know where you're staying in Paris and I'll call you and tell you where you can find me."

"I think we can use a drink," Billy said.

"I think so, too," said Wesley.

The next day they drove together to Nîmes, where Billy would turn north toward Paris. Billy sat at the wheel in silence under the shade of a poplar while Wesley got his backpack out of the car and slung it over his shoulder. They had agreed that Billy would send him a telegram at Poste Restante in Saint-Tropez to let Wesley know in what hotel he was staying in Paris.

"Well," Wesley said, "take care of yourself."

"You, too," Billy said. "You're not going to do anything foolish while I'm gone, are you?"

"No. I promise." They shook hands. "I'm going to miss the tennis." Billy grinned.

"You'll remember," Billy said, "that they play very little tennis in French jails."

"I'll remember," Wesley said and stepped back.

Billy started the motor and waved as the car, built for holidays and sunshine, spurted onto the road from beneath the shadow of the poplar tree. In the rearview mirror he saw the tall, lean figure start trudging in the direction of Cannes.

When he got to Paris, the first thing Billy did after checking into a hotel on the Left Bank was put in a call to America. When Rudolph came to the phone, Billy said,

"Uncle Rudolph, this is Billy Abbott. I'm in Paris at the Hôtel Alembert. I need help. Bad. Something awful is going to happen to Wesley—and maybe to me, too, unless . . ." He stopped.

"Unless what, Billy?" Rudolph said.

"Unless we can stop certain things from happening," Billy said. "I can't tell you over the phone."

"I'll be in Paris tomorrow," Rudolph said.

"God," Billy said, "those're sweet words."

He lay back on the bed wearily and a minute later he was asleep.

CHAPTER 9

"Now," RUDOLPH SAID to Billy as they turned onto the auto route that led from the airport toward Paris, "explain."

"It's Wesley," Billy said, driving carefully. It was raining and the headlights of the late evening traffic glared off the wet surface of the road. "He's down in the south of France now looking for the man he says was behind the murder." He pulled at the wheel to swerve into the right lane because the driver of the car behind him was blinking his lights impatiently at him. The car passed in a whoosh, throwing up a curtain of rain that made the windshield opaque for several seconds. "Bastard," Billy said, grateful to have something else to worry about, even for a moment.

Rudolph pushed his hat back on his head and ran his hand across his forehead, as though relieving pain there. "How do you know all this?" he asked, his voice dull.

"He told me," Billy said. "We became very close in Spain. I was glad we could become such good friends. He shared my room with me. He slept as though he were in a foxhole, with the artillery hitting nearer to him all the time. I could see something was psyching him out and it worried me and I finally asked him and he told me."

"Do you think he's serious?" Rudolph asked.

"Absolutely," Billy said. "There're no jokes in that kid's repertoire. There's even something scary about the way he plays tennis. He's not like any other boy I've ever known. Or man, for that matter."

"Is he sane?"

"Except for this," Billy said.

"Do you think a psychiatrist would help?"

Billy thought for a moment. "It wouldn't do any harm," he said. "If you could get him to sit still for it for maybe a year or so. Only you couldn't get him to do it."

Rudolph grunted. "Why didn't you stay with him?" He sounded accusing.

"Well . . ." Billy said uncomfortably. "That's another part of the story. I said I'd help him."

"How?"

Billy shifted uneasily in the bucket seat and changed his grip on the wheel. "I said I'd try to figure some way of our doing the job together," he said, "some way of getting away with it without being caught. What with my training as a soldier and all."

"Are *you* sane?" Rudolph's voice was sharp.

"I've always thought so."

"Did you *mean* what you said?"

"I don't know what I meant, really," Billy said flatly. "If it comes to the sticking point, I guess I mean it now. You don't have to sound like a cop interrogating a prisoner, Rudolph."

Rudolph made an exasperated noise. "Two nuts," he said, "two young nuts off the same tree."

"All in the family," Billy said, offended by Rudolph's estimate of him. "Welcome to Nutsville, European division, Uncle."

"Why're you in Paris while he's down there getting into God knows what kind of idiotic trouble?" Rudolph's voice rose in anger as he spoke.

"I told him I had a gun in Paris with a silencer and that I would bring it to him," Billy said.

"*Do* you have a gun with a silencer?"

"Yes."

"God damn it, Billy," Rudolph said, "what the hell have you been messed up with these last few years?"

Again Billy shifted uneasily in the bucket seat. "I'd rather not say. And it's better for you—and for me—if you don't know."

Rudolph took a deep breath and then sighed. "Are the police after you?"

"No. At least not that I know of," Billy said, glad that he had to keep his eyes on the road so that he couldn't see the expression on his uncle's face.

Rudolph rubbed his face wearily, the gesture making a rasping sound on his unshaven cheek. "You'd better give me that gun," he said.

"I told Wesley I'd bring it down to him in a day or so," Billy said.

"Listen, Billy," Rudolph said, trying to keep his voice even, "you asked me to come over here to help. I took the next plane. Either you're going to do what I say or . . ." He stopped.

"Or what?" Billy asked.

"I don't know. Yet. Something. Just exactly where is Wesley now? Today? This minute?"

"Saint-Tropez. We agreed I'd send him a wire telling him where he could call me in Paris and arrange for where and when we'd meet down south."

"*Did* you send the wire?"

"This morning."

"What was your rush? Why didn't you wait until I got here? Maybe it would be better if he didn't know where to find you."

"He's suspicious enough of me as it is," Billy said, defending himself. "If I don't come through with my half of the bargain, he'll just go off on his own and that will be the end of Wesley Jordache."

"Ah, maybe you're right," Rudolph said. "Maybe. Has he called you yet?"

"No."

"All right," Rudolph said. "When he does call don't tell him I'm in Europe. And tell him it's taking more time than you thought to lay your hands on that goddamn gun."

"What good will that do?"

"It'll give me some extra time to come up with something, that's what it will do," Rudolph said angrily. "And you could use some time to do a little thinking, too. Now don't talk for a while. I'm bushed from the trip and I want to close my eyes for a few minutes and hope that either you or I will be struck by lightning or at least one single useful thought before we get to the hotel."

Just before they said good night Rudolph said, "Remember, I want that gun tomorrow. And one thing is sure—Wesley's never even going to *see* it."

"Then he'll use a knife or a club or maybe his bare hands," Billy said. "You don't know what he's like."

"That's true," said Rudolph. "And I'm sorry I'm finding out now."

"Listen," Billy said, "if you don't really want to get mixed up in this, I'll try to handle it myself. You can always forget what I've told you, you know."

Rudolph looked thoughtfully at Billy, as though he was considering the disadvantages of not forgetting, then shook his head. "Maybe," he said, "I should have been the one to go looking for Mr. Danovic. Long ago. Only it never occurred to me until tonight. No, I don't think forgetting is the answer. Good night, Billy. If you have any good ideas during the night, call me. I don't think I'll be sleeping all that well, anyway."

He wiped his face with his hands again and walked slowly and heavily toward the elevator.

I never thought about how old he is before this, Billy thought, as the elevator door opened and then shut behind his uncle.

The next morning they had breakfast together in the hotel dining room. Rudolph looked haggard, with puffs under his eyes, and he ate without speaking, drinking one cup of coffee after another.

"You go get the—the object—this afternoon," he said finally, "and hand it over to me."

"Are you sure you want to . . ." Billy began.

"One thing I'm sure of," Rudolph snapped, "is that I don't want any more arguments from you."

"Okay," Billy said, "you're the boss." He felt relieved to be able to say it, the responsibility for decision no longer only in his hands.

The concierge came into the dining room and approached Billy. "There's a telephone call for you, Mr. Abbott," he said in French. "In the hall booth."

"Thank you." Billy stood up. "It must be him," he said to Rudolph. "Nobody else knows I'm here."

"Be smart about how you talk to him," Rudolph said. "Make everything sound plausible."

"I'll do my best. I'm not guaranteeing anything when it comes to that boy," Billy said and started out of the dining room. The coffee he had drunk suddenly tasted sour in his mouth as he went into the hall and entered the booth and picked up the phone.

"Billy," Wesley said, his voice thin over the wire, "can you talk?"

"Not really."

"I'm at the Les Pinèdes in Saint-Tropez. When will you get here?"

"Not for a few days, I'm afraid, Wesley. There've been some complications about getting the stuff." His own voice sounded fake to him as he spoke.

"What sort of complications?" Wesley said harshly.

"I'll tell you when I see you."

"Are you going to get it or aren't you going to get it?"

"I'm going to get it all right. It's just going to take a little time."

"What's a little time?"

"Four, five days."

"If I don't see you in the next five days, I'm going on to Cannes," Wesley said. "Alone. Do you understand what I'm saying?"

"Keep your cool, Wesley. I'm doing the best I can."

"I think you're stalling, Billy."

"I'm not stalling," Billy said. "It's just that certain things have come up."

"I bet," Wesley said and hung up.

Billy walked slowly back into the dining room. "He's at Les Pinèdes in Saint-Tropez," he said as he sat down. "And he's not happy. He gave me five days."

Rudolph nodded. "You didn't tell him I was here, did you?"

"No."

"I'll take the train down to Antibes tonight," Rudolph said. "I don't want to go through the check at the airport. I'll be at the Colombe d'Or at Saint-Paul-de-Vence if you want to reach me."

"Did you come up with any ideas during the night?" Billy asked.

"Maybe." Rudolph smiled grimly.

"Do you want to tell me what they are?"

"No. As you said last night, I'd rather not say. And it's better for you and for me if you don't know."

"We're a great family at keeping secrets from one another, aren't we?"

"Up to a certain point." Rudolph stood up. "I'm going to enjoy the city of Paris today. I may even go to the Louvre. I'll meet you back here at five o'clock. Don't do anything foolish until then."

"I'll try not to," Billy said. "Until five o'clock."

After his uncle had gone, Billy took a taxi to the bank on the corner of the rue St. Dominique. He didn't want anyone noticing the convertible Peugeot and perhaps taking down the number on the license plate. He took his tennis bag along with him, and when the attendant in the vault had turned the two keys and had gone back to his desk, Billy slipped the automatic and the extra clips into the bag and what remained of the ten thousand francs and went upstairs and told the clerk he was giving up the *coffre-fort* and handed over his key.

Then, carrying the bag, he took a taxi back to the hotel and put the bag on the bed. He sat there looking at it until five o'clock.

Rudolph got off the train into the southern morning sunlight at Antibes. The car he had ordered from Hertz was waiting for him at the station. As he signed for it he kept one leg pressed against his locked bag.

When he drove up to the Colombe d'Or he carried the bag with him to the hotel and after checking in followed the porter who carried the bag.

After the porter had left he telephoned the old lawyer in Antibes and made a date for eleven o'clock in his office. Rudolph shaved and had a bath, in which he drowsed for a long time. It was two o'clock in the morning in New York and his body knew it. He moved lethargically as he put on fresh clothes and ordered a big cup of coffee to be sent to his room. It was the same room he had had before. Jeanne had visited him there and the memory of the times with her stirred old desires. He took out a sheet of paper and wrote, "Dear Jeanne, I'm back at our hotel and wonder if you're free—" He stopped writing and crumpled the sheet of paper. It had been too long ago. Over.

At ten-thirty he locked his bag and went down to the rented car and drove carefully to Antibes.

The old man was waiting for him at the large polished table with the sunny blue sea framed in the big window behind him.

"It's safe to talk in here, isn't it?" Rudolph asked as he sat down.

"Completely," the lawyer said.

"I mean, there are no tape recorders in the desk or anything like that?"

"There is one," the lawyer admitted, "but it is not turned on. I only use it when the client demands it."

"I hope this doesn't offend you, sir," Rudolph said, "but I would like you to put it on the desk so that we both can be sure it is not recording."

The old man wrinkled his face into a frown. "If you wish, sir," he said coldly. He pulled open a drawer and put the little machine on the desk, to one side.

Rudolph stood up to look at it. It was not turned on. "Thank you, sir," he said and sat down again. "I would also appreciate it," he said, "if you didn't take any notes either now or after I've left."

The old man nodded. "No notes," he said.

"The matter I'm here for is a very delicate one," Rudolph said. "It concerns the safety of my nephew, the son of my brother who was killed."

The old man nodded again. "A sad affair," he said. "I trust the wounds have healed somewhat."

"Somewhat," Rudolph said.

"And," the lawyer said, "that the estate was divided with a minimum of—ah—acrimony."

"Maximum," Rudolph said grimly.

"Alas," the old man said. "These family matters."

"My nephew is in the south of France," Rudolph said. "He doesn't know that I'm in the country and I would prefer it if he didn't learn about my presence for the time being."

"Very well."

"He is here to find out where he can reach Mr. Danovic."

"Ah," the old man said gravely.

"He intends to kill the man when he finds him."

The old man coughed, as though something were stuck in his throat. He took out a large white handkerchief and wiped his lips. "Forgive me," he said. "I see what you mean when you say it is a delicate matter."

"I don't want him ever to find Danovic."

"I understand your position," the lawyer said. "What I don't understand is how I can be of any help."

Rudolph took a deep breath. "If Danovic is killed—by other means, let us say—before my nephew learns of his whereabouts, the problem would be solved."

"I see," the old man said thoughtfully. He coughed again and once more produced the handkerchief. "And just how do you believe I can help achieve this desirable result?"

"In your time, sir," said Rudolph, "you must have handled cases that involved members of the *milieu* along this coast. . . ."

The lawyer nodded. "In my time," he said softly, "yes."

"If you would introduce me to a man who knew where Danovic could be found," Rudolph said, "and who could be persuaded to undertake the job, I'd be prepared to pay very well for his—his services."

"I see," the lawyer said.

"Naturally," Rudolph said, "I'd be prepared to deposit a considerable sum in your Swiss account for *your* services."

"Naturally," the lawyer agreed. He sighed. Rudolph could not tell whether it was because of the risks that might have to be run or at the thought of the considerable sum in the Swiss account.

"It would have to be done very soon," Rudolph said. "The boy is impatient and foolish."

The lawyer nodded. "I sympathize with your position, *Monsieur* Jordache," he said, "but as you can imagine, it is not something that can be arranged overnight, if at all. . . ."

"I'm prepared to go as high as twenty thousand dollars," Rudolph said steadily.

Again the lawyer coughed. Again he wiped his mouth with the handkerchief. "I have never smoked in my life," he said, almost petulantly, "and yet this cough pursues me." He swung around in his chair and looked out at the calm sea, as though some fruitful answer could be found there for the questions that were troubling him.

There was silence in the room for a long moment. In the silence Rudolph reflected painfully on what he was doing. He was committing an evil act. All his life he had believed in goodness and morality and he was now committing an evil act. But what was he doing it for? To prevent an even more evil act. Morality can be a trap, he thought, just like a lot of other noble words. The question is—what comes first, your principles or your own flesh and blood? Well, he had answered the question, at least for himself. He would suffer for this later, if he had to.

The silence in the room was broken when, without turning to face Rudolph, the lawyer said, "I will see what I can do. At the very best, I can only hope to communicate with a gentleman who might just possibly be interested and have him get in touch with you. I hope you understand that would have to be the beginning and the end of the matter for me."

"I understand," Rudolph said. He stood up. "I am staying at the Colombe d'Or in Saint-Paul-de-Vence. I will be waiting for a telephone call."

"I promise nothing, dear *monsieur*," said the lawyer. He turned around, and with his back to the sea, smiled wanly at Rudolph. "To be perfectly honest with you, I would prefer it if you could persuade your nephew to abandon his rash scheme."

"So would I," Rudolph said. "But I doubt that I could do so."

The lawyer nodded somberly. "Young men," he said. "Ah, well, I shall do what I can do."

"Thank you." Rudolph stood up. As he went out of the room the lawyer was looking out at the sea again. They had not shaken hands as they said good-bye.

The power of money, Rudolph thought, as he drove along the port. Would Hamlet have paid Rosencrantz and Guildenstern to do the job on his uncle, the king, if he had had the florins?

When he got to the Colombe d'Or, he called the Hôtel Alembert, in Paris. Luckily, Billy was in. What Rudolph didn't know was that Billy hadn't left the hotel, except for the one trip to the bank the day before.

"Billy," Rudolph said, "there's a ray of hope. I can't tell you about it, and don't ask what it is—now—or ever. But it's there. What we have to do is buy time. What you have to do is keep Wesley pacified. Can you hear me clearly?"

"Too clearly," Billy said. "What am I supposed to do to keep him pacified?"

"Get to Saint-Tropez on the fifth day. Make up some story—any story—you're a clever fellow. . . ."

"That's what they tell me," Billy said bleakly.

"Just hang in there with him," Rudolph said. I don't want him disappearing into the blue. We've got to know where he is at all times. Got it?"

"Got it," Billy said, without enthusiasm.

"If necessary," Rudolph said, "you can tell him where I am. I'd rather he didn't know, but if that's the only way we can put him off, I'll chip in on the holding process. And keep me posted."

"How long do I have to keep him pacified?" Billy asked.

"As long as it takes."

"That's a nice round figure," Billy said.

"No witticisms, please," Rudolph said severely. "I'm doing my share, you do yours."

"Yes, sir," Billy said. "I'll spend the next couple of days making up a story."

"That's a good boy."

"Making that crazy man believe it is another story," Billy said.

"Get lucky," Rudolph said and hung up.

The *Clothilde* was moored not far from the Chris-Craft that Bunny was crewing in the port of Saint-Tropez, and Wesley and Bunny went over to take a look at it. Bunny hadn't wanted him to go. "You've seen enough of that boat," he said.

"Don't worry, Bunny," Wesley said. "I won't break into tears or hit anybody. It was the only home I ever had that I felt good in. I'll just look at it and remember that, how it was when my old man was on it. I've been looking at a lot more depressing things since then. . . ." He had spent the days and nights of waiting for Billy prowling around the ports of Saint-Tropez and Cannes and going in and out of the nightclubs in both places. He couldn't ask Bunny if Danovic was around, because Bunny would start arguing with him. He couldn't ask anyone else, either, about Danovic because he couldn't let Danovic, or eventually the police, know that he was after him, but he could look. He had looked and hadn't found the man, but he was certain that, given enough time, Danovic would surface. Well, he had plenty of time. Surprisingly, being around the ports in the quiet month or so before the season began had calmed him. He even slept more quietly and the violent dreams that had plagued him for so long did not recur.

When they reached the place where the *Clothilde* was tied up, they stood looking at it, without talking. The ship looked old-fashioned and comfortable and Wesley was pleased that it was clean and well-kept. It would have hurt him if the ship was messy or looked neglected.

"They keep it up nice, don't they?" he said to Bunny.

"They're Germans," Bunny said; "you could eat off the deck. You want to go on and take a look around? They put in an automatic pilot."

Wesley shook his head. "No. This is enough. I'm glad I saw it, but it's enough."

They went back to the Chris-Craft, where Wesley had a fish stew going on the range for lunch. There would be three for lunch, because Bunny had taken up with a girl who worked in one of the boutiques on the port and she lunched with him every day. She was a pretty, small, dark-haired girl who spoke fairly good English and Bunny was crazy about her and as far as Wesley could tell, she was crazy about him. She came over to the Chris-Craft after work, too, and sometimes spent the night with Bunny. Bit by bit, Bunny was losing some of his womanish gestures, Wesley noticed. Bunny and she were talking about getting married and signing on as a couple in a bigger ship. Bunny, Wesley noticed, was not only taking on some of the mannerisms of Tom, he was moving consciously or unconsciously toward the sort of life his father and Kate had had together.

Wesley was pleased by that, too—it was a tribute, he recognized, to the value of his father, a tribute from the man who had known him better than anyone else alive. It made up for a lot of the things Wesley had heard about his father from Teddy Boylan and from Schultzy, in the Hebrew Home for the Aged in the Bronx.

The lunch was a good one, with a bottle of cold wine. Wesley had asked Bunny not to tell anybody that he was acting in a picture that was going to be down in Cannes, but when the girl, whose name was Nadine, asked Wesley what his profession was, Bunny blurted out, "He's a goddamn movie actor. How do you like that—my old shipmate?"

Well, Wesley thought, if it gives Bunny points with his girl, what harm can it do?

"Is that true?" Nadine looked at him incredulously.

"I'm afraid so," Wesley said. "After the picture comes out I may be an ex-movie actor."

"Are you two fellows pulling my leg?" Nadine asked.

"You can see for yourself," Bunny said. "He's the star of a movie they're going to show at the festival."

"Not the star," Wesley protested. "It's just a bit part."

Nadine looked at him closely. "I thought you were too good looking just to be *nobody*."

"A dime a dozen," Wesley said. "I'm really just a seaman at heart."

"There's a girl who works with me," Nadine said, "actually my best friend, she's crazy about the movies, she's awfully cute, why don't I bring her to dinner tonight?"

"I'm just staying in Saint-Tropez a little while," Wesley said uneasily. Remembering Alice's promise to try to come over to Europe for at least two weeks, he didn't want to be tempted by an awfully cute French girl.

"She speaks good English," Nadine said.

"Actually," Wesley said, "I have a date for tonight." It was the fifth day and he wanted to be at the hotel if and when Billy showed up.

"How about tomorrow night?" Nadine persisted.

"I'll probably be in Cannes tomorrow night," Wesley said. "Maybe some other time."

"Are you coming back from Cannes after the festival?" Nadine asked.

"That depends," Wesley said.

"She just broke up with her boyfriend," said Nadine. "You'd be just the thing to cheer her up."

"I'm not much good at cheering people up," Wesley said. "Ask Bunny."

"He's a serious boy," Bunny said. "He can stand some cheering up himself."

"If we come to Cannes," Nadine said, "can you get us tickets to see your film?"

"I guess so. I'll let Bunny know where I'm staying." Christ, Wesley thought, that's all I need, two French girls hanging around my neck just as I bump into that sonofabitch Danovic.

"You won't forget now?" Nadine said, as she prepared to go back to her boutique.

"I won't forget," Wesley lied.

Nadine kissed Bunny, and they both watched her walk swiftly down the quay, a curvy small girl with a swinging walk.

"What do you think of her?" Bunny asked. He had not asked before.

"She's pretty as can be," Wesley said.

"Do you think she's too flighty to make a good wife?" Bunny asked anxiously.

"I think she's fine, Bunny," Wesley said. He didn't want to be responsible in any way for a decision as grave as marriage for Bunny. "I hardly know her."

"I tell you something," Bunny said, "with your looks and what you learned from your father and now, with being a movie actor and all, I bet you know a hundred times more than I do about women. That's never been my strong point and I don't want to kid myself about that." He hesitated. "Did you get the impression she was flirting with you or anything like that?"

"Come on, Bunny." Wesley was honestly shocked.

"I wouldn't want to get hooked up with any woman who made passes at my friends," Bunny said.

"Rest easy, mate," Wesley said. "There wasn't the flicker of an eyelash."

"I'm glad to hear that," Bunny said. "Now—about you—"

"What about me?"

"I got the feeling you didn't come down to the Côte d'Azur just to see your old shipmate or to go to any goddamn movie. . . ."

"You're just imagining things. I just . . ."

"I'm not imagining anything," Bunny said. "I have feelings about you. When you're on the level. When you're hiding something. You're hiding something right now. I keep watching you when you don't know I'm looking and I don't like what I see, Wesley."

"Crap," Wesley said roughly. "Stop being an old lady."

"I know one thing," Bunny said. "Your father would hate to see you get into trouble—bad trouble—especially if it's because of that Danovic fellow. Are you listening to me, Wesley?"

"I'm listening."

"He loved you and the thing he wanted most was for you to have a good life. And that goes almost ditto for me. I don't want to have to visit you in prison or in a hospital or in a morgue."

"Don't make me feel sorry I came to see you, Bunny," Wesley said quietly.

"I don't care if you never see me again," Bunny said, "if I can hammer some sense into your head. You've got a great life ahead of you—don't ruin it. Your father's dead and that's that. Respect his memory, is all I'm asking from you."

"I've got to get back to my hotel," Wesley said; "I'm expecting a call."

Bunny was standing at the stern of the Chris-Craft staring coldly at Wesley as Wesley mounted the one-cylinder bicyclette he had rented and chugged off toward his hotel.

When Wesley reached the hotel, he saw the open Peugeot standing in the parking lot. He hurried into the hotel. "There's a gentleman waiting for you in the bar," the concierge told him as he gave Wesley his key.

Billy was sitting alone in the empty bar, sipping at a beer and staring out at the inlet of the bay on which the hotel was built. He looked small and disconsolate, slumped in his chair. His clothes were rumpled and he hadn't bothered to comb his hair, which had been whipped by the wind on his journey. The long trip to Paris and back in the open car had made his normally dark complexion two or three shades darker. He looks like a shifty little Arab, Wesley thought as he went up to him. Billy stood up as Wesley approached, and they shook hands.

"Well, Cousin," Wesley said, "it's about time."

"For Christ's sake," Billy said querulously, "are you going to start like that?"

"Let's go to my room," Wesley said, looking over at the barman who was peeling lemons at the other side of the room. "We can talk there."

"You might let me finish my beer," Billy said. "And you look as though you could use one yourself."

"There's a lot of things I could use more," Wesley said. "Drink up."

Billy looked around him. "This is a pretty fancy place," he said. "It must cost a fortune."

"I thought I was only going to be here a couple of days," Wesley said. "I didn't think I'd have to stay here the whole season. You finished with your beer?"

"I suppose so," Billy said, "but I have to pay."

"Put the gentleman's drink on my bill, please," Wesley called to the bartender at the other end of the room.

"Thanks," Billy said as he followed Wesley out of the bar.

"It's the least I could do," Wesley said sardonically, "for my true-blue cousin."

In his room, Wesley turned on Billy. "Have you got it?" he asked harshly.

"You have to let me explain," Billy said. "The man who was holding it for me is on the lam. He wasn't in Paris and his girlfriend said she didn't know where he is. But she said he would call her and . . ."

"When?" Wesley asked. "When is he going to call her?"

"She couldn't say. Soon, she thinks."

"Soon? The fourth of July? Christmas?"

"Jesus," Billy said aggrievedly, "there's no call for you to talk to me like that. I did my best. It's not like going into a store and buying a box of candy."

"You know what I think, Billy," Wesley said levelly, "I think you're lying to me."

"Don't be so goddamn suspicious. I volunteered, didn't I, for Christ's sake? Nobody put a gun to my head. All I was doing was trying to help."

"Balls," Wesley said. "You know where that gun is—if there ever was a gun . . ."

"There's a gun." Billy said. "I swear it."

"Then you're going to tell me where it is. And you're going to tell me right now." With a sudden, feline motion, Wesley leaped at Billy and began to choke him. Billy struggled, clawing at the hands around his throat and trying to use his knee to Wesley's groin. But Wesley outweighed him by forty pounds. Soundlessly, they struggled around the room. Billy slipped and was on the floor, with Wesley kneeling on him, his face calm, his hands pressing maniacally on Billy's throat. Just before Billy was about to black out, the hands relaxed.

"You going to tell me or not?" Wesley whispered.

"Christ," Billy gasped, "you could have choked me to death."

"Highly possible." Wesley's hands began to press a little harder.

"Rudolph . . ." Billy said brokenly. "He's in Saint-Paul-de-Vence . . . the Hôtel Colombe d'Or. Now will you get off my chest?"

Slowly, Wesley released his grip and stood. He helped Billy up and Billy fell into a chair, feeling his throat with his hands. "You're too fucking strong for your own good," he said.

Wesley stood over him, still threateningly. "How did Uncle Rudolph come into the picture?" he asked. "And no more fairy tales, Billy."

"I called him in New York. I thought if anybody could help you, he could. I did it for you. You don't think I did it for myself, do you?"

"You chickened out," Wesley said contemptuously. "And you called in Santa Claus. I should have known. What the hell would you expect from a tennis player? Go back to your fancy ladies, you bastard. What a royal fucking runaround."

"You go to Saint-Paul-de-Vence, you murdering idiot," Billy said, "and you try to choke your Uncle Rudolph."

"Maybe I'll just try that," Wesley said. "And now you get out of my room. And out of town. If I see you around I might be sorry I ever let up on you."

"The next time I see you," Billy said as he stood up. "I'm going to have a knife on me. I warn you."

"Thanks," Wesley said, "I'll keep that in mind."

At the door, Billy turned. "One last word," he said, "I'm your friend, no matter what you think."

Wesley nodded somberly and Billy opened the door and went out.

When he got downstairs he called Saint-Paul-de-Vence. When Rudolph came to the phone, Billy told him what had happened.

"Oh, Lord," Rudolph said. "He's as bad as that?"

"Worse," said Billy. "Demented. You'd better move to another hotel, if you don't want another choking session in the family."

"I'm not moving anywhere," Rudolph said calmly. "Let him come."

"Just don't see him alone," Billy said, admiring his uncle's serenity. "With that boy you need plenty of witnesses."

"I'll see him any way he wants."

"Have you come up with anything?"

"Maybe," Rudolph said. "We'll see."

"If I can give you some advice," Billy said, "I'd get rid of the thing before he gets there. Throw it in the sea."

"No," Rudolph said thoughtfully, "I don't believe I want to do that. It may come in handy. In the not too distant future."

"Good luck," Billy said.

"I'll see you next week in Cannes, at the festival," Rudolph said. "I've reserved rooms at the Hôtel Majestic for all of us. I put you in a room with Wesley. Given the circumstances . . ." He chuckled oddly. "Given the circumstances, I think I'll put you on another floor."

"You think of everything, don't you, Rudolph," Billy said sarcastically.

"Almost everything," Rudolph said.

Billy hung up and went over to the concierge's desk and said, "Please put the call on Mr. Abbott's bill."

Wesley didn't call that day or the next, but the lawyer from Antibes did.

"I may have some news," the lawyer said. "The gentleman I have in mind to apply for the position you spoke to me about the other day is not available for the moment. He happens to be in prison in Fresnes. But he is due to get out in two weeks and he is expected at his home in Marseilles shortly after that. I will be in touch with him and will tell him where he can reach you."

"I'll be at the Hôtel Majestic in Cannes," Rudolph said.

"I'm sorry about the delay," the lawyer said.

"It can't be helped," Rudolph said. "Thank you for your trouble. I'll be expecting the call."

It can't be helped, Rudolph thought as he hung up. That would be a good title for the story of my life. It can't be helped.

CHAPTER 10

THE PUBLICITY MAN at the festival for Gretchen's movie had put out a story about the woman whose first picture as a director had been chosen as one of the American entries to be shown in Cannes, so there were photographers at the Nice airport when Gretchen's plane came in. The photographers took pictures of Gretchen getting off the plane and then again as she greeted Billy and Rudolph after going through customs. She was near tears as she kissed Billy and hugged him, hard. "It's been so long," she whispered.

Billy was embarrassed at the show of maternal emotion with flashbulbs popping off and extricated himself, gently but firmly, from his mother's embrace. "Mother," he said, "why don't we save the reunion scene for later?" He didn't like the idea of a photograph of himself being clutched in a domestic stranglehold appearing in the papers, publicity or no publicity.

As Gretchen stepped back Billy saw her lips set in the cold line that was all too familiar to him. "Billy," she said, her tone formal, "let me introduce you to Mr. Donnelly. He did the sets for our picture."

Billy shook hands with the red-bearded young man. "Glad to meet you, sir," he said. Another one, he thought. She never gives up. He had noticed the possessive, protective way the man had held his mother's arm as they came through the small crowd grouped around the exit from the customs. He had intended to be warm and responsive at this first meeting after so long, but the sight of his mother, as beautiful as ever in her smart blue traveling suit, being squired ostentatiously off the plane by a man who seemed not much older than himself had disturbed him.

Then he felt ashamed for allowing himself to be annoyed. After all, his mother was a big grown woman and what she did on her own time and her taste in partners was none of his business. As he walked beside her toward the chauffeured car that had been sent for her, he squeezed her hand affectionately, to make up for the remark about the reunion scene. She looked at him, surprised, then smiled widely. "We're going to have a great two weeks," she said.

"I hope so," he said. "I can't wait to see the picture."

"The omens are good," she said. "The people who've seen it so far seem to like it a great deal."

"A lot more than a great deal," Rudolph said. "People're raving about it. I've already been offered a hundred percent profit on my share of it and I've turned it down."

"Faithful brother," Gretchen said lightly. "He puts his money where his heart is." Then she frowned. "Rudy," she said, "you don't look well. You look as though you haven't slept in weeks. What's the matter?"

Rudolph laughed uneasily. "Nothing. Maybe I've been staying up too late at the casino."

"Have you been winning?"

"As always," Rudolph said.

As the porter and the chauffeur were putting the bags in the car, Gretchen said, "I'm a little disappointed."

"Why?" Rudolph asked.

"I'd hoped that Wesley would come to meet me, too."

Rudolph and Billy exchanged glances.

"Isn't he staying at the hotel with us?" Gretchen asked.

"No," said Rudolph.

"He's in Cannes, isn't he? After the picture's shown, he's going to be mobbed by the papers and TV people for interviews. He's got to *behave* like an actor even if he doesn't think he is one."

"Gretchen," Rudolph said softly, "we don't know where he is. He was in Saint-Tropez the last we knew, but he's disappeared."

"Is there anything wrong?"

"Not that we know of," Rudolph lied. "Don't worry, I'm sure he'll turn up."

"He'd better," Gretchen said, as she and Donnelly got into the car. "Or I'll send out a missing persons alarm."

With all the baggage there was no room in the car for Rudolph. He and Billy went toward where the Peugeot was parked. "We'd better cook up *some* kind of story for her about Wesley," Rudolph said as they got into the Peugeot.

"*You* cook up the story this time," Billy said, as they drove out of the parking lot. "The last story I cooked up nearly got me killed."

"Maybe when he sees Gretchen's picture in the papers, he'll come around," Rudolph said. "He grew very fond of her while they were shooting."

"I know. He told me so. Still, I wouldn't be too hopeful. What he's really fond of these days is finding a certain Yugoslav." He turned his head and peered curiously at Rudolph. "Anything new on your front?"

"I won't know for a few days yet."

"You still don't want to tell me what it might be?"

"No," Rudolph said decisively. "And don't pry."

Billy devoted himself to his driving for a minute or so. He had had the car washed and he had dressed in clean, neat clothes for his mother's arrival. He was sorry that Wesley's absence had cast a shadow over the occasion. "I hope," he said, "that wherever he is or whatever he does, he doesn't spoil my mother's big moment. She seemed in great spirits at the airport."

"Except when you made that snide crack about the reunion," Rudolph said sourly.

"Force of habit."

"Well, break the habit."

"I'll try," Billy said. "Anyway, for your information, I made up for it on the way to the car."

"You think she's tough," Rudolph said. "Well, let me tell you something—she isn't. Certainly not about you."

"I'll try, I said." Billy smiled. "She looks beautiful, doesn't she?"

"Very."

Again, Billy turned his head to peer at Rudolph. "What's there between her and that Donnelly fellow?"

"Nothing that I know of," Rudolph said curtly. "They worked well together and he's now a business associate of mine, too. Don't pry into that, either."

"I was just asking," Billy said. "A son's natural concern for his mother's welfare. What sort of guy is he?"

"One of the best," Rudolph said. "Talented, ambitious, honest, with a drinking problem."

"She ought to be used to that," Billy said, "after her life with my father. The drinking part, I mean."

"She invited your father to come over, too," Rudolph said. "He said he had a new job and couldn't leave Chicago. Maybe he's taking hold of himself at last."

"I wouldn't bet on that," said Billy. "Well, he's done at least one useful thing for his son."

"What's that?"

"He turned me off drink." Billy chuckled. "Say—I have an idea. Not about my father or my mother—about Wesley."

"What's that?"

"You know, the police pick up those forms you have to fill in when you check into a hotel . . ."

"Yes."

"I don't think Wesley knows anybody he could stay with in Cannes," Billy went on earnestly, "so he's most probably in a hotel in the town. We could go to the police and ask for information. After all, he's in the picture and we could say he's needed for press photographs and interviews, stuff like that."

"We could, but we won't," Rudolph said. "The less interest the police take in Wesley, the better it will be for all of us."

"It was just an idea."

"We'll just have to find him ourselves. Hang around the port, go to the nightclubs, generally keep our eyes open," Rudolph said. "Meanwhile, you can tell your mother that he told you he's shy about any publicity before the picture is shown, he's afraid he's no good in it and that people will laugh at him, he'd rather not be around if that happens . . ."

"Do you think she'll go for that?" Billy said doubtfully.

"Maybe. She knows he's a strange young man. She'll probably say it's just what you could expect from him."

"What I'm surprised at," Billy said, "is that he never called you or came to see you."

"I was almost sure he wouldn't," Rudolph said. "He knows that he'd never get what he was looking for out of me."

"Have you still got it?" Billy asked. "The gun?"

"Yes."

Billy chuckled again. "I bet you're the only one at this festival with a gun with a silencer in his hotel room."

"It's a distinction I would gladly renounce," Rudolph said bleakly.

When they drove down the Croisette in Cannes, Rudolph saw that among the posters advertising the movies to be shown in the next two weeks there was one for *Restoration Comedy* and that Gretchen's name was prominently displayed.

"She must have gotten a kick seeing that," Rudolph said. "Your mother."

"Now," Billy said, joking, "with all the other things I have to worry about her for, I'll have to figure out how to handle being the son of a famous mother. What do I say if they interview me and ask me how it feels?"

"Say it feels great."

"Next question, Mr. Abbott," Billy said. "Did your mother, in your opinion, neglect you in the interest of her career? Answer—only for ten or fifteen years."

"You can joke like that with me," Rudolph said sharply, "but not with anyone else. You understand that?"

"Yes, sir. Of course I was kidding."

"Anyway," said Rudolph, "she's not famous yet. In a place like this, you can be famous one day and nonfamous the next. It's a tricky emotional time for your mother and we've got to be very careful with her."

"I will be steadfast as an oak in her support," Billy said. "She will not recognize her wayward son and will look at me in amazement."

"You may not drink like your father, Billy," Rudolph said, "but you seem to have inherited his lack of ability to make anyone believe he ever took anything seriously."

"A protective device," Billy said lightly, "passed on from father to son, to hide the quivering, tender soul hidden beneath."

"Let it show once in a while," Rudolph said. "It won't kill you."

When they went into the lobby of the hotel, Rudolph asked if there were any messages for him. There were no messages.

Gretchen was in a corner of the lobby, surrounded by journalists and photographers. The big guns had not yet arrived in Cannes and the publicity man for *Restoration Comedy* was making the most of it. Rudolph saw that Gretchen was talking smoothly, smiling and at ease.

Gretchen saw them and gestured for them to join her, but Billy shook his head. "I'm going out," he said to Rudolph. "I'll take a swing around the port looking for our lost angel child. Tell my mother I love her but I had an errand to run."

Rudolph went over to Gretchen and she introduced him as her brother and a backer of the film. She didn't inquire where Billy had gone. In a lull in the questioning, when a photographer asked Grechen to pose with Rudolph, Rudolph asked her where Donnelly was.

"One guess," she said, smiling up at Rudolph for the photograph.

Rudolph went to the bar and saw Donnelly hunched over it gloomily, a glass of whiskey in front of him.

"Enjoying the fun and frolic of the famous festival?" Rudolph asked.

Donnelly scowled at him. "I'll add another f. I shouldn't have fucking come," he said.

"Why not?" Rudolph asked, surprised.

"That kid," Donnelly said. "Her son, Billy. He gave me the old cold eye at the airport."

"You're imagining things."

"I didn't imagine this. I'm afraid he's going to make Gretchen's life miserable on account of me. What is he—jealous?"

"No," Rudolph said. "Maybe he's worried that you're so much younger than she and that she'll get hurt."

"Did he tell you that?"

"No," Rudolph admitted. "He didn't say anything."

"She's told me about him." Donnelly drank what was left in his glass and signaled for another. "He's been a pain in the ass since he was a kid."

"He's turned over a new leaf, he told me."

"He wasn't turning over any new leaves at the Nice airport, I'll tell you that. And where's the other kid—Wesley? The two of them were supposed to drive up together from Spain, according to Gretchen."

"He's around," Rudolph said vaguely.

"Where around?" Donnelly demanded. "He wasn't around when we got in and he damn well should have been, after all Gretchen did for him." He sipped thirstily from the second glass. "I'll bet a dollar against a plugged nickel that son of hers has something to do with it."

"Don't be neurotic about one look at an airport," Rudolph said. "I guarantee that everything will be all right."

"It better be," Donnelly said. "If that kid ruins these next two weeks for his mother, I'll break his back for him. And you can tell him that for me. You can also tell him I've asked his mother to marry me."

"What did she say?"

"She laughed."

"Congratulations."

"I'm just so crazy about her I can't see straight," Donnelly said gloomily.

"You'd see straighter . . ." Rudolph tapped the glass on the bar lightly, "if you laid off this stuff a bit."

"Are *you* going to bitch about it, too?"

"I imagine Gretchen must have mentioned something of that nature in passing."

"So she did. I promised her that if she married me I'd go the wine route only."

"What did she say to that?"

"She laughed."

Rudolph chuckled. "Have a good time in Cannes," he said.

"I will," Donnelly said, "but only if Gretchen does. By the way, the day before we left New York, our lawyer called and said that he thinks there's a good chance we can settle the Connecticut business before the year's out."

"Everything's going our way, lad," Rudolph said. "Stop looking so darkly Irish."

"The Celtic twilight on the Côte d'Azur," Donnelly said, breaking into a smile. "I see demons in the Gallic dusk. Pay it no heed, man.''

Rudolph patted Donnelly's arm in a comforting, friendly gesture and left the bar. In the hall he saw that the press conference was over, although the publicity man was still there, assembling papers. The publicity man was an American by the name of Simpson who worked out of Paris for various movie companies.

"How did it go?" Rudolph asked him.

"Fine," the man said. "She knows how to use her charm with those guys. You know, I saw the picture at a screening in Paris and I think we've got a winner there."

Rudolph nodded, although he'd never heard of a publicity man who said he had a loser the first week on the job. "I'd like you to make a special effort," he said, "to get Wesley Jordan's photograph spread around."

"No sweat," the man said. "The word's out already that he's something special. His looks won't hurt, either."

"He's missing in action somewhere in the neighborhood," Rudolph said, "and I want people to recognize him so that we can find him for background stories before the picture's shown."

"Will do," the publicity man said. "I could use some personal stuff on him myself."

"Thanks," Rudolph said and went up to his room. The bag was where he had left it on a chair. He twirled the combination lock and opened it. The automatic was still there. What an ugly piece of furniture, he thought, as he closed and locked the bag again. He found himself going to his room and looking into the bag ten times a day.

He went into the bathroom and took two Miltowns. Ever since he had arrived in Paris he had been jittery and had developed the first tic of his life, a twitching of the right eyelid that he tried to hide when he was with anybody else by rubbing at the eye as though he had something caught in it. The Miltown helped each time for an hour or two.

The phone was ringing when he went back into the bedroom. He picked it up and heard a woman's voice saying, "Mr. Rudolph Jordache, please."

"Speaking," he said.

"You don't know me," the woman said. "I'm a friend of Wesley's. My name is Alice Larkin."

"Oh, yes," Rudolph said. "Wesley's spoken about you. Where're you calling from?"

"New York," Alice said. "Is Wesley with you?"

"No."

"Do you know where I can reach him?"

"Not at the moment, I'm afraid."

"He was supposed to call me last week," Alice said. "I was trying to get my vacation moved up so that I could come over to Cannes for a few days. I think I can manage it. I'll be told definitely tomorrow and I'd like to know if he still wants me to come."

"I think you'd better wait before making any decision," Rudolph said. "To be honest with you, Wesley's disappeared. If he turns up, I'll tell him to call you."

"Is he in trouble?" Alice asked anxiously.

"Not that I know of." Rudolph spoke carefully. "Although it's hard to tell with him. He's an unpredictable boy."

"You can say that again." Now the girl sounded angry. "Anyway, if you do happen to see him, tell him that I wish him all sorts of success."

"I'll do that," Rudolph said. He put the phone down slowly. He wished the Miltowns would start working quickly. The burden of Wesley's obsession was wearing him down. Maybe, he thought, when I do find him I'll give him the goddamn gun and wash my hands of the whole thing. He went over to the window and looked out at the sea, calm and blue, and the people walking below on the Croisette, enjoying the sunshine, with the flags above their heads snapping festively in the warm breeze.

Momentarily he envied each and every stroller on the broad avenue below, just for not being him.

Billy got back to his room at dusk. He had patrolled the old port all afternoon, peering at the boats and going into the bars and restaurants. Wesley had not been on any of the boats or in any of the bars or restaurants. He called his mother's room, but the operator said that she was not taking any calls. Probably in the sack, he thought, with that fellow with the beard. Best not to think about it.

He undressed and took a shower. It had been a long hot day and he luxuriated under the needle-sharp cold spray, forgetting everything but the delicious tingling of his skin.

When he got out of the shower he heard a knock on the bedroom door. He wrapped a towel around his waist and, leaving wet footprints on the carpet, he went to the door and opened it. Monika stood there, smiling, in one of the pretty cotton gowns he had seen her wearing in Spain.

"Good Lord," he said.

"I see you're dressed to receive guests," she said. "May I come in?"

He peered past her into the corridor to see if she was alone.

"Don't worry," she said, "this is a social visit. There's nobody with me." She brushed past him and he closed the door. "My," she said, looking around at the large, handsomely furnished room, "we're moving up in the world, aren't we? This beats Brussels by a mile, doesn't it? Capitalism becomes you, laddy."

"How'd you find me?" Billy asked, ignoring what she had said about the improvement over Brussels.

"It was easy," she said. "This time you left a forwarding address."

"I must remember never to do that again," he said. "What do you want?" He felt foolish, standing there soaking wet, with the towel precariously draped around him.

"I just wanted to say hello." She sat down and crossed her legs and smiled up at him. "Do you mind if I smoke?"

"What would you do if I said I *did* mind?"

"I'd smoke." She laughed and took a cigarette out of her bag but didn't light it.

"I'll put some clothes on," he said. "I'm not used to entertaining strange ladies naked." He started past her toward the bathroom, where his pants and shirt were hanging.

She dropped the cigarette and reached out and held his arm. "No need," she said. "I'm not as strange as all that. Besides—the less you're wearing the better you look." She took her hand off his arm and reached around and held him, encircling his legs. She tilted her head and looked up at him. "Give me a kiss."

He pulled against the pressure of her arm, but she held him tight. "What're you up to now?" he said harshly, although he could feel the familiar stirrings in his groin.

She chuckled. "The same old thing," she said.

"It wasn't the same old thing in Spain," he said, cursing the sudden erection that plainly bulked under the towel.

"I had other things on my mind in Spain," she said. "And I wasn't alone then, if you remember. Now I'm alone and on holiday and it's the same old thing. I think I told you once that orgasms are few and far between on the New Left. That hasn't changed." With a swift motion, she reached under the towel and put her hand on his penis. She chuckled again. "I see this hasn't changed either." She caressed him gently, her hand moving with remembered deftness.

"Oh, Christ," he said, sure that he was finally going to regret what he was saying, "let's get into bed."

"That was my general idea," she said. She stood up and they kissed. "I missed you," she whispered. "Just lie down while I get these clothes off."

He went over to the wide bed and lay down, the towel still draped around him, and watched as she pulled the pretty dress over her head. She wasn't wearing a brassiere and the sight of the lovely small breasts made him ache with pleasure. He closed his eyes. One last time, he thought, what the hell? His mother was probably doing the same thing one floor above. Like mother, like son. A big evening for the family. He heard Monika moving barefooted toward the bed, and the click of a switch as she turned off the light. He threw off the towel. She fell on top of him with a low moan and he put his arms around her.

Later, in the warm darkness, he was lying on his back, his arm under her neck, as she snuggled against him, her head on his shoulder, one leg thrown across him. He sighed. "The best," he said, "the very goddamn best. All in favor say, Aye."

"Aye," Monika said. "From now on always remember to leave a forwarding address."

"Aye," he said, although he wasn't sure he meant it. He had been through too much with her and the only place he felt safe with her was in bed. "What's *your* address now?"

"What do you have to know that for?"

"I might just happen to be passing your hotel," he said, "and be suddenly overcome with an irresistible urge."

"I'll see you here," she said, "when *I* happen to be overcome with an irresistible urge. I don't want to be seen with you. You'll see me often enough. But only in this room."

"Dammit." He wriggled his arm free from under her neck and sat up. "Why do you always have to be the one who calls the signals."

"Because that's the way I like to operate," she said.

"Operate," he said. "I don't like that word."

"Learn to live with it, laddy," Monika said. She sat up, too, and searched for the pack of cigarettes she had put on the bedside table. She took out a cigarette and lit it, the small flare of the match illuminating her face and eyes.

"I thought you said you were on holiday," Billy said.

"Holidays end."

"If you don't tell me where I can get hold of you, *this* is the end," Billy said angrily.

"I'll see you here," she said, inhaling smoke, "same time tomorrow."

"Bitch."

"I've always been amused by your vocabulary." She got out of bed and began dressing, the glow of her cigarette the only light in the dark room. "By the way, I saw your cousin coming out of a hotel this afternoon. You know, the boy you used to play tennis with."

"You did?" Billy said. "Who told you he was my cousin?"

"I looked him up in *Who's Who*."

"Funny as usual, aren't you? What hotel was it?"

Monika hesitated. "Isn't he staying here with you?"

"No. What hotel? We have to find him."

"Who's we?"

"What difference does that make to you?" Billy tried to keep his voice down.

"You never can tell what difference it might make to me. Who's we?"

"Forget it."

"Actually," Monika said, "I don't remember the name of the hotel."

"You're lying."

She laughed. "Perhaps. Maybe if you're here, like a good boy, tomorrow evening, I might remember it."

"Did you talk to him?"

"No. I'm interested in another member of the family."

"God," Billy said, "you know how to make sex complicated."

"Sex?" she said. "Once upon a time you used to use the word love."

"Once upon a time," Billy said grimly.

"Have it your own way, laddy," Monika said lightly. "For the moment. One last compliment—you're better in bed than on a tennis court."

"Thanks."

"*Pour rien*, as the French say." She threw away her cigarette and came over to the bed and bent and kissed his cock, briefly. "Good night, laddy," she said, "I have to go now."

As the door closed behind her Billy lay back against the pillows, staring up at the dark ceiling. Another problem. He had to decide whether or not to tell Rudolph that Wesley had been seen coming out of a hotel in Cannes that day, but that he didn't know the name of the hotel, although he might find out tomorrow. But then he'd have to explain how he had heard it and why he had to wait for tomorrow. And he couldn't explain anything, without at least mentioning Monika. And then he'd have to explain something, at least, about Monika. He shook his head irritably against the pillow. Rudolph had enough on his mind without having to worry about Monika.

The phone rang. It was Rudolph to tell him that they would all meet at the bar downstairs in a half hour before going to dinner. After he hung up, Billy went in and took another shower. He didn't want to go to dinner smelling as though he had been in an orgy. He wondered if his mother was upstairs now also taking a shower.

CHAPTER 11

"No," Gretchen was saying, "I don't want any party after the showing. I'm exhausted and all I want to do is fall into bed and sleep for forty-eight hours." She was in the salon of her small suite with Donnelly and Rudolph. It had been Rudolph's suggestion that after the evening performance of *Restoration Comedy* they should celebrate by having a gala supper, inviting the festival judges and some of the representatives of the major distribution companies as well as several of the newspapermen with whom Gretchen and Rudolph had become more or less intimate in the last few days. Gretchen was showing increasing signs of tensions as the date approached. A party might help her unwind.

"If there was anyone else but us three here," Gretchen said, "maybe a party would be called for. But I don't want to be the only one to accept the kudos, if there *are* going to be any kudos to accept, or the only one to see the long faces of all those people if the picture flops. If Frances Miller and Wesley were here, I'd say yes, but that little bitch couldn't take the trouble to come and you can't find Wesley for me and I'm too old for parties anyway. . . ."

"Okay," Rudolph said. "No party. We'll have a nice little foursome for supper—us three and Billy—and congratulate each other." He looked at his watch. "It's getting late," he said. "I suggest you go to bed and try to get some sleep." He kissed Gretchen good night and started toward the door.

"I'll go along with you," Donnelly said, "I need some sleep, too. Unless you want me to stay, Gretchen . . ."

"No, thanks," Gretchen said. "See you in the morning."

In the corridor, on the way to the elevator, Donnelly said, "I have to talk to you about her, Rudy. I'm worried. She's taking it too hard. She can't sleep and she's dosing herself with pills and she has crazy crying fits when she's alone with me and I don't know how to stop her."

"I wish I were a woman," Rudolph said. "I'd like to break down and cry myself."

"I thought you felt fine about the picture." Donnelly sounded surprised.

"I do," Rudolph said. "It's not that. It has nothing to do with the picture."

"What then?"

"Some other time," Rudolph said.

"Can I help?"

"Yes," said Rudolph. "Take care of Gretchen."

"Maybe," Donnelly said, "it would be a good idea, after the showing, if I got into a car with her and took her on a little sight-seeing trip—get out of this madhouse for a couple of days."

"I'd be for that," Rudolph said, "if you could convince her."

"I'll try in the morning."

"Good man," Rudolph said, as the elevator door opened. "Good night, David. Sleep well." Donnelly walked back along the corridor and stopped in front of the door to Gretchen's salon. There was no sound from the room. Donnelly put out his hand to rap on the door, then stopped himself. Tonight, he thought, it's probably better if she sleeps alone. He went back toward the elevator and took it down to the ground floor where he strode into the bar. He hesitated when the bartender asked him what he wanted. He ordered a whiskey and soda. The wine route could wait for another time.

The phone was ringing when Rudolph unlocked the door to his room. He hurried over to the phone and picked it up to say hello. "*Monsieur* Jordache . . ." It was a man's voice.

"Yes."

"*L'avocat d'Antibes*," the man said, "*m'a dit que vous voulez me parler . . .*"

"Do you speak English?" Rudolph said. If it was the man he thought it was he had to understand every word he said. He might just barely be able to arrange a murder in English, but never in high-school French.

"A leetle," the man said. He had a hoarse, low voice. "The lawyer of Antibes, he say per'aps we do a leetle business together . . ."

"When can we meet?"

"Now," the man said.

"Where?"

"*A la gare*. Z' station. I stand by z' bar in z' buffet."

"Ten minutes," Rudolph said. "How will I recognize you?"

"I am dressed z' following," the man said. "Blue pantalons, jacket brown, I am small man, w'z grand belly."

"Good," Rudolph said. "Ten minutes." He hung up. Blue pants, brown jacket, big belly. Well, he wasn't picking the man for his beauty or his taste in clothing. He unlocked his bag, peered in. The automatic was still there. He closed the bag, locked it and went out.

Downstairs, he went into the cashier's room behind the desk and had his safe-deposit box opened. He had had ten thousand dollars sent over from his bank in New York and had converted them into francs. Whatever was going to happen, good or bad, he knew would cost money. He looked down at the neat bundles of bills, considered for a moment, then took out five thousand francs. He put the remaining bundles back in the box and locked it. Then he went out of the hotel and got into a taxi. "*La gare*," he said. He tried to think of nothing on the short trip to the station. He fumbled as he pulled some ten-franc notes out of his pocket and his hand was shaking as he took the change and tipped the driver.

He saw the fat little dark man in the blue pants and brown jacket standing at the bar, a glass of pastis in front of him. "Good evening, *monsieur*," he said as he went up to the man.

The man turned and looked soberly at him. He was dark, with a fat face and small, deep-set black eyes. His lips were thick and wet. An incongruous baby-blue cotton golf hat that was too small for him sat back from his domed and wrinkled forehead. It was not a prepossessing face or one that in other circumstances Rudolph would have been inclined to trust. "Per'aps we go for walk," the man said. He had a strong Provençal accent. "Z' light here bad for z' eyes."

They went out together and walked away from the station and along a narrow, dark, deserted street. It could have been a thousand miles away from the bright, crowded bustle of the festival.

"I listen proposal," the man said.

"Do you know a man called Danovic?" Rudolph asked. "Yugoslav. Small-time hoodlum."

"'oodlum?" the man said. "What z' 'oodlum?"

"*Voyou,*" Rudolph said.

"Ah."

"Do you know him?"

The man walked ten paces in silence. Then he shook his head. "Per'aps under different name. Where you t'ink 'e z'?"

"Cannes, most likely," Rudolph said. "Last time he was seen it was in a nightclub here—La Porte Rose."

The man nodded. "Bad place," he said. "Varry bad."

"Yes."

"If I find him, what 'appens?"

"You will get a certain number of francs if you dispose of him."

"Dispose?" the man said.

"Kill." Good God, Rudolph thought, is it me who is saying this?

"*Compris,*" the man said. "Now we talk money. What you mean certain number of francs?"

"Say—fifty thousand," Rudolph said. "About ten thousand dollars, if you want it in dollars."

"'ow much advance? Now? To find z' man."

"I have five thousand francs on me," Rudolph said. "You can have that."

The man stopped. He put out a pudgy hand. "I take money now."

Rudolph took out his wallet and slipped out the bills. He watched as the man carefully counted them by the dim light of a streetlamp thirty feet away. I wonder what he would say, Rudolph thought, if I asked him for a receipt. He almost laughed aloud at the thought. He was dealing with a world where the only guarantee was vengeance.

The man stuffed the bills into an inside pocket of his coat. "When I find him," he said, "'ow much I get?"

"Before or after the . . . the job?"

"Before."

"Twenty thousand," Rudolph said. "That would make half the total."

"*D'accord,*" the man said. "And after, how I make sure I am paid?"

"Any way you want."

The man thought for a moment. "When I say I find him," he said, "you put twenty-five thousand in hands of lawyer. The lawyer read in *Nice-Matin* he is . . . what word you used?"

"Disposed of," Rudolph said.

"Dispose," the man said, "and a friend of me go to lawyer office for rest of money. We shake on deal?"

Rudolph had shaken hands on a variety of deals in the past and had celebrated after. There would be no celebration after this handshake.

"Stay near z' telephone," the man said and turned and walked quickly back in the direction of the station.

Rudolph took a deep breath and started walking slowly toward the Croisette and his hotel. He thought of the two men who had ambushed him in the hallway of the house in New York and who had been so furious that a man who looked as prosperous as he did had only a few dollars on him to reward them for their trouble. If anybody mugged him tonight on the dark streets of Cannes, they'd probably leave him for dead after they'd searched his pockets. He didn't have much more than cab fare left.

Billy was awakened by a knocking on his door. He got sleepily out of bed and barefooted and in pajamas he went over to the door and opened it. Monika was standing there, smoking a cigarette, a raincoat draped over her shoulders like a cape. She came in quickly and he closed the door and switched on a lamp.

"Hello," Billy said, "I was wondering when you would turn up." It had been four days since her visit.

"Did you miss me?" She threw off her coat and sat on the rumpled bed, facing him, smiling.

"I'll tell you later," Billy said. "What time is it?"

"Twelve-thirty," Monika said.

"You keep some weird office hours."

"Better late than never," she said. "Wouldn't you agree?"

"I'll tell you later about that, too," he said. "The fact is, I like afternoons better."

"How European you've become."

"What the hell do *you* do with your afternoons?"

Monika smiled demurely up at him. "Curiosity killed the cat," she said.

Billy grunted. "I see this is your night for clichés," he said. "Did you remember the name yet of the hotel where you saw my cousin?"

"I am trying hard," Monika said. "Sometimes it seems to be almost on the tip of my tongue."

"Oh, balls," Billy said.

"What a nice word," she said. She threw her cigarette to the floor and ground it into the carpet. Billy winced. Her manner of dressing had improved considerably but her housewifely instincts were still at the Brussels level. She stood up and came over to him and put her arms around him and kissed him, her tongue sliding softly inside his mouth. His erection was immediate. He tried to think of other things, whether it was time to have the oil changed in his car, whether he wanted to play tennis the next day or not, if he had to get his dinner jacket pressed for the evening performance of *Restoration Comedy* two nights from then, but it was no good. "Let's go to bed," he muttered.

"I was wondering how long it was going to take you to say that." She chuckled, sure of the hold she had on him.

An hour later she said, "It's not too bad at night, either, is it?"

He kissed her throat. She wriggled out of his arms and slid from the bed and stood up. "I have to go now," she said.

"Why the hell can't you stay the night?" he said, disappointed. "At least once."

"Previous engagements." She began to dress. It didn't take her long. She put on her panties, girlishly plain and white, over her tan, shapely legs and slipped her dress over her head. He watched her, feeling deprived, as she pulled on her ballet slippers and combed her hair in front of the mirror. "By the way," she said, "we decided to call in our debts."

A cold chill went over him and he drew the blankets over him. "What do you mean by that?" he said, trying to keep his voice calm.

"The Paris debt," she said, still combing her hair. "You remember that, I imagine?"

He said nothing and lay absolutely still.

"I'll tell you what you're going to do," she went on, tugging at her tangled hair with the comb. "Two nights from now, you're going to go to a bar called the Voile Vert on the rue d'Antibes at six P.M. There will be a man waiting for you. He will have two magazines with him, *L'Express* and *Le Nouvel Observateur*. He will be reading *L'Express* and the *Observateur* will also be on the table in front of him. You will sit down at the table with him and you will order a glass of wine. He will reach under the table and will pick up a sixteen-millimeter movie camera."

"Only it won't be a sixteen-millimeter movie camera," Billy said bitterly.

"You're learning," Monika said.

"Will you for Christ's sake stop combing your hair?" Billy said.

"You will take the camera and when you go into the Festival Hall that evening you will open it and take out what you find in it and hide it in an inconspicuous place. It will be timed to go off at nine forty-five." Monika finally put the comb down and pushed at her hair with her hands, twisting her body so that she could look at her reflection from the side.

"You must be out of your mind," Billy said, still with the blankets pulled up under his chin. "At nine forty-five they'll be running my mother's picture."

"Exactly," Monika said. "No one will suspect you. There will be dozens of photographers with all sorts of cameras. You can wander all over the building without anyone questioning you. That's why you were chosen for the job. Don't worry. Nobody's going to be hurt."

"You mean it's going to be a nice, harmless, friendly type of bomb?"

"You should know enough by now not to be sarcastic with me." Monika turned away from the mirror and faced him. "The police will be called at nine o'clock and told there is a bomb somewhere in the building. They'll clear the place in five minutes. We're not out to kill anybody. This time."

"What *are* you out to do?" Billy was ashamed of the quaver in his voice.

"A demonstration," Monika said evenly, "a demonstration which will have the greatest kind of publicity, with newspapermen, television crews all over the place and internationally famous people falling all over themselves to get out of there. If anything represents the rot of the whole system better than this disgusting fat circus, we haven't heard of it."

"What if I say no, I won't do it?"

"You will be dealt with," Monika said quietly. "When it is done to our satisfaction, I believe I'll remember what hotel your cousin is at. In the meanwhile I trust *you'll* remember—the Voile Vert, the two magazines, six P.M. Good night, laddy." She picked up her bag, threw her raincoat over her shoulders and went out the door.

As Billy went up the steps of the Festival Hall for the morning showing of *Restoration Comedy* with Gretchen and Donnelly and Rudolph, he said, "I think I'd like to sit downstairs in the orchestra with the peasants." The others had reserved seats in the balcony. He kissed his mother and whispered, *"Merde."*

"What's that?" Gretchen asked, surprised.

"It's French show-business for good luck," he said.

Gretchen smiled and gave him another quick kiss. "I hope you like the picture," she said.

"I hope so, too," he said gravely. He showed his ticket to the man at the door and went into the auditorium. It was already crowded, although the picture was not scheduled to start for another ten minutes. An inconspicuous place, he thought, an inconspicuous place. Everywhere he looked seemed like a highly conspicuous place to him. He went to the men's room. At the moment it was empty. There was a trash basket for paper towels. It would be possible, given thirty seconds alone, to open the back of the camera, take out the bomb and hide it. If he could manage thirty seconds alone.

The door to the men's room opened and a man in a flowered shirt came in and went over to the urinals. Billy ostentatiously washed his hands, pulled out a paper towel and dried them. Then he went out and found a seat near the front of the auditorium, where there were still a few vacant places. In the state he was in he didn't know whether or not he would be able to sit through the picture, which was another reason for not sitting beside his mother for the showing. But when the picture started he found himself immediately engrossed and even laughed with the rest of the audience at the humorous scenes. And Wesley's performance astonished him. It was Wesley all right, but a Wesley who had somehow blended someone else's character with his own, to become a boy hidden and besieged, revealing bits and pieces of himself at rare, emotional moments, by a glance, a movement of his head, a mumbled monosyllable, and through it all looking brutally handsome while suggesting sweetness and vulnerable sensitivity, even when the script demanded violence and cynical behavior from him.

After the final fade-out, the applause was loud and sustained, greater than that at any of the other movies Billy had heard about since the festival opened. Then people began turning around and applauding, and he saw that they were applauding his mother, who was standing, smiling tremulously, at the railing of the balcony. Billy, near tears himself, clapped with the heartiest of the people around him. As he filed out of the hall, moved by his mother's accomplishment, he wondered what had driven him to be such a bastard with his mother for all those years.

Outside, on the Croisette, he saw a cluster of young people getting autographs from a man who was standing with his back toward him. Whoever it was, he was almost obscured by a tall, bulky boy in blue jeans. Curiously, Billy went toward the group. Then he stopped. The man who was autographing programs and notebooks and scraps of paper was Wesley. Billy grinned. The ham, he thought, I should have known he couldn't resist seeing himself. He pushed his way, as politely as possible, through the little crowd around Wesley, who was bending over, signing a notebook held out to him by a short girl in a gypsy skirt. "Mr. Jordan," Billy said, lisping in a high, feminine voice, "will you sign my program for me? I think you're just wonderful."

Wesley looked up from the notebook. "Go fuck yourself, Billy," he said. But there was a pleased smile on his face.

Billy took Wesley's arm firmly. "That's all for the moment, boys and girls," he said loudly. "Mr. Jordan has to go upstairs for the press conference. Come with me, sir." He started off, still holding Wesley's arm. Wesley held back for a moment, then walked beside him. "You're just what my mother needs today," Billy said, "and you can't let her down."

"Yeah," Wesley said. "Jesus, she's a wonder, isn't she?"

"A wonder," said Billy. "And you're going to tell her so. You were pretty wonderful yourself in there, too, you know."

"Not too bad," Wesley said complacently, the smile now permanently glued on his face.

As they waited for the elevator to take them up to the conference room, Billy said in a low voice, "Any luck in finding the man?"

Wesley shook his head.

"Don't you think it's about time you forgot all about it?"

Finally, Wesley stopped smiling. "No, it's not time."

"Movie stars don't go around murdering people," Billy said.

"I'm not a movie star," Wesley said shortly.

"Everybody in Cannes knows your face by now," said Billy. "You won't be by yourself long enough to swat a fly without witnesses, let alone kill a man." Then he had to keep quiet because two other people joined them waiting for the elevator.

Gretchen was just beginning to speak in the conference room, crowded with journalists and cameramen, as Billy and Wesley came in. She saw them immediately and broke off what she was saying. "Ladies and gentlemen," she said, her voice not under full control, "I have just had a most pleasant surprise. One of the most promising young actors I have ever seen has just walked into the room. Wesley, will you come up here, please."

"Oh, Christ," Wesley muttered under his breath.

"Get up there, idiot." Billy pushed him toward the raised platform where Gretchen was standing. Slowly, Wesley made his way through the crowd and stepped onto the platform. Gretchen kissed him and then, addressing the room, said, "I have the honor to introduce Wesley Jordan."

There was hearty applause and flashbulbs going off everywhere and the smile, now a little glassy, reappeared on Wesley's face. Billy slipped out of the room. He could hear the applause continuing as he walked quickly toward the elevators.

Outside, he left the Croisette and went into a café and ordered a beer, took a sip, asked for a token for the telephone, then went downstairs, where the booth was located. He looked in the directory for the *préfecture de police,* found the number and dialed it. A man's voice said, *"Allo."*

"This evening at six o'clock at a café called Voile Vert, on the rue d'Antibes," Billy said in French, with a harsh Midi accent, which he had only used before to amuse people at parties, "you will find a man sitting at a table with a copy of *L'Express* in his hands and a copy of *Le Nouvel Observateur* on the table in front of him . . ."

"One moment." The policeman's voice was excited and he stumbled over the words. "Who is this? What do you want?"

"On the floor under the table," Billy went on, "you will find a bomb."

"A bomb!" the man shouted. "What are you saying? A bomb for what?"

"It will be timed to go off at nine forty-five tonight," Billy said. "Six this evening, the Voile Vert."

"Wait a minute. I must . . ." the policeman shouted more loudly.

Billy hung up the phone and went up to the bar and finished his beer.

They were in Gretchen's salon after the evening showing of the picture, drinking champagne, and Simpson, the publicity man, was saying, "We're going to take home everything—best picture, best actress, best supporting actor. I guarantee it." He was a tall gaunt man, with a mournful, seamed face and he waved his hands as he talked. "I usually have a tendency to look at the worse side of things, but this time . . ." He shook his head wonderingly, as though the immensity of the treasure entrusted to him was beyond his comprehension. "I've been coming to Cannes for fifteen years and I tell you that was one of the most enthusiastic audiences I've ever seen down here. As for you, young man," he turned to Wesley, who was sitting next to Billy on a small sofa, dressed in a dinner jacket that was too tight and too short that the publicity man had borrowed for him for the evening, "as for you, I'd bet my left nut that you're going home with a prize."

Wesley just sat there, a glass of champagne in his hand, the permanent glassy smile on his face. Billy got up and poured himself his fifth glass of champagne. He had sat through the beginning of the picture staring blankly at the screen. The images had made no sense to him and the dialogue had seemed to come out of the actors' mouths in spurts of nonsense syllables. He had kept looking at his watch until nine forty-five and then had slumped in his seat and closed his eyes.

Gretchen looked pale and drawn, nervously pulling a ring on and off her finger. The champagne that Billy had poured for her lay untouched in the glass on the end table beside her. She had said hardly a word all night. From time to time Rudolph, who was sitting next to her on the sofa, reached out and patted her arm soothingly. Donnelly, standing leaning against the fireplace, tugged at his beard and seemed annoyed at the publicity man's effusions.

"Tomorrow," Simpson said, "is going to be a full day for you, Gretchen, and for Wesley. Everybody, but *everybody,* will be wanting to talk to you and take photos. I'll give you the schedule at nine in the morning and . . ."

Rudolph and Donnelly exchanged glances and Rudolph stood up and broke in on Simpson. "If it's going to be a big day I think Gretchen had better get some rest. We all ought to leave her alone now."

"I think that's a good idea," Donnelly said.

"Of course," said Simpson. "It's just that I'm so excited with what we have here that . . ."

"We understand, old man," Rudolph said. He bent and kissed Gretchen. "Good night, Sister," he said.

She smiled wanly up at him. As they all prepared to leave she stood up and went over to Donnelly and took his hand. "David," she said, "could you stay on for a little while?"

"Of course," Donnelly said. He stared sternly at Billy.

Billy tried to smile, then kissed Gretchen's cheek. "Thanks, Mother," he said, "for a marvelous day."

Gretchen gripped his arm, briefly, then broke into a sob. "Forgive me," she said. "It's just that it's—well—it's all too much for me. I'll be all right in the morning." Wesley opened the door and was about to go out when Gretchen called to him. "Wesley, you're not going to disappear again, are you?"

"No, ma'am," Wesley said. "I'm just two floors down if you need me." Rudolph had tried to put him in the same room with Billy, but Billy had said he was afraid of sleeping in the bed next to Wesley's, there was no telling what that crazy boy might do, even on a night like this. He hadn't told Rudolph what he really was afraid of and with any luck Rudolph would never find out.

As the door closed behind the four men and they went down the corridor, Rudolph said, "I'm not sleepy. I have a bottle of champagne in my room, too. Would you like to help me with it?"

"I have some people to see about tomorrow," Simpson said, "but you boys drink hearty." He stood against the back of the elevator wall, gaunt and mournful, doomed to praise other people and never himself all his life, as he raised an eloquent hand in a parting salute to the uncle and two nephews who were going to continue the evening's celebration with a bottle of champagne while he prepared the morning.

As Rudolph wrestled with the cork of the champagne bottle, he noticed Wesley eyeing the locked bag on the chair near the window. "I bet," Wesley said, as the cork popped and Rudolph began to pour, "I bet it's right in there."

"What's right in there?" Rudolph said.

"You know what I'm talking about," Wesley said.

"Drink your champagne." Rudolph raised his glass.

Wesley put his glass down deliberately and reached into the pocket of the borrowed dinner jacket and brought out a small pistol. "I don't need it anymore," he said evenly. "Keep it as a souvenir."

"Crazy as ever," Billy said.

"I'll drink to that," Wesley said.

They drank.

Wesley put the pistol back in his pocket.

"So," Rudolph said, "you were sitting there in the hall watching yourself act and taking bows with that thing on you all night."

"Yep," Wesley said. "You never know when a target might show up."

Rudolph paced around the room, frowning. "Wesley," he said, "what if I told you that the matter will be taken care of without your having to do anything about it?"

"What does that mean? Taken care of?"

"It means that right now, as we drink champagne in this room, a professional killer is looking for your man."

"I'd say I don't want anybody to do the job for me," Wesley said coldly, "and I don't want any more gifts from you or anyone else."

"I intend to stay here in Cannes until the end of the festival," Rudolph said. "That's only ten days. If the job isn't done by then, I'm going home and calling it quits. All I want from you is a promise that you won't do anything until then. After that, you're on your own."

"I'm not promising anything," Wesley said.

"Wesley . . ." Billy said.

Wesley turned on him sharply. "You keep out of this. You've meddled enough already."

"Calm down," Rudolph said. "Both of you. Another thing, Wesley. Your friend

Miss Larkin called the other day. You owe her a lot, too."

"More than you know," Wesley said. "What did she have to say?"

"She wants to come over here. She thinks she can get leave from the magazine for two weeks. She's waiting for a call from you."

Wesley finished his glass of wine. "Let her wait," he said.

"She said you knew she might come over. That you wanted her to come."

"I thought the whole thing would be over by now," Wesley said. "Well, it isn't over. I'll see her some other time."

"Ah, the hell with it," Rudolph said. "I'm not going to play Cupid with all the other things I'm doing. Let's finish the bottle. I'm going to get some sleep."

"What're you going to do now?" Billy asked Wesley when they were alone in front of the hotel.

"Night patrol," Wesley said. "Want to come along?"

"No."

Wesley looked quizzically at Billy. "What do you think of all this?" he asked.

"I'm scared shitless," Billy said. "For all of us."

Wesley nodded solemnly.

"I'll walk with you as far as the parking lot," Billy said. "I forgot to put the top up on the car and it looks as though it might rain."

Wesley helped as they put the top up and Billy rolled up the windows. "Wesley," Billy said, "it still would be a nice idea if we two drove up to Paris, with a few stops for tennis and feasts along the way. You could ask your girl to meet you there. They'll drive you bats down here in the next ten days. How much harm can another ten days do after all this time?"

"I'll play tennis all right with you, Billy," Wesley said. "Down here. Good night, pal."

Billy watched the tall figure in the dark suit with the little bulge in the pocket stride off. He shook his head and walked back to the hotel. In his room he doublelocked the door.

The next morning he awoke early and sent down for the newspapers. Along with the special sheets put out for the festival, the bellboy brought a copy of *Nice-Matin*. On the front page there was a photograph of a man who looked familiar. The man was wearing dark glasses in the photograph and he was between two policemen. It was Monika's frozen-food friend from Düsseldorf. In the accompanying story, Billy read that he had been arrested on an anonymous tip over the telephone and that he had been caught with a bomb in his possession hidden in a motion picture camera case. The man who had phoned in the tip, the article continued, had spoken in a pronounced Midi accent.

Billy smiled as he read that. Wesley, he thought, was not the only actor in the family.

They played tennis the next morning, driving over to a quiet club in Juan-les-Pins in the little open car, Wesley, in blue jeans and faded cotton shirt and a tweed jacket with frayed cuffs, not looking so much like an actor who had been acclaimed in the press as a man with an exciting career ahead of him. Billy had touched the little bulge in the pocket with distaste and had said, "Can't you leave that damn thing at home even when you play tennis? It gives me the willies. I have the feeling you'll take it out and shoot me if I ace you once too often."

Wesley smiled benignly. "Where I go, it goes," he said. And when they went out to the court he wore the jacket over his tennis clothes and before they started to play laid it carefully over a bench near the net, where he could see it at all times.

The first day Wesley played with the same old wild abandon, hitting the ball savagely, more often than not into the net or to the backstop. After two hours of that Billy said, "That's enough for today. If you *acted* like that they wouldn't let you as much *see* a movie even if you paid for the ticket."

Wesley grinned. "Youthful high spirits," he said, putting on the tweed coat over his soaked shirt. "I promise to reform."

"Starting when?"

"Starting tomorrow," Wesley promised.

When they went in to take their showers, although there was nobody else in the locker room, Wesley insisted that Billy stay in the room and watch his jacket while he took the first shower.

"I've done some foolish things in my time," Billy complained, "but this is the first time I've hired out as a coat watcher." He sat down on the bench in front of the lockers as Wesley stripped, the big muscles of his back standing out clearly, the long legs heavy, but perfectly proportioned. "If I had a build like yours," Billy said, "I'd be in the finals at Wimbledon."

"You can't have everything," Wesley said. "You have brains."

"And you?"

"None to brag about."

"You'll go far in your chosen profession," Billy said.

"If I choose it," Wesley said, as he went into the shower room.

A moment later, Billy heard, over the splash of the water, Wesley's voice, singing, "Raindrops keep falling on my head . . ." He had a strong, true voice and an accurate talent for phrasing on the lyrics. That, too, Billy thought, along with everything else he has. There was one sure thing, Billy thought, if anyone came into the locker room and saw and heard him, as though he hadn't a care in the world, they'd never guess in a million years that he carried a pistol around with him day and night.

As they went to where the car was parked behind the clubhouse in the shadow of the trees there, Billy said, "If you piss it all away, my mother will never forgive you. Nor will I."

Wesley didn't say anything, but just plumped himself down in the bucket seat, whistling a melody from the score of his picture.

The next day Wesley kept his promise and played more calmly. Suddenly, he seemed to have found a sense of the tactics of the game and mixed up his shots, playing the percentages and not trying to kill every ball. At the end of the two hours Billy was exhausted, even though he had won all four sets. Wesley wasn't even breathing hard, although he had run twice as much as Billy. And once again, he made Billy watch his coat while he took his shower.

The third day they could only play an hour because Billy had promised to get back early so that Donnelly and Gretchen could have the car to drive to Mougins for a quiet lunch. Since the running of the picture there was no chance of even a quiet fifteen minutes in Cannes for Gretchen, and she was showing the strain.

It took the whole hour just to play one set and Billy had to fight for every point, even though he won six-three. "Whew," he said as they walked toward the locker room, "I'm beginning to feel sorry I asked you to calm down. You'll wear me down to the bone if you keep this up."

"Child's play," Wesley said complacently.

They were dressing after their showers when they heard the explosion outside.

"What the hell was that?" Billy asked.

Wesley shrugged. "Maybe a gas main," he said.

"That wasn't any gas main," Billy said. He felt shaky and had to sit down for a moment. He was sitting there shirtless when the manager of the club came running into the locker room. *"Monsieur* Abbott," he said, babbling, his voice high and frightened, "you'd better come quick. It was your car. . . . It's horrible."

"I'll be right there," Billy said, but didn't move for a moment. In the distance, there was the sound of a police siren approaching. Billy put on his shirt and meticulously and slowly began to button it as Wesley rushed into his jeans. "Wesley," Billy said, "don't you go out there."

"What do you mean, don't go out there?"

"You heard me. The police'll be there in a few seconds," Billy spoke swiftly, biting out his words. "You'll be all over the papers. Just stay right here. And hide that fucking pistol of yours. In an inconspicuous place. And if anybody asks you anything, you don't know anything."

"But I don't know anything . . ." Wesley said.

"Good," said Billy. "Stay that way. Now I have to go and see what happened." He finished buttoning his shirt and walked, without hurrying, out of the locker room.

People from the nearby apartment buildings had begun to stream toward the trees behind the clubhouse where the car had been parked. A small police car, its siren wailing, sped through the club gates and squealed to a halt on the driveway. Two policemen got out and ran toward the car. As Billy approached he saw that the car was torn apart, its front wheels blown off and the hood lying some feet from the body of the car. Billy's view of the scene was blocked by the people standing around it, but he could see and hear a woman gesticulating wildly and screaming at the policemen that she had been walking past the gates and had seen a man bending over the front of the car with the hood up and then a few seconds later, after she had passed the gate, had heard the explosion.

In the high babble of excited conversation, Billy could hear one of the policemen asking the manager of the tennis club who owned the car and the manager answering and turning to point at Billy. Billy pushed through the crowd and only then saw the body of a man lying facedown, mangled and bloody, next to what had been the radiator of the Peugot.

"*Messieurs,*" Billy said, "it is my car." If the manager, who knew he spoke French, had not been there, he would have pretended he only spoke English.

As the two policemen started to turn the dead man's body, Billy turned his head. The people in the crowd recoiled and there was a woman's scream.

"*Monsieur,*" one of the policemen said to Billy, "do you recognize this man?"

"I prefer not to look," Billy said, with his head still turned away.

"Please, *monsieur,*" the policeman said. He was young and he was pale with fright and horror. "You must tell us if you know this man. If you don't look now you will be forced to come to the morgue later and look then."

The second policeman was kneeling over the dead man, searching what remained of his pockets. The policeman shook his head and rose. "No papers," he said.

"Please, *monsieur,*" the young policeman pleaded.

Finally, turning his head slowly, conscious first of looking at the stricken faces of the onlookers, of the tops of trees, of the blue of the sky, Billy made himself look down. There was a gaping red hole where the chest had been and the face was torn and there was a crooked grimace that bared broken teeth between charred lips, but Billy still could recognize the face. It was the man he had known as George in Brussels.

Billy shook his head. "I'm sorry, *messieurs,*" he said, "I've never seen this man before."

Part Four

<u>CHAPTER 1</u>

BILLY WAS SITTING at his desk in the almost deserted city room, staring at his typewriter. It was late at night and he had done his work for the day and he was free to go home. But home was a nasty little one-room studio near the university and there was no one there to greet him. This was by choice. Since Juan-les-Pins he had avoided company of all kinds.

On his desk, there was a bulky letter from his Uncle Rudolph, from Cannes. It had been on his desk, unopened, for three days. His uncle wrote too many letters, with tempting descriptions of the fascinating life at high pay for bright young men in Washington, where Rudolph now spent a good part of his time, doing some sort of unpaid but seemingly important work for the Democratic Party. At least his name had begun to appear in the newspaper stories from Washington, linked sometimes with that of Helen Morison and that of the senator from Connecticut with whom he traveled on missions to Europe.

Billy was reaching for his uncle's letter when the telephone on his desk rang. He picked it up and said, "Abbott speaking."

"Billy, this is Rhoda Flynn." It was a woman's voice, with the sound of music and conversation in the background.

"Hello, Rhoda," he said. She was a cub reporter on the paper, a pretty girl who was doing a lot better than he was, who already had a by-line and who tried to flirt with him whenever they bumped into each other in the office.

"We're having a little party over at my house," the girl said, "and we could use some extra men. I thought, if you weren't doing anything . . ."

"Sorry, Rhoda," Billy said. "I'm still working. Some other time, maybe."

"Some other time." She sounded disappointed. "Don't work too hard. I know what they're paying you and you shouldn't spoil them."

"Thanks for the advice," he said. "Although there're no visible signs that they think I'm spoiling them. Have a good time."

After he had put down the phone he stared at his typewriter, only the clatter of a distant teletype machine breaking the silence, the sounds of gaiety and companionship he had heard on the telephone still echoing in his ears. He would have liked to go to the party, talk freely to a pretty girl, but what he really wanted to say he couldn't say.

What the hell, if I can't talk to anybody else, I can still talk to myself.

He put a sheet of paper in the typewriter and began to tap on it.

This is for the 1972 notebook. For various reasons I haven't done anything on it since Spain and I'm alone and anonymous and afraid in the city of Chicago and I think there are some things that should be said by a man of my generation and my peculiar career that might eventually be read with interest in the future by other young men. As the Colonel said in Brussels, "We're on the firing line of civilization," which if it was true of Brussels, must be equally true of Chicago. Messages from such an important position should be left where survivors, if there are any, might be able to find them.

He paused, reread what he had written, remembered that he had heard that the Colonel had been passed over for his star and had retired to Arizona, where he could play tennis all year. Then he began to type, very fast.

I am getting neurotic. Or maybe not. I think that I am being constantly followed. I think I see men and women whom I have never seen before staring intently at me in restaurants, I have gotten into the habit of turning unexpectedly around when I walk in the street, I have moved four times in six months. Up to now, I have not caught anybody in the act. Perhaps my mind is prescient and is warning me of my future. Maybe time is a circle and not a spiral and somebody is on the circle, coming the other way. William Abbot, Jr.'s, neurosis, heretofore unrecognized by science.

If I am killed or die in a curious way, the person who will be responsible is a woman who called herself Monika Wolner when she worked at NATO as an interpreter while I was in the army in Brussels, and Monika Hitzman when I saw her later at the El Faro Club near Malaga in Spain. She was, and I suppose still is, a member of a terrorist organization which operated and probably still operates all over Europe, with connections, perhaps, with similar organizations in America.

The man who was found dead after accidentally blowing himself up while placing a bomb in my car in Juan-les-Pins, France, was a man known to me only as George and was the leader of the cell to which Monika Wolner-Hitzman belonged. He was an expert with small arms and until the accident which caused his death, was considered an expert in the manufacture of explosive devices.

I am writing this in the city room of the Chicago Tribune, *where I have been employed for the last six months, as a result of the friendship of my father with one of the editors. My father will know where to find this quite lengthy notebook. Along with some books and papers and old clothes and various pieces of junk I have accumulated in my travels, I keep my notebook in a foot locker in the basement of his apartment, as there's no space for it in my tiny room. He knows that in the footlocker I have some stuff I've written, but he hasn't read any of it. I have led him to believe that it is an outline for the novel which he is constantly encouraging me to write.*

Since I left Cannes, where I underwent a quite rigorous interrogation by the French police, who rightly suspected some sort of connection between the man I knew as George and myself, but who could prove nothing, I have not seen any members of my family, more out of fear of what could happen to them in my company than any lack of affection. The thought that just some twenty minutes after the bomb went off I was to lend my car to my mother and her friend for a luncheon date haunts me, although this is the first time I have been able to bring myself to write about what happened on the Cote d'Azur.

Once again he stopped typing and remembered the hours with the two detectives who had interrogated him, first politely and sympathetically and then harshly and with open hostility. They had threatened to arrest him but he knew they were bluffing and had held out, saying over and over again, "I can only repeat, in answer to your questions, that I am here in Cannes only to see my mother's movie and I never saw the man before and I have no enemies that I know of. I can only guess that the man made some sort of tragic mistake."

Finally, they had broken off and let him go, with a last warning that the case was not closed and that there was an extradition treaty between France and the United States.

Rudolph had looked at him queerly, but that was to be expected, after the business with the gun and silencer.

"You're a lucky man," Rudolph had said at the airport the next day, just before he boarded the plane to New York. "Just keep it that way."

"Never fear," he had said.

Wesley, who was with them and who had lost his smile, shook his hand soberly, but had said nothing.

Gretchen had not been able to come. When she had heard about the bombing—there was no way of keeping it from her—she had collapsed and gone to bed. The doctor they had called for her had discovered that she had a raging fever, although he couldn't diagnose her ailment. He had ordered her to stay in bed for at least five days.

When Billy had gone to her room to say good-bye to her he was shocked at her appearance. Her face was a bluish-white and she had seemed to diminish in the space of a few hours and her voice was almost inaudible when she said, "Billy, please—for my sake—take care of yourself."

"I will," he said and leaned over and kissed the hot forehead as she lay propped up against the pillows of the bed.

Billy shook his head at the flood of memories, then started typing again.

If I could have told the whole truth to the cops, they might have given me the Legion of Honor. After all, I was instrumental in breaking up or at least depleting a gang of assassins that was terrorizing all Europe. Of course, I did it by accident, but accidents count, too, maybe more than anything else. The entire history of the family is one of accidents, good and bad. Maybe of all families.

Despite the fact that I seem to be avoiding any meetings with my relatives, they write me often and keep me abreast of their affairs. I write cheerful and chatty letters in return, pretending that my father is sober most of the time and that I am doing splendidly on the paper. Since I cover police headquarters and small crimes in the local courts, this is hardly the case. While I do not pretend to my father that the novel I am theoretically outlining will be another War and Peace *or even* The Great American Novel, *I confide to him that I believe it is shaping up to my satisfaction.*

My Uncle Rudolph, who is the cement, the saviour, the conscience and ministering angel of the family, even though he now, in his eternal search for good deeds to be done, commutes between Long Island, Connecticut, Washington and the capitals of Europe, finds time to send out long letters of admonition and advice, which none of us follow. He is the most ardent of letter writers and it is through him that I hear of the various activities of himself, my mother, who is now Mrs. Donnelly, and my Cousin Wesley, who has remained in Cannes, having found himself a job as a deckhand on a yacht. Uncle Rudolph finds the time to visit Wesley in Cannes, in connection with an affair that . . .

He stopped typing, stood up and walked around the desk. Then he sat down again, stared at the sheet of paper in the machine and began to type again, more slowly than before.

Even now, I think it would be wiser not to go into the subject of Wesley's obsession. All of us, my mother, my uncle and myself, have tried to get Wesley away from the Cote D'Azur. None of us have happy memories of the place, to put it mildly. Even the festival turned out to be a disappointment. Contrary to what the publicity man on the picture predicted, nobody was voted anything by the jury and it's lucky for Mr. Simpson that nobody took him up on the bet of his left nut that Wesley would go home with a prize. According to my mother, who is about to start shooting her second picture, Wesley has refused her offer of a part, with a lot of money attached to it, as well as offers of important roles by other companies. As of now, Wesley is undoubtedly potentially the richest deckhand on the Mediterranean. In his last letter to me, Wesley wrote me that when he gets through with what I still have to call his affair on the Cote, he will do enough work in the movies to save up for a boat and set himself up, as his father did, as a charter captain. He sounds cheerful enough in his letters, but he may be lying, as I do, when I write to the family. Still, he's got something that I haven't got to be cheerful about. At eighteen he came into about thirty thousand dollars minus a big bite for the tax people, and his girl wangled herself a job in the Paris bureau of Time *and flies down to Cannes to see him as often as possible. He also writes that he gets in a lot of tennis, except for the summer months, and believes he could swamp me if he played me now. I haven't touched a racket since Juan-les-Pins.*

The police never did find out what George's real name was or where he came from. I can't get over the feeling that one day I will look up from my desk and see Monika standing there. I dream about her constantly and the dreams are erotic and happy and leave me desperate when I wake up.

Billy stopped typing, frowned. "Oh, hell," he said aloud. He took the sheet of paper out of the machine and put it with the other two sheets of paper into a large envelope to take home with him. He stood up and put on his jacket and was about to leave when he glanced down and saw the bulky envelope his uncle had sent him from Cannes. Might as well, he thought. I'll have to read it *sometime*. He tore open the envelope. There was a note clipped to a page of newsprint that had been folded many times. There was a second note clipped to the back of the newspaper page. "Read the item circled in red," was written in his uncle's handwriting, "and then read the note on the other side."

Billy shook his head annoyedly. Games, he thought. It wasn't like Rudolph. Curious, he sat down so that he could put the newspaper page under the light. At the top left-hand corner of the page MARSEILLES was printed in block letters and in smaller letters, *Page Deux*. The column headed *Faits Divers* was circled in red crayon.

Mort d'un Voyou, he read, his French still serviceable. Then the story:

> Last night, the body of a man, later identified by the police as that of Janos Danovic, a Yugoslav national, was found on a pier in the Vieux Port. He had been shot twice through the head. He was known to belong to the *milieu* along the Côte d'Azur and in Marseilles and was arrested several times for pimping and armed robbery, although he was never convicted of the crimes. Police believe that it was another incident in the settling of accounts that has been keeping them occupied in Marseilles in recent weeks.

Billy slowly put the paper down. Christ, he thought, Rudolph must be crazy to send something like this through the mails. If it had gone astray or if it had been opened accidentally, some curious bastard would have wondered why an adviser to an American senator would be interested in the murder of a small-time murderer in Marseilles, and started to make unpleasant inquiries. He was about to tear the page into small pieces when he remembered the note on the back.

He turned the page over and slipped the note out of the clip. "Look at the date on the newspaper," his uncle had written. Billy looked at the top of the page. It was page one of *Le Meridional* and it was dated Samedi, 24 Octobre, 1970.

1970. Danovic had been dead over six months before Wesley had gone back to Europe. Billy leaned over his desk, his elbows on it, and put his head in his hands. He began to laugh. The laughter grew hysterical. When he finally could make himself stop, he picked up the phone and asked the night operator for Rhoda Flynn's phone number. When she answered the phone, he said, "Hi, Rhoda, is the party still on?"

"If you can make it," Rhoda said, "yes."

"I'm on my way," he said. "What's the address?"

She told him the address and he said, "Ten minutes. Make me a stiff drink. I need it tonight."

As he walked out of the Tribune Building and went along Michigan Avenue, looking for a taxicab, he had the feeling he was being followed. He turned around and looked, but there were just two couples half a block behind him.

Maybe, he thought, it would be a good idea if I asked Rudolph if he still has that gun. It might come in handy.

Then he saw a taxi and hailed it and got in and went to the party.

Nightwork

TO GERDA NIELSEN

CHAPTER 1

It was night and I was alone, behind the locked door, the bulletproof glass. Outside, the city of New York was in the black grip of January. For the last two years, six times a week, I'd come in an hour before midnight and left at eight in the morning. I was neither content nor discontent. The room I worked in was warm, the work untaxing, the necessity to speak infrequent.

My duties left me time for my own amusements, with no one to give me orders or change the routine of the night. I spent an hour on the *Racing Form,* preparing my bets for the next day. It was a lively paper, written with brio, confident of the future, renewing hope with each edition.

Finished with my calculations of times, weights, distances, sunshine, and rain, I read, making sure always to have a supply of books on hand to suit my tastes. For other nourishment there was a sandwich and a bottle of beer that I picked up on the way to work. Twice during the night I did isometric exercises, for the arms, the gut, the legs. Despite my sedentary occupation, at the age of thirty-three I was stronger and in better conditon than I had been at twenty. I'm just short of six feet tall and weigh one hundred and eighty-five pounds. People are surprised when they hear I weigh that much. I'm vain enough to be pleased by this. But I wish I were taller. Some women have told me I look boyish, which I don't take as a compliment. I have never longed for a mother. Like most men I would prefer to resemble the sort of man who is cast on televison as a captain in the Marines or the leading figure in a desperate enterprise.

I was working on an adding machine, preparing the previous day's accounts for the day staff. The machine made a noise like a large, irritated insect as I hit the keys. The sound, which had at first annoyed me, was now familiar and rhythmic, soothing. Beyond the glass, the lobby of the hotel was dark. The management saved on electricity, as on everything else.

The bulletproof pane had been put in over the front desk after the last night man had been held up for the second time. Forty-three stitches. The night man had taken up another profession.

I owed my position to the fact that, at the urging of my mother, I had taken a year's course in business procedures in college. She had insisted that I learn at least one useful thing, as she put it, in those four years. I had finished college eleven years ago and my mother was now dead.

The name of the hotel was the St. Augustine. What yearning for the South the name represented for the original owner or what obscure religious whim would have been hard to say. There were no crucifixes on any of the walls, and only the four potted rubber plants in the worn lobby had any conceivable connection with the Tropics. Although it looked respectable enough on the outside, the hotel had seen better days. As had its clientele. They paid modestly for their accommodations and expected little in return. Except for two or three guests who wandered in late, I hardly had to talk to anybody. I hadn't taken the job for its opportunities for conversation. Often whole nights went by without a single light showing on the switchboard.

I was paid one hundred and twenty-five dollars a week. Home was one room with kitchenette and bath on East Eighty-first Street.

Tonight I had been interrupted only once, by a prostitute who had come down from upstairs a little after one o'clock and had to be let out of the front door. I hadn't been on duty when she came in so I had no idea which room she had been visiting. There was a buzzer by the side of the door that was designed to open it automatically, but it had been broken for a week. I sniffed the cold night air briefly and was happy to close the door and get back to the office.

The *Racing Form* was open on my desk to the next day's program at Hialeah. The warm holidays of the South. I had made my choice earlier. Ask Gloria in the second. The filly had finished out of the money in its last three outings, but had had a good race up North in the autumn and was dropping down in class. The probable odds were fifteen to one.

I had always been a gambler. I had paid a good part of my way through college in fraternity poker games. When I still was working in Vermont, I played in a weekly poker game and figured I was ahead by several thousand dollars by the time I left. Since then I had not been particularly lucky.

In fact, it was my devotion to gambling that had led me to the Hotel St. Augustine. When I first drifted into New York, I had happened to meet a bookie in a bar. He lived in the hotel, and paid off there. He gave me a line of credit and we settled at the end of each week. The hotel was cheap and convenient, and my financial situation did not permit me to demand luxury. When I ran up a five-hundred-dollar debt to the bookie, he had cut me off. Luckily, he said, the old night clerk had just quit his job and the manager was looking for a new man. I looked and sounded like a college graduate, the bookie said, and he knew I could add and subtract. I took the job, but moved out to a place of my own. Twenty-four hours a day at the St. Augustine was more than anybody could stomach. I paid the bookie off in weekly installments from my salary. I had cleared my original debt with him and was on credit again. I was only a hundred and fifty dollars down on this night.

As we had arranged in the beginning, I would write out my choice or choices for the day, and put them in an envelope in the bookie's box. He never awoke before eleven in the morning. I decided to bet five dollars. If the filly came in it would cut my debt by half.

Lying on top of the *Racing Form* was a Gideon Bible, open to the Psalms. I come from a religious family and had been reared on the Bible. My faith in God was not what it once was, but I still enjoyed reading the Bible. Also on the desk were *Vile Bodies,* by Evelyn Waugh and Conrad's *Almayer's Folly.* In the two years I had been working behind the desk, I had given myself a liberal education in English and American literature.

As I sat down once more in front of the adding machine, I glanced over at the Bible lying open on top of the *Racing Form. "Praise him for his mighty acts,"* I read; *"praise him according to his excellent greatness, praise him with the sound of the trumpet; praise him with the psaltery and harp. Praise him with the timbrel and dance; praise him with stringed instruments and organs."*

All right for Jerusalem, I thought. Could a timbrel be found in New York? High above, penetrating stone and steel, there was the whining noise of a jet, crossing New York. Descending from the pole, outward bound to Karachi. I listened, thinking of the quiet flight deck, the silent men at the controls, the flicker of the dials, the radar scanning the night sky. "Christ," I said aloud.

Finished with the adding machine, I pushed my chair back, took a sheet of paper, held it on my thighs, looked straight ahead at a calendar on the wall. Then I moved the sheet of paper up, bit by bit. Only when it was high up on my chest, almost to my chin, did it come within the limit of my vision. No miracle had happened that night.

"Christ," I said again and crumpled the sheet of paper and threw it into the wastebasket.

I made a neat, small pile of the bills I had prepared and began filing them in alphabetical order. I had been working automatically, my mind on other things, and I hadn't paid any attention to the date on the bills on my desk. Now it struck me. The date on the bills was January 15. It was now several hours before dawn on January 16. An anniversary. Of a kind. I grinned. Painfully. Three years ago, to the day, it had happened. . . .

CHAPTER 2

IT HAD BEEN overcast in New York, but when we passed Peekskill, flying north, the skies cleared. The snow glistened in the sunshine on the rolling hills below. I had flown the little Cessna down to Teterboro Airport early to pick up the New Jersey charter, and I could hear my passengers behind me congratulating each other on the blue skies and the fresh powder. We were flying low, only six thousand feet, and the fields made clearly defined checkerboard patterns, with stands of trees black against the clean white of the snow. It was a flight I always liked to make. Recognizing individual farmhouses and road intersections and the course of a small stream here and there made the short voyage cosy and familiar. Upstate New York is beautiful at ground level, but on a fine day in early winter, from the air, it is one of the loveliest sights a man can hope to see. Once again, I was grateful that I had never been tempted to take a job on one of the big airlines, where you spent the best part of your life at an altitude of over thirty thousand feet, with the world below you just a vast sea of cloud or a remote and impersonal map unrolling slowly beneath you.

There were only three passengers, the Wales family, mother and father and a plump girl with buckteeth of about twelve or thirteen called Didi. They were enthusiastic skiers and I had flown them up and back four or five times. There was a regular airline to Burlington, but Mr. Wales was a busy man, he said, and took off when he could find the time and didn't like being tied down to a schedule. He had an advertising firm of his own in New York and he didn't seem to mind throwing his money around. Flatteringly, when he called for a charter he always asked for me. Part of the reason, or maybe the whole reason for this was that I skied with them from time to time at Stowe and Sugarbush and Mad River and led them down the trails, which I knew better than they did, and occasionally threw in a little tactful instruction about how they could improve their performance. Wales and his wife, a hard-looking, athletic New York woman, were fiercely competitive with each other and went too fast, out of control a good deal of the time. I predicted to myself that there would be a broken leg in the family one of these days. I could tell when they were furious with each other by the different tones in which they called each other "Darling" at various moments.

Didi was a serious and unsmiling child, always with a book in her hands. According to her parents, she started reading as soon as she was strapped into her seat and only stopped when the plane rolled to a halt. On this flight she was engrossed in *Wuthering Heights*. I had been an omnivorous reader, too, as a boy—when my mother was displeased with me she would say, "Oh, Douglas, stop acting like a character in a book"—and it amused me to keep track of what Didi was reading from one winter to another.

She was by far the best skier in the family, but her parents made her bring up the rear on all descents. I had skied alone with her one morning in a snowstorm, when the older Waleses were hung over from a cocktail party, and she had been a changed girl, smiling blissfully and fleeing joyfully down the mountain with me, like a small wild animal suddenly let loose from a cage.

Wales was a generous man and made a point of giving me a gift after each flight—a sweater, a new pair of fancy poles, a wallet, things like that. I certainly made enough money to be able to buy anything I needed, and I didn't like the idea of being tipped, but I knew he would have been insulted if I had ever refused to take his offerings. He was not an unpleasant man, I had decided. Just too successful.

"Beautiful morning, isn't it, Doug?" Wales said behind me. He was a restless man and even in the small plane seemed always on the prowl. He would have made a terrible pilot. He brought a smell of alcohol into the cockpit. He always traveled with a small, leather-bound flask.

"N . . . not bad," I said. I had stuttered ever since I was a boy and as a result tried to talk as little as possible. Sometimes I couldn't help but speculate about what my life would have been like if I hadn't suffered from this small affliction, but I didn't allow myself to sink into gloom because of it.

"The skiing ought to be marvelous," Wales said.

"Marvelous," I agreed. I didn't like to talk while I was at the controls, but I couldn't tell Wales that.

"We're going to Sugarbush," Wales said. "You going to be there this weekend?"

"I . . . I b . . . believe so," I said. "I t . . . told a girl I'd ski with her up . . . up there." The girl was Pat Minot. Her brother worked in the airline office and I had met her through him. She taught history at the high school, and I had arranged to pick her up at three o'clock when school let out. She was a good skier and very pretty besides, small and dark and intense. I had known her for more than two years and we had had what was a rather desultory affair for fifteen months now. At least it was desultory as far as she was concerned, since for weeks on end she would put me off with one excuse or another and hardly notice me when we met by accident. Then suddenly she would relent and suggest we go off together somewhere. I could tell by the particular kind of smile on her face when, for whatever reason, she was entering into a nondesultory phase.

She was a popular girl, stubbornly unmarried; at one time or another, according to her brother, almost every friend of his had made a pass at her. With what success I never did find out. I have always been shy and uneasy with girls and I could not say that I pursued her. I couldn't say, either, that she had pursued me. It had just, well, happened, when we found each other skiing together on a long weekend at Sugarbush. After the first night, I had said, "This is the best thing that ever happened to me."

All she had said was, "Hush."

I never made up my mind whether or not I was in love with her. If she hadn't badgered me continually about curing my stutter, I think I would have asked her to marry me. The coming weekend, I felt, was going to rise—or fall—to some sort of climax. I had decided to be cautious, leaving all options open.

"Great," Wales was saying. "Let's all have dinner together tonight."

"Thanks, G . . . George," I said. He had insisted from the first time I met him that I call him and his wife by their first names. "Th . . . that w . . . would be very nice." Dinner with another couple would postpone decisions, give me time to sound out Pat's mood and reassess my own feelings.

"We're driving up as soon as we land," Wales said. "We can get in a few runs this afternoon. How about you? Should we wait for you at the inn?"

"I . . . I'm afraid n . . . not. I have my six-m . . . month physical checkup at the doc's and . . . and I don't know when I c . . . can split."

"Dinner, then?" Wales said.

"D . . . dinner."

"Doug," Wales said, "do you ever get three weeks off at a time? In the winter, I mean?"

"N . . . not really," I said. "It's a busy season. Wh . . . Why?"

"Beryl and I're going over on a charter flight to Zurich the first of February." Beryl was his wife. "We always try to manage three weeks in the Alps. . . . You ever ski in the Alps?"

"I've never b . . . been out of the country. Except Canada for a f . . . few days."

"You'd flip," he said. "The slopes of Heaven. We've been talking it over and we'd love to have you with us. There's this club I belong to. It's surprisingly cheap. Under three hundred dollars round trip. The Christie Ski Club. It's not just the money, of course. It's the people. The nicest bunch of people you could ever travel with and all the free booze you can drink. And no worrying about a baggage allowance or Swiss customs. They just wave you through with a smile. You're supposed to belong at least six months in advance, but they're not sticky about it. There's a girl in the office I know, her name's Mansfield, and she fixes everything. Just tell her you're a friend of mine. They have flights just about every week in the winter. We made St. Moritz last and we're doing St. Anton this year. You'll dazzle the Austrians."

I smiled. "I b . . . bet," I said.

"Think it over," Wales said. "You'd have the time of your life."

"S . . . stop t . . . tempting a working man," I said.

"What the hell," Wales said. "Everybody needs a vacation."

"I . . . I'll think it o . . . over," I said.

He went back to his seat, leaving the smell of whiskey in the cockpit. I kept my eyes on the horizon, sharp against the bright blue of the winter sky, trying not to be jealous of a man who was as untalented on the slopes as Wales, but who could take three weeks off from work to spend thousands of dollars to ski in the Alps.

After I checked into the airline office and confirmed that there was nothing for me that weekend, I drove into town in my Volkswagen for the biannual ritual of the physical examination. Dr. Ryan was an eye-specialist but kept up a limited general practice on the side. He was a slow-moving, gentle old man who had been listening to my heart, taking my blood pressure, and testing my eyes and reflexes for five years. Except for one occasion when I had come down with a mild case of grippe, he had never prescribed as much as an aspirin for me. "In shape for the Derby," he would say each time when he finished with me. "Ready to run for the roses." He shared my interest in the horses and was an impressive student of form. Every once in a while he would call me at my home when he would discover a horse that was outrageously underpriced or carrying, in his opinion, much too little weight.

The examination followed its usual routine, with the doctor nodding comfortably after each stage. It was only when he came to my eyes that his expression changed. I read the charts all right, but when he used his instruments to look into my eyes, his face became professionally sober. His nurse came into the office twice to tell him that there were patients in the waiting room with appointments, but he brusquely waved her aside. He gave me a whole series of tests that he had never used before, making me stare straight ahead while he kept his hands in his lap, then slowly lifting his hands and asking me to tell him when they came into my field of vision. Finally, he put away his instruments, sat down heavily behind his desk, sighed and passed his hand wearily across his face.

"Mr. Grimes," he said finally, "I'm afraid I have bad news for you."

The news old Dr. Ryan had for me on that sunny morning in his big, old-fashioned office changed my whole life.

"Technically," he said, "the name of the disease is retinoschisis. It is a splitting of the ten layers of the retina into two portions, giving rise to the development of a retinal cyst. It is a well-known condition. Most often it does not progress, but as far as it goes it's irreversible. Sometimes we can arrest it by operating by laser beam. One of its manifestations is a blocking out of peripheral vision. In your case downward peripheral vision. For a pilot who has to be alert to a whole array of dials in front of him, below, around him on all sides, as well as the horizon toward which he is speeding, it is essentially disabling. . . . Still, for all general purposes, such as reading, sports, et cetera, you can consider yourself normal."

"Normal," I said. "Boy, oh, boy, normal. You know the only thing that's normal for me, Doc. Flying. That's all I ever wanted to do, all I ever prepared myself to do. . . ."

"I'm sending the report over today, Mr. Grimes," Ryan said. "With the greatest regret. Of course, you can go to another doctor. Other doctors. I don't believe they can do anything to help you, but that's only my opinion. As far as I'm concerned, you're grounded. As of this minute. For good. I'm sorry."

I fought to hold back the surge of hatred I felt for the neat old man, seated among his shining instruments, signing papers of condemnation with his scrawly doctor's handwriting. I knew I was being unreasonable, but it was not a moment for reason. I lurched out of the office, not shaking Ryan's hand, saying, "Goddamnit, goddamnit," aloud over and over to myself, paying no attention to the people in the waiting room and on the street who stared curiously at me as I headed for the nearest bar. I knew I couldn't face going back to the airfield and saying what I would have to say without fortification. Considerable fortification.

The bar was decorated like an English pub, dark wood and pewter tankards on the walls. I ordered a whiskey. There was a thin old man in a khaki mackinaw and a hunter's red cap leaning against the bar with a glass of beer in front of him. "They're polluting the whole lake," the old man was saying in a dry Vermont accent. "The paper mill. In five years it'll be as dead as Lake Erie. And they keep putting salt on the roads so those idiots from New York can go eighty miles an hour up to Stowe and Mad River and Sugarbush, and, when the snow melts off, the salt goes into all the ponds and rivers. By the time I die there won't be a fish left anywhere in the whole state. And nobody does a goddamn thing about it. I tell you, I'm glad I won't be around to see it."

I ordered another whiskey. The first one hadn't seemed to do anything for me. Nor did the second. I paid and went out to my car. The thought that Lake Champlain, in which I had swum every summer and on which I had spent so many great days sailing and fishing, was going to die, somehow seemed sadder than anything that had happened to me for a long time.

When I got to the office I could tell by the look on Cunningham's rough old face that Dr. Ryan had already called him. Cunningham was the president and sole owner of the little airline and was a World War Two-vintage fighter pilot and I guess he knew how I felt that afternoon.

"I'm ch . . . checking out, Freddy," I said. "You know wh . . . why."

"Yes," he said. "I'm sorry." He fiddled uncomfortably with a pencil on his desk. "You know, we can always find something for you here. In the office, maybe . . . maintenance . . ." His voice trailed off. He stared at the pencil in his big hand.

"Thanks," I said. "It's nice of you, but forget it." If there was one thing I knew it was that I couldn't hang around like a crippled bird, watching all my friends take off into the sky. And I didn't want to get used to the look of pity I saw on Freddy Cunningham's honest face, or on any other face.

"Well, anyway, Doug, think it over," Cunningham said.

"No n . . . need," I said.

"What do you plan to do?"

"First," I said, "leave town."

"For where?"

"Anywhere," I said.

"Then what?"

"Then try to figure out what I'm going to do with the rest of my life." I stuttered twice on the word life.

He nodded, avoiding looking at me, deeply interested in the pencil. "How're you fixed for dough?"

"Sufficient," I said. "For the time being."

"Well," he said. "If you ever . . . I mean you know where to come, don't you?"

"I'll keep that in mind." I looked at my watch. "I have a date."

"Shit," he said loudly. Then stood up and shook my hand.

I didn't say good-bye to anyone else.

I parked the car and got out and waited. There was a peculiar muted hum coming from the big red-brick building with the Latin inscription on the facade and the flag flying above it. The hum of learning, I thought, a small decent music that made me remember my childhood.

Pat would be in her classroom, lecturing the boys and girls on the origins of the Civil War or the succession of the kings of England. She took her history seriously. "It is the most relevant of subjects," she had told me once, using the word that cropped up in every conversation about education in those days. "Every move we make today is the result of what men and women have been doing with each other and to each other since before recorded time." As I remembered this, I grinned sourly. Had I been born to stutter or lived to be a discarded airman because Meade had repulsed Lee at Gettysburg, or because Cromwell had had Charles beheaded? It would be an interesting point to discuss when we had an idle moment to spare.

Inside the building a bell clanged. The hum of education swelled to a roar of freedom, and a few minutes later the students began to pour out of the doors in a confused sea of brightly colored parkas and brilliant wool hats.

As usual, Pat was late. She was the most conscientious of teachers, and there were always two or three students who clustered around her desk after class, asking her questions she patiently answered. When I finally saw her, the lawn was deserted, the hundreds of children vanished as if melted away by the pale Vermont sun.

She didn't see me at first. She was nearsighted, but out of vanity didn't wear her glasses except when she was working or reading or going to the movies. It had been a little joke of mine that she wouldn't find a grand piano in a ballroom.

I stood, leaning against a tree, without moving or saying anything, watching her walk down the cleared walk toward me, carrying a leather envelope that I knew contained test papers, cradled against her bosom, schoolgirl fashion. She was wearing a skirt and red wool stockings and brown suede after-ski boots and a short, blue cloth overcoat. Her way of walking was concentrated, straight, uncoquettish, always brisk. Her small head with its dark hair pulled back was almost half obscured by the big, upraised collar of her coat.

When she saw me, she smiled, a nondesultory smile. It was going to be even more difficult than I had feared. We didn't kiss. You never knew who was looking out of a window. "Right on time," she said. "My stuff's in the car." She waved toward the parking lot. She had a battered old Chevy. A good part of her salary went for Biafra refugees, starving Indian children, political prisoners in various parts of the world. I don't think she owned more than three dresses. "I hear the skiing's great," she said, as she started toward the parking lot. "This ought to be a weekend to remember."

I put my hand out and held her arm. "W . . . wait a min . . . minute, Pat," I said, trying not to notice the slight strained look that invariably crossed her face when I stuttered. "I have some . . . something to tell you. I . . . I'm not going up there th . . . this weekend."

"Oh," she said, her voice small. "I thought you were free this weekend."

"I am f . . . free," I said. "But I'm not going skiing. I'm leaving town."

"For the weekend?"

"For good," I said.

She squinted at me, as though I had suddenly gone out of focus. "Has it got something to do with me?"

"N . . . nothing."

"Oh," she said harshly, "nothing. Can you tell me where you're going?"

"No," I said. "I don't know wh . . . where I'm g . . . going."

"Do you want to tell me why you're going?"

"You'll hear s . . . soon enough."

"If you're in trouble," she said, her voice soft now, "and I could help . . ."

"I'm in t . . . trouble," I said. "And you can't help."

"Will you write me?"

"I'll try."

She kissed me then, not worrying who might be at a window. But there were no tears. And she didn't tell me that she loved me. It might have been different if she had, but she didn't. "I have a lot of work to catch up on over the weekend anyway," she said, as she stepped back a pace. "The snow'll last." She smiled a little crookedly at me. "Good luck," she said. "Wherever."

I watched her walk toward the old Chevy in the parking lot, small and neat and familiar. Then I got into the Volkswagen and drove off.

I was out of my small furnished apartment by six o'clock that evening. I had left my skis and boots and the rest of my skiing equipment except a padded parka, which I liked, in a duffel bag to be delivered to Pat's brother, who was just about my size, and had told my landlady that she could have all my books and whatever else I left behind me. Traveling light, I headed south, leaving the town where, I realized now, I had been happy for more than five years.

I had no destination. I had told Freddy Cunningham that I was going to try to figure out what I was going to do with the rest of my life and one place was as good as another for that.

CHAPTER 3

FIGURE OUT MY life. I had plenty of time to do it. As I drove south, down the entire East Coast of America, I was alone, unfettered, free of claims, with no distractions, plunged in that solitude that is supposed to be the essential condition of philosophic speculation. There was Pat Minot's cause and effect to be considered; also not to be overlooked was the maxim I had been taught in English lit courses that your character was your fate, that your rewards and failures were the result of your faults and virtues. In *Lord Jim,* a book I must have read at least five times since I was a boy, the hero is killed eventually because of a flaw in himself that permitted him to leave a shipload of poor beggars to die. He pays for his cowardice in the end by being killed himself. I had always thought it just, fair, inevitable. At the wheel of the little Volkswagen, speeding down the great highways past Washington and Richmond and Savannah, I remembered *Lord Jim.* But it no longer convinced me. I certainly was not flawless, but, at least in my opinion, I had been a decent son, an honorable friend, conscientious in my profession, law-abiding, careful to avoid cruelty or spite, inciting no man to be my enemy, indifferent to power, abhorring violence. I had never seduced a woman nor cheated a shopkeeper, had not struck a fellow human being since a fight in the schoolyard at the age of ten. I had definitely never left anyone to die. Yet . . . Yet there had been that morning in Dr. Ryan's office.

If character was fate, was it the character of thirty million Europeans to die in World War II, was it the character of the inhabitants of Calcutta to drop in the streets of starvation, was it the character of thousands of citizens of Pompeii to be mummified in a flood of lava?

The ruling law was simple—accident. The throw of dice, the turning of a card. From now on I would gamble and trust to luck. Maybe, I thought, it was in my character to be a gambler and fate had neatly arranged it so that I could play out my destined role. Maybe my short career as a man who traveled the Northern skies was an aberration, a detour and only now, back to earth, was I on the right path.

When I got to Florida, I spent my days at the tracks. In the beginning, all went well; I won often enough to live comfortably and not have to worry about taking a job. There was no job that anyone could offer me that I could imagine accepting. I kept by myself, making no friends, approaching no women. I found, mildly surprised, that all desire had left me. Whether this was temporary or would turn out to be permanent did not bother me. I wanted no attachments.

I turned, with bitter pleasure, into myself, content with the long sunny afternoons at the track and the solitary meals and the evenings spent studying the performances of thoroughbreds and the habits of trainers and jockeys. I also had time now for reading, and indiscriminately devoured libraries of paperbacks. As Dr. Ryan had assured me, the condition of my eyes did not interfere with my ability to read. Still, I found nothing in any of the books I read that either helped or harmed me.

I lived in small hotels, moving on from one to another when other guests, to whom I had become a familiar presence, attempted to approach me.

I was ahead of the game by several thousand dollars when the season ended and I drifted up to New York. I no longer went to the track. The actual running of a race now bored me. I continued betting, but with bookies. For a while I went often to the theater, to the movies, losing myself for a few hours at a time in their fantasies. New York is a good city for a man who prefers to be alone. It is the easiest city in the world to enjoy solitude.

My luck began to change in New York and with the onset of winter I knew that I would have to look for some kind of job if I wanted to continue eating. Then the night man at the St. Augustine was held up for the second time.

I put the last of the January 15 bills in the file. It was now three hours into January 16. Happy Anniversary. I got up and stretched. I was hungry and I got out my sandwich and the bottle of beer.

I was unwrapping my sandwich when I heard the sound of the door from the fire emergency stairs opening into the lobby and quick woman's footsteps. I reached for the switch and the lobby was brightly lit. A young woman was hurrying, almost running toward the desk. She was unnaturally tall, with those thick soles and exaggerated high heels which made women look like so many displaced Watusis. She had on a white fake fur coat and a blonde wig that wouldn't fool anybody. I recognized her. She was a whore who had come in just after midnight with the man in 610. I glanced at my watch. It was just after three o'clock. It had been a long session in 610 and the woman looked it. She ran to the front door, pushed futilely at the broken buzzer, then clattered over to the desk.

She knocked sharply on the glass over the desk. "Open the door, mister," she said loudly. "I want to get out of here."

I took the key from the drawer under the desk in which the pistol was kept and went through the little room next to the office where there was a huge old safe against the wall, lined with safety-deposit boxes. The safety-deposit boxes were relics of a richer day. None was in use now. I unlocked the door and stepped out into the lobby. The woman followed me across the lobby toward the front door. She was gasping for breath. Her profession didn't keep her in shape for running down six flights of steps in the middle of the night. She was somewhere around thirty years old, and by the look of her they hadn't been easy years. The women who came in and out of the hotel at night made a strong argument for celibacy.

"Why didn't you take the elevator down?" I asked.

"I was waiting for the elevator," the woman said. "But then this crazy, naked old man popped out of the door, making all kinds of funny noises, grunting, like an animal, and waving something at me. . . . "

"Waving wh . . . wh . . . *what?*"

"Something. It looked like a club. A baseball bat. It's dark in that hall. You bastards certainly don't waste much money on lights in this hotel." Her voice was whiskey-hoarse, set in city cement, praising nothing. "I didn't wait around to see. I just took off. You want to find out, you go up to the sixth floor and see for yourself. Open the goddamn door, will you? I have to go home."

I unlocked the big, plate-glass front door, reinforced by a heavy, cast-iron grill. For a shabby old hotel like the St. Augustine, the management was nervously security conscious. The woman pushed the door open impatiently and ran out into the dark street. I took a deep breath of the cold night air as the clatter of heels diminished in the direction of Lexington Avenue. I stood at the door another moment, looking down the street, on the chance that a prowl car might be cruising past. I would have felt better about going up to see what was happening on the sixth floor if I had a cop with me. I was not paid for solitary heroics. But the street was empty. I heard a siren in the distance, probably on Park Avenue, but that was no help. I closed the door and locked it and walked slowly back across the lobby toward the office, thinking, Am I going to spend the rest of my life ushering whores to and from anonymous beds?

Praise him with stringed instruments and organs.

In the office I took the passkey out of the drawer, looked for a moment at the pistol. I shook my head and shut the drawer. Having the pistol there wasn't my idea. It hadn't helped the other night man when the two junkies came in and walked off with all the cash in the place, leaving the night man lying in his blood on the floor with a bump the size of a cantaloupe on his head.

I put my jacket on, somehow feeling that being properly dressed would give me more authority in whatever situation I would find on the sixth floor, and went out into the lobby again, locking the office door behind me. I pushed the elevator button and heard the whine of the cables as the elevator started down the shaft.

When the door creaked open, I hesitated before going in. Maybe, I thought, I just ought to go back into the office, get my overcoat and my sandwich and my beer, and walk away from here. Who needs this lousy job? But just as the door began to slide shut, I went in.

When I reached the sixth floor, I pushed the button that kept the elevator door open, and stepped out into the corridor. Light was streaming from the doorway of the room diagonally across from the elevator, number 602. On the worn carpet of the corridor, half in and half out of the light, was a naked man, lying on his face, his head and torso in shadow, old man's wrinkled buttocks and skinny legs sharply, obscenely illuminated. The left arm was stretched out, the fingers of the hand curled, as though the man had been trying to grab at something as he fell. His right arm was under him. He lay absolutely still. Even as I bent to turn the man over, I was sure that nothing I could do and nobody I could call would do any good.

The man was heavy, with a big loose paunch that belied the thin legs and buttocks, and I grunted as I pulled the body over onto its back. Then I saw what the whore had said the man had been waving at her, that might have been a club. It wasn't a club, but a long cardboard tube tightly wrapped in brown paper, the kind artists and architects use to carry rolled-up prints and building plans. The man's hand was still clutching it. I didn't blame the whore for being frightened. In the dim light of the corridor I'd have been frightened, too, if a naked man had suddenly sprung out waving the thing menacingly at me.

I stood up, feeling a chill on my skin, nerving myself to touch the body once more. I stared down at the dead face. The eyes were open, staring up at me, the mouth in a last tortured grimace. Grunting animal sounds, the whore had said. There was no blood, no sign of a wound. I had never seen the man before, but that was not unusual with my working hours, coming in after guests had checked in for the night and leaving before they came down in the morning. It was a round, fat, old man's face, with a big fleshy nose and wispy gray hair on the balding skull. Even in the disarray of death, the face gave the impression of power and importance.

Fighting down a rising feeling of nausea, I knelt on one knee and put my ear to the man's chest. His breasts might have been those of an old woman, with just a few straggles of damp white hair and nipples that were almost green in the bare light. There was the sour, living odor of sweat, but no movement, no sound. Old man, I thought, as I stood up, why couldn't you have done this on somebody else's time?

I bent down again and hooked my hands under the dead man's armpits and dragged him through the open doorway into room 602. You couldn't just leave a naked body lying in the corridor like that. I had been working in the hotel business long enough to know that death was something you kept out of the sight of paying guests.

As I pulled the body along the floor of the little hallway that led into the room proper, the cardboard tube rolled to one side. I got the body into the room, next to the bed, which was a tangle of sheets and blankets. There was lipstick smeared all over the sheets and pillows. The lady I had let out around one o'clock, probably. I looked down with something like pity at the old body naked on the threadbare carpet, the flaccid dead flesh outlined against a faded floral pattern. One last erection. Joy and then mortality.

There was a medium-sized but expensive-looking leather suitcase open on the little desk. A worn wallet lay next to it and a gold money clip, with some bills in it. In the bag three clean shirts were to be seen, neatly folded.

Strewn on the desk were some quarters and dimes. I counted the money in the clip. Four tens and three ones. I dropped the clip back on the desk and picked up the wallet. There were ten crisp new hundred-dollar bills in it. I whistled softly. Whatever else had happened that night to the old man, he had not been robbed. I put the ten bills back into the wallet and carefully placed it back on the desk. It never occurred to me to take any of the money. That was the sort of man I used to be. *Thou shalt not steal.* Thou shalt not do a lot of things.

I glanced at the open suitcase. Along with the shirts there were two pair of old-fashioned button shorts, a striped necktie, two pairs of socks, some blue pajamas. Whoever he was, number 602 was going to stay in New York longer than he had planned.

The corpse on the floor oppressed me, made uncertain claims on me. I took one of the blankets from the bed and threw it over the body, covering the face, the staring eyes, the mutely shouting lips. I felt warmer, death now only a geometric shape on the floor.

I went back to the corridor to get the cardboard tube. There were no labels or addresses or identification of any kind on it. As I carried it into the room, I saw that the heavy brown paper had been torn raggedly away from the top. I was about to put it on the desk, next to the dead man's other belongings, when I caught a glimpse of green paper, partially pulled out of the opening. I drew it out. It was a hundred-dollar bill. It was not new like the bills in the wallet, but old and crumpled. I held the tube so that I could look down into it. As far as I could tell, it was crammed with bills. I remained immobile for a moment, then stuffed the bill I had taken out back in and folded the torn brown paper as neatly as I could over the top of the tube.

Holding the tube under my arm, I went to the door, switched off the light, stepped out into the corridor and turned the passkey in the lock of room number 602. My actions were crisp, almost automatic, as though all my life I had rehearsed for this moment, as though there were no alternatives.

I took the elevator down to the lobby, went into the little windowless room next to the office, using the key. There was a shelf running along above the safe, piled with stationery, old bills, ragged magazines from other years that had been recuperated from the rooms. Pictures of extinct politicians, naked girls who by now were no longer worth photographing—the momentarily illustrious dead, the extremely desirable women, monocled assassins, movie stars, carefully posed authors—a jumble of recent and not-so-recent American miscellany. Without hesitation I reached up and rolled the tube back toward the wall. I heard it plop down onto the shelf, out of sight, behind the dog-eared testimony of scandals and delights.

Then I went into the lighted office and called for an ambulance.

After that I sat down, finished unwrapping my sandwich, opened the bottle of beer. While I ate and drank, I looked up the register. Number 602 was, or had been, named John Ferris, had booked in only the afternoon before, and had given a home address on North Michigan Avenue, Chicago, Illinois.

I was finishing my beer when the bell rang and I saw the two men and the ambulance outside. One of the men was dressed in a blue uniform and was carrying a rolled-up stretcher. The other was in a white coat and was carrying a black bag, but I knew he wasn't a doctor. They don't waste doctors on ambulances in Manhattan, but dress up an orderly who is something of a medical technician, good enough to give first aid, and can usually be depended upon not to kill a patient on the spot. As I was opening the door, a prowl car drove up and a policeman got out.

"What's wrong?" the policeman asked. He was a heavyset, dark-jowled man, with unhealthy rings under his eyes.

"An old man croaked upstairs," I said.

"I'll go along with them, Dave," the policeman said to his partner at the wheel. I could hear the car radio chattering, dispatching officers to accidents, cases of wife beating, suicides, to streets where suspicious-looking men had been reported entering buildings.

Calmly, I led the group through the lobby. The technician was young and kept yawning as though he hadn't slept in weeks. People who work at night all look as though they are being punished for some nameless sin. The policeman's shoes on the bare floor of the lobby sounded as though they had lead soles. Going up in the elevator nobody spoke. I volunteered no information. A medicinal smell filled the elevator. They carry the hospital with them, I thought. I would have preferred it if the prowl car hadn't happened along.

When we got out on the sixth floor, I opened the door to 602 and led the way into the room. The technician ripped the blanket off the dead man, bent over him, and put his stethoscope to the man's chest. The policeman stood at the foot of the bed, his eyes taking in the lipstick-smeared sheets, the bag on the desk, the wallet and money clip lying next to it. "Who're you, Jack?" he asked me.

"I'm the night clerk."

"What's your name?" The way he asked was full of accusation, as though he was sure whatever name I gave would be a false one. What would he have done if I had answered, "My name is Ozymandias, King of Kings"? Probably taken out his black book and written, "Witness asserts name is Ozymandias. Probably an alias." He was a real nighttime cop, doomed to roam a dark city teeming with enemies, ambushes everywhere.

"My name is Grimes," I said.

"Where's the lady who was here with him?"

"I have no idea. I let a lady out around one o'clock. It might have been this one." I was surprised that I wasn't stuttering.

The technician stood up, taking the stethoscope plugs out of his ears. "DOA," he said flatly.

Dead on arrival. I could have told that without calling for an ambulance. I was discovering that there is a lot of wasted motion about death in a big city.

"What was it?" the cop asked. "Any wounds?"

"No. Coronary, probably."

"Anything to be done?"

"Not really." the technician said. "Go through the motions." He bent down again and rolled back the dead man's eyelids and peered into the rheumy eyes. Then he felt around the throat for a pulse, his hands gentle and expert.

"You seem to know what you're doing, friend," I said. "You must get a lot of practice."

"I'm in my second year in medical school," he said. "I only do this to eat."

The policeman went over to the desk and picked up the money clip. "Forty-three bucks," he said. "And in the wallet—" His thick eyebrows went up as he inspected it. He took out the bills and riffled them, counting. "An even grand," he said.

"Holy man!" I said. It was a good try, but from the way the cop looked at me, I wasn't fooling him.

"How much was there in it when you found him?" he asked. He was not a friendly neighborhood cop. Maybe he was a different man when he was on the day shift.

"I haven't the faintest idea," I said. Not stuttering was a triumph.

"You mean to say you didn't look?"

"I didn't look."

"Yeah. Why?"

"Why what?" This was a good time to look boyish.

"Why didn't you look?"

"It didn't occur to me."

"Yeah," the cop said again, but let it go at that. He riffled the bills again. "All in hundreds. You'd think a guy with that much dough on him would pick a better place to knock it off than a creep joint like this." He put the bills back into the wallet. "I guess I better take this into the station," he said. "Anybody want to count?"

"We trust you, Officer," the technician said. There was the faintest echo of irony in his voice. He was young, but already an expert at death and despoliation.

The policeman looked through the wallet compartments. He had thick hairy fingers, like small clubs. "That's funny," he said.

"What's funny?" the intern asked.

"There's no credit cards or business cards or driver's license. A man with more than a thousand bucks in cash on him." He shook his head and pushed his cap back. "You wouldn't call that normal, would you?" He looked aggrieved, as though the dead man had not behaved the way a decent American citizen who expected to be protected in death as in life by his country's police should have behaved. "You know who he is?" he asked me.

"I never saw him before," I said. "His name is Ferris and he lived in Chicago. I'll show you the register."

The policeman put the wallet into his pocket, went quickly through the shirts and underwear and socks in the bag, then opened the closet door and searched the pockets of the single dark suit and overcoat that were hanging there. "Nothing," he said. "No letters, no address book. Nothing. A guy with a bad heart. Some people got no more sense than a horse. Look, I got to make a inventory. In the presence of witnesses." He took out his pad and moved around the room, listing the few possessions, now no longer possessed, of the body on the floor. It didn't take long. "Here," he said to me, "you have to sign this." I glanced at the list. One thousand and forty-three dollars. One suitcase, brown, unlocked, one suit and overcoat, gray, one hat . . . I signed, under the patrolman's name. The cop put his thick black pad into a back pocket. "Who put the blanket over him?" he asked.

"I did," I said.

"You find him there on the floor?"

"No. He was out in the corridor."

"Starkers—like that?"

"Starkers. I dragged him in."

"What did you want to do that for?" The policeman sounded plaintive now, faced with a complication.

"This is a hotel," I said. "You have to keep up appearances."

The policeman glowered at me. "What are you—trying to be smart?" he said.

"No, Officer, I'm not trying to be smart. If I'd left him out where I found him and somebody had come along and seen him, I'd have had my ass chewed down to the bone by the manager."

"Next time you see a body laying anyplace," the policeman said, "you just let it lay until the law arrives. Just remember that, see?"

"Yes, sir," I said.

"You alone in this hotel all night?"

"Yes."

"You work in the office all by yourself?"

"Yes."

"How'd you happen to come up here? He telephone down or something?"

"No. A lady was leaving the building and she said there was a crazy old naked man up on the sixth floor who was making advances toward her." Objectively, almost as though I were listening to myself on a tape, I noted that I hadn't stuttered once.

"Sexual advances?"

"She implied that."

"A lady? What sort of lady?"

"I would think she was a whore," I said.

"You ever see her before?"

"No."

"You get a lot of lady traffic in this hotel, don't you?"

"Average, I would say."

The policeman stared down at the contorted bluish face on the floor. "How long you think he's been dead, bud?"

"Hard to tell. Anywhere from ten minutes to a half hour," the technician said. He looked up at me. "Did you call the hospital as soon as you saw him? The call came in at three fifteen."

"Well," I said, "first I listened to see if I could get a heartbeat, then I pulled him in here and covered him and then I had to go down to the office and phone."

"Did you try mouth-to-mouth resuscitation?"

"No."

"Why not?" The technician wasn't being inquisitive; it was too late at night and he was too tired for that; he was just going through a routine.

"It didn't occur to me," I said.

"A lot of things didn't occur to you, mister," the policeman said darkly. Like the intern he was going through a routine. Suspicion was his routine. But his heart wasn't in it and he sounded bored already.

"Okay," the intern said, "let's take him away. No sense wasting any time. When you find out what the family wants to do with the body," he said, addressing me, "call the morgue."

"I'll send a telegram to Chicago right away," I said.

The two ambulance men lifted the body onto the stretcher. "He's a heavy old sonofabitch, isn't he?" the driver said, as he let the cadaver down. "I bet he ate good, the old goat. Sexual advances. With a droopy old cock like that." He draped a sheet over the body and strapped the ankles to the foot of the stretcher while the technician buckled a strap across the chest. The elevator was too small to handle the body lying flat and they would have to stand the stretcher up to fit in it. They took the stretcher out into the hall, following the policeman. I took a last look around the room and put out the light before closing the door.

"Had a busy night?" I asked the technician pleasantly, as the elevator started down. Be matter-of-fact, normal, I told myself. Obviously it was perfectly normal for all three of these men to carry dead men out of hotels in the middle of the night, and I tried to fit into their standards of behavior.

"This is my fourth call since I came on," he said. "I'll trade jobs with you."

"Yeah," I said. "I'll still be sitting here all night working an adding machine while you're raking in loot year after year." Now, I thought, why did I use the word loot? "I read the papers," I said quickly; "doctors make more than anybody else in the country."

"God bless America," the technician said as the elevator came to a stop and the door opened. He and the driver picked up the stretcher, and I led the way across the lobby. I opened the door for them with my key and watched as they put the body into the ambulance. The policeman at the wheel of the car was asleep, snoring softly, his cap off and his head lolling back.

The technician got into the ambulance with the corpse, and the driver slammed the door shut. He went around to the front and started the motor, reviving it loudly. He had the siren going while he was still in first gear.

"What the hell is his hurry?" the policeman standing on the sidewalk with me said. "They're not going anywhere."

"Aren't you going to wake your pal up?" I asked.

"Nah. He wakes up if a call comes for us. He's got the instinct of a animal. Might as well let him get his beauty rest. I wish I had his nerves." He sighed, weighed down by cares which his own nerves were not strong enough to support. "Let's get a look at the register, mister." He followed me back into the hotel, his tread heavy, the law weighty.

I unlocked the office door. I didn't look up at the shelf over the safe, where the cardboard tube lay hidden behind the boxes of stationery and the piles of old magazines. "I have a bottle of bourbon in here, if you'd like a slug," I said, as we went into the front office. Even as I spoke I admired the absolutely matter-of-fact way in which I was behaving. I was running on computers; all the cards were correctly punched. Data input. But it had been an effort not to look up at the shelf.

"Well, I'm on duty, you know," the policeman said. "But one small slug . . . "

I opened the register and pointed out the entry for room 602. The policeman slowly copied it out into his black book. The history of the city of New York, faithfully recorded in twenty thousand handwritten pages by the graduates of the police academy. An interesting archaeological discovery.

I got out the bottle and uncorked it. "Sorry, I don't have a glass," I said.

"I drunk out of bottles before this," the policeman said. He raised the bottle. "Well, *L'chaim*," he said, and took a long swig.

"You Jewish?" I asked as the policeman gave me the bottle.

"Nah. My partner. I caught it from him."

L'chaim. To life, I remembered from the song in *Fiddler on the Roof.* "I think I'll join you," I said, raising the bottle. "I can use it. A night like this can leave a man a little shaky."

"This is nothing," the cop said. "You oughta see some of the things we run into."

"I can imagine, I said. I drank.

"Well," the policeman said, "I gotta be going. There'll be an inspector around in the morning. Just keep that room locked until he gets here, understand?"

"I'll pass the word on to the day man."

"Night work," the policeman said. "Do you sleep good during the day?"

"Fair."

"Not me." The policeman shook his head mournfully. "Look at the rings under my eyes."

I looked at the rings under the policeman's eyes. "You could use a good night's sleep," I said.

"You ain't kidding." The man dug a knuckle into his eye, viciously. *If thy eye offend thee* . . . "Well, at least there ain't been no crime committed. Be thankful for small mercies," he said surprisingly. Unsuspected depths, a vocabulary that included the word mercy.

I accompanied him to the front door, opened it politely.

"Have a good day," the policeman said.

"Thanks. You, too."

"Hah," he said.

I watched the heavy, slow-moving man climb into the prowl car and wake up his partner. The car went slowly down the silent street. I locked the door and went back to the office. I picked up the telephone and dialed. I had to wait for at least ten rings before the connection came through. This country is in full decay, I thought, waiting; nobody moves.

"Western Union," the voice said.

"I want to send a telegram to Chicago," I said. I gave the name and address, spelling out Ferris slowly and clearly. "Like wheel," I said.

"What's that?" The voice of Western Union was irritated.

"Ferris wheel," I said. "Amusement parks."

"What is the message, please?"

"Regret to inform you that John Ferris, of your address," I said, "died this morning at three fifteen A.M. Please get in touch with me immediately for instructions. Signed, H. M. Drusack, Manager, Hotel St. Augustine, Manhattan." By the time the reply came in, Drusack would be on duty and I would be somewhere else, safely out of the way. There was no need for the family in Chicago to know my name. "Charges please?"

The operator gave me the charges. I noted them on a sheet of paper. Good old Drusack would put them on Ferris' bill. I knew Drusack.

I took another slug of bourbon, then settled down in the swivel chair and picked up the Bible. I figured I could get well into Proverbs before the day man came on to relieve me.

CHAPTER 4

I TOOK A taxi home after telling the day man what had happened, or most of what had happened. I left the envelope for my bookie friend, as usual, with the note inside telling him I was betting five dollars on Ask Gloria at Hialeah in the second. For as long as possible it was wise to make it seem that today was just like every other day.

Even in the East Eighties where I lived, muggings at all hours were not infrequent. The taxi was a luxury, but this was no day to be mugged. I had gotten the tube down from the shelf when the day man was busy in the front office. There had been no one in the lobby when I went out, and, even if there had been, there was nothing remarkable about a man carrying a cardboard tube wrapped in brown paper in broad daylight.

My head was clear and I wasn't in the least bit sleepy. Ordinarily, when the weather was good I would walk the thirty-odd blocks to my apartment, stopping for breakfast at a coffee shop on Second Avenue, before getting into bed and sleeping until two o'clock in the afternoon. But today I knew I couldn't sleep, had no need of sleep.

When I opened the door of the one-room apartment, its windows gray in the cold north light, I went to the refrigerator in the kitchenette and took out and opened a bottle of beer. I didn't bother to take off my overcoat. Then, occasionally taking a sip of beer, I tore the paper from the cardboard tube. Using a knife, I managed to slit the tube down one side. It was stuffed from top to bottom with one-hundred-dollar bills.

I took the bills out one by one, smoothed them, and arranged them in piles of ten on the kitchen table. When I finished, there were a hundred piles. One hundred thousand dollars. They covered the table.

I stared silently at the bills spread out on the table. I finished the beer. I wasn't conscious of feeling any emotion, not fear, or exhilaration, or regret. I looked at my watch. It was just eight forty. The banks wouldn't open for another twenty minutes.

I got a small bag from the closet and stacked the money in it. There was no one else who had a key to the apartment, but there was no sense in taking any chances. Carrying the bag, I went downstairs and walked to the avenue. There was a stationery store on the next block and I bought a packet of rubber bands and three thick manila envelopes, the largest in the shop.

Then I went back to the apartment, locked the door, took off my overcoat and jacket, and methodically slipped the rubber bands around each batch of bills before putting it into one of the manila envelopes. I kept one thousand dollars, which I put in my wallet, for immediate use.

I sealed the envelopes, grimacing at the taste of the glue as I licked the flaps. Then I took another bottle of beer from the refrigerator, poured the beer into a glass, and sipped at it, sitting in front of the table, in front of the neat pile of thick brown envelopes.

I had taken the apartment furnished and only the books in the room were mine. And there weren't many of those. When I finished a book, I usually threw it away. There was never enough heat and when I sat in the one frayed easy chair to read, I usually wore the padded ski jacket that hung on a hook on the back of the front door. This morning, while it was as cold as usual, and even though I was now in my shirt-sleeves, I felt perfectly comfortable.

I knew that I was going to have to move out. And quit the job. And get out of the city. I had no plan beyond that, but I knew that one day or another somebody was going to appear, looking for one hundred thousand dollars.

At the bank I had to write out two specimen signatures on separate cards. My hand was absolutely steady. The sealed manila envelopes with the money in them lay on the desk at which I was sitting, facing the young assistant manager who was serving me. He had the bland, sexless face of a seminarian. The conversation between us was short and businesslike. I'd shaved and was neatly dressed. I still had a couple of decent suits left over from the old days, and today I had put on a sober, quiet, gray Glen plaid with a blue oxford shirt and solid blue tie. I wanted to give the impression of being a solid citizen, perhaps not wealthy, certainly not wealthy, but modestly prosperous, a careful, industrious man who might have some bonds and some legal papers that were too valuable to leave lying around the house.

"Your address, please, Mr. Grimes," the assistant manager was saying.

I gave him the address of the St. Augustine. If anybody got as far as the bank in the search for me, which was unlikely in any case, there would be no useful information to be found.

"Will you be the sole person authorized to have access to the safety-deposit box?" That's for sure, brother, I thought. But all I said was, "Yes."

"That will be twenty dollars for the year. Do you wish to pay by cash or by check?"

"Cash." I gave him a hundred-dollar bill. His expression did not change. Obviously, he thought that I looked like a man who might normally carry a hundred-dollar bill loose in his pocket. I took this as a good sign. The assistant manager smoothed the bill carefully, with a churchly gesture, went over to a teller's window to break the bill down into smaller denominations.

I sat relaxedly at the desk, touching one of the manila envelopes with the tips of my fingers. I hadn't stuttered once all morning.

The assistant manager came back and handed me my change and made out a receipt. I folded it neatly and put it into my wallet. Then I followed the man down to the vault. There was a hygienic, almost religious hush there that made you hesitate to speak above a whisper. Stained-glass windows would not have been out of place. The parable of the talents. The vault attendant gave me a key and led me down a silent aisle of money.

With the three thick manila envelopes under my arm. I couldn't help wondering how all the treasure lying in those locked boxes, the greenbacks, the stocks and bonds, the jewelry, had been accumulated, what sweat expended, what crimes enacted, through whose hands all those stones and all that luxuriously printed paper had passed before coming to rest in this sanctified, cold steel cave. I looked at the attendant's face as he used the two keys, his and mine, and pulled out a box for me. He was an old man, pale from his underground existence. He didn't look as though he had ever speculated about anything. Perhaps such people were chosen for their lack of curiosity. A curious man would go mad here. I followed the attendant back to a little curtained cubbyhole with a desk in it, and the attendant left me there with my box, respecting the privacy of wealth.

I tore open the manila envelopes and laid the piles of bills in the box. I looked at the neatly stacked notes, trying without success to foresee what they finally would mean for me. It was like looking at a huge engine, quiet now, but capable of sudden, brutal force. I closed the box with a decisive little click. I tossed the envelopes into a wastepaper basket and went back along the row of safes with the attendant and watched him slide the box into my own slot. The attendant used both keys once more to lock the safe. I dropped my key into my pocket, said, "Thank you," to the man. "Have a good day," courteous as any policeman.

"Hah," the man said. He hadn't had a good day since he was twelve.

I went up the steps and out onto the sunny, cold avenue. Okay for today, I thought. Chemical Bank and Trust, with all my worldly goods I thee endow.

I walked home briskly and packed. Beside the small bag I had carried the money in, I had a flight bag and everything I owned fitted in, with room to spare. I left the old parka hanging in the closet. Whoever moved in next would need it more than I. Then I wrote a note to the landlord saying that I was giving up the apartment. I had no lease and was on a month-to-month arrangement, so there wouldn't be any difficulties there. I folded the note and stuck it in an envelope and dropped the key in with the note. Downstairs I put the envelope in the landlord's mailbox. Carrying the two bags, I left the building without looking back. I wouldn't ever again have to worry about keeping warm at that particular address.

I hailed a cab and gave the driver the name of a hotel on Central Park West. It was a neighborhood I had never lived in and had only rarely visited. Even with my nighttime job and my reclusive habits, in my old neighborhood on the East Side there were bound to be people who had come to recognize me, my bookie, the bartender in the saloon around the corner I sometimes drank in, a waitress in a nearby Italian restaurant, others, who could point me out to someone who might come around making inquiries about me. Eventually, I knew, I would put a great deal more distance behind me, but for the time being crossing Central Park would have to do. But I didn't want to flee blindly. I knew that I needed at least one day to think and plan.

The hotel was a busy one, but middle class and commercial, and not the sort of place a man who had entered into sudden wealth would choose to celebrate in.

I asked for a single room with bath, registered under the name of Theodore Brown, gave as my home address Camden, New Jersey, a city I had never visited, and followed the bellboy with the bags into the elevator. On the way up, I studied the man's sullen, narrow face. He was young, but there was no trace of innocence in the guarded eyes, the tightly closed lips. It was a face designed specifically by nature for corruption. What wonders a man with a face like that could perform with a hundred thousand dollars.

In the room, which overlooked the park, the bellboy put the big bag in a chair, turned on the light in the bathroom, ostentatiously earning his tip.

"I wonder if you could do me a favor," I said, taking out a five-dollar bill.

The boy eyed the bill. "Depends on what the favor is," the bellboy said. "The management don't like whores coming in and out."

"Nothing like that," I said. "I'd just like to make a bet on a horse and I'm new in town and . . . " I had entered a new life, but I was taking some baggage along with me. Ask Gloria cantered out of the stables of my past.

The bellboy showed his teeth in what he imagined was an accommodating smile. "We have a house bookie," he said. "I can have him up here in fifteen minutes."

"Thanks." I gave him the five-dollar bill.

"Very good of you, sir," the bellboy said. The bill disappeared. "Do you mind telling me what you're going to play?"

"Ask Gloria in the second," I said. "At Hialeah."

"It's a fifteen-to-one shot," he said. He was a student of the sport.

"So it is," I said.

"Interesting," he said. There was no doubt about what he was going to do with my five dollars. Dishonest as he was, he would live and die a poor man.

When he left the room, I loosened my tie and lay down on the bed, although I still wasn't tired. Try money, I thought, grinning, for that run-down feeling, that mid-morning sag. More and more, thinking these days is in the form of a television commercial.

The house bookie appeared promptly. He was a huge fat man in a rumpled suit, with three ball-point pens clipped into the breast pocket of his jacket. He panted when he moved and spoke in a high, almost soprano voice, surprising coming out of all that bulk. "Hi, pal," he said as he came into the room. He looked around the room swiftly, taking everything in. He was a man prepared for ambush. Although he performed in daylight, he lived in the same world as the cop in the prowl car. "Morris said you were looking for a little action."

"A little," I said. "I like Ask Gloria for . . . " I hesitated for a moment. "For three hundred to win in the second at Hialeah. The morning line has her at fifteen to one." I had a peculiar feeling of lightheartedness, as though I were in an open plane, without oxygen, and had suddenly climbed from the deck to twenty thousand feet.

The fat man took a creased sheet of paper from his pocket, unfolded it, ran a finger down it. "I can give you twelve to one," he said.

"Okay," I said. I gave him three bills.

The bookie took the bills, examined them closely, glanced briefly at me. I detected respect, a certain delicate wariness.

"My name is . . . " I started to say.

"I know your name, Mr. Brown. Morris told me," the bookie said. He made a note with one of the pens on the sheet of paper. "I pay off at six o'clock in the bar downstairs."

"See you at six," I said.

"You hope," the fat man said, without smiling. He placed the notes that I had given him on the outside of a roll of bills, snapped a rubber band deftly around it. He had small, fat, nimble hands. "Morris always knows where to find me, Mr. Brown," he said as he went out.

After that, I unpacked and started to put my clothes away. As I was taking my toothbrush and shaving things out of the kit, my razor fell to the floor and skidded beneath the chest of drawers. I knelt to retrieve it, running my hand under the chest. Along with the razor and a small pile of dust, I brought out a coin. It was a silver dollar. I blew the dust off the coin and put it in my pocket. They don't clean very thoroughly in this hotel, I thought. Good for them. Today, I was definitely ahead of the game.

I looked at my watch. It was almost noon. I picked up the telephone and gave the number of the St. Augustine to the operator. As usual, it was nearly thirty seconds before there was an answer. Clara, the operator, regarded all calls as wanton interruptions in her private life, which consisted, as far as I could ever tell, of reading magazines on astrology. She used delay as a means of protest and punishment for electronic interrupters of her search for the perfect horoscope, wealth, fame, a young and handsome dark stranger.

"Hello, Clara," I said. "Is Mr. Drusack there?"

"He sure is," Clara said. "He's been on my neck all morning to call you. What the hell is your number anyway? I couldn't find it anywhere. I called the hotel we have here as your address and they say they never heard of you."

"That was two years ago. I moved." Actually, I had moved four times since then. A typical American, I had continually pushed toward new frontiers, always farther north. The wealth of the Yukon, by way of the East Eighties, Harlem, Riverdale, the frozen tundra. "I don't have a number, Clara."

"What do you mean, you don't have a number?"

"I don't have a telephone."

"You're a lucky man, Mr. Grimes."

"You can say that again, Clara. Now give me Mr. Drusack."

"My God, Grimes," Drusack said when he got on the phone, "you sure left me a mess. You better get right on down here and help me straighten it out."

"I'm very sorry, Mr. Drusack," I said. I tried to sound genuinely grieved. "I'm busy today. What's the matter?"

"What's the matter?" Drusack was shouting now. "I'll tell you what's the matter. The goddamn Western Union called at ten o'clock. There's no John Ferris at that address you gave them, that's what's the matter."

"That's the address he registered under."

"You come and tell that to the police. They were in here for an hour this morning. And there were two characters in here asking for him, and if they weren't packing guns I'm Miss Rheingold of 1983. They talked to me as if I was hiding the sonofabitch or something. They asked me if the guy left a message for them. *Did* he leave a message?"

"Not that I know of."

"Well, they want to talk to you."

"Why me?" I asked, although I knew why.

"I told them the night man found the guy. I told them you'd be in at eleven P.M., but they said they couldn't wait that long, what was your address. Grimes, do you know that nobody in this goddamn hotel knows where you live? Naturally, those two fuckers wouldn't believe *that*. They said they're coming back here at three o'clock and I'd better damn well produce you. Scary. They weren't any small-time hoods. Short hair, dressed like stockbrokers. Quiet. Like spies in the movies. They weren't kidding. Not at all kidding. So you be here. Because I'm going to be out on a long, long lunch."

"That's what I wanted to talk to you about, Mr. Drusack," I said smoothly, enjoying a conversation with the manager for the first time since I started working for him. "I wanted to say good-bye."

"What do you mean, good-bye?" Drusack was really shouting now. "Good-bye, good-bye, who says good-bye like that?"

"I do, Mr. Drusack. I decided last night I don't like the way you run your hotel. I'm quitting. . . . I *have* quit."

"Quit! Nobody quits like that. For Christ's sake, it's only Tuesday. You got things here. You got a half bottle of bourbon, you got your goddamn Bible, you . . . "

"I'm donating it to the hotel library," I said.

"Grimes," Drusack roared. "You can't do this to me. I'll have the police bring you in. I'll . . . "

I put the telephone gently down on its cradle. Then I went out to lunch. I went to a good seafood restaurant near Lincoln Center and had a large grilled lobster that cost eight dollars, with two bottles of Heineken.

As I sat there in the warm restaurant, eating the good food and drinking the imported beer, I realized that it was the first moment since the whore had come running down from the sixth floor of the hotel that I had time to think about what I was doing. Everything up to now had been almost mechanical, act following act unhesitatingly, my movements ordered and precise, as though I had been following a program learned, assimilated, long ago. Now I had to make decisions, consider possibilities, scan the horizon for danger. Even as I was thinking this, I saw that something in my subconscious had made me choose a table where I could sit with my back against the wall, with a clear view of the entrance to the restaurant and of everybody who came in. I was amused by the realization. Given half a chance, every man becomes the hero of his own detective story.

Amusement or not, the hour had come to take stock, think about my position. I could no longer depend on simple reflexes or on anything in my past to guide me for the future. I had always been completely law-abiding. I had never done anything to make enemies. Certainly not enemies like the two men who had frightened Drusack that morning. Naturally, I thought, men who came to a hotel where they expected to receive a hundred thousand dollars in cash from someone who was registered most probably under a false name and certainly with a false address might very likely be carrying guns or at least *look* like men who were in the habit of carrying guns. Drusack might have been a little hysterical that morning, but he was no fool and he had been in the hotel business a long time and had a feeling about who meant trouble when he arrived at the front desk and who didn't. Drusack couldn't possibly know just what trouble the two men represented and in all probability would never know.

One thing was sure, or almost sure—the police wouldn't be brought in, although an individual crooked policeman here or there might be in on it. So I wouldn't have that to worry about. There was no possibility that the man who had registered under the name of John Ferris and the two men who had come to meet him at the hotel were engaged in a legal business transaction. It had to be bribery of some sort, a payoff, blackmail. This was when the scandals of the second Nixon Administration were just beginning to surface, when we all discovered that perfectly respectable people, pillars of the community, had developed the habit of secretly carrying huge sums of money around in attaché cases and stuffing hundreds of thousands of dollars in office desks, so it didn't occur to me, as it could have later, that I might have stumbled on an amateurish and comparatively undangerous political technique. What I had to deal with, I was sure, was grim professionalism, men who killed for money. Like spies in the movies, Drusack had said. I discounted that. I had seen the body.

Gangsters, I thought. The Mob. Despite the occasional movies and magazine pieces about the underworld I had seen and read, like most people, I had only the vaguest notion of what was meant by the Mob and a perhaps exaggerated respect for its omnipotence, its system of intelligence, its power to seek out and destroy, the lengths it was likely to go to exact vengeance.

One thing I was sure of. I was on its side of the fence now, whoever it might turn out to be, and I was playing by its rules. In one moment in the tag end of a cold winter night, I had become an outlaw who could look only to himself for safety.

Rule one was simple. I could not sit still. I would have to keep moving, disappear. New York was a big city and there were undoubtedly thousands of people hiding out in it successfully for years, but the men who even now were probably on my trail would have my name, my age, a description of my appearance, could, without too much trouble and with a minimum of cunning, discover where I had gone to college, where I had worked before, what my family connections were. Lucky me, I thought, I am not married, there are no children, neither my brothers nor my sister have the faintest notion of where I am. Still, in New York, there was always the chance of running into someone I knew, who would somehow be overheard saying the wrong thing to the wrong man.

And just this very morning, there was the bellboy. I had made my first mistake there. He would remember me. And from the look of him, he would sell his sister for a twenty-dollar bill. And the bookie in the hotel. Mistake number two. I could easily imagine what sort of connections *he* had.

I didn't know what I was eventually going to do with the money now lying in the hush of the vault, but I certainly intended to enjoy it. And I wouldn't enjoy it in New York. I had always wanted to travel, and now traveling would be both a pleasure and a necessity.

Luxuriously, I lit a cigar and leaned back in my chair and thought of all the places I would like to see. Europe. The words London, Paris, Rome rang pleasantly in my mind.

But before I could cross the ocean I had things to do, people to see, closer to home. First I would have to get a passport. I had never needed one before, but I was going to need one now. I knew I could get it at the State Department office in New York, but whoever might be looking for me could very well figure out that that would be the first place I would go and could be there waiting for me. It was an outside chance but I was in no mood to take even that.

Tomorrow, I decided, I would go to Washington. By bus.

I looked at my watch. It was nearly three o'clock. The two men who had confronted Drusack that morning would be approaching the St. Augustine, eager to ask questions and no doubt with the means to compel answers. I flicked the ashes off the end of my cigar and smiled gently. Why, this is the best day I've had in years, I thought.

I paid my bill and left the restaurant, found a small photographer's shop and sat for passport photos. The photographer told me they would be ready at five thirty, and I spent the time watching a French movie. I might as well start getting used to the sound of the language, I thought, as I settled comfortably in my seat, admiring the views of the bridges across the Seine.

When I got back to my hotel with the photographs in my pocket (I looked boyish), it was nearly six o'clock. I remembered the bookie and went into the bar to look for him. The bookie was in a corner, alone, sitting at a table, drinking a glass of milk.

"How'd I do?" I asked.

"Are you kidding?" the bookie said.

"No. Honest."

"You won," the bookie said. The silver dollar had been a reliable omen. Speak again, Oracle. My debt to my man at the Hotel St. Augustine was reduced by sixty dollars. All in all a useful afternoon's work.

The bookie did not look happy. "You came in by a length and a half. Next time tell me where you get your information from. And that little shit, Morris. You had to let him in on it. That's what I call adding insult to injury."

"I'm a friend of the working man," I said.

"Working man." The bookie snorted. "Let me give you a piece of advice, brother, about that particular working man. Don't leave your wallet where he can spot it. Or even your false teeth." He took a few envelopes out of his pocket, shuffled through them, gave me one and put the rest back in his pocket. "Thirty-six hundred bucks," the bookie said. "Count it."

I put the envelope away. "No need," I said. "You look like an honest man."

"Yeah." The bookie sipped at his milk.

"Can I buy you a drink?"

"I can only stand so much milk," the bookie said. He belched.

"You're in the wrong business for a man with a bad stomach," I said.

"You can say that again. You want to bet on the hockey game tonight?"

"I don't think so," I said. "I'm not really a gambling man. So long, pal."

The bookie didn't say anything.

I went over to the bar and had a Scotch and soda, then went out into the lobby. Morris, the bellboy, was standing near the front desk. "I hear you hit it big," he said.

"Not so big," I said airily. "Still, it wasn't a bad day's work. Did you take my tip?"

"No," the bellboy said. He was a man who lied for the sheer pleasure of lying. "I was too busy on the floors."

"That's too bad," I said. "Better luck next time."

I had a steak for dinner in the hotel dining room, and another cigar with the coffee and brandy and then went up to my room, undressed, and got into bed. I slept without dreaming for twelve hours and woke up with the sun streaming into the room. I hadn't slept that well since I was a small boy.

CHAPTER 5

IN THE MORNING I packed my bags and carried them myself to the elevator. I didn't want to have any more conversations with Morris, the bellboy. I checked out, paying with some of the money I had won on the second race at Hialeah. Under the hotel canopy I looked around carefully. There was nobody as far as I could see who was waiting for me or who might follow me. I got into a cab and drove to the bus terminal where I could board a bus to Washington. Nobody would dream of looking in a bus terminal for a man who had just stolen a hundred thousand dollars.

I tried the Hotel Mayflower first. As long as I was in Washington I thought I might as well take the best of what the city had to offer. But the hotel was full, the man at the desk told me. He gave me the impression that in this center of power one had to be *elected* to a room by a large constituency, or at least appointed by the President. I resolved to buy a new overcoat. Still, he was polite enough to suggest a hotel about a mile away. It usually had rooms, he said. He said it the way he might have said of an acquaintance that he usually wore soiled shirts.

He turned out to be right. The building was new, all chrome and bright paint and looked like a motel on any highway in America, but there were vacancies. I registered under my own name. In this city, I felt, I didn't have to go to extreme lengths to remain anonymous. Remembering what I had heard about crime in the streets of the capital, I prudently put my wallet in the hotel's vault, keeping out only a hundred dollars for the day's expenses. Avoid the chambers of the mighty. Danger lurks at their doorsteps. The Saturday Night Special lays down the final law.

The last time I had been in Washington had been when I'd flown a charter of Republicans down from Vermont for the Inaugural of Richard Nixon in 1969. There had been a lot of drinking among the Republicans on the plane, and I had spent a good part of the flight arguing with a drunken Vermont State Senator who had been a B-17 pilot during World War Two and who wanted to be allowed to fly the plane after we crossed Philadelphia. I hadn't gone to the Inaugural or to the ball for which the Republicans had found me a ticket. At that time I considered myself a Democrat. I didn't know what I considered myself now.

I had spent the day of the Inaugural at Arlington. It seemed a fitting way to celebrate the installation of Richard Nixon as President of the United States.

There was a Grimes buried in the cemetery, an uncle, who had died in 1921 from the effects of a dose of chlorine gas in the Argonne Forest. Myself, I would never be buried in Arlington. I was a veteran of no wars. I had been too young for Korea and by the time Vietnam came around I was set in the job with the airline. I had not been tempted to volunteer. Walking among the graves, I experienced no regret that I finally would not be laid to rest in this company of heroes. I had never been pugnacious— even as a boy I had had only one fistfight at school, and although I was patriotic enough and saluted the flag gladly, wars had no attraction for me. My patriotism did not run in the direction of bloodshed.

When I went out of the hotel the next morning, I saw there was a long line of people waiting for taxis, so I started to walk, hoping to pick up a taxi along the avenue. It was a mild day, pleasant after the biting cold of New York, and the street I was on gave off an air of grave prosperity, the passersby well-dressed and orderly. For half a block I walked side by side with a dignified, portly gentleman wearing a coat with a mink collar who looked as though he could well be a Senator. I amused myself by imagining what the man's reaction would be if I went up to him, fixed him, like the Ancient Mariner, who stoppeth one of three, and told him what I had been doing since early Tuesday morning.

I stopped at a traffic light and hailed a cab which was slowing to a stop there. It was only after the cab had come to a halt that I saw that there was a passenger in the back, a woman. But the cabby, a black man with gray hair, leaned over and turned down the window. "Which way you going, mister?" the cabby asked.

"State."

"Get in," the cabby said. "The lady is on the way."

I opened the back door. "Do you mind if I get in with you, ma'am?" I asked.

"I certainly do," the woman said. She was quite young, no more than thirty, and rather pretty, in a blonde, sharp way, less pretty at the moment than she might ordinarily have been, because of the tight, angry set of her lips.

"I'm sorry," I said apologetically and closed the door. I was about to step back on the curb when the cabby opened the front door. "Get in, suh," the cabby said.

Serves the bitch right, I thought, and, without looking at the woman, got in beside the driver. There was a bitter rustle from the back seat, but neither the cabby nor I turned around. We drove in silence. When the cab stopped in front of a pillared government building, the woman leaned forward. "One dollar and forty-five cents?" she said.

"Yes, ma'am," the cabby said.

The woman yanked open her purse, took out a dollar bill and some change, and put it down on the back seat. "Don't expect to find a tip," she said as she got out. She walked toward the big front doors, her back furious. She had nice legs, I noted.

The cabby chuckled as he reached back and scooped up his fare. "Civil servant," he said.

"Spelled c-u-n-t," I said.

The cabby chuckled again. "Oh, in this town you learn to take the fat with the lean," he said.

As he drove, he shook his head, chuckling to himself, over and over again.

At State, I gave the man a dollar tip. "I tell you, suh," the cabby said, "that little blonde lady done made my day."

I went into the lobby of the building and up to the information desk.

"I'd like to see Mr. Jeremy Hale, please," I said to the girl at the desk.

"Do you know what room he's in?"

"I'm afraid not."

The girl sighed. Washington, I saw, was full of tight-assed women. While the girl thumbed through a thick alphabetical list for Jeremy Hale I remembered how I had once said to Hale, long ago, With a name like that, Jerry, you *had* to wind up in the State Department. I smiled at the memory.

"Is Mr. Hale expecting you?"

"No." I hadn't spoken to Hale or written him in years. Hale certainly wasn't expecting me. We had been in the same class at Ohio State and had been good friends. After I took the job in Vermont we had skied together several winters, when Hale wasn't on a post overseas.

"Your name, please?" the girl was saying.

I gave her my name and she dialed a number on the desk telephone.

The girl spoke briefly on the phone, put it down, scribbled out a pass. "Mr. Hale can see you now." She handed me the pass and I saw she had written on it the number of the room I was to go to.

"Thank you, miss," I said. Too late, I saw the wedding ring on her finger. I have made another enemy in Washington, I thought.

I went up in the elevator. The elevator was nearly full, but it rose in decorous silence. The secrets of state were being well-guarded.

Hale's name was on a door that was exactly the same as a long row of identical doors that disappeared in diminishing perspective down a seemingly endless corridor. What can all these people possibly be doing for the United States of America eight hours a day, two hundred days a year? I wondered, as I knocked.

"Come in," a woman's voice called.

I pushed the door open and entered a small room where a beautiful young woman was typing. Good old Jeremy Hale.

The beautiful young woman smiled radiantly at me. I wondered how she behaved in taxicabs. "Are you Mr. Grimes?" she said, rising. She was even more beautiful standing up than sitting down, tall and dark, lissome in a tight blue sweater.

"I am indeed," I said.

"Mr. Hale is delighted you could come. Go right in, please." She held the door to the inner office open for me.

Hale was seated at a cluttered desk, peering down at a sheaf of papers in front of him. He had put on weight since I had last seen him, and had added statesmanlike solidity to the mild polite face. On the desk in a silver frame was a family group, a woman and two children, a boy and a girl. Everything in moderation. Zero population growth. An example to the heathen. Hale looked up when I came in and stood, smiling widely. "Doug," he said, "you don't know how glad I am to see you."

As we shook hands, I was surprised at how moved I was by my friend's greeting. For three years now, no one had been genuinely glad to see me.

"Where've you been, where've you been, man?" Hale said. He waved to a leather sofa along one side of the spacious office and as I sat down pulled a wooden armchair close to the sofa and sat down himself. "I thought you'd disappeared from the face of the earth. I wrote three times and each time the letters came back. Haven't you learned anything about forwarding addresses yet? And I wrote your girl friend, Pat, asking about you and she wrote back and said she didn't know where you'd gone." He scowled at me. He was agreeable-looking, tall, comfortably built, soft-faced, and the scowl was incongruous on him. "And you don't look so almighty great, either. You look as though you haven't been out in the open air for years."

"Okay, okay," I said, "one thing at a time, Jerry. I just decided I didn't like flying anymore and I moved on. Here and there."

"I wanted to ski with you last winter. I had two weeks off and I heard the snow was great. . . ."

"I haven't been doing much skiing, to tell the truth," I said.

Impulsively, Hale touched my shoulder. "All right," he said. "I won't ask any questions." Even as a boy in college he had always been quick and sensitive. "Well, anyway, just one question. Where're you coming from and what're you doing in Washington?" He laughed. "I guess that's two questions."

"I'm coming from New York," I said, "and I'm in Washington to ask you to do a little favor for me."

"The government is at your disposal, lad. Ask and ye shall receive."

"I need a passport."

"You mean you never had a passport?"

"No."

"You've never been out of the country?" Hale sounded amazed. Everybody *he* knew was out of the country most of the time.

"I've been in Canada," I said. "That's all. And you don't need a passport for Canada."

"You said you were in New York," Hale looked puzzled. "Why didn't you get it there? Not that I'm not delighted you finally had an excuse to visit me," he added hastily. "But all you had to do was go to the office on Fifth Avenue . . . "

"I know," I said. "I just didn't feel like waiting. I'm in a hurry and I thought I'd come to the fountainhead, from which all good things flow."

"They *are* swamped there," Hale said. "Where do you intend to go?"

"I thought Europe, first. I came into a little dough and I thought maybe it was time I ought to get a dose of Old World culture. Those postcards you used to send me from Paris and Athens gave me the itch." Deception, I found, was coming easily.

"I think I can run the passport through for you in a day," Hale said. "Just give me your birth certificate. . . . " He stopped when he saw the frown on my face. "Don't you have it with you?"

"I didn't realize I needed it."

"You sure do," Hale said. "Where were you born—Scranton, wasn't it?"

"Yes."

He made a face.

"What's the matter?" I asked.

"Pennsylvania's a bore," he said. "All the birth certificates are kept in Harrisburg. The state capital. You'd have to write there. It'd take at least two weeks. If you're lucky."

"Balls," I said. I didn't want to wait *anywhere* for two weeks.

"Didn't you get your birth certificate when you applied for your first driver's license?"

"Yes," I said.

"Where is it now? Have you any idea? Maybe somebody in your family? Stashed away in a trunk somewhere."

"My brother Henry still lives in Scranton," I said. I remembered that after my mother died he had taken all the accumulated family junk, old report cards, my high school diploma, my degree from college, old snapshot albums and stored them in his attic. "He might have it."

"Why don't you call him and have him look. If he finds it tell him to send it to you special delivery, registered."

"Even better," I said. "I'll go down there myself. I haven't seen Henry for years and it's time I put in an appearance, anyway." I didn't feel I had to explain to Hale that I preferred not to have Henry know where I was staying in Washington or anywhere else.

"Let's see," Hale said. "This is Thursday. There's a weekend coming up. Even if you find it, you couldn't get back in time to do anything until Monday."

"That's okay," I said. "Europe's waited this long, I guess it can wait another couple of days."

"You'll need some photographs, too."

"I have them with me." I fished the envelope out of a pocket.

He slid one out of the envelope and studied it. "You still look as though you're just about to graduate from high school." He shook his head. "How do you manage it?"

"A carefree life," I said.

"I'm glad to hear they're still available," Hale said. "When I look at pictures of myself these days, I seem to be old enough to be my own father. The magic of the cameraman's art." He put the photograph back in its envelope, as though the one glimpse of it would do him for a long, long time. "I'll have the application ready for you to sign Monday morning. Just in case."

"I'll be here."

"Why not come back and spend the weekend here?" Hale said. "Washington is at its best on the weekends. When government grinds to a halt. We have a poker game on Saturday night. You still play poker?"

"A little."

"Good. One of our regulars is out of town and you can have his place. There're a couple of eternal pigeons in the game who'll donate their dough with pathetic generosity." He smiled. He hadn't been a bad poker player himself in college. "It'll be like old times. I'll arrange everything."

The phone rang and Hale went over to the desk, picked up the instrument, and listened for a moment. "I'll be right over, sir," he said and put the phone down. "I'm sorry, Doug, I have to go. The daily eleven A.M. crisis."

I stood up. "Thanks for everything," I said, as we walked toward the door.

"Nada," Hale said. "What're friends for? Listen, there's a cocktail party at my house tonight. You busy?"

"Nothing special," I said.

"Seven o'clock." We were in the outer office now. "I've got to run. Miss Schwartz will give you my address." He was out of the door, moving fast, but still preserving a statesmanlike decorum.

Miss Schwartz wrote on a card and gave it to me, smiling radiantly, as though she were ennobling me. Her handwriting was as beautiful as she was.

I awoke slowly as the soft hand went lightly up my thigh. We had made love twice already, but the erection was immediate. The lady in bed with me was profiting from my years of abstinence.

"That's better," the lady murmured. "That's much better. Don't do anything for the moment. Just lie back. Don't move."

I lay back. The expert hands, the soft lips, and lascivious tongue made remaining motionless exquisite torture. The lady was very serious, ritualistic almost, in her pleasures, and was not to be hurried. When we had come into her bedroom at midnight, she had made me lie down and had undressed me slowly. The last woman who had undressed me had been my mother, when I was five, and I had the measles.

It was not the way I had expected the evening to end. The cocktail party in the nice Colonial house in Georgetown had been polite and sober. I had arrived early and had been taken upstairs to admire the Hale children. Before the other guests came, I had chatted desultorily with Hale's wife, Vivian, whom I had never met. She was a pretty, blondish woman with an overworked look about her. It turned out that through the years Hale had told her quite a bit about me. "After Washington," Mrs. Hale had said, "Jerry said you were like a breath of fresh air. He said he loved skiing with you and your girl—Pat—am I right, was that her name?"

"Yes."

"He said—and I hope you won't think it's condescending—he said that both of you were so transparently decent."

"That's not condescending," I said.

"He was worried about you when he found out that you weren't, well—together— anymore. And that you'd just vanished." Mrs. Hale's eyes searched my face, looking for a reaction, an answer to her unspoken question.

"I knew where I was," I said.

"If I hadn't met Jerry," Mrs. Hale said, candor making her seem suddenly youthful, "I'd have nothing. Nothing." The doorbell rang. "Oh, dear," she said, "here comes the herd. I do hope we'll see a lot of you while you're here. . . ."

The rest of the party had been something of a blur, although not because of drink. I never drank much. But the names had been flung at me in such quick succession, Senator So-and-So, Congressman This, Congressman That, His Excellency, the Ambassador of What Country, Mr. Blank, he works for *The Washington Post*, Mrs. Whoever, she's ever so important at Justice, and the conversation had been about people who were powerful, famous, despicable, conniving, eloquent, on the way to Russia, introducing a bill that would make your hair stand on end.

Even though I knew next to nothing about the social structure of the capital, I could tell that there was a lot of power assembled in the room. By Washington standards everybody there was more important than the host, who while obviously on the way up, was still somewhere in the middle ranks of the Foreign Service, and who couldn't have afforded many parties like this on his salary. But Vivan Hale was the daughter of a man who had been a Senator for two terms and who owned a good part of North Carolina besides. My friend had married well. I wondered what I would have turned into if I had married a rich wife. Not that I ever had the offer.

I had merely stood around, wincing a little as the drinks began to take effect on the rising curve of conversation, a glass tactfully in my hand at all times, smiling manfully, like a small boy at dancing school. I wondered how Hale could bear it.

Mrs. Whoever, whose hand and lips were now caressing me, had turned out to be the lady who was ever so important at Justice. She looked thirty-five years old, but a very handsome thirty-five, full bodied, with glowing skin, large dark eyes, and soft dark blonde hair, almost the color of mine, that fell to her shoulders. We had found ourselves in a corner together and she had said, "I've been watching you. Poor man, you look marooned. I take it you're not an inmate."

"An inmate?" I had asked, puzzled. "Of what?"

"Washington."

I had grinned. "Does it show that badly?"

"It does, man, it does. Don't worry about it. I leap at the opportunity to talk to someone who isn't in the government." She had looked at her watch. "Forty-five minutes. I have done my duty. Nobody can spread the rumor that I don't know how to behave in polite society. Time for chow. Grimes, are you busy for dinner?"

"No." I was surprised that she had remembered my name.

"Shall we leave together or leave separately?"

I laughed. "That's up to you, Mrs. . . . "

"Coates, Evelyn." She had smiled widely. I decided she had a mouth for smiling. "Together. I'm divorced. Do you consider me forward?"

"Yes, ma'am."

"Excellent man." She had touched my arm lightly. "I'll wait for you in the front hall. Say good-bye to your hosts, like a good boy."

I had watched her sweep through the crowded room, imperious and confident. I had never met a woman like that before. But even then I hadn't imagined for a moment that the evening would end up as it did. I had never in my life gone to bed with a woman the first time I had met her. What with my stutter and ridiculously youthful appearance, I had always been rather shy, not sure that I was particularly attractive, and had felt that I was clumsy with women. I was resigned to the fact that other men got the beauties. I had never gotten over wondering why Pat, who was exceptionally attractive, had had anything to do with me. Luckily for my ego, I had no taste for the ordinary kind of male conquest, and the remnants of my religious upbringing had kept me from promiscuity, even if I could have indulged in it.

The restaurant Mrs. Coates had taken me to was French and, as far as I could tell, very good. "I hope you're enormously wealthy," she had said. "The prices here are ferocious. Are you enormously wealthy?"

"Enormously."

She had squinted at me across the table, studying me. "You don't look it."

"It's old money," I had said. "The family likes to pretend to be slightly shabby."

"What old family?"

"Some other time." I had turned her off.

She had talked about herself, though, without any urging from me. She was a lawyer, she worked in the antitrust division of the Justice Department, she had been in Washington eleven years, her husband had been a commander in the Navy and was an absolute beast, she had no children and wanted none, she went to the Hamptons on Long Island whenever she could and swam and puttered around a garden, her boss had been trying to lay her for five years, but was otherwise a dear, she was determined to run for Congress before she died. Along with all that, all spoken in an incongruously low, melodic voice, she had entertained me through dinner by interrupting herself to point out other guests and describing them by function and character in short, malicious sketches. There was a Senator with whom a girl wasn't safe if they were in an elevator together, a second secretary at an embassy who ran dope in the diplomatic pouches, a lobbyist who had blocs in both Houses in his pocket, a CIA operator who was responsible for murders in several South American countries. I had enjoyed myself, allowing her to pick the wine, although I would have preferred beer, and order for both of us, saying, "I'm just a simple country boy and I trust myself to your hands." It was exhilarating to be able to talk to a handsome woman without stuttering. A whole new world seemed to be opening up before me.

"Is your entire enormously wealthy, slightly shabby family composed of simple country boys like you?"

"More or less," I had said.

She had stared at me quizzically. "Are you a spook?"

"A what?"

"A spook. CIA?"

I had shaken my head, smiling. "Not even."

"Hale told me you were a pilot."

"Once. Not anymore." I wondered when she had had time, in all the confusion of the party, to question Hale about me. For a moment, the woman's inquisitiveness had bothered me and I half-decided to put her in a cab after dinner and let her go home herself. But then I had thought, I mustn't get paranoid about the whole thing and settled back to enjoy the evening. "Don't you think we need another bottle?" I had asked.

"Definitely," she had said.

We had been the last ones left in the restaurant, and I was pleasantly drunk from the unaccustomed wine when we got into the taxi. We sat in the taxi without touching each other, and when the taxi stopped in front of the apartment building in which Mrs. Coates lived, I had said, "Hold it, driver, please; I'm just seeing the lady to the door."

"Forget it, driver," Mrs. Coates had said. "The gentleman is coming in for a nightcap."

"That's just what I need," I had said, trying not to mumble, "a nightcap." But I had paid the driver and gone in with her.

I hadn't discovered what the apartment was like, because she didn't switch on the lights. She merely put her arms around me as I shut the door from the hall and kissed me. The kiss was delicious.

"I am now seducing you," she had said, "in your weakened state."

"Consider me seduced."

Chuckling, she had led me by the hand through the dark living room and into the bedroom. A thin shaft of light from the partially open door to a bathroom was enough so that I could make out the shapes of pieces of furniture, a huge desk piled with papers, a dresser, a long bookcase against one wall. She had led me to the bed, turned me around, then given me a sharp push. I had fallen backward on the bed. "The rest," she had said, "is my job."

If she was as good at Justice as she was in bed, the government was getting its money's worth.

"Now," she said, sliding up on me, straddling me, using her hand to guide me into her. She moved on me, first very slowly, then more and more quickly, her head thrown back, her arms rigid behind her, her hands spread out on the bed, supporting her. Her full breasts loomed above me, pale in the dim light reflected off a mirror. I put up my hands and caressed her breasts and she moaned. She began to sob, loudly, uncontrollably, and when she came she was weeping.

I came immediately after, with a long, subdued sigh. She rolled off me, lay on her stomach beside me, the weeping slowly coming to an end. I put out my hand and touched the firm, rounded shoulder. "Did I hurt you?" I asked.

She laughed. "Silly man. Lord, no."

"I was afraid I . . ."

"Didn't a lady ever cry while you were fucking her?"

"Not that I remember," I said. And none of the ladies ever called it that either, I could have added. They obviously called a spade a spade at Justice.

She laughed again, twisted around, sat up, reached for a cigarette, lit it. Her face was calm and untroubled in the flare of the match. "Do you want a cigarette?"

"I don't smoke cigarettes."

"You'll live forever. So much the better. How old are you anyway?"

"Thirty-three."

"In the prime of life," she said. "The dear prime of life. Don't go to sleep. I want to talk. Do you want a drink?"

"What time is it?"

"Drink time." She got out of bed and I saw her put a dressing gown on. "Whiskey okay?"

"Whiskey is fine."

She went into the living room, her robe making a soft rustling sound. I looked at my watch. She had taken it off, the last item, when she had undressed me and put it neatly on the bedside table. She was an orderly woman. The luminous dial of the watch showed that it was past three. Everything in its time, I thought, lying back luxuriously, remembering other three o'clocks, the noise of the adding machine, the bullet-proof glass, the bedraggled women asking me to unlock the front door.

She came back with the two glasses, handed me mine, sat on the edge of the bed, her profile outlined against the light from the bathroom. The silhouette was bold and sharp. She drank heartily. She was a hearty as well as an orderly woman. "Most satisfactory," she said. "You were, too."

I laughed. "Do you always rate your lovers?"

"You're not my lover, Grimes," she said. "You're a nice-looking, youngish man with good manners whom I happened to take a slight shine to at a party and who had the great virtue to be passing briefly through town. Briefly is the operative word in that sentence, Grimes."

"I see," I said, sipping at the whiskey.

"You probably don't and I won't bother to explain."

"You don't have to explain anything to me," I said. "Sufficient unto the night are the pleasures thereof."

"You don't do this sort of thing often, do you?"

"Frankly, no." I laughed again. "Frankly, never. Why—does it show?"

"Like a neon sign. You're not at all like what you look like, you know."

"What do I look like?"

"You look like those young men who play the villains in Italian movies—bold and dark and unscrupulous."

Nobody had ever said anything like that to me before. I had gotten used to hearing that I reminded people of somebody's kid brother. Either I had changed drastically or Evelyn Coates was not deceived by surfaces, could see through to the wished for inner man. "Is that a good way to look?" I asked. I was a little worried by the "unscrupulous."

"It's a very nice way to look. In certain situations."

"Like tonight, for example?"

"Like tonight."

"I might be coming back to Washington in a few days," I said. "Should I call you?"

"If you have nothing better to do."

"Will you see me again?"

"If *I* have nothing better to do."

"Are you as tough as you pretend to be?"

"Tougher, Grimes, much tougher. What would you be coming back to Washington for?"

"Maybe for you."

"Try that once more, please."

"Maybe for you."

"You *do* have nice manners. Maybe for what else?"

"Well," I said slowly, thinking, this is as good a place and as good a time to dig for information, "supposing I was looking for somebody . . ."

"Somebody in particular?"

"Yes. Somebody whose name I know, who's dropped out of sight."

"In Washington?"

"Not necessarily. Somewhere in the country, or maybe even out of the country. . . ."

"You *are* a mysterious man, aren't you?"

"Someday I may tell you the whole story," I said, sure that I never would, but pleased that luck had put me into the bed of a woman who was in on the secrets of government, and whose job, partially, at least, must involve tracing people down, people usually who did not want to be traced down. "It's a private, delicate matter. But suppose I had to find this hypothetical friend, how would I go about it?"

"Well, there are a lot of places you could look," she said. "The Internal Revenue Service—they'd know his address at the time he sent in his last return. The Social Security people. They'd have a record of whom he was working for. The Selective Service people, although that would probably be outdated. The FBI. You never know what you can pick up in *that* factory. The State Department. It would all depend upon whether or not you knew the right people."

"Take it for granted that I would get to know the right people," I said. For a hundred thousand dollars, I could take it for granted *somebody* would be able to reach the right people.

"You probably would eventually be able to pick up your friend's trail. Say, are you a private detective or something?"

"Or something," I said ambiguously.

"Well, everybody comes to Washington eventually," she said. "Why not you? It's America's *real* living theater. Standing room only at every performance. Except that it's a peculiar audience. The good seats are all filled by actors."

"Are you an actress?"

"You bet your life. I'm playing a role that can't be beat. The dauntless Portia striking deadly blows at the malefactors of great wealth. Women's Lib at Justice and Injustice. I've gotten rave reviews in the best beds in town. Do I shock you?"

"A little."

"While on the subject," she said, "let me give you a t.l."

"What's a t.l.?"

"Where have you been, you poor innocent?" She reached over and pinched my cheek. "T.l. stands for trade last. A compliment. You gave almost the best performance of anyone I've slept with in this town. You were even as good as a certain Senator from a Western state whom I shall not name, who used to be at the head of the list. Until the poor dear was beaten at the last election."

"I didn't realize I was giving a performance." I had no desire to hear the defeated Senator's name.

"Of course you were. Otherwise you wouldn't be in Washington. And every performance calls on enormous talent here. We all have to pretend we live our roles."

"Are you like that, too?"

"You must be kidding, honey. Of course. I'm a big, grown woman. Do you think that if I went into that office every day for the next hundred years, it would make the slightest difference to you or General Motors or the United Nations or anybody's pet dog? I just play the game, honey, and have fun like everybody else, because this town is the best place to have fun anybody's found for people like us. Actually, what I believe is that, if everyone here, from the President down to the janitor at Indian Affairs, would only be allowed to operate two weeks a year, America would turn out to be the greatest country in the world."

I had finished the whiskey by now and felt an overwhelming desire to sleep. I barely suppressed a yawn.

"Oh," she said. "I'm boring you."

"Not at all." I said truthfully. "But aren't you tired?"

"Not really." She put her glass down, slipped out of her robe, and got into bed beside me. "Sex invigorates me. But I have to get up early and it doesn't do for me to look debauched when I get to the office in the morning." She snuggled up to me and kissed my ear. "Good night, Grimes. Of course call me when you come back."

When I awoke, it was nearly ten o'clock and I was alone. The curtains let enough sun through for me to see that it was a nice day. There was a note on the dresser, where she had put my money clip the night before. "Dear Guest: Off to work. You were sleeping like a baby and I hadn't the heart to wake you. I am happy to see such evidence of a clear conscience in this naughty world. There's a razor and shaving cream in the medicine cabinet and a big glass of orange juice in the refrigerator and a pot of coffee on the stove. The good servant deserves his hire. I hope you find your friend. E.C."

I grinned at the last sentence, then went into the bathroom and shaved and showered. The cold shower woke me up completely and I felt fresh and cheerful. And, I had to admit, pleased with myself. I looked carefully at myself in the mirror. My color had improved.

As I went into the living room, I smelled bacon frying. I pushed open the door to the kitchen and saw a young woman sitting at a table in slacks and a sweater, with a scarf around her head, reading the newspaper and munching on a piece of toast.

"Hi," the young woman said, looking up. "I wondered if you were going to sleep all day."

"I . . . I'm terribly sorry . . ." I said, flustered. "I didn't mean to disturb you."

"You're not disturbing me." She got up and opened the refrigerator and took out a glass of orange juice. "Evelyn left this for you. You must be thirsty." She didn't say why she thought I must be thirsty. "Do you want bacon and eggs?"

"I don't want to be any trouble."

"No trouble. Breakfast comes with the deal." She stripped off three slices of bacon from an open package and put it in the pan with the others. She was tall and slender in her slacks. "Sunny-side-up?"

"Any way you're having them."

"Sunny-side-up," the woman said. She put a slab of butter in another pan and cracked four eggs into the pan, her movements swift and authoritative. "I'm Brenda Morrissey," she said. "I share the apartment with Evelyn. Didn't she say anything about me?"

"Not that I remember," I said. I sipped at the chilled orange juice.

"I guess Evelyn was busy at the time," the woman said flatly. She poured two cups of coffee, indicated the cream and sugar on the table. "Sit down. You're not in a hurry, are you?"

"Not really." I sat down.

"Neither am I. I run an art gallery. Nobody ever buys a picture before eleven o'clock in the morning. It's a dream job for a girl like me. Evelyn neglected to tell me your name."

I told her my name.

"How long have you known Evelyn?" she asked, as she stood at the stove, shaking the pan with the eggs in it with one hand and feeding slices of bread into the toaster with the other hand.

"Well," I said, embarrassed, "truth is we just met last night."

She gave a short, sharp chuckle. "That's Washington. You collect votes wherever you can find them. Any kind of votes. Maybe this is the nicest kind. Dear Evelyn," she said, but without malice. "I heard you at your revels."

I felt myself blushing. "I had no idea there was anyone else in the house."

"That's all right. Actually, I keep meaning to buy earplugs and then I forget from one time to the next." She slid the eggs onto plates and put the bacon over them. She sat across from me on the other side of the little table, clear greenish eyes staring at me steadily. She was wearing no lipstick and her lips were light pink, her cheeks just a little flushed from the heat of the stove. She had a long face, the bones all showing, and the scarf around her head make her look severe. "Evelyn's not one to keep her enjoyment to herself when she's being amused," she said, as she broke a piece of bacon and started eating it with her fingers. "I had to use all my maidenly restraint to keep from coming and joining the fun."

I felt my face go rigid and I ducked my eyes. The woman laughed. "Don't worry," she said, "it hasn't happened yet. Whatever else we do around here, we do not go in for orgies. Still," she said evenly, "if you're going to be in Washington tonight and if you tell me what hotel you're staying at, you might like to buy me a drink."

I won't say that I wasn't tempted. The night had reawakened all the sensuality in me that had lain dormant for so long. And the cool impersonality of the invitation was intriguing. At least for its novelty. Things like that had happened to friends of mine, or at least so they had said, but never to me. And after what I had done in room 602 of the St. Augustine Hotel, I could hardly refuse on moral grounds to sleep with the friend of a lady I had only just met the night before. Let the accidents happen. But there was the business of the birth certificate. "I'm sorry," I said. "I'm leaving town this morning."

"What a pity," the woman said tonelessly.

"But I'll be back at my hotel . . ." I hesitated, remembering Jeremy Hale's poker game on Saturday night. First things first. "I'll be back on Sunday."

"What hotel are you staying at?"

I told her.

"Perhaps I'll call on Sunday," she said. "I have nothing against Sundays."

Money in the bank, I thought, as I was leaving the apartment building, even money in a bank two hundred and fifty miles away must give off an irresistible sexual aroma.

I tried to examine just how I felt that morning. Springy and light-footed. Light-hearted, I decided. Wicked. It was an old-fashioned word, but it was the word that came to mind. Was it possible that for thirty-three years I had miscalculated absolutely what sort of man I was? I looked carefully at the ordinary faces of the men and women on the street. Were they all on the edge of crime?

At the hotel I rented a car and took my wallet out of the vault. I was beginning to feel deprived if I wasn't carrying a certain number of hundred-dollar bills on me.

The roads through Pennsylvania were icy and I drove carefully. A car crash was one accident I wanted to avoid. This was no time to be laid up, immobilized and helpless, in a hospital for weeks or maybe months on end.

CHAPTER 6

"MAY I SPEAK to Mr. Grimes, please," I said to the girl on the phone. "Mr. Henry Grimes."

"Who's calling, please?"

I hesitated. I was getting more and more reluctant to give my name to anyone. "Say his brother is calling," I said on the phone. Since there were three brothers in the family, this could leave at least a small margin of doubt.

When I heard my brother's voice on the phone, I said, "Hello, Hank."

"Who's this? No, I don't believe it! Doug! Where the hell are you?" Once again I felt the same quick gratitude that had swept over me in Jeremy Hale's office because someone was so obviously glad to hear the sound of my voice. My brother was seven years older than I and when we had been growing up had regarded me as a pest. Since I had moved away from Scranton, we had only seen each other rarely, but there was no mistaking the warmth in the greeting.

"I'm in town. At the Hilton Inn."

"Take your bag and come on over to the house. We've got a guest room. And the kids won't wake you until six thirty in the morning." Henry laughed at his own invitation. Behind the deep, remembered voice, there was the clatter of office machines. Henry worked in a firm of accountants and the mechanical noise of the symbols of money coming in and going out was the music of his working day. "I'll call Madge," Henry was saying, "and tell her to expect you for dinner."

"Hold it a minute, Hank," I said. "I have to ask you for a favor."

"Sure, kid," he said. "What is it?"

"I'm applying for a passport," I said, "and I need my birth certificate. If I write Harrisburg it'll take weeks and I'm in a hurry . . ."

"Where you going?"

"Abroad."

"Where abroad?"

"No matter. Do you think that in the stuff you took from Mom's house you might find my birth certificate?"

"Come on over to the house for dinner and we'll look for it together."

"I'd rather Madge didn't know I was in town, Hank," I said.

"Oh." The worry set in immediately.

"Do you think you might see if you could find it this afternoon and then come over to the Hilton and have dinner with me. Alone?"

"But why . . .?"

"I'll explain later. Can you manage it?"

"I'll be there a quarter after six."

"In the bar."

"That's no hardship." Henry chuckled. It was a drinker's chuckle.

"See you then," I said and hung up. I sat on the edge of the single bed in the hotel room, my hand on the telephone, wondering if it wouldn't have been better to have written Harrisburg and waited the two weeks and never have come back to Scranton, never have said anything to my brother. I shook my head. If you wanted to figure out what your future was going to be, you had to have a firm grasp on your past. And my brother Henry was a big part of my past.

Because our father had died when Henry was twenty and all the other children much younger, and Henry had taken on the responsibility of the male head of the family automatically, without fuss, I had learned to respect him and depend on him. It was easy to depend on Henry. He was an outgoing, uncomplicated, clever boy, quick in his studies (he always led his class, always was elected class president, and got a scholarship to the University of Pennsylvania). He had a knack for business, too, and was generous to the other children, especially to me, with the money he made after school and in the summers. As our mother kept repeating, he was the one of her children who was born to be rich and successful. It was Henry who fought our mother and overcame her objections when I decided I wanted to learn to fly. Henry had also financed the flying school. By that time he was a certified public accountant, doing fairly well for his age, and already married.

Through the years, I had paid back the money Henry had lent me, although Henry had never once asked me for a penny. But we had not seen each other often. We lived in different parts of the world, and Henry was involved with his growing family and his wife, Madge. Because of the scandal of my younger brother, Bert, the few times that we had all been together Madge had been uncomfortably persistent in trying to find out why I was not yet married.

Because of everything, my brother Henry was one of the people in my life who somehow made me feel guilty, lacking in feeling. I knew that I had received much more than I had given and the imbalance disturbed me. I was glad now that the bureaucracy in Harrisburg had forced me to come to my home town and once more ask my brother to help me.

I was shocked when I saw him come into the bar. I had not seen him for five years, and Henry had been a powerfully built, erect, confident-seeming man then. Now he looked as though the five years had ravaged him. He seemed diminished, bent. His hair had thinned and what was left was stringy, yellowish-gray. He wore thick, gold-rimmed spectacles that bit deep into the bridge of his nose. He had always had fine eyes, deep-colored, like all the family, and keen of sight, and the glasses did not become him. Even in the half-light of the bar, Henry reminded me of a small, worried animal peering fearfully out of a hole, ready to scuttle back at the first sign of danger.

"Over here, Hank," I said, standing up.

We shook hands wordlessly. I was sure Henry knew the changes that had taken place in him were apparent and that I was trying to hide my reaction to them.

"You're in luck," Henry said. "I found it right off." He reached into his pocket and took a yellowed envelope and gave it to me. I slipped out the certificate. There it was. My identity was confirmed. Douglas Traynor Grimes, citizen, born in America, son of Margaret Traynor Grimes, heir to the continent.

While I was examining the frail piece of aging paper, Henry was fussily taking off his coat and folding it on a chair. The coat was worn at the cuffs and elbows.

"What'll it be, Hank?" I asked, overly hearty, false.

"An old-fashioned will do it." His voice had somehow remained the same, full and deep, like a cherished and lovingly polished relic from better days.

"The same," I said to the waiter, who was standing at the table.

"Well, boy, well," Henry said. "The Prodigal returns." If I closed my eyes the voice was still my brother.

"Not exactly. More of a refueling stop, I would say."

"You're not flying anymore?"

"I wrote you that."

"*That's* the only thing you wrote me," Henry said. "I'm not complaining, you understand." He spread his hands in a placating gesture. I noticed that the hands shook a little. Holy God, I thought, he's only forty years old. "The world's a busy place," Henry said. "Communication is difficult. Time passes. Brothers go their different ways."

We toasted each other when the drinks came. Henry drank greedily, half the glassful in one gulp. "After a day in the office," he said, catching my glance. "Those're long days in that office."

"I can imagine," I said.

"Now tell me the news," Henry said.

"You tell *me* the news," I said, "Madge, the kids et cetera, et cetera."

There were two more drinks for Henry while he told me about Madge and the kids. Madge was fine, a little run down taking care of everything with no help and the PTA and teaching a stenographic course at night, the three daughters were lovely, the oldest at fourteen something of a problem, high-strung, the way kids that age these days were likely to be, and having a little psychiatric help. The photographs came out of the wallet, the family beside a lake in the Poconos, all the females brown, robust, and cheerful, Henry, in a pair of bathing trunks that were too big for him, pale and worried-looking, as though a drowning was imminent. The news of our brother Bert was not surprising. "He's a fag radio announcer out in San Diego," Henry said. "We should have seen it coming. Did you see it coming?"

"No."

"Well, these days, it's not so bad, I suppose," Henry said with a sigh. "Still, in our family . . . Pa would have split a gut. He's got a good heart, Bert, he always sends the kids gifts on Christmas from California, but I wouldn't know what to do with him if he ever showed up here."

Our sister Clara, the youngest of the family, was married, in Chicago, with two kids, did I know that?

"I knew about her being married. Not about the kids."

"We don't see much of her either," Henry said. "Families sort of just disintegrate, don't they? In a few years I suppose my kids'll go off, too, and Madge and I'll be sitting home looking at the television together." He laughed ruefully. "Happy thoughts. Still, there's one good thing. The bastards'll never to able to drag any son of mine off and kill him in one of their goddamn wars. What a country, where you thank God you don't have a son. More happy thoughts." He shook himself, as though the conversation had gotten away from him onto subjects that would have been better left unexamined. "Don't you think it's time for another drink?"

I still had my first glass almost full in front of me, but he ordered two more. In a little while Henry would be drunk. Maybe that explained it all, although I knew it never explained it all.

"Clara's doing all right," Henry was saying. "At least that's what she writes us. *When* she writes us. Her husband's a big shot in a brokerage firm out there. They have a boat on the lake. Imagine that—a Grimes with a yacht. Okay, enough about all of us. What about you?"

"Over dinner," I said. By now it was obvious that Henry had to get some food in him—fast.

In the dining room, Henry ordered a big meal. "How about a bottle of wine?" he said, smiling widely, as though he had just thought of a brilliant and original idea.

"If you want," I said. I knew that Henry would be much the worse for wine, but I had been in the habit all my boyhood and youth of taking orders from him, not the other way around, and the habit, I saw, persisted.

Henry neglected his food, but paid a great deal of attention to the wine during dinner. He had flashes of sobriety, when he would sit very erect and peer fiercely across the table at me and speak almost sternly, as though suddenly remembering his position as the head of the family. "Now let's have it, son," he said, during one of these periods. "Where've you been, what have you done, what brings you here? You need help, I imagine. I don't have much, but I guess I could manage to scrape up a couple of . . ."

"Nothing like that, Hank," I said hastily. "Really. Money isn't the problem."

"That's what you think, brother." Henry laughed bitterly. "That's what you think."

"Listen carefully, Hank." I said, leaning forward, speaking in a low voice, trying to freeze his attention, "I'm going away."

"Going away? Where?" Henry asked. "You've been going away all your life."

"This is different. Maybe for a long time. To Europe first."

"Do you have a job in Europe?"

"Not exactly."

"You don't have a job?"

"Don't ask any questions, please, Hank," I said. "I'm going away. Period. I don't know when I'll ever be able to see you again. Maybe never. I wanted to touch some of the bases before I took off. And I want to thank you for what you've always done for me. I want to tell you that I realize it and I'm grateful for it. I was a snotty little kid and I guess I used to think gratitude was effeminate or degrading or un-British or something equally idiotic."

"Oh, shit, Doug," Henry said. "Forget it, will you?"

"I won't forget it. Another thing. Pa died when I was thirteen years old. . . ."

"He left a nice little piece of insurance." Henry nodded approvingly. "Yessirree, a very nice little piece of insurance. You'd never have expected it—a man who worked as a foreman in a machine shop. A man who worked with his hands. His thought was only for his family. Where would we all be today if it wasn't for that nice little piece of insurance . . .?"

"I'm not talking about that part of it."

"Talk about that part of it. Listen to an accountant when it comes to death and insurance."

"What do you remember about him? That's what I want to talk about. I was just a kid, it seems to me I hardly ever saw him; he was just somebody who came in for meals mostly. I still have dreams about him, but I never get the face right. But you were twenty. . . ."

"His face," Henry said. "His face was the face of an honest rough man who never had any doubt about himself. It was a face out of another century. Duty and honor were written plain on those simple features." Henry was mocking himself, mocking our father's memory now. "And he gave me bad advice," Henry said, almost sober for the moment. "Also out of another century. He said, Marry early, boy. You know how he was always reading the Bible, and making us all go to church. It's better to marry than to burn, he said. I married early. I have a bone to pick with good old dad; insurance or no insurance, burning is better."

"Will you for Christ's sake stop talking about insurance?"

"Whatever you say, boy. It's your dinner. I take it it *is* your dinner?"

"Of course."

"Forget Pa. He's dead. Forget Mom. She's dead. They worked their fingers to the bone and worried night and day and got the old royal American screwing and raised a family, one who's a fag radio announcer in San Diego, the other who's a drunken accountant in Scranton working *his* fingers to the bone to raise a family, who in turn will work *their* fingers to the bone to raise *their* families. I'll say this for our dad, he had his religion. Clara has her yacht. Bert has his beach boys. I have my bottle." He smiled owlishly. "What have you got, brother?"

"I don't know yet," I said.

"You don't know yet?" Henry cocked his collapsed, pale head to one side and grimaced. "You're what—thirty-two, thirty-three? And don't know yet? You're a lucky man. The future is all ahead of you. I got something beside the bottle. I got a pair of eyes that are no good for anything and steadily getting worse."

"What?"

"You heard me. Did you ever hear of a blind accountant? In five years I'll be out in the street on my naked ass."

"Jesus," I said, shaken by the coincidence. "That's why *I* was grounded. My eyes started to go bad."

"Aha," Henry said. "I thought you'd run a plane into a hill or screwed the boss's wife."

"No. Just a little failure of the retina. Nothing much," I said bitterly. "Just enough."

"We none of us ever did see clearly, I guess." Henry laughed foolishly. "The fatal flaw of the Grimeses." He took off his glasses and wiped his eyes, which were watering. The marks of the frames on his nose were like small deep wounds. His eyes without the glasses looked almost blank. "But you said you were traveling, you were going to Europe. What've you got—a rich woman to support you?"

"No."

"Take my advice. Find one." Henry put his glasses on. They fitted automatically into the slots on each side of his nose. "Romance yourself no romance. That's another thing I have." He was off ranting again. "I have a wife who despises me."

"Oh, come on now, Hank." In the photograph Madge hadn't looked like a woman who despised anyone, and the few times I had met her she had seemed like a good-natured, even-tempered woman, solicitous at all times of her husband's welfare.

"Don't say come on now, brother," Henry said. "You don't know. *I* know. She despises me. You know *why* she despises me? Because by her high American standards I am a failure. She does not get new dresses when her friends get new dresses. I can't afford to pay for a psychiatrist for the older kid *and* send her off to a private school and she's afraid the Blacks at the high school will rape her between lunch and gym class. The house hasn't been painted for ten years. We're behind on our payments for the television set. Our car is six years old. I am not a partner in the firm. I keep track of other people's money. You know what the worst thing in the world is? Other people's money. I . . ."

"That's enough, Hank, please." I couldn't stand the wave of self-hatred at the dinner table, even though there was nobody near enough but myself to hear any of it.

"Permit me to continue, brother," Henry said. "My teeth are bad and they smell, she says, because I can't afford to go to the dentist. I can't afford to go to the dentist because all three goddamn kids go to the dentist every week to have their braces worked on so that they'll all look like movie stars when they grow up. And she despises me because I haven't been able to fuck her for five years."

"Why not?"

"I'm impotent," Henry said with a crazy smile. "I have every reason to be impotent and I'm impotent. Do you remember when you came home that Saturday afternoon and you found me in bed with that girl? What was her name?"

"Cynthia."

"That's it—Cynthia. Cynthia of the big tits. She let out a shriek when she saw you that I can hear to this day. And she slapped me because I laughed. What did you think of your big brother then?"

"I didn't think anything. I didn't know what you were doing."

"You know now, don't you?"

"Yes."

"I wasn't impotent then, was I?"

"How the hell would I know?"

"Take your brother's word for it. Glad you came back to Scranton, Doug?"

"Listen to me, Hank." I grabbed both his hands and pressed them hard. "Are you sober enough to understand what I'm saying?"

"Approximately, kid, approximately." Henry chuckled, then frowned. "Give me back my hands."

I let go of his hands. I took out my wallet and counted out ten bills. "This is a thousand dollars, Hank," I said. I leaned over and stuffed it into my brother's breast pocket. "Don't forget where I put it."

Henry let out his breath noisily. He fumbled at his pocket, took out the bills, smoothed them out on the table. "Other people's money," he said. He sounded dead sober.

I nodded. "There's more where that came from. Now, I'm going away tomorrow. Out of the country. I won't tell you where, but from time to time you'll hear from me, and if you need more there'll be more. Do you understand that?"

Henry slowly folded the bills and put them in his wallet. Then the tears started, silently rolling down the pallid cheeks out from under the glasses.

"For Christ's sake, Hank, don't cry," I pleaded.

"You're in trouble," Henry said.

"Maybe," I said. "Anyway, I have to keep on the move. If anybody ever comes to you and asks you if you know where I am, you don't know anything. You got that?"

"I got it." Henry nodded. "Let me ask you a question, Doug." He *was* sober now, sobered by money. "Is it worth it? Whatever you're doing?"

"I don't know yet. I'll let you know when I find out. I think we can skip coffee, can't we?"

"I don't need any coffee. I can get coffee in my happy home from my happy wife."

We stood up and I helped Henry put on his coat. We walked out together, after I had paid the waiter. Henry walked in a straight line, a bent, oldish figure, then stopped for a moment, as I was pushing at the door. "Just before he died," Henry said, "do you know what Pa said to me? He said, of all his sons he loved you best. He said you were the purest." His voice sounded petulant, almost childish. "Now why would a man on his deathbed want to tell his oldest son something like that?" He started walking again, and I opened the door for us, thinking, I am an opener of doors.

It was cold outside, the night wind gusting. Henry shivered a little, settling deeply into his coat. "Beautiful old Scranton, where I live and die," he said.

I kissed him on the cheek, hugging him, feeling the wetness of his tears. Then I put him in a cab. But before the cabby could start off, Henry tapped him on the shoulder to stop him and rolled down the window on my side. "Hey, Doug," he said. "I just noticed; I knew something was peculiar about you all evening and I couldn't put my finger on it. You don't stutter anymore."

"No," I said.

"How'd it happen?"

"I went to a speech doctor," I said. It was as good an explanation as any.

"Why, that's great, that's wonderful. You must be a happy man."

"Yep," I said. "I'm a happy man. Get a good night's sleep, Hank."

He rolled up the window and the cab started away. I watched its tail-lights go down the street, disappear around a corner, carrying away the brother of whom our mother had said that of all her children he was the one who was born to be rich and successful.

I took a deep breath of the icy night air, shivered, remembered the warm beds of Washington. Then I went in and took the elevator to my room and watched the television for hours. Many objects were advertised that I would never buy.

I slept badly that night, tantalized by fleeting visions of women and funerals.

The ringing of the telephone on the bedside table put a welcome stop to my dreams. I looked at my watch. It was only seven thirty. "Doug . . ." It was Henry on the phone. It couldn't have been anyone else. Nobody else in the whole world knew where I was. "Doug . . . I have to see you."

I sighed. I felt as though we had exhausted each other the night before, that there was no need to see each other for another five years. "Where are you?" I asked.

"Downstairs. In the lobby. Have you had your breakfast?"

"No."

"I'll wait for you in the dining room." He hung up before I could say yes or no.

He was drinking a cup of black coffee, alone in the dining room. It was still dark outside. Henry had always been an early riser. It was another one of his virtues that my parents had praised.

"I'm sorry if I woke you," he said, as I sat down across from him. "I wanted to make sure I got hold of you before you left town."

"That's okay." Half-remembering my dreams, I said, "I wasn't particularly enjoying my sleep."

The waitress came over to us and I ordered breakfast. Henry asked for a second cup of coffee.

"Listen, Doug," he said, when the waitress had gone, "last night, you said something. When you . . . when you gave me all that money. Don't think that I'm not grateful . . ."

I waved my hand impatiently. "Forget it," I said. "Let's not talk about it."

"You said . . . and I can't forget it . . . you said, if I needed it, there's more where that came from."

"That's what I said."

"Did you mean it?"

"I wouldn't have said it if I didn't mean it."

"Did you mean as much as twenty-five thousand?" He flushed, as though the effort of getting the question out had been enormous.

I hesitated only a moment. "Yes," I said. "I meant that. If you need it."

"Don't you want me to tell you what I'm going to do with it?"

"Only if you want to tell me," I said. I was sorry I hadn't left town last night.

"I want to tell you. It's not only for me, it's for both of us. It's a . . ." he began, then stopped, as the waitress came over with my juice and coffee and toast. He watched her tensely as she poured him a second cup. When she'd finished and moved off, he gulped a steaming mouthful. I saw that he was sweating.

"Here it is," he said. "There's an account I handle in the office. A small new company. A couple of very smart young guys. Two kids out of MIT. They're on to something. Something that can be very big. Big. *Big.* They've got a patent pending for a new system of miniaturization. For all sorts of electronic systems. But they're just about busted. They need about twenty-five thousand to tide them over. They've been to the banks and they've been refused. I know their situation because I know their books inside out. And I've talked to them about it. I can buy in. With a little pushing, for twenty-five thousand I could have a third of the stock. And I could become an officer of the company, treasurer, to protect our interests. Once they go into production, they'd go on the board on Amex . . ."

"What's Amex?" I asked.

"American Exchange." He looked at me oddly. "Where the hell have you been all these years?"

"No place," I said.

"There's no limit to how high the stock would go. I'd take a third of the thirty-three percent and you'd get two-thirds. Does that seem unfair to you?" he asked anxiously.

"No." I had already kissed the twenty-five thousand good-bye. None of it was real to me anyway. Stacks of paper in a vault.

"You're noble, Doug, noble." Henry's voice was quivering with emotion.

"Oh, cut it out, Hank," I said sharply. I didn't feel noble. "Can you be in New York Wednesday?"

"Sure."

"I'll have the money ready for you. In cash. I'll call you at your office Tuesday and tell you where to meet me."

"In cash?" Henry looked puzzled. "What's the matter with a check? I hate to carry that much cash around with me."

"You'll just have to bear the burden," I said. "I don't write checks." I could see his face working. He wanted the money—badly, badly—but he was an honest man and no fool and there was no doubt in his mind that whatever else the money was, it wasn't honest. "Doug," he said, "I don't want you to get into trouble on my account. If it means . . ." He was pushing himself and I appreciated what it cost him. "Well, I'd rather do without it."

"Let me handle my end," I said curtly. "You handle yours. Just be in your office Tuesday morning for my call."

He sighed, an old man's resigned, weary sigh, honesty too difficult a position to maintain. "Baby brother," was all he said.

I was glad to get out of Scranton and back on the icy road to Washington. At the wheel, I thought of the poker game that night and touched the silver dollar in my pocket.

I was stopped for speeding in Maryland, where the ice ran out, and bribed the cop with a fifty-dollar bill. Mr. Ferris, or whatever his name really was, was spreading the wealth all through the American economy.

CHAPTER 7

IT WAS LATE in the afternoon when I arrived in Washington. The monuments to Presidents, generals, justice, and law, all the ambiguous Doric-American pantheon, were wavery in a soft, twilight Southern mist. Scranton could have been in another climate zone, another country, a distant civilization. The streets were almost empty, and the few people walking there in the quiet dusk moved slowly, peacefully. Jeremy Hale had said Washington was at its best on weekends, when the mills of government ground to a halt. In the capital, between Friday afternoon and Monday morning, it was possible to believe in the value and decorum of democracy. I wondered idly what the blonde lady whose taxicab I had shared was doing with her holiday.

There was no message for me at the desk of the hotel, and when I went up to my room, I called Hale at his home. A child answered, her voice bell-like and pure, and I had a sudden, unexpected moment of jealousy because there was no child to answer for me and to call, with uncomplicated love, "Daddy, it's for you."

"Is the game still on?" I asked Hale.

"Good," Hale said. "You got back. I'll pick you up at eight."

It was only five o'clock and I played with the idea of calling Evelyn Coates's number to see which one of the ladies was at home. But then what would I say? "Listen, I have two hours to spare." I was not that sort of man and never would be. So much the worse for me.

I shaved and took a long hot bath. Lying there, luxuriously steaming myself, I counted my blessings. They were not insignificant. "Peter Piper picked a peck of pickled peppers," I said aloud in the clouded bathroom. I hadn't stuttered once in five days and nights. In a minor way it was like being able to throw down your crutches and stride away from the spring at Lourdes. Then there was the money in the vault in New York, of course. Again and again, I found myself thinking of it, the neat stacks of bills lying in the steel box, laden with infinite promise. The twenty-five thousand dollars I was going to give Hank was a small price to pay for freeing me from the guilt about my brother that had lain somewhere in my subconscious for so many years.

And Evelyn Coates . . . Old man, I thought, remembering the flaccid body in the corridor, you have not died in vain.

I got out of the bath, feeling fit and rested, put on some fresh clothes and went down and had a leisurely dinner by myself, without liquor. Not before a poker game.

I made sure I had the silver dollar in my pocket when Hale came to get me. If there ever was a gambler, dead or alive, who was not superstitious, I haven't heard of him.

Silver dollar or no silver dollar, Hale nearly got us killed driving to the hotel in Georgetown, where the weekly poker game was played. He went through a stop sign without looking, and there was a wild screech of brakes as a Pontiac swerved to avoid hitting us. From the Pontiac somebody screamed, uncomprehensibly, "Goddamn niggers."

Hale had been a careful driver in college. "Sorry," he said. "People drive like maniacs on Saturday night." He must have smoked six cigarettes on the short trip. If gambling did that to me, I thought, I wouldn't play. But I didn't say anything.

There was a big round table covered by a green cloth set up in one of the small private dining rooms of the hotel, and an array of bottles, ice, and glasses on a sideboard, all under a strong light. Very professional. I looked forward to the evening. There were three other men already in the room and one woman, standing with her back to the door fixing herself a drink as we came in. Hale introduced me to the men first. I found out later that one of them was a well-known columnist, one a Congressman from upstate New York, who looked like Warren Gamaliel Harding, white-haired, benign, falsely presidential. The last player was a youngish lawyer by the name of Benson who worked at the Department of Defense. I had never met a columnist or a Congressman before. Was I going up or down on the social scale?

When the woman turned around to greet us, I saw that it was Evelyn Coates. Somehow, I wasn't surprised. "Yes," she said, without smiling, as Hale started to introduce us, "I know Mr. Grimes. I believe I met him at a party the other night at your house, Jerry."

"Of course," Hale said. "I must be losing my mind." He did seem distracted. I noticed that he kept rubbing the side of his jaw with the palm of his hand, as though he had an intermittent itch there. I made a small bet with myself that he would wind up losing that night.

Evelyn Coates was dressed in dark blue slacks, not too close fitting, and a loose beige sweater. Working clothes, I thought. Dyke? I dismissed the idea. Probably when she was younger she was one of those girls who played touch football with the boys on the block. I wondered if her roommate had told her about me.

She was the only one in the room who had a drink in her hand as we sat down at the table and started counting our chips. She piled her chips expertly, her long hands deft, pale fingers, pale polished nails.

"Evelyn," Benson said as the Congressman began to throw cards for the first ace to deal, "tonight you must be merciful."

"Without fear or favor," she said.

The lawyer, I noticed, seemed to have a special, teasing relationship with her. I put it out of my mind. I didn't like his voice either, round and self-satisfied. I put that out of my mind, too. I was there to play cards.

Evelyn took the game very seriously, and there was almost no conversation except for the usual postmortems between hands. Hale had told me the game was a moderate one. Nobody had ever lost more than a thousand dollars on any one night, he said. If he hadn't been married to a rich wife, I doubt that he would have called it moderate.

Evelyn Coates was a tricky player, unpredictable and hard-nosed. She won the second biggest pot of the night on a pair of eights. In other days you would have said she played like a man. Her expression was the same whether she won or lost, cool and businesslike. It was hard for me to remember, as I faced her across the table, that I had ever been in her bed.

I won the biggest pot of the night on a low straight. I had never had as much money to back me up in any of the games I had been in before, but, as far as I could tell, I played as I always did. My newfound fortune wasn't reflected in my betting. I folded early a good deal of the time.

The newspaper columnist and the Congressman were the eternal pigeons Hale had promised me. They played out of hope and optimism, and were around at the end of almost every pot. Inevitably, it made me doubt their wisdom in other fields. I knew I would read the columnist from then on with great reservations, and I trusted the Congressman wasn't in on any important legislative decisions.

It was a friendly game and even the losers were good-natured about their bad luck. I enjoyed playing poker again after the three-year hiatus. I would have enjoyed it more if Evelyn Coates hadn't been there. I kept looking for a wink, a secret, conspiratorial smile, but it never came. I couldn't help beginning to feel resentful. I didn't let it affect my game, but I felt a little extra satisfaction when I took a pot away from her.

She and I were the only winners at two o'clock, when we finished. While the Congressman, as banker, bent over the accounts, I fingered the silver dollar in my pocket. The go-ahead sign from Central Park West.

A waiter had brought in some sandwiches, and we started on them while the Congressman worked at the table. I couldn't help but think how pleasant it all was, a game that continued, in the same room, with the same friends, week after week, everybody knowing everybody's telephone number, everybody's address, everybody's mannerisms and jokes. Whom would I be seeing next week, what numbers would I dare call, what game would I be playing? For a moment I was on the verge of saying that I would be available next week to give them all the chance to get back their money. Put down my roots in a deck of cards, in the mulch of government. How fast did I have to run? If Evelyn Coates had as much as smiled at me, I believe I would have spoken. But she didn't even glance in my direction.

To give her a chance to say a few words to me away from the others, I went over to a window at the far corner of the room and opened it, pretending I was warm and that the cigarette smoke was bothering me, but she still did not make a gesture toward me, didn't even seem to notice that I had moved.

The bitch, I thought, I won't give her the satisfaction of calling when I get back to my hotel. I imagined her in her place with the young lawyer, smooth and tallow-faced, and the phone ringing and Evelyn Coates saying, "Hell, let it ring," and knowing who it was on the other end and smiling secretly to herself. I wasn't used to hard women. To any kind of women, if I wanted to be honest with myself. One thing, I decided, as I closed the window with a sharp little click, insisting on my presence, one thing I'm going to do from now on is learn how to handle women.

The columnist and the lawyer began a long discussion about what was happening in Washington. The columnist accused the President of trying to destroy the American press, raising postal rates to drive newspapers and magazines into bankruptcy, jailing reporters for not disclosing their sources, threatening to lift the franchises of television stations that broadcast material which displeased the Administration, all stuff that I had read in his columns whenever I had happened to come across them. Even I, who barely read any newspaper but the *Racing Form*, was overexposed to all possible opinions. I wondered how anyone in that room, battered by arguments from all sides, ever managed to vote yes or no on anything. The Congressman, working on a scratch pad, his forehead sweating from the effort, never even looked up. He had showed himself an amiable man throughout the game, and I supposed he voted as he was told, his attention always on party instructions and on the next election. He had said nothing to indicate whether he was a Republican, a Democrat, or a follower of Mao.

When Evelyn Coates brought up the subject of the Watergate break-in and said it meant grave trouble for the President ahead, the columnist said, "Nonsense. He's too smart for that. It'll all just be kicked under the rug. Mark my words. By May, if you ask anybody about it, they'll say, Watergate? What's that? I'll tell you," said the columnist, his deep voice and meticulous speech resonant with the assurance of a man who was accustomed to being listened to attentively at all times, "I tell you we're witnessing the opening moves toward Fascism."

As he spoke, he munched on a corned beef sandwich, washed down with Scotch. "The skinheads are preparing the ground. I won't be surprised if they're not called in to run the whole show. One morning we'll wake up and the tanks will be rolling down Pennsylvania Avenue and the machine guns will be on every roof." *That* hadn't been in any of his columns that I had read. Come to Washington and get the real, authentic, scary dope.

The lawyer didn't seem to be at all ruffled by the charges. He had the calm, good-natured imperturbability of the pliant Company Man. "Maybe it wouldn't be such a bad idea," he said. "The press is irresponsible. It lost the war in Asia for us. It churns up the public against the President, the Vice President, it holds up all authority to scorn, it's making it more and more impossible to govern the country. Maybe putting the skinheads, as you call them, in control for a few years might be the best thing that happened to this country since Alf Landon."

"Oh, Jack," Mrs. Coates said. "The true believer. The voice of the Pentagon. What crap!"

"If you saw what passed over my desk day after day," the lawyer said, "you wouldn't call it crap."

"Mr. Grimes . . . " She turned toward me, a little cool smile on her lips. "You're not in the mess here in Washington. You represent the pure, undefiled American public here tonight. Let's hear the simple wisdom of the masses . . . "

"Evelyn," Hale said warningly. I half-expected to hear him say, Remember, he's our guest. But he let it go with the Evelyn.

I looked at her, annoyed with her for taunting me, feeling that she was testing me somehow, for some not quite innocent purpose of her own. "The pure, undefiled representative of the American public here tonight," I said, "thinks it's all bullshit." I remembered the speech she had made to me, naked, a glass of whiskey in her hand, sitting on the side of the big soft bed in the darkened room, about everybody in Washington being an actor. "You people aren't serious," I said. "It's all a game for you. It's not a game for me, the pure, undefiled et cetera, it's life and death and taxes, and other little things like that for me, but it's just a pennant race for you. You depend upon each other to have different opinions, just the way baseball teams depend upon other teams to have different color uniforms. Otherwise nobody would know who was leading the league. In the end, though, you're all playing the same game." I was surprised at myself even as I spoke. I didn't even know that I had ever thought like this before. "If you get traded to another team, you'll just take off the old suit and put on another one and you'll go out there and try to boost your batting average so you can ask for a raise the next year."

"Let me ask you something, Grimes," the lawyer said affably. "Did you vote in the last election?"

"I did," I said. "I got fooled. The papers printed the sports news on the editorial pages. I don't intend to vote again. It's an undignified occupation for a grown man." I didn't tell them that where I expected I'd be by the time of the next elections, there wouldn't be a chance I'd be able to vote.

"Forgive me, folks," Evelyn Coates said, "I didn't realize I had introduced a homespun political philosopher into our midst."

"I'm not absolutely against what he said," the lawyer said. "I don't see where it's so wrong to be loyal to the team. If the team's winning, of course." He chuckled softly at his own joke.

The Congressman looked up from his accounts. If he had heard a word of the discussion, or any discussion for the last ten years, for that matter, he didn't show it. "Okay," he said, "it all comes out even. Evelyn, you won three hundred and fifty-five dollars and fifty cents. Mr. Grimes, you won twelve hundred and seven dollars. Everybody else get out their checkbooks."

While the losers were finding out how much they owed, there were the usual jokes, directed at Hale, for bringing a ringer, me, into the game. Evelyn Coates made no jokes. There was no hint in the way anyone else talked that anything like an argument had just taken place.

I tried to look offhand as I put the checks into my wallet. Luckily, they were all on Hale's Washington bank. He endorsed them for me so that I wouldn't have any trouble cashing them.

We all left together, and there was a jumble of good-byes as the Congressman and the columnist got into a taxi together. The lawyer took Evelyn by the arm, saying, "You're on my way, Evelyn, I'll drop you." Hale was inside getting a pack of cigarettes from the machine, and I stood alone for a moment watching the lawyer and Evelyn Coates walk off into the darkness of the parking lot. I heard her low laugh at something he had said as they disappeared.

Hale drove silently for a little while. "How long do you plan to stay in town?" he asked, as we were stopped for a light.

"Just until I get my passport. Monday, Tuesday . . . "

"Then where?"

"Then I'll look at a map. Somewhere in Europe."

He started the car with a jerk as the light changed. "God, I wish I was coming along with you. Wherever you're going." The intensity in his voice was disturbing. He sounded like a prisoner speaking to a man who was about to be freed in the morning. "This town," he said. "Total swamp." He turned a corner recklessly, the tires squealing. "That miserable, smooth molasses-talking Benson bastard . . . It's a lucky thing you're not in the government. . . . "

"What're you talking about?" I was really honestly puzzled.

"If you were—in the government, I mean—by Monday night, somebody in your department—somebody *higher* in your department—would get a little poison in his ear about you."

"You mean because of what I said about voting and changing uniforms, that stuff?" I tried not to sound incredulous, as though I were really taking him seriously. "Actually, I hardly meant it. I was joking, or anyway, half-joking."

"You don't joke in this town, friend," Hale said somberly. "At least not in front of guys like him. I've been trying to get him out of the game for six months and nobody's got the guts to do the job. Including me. You may have been joking, but he for sure wasn't."

"At one point in the evening," I said, "I was on the point of saying I'd hang around till next Saturday."

"Don't. Blow. Blow as fast as you can. I wish to hell I could."

"I don't know how it works in your department," I said, "but can't you ask for an assignment someplace else?"

"I can ask," Hale said. "That's about as far as it would go." He fumbled at a cigarette. "They have me pegged as unreliable in the service, and they're making sure they can keep an eye on me twenty-four hours a day. . . . "

"You? Unreliable?" It was the last thing I'd ever guess anybody would think about him.

"I was in Thailand for two years. I sent you a letter. Remember?"

"I never got it, I've been moving around a lot. . . ."

"I wrote a couple of reports that didn't exactly go through channels." He laughed bitterly. "Channels! Sewers. Well, they yanked me—politely—and gave me a nice office with a beautiful secretary and a raise in salary and some memos to shuffle that you might just as well paper the walls with. And the only reason they're being so kind to me is because of my goddamn father-in-law. But the message was clear—and I got it. Be a good boy or else. . . . God!" He laughed again, a harsh, croaking sound. "When I think that I celebrated when I found out I passed the Foreign Service exam! And it's all so senseless—those reports I wrote . . . I was patting myself on the back—the intrepid truth-seeker, the brave little old truth-announcer. Christ, there wasn't anything in those pages that hadn't been spread over every newspaper in the country since then." He scraped his cigarette out savagely in the ashtray on the dashboard. "We live in the age of the Bensons, the smooth poison-droppers, who know from birth that the way up is through the sewer. I'll tell you something peculiar—a physiological phenomenon—somebody ought to write it up in a medical journal—I have days when I have the taste of shit in my mouth all day. I wash my teeth, I gargle, I get my secretary to put a bowl of narcissus on my desk—nothing helps. . . . "

"Jesus," I said, "I thought you were doing great."

"I put on a good act," Hale said lifelessly. "I have to. I'm a dandy little old liar. It's a government of liars and you get plenty of practice. Happy civil servant, happy husband, happy son-in-law, happy father of two. . . . Ah, Christ, why am I letting it all out on you? I imagine you have troubles enough of your own."

"Not at the moment," I said. "If it's so bad, why don't you quit? Go into something else?"

"Into what?" he said. "Selling neckties?"

"Something would be bound to turn up." I didn't tell him that there might be a job open as a night clerk in New York. "Take a few months off and look around and . . ."

"On what?" He made a derisive sound. "I haven't a penny. You saw how we live. My salary's just about half of it. My sainted father-in-law kicks in the rest. He nearly had apoplexy when I got sent home from Asia. He'd burn the house down over my head if I told him I was quitting. He'd have my wife and the kids back living with him in two months after I went out the door. . . . Ah, forget it, forget it, I don't know why I suddenly went off the handle like this. That sonofabitch Benson. I see him multiplied by a thousand every time I come to work in the morning. What the hell—I don't *have* to play in that poker game anymore. At least that'll be *one* Benson I won't have to talk to." He laughed softly. "Maybe if I'd won tonight, I'd be telling you what a great life it is right this minute in this dandy little old town of Washington." He was driving more and more slowly, as though he didn't want to be left alone or have to go home and face the concrete facts of his wife, his children, his career, his father-in-law. I wasn't so anxious to get to my hotel room either. I didn't want to put on the light and look at the telephone on the bedside table and fight down the temptation to pick it up and ask for Evelyn Coates's number.

"I wonder if you'd do me a favor, Doug?" he said, as we neared my hotel.

"Of course." But even as I said it, I made strong mental reservations. After the conversation in the car, I didn't have any inclination to get mixed up more than was absolutely necessary with the life and problems of my old college buddy, Jeremy Hale.

"Come out to dinner tomorrow night," he said, "and somehow get onto the subject of skiing and say you're thinking of going skiing in Vermont the first two weeks next month and why don't I join you?"

"I don't think I'll even be in the country by then," I said.

"That makes no difference," he said calmly. "Just say it. Where my wife can hear it. I have some time coming to me and I can get away then."

"You mean you have to make excuses to your wife if you want to . . . ?"

"Not really." He sighed, at the wheel. "It's more complicated than that. There's a girl . . ."

"Oh."

"That's it." He laughed uneasily. "Oh. That doesn't sound like me either, does it?" He said it pugnaciously, as though somehow he was accusing me of something.

"Frankly, no," I said.

"It *isn't* like me. This is the first time since I've been married . . . I never thought it would happen. But it *did* happen and it's driving me crazy. We've just had a few times . . . a few minutes, an hour, here and there. Sneaking around. It's killing both of us. In a town like this, with people snooping around like bird dogs after everybody. We need some time together—*real* time. God knows what my wife would do if anybody said anything to her. I didn't want it to happen, I swear to God, but it happened. I feel as though the top of my head is going to blow off. I can't talk to anyone in this town. It's like living with a stone on my chest, day in, day out. I never knew I could feel like this about any woman. . . . You might as well know who it is. . . ."

I waited. I had the terrible feeling that the name he was going to come out with would be Evelyn Coates.

"It's that girl in my office," he said, whispering. "Miss Schwartz. Miss Melanie Schwartz. God, what a name!"

"Name or no name," I said, "I can understand. She's beautiful."

"She's a lot more than that. I'm going to tell you something, Doug—if it keeps going on the way it's been going—I don't know what I'm liable to do. We've got to get out of this town together . . . a week, two weeks, a night . . . But we've got to . . . I don't want a divorce. I've been married ten years, I don't want . . . Oh, hell, I don't know why I should drag you into it."

"I'll come to dinner tomorrow night," I said.

Hale didn't say anything. He stopped in front of the hotel. "I'll expect you around seven," he said calmly, as I got out of the car.

In the elevator on the way up to my floor, I thought, Scranton isn't all that far from Washington after all.

As I got ready for bed I kept away from the telephone in my room. I took a long time getting to sleep. I guess I was waiting for the phone to ring. It didn't ring.

I couldn't tell whether it was the telephone that awoke me or if I had opened my eyes just before it began to ring. I had had a nasty, jumbled dream in which I was hiding out, running, from unseen and unknown pursuers, through dark, forested country, then suddenly in glaring sunlight between rows of ruined houses. I was glad to be awake and I reached over gratefully for the telephone.

It was Hale. "I didn't get you up, did I?" he asked.

"No."

"Listen," he said, "I'm afraid I have to cancel the dinner tonight. My wife says we're invited out." He sounded offhand and untroubled.

"That's okay," I said, trying not to let my relief show in my voice.

"Besides," he said, "I talked to the lady in question and—" The rest of the sentence was muffled by a deep crescendo of sound.

"What's that noise?" I asked. I remembered what he had said about phones being tapped in Washington.

"It's a lion roaring," he said. "I'm in the zoo with my kids. Want to join us?"

"Some other time, Jerry," I said. "I'm still in bed." After the outburst in the car after the poker game, I didn't relish the idea of watching him play the role of the dutiful father devoting his Sunday morning to his children. I have never been expert at complicity and didn't relish the thought of being used to deceive infants.

"See you in the office tomorrow," he said. "Remember to bring your birth certificate."

"I'll remember," I said.

The lion was roaring as I hung up.

I was in the shower when the phone rang again. Streaming and soapy, grabbing a towel to wrap around my middle, I picked up the phone.

"Hello," the voice said. "I waited as long as I could." It was Evelyn Coates. Her voice was half an octave lower on the phone. "I have to leave the house. I thought you might have been tempted to call last night, after the game. Or this morning." Her self-confidence was irritating.

"No," I said, leaning back, trying to keep the water from dripping onto the bed. "It didn't occur to me," I lied. "Anyway, you seemed somewhat preoccupied."

"What are you doing today?" she asked, ignoring my complaint.

"At the moment I'm taking a shower." I felt at a disadvantage trying to cope with that low, bantering voice, the water dripping coldly down my back from my wet hair and my eyes beginning to smart because I had gotten some soap in them.

She laughed. "Aren't you polite?" she said. "Getting out of a shower to answer the phone. You knew it was me, didn't you?"

"The thought may have crossed my mind."

"Can I take you to lunch?"

I hesitated, but not for long. After all, I had nothing better to do that afternoon in Washington. "That would be fine," I said.

"I'll meet you at Trader Vic's," she said. "It's a Polynesian place in the Hilton. It's nice and dark, so you won't see the poker rings under my eyes. One o'clock?"

"One o'clock," I said. I sneezed. I heard her laugh.

"Go back to your shower and then dry yourself thoroughly, like a good boy. We don't want you spreading cold germs among the Republicans."

I sneezed again as I hung up. I fumbled my way back to the bathroom with my eyes smarting from the soap. A dark room would suit me, too, because I knew my eyes would be bloodshot the better part of the afternoon. Somehow, I was beginning to have the feeling that I would have to be at my best, physically and mentally, anytime I had anything to do with Evelyn Coates.

"Grimes," she said to me as we were finishing lunch in the dimly lit room, watching the Chinese or Malayan or Tahitian waiter pour flaming rum into our coffee, "you give me the impression of being a man with something to hide."

It came as a complete surprise to me. Until then our conversation had been almost absolutely impersonal—about the food, the drinks (she had had three enormous rum concoctions, with no apparent effect)—about the poker game the night before (she had complimented me on the way I played and I had complimented her)—about the various social strata in Washington and where the people of the night before fitted in, all the small, polite kind of talk with which a courteous and worldly woman might fill an hour to entertain a visitor from afar who had been asked to look her up by some mutual friend. She was dressed charmingly, in a loose tweed suit and a plain blue blouse, high at the throat, and had her dark blonde hair pulled back and tied with a blue ribbon in girlish fashion. I had spoken little, and if I wondered why she had bothered to call me, I hadn't shown it. She hadn't mentioned the night we had spent together, and I had made up my mind not to be the first to bring it up.

"Something to hide," she repeated. My questions to her the night I had met her, I realized, had not been forgotten. Had been filed away in that sharp, suspicious mind for future reference.

"I don't know what you're talking about," I said. But I avoided her eyes.

"Yes, you do," she said. She watched the waiter finish with his performance and place the mugs of hot coffee, smelling of rum and orange and cinnamon sticks, in front of us. "I've seen you three times now—and this is what I don't know about you—where you come from, where you're going, what you're doing in town, what business you're in, why you didn't call me after the other night." She sipped at her drink, smiling demurely over the rim of the mug. "Every other man I've ever seen three times in one week has regaled me with his complete biography—how his father didn't communicate with him, how important he is, what stocks he's bought, all the influential people he knows in town, what problems he has with his wife . . . "

"I'm not married."

"Bravo," she said. "I am in possession of a fact. Mind you, I'm not digging for information. I'm not all that curious about you. It just occurred to me all of a sudden that you must be hiding something. Please don't tell me what it is—" She held up her hand as though to stop me from saying anything. "You might turn out to be a lot less interesting than I think you are. There's only one thing I'd like to ask you, if you don't mind."

"I don't mind." I could hardly say less.

"Are you staying in Washington?"

"No."

"According to Jerry Hale you're going abroad."

"Eventually," I said.

"What does that mean?"

"Soon. In a week or so."

"Are you going to Rome?"

"I imagine so."

"Are you prepared to do me a favor?"

"If I can."

She looked at me consideringly, tapping a fingernail absently on the wood surface of the table. She seemed to come to some decision. "In the course of my duties," she said, "I have come across certain private memorandums of considerable interest. I've taken the liberty of Xeroxing them. The Xerox is Washington's secret weapon. No man is safe if there's one in the office. I happen to have a small sampling of records of delicate negotiations that someday may prove to be very useful to me. And to a friend—a very good friend. He used to work with me, and I'd like to protect him. He's in the embassy in Rome. I want to get some papers to him—some papers very important to me and to him—safely. I don't trust the mails here. And I certainly don't trust them in Rome. My friend has told me he thinks his correspondence is being tampered with, both in the embassy and at his home. Don't look so surprised. If you'd been in this city as long as I have . . . " She didn't finish the sentence. "There's not a soul here I really trust. People talk incessantly, pressures are applied, mail is opened, as I said, phones are bugged . . . I imagine your good friend Jeremy Hale intimated as much to you."

"He did. You think you can trust me?"

"I think so." Her voice was hard, almost threatening. "For one thing, you won't be in Washington. And if you're hiding something important of your own, as I believe . . . Do you deny it?"

"Let it pass," I said. "For the moment."

"For the moment." She nodded, smiling pleasantly at me. "As I said, if you're hiding something important of your own, why couldn't you undertake a little secret errand for a friend? Something that wouldn't take up more than a half hour of your time—and keep quiet about it?" She dug in the big leather handbag that she had on the floor under the table and produced a thick, business-size envelope, sealed with Scotch tape. She slapped it down on the table between us. "It doesn't take up much space, as you can see."

"I don't know when I'm going to be in Rome," I said. "Maybe not for months."

"There's no rush," she said deliberately. She pushed the envelope a half-inch closer to me across the table with her fingernail. She was a hard woman to say no to. "Any time before May will do."

There was no name or address on the envelope. She took out a small gold pencil and a notebook. "Here's the address and telephone number of my friend," she said. "Call him at home. I'd rather you didn't deliver this at the embassy. I'm sure you'll like him. He knows everybody in Rome and you might meet some interesting people through him. I'd appreciate it if you dropped me a line after you've seen him to let me know the deed's been done."

"I'll write you," I said.

"There's a nice boy." She pushed the envelope still closer to me. "From all indications," she said evenly, "you would like to see me from time to time. Am I right?"

"Yes, you're right."

"Who knows?" she said. "If I knew where you were and I had a few weeks of holiday, I might just turn up . . . "

It was pure blackmail and we both knew it. But it was more than that, too. I was going abroad with the intention of losing myself. I had told Hank that I would get in touch with him from time to time, but that was different. He would never know where I was. Looking across the table at this baffling, desirable woman, I realized that I did not want to lose myself completely, cut all ties to America, have no one in my native country who could, *in extremis,* reach me with a message, even if the message were only Happy Birthday or Will you lend me a hundred dollars?

"If you're tempted to open this"— she touched the envelope—"and read what's in it, by all means do so. Naturally, I'd rather you didn't. But I promise you there is nothing there that'll make the slightest sense to you."

I picked up the envelope and put it in my inside pocket. I was connected to her, even if it was only by the memory of a single night, and she knew it. Just how deeply she was connected to me was another matter. "I won't open it."

"I was sure I could depend on you, Grimes," she said.

"Use my first name, please," I said, "the next time we meet."

"I'll do that," she said. She looked at her watch. "If you're finished with your coffee," she said, "I'll pay and we'll leave. I have a date in Virginia."

"Oh," I said, trying not to sound disappointed. "I thought we might spend the afternoon together."

"Not this time, I'm afraid," she said. "If you're lonely, I believe my roommate, Brenda, isn't doing anything this afternoon. She said she thought you were very nice. You might give her a call."

"I might," I said. I was glad the room was dimly lit. I was sure I was blushing. But I was stung by the callousness of her offer. "Do your lovers always go with the apartment?" I asked.

She looked at me evenly, undisturbed. "I think I told you once before that you are not my lover," she said. Then she called to the waiter for the check.

I didn't phone Evelyn's roommate. By some perverse reasoning that I didn't really try to understand, I decided that I would not give Evelyn Coates *that* satisfaction. I spent the afternoon walking around Washington. Now that I knew, at least fragmentarily, what went on behind those soaring columns, off the long corridors, in those massive copies of Grecian temples, I was not as impressed as I otherwise would have been. Rome, I thought, just before the arrival of the Goths. It occurred to me that I probably was never going to vote again, but I was not saddened by the idea. But for the first time in three years I felt unbearably lonely.

As I entered the lobby of my hotel in the dusk, I made up my mind to leave Washington the next day. The sooner I arranged to get out of the country the better. As I packed my bags I remembered George Wales' ski club. What was its name? The Christie Ski Club. No worrying about baggage allowance, no worrying about the Swiss customs, all the free booze you could drink. I had no intention of arriving economically drunk when I set foot on European soil, but with the freight I would be carrying, being waved through Swiss customs with a smile had obvious attractions. Besides, if anybody was watching for the clerk who had fled the Hotel St. Augustine with a hundred thousand dollars in hundred-dollar bills, I reasoned, the last place they'd think to look would be the counter where some three hundred and fifty hilarious suburbanites were embarking for a holiday in the snow from which they would all return en masse in three weeks to the United States.

I was just about to close my second bag when the phone rang. I didn't want to speak to anybody and I let it ring. But it rang on persistently and finally I picked it up.

"I know you're there . . . " It was Evelyn Coates's voice. "I'm in the lobby and I asked at the desk if you were in."

"How was Virginia?" I said flatly.

"I'll tell you when I see you. May I come up?" She sounded hesitant, uncertain.

"I suppose so," I said.

She chuckled, a little sadly, I thought. "Don't punish me," she said. And hung up.

I buttoned the collar of my shirt, pushed the tie into place, and put on my jacket, ready for all formalities.

"Ghastly," she said, when she came through the door and looked around her at my room. "Chromium America."

I helped her off with her coat, because she stood there with her arms out as though expecting it. "I don't intend to spend the rest of my life here," I said.

"I see," she said, glancing at the packed bag on the bed. "Are you on your way?"

"I thought I was."

"Past tense."

"Uh-huh." We were standing stiffly, confronting one another.

"And now?"

"I'm not in all that much of a hurry." I did nothing to make her comfortable. "I thought you said you were busy today. . . . In Virginia."

"I was," she said. "But during the course of the afternoon, it occurred to me I wasn't fond of Virginia. It occurred to me that there was one person I desperately wanted to see and that he was in Washington. So here I am." She smiled experimentally. "I hope I'm not intruding."

"Come on," I said.

"Are you going to ask me to sit down?"

"I'm sorry," I said. "Of course. Please."

She sat down, with neat, womanly grace, her ankles primly crossed. She must have been walking in the cold in Virginia because the color was heightened along her cheekbones.

"What else occurred to you?" I asked, still standing, but at a good distance from her.

"A few other things," she said. She was wearing brown driving gloves, and she pulled them off and dropped them in her lap. Her long fingers, nimble with cards, deft with men, shone in the light of the lamp on the desk beside her. "I decided I didn't like the way I talked to you at lunch."

"I've heard worse," I said.

She shook her head. "It was pure, hard-boiled Washingtonese. Defend yourself at all times. Professional deformation of speech habits. No reason to be used on you. You don't have to be defended against. I'm sorry."

I went over to her and kissed the top of her head. Her hair smelled of winter countryside. "There's nothing to be sorry about. I'm not as tender as all that."

"Maybe I think you are," she said. "Of course you didn't call Brenda."

"Of course not," I said.

"What a stupid, patronizing thing for me to have said." She sighed. "On weekends," she said, "I must learn to leave my armor at home." She smiled up at me, her face soft and young in the subdued glow of the lamp. "You'll forget I said it, won't you?"

"If you want. What else occurred to you in Virginia?"

"It occurred to me that the only time we made love, we both had had too much to drink."

"That's for fair."

"I thought how nice it would be if we made love stone-cold sober. Have you had anything to drink since lunch?"

"No."

"Neither have I," she said, standing up and putting her arms around me.

This time she allowed me to undress her.

Sometime in the middle of the night she whispered, "You must leave Washington in the morning. If you stay another day, maybe I'll never let you out of the city again. And we can't have that, can we?"

When I woke in the morning, she was gone. She had left a note on the desk in her bold, slanted handwriting. "Weekend blues. It's Monday now. Don't take anything the lady said seriously, please. E."

She had put on her armor for the day's work. I crumpled the note and threw it in the wastebasket.

CHAPTER 8

I GOT MY passport that morning. Mr. Hale was not in his office, but he had left all the necessary instructions, Miss Schwartz said. I was fairly certain that Mr. Hale was not in his office because by the end of the weekend he had come to the conclusion that he wouldn't be comfortable seeing me again. Not in the presence of Miss Schwartz. It wás not the first time that a man had regretted in daylight the dark confidences of midnight.

Miss Schwartz was as beautiful and melodious as ever, but I didn't envy Jeremy Hale.

I cashed the checks from the poker game, and with the bills in my pocket went to a department store and bought two strong, but lightweight suitcases. They were handsome pieces of luggage, dark blue with red piping, one large, the other an overnight bag. They were expensive, but I was looking for security, not bargains, at the moment. I also bought a roomy leather attaché case, with a sturdy lock. The case fit snugly into the larger of the two bags. I was now armed for travel, Ulysses with the black ships caulked and a fair wind behind him, unknown perils beyond the next promontory.

The salesman asked what numbers I wanted to put into the combination. "It's advisable," he said, "to use a number that means something to you, that you won't forget."

"Six-O-Two," I said. It was a number that meant quite a bit to me and I doubted that I ever would forget it.

With the new bags in the trunk of the rented car, I was on my way toward New York by three o'clock in the afternoon. I had called my brother and told him to meet me outside my bank at ten o'clock the next morning.

I stopped at a motel on the outskirts of Trenton for the night. I wasn't going to stay in New York any longer than I had to.

Knowing that I was doing the wrong thing, accumulating regrets for the future, I called Evelyn's number in Washington. I didn't know what I could say to her, but I wanted to hear the sound of her voice. I let the phone ring a dozen times. Luckily, there was no one home.

When I drove through the New York City traffic up Park Avenue, toward the bank, I was stopped at a light at the corner of the cross street on which the St. Augustine was located. On an impulse, when the light turned green, I turned down the street. I could feel the skin on the back of my neck prickling as I drove slowly past the falsely impressive canopied entrance, and I even played with the idea of going in and asking for Drusack. It was not a case of nostalgia. There were some questions that he might be able to answer by now. And his predictable rage would have brightened my morning. If there had been a place to park, I think I would have been foolish enough to go in. But the whole street was solidly blocked and I drove on.

Hank was huddled down into his overcoat, with the collar turned up, looking cold and miserable in the biting wind, when I walked up to the bank. If I were a policeman, I thought, I would suspect him of *something,* a small, mean crime, petty forgery, abuse of a widow's confidence, peddling fraudulent jewelry.

His face lit up when he saw me as though he had doubted that I would ever arrive, and he took a step toward me, but I didn't stop. "Meet me at the next corner uptown," I said as I passed him. "I'll only be a minute." Unless someone had been standing near and watching closely, it couldn't have seemed that there was any connection between us. I had the uncomfortable feeling that the city was one giant eye, focused on me.

In the vault, the same old man, paler than ever, took my key and, using his own along with it, opened my safe and handed me the steel box. He led me back to the curtained cubicle and left me there. I counted out the two hundred and fifty hundred-dollar bills and put them in a manila envelope that I had bought in Washington. I was becoming an important consumer of manila envelopes and was no doubt giving a lift to the entire industry.

Hank was waiting for me at the corner, in front of a coffee shop, looking colder than ever. He eyed the manila envelope under my arm fearfully, as though it might explode at any instant. The plate-glass window of the shop was steamed over, but I could see that the place was almost empty. I motioned for Hank to follow me and we went in. I chose a table in the rear and put the manila envelope down and took off my coat. It was suffocatingly hot in the restaurant, but Hank sat down opposite me without taking off his coat or the old, sweat-stained gray slouch hat he was wearing, set squarely and unfashionably on his head. His eyes behind the glasses that dug into the sides of his nose were leaking tears from the cold. He had an old commuter's face, I thought, the kind of face, weathered by years of anxiety and stale indoor air, that you see on men standing on windy station platforms on dark winter mornings, patient as donkeys, weary long before the day's work ever begins. I pitied him and could hardly wait to get rid of him.

Whatever happens, I thought, I am not going to look like that when I'm his age. We still didn't say a word to each other.

When the waitress came over, I asked for a cup of coffee.

"What I need is a drink," Hank said, but he settled for coffee, too.

Against the partition at the end of the small table, there was a small slot for coins and a selector for the jukebox near the entrance. I put in two dimes and jabbed the selector at random. By the time the waitress came back with our coffees, the jukebox was playing so loudly that nobody could have heard me at the next table unless I shouted.

Hank drank his coffee greedily. It did not smell of cinnamon or rum or oranges. "I puked twice this morning," he said.

"The money is in there." I tapped the envelope.

"Christ, Doug," Hank said, "I hope you know what you're doing."

"So do I," I said. "Anyway, it's yours now. I'll leave first. Give me ten minutes and then you can go." I didn't want him to see my rented car and note the license number. I hadn't planned any of this and didn't believe it was really necessary, but caution was becoming automatic with me.

"You'll never regret this," he said.

"No, I won't," I said.

With a crumpled handkerchief he wiped at the cold tears streaming from his eyes. "I told the two fellows that I was coming up with the money this week," he said. "They're delirious with joy. They're going for the deal. They didn't say boo." He opened his overcoat and fished past an old gray muffler that hung around his neck like a dead snake. He brought out a pen and a small notebook. "I'll write a receipt."

"Forget it," I said. "I know I gave you the money and you know you got the money." He had never asked for a receipt for any of the sums he had lent me or given me.

"Inside of a year you'll be a rich man, Doug," he said.

"Good," I said. His optimism was forlorn. "I don't want anything on paper. Not anything. As an accountant, I imagine you know how to arrange to check off whatever may be coming to me without any records being kept." I remembered what Evelyn Coates had said about Xeroxes. I was reasonably sure there were Xeroxes in Scranton, too.

"Yes, I imagine I do." He said it sadly. He was in the wrong profession, but it was too late now to do anything about it.

"I don't want the Internal Revenue Service looking for me."

"I understand," he said. "I can't say I like it, but I understand." He shook his head somberly. "You're the last man in the world I'd . . ."

"That's enough of that, Hank," I said.

The first record on the jukebox ended with an earshattering climax, and the voice of the waitress giving an order to the counterman sounded unnaturally loud in the lull. "Eggs and bacon, up. One English."

I took another gulp of my coffee and got up, leaving the envelope on the table. I put on my coat. "I'll be calling you. From time to time."

He smiled up at me wanly as he put his hand on the envelope. "Take care of yourself, kid," he said.

"You, too." I touched his shoulder and went out into the cold.

* * * * * * * * * * * * * * * * *

The flight wasn't scheduled to leave until eight Wednesday night.

On Wednesday afternoon, at two thirty, I left a hundred-dollar bill in the safety-deposit box and walked out of the bank with seventy-two thousand, nine hundred dollars in the attaché case I had bought in Washington. I was through with manila envelopes. I couldn't have explained even to myself, why I had left the hundred dollars behind. Superstition? A promise to myself that one day I would come back to the country? In any event, I had paid in advance for the rental of the box for a year.

This time I was staying at the Waldorf Astoria. By now, anybody who was looking for me must have decided that I had left the city. I went back to my room and opened the attaché case and took out three thousand dollars, which I put into the new sealskin wallet I had bought for myself. It was large enough to hold my passport and my round-trip charter ticket. At the Christie Ski Club office on Forty-seventh Street, where I had gone after I left Hank in the coffee shop, I had asked for Wales's friend Miss Mansfield, and the girl had filled out my application form and predated it automatically. She told me I had been lucky to come in just then, as they had two cancellations that morning. Off-handedly, I asked her if the Waleses were also making the flight. She checked her list and to my relief said that they weren't on it. I still had plenty of cash from my winnings on Ask Gloria and the Washington poker game. Even without the money in the attaché case and after the expenses of the hotels in Washington and Scranton and what it had cost me when I returned the rented car, I still had more money on me than I ever had carried at one time in my whole life. When I checked in at the desk at the Waldorf, I didn't bother to ask what the room cost. It was a pleasant experience.

I gave Evelyn Coates's address in Washington as my residence. Now that I was completely alone, all my jokes had to be private ones.

There had been very little opportunity for any kind of laughter at all in the last few days. Washington had been a sobering experience. If, as so many people believed, wealth made for happiness, I was a neophyte at the job. I had made a poor choice of companions in my new estate—Hale, with his blocked career and nervous love affair; Evelyn Coates, with her complex armor; my poor brother.

In Europe, I decided, I was going to seek out people without problems. Europe had always been a place to which the American rich had escaped. I now considered myself a member of that class. I would let others who had preceded me teach me the sweet technique of flight. I would look for joyful faces.

But Tuesday night I stayed in my room, alone, watching television. On this last night in America there was no sense in taking unnecessary risks.

As a last gesture, I put a hundred and fifty dollars in an envelope with a note to the bookie at the St. Augustine that read, "Sorry I kept you waiting for your money," and signed my name. There would be one man in America who would vouch for my reputation as an honest man. I mailed the note as I checked out of the hotel.

I got to the airport early, by taxi. The attaché case, with the money inside it, was in the big blue bag with the combination lock. The money would be out of my hands, in the baggage compartment, while we crossed the Atlantic, but there was nothing to be done about it. I knew that every passenger was searched and his hand luggage opened and examined before boarding the plane, as a precaution against hijackers, and it would have been awkward, to say the least, to have to try to explain to an armed guard why I needed more than seventy thousand dollars for a three-week skiing trip.

Wales had been right about the overweight, too. The man at the desk never even looked at the scale as the skycap swung my two bags onto it.

"No skis or boots?" he asked.

"No," I said. "I'm going to buy them in Europe."

"Try Rossignols," he said. "I hear they're great." He had become an expert on equipment at a departure desk at Kennedy.

I showed him my passport, he checked the manifest list and gave me a boarding pass and the formalities were over. "Have a good trip," he said. "I wish I was going with you." The other people on the line with me had obviously started celebrating already, and there was a loud holiday air about the entire occasion, with people embracing and calling to each other and skis clattering to the floor.

I was early and went into the restaurant for a sandwich and a glass of beer. I hadn't eaten lunch and it would be a long time before they served us anything on the plane and I was hungry.

As I ate and drank my beer, I read the evening paper. A policeman had been shot in Harlem that morning. The Rangers had won the night before. A judge had come out against pornographic films. The editors were firmly in favor of impeaching the President. There was talk of his resigning. Men who had had high positions in the White House were being sent to jail. The envelope Evelyn Coates had given me to deliver in Rome was in my small bag, now being stowed into the hold of the airplane. I wondered if I was helping to put someone in jail or keeping him out. America. I reflected on my visit to Washington.

There was a pay telephone on the wall near where I was sitting and I suddenly had the desire to speak to someone, make one last statement, make one ultimate connection with a familiar voice, before I left the country. I got up and dialed the operator and once more called Evelyn Coates's number.

Again, there was no answer. Evelyn was a woman who was more likely to be out than in at any given moment. I hung up and got my dime back. I was about to return to my table, where my half-eaten sandwich was waiting for me, when I stopped. I remembered driving down the street past the St. Augustine Hotel and nearly stopping. This time there would be no danger. I would be climbing into international jet space within forty minutes. I put the dime back into the machine and dialed the number.

As usual, the phone rang and rang before I heard Clara's voice. "Hotel St. Augustine," she said. She could manage to get her discontent and her irritation with the entire world even into this brief announcement.

"I'd like to speak to Mr. Drusack, please," I said.

"Mr. Grimes!" My name came out in a shriek. She had recognized my voice.

"I would like to speak to Mr. Drusack, please," I said, pretending that I hadn't heard her or at least hadn't understood her.

"Mr. Grimes," she said, "where are you?"

"Please, miss," I said, "I would like to speak to Mr. Drusack. Is he there?"

"He's in the hospital, Mr. Grimes," she said. "Two men followed him in his car and beat him up with a pistol. He's in a coma now. They think his skull is fractured and . . ."

I hung up the phone and went back to my table and finished the sandwich and the beer.

The seat belt and no smoking signs went on and the plane started the descent from the zone of morning sunlight. The snow-capped peaks of the Alps glittered in the distance as the 747 slanted into the gray bank of fog that lay on the approaches of Kloten Airport.

The large man in the seat next to mine was snoring loudly. By actual count, between eight and midnight, when I had given up keeping track, he had drunk eleven whiskies. His wife, next to him on the aisle, had kept her own pace, at the ratio of one to his two. They had told me they planned to catch the early train from Zurich to St. Moritz and intended to ski the Corvatch that afternoon. I was sorry I couldn't be there to watch their first run down the hill.

The flight had not been restful. Since all the passengers were members of the same ski club, and a great many of them made the trip together every winter, there had been a good deal of loud socializing in the aisles, accompanied by hearty drinking. The passengers were not young. For the most part they were in their thirties or forties, the men seeming to belong to that vague group that goes under the label of the executive class and the women carefully coiffed suburban housewives who were damned if they couldn't hold their liquor as well as their husbands. A certain amount of weekend wife-swapping could be imagined. If I had to make a guess, I would have said that the average income per family of the passengers on the plane was about thirty-five thousand dollars a year and that their children had nice little trust funds set up by Grandpa and Grandma, craftily arranged to avoid the inheritance tax.

If there were any passengers on the plane who were reading quietly or looking out the windows at the stars and the growing dawn, they were not in my part of the aircraft. Sober myself, I regarded my boisterous and boozy fellow-travelers with distaste. In a more restrictive state than America, I thought, they would have been prevented from leaving the country. If my brother Hank had been on the plane, I realized with a touch of sorrow, he would have envied them.

It had been warm in the plane, too, and I hadn't been able to take off my jacket, because my wallet with my money and passport was in it and the wallet was too bulky to fit in my trouser pocket.

The plane touched down smoothly and I had a moment of envy of the men who piloted those marvelous machines, confidently at work on the flight deck forward. For them only the voyage mattered, not the value of the cargo. I made sure that I was one of the first travelers out of the plane. At the terminal building I went through the door reserved for passengers with nothing to declare. I was lucky enough to see my two bags, both blue, one large, one small, come out in the first batch. I grabbed one of the wire carts and threw the bags on it and rolled the cart out of the customs room without being stopped. The Swiss, I saw, were charmingly tolerant toward prosperous visitors to their country.

I got into a waiting taxi and said, "The Savoy Hotel, please." I had heard that it was a good hotel in the center of the business district.

I had not changed any money into Swiss currency, but when we arrived at the hotel, the driver agreed to accept two ten-dollar bills. It was a few dollars more than it would have been if I had had francs, but I didn't argue with the man.

While I was registering, I asked the clerk for the name and telephone number of the nearest private bank. Like most Americans of this age I had only the vaguest notions of just what Swiss private banks might be like, but had a firm belief, nourished by newspaper and magazine articles, in their ability to conceal money safely. The clerk wrote down a name and a number, almost as if that were the first service demanded of him by every American who signed in at his desk.

Another clerk showed me up to my room. It was large and comfortable, with heavy, old-fashioned furniture, and as clean as I had heard Swiss hotel rooms were likely to be.

While waiting for my luggage to come up, I picked up the phone and gave the operator the number the clerk had given me. It was nine thirty, Swiss time, four thirty in the morning New York time, but even though I had not slept at all on the plane, I wasn't tired.

A voice on the phone said something in German. "Do you speak English?" I asked, regretting for the first time that my education had not equipped me even well enough to say "Good morning" in any language but my own.

"Yes," the woman said. "Whom do you wish to speak to?"

"I would like to make an appointment to open an account," I said.

"Just a moment, please," she said. Almost immediately a man's voice said, "Dr. Hauser here. Good morning."

So. In Switzerland men who were entrusted with money were doctors. Why not? Money was both a disease and a cure.

I gave the good doctor my name and explained once more that I wanted to open an account. He said he would expect me at ten thirty and hung up.

There was a knock on the door and the porter came in with my bags. I apologized for not having any Swiss money for his tip, but he merely smiled and said, "Thank you," and left. I began to feel that I was going to like Switzerland.

I twirled the three tumblers on the combination lock of the big bag and pushed on the lever to open it. The lever did not budge. I tried once more. It still didn't open. I tried again, with the same result. I was sure I was using the correct numbers. I picked up the small bag, which had the same combination, and twirled the tumblers and pushed at the lever. It opened smoothly.

"Damn it," I said under my breath. The big bag had probably been handled roughly at one end of the flight or the other and the lock had jammed. I had nothing with me with which to force the lock. I didn't want anyone else meddling with the bag, so I went down to the desk and asked for a big screwdriver. The concierge's English vocabulary did not include the word screwdriver, but I finally got him to understand by the use of elaborate gestures what I wanted. He said something in German to an assistant and two minutes later the man reappeared with a screwdriver.

"He can go up with you," the concierge said, "and assist you, if you want."

"That won't be necessary, thank you," I said, and went back to my room.

It took five minutes of scraping and prying to force the lock, and I mourned for my handsome, brand-new bag as it broke open. I would have to get a new lock put on, if that were possible.

I lifted the lid. On the top of whatever else was in the bag there was a loud, houndstooth sport jacket. I had never owned a jacket like that in my life.

I had taken the wrong bag at the airport. One that looked exactly like mine, the same size and make, the same color, dark blue with red piping. I swore softly at the chain-belt system of manufacturing and selling in America, where everybody makes and sells a million identical copies of everything.

I let the lid drop on the bag and flipped the clasps on each side of the lock shut. I didn't want to disturb anybody else's belongings. It was bad enough that I had broken open the lock. Then I went down to the concierge's desk again. I gave him back the screwdriver and explained what had happened and asked him to call the airport for me to find out if one of the other travelers on my plane had reported that a mistake had been made and, if so, where and how I could pick up my own bag.

"Do you have your baggage checks?" he asked.

I searched through my pockets while the concierge looked on condescendingly. "Accidents happen. One must foresee," he said. "When I travel, I always paste a large colored etiquette with my initials on it on all my luggage."

"A very good idea," I said. "I will remember it in the future." I didn't have the baggage checks. I must have thrown them away when I went through customs and saw I didn't need them. "Can you call, now, please? I don't know any German and . . ."

"I shall call," he said. He picked up the phone and asked for a number.

Five minutes later, after a good deal of agitated Swiss-German, interrupted by long waits which the concierge filled with rapid drumming of his fingertips on his desk, he hung up. "Nothing has been reported," he said. "They will call you here when there is any news. When the passenger who has your bag gets to his hotel, he will undoubtedly discover that there has been an exchange and will make inquiries at the airport."

"Thank you," I said.

"For nothing." He bowed. I did not bow back. I went up to my room.

When the passenger gets your bag to his hotel, the concierge had said. I had overheard some of the conversations on the plane. There were probably five hundred ski resorts in Europe, and from what I had heard my bag might even at that minute be on its way to Davos or Chamonix or Zermatt or Lech or . . . I shook my head despairingly. Whoever it was who had my bag might not try to open it until the next morning. And when he did, he probably would do exactly as I had done and break open the lock. And he might not be as fastidious as I had been about disturbing a stranger's affairs.

I lifted the lid of the bag on the bed and stared down at the houndstooth jacket. I had a premonition that I was going to have trouble with the man who would wear a jacket like that. I knocked the lid back hard.

I picked up the telephone and gave the number of the bank. When I got an answer, I asked for Dr. Hauser again. He was very polite when I told him that I found that I could not come in today. A specialist in the fever regions of international currency, he was calm in the face of ups and downs. I said I would try to call him tomorrow for an appointment. "I will be in my office all day," he said.

After he had hung up, I sat staring at the telephone for a long time. There was nothing I could do but wait.

Accidents happen, the concierge had said. One must foresee.

He had been a little late with his advice.

CHAPTER 9

IN THE NEXT two days I had the concierge call the airport half a dozen times. The conversation was always the same. No one from the ski club had reported having taken a wrong bag.

Pacing up and down in the gloomy room, my nerves twanging like overtuned guitar strings, I remembered the old saw—accidents go in threes. There had been Ferris on the floor, Drusack in the hospital, now this. Should I have been more wary? I knew I was a superstitious man and I should have paid more honor to superstition. The hotel room, which had seemed at first glance to be cosy and welcoming, now only added to my depression, and I took long random walks around the city, hoping to tire myself at least enough so that I could sleep at night. The climate of Zurich in the winter is not conducive to gaiety. Under the leaden sky, even the lake looked as though it had lain in a vault for centuries.

On the second day I recognized defeat and finally unpacked the suitcase I had carried away from Kloten. There was nothing in it to identify its owner, no address books, no checkbooks, no books of any kind, with or without a name on the flyleaf, no bills or photographs, signed or unsigned, and no monograms on anything. The owner must have been inordinately healthy—in a leather shaving kit, there were no medicine bottles that might have had a name on a label—just toothpaste, toothbrush, a safety razor, a bottle of aspirin, after-shaving talcum powder, and a bottle of eau de cologne.

I began to sweat. It was room 602 all over again. Was I going to be haunted forever by ghosts who slipped into my life for a moment, changed it, and then slipped out, eternally unidentified?

Remembering detective stories I had read, I looked for tailors' labels on the jackets of suits. While the clothes were presentable enough, they all seemed to come from big clothing manufacturers who distributed to stores all over the United States. There were laundry symbols on some of the shirts. Perhaps, given time, the FBI would have been able to track them down, but I couldn't see myself approaching the FBI for help.

There was a pair of crimson ski pants and a lemon yellow nylon lightweight parka. I shook my head. What could you expect of a man who would appear on the slopes looking like the flag of a small hot country? It was in keeping with the houndstooth jacket. I would keep my eyes open for bright spots of color coming down the hill.

There was one clue, if it could be called that. Along with the two suits and the flannel slacks and the houndstooth sport jacket, there was a tuxedo. It might mean that my man had intended to spend at least part of his time at a plush resort where people dressed for dinner. The only place I had ever heard of like that was the Palace Hotel in St. Moritz, but there probably were a dozen others. And the presence of the tuxedo could also mean that its owner intended to go to London or Paris or some other city where dress might occasionally be formal while he was in Europe. Europe was just too goddamn enormous.

I thought of calling the ski club office in New York, explaining that there had been an innocent mix-up at the Zurich airport and asking for a copy of the manifest with the names of the people on board my plane and their home addresses. For a little while I entertained the notion of sending letters to each and every one of the more than three hundred passengers with my story of the mistake about the luggage and asking the recipients of the letter to let me know whether or not they had lost theirs, so that I could return the bag in my possession to its rightful owner. But thinking about this plan for just a minute or two, I realized how hopeless it would be. After the two fruitless days, I was sure that whoever had my bag would not be inclined to advertise.

Trying to get some idea of what the thief (which was how I now described the man to myself) might look like, I tried on some of his clothes. I put on one of his shirts. It fit me around the neck. I have a sixteen-and-a-half-inch neck. The sleeves were about an inch too short for me. Could I carry a tape measure and invent some plausible reason for measuring the necks and arms of all the Americans in Europe for the winter? There were two pairs of good shoes, one brown, one black, size ten. Whitehouse & Hardy. Stores in almost every big city in the United States. No footprint there. I tried them on. They fit me perfectly. My feet would be dry this winter.

The houndstooth jacket fit me well enough, too—a little loose around the middle but not much. No middle-aged paunch there, but then, again, the man was a skier and probably in good condition, no matter how old he was. The slacks were a little short, too. So the man was slightly shorter than I, say five foot ten or eleven. At least I wouldn't have to waste my time on giants or fat men or midgets.

I hoped that the thief would turn out to be as thrifty as I intended to be and wear the clothes he had no doubt by now found in my bag, even though they would only fit him approximately, as his fit me. I was sure that if I saw a suit of mine go past I would recognize it. I realized I was grasping at straws—with seventy thousand dollars in his pocket he was probably being measured at that moment by some of the best tailors in Europe. I had the same sense of pain that I imagined a husband might have knowing that at that moment his beautiful wife was in bed with another man. With anguish I realized I was *married* to a certain number of hundred-dollar bills. It wasn't rational. After all, I was richer than I had been only two weeks before. But there it was. I was beyond rationality.

Meanwhile I had about five thousand dollars in cash on me. I had five thousand dollars worth of time to find a man with a sixteen-and-a-half neck, thirty-four-inch arms, a size ten shoe, and no intention of returning seventy thousand dollars that had fallen, almost literally, from the heavens into his hands.

As I repacked the bag carefully, putting the gaudy jacket on top, the way I had found it, I thought, Well, at least there's one consolation—I won't have to spend any money on a new wardrobe to replace the one I had lost. The Lord giveth and the Lord taketh away. I don't know what I would have done if the bag had been full of women's things.

I paid my bill and took a taxi to the Bahnhof and bought a first-class ticket for St. Moritz. The only people I had spoken to on the plane coming over were the couple who were going to ski the Corvatch at St. Moritz. They hadn't told me their names or where they were going to stay. I knew the chances of their being able to give me any useful information if I did find them were almost infinitesimal. But I had to start somewhere. Zurich had no further charms for me. It had rained the two days I had been there.

At Chur, an hour-and-a-half ride from Zurich, I had to change for the narrow-gauge railroad that mounted into the Engadine. I went down the first-class car until I saw an empty compartment and went in and put my coat and two bags on the rack over the seats.

The atmosphere on the new train was considerably different from the one on the express from Zurich, which had been businesslike and quiet, with solid, heavy types reading the financial pages of the *Zurcher Zeitung*. Getting into the toylike cars en route to the Alpine resorts, there were a lot of young people, many of them already in ski clothes, and expensively dressed pretty women in furs, with appropriate escorts. There was a feeling of holiday that I was in no mood to share. I was hurting and I wanted to think and I hoped that no one would come into my compartment to disturb me. Undemocratically, I closed the sliding door of the compartment, as a deterrent to company. But just before the train started, a man pulled the door open and asked, in English, politely enough, "Pardon me, sir, are these seats taken?"

"I don't think so," I said as ungraciously as possible.

"Honey," the man called down the corridor. "In here." A fluffy blonde, considerably younger than the man, wearing a leopard coat and a hat to match, came into the compartment. I grieved briefly for all prowling animals threatened with extinction. The lady was carrying a handsome leather jewel case and smelled strongly of a musky perfume. A huge diamond ring graced the finger over her wedding band. If the world were better organized, there would have been a riot of porters and any other workers within a radius of ten blocks of the station platform. Unthinkable in Switzerland.

The man had no luggage, just some magazines and a copy of the *International Herald Tribune* under his arm. He dropped the magazines and paper on the seat opposite me and helped the lady off with her coat. Swinging it up to put it on the rack, the hem of the coat brushed against my face, tickling me and swamping me in a wave of scent.

"Oh," the woman said, "excuse, excuse."

I smiled glumly, restraining myself from scratching at my face. "It's a pleasure," I said.

She rewarded me with a smile. She couldn't have been more than twenty-eight years old, and up to now she had obviously had every reason to feel that a smile of hers was indeed a reward. I was sure that she was not the man's first wife, maybe not even the second. I took an instant dislike to her.

The man took off the sheepskin coat that he was wearing, and the green, furry Tyrolean hat, with a little feather in the band, and tossed them up on the rack. He had a silk foulard scarf tied around his throat, which he didn't remove. As he sat down he pulled out a cigar case.

"Bill," the woman said, complaining.

"I'm on a holiday, honey. Let me enjoy it." Bill opened the cigar case.

"I hope you don't mind if my husband smokes," the woman said.

"Not at all." At least it would kill some of the overpowering aroma of the perfume. The man pushed the cigar case toward me. "May I offer you one?"

"Thank you, no. I don't smoke," I lied.

He took out a small gleaming clipper and cut off the end. He had thick, brutal, manicured hands that went with his high-flushed, fleshy face and hard blue eyes and jaw. I would not have liked to work for him or be his son. I figured he was over forty years old. "Pure Havana," he said. "Almost impossible to find back home. The Swiss are neutral about Castro, thank God." He used a thin gold lighter to start the cigar and leaned back, puffing comfortably. I looked out the window morosely at the snowy countryside. I had thought I was going to be on holiday, too. For the first time it occurred to me that perhaps I ought to turn around at the next station and start for home. Except where was home? I thought of Drusack, who was not going to St. Mortiz.

The train went into a tunnel and it was absolutely dark in the compartment. I wished the tunnel would go on forever. Self-pityingly, I remembered the nights at the St. Augustine and thought, Darkness is my element.

Sometime after we emerged from the tunnel, we were in sunlight. We had climbed out of the gray cloud that hung over the Swiss plain. The sunlight was somehow an affront to my sensibility. The man was dozing now, his head thrown back, the cigar dead in an ashtray. His wife had the *Herald Tribune* and was reading the comic strips, a rapt expression on her face. She looked foolish, her mouth pursed, her eyes childish and bright under the leopard hat. Was that what I had thought money was going to buy for me?

She became conscious that I was staring at her, looked up at me, giggled coquettishly. "I'm a pushover for comic strips," she said. "I'm always afraid Rip Kirby is going to get killed in the next installment."

I smiled inanely, looked at the diamond on her finger, earned, I was sure, in honest matrimony. She peered obliquely at me. I guessed that she never looked at anyone straight on. "I've seen you someplace before," she said. "Haven't I?"

"Perhaps," I said.

"Weren't you on the plane Wednesday night? The club plane?"

"I was on it," I said.

"I was sure I knew you from someplace before that. Sun Valley maybe?"

"I've never been in Sun Valley," I said.

"That's the wonderful thing about skiing," she said, "you get to meet the same people all over the world."

The man groaned a little, awakened by the sound of our voices. Coming out of sleep, his eyes stared at me with blank hostility. I had the feeling that hostility was his natural and fundamental condition and that I had surprised him before he had time to arrange himself for the ordinary traffic of society.

"Bill," the woman said, "this gentleman was on the plane with us." From the way she said it, it sounded as though it had been an extraordinary pleasure for us all.

"Is that so?" Bill said.

"I always feel it's lucky to find Americans to travel with," the woman said. "The language and everything. Europeans make you feel like such a dummy. I think this calls for a drink-drink." She opened the jewel case, which she had kept on the seat beside her, and brought out an elegant silver flask. There were three small chromium cups, one inside the other, over the cap, and she gave one to me and one to her husband and kept one for herself. "I hope you like cognac," she said, as she poured the liquor carefully into our cups. My hand was shaking, and some of the cognac spilled over on it. "Oh, I'm so sorry," she said.

"Nothing," I said. The reason my hand was shaking was that the man had taken off the foulard scarf around his neck and for the first time I saw the tie he was wearing. It was a dark red woolen tie. It was either the tie that I had packed in my bag or one exactly like it. He crossed his legs and I looked down at his shoes. They were brown, plain-toed, with gum soles. They were not new. I had had just such a pair of shoes in my bag.

"Here's to the first one to break a leg this year," the man said, raising his chromium cup. He laughed harshly. I was sure he had never broken anything. He was just the sort of man who had never been sick a day in his life and didn't carry anything stronger than aspirin with him when he traveled.

I drank my cognac in one gulp. I needed it. And I was glad when the lady refilled my cup immediately. I raised the cup gallantly to her and smiled widely and falsely, hoping the train would be wrecked and both she and her husband crushed, so that I could search them and their baggage thoroughly. "You people certainly know how to travel," I said, with an exaggerated, admiring shake of the head.

"Be prepared in foreign lands," the man said. "That's our motto. Say . . . " He extended his hand. "My name's Bill. Bill Sloane. And the little lady is Flora."

I shook his hand and told them my name. His hand was hard and cold. The little lady (weight one twenty-five, I figured) smiled winsomely and poured some more cognac.

By the time we reached St. Moritz we were a cosy threesome. I had learned that they lived in Greenwich, Connecticut, that Mr. Sloane was a three-handicap golfer, that he was a building contractor and a self-made man, that, as I had guessed, Flora was not his first wife, that he had a son at Deerfield, who, thank God, did not wear his hair long, that he had voted for Nixon and had been to the White House twice, that the Watergate fuss would die down in a month with the Democrats sorry they had ever started it, that this was their third visit to St. Moritz, that they had stopped over in Zurich for two days so that Flora could do some shopping, and that they were going to stay at the Palace Hotel in St. Moritz.

"Where're you staying, Doug?" Sloane asked me.

"The Palace," I said without hesitation. I certainly couldn't afford it, but I was not going to let my new friends out of my sight at any cost. "I understand it's fun."

When we got to St. Moritz, I insisted on waiting with them until their luggage came out of the baggage car. Neither of them changed expression when I swung the big blue bag off the rack. "Do you know your bag's unlocked?" Sloane asked.

"The lock's broken," I said.

"You ought to get it fixed," he said, as we left the compartment. "St. Moritz is full of Italians." His interest could mean something. Or nothing. The two of them might be the best actors in the world.

They had eight bags between them, all brand new, none of them the twin of mine. That again could mean nothing. We had to hire an extra taxi for the baggage, and it followed us up the hill through the busy, snowy streets of the town to the hotel.

The hotel had a tantalizing, faint, indefinable aroma. Its source was money. Quiet money. The lobby was like an extension of the bank vault in New York. The guests were treated by the help in a kind of reverential hush, as though they were ikons of great age and value, frail and worthy of worship. I had the feeling that even the small exquisitely dressed children with their English nannies, who walked decorously along the deep carpets, knew I didn't belong there.

Everybody at the reception desk and at the concierge's desk shook Mr. Sloane's hand and bowed to Mrs. Sloane. The tips had obviously been princely in the preceding years. Would a man like that, who could afford a wife like Flora and a hotel like the Palace, walk off with somebody else's seventy thousand dollars? And wear his shoes in the bargain? The answer, I decided, was probably yes. After all, Sloane had confessed he was a self-made man.

When I told the clerk at the reception desk that I had no reservation, his face took on that distant no-room-at-the-inn look of hoteliers in a good season. He had pierced my disguise instantly. "I'm afraid, sir," he began, "that . . . "

"He's a friend of mine," Mr. Sloane said, coming up behind me. "Fit him in please."

The clerk made an important small business of checking the room chart and said, "Well, there's a double room. I might . . . "

"That's fine," I said.

"How long will you be staying, Mr. Grimes?" the clerk asked.

I hesitated. Who knew how long five thousand dollars would last in a place like that? "A week," I said. I would skip orange juice in the mornings.

We all went up in the elevator together. The clerk had put me in the room next to the Sloanes. It would have been convenient if the walls had been thinner or I had been trained in electronic bugging equipment.

My room was a large one, with a great double bed with a pink satin spread and a magnificent view of the lake and the mountains beyond, pure and clear in the late afternoon sunlight. Under other conditions it would have been exhilarating. Now it merely seemed as if nature was being callous and expensive. I closed the blinds and in the gloom lay down fully dressed on the soft bed, the satin rustling voluptuously under my weight. I still seemed to smell Flora Sloane's perfume. I tried to think of some way in which I could find out quickly and surely if Sloane was my man. My mind was flat and tired. The two days in Zurich had exhausted me. I felt a cold coming on. I could think of nothing except to hang on and watch. But then if I *did* find out that it was my tie he was wearing, my shoes he was walking around in, what would I do? My head began to ache. I got up off the bed and dug in the leather shaving kit for the tin of aspirin and swallowed two.

I dozed fitfully after that, dreaming disconnectedly. There was a man who appeared and disappeared at the edge of my dreams who might have been Sloane or Drusack, jangling keys.

I was awakened by the ringing of the telephone. It was Flora Sloane, inviting me to dinner. I made myself sound enthusiastic as I accepted. I didn't have to dress for dinner, she said; we were dining in town. Somehow, Bill had forgotten to pack his tuxedo, and it was being flown from America but hadn't arrived yet. I said I preferred not dressing myself and went in and took a cold shower.

We met for drinks at the bar of the hotel. Sloane was wearing a dark gray suit. It was not mine. He had changed his shoes. There was another couple at the table who had been on our plane coming over and who were also from Greenwich. They had been out skiing that day and the wife was already limping. "Isn't it marvelous?" she said. "I can just go up to the Corveglia Club every day for the next two weeks and just lie in the sun."

"Before we were married," her husband said, "she used to tell me how much she loved to ski."

"That was before we were married, dear," the woman said complacently.

Sloane ordered a bottle of champagne. It was finished quickly and the other man ordered a second one. I would have to get out of St. Moritz before it was my turn to reciprocate. It was easy to love the poor in that atmosphere.

We went to dinner in a restaurant in a rustic chalet nearby and drank a great deal more champagne. The prices on the menu were not rustic. During the course of the meal I learned more than I ever wanted to know about Greenwich—who was nearly thrown out of the golf club, what lady was doing it with what gynecologist, how much the new addition to the Powells' house cost, who was leading the brave fight to keep black children from being bussed into the town schools. Even if I had been guaranteed that I would get my seventy thousand dollars back before the end of the week, I wondered if I could endure the necessary dinners.

It was worse after dinner. When we got back to the hotel, the two men went to play bridge and Flora asked me to take her dancing in the Kings Club downstairs. The lady with the limp came along with us to watch. When we were seated at a table, Flora asked for champagne, and this time it was fairly and truly on my bill.

I never liked to dance, and Flora was one of those women who clutch their partners as if to cut off any possible movement to escape. It was hot in the room and infernally noisy and my flannel blazer was heavy and too tight under the arms and I was swamped in Flora's perfume. She also hummed amorously into my ear as we danced.

"Oh, I'm so glad we found you," she whispered. "You can't *drag* Bill onto a dance floor. And I'll bet you're a great skier, too. You move like one." Sex and all other human activities were clearly inextricably entwined in Mrs. Sloane's mind. "Will you ski with me tomorrow?"

"I'd love to," I said. If I could have chosen a list of people whom I could suspect of having stolen my suitcase, the Sloanes would have been far down at the bottom.

It was after midnight, with two bottles of champagne gone, when I finally managed to call a halt. I signed the check and escorted the two ladies upstairs to where their husbands were playing bridge. Sloane was losing. I didn't know whether I was glad or sorry. If it was my money, I would have wept. If it was his, I'd have cheered. Aside from his friend from Greenwich, there was a handsome, graying man of about fifty at the table, and an old lady encrusted with jewelry, with a harsh Spanish accent, like the cawing of a crow. The Beautiful People of the International Set.

While I was watching, the handsome, gray-haired man made a small slam. "Fabian," Sloane said, "every year I find myself writing out a check to you."

The man Sloane had called Fabian smiled gently. He had a charming smile, almost womanish in sweetness, with laugh wrinkles permanently around his liquid dark eyes. "I must admit," he said, "I'm having a modest little run of luck." He had a soft, husky voice and an accent that was a little strange. I couldn't tell from the way he spoke where he came from.

"Modest!" Sloane said. He wasn't a pleasant loser.

"I'm going to bed," Flora said. "I'm skiing in the morning."

"I'll be right up," Sloane said. He was shuffling the cards as though he was preparing to use them as weapons. . . .

I escorted Flora to her door. "Isn't it comfy," she said, "we're just side by side?" She kissed my cheek good night, giggled, and said, "Night-night," and went in.

I wasn't sleepy and I sat up and read. I heard footsteps about a half hour later and the door to the Sloanes' room open and shut. There were some murmurs through the wall that I couldn't make out and after a while silence.

I gave the couple another fifteen minutes to fall asleep then opened the door of my room silently. All along the corridor, pairs of shoes were placed in front of the bedroom doors, women's and men's moccasins, wing tips, patent leathers, ski boots, in eternal sexual order. Two by two, entries to the Ark. But in front of the Sloanes' door, there were only the dainty leather boots Flora Sloane had worn on the train. For whatever reason, her husband had not put out the brown shoes with the gum soles, possibly size ten, to be shined. I closed my door without a sound, to ponder the meaning of this.

CHAPTER 10

"I'M WORRIED ABOUT my husband," Flora Sloane said to me. We were having a drink before lunch, seated in the sunshine on the terrace of the Corveglia Club, among the maritime Greeks, the Milanese industrialists, the people who were photographed beside pools at Acapulco, and the ladies of various nationalities who preyed on them all. Flora Sloane, who obviously had not been what has in other times been called "gently reared" and who lapsed, when excited, into a language and an accent you might expect to hear from a waitress in a diner in New Jersey patronized almost exclusively by truck drivers, was completely at home here and accepted all attention or deference with regal aplomb. I, on the other hand, felt like a man who had just been dropped behind enemy lines.

The temporary membership had cost me a hundred and twenty francs for two weeks, but where the Sloanes went I had to follow. Not that Sloane himself was very much in evidence. In the mornings, according to Flora, he was on the phone back to his office in New York for hours on end and in the afternoon and evening he played bridge.

"He won't even have a *tan* when we get back to Greenwich," she complained. "People won't believe he's ever *seen* an Alp."

Meanwhile, I had the honor of leading Flora Sloane down the hill and buying her lunch. She was a fair skier, but one of those women who squealed when she came to a steep bit and constantly complained of her boots. I spent quite a bit of time kneeling in the snow, loosening the hooks, then tightening them again after three turns. I had refused to be seen in the red pants and the lemon yellow parka I had found in the suitcase and had bought myself a sensible navy blue outfit. At great expense.

At night, there was the inevitable sweaty dancing and the champagne. Madame Sloane was becoming progressively more amorous, too, and had a nasty habit of sticking her tongue in my ear while we danced. I wanted to get into the Sloanes' room and search it, but not that way. There was a choice of reasons for my coolness, not the least of which was the total lack of all response to any sexual stimulation, dating from the moment I had realized that my seventy thousand dollars had disappeared. Money was power. That I knew. It had not occurred to me that its absence involved impotence. Any attempt at performance on my part, I was sure, would be grotesquely inadequate. Flora Sloane's flirtatiousness was trying enough. Her derision would be catastrophic. I foresaw years of psychiatry ahead of me.

My efforts at detective work had been pathetically useless. I had knocked at the Sloanes' door several times on one pretext or another in the hope of being invited in so that I at least could take a quick surreptitious look around their room, but whether it was the wife or the husband who responded, all conversations took place on the threshold, the door just barely ajar.

I had opened my door every night when the hotel slept, but the brown shoes had never been in the corridor. I had begun to feel that I had been the victim of a hallucination in the train compartment—that Sloane had never worn brown shoes with gum soles and never had a red wool tie around his neck. I had brought up the subject of the confusion of luggage at airports these days, but the Sloanes had shown no interest. I would stay the week, I had decided, on the off chance that something would happen, and then I would leave. I had no idea of where I would go next. Behind the Iron Curtain, perhaps. Or Katmandu. Drusack haunted me.

"Those miserable bridge games." Flora Sloane sighed over her Bloody Mary. "He's losing a fortune. They play for five cents a point. Everybody knows Fabian's practically a professional. He comes here for two months each winter and walks away rich. I try to tell Bill that he's just not as good a bridge player as Fabian, but he's such a stubborn man he refuses to believe that anybody is better than him at *anything*. Then when he loses he gets furious at me. He's the worst loser in the world. You wouldn't believe some of the things he says to me. When he comes up to the room after one of those awful games, it's nightmare time. I haven't had a decent night's sleep since I came up here. I have to *drive* myself to put on my ski boots in the morning. By the time I leave here, I'll be a worn-out old hag."

"Oh, come now, Flora." I made the awaited objection. "You couldn't look like a hag if you tried. You look blooming." This was true. At all hours of the day and night, in no matter what clothes, she looked like an overblown peony.

"Appearances are deceiving," she said darkly. "I'm not as strong as I look. I was *very* delicate as a child. Frankly, honey, if I didn't know you were waiting for me downstairs every morning, I think I'd just stay in bed all day."

"Poor girl," I said sympathetically. The thought of Flora staying in bed was delicious, but not for the reason that Flora herself might have believed. With her off the hill I could give back my rented skis and boots and never have to go up the mountain again that winter. Even with the welcome discovery that my eyes served me adequately when skiing, after Vermont the sport had no joys for me.

"There's a gleam of hope," Flora said. She looked at me obliquely in that sidelong, automatically provocative way I had learned to hate. "Something has come up and Bill may have to go back to New York next week. Then we could spend *all* the time together." The *all* had a thunderous emphasis that made me look around uneasily to see if anyone on the terrace happened to be listening to us. "Wouldn't that be just beautiful?"

"B . . . bu . . . beautiful," I said. It was the first time I had stuttered since I left the St. Augustine. "Let's . . . let's go in for lun . . . lunch."

That afternoon she presented me with a watch. It was a great, thick model, guaranteed for accuracy under three hundred feet of water or when dropped from the roofs of tall buildings. It had a stopwatch attachment and all sorts of dials. It did everything but play the Swiss national anthem. "You shouldn't have," I said faintly.

"I want you to think of this marvelous week whenever you look at the time," she said. "Don't I get just a little kiss for it?"

We were in a *stubli* in the middle of town where we had stopped on the way to the hotel after the afternoon's skiing. I liked it because there wasn't a bottle of champagne in the house. The place smelled of melted cheese and wet wool from the other skiers who crowded the room, drinking beer. I pecked at her cheek.

"Don't you like it?" she asked. "The watch, I mean."

"I love it," I said. "Hon . . . honestly. It's just so extravagant."

"Not really, honey," she said. "If you hadn't come along and just *pampered* me, I'd have had to hire a ski teacher and you know what ski teachers cost in a place like this. And you have to buy them lunch besides. And the way they eat! I think they just dine on potatoes all the rest of the year and stock up in the winters." She was a flighty woman, but she had a strong feeling for economics. "Here," she said, "let me put it on you." She slipped it on my wrist and clipped on the heavy silver band. "Isn't it just absolutely *male?*"

"I suppose you could describe it like that," I said. When I finally rid myself of the Sloanes, man and wife, I would take it back to the jeweler's and sell it back. It must have cost at least three hundred dollars.

"Just don't tell Bill about it," she said. "It's a little secret between you and me. A little darling secret. You'll remember, won't you, honey?"

"I'll remember." That was one promise I definitely would keep.

The crisis arrived the next morning. When she came down into the hall where I was waiting for her as usual at ten o'clock, she wasn't in ski clothes. "I'm afraid I can't ski with you this monring, honey," she said. "Bill has to go to Zurich today and I'm taking him to the train. The poor man. With all this beautiful snow and gorgeous weather and all." She giggled. "And he has to stay overnight, too. Isn't it just too bad?"

"Awful," I said.

"I hope you won't be lonesome, skiing by yourself," she said.

"Well, if it can't be helped, it can't be helped," I said manfully.

"Actually," she said, "I don't feel much like skiing today either. I had an idea. Why don't you go up now and get your exercise and come down by one o'clock and we'll have a cosy little lunch somewhere? Bill's train leaves at twenty to one. We can have a perfectly dreamy afternoon together . . ."

"That's a great idea," I said.

"We'll start with a scrumptious cold bottle of champagne in the bar," she said, "and then we'll just see how things work out. Does that sound attractive to you?"

"Scrumptious."

She gave me one of her significant smiles and went back upstairs to her husband. I went out into the cold morning air feeling a frown beginning to freeze on my face. I had no intention of skiing. If I never saw a pair of skis again it would be all the same to me. I regretted ever having listened to Wales about the ski club plane, which was the beginning of the chain of events that was leading Mrs. Sloane inexorably into my bed. Still, I had to admit to myself, if I had crossed the ocean on a regular flight and my bag had been stolen, I'd have had *no* notion at all of where I might look for it. And through the Sloanes I had met quite a few of the other passengers on the plane and had been able to try my lost luggage gambit on them. True, it had yielded nothing so far, but one could always hope that on the next hill or in the next Alpine bar, a face would leap out, an involuntary gasp or heedless word would put me on the track of my fortune.

I thought of leaving St. Moritz on the same train with Sloane, but when we got to Zurich what could I do? I couldn't trail him around the city spying on him.

I contemplated the perfectly dreamy afternoon ahead of me, starting with a scrumptious bottle of champagne (on my bill) and groaned. A young man, swinging ahead of me down the street on crutches, his leg in a cast, heard me and turned and stared curiously at me. Everyone to his own brand of trouble.

I turned and looked into a shop window. My reflection stared back at me. A youngish-looking man in expensive ski clothes, on holiday in one of the most glamorous resorts in the world. You could have taken my picture for an advertisement for a chic travel magazine. Money no object. The vacation of your dreams.

Then I grinned at myself in the window. An idea had come to me. I started down the street, after the man on crutches. I was limping a little. By the time I passed him I was limping noticeably. He looked at me sympathetically. "You, too?" he said.

"Just a sprain," I said.

By the time I reached the small private hospital, conveniently located in the center of town, I was giving a fair imitation of a skier who had fallen down half the mountain.

Two hours later I came out of the hospital. I was equipped with crutches and my left leg was in a cast above the knee. I sat in a restaurant for the rest of the morning, drinking black coffee and eating croissants, happily reading the *Herald Tribune* of the day before.

The young doctor at the hospital had been skeptical when I told him I was sure I had broken my leg—"A hairline fracture," I told him. "I've done it twice before." He was even more skeptical when he looked at the X rays, but when I insisted he shrugged and said, "Well, it's *your* leg."

Switzerland was one country where you could get any kind of medical attention you paid for, necessary or not. I had heard of a man who had a slight fungous growth on his thumb and had become obsessed with the idea that it was cancer. Doctors in the United States, England, France, Spain, and Norway had assured him it was only a slight fungous infection that would go away eventually and had prescribed salves. In Switzerland, for a price, he had finally managed to have it amputated. He now lived happily in San Francisco, thumbless.

At one o'clock I took a taxi back to the Palace. I accepted the sympathy of the men at the desk with a wan smile, and I fixed a look of stoic suffering on my face as I clumped into the bar.

Flora Sloane was seated in a corner near the window, with the unopened bottle of champagne in a bucket of ice on the table in front of her. She was dressed in skintight green slacks and a sweater that made the most of her generous, and I must admit, well-shaped bosom. Her leopard coat was on a chair beside her, and the aroma of her perfume made the bar smell like a florist's shop full of exotic tropical plants.

She gasped when she saw me stagger in, using the crutches clumsily. "Oh, shit," she said.

"It's nothing," I said bravely. "Just a hairline fracture. I'll be out of the cast in six weeks. At least that's what the doctor says." I collapsed on a chair with a sound that sensitive ears would have distinguished as a smothered groan, and put the cast up on the chair across from me.

"How in hell did you do it?" she asked crossly.

"My skis didn't open." That much was true. I hadn't touched them that day. "I crossed my skis and they didn't open."

"That's damned peculiar," she said. "You haven't fallen once since you've been here."

"I guess I wasn't paying attention," I said. "I guess I was thinking about this afternoon and . . ."

Her expression softened. "You poor dear," she said. "Well, anyway, we can have our champagne." She started to signal the barman.

"I'm not allowed to drink," I said. "The doctor was most specific. It interferes with the healing process."

"Everybody else I know who's broken bones went right on drinking," she said. She was not a woman who liked to be deprived of her champagne.

"Maybe," I said. "I have brittle bones, the doctor said." I grimaced in pain.

She touched my hand lightly. "It hurts, doesn't it?"

"A little," I admitted. "The morphine's beginning to wear off."

"Still," she said, "we can at least have lunch. . . ."

"I hate to have to disappoint you, Flora," I said, "but I'm a bit woozy. Actually, I feel like throwing up. The doctor said I'd better stay in bed today, with my leg up on some pillows. I'm terribly sorry."

"Well, all I can say is you sure picked the wrong day to crash." She brushed at her cashmere bosom. "And I got all dressed up for you."

"Accidents happen when they're fated to happen," I said philosophically. "And you *do* look beautiful." I heaved myself to my feet. Or rather my foot. "I think I'd better go upstairs now."

"I'll come with you and make you comfy." She started to rise.

I waved her back. "If you don't mind, for the moment I'd rather be alone. That's the way I've always been when something is wrong with me. Ever since I was a kid." I didn't want to be lying helpless on a bed with Flora Sloane loose in the room. "Drink the champagne for both of us, dear. Please put this bottle on my bill," I called to the barman.

"Can I come and see you later?" she asked.

"Well, I'm going to try to sleep. I'll call you later if I wake up. Just don't worry about me, dear."

I left her there, the brightest and fullest flower in the garden, splendid and pouting in her tight green slacks and snug sweater, as I maneuvered out of the bar.

Just as the last light of the afternoon sun was dying in a pink glow on the farthest peaks I could see from my window, the door of my room opened softly. I was lying in bed merely staring brainlessly but comfortably at the ceiling. I had had lunch sent up and had eaten heartily. Luckily, the waiter had been in to take away the tray, because it was Flora Sloane who poked her head around the door.

"I didn't want to disturb you," she said. "I just wanted to see if you needed anything." She came into the room. I could barely see her in the dusk, but I could smell her. "How are you, honey?"

"Alive," I said. "How did you get in here?" Being an invalid excused me from gallantry.

"The floor maid let me in. I explained." She came over to the side of my bed and touched my forehead in a Florence Nightingale gesture. "You have no fever," she said.

"The doctor says I can expect it at night," I said.

"Did you have a good afternoon?" she asked, seating herself on the edge of the bed.

"I've had better." This was not true—at least for the time I had been at St. Moritz.

Suddenly, she swooped down and kissed me. Her tongue, as ever, was active. I twisted, so as to be able to breathe, and my bad leg (as I now considered it) dropped off the edge of the bed. I groaned realistically. Flora sat up, flushed and breathing hard. "I'm sorry," she said. "Did I hurt you?"

"Not really," I said. "It's just . . . well, you know . . . sudden movements."

She stood up and looked down at me. It was too dark in the room for me to see her face clearly, but I got the impression of the birth of suspicion. "You know," she said, "a friend of mine picked up a young man on the slopes at Gstaad and they arranged to meet that night and, well . . . *do* it, and he broke his leg at three o'clock, but he didn't let it stop him. By ten o'clock that night, they *did* it."

"Maybe he was younger than I am," I said lamely. "Or he had a different kind of break. Anyway, the first time . . . with you, I mean . . . I wouldn't like it to be anything but perfect."

"Yeah," she said. Her voice was flat and unconvinced. "Well, I better be going. There's a party tonight and I have to get ready." She leaned over and kissed me chastely on the forehead. "If you want, though," she said, "I can look in after the party."

"I don't think it would be a wise idea, really."

"Probably not. Well, sleep well," and she left the room.

I lay back and stared once more at the dark ceiling and thought of the heroic young man at Gstaad. One more day, I thought, and I'm getting out of here, crutches or no crutches. Still, Flora Sloane had given me an idea. Without a key to my room, she had had the door opened. The floor maid . . .

That evening I dined alone, late. I had seen Flora Sloane, in a blazing evening gown, at a distance, sweeping off to her party with a group of people, some of whom I recognized, some of whom I didn't, any one of whom might have my seventy thousand dollars in the bank. If Flora saw me, she gave no sign. I took my time over dinner, and, when I went up to my floor, I deliberately avoided asking for my key at the desk. The corridor on which my room was located was empty, but after a moment I spied the night maid coming out of a room farther down. I stepped in front of the Sloanes' door and called to the maid. "I'm terribly sorry," I said, moving heavily toward the woman on my crutches, "but I seem to have forgotten my key. Will you let me in, please?" I had never seen her before.

She took a key out of her apron pocket and opened the door. I said thank you and went in, closing the door behind me. The room had already been made up for the night, and the bed was turned down, two bedside lamps softly lit. The scent of Flora Sloane's perfume was everywhere. Except for that, it could have been any room in the hotel. I was breathing heavily, moving with care. I went over to the big wardrobe and opened the door. Women's clothes. I recognized various dresses, ski outfits. I opened the next door. A long array of suits, stacked shirts. On the floor six pairs of shoes. The brown shoes Sloane had worn on the train were the last in line. I bent down clumsily, nearly toppling, and picked up the right shoe. Then I sat on a little straight-backed chair and took off my right shoe. My left foot was encased in plaster. I tried to put my foot into the brown shoe. I could hardly get halfway in. It must have been two sizes smaller than mine—size eight. I sat there for a moment, holding the shoe in my hand, staring at it numbly. I had wasted almost a week, precious time, and a small fortune, on a false trail. I was sitting like that, in the softly lit room, stupidly holding the shoe in my hand, when I heard the rattle of a key in the door. The door opened and Bill Sloane, dressed for traveling and holding a small bag in his hand, came into the room.

He stopped when he saw me and dropped the bag. It made a small, luxurious thump on the thick carpet. "What the hell . . . ?" he said. He didn't sound angry. He hadn't had time to be angry.

"Hello," I said foolishly. "Hello, Bill. I thought you were in Zurich."

"I'll bet you did." His voice was beginning to rise. "Where the hell is Flora?" He switched on the overhead light, as though his wife might be lurking in the shadows.

"She went to a party." I didn't know whether I ought to get up or stay where I was. Getting up presented problems, with the cast and my stockinged foot.

"Went to a party." He nodded grimly. "And what the fuck are you doing here?"

"I forgot my key," I said, realizing as I said it how improbable the whole scene was.

"I asked the maid to open the door to my room and I wasn't looking . . ."

"What're you doing with my shoe?" Each question was an arc on a constantly rising curve.

I looked at the shoe as though I had never seen it before. "I honestly don't know," I said. I dropped it to the floor.

"The watch," he said. "The goddamn watch."

I looked at it automatically. It was ten minutes past ten.

"I know where you got that goddamn watch." There was no mistaking the menace in his tone now. "My wife. From my stupid, goddamn wife."

"It was . . . well . . . a kind of private little joke." Nothing in my life until then had prepared me for a situation like this, and I realized bitterly that my improvisations at the moment were far from brilliant.

"Every year she gets a crush on some idiotic ski teacher and she gives him a watch. For openers," he said. "Just for openers. So—this year, you're elected. This is her year for amateurs. The St. Moritz Open."

"It's only a watch, Bill," I said.

"She's the shiftiest little bitch in the business," Sloane said, looming over me. "And I thought, well, this year, finally, she's out there with someone I can trust." He began to cry. It was terrifying.

"Please, Bill," I pleaded. "Don't cry. I swear nothing's happened." I wished I could explain to him that I hadn't had the slightest twinge of sexual desire or the least hope of consummation in the last seven days.

"You swear," he growled, weeping. "You swear. They all swear." With a surprisingly swift movement he bent and grabbed my arm and yanked at it. "Give me back that goddamn watch, you son of a bitch."

"Of course," I said, with considerable dignity. I unclasped it and gave it to him. He glared down at it, then strode over to the window, opened it, and hurled the watch out into the night. I took advantage of his trip to get up and balance on my crutches. He wheeled and came back to me, very close to me. I could smell the whiskey on his breath. "I ought to hammer you into the deck. Only I don't hit cripples." He kicked my cast, not very hard, but enough to make me teeter. "I don't know what the fuck you were doing in here and I don't want to know. But if you're not out of this hotel and out of this town by tomorrow morning, I'm going to have you thrown out bodily. When the Swiss police get through with you, you'll be sorry you ever saw a mountain." He swooped down again and grabbed my single shoe from the floor and swept across the room with it and threw it out the window after the watch. It was the weirdest act of revenge I'd ever heard of. He was still weeping. There was no doubt about the fact that, appearances to the contrary (all that telephoning in the morning and all that bridge), he was linked with a high and unusual passion, for a man his age and temperament, to his wife.

He was seated, like a great tragic bear, his head bent into his hands, sobbing, as I left the room on my crutches.

CHAPTER 11

THE NEXT MORNING, early, I was on the train to Davos. Davos is a ski resort some two hours away from St. Moritz, famous for long runs that I had no intention of exploring. I had begun to hate winter and the sight of ruddy, happy faces, the sound of boots on snow, the tinkle of sleigh bells, the bright colors of ski caps. I yearned for the comfort of soft Southern weather, a climate where decisions could be put off until tomorrow. Before I bought my ticket at the railroad station, itself a loathsomely picturesque structure on the valley floor, I had played with the idea of surrender, of heading for Italy, Tunisia, the Mediterranean coast of Spain, in one last destructive splurge. But the first train into the station was going in the direction of Davos. I had taken it as an omen and, helped by a porter, had clambered aboard. I was doomed for the winter to cold country.

The train wound its way through some of the most magnificent mountain scenery in the world, soaring peaks, dramatic gorges, high spidery bridges across foaming streams. The sun shone brightly over it all in a clear blue sky. I appreciated none of it.

When I reached Davos I got into a taxi and went directly to the hospital and had the cast taken off my leg, resisting all attempt by two doctors to have me X-rayed. "Just when and where, sir," one of the doctors asked, as he saw me hop jauntily off the table, "was this cast put on?"

"Yesterday," I said. "In St. Moritz."

"Ah," he said, "St. Moritz." He and the other doctor exchanged significant looks. Obviously *they* would never choose St. Moritz for medical attention.

The younger of the two doctors accompanied me to the cashier's desk at the door to make sure I paid for the operation. One hundred Swiss francs. A bargain. The doctor watched me puzzledly as I opened the big bag that I had left at the entrance and took out a sock and a shoe and put them on. As I went out the door, carrying my bags, I was sure I heard him say, "Amerikanisch," to the cashier, as though that explained all eccentricities.

There was a taxi at the door, discharging a child in a cast. I was in the zone of broken bones. It suited the mood I was in. I got into the taxi and, after a short struggle with the German language, managed to make the driver understand that I wanted to be taken to a reasonably priced hotel. Driving through the town, we passed one hotel after another, with large individual balconies for each room, which at other times had been used to air the invalids who had made prewar Davos the tuberculosis capital of the world. Now, the institutions had all been renamed sport hotels, but in my present circumstances all I could think of as we drove past these endless empty balconies was the vanished thousands of bundled figures, lying in rows in the cold sunlight, coughing blood.

The chauffeur of the taxi drove me to a small place, owned by his brother-in-law, with a good view of the railroad tracks. The brother-in-law spoke English and our negotiations were amiable. The price of a single room with a bath down the hall was not exactly amiable, but after the ravages of the Palace it was friendly.

The narrow bed was not covered in silk and the room was so small that there was no place in it for my big bag. The owner explained that, after I unpacked, I could leave it out in the hall, with whatever clothes would not fit into the tiny closet and the minute dresser. It would be safe, he said; there were no thieves in Switzerland. I did not laugh.

I unpacked haphazardly, cramming the stranger's suits into the closet. I left the tuxedo in the bag. I had worn it several times in St. Moritz, when necessary, and the memories associated with it were not of a nature to induce nostalgia. If a thief finally showed up in Switzerland and happened to take a liking to it, he would be welcome to it.

I took a hot bath, scrubbing the shaved leg that had been in the cast. The leg had begun to itch. Back in my room, I put on a pair of the shorts I had found in the bag. They were made of silk and were pale blue and I had to fold them over at the top to keep them on me, but I had refused to send any laundry out at the Palace, and the few pieces of clothing I had had in my small bag all needed washing. The jacket I had worn across the ocean and in Zurich and St. Moritz, when I hadn't worn the tuxedo, was crumpled. I hesitated for a moment, then picked the houndstooth jacket off the hanger and put it on, hoping nobody I knew would chance to be in Davos to see it on me. I put my wallet, containing all that was left of my fortune, into the inside breast pocket. There was a small crinkling sound as I did so. I reached down and pulled out a folded sheet of paper. It was rose colored and perfumed and was covered with a woman's handwriting.

My hands began to shake and I sat down heavily on the bed and began to read. There was no address or date on the luxuriously tinted sheet of paper.

"Love," the letter began, "Oh, dear! I hope you won't be too frantically disappointed. I can't make it to St. Moritz this year. . . ." I felt a tremor go through my body as I read this, as though an avalanche had dropped down the side of one of the surrounding peaks and shaken the foundations of the city. "Poor old Jock fell off his trusty steed hacking home from a hunt three days ago and broke his hip and has been in *agony* ever since. The local witch doctor, whose practice dates back to the Crimean War, just made pitiful little cries when asked for a diagnosis, so we've moved Jock down to London. The surgeons here are debating whether or not to operate and don't seem to be able to make up their minds and meanwhile the poor old darling just lies there groaning on his bed of pain. Naturally, dear little wifey can't go swinging off to the Alps while the drama is so hideously fresh. So I'm back and forth to the hospital, carrying flowers and gin and soothing the fevered brow and telling him he'll be able to hunt again next year, which, as you know, is his chief and practically single occupation in life.

"However, all is not lost. I have promised to visit my sweet old Aunt Amy in Florence, arriving on Feb Quatorze. The situation should have subsided by then and I'm sure dear old Jock will insist I go. Aunt Amy has a house full of guests, so I'll be staying at the Excelsior. Which is just as well. Or even better. I'll look for your beaming, welcoming face in the bar. Longingly, L."

I read the letter again, getting a clear and not very flattering impression of the lady who had written it. I considered it an affectation on her part not to put an address or a date on her letter, writing Quatorze instead of the honest English fourteen and signing it only with her initial. I tried to picture what she probably looked like. A cold, fashionable English beauty between thirty and forty, with lofty airs, and a manner that owed a great deal to the works of Sir Noel Coward and Michael Arlen. But whatever she looked like and however she behaved, I would be at the Hotel Excelsior in Florence to greet her, along with her paramour, on February fourteenth. St. Valentine's Day, I remembered, anniversary for lovers and massacre.

I tortured myself briefly with the thought that I might have brushed shoulders with the adulterer in the dining room of the Palace Hotel or on the slopes of St. Moritz and even thought for a moment of returning there. The idea of Madam L.'s friend squandering my money undisturbed in St. Moritz for another full week was harrowing. But if I hadn't found him before, there was no reason to suppose that I could find him now. The only clue to his identity in the letter was that he was probaby not married or at least was not accompanied by a wife on this trip to Europe, that he could count in French, at least up to fourteen, and that in the presence of his partner in sin he would be expected to have a beaming and welcoming face. It was information that was of no practical value at the moment. I would have to be patient and wait seven days.

I left Davos, with its regiments of coughing ghosts, happy to be able to get out of the regions of snow. The train from Zurich to Florence passed through Milan, and I got off and spent the night there, using my time to go see *The Last Supper,* fading sadly into the past on its stone wall in the ruined church. Leonardo da Vinci helped me feel that there was an escape possible from comedy. Milan was covered in fog and I soaked myself in healing melancholy.

I had one moment of uneasiness, when I was followed through the vaulted gallery which presides over the center of Milan by a swarthy youngish man in a long overcoat, who waited across from the door of a café I went into for an esprèsso. I had felt safe, although uncomfortable, in Switzerland, but here I couldn't help remembering what I had read about the Italian connections to organized crime in America. I ordered another esprèsso and drank it slowly, but the man didn't budge. I couldn't wait in the café forever, so I paid and left the place, walking rapidly.

The man in the long overcoat crossed the arcade swiftly and cut me off. He grabbed my elbow. He had one walleye, which somehow made him seem extremely menacing, and the grip on my elbow was like a steel clamp.

"Hey, boss," he said, walking along with me. "What's a da hurry?"

"I'm late for an appointment." I tried to tug away, but it was useless.

He put his other hand in his pocket and I feared the worst.

"Wanna buy beautiful piece genuine jewelry?" he said. "Big bargain." He let go of me then and produced something that clinked and was wrapped in tissue paper. "Beautiful gift for lady." He pulled back the tissue paper and I saw a gold chain.

"I have no lady," I said, beginning to walk again.

"Interesting piece." Now he was pleading. "You would pay twice, three times, in America."

"Sorry," I said.

He sighed, and I left him rewrapping the chain and putting it back in his pocket.

As I walked away, I realized that any hope I might have had of fading unnoticed into the population of Europe was derisive. Wherever I went I would be picked out, by anyone who had the slightest interest in me, as an American. I considered growing a beard.

The next day, feeling that perhaps I would never pass this way again, I took the *rapido* to Venice, a city that I believed, rightly it turned out, would be even sadder at that season than Milan. The misty canals, the sad hooting of boat horns, the black water and mossy pilings in the gray Adriatic winter light did much to restore the sense of my own dignity and erase the memory of the athletic frivolity of St. Moritz. I read, with satisfaction, that Venice was sinking into the sea. I lingered on, in a cheap pensione, visiting churches, drinking a light white wine called Soave in bare cafés along the sides of the Piazza San Marco and watching Italians, an occupation that I found I enjoyed. I avoided Harry's Bar, which I feared would contain a hard core of Americans, even at that season. There was only one American I wanted to see and I had no reason to believe he would be found in Venice that week.

The little excursion had done me a great deal of good. My nerves, which had been shattered in Switzerland, now seemed dependable. I arrived at the Hotel Excelsior in Florence on the evening of the thirteenth of February confident that I would handle myself capably when the moment of confrontation arrived.

After an excellent dinner I wandered through the streets of Florence, stood awhile before the monumental copy of Michelangelo's statue of David in the Piazza della Signoria, musing on the nature of heroism and the defeat of villainy. Florence, with its history of plots and vendettas, its Guelphs and Ghibellines, was a fitting city in which to meet my enemy.

Not unnaturally, I slept badly and was up before the light of dawn broke over the swollen Arno beneath my window.

Even before I had my breakfast I questioned the concierge about the schedules of flights from London to Milan and the most convenient rail connection from Milan to Florence. By my calculation the lady would arrive at five thirty-five.

I would be in the lobby of the hotel at that hour, strategically placed so as to be able to observe any female who signed in at the reception desk. And any man, slightly shorter than myself, who might accompany her or move to greet her.

I drank a great deal of black coffee all that day, but no alcohol, not even a beer. Out of a sense of duty to my role as a tourist, I wandered through the Uffizi Gallery, but the glorious display of Florentine art spread through the great halls made no impression on me. I would come back at another time.

I made one purchase, at a little souvenir shop, a letter opener, shaped like a stiletto, with a chased silver hilt. I refused to think of the exact reasons for the purchase, and pretended to myself that I had merely taken an idle and innocent fancy to it when I had happened to see it lying in the display window.

Late in the afternoon I bought the *Rome Daily American* and installed myself in one of the ornate chairs in the hotel lobby, not too ostentatiously close to the entrance and the reception desk, but with a clear view of the critical area. I was wearing my own clothes. I didn't want to warn anyone off with the houndstooth jacket or any of the brightly striped shirts that had come along with it.

By six o'clock I had read the newspaper over twice. The only arrivals at the hotel had been an American family, stout, loud father, weary mother in sensible shoes, three lanky, pale children in identical red, white, and blue anoraks. They had driven up from Rome, I overheard; the roads were icy. By an act of will, I restrained myself from going over to the concierge to ask him to find out if the train from Milan was running late.

I was reading the column of social notes, which I had skipped before, and learned that in Parioli someone I had never heard of had given a party for someone else I never had heard of, when a hatless blonde woman of about thirty came through the door, followed by a quantity of expensive-looking luggage. I made a conscious effort to control my breathing. The woman, I noted automatically, was pretty, with a long, aristocratic nose and a bright slash of a mouth and was wearing a heavy wraparound brown cloth coat that was, even to my inexperienced eye, beautifully tailored. She strode over to the reception desk with the air of a woman who had been used to five-star hotels all her life, but just as she was about to give her name to the clerk behind the desk, two of the three American children, who had remained in the hall, broke into a loud argument about whose turn it was to go up to their room and take the first bath. So I couldn't hear the name that the lady gave the clerk. If I ever had children, I thought grimly, I would never travel with them.

I sat glued to my chair while the lady signed the hotel registration card and threw down her passport. I could not see its color. Finished at the desk, the lady didn't go toward the elevators, but strode directly into the bar. I touched the silver coin in my pocket and stood up and started toward the bar. But just as I reached it, she came out. I stepped back to let her pass me, and made a little hint of a polite bow, but she paid no attention to me. I could not tell what the expression on her face meant.

I sat in a corner of the bar and ordered a Scotch and soda. The bar was empty and dark. There was nothing I could do for the moment but wait.

I was still there at seven o'clock, when she came back. She was wearing a severe black dress with two strands of pearls looped around her throat and was carrying her brown coat. Obviously she intended to go out. She stopped at the door and scanned the room. The American family was seated around a table, the mother and father drinking martinis, the children Coca-Colas, the father from time to time saying, "For God's sake, will you kids stop yelling?"

An elderly English couple was seated across the room from me, the gentleman reading a three-day-old copy of the London *Times,* the woman, in a billowing flowered print, staring vacantly into space.

An Italian group near the bar itself chattered continuously, and I could make out the word "disgrazia" which they had been using over and over again, with great intensity, ever since they had sat down fifteen minutes before. There was no way of my telling who or what was disgraceful.

No one but myself was sitting alone.

A little grimace twisted the generous red mouth of the woman at the door. Her skin was pale, with a delicate pink flush over the prominent cheekbones. The eyes were dark blue, almost violet, the figure, frankly revealed by the sober dress, willowy, the legs slender and finely shaped. I decided she was not pretty, but beautiful. Just the sort of woman a man who was bold and shameless enough to steal seventy thousand dollars at the Zurich airport would be likely to take away on an illicit holiday from an adoring and crippled husband.

She noticed me looking at her and frowned slightly. Frowning became her. I lowered my eyes. Then she came across the room and sat down at the table next to mine, throwing her coat over the other chair at her table and dragging a pack of cigarettes and a heavy gold lighter out of her bag.

The waiter on duty hurried over to her and lit her cigarette. She was the sort of woman who is served immediately on all occasions. The waiter was a handsome, dark young man with the soft, watchful eyes of a fighting bull, and he showed splendid teeth in a wide smile as he bent gracefully over the lady's table to take her order.

"A pink gin, *per favore,*" she said. "No ice." British.

"Another Scotch and soda, please," I said to the waiter.

"*Prego?*" The smile on the waiter's face vanished as he faced me. He had not questioned me when I had ordered before.

"*Ancora un whiskey con soda,*" the lady said impatiently.

"*Si, signora.*" The smile appeared once more. "*Molto grazie.*"

"Thank you for helping out," I said to the lady.

"He understood you perfectly well," she said. "He was just being Italian. You're American, aren't you?"

"I guess it sticks out all over," I said.

"Not to be ashamed," she said. "People have a right to be American. Have you been here long?"

"Not long enough to learn the language." I felt my pulse quickening. Things were going along infinitely better than I had dared hope. "I just arrived last night."

She made an impatient gesture. "I mean here in the bar."

"Oh. For about an hour."

"An hour." She had a clipped manner of talking but the voice was musical. "Did you by any chance see another American gentleman wander through? A man of about fifty, though he looks younger. Very fit. A little gray in the hair. Perhaps with a questing look in his eyes. As though he was looking for someone."

"Well, let me think," I said craftily. "What would his name be?"

"You wouldn't know his name." She looked hard at me. Adulteresses, even British ones, I had just discovered, weren't anxious to broadcast the names or exact locations of their lovers.

"I wasn't paying any particular attention," I said innocently, "but I seem to have noticed somebody who might answer to your description at the door. Around six thirty, I would guess." I wanted to keep the conversation going at any cost, and I wanted to keep the lady in the bar as long as possible.

"What a bore," she said impatiently. "The mails these days."

"I'm sorry," I said, touching the letter in my pocket, "I didn't quite get that. I mean, what about the mails?"

"No matter," she said. The waiter was putting the drink on the table in front of her. I would not have been surprised if he had knelt to do so. My own drink was put before me without ceremony. The lady raised her glass. "Cheers," she said. She plainly had no girlish prejudices against talking to strangers in bars.

"Are you here for long?" I asked.

"One never knows, does one?" She left a lipstick stain on her glass. I longed to ask her name, but something told me not to rush matters. "Beautiful old Firenze. I've been in gayer towns." As she talked, she kept turning her head toward the door. A German couple came in and she frowned again. She looked impatiently at her watch. "You're sunburned," she said to me. "Have you been skiing?"

"A little."

"Where?"

"St. Moritz, Davos." It was a small lie.

"I adore St. Moritz," she said. "All those amusing cheap people."

"Have you been there?" I asked. "This season, I mean."

"No. Disaster intervened." I would have liked to ask her about the health of her husband, to keep the conversation going on a friendly basis, but thought better of it. She looked around her with distaste. "This place *is* gloomy. They must have buried Dante in the front hall. Do you know of any brighter spot in town?"

"Well, I had a very good meal in a restaurant called Sabattini's last night. If you'd care to join me tonight I'd be . . ."

At that moment a page came in, calling "Lady Lily Abbott, Lady Lily Abbott . . ." *Longingly, L.,* I remembered, as she crooked a finger at the page. *"Telefono per la signora,"* the page said.

"Finalmente," she said loudly and stood up and followed the boy into the lobby. She left her handbag on the chair, and I wondered how I could manage to look through it while she was busy on the phone without being arrested for theft. The German couple kept staring at me. Oddly, I thought. They would certainly report all suspicious activities to the proper authorities. I didn't touch the bag.

She was gone about five minutes, and, when she came striding back into the bar, her expression could have been described as peevish if it had been on the face of another woman. On her it was noble displeasure. She slumped down in her chair, her feet sticking out straight under the table.

"I hope it wasn't bad news," I said.

"It wasn't good." She sounded grim. "Absent me from felicity awhile. Rearrangements of schedules. Someone will suffer." She slugged down her gin and began to stuff her cigarettes and lighter into her bag.

"If that means you're free . . ." I began. "What I was saying, when you were called to the phone, Lady Abbott . . ." It was the first time in my life that I had called anybody Lady Anything and I nearly stuttered over the words. "Well, I was about to invite you to have dinner with me at this very nice . . ."

"Sorry," she said. "That's sweet of you. But I'm not free. I'm taken for dinner. There's a car waiting for me outside." She stood up, gathering in her coat and bag. I stood up gallantly. She looked hard at me, squarely in the eyes. A decision was made. "The dinner will be over early," she said. "All the poor old dears have to go beddy-bye. We can have a nightcap, if you'd like that."

"I'd like it very much."

"Shall we say eleven? Here, in the bar?"

"I'll be here."

She swept out of the bar, leaving waves of sensuality quivering in the air behind her, like the reverberations of the last notes of an organ in a cathedral.

I spent the night in her room. It was as simple as that. "I came to Florence all primed to sin," she said as she undressed, "and sin I shall." I don't believe she even asked my name until about 2:30 A.M.

Despite her imperious manner, she was a gentle and charming lover, undemanding, grateful, and pleasantly lacking in chauvinism. "There is a large, untapped reservoir of sexual talent in America," she said at one point. "The New World to the aid of the diminishing Old. Isn't that nice?"

I was happy to discover that my fears about impotence, nourished by the dreadful Mrs. Sloane, were unfounded. I did not think I had to mention to Lady Abbott that my pleasure in her company was heightened by perverse overtones of vengeance.

She was the least curious of women. We talked little. She asked me no questions about what I did, why I was in Florence, or where I was going.

Just before I left her room (she insisted I get out before the help started stirring about), I asked her if she would lunch with me that day.

"If I don't have a telephone call," she said. "Kiss the lady good night."

I bent over and kissed the wide, dear mouth. Her eyes were closed, and I had the impression that she was asleep before I went through the door.

As I went through the baronial halls of the hotel to my room, I felt a surge of optimism. Through Zurich, St. Moritz, Davos, Milan, and Venice, nothing good had happened to me, no voice had spoken to me reassuringly. Until this night. The future was far from certain, but there were gleams of hope.

Sweet St. Valentine's Day.

Exhausted by the fitful wakefulness of my first night in Florence and my recent exertions, I fell into bed and slept soundly until amost noon.

When I awoke I lay still, staring at the ceiling, enjoying the feel of my body, smiling softly. I reached for the phone and asked for Lady Abbott. There was a long pause and then I heard the voice of the concierge. "Lady Abbott checked out at ten A.M. No, she left no message."

It cost me ten thousand lire and a lie to extract the forwarding address of Lady Abbott from one of the assistants behind the concierge's desk. Lady Abbott had left word that, while she wanted messages sent on to her, she did not want the address given out. As I slid the ten-thousand-lire note across to the man, I intimated that the lady had left a piece of jewelry of great value in my room and that it was imperative that I return it to her in person.

"*Bene, signore,*" the man said. "It is the Hotel Plaza-Athénée, in Paris. Please explain the special circumstances to Lady Abbott."

"I certainly shall," I said.

I was in Paris, checking in at the Plaza-Athénée the next day at noon. Before I had time to ask the price of the room, I saw Lady Abbott. She was coming through the lobby on the arm of a hatless, graying man with a busy British moustache who was wearing dark glasses. They were laughing together. I had seen the man before. It was Miles Fabian, the bridge player from the Palace Hotel in St. Moritz.

They did not look in my direction, and went out through the front doors into the expensive sunlight of the Avenue Montaigne, two lovers in the city for lovers, on the way to an exquisite lunch, oblivious of the rest of the world, oblivious of me, standing just a few feet from where they had passed, with a stiletto in my overnight bag and murder in my heart.

CHAPTER 12

THE NEXT MORNING I was in the lobby at eight thirty. Two hours later she came through the lobby and went out. In Florence I had never seen her in daylight. She was more beautiful than I remembered. If ever there was a lady made for an American's dream of a wicked weekend in Paris, it was Lily Abbott.

I made sure she didn't see me, and after she was gone I went up to my room. There was no way of my knowing how long she would be gone from the hotel. So I moved quickly. I had packed Fabian's bag, with all his belongings, the houndstooth jacket on top, as I had found it. I called down to the concierge's desk and asked for a porter to come to my room and pick up a suitcase to take to Mr. Fabian's room.

I had the stiletto letter-opener in its leather sheath in my pocket. The adrenalin was pumping through my system and my breathing was shallow and rapid. I had no plan beyond getting into Fabian's room and confronting him with his suitcase.

There was a knock on the door and I opened it for the porter. I followed him as he carried the suitcase to the elevator. He pushed the button for the sixth floor. Everything happens on the sixth floor, I thought, as we rose silently. When the elevator stopped and the door opened, I followed him down the corridor. Our footsteps made no sound on the heavy carpet. We passed nobody. We were in the hush of the rich. The man set the bag down at the door of a suite and was about to knock when I stopped him. "That's all right," I said, picking up the bag myself, "I'll take it in. Mr. Fabian is a friend of mine." I gave the porter five francs. He thanked me and left.

I knocked gently on the door.

The door opened and there was Fabian. He was completely dressed, ready to go out. At last we were face to face. Myself and Sloane's nemesis, riffling cards, afternoon and evening, at home in the haunts of wealth. Thief. He squinted slightly, as though he couldn't see me clearly. "Yes?" he said politely.

"I believe this belongs to you, Mr. Fabian," I said and bulled past him, carrying the suitcase down a hall that led into a large living room which was littered with newspapers in several languages. There were flowers in vases everywhere. I dreaded to think of what he was paying each day for his lodgings. I could hear him closing the door behind me. I wondered if he was armed.

"I say," he said, as I turned to him, "there must be some mistake."

"There's no mistake."

"Who are you anyway? Haven't we met somewhere before?"

"In St. Moritz."

"Of course. You're the young man who attended to Mrs. Sloane this year. I'm afraid I don't remember your name. Gr-Grimm, isn't it?"

"Grimes."

"Grimes. Forgive me." He was absolutely calm, his voice pleasant. I tried to control my breathing. "I was just about to go out," he said, "but I can spare a moment. Do sit down."

"I'd rather not, if you don't mind." I gestured toward the suitcase, which I had deposited in the middle of the room. "I'd just like you to open your bag and check that nothing's missing. . . ."

"My bag? My dear fellow, I never . . ."

"I'm sorry about the broken lock . . ." I kept on talking. "I did it before I realized I had the wrong one."

"I just don't know what you're talking about. I never saw that bag before in my life." If he had rehearsed a year for this moment, he couldn't have been more convincing.

"When you've finished and you're satisfied that I've taken nothing," I said, "I'd be obliged if you brought out *my* bag. With everything that was in it when you picked it up in Zurich. *Everything*."

He shrugged. "This is absolutely bizarre. If you want, you can search the apartment and see for yourself that . . ."

I reached into my pocket and took out Lily Abbott's letter. "This was in your jacket," I said. "I took the liberty of reading it."

He barely glanced at the letter. "This is getting more and more mysterious, I must say." He made a charming, deprecating gesture, too much of a gentleman to read another man's mail. "No names, no dates." He tossed the letter on a table. "It might have been written to anyone, by anyone. Whatever gave you the idea that it had anything to do with me?" He was beginning to sound testy now.

"Lady Abbott gave me the idea," I said.

"Oh, really," he said. "I must confess, she *is* a friend of mine. How is she anyway?"

"Ten minutes ago, when I saw her in the lobby, she was well," I said.

"Good God, Grimes," he said, "don't tell me Lily is here in the hotel?"

"That's enough of that," I said. "You know what I'm here for. Seventy thousand dollars."

He laughed, almost authentically. "You're joking, aren't you? Did Lily put you up to this? She *is* a joker."

"I want my seventy thousand dollars, Mr. Fabian," I said. I made myself sound as menacing as possible.

"You must be out of your mind, sir," Fabian said crisply. "Now I'm afraid I must go."

I grabbed him by the arm, remembering the walleyed man in the arcade in Milan. "You're not leaving this room until I get my money," I said. My voice rose and I was ashamed of the way I sounded. It was a situation for a basso and I was singing tenor. High tenor.

"Keep your hands off me." Fabian pulled away and brushed fastidiously at his sleeve. "I don't like to be touched. And if you don't get out right away, I'm calling the management and asking for the police. . . ."

I picked up a lamp from the table and hit him on the head. The lamp shattered with the blow. Fabian looked surprised as he sank slowly to the floor. A thin trickle of blood ran down his forehead. I took out my paper knife and knelt beside him, waiting for him to come to. After about fifteen seconds he opened his eyes. The expression in them was vague, unfocused. I held the sharp, needle-like point of the stiletto to his throat. Suddenly, he was fully conscious. He didn't move, but looked up at me in terror.

"I'm not fooling, Fabian," I said. I wasn't, either. At that moment, I would have happily killed him. I was trembling, but so was he.

"All right," he said thickly. "There's no need to go to extremes. I took your bag. Now let me up."

I helped him to his feet. He staggered a little and sank into an easy chair. He felt his forehead and looked apprehensively at the blood smeared on his hand when he took it away. He pulled a handkerchief from his breast pocket and dabbed at his forehead. "Good God, man," he said weakly, "you could have killed me with that lamp."

"You're lucky," I said.

He managed a little laugh, but he kept looking at the stiletto in my hand. "I've always detested knives," he said. "You must be awfully fond of money."

"Average fond," I said. "About like you, I guess."

"I wouldn't kill for it."

"How do you know?" I asked. I stroked the blade of the little weapon with my left hand. "I never thought I would either. Until this morning. Where is it?"

"I don't have it," he said.

I took a step toward him, threateningly.

"Stand back. Please stand back. It's . . . well . . . Shall we say that I don't have it at the moment, but that it's *available?* Please don't wave that thing around anymore. I'm sure we can come to terms without further bloodshed." He dabbed at his forehead again.

Suddenly the reaction set in. I started to shake violently. I was horrified at what I had done. I had actually been on the point of murder. I dropped the stiletto on the table. If Fabian had said at that moment that he refused to give me a cent, I would have walked out the door and forgotten the whole thing. "I suppose," he said quietly, "at the back of my mind I realized that one day someone would come in and ask me for the money." There was an echo there that I could not help but recognize. How had Drusack behaved in his desperate hour? "I've taken very good care of it," Fabian said, "only I'm afraid you'll have to wait awhile."

"What do you mean—wait awhile?" I tried to keep my tone menacing, but I knew I wasn't succeeding.

"I've taken certain liberties with your little nest egg, Mr. Grimes," he said. "I've made some investments." He smiled like a doctor announcing an inoperable cancer. "I don't believe in letting money lie idle. Do you?"

"I haven't had any money to let do anything before this."

"Ah," he said. "Recent wealth. I thought as much. Would you mind if I went into the bathroom and washed off some of this gore? Lily is likely to come in at any moment and I wouldn't like to frighten her."

"Go ahead." I sat down heavily. "I'll be right here."

"I'm sure you will." He got up from his chair and walked unsteadily into the bedroom. I heard water running. There was undoubtedly a door leading from the bedroom into the corridor, but I was convinced he wouldn't leave. And if he had wanted to I wouldn't have done anything to prevent him. I felt numb. Investments. I had imagined various possible scenes while on the trail of the man who had taken my money, but I had never thought that when I finally caught up with him our meeting would take the shape of a business conference.

Fabian came out of the bedroom, his hair wet and freshly combed. His step was firm now and there was no indication that just a few minutes before he had been lying on the floor, senseless and bloody. "First," he said, "would you like a drink?"

"Yes," I said.

"I believe we can both use one." He went over to a sideboard and opened it and poured from a bottle of Scotch into two glasses. "Soda?" he asked "Ice?"

"I'll take it neat."

"Capital idea," he said. He slipped in and out of being British. White's Club, the Enclosure at Epsom. He handed me the whiskey and I gulped it down. He drank more slowly and sat opposite me in the easy chair, twirling the glass in his hand. "If it hadn't been for Lily," he said, "you probably never would have found me."

"Probably not."

"Women." He sighed. "Have you slept with her?"

"I'd rather not answer that question."

"I suppose you're right." He sighed again. "Well, now . . . I imagine you'd like me to begin at the beginning. Do you have the time?"

"I have plenty of time," I said.

"May I make one proviso before I start?" he asked.

"What's that?"

"That you don't tell Lily anything about . . . well, about all this. As you might have gathered from the letter, she thinks highly of me."

"If I get my money back," I said, "I won't say a word."

"That's fair enough." He sighed again. "First, if you don't mind, I'd like to tell you a little about myself."

"I don't mind."

"I'll make it brief," he promised.

As it turned out, it wasn't as brief as all that. He started with his parents, who were poor, the father a minor employee in a small shoe factory in Lowell, Massachusetts, where he was born. There was never enough money around the house. He had not gone to college. During World War Two he was in the Air Force, stationed outside London. He had met an English girl from a rich family. Actually, the family lived in the Bahamas, where they were reputed to have large estates. He had been demobilized in England and there, after a hasty courtship, had married the girl. "Somehow," he said, explaining the union, "I had developed expensive tastes. I had no desire to work and no other prospects for leading the kind of life I wanted any other way."

He had moved to the Bahamas with his new wife and taken up British citizenship. His wife's family weren't miserly toward him, but they were not generous either, and he had begun to gamble to eke out his allowance. Bridge and backgammon were his games. "Alas," he said, "I fell into associated vices. Ladies." One day there had been a family meeting and the divorce had followed immediately. Since that time, he had made do with his gambling winnings. For the most part he had lived fairly comfortably, although with many anxious moments. During part of the winter season the pickings were not bad in the Bahamas, but he was forced to keep traveling. New

York, London, Monte Carlo, Paris, Deauville, St. Moritz, Gstaad. Where the money was. And the games.

"It's a hand-to-mouth existence," he said. "I never got far enough ahead to take even a month off without worrying. I saw opportunities around me constantly that would have made me a rich man if I had even a modest amount of capital. I won't say that I was bitter, but I certainly was discontented. I had just turned fifty a few days before the flight to Zurich, and I was not pleased with what the future might have in store for me. It is rasping to the soul to be committed to the company of the rich without being rich yourself. To pretend that losing three thousand dollars in one evening means as little to you as to them. To go from one great palace of a hotel to another while you're on duty, so to speak, and to hide in dingy out-of-the-way boardinghouses when you're on your own."

The ski club group had been particularly lucrative. Almost permanent games had been set up from year to year. He had made himself well-liked, did a minimum amount of skiing to establish his legitimacy, paid his debts promptly, gave his share of parties, never cheated, was agreeable with the ladies, and was introduced to likely prey among the abundant Greek, South American, and English millionaires, all gamblers by nature, proud of their games and careless in their play.

"There was also the possibility," he said, "of meeting widows with independent fortunes and young divorcées with handsome settlements. Unfortunately," he said, with a sigh, "I am terribly romantic, a failing in a man my age, and what was offered I wouldn't have and what I would have wasn't offered. At least," he said, with a touch of vanity, "not on a financially acceptable basis. I know that I am not painting a very heroic picture of myself . . ." he said.

"No," I said.

" . . . but I would like you to believe that I tell the truth, that you can trust me."

"Go on," I said. "I don't trust you yet."

"So," he said, "that was the man who tried to open a bag that was ostensibly his in the overpriced room at the Palace Hotel in St. Moritz and found that the combination didn't work."

"So you sent down for something to break it open with," I said grimly, remembering my own experience.

"I had the desk send a man up. When he got the bag open, I saw immediately that it wasn't mine. I don't know why I didn't tell him that the bag belonged to somebody else. Some sixth sense, perhaps. Or maybe the sight of the brand-new attaché case lying on top of everything else. People don't usually pack a case like that in their luggage, but usually carry it by hand. In any event, I thanked the man and tipped him. . . . Incidentally, I didn't have the heart to throw the case away. It's in the bedroom and of course I'll be pleased to give it back to you."

"Thank you."

"You're welcome," he said. Without irony. "Of course," he said, "when I counted the money, I realized that it had been stolen."

"Of course."

"It changes the morality of the affair a bit, doesn't it?"

"A bit."

"It also meant that whoever had carried it across the ocean would not go crying to Interpol to recover it. Would my reasoning seem inaccurate to you?"

"No."

"I went through the bag very carefully. I hope you'll forgive me if I tell you that I found nothing there to make one believe that the owner of the bag was in anything but the most modest circumstances."

I nodded. "You can say that again, brother," I said.

"I also found no indication of who the owner was. No address books, letters, et cetera. I even looked in the shaving kit to see if there were any medicines with a name on it."

I laughed, despite myself.

"You must be an extraordinarily healthy man," Fabian said, approvingly.

"About the same as you," I said.

"Ah," he said, beaming, "you had the same experience."

"Exactly."

"I spent the next hour," he went on, "trying to recall if there was anything in *my* bag which had my name on it. I decided there was nothing. I had forgotten about Lily's letter, of course. I thought I had thrown it away. Even so, with her usual caution, I knew no names would be committed to the page. The next step was obvious."

"You stole the money."

"Let's say I put it to use."

"What do you mean, use?"

"Let me go step by step. I had never been in a position before to risk enough to make any coup really conclusive. In view of the circles in which I moved, the amounts I *could* risk were derisive. So that even when I won, as I have more often than not, I never reaped the full benefits of my luck. Do you follow me, Grimes?"

"Partially," I said.

"For example, until now, I have never dared to play bridge at more than five cents a point."

"Mrs. Sloane told me that you were playing with her husband at five cents a point."

"That was true. The first night. After that we went up to ten cents a point. Then to fifteen. Naturally, since Sloane was losing rather heavily, he lied to his wife."

"How much?"

"I'll be frank with you. When I left St. Moritz, I had Sloane's check for twenty-seven thousand dollars in my wallet."

I whistled and looked at Fabian with growing respect. My own poker exploits in Washington dwindled to a pinpoint. Here was a gambler who really knew how to ride his luck. But then I remembered it was *my* money he was risking, and I began to get angry all over again. "What the hell good does that do *me?*" I asked.

Fabian put up his hand placatingly. "All in due time, my dear fellow." I had never expected to be called a dear fellow by a man who had grown up in Lowell, Massachusetts. "I also did quite well, I am happy to say, at backgammon. Perhaps you remember that handsome young Greek with the beautiful wife?"

"Vaguely."

"He was delighted when I suggested raising the stakes. A little over nine thousand dollars."

"What you're telling me," I said harshly, "is that you ran my stake up thirty-six thousand dollars. Goody for you, Fabian; you're in the chips and you can give me back the seventy and we'll shake hands and have a drink on it and we're both on our way."

He shook his head sadly. "It isn't quite as simple as that, I'm afraid."

"Don't abuse my patience, man. You either have the money or you don't. And you'd better have it."

He stood up. "I believe we both could use another drink," he said. I glowered at him as he went over to the sideboard. Having refrained from killing him when I had the chance, any lesser threats had depreciated greatly in value. It also occurred to me as I watched his well-tailored back (not my clothes, but from any one or two or three other bags he probably traveled with at all times) that it might all be a lie, a cock-and-bull story to keep me tamped down until somebody—a maid, Lily Abbott, a friend, came into the room. There would be nothing to stop him then from accusing me of annoying him, dunning him for a loan, trying to sell him dirty postcards, anything, and having me thrown out of the hotel. As he gave me a drink, I said, "If you're lying to me, Fabian, the next time I see you I'm going to be carrying a gun." I had no idea, of course, of how you went about getting a gun in France. And the only guns I fired were .22 rifles at shooting galleries at town fairs.

"I wish you would believe in me," Fabian said as he sat down again with his drink, after pouring soda into it with a steady hand. "I have plans for us two that will require mutual trust."

"Plans?" I felt childishly manipulated, cunningly outmaneuvered by this man who had lived by his wits for nearly thirty years and whose hand could be so steady just a few minutes after he had escaped violent death. "Okay, go on," I said. "You're thirty-six thousand dollars richer than you were three weeks ago and you say it isn't simple to give me back the money you owe me. Why not?"

"For one thing, I have made certain investments."

"Like what?"

"Before I go into detail," Fabian said, "let me outline in general what sort of a plan I'd like to suggest." He took a long sip of his drink, then cleared his throat. "I suppose you have some right to be angry at what I've done . . ."

I made a small, choking noise, which he ignored. "But in the long run," he said, "I have every reason to believe you'll be deeply grateful." I started to interrupt, but he waved me to silence. "I know that seventy thousand dollars in one lump seems like quite a bit of money. Especially to a young man like you, who, I can guess, was never particularly prosperous."

"What are you driving at, Fabian?" I could not get over the feeling that moment by moment a web was being spun around me and that, in a very short time, I would be unable to move or even utter a sound.

The voice went on, gentle, almost-British, confident, persuasive. "How long would it last you? A year, two years. Three years, at the most. As soon as you surfaced, you would be the prey of conniving men and rapacious women. I take it that you have very little experience, if any, in handling large sums of money. Just the primitive—and if I may permit myself a small criticism—the fairly careless way in which you attempted to transfer your hoard from the States to Europe is plain evidence of *that*. . . ."

I certainly was in no position to contradict him about my ineptitude, so I remained silent.

"I, on the other hand," he went on, thoughtfully twirling the ice in his glass and looking me frankly and directly in the eye, "have been handling considerable sums for nearly thirty years. Where you, in three years, say, would be stranded, penniless, in some backwater of Europe—I take it that you don't think it would be healthy to return to America. . .?" He looked at me quizzically.

"Go on," I said.

"I, with any luck, given this start, would not be surprised if I wound up with well over a million . . ."

"Dollars?"

"Pounds," he said.

"I must admit," I said, "I admire your nerve. Still, what would that have to do with me?"

"We would be partners," he said calmly. "I would handle the . . . uh . . . investments and we would share the profits fifty-fifty. Starting, I would like to say with the check of Mr. Sloane and the contribution of the handsome young Greek. Could anything be fairer than that?"

I made myself think hard. The low, polite voice was hypnotizing me. "So—in exchange for my seventy thousand dollars, I'd get half or thirty-six?"

"Minus certain expenses," he said.

"Like what?"

"Hotels, travel, entertainment. That sort of thing."

I looked around at the room full of flowers. "Is there anything left?"

"Quite a bit." He put his hand up again. "Please hear me out. To be more than fair—after one year, you would be permitted to withdraw your original seventy thousand dollars, if you so desired."

"What if during the year you *lost* the whole thing?"

"That is a risk we'd both have to run," he said. "I believe that it is worth taking. Now let me ask you to consider other advantages. You, as an American, are fully liable to the American income tax. Am I right?"

"Yes, but . . ."

"I know what you are going to say—you do not intend to pay it. I take it for granted that you have not declared the seventy thousand dollars that is the subject of our discussion. If you merely *spend* it, you would not be in any difficulty. But if you *increased* it, in legal or even semi-legal ways, you would have to beware of the legion of American agents all through Europe, of informers in banks and business houses. . . . You would always have the fear of confiscation of your passport fines, criminal prosecution . . ."

"And you?" I asked, feeling locked in a corner by his logic.

"I am a British subject," he said, "domiciled in the Bahamas. I don't even fill out a form. Just one quick example—You, as an American, are not legally permitted to trade in gold, although your government is making certain noises that indicate that will be changed eventually. But there is no such restriction on me, and the gold market these days is most seductive. In fact, even while I was amusing Mr. Sloane and my Greek with our little games, I put in an order for a tidy amount. Have you been following the rate of gold recently?"

"No."

"I am ahead—*we* are ahead—ten thousand dollars on our investment."

"In just three weeks?" I asked incredulously.

"Ten days, to be exact," Fabian said.

"What else have you done with my money?" I still clung to the singular possessive pronoun, but with diminishing vigor.

"Well . . ." For the first time since he had come out of the bathroom, Fabian looked a little uneasy. "As a partner, I don't intend to hide anything from you. I've bought a horse."

"A horse!" I couldn't help groaning. "What kind of horse?"

"A thoroughbred. A racehorse. Among other reasons, which I'll come to later, that was why I didn't appear as scheduled in Florence. Much to Lily's annoyance, I must admit. I had to come to Paris to complete the deal. It is a horse that took my eye at Deauville last summer, but which I was not in a position to buy at that time. Also—" He smiled. "It wasn't for sale then. A friend of mine who happens to own a racing stable and a breeding farm in Kentucky expressed an interest in the colt—a stallion, by the way, and potentially quite valuable later on at stud—and I am sure he would show his gratitude in a substantial way if I were to let him know that I am now the owner of the animal. Out of friendship, I plan to indicate to him, I'd be ready to part with it."

"What if he indicates to you that's he's changed his mind?" By now, almost insensibly, I had been swept into what just fifteen minutes before I would have considered a gambler's insane fantasies. "That he doesn't want to buy it anymore?"

Fabian shrugged, rubbed lovingly at the ends of his moustache, a gesture I was to come to recognize as a tic, useful to gain time when he didn't have a ready answer to a question. "In that case, old man," he said, "you and I would have a fine start toward a racing stable. I haven't chosen any colors as yet. Do you have any preferences?"

"Black and blue," I said.

He laughed. He had a hearty, Guards' officer kind of laugh. "I'm glad to see you have a sense of humor," he said. "It's a bore doing business with the glum."

"Do you mind telling me what you've paid for this brute?" I asked.

"Not at all. Six thousand dollars. He broke down in training last autumn with something called splints, so he comes as a bargain. The trainer's an old friend of mine"— I was to find out that Fabian had old friends all over the globe and in all professions—"and he assures me he's as right as a dollar now."

"Right as a dollar." I nodded, in pain. "While we're at it, Fabian," I said, "are there any more . . . uh . . . investments that I happen to have in my portfolio?"

He played with his moustache again. "As a matter of fact, yes," he said. "I hope you're not overwhelmingly prudish."

I thought of my father and his Bible. "I would say medium," I said. "Why?"

"There's a delightful French lady I make a point of looking up every time I come to Paris." He smiled, as though welcoming the delightful French lady into his dreams. "Interested in films. Been an actress in her time, she says. On the producing side now. An old admirer has been staking her. Not sufficiently, I gather. She's in the middle of making a picture at the moment. Quite dirty. Quite, quite dirty. I've seen some of the—I think they call them dailies in the industry. Most amusing. Have you any idea what a movie like *Deep Throat* has brought in for its backers?"

"No."

"Millions, lad, millions." He sighed sentimentally. "My delightful little friend has let me read the script, too. Most literate. Full of fancy and provocation. Essentially innocent in my opinion. Almost decorous from a sophisticated point of view, but a little bit of everything for every taste. Something like a combination of Henry Miller and the Arabian Nights. But my delightful lady friend—she's directing it herself, by the way—she got the script almost for nothing from a young Iranian who can't go back to Iran—but even though she's making it on a shoestring—some of the most lucrative of these particular works of art are made for under forty thousand dollars—I think *Deep Throat* cost no more than sixty—as I was saying, her bookkeeping doesn't quite match her talent—she's just a slip of a woman—and when she told me she needed fifteen thousand dollars to complete the picture . . ."

"You said you'd give it to her."

"Exactly." He beamed. "Out of gratitude she offered me twenty percent of the profits."

"And you said you'd take it?"

"No, I held out for twenty-five." He beamed again. "I may be a friend, but I'm a businessman first."

"Fabian," I said, "I don't know whether to laugh or cry."

"In the long run," he said, "you'll smile. At least smile. They're having a screening of what they've shot thus far this evening. We're all invited. I guarantee you'll be impressed."

"I've never seen a pornographic movie in my life," I said.

"Never too late to begin, lad. Now," he said briskly, "I suggest we go down to the bar and wait for Lily. She can't be too long. We can cement our partnership in champagne. And I'll treat you to the best lunch you've ever eaten. And after lunch we'll take in the Louvre. Have you ever been to the Louvre?"

"I just arrived in Paris yesterday."

"I envy you your initiation," he said.

We had just about finished a bottle of champagne when Lily Abbott strode into the bar. When Fabian introduced me as an old friend from St. Moritz, she did not show, by as much as the blink of an eye, that we had ever gone so far as to shake hands in Florence.

Fabian ordered a second bottle.

I wished I liked the taste.

CHAPTER 13

WE WERE EIGHT in the small screening room. My feet ached from the Louvre. The room smelled of twenty years of cigarettes and sweat. The building on the Champs Élysées was a shabby one with creaky, old-fashioned elevators. The peeling signs of the businesses on the floors we passed all looked like advertisements for concerns that were well into bankruptcy and minor evasions of the criminal code. The corridors were dimly lit, as though the people who frequented the building did not wish to be clearly observed as they came and went. With Fabian, Lily, and myself were Fabian's delightful French lady, whose name was Nadine Bonheur. At the console in the rear was the cameraman on the picture, a weary, gray professional of about sixty-five who wore a beret and a permanent cigarette hanging from his lip. He looked too old for this sort of work and kept his eyes almost completely closed at all times, as though he did not want to be reminded too definitely of what he had recorded on the film we were about to see.

Seated together on the far aisle were the two stars of the film, a slender dark young man, probably a North African, with a long, sad face, and a pert, pretty young American girl by the name of Priscilla Dean, with a blonde ponytail, an anachronistic, fresh-faced relic of an earlier generation of Midwestern virgins. She was primly dressed and looked as proper as a starched lace apron. "It's a pleasure, I'm sure," she said, her voice pure Iowa. I was introduced without ceremony to the others, the atmosphere businesslike. We might have been assembled for a lecture on the marketing of a breakfast food.

A bearded, long-haired man sitting apart, who was wearing a soiled denim jacket and who looked as though he had just bitten into something extremely distasteful, merely grunted when I said hello.

"He's a critic," Fabian whispered to me. "He belongs to Nadine."

"'Appy to make the acquaintance," Nadine Bonheur said to me, looking up from a clipboard and extending her hand. Her hand was silky. She was small and slight, but with a perky full bosom, half of which could be seen over her low-cut black dress. She was tanned a beautiful even shade of brown. I imagined her lying naked on the beach at St. Tropez, surrounded by equally unclothed dissolute young men. "See what the hassole of a projectionist is doing," she said to the cameraman. "We only 'ave the room for teartty minutes." Her accent in English was the sort that sounds charming to Americans.

The cameraman shouted something in French into a telephone on the desk in front of him and the lights dimmed.

For the next thirty minutes I was pathetically grateful that the room was dark. I was blushing so furiously that I felt that although nobody could see me, the raw animal heat of the blood in my face must be raising the temperature of the room like a huge infrared lamp. The goings-on on the screen, in color, were what my father would have described as indescribable. There were couplings of all sorts, in all positions, in a variety of backgrounds. There were triplings and quadruplings, animals, including a black swan, lesbian dalliance, and those caresses which we have been taught by *Playboy* to call fellatio and cunnilingus. There was sadism and masochism and behavior for which I, for one, had no name. As Fabian had said, there was something for everybody. The period seemed to be some time in the middle of the nineteenth century, as some of the men wore top hats and frock coats and the women wore crinolines and bustles, briefly. There were hussars' uniforms, boots and spurs, and an occasional shot of a castle, with buxom peasant girls being led behind bushes. Nadine

Bonheur, scantily dressed, with her mischievous, incorruptible schoolgirl face topped by a long black wig, played a kind of mistress of the revels in the film, arranging bodies with the cool grace of a hostess preparing flowers in a salon before the arrival of her guests. Fabian had told me the script was literate, but since there was no sound or dialogue it was difficult for me to judge just how accurate his estimate was. The film was to be dubbed later, he told me. From time to time, there was a shot of an angelic-faced young man in a long pink robe, trimmed with fur, clipping hedges. Occasionally he stared soulfully off screen. He was also to be seen seated on a thronelike gilt chair in a stone hall lit by candelabra observing various combinations of the sexes in the throes of orgasm. He never changed his expression, although once, as the action reached a climax, he languidly picked up a long-stemmed rose and sniffed at it.

To her credit, I heard Lily, seated on the other side of Fabian, suppress a giggle.

"The story's simple," Fabian explained to me in a whisper. "It takes someplace in Mittel-europa. The young man in the robe with the clippers is a prince. The working title, by the way, is *The Sleeping Prince*. He has just been married to a beautiful foreign princess. His father, the king—that's going to be shot next week—wants an heir. But the boy's a virgin. He's not interested in girls. All he's interested in is horticulture."

"That explains the clippers," I said, hoping that proof that I was still capable of speech would somehow pale my blushes.

"Naturally," Fabian said impatiently. "His aunt, that's Nadine, has been commissioned by her brother, the king, to stimulate his libido. The princess, his wife, awaits him, weeping in one of the towers of the castle, lying in the unused wedding bed garlanded with flowers. But nothing—and, as you see, every possible attraction is tried—nothing arouses him. He looks on with glazed eyes. Everybody is desperate. Then, as a last resort, his aunt, Nadine, dances alone in a diaphanous gown before him, holding a red rose between her teeth. His eyes lose their glaze. He sits up. He drops his clippers. He moves down from the throne. He takes his aunt in his arms. He dances. He kisses her. They fall to the turf together. They make love. There is cheering in the castle. The king declares the marriage to the princess annulled. The prince marries his aunt. There is a three-day orgy in the castle and behind the bushes to celebrate. Nine months later, a son is born. Every year, to commemorate the occasion, the prince and his aunt repeat the dance, in their original robes, as the church bells ring out. It's all pretty Iranian, if you tell it baldly like this, but it has an earthy charm. There's a subplot, of course, with a villain who is plotting for the throne himself and has a thing about whips, but I won't bother you with that . . ."

The lights went up. I made believe I had a coughing attack to explain the blaze of my cheeks.

"That's it," Fabian said, "in a nutshell. It's camp and it's not camp, if you get what I mean. We'll get the intellectuals, as well as everybody else."

"Miles," Nadine Bonheur, switching smoothly from her role of incestuous seductress to serious businesswoman, stood up from her chair two rows in front of us and faced us, "'ow you like it, eh? It will lay them in the haisles, no?"

"It's jolly," Fabian said. "Very jolly. We're bound to make a packet."

I avoided looking at anybody as we trooped out to the elevator. I took especial care not to glance at the American girl, who had featured prominently in all the most lurid scenes, and whom I would recognize, even with a sack over her head, on any nudist beach in the world. Lily, I saw, also showed an intense interest in the floor of the elevator.

As we walked down the Champs Élysées toward an Alsatian brasserie for refreshments, Nadine took my arm. "The little girl," she said to me. "What you think of 'er? Talented, eh?"

"Extremely," I said.

"She only does these on the side," Nadine said. "She is paying 'er way through the Sorbonne. Comparative literature. American girls 'ave more character than European girls. You think so?"

"I'm not much of an expert," I said. "I've only been in Europe a few weeks."

"You think it will be big success in America?" She sounded anxious.

"I'm very optimistic," I said.

"I'm just afraid maybe we 'ave too much what you call class for the general audience."

"I wouldn't worry," I said.

"Miles, too," Nadine said. She squeezed my arm, her motives ambiguous. "He is wonderful on the set. A smile for everybody. You must come on the set, too. The ambiance is beautiful. One for all and all for one. 'Ow they work! Overtime, double overtime, nevair a complaint. Of course, the salaries are very small and the stars are on percentages and that 'elps. Will you come tomorrow? We 'ave a scene where Priscilla is dressed as a nun . . ."

"I'm afraid I'm in Paris on business," I said. "I'm awfully busy."

"Welcome hany time. Do not 'esitate."

"Thank you," I said.

"Do you think it will pass the censors in America?" Again she sounded anxious.

"I imagine so. From what I hear they have to pass everything these days. There's always the chance, of course, that a picture can run into trouble with some local police chief, who can get a theater closed down for a while." Even as I said it I realized that I was giving myself something else to worry about. If I were a local police chief I'd have the film burned, law or no law. But I wasn't a policeman. I was whether I liked it or not, an investor. To the tune of fifteen thousand dollars. I tried to sound offhand. "How about France?" I asked. "Will it pass here?"

"It is terrible here." She squeezed my arm illogically again. "You never can tell. A old fart of a bishop makes a speech one Sunday and hall the theaters go dark the next day. And if the wife of the president or a cabinet minister 'appens to walk by and see a poster . . . You 'ave no hidea how narrow-minded French people can be about hart. Luckily, there is halways a new scandal next week to take the pressure hoff." Suddenly, she stopped, releasing my arm. She moved off two steps and looked searchingly at me. "To the naked heye," she said, "you look very nicely built. Ham I wrong?"

"I used to ski a lot," I said.

"We 'ave not yet cast the role of the villain," Nadine said. "'E has two very interesting scenes. One with Priscilla alone and one with Priscilla and a Nubian girl . . . Maybe it would hamuse you."

"She's offering you a job, Douglas," Miles said. His voice seemed to boom out over all the noise of the avenue traffic. "Protect your investment."

"It's very good of you madame," I said to Nadine, "but if my mother in America ever saw it, I'm afraid . . ." I was ashamed to bring my dead mother into this affair, but at the moment it seemed like the quickest way to end the conversation.

"Priscilla 'as a mother in America, too," Nadine said.

"There are mothers and mothers in America. I'm an only son," I said idiotically.

"Oh, take it," Lily said. "I'll go over your lines with you on the set. And we could rehearse the difficult bits back at the hotel."

"Sorry," I said glaring at her, "I'd really love to do it. But I may be called out of Paris at any time."

Nadine shrugged. "The trouble with this business," she said, "there hare nevair henough new faces. Halways the same hequipment, the same horgasms. Some hother time, maybe. You have something—ha kind hof underground sexiness, like a young curé. . . . Ham I right, Lily?"

"Absolutely," Lily said.

"It would be beautifully perverse," Nadine said. "Hinnocently rotten. A new dimension. The bishops would gnash their teeth."

"Some other time," I said firmly.

"I will work hon you." Nadine smiled her incorruptible school-girl smile.

The two beers he drank one after the other in the brasserie seemed to have aroused the critic with the beard. He began to speak excitedly in French to Nadine.

"Philippe," Nadine said, "speak Henglish. We have guests."

"We are in France," Philippe said loudly through his beard. "Why shouldn't they speak French?"

"Because we're stupid Anglo-Saxons, dearie," Lily said, "and, as every Frenchman knows, undereducated."

"'E speaks Henglish very good," Nadine said. "Very good. 'E was in Hamerica two years. 'E was in 'Ollywood. 'E wrote criticisms for Cahiers du Cinema."

"Did you like Hollywood?" Fabian asked.

"I hated it."

"Did you like the pictures?"

"I hated them."

"Do you like French pictures?" Lily asked.

"The last one I liked was *Breathless*." Philippe swigged at his beer.

"That was ten years ago," Lily said.

"More than that," Philippe said complacently.

"'E is very particular," Nadine said. "Halso political."

"How many times . . ." He turned angrily on her. "How many times have I told you the two invariably go together?"

"Too many times. Don't be an *emmerdeur,* Philippe. He likes China," Nadine explained to us.

"Do you like Chinese films?" Lily asked. She seemed to take delight in baiting the man, in her offhand, ladylike way.

"I haven't seen any—yet," the man said. "I wait. Five years. Ten years." His English was heavily accented, but fluent. His eyes glittered. He was the sort of man who would debate happily in Sanskrit. I had the impression that if he ever got into a conversation with anybody who agreed with him he would jump up and storm out of the room.

"Tell me, old man," Fabian said, hearty and friendly, "what do you think of our little opus so far?"

"*Merde*. A piece of shit."

"Really?" Lily sounded surprised.

"Philippe," Nadine said warningly. "Priscilla hunderstands English. You don't want to hundermine her performance, do you?"

"That's all right," Priscilla said, in her pure, corn-fed, high-school soprano, "I never take what a Frenchman says seriously."

"We are in the city where Racine presented *Phédre*, where Molière died," the critic recited, "where Flaubert went to court to defend *Madame Bovary*, where they rioted in the streets after the first performance of Hernani, where Heine was welcomed because of his poetry in another language, and Turgenev found a home." Philippe's beard was electric with argument, the great names luscious on his tongue. "In our own time, in the same medium—film—we have to our credit at least *Grand Illusion, Poli de Carotte, Forbidden Games*. And what have we gathered tonight to discuss? A comic and distasteful attempt to arouse our basest emotions . . ."

"Do not sound, *chéri*," Nadine Bonheur said calmly, "as though you are too fine to fuck. I could gather testimony."

The critic glowered at her and waved for another beer. "What have you shown me? The rutting of an empty-faced American *poupée* and a Moroccan pimp, the . . ."

"*Chéri,*" Nadine said, more sharply now, "remember, you are halways signing petitions against racism."

"That's all right, Nadine," Priscilla said. She was spooning away at a huge bowl of ice cream with chocolate sauce. "I never take what a Frenchman says seriously."

The Moroccan smiled benignly, his English obviously not up to complicated observations on aesthetics in that language.

"Made in France," the critic said, "written in France, composed in France, painted in France— You remember—" He pointed an accusing finger at Nadine. "I ask you to remember what that used to mean. Glory. Devotion to beauty, to art, to the highest aspirations of the human race. What does *your* Made in France mean? A tickling of the balls, a lubricity of the vagina . . ."

"Hear, hear," Lily said.

"English lightness of charactrer," the critic said, leaning forward over the table, jutting his beard fiercely at Lily. "The Empire is gone. Now we will emit a Buckingham Palace snicker."

"Old man," Miles said amiably, "if I may say so, I think you're missing the point."

"If I may say so, sir," Philippe said, "I think I am missing nothing. What is the point?"

"For one thing, the point is to make a dollar or two," Miles said. "From what I've heard, that isn't *completely* against the French character."

"That is not the French character. That is capitalism in France. They are two different things, monsieur."

"All right," Fabian said good-naturedly, "let's leave money out of it for the time being. Although permit me to point out in passing that the greatest number of pornographic films and the most—ah—explicit ones—come out of Sweden and Denmark, two Socialist countries, if I have my facts straight."

"Scandinavians," the critic said. He snorted, dismissing the North. "A mockery of the word Socialism. I piss on such Socialism."

Fabian sighed. "You're a hard man to do business with, Philippe."

"I have my definitions," Philippe said. "I define Socialism."

"China, again," Nadine said. She made a small, wailing sound.

"We can't all live in China, now, can we?" Fabian spoke reasonably. "Whether we like it or not, we live in a world that has a different history, different tastes, different needs."

"I piss on a world that needs *merde* like the *merde* we saw tonight." Philippe called for another beer. He would have a belly like a barrel by the time he was forty.

"I went to the Louvre with my young friend this afternoon." Fabian waved in my direction, his voice gentle. "And yesterday I treated myself to a visit to the Jeu de Paume. Where the Impressionists are collected."

"I do not have to have the museums of Paris described to me, monsieur," Philippe said coldly.

"Forgive me," Fabian said. "Tell me, monsieur, do you disapprove of the works of art in these museums?"

"Not all of them," Philippe said reluctantly. "No."

"The nudes, the embracing figures, the busty madonnas, the goddesses promising all sorts of carnal pleasures to the poor mortals below, the beautiful boys, the reclining princesses . . . Do you disapprove of all that?"

"I do not gather what you are heading for, monsieur," Philippe said, sprinkling beer on his beard.

"What I'm getting at," Fabian said, all patience and bonhomie, "is that throughout our civilization artists have presented objects of sexual desire, in one form or another, sacred, profane, lowly, elevated—the stuff of sensual fantasy. For example, yesterday in the Jeu de Paume, I saw, with pleasure, for perhaps the tenth time, the large canvas by Manet, *Le déjeuner sur l'herbe,* the one with the two superb ladies lolling naked on the grass with their fully dressed gentlemen friends watching admiringly and . . ."

"I am familiar with the work," Philippe said flatly. "Continue."

"Obviously," Fabian said with relish, "Monsieur Manet did not mean for the viewer to understand that nothing went before that moment and that nothing would happen *after* that moment. The impression *I* get, at least, is one of delicious familiarity, with all that that connotes. . . . Are you beginning to follow me?"

"I understand." Philippe was surly now. "I do not follow."

"Perhaps," Fabian said, "if Manet had had the time, he would have painted some scenes of what went on before that peaceful, suspended moment and what would go on after it. And they might not be so terribly different from some of the scenes that were screened for us tonight. Shall we admit that dear Nadine is perhaps not as great an artist as Manet and that sweet little Priscilla might not be as agelessly attractive as the ladies in the painting, but that in its modest way, Nadine's film springs from some of the same basic motives as Manet's oil . . . ?"

"Bravo," Nadine said. "He's halways trying to get me to fuck him hout in the hopen hair. Don't deny hit, Philippe. Remember Brittany last summer? Hall that sand up my hassole."

"I deny nothing," Philippe said unhappily.

"Sex, love, whatever you call it," Fabian rolled on sonorously, "is never just plain flesh. There is always an element of fantasy involved. Each age looks to its artists for the fantasies that deepen or improve or even make possible the actual act. Nadine, once again in her modest way—forgive me, dear . . ." He leaned over and patted Nadine's hand in a fatherly way. "Nadine is trying to enrich the fantasies of her fellowmen and women. In this dark, joyless, imaginatively stunted age, I would say that she should be saluted, not criticized."

"Talk the hind leg off a donkey," Lily said, in full Cockney, "that one would."

"You can say that again, sister," I said, remembering what Fabian had already talked me into in the space of one afternoon. It suddenly occurred to me that he must be a disbarred lawyer. Disbarred for a very good reason, no doubt.

"Someday, monsieur," Philippe said, with dignity, "I would like to have a discussion with you in my native language. I am at a disadvantage in English." He stood up. "I have to rise early in the morning. Pay the bill, Nadine, and let us find a taxi."

"That's all right, Nadine," Fabian said, waving his hand, although she had made no move toward her purse. "The refreshments are on us." The plural did not escape me. "And thank you for a jolly evening."

We all stood up and Nadine kissed Fabian on both cheeks. She merely shook my hand. I was a little disappointed. The film had had its effect on me, blushes or no blushes. The touch of her lips would have been bracing. I wondered how the Moroccan boy, who had disported with her as her undeniably willing partner in at least two long scenes, could stand meekly aside and watch her go off with another man. Actors, I thought. They must divide themselves into compartments.

"Do you live near here?" Fabian asked Miss Dean.

"Not far."

"Perhaps you'd like us to escort you home—"

"No, thanks, I'm not going home," Priscilla said. "I have a date with my fiancé." She put out her hand to me and I shook it. "G'bye, see you in church," she said. I felt a small, rolled-up piece of paper in my palm. For the first time I looked directly at her. There was a little smudge of chocolate at the corner of her mouth, but her eyes were a deep sea blue, the tide coming in rapidly, bringing incalculable sunken treasure.

"See you," I mumbled and closed my hand over the bit of paper as she stepped away.

Outside, on the avenue, in the soft wet air of the February Paris night, after we parted with Priscilla and the Moroccan and the cameraman, I dug into my pocket where I had dropped the piece of paper. I unrolled it and by the light of a streetlamp, saw that it had a telephone number written on it. I put the piece of paper back in my pocket and hurried after Fabian and Lily, who were walking ahead of me.

"Glad you came to Paris, Douglas?" Fabian asked.

"It's been a lively day," I said. "Most educational."

"It's only the beginning," said Fabian. "There are vistas ahead of you, vistas."

"Did you believe all that stuff you were spouting back there?" I asked. "About Nadine and Manet and so on?"

Fabian laughed. "Not at the start maybe," he said. "I was just giving in to my normal reaction when I hear a Frenchman start orating about Racine and Molière and Victor Hugo. But by the end I damn near had myself convinced that I was a patron of the arts. That includes you, of course," he added hastily.

"You're not going to put your name—*our* name—on it, are you?" I said, alarmed.

"No." Fabian sounded almost regretful. "I suppose that would be going too far. We'll have to find a company name. Have you any ideas, Lily? You've always been the clever girl."

"Up, Down, and Over Productions," Lily said.

"Don't be vulgar, dear," Fabian said prissily. "Remember, we want a review in *The Times*. We'll have to put our minds to it in the calm light of day. Oh, by the way, Douglas, get a good night's sleep. We'll be up at five. We have to drive out to Chantilly for the workouts."

"What workouts?" I had no idea where Chantilly was and for a moment I thought that it was a special place where actors in pornographic movies kept in shape. From what I had seen that evening, a day's shooting involved as much physical expenditure for man and woman alike as ten fast rounds with a bantamweight prizefighter.

"Our horse," Fabian said. "There was a cable waiting for me at the desk when we got back from the Louvre this afternoon—By the way, you did enjoy the Louvre, didn't you?"

"Yes. What about our horse?"

"The cable was from my friend in Kentucky. Somehow, he found out about the splints. He's not ready to buy at the moment . . ."

"Oh, God," I said.

"Not to fret, dear boy," Fabian said. "My friend in Kentucky wants the animal to run in one decent race before he puts his money down. You can't blame the man, can you?"

"No. But I can blame you."

"I'm afraid you're starting our relationship on the wrong note, Douglas," Fabian said, hurt. "We just have to explain matters to the trainer. He has great faith in the horse, great faith. All he has to do is to make sure the horse is fit and pick the appropriate race to enter him in. The trainer's name is Coombs. An English name, but his family's been in Chantilly since the Empress Josephine. He's a wizard at picking appropriate races, an absolute wizard. He's won races with animals they were about to sell to pull junk wagons. Anyway, you'll love Chantilly. No lover of horses should come to Paris without seeing Chantilly."

"I'm no lover of horses," I said. "I hate horses. I'm scared stiff of them."

"Ah, Douglas," Fabian said as we reached the hotel, "you have a long way to go, a long, long way." He tapped me, old comrade, on the shoulder, as we went in. "But you'll make it, I guarantee you'll make it."

I went up to my room, looked at the bed, turned down for the night, and stared at the telephone. I remembered some of the scenes in the movie I had seen that evening and decided I wasn't sleepy. I went down to the bar and ordered a whiskey and soda. I drank it slowly, then took out the slip of paper Priscilla Dean had put in my hand and spread it out before me on the bar. "Is there a telephone here?" I asked the barman.

"Downstairs," he said.

I went downstairs and gave the number to the girl who was on duty there and went into the booth she indicated to me and picked up the phone. There was a moment's silence, then a busy signal. I listened to the signal for thirty seconds, then replaced the phone. So be it, I thought.

I went back to the bar, paid for my drink. Ten minutes later I was in my bed. Alone.

The name of the horse was Rêve de Minuit. Lily, Fabian, and I were standing with Coombs, the trainer, in the morning mist at the head of one of the *allées* in the forest of Chantilly, watching the exercise boys gallop in pairs and trios. It was seven in the morning and cold. My shoes and the cuffs of my trousers were muddy and wet through. I was hunched in my old, sooty, greenish overcoat, the same one I had when I was at the St. Augustine, and I felt citified and out of place in the dripping woods, with the smell of wet foliage and steaming horses all around me. Fabian, ready for an occasion, was wearing jodhpur boots and a smart, short, canvas hunting coat over his houndstooth jacket and corduroy pants. An Irish tweed cap sat squarely on his head and moisture glinted on his moustache. He looked as though dawn was his favorite time of day and as if he had owned a string of thoroughbreds all his life. Anyone seeing him there for the first time would be sure that no trainer would be able to pull any crafty trainer's tricks on him.

Lily, too, was dressed for the scene, in high brown boots and loose belted polo coat, her English complexion brought to its genetic perfection by the dank atmosphere of the forest. If I intended to remain in their company—and by now I would have been hard put to figure out how I could disentangle myself—I would have to rethink my wardrobe.

Coombs, a booted, ruddy-faced, sly-looking, tiny old man with a gravelly outdoor voice, had pointed out our horse to us. He looked like every other brownish horse to me, with wild rolling eyes and what seemed to me dangerously thin legs. "He's coming along nicely, the colt, nicely," Coombs said. Then we all had to duck behind some trees as one of the other horses started running backward toward us, almost as fast as if it had been going forward. "They're a little nervy these cold mornings," Coombs said indulgently. "That one's only a wee two-year-old filly. Playful at that age."

The exercise boy finally got the creature under control and we could come out from behind the trees. "How are the splints, Jack?" Fabian asked. The connoisseur of paintings and sculpture who had led me around the Louvre and who had discoursed on Manet to the critic the night before was gone now, replaced by a knowing horseman, expert on the fine points and obscure ailments of the equine race.

"Ah, I wouldn't worry, man," Coombs said. "He's coming along something splendid."

"When will he be ready to run?" I said, the first words I had uttered since I had been introduced to the trainer. "I mean in a regular race?"

"Ah, man," Coombs wagged his head ambiguously. "Ah, man, that's another question altogether, isn't it? You wouldn't want to push the colt, now, would ye? You can see he's not totally hardened yet, can ye not?" He had the damndest Irish-English way of talking for a man whose family had lived in France since the Empress Josephine.

"He does look as though another couple of weeks of work wouldn't do him any harm," Fabian said.

"He still seems to be favoring his off foreleg a bit," Lily said.

"Ah, ye noticed, ma'am," Coombs beamed at her. "It's more psychological than anything else, you understand. After the firing."

"Yes," Lily said. "I've seen it before."

"Ah, and a pleasure it is not to be having to hold the hand of an anxious owner." Coombs beamed more widely.

"Could you give us an estimate?" I asked stubbornly, remembering the six thousand dollars invested in Rêve de Minuit. "Two weeks, three weeks, a month?"

"Ah, man," Coombs said, head wagging again, "I don't like to be pinned down. It's not my way to raise an owner's hopes and then have to disappoint the good man."

"Still, you could make a guess," I persisted.

Coombs looked at me steadily, his little gray eyes, set in a thousand wrinkles, suddenly winter-cold. "Ay, I could guess. But I won't. *He'll* tell me when he's ready to run." He smiled jovially, the ice in his eyes melting instantaneously. "Well, we've seen enough for the morning, wouldn't ye say? Now let's go and have a bit of breakfast. Ma'am . . ." Gallantly, he offered Lily his arm and led the way out of the forest with her.

"You've got to be careful with these fellows, Douglas," Fabian said in a low voice as we followed along a path through the woods. "They can be touchy. He's one of the best in the business. We're lucky to have him. You've got to let these old boys make the pace themselves."

"It's our horse, isn't it? Our six thousand bucks?"

"I wouldn't talk like that where he could hear you, old man. Ah, it's going to be a lovely day." We were out of the forest by now and the sun was breaking through the mist, shining on the coats of the horses that were ambling in slow strings back toward the barns. "Doesn't this lift your heart?" Fabian said, throwing his arms wide in an expansive gesture. "This ancient, glorious countryside in the fresh sunshine, these beautiful, delicate animals . . ."

"Delicate is the word," I said ungraciously.

"I am full of confidence," Fabian said firmly. "What's more, I will make a prediction. Before we're through, we'll make our mark on the sport. And not with only one six-thousand-dollar reject. Wait until you come to Chantilly and see twenty horses working out and know they're all yours. Wait until you're sitting in an owner's box at Longchamps and see your colors parade by before a race. . . . Wait until . . ."

"I'll wait," I said sourly. "Happily." But although I carefully kept from showing it, I, too, felt the attraction of the place and the horses and the canny old trainer. I couldn't go along with Fabian's manic optimism, but I felt the power of his dream.

If speculating in gold and risking huge sums on lunatic pornographic films written by an Iranian and starring a nymphomaniac Midwestern student of comparative literature at the Sorbonne could result in thirty mornings a year like this one, I would follow Fabian gratefully. Finally, the money I had stolen had achieved a concrete good. I breathed deeply of the sharp country air before I went into breakfast at a long table in the Coombses' dining room, where the shelves and walls were reassuringly covered with cups and plaques the stable had won through the years. The old man poured each of us a generous shot of Calvados before we sat down at the long table with his plump and rosy wife and eight or nine jockeys and exercise boys and girls. The aroma of coffee and bacon in the room was mixed with the smell of tack and boots. It was a simpler and heartier world than I had imagined still existed anywhere on the surface of the earth, and when Coombs winked at me across the table and said, "*He'll* tell me when he wants to run, man," I winked back at him and raised my mug of coffee to the old trainer in return.

CHAPTER 14

"I THINK IT is time we thought of Italy," Fabian said. "What do you think of Italy, dear?"

"I like it," Lily said.

We were sitting in a restaurant called the Chateau Madrid, high up on a cliff overlooking the Mediterranean. The lights of Nice and the coastal settlements far below us twinkled in the lavender evening air. We were waiting for our dinner and drinking champagne. We had also drunk a considerable amount of champagne on the Train Bleu down from Paris the night before. I was beginning to develop a taste for Moët & Chandon. Old man Coombs had been with us on the train and most of the afternoon. After more than two weeks of workouts, Rêve de Minuit had finally told the trainer he was ready to run. And run he had. He had come in first by a neck that afternoon in the fourth race at Cagnes, the track outside Nice, where they had a winter meeting. The purse had been a hundred thousand francs, about twenty thousand dollars. Jack Coombs had lived up to his reputation for picking appropriate races. Unfortunately, he had had to fly back to Paris immediatey after the race, so we were denied the pleasure of his company at dinner. I was curious to see just how many bottles of champagne, interspersed with shots of cognac the old man could down in one full day.

We had also bet five thousand francs on the nose of Rêve de Minuit, at six to one. "For sentiment's sake," Fabian had said, as we went to the window. In New York I had been gambling for my life with every two-dollar bet. Obviously, as a guiding principle, sentiment was more profitable than survival at a racetrack.

When we had gone back to our hotel in Nice to change our clothes for dinner, Fabian had called Paris and Kentucky. From Paris he had learned that *The Sleeping Prince* had finished shooting that evening and that, after a showing of the incomplete rough cut the night before, representatives of distributors in West Germany and Japan had already put in substantial bids. "More than enough," Fabian told me with some satisfaction, "to cover our investment. And with the rest of the world still to go. Nadine is ecstatic. She is even contemplating starting on a *clean* picture." As an afterthought, he mentioned to me that the price of gold had gone up five points that day.

His friend in Kentucky had been impressed with the news of Rêve de Minuit's victory, but wanted to consult a partner before making a firm offer. He would call back later, at the restaurant.

The champagne, the view, the triumph of the afternoon, the price of gold, the news from Nadine, the prospect of a splendid meal, the company of Lily Abbott, sitting between us in all her beauty, made me feel an enormous friendliness toward the entire world, with an especial warmth toward the man who had stolen my bag at the Zurich airport. Enemies and allies, I was discovering, as in the case of the German and Japanese movie people, were interchangeable entities.

If Rêve de Minuit hadn't won, I suppose I would have been ready to toss Fabian over the cliff into the sea a thousand feet below. But the horse had won and I looked across the table fondly at the handsome, moustached face.

"Did you mention a possible price to Kentucky?" I asked.

"I said in the neighborhood of fifty," Fabian said.

"Fifty what?"

"Thousand dollars." He sounded annoyed.

"Don't you think that's a little steep for a six-thousand-dollar horse?" I asked. "We don't want to scare him off."

"Actually, Douglas," Fabian sipped appreciatively at his glass, "he's not a six-thousand-dollar horse. I have a little confession to make. I paid fifteen thousand for him."

"But you told me . . ."

"I know I told you. I just thought at the time that it might be wiser to lead you along gently. If you doubt me, I can show you the bill of sale."

"I no longer doubt you," I said. It was almost true.

"How about the fifteen thousand for the picture? Were you leading me along gently on that, too?"

"On my honor, old man." He raised his glass. "To Rêve de Minuit." We all clinked glasses happily. I had grown attached to the animal in the time that it took him to come from dead last at the turn, and then go on to lead the pack in the final three strides, and I told Fabian I hated to see him go.

"I'm afraid you have the instincts of a bankrupt, my friend," Fabian had said. "You are not yet sufficiently rich to love horses enough to hold onto them. The same I may say, goes for ladies." He looked meaningfully at Lily. There had been a noticeable tension between them in Paris. He had had three or four business conferences too many at odd hours with Nadine Bonheur. For myself, I had carefully avoided going to the studio where the movie was being shot and had not seen any of the people involved in it again. The busy signal on the telephone still tolled its message to me.

"What we'll do," Fabian was saying, "is buy a car. Do you have any objection to Jaguars?"

Neither Lily nor I had any objection to Jaguars.

"A Mercedes might be too flashy," he said. "We do not wish to appear *nouveau riche*. Anyway, I like to do what I can for the poor old Brits."

"Hear, hear," Lily said.

The waiter came with the caviar. "Just lemon, please," Fabian said, waving away the platter with chopped hard-boiled eggs and onion on it. "Let us not dilute the pleasure."

The waiter spooned mounds of grayish pearls on our plates. This was only the fourth time in my life that I had tasted caviar. I remembered the other three times clearly.

"We will fly to Zurich," Fabian said. "I have a little business to do in that fair city. We'll pick up the car there. I think the only honest automobile dealers in the world can be found in Switzerland. Besides, there's a first-class hotel there I'd like Douglas to see."

Baby, I thought, if they could see good old Miles Fabian back in Lowell, Massachusetts, now. Or if Drusack could see me. Then I was sorry I had thought of Drusack. Fabian had not yet asked me how I had come to be carrying seventy thousand dollars in my suitcase and I hadn't told him. Actually, there were many things we had to talk about. In Paris Fabian had spent most of his time around the movie set. Watching the shop, as he put it, while I wandered around sight-seeing, sinking blissfully into the city. When we were together, Lily was almost always present and neither of us, I was sure, wanted her to hear about the details of our partnership, as I now thought of it. As for her, if she considered it odd that her lover of one night in Florence had turned up promptly in another country as the close friend and associate of her lover of some years, she gave no sign. As I was to find out, as long as she was fed and admired and taken to interesting places, she asked no questions. She had an aristocratic disregard for the machinery behind events. She was the sort of woman you could never imagine in a kitchen or an office.

"I would like to bring up a delicate subject," Fabian said, expertly loading a portion of caviar on his toast, not losing a single egg. "It is a question of numbers. Three to be exact." He looked first at Lily, then at me. "Do you get my drift?"

"No," I said.

Lily said nothing.

"It is the wrong number for traveling," Fabian went on. "It can lead to division, subterfuge, jealousy, tragedy."

"I see what you mean," I said, feeling a hot flush begin at my collar.

"I suppose you agree, Douglas, that Lily here is a beautiful woman."

I nodded.

"And Douglas is a most attractive young man," Fabian said, his tone paternal and kindly. "And will become more so as he becomes accustomed to wealth and after we supply him with a fresh wardrobe, which I intend to do as soon as we reach Rome."

"Yes," Lily said. She looked demurely down at her plate.

"We must face the truth. I am an older man. I hope nobody is going to contradict me."

Nobody contradicted him.

"The chances of mischief are plain." Fabian helped himself to more caviar. "If there is a lady you have in mind as a fit traveling companion, Douglas, why don't you get in touch with her?"

The image of Pat came immediately to my mind, in a wave of tenderness, mingled with regret. I had rarely even thought of her during the years at the St. Augustine. The protective, icy numbness that had come over me that last day in Vermont was melting fast in the company of Lily and Fabian. I had to recognize that, like it or not, I was once again exposed to old emotions, old loyalties, to the memories of distant pleasure. But even if Pat were free, I couldn't imagine her accepting my relationship with Fabian, whatever it was or turned out to be, or his blatantly high style of living. The girl who donated a portion of her small salary as a schoolteacher to the refugees of Biafra could hardly be expected to approve of the man sitting at the table spooning up caviar. Or of me, for that matter. Evelyn Coates was a more likely candidate for our little group and would be an interesting match for both Lily and Fabian, but who knew which Evelyn Coates would turn up—the surprisingly gentle woman of that last Sunday night in my hotel room or the abrasive Washington operator and businesslike rapist I had met at the Hale's cocktail party? I also had to consider the possibility that one way or another, Fabian and I might eventually be exposed. It would hardly do her career as a government lawyer any good if one day she was publicly branded as the consort of a pair of thieves.

"I'm afraid there's nobody I can think of at the moment," I said.

I thought I detected the ghost of a smile pass across Lily's face.

"Lily," Fabian said, "what is your sister Eunice doing these days?"

"Going through the Coldstream Guards in London," Lily said. "Or the Irish Guards. I forget who's on duty at the palace."

"Do you think it would amuse her to join our party for a while?"

"Indeed," Lily said.

"Do you think that if you sent her a wire she'd be prepared to meet us tomorrow night at the Hotel Baur au Lac in Zurich?"

"Very likely," Lily said. "Eunice travels light. I'll send the wire when we get back to the hotel."

"Is that okay with you, Douglas?"

"Why not?" It seemed terribly cold-blooded to me, but I was in cold-blooded company. When in Rome. Caviar and circuses.

The maître d'hôtel came over to our table to tell Fabian that there was a call for him from America. "What do you say, Douglas?" Fabian asked as he got up from the table. "How low are you ready to go? How about forty, if necessary?"

"I'll leave it up to you," I said. "I've never sold a horse before."

"Neither have I." Fabian smiled. "Well, there's a first time for everything."

He followed the maître d'hôtel off the terrace.

The only sound was the crunching of Lily's teeth on her toast, ladylike, but firm. The sound made me nervous. I could feel her looking speculatively at me. "Were you the one," she asked, "who broke the lamp on Miles' head?"

"Did he say I did?"

"He said there'd been a slight misunderstanding."

"Why don't we let it go at that?"

"If you say so." There was more crunching. "Have you told him about Florence?"

"No. Have you?"

"I'm not an idiot," she said.

"Does he suspect?"

"He's too proud to suspect."

"And where do we go from here?"

"To Eunice," Lily said calmly. "You'll like Eunice. Every man does. For a month or so. I look forward to our holiday."

"When do you have to go back to Jock?"

She glanced at me sharply. "How do you know about Jock?"

"Never mind," I said. She had hurt me with her debonair assignment of me to her sister and I wanted to get a little of my own back.

"Miles says he's never going to play bridge or backgammon again. Do you know anything about that?"

"I have a general idea," I said.

"But you're not going to tell me what it is."

"No."

"He's a complicated man, Miles," she said. "He has an abiding fondness for money. Anybody's money. Be careful of him."

"Thanks. I shall be."

She leaned over and touched my hand. "I had a lovely time in Florence," she said softly.

For a tortured moment I wanted to grab her and plead with her to get up from the table and flee with me. "Lily . . ." I said thickly.

She withdrew her hand. "Don't be oversusceptible, love," she said. "Remember that."

Fabian came back, his face grave. "I had to come down," he said as he took his seat. He helped himself to more caviar. "All the way to forty-five." He grinned boyishly. "I think we need another bottle of champagne."

I was at the big, carved, oak desk in my room at the hotel. I had said good night at my door to Lily and Fabian. They had the suite next to me. We both overlooked the Mediterranean. Lily had kissed me on the cheek and Fabian had shaken my hand. "Get a good night's sleep, old boy," he had said. "I want to do some sight-seeing in the morning, before we take off for Zurich."

I was feeling a little giddy from all the champagne, but I didn't feel like sleeping. I took a sheet of the hotel stationery from the drawer of the desk and began to write on it almost at random.

Stake, I wrote, 20,000. Gold—15,000. Bridge and backgammon—36,000 . . . Movie?

I stared at what I had written, half-hypnotized. Before this, even when I was making a comfortable living at the airline, I had never bothered to add up my checkbook and certainly had not known within a hundred dollars what I was worth or even how much I had in my pocket at any given time. Now I resolved to keep an accounting every week. Or, with the way things were going, every day. I had discovered one of the deepest pleasures of wealth—addition. The numbers on the page gave me a greater satisfaction than I could hope to get from buying anything with the money the numbers represented. Briefly, I wondered if I should consider this a vice and be ashamed. I would wrestle with this at a later time.

I heard an unmistakable sound from the next room and winced. How far could I trust Fabian? His attitude toward money, his own and that of others, was, to say the least, cavalier. And there was nothing in what I knew of his character and background that suggested an unwavering commitment to fiscal honesty. Tomorrow I would demand that we write out a firm legal document. But no matter what we had on paper, I knew I would have to keep him in sight at all times.

When I finally fell asleep, I dreamed of my brother Hank, sad at his adding machines, working on other people's money.

In the morning we finally had a chance to talk. Lily was going to the coiffeur to get her hair done and Fabian said he wanted to take me to see the Maeght Museum at St.-Paul-de-Vence.

We set out from Nice, with Fabian at the wheel of the rented car. There was little traffic, the sea was calm on our left, the morning bright. Fabian drove safely, taking no risks, and I relaxed beside him, the euphoria of the evening before not yet dispelled by daylight. We drove in silence until we got out of Nice and past the airport. Then Fabian said, "Don't you think I should know the circumstances?"

"What circumstances?" I asked, although I could guess what he meant.

"How the money came into your hands. Why you felt you had to leave the country. I imagine there was some danger involved. In a way, now, I may be equally endangered, wouldn't you say?"

"To a certain extent," I said.

He nodded. We were climbing into the foothills of the Alpes-Maritimes, the road winding through stands of pine, olive groves, and vineyards, the air spiced and fragrant. In that innocent countryside, under the Mediterranean sun, the idea of danger was incongruous, the haunted dark streets of nighttime New York remote, another world. I would have preferred to keep quiet, not because I wanted to hide the facts, but from a desire to enjoy the splendid present, unshadowed by memory. Still, Fabian had a right to know. As we drove slowly, higher and higher into the flowered hill, I told him everything, from beginning to end.

He listened in silence until I had finished, then said, "Supposing we were to continue to be as successful in our—our operations"— he smiled—"as we have been until now. Supposing after a while we could afford to give back the hundred thousand and still have a decent amount left for our own use. . . . Would you be inclined to try to find out who the original owner was and return the money to his heirs?"

"No," I said. "I would not be inclined."

"An excellent answer," he said. "I don't see how it could be done without putting someone on your trail. On *our* trail. There must be a limit to wanton curiosity. Has there been any indication that people have been searching for you?"

"Only what happened to Drusack."

"I would take that as fair warning." Fabian made a little grimace. "Have you ever had anything to do with criminals before this?"

"No."

"Neither have I. That might be an advantage. We don't know how they think, so we won't fall into the dangerous pattern of trying to outwit them. Still, I feel that so far you've done the right thing. Keeping constantly on the move, I mean. For a while, it would be wise to continue. You don't mind traveling, do you?"

"I love it," I said. "Especially now that I can afford it."

"Did it ever occur to you that the people involved might not have been criminals?"

"No."

"I read in the newspapers some time back about a man who was killed in an airplane crash and was found with sixty thousand dollars on him. He was a prominent Republican and he was on his way to Republican headquarters in California. It was during Eisenhower's second campaign. The money you found might have been a campaign contribution that had to be kept secret."

"Possibly," I said. "Only I don't see any prominent Republican coming into the Hotel St. Augustine for any reason whatsoever."

"Well . . ." Fabian shrugged. "Let's hope that we never find out whose money it was, or who was supposed to get it. Do you think you'll ever see the twenty-five thousand dollars you loaned your brother?"

"No."

"You're a generous man. I approve of that. That's one of the nicest things about wealth. It leads to generosity." We were entering the grounds of the museum now. "For example, this," Fabian said. "Superb building. Glorious collection, marvelously displayed. What a satisfactory gesture it must have been to sign the check that made it all possible."

He parked the car and we got out and started walking up toward the severely beautiful building set on the crest of a hill, surrounded by a green park in which huge angular statues were set, the rustling foliage of the trees and bushes all around them making them seem somehow light and almost on the verge of moving themselves.

Inside the museum, which was nearly deserted, I was more puzzled than anything else by the collection. I had never been much of a museum-goer, and what taste I had in art was for traditional painters and sculptors. Here I was confronted with shapes that existed only in the minds of the artists, with splotches on canvas, distortions of everyday objects and the human form that made very little sense to me. Fabian, on the other hand, went slowly from one work to another, not speaking, his face studious, engrossed. When we finally went out and started toward our car, he sighed deeply, as though recovering from some tremendous effort. "What a treasure-house," he said. "All that energy, that struggle, that reaching out, that demented humor, all collected in one place. How did you like it?"

"I'm afraid I didn't understand most of it."

He laughed. "The last honest man," he said. "Well, I see that you and I are going to put in a lot of museum time. You eventually cross a threshold of emotion—mostly just by looking. But it's like almost any valuable accomplishment—it has to be learned."

"Is it worth it?" I knew I sounded like a Philistine, but I resented his assumption that it was my duty to be taught and his to teach. After all, if it hadn't been for my money, he wouldn't have been on the coast of the Mediterranean that morning, but back in St. Moritz, scrambling at the bridge table and the backgammon board for enough money to pay his hotel bill.

"To me it's worth it," he said. He put his hand on my arm gently. "Don't underestimate the joys of the spirit, Douglas. Man does not live by caviar alone."

We stopped at a café on the side of the square of St.-Paul-de-Vence and sat at a table outside and had a bottle of white wine and watched some old men playing *boules* under the trees in the square, moving in and out of sunlight, their voices echoing hoarsely off the old, rust-colored wall behind them that had been part of the fortifications of the town in the Middle Ages. We sipped the cold wine slowly, rejoicing in idleness, in no hurry to go anywhere or do anything, watching a game whose outcome would bring no profit or pain to anyone.

"Do not dilute the pleasure," I said. "Do you remember who said that?"

Fabian laughed. "I do indeed." Then, after a moment, "On that subject—let me ask you a question. What is your conception of money?"

I shrugged. "I guess I never really thought about it. I don't think I *have* a conception. That's peculiar, isn't it?"

"A little," Fabian said.

"If I asked you the same question, what would your answer be?"

"A conception of money," Fabian said, "doesn't exist in a pure state. I mean you have to know what you think of the world in general before you can hope to have a clear notion about money. For example, your view of the world, from what you've told me, changed in one day. Am I right?"

"The day in the doctor's office," I said. "Yes."

"Wouldn't you say that before that day you had one conception of what money meant to you and after it another?"

"Yes."

"I haven't had any dramatic changes of outlook like that," Fabian said. "A long time ago I decided that the world was a place of infinite injustice. What have I seen and lived through? Wars in which millions of the innocent perished, holocausts, droughts, failures of all kinds, corruption in high places, the enrichment of thieves, the geometric multiplication of victims. And nothing I could possibly do to alter or alleviate any of it. I am not a painseeker or reformer, and even if I were, no conceivable good would come out of my suffering or preaching. So—my intention has always been to try to avoid joining the ranks of the victims. As far as I could ever see, the people who avoided being victims had at least one thing in common. Money.

So my conception of money began with that one thing—freedom. Freedom to move. To be one's own man. Freedom to say, Screw you, Jack, at the appropriate moment. A poor man is a rat in a maze. His choices are made for him by a power beyond himself. He becomes a machine whose fuel is hunger. His satisfactions are pitifully restricted. Of course there is always the exceptional rat who breaks out of the maze, driven most often by an exceptional and uncommon hunger. Or by accident. Or luck. Like you and me. Well, I don't pretend that the entire human race is—or should be—satisfied with the same things. There are men who want power and who will abase themselves, betray their mothers, kill for it. Regard certain of our presidents and the colonels who rule most of the world today. There are saints who will commit themselves to the fire rather than deny some truth that they believe has been vouchsafed them. There are men who wear themselves out with ulcers and heart attacks before the age of sixty for the ludicrous distinction of running an assembly line, an advertising agency, a brokerage house. I'll say nothing about the women who allow themselves to become drudges for love, or whores out of pure laziness. When you were earning your living as a pilot, I imagine you believed yourself happy."

"Very," I said.

"I dislike flying," Fabian said. "I am either bored in the air or frightened. Everyone to his own satisfactions. Mine, I'm afraid, are banal and selfish. I hate to work; I like the company of elegant women; I enjoy traveling, with a certain emphasis on fine, old-fashioned hotels; I have a collector's instinct, which up to now I have had to suppress. None of this is particularly admirable, but I'm not running as an admirable entry. Actually, since we're partners, I'd prefer it if we could share the same tastes. It would reduce the probability of friction between us." He looked at me speculatively. "Do you consider yourself admirable?"

I thought for a moment, trying to be honest with myself. "I guess I never thought about it one way or another. I guess you could say it never occurred to me to ask myself if I was either admirable or unadmirable."

"I find you dangerously modest, Douglas," Fabian said. "At a crucial moment you may turn out to be a dreadful drag. Modesty and money don't go well together. I like money, as you can guess, but I am rather bored by the process of accumulating it and am deeply bored by most of the people who spend the best part of their lives doing so. My feeling about the world of money is that it is like a loosely guarded city which should be raided sporadically by outsiders, noncitizens, like me, who aren't bound by any of its laws or moral pretensions. Thanks to you, Douglas, and the happy accident that led you and myself to buy identical bags, I may now be able to live up to my dearest image of myself. Now—about you— Although you're over thirty, there's something—I hope you won't take this unkindly—something youthful, almost adolescent—unformed, perhaps—that I sense in your character. If I may say so, as a man who has always had a direction, I sense a lack of direction in you. Am I unfair in saying that?"

"A little," I said. "Maybe it's not a lack of direction, but a confusion of directions."

"Perhaps that's it," Fabian said. "Perhaps you're not yet ready to accept the consequences of the gesture that you have made."

"What gesture?" I asked, puzzled.

"The night in the Hotel St. Augustine. Let me ask you a question. Supposing you had come across that dead man, with all that money in the room, before your eyes went bad, while you still were flying, still were playing with the idea of marriage—would you have done what you did?"

"No," I said. "Never."

"There's one thing you can always depend on," Fabian said. "The wrong man will always be in the wrong place at the right moment." He poured some more wine for himself. "As for me—there was never a time in my whole life that I would have hesitated for a second. Well, all that's in the past. We want to move as far away as possible from the original source, to cover it up, so to speak, with so much fresh capital, that people will never speculate about just how we started in the first place. Don't you agree?"

"In principle, yes," I said. "But just how do you propose to do it? We can't depend upon buying winning horses every day. . . ."

"No," Fabian said, "I must admit, we have to regard that as unusual."

"And you've told me you're never going to play bridge or backgammon again."

"No. The people I had to associate with depressed me. And the deception I had to practice made me a little ashamed of myself. Duplicity is unpleasant for a man who, by his own lights, would like to have a high opinion of himself. I sat down every night with the cold intention of taking their money away from them and nothing more—but I had to pretend to be friendly with them, be interested in them and their families, enjoy dining with them. . . . I really was getting too old for all that. Money . . ." He pronounced the word as though it were a symbol for a problem in mathematics that had to be solved. "To get the most pleasure out of money, it is best not to have to think about it most of the time. Not to have to keep on making it, with your own efforts or your own luck. In our case, that would mean investing our capital in such a way as to ensure us a comfortable income over the years. By the way, Douglas, what is your notion of a comfortable yearly income?"

"Fifteen, twenty thousand dollars," I said. "Thirty, maybe."

"Fabian laughed. "Come, come, man, raise your sights a little."

"What would *you* say?"

"One hundred, at least," Fabian said.

"That'll take some doing," I said.

"Yes, it will. And entail some risks. From time to time it will also take nerve. And no matter what happens, no recriminations. And certainly no more stilettos."

"Don't worry," I said, hoping I sounded more confident of the future than I actually was. "I'll go along."

"We share all decisions," Fabian said. "I'm saying this as a warning to both of us."

"I understand. Miles," I said, "I'd like something in writing."

He looked at me as though I had slapped him. "Douglas, my boy . . ." he said sorrowfully.

"It's either that," I said, "or I'm getting out right now."

"Don't you trust me?" he asked. "Haven't I been absolutely honest with you?"

"After I hit you over the head with a lamp," I said. Tactfully, I didn't bring up the subject of the six-thousand-dollar horse that had actually cost fifteen thousand. "Well, what's it to be?"

"Putting something in writing always leads to ugly differences of interpretation. I have an instinctive distaste for documents. I prefer a simple, candid, manly handshake." He extended his hand toward me across the table. I kept my hands at my sides.

"If you insist." He withdrew his hand. "In Zurich, we'll put it all into cold legal language. I hope neither of us lives to regret it." He looked at his watch. "Lily will be waiting for us for lunch." He stood up. I took out my wallet to pay for the wine, but he stopped me and dropped some coins on the table. "My pleasure," he said.

CHAPTER 15

"WELL, DONE AND done," Fabian said as he and I left the lawyer's office and stepped out into the slush of the Zurich street. "We are now bound together by the chains of law." The agreement between us had just been notarized and the lawyer had promised to have us incorporated in Liechtenstein within the month. Liechtenstein, I had discovered, which imposes no taxes and where corporate income and outlay are closely guarded state secrets, had an irresistible attraction for lawyers.

There were to be two shares outstanding in the corporation—one owned by Fabian, the other by myself. There was a simple justification for this that I did not understand. For some reason which had to do with the intricacies of Swiss law, the lawyer had appointed himself president of the corporation. We had to choose a name for it and I had offered Augustine Investments, Inc. There had been no dissenting votes. Various fees had been paid.

Fabian had gallantly volunteered to include in the agreement the clause guaranteeing me the right to withdraw my original seventy thousand dollars at the end of a year. We had been to the private bank where Fabian already had a numbered account, and we made it a joint one, so that neither of us could take out any money without the consent of the other.

We each deposited five thousand dollars in our own names in an ordinary checking account in the Union Bank of Switzerland. "Walking-around money," Fabian called it.

If either of us were to die, the full assets of the company and the balance in the bank went to the survivor. "It's a little macabre, I know," Fabian had said to me as I read the clause, "but one can't afford to be finicky in matters like this. If you have any misgivings, Douglas, I could point out that I'm considerably older than you and can be expected to be the first to leave the scene."

"I realize that," I said. I didn't tell him that it had occurred to me as I read the document that it also offered him the temptation to push me off a cliff or poison my soup. "Yes, it's very fair."

"Are you satisfied now?" Fabian asked, as we picked our way around a puddle. "Do you feel protected?"

"From everything," I said, "except your optimism." We had been in Zurich six days under a gray and sullen sky and in those six days Fabian had bought twenty thousand dollars more worth of gold, had been in and out of the sugar market, on margin, in Paris, twice, and had acquired three abstract lithographs by an artist I had never heard of, but who was going to skyrocket, as Fabian put it, in the next two years. As he told me, he did not like to allow money to lie idle.

Fabian had discussed all our deals with me and had patiently explained the working of the commodity markets, where fluctuations were so erratic that fortunes could be made or lost in the space of an afternoon and where we had done incredibly well in sugar between Thursday and Friday. I understood, but when asked for an opinion could only leave decisions up to him. My own naïveté shamed me and I felt the way I had as a small boy in an arithmetic class when I was called on by the teacher for a question which every pupil but myself was prepared to answer. It all seemed so complicated and dangerous that I was beginning to wonder how I had been able to survive in the same world as Miles Fabian for thirty-three years.

By the end of the six days I wasn't sure anymore that I could stand the daily wear and tear on my nerves. There was cold sweat on the palms of my hands every morning.

As for Fabian, nothing seemed to disturb him. The bigger the risk he was taking, the more serene he became. If there was one lesson I would have liked to learn from him, it was that. For the first time since I was a child, I began to suffer from my stomach. As I swallowed Alka-Seltzer after Alka-Seltzer, I tried to tell myself that it wasn't nerves, but the rich food that we were eating twice a day in the fine restaurants in the city, and all the wines that Fabian kept ordering. But neither he nor Lily, nor Lily's sister Eunice, complained of any distress, even after a most elaborate dinner at the Kronenhalle, a Helvetian monument to hearty food and Swiss digestion, where we had smoked trout, saddle of venison with Spätzle and preiselberry sauce, washed down first with a bottle of Aigle and later a heavy Burgundy, followed by slabs of

Vacherin cheese and a chocolate soufflé.

I was beginning to worry about my weight, too, and my trousers were getting uncomfortably tight around my waist. Lily didn't change by as much as an ounce, remaining gloriously slender, although she actually ate more than either Fabian or myself. Eunice, who was chubby and cuddly, remained chubby and cuddly. Fabian, by some miracle, was losing weight, and looked much the better for it, as though the sudden injection of money into his life had drastically improved his metabolism. No matter how much he ate and drank his eyes remained clear, his skin an even healthy pink, his gait springy, his moustache bristling with virility. Generals who had endured long years of peacetime obscurity must react similarly, I thought, when suddenly put in command of armies for enormous, bloody battles. Looking at him, I had the gloomy presentiment that, like a private in the ranks, I was going to do the suffering for the two of us.

Eunice had turned out to be a pretty, pleasant girl with an upturned nose, vulnerable blue eyes, the flowery coloring of a springtime mountain meadow, a sprinkling of freckles, a figure that would have been more fashionable in the age of Victoria than it was in the 1970s, and a soft, almost hesitant manner of speaking that was the result, it was easy to imagine, of the crisp and authoritative speech of her older sister. It was hard to conceive of her going through the Coldstream Guards, as Lily had suggested, or any other regiment.

Whenever the four of us went anyplace together, the two women invariably drew intense looks of admiration from the other men in the room, with Eunice getting just about the same time and an equal coefficient of lust as her more spectacular sister. Under other circumstances I would undoubtedly have been attracted to the girl, but confronted with Fabian's semi-innocent voyeurism and raked by Lily's cold, Florentine eye, I could not bring myself to voice any proposals, or even indicate that they might be welcome if they came from Lily's sister. I had been brought up to believe that sex was a private aberration, not a public enterprise, and it was too late to change now. Chastely, ever since her arrival, Eunice and I had said good night in the elevator, without as much as a kiss on the cheek. Our rooms were on different floors.

It was with something like relief that I listened to the complaints of the two ladies about staying on in Zurich. They had exhausted the shopping, they said, the climate oppressed them, and they didn't know what to do with themselves in the long hours Fabian and I sat talking in offices or in the lobby of the hotel with the various businessmen, bankers, and brokers Fabian collected from the financial center of the city, all of whom spoke, or rather whispered, English in a variety of accents, but whom I didn't understand any better than either Eunice or Lily would have done if they had been in my place. Unfortunately, I had to stay, both at Fabian's request and because of my grim resolve to be present at all transactions. But the two sisters had entrained for Gstaad, where the sun, according to the weather reports, was shining, the snow good, and the company welcoming. We would follow, Fabian promised, as soon as our business was finished in Zurich, which would not be long, he said, and then on to Italy. Fabian gave them the equivalent in Swiss francs of two thousand dollars from our joint account. Walking-around money, he called it, in a phrase I had come to dread. For a man who had led a precarious existence for most of his life, he had lordly habits.

Once the sisters were out of the way, Fabian managed to find time for some of the other attractions of the city. We spent long hours in the art museum, with especial attention to a Cranach nude that Fabian visited, he said, every time he passed through Zurich. He never tried to explain his particular tastes to me, but seemed content enough if I merely accompanied him on his rounds of the art galleries of the city. We went to a concert where we heard a program of Brahms, but all he said about it was, "In Mittel-europa, you must listen to Brahms."

He even took me to the cemetery where James Joyce, who died in Zurich, was buried, the grave marked by a statue of the writer, and there wrung from me the admission that I had never read *Ulysses*. When we got back to town, he took me directly to a bookstore and bought me a copy. For the first time I had an inkling of the fact that the prisons of the world might be filled with men who had read Plato and appreciated music, literature, modern painting, fine wines, and thoroughbred horses.

The thought had crossed my mind that he was attempting, for some private reason of his own, to corrupt me. But if so, he was doing it in a most peculiar way. Ever since we had left Paris, he had treated me in a semiaffectionate, semicondescending manner, like a sophisticated uncle entrusted for a short while with the worldly education of an untutored nephew from a backward part of the world. Things had moved so fast, and the future he outlined seemed so bright, that I had had neither the time nor the inclination to complain. The truth was that, during those first days, despite my moments of panic, I felt myself lucky to have lost my suitcase to him. I hoped that before long I could manage to behave very much as he did. In other eras the virtues for which heroes were celebrated were such commonplaces as courage, generosity, guile, fidelity, and faith, and hardly ever included, as far as I could remember, aplomb. But in our uneasy time, when most of us hardly know where we stand, cannot say with confidence whether we are rising or falling, advancing or retreating, whether we are loved or hated, despised or adored, aplomb attains, at least for people like myself, a primary importance.

Whatever Miles Fabian may have lacked, he had aplomb.

"Something has come up," Fabian said. "In Lugano." We were in the living room of his suite, littered, as usual, with American, English, French, German, and Italian newspapers, all opened to the financial pages. He was still in his bathrobe, having his morning coffee. I had had my morning Alka-Seltzer in my room on the floor below.

"I thought we were going to Gstaad," I said.

"Gstaad can wait." He stirred his coffee vigorously. For the first time I noticed that his hands looked older than his face. "Of course, if you want, you can go to Gstaad without me."

"Is it business in Lugano?"

"Of a sort," he said carelessly.

"I'll go to Lugano with you."

He smiled. "Partner," he said.

We were in the new blue Jaguar an hour later, with Fabian at the wheel, heading for the San Bernardino Pass. He drove swiftly, even when we climbed into the Alps, and hit patches of ice and snow. He said hardly a word until we had gone through the enormous tunnel and emerged on the southern slopes of the mountain range. He seemed abstracted, and I knew him well enough by now to understand that he was working something out in his head, probably just how much he wanted to tell me about the day's business and how much he wanted to leave out.

It had been overcast all the way from Zurich, but we hit another weather pattern when we got out of the tunnel, and the sun was shining brightly, only occasionally obscured by high, fast-moving white clouds. The sun seemed to change Fabian's mood, and he whistled softly to himself as he drove. "I suppose," he said, "you would like to know why we're going to Lugano."

"I'm waiting," I said.

"There's a German gentleman of my acquaintance," he said, "who happens to live in Lugano. There has been a great influx of Germans, wealthy ones, in that section since the German Economic Miracle. The climate of the Ticino appeals to them. And the banks. You've heard of the German Economic Miracle?"

"Yes. What does the German gentleman of your acquaintance do?"

"Hard to say." Fabian was dissimulating now and we both knew it. "A little of everything. Dabbles in old masters. Adds to his fortune. We have had one or two minor dealings. He called me in Zurich last night. He mentioned a small favor I might do for him. He would show his gratitude. Nothing is fixed as yet. It's still very vague.

Don't worry—if it amounts to anything, you'll be in on every detail."

When he talked like that, there was no use in asking any more questions. I turned on the radio and we descended into the green Ticino to the accompaniment of a soprano singing an aria from *Aida*.

In Lugano we checked into a new hotel situated on the lake shore. There were flowers everywhere. The spiky fronds of palm trees waved gently in the southern breeze, and people in summery clothes were sitting out on the terrace having tea. It was almost Mediterranean, and I could understand why the climate of the Ticino might appeal to a northern and refrigerated race. In the glassed-in swimming pool adjoining the terrace, a robust blonde woman was methodically swimming lap after lap.

"All the hotels have had to put in pools," Fabian said. "You can't swim in the lake anymore. Polluted."

The lake stretched out blue and sparkling in the warm sunshine. I remembered the old man in the bar in Burlington complaining that Lake Champlain would be dead as Lake Erie in five years.

"When I first came to Switzerland after the war," Fabian said, "you could swim in every lake, in every river, even." He sighed. "Times do not improve. Now, if you'll ask the waiter for a bottle of Dezaley for us, I'll go in and call my friend and make the necessary arrangements. I won't be long."

I ordered the wine and sat in the late-afternoon sunshine, enjoying the view. The necessary arrangements Fabian was making on the telephone must have been complicated because I had drunk almost half the bottle of wine before he came back. "Everything in order," he said cheerfully, as he sat down and poured himself a glass. "We have a date to see him at six o'clock at his villa. His name, by the way, is Herr Steubel. I won't tell you anything more about him just yet. . . ."

"You haven't told me *anything* so far," I reminded him.

"Just so. I don't want you to have any preconceptions. You have no prejudices against Germans, I trust?"

"Not that I know of."

"Good," he said. "Too many Americans are still fighting World War II. Oh, incidentally, to explain your presence to Herr Steubel, I said that you were Professor Grimes of the Art Department of the University of Missouri."

"Good God, Miles!" I spluttered over my wine. "If he knows *anything* about art, he'll catch on in ten seconds that I'm an absolute ignoramus." Now I realized why Fabian had been so quiet and thoughtful on the first half of our journey. He had been cooking up a useful identity for me.

"I wouldn't worry," Fabian said. "Just look grave and judicious if he shows us anything. And when I ask your opinion, hesitate . . . you know how to hesitate, don't you?"

"Go on," I said grimly. "What do I do after I hesitate?"

"You say, 'At first glance, my dear Mr. Fabian, it would seem to be authentic.' But you would like to come back tomorrow and study it more carefully. In the light of day, so to speak."

"But what's the sense in it?"

"I want him to spend a nervous night," Fabian said calmly. "It will make him more generous in his arrangements tomorrow. Just remember not to show any undue enthusiasm."

"That'll be the easiest thing I've done since I met you," I said sourly.

"I know I can depend on you, Douglas."

"How much is all this going to cost us?"

"That's the beauty of it," Fabian said gaily. "Nothing."

"Explain." I sat back in my chair and crossed my arms.

"I'd really rather not at the moment," Fabian said. He sounded annoyed. "It would be much better if we just let things work themselves out. I expect a certain amount of taking on trust between us . . ."

"Explain or I don't go," I said.

He shook his head irritably. "All right," he said, "if you insist. For reasons of his own, Herr Steubel is breaking up a family collection. He believes that by doing it this way he can avoid lawsuits from distant members of the family. And, naturally, he prefers not to pay the grotesque taxes imposed by various governments on this kind of transaction. To say nothing of the difficulties with customs officials when one attempts to ship national art treasures out of one country and into another. . . ."

"Are you suggesting that you and I are going to smuggle whatever this art treasure is out of Switzerland?"

"You know me better than that, Douglas." His tone was reproachful.

"Tell me," I said, "what are we doing? Are we buying or selling?"

"Neither," Fabian said. "We are simply agents. Honest agents. There is a South American of great wealth, who happens to be an acquaintance of mine . . ."

"Another acquaintance."

"Exactly." Fabian nodded. "I happen to know that he is a lover of Renaissance painting and is willing to pay handsomely for authentic examples. South American countries are noted for their discretion in their handling of the importation of art treasures. There are perhaps thousands of great European pictures that have sailed quietly across the ocean and are now hanging safely on South American walls that no one will ever *hear* of for the next hundred years."

"You said we weren't taking anything out of Switzerland," I said. "The last time I looked at a map, Switzerland was not in South America."

"Don't be witty, Douglas, please," Fabian said. "It ill becomes you. The particular South American I have in mind is at present in St. Moritz, where all good things abound. He is a dear friend of his country's ambassador, and the diplomatic pouch is always available for his use. He hinted that he is willing to go as high as one hundred thousand dollars. And I believe that Herr Steubel could be influenced to pay a fair percentage of that as our commission."

"What's a fair percentage in this kind of deal?" I said.

"Twenty-five percent," Fabian said promptly. "Twenty-five thousand dollars for merely taking a five-hour, absolutely legal drive through the picturesque scenery of beautiful Switzerland. Now do you understand why I told you in Zurich that Gstaad could wait?"

"Yes," I said.

"Don't say it so glumly," Fabian said. "Oh—incidentally—the painting that we are going to see is a Tintoretto. As a professor of art you should be able to recognize it. You will remember the name, won't you?"

"Tintoretto," I said.

"Excellent." He beamed at me. He drained his glass. "This wine is delicious." He poured for both of us.

It was dark when we reached the villa of Herr Steubel. It was a squat, two-story house built of stone, perched high on an unlit, narrow road overlooking the lake. No lights could be seen through the closed shutters on the windows.

"Are you sure this is the place?" I asked Fabian. It did not look like the mansion of a man who was in the process of breaking up a family collection of old masters.

"Positive," Fabian said, as he turned off the ignition of the car. "He gave me explicit instructions."

We got out of the car and walked on a path through a small overgrown garden to the front door. Fabian pushed the bell. I heard nothing from within. I had the feeling that we were being watched from somewhere. Fabian pushed the bell again and the door finally creaked open. A tiny old lady in a lace cap and an apron said, *"Buona sera."*

"*Buona sera,* signora," Fabian said, as we went in. The old lady led the way, limping, down a dimly lit hall. There were no pictures on the walls.

The old lady opened a heavy oak door and we went into a dining room lit by a heavy crystal chandelier over the table. A huge bald man with a heavy paunch and a beard like a New Bedford whaling captain's was standing waiting for us, dressed in a creased corduroy suit that included a pair of short knickers, under which the man's massive calves were brilliant in red wool stockings. Behind him, unframed, lit by the chandelier, hung a dark painting pinned by artist's tacks to the plain, yellowish wall. The painting was of a madonna and child, perhaps thirty inches wide and a yard long.

The man greeted us in German, with a little bow, as the old lady went out, closing the door behind her.

"Unfortunately, Herr Steubel," Fabian said, "Professor Grimes does not understand German."

"In that case, we will speak English, of course," Herr Steubel said. He spoke with an accent, but it was not heavy. "I am happy you could come. Could I offer you gentlemen some refreshment?"

"It's good of you, Herr Steubel," Fabian said, "but I'm afraid we haven't the time. Professor Grimes has a call to make at seven o'clock to Italy. And after that to America."

Herr Steubel blinked and rubbed the palms of his hands together, as though they were sweating. "I trust the professor can get through to Italy promptly," he said. "The telephone system in that misguided country . . ." He didn't finish his sentence. I had the distinct impression that he didn't want anybody to call anywhere.

"If I may," I said, taking a step toward the painting on the wall.

"Please." Herr Steubel stepped out of the way.

"You have the documents, of course?" I said.

He rubbed his hands together again, only harder this time. "Of course. But not with me. They are in my . . . my home in . . . in Florence."

"I see," I said coldly.

"It would be a matter of a few days," Steubel said. "And I understood from Herr Fabian that there is a time element . . ." He turned toward Fabian. "Didn't you tell me the gentleman in question was scheduled to leave by the end of the week?"

"I may have," Fabian said. "I honestly don't remember."

"In any case," Herr Steubel said, "here is the painting. I am sure I do not have to tell the professor that it speaks very eloquently for itself."

I could hear him breathing heavily as I stepped up to the painting and stared at it. If it was Fabian's plan to make the man nervous, he was succeeding admirably.

After about a minute of silent scrutiny, I shook my head and turned around. "Of course I may be wrong," I said, "but after the most superficial inspection, I would have to say that it is not a Tintoretto. It may be the *school* of Tintoretto, but I doubt even that."

"Professor Grimes!" Fabian said, his voice pained. "Surely you can't believe—in one minute—in artificial light . . ."

Herr Steubel's breath was coming in short, labored gasps and he was leaning against the dining-room table for support.

"Mr. Fabian," I said crisply, "you brought me along to give my opinion. I've given it."

"But we owe it to Herr Steubel . . ." Fabian was hunting for words and pulling furiously at his moustache. "Out of common courtesy . . . I mean . . . give it a few hours' thought. Come back tomorrow. In daylight. Why . . . why . . . this is frivolous. Frivolous. Herr Steubel says he has documents . . ."

"Documents," Herr Steubel moaned. "Berenson himself has attested to this painting. Berenson . . ."

I had no notion who Berenson was, but I took a chance. "Berenson is dead, Herr Steubel," I said.

"Ven he wass alife," Herr Steubel said.

The chance had paid off. My credentials as an art expert had been confirmed.

"Of course, you could seek other opinions," I said, "I could give you a list of certain colleagues of mine."

"I haff no need of any damned colleagues of yours, Professor," Herr Steubel shouted. His accent had thickened considerably. He loomed over me. For a moment I thought he was going to hit me with one of his huge, clublike hands. "I know what I know. I don't need any damned small-time, barbaric Americans to tell me about Tintoretto."

"I'm afraid I must leave now," I said. "As you remarked, it is difficult to put calls through to Italy and there may be delays. Are you coming with me, Mr. Fabian?"

"Yes, I'm coming with you." Fabian made it sound like a curse. "I'll call you later, Herr Steubel. We'll arrange something for tomorrow, when we can speak more calmly."

"Come alone," was all that Herr Steubel said as we opened the dining-room door and went out into the dark hall. The little old lady in the lace cap was standing just a few feet away, as though she had been trying to listen to what had been said in the dining room. She let us out of the house without a word. Even if she couldn't have understood what had been spoken in the dining room, the tones she had overheard and the brevity of the conference must have made an impression on her.

Fabian slammed the car door behind him when he got behind the wheel of the Jaguar. I closed my door gently as I slid into my seat. Fabian didn't say anything as he started the engine and revved it savagely. He had to back into a driveway to make the turn to go down the hill toward the lake. I heard the tinkling of glass as he slammed the rear light into a low stone fence. I said nothing. He didn't say a word either until we reached the lake. Then he parked the car and turned the motor off. "Now," he said, keeping his voice even with an obvious effort, "what was all that about?"

"What was what about?" I asked innocently.

"How the hell do you know whether a Tintoretto is a fake or not?"

"I don't," I said. "But I was getting bad vibes from that fat Herr Steubel."

"Vibes! We risk losing twenty-five thousand dollars and you talk about vibes!" Fabian snorted.

"He's a crook, Herr Steubel."

"What're you and I? Trappist monks?"

"If we've turned out to be crooks, it's by accident," I said, not completely honestly. "Herr Steubel's a crook by birth, by inclination, and by training."

"You say that." Fabian was on the defensive now. "You see a man for three minutes and you invent a whole history for him. I've done business with him before and he's always fulfilled his obligations. If we'd gone through with the deal, I guarantee you he would have come across with our money."

"Probably," I admitted. "We might also have wound up in jail."

"For what? Transporting a Tintoretto, even a fake one, across Switzerland, isn't a criminal offense. One thing I can't stand in a man, Douglas, and I must tell you to your face, is timidity. And if you want to know, I happen to believe the man's telling the truth. It *is* a Tintoretto, Professor Grimes of the University of Missouri."

"You through, Miles?" I asked.

"For the moment. I'm not guaranteeing the future."

"Transporting a Tintoretto, even a fake one, isn't, as you say, a criminal offense," I said. "But arranging for the sale of a *stolen* Tintoretto is. And I'm not having any of it."

"How do you know it's stolen?" Fabian was sullen now.

"In my bones. You do, too."

"I don't know anything," Fabian said defensively.

"Did you ask?"

"Of course not. That doesn't concern me. And it shouldn't concern you. What we don't know can't hurt us. If you've decided to back out, back out now. I'm going into the hotel and I'm calling Herr Steubel and I'm telling him I'll be there tomorrow morning to pick up the painting."

"You do that," I said levelly, "and I'll have the police waiting for you *and* that old art lover, Herr Steubel, at his ancestral mansion when you arrive."

"You're kidding, Douglas," Fabian said incredulously.

"Try me and see. Look—everything I've done since I left the Hotel St. Augustine has been legal, or approximately legal. Including everything I've done with you. If I'm a criminal, I'm a onetime criminal. If they ever can pin anything on me, it will only be evasion of income tax and nobody takes that seriously. I'm not going to jail for anybody or anything. Get that absolutely straight."

"If I can prove to you that the picture is legitimate and that it isn't stolen . . ."

"You can't and you know you can't."

Fabian sighed, started the motor. "I'm calling Steubel and I'm telling him I'll be at his house at ten A.M."

"The police will be there," I said.

"I don't believe you," Fabian said, staring ahead at the road.

"Believe me, Miles," I said. "Believe me."

When we got to the hotel, we didn't say a word to each other. Fabian went off to the telephone and I went to the bar. I knew he would finally have to join me. I was on my second whiskey when he came into the bar. He looked more sober than I had ever seen him. He sat down on a stool next to mine at the bar. "A bottle of Moët and Chandon," he said to the barman. "And two glasses." He still didn't say anything to me, lifting his glass. "To us," he said. He was smiling broadly. "I didn't talk to Herr Steubel," he said.

"That's good," I said. "I haven't called the police yet."

"I spoke to the old lady in Italian," he said. "She was crying. Ten minutes after we left, the police came and arrested her boss. They took the painting. It was a Tintoretto, all right. It was stolen sixteen months ago from a private collection outside Winterthur." He laughed wildly. "I knew there had to be some reason I took you with me to Lugano, Professor Grimes."

We clinked glasses and again Fabian's maniacal laughter rang out, making everyone in the bar stare at him curiously.

CHAPTER 16

OUR BUSINESS DONE in Lugano, we set out the next morning in the new dark blue Jaguar for Gstaad. I drove this time and enjoyed the sweet performance of the purring machine as we made our way back over the mountains and then sped through winter sunshine through the gentle rolling hills between Zurich and Bern. Fabian sat beside me, contentedly humming a theme that I recognized from the Brahms concerto we had heard a few nights before. From time to time he chuckled. I imagine he was thinking of Herr Steubel in the Lugano jail.

The towns we passed through were clean and orderly, the fields geometrically precise, the buildings, with their great barns and sweeping, slanted eaves, witnesses to a solid, substantial, peaceful life, firmly rooted in a prosperous past. It was a landscape for peace and continuity, and you could not imagine armies charging over it, fugitives fleeing through it, creditors or sheriffs scouring it. I firmly shut out the thought that, if the policemen we occasionally passed and who politely waved us through the immaculate streets knew the truth of the history of the two gentlemen in the gleaming automobile, they would arrest us on sight and escort us immediately to the nearest border.

Since there was no possible way Fabian could risk any more of our money while we were on the road, I was freed, at least for the day, from the erratic nervousness, that fluctuation between trembling hope and taut anxiety that came over me when ever I knew that Fabian was near a telephone or a bank. I hadn't had to take an Alka-Seltzer that morning and knew that I was going tó be pleasantly hungry at lunchtime. As usual, Fabian knew of a beautiful restaurant in Bern and promised me a memorable meal.

The gliding, steady motion of the car, as it so often does, set up agreeable sexual currents in my groin, and as I drove I rehearsed in my mind the gentler moments of my night in Florence with Lily and remembered with pleasure the soft voice of Eunice awaiting me at the end of the day's journey, the childish freckles across her tilted British nose, her slender throat and nineteenth-century bosom. If she had been at my side at the moment, instead of Fabian, I was sure I would not have hesitated to drive into the courtyard of one of the charming timbered inns that we kept passing, with names like Gasthaus Lowen and Hirschen and Hotel Drei Koenig, and take a room for the afternoon. Well, I comforted myself, pleasure delayed is pleasure increased, and stepped a little harder on the accelerator.

As I glimpsed snow on fields high up from the road, I realized that I was even looking forward to skiing again. The days in the heavy atmosphere of Zurich and the dealings with lawyers and bankers had made me long for clear mountain air and violent exercise.

"Have you ever skied in Gstaad?" Fabian askcd me. The sight of the snow must have set his thoughts going along the same track as mine.

"No," I said. "Only Vermont and St. Moritz. But I've heard it's rather easy skiing."

"You can get killed there," he said. "Just like anyplace."

"How do the girls ski?"

"Like English," he said. "Once more into the breach, dear friends . . ." He chuckled. "They'll keep you moving. They're not like Mrs. Sloane."

"Don't remind me of her."

"Didn't quite work out, did it?"

"That would be one way of putting it."

"I wondered what you bothered with her for. I must say, even before I knew you at all, I didn't think she was your type."

"She isn't. Actually," I said, "it was your fault."

Fabian looked surprised. "How was that?"

"I thought Sloane was you," I said.

"What?"

"I thought he'd taken my bag." I explained about the brown shoes and the red wool tie in the train from Chur.

"Oh, you poor man," Fabian said. "A week out of your life with Mrs. Sloane. I do feel guilty now. Did she stick her tongue in your ear?"

"More or less."

"I had three nights of that, too. Last year. How did you find out it *wasn't* Sloane?"

"I'd rather not say." As far as I was concerned the story of Sloane's discovering me, with a cast on my perfectly sound leg, trying to put my foot into his size-eight shoe and throwing *my* shoe and Mrs. Sloane's watch out into the Alpine night was going to die with me.

"You'd rather not say." Fabian sounded pettish. "We're partners, remember?"

"I remember. Some other time," I said. "Perhaps. When we both need a good laugh."

"I imagine that time will come," he said softly.

He was silent for a while. We sped along through admirably preserved Swiss pine forests.

"Let mc ask you a question, Douglas," he said finally. "Have you any ties in America?"

I didn't answer immediately. I thought of Pat Minot, of Evelyn Coates, my brother

Hank, of Lake Champlain, the hills of Vermont, room 602. As an afterthought, of Jeremy Hale and Miss Schwartz. "Not really," I said. "Why do you ask?"

"Frankly," he said, "because of Eunice."

"What about her? Has she said anything?"

"No. But you must admit—to say the least—you've been most reticent."

"Has she complained?"

"Not to me anyway," he said. "But Lily has hinted that she's puzzled. After all, she flew all the way from England . . ." He shrugged. "You know what I mean."

"I know what you mean." I was beginning to feel uncomfortable.

"You do *like* girls, Douglas?"

"Oh, come on, now." I thought of my brother in San Diego and took a turn in the road more sharply than necessary.

"Just asking. These days one never knows. She *is* an attractive girl, don't you think?"

"I think. Listen, Miles," I said, more hotly than I would have wished, "as far as I understand, our partnership doesn't include my hiring out to stand at stud."

"That's a crude way of putting it." Surprisingly, he chuckled. "Although, I must confess, in my own case, from time to time I haven't been averse to the practice myself."

"Christ, Miles," I said, "I've only known the girl a few days." Even as I said it I mourned for the hypocrisy into which he was forcing me. I had only known Lily four hours before I had gone to her room in Florence. As for Evelyn Coates . . . "If you must know," I said, "I don't like the role of public fucker." Finally, I was approaching the truth. "I guess I was brought up differently from you."

"Come now," he said. "Lowell, Massachusetts, isn't all that different from Scranton."

"Who're you kidding, Miles?" I snorted. "They wouldn't find a trace of Lowell in you if they went in with drills."

"You'd be surprised," he said softly. "You really would be surprised. Douglas," he asked, "do you believe me when I tell you that I've grown fond of you, that I have your best interests at heart?"

"Partially," I said.

"To put it more cynically," he said, "especially when they coincide with my best interests?"

"I'll go along with that," I said. "Part of the way. What are you driving at now?"

"I think we ought to put you in the marriage market." His tone was flat, as though it was a decision that he had worked over and had come to after hard thought.

"You're missing a lot of beautiful scenery," I said.

"I'm serious. Listen to me carefully. You're thirty-three, am I right?"

"Right."

"One way or another in the next year or two you're bound to get married."

"Why?"

"Because people do. Because you're fairly good-looking. Because you're going to seem like a rich young man. Because some girl will want you as her husband and will pick the right moment to make her move. Because as you've told me, you've had enough of being lonely. Because you'll finally want children. Does all that sound reasonable?"

I remembered, painfully, the sense of deprivation, jealousy, loss that I had felt when I had called Jeremy Hale's home and his daughter had answered the phone and the pure young voice had called, "Daddy, it's for you."

"Reasonable enough," I admitted.

"All I'm suggesting is that you shouldn't leave it to blind chance, as most idiots do. Control it."

"How do you do that? Will you go out and arrange a match for me and sign a marriage contract? Is that the way it's done in the Principality of Lowell these days?"

"Make your jokes if you want to," Fabian said placidly. "I know they come out of a sense of embarrassment and I forgive them."

"Don't be so goddamn superior, Miles," I warned him.

"The key word, I repeat, is control." He ignored my little outburst.

"You married for money, if I remember correctly," I said, "and it didn't turn out to be so god-awful wonderful."

"I was young and greedy," he said, "and I didn't have a wiser, older man to guide me. I married a shrew and a fool because she was rich and available. I would do everything in my power to prevent you from making the same mistake. The world is full of lovely, lovable girls with rich, indulgent fathers, who want nothing better in life than to marry a handsome, well-mannered, and well-educated young man who is obviously wealthy enough not to be after their money. In a word, you. Good grief, Douglas, you know the old saw—it's just as easy to love a rich girl as a poor one."

"If I'm going to be as rich as you say," I insisted, "what do I have to bother with the whole thing for?"

"Insurance," Fabian said. "I am not infallible. True, we have what seems to you like a substantial sum to dabble with at the moment. But in the eyes of men of real wealth, we're paupers. Paupers, Douglas, playing in a penny-ante poker game."

"I have faith in you," I said, with just a little irony. "You'll keep us both out of the poorhouse."

"Devoutly to be wished," he said. "But there are no guarantees. Fortunes come and go. We live in an age of upheaval. Just in my own lifetime . . ." Contemplating his lifetime in the speeding car, he shook his head sorrowfully. "We are caught in cycles of catastrophe. Perhaps right now we are in the lull before the storm. It is best to take what small precautions we can. And without wishing to harp on ugly matters, you're more vulnerable than most. There's no way of being sure that you'll be able to go forever unrecognized. At any moment, some extremely unpleasant chap may present you with a bill for one hundred thousand dollars. It would be cosier if you could pay it promptly, wouldn't it?"

"Cosier," I said.

"A wealthy, pretty wife from a good family would be an excellent disguise. It would take a leap of imagination on anyone's part to guess that the well-mannered young man, moving easily in the cream of international society and married to solid old English money got his start by swiping a packet of hundred-dollar bills from a dead man in a sleazy hotel in New York. Do I make sense?"

"You make sense," I said reluctantly. "Still—you were talking about mutual interests. What'd be in it for you? You wouldn't expect me to pay an agent's commission on my imaginary wife's dowry, would you?"

"Nothing as crass as that, old man," Fabian said. "All I'd expect would be that our partnership wouldn't be allowed to lapse. The most natural thing in the world would be that your wife would be pleased if you would relieve her of the burden of handling her money. And if I know women, and I believe I do, she'd much prefer to have you do it than the usual gaggle of brokers and trustees and hard-eyed bankers women usually have to depend on."

"Is that where you come in?"

"Exactly." He beamed, as though he had just presented me with a gift of great value. "Our partnership would continue as before. Whatever new capital you brought in would of course still be reserved to you. The profits would be shared. As simple and equitable as that. I hope I've proved to your satisfaction that I am of some use in the field of investments."

"I won't even comment on that," I said.

"The workman is worthy of his hire," he said sententiously. "I don't think you'd have any trouble explaining that to your wife."

"That would depend on the wife."

"It would depend on *you*, Douglas. I would expect you to choose a wise girl who trusted you and loved you and was anxious to give you substantial proof of her devotion to you."

I thought back over my history with women. "Miles," I said, "I think you have an exaggerated notion of my charms."

"As I told you once before, old man," he said, "you're much too modest. Dangerously modest."

"I once took out a pretty waitress in Columbus, Ohio, for three months," I said, "and all she ever let me do was hold her hand in the movies."

"You're moving up in class now, Douglas," Fabian said. "The women you're going to meet from now on are attracted by the rich, so inevitably they are surrounded by older men, men who are engaged almost twenty-four hours a day in great affairs, who have very little time for women. Along with them there are the men who *do* have time for women but whose masculinity very often is ambiguous, to say the least. Or whose interests are transparently pecuniary. Your waitress in Columbus wouldn't even enter a movie house with any of them. In the circles in which you're going to move now, any man under forty with an obvious income of his own and who shows the slightest evidence of virility and who has the leisure to have a three-hour lunch with a lady is greeted with piteous gratitude. Believe me, old man, just by being your normal, boyish self, you will be a smashing success. Not the least of the benefits I mean to shower on you is a new conception of your worth. I trust you will ask me to be the best man at your wedding."

"You're a calculating bastard, aren't you?" I said.

"I calculate," he said calmly, "and I intend to teach you to calculate, too. It's absurd that the perfectly good verb, to calculate, should have a bad reputation in the modern world. Let schoolgirls and soldiers wallow in romance, Douglas. You calculate."

"It all seems so—so immoral," I said.

"I had hoped you would never use that word," he said. "Was it moral to abscond with all that money from the St. Augustine Hotel?"

"No."

"Was it moral for me to hold onto your suitcase when I saw what was in it?"

"I should say not."

"Morality is indivisible, my boy. You can't select certain chunks of it, as though it were a pie waiting on a table to be cut up and served. Let's face it, Douglas, you and I are no longer permitted the luxury of morality. Let's understand each other, Douglas; it wasn't morality that made you run from Herr Steubel—it was a huge reluctance to share a cell with him."

"You've got a fucking argument for everything," I said.

"I'm happy you think that," he said, smiling. "Let me present some further arguments. Forgive me if I repeat myself in assuring you that whatever I suggest is in your best interests. I haven't hidden from you that your best interests are my best interests. I am thinking of the quality of life that you and I are eventually going to lead. You agree, I imagine, that, no matter what we do, we will have to do it together—that we will always have to be close together. Just like partners in any enterprise, we will have to be in constant communication. Practically on a day-to-day basis. You do agree, don't you?"

"Yes."

"For the moment, except for the little disagreement in Lugano, it has been quite pleasant to wander about as we've been doing."

"Very pleasant." I hadn't told him about the Alka-Seltzers and the tightness around my waist.

"Eventually, though, it will begin to pall. Going from hotel to hotel, even the best ones in the world, and living out of a suitcase is finally dreary. Traveling is only amusing when you have a home to return to. Even at your age . . ."

"Please don't make me sound as though I'm ten years old," I said.

He laughed. "Don't be so sensitive. Naturally, to me, you seem enviably young."

He became more serious. "Actually, our differences in age are an asset. I doubt if we would be able to continue for long if we were both fifty or both thirty-three. Rivalries would develop, differences in temperament would arise. This way you can be impatient with me and I can be patient with you. We achieve a useful working balance."

"I'm not impatient with you," I said. "Just scared shitless from time to time."

He laughed again. "I take that as a compliment. By the way, has either Lily or Eunice asked you about what you do for a living?"

"No."

"Good girls," he said. "Real ladies. Has *anybody* asked you? I mean, since the happening in the hotel?"

"One lady. In Washington." Good old Evelyn Coates.

"What did you answer?"

"I said my family had money."

"Not bad. At least for the time being. If the question arises in Gstaad, I suggest you tell the same story. Later on, we can invent a new one. Perhaps you can say you're a managerial consultant. It covers a multitude of murky activities. It's a favorite cover for CIA agents in Europe. It won't do any harm in most circles if that's what people believe. You have such an honest face, no one will be inclined to doubt anything you say."

"How about *your* face?" I asked. "After all, people will be seeing us together all the time. Finally, we'll be held responsible for each other's faces."

"My face," he said reflectively. "Quite often I study it for hours on end in a mirror. Not out of vanity, I assure you. Out of curiosity. Frankly, I'm not quite sure I know *what* I look like. Moderately honest, perhaps. What's your opinion?"

"Aging playboy, maybe," I said cruelly.

He sighed. "Sometimes, Douglas," he said, "frankness is not the virtue it's cracked up to be."

"You asked me."

"So I did. I asked you," he said. "I'll remember not to ask you again." He was silent for a moment. "I've made a conscious effort through the years in a certain direction."

"What direction?"

"I have tried to make myself look like a semi-retired, English gentleman farmer. Obviously, at least as far as you're concerned, I haven't succeeded."

"I don't know any retired, English gentlemen farmers. We got very few of them at the Hotel St. Augustine."

"Still, you didn't guess that I was an American by birth?"

"No."

"A step in the right direction." He smoothed his moustache gently. "Have you ever thought of living in England?"

"No. Actually, I haven't thought of living anyplace. If my eyes hadn't gone wrong, I suppose I'd have been happy staying in Vermont. Why England?"

"Many Americans find it attractive. Especially in the country, perhaps an hour or so away from London. A polite, uninquiring race of people. No hustle or bustle. Hospitable to eccentrics. First-class theater. If you like horses or salmon fishing . . ."

"I like horses all right. Especially since Rêve de Minuit."

"Brave animal. Although I wasn't thinking in exactly those terms. Eunice's father, for example, rides to the hounds three times a week."

"So?"

"He has a handsome estate which happens to be just about one hour from London . . ."

"I'm beginning to catch on," I said flatly.

"Eunice is quite independent in her own right."

"What a surprise."

"For myself," he said, "I find her extraordinarily pretty. And when she isn't under the dominating influence of her sister, a lively and intelligent girl. . . ."

"She's barely looked at me since she arrived," I said.

"She'll look at you," he said. "Never fear."

I didn't tell him about the lascivious thoughts that had crossed my mind, with Eunice as target, as we drove steadily through the neat countryside. "So," I said, "that's why you asked Lily if she thought Eunice would join us?"

"The notion might have flickered through my subconscious," he said. "At the time."

"And now?"

"And now I would advise you to consider it," he said. "There's no great hurry. You can weigh the pros and cons."

"What would Lily have to say about it?"

"From what she's let drop here and there, I would say that on the whole Lily would react favorably." He slapped his hands briskly together. We were approaching the outskirts of Bern. "Let's say no more about it. For the time being. Let us say we'll allow matters to take their natural course." He reached forward and took the auto-mobile map out of the glove compartment and studied it for a moment, although wherever we went he seemed to know every turn in the road, every street corner. "Oh, by the way," he said offhandedly, "did Priscilla Dean slip you her telephone number that night, too?"

"What do you mean, *too?*" I nearly stuttered.

"She did to me. I'm not vain enough to suppose she was all that choosy. After all she's an American. Unfailingly democratic."

"Yes, she did," I admitted.

"Did you use it?"

I remembered the busy signal. "No," I said, "I didn't."

"Lucky man," Fabian said. "She gave the Moroccan the clap. You turn right at the next corner. We'll be at the restaurant in five minutes. They make excellent martinis. I think you can indulge yourself in one or two. And have wine with lunch. I'll drive the rest of the afternoon."

CHAPTER 17

WE ARRIVED IN Gstaad in the early dusk. It had begun to snow. The lights were just being lit in the chalets scattered along the hills, their glow behind curtained windows cosy and warm in the twilight. In this weather and at this time of day, the town looked magical. There was an instant of nostalgia for the harsher slopes of Vermont, for store signs in English rather than German. I wondered what Pat was doing at this moment.

Fabian had not brought up the subject of Eunice again on the trip from Bern, and I was grateful to him for it. It was a problem I was not yet ready to face. The lunch in Bern had been as good as he had promised, and I had had the two martinis and half a bottle of wine and had felt that my defenses were weakened and I could too easily have been persuaded to take a course of action I might later regret.

We had to slow down on the main street for a group of boys and girls, all in jeans and brightly colored parkas, who were streaming out of a *confiserie,* their laughter ringing bell-like in the icy air. It was easy to imagine the heaps of chocolate cakes and mounds of whipped cream they had just consumed in preparation for dinner.

"That's the nice thing about this place," Fabian said, as he maneuvered around them. "The kids. There're three or four international schools here. A ski resort needs young people. It gives an atmosphere of innocence to the sport. And the clothes are designed for youthful bottoms and the climate for adolescent complexions. You'll see them all over the hills tomorrow and you'll mourn that you had to go to school in Scranton."

The car climbed a twisting hill, the wheels spinning erratically in the new snow. On top of the hill, dominating the town, was the huge fake castle of the hotel. Inside and out, the hotel gave no impression of innocence. "The standard joke runs," Fabian said, "that Gstaad is trying to be St. Moritz and will never make it."

"That's okay with me," I said. I had no desire ever to see St. Moritz again.

We signed in. As usual, everybody at the reception and behind the concierge's desk knew Fabian and seemed deeply pleased to see him. He moved from place to place in waves of welcome.

"The ladies," the concierge said, "left a message. They are in the bar."

"What a surprise," Fabian said.

The bar was a large dark room, but not so dark that I couldn't see Lily and Eunice at the other end. They were still in ski clothes and they were seated at a table with five men. There was a magnum of champagne on the table and Lily was telling a story which I couldn't hear, but which ended with a loud burst of laughter that made the other people in the bar turn and look at their table.

I stopped at the door. I doubted that either Fabian or I would be greeted with pleasure. "They haven't been wasting their time, have they?" I said.

"I didn't doubt that they would." He was undisturbed as usual.

"I think I'll go up to my room and take a bath," I said. "Call me when you're ready for dinner."

Fabian smiled slightly. "Faint heart," he said.

"Up yours," I said. As I left the bar, there was another burst of male laughter. Fabian strolled toward the table.

As I went up to the concierge's desk, a group of youngsters came out into the hall from a doorway that led to a bowling alley. They were a mixed bunch of girls and boys, the boys with long hair, some of them with beards, although the oldest couldn't have been more than seventeen. There was a high-pitched gabble of conversation in French and English. I remembered what Fabian had just said about going to school in Scranton. I felt the wrong age, in the wrong place. One of the girls, the prettiest of the lot, stared at me. She had long, uncared-for blonde hair that almost hid a tiny pink face, and she was wearing skintight jeans with flowers embroidered in pastel colors over babyish full hips. She pushed her hair back from her eyes in a languid, womanly gesture. She wore green eye shadow, but no lipstick. Her gaze made me uneasy, and I turned my back to ask for the key.

"Mr. Grimes . . ." The voice was hesitant, high-pitched, childish.

I looked around. She had let the other boys and girls in her group go out the front door and was alone now. "You *are* Douglas Grimes, aren't you?" she said.

"Yes."

"You're the pilot."

"Yes." I didn't see the need of correcting the tense.

"You don't remember me, I suppose?"

"I'm afraid not, miss."

"I'm Didi Wales. Dorothea. Of course it was ages ago. Three years. I had buckteeth and had braces that I wore at night." She shook her head and the long blonde hair obscured her face. "I wouldn't expect. Nobody remembers a thirteen-year-old brat." She threw her hair back and smiled, showing that she no longer needed braces. Her teeth were nice, white, young-American teeth. "Stowe," she said. "You used to ski once in a while with my mother and father."

"Of course," I said, remembering. "How are they? Your mother and father."

"They're divorced," she said. Of course I thought, I could have bet on it. "My mother is recovering from her heartbreak in Palm Beach. With a tennis player." The girl giggled. "And I'm stashed away here."

"It doesn't seem like such a hardship," I said.

"If you only knew," she said. "I used to like to watch you ski. You never showed off, like the rest of the boys."

Boy, I thought. Miles Fabian was the only other person who had called me a boy since I was twenty.

"I could tell it was you," the girl went on, "even a mile away on the slope. You used to ski with a very nice pretty lady. Is she with you?"

"No," I said. "You were reading *Wuthering Heights* the last time I saw you."

"Kid stuff," she said. "You once led me down Suicide Six in a snowstorm. Do you remember?"

"Of course," I said, lying.

"It's nice of you to say so. Even if you don't. It was my accomplishment of the year. Have you just arrived?"

"Yes." She was the first person who had recognized me since I had come to Europe and I hoped the last.

"Are you going to stay here long?" She sounded like a little girl who was afraid to stay alone at night when her parents were going out.

"A few days."

"Do you know Gstaad?"

"This is my first time."

"Maybe I could lead *you* this time." Again there was the languid gesture of pushing her hair back.

"That's very kind of you, Didi," I said.

"If you're not otherwise occupied," she said formally.

A boy with a beard came back through the door and shouted, "Didi, are you going to stand there gabbing all night?"

She made an impatient gesture of her hand. "I'm talking to an old friend of my family. Screw off." She smiled gently at me. "Boys these days," she said. "They think they own you body and soul. Hairy beasts. You never saw such a spoiled bunch of kids. I fear for the world when they finally grow up."

I tried not to smile.

"You think I'm peculiar, don't you?" It was an accusation, sharp and clear.

"Not at all."

"You ought to see them arriving in Geneva after holidays," she said. "In their fathers' private Lear jets. Or driving up to the school in Rolls-Royces. A royal pageant of corruption."

This time I couldn't help smiling.

"You think the way I talk is funny." She shrugged. "I read a lot."

"I know."

"I'm an only child," she said, "and my parents were always someplace else."

"Have you been analyzed?" I asked.

"Not really." She shrugged again. "Of course, they tried. I didn't love them enough, so they thought I was neurotic. *Tant pis* for them. Do you speak French?"

"No," I said. "But I guess I could figure out what *tant pis* means."

"It's an overrated language," she said. "Everything rhymes with everything else. Well, I've enjoyed our little conversation. When I write home, whom should I send your regards to, my mother or my father?"

"Both," I said.

"Both," she said. "That's a laugh. There is no both. To be continued in our next. Welcome to never-never land, Mr. Grimes." She put out her hand and I shook it. The hand was small and soft and dry. She went through the door, the embroidered flowers on her plump buttocks waving.

I shook my head, pitying her father and her mother, thinking, maybe going to school in Scranton wasn't so bad after all. I took the elevator and went upstairs and ran a hot bath. As I soaked, I played with the idea of writing a short note to Fabian and quietly getting on the next train out of Gstaad.

*   *   *   *   *   *   *   *   *   *   *   *   *   *   *   *   *

At dinner that night, there were only the four of us, Lily, Eunice, Fabian, and myself. As unostentatiously as possible, I kept studying Eunice, trying to imagine what it would be like sitting across the breakfast table from her ten years from now, twenty years from now. Imagining sharing a bottle of port with her father, who hunted three times a week. Standing at the baptismal font with her, as our children were christened. Miles Fabian as godfather? Visiting our son at what would it be—Eton? All I knew about English schools had been gleaned from books by men like Kipling, Waugh, Orwell, Conolly. I decided against Eton.

The few days of skiing had given Eunice's complexion a pretty, flush, summery color. She was wearing a figured silk dress that clung to her figure. Buxom today, would she be stately later? The old saw had it, as Fabian had pointed out, that it was just as easy to love a rich girl as a poor one. But was it?

The sight and sound of her and Lily surrounded by lolling, arrogant young men (at least they seemed so to me) at the table with the magnum of champagne on it had made me flee from the bar. There was no denying that she was a pretty girl, and there would undoubtedly always be young men of that caliber and class in attendance. How would I take that if she were my wife? I had never really thought about what class I belonged to or what class *other* people might think I belonged to. Miles Fabian could leave Lowell, Massachusetts, behind him and pretend to be an English squire. I doubted that I could ever get rid of Scranton, Pennsylvania, and pretend to be anything but what I was—a grounded pilot, a man trained as a kind of superior technician, dependent on a payroll. What would the guests at the wedding be whispering about me as I stood beside the altar of the English country church waiting for the bride to descend the aisle? Could I invite my brother Hank and his family to the wedding? My brother in San Diego?

Fabian could educate me to a degree, but there were limits, whether he recognized them or not.

As for sex . . . Still affected by my reveries at the wheel that afternoon I was sure that it would be, at the very least, agreeable. But the passionate desire which I couldn't help but believe was the only true foundation of any marriage—would I ever be stirred to anything even approximating it by this placid, foreign, hidden girl? And what about the ties of family? Lily, as sister-in-law, with the memory of the night in Florence as a permanent ghost at every reunion? At that very moment I knew I wished the room would empty, leaving Lily and myself alone, untrammeled. Was I doomed always to get close to what I wanted, but never *exactly* what I wanted?

"This really has turned into a smashing holiday," Eunice was saying, as she buttered her third roll of the meal. Like her sister, she had a splendid appetite. No matter what else might finally turn out wrong with the children, they would be born with at least half a chance of having marvelous digestions. "When I think of all the poor folk back in bleakest London," Eunice said, "I could cheer. I have a lovely idea . . ." She looked around the table with her innocent, blue, childish eyes. "Why don't we all just stay here in the beautiful sunshine until everything melts?"

"The concierge says it's going to snow again tomorrow," I said.

"Just a manner of speaking, Gentle Heart," Eunice said. She had begun calling me Gentle Heart the second day in Zurich. I hadn't figured out what it meant yet. "Even when it's snowing here, you have the feeling the sun is shining, if you know what I mean. In London in winter it's as though the sun has wandered away permanently."

I wondered if she would have been so eager to continue the quadruple holiday with old Gentle Heart and his friends if she had been able to overhear the cold-blooded conversation about her future that had taken place in the car on the road to Bern.

"It seems like such a waste to go rushing off to crumbling, noisy Rome when we're having such a lovely time here," Eunice said, the roll now thoroughly buttered. "We've all *been* in Rome, after all."

"I haven't," I said.

"It'll still be there in the spring," she said. "Don't you agree, Lily?"

"It's a good bet," Lily said. She was eating spaghetti. She was perhaps the only woman I had ever met who could look graceful eating spaghetti. The sisters had come into my life in the wrong order.

"Miles," Eunice said, "are you absolutely frantic to get to Rome?"

"Not really," Fabian said. "There's a couple of things I want to look into here anyway."

"Like what?" I asked. "I thought we were here on a holiday."

"We are," he said. "But there're all sorts of holidays, aren't there? Don't worry, I won't interfere with your skiing."

By the time the meal was over we had decided that we'd stay in Gstaad at least another week. I said I wanted some air and asked Eunice if she would like to take a walk with me, feeling that perhaps if we were alone for once we could make some sort of overt move toward one another, but she yawned and said that the exercise and the cold air all day had left her exhausted and she just had to fling herself into bed. I escorted her out of the dining room to the elevator and kissed her on the cheek and said good night. I didn't go back to the dining room, but got my coat and took a walk alone, with the snow whirling down around me out of the black night.

The concierge had been wrong. It wasn't snowing in the morning, but clear, blue, and cold. I rented skis and boots and had some wild runs down the mountain with Lily and Eunice, both of whom skied with a devoted British recklessness that was certain to land them in the hospital eventually. Fabian wasn't with us. He had some telephone calls to make, he said. He didn't tell me to whom or what subject, but I knew I'd find out soon enough and did my best not to speculate just how much more of our joint fortune would be engaged in perilous enterprises before we met for lunch. He had told us he'd meet us around one thirty at the Eagle Club, on a mountain called the Wassengrat, so that we could eat together. It was an exclusive club, with rules about membership, but Fabian naturally had arranged for us all to be accepted there as guests for our stay in Gstaad.

It was a marvelous morning, the air glittering, the snow perfect, the girls graceful and happy in the sunshine, the speed intoxicating. By itself, I thought at one moment, it made everything that had happened to me since the night in the Hotel St. Augustine almost worthwhile. There was only one slightly annoying development. A young American, hung with cameras, kept taking photographs of us again and again, getting onto the lifts, adjusting our skis, laughing together, starting off down the hill.

"Do you know that fellow?" I asked the girls. I didn't recognize him as one of the men at the table in the bar with them the evening before.

"Never saw him before," Lily said.

"It's a tribute to our beauty," Eunice said. "All three of us."

"I don't need any tributes to my beauty," I said. At one point, when Eunice had fallen and I was climbing back to help her up and put her skis on again, the man appeared and began snapping pictures from all angles. As politely as possible, I said, "Hey, friend, don't you have enough by now?"

"Never have enough," the man said. He was a gaunt, easy-speaking young man in baggy old clothes and he continued to click away. "Back at the paper they like to have a wide choice."

"Paper?" I said. "What paper?"

"*Women's Wear Daily*. I'm doing a story on Gstaad. You're just what I need. Chic and photogenic, with your skis together. Happy people, in the height of fashion, not a care in the world."

"You think," I said sourly. "There's lots of other people around who answer to that description. Why don't you work on them?" I didn't relish the idea of having my photograph all over a newspaper in New York with a circulation of maybe a hundred thousand. Who knew what paper the two men who had visited Drusack read every morning?

"If the ladies object," the man said pleasantly, "of course I'll stop."

"We don't object," Lily said. "If you'll send us copies. I adore pictures of myself. If they're flattering."

"They could only be flattering," the young man said gallantly. I suppose he'd taken pictures of a thousand beautiful women in his career and I was sure he hadn't been shy to begin with. Meanly, I envied him.

But he did ski off, loose and careless over the bumps, and we didn't see him again until we were on the terrace of the club, having a Bloody Mary, waiting for Fabian to appear.

By that time another complication had arisen. Just at noon I noticed a small figure following us at a distance. It was Didi Wales. She never came within fifty yards of us, but wherever we went, there she was, skiing in our tracks, stopping when we stopped, moving when we moved. She skied well, lightly, and surely, and even when I put on a real burst of speed, which made Lily and Eunice fly down the hill completely out of control, to keep me in sight, there was that small figure faithfully on our trail as though attached to us by a long, invisible cord.

On the last run down, just before lunch, I purposely waited at the bottom of the lift, allowing Lily and Eunice to go up together, in one of the two-seater chairs. Didi came into the lift building, her long blonde hair now caught in a bow of ribbon at the nape of her neck and falling down her back. She was still wearing the flowered blue jeans and a short, bulky orange parka.

"Let's take this one up together, Didi," I said as the chair swung into place and she clumped up in her heavy boots.

"I don't mind," she said. She sat quietly as we swung up out into the open sunlight. The chair mounted silently and we got a view of the whole town spread out in the sunlight. The jagged white peaks, stretching everywhere, were like white cathedrals in the distance.

"Do you mind if I smoke?" she said, starting to get a package of cigarettes out of a pocket.

"Yes," I said.

"Okay, Daddy," she said. Then giggled. "Having a nice day?" she asked.

"Wonderful."

"You're not skiing as well as you used to," she said. "More effort."

I knew this was true but wasn't pleased to hear it. "I'm a little rusty," I said with dignity. "I've been busy."

"It shows," she said matter-of-factly. "And those ladies with you." She made a peculiar little noise. "They'll kill themselves one day."

"So I've told them."

"I bet when there's no men with them, if they ever go *anywhere* without a man, they snowplow all the way down. They sure have fancy clothes though. I saw them in the stores the day they came, buying up everything in sight."

"They're pretty women," I said defensively, "and they like to look their best."

"If their pants were one inch tighter," she said, "they'd strangle to death."

"Your pants aren't so loose either."

"That's my age group," she said. "That's all."

"I thought you said you were going to lead me in Gstaad."

"If you weren't occupied," she said. "Well, you sure look occupied."

"Still, you could have joined us," I said. "The ladies would have been pleased."

"*I* wouldn't," she said flatly. "I bet you're all going to have lunch at the Eagle Club."

"How do you know?"

"You are, aren't you?"

"It happens, yes."

"I knew." There was a note of scornful triumph in her voice. "Women who dress like that always have lunch there."

"You don't even know them."

"This is my second winter in Gstaad. I keep categories."

"Do you want to join us for lunch?"

"Thank you, no. That's not for me. I don't like the conversation. Especially the women. Nibbling away at reputations. Stealing each other's husbands. I'm a little disappointed in you, Mr. Grimes."

"You are? Why?"

"Being in a place like this. With ladies like that."

"They're perfectly nice ladies," I said. "Don't be censorious. They haven't nibbled a reputation yet."

"I *have* to be here," she went on stubbornly. "It's my mother's idea of where a well-bred young lady ought to be while she pursues her education. Education. Hah! How to grow up useless in three languages. And expensive."

The bitterness in her voice was disturbingly adult. It was not the sort of conversation one would expect to have with a pretty, plump, little sixteen-year-old American girl while rising slowly in the sunshine over the fairy-tale landscape of the winter Alps. "Well," I said, knowing it sounded lame, "I'm sure *you're* not going to grow up useless. In no matter how many languages."

"Not if it kills me," she said.

"Do you have any plans?"

"I'm going to be an archaeologist," she said. "I'm going to dig in the ruins of old civilizations. The older the better. I want to get as far away as I can from twentieth-century civilization. At least, my mother's and father's version of twentieth-century civilization."

"I think you're being a little harsh on them," I said. I was defending myself, I suppose, as well as her parents. After all, they belonged almost to the same generation as I did.

"I'd rather not talk about my parents, if you don't mind," she said. "I'd rather talk about you. Are you married yet?"

"No."

"I don't plan to get married either." She looked at me challengingly, as though daring me to comment on this.

"I hear it's going somewhat out of style," I said.

"With good reason," she said. We were approaching the top now and prepared to debark. "If you want to ski with me sometime, *alone* . . ." She accented the word. "Leave a note for me in your box at the hotel. I'll pass by." We got off the chair and took our skis. "Though if I were you," she said as we walked out of the shed into the sunlight, "I wouldn't stay here too long. It isn't your natural habitat."

"What do you think is my natural habitat?"

"I'd say Vermont." She bent and started to put on her skis, limber and competent. "A small town in Vermont, where people work for a living."

I put my skis over my shoulder. The club was just about fifty yards away, on the same level with the top of the lift, and a path was cleared through the snow to the entrance.

"Please don't resent me," she said, straightening up. "I made a decision recently to speak my mind on all occasions."

On an impulse that I didn't understand, I leaned over and kissed her cheek, cold and rosy. "Well, that's very nice," she said. "Thank you. Have a *smashing* lunch." She had obviously overheard Eunice and Lily talking. Then she was off, skating expertly on her skis, toward the bottom of the T-bar that led higher up the mountain. I shook my head as I watched the bulky, little, brightly colored figure moving swiftly across the slope. Then, carrying my skis, I walked toward the massive stone building that housed the club.

Fabian appeared while Eunice, Lily, and I were having our second Bloody Mary on the terrace of the club. He was not dressed for skiing, but looked very smart in a turtleneck sweater and blue, boiled-wool Tyrolean jacket, sharply pressed fawn-colored corduroy pants, and high suede after-ski boots. I was wearing the pair of ski pants and plain blue parka that I had bought off the rack in St. Moritz because they had been the cheapest things in the store, and I felt dowdy next to him. The pants already bagged pathetically in the seat and at the knees. I was sure that the other elegant people on the terrace were whispering about us, wondering what someone who looked and dressed like me was doing with such a group. Didi Wales' remark about my natural habitat had had its effect.

High above, in the brilliant blue sky, a large bird soared on motionless wings. It might well have been an eagle. I speculated on what prey it might find to live off in this glossy valley.

"Have a good morning?" I asked Fabian as he kissed the girls and ordered a Bloody Mary for himself.

"Only time will tell," he said. He enjoyed his little mysteries, Fabian.

I tried not to look worried.

"I hope you don't mind, Douglas," he said. "I've made an appointment in town for us after lunch."

"If the ladies will excuse me," I said.

"I'm sure they'll find some other young man to ski with," Fabian said.

"I'm sure," I said.

"There's a big party tonight," Lily said. "We have to go to the hairdresser, any-way. . . ."

"Am I invited?" I asked.

"Of course," she said. "I've let it be known that we're inseparable."

"Thoughtful of you," I said.

She looked at me sharply. "I'm afraid old Gentle Heart is not having as good a time as he should." Now she was calling me Gentle Heart, too. "Perhaps he prefers the company of younger ladies." She hadn't said anything, but my trip up on the chair lift with Didi Wales hadn't gone unnoticed.

"She's the young daughter of old friends of mine from back home," I said with dignity.

"Ripe for havoc," Lily said. "Let's go in and have lunch. It's cold out here."

The appointment Fabian had arranged was with a real estate dealer with a small office on the main street of the town. Before we went in he explained that he had been looking that morning at plots of land that were for sale. "It might be an interesting investment for us," he said. "As you may have caught on by now, my philosophy is simple. We live in a world in which certain primary elements are becoming scarcer and scarcer. Soybeans, gold, sugar, wheat, oil, et cetera. The economy of the planet is suffering from overpopulation, fright, wars, a bad conscience, and an overabundance of available cash. Put these things together and the moderately sensible, ordinarily pessimistic man knows that the scarcity can only get worse and buys accordingly. Switzerland is a tiny country with a stable government and practically no possibility of getting involved in military adventures. Soon they will be selling land here to frightened money almost by the ounce. Among my own friends and acquaintances I know dozens who would long to own even the smallest bit of it. At the moment, because of Swiss law, they are not permitted to buy. But we have a Swiss company, or a Liechtenstein one, which amounts to the same thing, and there is nothing to stop us from buying an option for six months, say, on a nice chunk of this beautiful country and letting it be known that we are considering building a luxurious nice-sized chalet with a number of fine apartments and renting them in advance for twenty-year leases, say. With the loan that we can swing from a bank, we can be the owners of a highly profitable piece of real estate which will cost us nothing finally and where we might even have a little *pied-à-terre* at no expense to ourselves for our own holidays. Does all this make sense to you?"

"As usual," I said. Actually, it made more sense than usual. I had seen how dizzily prices had risen for small sections of abandoned farmland in Vermont, when ski lifts were put in.

"Dear partner," Fabian said, smiling. "Old Gentle Heart."

By the end of the afternoon we had made an offer for a six-month option on a hilly stretch of ground off the road, about five miles from Gstaad. It would take some time, the agent told us, to arrange the formalities and draw up the contract, but he was sure there would be no important obstacles in our way.

I had never owned anything except the clothes I stood in, but by the time we went back to the hotel for tea I was practically assured, or so Fabian said, of being half-owner of a building that within a year would be worth well over a half-million dollars. The knuckles of my hands showed white with tension as I drove the Jaguar through the town that I now looked at with a new proprietary interest. Fabian merely looked quietly pleased with the day's work. "We are just beginning, Gentle Heart," was all he said, as I parked the car in the lot in front of the hotel.

I was getting dressed for the party when the telephone rang. It was Fabian. "Something's come up," he said. "I can't go with you. Do you mind taking the girls?"

"What is it?"

"I met Bill Sloane in the lobby just now."

"Oh. That's all I need." I felt a prickling at the back of my neck. Bill Sloane had not contributed to my finest hours in Europe.

"Someday you must tell me just what went on between you two."

"Someday," I said.

"He's alone. He sent his wife back to America."

"That's the smartest thing he's done all year. Still," I said, "what's he got to do with your not coming with us?"

"He wants to play cards this evening. Starting just about now."

"I thought you said you were off bridge for life?" Now that Fabian had introduced me to the science of high finance, bridge playing seemed unnecessarily risky. A deck of cards was not like gold ingots or soybean futures or an acre of land in Switzerland.

"He doesn't want to play bridge," Fabian said. "He's got the message about bridge, he says."

"What does he want to play?"

"Head-to-head poker," Fabian said. "In his room."

"Oh, Christ, Miles! Can't you tell him you're busy?"

"I've taken so much loot from him," Fabian said, "I feel I owe him an evening. And I also owe something to my reputation as a gentleman."

"Not to me, you don't."

"Have confidence in me, Gentle Heart," Fabian said.

"What sort of poker player are you?"

"Don't sound so worried. I can take care of myself. Especially with Bill Sloane."

"Famous last words," I said. "Anybody can get lucky for one night."

"If you're so worried, you can come and watch."

"My nerves aren't that good," I said. "And I doubt that Mr. Sloane would be charmed by my presence."

"Anyway, explain to the girls, will you?"

"I'll explain," I said, without grace.

"There's a dear fellow. Really, Douglas, if you're so skeptical, I'll do it on my own. I'll stake myself."

I hesitated, tempted, then felt ashamed. "Forget it," I said. "I'm in for half, win or lose."

"Smashing," he said.

"Yeah," I said. As I hung up I knew the party would have to be one of the greatest social events of the year if I was going to enjoy the evening.

CHAPTER 18

THERE WERE FIFTY guests at the party, with tables set for groups of six and eight in the enormous living room of the chalet, which was furnished in a cottagy and comfortable style, despite its great size. For dinner, there were fresh lobsters flown in that afternoon from Denmark. Two Renoirs and a Matisse, not particularly cottagy, hung on the walls. The lighting was low, to flatter the ladies, but not dim enough to make you feel that you were addressing a shadow when you spoke to your dinner partner. The ladies needed no flattering. They all looked as though at one time or another they had been photographed by my cameraman friend from *Women's Wear Daily*. The acoustics of the room must have been expertly planned, since, even when everybody seemed to be talking at once, the total sound in the room never rose above a polite and pleasant hum.

The host, a tall, gray-haired, hawkish-looking man, I was told, was a retired banker from Atlanta. A soft, agreeable Southern cadence mellowed his speech, and both he and his young wife, a dazzling Swedish lady, seemed genuinely pleased that I had been able to come to their party. It turned out they were celebrating their fifteenth wedding anniversary. If Didi Wales had been invited, she might have revised her ideas about marriage.

There was a general air of sunburned health and off-hand camaraderie among the guests, and through the course of the evening, during which I listened to a good deal of random conversation, I heard no one nibbling away at anybody else's reputation. While I wondered secretly how so many grown men could find the time away from their jobs to achieve the mountaineer bronze that was the standard male complexion, I asked no questions and was asked no question about my profession in return.

Looking around the candlelit room at the immaculate men and the perfectly turned out women, all of them imperiously privileged and at ease with fortune, I felt with added intensity the power of Miles Fabian's arguments in favor of wealth. If there were rifts, divisions, jealousies here, they were not evident, at least to me. Assembled for celebration, the guests were a joyous company of equal friends, secure against disaster, above petty care. As I seated myself next to Eunice, who was radiant in silk, the peer in beauty and grace of manner of any of the beauties in the room, I regarded her with new calculation. I squeezed her hand under the table and got a warm, sensual smile in return.

The talk at the table at which Eunice and I found ourselves was for the most part inconsequential—the usual anecdotes about snow and broken legs that are standard at all ski resorts, interspersed with criticisms of the theater in Paris, London, and New York and the appreciation of recent movies in various languages. The dicta expressed around the table even in the space of a half hour represented an impressive amount of multilingual traveling.

I had seen none of the plays and few of the movies and kept a public silence, whispering from time to time to Eunice, who had also seen all the plays in London and Paris and spoke with authority about them and was listened to respectfully. Lily was at another table, and in her absence Eunice spoke with much more freedom and assurance than usual. It turned out that she had at one time wanted to be an actress and had studied, for a short period, at the Royal Academy of Dramatic Arts. I observed her with fresh interest. If she had neglected to tell me this rather important fact about her life, what other surprises might be in store for me?

The subject of politics came up with the dessert, a lemon sherbet floating in champagne. (I figured, at a rough guess, that the evening must have cost our host at least two thousand dollars, but was slightly ashamed of myself for even thinking in such terms.) Among the men at the table there was a plumpish, smooth-faced American of about fifty who was the head of an insurance company, a French art critic with a sharp black beard, and a burly English banker. The current governments of the three nations were gently but firmly deplored by all three gentlemen. Chauvinism was conspicuous by its absence. If patriotism is the last refuge of scoundrels, there wasn't a scoundrel at the table. The Frenchman complained in nearly perfect English about France, "The foreign policy of France combines the worse elements of Gaullism—egotism, evasiveness, and illusion"; the English banker matched him with, "The English workingman has lost the will to work. And I don't blame him"; the American insurance man contributed, "The doom of the capitalist system was sealed the day the United States sold two million tons of wheat to the Soviet Union."

They all ate their lobster with relish and kept the waiter busy pouring from a seemingly inexhaustible store of bottles of exquisite white wine. I stole a look at the label on one of the bottles—Corton-Charlemagne—and noted it for future great occasions.

I kept silent, although I nodded gravely in agreement from time to time to show that I, too, belonged at the feast. I hesitated to talk, fearing that I somehow would betray my outsiderness, that a single uneasy word might sound a warning among the other guests, unmasking me as a visitor from the lower classes, contemplating revolution perhaps, the dangerous stain of the Hotel St. Augustine, that I had up to now managed to hide, suddenly detectable.

There was dancing after dinner in a huge playroom in the basement. Eunice, who loved to dance, went from partner to partner, while I stood at the bar, drinking, looking at my watch, feeling gloomy and deprived. I had always been a hopeless dancer and had never enjoyed it and certainly wasn't going to make a show of myself on the floor among all those swooping, graceful figures who all seemed to be trained in the latest fashionable steps. I was just on the verge of slipping out and going back to the hotel when Eunice broke away from her partner and came over to me. "Old Gentle Heart," she said. "You're not having a good time."

"Not really."

"I'm sorry. Do you want to go home?"

"I was thinking of it. You don't have to go, you know."

"Don't be a martyr, Gentle Heart. I hate martyrs. I've had enough dancing anyway." She took my hand in hers. "Let's go." She led me around the edge of the dance floor, avoiding Lily. Upstairs, we got our coats and left without saying good-bye to anyone.

We walked along the snowy path, the night cold and crackling around us, the piny air exhilarating after the warmth and noise of the party. When we had gone about two hundred yards and the chalet was only a small glow of light behind us, we stopped as though a signal had passed between us and faced each other and kissed. Once. Then, walking unhurriedly, we went to the hotel.

We picked up our keys and got into the elevator. Without a word Eunice got off at my floor with me. We made a slow, formal parade of our walk down the carpeted hallway. It was as though she, like myself, wanted to savor every moment of the evening.

I opened the door to my room and held it so that Eunice could go in before me. She brushed past me, the cold fur of her coat electric against my sleeve. I went in after her and turned on the lamp in the small hallway.

"Oh, my God!" Eunice cried.

Lying on the big bed, outlined by the light from the hall, was Didi Wales. Asleep. And naked. Her clothes were neatly draped across a chair, with her snow boots primly together beneath it. Her mother, whatever her other failings, had obviously taught her child to be neat.

"Let me out of here," Eunice said in a whisper, as though afraid of what would happen if she wakened the sleeping girl. "This is your baby."

"Eunice . . ." I said forlornly.

"Good night," she said. "Enjoy yourself." She pushed past me and was gone.

I stared down at Didi. Her long blonde hair half-covered her face and her even breathing stirred the ends gently. Her skin in the lamplight was childishly rosy except for her throat and face, darkened by the sun. Her breasts were small and plump, her legs sturdy, athletic, schoolgirl's legs. There was red polish on her toenails. She could have posed for an advertisement for baby food, although somewhat more fully clothed and without the nail polish. Her belly was a little soft mound and the hair beneath it a fuzzy shadow. She slept with her arms rigidly at her sides. It gave her a curious air of lying at attention. If it had been a painting instead of a live, sixteen-year-old girl, it would have been the essence of nude innocence.

But it wasn't a painting. It was a sixteen-year-old girl whose mother and father were, at least technically, friends of mine, and there was no possibility that her intentions in breaking into my room and lying on my bed were in any way innocent. I had the cowardly impulse to steal quietly out of the room and leave her there for the night. Instead, I took off my coat and covered her with it.

The movement awakened her. She opened her eyes slowly and stared up at me, pushing the hair away from her face. Then she smiled. The smile made her look about ten years old.

"God damn it, Didi," I said, "what the hell kind of school do you go to here?"

"It's the kind of school where the girls climb out of the window at night," she said. "I thought it would be nice to surprise you." She was much more in control of her voice than I was.

"You surprised me, all right."

"Aren't you pleased?"

"No," I said. "Definitely not,"

"When you get used to the idea," she said, "maybe you'll change your mind."

"Please, Didi . . ."

"If you're worried because you think I'm a virgin," she said loftily, "you can disabuse yourself. I've already had an affair with a man a lot older than you. A lecherous old Greek."

"I don't want any fancy talk," I said. "I want you to get up off that bed and get dressed and get out of here and go climb back through that window of yours."

"I know you don't really mean that," she said calmly. "You're just making proper noises because you knew me when I was thirteen years old. I'm not thirteen years old anymore."

"I know how old you are," I said, "and it isn't enough."

"Nothing bores me more than having people make-believe I'm a child." Aside from the gesture to push back her hair, she still hadn't moved on the bed. "What's the magic date for you? Twenty, eighteen?"

"There is no magic date, as you call it." I heard my voice go higher and higher with exasperation and sat down across the room from her to retain my dignity and show that I was prepared to be reasonable. "I'm just not in the habit of going to bed with girls of any age after talking to them for ten minutes."

"And I thought you were sophisticated." She put as much scorn into the word as she could manage. "With those fancy ladies and that Jaguar."

"Okay," I said, "I'm not sophisticated. Now will you get up and get dressed?"

"Don't you think I'm pretty? People have told me my body is delectable. Connoisseurs."

"I think you're very pretty. Delectable, if you like. That has nothing to do with it."

"Half the boys in town are trying to get me in bed with them. And plenty of men, if you want the truth."

"I'm sure, Didi. It still has nothing to do with it."

"You talked to me for a lot more than ten minutes, so that's no excuse. We had a long conversation on Suicide Six. I remember, even if you don't."

"This is a ridiculous scene," I said, as firmly and maturely as I could. "I'm ashamed for both of us."

"There's nothing ridiculous about love."

"Love, Didi!" I exploded.

"I was in love with you three years ago . . ." Her voice began to quaver and tears, real or forced, appeared in her eyes, glistening in the lamplight. "And then when I saw you again. I suppose you think you're too old and too worn out to believe in love?"

"I'm nothing of the kind." I decided to try cruelty. "I just happen to have a certain code. And it doesn't include fornicating with silly little girls who throw themselves at my head."

"That's an ugly word for a beautiful emotion." Now she was frankly crying. "I didn't think you were capable of talking like that."

"I'm capable of feeling angry," I said loudly, "and feeling foolish. And I feel both this minute."

"It would serve you right," she said, through sobs, "if I started yelling at the top of my voice and got the whole hotel in here and told everybody you tried to rape me."

"Don't be monstrous, young lady." I stood up now to threaten her. "Just for your information, when I came into the room I was with a friend . . ."

"A friend," she said. "Hah! One of those old bags."

"No matter. If you try anything, she'll tell everybody what she saw when she came into the room—you sleeping naked on the bed. That would fix you and your rape. You'd have to leave town in disgrace."

"I want to leave this miserable town anyway. And disgrace is something you feel yourself, and I wouldn't feel it."

I tried another tack. "Didi, Baby . . ."

"Don't call me Baby. I'm not a baby."

"Okay, I won't call you Baby." I smiled gently at her. "Didi, don't you want me to be your friend?"

"No. I want you to be my lover. Everybody else gets what they want," she wailed. "Why can't I?"

I handed her my handkerchief to wipe away her tears. She also blew her nose. I was glad that there was an automatic lock on the door so that nobody could come into the room and see us. I refrained from telling her that when she reached my age she would find out everybody didn't get what they wanted. Not by a long shot.

"You kissed me on the hill today, when we got off the lift," she cried. "What did you do that for if you didn't mean it?"

"There are kisses and kisses," I said. "I apologize if you misunderstood."

Suddenly she threw the coat off her and sat up in the bed. She put out her arms. "Try it once more," she said.

I took a step back, involuntarily. "I'm leaving," I said, as convincingly as I could. "If you're still here when I get back, I'm going to call your school to come and get you."

She laughed. "Coward," she taunted me, "coward, coward."

In full possession of the field, she was still repeating the word when I got out of the door.

*   *   *   *   *   *   *   *   *   *   *   *   *   *   *   *   *

I went down to the bar. I needed a drink. Luckily, there was no one I knew there and I sat on a stool in the dim light, staring into my glass. I had thought I could live by accident, taking everything that was offered as it came along—the long tube on the floor of room 602; Evelyn Coates in Washington; Lily in Florence; the outlandish proposition of that not quite certifiably sane man, Miles Fabian, slightly bloodied from where I had broken the lamp over his head; buying a racehorse; investing in a dirty French movie; dabbling in gold and soybeans; saying, Why not? when Fabian had suggested inviting an unknown British girl to join us; venturing into Swiss real estate; backing him for half, even as I sat there, in a head-to-head poker game against a rich and vengeful American gambler.

But there were limits. And Didi Wales had reached them. I told myself I had behaved honorably—no decent man would take advantage of the freakish, adolescent passion of an unhappy child. But I was nagged, in the quiet of the midnight bar, by a small, disturbing doubt. If Eunice hadn't gone into the room with me to discover Didi lying there, would I be in the bar now? Or still in my room? In retrospect, sitting alone staring into a glass, I had to admit that the girl had been marvelously attractive. Regret played in a little scudding cloud at the outer reaches of my conscience. What would Miles Fabian have done, confronted with a similar situation? Chuckled good-naturedly, said, "What a charming visit?" Thought, this is my lucky year, and climbed into bed? No doubt.

I resolved not to tell him a word about it. His scorn, tempered only by pity for my scruples, would be unbearable. I could just hear him say, mildly, paternally, "Finally, Douglas, one *must* learn the rules of the game."

Eunice. I broke into a light sweat as I thought of the next morning's breakfast, with Lily and Miles Fabian, and Eunice saying, over the orange juice and coffee cups, "The most extraordinary thing happened last night when old Gentle Heart and I got back from the party . . ."

I finished my drink, signed for it, and started toward the door. Just as I reached it, Lily came in with three enormous men, not one of them under six feet four. I had noticed them at the party and had seen Lily dancing with one of them. This seemed to be her night for size and quantity. She stopped when she saw me. "I thought I saw you go off with Eunice," she said.

"I did."

"And now you're alone?"

"I am."

She shook her head. There was an amused glint in her eye. "Peculiar man," she said. "Do you want to join us?"

"I'm not large enough," I said.

The three men laughed, their laughter resounding like bowling balls off the bottles behind the bar. "Have you seen Miles?" Lily asked.

"No."

"He said he'd try to make it for a nightcap by one." She shrugged. "I guess he's so immersed in stripping that desperate oaf Sloane of his last penny he can't be bothered with poor little me. Did you like the party?"

"Smashing," I said.

"It was almost like being in Texas," she said ambiguously. "Shall we drink, chaps?"

"I'll order the champagne," the tallest of the men said, lurching along the tables toward the bar like an ocean liner pulling out of a slip.

"Night, Gentle Heart," Lily said. "Persist." She leaned over and kissed my cheek. Instant memories. I bowed a little and went out.

Ripe for havoc, she had said about Didi Wales. How right she was.

A minute later I was at the door of Eunice's room. I listened, but there was no sound inside. I didn't know what I expected to hear. Weeping? Laughter? Sounds of revelry? I knocked, waited, knocked again.

The door opened. Eunice was standing there in a lace dressing gown. "Oh, it's you," she said. Her tone was neither welcoming nor unwelcoming.

"May I come in?"

"If you want."

"I want."

She held the door wider and I went in. Her clothes were piled haphazardly all over the room. The window was open and a cold Alpine breeze was whistling in. I shivered a little, my resistance to the elements weakened by the events of the night. "Aren't you cold?" I asked.

"Remember, I'm English," she said. But she closed the window. Full-bodied, barefooted, rustling of lace.

"May I sit down?"

"If you wish." She indicated a little upholstered chair. "Throw those clothes anywhere."

I picked up the silk dress she had worn at the party. I imagined it was still warm from her skin. I laid it gently across a little writing desk. I sat down on the chair and she lay back against the piled pillows on the bed, her legs revealed as the dressing gown fell away. She had long legs like her sister, but fuller. Shapelier, I thought. I smelled lightly scented soap. She had scrubbed her face when she undressed, and her skin glowed in the light of the bedside lamp.

I mourned for the evening.

"Eunice," I said, "I came to explain."

"You don't have to explain. Somebody got their appointments mixed, that's all."

"You don't think I asked that little girl to come up to my room, do you?"

"I don't think *anything*. She was just there. And she's not that little. Well-developed, I'd call it." Her tone was flat, weary. "One of us was *de trop*. I happened to think it was me."

"Tonight," I said, "I thought, finally . . ."

"That was my impression, too." She smiled wryly.

"I wish I could have been bolder," I said, "I mean even before tonight. Only I'm not built that way." I made a small helpless gesture with my hands. "And then there were always Miles and your sister."

"Miles and my sister. Didn't my sister tell you there were no preliminaries necessary with me?" Her voice took on a sudden harshness.

"I won't say what your sister told me."

"She likes to give the impression that I'm the wildest girl in London. Bitch," she said. "On the fingers of one hand."

"What's that?" I asked, puzzled.

"Never mind." She lay back in the piled pillows and crossed her arms over her face. She talked, muffled, through soft flesh. "If you must know, I didn't come to Zurich for you. Whoever you might have turned out to be. Though you turned out to be much dearer than I had ever imagined an American could be, Gentle Heart."

"Thanks," I said.

"I'm sorry if you're disappointed."

"We could forget the little accident in my room, you know."

I could see her head shaking behind her arms. "Not me. I should really be grateful to that naked fat girl. Because I was coming up to your room for all the wrong reasons."

"What do you mean by that?"

"I wasn't doing it for you. Or for me."

"Who, then?"

"For Miles Fabian," she said bitterly. "I was going to have the most blatant, sexy, public affair with you anyone could imagine—to show him—"

"To show him what?"

"To show him that I didn't care a penny's worth for him anymore. That I could be as fickle and callous as he was." She was weeping now behind her arms. It had turned out to be my night for feminine tears.

"I think you had better explain, Eunice," I said slowly.

"Don't be dense, American," she said. "I'm in love with Miles Fabian. Have been since the day I met him. I asked him to marry me years ago. So he fled. Into the arms of my bitch sister."

"Oh." For the moment, it was all I could say.

She took her arms away from her face. The tears had made gleaming silvery streaks on her cheeks. But her expression was calm, relieved. "If you hurry," she said, "maybe that little fat girl will still be there. So the evening won't be a total waste."

But Didi had already gone, leaving a note in schoolgirl handwriting on the desk. "I took your coat. So I would have a memento. Maybe one day you'll want to get it. You know where I am. Love. Didi."

As I was finishing reading, the phone rang. I nearly didn't answer it. It was not a night on which I could expect good news over the telephone.

I picked it up.

"Douglas?" It was Fabian.

"Yes?"

"I hope I didn't interrupt you at anything serious," he said with the hint of a chuckle.

"No."

"I thought you might like to hear how it went tonight."

"I certainly would."

There was a little sigh on the phone. "I'm afraid I didn't do so well, old chap. Sloane had a phenomenal streak of luck. We'll have to do some banking in the morning."

"How much?"

"Around thirty thousand," Fabian said matter-of-factly.

"Francs?"

"Dollars, Gentle Heart."

"Son of a bitch," I said, and hung up.

CHAPTER 19

THE NEXT MORNING the following things happened to me.

On my breakfast tray, which I called for at ten o'clock, because I hadn't been able to fall asleep until nearly dawn, there was a note from Eunice. "Dear Gentle Heart, I am taking the nine o'clock train out of Gstaad. I'm sure you understand why I'm doing this. Love."

I understood.

Miles Fabian called on the telephone and asked me to meet him in town in front of the Union Bank of Switzerland at eleven o'clock.

I was arrested. Or at the time, it seemed that I was arrested.

I was shaving, looking with distaste at my yellowed eyes in the mirror, when there was a knock at the door. With the lather still on my face, I went to the door. One of the assistant managers was standing there, correct in his dark suit and white shirt, with a squat man in a belted dark overcoat and a porcupine head of gray hair, cut short.

"Mr. Grimes," the assistant manager said, "may we come in?"

"I'm shaving," I said. "And as you see, I'm not dressed." All I had on was the bottom of my pajamas and I was barefooted. "Can't it wait a few minutes?"

The assistant manager spoke rapidly in German to the gray-haired man, who said only one word. *"Nein."*

"Police Officer Brugelmann says it can't wait," the assistant manager said apologetically.

Police Officer Brugelmann walked past me into the room.

"After you, Mr. Grimes." The assistant manager bowed a little.

I went into the bathroom, got a towel, and wiped the lather off my face and put on a bathrobe. Police Officer Brugelmann stood in the middle of the room, his eyes roaming icily over the bureau, on top of which I had my wallet and money clip and watch, then onto the two suitcases set on stands under the windows.

Didi, I thought; oh, my God, they've found out about Didi. Or believe they've found out. I had no idea what the age of consent was in Switzerland. Probably it varied from canton to canton, like everything else in the country. We were in the canton of Bern. It could be anything up to twenty-one, with all those girls' schools.

"I consider this an intrusion," I said coldly. "And I'd like an explanation immediately."

Again, the assistant manager spoke rapidly in German to the policeman. The policeman nodded. He had an extremely stiff mechanical nod. His neck was thick and rolled over his collar.

"Police Officer Brugelmann has authorized me to explain," the assistant manager said. "Briefly, Mr. Grimes, a robbery has been committed. Last night. On floor number five of the hotel. A valuable diamond necklace has been reported missing."

Eunice's room had been on the fifth floor. "What's that got to do with me?" I asked, relieved. At least Didi Wales wasn't involved.

There was another exchange in German. Before I leave for anywhere next time, I thought, I'm going to Berlitz.

"You have been noticed last night, late, prowling in the halls of the hotel," the assistant manager said.

"I was visiting a friend," I said. "I was not prowling."

"I was merely translating," the assistant manager said unhappily. He was not enjoying the task and was probably regretting he had ever bothered to learn English.

The police officer said something softly.

"The lady you were visiting," the assistant manager said, "checked out of the hotel at eight thirty this morning. Do you happen to know her destination?"

"No," I said. Almost honestly. I had never asked Eunice for her address. The note she had sent me was crammed into the pocket of my bathrobe. I hoped it didn't show.

The police officer rattled out several sentences that sounded unpleasant.

"The police officer asks permission to search the premises," the assistant manager said. The words seemed to strangle in his throat.

"Does he have a warrant?" I asked, American to the last civil rights, *amicus curiae,* Supreme Court brief.

There was another exchange in German.

"There is no warrant. As yet," the assistant manager said. "If you insist on a warrant, Police Officer Brugelmann says he will have to take you to the bureau of police and keep you there until the warrant is made out. He warns that it may take a long time. Maybe two days. There will be no avoiding publicity, he says. There are always many foreign newspapermen here. Because of the quality and prominence of our guests."

"Did *he* say all that?" I asked.

"I added some on my own," the assistant manager admitted. "So that you can have a proper basis for action."

I stared at Police Officer Brugelmann. He stared back glacially. It was warm in the room, but he hadn't unbuttoned his overcoat. He was a naturally cryogenic man. Snakes and birds were his blood cousins. "All right," I said. I seated myself in an easy chair. "I have nothing to hide. Let him start looking. But please make it quick. I have an appointment at eleven."

The assistant manager translated and Police Officer Brugelmann nodded stiffly in satisfaction. Then he motioned for me to stand up.

"What does he want now?" I asked.

"He wants to look at the chair."

I stood up, admiring, despite myself, the talent for his profession of Police Officer Brugelmann. Naturally, if the necklace was hidden in the chair, I would immediately sit on it. I moved away and watched the police officer run his hand over the cushion, then pick it up and poke down into the upholstery. Then he put the cushion back, patting it neatly, and motioned politely that I could seat myself again.

After that, he went swiftly through all my belongings. When he had gone through the closet, he took out my ski pants and held them up, saying something to the assistant manager, obviously, from his tone, a question. The assistant manager fidgeted nervously with the button of his jacket as he translated. "Police Officer Brugelmann wishes to know," he said, "if these ski trousers are the only ones you have brought with you."

"Yes," I said.

"Where it wass you wass before?" The police officer was getting impatient with the business of translation and now showed that he could speak a variant of English.

"St. Moritz," I said, "Davos."

"St. Moritz? With only *these?*" The police officer sounded incredulous. "And now Gstaad, too?"

"They do the job," I said.

"How long you plan the entire holiday iss to endure, Mr. Grimes?"

"Three weeks. Perhaps more."

Solemnly, the police officer hung the pants back in the closet. Then he turned back to me, taking out a black, plastic-covered pad as he did so, and seating himself at the small desk, so that he could write comfortably. "Now I am afraid I must some questions ask," he said. "Permanent address in the United States?"

I nearly said the Hotel St. Augustine, then gave him the address on East Eighty-first Street. It was as permanent as anything else and if Interpol, or whoever it might be, inquired, at least they couldn't accuse me of lying.

"Profession?" The police officer kept his head down as he laboriously wrote in his pad.

"Private investor," I said briskly.

"Bank?"

From the expression on his face I knew that sooner or later I would have to explain this more fully.

The water was getting deep. "Union Bank of Switzerland. Zurich." I thanked Miles Fabian in my heart as I said this for having insisted on our opening separate accounts in each of our names there for what he called walking-around money.

"In America?"

"I've given up banking in America," I said. "I'm considering moving to Europe. The economy . . ."

"Have you ever been arrested before?" The police officer said.

"Now, see here," I appealed to the assistant manager. "I'm a guest in this hotel. It's supposed to be one of the best hotels in Europe. I don't have to answer insulting questions like that."

"It is only standard police procedure." The button on the assistant manager's coat was almost off by now. "It is not personal. Others are being questioned, too."

The policeman didn't look up from his pad, writing and talking at the same time.

"You know Mr. Miles Fabian, don't you?" I said.

"Of course. Mr. Fabian is an old and honored guest of ours," said the assistant manager.

"Well, he's my good friend. Why don't you call him and ask him about me?"

The assistant manager spoke in swift German. The police officer nodded and said, "Before haff you ever been arrested?"

"No, by God!"

"One thing more." The police officer stood up. "I would like your passport."

"What do you need my passport for?"

"To make sure you remain in Switzerland, Herr Grimes."

"What if I don't give my passport?"

"Then other measures I would have to take. Like confining you. Swiss prisons are of a good reputation. But they are still prisons."

"Please, Mr. Grimes," the assistant manager said.

I went over to my wallet and took out my passport. "I am going to see a lawyer," I said to Officer Brugelmann, as I gave him the passport.

"You are at liberty," he said, stuffing the passport into an inside pocket of his black coat. "Please, keep yourself free for other questions. I belieff that iss all for the moment." He nodded, working the stiff hinge of his powerful cantonal neck, and went out.

The assistant manager wrung his hands. "I offer you the sincere apologies of the management. This is terribly embarrassing for all of us."

"Us?" I said. I had no intention of making things easy for him.

"It is these careless rich women," he said. "They have no idea of the value of money. They leave eighty thousand dollars worth of jewelry in the train and then there is hysteria for days while we try to recover it. Luckily, we are in Switzerland . . ."

"You have no idea how lucky I feel to be in Switzerland, brother," I said. I now regretted bitterly the option we had taken on the land for the condominium the day before.

"Anything the management can do, Mr. Grimes . . ." the assistant manager said piously. "We will leave no stone unturned."

"The management can get my passport back," I said. "That's what the management can do. I want to leave the country. Fast."

"I understand." He bowed. "The foehn is blowing." He touched his forehead as though ascertaining the degree of fever he was running. "The south wind. Everybody behaves curiously. Let me say something personal, Mr. Grimes. I, myself, do not believe you are a criminal."

"Thanks," I said.

"Enjoy your day's skiing," he said automatically.

"I'll do my best," I said.

He backed out, twisting at his button.

Fabian was waiting for me in front of the bank in his dapper Tyrolean outfit. He was as healthy-looking as ever and no one could have suspected that he had sat up half the night losing thirty thousand dollars. He smiled charmingly as I walked up to him, then frowned at what must have been the expression on my face. "I say, old man, is something wrong?" he said.

I didn't know where to begin, so I said, "Everything is dandy."

"I heard about Eunice. Leaving, I mean. I imagine that was a blow to you." He was the essence of discreet sympathy.

"First things first," I said. "Let's do our banking." I would discuss Eunice with him another time, when I had cooled down and there was no danger that I would hit him on the jaw.

"Sorry about that," he said, as he took me by the elbow and guided me into the bank. "Sloane had a lifetime's worth of luck last night. I gave him an IOU. He wants it all in cash. I promised it by four this afternoon. I've already called Zurich to send it over, but there are certain formalities . . ." He shrugged. "Swiss bankers."

We went in and were quizzed by a young man in a back room, who then called our bank in Zurich and spoke lengthily in German. He kept looking up from the phone at Fabian and myself, and I gathered that he was describing us minutely. He asked me for my passport number and luckily I remembered it. After about fifteen-minutes' conversation with Zurich, he hung up and said, "Very good, gentlemen; the money will be ready at four o'clock."

When we were out of the bank, Fabian said, "I promised Lily I'd ski with her this afternoon. No need to let her in on the drama, is there?"

"No," I said.

"I could use a little air and exercise after last night," he said. "It wasn't exactly a health cure." It was the one intimation that the hours of play had not been completely enjoyable. He stopped as we reached the car, which he had parked a few yards away from the bank. "I say, Douglas, I'm concerned about you. You *do* look glum. It's only money, after all. We're still far ahead of the game . . ."

"That's not why I look so glum," I said, and told him about the visit of the policeman. I didn't tell him about Didi Wales or Eunice or prowling around the halls.

He chuckled, as though I had told him a mildly funny story. "*Did* you take the necklace?" he asked.

"God damn it, Miles," I said, "what sort of man do you think I am?"

"I'm beginning to know you, old boy," he said. "And after all, you *have* been around hotels for quite a few years."

"One hotel," I said. "And the most anyone could pick up there would be a pair of dime-store cuff links."

"May I remind you that you did better than that?" he said coolly. For the first time I realized that he could believe that I might have done it. "Considerably better than that."

"Oh, shit," I said. "Let's go skiing."

We didn't speak in the car driving back to the hotel. It was not the happiest day of our partnership.

Fabian skied fairly well, making the right movements just a little bit wrongly. He had obviously had a good deal of instruction. He was not reckless, and I kept far enough ahead of him and Lily so that there was no conversation possible between us. Lily had started to ask me about Eunice. "Really, Gentle Heart," she said, "what in the world did you do to my poor little sister to make her skulk away like a thief in the night?"

"Ask your sister," I said. "If you ever see her again."

"Oh, this foehn," Lily said. "It makes everybody so grumpy."

She, too, with the south wind.

Sloane came into the club while we were eating lunch. He came over to our table promptly, his ski boots making even more noise than ski boots usually make. His face was florid and triumphant and he looked as though he had been drinking. I could hear his heavy breathing two yards away. I put down my knife and fork. Any desire to eat had suddenly left me.

"Hello, folks," Sloane said. "Isn't this a great day?"

"Great," Fabian said, sipping at his wine.

"Aren't you going to invite me to sit down with you for lunch?" Sloane said.

"No," said Fabian.

Sloane grinned, his eyes eternally, congenitally hostile. "That's what I like," he said, "a bad loser." He dug into his pocket and dug out a piece of the hotel stationery, with a few lines written on it. "Fabian," he said, "you're not going to forget this, are you?"

"Don't be rude," Fabian said coldly. "There's a lady present."

"Good day, ma'am," Sloane said, as though he was noticing Lily for the first time. "I believe we met. Last year at St. Moritz."

"I remember you well, sir," Lily said, abruptly eighteenth century.

Sloane folded the sheet of paper carefully and put it back into his pocket. Then he turned his attention to me. He tapped me heavily on the shoulder. "What the hell are you doing here, Grimes? I thought you broke your goddamn leg."

"It was a mistaken diagnosis," I said.

"Break into any more hotel rooms lately, Smart Boy?"

I looked around uneasily. Sloane's voice was loud and clear, but nobody seemed to be listening. "Only last night," I said.

"Full of jokes, this boy," Sloane said. "He's a shoe fetishist." He laughed hoarsely, his eyes venomous and bloodshot in their wrinkled pouches. He was the sort of man who could destroy relations between friendly nations in the space of a half hour. The thought of our having to hand over thirty thousand dollars to this American peasant at four o'clock that afternoon made me ache.

"How's the watch trade, boy?" he boomed. "Just as thriving as on the other side of Switzerland?"

"Fuck off, Sloane," I said. As I spoke, I felt new blood coursing happily through my veins and my appetite returning.

He laughed, uninsultable, at least for today. "Be careful of this feller," he said to Fabian. "He's quirky." He laughed hollowly. "Well," he said, "if I'm not invited to the party, I might as well ski. I stayed up late last night and I have to blow the cobwebs out. See you at four o'clock at the hotel, Fabian." His tone was no longer joking.

He clumped out of the room. Fabian sighed. "The people you have to do business with," he said.

"Americans," Lily said. Then she put her hand on my arm. "Forgive me, Gentle Heart. I didn't mean you."

"Americans are like anyone else," Fabian said. "Some don't export well. I've seen some English in my time . . ."

"As have I," Lily said.

"I forgive everybody," I said. "Don't you think we ought to have another bottle of wine?" My nerves needed some soothing, and if I was going to ski after lunch, a good dose of alcohol might prevent me from breaking something. Also, sitting at the table with Fabian and Lily, calmly and composedly working at their food, I felt myself on the verge of launching into a bitter harangue against them both, blurt out the confession of the meeting in Florence, the details of what Eunice had told me in her cold room the night before. The temptation to tell Fabian that I was through with him once and for all was strong and would have given me immense immediate satisfaction, but our affairs were so hopelessly intertwined that to disentangle them would probably take years, if it ever possibly could be done. The gesture would only make it more difficult. So I concentrated on my food and on the new bottle of wine when it came and hardly listened as Fabian and Lily chatted away.

"Mr. Fabian, Mr. Fabian . . ." It was a young ski instructor hurrying into the restaurant, his voice strained and high. Ordinarily the ski instructors did not eat in the same room with the guests, and the people at the other tables looked up in nondemocratic disapproval from their meals as the ski instructor ran down the aisle.

"Yes?" Fabian motioned for the boy to keep his voice down. "What is it?"

"Your friend," the instructor said. "Mr. Sloane. You'd better come. He was just bending down to put on his skis . . ."

"Not so loud, please, Hans," Fabian said. He knew everybody's name. It was one of the things about him that made him so popular with waiters and concierges. "What is it?"

"He just went *poomp*," the instructor said. "He dropped like a log. I think he's dead."

Fabian looked across at me, a peculiar expression in his eyes. I could have sworn it was amusement.

"Nonsense, Hans," he said sharply. "I believe I'd better take a look. Lily, I think perhaps you should stay here. Douglas, may I ask you to come along with me?" He got up and walked swiftly, his face grave, with all eyes upon him, toward the door. I followed. Our ski boots sounded like a company of infantry crossing a bridge. A drum roll for a loud American, with an IOU for thirty thousand dollars in his pocket.

A small crowd was grouped around the exit of the chair lift, where people put on their skis to traverse to the T-bar. The afternoon was suddenly very quiet. Sloane was lying on his back, staring up at the sky. Another ski teacher was rubbing snow on his face, which was a terrible purple and green. Fabian got down on one knee beside the body and tore open the zipper of Sloane's anorak and pulled up the sweater and shirt underneath. Sloane's chest was hairy and white. I started to shake in cold, involuntary shudders. I could feel my teeth set like clamps in my jaws. Fabian leaned over and put his ear to Sloane's chest. It seemed hours before Fabian lifted his head. Slowly he pulled Sloane's shirt and sweater down and zipped up the anorak. "I think we'd better take him down to the hospital," Fabian said to the two instructors. "As quickly as possible." He stood up, rubbing his face as if to hide his sorrow. "Poor man," he said, "he was a heavy drinker. The altitude and the sudden cold . . . If you'll carry him to the lift," he said to the instructors, "I'll go down with him. Just call for an ambulance to be waiting at the bottom. Douglas, may I speak to you for a moment . . .?" He put his arm around my shoulders and led me to one side, two friends of the newly departed seeking a moment alone to soften the blow of the tragic loss of a comrade. Right out of an old wartime B movie, I thought, playing my part with conviction. The crowd, which had now grown larger, parted respectfully.

"Douglas, my boy," Fabian whispered, patting my shoulder as if to console me, "I will not leave the corpse. I'll get the IOU out of his pocket on the way down. Do you remember which side it was on?"

"That's what I call showing a decent respect for the dead," I said. "Left."

"I admire your attitude, Gentle Heart." He pulled me to him in a manly embrace, as though to keep me from breaking down. "I must say, old chap," he said, "you *are* Johnny-on-the-spot when it comes to heart attacks." Then he dropped his arm and said aloud, so that everybody could hear what he was saying. "I'll leave you to break the news to Lily. She'll be undone. Give her a stiff brandy."

Then he walked, his head down, along the snowy path to the lift, where the two ski instructors were securely strapping the corpse onto one of the two-seater chairs. Fabian got into the second seat and put his arm protectively around the dead man. He gave a signal and the chair began to move slowly down the hill.

The two ski teachers took the next chair down. Honorary pallbearers, in bright jackets, descending into the valley to help dispose of the dead.

I went back into the club, where Lily was finishing her coffee, and ordered two brandies.

CHAPTER 20

WHEN I GOT back to the hotel, I was told by the concierge that Mr. Fabian expected me to come up to his room. It was late in the afternoon. Lily and I had had several more brandies, sitting in silence as the restaurant slowly emptied. Death makes for long lunches.

I had left Lily at the hairdresser's. "No sense," she had said, "in wasting the whole afternoon." We had taken the chair lift out of a sense of decorum. Skiing down, we agreed, after what had happened, would have seemed frivolous. Neither of us had spoken of Eunice.

"What was the last thing you said to the man?" Lily asked as we swung slowly toward the shadowed valley.

"Fuck off," I said.

She nodded. "That's what I thought you said. Hail and Farewell." She gestured toward the peaks in the distance, still glowing in sunlight. The eagle, if that was what it was, was back on station, patrolling the neutral Helvetian air. "There are worse places to die." She chuckled. "And worse last words. If there's any justice, he cut that wife of his out of his will."

"I'm sure he didn't."

"I said, if there's any justice."

"Do you think your husband has cut you out of *his* will?"

"Don't be so American," she said.

We left it at that.

On the way back to the hotel I stepped off at a shop and bought myself a topcoat. Didi Wales was welcome to her memento. It was a small price to pay for her absence.

Fabian was packing when I arrived at the suite he shared with Lily. He did not travel light. There were four big suitcases scattered around the two rooms. As usual, there were newspapers everywhere, opened to the financial pages. He packed swiftly and neatly, shoes in one bag, shirts in another, in crisp perfect piles. "I'm accompanying the body home," he said. "It's the least I can do, don't you think?"

"The least," I said.

"You were correct," he said. "The IOU was in the left pocket. The formalities will all be taken care of before this evening. The Swiss are very efficient when it comes to getting a dead foreigner out of the country. He was only fifty-two. A choleric man. Premature destruction. A lesson for us all. I called his wife. She took the news bravely. She's going to meet us—the coffin and myself—at Kennedy tomorrow. She's making the necessary dreary arrangements. By the way, do you happen to know where Lily is?"

"Getting her hair done."

"Unflappable girl. I admire that in her." He picked up the phone and asked for the hairdresser's. While he was waiting for the call to be put through, he said, "Would you mind driving us down to Geneva tomorrow?"

"If the police let me out of town," I said. "They still have my passport."

"Oh," Fabian said, "I nearly forgot." He took my passport out of his pocket and tossed it onto a table. "Here it is."

"How did you get it?" Somehow I was not surprised that he had it. Partially against my will he had established himself in my imagination as a looming father-figure, capriciously powerful, solver of problems and mysteries, mover of men and laws. I thumbed through the passport to see if there was anything added or missing. I could see nothing to indicate that I had been suspected of crime.

"The assistant manager gave it to me when I came in," Fabian said carelessly. "They found the necklace."

"Who stole it?"

"Nobody. The lady had it stuffed in a ski boot for safekeeping and forgot where she'd put it. Her husband found it this afternoon. The assistant manager was writhing in apology. There's a large bouquet of flowers and a magnum of champagne waiting for you in your room as a sign of the hotel's mortification. Hello, hello," he said into the phone, "may I speak to Lady Abbott, please?" Then to me. "You don't mind being left alone for a few days, do you?"

"Frankly," I said, "nothing could please me more."

He arched his eyebrows. "Well . . ." he said.

"I feel as though I've been running cross-country for weeks," I said. "I could use a little holiday."

"I thought you were enjoying yourself." There was a touch of reproach in his voice.

"Everybody to his own opinion," I said.

"Lily," Fabian said into the phone, "I have to go to America tomorrow. Two or three weeks, at the outside. Do you want to come?" He listened for a moment, smiled. "That's my girl," he said. "You'd better get back rather quickly and start packing."

He hung up. "She loves New York," he said. "We'll be staying at the St. Regis. In case you want to keep in touch."

"Roughing it, aren't you?"

He shrugged, went back to his packing. "It's convenient," he said. "And I like the bar. Actually, even if this hadn't come up, I would have had to fly over in a day or two anyway. I want to put together the chalet deal and just about everybody I can think of is on the East Coast. I may have to go down to Palm Beach for a week or so, too. After the funeral."

"Rough country."

"I sense a certain resentment on your part, Douglas." He frowned at a cashmere sweater he was folding. "I don't think I'll need this, do you?"

"Not in Palm Beach, you won't."

"You make it sound as though I'm going on this trip for pleasure." Again I heard a mild reproach. "I assure you I'd much rather go down to Italy with you. As a matter of fact, there's something I'd like you to do for me—for us—after you get to Rome. I've been in touch with a charming Italian gentleman. Name of Quadrocelli. Italians have all the luck when it comes to choosing names, don't they? I'll send the dottore a wire to expect you. A nice little enterprise that's waiting to be wrapped up."

"What's that?"

"Don't sound so suspicious."

"You must admit your last enterprise was hardly a howling success."

"It worked out all right in the end, didn't it?" Fabian said cheerfully.

"I don't think we can count on *everybody* we do business with dropping dead on payday."

Fabian laughed, showing his excellent teeth beneath the neat moustache. "Who can tell? I myself am now approaching the crucial age."

"It would take an ax to do you in, Miles," I said. "And you know it."

He laughed again. "Anyway, you can explain the circumstances to Dottore Quadrocelli. Why I couldn't come in person. You'll find him in Porto Ercole. That's just about two hours north of Rome. It's a delightful place. I had hoped to spend at least two weeks there. There's a first-class small hotel overlooking the Med. It's called the Pellicano. An ideal place to hide out with a girl." He sighed, regretting the first-class small hotel overlooking the Med. "Lily adores it. Later in the year, perhaps. Ask for the room with the big terrace. The good dottore has a villa not far from there."

"What have you got going *this* time?"

"I wish you wouldn't sound so surly, old man. I like contented partners."

"My nerves aren't as strong as yours."

"No, I suppose they're not. Wine."

"What?"

"You asked me what I had going this time. What I have going is wine. With the way the world's drinking these days, being in wine is like having a license to steal. Have you noticed how the prices for any kind of bottle have been going up? Especially in America."

"I can't say I have."

"Trust me, they have. Quadrocelli has a small estate outside Florence. He makes a delicious Chianti. So far, on a very small scale. Just for himself and his friends. He's surrounded by a lot of small farmers who also grow wine of the same quality. We played with the idea last summer of contracting to buy the crop of his neighbors, having a pretty label drawn up, and bottling it under his name and selling it in the States directly to restaurant chains. Eliminate all the middlemen. You can imagine the advantages."

"I can't really," I said. "I've never eliminated a middleman in my life. But I suppose it's enough if *you* can."

"Believe me," he said. "It would take a little capital, of course. Mr. Quadrocelli doesn't have the necessary and last summer, as you can imagine, neither did I."

"And now you have."

"*We* have. First person plural, old man." He patted my arm in a brotherly gesture. "Forever and a day. I've been in touch with Mr. Quadrocelli and he's working out a set of figures. I'd appreciate it if you'd look them over and call me in New York so we can discuss it. In fact, I think it would be a good idea if you called me every few days, say at ten o'clock New York time. There's always something coming up."

"That's no lie," I said.

"Keeps the blood circulating," he said airily. "Tell Mr. Quadrocelli that on my side I'll be lining up restaurants in the States. Luckily, I have some dear friends who are in the business. Very much in the business. In fact, they've been after me to come in with them as vice-president in charge of public relations. But it would mean going to an office every day. Unthinkable. No matter what the money is. It would also mean smiling all the time. Not my cup of tea, at all. But they'd absorb a lot of wine."

"Miles," I said, "how many other schemes have you got at the back of your head that you're going to spring on me one at a time?"

He laughed. "I don't like to worry you about projects until they ripen, Gentle Heart. You should thank me."

"I thank you," I said.

"After dinner," he said, "I'll give you Quadrocelli's address and telephone number. Also the address of my tailor in Rome. Tell him you're a friend of mine. I suggest a complete wardrobe. I'll also give you the address of a very good shirtmaker. I also suggest throwing away your present wardrobe. It does nothing for our mutual image, if you get what I mean. I hope I'm not hurting your feelings."

"On the contrary," I said. "I understand. By the time you see me again, I'll be a credit to you."

"That's better," he said. "Would you like the telephone numbers of some lovely Italian girls?"

"No, I'll do it alone, thank you, if you don't mind."

"I just thought you might like to save a little time."

"I'm in no hurry."

"Finally," he said, "we'll have to try to uproot the old Puritan in you. Meanwhile I suppose I'll have to take you as you come."

"The way I take you."

He had been going in and out of the bedroom through all this, coming out with various articles of clothing that he stowed in one bag or another. Now he emerged with the pretty blue Tyrolean jacket. "This would look very good on you, Douglas," he said. "It's a little large for me. Would you like it?"

"No, thanks. I've had my skiing for the year," I said.

He nodded soberly. "I understand. What happened today took the edge off Alpine joys a bit."

"I never wanted to come here in the first place."

"Sometimes you have to do things to please the ladies," Fabian said. "Apropos of that. Do you want to tell me why Eunice decamped?"

"Not particularly."

"I regret you didn't see fit to take my advice," Fabian said. "It was good advice."

"Oh, come on, now, Miles! Enough is enough. She told me everything." Somehow, the sight of this handsome, completely composed man, every hair in place, his trousers and shirt fitting him perfectly, his shoes with a high mahogany shine, deftly packing his array of bags, the perfect traveler for the jet age, suddenly infuriated me. "All about you. Or at least enough about you."

"I haven't the faintest notion of what you're talking about, old man." He tucked a half-dozen pairs of socks neatly into a corner of a suitcase. "What in the world would there be to tell about me?"

"She's in love with you."

"Oh, dear," he said.

"You had an affair with her. I'm not in the business of accepting hand-me-downs."

"Oh, dear," he said again. "She said that?"

"And more."

"Ever since I've met you," he said, "I've worried about your innocence. You have a terribly low threshold of shock. People have affairs. It's a fact of life. People you're associated with. More or less permanently. Good God, man, have you ever been to a wedding at which the bride hasn't had an affair with at least one of the guests?"

"You might have told me," I said, knowing it sounded foolish.

"What good would that have done? Be reasonable. I suggested her to you with the best intentions in the world. For both you and her. I can vouch for the fact that she's a marvelous girl. In bed and out, not to put too fine a point on it."

"She wanted to marry *you*."

"A passing whim. I'm much too old for her, for one thing."

"Oh, come now, Miles. Fifty's not all that old."

"I'm not fifty. I'm long past that, if you must know."

I looked at him incredulously. If he hadn't told me when we first met that he was fifty, I'd have found it hard to believe that he was much over forty. I knew he found it easy to lie, but I couldn't see why he would pretend to be older than he was. "How much past?" I asked.

"I'll be sixty next month, old man."

"You must tell me your secret," I said. "Someday."

"Someday." He snapped a suitcase shut decisively. "Women like Eunice have no sense of the future. They look at a man they've taken a fancy to and they see only their lover, ageless with passion, not an old man sitting by the fire in slippers a few years from then. There's no need to tell anyone what you've just learned, of course."

"Does Lily know."

"Not on your life," he said briskly. "So, you see, I rather thought I was doing both you and Eunice a good turn."

"It didn't quite work," I said.

"Sorry about that."

I almost told him about Didi Wales lying naked on my bed, but realized in time that it would not increase his esteem for me appreciably. "Anyway," I said, "I think it's better for all concerned that Eunice went home."

"Perhaps you're right," he said. "We'll never know, shall we? By the way, is there anybody you'd like me to call or see while I'm in America? Any messages?"

I thought for a moment. "You might telephone my brother in Scranton," I said. I wrote down his address. "Ask him how he's doing. And tell him all is well. I've found a friend."

Fabian smiled, pleased. "You certainly have. Anybody else?"

I hesitated. "No," I said finally.

"I look forward to it." Fabian put the slip with Henry's address on it in his pocket. "Now, if you don't mind, I have to do my yoga exercise before my bath. I imagine you're going to change for dinner?"

Yoga, I thought, as I left the suite. Maybe that's what I ought to take up.

I watched the big plane take off from Cointrin, the Geneva airport, with Fabian and Lily and the coffin on it. The sky was gray and it was drizzling. I had said that nothing would please me more than being left alone for a few days and I had thought that I would be relieved at seeing them finally on their way, like a schoolboy at the beginning of a holiday, but I felt lonely, depressed. I had a slip of paper with Mr. Quadrocelli's address and telephone number in my wallet and the addresses of the tailor and shirtmaker in Rome and a list that Fabian had made out for me of good restaurants and churches that I was not to miss on my route south. But it was all I could do to keep from going over to the ticket counter and buying passage on the next plane to New York. As the plane disappeared westward, I felt deserted, left behind, the only one not invited to the party.

What if the plane crashed? No sooner had I thought of it than it seemed to me to be probable. Otherwise, why would I have thought of it? As a pilot I had always taken a macabre professional interest in crashes. I knew how easily things could go wrong. A stuck valve, unexpected clear air turbulence, a flock of swallows . . . I could almost see Fabian calmly dropping through the deadly air, imperturbably drowning, perhaps at the last moment, before the ocean swallowed him, finally telling Lily his correct age.

I had been involved in two deaths already since the beginning of my adventure— the old man in the St. Augustine and Sloane, now flying to his grave. Would there be an inevitable third? Was there a curse on the money I had stolen? Should I have let Fabian leave? What would the rest of my life be like without him? If there had been any way I could have done either, I would have had the plane recalled, run out to greet it, all reticence and reason gone, before it even rolled to a halt.

In the gray weather, Europe seemed suddenly hostile and full of traps. Maybe, I thought, as I walked toward where the Jaguar was parked, Italy will cure me. I wasn't hopeful.

CHAPTER 21

ON THE TRIP down from Geneva to Rome, I dutifully visited most of the churches on the list that Fabian had given me and ate in the restaurants he had suggested, the slow drive south a confused mingling of stained glass, madonnas, martyred saints, and heaped plates of spaghetti a la vongole and fritto misto. There had been no reports of any planes falling into the Atlantic Ocean. The weather was good, the Jaguar performed nobly, the country through which I drove was beautiful. It was just the kind of voyage I had dreamed of since I was a boy, and I should have savored every moment of it. But as I entered Rome and drove across the broad reaches of the Piazza del Popolo, I realized that for the first time in my life I was miserably lonely. At the end, Sloane had had his revenge.

Using a map, I drove slowly toward the Grand Hotel, another of Fabian's choices. The traffic seemed insane, the other drivers wildly hostile. I felt that if I made one wrong turn I would be lost for days in a city of enemies.

The room I was given in the Grand was too large for me, and, although it was sunny outside, dark. I hung up my clothes carefully. Fabian had told me that Quadrocelli was traveling and didn't expect to be back in Porto Ercole until the weekend. It was only Monday. I had four days to enjoy Rome or despair in it.

At the bottom of my overnight bag, as I cleared it, I saw the thick envelope Evelyn Coates had given me to deliver to her friend at the embassy. I had his name and address and telephone number in a notebook. I looked it up. Lorimer, David Lorimer. Evelyn had asked me not to call him at the embassy. It was just past one o'clock. There was a chance he would be home for lunch. I had been alone for almost a week, walled off from all but the most primitive communication by the barrier of language. I hoped Mr. Lorimer would invite me to lunch. The contented unsociability of my nights at the St. Augustine had vanished. I missed Fabian and Lily, I missed the sound of voices speaking English, I missed a lot of other things, many of them vague and indefinable.

I gave the number to the operator. A moment later, a man's voice said, *"Pronto."*

"This is Douglas Grimes," I said, "Evelyn . . ."

"I know," the man said quickly. "Where are you?"

"At the Grand," I said.

"I'll be there in fifteen minutes. Do you play tennis?"

"Well . . ." I wondered if he were speaking in code. "A bit."

"I was just leaving for my club. We need a fourth."

"I haven't any stuff with me . . ."

"We'll find gear for you at the club. And I have an extra racquet. I'll meet you in the bar. I have red hair. You can't miss me." He hung up abruptly.

The lanky man with red hair came into the bar, his stride loose and energetic. His hair was quite long, at least for a diplomat, his face craggy, with thick bushy eyebrows, also red, and a bold nose. As he had said, you couldn't miss him. We shook hands. He seemed about my own age. "I found an old pair of sneakers," he said. "What size do you wear?"

"Ten," I said.

"Good. They'll fit."

His car, a sleek little blue, open two-seater Alfa Romeo was parked just outside the hotel, constricting traffic. A policeman was standing beside it, a look of pain on his face. The policeman remonstrated gently with Lorimer, his voice musical, as we climbed into the car. Lorimer waved him off good-naturedly and we headed into the traffic. He drove zestfully, like his fellow Romans, and we nearly scraped fenders a dozen times before we reached the tennis club, situated on the banks of the Tiber. Driving, especially at his speed, seemed to require all his attention, so there was no conversation. He spoke only once. "This is the Borghese Gardens," he said as we turned into a green park. "You ought to look in at the museum."

"I will," I said. By now I had acquired a small addiction to museums. It would please Fabian when I reported that I had been to the Borghese. He, too, had told me to visit it. "Pay special attention to the Titians," Fabian had instructed.

When we swung through the gates of the club, Lorimer parked the car in the shade of some poplars. There were other cars parked along the road, but nobody to be seen. I started to open the door on my side, but Lorimer put out his hand and touched my arm to stop me.

"Have you got it?"

"Yes." I reached into the inside pocket of my jacket and pulled out the bulky envelope. I handed it to Lorimer. Without examining it, Lorimer stuffed it into the inside pocket of his jacket.

"Evelyn told me you'd turn up eventually," Lorimer said. "Thanks for not calling me at the embassy."

We got out of the car, Lorimer reaching in for a battered old tennis bag. As we walked toward the clubhouse, he said, "I'm glad you could come. It's hard to arrange games at this hour. I like to play *before* lunch and Italians like to play after lunch. Fundamental differences in two civilizations. Never to be reconciled. We call to each other from opposite sides of an abyss." He saluted two small dark men who were playing on one of the courts. "In a minute," he shouted.

The two men were only rallying, but they looked pretty good. "I'm afraid I'm going to slow down your game a bit," I said, watching them. "I haven't played in years."

"Don't give it a thought," he said. "Just keep moving up to the net. They crack under pressure." He grinned. He had a nice, friendly, wolfish grin.

The sneakers fit me comfortably and the shorts and shirt approximately, flopping around me a bit, but playable.

"Take your valuables with you to the court," Lorimer said. "You could leave them at the desk, but there have been incidents. And don't leave your passport lying around anywhere, or one day you will be surprised to read that a Sicilian by the name of Douglas Grimes has been arrested for smuggling heroin." I saw that along with his wallet and loose change and his watch, he also took Evelyn's envelope out to the court with him.

I doubt that the two men we played with ever heard my name. Lorimer introduced us, but spoke in mumbled Italian, and I never got *their* names.

I enjoyed the game more than I thought I would. The skiing I had done that winter had kept me in shape and my reflexes were still there. And as Dr. Ryan had promised, my eyes were adequate for the sport. Lorimer loped all over the court, blasting everything. He was wild, but intermittently very effective. We split the first two sets with the Italian gentlemen, who, as Lorimer had predicted, cracked under pressure. I developed a blister on my thumb in the third set and had to quit. The blister was a small price to pay for the pleasure of playing in the balmy Roman sunshine alongside the river which Shakespeare had insisted Caesar had swum with all his armor on. It had been a dry season and the river looked small and innocent and as though I could have swum it, too.

While we were dressing, after our showers, the Italians invited us to lunch, which they were having at the club, before going back to their offices. "Tell me, partner," Lorimer said to me, "is this your first time in Rome?"

"First day," I said.

"We won't eat here then. We'll go to a tourist place. The Tre Scalini in the Piazza Navona." I nodded. That was on Fabian's list, too. "Whenever anybody comes to Rome," Lorimer said, "I tell them not to pretend to be anything else but a tourist. Do and see all the standard things. The Vatican, the Sistine Chapel, the Castel Sant' Angelo, the Moses, the Forums, et cetera. They haven't been put in guidebooks for hundreds of years for nothing. Later on, you can pick your own way. For reading, I suggest Stendhal. Do you read French?"

"No."

"Pity."

"I wish I could go back to school all over again."

"Don't we all?" he said.

"How do you like your lunch?" Lorimer asked. We were sitting out on the terrace looking across at the great fountain, with the four enormous carved feminine figures of the Rivers. It was certainly a better idea than having a sandwich and a beer at the bar of the tennis club.

"I like it fine," I said.

"Don't spread it around," Lorimer said. "In certain high-toned circles it is accepted doctrine that the food is inedible." He grinned. "You'll be marked as a crude yokel for life and you'll only get to meet a *principessa* with difficulty."

"Well, I can say I liked the view, can't I?"

"Say you just happened to be strolling through the Piazza Navona by accident. At night. If the subject comes up." He stared thoughtfully at the fountain. "Dwarfing, isn't it?"

"What's dwarfing?"

"Those big girls. That's one of the reasons I prefer Rome to New York, say. Here you're dwarfed by art and religion, not by the steel and glass fantasies of insurance companies and stockbrokers."

"Have you been here long?"

"Not long enough. And the sons of bitches are trying to move me out." He tapped the bulge in his jacket made by the envelope I had given him. He had taken it out, slit it open, and glanced through the pages hastily while we were waiting to be served. When the first course and the wine appeared, he had jammed the pages back into his pocket without comment. "That's what this is all about," he said, tapping the jacket for the second time. "They're after me. I know it and they know I know it and we're all waiting for someone to make the wrong move. I sent along some recommendations that were not received—ah—with enthusiasm in certain quarters. I pushed through some contracts. Evelyn was in on it, too, in Justice and her head is on the block, too. We tried to get the money to the right people in this beautiful, lamentable country, with its desperate inhabitants, not the wrong people. A difference of opinion.

Possibly fatal. Don't boast that you know me. There're spies everywhere. When I get back to my desk, the papers will have been moved. Do I sound paranoid?"

"I wouldn't know," I said, "although Evelyn hinted . . ."

"It happened before," Lorimer said, "and it sure as hell can happen again, with what's going on in Washington. What McCarthy did to the old China hands for coming in with an unpopular message will look like a tea party compared to what that bunch in the White House are capable of pulling off. Orwell was wrong. It shouldn't have been nineteen eighty-four. It should have been nineteen seventy-three. Do you think they'll get that second-story man out of the White House?"

I shrugged. "I haven't been following it closely," I said.

Lorimer looked at me oddly. "Americans." He shook his head sadly. "My bet is he'll still be there till the next election. With his foot on all our necks. My next post will probably be in some small African country where they have a *coup d'état* every three months and shoot American ambassadors. Come and visit me." He grinned and poured himself a full glass of wine. Whatever he was, he wasn't frightened. "I'm afraid I won't be able to devote any time to you this week. I have to go to Naples for a few days. But I can get back for tennis again on Saturday and there's a poker game on Saturday night, mostly newspapermen, nobody from the embassy. . . . Evelyn wrote you were a devout poker player. . . ."

"I'm sorry," I said. "I won't be here. I have to be in Porto Ercole Saturday."

"Porto Ercole?" he said. "The Pellicano?"

"As a matter of fact, I have a reservation there."

"For a fellow who's just arrived in Italy, you know your way around. The Grand in Rome, the Pellicano in Porto Ercole."

"I've been briefed by a friend," I said. "He knows his way around everywhere."

"You'll love it," Lorimer said. "I go up there for weekends whenever I can. They have a nice tennis court. I envy you." He looked at his watch, then started to pull out his wallet to pay.

"Please," I said. "On me."

He put his wallet back. "Evelyn wrote you were independently wealthy. Is that true?"

"More or less," I said.

"Three cheers for you. In that case, it's your lunch." He stood up. "Do you want me to drive you back to the hotel?"

"I think I'd like to walk."

"Well thought out," he said. "I wish I had the time to walk with you. But the executioners await. *Arrivederci,* chum." He strode off toward his car, brisk and American, the statues looming over him, toward the desk on which the papers had been moved in his absence.

I finished my coffee slowly, paid, and walked leisurely in the general direction of the hotel, reflecting that Rome, as seen by a pedestrian, was a different and much better city than Rome seen from an automobile. For that afternoon, at least. Lorimer's description of Italy as a beautiful, lamentable country, peopled with desperate inhabitants, seemed only partially correct.

I found myself on a narrow busy street, the via del Babuino, where there were several art galleries. Faithful to Fabian, I peered in through the windows. In one of the windows there was a large oil of a deserted street in a small town in America, the familiar drugstore, barbershop, fake Colonial bank, a clapboard newspaper office, all in what looked like the last faded light of a cold evening in the middle of flat prairie country. It was painted realistically, but realism heightened by an obsessed attention to every smallest detail, which gave the impression of a distorted, fanatical vision of the country, loving and furious at the same time. The name of the painter who was having the one-man show in the gallery was not an American one—or perhaps half an American one, Angelo Quinn. Out of curiosity I went into the gallery. Aside from the man who ran the place, a wispy, gray-haired sexagenarian in a high collar, and a youngish, sloppily dressed man in need of a shave who sat in a corner reading an art magazine, I was the only one in the shop.

All the paintings were of small towns or dilapidated old sections of cities, with here and there a weather-worn farmhouse set on a bleak, windy hill, or a rusted line of railroad tracks, with frozen puddles reflecting a dark sky, the tracks looking as though they were going nowhere and as if the last train had passed that way a century before.

There were no little red stamps on the frames to indicate that any of the paintings had been sold. The owner of the gallery did not follow me around or offer to talk to me, but merely gave me a sad little dental-plate smile when he caught my eye. The young man with the art magazine never looked up.

I left the gallery saddened, but somehow also uplifted. I wasn't certain enough about my taste to be able to pronounce whether or not the paintings were good or bad, but they had spoken to me directly, had reminded me, elusively but surely, of something I didn't want to forget about my native country.

I walked slowly through the bustling street, puzzling over the experience. It was very much like what I had felt about books at the age of thirty, when I had begun to read seriously, the sense that something enormous and enigmatic was being tantalizingly revealed to me. I remembered what Fabian had said the morning we had visited the Maeght Museum in St.-Paul-de-Vence—that after I had *looked* enough I would pass a certain threshold of emotion. I resolved to come back again the next day.

Near my hotel, by accident, I noticed that I was passing the shop that Fabian had told me was the place I should get my suits made. I went in and spent an interesting hour looking at materials and talking to the head tailor, who spoke a kind of English. I ordered five suits. I would dazzle Fabian when I saw him next.

The next day I got a directory of the art galleries in Rome that were having exhibitions that week and I visited all of them before going back to Quinn's show. I wanted to see how the other contemporary works of art on view in the city affected me. They affected me not at all. Realistic, surrealist, abstract, my eye remained unmoved. Then I went back to the gallery on the via del Babuino and slowly drifted from painting to painting, studying each one carefully and critically, to make sure that what I had felt the afternoon before had not been the result of its having been my first day in Rome, following a good lunch with plenty of wine and the pleasure of conversation with a knowing young American after a week of silence.

The effect on me was, if anything, greater than it had been the day before. The gallery owner and the young man with the art magazine were again the only ones in the shop, looking as though they had not moved in the last twenty-four hours. If they recognized me, they gave no sign that they did so. If I can afford to buy suits, I decided suddenly, I can afford to buy a painting. I had never bought even as much as a print before and was unsure about how one went about it. Fabian had haggled with the dealer in Zurich, but I knew I wasn't up to that.

"Excuse me," I said to the wispy old gallery owner, who smiled automatically at me, "I'm interested in the painting in the window. And maybe this one, too." I was standing in front of the oil of the disused railroad tracks. "Could you give me some idea of how much they might be?"

"Five hundred thousand lire," the old man said promptly. His voice was strong and steady.

"Five hundred thousand . . . Uh . . ." It sounded monumental. I still suffered from fits of apprehension when dealing with the Italian decimal system. "How much is that in dollars?" Tourist, tourist, I though bitterly as I asked the question.

"About eight hundred dollars." he shrugged despondently. "With the ridiculous rate of exchange, less."

I was paying two hundred and fifty dollars for each of the five suits. They would never give me as much pleasure as either of the paintings. "Will you take a check on a Swiss bank?"

"Certainly," the old man said. "Make it out to Pietro Bonelli. The show closes in two weeks. We can deliver the paintings to you then at your hotel, if you wish."

"That won't be necessary," I said. "I'll pick them up myself." I wanted to walk out of the shop with the treasures under my arm.

"There should be a deposit, of course," the old man said. "To confirm . . ."

I looked in my wallet. "Would ten thousand lire do the trick?"

"Twenty thousand would be more normal," he said smoothly. I gave him twenty thousand lire and told him my name and he wrote out a receipt for me in flowing Italian script. It was Pietro Bonelli. Through all this the shaggy young man had not looked up from his magazine.

"Would you like to meet the artist?" the old man asked.

"If it's not too much trouble."

"Not at all. Angelo," he said, "Mr. Grimes, who is a collector of your work, would like to say hello."

The young man finally looked up. "Hi," he said. "Congratulations." He smiled. He seemed even younger when he smiled, with brilliant teeth and deep, dark eyes, like a mournful Italian child. He stood up slowly. "Come on, Mr. Grimes, I'll buy you a coffee to celebrate."

Bonelli was pasting the first red tab on the frame of the painting in the window as we went out of the shop.

Quinn led me to a café down the street and we stood at the bar as he ordered coffee. "You're American, aren't you?" I asked.

"As apple pie." His accent was from no particular place in the States.

"Did you just come over?"

"I've been here for five years," Quinn said. "Studying the Italian scene."

"Did you do all those paintings in the gallery more than five years ago?"

He laughed. "No. They're all new. They're from memory. Or inventions. Whatever you want to call them. I paint out of loneliness and nostalgia. It gives a certain original aura to the stuff, don't you think?"

"I would say so."

"When I go back to the States I'll paint Italy. Like most painters I have a theory. My theory is that you must leave home to know what home is like. Do you think I'm crazy?"

"No. Not if that's the way they come out."

"You like them, eh?"

"Very much."

"I don't blame you." He grinned. "The Angelo Quinn *optique* on his native land. Hold onto them. They'll be worth a lot. Someday."

"I intend to hang on," I said. "And not for the dough."

"Nice of you to say so." He sipped at his coffee. "If it was only for the coffee," he said, "I wouldn't consider my time in Italy wasted."

"Where did you get the name Angelo?"

"My mother. She was an Italian war bride. My father brought her home. To a variety of homes. He was a smalltime newspaperman. He'd get tired of one job and he'd move on to another god-forsaken, two-bit town until he got tired of that. I paint my father's wanderings. *Are* you a collector, as old man Bonelli said."

"No," I said. "To tell the truth, this is the first time in my life I ever bought a painting."

"Holy man," Quinn said. "You broke your maiden. Keep at it. You've got a good eye, though I'm not the one who should say so. Have another coffee on me. You've made my day."

I took the check around to Bonelli's the next day and had a good half hour looking at the pictures I'd bought. Bonelli promised to hold them for me if I couldn't get back in time to claim them when the show closed. All in all, I thought, as I drove up toward Porto Ercole on Friday afternoon, I had to consider my first visit to Rome a successful one.

CHAPTER 22

THERE WERE FEW guests at the Pellicano and I was given a large airy room, fronting on the sea. I had the girl at the desk call the Quadrocelli home. Mr. Quadrocelli was not expected back until tomorrow morning, she told me. I told her to leave word that I would be at the hotel all day.

I had bought some tennis things in Rome and my blister had healed and the next morning I played polite mixed doubles with some elderly English people who were staying at the hotel. After the tennis and a shower, I was sitting on the terrace overlooking the Mediterranean when the girl from the desk came out with a short dark man dressed in shapeless corduroy pants and a sailor's high-necked, navy blue sweater. "Mr. Grimes," the girl said, "this is Dottore Quadrocelli."

I stood up and shook hands with Dottore Quadrocelli. His hand was hard and callused, like a laborer's. He looked like a peasant, deeply tanned, with a round strong body. His hair and eyes were deep black, his movements quick and vivacious. There were deep lines around his eyes as though he had laughed a great deal in his lifetime. I guessed that he was about forty-five.

"Welcome, welcome, my dear friend," he said. "Sit down, sit down. Enjoy the morning. What do you think of our magnificent view?" He said it as though the view, the rocky sweep of the coast of the Argentario Peninsula, the sunlit sea, and the island of Giannutri that bulked in the distance were all part of his personal estate. "May I offer you a drink?" he asked as we seated ourselves.

"Not yet, thank you," I said. "It's a little early for me."

"Ah, excellent," he said. "You are going to present me with a good example." His English had almost no trace of an accent and he spoke rapidly, as though his thoughts tumbled over each other in his head and he could only keep up with himself by speaking at top speed. "And how is the delightful Miles Fabian? What a pity he couldn't come with you. My wife is desolate. She is hopelessly in love with him. Also my three daughters." He laughed gaily. His mouth was small, the lips curved, almost like a girl's, but his laughter was loud and robust and masculine. "Ah, what a history of amour his life must be. And unmarried, to boot. Wisdom, wisdom. He has the sagacity of a philosopher, our friend Miles. Wouldn't you agree, Signore Grimes?"

"I don't know him all that well," I said. "We've only met recently."

"Time only improves him. As compared to the rest of us poor mortals." Quadrocelli laughed again. "Are you here alone?"

"I'm afraid so."

He made a little sad grimace. "You have my pity. In a place like this . . ." He made a wide gesture, saluting the glory of our surroundings. "You are not married?"

"No."

"I will introduce you to my three daughters. One is beautiful, even if it is a doting father who says so, and the others have character. Each soul to its own virtues. But I treat them equally. When Miles called me on the telephone from Gstaad, he spoke very highly of you. He said that you were the best of companions. You possessed intelligence and rectitude, he said. Two characteristics that do not often go together in one person in these naughty days. I would say the same about Miles."

I didn't think I had to inform my new friend that he was too generous by half in his judgment.

"How did you happen to meet Miles?" Quadrocelli asked.

"We were on the plane together coming from New York." This was true, even though I hadn't seen him on the flight and he had never mentioned having seen me. But it would help stop further questions.

"And you hit it off together just like that?" Quadrocelli snapped his fingers.

Hit was the appropriate word, I thought, remembering the lamp I broke on Fabian's head. "Just like that," I said.

"Like marriages," Quadrocelli said, "partnerships are made in heaven. Have you any experience in wine, Mr. Grimes?"

"None. Until I came to Europe, I hardly ever touched it. Beer was my drink."

"Of no importance. Miles has the palate for all three of us. I tell you, it was a day of great honor for my wine when Miles suggested he would be interested in sending it out into the world with my name on the bottle. Every time an American will say, 'I would like to order a Chianti Quadrocelli,' I will have a little thrill of pride. I am not a vain man, but vanity is not unknown to me. And it will be an honest wine. That I promise you. It will not be mixed with Greek rotgut or Sicilian acid. Ah, the things they do here in Italy. Bull's blood, chemicals. I am ashamed for my country. So much of our wine is like so much of our politics. Debased. Devalued, like our lire. And not only Italy. If the truth would get out about France! You and I and our friend Miles will be able to look any man in the face and say, 'You have not been deceived in buying our product.' And we will be enriched in the process. Greatly enriched, my dear friend. The thirst is insatiable. I will show you the figures after lunch—you will have lunch with me and my wife, please—"

"Thank you," I said.

"It is one of the few things our idiotic government cannot ruin," Quadrocelli said. "My wine. I have a printing business in Milan. You have no idea of how difficult they make it just to keep the head above water. Taxes, strikes, red tape . . . Bombings." His face grew sober. "*Dolce Italia*. I have to have an armed guard at my plant in Milan twenty-four hours a day. I print, at cost, some harmless tracts for some Socialist friends of mine and I am constantly being threatened. Do not believe it, Mr. Grimes, when you are told Mussolini is dead. My father had to flee to England in 1928—there was one consolation, of course—I learned your beautiful language—and I would not be surprised if one day *I* will have to flee, too. From the right, from the left, from above, from below." He made an impatient gesture, as though he was annoyed at himself for this show of pessimism. "Ah, you must be careful not to take everything I say too seriously. I swing from extreme to extreme. My family came from the South. In our family, we all cried and laughed on the same day." He laughed gaily, fond of his family's range of emotions. "You are here to talk about wine, not our insane politics. The eternal grape. Not even the politicians and the bully boys can keep grapes from growing. And the yeasts never go on strike. You and Miles have picked the one business that might be considered a reasonable risk in all of Italy. When Miles spoke to me on the phone, he talked of a death."

I began to see that I would have to be on the alert for sudden switches of subjects in Mr. Quadrocelli's conversation. "A friend of ours," I said.

"Ah," he said, "we are all mortal." He hugged himself, as if to reassure himself that his body was still there. "Let us talk of more cheerful things. Have you ever been in Italy before?"

"No." I didn't think I had to count the trip to Florence hunting for Miles Fabian.

"I will be your guide. It is a wonderful country, full of surprises. Some of them even happy ones." He laughed. He was not shy at laughing at his own jokes. I had begun to like the man already, his vitality and bouncing health and cynical honesty. "We are no longer great, but we are the inheritors of greatness. We are poor caretakers, but everything is all there, even if it is crumbling a little. I will take you to my home near Firenze. You will see the vineyards with your own eyes. You will drink your wine in the place where it is grown. I have some bottles in my cellar that will make the tears come to your eyes. That I promise you. Do you like the opera?"

"I've never been."

"I will take you to La Scala, in Milan. You will be introduced to rapture. Do you plan to stay long in Italy?"

"That depends somewhat on Miles."

"Do not be in a hurry to leave, I beg of you. I do not want our relationship to be merely a business one," he said earnestly. "I know it sounds foolish, but it will be bad for the wine. Are you a good sailor?"

"I've only been in small boats on a lake back home."

"I have a twenty-five-foot little power cruiser in the harbor. We will visit Giannutri." He gestured toward the island, which now looked like a small, wispy cloud on the horizon. "It is still wild and unspoiled. That is a great deal to say about a place in these naughty days. It is too bad it is too cold to swim. The water is like sapphires. We will take a picnic and get sunburned. You will want to live the rest of your life here. Where is your home in America?"

I hesitated. "In Vermont. But I move around a lot."

"Vermont." He shivered. "I never can understand why people who do not have to do it live in ice and snow. Like Miles, with his crazy skiing. I have told him that there is a house just next to mine that is for sale. A beautiful house and I could get it at a price. And with his Italian . . . He could live like a king. At his age there is a good chance he could live his life out before everything went down in ruins. He seems to have come into some money . . ." Quadrocelli looked at me shrewdly, his eyes narrowing. "Am I right or wrong?"

"I don't know," I said. "As I told you I only met him recently."

"Ah, good," he said, "you are a discreet gentleman. If Miles wishes to tell me, he can tell me himself. Is that it?"

"More or less."

"If I may ask, Mr. Grimes . . . Ah!" He made an impatient gesture. "What is your first name?"

"Douglas."

"And I am Giuliano. so that is settled. If I may ask, Douglas, what is your business?"

"Mostly investments," I said.

"I will not pry." Quadrocelli put his hands out in front of him in a braking motion, as though physically stopping himself from going to far. "You are a friend of Miles and that is enough for me. Or any man." He stood up. "And now it is time for lunch. Pasta and fresh fish. Simple fare. I have never had a stomachache since the day I married my wife. I am overweight, my doctor says, but I tell him I do not plan to be a movie star." He laughed again.

I got up and he linked my arm in his as we started toward the door of the hotel. But before we reached it, the door opened and out into the bright Italian sunshine stepped Evelyn Coates.

"Lorimer called me," she said. "He told me you might be here. I hope I'm not intruding."

"You're not intruding," I said.

It might have been the springtime Mediterranean weather or the fact that she was on a holiday or merely being away from Washington, but whatever the reason, Evelyn was a changed woman. The harshness and abrasive authority that had offended me in my first introduction to her were no longer in evidence. She was gentler, careful not to wound, relaxed. When we made love, I no longer had the feeling that she was on a desperate search for something she would never find. Even on the last Sunday night in Washington, with all the tenderness, I realized now, there had been the same underlying tension. We spent hours alone together, basking in the sun, holding hands, talking desultorily, laughing easily, childishly, at little things, like our attempts to talk Italian to a waiter or posing for each other in extreme positions in snapshots that we took with a camera that Evelyn had brought along with her.

When she arrived, Mr. Quadrocelli had left us tactfully alone, saying, "You must have many things you wish to talk about with your beautiful American friend. We can have lunch tomorrow, instead of today. My wife will understand. And my three daughters." He laughed, his rumbling, robust laugh. "I do not pity you anymore, Douglas." He winked as he said it. "Not at all."

Then he had called during the afternoon, full of apologies, to say that he had received a telephone call, that he had to fly to Milan that evening, there had been sabotage at the plant. "Imagine," he said, "even on Saturday." But he would return as soon as possible, he said. I was to give his salutations to the beautiful American. His call had come after lunch, when Evelyn and I were in bed together, in the warm, pretty room overlooking the sea, all our hungers for the moment sated. Although I was sorry Quadrocelli's plant had been sabotaged, I was not sorry that I wouldn't have to spend time with him, nice as he was, time that I otherwise could devote to Evelyn.

The hotel was practically empty in this off season, and it was like having a luxurious country house, equipped with a friendly and highly efficient staff, all to ourselves. The large terrace that came with our room was shielded from observation, and we lay naked side by side for hours in the warm sunshine, tanning ourselves. It seemed to me that Evelyn's body had grown softer and rounder. In Washington it had been hard and taut, trained for competition, the body of a woman who religiously went through strenuous calisthenics and expensive massages daily to keep in shape. We talked of many things, but never about Washington or her work there. I didn't ask her how long she could stay with me and she didn't mention when she would have to leave. I did not report my conversation with Lorimer at the Tre Scalini.

It was a marvelous, in-between kind of time, sensual and carefree, untroubled by clock or calendar, in a beautiful country whose language we could not speak and whose problems were not our problems. We read no newspapers and never listened to the radio and made no plans for the future. Fabian called me several times to say things were going swimmingly in New York and that we were growing richer daily but that because of certain complications that he wouldn't bother to explain to me over the phone he would have to stay in the States longer than he had expected. Quadrocelli had sent over the figures on the wine deal before he had left, and I had mailed them to Fabian without looking at them. They were fine, Fabian said, and when Quadrocelli got back to Porto Ercole, I could tell him his terms were acceptable.

"Incidentally," I said, "how was the funeral?"

"Pure pleasure," Fabian said. "Oh—I nearly forgot—your brother came to New York to visit me. He's a very different kettle of fish from you, isn't he?"

"I guess, you might put it that way," I said.

"Still, he says the company you and he are in on looks very promising. He told me about his eyes and I sent him to my man in New York and he's being treated with some new drug and the doctor says he'll be fine. Lily sends her love."

It was a week in which nothing could go wrong.

We drove down to Rome to get my five suits and stayed at a hotel overlooking the Spanish Steps and like good tourists we walked everywhere, had lunch in the Piazza Navona and drank the wine of Frascati and visited the Vatican and the Forum and the Borghese Museum and heard *Tosca* at the opera. Evelyn said she admired my suits and pretended that all the girls we passed looked longingly at me. I was not blind to the fact that practically all the Italian men we passed looked longingly at *her*.

On one of our walks I steered her to Bonelli's gallery. The painting of the American small-town main street was still in the window, with my little red tab on the frame. I didn't tell Evelyn that it belonged to me. I was curious about what she thought about it. She was much more sophisticated than I and, sharing an apartment with a gallery-owner, she must have been exposed, even if it was only by this association, to a good deal of modern art. I stood silently by her side as we both studied the painting. If she said it was worthless, I probably would never claim the painting and never admit that I had bought it.

"What do you think of it?" I finally asked.

"It's beautiful," she said. "Absolutely beautiful. Let's go in and see the whole show. I must write Brenda about this man."

But it was lunch hour or hours and the gallery was closed, so we couldn't go in. It was just as well, I thought. She might not have liked any of the other paintings and Bonelli would have undoubtedly spoken to me, thanking me for the check I had given him and I would have felt diminished in her eyes. I knew that after the days we had spent together since she had arrived at Porto Ercole I wanted her always to have a high opinion of me. In all fields.

The next day, I went down to the gallery to collect the two paintings. Evelyn had an appointment with a friend at the embassy and I was alone. Bonelli seemed happier than when I had last seen him. There were three more red tabs on the paintings on the walls and I supposed that accounted for the improvement in his spirits. As he wrapped my canvas he hummed a tune that I recognized as an aria from *Tosca*. Quinn was not there. "He has had a sudden seizure of talent," Bonelli said when I asked about him. "Since you talked to him, he has been home painting night and day."

Further wanderings of father, I thought, coming up.

"I think you must take some of the credit, Mr. Grimes," Bonelli said. "He was very despondent, sitting around here from opening to closing, looking at more than a year's work on the walls and nothing happening, nothing. An artist, especially a young artist, becomes desperate for a little encouragement."

"Not only artists," I said.

"Of course you're right," Bonelli agreed. "Despondency is not only the privilege of artists. I myself sometimes have days when I wonder if I had not totally wasted my life. Even in America, I suppose . . ." He shrugged, leaving the sentence unfinished.

"Even in America," I said.

When I got back to the hotel, Evelyn had not yet returned, and I put the paintings side by side on the mantelpiece, with a note on which I merely wrote, "To Evelyn. In gratitude, Rome," and the date. Then I went out and walked down to the Via Veneto and sat at Donet's on the terrace, drinking coffee and watching the crowds walk by. I wanted Evelyn to see the pictures and the note without me.

When I got back to the hotel, she was lying on the bed, propped up against the pillows, staring at the paintings. She was crying. Without saying anything, she motioned for me to come over to her and pulled me down beside her and kissed me.

After a while, she said, "I'm a bitch."

"Oh, come on, now," I said.

She pulled away from me and sat up. "I have to tell you why I came over here. To Italy."

"I'm delighted you came," I said. "Let's leave it at that. And I don't want to hear why you think you're a bitch."

"I'm pregnant," she said. "By you. I ran out of the pill the day I met you. You don't have to believe me if you don't want to."

"I believe you," I said.

"I was all ready to have an abortion," she said, "when Lorimer called me."

"I'm glad he did."

"I've always said I didn't want children," she said. "But when David told me where you were . . . I suddenly realized I'd been fooling myself. About that. And about a lot of other things, too. I've quit my job. No more government for me. I was destroying myself in Washington. Along with just about everybody else I knew there. I had a cold-blooded lawyer's proposition I was going to put to you. . . ."

"What was that?"

"I was going to ask you to marry me," she said.

"That's not so awfully cold-blooded," I said.

"I was going to tell you we could get a divorce after the baby was born. I didn't want an illegitimate child. Big, hotshot, hard-boiled, liberated woman that I am, the scourge of the Department of Justice." She laughed miserably. "And I was ready to behave just like a brainless, marshmallowy little flirt just out of finishing school. But then, after the week we've had . . . " She gestured helplessly. "You've been so *good*, The pictures were the final touch. I'll handle it by myself."

I took a deep breath. "I have a better idea," I said. "Why don't we get married and have the baby and *not* get divorced?" As I said it I knew I was wrong to have done so. There were shadows hanging over me, shadows that had to be dissipated before I could marry anyone. Chief among the shadows was that of Pat. I had almost asked her to marry me, too, and that had come to nothing. I had tried to forget her, but had I? More often than I liked to admit I dreamed about her. Even in bed, with Evelyn sleeping beside me, I had dreamed about her.

It was with relief that I heard Evelyn say, "Not so fast. Not so fast. First of all, I might be lying . . . "

"About what?"

"About who's the father of the child, for instance."

"Why would you do that?"

"Women do, you know."

"*Are* you lying?"

"No."

"That's good enough for me," I said.

"Even so," she said, shaking her head, "not so fast. I want no repenting in leisure in my house. No long faces of regret year after year. Save your spontaneous gestures of generosity for lesser events. Think it over for a while. Let's both think *everything* over for a while. Let's both be sure we know what we're doing. Let's give ourselves a couple of weeks."

"But you said . . . " Her sudden resistance made me irrationally stubborn. "The reason you came to Italy . . . "

"I know what I said. I know the reason I came to Italy. It's no longer operative. That's a word that's very popular in Washington these days."

"Why is it no longer operative?"

"Because I've changed," Evelyn said. "You were a stranger I was going to use. You're not a stranger any longer and I can't use you."

"What am I now?"

She laughed, a little sad laugh. "I'll tell you another time." She stood up. "Let's go and have a drink," she said. "I need one."

"Remember what you told me the first night in Washington?" Evelyn was saying. We were walking down the Via Condotti, peering idly into the windows. Since the scene in the room in the hotel, we had avoided the subject of marriage. We behaved as though the conversation had never taken place. Or almost as if it hadn't. We were more tender with each other than before, gentler. Our lovemaking had an edge of sorrow to it.

"What did I tell you in Washington?"

"That you were a simple country boy from an enormously wealthy family."

I nodded. "Did you believe it?"

"No."

"You were right."

She smiled. "Remember," she said, "I'm a trained lawyer. Just what do you do? As your possible future wife I suppose I ought to know, don't you think?"

"Worry not," I said. "I make enough to support you." Without reflecting on it, I kept up the pretense that I was still committed to what I had said to her. I knew it was foolish, unrealistic, but it was the easiest path to follow. At least for the moment.

"I'm not worrying about anyone supporting me," she said. "I have money of my own, and wherever we go I can always make a living. Lawyers hardly starve in America."

"Why America? What's wrong with living in Europe?"

She shook her head. "Europe's not for me. I like to come on holidays and all that, but not permanently." She looked at me shrewdly. "Is there a reason you don't want to go back?"

"No."

"You're lying to me." She stopped walking.

"Maybe," I admitted. A man coming out of a leather shop bumped into me and said, "*Scusi.*"

"Would that be a good way to start a marriage?"

"I'm not asking *you* any questions."

"Ask," she said.

"I'd rather not."

"I have a nice small house near the bay in Sag Harbor," she said. "My parents left it to me. I like it there. I could set up a law practice and make a living without running myself into the ground. Whatever your business is, could you handle it living there?"

"Maybe."

"If I said that the *only* place I would live after we got married was there, would you still want to marry me?"

"*Are* you saying that?"

"I am," she said. It was the first time since she had appeared on the terrace at the hotel in Porto Ercole that the Washington tone had come into her voice. Plainly, she was going to be no man's meek little wife. We were walking again and I was silent for twenty yards. "Are you going to answer me?"

"Not right now," I said.

"When?"

"Tonight, in a few days, in a month . . . " She was making me think about America and I was angry with her for it. Angelo Quinn's paintings back in the hotel room were having their effect on me. Ever since I had first seen them, with their harsh and melancholy statement about my native country, I had been fighting the realization that one day I would have to go back. Some people, I had found out, are born to be aliens, luxuriate in being aliens. Not I. That was one thing the paintings had proved to me. Hell, I had thought, I'll never learn another language. Not even one other language. Perhaps it had been an accident that I had gone into Bonelli's gallery that day and perhaps it had been an accident that the paintings had been as good as they were, but paintings or no paintings, in the long run, I now knew, whether it was with Evelyn or without her, I would go back. I was sure Fabian would disapprove. I could hear his arguments in advance. "Good God, man, you'll wind up with a bullet in your head." But I couldn't spend my life seeking Miles Fabian's approval.

"I'm not saying I won't live in America," I said. "In your house in Sag Harbor, if you want. But, everything else being equal, if I told you that there are reasons that I don't want to explain for my preferring to live abroad, reasons I might never tell you, would you still want to marry me?"

"I don't like to accept people on faith," she said. "Even you. I don't have all that much faith."

"Now I'm the one that's asking the question. Would you still want to marry me?"

"I won't answer that now." She laughed. The laugh was harsh.

"When?" I asked.

"Tonight, in a few days, in a month . . ."

We walked in silence again. Crossing the street we were nearly run over by a large Mercedes, speeding to catch a light. Suddenly, I had had enough of Rome.

"By the way," Evelyn said, "who's Pat?"

"How do you know anything about Pat?"

"I know that you know a girl called Pat."

"How do you know it's a girl?" I had been taken by surprise and stalled for time. I had never mentioned Pat to Evelyn. "It's a man's name."

"Not the way you said it," Evelyn said.

"When did I say it?"

"Twice. Last night in your sleep. And the way you said it, it couldn't be a man."

"Oh." I had stopped walking.

"Uh-huh. Oh."

"It's a girl I know. Knew," I corrected myself.

"You sounded as if you knew her very well."

"Did I?"

"Were you in love with her?"

"I thought so. Some of the time."

"When was the last time you saw her?"

"Three years ago."

"But you still call out to her in your sleep."

"If you say so," I said.

"Do you still love her?" She smiled. "Some of the time?"

I waited a long time before answering. "I don't know," I said.

"Don't you think you'd better see her and find out?"

"Yes," I said.

CHAPTER 23

THE TRIP BACK to Porto Ercole the next morning was a quiet one. Neither of us spoke much. I was busy with my own thoughts and I suppose Evelyn was busy with hers. She sat far over on her side of the car, her hands in her lap, her face composed and grave. Pat, unmentioned and thousands of miles away in snowbound Vermont, was a dark presence in the sunny Italian morning. I had told Evelyn I would go and see her. "The sooner the better," Evelyn had said. I would have to call Fabian and tell him I was arriving in New York. By way of New England.

When we got to the Pellicano, they told me that Quadrocelli had been in looking for me the night before. I asked the girl at the desk to get him for me on the phone. "Welcome home," he said, when the connection was made. "Did you enjoy Rome?"

"Moderately," I said.

"You are becoming blasé." He laughed. He did not sound like a man whose plant had recently been sabotaged. "It is a beautiful morning," he said. "I thought today would be nice for the trip to Giannutri. The sea is gentle. Would you like to go?"

"I have to ask my friend." Evelyn was standing beside me at the desk. "He wants to take us for a ride on his boat. Do you want to go?"

"Why not?" Evelyn said.

"We'd be delighted," I said into the phone.

"Fine. My wife will pack us a picnic hamper. She will not accompany us. She despises boats. She has transmitted this trait to her daughters, alas." His voice was cheerful as he described the nonadmiration for life at sea of the women of his family. "I must always be on the lookout for other companionship. Do you know where the Yacht Club is in the harbor?"

"Yes."

"Can you be there in an hour?"

"Whenever you say."

"An hour. I will be there getting the boat ready. Bring sweaters. It can get cold . . ."

"By the way, how bad was the damage at the plant?" I asked.

"Normally bad," he said. "For Italy. Do you know anybody who wants to buy a highly up-to-date, slowly failing printing establishment?"

"No," I said.

"Neither do I." He was laughing merrily as he hung up.

The idea of sailing to the island on the horizon attracted me. Not so much for the cruise itself as for the fact that for a full afternoon Evelyn and I would not be alone together. I decided to invite Quadrocelli and his wife to dinner with us. That would take care of the evening, too.

Evelyn went up to our room to change for the outing and I put in a call for Fabian. While waiting for the call to come through, I read the morning's *Rome Daily American*. In a column of social notes, there was an item about David Lorimer. He was being transferred to Washington. A farewell party was being arranged in his honor. I threw the paper away. I didn't want Evelyn to read it.

"Holy God, man," Fabian said, when I finally reached him. "Do you know what time it is?"

"Noon."

"In Italy," Fabian complained. "It's six o'clock in the morning here. What civilized human being wakes up a friend at six in the morning?"

"Sorry about that," I said. "I just didn't want to make you wait for the good news."

"What good news?" His voice was suspicious.

"I'm coming back to the States."

"What's so good about that?"

"I'll tell you when I see you. Private business. Can you hear me? This connection is lousy."

"I can hear you," he said. "All too well."

"The real reason I'm calling is to find out where you want me to leave the car."

"Why don't you wait where you are and I'll come over and we can discuss this calmly."

"I can't wait," I said. "And I'm calm right now."

"You can't wait." I could hear him sigh at the other end of the wire. "All right—can you drive the car to Paris? Tell the concierge at the Plaza-Athénée to put it in a garage for me. I have some business to look into in Paris."

He could have said someplace more convenient—like Fiumicino. He was a man who had some business to look into everywhere—Rome, Milan, Nice, Brussels, Geneva, Helsinki. He was being purposely inconvenient to discipline me. But I was in no mood to argue with him.

"Okay," I said. "Paris it will be."

"You know you've ruined my day, don't you?"

"There'll be other days," I said pleasantly.

When we drove down to the harbor and parked the car, I could see Quadrocelli coiling rope on the deck of his little white cabin cruiser, tied fore and aft to the dock of the Yacht Club. Most of the other boats in the harbor were still fitted out with their winter tarpaulins and the dock was deserted except for him.

"Sailing, sailing, over the bounding main," Evelyn sang as we walked toward the dock. She had made me stop at a pharmacy and buy some Dramamine. I had the feeling she shared Mrs. Quadrocelli's low opinion of the sea. "Are you sure you're not going to drown me when you get me out on the water?" she said. "Like what's-his-name in *An American Tragedy* when he finds out Shelly Winters is pregnant.

"Montgomery Clift," I said. "I'm not Montgomery Clift and you're not Shelley Winters. And the picture wasn't called *An American Tragedy*. It was *A Place in the Sun*."

"I just said it for laughs." She smiled sweetly at me.

"Some laughs." But I smiled back. It wasn't much of a joke, but it was a joke. At least it was a sign she was ready to make an effort not to be gloomy for the rest of our time in Europe. The long haul through France would have been hard to take if she just sat in her corner of the car, silent and withdrawn, as she had done on the trip that morning from Rome. After the phone call to Fabian I had told her I had to drive to Paris and asked her if she wanted to come along.

"Do you want me to?" she said.

"I want you to."

"Then so do I," she had said flatly.

Quadrocelli saw us as we approached the dock and jumped off the boat spryly and hurried to meet us, robust and nautical in his shapeless corduroys and bulky blue seaman's sweater. "Come aboard, come aboard," he said, bending to kiss Evelyn's hand, then shaking mine heartily. "Everything is ready. I have arranged all. The sea, as you notice, is calm as a lake and the well-advertised blue. The picnic basket is secured. Cold chicken, hard-boiled eggs, cheese, fruit, wine. Adequate nourishment for seagoing appetites . . ."

We were about twenty yards away from the boat when it blew up. Bits and pieces of wood and glass and wire flew around us as we all dove to the pavement. Then everything became deadly quiet. Quadrocelli stood up slowly and stared at his boat. The stern line had been torn away and the stern was drifting at an odd angle from the dock, as though the boat had been broken in two just aft of the helm.

"Are you all right?" I asked Evelyn.

"I think so," she said in a small voice. "How about you?"

"Okay," I said. I stood up and put my arm around her. "Giuliano . . ." I began.

He did not look at me. He kept staring at his boat. "*Fascisti,*" he whispered. "Miserable *Fascisti.*" People were now streaming out of the building across the wide quay and we were surrounded by a crowd of citizens, all talking at once, asking questions. Quadrocelli ignored them. "Take me home, please," he said to me quietly. "I do not believe I trust myself to drive. I want to go home."

We shouldered our way through the crowd to our car. Quadrocelli never looked back at his pretty little boat, which was sinking slowly now into the oily waters of the harbor.

In the car, he began to shiver. Violently, uncontrollably. Under his tan, his face took on a sickly pallor. "They could have killed you, too," he said, his teeth chattering. "If you had arrived two minutes earlier. Forgive me. Forgive all of us. *Dolce Italia.* Paradise for tourists." He laughed eerily.

When we reached his house, he wouldn't let us go in with him, or even get out of the car. "Please," he said, "I must have a discussion with my wife. I do not wish to be rude, but we must be alone."

We watched him walk slowly, looking old, across the driveway and to the door of his house. "Oh, the poor man," was all that Evelyn said.

We drove back to our hotel. We didn't say anything about what had happened to anyone. They would find out soon enough. We each had a brandy at the bar. Two dead, I thought, one in New York, one in Switzerland and one near miss in Italy. Evelyn's hand was steady as she picked up her glass. Mine wasn't. "To sunny Italy," Evelyn said. "*O sole mio.* Time to go, I'd say. Wouldn't you?"

"I would," I said.

We went up and packed our bags and were paid up and out of the hotel and on the road north in twenty minutes. We didn't stop, except for gas, until after midnight, when we had passed the border and were in Monte Carlo. Evelyn insisted on seeing the casino and playing at the roulette table. I didn't feel like gambling, or even watching, and sat at the bar. After a while she came back, smiling and looking smug. She had won five hundred francs and paid my bar bill to celebrate. Whoever would finally marry her would marry a woman with sound nerves.

*   *   *   *   *   *   *   *   *   *   *   *   *   *   *   *   *

Evelyn drove out to Orly with me in the rented car with a chauffeur. The Jaguar was in the garage, waiting for Fabian. Evelyn was going to stay in Paris a few more days. She hadn't been in Paris for years and it would be a shame just to pass through, she said. Anyway, I was going to Boston and she was going directly to New York. She had been carefree and affectionate on the trip through France. We had driven slowly, stopping often to sight-see and indulge in great meals outside Lyon and in Avallon. She had taken my picture in front of the Hospice de Beaune, where we toured the wine cellars, and in the courtyard at Fontainebleau. We had spent the last night of the trip just outside Paris at Barbizon, in a lovely old inn. We had dined gloriously. Over dinner I had told her everything. Where my money had come from, how I had met up with Fabian, what our arrangement was. Everything. She had listened quietly. When I finally stopped talking, she laughed. "Well," she said, "now I know why you want to marry a lawyer." She had leaned over and kissed me. "Finders keepers, I always say," she said, still laughing. "Don't worry, dear. I am not opposed to larceny in a good cause."

We slept all night in each other's arms. Without saying it to each other, we both knew a chapter in our lives was coming to an end and tacitly we postponed the finish. She asked no more questions about Pat.

When we reached Orly, she didn't get out of the car. "I hate airports," she said, "and railway stations. When it's not me that's going."

I kissed her. She patted my cheek maternally. "Be careful in Vermont," she said. "Watch out for changes in the weather."

"All in all," I said, "it's not been a bad time, has it?"

"All in all, no," she said. "We've been to some nice places."

My eyes were teary. Hers were brighter than usual, but dry. She looked beautiful, tanned and refreshed by her holiday. She was wearing the same dress she had worn when she arrived in Porto Ercole.

"I'll call you," I said, as I got out of the car.

"Do that," she said. "You have my number in Sag Harbor."

I leaned into the car and kissed her again. "Well, now," she said softly.

I followed the porter with my luggage into the terminal. At the desk, I made sure I had all the checks for my bags.

I caught a cold on the plane and was sniffling and running a fever when we landed in Logan. The customs man who came up to me must have taken pity on my condition because he merely waved me on. So I didn't have to pay any duty on the five Roman suits. I took it as a favorable omen to counterbalance the cold. I told the taxi driver to take me to the Ritz-Carlton, where I asked for a sunny room. I had learned the Fabian lesson of the best hotel in town, if I had learned nothing else. I sent down for a Bible and the boy brought up a paperback copy. The next three days I spent in the room, drinking tea and hot rum and living on aspirin, shivering, reading snatches from the Book of Job, and watching television. Nothing I saw on television made me happy I had returned to America.

On the fourth day my cold had gone. I checked out of the hotel, paying cash, and rented a car. The weather was wet and blustery, with huge dark clouds scudding across the sky, not a good day for driving. But by then I was in a hurry. Whatever was going to happen I wanted to happen soon.

I drove fast. The countryside in the changing northern season was dead, desolate, the trees bare, the fields muddy, shorn of the grace of snow, the houses closed in on themselves. When I stopped once for gas, a plane flew overhead, low, but unseen in the thick cloud. It sounded like a bombing raid. I had crossed this stretch of the country, at the controls of a plane, hundreds of times. I touched the silver dollar in my pocket.

I reached Burlington just before three o'clock and went directly to the high school. I parked the car across the street from the school and turned the motor off and waited, with the windows all turned up to keep out the cold. I could hear the three o'clock bell ring and watched the flood of boys and girls surge through the school doors. Finally, Pat came out. She was wearing a big, heavy coat and had a scarf around her head. With her myopic eyes I knew my car, forty yards away from her, was only a blur to her and that she couldn't tell whether anyone was in it or not. I was about to open the door and get out and cross over to her when she was stopped by one of the students, a big fat boy in a checkered mackinaw. They stood there in the gray afternoon light, talking, with the wind whipping at her coat and the ends of her scarf. The window on my side was beginning to mist over from the condensation of my breath in the cooling car, and I rolled it down to see her better.

She and the boy seemed in no hurry to be on their way, and I sat there looking at her for what seemed like a very long time. Consciously, I made myself assess, at that one moment, what I felt, on the deepest level, as I watched her. I saw a nice enough little woman, ordinarily pretty, who in a few years would look austere, who had no connection with me, who could not move me to joy or sorrow. There was a faded, almost obliterated memory of pleasure and regret.

I turned on the ignition and started the car. As the car moved slowly past her and the boy, they were still talking. She did not look at the car. They were still standing there, on the windswept, darkening street, when I took a last look back in the rearview mirror.

I drove to the Howard Johnson Lodge and put in a call for Sag Harbor.

"Love, love!" Fabian was saying disgustedly. We were in the living room of his suite in the St. Regis. As usual, as in anyplace he lived even for a day, it was littered with newspapers in several languages. We were alone. Lily had had to go back to England. I had driven directly to New York. I had told Evelyn on the phone that I would get to Sag Harbor the next day. "I thought that you had at least gotten over *that*," Fabian was saying. "You sound like a high-school sophomore. Just when everything is going so smoothly, you've got to blow up the whole thing. . . ."

Remembering the morning on the dock at Porto Ercole, I was displeased with his choice of words. But I said nothing. I was going to let him talk himself out.

"Sag Harbor, for Christ's sake," he said. He was pacing up and down, from one end of the big room to another. Outside there was the sound of the traffic on Fifth Avenue, reduced to a rich hum by thick walls and heavy drapes. "It's just a couple of hours from New York. You'll wind up with a bullet in your head. Have you ever been in Sag Harbor in the winter, for God's sake? After the first fine flush of passion dies down, what do you expect to do there?"

"I'll find something," I said. "Maybe I'll just read. And let you work for me." He snorted and I smiled.

"Anyway," I said, "I'll probably be safer in America surrounded by millions of other Americans than in Europe. You saw for yourself—I stick out like a lighthouse among Europeans."

"I had hoped to be able to teach you to blend into the scenery."

"Not in a hundred years, Miles," I said. "You know that."

"You're not that unteachable," he said. "I saw certain signs of improvement even in the short time we were together. By the way, I see you went to my tailor."

I was wearing one of the suits from Rome. "Yes," I said. "How do you like it?" I flipped the lapel of the jacket.

"A welcome change," he said, "from the way you looked when I met you. You got a haircut in Rome, too, I see."

"You never miss anything, do you?" I said. "Good old Miles."

"I dread to think of what you're going to look like after a visit to the barber at Sag Harbor."

"You make it sound as though I'm going to live in the wilderness. That part of Long

Island is one of the swankiest places in the United States."

"As far as I'm concerned," he said, still pacing, "there are no swanky places, as you so elegantly put it, in the United States."

"Come on, now," I said. "I remember you come from Lowell, Massachusetts."

"And you come from Scranton, Pennsylvania," he said, "and we both should do our damndest to forget the two misfortunes. Righto, marriage. I grant you that. You're pleased at the prospect of having a son. I'll grant you *that,* even though it's against all my principles. Have you ever taken a good look at American kids today?"

"Yes. They're endurable."

"That woman must have bewitched you. A lady lawyer!" He snorted again. "God, I should have known I should never have left you alone. Listen, has she ever been to Europe? I mean before this—this episode?"

"Yes," I said.

"Why don't you make this proposition to her— You get married. Righto. But she tries living in Europe with you for a year. American women love living in Europe. Men chase them until they're seventy—especially in France and Italy. Let her talk to Lily. Then she can decide. Nothing could be fairer than that, could it? Do you want me to talk to her?"

"You can talk to her," I said, "but not about that. Anyway, it's not only the way she feels. It's the way *I* feel. I don't want to live in Europe."

"You want to live in *Sag Harbor.*" He groaned melodramatically. "Why?"

"A lot of reasons—most of them having very little to do with her." I couldn't explain to him about Angelo Quinn's paintings and I didn't try.

"At least can I meet the lady?" he asked plaintively.

"If you don't try to convince her," I said. "About anything."

"You're some dandy little old partner, partner," he said. "I give up. When can I meet her?"

"I'm driving out tomorrow morning."

"Don't make it too early," he said. "I have some delicate negotiations starting at ten."

"Naturally," I said.

"I'll explain everything I've been doing over dinner. You'll be pleased."

"I'm sure I will," I said.

And I was, as he talked steadily across the small table late that evening at a small French restaurant on the East Side, where we had roast duckling with olives and a beautiful, full Burgundy. I was considerably richer, I learned, than when I had watched his plane take off from Cointrin with Sloane's coffin in the hold. And so, of course, was Miles Fabian.

It was nearly six o'clock by the time we got to Evelyn's house, the rural, gentle landscape through which we passed neat in the seaside dusk. Fabian had checked into a hotel in Southampton on the way, and I had waited for him while he bathed and changed his clothes and made two transatlantic telephone calls. I had told him that Evelyn expected him and was readying a guest room for him, but he had said, "Not for me, my boy. I don't relish the idea of being kept awake all night by sounds of rapture. It's especially disturbing when one is intimate with the interested parties."

I remembered Brenda Morrissey reporting at breakfast on the same phenomenon in Evelyn's apartment in Washington and didn't press him.

As we drove up to the house, the outside lamp beside the door had snapped on. Evelyn was not going to be taken by surprise.

The lamp shed a mild welcoming light on the wide lawn in front of the house, which was built on a bluff overlooking the water. There were copses of second-growth scrub oak and wind-twisted scraggly pine bordering the property, and no other houses could be seen. In the distance there was a satiny last glow of evening on the bay. The house itself was small, of weathered, gray, Cape Cod shingle, with a steep roof and dormer windows. I wondered if I would live and die there.

Fabian had insisted upon bringing two bottles of champagne as a gift, although I had told him that Evelyn liked to drink and was sure to have liquor in the house. He did not offer to help as I unloaded my bags and picked them up to carry them into the house. He considered two bottles of champagne the ultimate in respectable burdens for a man in his position.

He stood looking at the house as though he were confronting an enemy. "It *is* small, isn't it?" he said.

"It's big enough," I said. "I don't share your notions of grandeur."

"Pity," he said, grooming his moustache. Why, I thought, surprised, he's nervous. "Come on," I said.

But he held back. "Wouldn't it be better if you went in alone?" he said. "I could take a little walk and admire the view and come back in fifteen minutes. Aren't there some statements you want to make to the lady alone?"

"Your tact does you credit," I said, "but it isn't necessary. I made all the required statements to the lady on the telephone from Vermont."

"You're sure you know what you're doing?"

"I'm sure." I took his arm firmly and led him up the gravel path to the front door.

I can't pretend that the evening was a complete success. The house was charming and tastefully although inexpensively furnished, but small, as Fabian had pointed out. Evelyn had hung the two paintings I had bought in Rome and they dominated the room, in a peculiar, almost threatening way. Evelyn was dressed casually, in dark slacks and a sweater, making the point, a little too clearly, I thought, that she wasn't going to go to any extra lengths to impress the first friend of mine she had ever met. She thanked Fabian for the champagne, but said she wasn't in the mood for champagne and started for the kitchen to mix martinis for us. "Let's save the champagne for the wedding," she said.

"There's more where that comes from, dear Evelyn," Fabian said.

"Even so," Evelyn said firmly, as she went through the door.

Fabian glanced thoughtfully at me, looked as though he was about to say something, then sighed and sank into a big leather easy chair. When Evelyn came back with the pitcher and glasses, he played with his moustache, ill at ease, and only pretended to enjoy his drink. I could see he had had his taste buds ready for the wine.

Evelyn helped me carry my bags upstairs to our bedroom. She was not one of those American women who believe that the Constitution guarantees that they will never be required to carry anything heavier than a handbag containing a compact and a checkbook. She was stronger than she looked. The bedroom was large, running almost the full width of the house, with a bathroom leading off one side of it. There was an oversized double bed, a vanity table, bookcases, and two cane and mahogany rocking chairs set in an alcove. I noticed that there were lamps, well placed for reading.

"Do you think you'll be happy here?" she asked. She sounded uncharacteristically anxious.

"Very." I took her in my arms and kissed her.

"*He's* not very happy, your friend," she whispered, "is he?"

"He'll learn." I tried to make my voice sound confident. "Anyway, he's not marrying you. I am."

"One hopes," she said ambiguously. "He's power-hungry. I recognize the signs from Washington. His mouth tightens when he's crossed. Was he in the Army?"

"Yes."

"A colonel? He seems like a colonel who's sorry the war ever ended. I bet he was a colonel. Was he?"

"I never asked him."

"I get the impression that you're very close."

"We are."

"And you never asked him what his rank was?"

"No."

"That's a funny kind of very close," she said, slipping out of my arms.

Fabian was standing in front of the mantelpiece, on which stood his half-drunk martini. He was staring at Angelo Quinn's painting of the main street. He made no comment when we came down the stairs and into the living room, but reached, almost guiltily, for his glass. "As for refreshments," he said, falsely hearty, "let me buy you two dear children a magnificent seafood dinner. There's a restaurant in Southampton I . . ."

"There's no need to go all the way to Southampton," Evelyn said. "There's a place right near here in Sag Harbor that serves the best lobsters in the world."

I saw Fabian's mouth tighten, but all he said was, "Whatever you say, dear Evelyn."

She went upstairs to get a coat and Fabian and I were alone for a moment. "I do like a woman," he said, a hard glint in his eye, "who knows her own mind. Poor Douglas."

"Poor nothing," I said.

He shrugged, touched his moustache, turned to look at the painting over the mantelpiece. "Where did she get that?" he asked.

"In Rome," I said. "I bought it for her."

"You did?" he said flatly, but with a hint of unflattering surprise. "Interesting. Do you remember the name of the gallery?"

"Bonelli's. It's on the via . . ."

"I know where Bonelli's is. Old man with sliding teeth. If I happen to be in Rome I may look in . . ."

Evelyn came down from the bedroom, with her coat over her arm, and Fabian was quick to help her on with it. Somehow, as was the case with any woman whom he considered attractive, his movements at moments like that were caressing, like a lover's, not a headwaiter's. I took it as a good sign.

The lobster turned out to be every bit as good as Evelyn had promised, and Fabian ordered a bottle of American white wine from Napa Valley that he said was almost as good as any white wine he had drunk in France. Then he ordered another bottle. By then, the atmosphere had relaxed considerably and he teased me gently about my Roman suits, praised my skiing to Evelyn and told her that she must allow me to teach her, mentioned Gstaad, St.-Paul-de-Vence, Paris, all very casually, told two funny, unmalicious anecdotes about Giuliano Quadrocelli, listened seriously as we described the blowing up of the boat in the harbor, did not bring up the names of Lily or Eunice, stayed away from the topic of business, deferred at all times when Evelyn wanted to say something, and in general behaved like the most charming and considerate of hosts. I could see that for better or worse he had decided to win over Evelyn and I hoped he would succeed.

"Tell me, Miles," Evelyn said as we were finishing our coffee, "in the war were you a colonel? I asked Douglas and he said he didn't know."

"Heavens no, dear girl," he laughed. "I was the lowliest of lieutenants."

"I was sure you were a colonel," Evelyn said. "At least a colonel."

"Why?"

"No particular reason," Evelyn said carelessly. She put her hand on mine on the table. "Just a kind of air of commanding the troops."

"It's a trick I learned, dear Evelyn," Fabian said, "to cover up my essential lack of self-confidence. Would you like a brandy?"

When he had paid the bill, he wouldn't hear of our driving all the way to take him to his hotel in Southampton. "And tomorrow morning," he said to me, "don't bother to get up early. I have to be in New York by noon and the hotel will find a limousine for me."

As the taxi drove up to the restaurant, now half-obscured by fog rolling in from the bay, he said, "What a lovely evening. I hope we will have many such. If I may, Gentle Heart . . ." I did not miss the echo . . . "If I may . . ." He leaned toward Evelyn. "I would love to kiss this dear girl good night."

"Of course," she said, not waiting for my permission, and kissed him on the cheek.

We watched him get into the taxi and the red taillights faded wetly into the fog.

"Whew!" Evelyn said, reaching for my hand.

That night and the next morning I was glad Fabian was in a hotel and not in Evelyn's house.

He did not make it to the wedding, as he was in England that week. But he sent a superb Georgian silver coffeepot as a gift from London, hand-carried by a stewardess he knew. And when our son was born, he sent five gold napoleons from Zurich, where he happened to be at the time.

CHAPTER 24

THE SOUND OF hammering woke me up. I looked at the clock on the bedside table. It was six forty. I sighed. Johnson, the carpenter who was working on the new wing of the house, insisted upon giving what he called an honest day's work for your money. Evelyn stirred in the bed beside me, but did not awake. She was breathing softly, the covers half-thrown back, her breasts bare. She looked delicious lying there, and I would have liked to make love to her. But she was cranky in the morning, and besides, she had worked late the night before on a brief she had brought home from the office with her. Later, I promised myself.

I got out of bed and parted the curtains to see what the weather was like. It was a fine summer morning and the sun was already hot. I put on a pair of bathing trunks and a terry-cloth bathrobe, got a towel, and left the room, barefooted and silent, congratulating myself for having had the good sense to marry a woman who came complete with a house on a beach.

Downstairs, I went into the guest room, which was now transformed into a nursery. I could hear Anna, the girl who looked after the baby, moving around in the kitchen. The baby was in his crib, gurgling over his morning bottle. I stared down at him. He looked rosy, serious, and vulnerable. He didn't resemble either Evelyn or myself; he just looked like a baby. I didn't try to analyze my feelings as I stood beside my son, but when I went out of the room, I was smiling.

I turned the bolt on the second lock that I had installed on the front door when I moved in with Evelyn. She had said that it was unnecessary, that in all the time she and her parents had the house there never had been any trouble. So far there had been no uninvited guests, but I still made certain the bolt was in place each night before I went to bed.

Outside, the lawn was wet with dew, cool and agreeable on my bare feet. "Good morning, Mr. Johnson," I said to the carpenter, who was putting in a window frame.

"Good morning, Mr. Grimes," Johnson said. He was a formal man and expected to be treated formally. The rest of the building crew wouldn't arrive until eight, but Mr. Johnson had told me he preferred working alone and that his early-morning labor, when nobody was around to bother him, was the best part of the day. Evelyn said the real reason he started so early was that he enjoyed waking people up. He had a

Puritanical streak and didn't approve of sluggards. She had known him since she was a little girl.

The new wing was almost finished. We were going to move the nursery into it and there would be a library where Evelyn could work and keep some books. Up to now she had had to work on the dining-room table. She had an office in town, but the phone was always ringing there, she said, and she couldn't concentrate. She had a secretary and a clerk, but she always seemed to have more work than she could comfortably handle between nine in the morning and six at night. It was amazing how much litigation went on in this peaceful part of the world.

I circled the house and crossed to the edge of the bluff. The bay stretched out below me, glittering and calm in the morning sunlight. I went down the flight of weathered wooden steps to the little beach. I took off the bathrobe and took a deep breath and ran into the water. It was still early in July and the water was shockingly cold. I swam out a hundred yards and then back and came out tingling all over and feeling like singing aloud. I took off my trunks and toweled myself dry. There was nobody else on the whole stretch of beach at that hour to be offended by momentary male nudity.

Back in the house, I turned on the kitchen radio for the early news as I made myself breakfast. There was speculation in Washington that President Nixon was going to be forced to resign. I thought of David Lorimer and his farewell party in Rome. I sat at the kitchen table and drank my fresh orange juice and lingered over bacon and eggs, toast and coffee. I pondered on the special, marvelous taste of breakfasts that you made for yourself on a sunny morning. In the fourteen months since we had been married, I had become addicted to domesticity. Often, when Evelyn came home tired from the office, I prepared dinner for both of us. I had made Evelyn swear never to tell this to a soul, especially not to Miles Fabian. On his subsequent visits, after the first touchy evening on which they had met, Evelyn and he had come to terms. They would never be friends, but they were not unfriendly.

Fabian had been in East Hampton for three weeks, helping me get ready for the opening. Early in the year, he had gone to Rome and had gotten in touch with Angelo Quinn and made a contract with him for all his output. He had done the same thing with the man whose lithographs he had bought in Zurich. Then he had come out to Sag Harbor and outlined a scheme that I had thought was insane at first, but which, surprisingly, Evelyn had approved of. The plan was to open a gallery in nearby East Hampton and have me run it. "You're not doing anything, anyway," he said, which was true at the time, "and I'll always be available to help you when you need it. You have a lot to learn, but you certainly picked a winner with Quinn."

"I bought two paintings for my girl," I said. "I didn't intend to start a career."

"Have I steered you wrong up to now?" he demanded.

"No," I admitted. Among the other things on which he had not steered me wrong, like gold and sugar and wine and Canadian zinc and lead and the land in Gstaad (the chalet would be built by Christmas and every apartment had been rented), there was also Nadine Bonheur's dirty movie, which had been playing to full houses for seven months, in New York, Chicago, Dallas, and Los Angeles amid cries of shame in church publications. Our names, happily, were not on anything connected with the picture except the checks we received each month. And they went directly to Zurich. My bank balances, both open and secret, were impressive, to say the least. "No," I said, "I can't say that you've steered me wrong up to now."

"This area is rich in three things," Fabian went on, "money, potatoes, and painters. You could have five shows a year just with local artists and you still wouldn't begin to tap the total product. People are *interested* in art here and they have the dough to invest in it. And it's like Palm Beach—people are on vacation and are free with their money here. You can get double the price for a picture that you'd have to sweat to get off the wall in New York. That's not to say that we'd just stick with this one place. We'll start modestly and see how it goes, of course. After that, we could look into the possibilities of Palm Beach, say, Houston, Beverly Hills, even New York. You wouldn't be against spending a month or so in Palm Beach in the winter, would you?" he asked Evelyn.

"Not completely," Evelyn said. "No."

"What's more, Douglas," he said, "it would launder a reasonable portion of your money for the tax hounds. You were the one who wanted to live in the States and they're bound to come after you. You could throw open your books and sleep at night. And you'd have a legitimate reason to travel in Europe, on the search for talent. And while you were in Europe you could make the occasional necessary visit to your money there. And, finally, for once you could do something for me."

"For once," I said.

"I don't expect gratitude," Fabian said aggrievedly, "but I do expect normal civility."

"Listen to the man," Evelyn said. "He's making sense."

"Thank you, my dear," Fabian said. Then, to me, "You don't object if something that is in both our interests happens to be a project that is dear to my heart, do you?"

"Not necessarily," I said.

"You *can* be ungracious, can't you?" he said. "Nevertheless—permit me to go on. You know me. You've tagged along with me through enough museums and galleries to have some notion of what I think about art. And artists. And not just what they mean in terms of money. I *like* artists. I would have liked to be one myself. But I couldn't. And the next best thing is to be mixed up with them, help them, gamble on my taste, maybe one day discover a great one." Part of this may have been true, part pure rhetoric, for the purpose of persuading me. I doubted if Fabian could have distinguished which was which himself. "Angelo Quinn is good enough," he went on, "but maybe one day some kid will walk in with a portfolio and I'll say, 'Now I can give up everything else. This is it, this is what I've been waiting for.'"

"Okay," I said. I had known from the beginning I couldn't hold out against him. "You've convinced me. As usual. I'll devote my life to the building of the Miles Fabian museum. Where do you want it? How about down the hill from the Maeght Museum in St.-Paul-de-Vence?"

"Wilder things have happened," Fabian said soberly.

We had rented a barn on the outskirts of East Hampton, painted it, cleaned up the interior, and put up our sign—The South Fork Gallery. I had refused to put my name on it. I wasn't quite sure whether my refusal was influenced by modesty or fear of ridicule.

Now, Fabian would be waiting for me there at nine o'clock that morning, surrounded by thirty paintings by Angelo Quinn that we had spent four days hanging on the barn walls. The invitations to the opening of the show had gone out two weeks in advance and Fabian had promised free champagne to about a thousand of his best friends who were in the Hamptons for the summer and we had arranged for two policemen to handle the parking problem.

I was finishing a second cup of coffee when the telephone rang. I went into the hall and picked it up. "Hello," I said.

"Doug," a man's voice said, "this is Henry."

"Who?"

"Henry. Hank. Your brother, for God's sake."

"Oh," I said. I had called him when I got married but hadn't seen or spoken to him since. He had written to me twice to say that the business still looked promising, which I took to mean that it was about to go under. "How are you?"

"Fine, fine," he said hurriedly. "Listen, Doug, I've got to see you. Today."

"I've got an awfully busy day, Hank. Can't it . . ."

"It can't wait. Look, I'm in New York. You can get here in two hours. . . ."

I sighed. I hoped inaudibly. "Not possible, Hank," I said.

"Okay. I'll come out there."

"I'm really jammed . . ."

"You're going to eat lunch, aren't you?" he said accusingly. "Christ, you can spare an hour every two years for your brother, can't you?"

"Of course, Hank," I said.

"I can be there by noon. Where do I meet you?"

I gave him the name of a restaurant in East Hampton and told him how to find it.

"Great," he said.

I hung up. This time I sighed aloud.

I went upstairs and dressed.

Evelyn was just getting out of bed and I kissed her good morning. For once she wasn't cranky at that hour. "You smell salty," she whispered as I held her. "Deliciously salty." I slapped her fondly on her bottom and told her I was busy for lunch, but that I'd call her later and tell her how things were going.

As I drove toward East Hampton I decided that I could give Hank ten thousand dollars. At the most, ten thousand. I wished he had chosen another day to call.

Fabian was prowling around the gallery, giving little touches to the paintings to straighten them, although they all looked absolutely straight to me. The girl from Sarah Lawrence we had hired for the summer was taking champagne glasses out of cases and arranging them on the trestle table we had set up at one end of the barn. The champagne would be delivered in the afternoon by the caterer Fabian had hired. The two paintings from our living room were on the walls. Fabian had put little red sold tabs on them. "To break the ice," he had explained. "Nobody likes to be the first one to buy. Tricks in every trade, my boy."

"I don't know what I'd do without you," I said.

"Neither do I," he said. "Listen, I've been thinking."

I recognized the tone. He was coming up with a new scheme.

"What is it now?" I asked.

"We're underpricing," he said.

"I thought we'd been through all that." We had spent days discussing prices. We had settled on fifteen hundred dollars for the larger oils and between eight hundred and a thousand for the smaller ones.

"I know we talked about it. But we set our sights too low. We were too modest. People will think we don't have any real confidence in the man."

"What do you suggest?"

"Two thousand for the big ones. Between twelve and fifteen hundred for the smaller ones. It'll show we're serious."

"We'll wind up the proud owners of thirty Angelo Quinns," I said.

"Trust my instinct, my boy," Fabian said grandly. "We're really going to put our friend on the map tonight."

"It's a good thing he won't be here," I said. "He'd swoon."

"It's a pity the young man wouldn't come. Give him a haircut and a shave and he'd be most personable. Useful for lady art lovers." Fabian had offered to pay Quinn's way across from Rome for the show, but Quinn had said he wasn't finished painting America yet. "So," Fabian said, "two thousand it is, right?"

"If you say so," I said. "I'll hide in the john when anybody asks what anything costs."

"Boldness is all, dear boy," Fabian said. "The breaks are coming our way. I was at a party last night and the art critic from *The Times* was there. He's down for the weekend. He promised to look in tonight."

I felt my nerves grow taut. Quinn had only gotten two lines in an Italian paper for his show in Rome. They had been appreciative, but they had only been two lines. "I hope you know what you're doing," I said. "Because I don't."

"The man will be stunned," Fabian said confidently. "Just look around you. This old barn is positively glowing."

I had looked so hard and so long at the paintings that I no longer had any reaction to them. If it had been possible, I would have driven out to the far edge of the island at Montauk Point and stayed there looking at the Atlantic Ocean until the whole thing was over.

There was a tinkle behind us and I heard the girl say, "Oh, dear." I turned and saw she had dropped a glass and broken it. I supposed they didn't have any courses on the handling of champagne glasses at Sarah Lawrence.

"Do not grieve, dearest," Fabian said as he helped pick up the pieces. "It's a lucky omen. In fact, I'm glad you did it. It reminds me we have a cold bottle of wine in the fridge."

The girl smiled gratefully at Fabian. In the three weeks she had been working for us, he had won her over completely. When *I* spoke to her, she seemed to be trying to catch a weak message being tapped through a thick wall.

Fabian went back into the little room we had partitioned off as an office and brought out the bottle of champagne. He had insisted upon having the refrigerator put in as an essential piece of the gallery's furniture. "It will pay its keep in the first week," he had said as he told the workmen where to install it.

I watched him expertly tear off the foil and unwind the wire. "Miles," I said, "I just had breakfast."

"What better time, old man." The cork popped out. "This is a great day. We must treat it with the utmost care." His life, I had discovered, was replete with great days.

He poured the champagne for the girl and myself. He raised his glass. "To Angelo Quinn," he said. "And to us."

We drank. I thought of all the champagne I had drunk since I had met Miles Fabian and shook my head.

"Oh, by the way, Douglas," he said, as he filled his glass again, "I nearly forgot. Another of our investments will be represented here tonight."

"What investment?"

"At the party last night, we had a distinguished guest." He chuckled reminiscently. "Priscilla Dean."

"Oh, my God," I said. A good part of the abuse heaped on our movie had been directed at the feminine lead. Her photograph, in the nude and in the most provocative positions, had appeared in two nationally circulated magazines. Crowds followed her in the streets. She had been booed by a section of the studio audience when she appeared on television. It had added to the receipts of the movie, but I was doubtful of what it would do for Quinn's reputation. "Don't tell me," I said, "that you invited her here tonight."

"Of course," Fabian said calmly. "We'll be in all the papers. Don't worry, Gentle Heart. I took her aside and told her that her—ah—her connection to us must remain a closely guarded secret. She swore by the head of her mother. Dora," he said, "you realize that anything we say here is never to be repeated anywhere."

"Of course, Mr. Fabian." She looked puzzled. "I really don't understand. Who is Priscilla Dean?"

"A low woman," Fabian said. "I'm glad to see that you don't go to the movies or read filthy magazines."

We finished the bottle of champagne without any more toasts.

Henry was waiting for me when I got to the restaurant a little after twelve. He was not alone. Seated next to him on the banquette was a very pretty young woman with long auburn hair. He stood up as I came over to the table and shook my hand warmly. He was not wearing glasses, his teeth were capped and even, he was tanned and healthy-looking and had put on weight. He had dyed his hair and he could have passed for a man of thirty. "Doug," he said, "I want you to meet my fiancée. Madeleine, my brother."

I shook hands with the lady, choking back questions. "Hank has told me so much about you," Madeleine said. She had a low, pleasant voice.

I sat down, facing them. I noticed that there were no drinks on the table. "Madeleine has never been out here," Henry said, "and she thought she'd like to take a look."

"I really wanted to meet you," she said, staring directly at me. She had big gray eyes that I guessed could be blue in some lights. She did not look like a woman who was engaged to a man who was reputed in some quarters to be impotent.

"This calls for a drink. Waiter . . ." I called.

"Not for us, thanks," Henry said. "I'm off the stuff." He sounded slightly defiant, as though challenging me to comment. I said nothing.

"And I've never been on it," Madeleine said.

"In that case, no drinks," I said to the waiter.

"Shall we order?" Henry said. "I'm afraid we're pressed for time."

Madeleine stood up and Henry and I stood up with her. "I won't be having lunch with you gentlemen," she said. "I know you have a lot to talk over. I'll take a walk and look around this pretty little town and come back and join you for coffee."

"Don't get lost," Henry said.

She laughed. "Not a chance," she said.

Henry's face as he watched her walk toward the door was curiously intense. She had slender legs, a good figure, and her walk was ladylike but sensual. Henry seemed to be holding his breath, as though he had momentarily forgotten to breathe.

"Holy man," I said, as the door closed behind her, "what is all this?"

"Isn't she something?" he said, as he sat down.

"She's a lovely girl," I said with conviction. I didn't say it to flatter either him or her. "Now, spill it."

"I'm getting a divorce."

I nodded. "It's about time, I guess."

"More than about time."

"Where are your glasses?" I asked.

He laughed. "Contact lenses," he said. "That friend of yours, Fabian, sure sent me to the right man. Give him my regards when you see him."

"You can do that yourself. I just left him."

"I'd love to. But I have to be back in New York by four."

"What were you doing in New York this morning?" Somehow, it had never occurred to me that it was possible for my brother to escape Scranton.

"I live there," Henry said. "Madeleine has an apartment there. And the business moved up to Orangeburg. That's just about thirty minutes from the city."

The waiter had come back by now with two glasses of water. Henry ordered shrimp cocktail and a steak. His appetite, as well as his appearance, had improved.

"I appreciate your coming all the way out here to see me, Hank," I said, "but what was the hurry? Why did it have to be today?"

"The lawyers want to have a handshake on the deal this afternoon," he said. "We've been working on it for three months and they've finally got everything together and they don't want to give the other side time to come up with more objections. You know how lawyers are."

"Not really," I said. "What deal?"

"I didn't want to bother you with it until it was definite," he said. "I hope you don't mind."

"I don't mind. Now if you'll begin at the beginning . . ."

"I told you the business looked promising . . ."

"Yes." Guiltily, I remembered that I had considered the word "promising" in his mouth as a synonym for failure.

"Well, it turned out to be a lot better than that." He was silent as the waiter put the shrimp cocktail and my salad in front of us. When the waiter had left, he said, "Better than any of us ever dreamed." He dug heartily into the cocktail. "We had to expand almost immediately. We have more than a hundred people working for us in the plant right now. The stock's not on any of the boards yet, but it's gone way up in value. We've had feelers from a half-dozen companies who want to buy us out. The biggest offer is from Northern Industries. It's a huge conglomerate. You must have heard of them. . . ."

"No," I said, "I'm afraid I haven't."

He looked at me disapprovingly, like a teacher at a pupil who neglected his homework in school. "Anyway, they're *huge*," he said. "Take my word for it. They're the people who're ready to give us the go sign today. They're ready to offer us—our company, that is—a half million dollars." He sat back and let this sink in. "Does the figure grab you?"

"It grabs me," I said.

"We should have the money within a couple of months," Henry said, resuming his meal. "What's more, we—the two boys who came up with the idea and myself—retain running control of the business for the next five years—now, listen to this—at three times the salaries we've been paying ourselves, plus stock options. You'd be in on the options, of course, along with me. . . ."

I wished Fabian was there at that lunch. It was the sort of thing he would wallow in.

The waiter brought Henry his steak and he began to wolf it down hungrily, eating a baked potato and a roll, both heavily buttered, along with it. Before long he would have to watch his diet. "Figure it out, Doug," he said, through a mouthful of food, "you put in twenty-five thousand. Our third of the stock will bring us thirty-three percent of half a million. That's one hundred and sixty-six thousand. Your two-thirds of that . . ."

"I can do arithmetic," I said.

"That's without taking into account the options," Henry said, continuing eating. Either the hot food or the chanting of enormous figures had made his face flush and he was sweating. "Even with today's inflation and all that crap . . ."

I nodded. "It's a nice bundle."

"I promised you you'd never regret it, didn't I?" he said harshly.

"So you did."

"No more other people's money," he said. He stopped eating and put his knife and fork down. He looked at me soberly. His eyes, through the contact lenses, were deep and clear. The little red furrows on the side of his nose had disappeared. "You saved me from drowning, Doug," he said in a low voice. "I can never thank you enough and I won't try."

"Don't try," I said.

"Are you all right?" he asked. "I mean—well—about everything?"

"Couldn't be better."

"You look good, kid, you really do."

"And so do you," I said.

"Well—" He shifted uneasily on the banquette. "The decision is finally up to you. Is it yes or no?"

"Yes," I said. "Of course."

He smiled widely and picked up his knife and fork again. He finished his steak and ordered blueberry pie a la mode for dessert.

"You'd better get some exercise, Hank," I said, "if you're going to eat like that."

"I'm taking up tennis again."

"Come on out here and play sometime," I said. "There're a thousand courts at this end of the island."

"That'd be nice. I'd like to meet your wife, too."

"Anytime." Then I began to laugh.

He looked at me suspiciously. "What're you laughing about?"

"On the way to town this morning," I said, "after you called, I made up my mind that when I saw you today I wasn't going to let you have one cent more than ten thousand dollars."

For a moment he looked hurt. Then he began to laugh, too. We were both laughing, a little hysterically, when Madeleine came back to the restaurant to join us for coffee.

"What's the joke?" Madeleine asked as she sat down.

"A family affair," I said. "Brother stuff."

"Henry will tell me later," she said. "He tells me everything. Don't you, Henry?"

"Everything," he said. He took her hand and kissed it affectionately. He had never been an open or demonstrative man, but that, too, I saw had changed, along with the eyes, the teeth, the appetite. If stealing a hundred thousand dollars from a dead old man could put the expression that I saw now on Henry's face, felony became a virtue and I would steal ten times over from ten dead men.

When I took them to their car, Madeleine gave me their address. "You must come and see us soon," she said.

"I will," I promised. None of us had any idea of how soon it was going to be.

The show, Fabian assured me, was a great success. At one time there must have been more than sixty cars parked outside the barn. The room remained crowded, as people came and went. The champagne got a good deal of serious attention, but so did the paintings. What comments I could overhear in the din of conversation were enthusiastic. "All on the plus side," Fabian whispered to me when we both found ourselves together for a moment at the bar. I didn't see the critic from *The Times,* but Fabian told me he liked the expression on the man's face. By eight o'clock, Dora had put red tabs on four of the big oils and six of the small ones. "Phenomenal," Fabian exulted as he passed me. "And a lot of people have told me they're coming back. What a pity Lily couldn't be here. She'd adorn the room. And she loves parties." His speech was a little thick. He hadn't eaten all day and he had a glass in his hand at all times. I had never seen him drunk before. I hadn't thought he *could* get drunk.

Evelyn seemed somewhat dazed by it all. Quite a few of the guests were theater and movie people, and there were four or five well-known writers whom she recognized but had never met. In Washington, she had never been impressed by the Senators or ambassadors she had known, but this was a world that was new to her and she was almost tongue-tied when she had to talk to a man whose book she admired or an actress who had moved her on the stage. I found it an endearing weakness. "Your friend, Miles," she said to me, shaking her head. "He knows *everybody.*"

"You don't know the half of it," I said.

Evelyn had to go home early, because she had promised Anna the night off. "Congratulations, darling," she said as I accompanied her outside to her car. "It's been splendid." She kissed me and said, "I'll be waiting up for you."

The night air was cool for a few minutes, enjoying the clear, unsmoky evening air. I saw a big Lincoln Continental drive up and Priscilla Dean get out with two graceful young men. The men were in dinner jackets and Priscilla was wearing a long black dress, with a bright red cape thrown over her bare shoulders. She didn't see me and I didn't think I had to go over to say hello to her. I followed them warily into the gallery. There was a little hush as she entered the room, and eyes turned in her direction, but the conversation rose quickly to normal pitch. It was a polite and well-mannered group, and I guessed that most of the people there, like Dora, were not the sort who patronized the kind of theaters in which *The Sleeping Prince* was playing, or subscribed to the magazines in which Priscilla Dean, unclothed, was so prominently featured.

Fabian himself escorted her to the bar. I didn't see her look at a single painting. By the time all the other guests had left, it was past ten o'clock and she was alone at the bar. Drunk. Very drunk. When there had still been a dozen or so people in the room, the two young men had tried to persuade her to leave. "We're expected for dinner, Prissy, darling," one of them had said. "We're way overdue. Come on. *Please.*"

"Fuck dinner," Priscilla said.

"*We* have to go," the other young man had said.

"Go," Priscilla said, steadying herself against the bar. Her cape had fallen to the floor and a generous portion of her excellent upper body was on view. "And fuck you, too. Tonight I'm an art lover. Fags. My old friend from Paris, Miles Fabian, will take me home, won't you, Miles?"

"Of course, dear," Fabian said, without enthusiasm.

"He's an old man," Priscilla said, "but oo la la. Nadine Bonheur has spread the word from Passy to Vincennes. A for effort. *Très bien*. That's French, you fags."

By now, the last of the guests had vanished. I gave silent thanks that Priscilla had arrived on the scene late and that Evelyn had had to go home to mind the baby. Dora was staring at Priscilla with her eyes wide and her mouth hanging open. She had told us when we interviewed her that she was looking for a quiet, clean job where she could catch up on her reading. I avoided Fabian's eyes.

"Stop hanging around, for shit's sake," Priscilla said to the two young men. "One thing I can't stand is people hanging around."

The two young men looked at each other and shrugged. They said good night civilly to Fabian and me and told us how much they had liked the paintings. "Incidentally," the older of the two said, "we're not homosexual. We're brothers." They made their exit with dignity, and a minute later I heard the Lincoln Continental start up and go off.

Fabian bent to pick Priscilla's cape from the floor. He staggered a little and almost fell, but recovered quickly. He put the cape over Priscilla's shoulders. "Time to go beddy-bye, dear," he said. "I shouldn't drive in my condition—" At least, I realized gratefully, he wasn't that far gone. "But Douglas will drive us nice and slowly."

"Your condition." Priscilla laughed raucously. "I know what your condition is, you old goat. Give me a kiss, Daddy." She held out her arms.

"In the car," Fabian said.

Priscilla held onto the table. "I won't budge until I get my kiss," she said.

With an uneasy glance at Dora, who had shrunk back against the wall, Fabian leaned over and kissed Priscilla. Priscilla wiped her mouth with the back of her hands, smudging her lipstick. "I heard you can do better than *that*," she said. "What's the matter—out of practice? Maybe you ought to go back to France." But she allowed Fabian to lead her to the door.

"Dora," Fabian called back, "put out the lights and lock the doors. We'll clean up in the morning."

"Yes, Mr. Fabian," Dora whispered.

We left her there, not moving, rigid against the wall, as we went out.

Priscilla insisted upon sitting between us in the front seat. "Cuddly," she said. She had spilled champagne down the front of her dress and the smell was unpleasant. I rolled down my window before I turned on the ignition.

"Now, dear," Fabian said, "where are you staying?"

"Springs," Priscilla said. "That's it. Springs."

"Where *exactly* in Springs, dear?" Fabian said patiently. "What road?"

"How the hell do I know what road?" Priscilla said. "Just drive. I'll show you the way."

"What's the name of the people you're staying with? We could call them and they could give us directions." Fabian sounded like a policeman trying to get information from a lost child on a crowded beach. "Surely, you must know the name of the people you're staying with."

"Of course I do. Levy, Cohen, McMahon, something like that. Who cares? A bunch of jerks." Priscilla leaned over and turned on the radio. The music from *The Bridge on the River Kwai* crashed through the car. "Come on, Mr. Clean," she said angrily to me, "get this crate moving. You know where Springs is, I hope."

"Go to Springs," Fabian said.

I started the car. But two minutes after we had passed the sign that read, Welcome to Springs, I knew it would be a miracle if we ever found the house that Priscilla was gracing with her presence that weekend. I slowed down at every fork and crossroad and every house we passed, but Priscilla only shook her head and said, "No, that's not it."

No matter how much money we were making from *The Sleeping Prince,* I thought, as I drove, it wasn't worth this.

"We're just wasting time," Priscilla said. "I got an idea. I have two girl friends in Quogue. On the beach. You can at least find the Atlantic Ocean in Quogue, can't you?" She didn't wait for an answer. "They're fantastic. Original swingers. You'll love them. Let's go to Quogue and have a gang bang."

"Quogue is an hour away from here," Fabian said. He sounded very tired.

"So Quogue is an hour away. So what?" Priscilla demanded. "Let's have some fun."

"We've had a very long day," Fabian said.

"Who hasn't?" Priscilla said. "On to Quogue."

"Perhaps tomorrow night," Fabian said.

"Fags," Priscilla said.

We were running through woods, on a small, dark back road that I didn't recognize, and I wasn't sure how I could get back to town without roaming all over the Hamptons for hours. I had just about decided to try to make my way back to East Hampton and find a hotel room for Priscilla and dump her on the sidewalk, if necessary, when my headlights picked up a car facing me, pulled over to the side of the road, with its hood up and two men looking down into the motor. I stopped the car and called out, "I wonder if you two gentlemen could tell me where . . ."

Suddenly I realized I was looking into the muzzle of a gun.

The two men came over to the car, walking slowly. I couldn't see their faces in the dark but could make out that they were both wearing leather jackets and fishermen's long-billed caps. "They have a gun," I whispered to Fabian, across Priscilla, whom I felt stiffening beside me.

"That's right, brother," the man with the gun said. "We have a gun. Now. Listen careful. Leave the key in the ignition, because we're going to take the loan of your car. And get out. Nice and easy. And the old guy, too. He gets out on his side. Also nice and easy. And leave the lady in the car. We're going to take the loan of the lady for a while, too."

I heard Priscilla gasp, but she sat absolutely still. The man stepped back a pace as I opened the door and got out. The other man went around to Fabian's side. I heard him say to Fabian, "Get over there with your partner." Fabian came around and joined me. He was breathing heavily.

Then Priscilla started to scream. It was the loudest, most piercing scream I had ever heard.

"Shut the bitch up," the man with the gun shouted to his partner. Priscilla was still screaming, but she was lying back, with her head on the wheel and kicking at the man, who was trying to hold onto her legs.

"For Christ's sake," the man with the gun said. He moved a little, as though he was going to get at Priscilla from the driver's side. His gun had drooped a little and Fabian lunged at him. There was an enormous noise as the gun went off. I heard Fabian grunt as I jumped on the man, dragging his gun hand down. Our combined weight was too much for him and he fell back, the gun clattering to the pavement. Priscilla was still screaming. I grabbed the gun just as the second man came around the front of the car in the glare of the headlights. I fired at him and he turned and ran off into the woods. The man who had had the gun was crawling away on his hands and knees, and I fired at him. He jumped off and ran into the darkness. Priscilla was still screaming.

Fabian was lying on his back now on the pavement, holding his chest with his two hands. He was breathing in loud, irregular gasps. There was a little light reflected off the road top from our headlights. "I think we'd better get me to a hospital, old man," he said, with long spaces between the words. "Fast. And tell Priscilla to please stop yelling."

I was trying to lift Fabian, as gently as possible, into the back seat of the car, when I became conscious of headlights approaching from behind me. "Sorry," I said to Fabian, who was half in and half out of the car now. "There's somebody coming." I picked up the gun again and stood between Fabian and the oncoming car. Priscilla had stopped screaming and was sobbing wildly in the front seat, hitting her head dementedly against the dashboard. I didn't know which was worse, her screaming or this.

As the car approached, I saw that it was a police car. I dropped the gun I was holding. The car came to a halt and two policemen jumped out, their revolvers in their hands.

"What's going on here?" the one in front asked harshly.

"There's been a holdup. Two men. They're in the woods somewhere. My friend's been shot. We've got to get him to a hospital right away."

"Whose gun is this?" The policeman asked, bending down to pick it up from where it was lying at my feet.

"Theirs."

"You jumped a guy with a gun?" the policeman said incredulously.

"Not me," I said. "Him."

"Holy man," the policeman said softly.

He helped me put Fabian into the rear of the car, while his partner, a thin man with glasses, who looked too young to be a policeman, went to inspect the car with the hood up that the two men had been examining when we drove up. "That's the car, all right," he said when he came back. "We've been looking for it. It was stolen last night at Montauk. We got a description from a gas station at Three Mile Harbor. Lucky for you."

"Real lucky," I said.

He looked curiously at Priscilla, who was still knocking her head against the dashboard, but he didn't say anything. "Follow us," he said. "We'll lead you to the hospital."

With the lights of the police car all flashing and the siren going, we sped down the dark roads. Coming the other way, I saw first one, then another police car racing past us toward the scene of the holdup. They must have sent out a call by radio from the car ahead of us.

The operation took three hours. Fabian had lapsed into unconsciousness before we reached the hospital in Southampton. An intern had taken one look at Priscilla and had her put in a bed under heavy sedation. I sat in the anteroom of the emergency ward, trying to answer the questions of the policemen about what the men looked like, the sequence in which things had happened, what we were doing on the road at that hour, who the lady was, whether or not I thought I had hit one or both of the men when I fired at them. It was hard to sort the things out. My mind felt numb, overwhelmed. It was hard to make the policemen understand who Priscilla Dean was and how it happened she didn't know where she lived. They were unfailingly polite and not suspicious, but they kept asking the same questions, in slightly different ways, over and over again, as though what had happened couldn't have happened the way I thought it had. I had called Evelyn as soon as they wheeled Fabian into the operating room and told her Fabian had had an accident but I was all right, not to worry. I told her I'd give her the details when I got home.

It was about midnight when the young policeman came back from using the phone to tell me the two men had given themselves up. "You didn't hit either one of them." He couldn't help grinning as he said it. I would have to go to the police station in the morning to identify them. And so would the lady, he added.

When Fabian was wheeled out on the operating table he looked calm and peaceful. The doctor, in his green smock and mouth mask, now hanging at his throat, looked grave as he pulled off his rubber gloves. "It's not so good," he said to me. "We'll know better in twenty-four hours."

"Twenty-four hours," I said dully.

"He's a good friend of yours?" the doctor said.

"A very good friend."

"Where did he get that long scar on his chest and abdomen?"

"Scar? I never saw a scar." I blinked. "I guess I never saw him except with his clothes on."

"It must have been something fierce," the doctors said. "It looks like shrapnel. Was he wounded in a war?" The doctor was young, too, no more than thirty-two or thirty-three, and I wondered, briefly, what he knew about wars.

"Yes," I said, "he was in a war. He never told me he was wounded though."

"Live and learn," the doctor said briskly. "Good night."

When I went out of the hospital, there was a flash in my eyes and I cringed. But it was only a photographer, taking my picture. Wait until tomorrow, friend, I thought, when they get dear old Priscilla Dean down to the police station. There'll be some pictures to be taken then.

I drove home slowly, the road blurring uncertainly before me. Evelyn was waiting up for me and we each had a Scotch as we sat in the kitchen and I told her the whole story of the evening. When I finished, she bit her lips and said, "That miserable woman. I could strangle her with my bare hands."

CHAPTER 25

IN THE MORNING, the story was in the Long Island papers, with my picture. And, of course, Priscilla's. Before I went to the police station, I called the hospital and was told Fabian was resting comfortably. I probably could come and visit him for a few minutes later in the morning. Priscilla got to the police station just ahead of me, with uniformed escort. There must have been ten photographers waiting for us. Inside, we both identified the two men, although how Priscilla could have seen what they looked like in the darkened car with all her screaming and thrashing around was beyond me. They had both confessed anyway, so the identification was really a formality.

The two men looked harmless in the light of day. They weren't men, really. Neither of them could have been much more than eighteen, scrawny and frightened, with bad adolescent complexions and fake-tough mouths that quivered when the cops addressed them. Punk kids, my policeman friend called them contemptuously. It was difficult to believe that just a few hours before they had shot a man and had tried to kill me and I had tried to kill them.

When I left the building, the photographers tried to get me to pose with Priscilla, but I just kept on walking. I had had enough of Priscilla Dean.

I talked to the doctor before I went in to see Fabian. The doctor was optimistic. "He came out of the operation much better than I thought he would. I think he'll be around for a while."

Fabian was lying flat in the neatly made bed, with tubes leading into his arm and somewhere in his chest under the covers. The room was sunny and there was the smell of newly cut grass through the open window. He smiled wanly as I came in and raised his hand in greeting.

"I just talked to the doctor," I said as I drew up a chair next to the bed, "and he says you're going to be all right."

"I'm glad to hear that." His voice was frail. "Imagine dying to save the honor of Priscilla Dean." He laughed faintly. "What we should have done was *introduce* her to those two boys." He laughed again, a little rasping noise. "They could have gone off to Quogue together and had themselves a hell of a night."

"Tell me, Miles," I said, "what possessed you to go for that goddamn gun?"

He shook his head gently on the pillow. "Who knows? Instinct? My better judgment blunted by drink? Maybe it was just a little bit of old Lowell, Massachusetts, sticking out."

"I guess that's as good an explanation as any," I said. "While we're on the subject, the doctor says you have a great big scar on your abdomen and chest. Where did you get that?"

"Souvenir of a previous engagement," he said. "I'd prefer not to talk about it right now, if you don't mind. Could you do me a favor?"

"Of course."

"Will you call Lily and ask her if she could possibly come over for a few days? I think old Lily would do me a lot of good."

"I'll call her today," I said.

"That's a good fellow." He sighed. "That was a nice evening, last night. All those polite people. You ought to cable Quinn and congratulate him."

"Evelyn is doing it this morning," I said.

"Thoughtful woman. She looked beautiful last night." I started to get up. "Don't go quite yet," he said. "I believe there's a pad and a pen in that drawer. Will you give it to me, please?"

I opened the drawer and gave him the pad and the pen. He wrote slowly and with difficulty. He tore the top sheet off the pad and gave it to me. "There's no telling what's going to happen, Douglas," he said, "so I . . . " He stopped, as though he was having difficulty choosing his words. "That note you have in your hand is to the private bank in Zurich. I have an account of my own there, as well as our joint one. The number's on there. And my signature. What I'm trying to tell you is that from time to time I . . . I, well—siphoned off a not inconsiderable sum. To put it plainly, Douglas, I was cheating you. That note will restore the money to you."

"Oh, Christ," I said.

"I warned you in the beginning," he said, "I was not running as an admirable man."

I patted his head gently. "It's only money, friend," I said. "The ride was worth it."

There were tears in his eyes. "Only money," he said. Then he laughed. "I was just thinking—it was a lucky thing I got shot. Otherwise nobody would have believed that it was anything but a publicity stunt to promote Priscilla Dean."

The nurse came in and looked at me sternly, so I got up to go. "Don't neglect the shop," Fabian said as I left the room.

Lily arrived the next afternoon. I met her at Kennedy to drive her out to the hospital. She was handsomely dressed for traveling, in the same brown coat I remembered from Florence. She was composed and quiet as we sped east down the highway. But she smoked cigarette after cigarette. I had to stop at a diner to get her two fresh packs. I had told her that the doctor believed that there was a good chance that Fabian would pull through. She had merely nodded.

"The doctor also said"— I broke the silence as we passed Riverhead—"that Miles has an enormous scar running down his chest and abdomen. He said it looked like shrapnel. Do you know anything about that? I asked Miles, but he said he preferred not to talk about it."

"I saw it, of course," Lily said. "The first time we went to bed together. He seemed almost ashamed of it. As though it somehow lessened him. He's vain about his body, you know. That's why he'd never go swimming and always wore a shirt and tie. I didn't press him about it, but after a while he told me. He was a fighter pilot—I suppose he told you that . . . "

"No," I said.

She smiled gently through the cigarette smoke. "He's a great one for selective information to selected people, our Miles. Well, he was a pilot. He must have been a very good one. I found out from older American friends of mine who had known him that he had almost every medal a grateful government could hand out." Her mouth twisted ironically. "In the winter of nineteen forty-four, he was sent on a mission over France. It was a ridiculous, hopeless mission in impossible weather, he told me. I wouldn't know anything about that, of course, but on something like that I tend to believe him. He said his wing commander was a stupid, murderous glory hunter. I'm not up on wars, but I have some idea what that means. Anyway, he and his best friend were shot down over the Pas de Calais. His friend was killed. Miles was taken by the Germans. They took care of him—in a nice, German way. That's where the scar came from. When the hospital he was in was finally overrun, he weighed a hundred pounds. That big man." She smoked in silence for a while. "That's when he decided, he told me, that he had done his last deed for humanity. That explains something of the way he lived. Or does it?"

"Something." I said. "Did you believe that English act?"

"Of course not. We laughed about it. I coached him on Britishisms. You were involved in quite a bit of business with him, weren't you?"

"A bit," I said.

"You remember I warned you about him when it came to money?"

"I remember."

"Did he cheat you?"

"A bit."

She chuckled. "Me, too," she said. "Dear old Miles. He's not an honest man, but he's a joyous one. And he gives joy to others. I'm not the one to say, but maybe one is more important than the other." She lit a fresh cigarette. "It's hard to think of his dying."

"Maybe he won't die," I said.

"Maybe."

We said no more until we reached the hospital. "I think I'd like to see him alone," Lily said, as we drove up to the door of the handsome red-brick building.

"Of course," I said. "I'll drop your bags at the hotel. And I'll be home if you need me." I kissed her and watched her go into the hospital, in her smart brown coat.

It was dark by the time I got home. There was a car I didn't recognize standing in front of the house. More reporters, I thought disgustedly, as I walked up the gravel path. Evelyn's car wasn't in the garage and I guessed that Anna had let whoever it was into the house. I opened the door with my key. A man was sitting in the living room, reading a newspaper.

He stood up when I came in.

"Mr. Grimes . . . ?" he said.

"Yes."

"I took the liberty of coming in and waiting for you here," he said politely. He was a thin, studious-looking man with sandy hair. He was neatly dressed in a lightweight, dark-gray summer suit with a white shirt and dark tie. He didn't look like a reporter. "My name is Vance." he said. "I'm a lawyer. I'm here on behalf of a client. I came for a hundred thousand dollars."

I went over to the sideboard where the whiskey was and poured myself a drink. "Would you like a Scotch?" I asked the man.

"No, thank you."

I carried my drink with me and sat down in an easy chair, facing Vance. He remained standing, a neat, small-boned, unmenacing, indoor type of man. "I was wondering when you'd come," I said.

"It took some time," he said. His voice was dry, low, and educated. It would bore a listener in a short while. "You were not easy to follow. Fortunately . . . " He made a little movement with the newspaper. "You've made yourself into quite a hero out here."

"So it seems," I said. "There's nothing like a good deed for shining in a naughty world."

"Exactly," he said.

He glanced around at the room. From the nursery came the sound of the baby crying. "A nice place you've got here. I admired the view."

"Yes," I said. I felt very tired.

"My client has instructed me to tell you that you have three days to deliver the money. He does not want to be unreasonable."

I nodded. Even that was an effort.

"I will be at the Blackstone Hotel. Unless you prefer the St. Augustine." He smiled, skull-like.

"The Blackstone will do," I said.

"In the same condition in which it was found, please," Vance said. "In one-hundred-dollar bills."

I nodded again.

"Well," he said, "that takes care of everything, I think. I must be on my way now." At the door, he stopped. "You haven't asked me whom I represent," he said.

"No."

"Just as well. I couldn't tell you if you had asked. Still, I can say that your . . . your escapade . . . was not without its benefits. It might ease the pain of having to return the money to know that it saved several distinguished people . . . *very* distinguished people from considerable embarrassment."

"That makes my day," I said.

It was nine o'clock when I went up in the elevator in the apartment building on East Fifty-second Street. I had left word with Anna to tell Mrs. Grimes that I had been called to the city suddenly on business and that I would be gone a day or two. I could have called Evelyn at her office, but I didn't want to have to explain anything.

Henry let me into the apartment. I had caught him just as he was about to go out. He and Madeleine had tickets for the theater, but when I said he would have to wait for me, he said, "I'll be here." He looked worried as he opened the door. Madeleine was in the living room, dressed for her night out in New York. She, too, looked worried.

"Maybe it would be better if you and I talked alone, Hank," I said.

But he shook his head. "I'd rather she stayed, if you don't mind."

"All right," I said. "It won't take long. I need a hundred thousand dollars, Hank. In hundred-dollar bills. I haven't time to collect it from Europe and I don't have it here. I have only three days. Can you get it for me in three days?"

Henry sat down suddenly. We had all been standing in the middle of the living room. He rubbed his eyes with the back of his hand, in a gesture that was a hangover from childhood. "Yes," he said, almost inaudibly. "Somehow. Of course."

It only took two days.

I called Vance's room from the lobby of the hotel. He was there. "I'm coming up," I said. I held the heavy suitcase in one hand while I held the telephone with the other.

"Excellent," he said.

I waited while he counted the bills. He did it slowly and carefully. I hadn't asked Henry where he had found the money and he hadn't told me. "That's it," said Vance, as he snapped a rubber band around the last bundle of bills. "Thank you."

"You can keep the bag," I said.

"That's kind of you." He escorted me to the door.

I drove fast. I wanted to look in at the hospital before it was too late for visitors. I had called at noon and spoken to Lily. Fabian was resting comfortably, she had said. I wanted to tell him that the man had come, as he had predicted, and asked for a hundred thousand dollars and that I had had to give it to him.

When I got to the hospital, the nurse at the front desk stopped me. "I'm afraid you're too late, Mr. Grimes," she said. "Mr. Fabian died at four o'clock this afternoon. We tried to reach you, but . . . "

"That's all right," I said. I was mildly surprised at how calm my voice sounded. "Is Lady Abbott here?"

The nurse shook her head. "I believe Mrs. Abbott has left town." Even at that moment her American distrust of titles prevented her from saying Lady Abbott. "She said there was nothing more she could do here. She thought she could catch a night plane back to London."

I nodded. "Very wise," I said. "Good night, Nurse. I'll be here in the morning to make the necessary arrangements."

"Good night, Mr. Grimes," she said.

I drove slowly toward East Hampton. There was no hurry now. I did not want to go home just yet. I drove to the barn, dark now, with the newly painted sign, The South Fork Gallery, in small, modest letters above the door. "Don't neglect the shop," Fabian had said. I took out my ring of keys and opened the door. I sat on a bench in the middle of the room, without turning on the lights, thinking of the joyous, dishonest, scarred, cunning man who had died that day, and who, by the terms of the contract we had signed that slushy day in the office of the lawyer in Zurich, now had left me free and absurdly wealthy. The tears came slowly.

I got off the bench and went over to the switch and turned on the lights. Then I stood in the middle of the room and looked at the paintings of the wanderings of Angelo Quinn's father, glowing on the walls.

Evening in Byzantium

TO SALKA VIERTEL

OVERTURE

Dinosauric, obsolete, functions and powers atrophied, dressed in sports shirts from Sulka and Cardin, they sat across from each other at small tables in airy rooms overlooking the changing sea and dealt and received cards just as they had done in the lush years in the rainfall forest of the West Coast when in all seasons they had announced the law in the banks, the board rooms, the Moorish mansions, the chateaux, the English castles, the Georgian town houses of Southern California.

From time to time phones rang, and hearty, deferential voices spoke from Oslo, New Delhi, Paris, Berlin, New York, and the card players barked into the instruments and gave orders that at another time would have had meaning and no doubt been obeyed.

Exiled kings on annual pilgrimage, unwitting Lears permitted small bands of faithful retainers, living in pomp without circumstance, they said, "Gin," and, "You're on the schneider," and passed checks for thousands of dollars back and forth. Sometimes they talked of the preglacial era. "I gave her her first job. Seventy-five a week. She was laying a dialogue coach in the Valley at the time."

And, "He brought it two and a half million over the budget, and we had to yank it in Chicago after three days, and now look at him, the pricks in New York say he's a genius. Shit."

And they said, "The future is in cassettes" and the youngest of them in the room, who was fifty-eight, said, "What future?"

And they said, "Spades. Double."

Below, on the terrace seven feet above sea level, open to the sun and wind, leaner and hungrier men spoke their minds. Signaling the hurrying waiters for black coffee and aspirin, they said, "It isn't like the old days."

They also said, "The Russians aren't coming this year. Or the Japanese," and, "Venice is finished."

Under shifting clouds, in sporadic sunlight, the shifty young men carrying lion cubs and Polaroid cameras wound among them, with hustlers' international smiles, soliciting trade. But after the first day the cubs were ignored except by the tourists, and the conversation flowed on, and they said, "Fox is in trouble. Big trouble," and, "So is everybody else."

"A prize here is worth a million," they said.

"In Europe," they said.

And, "What's wrong with Europe?" they said.

"It's a Festival-type picture," they said, "but it won't draw flies in release."

And they said, "What are you drinking?" and, "Are you coming to the party tonight?"

They spoke in English, French, Spanish, German, Hebrew, Arabic, Portuguese, Rumanian, Polish, Dutch, Swedish, on the subject of sex, money, success, failure, promises kept and promises broken. They were honest men and thieves, pimps and panderers, and men of virtue. Some were talented, or more than that, some shrewd, or less than that. There were beautiful women and delicious girls, handsome men and men with the faces of swine. Cameras were busy, and everybody pretended he didn't know that photographs were being taken.

There were people who had been famous and were no longer, people who would be famous next week or next year, and people who would die unknown. There were people going up and people going down, people who had won their victories easily and people unjustly flung aside.

They were all gamblers in a game with no rules, placing their bets debonairly or in the sweat of fear.

At other places, in other meetings, men of science were predicting that within fifty years the sea that lapped on the beach in front of the terrace would be a dead body of water and there was a strong probability that this was the last generation to dine on lobster or be able to sow an uncontaminated seed.

In still other places bombs were being dropped, targets chosen, hills lost and taken; there were floods and volcanic eruptions, wars and the preparation for wars, governments shaken, funerals and marches. But on the terrace for two weeks in springtime France, all the world was printed on sprocketed strips of acetate that passed through a projector at the rate of 90 feet per minute, and hope and despair and beauty and death were carried around the city in flat, round, shining tin cans.

CHAPTER 1

THE PLANE BUCKED as it climbed through black pillars of cloud. To the west there were streaks of lightning. The seat-belt sign, in English and French, remained lit. The stewardesses served no drinks. The pitch of the engines changed. The passengers did not speak.

The tall man, cramped in next to the window, opened a magazine, closed it. Drops of rain made pale, transparent traces, like ghostly fingers, along the Plexiglas portholes.

There was a muffled explosion, a ripping noise. A ball of lightning rolled down the aisle, incredibly slow, then flashed out over the wing. The plane shuddered. The pitch of the engines changed again.

How comfortable it would be, the man thought, if we crashed, how definitive.

But the plane steadied, broke out of the clouds into sunlight. The lady across the aisle said. "That's the second time that's happened to me. I'm beginning to feel I'm being followed." The seat-light signs went off. The stewardesses started to push the drink cart down the aisle. The man asked for a Scotch and Perrier. He drank appreciatively as the plane whispered south, high across the clouded heart of France.

Craig took a cold shower to wake himself up. While he didn't exactly have a hangover, he had the impression that his eyes were fractionally slow in keeping up with the movements of his head. As usual on such mornings he decided to go on the wagon that day.

He dried himself without bothering to towel his hair. The cool wetness against his scalp was soothing. He wrapped himself in one of the big rough white terrycloth bathrobes the hotel supplied and went into the living room of the suite and rang for breakfast. He had flung his clothes around the room while having a last whisky before going to bed, and his dinner jacket and dress shirt and tie lay crumpled on a chair. The whisky glass, still half-full, was beaded with drops of moisture. He had left the bottle of Scotch next to it open.

He looked for mail in the box on the inside of the door. There was a copy of *Nice-Matin* and a packet of letters forwarded from New York by his secretary. There was a letter from his accountant and another from his lawyer in the packet. He recognized the monthly statement from his brokers among the other envelopes. He dropped the letters unopened on a table. With the way the market was going, his brokers' statement could only be a cry from the abyss. The accountant would be sending him unpleasant bulletins about his running battle with the Internal Revenue Service. And his lawyer's letter would remind him of his wife. They could all wait. It was too early in the morning for his broker, his accountant, his lawyer, and his wife.

He glanced at the front page of *Nice-Matin.* An agency dispatch told of more troops moving into Cambodia. *Cambodge,* in French. Next to the Cambodian story there was a picture of an Italian actress smiling on the Carlton terrace. She had won a prize at Cannes some years before, but her smile revealed that she had no illusions about this year. There was also a photograph of the president of France, M. Pompidou, in Auvergne. M. Pompidou was quoted as addressing the silent majority of the French people and assuring them that France was not on the brink of revolution.

Craig dropped *Nice-Matin* on the floor. Barefooted, he crossed the carpeted, high-ceilinged white room, furnished for liquidated Russian nobility. He went out on the balcony and regarded the Mediterranean below him on the other side of the Croisette. The three American assault ships that had been in the bay had departed during the night. There was a wind, and the sea was gray and ruffled, and there were whitecaps. The beach boys had already raked the sand and put out the mattresses and umbrellas. The umbrellas trembled unopened because of the wind. A choppy surf beat at the beach. One brave fat woman was swimming in front of the hotel. The weather has changed since I was last here, he thought.

The last time had been in the autumn, past the season. Indian summer, on a coast that had never known Indians. Golden mist, muted fall flowers. He remembered Cannes when pink and amber mansions stood in gardens along the sea front. Now the garish apartment buildings, orange and bright blue balconies flying, disfigured the littoral. Cities rushed to destroy themselves.

There was a knock at the door.

"*Entrez,*" he called without turning, still judging the Mediterranean. There was no need to tell the waiter where to put the table. Craig had been there three days already, and the waiter knew his habits.

But when he went back into the room, it was not the waiter standing there but a girl. She was small, five feet three, four, he guessed automatically. She was wearing a gray sweat shirt, too long and many sizes too large for her. The sleeves, which seemed to have been made for a basketball player, were pushed up from her narrow tan wrists. The sweat shirt hung almost halfway to her knees over wrinkled and faded blue jeans, stained with bleach. She wore sandals. Her brown hair was long and careless, streaked with sun and salt and hanging down in a mat below her shoulders. She had a narrow triangular face cut into a curious owl-like puzzle by huge, dark sunglasses behind which he could not see her eyes. An Italian leather pouch hung, brass-buckled and incongruously chic, from a shoulder. She slouched as she faced him. He had the feeling that if he looked down at her bare feet, he would discover that she had not bathed for some time, at least not with soap.

American, he thought. It was the reverse of chauvinism.

He pulled the robe around him. It had no sash, and it was not designed for social occasions. At the slightest movement everything dangled out.

"I thought it was the waiter," he said.

"I wanted to be sure to get you in," the girl said. The voice was American. From anywhere.

He was annoyed that the room was so sloppy. Then annoyed at the girl for breaking in like that when he was expecting the waiter.

"Most people call," he said, "before they come up."

"I was afraid you wouldn't see me if I called first," she said.

Oh, Christ, he thought, one of those. "Why don't you start all over again, miss?" he said. "Why don't you go downstairs and give the concierge your name and let him announce you and . . ."

"I'm here, now." She wasn't one of those smiling, oh-you-great-man type of girls. "I'll announce myself. My name is McKinnon, Gail McKinnon."

"Am I supposed to know you?" You never could tell at a place like Cannes.

"No," she said.

"Do you always barge in on people when they're undressed and waiting for breakfast?" He felt at a disadvantage, gripping the robe to hide his private parts and with his hair still dripping and the graying hair on his chest visible and the room a mess.

"I have a purpose," the girl said. She didn't move any closer to him, but she didn't retreat. She just stood there wriggling her bare toes in her sandals.

"I have a purpose, too, young lady," he said, conscious of water dripping down from his wet hair over his forehead. "I propose to eat my breakfast and read my paper and silently and singularly prepare for the terrors of the day."

"Don't be a drear, Mr. Craig," she said. "I mean you no permanent harm. You *are* alone?" She looked meaningfully at the door to the bedroom, which was ajar.

"My dear young lady . . . " I sound ninety years old, he thought, irritated.

"I mean I've been watching you," she said, "for three days, and you haven't been with anybody. Any female body, I mean." While she spoke, the dark glasses swept the room. He was conscious that her glance held for an extra fraction of a second when she saw the script on the desk.

"What are you?" he asked. "A detective?"

The girl smiled. At least her teeth smiled. There was no way of telling what her eyes were doing. "Have no fear," she said. "I'm a kind of a journalist."

"There's no news in Jesse Craig this season, miss. I bid you good morning." He took a step toward the door, but she did not move.

There was a knock, and the waiter came in carrying the tray with the orange juice and coffee, croissants and toast, and the little folding table.

"*Bonjour, m'sieur et 'dame,*" the waiter said with one swift look at the girl. The French, Craig thought, can leer instantaneously and without the slightest change of expression. He was conscious of the girl's costume, fought down an impulse to correct the leer. Shamelessly, he wanted to say to the waiter, "I can do better than *that,* for God's sake."

"I sought zere eez on'y wan breakfast," the waiter said.

"There is only one breakfast," Craig said.

"Why don't you break down, Mr. Craig," the girl said, "and ask for another cup?"

Craig sighed. "Another cup, please," he said. He had been ruled all his life by his mother's instructions about manners.

The waiter set up the table and arranged two chairs. "Eeen wan moment," he said, and left to get the second cup.

"Please be seated, Miss McKinnon," Craig said, hoping that the girl would realize that the formality was ironic. He held the chair for her with one hand while he clutched the robe closed with the other. She looked amused. At least from the nose down she looked amused. She dropped into the chair, placing her bag on the floor beside her. "And now, if you'll forgive me," he said, "I'll go and put on some clothes more suitable for the occasion."

He picked up the script and tossed it into the desk drawer, refused to collect his jacket and shirt, and went into the bedroom, closing the door firmly behind him. He dried his hair and brushed it back, ran his hand over his jaw, thought of shaving and shook his head. He put on a white tennis shirt and blue cotton slacks and stepped into a pair of moccasins. He looked at himself briefly in the mirror, not liking the opaque ivory of the whites of his eyes.

When he went back into the living room, the girl was pouring coffee for both of them.

He drank his orange juice in silence. The girl seemed in no hurry. How many women, he thought, have I sat at a breakfast table with in my life not wanting them to talk. "Croissant?" he asked.

"No, thank you," she said. "I've eaten."

He was glad he had all his teeth as he bit into a piece of toast.

"Well, now," the girl said, "Isn't this friendly? Gail McKinnon and Mr. Jesse Craig at a relaxed moment in the wild whirl of Cannes.

"Well . . ." he said.

"Does that mean I am to begin asking you questions?"

"No," he said, "it means I am going to begin asking you questions. What sort of journalist are you?"

"I'm a radio journalist. Part of the time," she said, holding her cup poised below her mouth. "I do five minute spots of people," she said, "on tape, for a syndicate that sells them to independent stations in America."

"What sort of people?"

"Interesting people. At least the syndicate hopes so." Her voice was flat and slurred, as though she was impatient with questions. "Movie stars, directors, artists, politicians, criminals, athletes, racing-car drivers, diplomats, deserters, people who believe that homosexuality should be legalized or marijuana, detectives, college presidents . . . Want any more?"

"No." Craig watched while she poured him more coffee, the lady of the house. "You said part of the time. What do you do the rest of the time?"

"I try to write interviews in depth for magazines. You're making a face. Why?"

"In depth," he said.

"You're right," she said. "Deadly jargon. You fall into it. It shall never pass my lips again."

"The morning has not been wasted," Craig said.

"Interviews like the ones in *Playboy*. Or that Falacci woman," she said. "The one who got shot by the soldiers in Mexico."

"I read a couple of hers. She cut up Fellini. And Hitchcock."

"Maybe they cut themselves up."

"Should I take that as a warning?"

"If you want."

There was something disturbing about the girl. He had the impression that she wanted something more than she was asking for.

"This town," he said, "is overrun at the moment by hordes of publicity-hungry folk who are dying to be interviewed. People your readers, whoever they are, drool for information about. I'm somebody nobody has heard from for years. Why pick on me?"

"I'll tell you some other time, Mr. Craig," she said. "When we get to know each other better."

"Five years ago," he said, "I would have kicked you out of this room ten minutes ago."

"That's why I wouldn't have interviewed you five years ago." She smiled again, owl-like.

"I'll tell you what," he said. "You show me some of the magazine pieces that you've done on other people, and I'll read them and decide if I want to take a chance on you."

"Oh, I couldn't do that," she said.

"Why not?"

"I haven't published any." She chuckled briefly, as though what she had said had delighted her. "You'll be my first."

"Good God, Miss," he said, "stop wasting my time." He stood up.

She remained seated. "I will ask fascinating questions," she said, "and you will give such fascinating answers that editors will tumble madly over themselves to publish the article."

"The interview is closed, Miss McKinnon. I hope you enjoy your stay on the Côte d'Azur."

Still she didn't move. "It can only do you good, Mr. Craig," the girl said. "I can help you."

"What makes you think I need help?" Craig said.

"In all these years you never came to Cannes for the Festival," the girl said. "All the years you were turning out one picture after another. Now, when you haven't had your name on a movie since 1965, you arrive, you install youself in a big plush suite, you're seen every day in the Hall, on the terrace, at the official parties. You want something this year. And whatever it is, a big splashy piece about you might just be the thing to help you get it."

"How do you know this is the first time I came for the Festival."

"I know a lot about you, Mr. Craig," she said. "I've done my homework."

"You're wasting your time, miss," he said. "I'm afraid I'll have to ask you to leave. I have a busy day ahead of me."

"What are you going to do today?" Infuriatingly, she picked up a croissant and took a small bite out of it.

"I am going to lie on the beach," he said, "and listen to the waves roll in from Africa. There's an example of the fascinating answers I'm likely to give you."

The girl sighed like a mother humoring a recalcitrant infant. "All right," she said. "It's against my principles, but I'll let you read something." She reached down into her bag and pulled out a batch of yellow paper covered with typescript. "Here," she said, offering him the pages.

He kept his hands behind his back.

"Don't be childish, Mr. Craig," she said sharply. "Read it. It's about you."

"I detest reading anything about myself."

"Don't lie, Mr. Craig," she said, impatient again.

"You have a remarkable way of ingratiating yourself with potential interviewees, miss," he said. But he took the pages and went over to the window where the light was better because he'd have had to put on his glasses to read in the shadowed room.

"If I do it for *Playboy*," the girl said, "what you have there will be in the form of an introduction, before the actual questions and answers begin."

At least, he thought, the girls in *Playboy* have their hair done before they present themselves.

"Do you mind if I pour myself another cup of coffee?" she asked.

"By all means." He heard the china clink of the spout against the cup rim as he began to read.

"To the general public," he read, "the word 'producer' usually has pejorative connotations. The cliché about a movie producer is that he is likely to be a portly Jewish gentleman with a cigar in his mouth, a peculiar vocabulary, and a distasteful penchant for starlets. Or for that small group who have been influenced by F. Scott Fitzgerald's romantic idealization of the late Irvin Thalberg in his unfinished novel *The Last Tycoon,* he is a mysteriously gifted dark figure, a benevolent Svengali, half-magician, half-master politician, who strangely resembles F. Scott Fitzgerald himself in his more attractive moments.

"The popular image of the theatrical producer is somewhat less colorful. He is less likely to be thought of as Jewish or fundamentally gross, although the admiration with which he is regarded is limited. If he is successful, he is envied as a lucky man who by chance one day picks up a script that happens to be lying on his desk, scrambles around for other people's money to back the production, and then coasts happily forward to fame and fortune on the talents of artists whose work he most often tries to corrupt in an attempt to please the Broadway market.

"Curiously enough, in a related field, that of the ballet, honor is given where honor is due. Diaghilev, who as far as is known never danced a step or choreographed a *pas de deux* or painted a dècor, is recognized everywhere as a giant innovator of the modern ballet. While Goldwyn (Jewish, whip-thin, no cigar) and Zanuck (non-Jewish, with cigar, wiry) and Selznick (Jewish, portly, cigarettes) and Ponti (Italian, plump, no cigar) are not perhaps what magazines like *Commentary* and the *Partisan Review* call seminal figures in the art that they served, the films that they have produced and that plainly bear their individual marks have influenced the thinking and attitudes of populations all over the world and certainly prove that they came to their tasks equipped with something more than luck and money or an influential family devoted to nepotism."

Well, he thought grudgingly, you can't fault her grammar. She's been to school *someplace*. But he was still irritated by the offhand manner in which Gail McKinnon had broken into his morning. And irritated even more by her cool assumption that he would perform obediently. Craig would have like to put the yellow pages down and order her from the room. But his vanity was aroused, and he wondered how she would place the name of Jesse Craig in her roster of heroes. He had to make an effort not to glance in her direction and examine her more closely. He read on.

"In the American theatre," he read, "the case is even clearer. In the 1920s Lawrence Langner and Terry Helburn, with their Theatre Guild, opened new horizons of drama, and as late as the 1940s, still functioning not as directors or writers but solely as producers, they transformed that most American of theatrical forms, the musical comedy, with *Oklahoma*. Clurman, Strasberg, and Crawford, the ruling trio of the Group Theater, while sometimes directors in their own right, made their chief contribution in their choice of controversial plays and the method of training actors in ensemble playing."

She wasn't lying, Craig thought. She had done her homework. She wasn't even born when any of this was going on. He looked up. "May I ask you a question?"

"Of course."

"How old are you?"

"Twenty-two," she said. "Does it make any difference?"

"It always makes a difference," he said. He read on with ungenerous respect. "More recent names are not hard to find, but there is no need to belabor the point. There was almost certainly someone, whatever he was called, who took on the task of assembling the talents for the festivals in which Aeschylus and Sophocles competed, and Burbage saw to it that the Globe Theatre was a running concern when Shakespeare brought in *Hamlet* for him to read.

"In this long and honorable list we now come to Jesse Craig."

Brace yourself, he thought. This is where the brick drops.

"In 1946," he read, "Jesse Craig, then aged twenty-four, first commanded attention when he presented *The Foot Soldier,* still one of the few viable dramatic works about World War Two. Between 1946 and 1965 Craig produced 10 more plays and 12 movies, a high proportion of them both critical and commercial successes. Since 1965 no production bearing his name has been seen either on the stage or screen."

The phone rang. "Excuse me," he said, picking it up.

"Craig speaking," he said.

"Did I wake you?"

"No." He glanced guardedly at the girl. She slouched in her chair, absurd in the oversized sweat shirt.

"Did you dream lascivious dreams of me all the terrible night?"

"Not that I remember."

"Brute. Are you having a good time?"

"Yes."

"Double brute," Constance said. "Are you alone?"

"No."

"Ah."

"You know better than that."

"Anyway, you can't talk at the moment?"

"Not exactly. How is Paris?"

"Sweltering. And the French as usual intolerable."

"Where are you calling from?"

"The office."

He could picture her in her office—a small, cramped room on the rue Marbeuf, usually crowded with a dozen young men and women who looked as though they had rowed across the Atlantic instead of arriving on the freighters and steamships and aircraft for student tours that her business was to arrange for them. Anyone under the age of thirty, in whatever state, seemed to be welcome there, and it was only when Constance got a whiff of marijuana that she would rise dramatically from the desk, point fiercely at the door, and clear the room.

"Aren't you afraid someone's listening?" he asked.

Constance was intermittently suspicious that her telephone was tapped—by the French tax people, by the American narcotics people, by ex-lovers highly placed in various embassies.

"I'm not saying anything the French don't know. They glory in being intolerable."

"How're the kids?"

"As usual. Well-balanced. One angelic. One devilish."

Constance had been married twice, once to an Italian, once to an Englishman. The boy was the result of the Italian and had been thrown out of four schools by the age of eleven.

"Gianni was sent home again yesterday," Constance said matter-of-factly. "He was organizing a gangbang in his art class."

"Come on, Constance." She was given to exaggeration.

"Actually, I think he tried to throw a little girl with glasses out of the window. He says she was looking at him. Anyway, something perfectly normal. He can go back in two days. I think they're going to give Philippa a copy of *The Critique of Pure Reason* as a term prize. They took her IQ, and they say she could be president of IBM."

"Tell her I'll bring her a navy blue sailor's jersey from here."

"Bring her a man to put inside it," Constance said. She was certain that her children, like herself, were swamped in sexuality. Philippa was nine. To Craig the girl didn't seem much different from his own daughters at that age. Except that she didn't stand up when grownups came into the room and that she sometimes used words from her mother's vocabulary that he would have preferred not to hear.

"How're things down there?" Constance asked.

"Okay."

Gail McKinnon got up politely and went out to the balcony, but he was sure she could still hear what he was saying.

"Oh," Constance said, "I put in a good word for you last night with an old friend of yours."

"Thanks. Who was it?"

"I had dinner with David Teichman. He always calls me when he comes through Paris."

"Along with ten thousand other people who always call you when they come through Paris."

"You wouldn't want a girl to have dinner alone, would you?"

"Never."

"Anyway, he's a hundred years old. He's coming down to Cannes. He says he's thinking of starting a new company. I told him you might have something for him. He's going to call you. Do you mind? At the worst, he's harmless."

"He'd die if he heard you say that." David Teichman had terrorized Hollywood for more than twenty years.

"Well, I did my bit." She sighed into the phone. "I had a bad morning. I woke up and reached out and said 'Damn him.'"

"Why?"

"Because you weren't there. Do you miss me?"

"Yes."

"You sound as though you're speaking from a police station."

"Something like that."

"Don't hang up. I'm bored. Did you have bouillabaisse for dinner last night?"

"No."

"Do you miss me?"

"I've already answered that."

"That's what a girl might call a very cool reply."

"It wasn't meant to be."

"Do you wish I was there?"

"Yes."

"Say my name."

"I'd rather not at the moment."

"When I hang up, I'm going to be prey to dark suspicions."

"Put your mind at rest."

"This call has been an almost total waste of money. I dread tomorrow morning."

"Why?"

"Because I'm going to wake up and reach out and you won't be there again."

"Don't be gluttonous."

"I'm a gluttonous lady. Well, get whoever it is out of the room and call me back."

"Will do."

"Say my name."

"Pest."

There was a laugh at the other end of the wire. Then the click as Constance hung up.

He put the phone down. The girl came back into the room. "I hope I didn't cramp your style," she said.

"Not at all," he said.

"You look happier than before the call," the girl said.

"Do I? I wasn't aware of it."

"Do you always answer the phone that way?"

"What way?"

"Craig speaking."

He thought for a moment. "I suppose so. Why?"

"It sounds so—institutional," the girl said. "Don't your friends object?"

"If they do," he said, "they don't tell me about it."

"I hate institutions," she said. "If I had to work in an office, I'd—" She shrugged and sat down in the chair at the breakfast table. "How do you like what you've read so far?"

"Early in my career I resolved never to make a judgment on unfinished work," he said.

"Do you still want to go on reading?"

"Yes," he said.

"I'll be still as the starry night." She slumped in the chair, leaning back, crossing her leg. Her sandalled feet were actually clean, he noticed. He remembered how many times over the years he had ordered his daughters to sit up straight. They still didn't sit up straight. The nonerect generation. He picked up the yellow pages that he had put down when he answered the telephone and began reading again.

"At the time of this interview," he read, "Craig received McK in the living room of his hundred-dollar-a-day suite in the Hotel Carlton, the pinkish gingerbread head-quarters for the VIPs of the Cannes Film Festival. He is a tall, slim, slow-moving, bony man with thick graying hair worn long and carelessly brushed back from a forehead deeply ridged by wrinkles. His eyes are a cold pale gray, deeply set in their sockets. He is forty-eight now, and he looks it. His glance is hooded, the eyelids characteristically almost half-shut. One gets the impression of a sentinel scanning the field below him through an aperture in a fortress wall. His voice, from which not all traces of his native New York have disappeared, is slow and husky. His manner is old-fashioned, distant, polite. His style of dress, in this town of peacock adornment for men and women alike, is conservative. He might be a Harvard professor of literature on a summer holiday in Maine. He is not handsome. The lines of his face are too flat and hard for that and his mouth too thin and disciplined. In Cannes, where a number of the assembled notables had either worked for him or with him and where he was greeted warmly at every appearance, he seemed to have many acquaintances and no friends. On two of his first three evenings at the festival he dined alone. On each occasion he drank three martinis before and a full bottle of wine with his meal, with no noticeable effect."

Craig shook his head and put the yellow pages down on the bookcase near the window. There were still three or four that he hadn't read.

"What's the matter?" the girl asked. She had been watching him closely. He had been conscious of her stare through the dark glassses and had carefully remained expressionless while he read. "You find a bubu?"

"No," he said. "I find the character unsympathetic."

"Read on," the girl said. "He improves." She stood up, slouching. "I'll leave it with you. I know what a strain it is reading something with the author watching you."

"Better take this stuff with you." Craig gestured toward the small pile of pages. "I am a notorious loser of manuscripts."

"Not to worry," the girl said. "I have a carbon."

The phone rang again. He picked it up. "Craig speaking," he said. Then he looked across at the girl and wished he hadn't said it.

"My boy," the voice said.

"Hello, Murph," he said. "Where are you?"

"London."

"How is it there?"

"Expiring," Murphy said. "Inside of six months they'll be turning the studios into feeding lots for Black Angus bulls. How's it down there?"

"Cold and windy."

"It's got to be better than here," Murphy said. As usual, he spoke so loudly that everybody in the room could hear him. "We're changing our plans. We're flying down tonight instead of next week. We're booked in at the Hotel du Cap. Can you have lunch with us tomorrow there?"

"Of course."

"Perfect," Murphy said. "Sonia says give him my love."

"Give her my love," Craig said.

"Don't tell anyone I'm coming," Murphy said. "I want a few days rest. I don't want to have to run into Cannes to talk to spitballing Italians three times a day."

"Your secret is safe with me," Craig said.

"I'll call the hotel," Murphy said, "and tell them to put the wine on ice."

"I was thinking of going on the wagon today," Craig said.

"Not on my time, my boy," Murphy said. "See you tomorrow."

"Tommorow," Craig said, and hung up.

"I couldn't help overhearing," the girl said. "That was your agent, wasn't it? Bryan Murphy?"

"How do you know so much?" Craig asked. His tone was sharper than he intended it to be.

"Everybody knows who Bryan Murphy is," the girl said. "Do you think he'd talk to me?"

"You'll have to ask him yourself, Miss," Craig said. "I'm not his agent, he's mine."

"I imagine he will. He's talked to everybody else," she said. "Anyway, there's no rush. We'll see how things work out. It'd be nice if I could listen in on you two talking for an hour or two. In fact, the best way to do the whole job," she went on, "would be to let me hang around with you for a few days. An admiring silent presence. You can introduce me as your niece or your secretary or your mistress. I'd put on a dress. I have a wonderful memory, and I won't embarrass you by taking notes. I'll just watch and listen."

"Please don't be so insistent, Miss McKinnon," Craig said. "I had a bad night."

"All right, I won't bother you anymore this morning," she said. "I'll just flee and let you read the rest of what I wrote about you and let you think it over." She slung her bag over her shoulder. Her movements were brusque, not girlish. She was not slouching now. "I'll be around. Everywhere. Wherever you turn, you'll see Gail McKinnon. Thanks for the coffee. Don't bother to see me out."

Before he could protest any further, she was gone.

CHAPTER 2

HE PACED SLOWLY around the room. Its appearance displeased him. It was a room for frivolous transients whose only decision each morning would be whether or not to go swimming and what restaurant to choose for lunch. He tapped in the top of the Scotch bottle and put the bottle away in a cabinet, then picked up his clothes and the sweating half-filled whisky glass. He took it all into the bedroom, dumped the clothes on the bed in which he had slept. The sheets and blankets were tangled. Uneasy sleeper. The second bed was neatly turned down. Whatever lady the maid had prepared it for had slept elsewhere. It made the room seem lonely. He went into the bathroom and emptied the whisky glass into the basin and rinsed it. The counterfeit of order.

He returned to the living room and carried the little folding table with the breakfast tray out into the hall. He locked the door behind him as he went back into the apartment.

There was an untidy pile of brochures and advertising throwaways for various films on the desk. He swept them all into the wastebasket. Other people's hopes, lies, talents, greed.

The letters he had tossed on the table lay next to Miss McKinnon's manuscript. He decided on the letters. Finally, they would have to be read and answered, anyway. He tore open the letter from his accountant. First things first. That primal concern—the income tax.

"Dear Jesse," his accountant wrote, "I'm afraid the 1966 audit is going to be a tough one. The agent on your case has been in and out of the office five times, and he's a bastard. I'm writing this from my home myself, on my own typewriter, so there won't be a copy, and I advise you to burn it when you've read it.

"As you know, we've had to waive the three-year limit of review on your 1966 return; 1966 was the last time you made any real money, and Bryan Murphy set up this deal with a European company because you shot most of the picture in France and the deal looked good to everybody because it seemed that the money your company borrowed against potential profits would be treated as capital gains rather than ordinary income. Well, the IRS is challenging the basis of the deal, and this agent is a real bloodhound.

"Also—and this is for your eyes only—this particular agent looks like a crook to me. He as much as intimated to me that if you did business with him, he'd O.K. the return as filed. For a price. He intimated that eight thousand dollars would do it.

"Now you know that I never touch anything like that. I know, too, that you've never gone in for any such shenanigans, either. But I felt that you had to know what the score was. If you want to do anything about it, you'd better come out here soonest and talk to the bastard himself. And don't tell me what you say to him.

"We could go to court and almost certainly win, as the deal is on the up and up and should stand scrutiny in any court of law. But I have to warn you that the legal costs would probably run you about $100,000. And considering who you are and your reputation, the papers would have a field day with a tax-avoidance case in which you were involved.

"I think we can settle with the bastard for between sixty and seventy-five thousand. My advice is to settle and get a job quick and make it up in a year or two.

"When you answer this, send your letter to my home address. I've got a big office, and you never know whom you can trust there. Aside from the fact that the Government is not averse to opening mail these days. Best regards, Lester."

Make it up in a year or two, Craig thought. It must have been sunny in California.

He tore the letter into small pieces and threw them into the wastebasket. Burning it, as the accountant had suggested, would have been too melodramatic. And he doubted that the Internal Revenue Service went as far as bribing the chambermaids of the Côte d'Azur to piece together the shreds of letters they found in wastebaskets.

Patriot, veteran, law-abider, taxpayer, he refused to think about how his sixty or seventy thousand dollars would be spent by Mr. Nixon, by the Pentagon, by the FBI, by Congress. There was a limit to the amount of moral agony a man could be expected to inflict upon himself when he was, theoretically at least, on holiday. Maybe I ought to let Gail McKinnon read my mail, he thought. The readers of *Playboy* would be fascinated. Diaghilev at the mercy of a postage stamp.

He reached for the letter from his lawyer, then thought better of it. He picked up the batch of yellow sheets, weighed them, held them indecisively over the wastebasket. He shuffled through the pages at random. *He is forty-eight now and looks it,* he read. What does a forty-eight-year-old man look like to a twenty-two-year-old girl? Ruins. The walls of Pompeii. The trenches of Verdun. Hiroshima.

He sat down at the desk, started reading from where he had left off when the girl had gone out of the room. See yourself as the world sees you.

"He does not seem like a self-indulgent man," he read, "and according to all reports he does not indulge in others.

"Because of this, in some quarters he has a reputation for ruthlessness. He has made many enemies, and among his former collaborators there are some who speak of what they call his disloyalty. In support of this it is cited that only once has he ever done more than one play by the same author and unlike other producers has never developed a favorite roster of actors. It must be admitted that when his last two films failed, for a total loss that is estimated at more than eight million dollars, there was little sympathy shown him in the movie colony."

The bitch, he thought, where did she get that? Unlike most other journalists who had interviewed him and who had rarely read anything more about him than they had gleaned from studio publicity handouts, the girl had arrived well prepared. Malevolently well prepared. He skipped two pages, dropping them on the floor, and read on.

"It is common knowledge that at least on one occasion he was offered the top position at one of the most prestigious studios in the industry. It is said he turned the offer down in a brief telegram: 'Have already deserted sinking ship. Craig.'

"His behavior might be explained by the fact that he is a rich man, or should be a rich man if he has handled the money he has earned in a resposible manner. A director he has worked with has put it differently. 'He's just a contrary son of a bitch,' is the way the director explained it. The actress Monica Browning has been quoted in an interview as saying, 'There is no mystery there. Jesse Craig is a simple, charming, homemade megalomaniac.'"

I need something to drink, he thought. He looked at his watch. It was ten twenty-five. So, it's only ten twenty-five, he thought. He got the bottle and went into the bathroom and poured a slug of whisky and ran a little water into the glass from the tap. He took a sip and carried the glass with him back into the living room.

Glass in hand, he continued reading. "Twice Craig has been invited to serve as a member of the jury in Cannes. Twice he refused the invitation. When it became known that he had made reservations for the entire festival this year, many eyebrows were raised. For five years, after the failure of his last film, he has kept away from Hollywood and was only intermittently seen in New York. He has kept his office open but has announced no new projects. He seems to have taken to wandering restlessly for good parts of the recent years around the Continent. The reasons for his retreat are obscure. Disgust? Disillusionment? Weariness? A feeling that his work was done and the time had come to enjoy its fruits in peace in places where he had neither friends nor enemies? Or was it a failure of nerve? Is the visitor to Cannes a spent man on a nostalgic voyage to a place where he can be reminded at every turn of his earlier vigor? Or is it the sallying forth of a man who has regrouped his forces and is intent once more on conquest?

"Does Jesse Craig, in his hundred-dollar-a-day suite overlooking the Mediterranean know the answers himself?"

The typing stopped in the middle of the page. He put the pages face down on the bookcase, sipped once more from his drink. Christ, he thought, twenty-two years old.

He went out on the balcony. The sun had come out, although the wind was as strong as ever. Nobody was swimming. The fat lady had disappeared. Having her hair done or drifted out to sea. Down below, on the terrace, there was already a sprinkling of customers around the tables. He saw the careless brown hair of Gail McKinnon, the oversized sweat shirt, the blue jeans. She was reading a newspaper, a bottle of Coca-Cola in front of her.

While he was watching, a man came up to her table and sat down across from her. She put away her newspaper. Craig was too high up to hear what she was saying.

"I saw him," she was saying to the man. "He'll bite. I've got the old bastard."

CHAPTER 3

HE TOOK A seat. The auditorium was filling rapidly. It was a young crowd, long-haired bearded boys with Indian bands around their heads and their accompanying barefooted girls dressed in fringed leather blouses and long multicolored skirts. They would have been at home in Constance's office. The movie that morning was going to be *Woodstock,* the American documentary about a rock festival, and the devotees, appropriately clad for revolt, had taken over the town. Craig wondered how they all would dress when they were his age. When he was *their* age, he had been happy just to shed his uniform and get into a gray suit.

He put on his glasses and spread his copy of *Nice-Matin.* He had awakened late, and since the movie was three and a half hours long, it had been scheduled to start at nine in the morning, and he hadn't had time for breakfast or the paper in the hotel.

In the warm, dull pinkish light he glanced at the front page of the newspaper. Four students had been shot and killed by the National Guard in Kent, Ohio. Murder continued, as usual, along the Suez Canal. The situation in Cambodia was confused.

A French naval missile had gotten out of control and turned inland and burst near Lavandou, some miles along the coast, destroying several villas. The mayors of the adjacent towns were protesting, pointing out, reasonably enough, that this military waywardness was detrimental to *le tourisme*. A French movie director explained, in an interview, why he would never submit a film of his to the Festival.

Somebody said, *"Pardon,"* and Craig stood up, still trying to read his newspaper. There was a rustle of a long skirt as somebody slid past him and sank into the seat beside him. He was conscious of a light scent of soap that was somehow childish.

"Welcome to the morning," the girl said.

He recognized the dark glasses masking most of the face. The girl's head was wrapped in a figured silk scarf. He was sorry that he hadn't taken the time to shave.

"Isn't it wonderful," the girl said, "how we are constantly thrown together?"

"Wonderful," he said. The voice, as well as the costume, was different today. Softer, without pressure.

"I was there last night, too," she said.

"I didn't see you."

"That's what they all say." The girl looked down at her program. "Were you ever tempted to do a documentary?"

"Like everybody else."

"People say this one is *wild*."

"Which people?"

"Just people." She let the program drop to the floor. "Did you cast an eye on the stuff I sent over?"

"I didn't even have time to order breakfast," he said.

"I like movies at nine in the morning," she said. "There's something perverse in it. It's in a big manila envelope. Further reflections on Jesse Craig. Cast an eye when you have time." She began to applaud. A tall young man with a beard was standing at the bottom of the aisle in front of the stage holding up his hand for silence. "That's the director," she confided.

"Do you know anything else he's done?"

"No." She applauded vigorously. "I'm a director buff."

The director was wearing a black armband, and he began his speech by inviting the members of the audience to do the same as a sign of mourning for the four students who had been killed at Kent State. In his final sentence he said that he was dedicating his film to their memory.

Although Craig did not doubt the young man's sincerity, the speech and the somber decoration made him vaguely uncomfortable. In another place, perhaps, he would have been touched. He certainly was as saddened by the death of the four youths as anybody there. After all, he himself had two children of his own who might be brought down in a similar massacre. But he was in an auditorium that was gilded and luxurious, seated among an audience that was festive and there to be amused. He could not rid himself of the feeling that the whole thing smacked of showmanship, not grief.

"Are you going to wear black?" the girl asked him, whispering.

"I don't think so."

"Nor I," she said. "I don't dignify death." She sat up, straight and alert, enjoying herself. He tried to pretend he didn't know she was sitting beside him.

As the house lights went down and the film began, Craig made a conscious effort to rid himself of all preconceptions. He knew that his distaste for beards and long hair was foolish and arose only because he had grown to manhood at a different time, accustomed to different styles. The manner of dress of the young people around him was at worst merely unsanitary. Fashions in clothes came and went, and a single glance at an old family album sufficed to show how ridiculous once thoroughly conservative garb could seem to later eyes. His father had worn plus fours on a holiday at the beach. He still remembered the photograph.

"Woodstock," he had been told, spoke for the young. If it actually did, he was ready to listen.

He watched with interest. It was immediately clear that the man who had made the picture had considerable talent. A professional himself, Craig appreciated the quality in others, and there was no hint of amateurism or idle playfulness in the way the film was shot and put together. The evidence of hard thought and painstaking labor was everywhere. But the spectacle of four hundred thousand human beings gathered together in one place, no matter who they were or in what place they had congregated, or for what purpose, was distasteful to him. There was a maniacal promiscuity reflected on the screen that depressed him more and more as the film went on. And the music and the performance, with the exception of two songs sung by Joan Baez, seemed coarse and repetitive to him and inhumanly loud, as though the whisper or even the ordinary tone of daily conversation had dropped from the vocal range of young Americans. For Craig the film was a succession of orgiastic howls without the release of orgasm. When the camera discovered a boy and a girl making love, undisturbed by the fact that their act was being recorded, he averted his eyes.

He watched in disbelief as one of the performers, like a cheerleader before a crowd at a football game, shouted out, "Give me an F!" Four hundred thousand voices gave him an F. "Give me a U!" Four hundred thousand voices gave him a U. "Give me a C!" Four hundred thousand voices responded with a C. "Give me a K!" Four hundred thousand voices gave him a K. "What's that spell?" the cheerleader shouted, his voice limitlessly magnified by the public address system.

"FUCK!" came the response in a hoarse, Nurembergrally tidal wave of sound. Then a wild cheering. The audience in the theatre applauded. The girl beside him, Craig noticed, sat with her hands primly clasped in her lap. He liked her the better for it.

He sat quietly in his seat but paid little attention to the film after that. Who could say what that gigantic many-throated FUCK! meant? It was a word like any other, and he used it himself, although not often. It was neither ugly nor beautiful in itself, and its use was now so widespread that it had almost no meaning or so many different meanings that it was no longer valid linguistic coin. In the voices of the giant choir of the young in the film it had a primitive derision, it was a slogan, a weapon, a banner under which huge destructive battalions could march. He hoped that the fathers of the four students who had been shot at Kent State would never see *Woodstock* and know that a work of art had been dedicated to their dead children contained a passage in which nearly half a million of their children's contemporaries had mourned their death by shouting FUCK! in unison.

The film had more than an hour yet to run when he left the theatre. The girl didn't seem to notice that he was going.

The sun was shining over the blue sea, and the flags of the nations represented in the festival snapped brightly at their poles on the theater's façade. Even with the continuous traffic of cars along the waterfront and the passage of the crowds on the sidewalk and promenade, it was blessedly quiet. For this morning, at least, Cannes remembered that it was supposed to look like a Dufy.

Craig went down to the beach and walked by the water's edge, unaccompanied, a private man.

He went up to his room to shave. In the mailbox there was the large manila envelope with his name scrawled on it in a slanting, bold woman's hand and a letter post-marked San Francisco from his daughter Anne.

He tossed the envelopes onto a table in the salon and went into the bathroom and shaved carefully. Then, his face pleasingly smarting from lotion, he went back into the salon and slit open Gail McKinnon's envelope.

There was a hand-written note on top of a pile of typed yellow pages.

"Dear Mr. Craig," he read, "I'm writing this late at night in my hotel room, wondering what's wrong with me. All my life people have been glad to see me, but this afternoon and evening, every time I as much as looked in your direction, on the beach and at lunch, in the lobby of the Festival Hall, at the bar, at the party, you made me feel as though I were Hurricane Gail on her way to lay waste the city. In your career you must have given hundreds of interviews. To people who were a lot more stupid than I am, I bet, and quite a few who were downright hostile. Why not to me?

"Well, if you won't talk to me about yourself, there are a lot of people who will, and I haven't been wasting my time. If I can't get the man whole, I'll get him refracted through a hundred different pairs of eyes. If he comes out not terribly happy about himself, that's his fault and not mine."

He recognized the reporter's usual gambit. If you won't tell me the truth, I will get your enemy to tell me lies. It was probably taught in the first year at all schools of journalism.

"Maybe," he read, "I'll do the piece in an entirely different way. Like a scientist observing the wild animal in his natural state. From afar, using stealth and a telescopic lens. *The animal has a well-developed sense of territory, is wary of man, drinks strong waters, has an inefficient instinct for survival, mates often, with the most attractive females in the herd.*"

He chuckled. She would be difficult to defeat.

"I lie in wait," the note finished. "I do not despair. I enclose some more drivel on the subject, neatly typed. It is now four A.M., and I will carry my pages through the dangerous dark streets of Gomorrah-by-the-sea to your hotel and cross your concierge's palm with silver so that the first thing you will see when you wake in the morning is the name of Gail McKinnon."

He put the note down and, without glancing at the typewritten yellow pages, picked up his daughter's letter. Every time he got a letter from either one of his daughters, he remembered the dreadful confession Scott Fitzgerald's daughter had written somewhere that whenever she got a letter from her father while she was in college, she would tear it open and shake it to see if a check would fall out and then toss the letter, unread, into a desk drawer.

He opened the letter. A father could do no less.

"Dear Dad," he read, in Anne's cramped, schoolgirlish handwriting, "San Francisco is Gloomstown. The college is just about closed down, and it might just as well be a war. The Huns are everywhere. On both sides. Springtime is for Mace. Everybody is so boringly convinced he's right. As far as I can tell, our black friends want me to learn about African tribal dances and ritual circumcision of young ladies rather than the Romantic poets. The Romantic poets are irrelevant, see. The professors are as bad as everybody else. On both sides. Education is square, chick. I don't even bother hanging around the campus anymore. If you do go there, twenty people ask you to lay your pure white body down in front of the Juggernaut for twenty different reasons. No matter what you do, you are a traitor to your generation. If you don't think Jerry Rubin is the finest fruit of young American manhood, your father is a bank president or a secret agent for the CIA or, God forbid, Richard Nixon. Maybe I'll take up simultaneous membership in the Black Panthers and the John Birch Society and show everybody. To paraphrase a well-known writer: Neither a student nor a policeman be.

"I know I was the one who wanted to go to college in San Francisco because after the years of school in Switzerland some insane superpatriot convinced me I was losing my American-ness, whatever that is, and that San Francisco was the town where the real action was. And I was planning to get a job as a waitress at Lake Tahoe this summer to see how the other half lives. I no longer give a damn how the other half lives. This may be temporary, I realize. I'm abashed how temporary so many of my ideas are. Most of them don't last till lunch. And I couldn't help being American, God help me, if I lived to be a hundred. What I'd like, if it wouldn't be too much of a burden on you, would be to get on a plane and come over to Europe for the summer and let them sort things out at the college without me before the fall term begins.

"If I do come to Europe, I'd like to avoid Mother as much as I can. I suppose you know she's in Geneva this month. She writes me dire letters about how impossible you are and that you are out to destroy her and that you're a libertine and suffering from the male menopause and I don't know what all. And ever since she found out I take the Pill, she treats me as though I'm Fanny Hill or a character out of the Marquis de Sade, and the evenings will be long on the banks of Lac Léman if I visit her.

"Your favorite daughter Marcia writes from time to time from Arizona. She is very happy there, she says, except for her weight. Obviously, no news gets through to the University of Arizona, and it is still like those old college musicals with panty raids and pillow fights you see on the Late Late Show. She is putting on weight, she says, because she eats compulsively because our happy home has been broken up. Freud, Freud, in the ice cream parlor.

"I've made a lot of jokes in this letter, I see, but Daddy, I don't feel funny. Love, Anne."

He sighed as he put his daughter's letter down. I will go someplace without an address, he thought, without a post office, without a telephone. He wondered what his letters home to his mother and father, written during the war, would sound like to him if he read them now. He had burned them all when he had found them in a trunk, neatly bound, after his mother's death.

He picked up Gail McKinnon's yellow pages. Might as well get all the day's reading done at one time before facing the day.

He carried the pages out to the balcony and sat down on one of the chairs in the sun. Even if he gained nothing else from the expedition to Cannes, he would have a suntan.

"Item" he read, "he is a formal man, a keeper of distances. Dressed in a slightly old-fashioned dinner jacket at a party in the ballroom off the Winter Casino, given after the evening showing, he seemed ambassadorial, remote. In the hothouse atmosphere of this place, where effusive camaraderie is the rule of the game, where men embrace and women kiss people they barely know, his politeness can be chilling. He spoke to no one for more than five minutes at a time but moved constantly around the room, not restlessly but with cool detachment. There were many beautiful women present, and there were two at least with whom his name had been linked. The two ladies, magnificently gowned and coiffed, seemed, to this observer, at least, to be eager to keep him at their side, but he allotted them only his ceremonial five minutes and moved on."

Linked, he thought angrily. *With whom his name has been linked.* Someone has been feeding her information. Someone who knows me well and who is not my friend. He had seen Gail McKinnon at the party across the room and had nodded to her. But he had not noticed that she had followed him around.

"It was not the economic condition of the Craig family that prevented Craig from going to college, as the family was comparatively well-off. Craig's father, Philip, was the treasurer of several Broadway theatres until his death in 1946, and while he was undoubtedly under some financial strain during the Depression, he certainly could have afforded to send his only child to college when he reached the age to apply. But Craig chose instead to enlist in the army shortly after Pearl Harbor. Although he served for nearly five years and rose to the rank of technical sergeant, he won no decorations aside from theatre and campaign ribbons."

There was an asterisk after this, indicating a footnote.

On the bottom of the page, under another asterisk, he read the footnote. "Dear Mr. C., this is all desperately dull stuff, but until you unbutton, all I can do is amass facts. When the time comes to put everything together, I shall mercilessly trim so as to keep the reader from dying of boredom."

He went back to the paragraph above the footnote. "He was lucky enough to come out of the war unscathed and even luckier to have in his duffel bag the script of a play by a young fellow enlisted man, Edward Brenner, which, a year after Craig's discharge from the army, he presented under the title *The Foot Soldier*. The elder Craig's theatrical connections undoubtedly aided considerably in allowing a very young and completely unknown beginner to manage so difficult a coup.

"Brenner had two more plays on Broadway in later years, both disastrous flops. One of them was produced by Craig. Brenner has since completely dropped out of sight."

Maybe out of your sight, young lady, Craig thought, but not out of his or out of mine. If he ever reads this, I will hear from my young fellow enlisted man.

"On the subject of his rarely working with creative people more than once, he is reputed to have said, not for quotation, 'It is generally believed in literary circles that everybody has at least one novel in him. I doubt that. I have found a few men and women who do have one novel in them, but the greatest number of people I have met have perhaps a sentence in them or at the very most a short story.'"

Where the hell did she get it? he thought angrily. He remembered having said something like that once as an abrasive joke to brush off a bore, although he couldn't remember where or when. And even if in a rough way he half-believed it, having it in print was not going to enhance his reputation as a lover of mankind.

She's goading me, he thought, the little bitch is goading me into talking to her, trading with her, bribing her to leave the antipersonnel mines unexploded.

"It would be interesting," the article continued, "to get Jesse Craig to make a list of the people he has worked with, categorizing them by the above standards. Worth a novel. Worth a short story. Worth a sentence. Worth a phrase. Worth a comma. If ever I get to speak to him again, I shall attempt to induce him to supply me with such a list."

She is out for blood, he thought. My blood.

The rest of the page was covered in handwriting. "Dear Mr. C., It's late now, and I'm getting groggy. I have tomes more to go but not tonight. If you wish to comment on anything you've read, I'm madly available. To be continued in the next installment. Yours, G. McK."

His instinct was to crumple the pages and toss them over the edge of the balcony. But he held onto them, reasonably. After all, as the girl had said, she had a carbon. And would have a carbon of the next installment. And the next.

A liner ws swinging at anchor out in the bay, and for a moment he thought of packing his bag and getting on it, no matter where it was going. But it wouldn't do any good. She'd probably turn up at the next port, typewriter in hand.

He went into the living room and tossed the yellow sheets onto the desk.

He looked at his watch. It was still too early for the Murphy's lunch. He remembered that yesterday he had promised Constance he'd phone her. She had said she wanted a blow-by-blow report. It had been partly due to her that he had come to Cannes. "Go on down there," she had said. "See if you can hack the action. You might as well find out now as later." She was not a woman who temporized.

He went into the bedroom and put in a call for Paris. Then he lay on the unmade bed and tried to doze while waiting. He had drunk too much the night before and had slept badly.

He closed his eyes but couldn't sleep. The thousand-fold amplified electric guitars of the movie he had just seen echoed in his ears, the orgiastic bodies writhed behind his hooded eyelids. If she's in, he thought, I'm going to tell her I'm taking the plane back to Paris this afternoon.

He had met her at a fund-raising party for Bobby Kennedy when he was on a visit to Paris in '68. He, himself, was registered to vote in New York, but a friend in Paris had taken him along. The people at the party had been attractive and had asked intelligent questions of the two eloquent and distinguished gentlemen who had flown from the United States to ask for money and emotional support for their man from Americans abroad, most of whom were not permitted to vote. Craig was not as enthusiastic as the others in the room, but he had signed a check for five hundred dollars, feeling that there was something mildly comic in his offering money to anybody in the Kennedy family. While the intense political discussion was still going on in the large handsome salon whose walls were splattered with dark, nonobjective paintings that he suspected would soon be sold at prices considerably lower than his hosts had paid for them, he went into the empty dining room where a bar had been set up.

He was pouring himself a drink when Constance followed him in. He had been conscious of her staring at him from time to time during the speeches. She was a striking-looking woman, dead pale, with wide greenish eyes and jet hair cut unfashionably short. At least it would have been unfashionable on anyone else. She was wearing a short lime-green dress and had dazzling legs.

"Are you going to give me a drink? I'm Constance Dobson. I know who you are," she said. "Gin and tonic. Plenty of ice." Her voice was husky, and she spoke quickly, in bursts.

He made the drink for her.

"What're you doing here?" she asked, sipping at her drink. "You look like a Republican."

"I always try to look like a Republican when I'm abroad," he said. "It reassures the natives."

She laughed. She had a rumbling laugh, almost vulgarly robust, unexpected in a woman as slender and as carefully put together as she was. She played with a long gold chain that hung down to her waist. Her bosom was youthful and high, he noticed. He had no idea how old she was. "You didn't seem as crazy as the others about the candidate," she said.

"I detect a streak of ferocity in him," Craig said. "I'm not partial to ferocious leaders."

"I saw you write out a check."

"Politics, as they say, is the art of the possible. I saw *you* write out a check."

"Bravado," she said. "I live from hand to mouth. It's because the young like him. Maybe they know something."

"That's as good a reason as any, I suppose," he said.

"You don't live in Paris."

"New York," he said, "if anyplace. I'm just passing through."

"For long?" She looked at him thoughtfully over the raised glass.

He shrugged. "My plans are indefinite."

"I followed you out here, you know."

"Did you?"

"You know I did."

"Yes." Surprised, he felt the trace of a blush.

"You have a brooding face. Banked fires." She chuckled, the disturbing, incongruous low sound. "And nice wide skinny shoulders. I know everybody else in the place. Do you ever come into a room and look around and say to yourself, 'My God, I know everybody here!' Know what I mean?"

"I think so," he said. She was standing close to him now. She had doused herself with perfume, but it was a fresh, tart smell.

"Are you going to kiss me now?" she said, "or are you going to wait for later?"

He kissed her. He hadn't kissed a woman for more than two years, and he enjoyed it.

"Sam has my phone number," she said. Sam was the friend who had brought him along. "Use it the next time you come through. If you want to. I'm busy this time. I'm shedding a fella. I have to go now. I have a sick child at home." The green dress flowed toward the hall where the coats were piled.

He stood alone at the bar and poured himself another drink, remembering the touch of her lips on his, the tart aroma of her perfume.

*   *   *   *   *   *   *   *   *   *   *   *   *   *   *   *   *

On the way home he had gotten her telephone number from his friend Sam, probed delicately for information, had not reported the full scene in the dining room.

"She's a man-killer," Sam had said. "A benevolent man-killer. She's the best American girl in Paris. She has some weird job with kids. Did you ever see such legs?" Sam was a lawyer, a solid man not given to hyperbole in his conversation.

The next time he came through Paris, after Bobby Kennedy had been killed and the election over, he had called the number Sam had given him.

"I remember you," she said. "I shed the fella."

He took her to dinner that night. Every night thereafter while he stayed in Paris.

She had been a great beauty out of Texas, had conquered New York, then Paris, a tall, slender, willful girl with a tilted, narrow dark head. Dear men, her presence demanded when she entered a room, what are you doing here, are you worth the time?

With her he saw Paris in its best light. It was her town, and she walked through it with joy and pride and mischief, lovely legs making a carnival of its pavements. She had small teeth, a dangerous temper. She was not to be taken lightly. She was a Puritan about work, her own and that of others. Fiercely independent, she scorned inaction, parasitism. She had come to Paris as a model, during, as she put it, the second half of the rule of Charlemagne. Unschooled, she was suprisingly bookish. Her age was anybody's guess. She had been married twice. Vaguely, she said. Both men, and others, had made off with money. She bore them no ill-will, neither the husbands nor the others. She had tired of modeling, gone with a partner, male, an ex-university professor from Maine, into the exchange-student business. "The kids have to know about each other," she said. "Maybe they finally won't be able to be talked into killing each other." A much older, beloved brother had been lost at Aachen, and she was furious against war. When she read the news from Vietnam, and it was particularly bad, she cursed in barracks language, threatened to move to the South Seas with her son.

As she had said the first night, she lived from hand to mouth, but dressed extravagantly. The couturiers of Paris loaned her clothes, knowing that in the places to which she was invited neither she nor their confections would go unnoticed. She left whatever bed she was in promptly at seven each morning to make breakfast for her children and send them off to school. Regardless of the night she had spent, she was at her desk promptly at nine A.M. Although Craig kept a suite in a hotel, the wide bed in her room overlooking a garden on the Left Bank became his true Paris address. Her children grew fond of him. "They're used to men," she explained. She had outgrown whatever morality she had been exposed to in Texas and ignored whatever conventions were in practice in the society or societies she adorned in Paris.

She was straightforward, funny, demanding, unpredictable, gloriously formed for lovemaking, affectionate, eager and enterprising, only serious at those moments that demanded seriousness. He had been dormant. He was dormant no longer.

He had fallen into the dull habit of not noticing or appreciating women as women. Now he was immediately conscious of beauty, a sensual smile, a way of walking; his eye had been re-educated, was youthful again, was quick and innocently lascivious for the flick of a skirt, the curve of a throat, womanly movements. Faithful to one, once more he enjoyed the entire sex. It was not the least of the gifts Constance had brought him.

She talked candidly of the men who had come before him, and he knew there would be others after him. He contained his jealousy. Now he knew that he had been suffering from deep wounds when he had met her. The wounds were healing.

In the quiet room, suffused only with the mild sound of the sea outside the window, he waited anxiously for the ring of the telephone, the darting, husky tones of her voice. He was preparing to say, "I am taking the first plane back to Paris," sure that if she had any other engagement that evening she would break it for him.

Finally the phone rang. "Oh, you," she said. The tone was not affectionate.

"Darling," he began.

"Don't darling me, Producer. I'm no little starlet wriggling her hot little ass for two weeks on a couch." He heard voices in the background—her office, as usual, was probably full, but she was not one to postpone rage because of an audience.

"Now, Connie . . . "

"Now, Connie balls," she said. "You said you were going to call me yesterday. And don't tell me you tried. I've heard that before."

"I didn't try."

"You haven't even got the grace to lie, you son of a bitch."

"Connie." He was pleading now.

"The only honest man in Cannes. Just my goddamn luck. Why didn't you try?"

"I was . . ."

"Save your goddamn excuses. And you can save your telephone calls, too. I don't have to hang around waiting for any goddamn phone to ring. I hope you've found somebody to hold your hand in Cannes because sure as Christ your franchise has run out in Paris."

"Connie, will you for God's sake be reasonable?"

"As of now. As of this minute I am purely, coldly, *glacially* reasonable. The phone's off the hook, laddie boy. Don't bother trying to get the number. Ever."

There was the angry sound as she slammed the instrument down six hundred miles away. He shook his head ruefully as he put the phone down in its cradle. He smiled a little, thinking of the dumb quiet that must have fallen among the young at her office and the frantic, professional eruption from the adjoining room of her partner, galvanized out of his usual somnolence by her tirade. It was not the first time she yelled at him. It would not be the last. From now on he would call her when he promised if it took hanging on the phone all day.

He went down to the terrace, had his photograph taken with a lion cub, wrote on it, "I have found a mate for you," and put it in an envelope and mailed it to her. *Express.*

It was time for his lunch with the Murphys, and he went out under the porte-cochère and asked for his car. The doorman was occupied with a peeling bald man in a Bentley and ignored Craig. The parking space in front of the hotel was crowded, with the best places reserved for the Ferraris, the Maseratis, and the Rolls-Royces. Craig's rented Simca was shunted around by the doorman to spots less exposed to public view, and sometimes, when the spate of expensive hardware was intense, Craig would find his car parked a block away on a side street. There had been a time in his life when he had gone in for Alfas and Lancias, but he had given all that up many years ago, and now, as long as a car carried him where he wanted to go, he was satisfied. But today, when the doorman finally told him that his car was parked behind the hotel and he trudged on the hunt for it past the tennis courts toward the corner where the whores loitered in the afternoon, he felt vaguely humiliated. It was as though the employees of the hotel had a subtle knowledge of him, that they were letting him know, in their scornful treatment of his humble rented car, that they did not believe he really belonged in the palace whose walls they guarded.

They will be surprised at the size of their tip when the time comes, he thought grimly as he turned the key in the ignition and started toward the Cap d'Antibes and his luncheon date with Bryan Murphy.

CHAPTER 4

MR. AND MRS. Murphy were down at their cabana, the concierge told him, and they were expecting him.

He walked through the fragrant piney park toward the sea, the only sound that of his own footsteps on the shaded path and the crackle of cicadas among the trees.

He stopped before he reached Murphy's cabana. The Murphys were not alone. Seated in the small patio in front of the cabana was a young woman. She wore a scanty pink bathing suit, and her long hair hung straight down her back, glistening in the sunlight. When she half-turned, he recognized the dark glasses.

Murphy, in flowered swimming trunks, was talking to her. Lying on a deck chair was Sonia Murphy.

Craig was about to go back to the hotel to call Murphy on the telephone and tell him to come up because he didn't like the company at the cabana when Murphy spotted him. "Hey, Jess," Murphy called, standing up. "We're over here."

Gail McKinnon did not turn around. She stood up, though, when he approached.

"Hi, Murph," he said, and went over and shook Murphy's hand.

"My boy," Murphy said.

Craig leaned over and kissed Sonia Murphy's cheek. She was fifty but looked about thirty-five, with a trim figure and a gentle, unlined, non-Hollywood face. She was covered with a beach towel and was wearing a wide-brimmed straw hat to keep from being sunburned. "It's been too long, Jesse," she said.

"It certainly has," Craig said.

"This young lady," Murphy said, gesturing toward Gail McKinnon, "tells me she knows you."

"We've met," Craig said. "Hello, Miss McKinnon."

"Hello." The girl took off her glasses. The gesture was deliberate, like the lowering of a disguise at a masquerade ball. Her eyes were wide, jewel-blue, but somehow evasive and uncertain, prepared for pain. Face grave and open, body not quite ripe, flesh satiny, she could have been sixteen, seventeen. He had a peculiar feeling that the rays of the sun were concentrated on her, a downfall of light, that he was looking at her from a distance, himself shadowed by a cloud with a dark promise of rain. She was perfect for the moment, poised quietly against the sea, the dazzle of the reflections from the water celebrating her youth, the richness of her skin, her almost-angular shapelinesss.

He had the troubling sense of having already been a witness at the scene—a girl perfect for a moment in bright sun with the sea behind her. He could not tell whether he was oppressed or exhilarated.

She reached down, not completely graceful, her long hair swinging, and he saw that there was a tape recorder at her feet. As she bent to the machine, he couldn't help but notice the soft roundness of her belly over the pink cloth of the tiny bikini, the adolescent jut of bones on generous hips. He wondered why she had disfigured herself the morning before with the absurd oversized sweat shirt, the affectation of the blank expanse of dark glass.

"She's been interviewing me," Murphy said. "Against my will."

"I bet," Craig said. Murphy was famous for giving interviews to anybody on any subject. He was a big, heavyset, squarely built man of sixty, with a shock of dyed black hair, a whisky complexion, shrewd, quick eyes, and an easy, bluff Irish manner. He was known as one of the toughest negotiators in the business and had done very well for himself while enriching his clients. He had no written contract with Craig, just a handshake, although he had represented Craig for more than twenty years. Since Craig had stopped making movies, they had only seen each other infrequently. They were friends. But, thought Craig meanly, not as close friends as when I was riding high.

"How're your girls, Jesse?" Sonia asked.

"When last heard from, they seemed okay," Craig said. "Or as okay as girls can be at that age. Marcia, I hear, has put on weight."

"If they're not up on a possession or pushing charge," Murphy said, "consider yourself a happy parent."

"I consider myself a happy parent," Craig said.

"You look pale," said Murphy. "Put on a suit and get some sun."

Craig glanced at the slender tan body of Gail McKinnon. "No, thanks," he said. "My season hasn't started yet. Sonia, why don't you and I take a walk and let them finish their interview in peace?"

"The interview is over," Gail McKinnon said. "He's been talking for a half hour."

"Did you give her anything she can use?" Craig asked Murphy.

"If you mean did I use any dirty words," Murphy said, "I didn't."

"Mr. Murphy was most informative," Gail McKinnon said. "He said the movie industry was bankrupt. No money, no talent, and no guts."

"That'll help a lot the next time you go in to make a deal," Craig said.

"Screw 'em," Murphy said. "I got my pile. What do I care? Might as well enjoy telling the truth while the mood is on me. Hell, there's a picture going into production that's been financed by a tribe of Apache Indians. What the hell sort of business are you in when you have to get script approval from Apache Indians? We ordered lobster for lunch. You got any objection to lobster?"

"No."

"How about you?" Murphy asked the girl.

"I love it," she said.

Oh, Craig thought, she's here for lunch. He sat down on one of the folding canvas chairs facing her.

"She's asked me a lot about you." Murphy jabbed a blunt finger in the direction of the girl. "You know what I told her? I told her one of the things wrong with the business is it's driven people like you out of it."

"I didn't know I had been driven out," Craig said.

"You know what I mean, Jess," Murphy said. "So it became unattractive to you. What's the difference?"

"He was most complimentary about you," Gail McKinnon said. "You would blush with pleasure."

"He's my agent," Craig said. "What do you expect he would say about me? Maybe you'd like to hear what my mother used to say about me when she was alive."

"I certainly would." The girl reached down toward the tape recorder. "Should I turn it on?"

"Not for the moment." He was conscious of the girl's small smile. She put the dark glasses on again. Once more she was an antagonist.

"Gail says you're being stony-hearted," Murphy said. It didn't take him long to call girls by their first names. "Why don't you give her a break?"

"When I have something to say," Craig said, "she'll be the first to hear it."

"I take that as a promise, Mr. Craig," the girl said.

"From what I heard my husband spouting for the last half hour," Sonia said, "you're wise to keep your thoughts to yourself, Jesse. If it was up to me, I'd put a cork in his mouth."

"Wives," Murphy said. But he said it fondly. They had been married twelve years. If they ever fought, they fought in private. The advantage, Craig thought, of late marriages.

"People ask too many questions," Sonia said. She had a quiet, motherly voice. "And other people give too many answers. I wouldn't even tell that nice young lady where I bought my lipstick if she asked me."

"Where do you buy your lipstick, Mrs. Murphy?" Gail McKinnon asked.

They all laughed.

"Jess," Murphy said, "why don't you and I wander down to the bar and leave the girls alone for a cozy little preluncheon slander session?" He stood up, and Craig stood, too.

"I'd like a drink, too," Sonia said.

"I'll tell the waiter to bring one for you," Murphy said. "How about you, Gail? What do you want?"

"I don't drink before nightfall," she said.

"Journalists were different in my day," Murphy said. "They also looked different in bathing suits."

"Stop flirting, Murphy," Sonia said.

"The green-eyed monster," Murphy said. He kissed his wife's forehead. "Come on, Jess. Apéritif time."

"No more than two," Sonia said. "Remember you're in the tropics."

"When it comes to my drinking," Murphy said, "the tropics begin just below Labrador for my wife." He took Craig's arm, and they started off together on the flagstone path toward the bar.

A plump woman was lying face down on a mattress in front of one of the cabanas, her legs spread voluptuously for the sun. "Ah," Murphy murmured, staring, "it's a dangerous coast, my boy."

"The thought has occurred to me," Craig said.

"That girl's after you," Murphy said. "Oh, to be forty-eight again."

"She's not after me for that."

"Have you tried?"

"No."

"Take an old man's advice. Try."

"How the hell did she get to see you?" Craig said. He had never liked Murphy's hearty approach toward sex.

"She just called this morning, and I said come along. I'm not like some people I know. I don't believe in hiding my light under a bushel. Then when I saw what she looked like, I asked if she had brought her bathing suit with her."

"And she had."

"By some strange chance," Murphy said. He laughed. "I don't fool around, and Sonia knows it, but I do like to have pretty young girls in attendance. The innocent joys of old age."

They were at the little service hut by now, and the uniformed waiter there stood up as they approached and said, *"Bonjour, messieurs."*

"Une gin fizz per la donna cabana numero quarantedue, per favore," Murphy said to the waiter. Murphy had been in Italy during the war and had picked up a little Italian. It was the only language besides English that he knew, and as soon as he left the shores of America, he inflicted his Italian on the natives, no matter what country he was in. Craig admired the blank self-assurance with which Murphy imposed his own habits on any environment he entered.

"Si, si, signore," the waiter said, smiling either at Murphy's accent or with pleasure at the thought of the eventual tip Murphy would leave him.

On the way to the bar they passed the swimming pool set in the rocks above the sea. A young woman with pale blond hair was standing on the side of the pool watching a little girl learning how to swim. The little girl had hair the same color as the woman's, and they were obviously mother and daughter. The mother was calling out instructions in a language that Craig could not identify. Her tone was soft and encouraging, with a hint of laughter in it. Her skin was just beginning to turn rosy from the sun.

"They're Danes," Murphy said. "I heard at breakfast. I must visit Denmark some day."

On inflated mattresses set back from the ladder leading to the sea two girls were lying face down, enjoying the sun. Their halters were discarded so that there would be no telltale strips of city-white skin across the tanned, beautiful young backs. Their brown rumps and long legs were smoothly shaped, appetizingly tinted. The bikini bottoms were merely a symbolic gesture toward public decorum. They were like two loaves of newly baked bread, warm, edible, and nourishing. Between them sat a young man, an actor Craig recognized from two or three Italian films. The actor was equally tanned, in swimming trunks that were hardly more than a jockstrap. He had a lean, muscular, hairless body, and a religious medal hung on a gold chain down his chest. He was darkly handsome, a superb animal with black hair and very white teeth, which he showed in a pantherish smile.

Craig was conscious of Murphy beside him staring down at the trio next to the sea.

"If I looked like that," Craig said, "I'd smile, too."

Murphy sighed loudly as they continued walking.

At the bar Murphy ordered a martini. He made no concessions to what his wife called the tropics. Craig orderd a beer.

"Well," Murphy said, raising his glass, "here's to my boy." He gulped down a third of his drink. "It's wonderful finally catching up with you. In person. You don't hand out much information in your letters, do you?"

"There's not much to say these days. Do you want me to bore you with the details of my divorce?"

"After all these years." Murphy shook his head. "I never would have thought it. Well, people have to do what they have to do, I suppose. I hear you've got a new girl in Paris."

"Not so new."

"Happy?"

"You're too old to ask a question like that, Murphy."

"The funny thing is I don't feel a day older than the day I got out of the army. Stupider but not older. Hell, let's get off that subject. It depresses me. How about you? What're you doing down here?"

"Nothing much. Lazying around."

"That kid, that Gail McKinnon, must have asked me in a dozen different ways what I thought you were after in Cannes. You want to work again?" Murphy glanced speculatively at him.

"Might be," Craig said. "If something good showed up. And if anybody was crazy enough to finance me."

"It's not only you," Murphy said. "Anybody'd have to be crazy to finance almost any movie these days."

"People haven't been knocking your door down asking you to get me to work for them, have they?"

"Well," Murphy said defensively, "you've got to admit you've sort of dropped out of things. If you really want to work, there's a picture I'm putting together . . . I might be able to swing it. I thought of you, but I didn't bother writing you until it was more definite. And there wouldn't be much money in it. And it's a lousy script. And it's got to be shot in Greece, and I know about you and your politics . . ."

Craig laughed at the torrent of Murphy's excuses. "It sounds just dandy," he said. "All round."

"Well," Murphy said, "I remember the first time you came to Europe, you wouldn't go to Spain because you didn't approve of the political situation there, and I . . ."

"I was younger then," Craig said. He poured some more beer into his glass from the bottle on the bar in front of him. "Nowadays, if you wouldn't shoot a picture in a country whose politics you didn't approve of, you wouldn't expose much film. You certainly wouldn't shoot a picture in America, would you?"

"I don't know," Murphy said. "My politics is take the money and run for the hills." He motioned to the bartender for another drink. "Well, then, if the Greek thing develops, do you want me to call you?"

Craig swished the beer around in the glass. "No," he said.

"This is no time to be proud, Jess," Murphy said somberly. "You've been out of it, so maybe you don't realize. The movie business is a disaster area. People who were getting seven hundred and fifty thousand a picture are offering to work for fifty. And getting turned down."

"I realize."

"If you're over thirty, it's don't call us, we'll call you." Murphy gulped at his drink. "Everybody is looking for some longhaired kid that nobody even heard of who'll make another *Easy Rider* for them for under a hundred thousand. It's like a sudden blight has fallen from the sky."

"It's only movies, Murph," Craig said. "Your best entertainment. Don't take it so hard."

"Some entertainment," Murphy said darkly. "Still, I worry about you. Listen, I don't like to bring up unpleasant matters, especially on a holiday, but I know you must be worrying about dough just about now . . ."

"Just about now," Craig said.

"Your wife's got lawyers all over the country, practically, and a pair of them have been in with a court order to look at my books to make sure I haven't smuggled any funds out to you that she can't get her hands on, and I know she's taking you for half, plus the house. And what you've got in the market . . ." Murphy shrugged. "You know what the market's like. And you've been living for five years with almost nothing coming in. Goddamn it, Jess, if I can swing the Greek thing, I'm going to make you do it. Just for walking around money until something breaks. Are you listening to me?"

"Of course."

"I'm making as much of an impression on you as on a stone wall," Murphy said gloomily. "You took it too hard, Jess. So you had a couple of flops. So what? Who hasn't? When I heard you were coming to Cannes, I was delighted. Finally, I thought, he's coming out of it. You can ask Sonia if I didn't say just that. But you just stand there giving me the fish eye when I try to talk sense." He drained his martini and motioned for another. "In the old days, if you had a flop, you'd come up with five new ideas that next morning."

"The old days," Craig said.

"I'll tell you what you have to do *these* days," Murphy said. "No matter how much talent you have or how much experience you have or how nice you are to your mother, you can't just sit back and wait for people to come to you begging you to take their ten million dollars to do a picture for them. You've got to get out and hustle up an idea. And develop it. Get a screenplay. And a damn good screenplay. And a director. And an actor. An actor somebody still wants to see. There're about two left. And a budget this side of a million dollars. Then I can go in and talk business for you. Not before. Those're the facts. Jess. They're not nice, but they're the facts. And you might as well face up to them."

"Okay, Murphy," Craig said. "Maybe I'm ready to do just that."

"That's better. That girl says she saw a script on the desk in your room."

"At this very moment," Craig said, "there are probably scripts on the desks of a hundred rooms in the Carlton Hotel."

"Let's talk about the one on yours," Murphy persisted. "What is it—a screenplay?"

"Uhuh. A screenplay."

"She asked me if I knew anything about it."

"What did you tell her?"

"What the hell could I tell her?" Murphy asked irritably. "I don't know anything. Are you interested in a screenplay?"

"I suppose you might say that," Craig said. "Yes."

"Whose?" Murphy asked suspiciously. "If it's been turned down by one studio, forget it. You're just wasting your time. The grapevine these days is run on laser beams."

"It hasn't been turned down yet," Craig said. "Nobody's seen it but me."

"Who wrote it?"

"A kid," Craig said. "You never heard of him. Nobody ever heard of him."

"What's his name?"

"I'd rather not say at the moment."

"Even to me?"

"Especially to you. You talk your head off. You know that. I don't want anybody getting to him."

"Well," Murphy said grudgingly, "that makes sense. Do you own it? The screenplay?"

"I have an option. For six months."

"What did it cost?"

"Peanuts."

"Is it about somebody under thirty years old with plenty of nude scenes?"

"No."

Murphy groaned. "Christ," he said. "Two strikes against you from the beginning. Well, let me read it, and then we'll see what we can do."

"Hold off for a few days," Craig said. "I want to go over it again and be sure it's ready."

Murphy stared hard at him without speaking, and Craig was almost sure that Murphy knew he was lying. Not just how he was lying, or where, or for what purpose, but lying.

"Okay," Murphy said, "When you want me, I'm here. In the meantime, if you're smart, you'll talk to that girl. At length. And talk to every newspaperman you can get hold of. Let people know you're alive, for Christ's sake." He drained his glass. "Now, let's go back for lunch."

They had lunch at the cabana. The cold langouste was very good, and Murphy ordered two bottles of Blanc-de-Blanc. He drank most of the wine and did most of the talking. He quizzed Gail McKinnon roughly but good-naturedly, at least at first. "I want to find out what the goddamn younger generation is about," he said, "before they come and slit my throat."

Gail McKinnon answered his questions forthrightly. Whatever she was, she was not shy. She had grown up in Philadelphia. Her father still lived there. She was an only child. Her parents were divorced. Her father had remarried. Her father was a lawyer. She had gone to Bryn Mawr but had quit in her sophomore year. She had gotten a job with a Philadelphia radio station and had been in Europe for a year and a half. Her base was in London, but her job allowed her to travel a good deal. She enjoyed Europe, but she intended to go back and live in the United States. Preferably in New York.

She sounded like a thousand other American girls Craig had met in Europe, hopeful, enthusiastic, and obscurely doomed.

"You got a boy friend?" Murphy asked.

"Not really," she said.

"Lovers?"

The girl laughed.

"Murph," Sonia Murphy said reproachfully.

"I'm not the one who invented the permissive society," Murphy said. "*They* did. The goddamn young." He turned again to the girl. "Do all the guys you interview make a pass at you?"

"Not all," she said, smiling. "The most interesting one was an old rabbi from Cleveland who was passing through London on his way to Jerusalem. I had to fight for my life in the Hotel Berkeley. Luckily, his plane left in an hour. He had a silky beard."

The conversation made Craig uncomfortable. The girl reminded him too much of his daughter Anne. He did not want to think of how his daughter talked to older men when he wasn't there.

Murphy rambled on about the decline of the movie industry.

"Take Warner's, for example," he said. "You know who bought Warner's? A cemetery business. How do you like that for crappy symbolism? And the age thing.

They talk about revolutions devouring their young. We've had a revolution out there, only it's devouring its old. I suppose you approve, Miss Smart-Face." He was becoming belligerent with the wine.

"Partially," Gail McKinnon said calmly.

"You're eating my lobster," Murphy said, "and you say partially."

"Look where the old have got us," Gail McKinnon said. "The young can't do any worse."

"I know that song and dance," Murphy said. "I don't have any children, thank God, but I listen to my friends' kids. The young can't do any worse. Let me tell you something, Gail Smart-Face, they can. They can do a lot worse. Put your tape recorder on again. I'll put that in the interview."

"Finish your lunch, Murph," Sonia said. "The poor girl's taken enough guff from you already."

"Seen and not heard," Murphy grumbled. "That's my motto. And now they're giving them the vote. The foundation's tottering."

Craig was relieved when the lunch was over. "Well," he said, standing, "thanks for the grub. I've got to be getting back."

"Jesse," Sonia said, "could you drive Miss McKinnon to Cannes with you? If she stays on and Murph talks to her anymore, the Immigration people will turn him back when he tries to get into the United States again."

Gail McKinnon looked at him soberly. He was reminded of his own daughters waiting for him to pick them up after a children's party.

"How did you get here this morning?" he asked ungraciously.

"A friend of mine drove me over. If you mind, I'll get a taxi."

"They charge outrageous prices," Sonia said. "It's sinful if you can get a ride with Jesse. Go in and get dressed, child," she said firmly. "Jesse will wait."

Gail McKinnon looked questioningly up at Craig. "Of course," he said.

She stood. "I won't be a minute," she said, and went into the cabana to change.

"Smart little girl," Murphy said, pouring the last drops of the wine from the bottle into his glass. "I like her. I don't trust her. But I like her."

"Don't talk so loud, Murph," Sonia whispered.

"Let 'em know my sentiments," Murphy said. "Let 'em know where I stand." He drained the wine. "Let me read that script, Jess. The sooner the better. If it's any good, I'll get it set up for you with two telephone calls."

Two telephone calls, Craig thought. No matter what he says, after lunch and two bottles of wine he thinks it's still 1960 when Bryan Murphy was still Bryan Murphy and Jesse Craig still Jesse Craig. He glanced worriedly toward the rear of the cabana where the girl was dressing behind a flimsy wooden wall. Murphy's voice carried. "Maybe in a couple of days, Murph," he said. "Don't broadcast until then, please."

"Still as a grave, my boy," Murphy said. "Grave as Warner's." He chuckled at the aptness of his simile. "I did have a good time today," he said. "Old friends and new girls and lobster for lunch and the Blue Mediterranean. Do you think the rich live better than we do, Jess?"

"Yes," Craig said.

Gail McKinnon came out, her bag swinging on its long strap from her shoulder. She had on white hip-hugger jeans and a short navy blue polo shirt. She wasn't wearing a brassiere, and Craig noted the small, round breasts jutting firmly out against the blue cotton cloth. She had put away the dark glasses for the moment. She looked nautical, sea-fresh, pure, and undangerous. She made her thanks to her hosts demurely and politely and bent to pick up the tape recorder, but Craig reached for it first and said, "I'll carry that."

Murphy was stretching out for his siesta as they started climbing the path toward the pool and the parking lot. The plump woman Craig and Murphy had passed on the way to the bar was still lying on her stomach absorbing the sun, her legs still widespread and inviting. With a sigh, as though she were suffering, the woman turned over. She stared peevishly at Craig and the girl, her privacy destroyed. Her face was thick and heavily made up. Dark blue mascara had run in the sweat of the sun. She was no longer young, and the features were marked by self-love, lust, greed, a sly and corrupt worldliness. The face made a shocking contrast with the healthy peasant fullness of the body. Craig found her hideous and averted his eyes. He couldn't have borne it if she had spoken aloud.

He let Gail McKinnon walk in front of him and followed her, protecting her. In her sandals she drifted noiselessly over the scoured stones. Her long hair blew cleanly in the sea wind. Suddenly he remembered what had troubled him when he first saw her in the Murphys' patio standing in sunlight with the sea behind her. She had reminded him of his wife Penelope on a June day on the Long Island shore, girlish and rosy, poised on a dune, outlined against the incoming tide.

The Danish mother was propped up against the rocks beside the pool reading, her child sitting with her blonde head on her mother's shoulder.

A dangerous coast.

Take an old man's advice. Try.

Walking to the car, Gail McKinnon put on the ridiculous dark glasses again.

CHAPTER 5

WHEN HE DROVE the car out of the gate of the hotel grounds, he turned, out of an old memory, in the wrong direction, toward Antibes, instead of toward Juan-les-pins and Cannes. The year after his marriage he had rented a villa for a summer on the coast between the Cap and Antibes, and the habit of turning toward it, he realized a little ruefully, had remained with him all this time.

"I hope you're not in a hurry," he said to the girl beside him. "I'm going the long way round."

"I have nothing better to do today," Gail McKinnon said, "than to go the long way round with Jesse Craig."

"I used to live down this road," he said. "It was nicer then."

"It's nice now."

"I suppose so. There're just more houses." He drove slowly. The road wound along the sea. A regatta of small sails glittered far out on the blue water. An old man in a striped shirt was fishing off the rocks. Above them a Caravelle was losing altitude, coming in to land at Nice.

"When were you here before?" Gail McKinnon asked.

"Quite a few times," he said. "In 1944, for the first time, when the war was still on . . ."

"What were you doing then?" she sounded surprised.

"You said you did your homework," he teased her. "I thought my past was an open book to you."

"Not that open."

"I was in a jeep," he said, "in an army camera unit. The Seventh Army had landed in the south of France, and we were sent down from Paris to make some film of the action down here. Our line was based near Menton, just a few miles from here. You could hear the artillery on the other side of Nice . . ."

Old soldier's maundering, he thought, and stopped. Ancient history. *Caesar ordered the camp to be set up on the hills overlooking the river. The Helvetti were in line of battle on the other bank of the river.* For the girl beside him Caesar's line and the line of young Americans before Menton were equally lost in the gulf of time. Did they even teach Latin anymore?

He looked sidelong at her. The glasses, which protected her and revealed him, annoyed him. Her youth annoyed him. Her ignorance, which was the innocent function of her youth, annoyed him. There were too many advantages on her side. "Why do you wear those damn things?" he asked.

"You mean my shades?"

"The glasses. Yes."

"You don't like them?"

"No."

With a single gesture she took them off and tossed them out of the car. She smiled at him. "That better?"

"Much."

They both laughed. He was no longer sorry Sonia Murphy had forced him into taking the girl along with him to Cannes.

"And what about that ghastly sweat shirt yesterday?" he asked.

"I experiment with different personalities," she said.

"What was today's personality?" He was amused now.

"Nice, scrubbed, virginally coquettish, in an up-to-date Women's Lib kind of way," she said. "For Mr. Murphy and his wife." She raised her arms as though to embrace the sea, the rocks, the pines shadowing the road, the entire Mediterranean afternoon. "I've never been here before, but I feel I've known this coast since I was a little girl." She pulled her legs up and turned in her seat to face him. "I'm going to come back here. Again and again and again. Until I'm an old lady with a big wide sun hat and a cane. When you were here during the war, did you ever think you'd come back?"

"When I was here during the war," he said, "all I thought about was getting home alive."

"Did you know then that you were going into the theatre and the movies?"

"I don't really remember." He tried to recall exactly that September afternoon long ago, the jeep moving toward the sound of the guns, the four helmeted soldiers with their cameras and carbines bumping along the lovely wild coast none of them had ever seen before, past the blown pillboxes and the camouflaged villas facing the sea. What were the names of the other three men in the jeep? The driver's name was Harte. He remembered that. Malcolm Harte. He had been killed in Luxembourg a few months later. He couldn't remember the names of the other two men. They had not been killed.

"I guess," he said, "I must have thought it was possible I'd have something to do with the movies after the war. After all, I had a movie camera in my hands. The army had taught me how to be a cameraman, and the Signal Corps was full of men who had worked in Hollywood. But I wasn't much of a cameraman. Just manufactured for the war. I knew I couldn't do *that* once the war was over." There was a melancholy pleasure in having an occasion to remember that distant time when he was a young man in the uniform of his country, in no danger, for that afternoon at least, of being shot at. "Actually," he went on, "my going into the theatre was an accident. On the troopship going back to the States from Le Havre I met Edward Brenner in a poker game. We became friendly, and he told me he'd written a play while he had been waiting in the redeployment depot at Reims to be shipped home. I knew a little about the theatre, of course, because of my father—he'd been taking me to see plays since I was nine years old—and I asked Brenner if I could read it."

"That was a lucky poker game," the girl said.

"I suppose so," Craig said.

Actually, it had not been during the poker game that they had come together but on deck, on a sunny day when Craig had been able to find a corner out of the wind and was reading a collection of the ten best American plays of 1944 that his father had sent him. (What was the APO number? It was an address he had thought he would never forget.) Brenner had passed him twice, had eyed the book in his hand, had finally crouched down, farmer-style, on his heels beside him, and had said, "How are they? The plays, I mean."

"Medium," Craig said.

They had begun to talk then. It turned out that Brenner was from Pittsburgh and had gone to Carnegie Tech and had taken the drama course there before he was drafted— he was older than he looked—and was interested in the theatre. The next day he had shown Craig his play.

Brenner was unprepossessing to look at—a gaunt, sallow boy with sad, dark eyes and a hesitant and guarded way of talking. Among the horde of jubilant, loud men sailing home from the war, he had been uncomfortable and unsoldierly in his ill-fitting uniform, his manner tentative, as though a little surprised that he had survived three campaigns and knew he could never survive a fourth. Craig had agreed to read his play with misgivings, trying in advance to compose anodyne comments that would not hurt Brenner's feelings. He was unprepared for the fierceness of the emotion, the harsh unsentimentality, the rigor of the construction of the infantry private's first dramatic work. While he himself had never done anything in the theatre, he had seen enough plays to be convinced, with youthful egotism, of the accuracy of his own taste. He had not measured his enthusiasm when he had discussed Brenner's play with him, and by the time they had passed the Statue of Liberty, the two men were firm friends and Craig had promised Brenner that through his father he would get the play into the hands of producers.

Brenner had to go to Pennsylvania to be discharged and then to resume at Carnegie Tech. Craig, who stayed in New York pretending to be looking for work, communicated with him only through the mails. There wasn't much to communicate. Craig's father had loyally approached the producers he knew, but the play had been turned down by all of them.

"Nobody, they say," Craig had written Pittsburgh, "wants to hear about the war. They are all idiots. Do not despair. One way or another this play will go on."

It went on, finally, because Craig's father died and left twenty-five thousand dollars. "I know it's a wild idea," Craig had written Brenner. "I don't know anything about producing, but I think I know more than the horse's asses who turned down your play. And by now I know an awful lot about your play. If you're willing to bet your talent, I'm willing to bet my dough."

Brenner was in New York two days later and never saw Pittsburgh again. Because he was practically penniless, he moved into the room in the Hotel Lincoln where Craig was living, and in the five months that it took to put the play on, they were together twenty-four hours a day. The year-long examination of the manuscript through the mails, with the testing and weighing of every line, had made the play their common property, and they were surprised when very occasionally their reactions to the people and ideas they had to deal with in the course of the production differed at all.

The director, a young man by the name of Baranis, who had had some experience in the theatre and who had thought he would be treated respectfully by the two neophytes, had complained one day when a pet notion of his had been calmly voted down, almost without discussion, by them. "Christ," Baranis had said, "I bet when you two guys go to sleep, you have the same dreams."

Curiously, the one time they had had a serious disagreement, it had been about Penelope Gregory, later to be Penelope Craig. She had been sent up to the office by an agent to read for a small part, and both Baranis and Craig had been favorably impressed by her beauty and by the soft, deep voice. But Brenner had been adamant. "Sure," he said, "she's beautiful. Sure, she has a great voice. But there's something I don't believe about her. Don't ask me why."

They had had Penelope up to read again, but Brenner refused to change his mind, and in the end they had compromised on a plainer girl.

During rehearsals Brenner became so nervous that he could not eat. It became part of Craig's duties, along with arguing with the scene designer, negotiating with the stagehands' union, and keeping the leading man from drinking, to lure Brenner into restaurants and get a minimum of nourishment into him to keep him alive until the curtain went up.

The day the signs were put in place outside the theatre, Craig found Brenner standing on the sidewalk in his dirty raincoat, the only coat he owned, looking wonderingly at the legend *"The Foot Soldier,* by Edward Brenner," and shaking as though he were suffering from a malarial attack. He laughed wildly when he saw Craig. "It's weird, Brother," he said, "just weird. I have the feeling somebody's going to tap me on the shoulder and I'm going to wake up and it's going to be Pittsburgh all over again."

Still shaking, he had allowed Craig to lead him to a drugstore and order a milk shake for him. "I've got a crazy double feeling," he confided over the milk shake. "I can't wait for the thing to open, and at the same time I hate to see it open. It's not only because I'm afraid it's going to flop. It's just that I don't want it all to end." He had gestured vaguely over the furniture of the soda fountain. "The rehearsals. The goddamn room in the Hotel Lincoln. Baranis. Listening to you snore at four o'clock in the morning. I know I'll never have anything like this again. Do you know what I mean?"

"Sort of," Craig said. "Finish your milk shake."

When the first reviews came in over the phone the night of the opening, Brenner had thrown up all over the floor of the hotel room, had apologized, had said, "I will love you until the day I die," had had eight Scotches, and passed out until Craig had awakened him the next day with the evening newspapers.

"What was he like then?" Gail McKinnon was saying. "Edward Brenner? When you first saw him?"

"Just another GI who had had a hard war," Craig said. He slowed the car down and pointed up the bluff to his left at a white villa set among the pine trees. "That's where I lived. The summer of 1949."

The girl stared at the broad, low building set behind a terrace on which an orange awning shaded some garden furniture from the intense sunlight. "How old were you then?"

"Twenty-seven."

"Not bad for twenty-seven," she said. "A house like that."

"No," Craig said. "Not bad."

What did he remember about that summer?

Scattered images.

Penelope water-skiing on the bay of La Garoupe, slim and tan, her hair flying, determinedly graceful in a one-piece black bathing suit as she broke through the wake of the speedboat. Brenner beside him in the boat taking home movies of Penelope clowning precarious ballet positions against the pull of the line and waving for the camera.

Brenner, himself, attempting to learn how to water-ski, trying doggedly again and again to stand up and never making it, a skinny, clumsy figure, all bones and knuckles, long, sad nose and starved shoulders burned painfully red from the sun, having to be fished out of the water finally, almost drowned from all the water he had swallowed, saying, "I am a goddamn useless intellectual," as Penelope, now aiming the camera at him like a weapon, laughed in the rocking boat.

Dancing in the open square on a velvety night in the walled town of Haut-de-Cagnes, moving to tinny French music in and out of the light of the lanterns hung along the old stone walls, Penelope, small, neat, and weightless in his arms, kissing him under the ear, smelling of sea and jasmine, whispering, "Let's not go back anywhere, *Ever.*" And Brenner sitting at a table, too self-conscious to dance, pouring wine and trying to communicate with a hardfaced French lady he had picked up the night before in the casino at Juan-les-Pines, saying, with effort, one of the ten French phrases he had learned since his arrival, *"Je suis un fameux écrivain à New York."*

Driving home in the green dawn from Monte Carlo where among them they had won 100,000 francs (at 650 francs to the dollar), Craig at the wheel of the small open car, Penelope between the two men, her head on Craig's shoulder, and Brenner shouting in his croaking voice into the wind, "Here we are, Scott, on the Grande Corniche," and all of them trying to sing "Les Feuilles Mortes," which they had heard for the first time the night before.

Lunch on the terrace of the white villa under a huge orange awning, all three of them fresh from the morning's swim, Penelope, trim in white cotton slacks and a sailor's blue jersey, her wet hair piled up on top of her head, softly and insistently sensual, rearranging the flowers in the vase on the white iron luncheon table with brown soft hands, touching the bottle of wine in the ice bucket to make sure it was cold enough, as the old lady who served as cook and who had come with the house shuffled out with the cold soup and salad on a big clay platter from Vallauris just down the coast. What was the old lady's name? Hélène? Perpetually in black, in mourning for ten generations of her family who had died within the walls of Antibes, and who fussed lovingly over the three of them whom she called *"Mes trois beaux jeunes Américains,"* none of whom had ever had a servant before then, and putting red, white, and blue flowers on the breakfast table for the Fourth of July and Bastille Day.

The piercing, sharp odor of the pine forest behind them in the noonday sun.

The siestas in the afternoons, Penelope in his arms in the great bed in the high-ceilinged, shadowed room, traversed here and there by light broken into thin lances by the shutters that were closed against the heat. The daily love-making complete, potent, accepting, tender, the two locked, grateful, familiar youthful bodies, cleansed and salty, the joys of double possession, equal surrender, the fruit smell of wine on their lips as they kissed, the low chuckles as they whispered in the fragrant gloom, the insidious, arousing touch of Penelope's long nails as they moved capriciously over the hard ridges of his belly.

The night in August, Penelope and he seated after dinner on the terrace, the sea smooth in the moonlight below them, the forest quiet, Brenner off somewhere with one of his girls, when Penelope had told him she was pregnant "Glad or sorry?" she had asked, her low voice tremulous. He leaned over and kissed her. "I guess that answers it," she said.

He went into the kitchen and brought out a bottle of champagne from the icebox, and they toasted themselves in the moonlight and decided to buy a house in New York when they went back because now that they would be a family the apartment in the Village would not be big enough for them. "Don't tell Ed," Penelope said.

"Why not?"

"He'll be jealous. Don't tell anybody. They'll all be jealous."

The routine of the mornings. After breakfast, he and Brenner sprawled in swimming trunks in the sun, the manuscript of Brenner's new play open on the table between them and Brenner saying, "What about as the curtain comes up on the second act, the stage is dark, and she comes in, goes over to the bar, you only see her in silhouette, she pours herself a drink, sobs, then knocks the whole drink down in one gulp . . .?"

Both of them squinting against the Mediterranean light, envisaging the dark stage, the actress moving in the hushed, full theatre on a cold winter's night in the welcoming city across the ocean as they worked on the revisions of Brenner's second play, which Craig had already announced for production in November.

Craig had produced two other plays since *The Foot Soldier,* and they had both been successes. One was still running, and he had rewarded himself with the season in

France as a belated honeymoon for himself and Penelope. Brenner had spent most of the royalties he had made on *The Foot Soldier,* which had not turned out to be all that much finally, and he was practically penniless again, but they had high hopes for the new play. Anyway, that year Craig had enough for everybody and was learning how to live luxuriously.

Behind them in the house there was the murmur of Penelope's voice working on her French with the cook and the occasional ringing of the telephone as friends called, or one of Brenner's girls, to be told by Penelope that the men could not be disturbed, they were working. It was surprising how many friends had found out where they were spending the summer and how many girls knew Brenner's telephone number.

At noon, Penelope coming out in her bathing suit, announcing, "Swim call." They swam off the rocks in front of the house in deep, cold, clear water, splashing each other, Penelope and Craig, who were good swimmers, hovering close to Brenner, who once had alarmingly begun to sink, thrashing his arms and blowing desperately, in need of rescue, the performance half-real, half-play-acting. "Oh," he had said when they had hauled him out, and he was lying, pink and slippery, beached on the rocks, "oh, you aristocrats who know how to do *everything,* who will never drown."

Images of pleasure.

Memory, of course, if given the opportunity, plays false. No time, even the month or the week that you remember later as the happiest of your life, is all of one piece, all pleasure.

There was the argument with Penelope that broke out late one night two or three weeks after they had moved into the villa. About Brenner. In the shuttered bedroom, so that they had to talk in whispers to keep Brenner from overhearing, although he was at the other end of the hall and the walls were thick. "Isn't that man ever going to leave?" Penelope demanded. "I'm getting tired of never being able to make a move without seeing that sad long face hanging over your shoulder."

"Keep it low, please," Craig said.

"I'm getting tired of having to keep everything low, too," Penelope said. She was sitting up on the edge of the bed naked, brushing her blonde hair. "As though I'm in somebody else's house."

"I thought you liked him," Craig said, surprised. He had been half-asleep, waiting for her to finish with her hair and turn out the lamp and get in beside him. "I thought you were friends."

"I like him." Penelope brushed savagely at her hair. "I'm his friend. But not twenty-four hours a day. When I married, I wasn't told I was marrying a team."

"It's not twenty-four hours a day," Craig said, knowing he sounded foolish. "Anyway, he'll probably leave when we finish getting the script ready."

"That script won't be ready until the day the lease runs out," Penelope said bitterly. "I know that man."

"That doesn't sound completely friendly, Penny."

"Maybe *he's* not so completely friendly," she said. "Don't think I don't know who it was that turned me down for the part in his play."

"He didn't even know you then."

"Well, he knows me now." Ten harsh strokes of the brush. "Don't tell me he thinks I'm the greatest actress to come to New York since Ethel Barrymore."

"We haven't discussed it," Craig said lamely. "Keep your voice down."

"I'll bet you haven't discussed it. I'll bet there're a lot of things you haven't discussed. Like the way whenever you're talking about anything seriously you ignore me. Just ignore me."

"That isn't true, Penny."

"You know it's true. The two great minds working as one, deciding the fate of the world, the Marshall Plan, the next elections, the atomic bomb, Stanislavsky . . ." The brush was going like a piston now. "Listening to me indulgently, as though I'm an idiot child . . ."

"You're absolutely irrational, Penny."

"I'm irrationally rational, Jesse Craig, and you know it."

He had to laugh then, and she laughed, too, and he said, "Throw that damned brush away and come to bed."

And a moment later she threw the brush away and turned out the light and came to bed. "Don't make me jealous, Jesse," she whispered, holding onto him. "Don't ever leave me out. Of anything."

And then days went by just as they had before, as though there had never been the midnight conversation on the edge of the bed, Penelope being sisterly and fond with Brenner, forcing him to eat, to put some meat on his poor bones, as she said, and being demure and quiet while the men talked and unostentatiously emptying ashtrays, bringing fresh drinks, teasing Brenner gently about the girls who called and the girls who sometimes stayed overnight and came down to breakfast the next morning asking if they could borrow a bathing suit for a dip before getting back to town.

"I'm a desirable sex object on the Côte d'Azur," Brenner said, embarrassed but pleased at the teasing. "It was never thus in Pennsylvania or Fort Bragg."

Then the bad evening at the end of August when Craig was packing to catch the night train up to Paris because he had to meet the head of a movie studio there to negotiate the terms for the sale of the play that was still running in New York. Penelope came in pulling a robe around her after a bath, her eyes, usually a soft brown, now harsh and dangerous. She watched him throw some shirts into his bag.

"How long're you going to be?" she asked.

"Three days. At the most."

"Take that son of a bitch with you."

"What are you talking about?"

"You know what I'm talking about. *Whom* I'm talking about."

"Sssh."

"Don't sssh me in my own house. I'm not going to play nursemaid to the one-play genius, that . . . that steel-town Don Juan, for three days while you go gallivanting around the nightspots of Paris . . ."

"I'm not going gallivanting anywhere, Penny," Craig said, trying to be patient. "You know that. And he's in the middle of the third act. I don't want him to interrupt . . ."

"I wish you'd be as thoughtful about your wife as you are about your holy scrounging friend. Has he bought us a dinner since he's been here? One single dinner?"

"What difference does that make? He's busted. You know that."

"I certainly do. He sure as hell makes that clear. Where does he get all the money to take those tarts out five times a week? What do you do—finance him for that, too? What is it, are you getting a vicarious kick out of his scrubby little conquests?"

"I have a great idea," Craig said quietly. "Why don't you pack and come along with me to Paris?"

"I'm not going to be driven out of my own house by any oversexed superior leech like Edward Brenner," Penelope said loudly, ignoring Craig's shushing gestures, "and let him turn this place into a whorehouse, with his cheap tarts running in and out just as near naked as the law allows. You better warn him—from now on he's got to behave himself. I'm through with behaving like the madame of a private bordello for him, taking down telephone numbers for him, saying, "Mr. Brenner is busy now, Yvette or Odile or Miss Big Tits, can he call you back?""

She's jealous, Craig thought, wonderingly. Go figure women out. But all he said was, "Don't turn bourgeoise on me, Penny. That went out with World War One."

"I'm bourgeoise. That's it." She began to cry. "Now you know it. Go complain to your elegant friend. He'll sympathize with you. The Great Bohemian Artist who never pays for aything will offer his condolences." She ran into the bathroom and locked the door and stayed in there so long that he was sure he was going to miss his train. But just when he heard Brenner toot warningly on the horn of the car outside, the bathroom door opened and Penelope came out, dry-eyed and smiling, full dressed. She squeezed Craig's arm and said, "Forgive the tantrum. I'm a little jittery these days," and they went out to the car together.

As the train pulled out of the Antibes station, with Craig leaning out the window of the wagon-lit, Penelope and Brenner were standing side by side on the platform in the dusk waving to him.

When Craig got back from Paris, Brenner gave him the finished copy of the play and said he had to leave for New York. They made plans to meet in New York at the end of September and had a farewell party, and when Craig and Penelope put him on the train, he said that he had never had a better time in his whole life.

With Brenner gone, Craig read the final version of the play Brenner had left him. As he read the familiar pages, he was conscious of a growing unease and at the end a vast, echoing emptiness. What had seemed, as he worked with Brenner, to be funny and alive and touching now was dead on the page before him, hopeless. He realized that until then he had been deceived by the beauty of the summer, his appreciation of his friends' real talent, the engulfing, optimistic joy of work. Now he was reading coldly and saw that the play was stillborn, irretrievable. It wasn't merely that he was sure the play would fail commercially but with the chance that it might perhaps find a small, perceptive audience that would give him some satisfaction in being connected with it. It was doomed, he was sure, to general oblivion. If it had been anybody else's play, he would have rejected it immediately. But with Brenner . . . Friend or no friend, he knew that if the play went on, Brenner would suffer. Badly.

Without telling Penelope his reaction, he gave her the script to read. She had heard them talking about it, of course, and knew what it was about, but she hadn't read a word of it. A mediocre actress, Penelope was a shrewd judge in the theatre, intuitive and tough-minded. When she had finished reading, Penelope said, "It won't go, will it?"

"No."

"They'll murder him. And you."

"I'll survive."

"What're you going to do?" she asked.

He sighed. "I'm going to put it on," he said.

She didn't mention it again. He was grateful for her tact. He didn't tell her, though, that he wasn't going to risk anybody else's money in it, that he was going to back it completely himself.

The rehearsals were disastrous. He couldn't get any of the actors he wanted or the director he wanted or even the scene designer he wanted because the play appealed to no one. He had to make do with worn-out hacks and inexperienced beginners, and he spent tortured nights trying to make up lies about the stream of refusals to protect Brenner's ego. So-and-so loved the play but had signed for Hollywood, so-and-so had promised to wait for the new Williams play, so-and-so was involved in television. Brenner remained serenely certain of success. His one triumph had made him feel inviolate. In the middle of rehearsals he even got married. To a plain, quiet woman by the name of Susan Lockridge who wore her straight black hair in a severe school-teacherly bun and who knew nothing about the theatre and who sat entranced through the rehearsals, thinking that was the way all rehearsals looked. Craig acted as best man at the wedding and gave the party and sweated as he acted the jolly, confident host, raising his glass again and again to toast the newlyweds and the success of the play. Penelope didn't appear for the party. She was in the fourth month of her pregnancy and was sick a good deal of the time and had a plausible excuse.

A week before the opening night Craig took Susan Brenner aside and told her they were heading for disaster and that the only sensible thing was to call the whole thing off. "How do you think Eddie will take it if I tell him this?" Craig asked her.

"He'll die," the woman said flatly.

"Oh, come on," Craig said.

"You heard what I said."

"Okay," Craig said wearily, "we'll open. Maybe there'll be a miracle."

But there wasn't any miracle. Only half the audience was left when the curtain came down on opening night. In Sardi's, where they went to wait for the reviews, Brenner said to Craig, "You son of a bitch. You sabotaged it. Susan told me what you told her. You never had any faith in it, and you did the whole thing on a shoestring, and it looks it . . ."

"Why would I want to sabotage it?" Craig asked.

"You know as well as I do, Brother," Brenner said, standing up. "Come on, Sue, let's get out of here."

It was only many years later, long after the birth of Anne and Marcia, that Craig had an inkling of what Brenner had been talking about that night. It was in the middle of an argument with Penelope, when things had been going badly between them for more than a year, after a party at which, Penelope said, he had been hanging all over a pretty and notorious young actress, that Penelope supplied the missing clue. In the three days he had been in Paris, the summer at Antibes, she had slept with Edward Brenner. She meant to hurt him, and she managed it.

He was at the wheel in the bright afternoon sunshine with the sea below him to his right and the white villa falling out of sight behind him. He turned and took a last look at the house.

Not bad for twenty-seven. Anne had been conceived there, in the great bed in the cool, high room overlooking the sea, the room that had been the haunt of pleasure for three dreamlike months. He didn't tell Gail McKinnon about Anne or Brenner or the three months or the death of friendship or the secret undermining of love.

What had happened to all the home movies they had taken that summer? He had no idea where the spools of aging, brittle film might be. Somewhere among the old theatre programs, old magazines, broken tennis racquets in the cellar of the house of Seventy-eighth Street he had bought so as to have room for the arrival of Anne, the house he had not visited since he had told Penelope he wanted a divorce, the house he would be able to walk through unerringly in total darkness until the day he died.

He stepped on the accelerator, and the villa disappeared beyond a bend of the road. *Lesson—Stay away from the places where you have been happy.*

The girl was silent for a moment. When she spoke, it was as though she knew exactly what he had been thinking of. "Murphy says your wife is a very beautiful woman."

"Was," Craig said. "Is, perhaps. Yes."

"Is it a friendly divorce?"

"As divorces go."

"The divorce in my family was silent and polite," Gail McKinnon said. "Obscene. My mother just wandered away. When I was sixteen. She had wandered away before. Only this time she didn't come back. When I was eighteen, I asked my father why. He said, "She is searching for something. And it isn't me."" The girl sighed. "She sends me a card at Christmas. From various parts of the world. I must look her up some day."

She was momentarily silent, leaning back now against the seat. Then she said, "Mr. Murphy's not what you expect a Hollywood agent to be like, is he?"

"You mean he's not small and fat and Jewish, with a funny way of talking?"

The girl laughed. "I'm glad to see you read me so carefully. Did you read what I left for you this morning?"

"Yes."

"Any comments?"

"No."

Again, she was quiet for a little while. "He's an intelligent man, Mr. Murphy," she said, "Before you came, he told me if your last picture were to come out today, it would be a hit. It was before its time, he said."

Craig paid attention to his driving, slowed down to avoid a family group in bathing suits crossing the road.

"I agreed with him," the girl said. "Maybe it wouldn't have been a hit, at least in Mr. Murphy's terms, but people would've recognized how original it was."

"You saw it?" Craig couldn't help sounding surprised.

"Yes. Mr. Murphy said the big mistake you made was not becoming a director. He says it's a director's business now."

"Maybe he's right."

"Mr. Murphy said it would have been easy any time until 1965 to get you a picture to direct . . ."

"That's probably true."

"Weren't you tempted?"

"No."

"Why not?"

"Laziness, maybe."

"You know that's not true." The girl sounded aggrieved at his evasiveness.

"Well, if you must know," Craig said, "I felt I didn't have the talent for it. At best, I would have just been pretty good. There would have been fifty better men than I at the job."

"Weren't there fifty better men working as producers?" Now her tone was challenging.

"Maybe five," he said. "And maybe if I was lucky, they would die off or go on the booze or lose their touch."

"If you had it to do all over again," the girl said, "would you do something else?"

"Nobody has it to do all over again," Craig said. "Now enjoy the scenery, please."

"Well, anyway," the girl said placidly, "it was a nice lunch."

After that, she asked no more questions, and they drove in silence along the sea and through the town of Antibes, sleepy in the sun, and on the busy highway back to Cannes.

He offered to drive her to her hotel, but she said it wasn't necessary, it was only two minutes from the Carlton, and she enjoyed walking.

There was a parking place open in front of the Carlton between a Jaguar and an Alfa. He swung the Simca into it and turned off the motor. He was sure it wouldn't be there when next he needed it.

"Thank you for the ride," the girl said, getting out of the car. "I like your friends the Murphys. And I'm sure I'd like you if I ever got the chance."

He smiled, rewarding her manners. "I'll be around," he said vaguely.

He watched her stride off along the Croisette carrying her tape recorder, Murphy isolated in a capsule. Her long brown hair shone over the blue polo shirt. Standing there in the bright sunshine, he felt deserted. He didn't want to be alone that afternoon, remembering what it had been like when he was twenty-seven. He had the impulse to hurry after her, touch her arm, walk beside her. But he fought the impulse down. He went into the bar, drank a pastis, then wandered fretfully over to the rue d'Antibes and saw half a dirty movie. It had been made in Germany and featured bosomy lesbian ladies in high leather boots in rural settings, glades and waterfalls. The theatre was crowded. He left and went back toward his hotel.

Two hard-faced whores on the corner near the tennis courts stared at him aggressively. Maybe I should do it, he thought. Maybe it would solve something.

But he merely smiled gently at the two women and walked on. There was applause coming from the tennis courts, and he went in. A tournament was being played, for juniors. The boys were wild but moved with dazzling speed. He watched for a few minutes, trying to remember the time when he had moved that fast.

He left the courts and went around the corner to the hotel, avoiding the terrace, which already had the beginning of the evening assembly of drinkers.

When he picked up his key, the concierge gave him some messages that had come in for him in his absence. He had to sign for a registered letter from his wife that had been forwarded from his hotel in Paris. He stuffed the messages and the letter into his pocket without reading them.

In the elevator a short man with a paunch wearing an orange shirt was saying to a pretty young girl, "This is the worst festival of all times." The girl could have been a secretary or a starlet or a whore or the man's daughter.

When he reached his apartment, he went out onto the balcony and sat down and regarded the sea for a while. Then he took the message out of his pocket and read them at random. He kept his wife's letter for last. Dessert.

Mr. B. Thomas and his wife would like to dine with Mr. Craig tonight. Would Mr. Craig be good enough to call back? They were at the Hotel Martinez and would be in until seven.

Bruce Thomas was a man whom he didn't know well but liked. He was a director and had had three hits in a row. He was about forty years old. He was one of the men Craig had been thinking about when he had told Gail McKinnon why he had never been tempted to direct. Tomorrow he would tell Thomas that he had returned to the hotel too late to call him back. He didn't want to dine that night with a man who had had three hits in a row.

Sidney Green had called and wanted to know if he could have a drink with Mr. Craig before dinner tonight. He would be in the bar at eight. Sidney Green was a man who had directed three or four movies and who had been hired by an independent company to prepare a series of pictures. The independent company had stopped operations a month before, and Green was in Cannes looking for a job, beseeching everyone he met to put in a good word for him. He would drink alone at the bar tonight.

Miss Natalie Sorel had called and would Mr. Craig please call back. Natalie Sorel had been one of the two magnificently gowned and coiffed ladies at the party the night before whom Gail McKinnon had noticed and celebrated. She was a fairly well-known movie actress, originally from Hungary, who played in three or four languages. She had been his mistress for a few months, five or six years ago, when he had been doing the picture in Paris, but he had lost sight of her. She was going on forty now, still lush and beautiful, and when he had seen her at the party, he had wondered why he had ever broken with her. They had spent a weekend together, he remembered, at Beaulieu, out of season, and it was one of the most satisfactory memories of his life. At the party she had told him she was getting married. Miss Natalie Sorel represented too many complications at the moment, he decided. Her phone would not ring.

There was a hand-written note from Ian Wadleigh. He and Wadleigh had had some drunken evenings together in New York and Hollywood. Wadleigh had written a novel that had been widely acclaimed in the early 1950s. At that time he had been a boisterous, witty man who argued loudly in bars with strangers. Since then he had written several disappointing novels and had worked on a lot of screenplays and had gone through three wives and become a drunk. Craig hadn't seen Wadleigh's name in print or on the screen for years, and he was surprised to see Wadleigh's signature on the envelope.

"Dear Jess," Wadleigh wrote in a loose scrawl, "I heard you were here and thought maybe it would be heart-warming to tie one on together, for old time's sake. I'm in a flea bag near the old port where the poor folk lead their short, nasty, brutish lives, but they're pretty good at taking messages. Call when you have the time. Ian."

Craig wondered what Wadleigh was doing in Cannes. But he wasn't curious enough to call the number Wadleigh had noted at the bottom of the page.

He opened his wife's registered letter. She had typed it herself. She was two days late in getting her monthly check, she wrote, and she was notifying her lawyer and his lawyer. If she did not receive the check within one day, she would instruct her lawyer to take the appropriate steps.

He stuffed all the loose bits of paper into his pocket and sat back and watched the darkening sea as the sun set.

The sky clouded over, and the sea turned a stony gray, and a light rain began to fall. The wind rose, and the fronds of the palm trees along the waterfront clashed with a mechanical dry noise. A white yacht, pitching in the swell, its running lights on, made for the old harbor.

He went in off the balcony and flicked the switch on the living-room wall. The lights came on, pale and watery. In the yellowish glow the room looked shabby and unwelcoming. He got out his checkbook and sat down at the desk and wrote out a check for his wife. He hadn't added up his balance in the checkbook for weeks, and he didn't do it now. He put the check in an envelope and wrote the address. Now a stranger's house, although still full of his books and papers and the furniture of half a lifetime.

He pulled open the drawer of the desk and took out the script, one of six copies that were lying there. It had no cover, and the title was on the top page—*The Three Horizons*. There was no author's name under the title. Craig took out a pen and leaned over the desk. He hesitated for a moment and then wrote, "by Malcolm Harte." It was as good a name as any. Let the work be judged entirely on its own merits, with an unknown name on its cover. The reactions would be purer. His friends would not be tempted to be lenient, his foes unaware of a new opportunity for derision. He recognized the cowardice there, but the good sense, too, the search for accuracy.

Methodically, he repeated the inscription, writing it neatly on the remaining five copies. He put a copy of the script in a manila envelope and wrote Bryan Murphy's name on it.

He thought of calling Constance. She should be home by now. And cooled down after the outburst of the morning. But if she weren't home, he knew it would sadden him, so he didn't pick up the telephone.

He went down to the crowded lobby, smiled without warmth at two people he knew but did not wish to talk to. At the concierge's desk he mailed the check to his wife and asked to have the script delivered immediately by messenger to Bryan Murphy at the Hotel du Cap. Then he wrote out a cable to Anne telling her to get on the next plane to Nice. If he was going to be unsettled by the young, it might as well be his own flesh and blood.

CHAPTER 6

HE WENT TO a small restaurant on the old port for dinner. Alone. He had spoken to enough people that day. The restaurant was one of the best in town, expensive and usually crowded. But tonight, except for himself and two loud parties of English, the men florid and excessively barbered, the women overdressed and bejeweled, the room was empty. The English groups were not connected with the Festival but were vacationing in Cannes. He had seen them all the night before at the casino, men and women alike playing for high stakes. The women were sopranoing about other holiday places, Sardinia, Monte, as they called it, Capri, St. Moritz, the compulsory stations of the rich. The men were complaining about the Labor government, currency restrictions, the bank rate, devaluation, their voices booming over the high trill of their wives.

There will always be an England, Craig thought as he ate his salade niçoise.

Pablo Picasso came in with a party of five, and the handsome woman who owned the restaurant fussed him into a table along the opposite wall. Craig looked at him once, admired the bull-like vitality radiating from the small stocky figure, the great naked head, the dark eyes that were somehow gentle and fierce at the same time. Then he averted his glance. Picasso, he was sure, enjoyed his fame, but he had the right to spoon his soup without having his every gesture noted by a middle-aged, prying American whose only claim to the artist's attention was that he had once hung a lithograph of a dove on the wall of a house he no longer owned.

The two English groups had stared briefly and incuriously at Picasso and his party as they entered the restaurant, then went back to their steaks and their champagne.

Later, the proprietress came over to his table. "You know who that is, don't you?" she said in a low voice.

"Of course."

"They . . ." There was a little sardonic gesture of her head for her British customers. "They don't recognize him," she said.

"Art is long," Craig said, "and recognition is fleeting."

"*Comment?*" The proprietress looked puzzled.

"An American joke," Craig said.

When he had finished his dinner, the proprietress gave him a brandy on the house with his coffee. If the English had recognized Picasso, he would have had to pay for his own brandy.

As he went out of the restaurant, he passed Picasso's table. Their eyes met briefly. He wondered what the old man's eyes really saw. An abstraction, an angular, ugly product of the American machine? A murderer standing over a slain Asian peasant counting bodies? A mournful, displaced clown at an alien, sad carnival? A lonely fellow human being moving painfully across an empty canvas? He deplored the conventions that ruled his conduct. How satisfactory it would be to go over to the man and say, "You have enriched my life."

He went out of the restaurant and crossed the street to the quay to walk past the moored yachts bobbing gently in the quiet, black water. Why are you not all at sea? he wondered.

As he neared the turn of the harbor, he saw a familiar figure approaching under the lamplights. It was Ian Wadleigh, walking, shambling loosely and wearily, his head down. At the last moment Wadleigh saw him and straightened up sprucely and smiled at him. Wadleigh had grown fat and bulged out of his unpressed clothes. His collar was open to accommodate the thick, flabby throat, and a tie hung, carelessly low and askew, down the rumpled shirt. He needed a haircut, and the uncombed thick hair, going in all directions over the high, bulging forehead, gave him a wild, prophetic air.

"Just the man I wanted to see," Wadleigh said loudly. "My friend, the boy wonder." Wadleigh had met Craig when he had just turned thirty. The phrase was now meant to hurt, and it did.

"Hello, Ian," Craig said. They shook hands. Wadleigh's palm was sweaty.

"I left a note for you," Wadleigh said accusingly.

"I was going to call you tomorrow."

"Who knows where I'm going to be tomorrow?" Wadleigh's voice was a little thick. He had been drinking. As usual. He had started to drink when his books had begun to go badly. Or his books had started to go badly when he had begun to drink. The cause and effect of Ian Wadleigh.

"Aren't you here for the whole festival?" Craig asked.

"I am nowhere for nothing," Wadleigh said. He was drunker than Craig had first thought. "What are you doing?"

"When?"

"Now."

"Just taking a walk."

"Alone?" Wadleigh peered around him suspiciously, as though Craig were hiding some dubious companion among the upturned dories and the fishing equipment on the dark quay.

"Alone," Craig said.

"The loneliness of the long-distance producer," Wadleigh said. "I'll walk with you. Two comrades, veterans of the retreat from Sunset Boulevard."

"Do you always talk in movie titles, Ian?" Craig asked. He was annoyed by the writer's assumption that they were linked in disaster.

"The Art of Now," Wadleigh said. "Print is dead. Read any Canadian philosopher. Lead me to the nearest bar, boy wonder."

"I've had enough to drink for tonight."

"Lucky man," Wadleigh said. "Anyway, I'll walk with you. You've got to be going in a better direction than I am."

They walked side by side, Wadleigh self-consciously straight-backed and springy. He had been a handsome man, with bold, lean features, but his face had been destroyed by drink and fat and self-pity. "Tell me all about yourself, boy wonder," he said. "What are you doing in this shit hole?"

"I thought it was time to see a couple of movies," Craig said.

"I live in London," Wadleigh said. "Did you know that?" He asked the question harshly, daring Craig to admit that he had lost interest in his one-time friend's activities.

"Yes," Craig said. "How is London?"

"The city of Shakespeare and Marlowe," Wadleigh said, "of Queen Elizabeth and Dickens, of Twiggy and Ian Wadleigh. Another shit hole. I'm supposed to be down here doing a piece on the Festival for an English fag magazine. On spec. They pay my hotel bill. If they take the piece, they throw me another couple of pounds. They want that old magic name Ian Wadleigh on their fag cover. When they read the piece, they'll probably puke. All I've seen here is shit. And I'm going to say so. There'll be a twitter in the dovecote. The fag entertainment editor never learned how to read, so he thinks movies are today's music of the spheres. The Art of Now. He thinks Jean-Luc Godard turns out a new Sistine Chapel four times a year. Christ, he thought *Blow-up* was a masterpiece! What do *you* think of the crap they're showing here?"

"Some good, some bad," Craig said. "I figure by the time the thing's over, we'll have seen at least six good pictures."

"Six!" Wadleigh snorted. "When you make up the list, send it to me. I'll include it in my piece. Freedom of the press. The half-dozen selections of a once-great mind."

"You'd better go back to your hotel, Ian," Craig said. "You're being a pain in the ass."

"I'm sorry." Wadleigh was genuinely contrite. "My manners have deteriorated the last few years. Along with everything else. I don't want to go back to my hotel. There's nothing there for me but a collection of fleas and half the manuscript of a book I'll probably never finish. I know I'm a bitter son of a bitch these days, but I shouldn't take it out on an old pal like you. Forgive me. You do forgive me, don't you, Jess?" He was pleading now.

"Of course."

"We were friends, weren't we?" He was still pleading. "We had some good times together, didn't we? We put down a lot of bottles together. There's still something left, isn't there, Jess?"

"Yes, there is, Ian," Craig said, although there wasn't.

"What kills me," Wadleigh said, "is what passes for writing these days. Especially in the movies. Everybody grunting and saying, Yeah, and, Like, you know, I dig you, baby, and, Let's fuck, and that's supposed to be dialogue, that's supposed to be how the noble human animal communicates with his fellow man under the eye of God. And the people who write like that get a hundred thousand a picture and win Oscars and all the girls they can handle, and I'm down to writing a crappy two-thousand-word piece on spec for a fag English magazine."

"Come on, Ian," Craig said. "Every artist has his ups and downs. Just about everybody goes in and out of fashion in his lifetime. If he lasts long enough."

"I will be back in fashion fifty years after I die," Wadleigh said. "Posterity's darling, Ian Wadleigh. And how about you? I haven't seen many articles in the Sunday papers recently saying how wonderful *you* are."

"I'm on sabbatical leave," Craig said, "from admiration."

"It's one hell of a long sabbatical leave," Wadleigh said.

"So it is."

"That reminds me," Wadleigh said. "There's a girl here by the name of McKinnon—she's some kind of reporter—who keeps trying to pump me about you. All sorts of questions. About women. Girls. Your friends. Your enemies. She seems to know more about you than I do. Have you been talking to her?"

"A bit."

"Be careful," Wadleigh said. "She has a funny light in her eye."

"I'll be careful."

A Fiat with two girls in it slowed down along the curve, and the girl nearest them leaned out the open window and said, *"Bonsoir."*

"Get the hell out of here," Wadleigh said.

"Sal juif," the girl said. The car spurted ahead.

"Dirty Jew," Wadleigh said. "Do I look *that* bad?"

Craig laughed. "You must learn to be more polite with French ladies," he said. "They've all been brought up in convents."

"Whores," Wadleigh said. "Whores everywhere. In the audience, on the screen, on the streets, in the jury room. I tell you, Jess, this is the living and eternal capital of whoredom for two weeks each year. Spread your legs and take your money. That ought to be printed on every letterhead under the seal of the city of Cannes. And look at that. Over there." He pointed across the boulevard where there were four young men smiling professionally at passing males. "How do you like that?"

"Not very much," Craig admitted.

"You can't tell the players without a program anymore," Wadleigh said. "Wait till you read my piece."

"I can't wait," Craig said.

"I'd better send you a copy of the manuscript," Wadleigh said. "Those fags'll never print it. Or maybe I'll turn whore, too, and write just what that fag entertainment editor wants to hear. If I don't get that dough, I don't know what I'll do."

"Maybe that's just what those girls in the car and those boys over there on the corner say to themselves every night," Craig said. "If I don't get that dough, I don't know what I'll do."

"You're just too fucking Christian tolerant, Jess," Wadleigh said. "And don't think it's a virtue. The world is going to the dogs on a sickening wave of tolerance. Dirty movies, dirty business, dirty politics. Anything goes. Everything's excused. There's always a half-dozen something that isn't bad."

"What you need, Ian," Craig said, "is a good night's sleep."

"What I need," Wadleigh said, stopping on the sidewalk, "is five thousand dollars. Have you got five thousand dollars for me?"

"No," Craig said. "What do you need five thousand dollars for?"

"There're some people making a movie in Madrid," Wadleigh said. "They have a lousy script, naturally, and they need a quick rewrite. If I can get there, it's almost sure the job's mine."

"It only costs about a hundred bucks to fly from here to Madrid, Ian."

"What'll I use for the hotel?" Wadleigh demanded. "And food? And for the time it takes to sign the contract? And before the first payment? And for my lousy third wife? At this moment she's attaching the books and typewriter I left in storage in New York for nonpayment of alimony."

"You've struck a responsive chord there, Brother," Craig said.

"If you go in to make a deal and the bastards know you haven't got a dime, they grind you to powder," Wadleigh said. "You've got to be able to get up and walk out and say, Up yours, friends. You know that. I figure five thousand is a minimum."

"Sorry, Ian," Craig said.

"Okay, can you give me three hundred? I can get to Madrid and give myself a couple of days on three hundred." The fat on his throat over his loose collar was quivering.

Craig hesitated. Unconsciously, he patted his coat over his wallet. He knew he had five hundred dollars in American money and about 2000 francs in the wallet. Superstitiously, in memory of the time he had been poor, he always carried a lot of money with him. Turning down requests for loans, even from people who were strangers, was invariably painful, almost impossible, for him. He regarded this trait, rightly, as a weakness in his character. He always remembered that in *War and Peace* Tolstoy had used Pierre Bezouchov's new-found ability to turn down supplicants for money as a sign of maturity and ripening intelligence. "All right, Ian," he said, "I can give you three hundred."

"Five thousand would do better," Wadleigh said.

"I said three hundred." Craig took out his wallet and extracted three one hundred dollar bills and gave them to Wadleigh.

Wadleigh stuffed the bills roughly into his pocket. "You know I'll never pay you back," he said.

"I know."

"I won't apologize," Wadleigh said fiercely.

"I'm not asking you to apologize."

"You know why I won't apologize? Because you owe it to me. You know why you owe it to me? Because once we were equals. And now you're something, and I'm nothing. Less than nothing."

"Have a good time in Madrid, Ian," Craig said wearily. "I'm going to bed. Good night."

He left Wadleigh standing there under the lamppost, with the whores cruising by him as he stared at Craig's retreating back.

By the time he had reached his hotel, Craig had caught a chill and was shivering a little. He went into the bar, which was nearly empty at this hour between dinner and the end of the showing in the Festival Hall. He sat at the bar and ordered a hot grog for his health's sake. While he was drinking it, the bartender showed him a photograph of his son. The son was dressed in the archaic uniform of the Escadre Noir of the French cavalry school at Saumur. In the photograph the young man was taking a fine black horse over a jump, his seat perfect, his hands secure. Craig admired the picture for the father's pleasure, thinking the meanwhile how wonderful it must be to devote your life to something as pretty and useless as a French cavalry squadron in 1970.

Still shivering a little and beginning to feel the advent of fever, he paid for his drink, said good night to the father of the cavalryman, and went to the lobby to get the key for his room. There was an envelope in his box, and he recognized Gail McKinnon's handwriting. Now he regretted not having asked her to have dinner with him. Wadleigh would not have spoken as he had if the girl had been at his side. Wadleigh had shaken him more than he cared to admit to himself. And he would have been three hundred dollars richer because Wadleigh wouldn't have brought himself to ask for money in front of a witness. Irrationally, too, he felt that the chill he was suffering from, and the mounting fever, could be traced to his encounter with the writer. The cold wind from the depths of Cannes.

In his room he put on a sweater and poured himself a whisky, again for his health's sake. It was too early to go to sleep, fever or no fever. He opened Gail McKinnon's envelope and in the yellowish glow of the glass chandelier read what she had written to him.

"Dear Mr. Craig," he read, "I persist. With optimism. This afternoon, at lunch and in the car, I sensed that you were becoming more friendly. You are not really as remote a man as you try to appear. As we passed the house where you told me you spent a summer on the Cap d'Antibes, I felt that you wanted to say more than you allowed yourself to say. Perhaps it was out of caution, not wanting to reveal something on the spur of the moment that you would regret later seeing in print. So what I'm doing here is writing out some questions that you can read at your leisure and then write out your replies to the ones you choose to answer in exactly the terms that please you. You can edit as you will, free of any fear of slips of the tongue that an unscrupulous newspaperman or newspaperwoman might take advantage of.

"Here goes—"

He read the first question and stopped. It was a simple one. "Why are you in Cannes?" Well, he thought, that's a good beginning. And a good end. Intelligent girl. The all-inclusive, everlasting inquiry. Why are you anyplace? *The answer to this question is to determine your general knowledge of the subject. You have thirty minutes, or twenty-four hours, or forty-eight years in which to complete the examination.*

Why are you in this city and not in another? Why are you in this bed with this woman and not another? Why are you alone here or in a crowd there? How have you come to be kneeling before this altar at this time? What has driven you to say no to that journey and yes to the one on which you find yourself? What has possessed you to cross that river yesterday, board this plane this morning, kiss this child this evening? What has driven you to this latitude? What friends, enemies, successes, failures, lies, truths, calculations of time and geography, what reading of maps, what detours and highways have deposited you in this room at this evening hour?

A fair question deserved a fair answer.

He went over to the desk and sat down and pulled out a sheet of paper and a pen. "Why am I in Cannes?" he wrote slowly. He hesitated. Then, without really thinking of what he was doing or writing, he wrote, almost automatically, "I am in Cannes to save my life."

CHAPTER 7

HE STARED AT the sentence that he had written. That is not my handwriting, he thought. He put the pen down. He knew he was not going to write anything more that night. *Anything you say may be used against you.* He leaned back in his chair and closed his eyes.

There was a brilliant, painful light shining, a wild, loud howling somewhere. He opened his eyes. Through the wet smear of the windshield wipers two damp moons were hurtling straight at him. His hands were still loosely on the wheel. He yanked at the wheel, slid past the other car by inches on the gleaming black road. The wail of the other car's horn faded like a funeral cry behind him. He felt calm, drove alertly, not stopping, peering carefully through the streaked glass at the curves ahead of him.

A few miles farther on his hands began to shake, his body to shiver uncontrollably. He pulled over to the side of the road, stopped his car, waited for the spasm to pass. He had no idea of how long it was before his hands stopped shaking. He was conscious of cold sweat on his forehead, icicles dripping down inside his clothing from his armpits. He took out his handkerchief, wiped his forehead, breathed deeply, four profound inhalations. The air in the car smelled sour. Where was he? The rows of black trees alongside the road told him nothing. He had crossed the French border not

so long ago, he remembered. He was somewhere between the Bidassosa River and
Saint Sebastian. He had started from Paris that morning, had not stopped except for
gasoline and a cup of coffee all day. *I have nearly died in sunny Spain.* He had
intended to drive without a halt until Madrid, sleep over, go farther south—to
Malaga—the next day. A man he knew, something of a friend, a matador, really the
friend of a friend, was fighting in Malaga the next afternoon. He had met the man in
Alicante the year before. There was a three-day *feria*. Mediterranean sunshine,
parading bands, fireworks, the costumes of the Spanish south, much drinking, long,
crowded hangovers, the amused irresponsibility of other people's celebrations,
companions, men and women he knew well enough to enjoy on a short holiday but
who meant nothing much to him, whom he only saw the four or five times in the year
when he happened to go to a bullfight.

The matador was too old for the bulls. He knew it. He was a rich man. There was no
sensible reason for him to go into an arena with animals who were devoted to killing
him. "What can I do?" the matador had said. "It is the only thing that deeply amuses
me. It is my only playground. I am lucky. I *have* a playground. Most people do not
have one. So—I cannot permit them to drive me from it."

There were many ways of dying in Spain. Horns, falling asleep at the wheel.

It was the third time that year he had fallen asleep driving at night. Once outside
Salzburg. Once on the *autostrada* near Florence. Tonight. He had been lucky. Or had
he been? Anyway, he had opened his eyes in time. In the last years he had taken to
driving nine hundred, a thousand miles at a stretch. What had he wanted to do in
Salzburg, what had he planned to see in Florence? His friend the matador would be
fighting in thirty different places all season. Why had he felt it was necessary to go to
Malaga? He no longer remembered. He liked driving at night, the solitude, the
numbing, hypnotic onrush of lights, the satisfaction of leaving a place he felt he had
been in too long, the pleasure of moving through the deserted, dark streets of a new
city, the accomplishment of distance.

Suicide was in every garage. He was sane enough to understand that.

He started the car, drove slowly into Saint Sebastian, found a hotel. He would not
reach Madrid that night.

A bar was open near the hotel. He ordered a brandy, then another. He wasn't
hungry. There were some men arguing at a table in Spanish. He listened. Their heads
were bent together over the table, their voices fell to a conspiratorial hush. They
might have been planning to murder Franco, free a priest, bomb the prefecture of
police, take a chance on a lottery. He did not understand the language. He was
soothed by his ignorance.

He called Paris from the hotel. It took a long time, and he undressed and got into
bed waiting for the call to be put through. Constance answered. He had left her early
in the morning. They had made love in the dawn. She had been sleepy and warm. Her
lovemaking was robust as usual, generous and easy. She gave freely, took without
stint, there were no favors exchanged, no debts to be paid off in bed. She never said,
"Why do you have to go?" when he announced without warning that he was off to
Zurich or the Côte Basque or New York. He would not have been able to answer her
truthfully if she had asked.

Every once in a while they went on trips together, but that was different. They were
holidays when she had time off from work. When he drove off by himself, it was not a
holiday. If she was in the car with him, he drove slowly, chatting with her, playing
word games, enjoying the scenery, stopping often for brandies. She liked to drive,
too. She was an erratic driver, but lucky. She had never had an accident, she boasted.
She should have had twenty. He had laughed once as they teetered around a curve on
the wrong side of the road. She hated being laughed at. She had stopped the car and
got out and said she wouldn't drive with him anymore and started walking back
toward Paris. He had waited, and she had come back a half hour later, trying
unsuccessfully to look imperious, and gotten into the car, and he had let her drive,

and she'd stopped the car at the first café, and they'd had a brandy.

That morning, when he had left her, he had gone back to his hotel and packed his bag and sped through the early-morning traffic toward the auto route south. Once she had asked him why he bothered keeping a hotel room since almost every night he was in Paris he stayed at her place. He had said, "I'm used to hotels." She hadn't asked again.

The phone rang on the table beside the bed. The room was an immense one, with dark, high furniture. He always went to the best hotel in town, avoiding the other guests. He didn't like the ordinary run of guests in the best hotel in any town.

"Are you in Madrid already?" she asked. He might have just awakened her, but you never could tell with Constance. Five seconds after she was roused, she sounded as though she had just come, bubbling and fresh, from a cold shower.

"No," he said, "I stopped in Saint Sebastian for the night."

"How is it in Saint Sebastian?"

"They're speaking Spanish," he said.

"What a surprise." She laughed. "What made you change your mind?"

If he had been honest, he would have said, "I didn't want to die tonight." Instead, he said, "It was raining."

Another year. Five years ago. He was standing in the lobby of a movie theatre in Pasadena. There had been a sneak preview of the last picture he had made. The movie had been shot in France, its hero a young lieutenant in the American army in Germany who had deserted and had a disastrous affair with a French woman before turning himself in. The director, Frank Baranis, was in the lobby with him, sunk in a large polo coat, depressed because the audience had coughed and been inattentive throughout the film. They had been friends ever since Baranis had directed Edward Brenner's play nearly twenty years before. Baranis had been the best man at Craig's wedding. During the shooting of the film, Craig had received an anonymous letter in a woman's handwriting saying that Baranis had been sleeping with Penelope before the marriage, the very day before, the letter had said, and probably for a long time after. Craig had ignored the letter, had said nothing about it either to Penelope or Baranis. On the strength of an anonymous letter, probably from a jilted and vengeful woman, you did not ask the man who was your friend and was working day and night for you on a complicated and demanding task whether or not he had slept with your wife the day before your wedding seventeen years ago.

Craig was suddenly aware of how old Baranis looked, like a fearful, wizened monkey. He was lightly pockmarked, but he had large liquid dark eyes and a disdainful, offhand way with women that was, Craig heard, effective.

"Well," Baranis said, "we bombed. What do we do now?"

"Nothing," Craig said. "That was the picture we wanted to make, and we made it."

A man and his wife, in the crowd coming out of the auditorium through the lobby, passed nearby. The woman was short and dowdy. If she had been on sale, you would have been able to find her in gross lots on the shelves of a supermarket at clearance prices. The man was burly, bursting out of his clothes, and looked like a football coach whose team had just lost a game and was furious with his players. His face was red and flushed, his eyes glared behind rimless glasses. "What a load of shit," he was saying as he passed the spot where Craig and Baranis were standing. "They think they can get away with anything these days."

"Harry," the woman said in her supermarket voice. "Your language."

"I repeat," the man said. "A load of shit."

Craig and Baranis looked silently at each other. They had worked for nearly two years on the picture.

After a while Baranis said, "Maybe it isn't a picture for Pasadena. Maybe it'll be different in New York."

"Maybe," Craig said. Then, since it was that kind of night, anyway, he said,

"Frank, a couple of months ago I got an anonymous letter that said you'd had an affair with Penelope before we were married. That you'd gone to bed with her the day before, even. Is that true?"

"Yes," Baranis said. It was still that kind of night.

"Why didn't you say something?"

"You never asked," Baranis said. "How the hell was I to know when it started you wanted to marry her?" He pulled the collar of the polo coat up around him, half-buried his face in it. He looked like a small, trapped, dying animal. "Anyway, if I had told you, you'd have married her just the same. You'd have forgiven her and hated me. You'd never have talked to me again."

"I suppose so," Craig said.

"Look at you and Ed Brenner," Baranis said. He sounded angry. "You never see *him* anymore, do you?"

"No."

"See?"

"You knew about Brenner and Penny?" Craig asked flatly.

"Everybody knew." Baranis shrugged impatiently. "So what good would it have done if I'd opened my big mouth?" Baranis sank deeper in his coat.

"No good." Craig nodded reasonably. "Come on, let's get out of here. I'll drive you home."

The picture didn't do much better in New York. It was before the time when movies about soldiers who were disillusioned with the American army were to the public taste.

He was sitting in his office signing checks on the scarred, fake mahogany desk. The office was small and shabby, two rooms, one for him and one for his secretary. Belinda Ewen had been with him since his first play. The furniture of the office also was the same he had started with back in 1946. Neither Belinda nor the furniture had improved with the passage of time. Belinda had been a small, dark, furiously energetic, almost pretty young woman when he had hired her. She was still small, dark, and energetic, but now was no longer almost pretty. Her face seemed to have been honed into severe angular lines by the abrasion of the years, her lips chipped out by a blunt knife. The desk had been fake mahogany in 1946. It just looked a little more fake now.

Penelope had campaigned to be allowed to choose a larger office for him and to decorate it herself. He had refused. He didn't like the offices of men whose wives had chosen the furniture, the thick rugs, the tasteful paintings on the walls. Penelope had also tried, at least once a year throughout their marriage, to get him to fire Belinda. "She runs the office as though it's hers, not yours," Penelope had said over and over again. "And besides, she's disrespectful to me." Among Penelope's complaints about Belinda Ewen was Belinda's style of dress. "It's grotesque," Penelope had said. "She looks as though she's gotten herself up to go to Coney Island with a sailor. What do you imagine people think about you when they come into the office for the first time and they see that woman decked out in all the colors of the rainbow?" He hadn't replied, as he might have, that people came to his office to work with Jesse Craig, not to pass judgment on the choice of his secretary's clothes. But he contented himself with saying, "When she marries, I'll get someone who dresses all in black."

"Married!" Penelope had sniffed. "While you're alive, that woman will never marry."

"I hope you're right," he had said. The discussion had taken place on one of the less pleasant evenings at home.

Even so, there were times when the clashing greens and purples of some new outfit that Belinda had put together made him shake his head in wonderment. Safely behind the closed door of his own office, of course.

Penelope had also suggested, in moments of anger, that he had had an affair—was still having an affair—with the secretary. He had never touched Belinda and believed that she would run screaming through the halls if he as much as brushed her cheek. And he saw no reason, if a woman did her work as efficiently as Belinda did hers, why she had to be respectful to her employer's wife.

And finally, he was superstitious. He had done well in the shabby little office with the unprepossessing, ludicrously dressed secretary; he had done better than he had ever hoped or dreamed he might do since the day when he had signed the first lease for eighty dollars a month. There was no sense in tempting fate with unnecessary signs of luxury. Although now, sitting at the old desk, in the late afternoon of an autumnal New York day, signing away at a torrent of checks after the disastrous preview in Pasadena and the neglected opening in New York, he could hardly argue that luck had made a permanent base in the bare room in which he had worked so long.

The checks he was signing were from his personal, not from his business account. For the most part they were for household bills, food, liquor, fuel, telephone, the salaries of the two maids, flowers, a bill for two thousand dollars for a sofa that Penelope had found at an antique dealer's on Madison Avenue, bills from Saks Fifth Avenue and Bergdorf Goodman for clothes that Penelope had bought, a two-hundred-dollar bill that came in monthly from Charles of the Ritz where Penelope had her hair done. There were other bills, too—tuition for Anne's school in Lausanne, tuition for Marcia's school in Maryland, insurance and garage rent for Penelope's car, a hundred-and-eighty-dollar bill for the masseuse who visited Penelope three times weekly, a savage bill from a doctor in Hollywood for treatment of Penelope's mother, who had come out to visit her daughter soon after the marriage when Craig had been making his first movie on the Coast and had immediately fallen mysteriously ill and was taking a long time to die in the most expensive place for dying in the world.

Craig had tried setting up a household account for Penelope to handle, but she was always overdrawn or neglected to pay the telephone bill so that suddenly it would be cut off, or she would pay bills twice or be too busy to bother for months on end, and there would eventually be dunning letters on his desk to annoy him. So now he had Belinda type up the checks, and once a month, in silent fury, he signed them himself. He wondered what Belinda thought as she typed out the checks for clothes that more than equaled her entire year's salary. She must also speculate, he thought, what anybody could do to a woman's hair that was worth two hundred dollars a month.

When he had finished with the last check, he threw down his pen and leaned back in his chair and looked out the streaked, dirty window of his office at the lighted windows across the street, behind which clerks and secretaries were working in the glare of neon tubes. If they had known what he had been doing at his desk for the last hour or so, they would have every right, he thought, to come storming out of their cubicles and into his office to tear his checkbook to bits. At the very least, the checkbook.

From time to time he had tried to remonstrate with Penelope about the bills she ran up, but Penelope invariably broke into tears at the mention of money. Quarreling about money was debasing. She had not dreamt when she married him that she was linking herself for life with a man who thought only in dollars and cents. In all her childhood and youth in Chicago she had never heard a word in her home about money. Listening to her, one would think that she came from a long line of landed aristocrats whose wealth was based in some illustrious, monarchal past in which plebeian matters such as debts and assets were handled only in backstairs obscurity by discreet underlings in frock coats. Actually, her father had been a traveling salesman in silks and ribbons who had died in want. Craig had had to pay for the old man's funeral.

As the discussions grew more heated, Penelope swore that she watched every cent, called on the names of wives of their friends who spent more on their clothes in one month than she did in a year, which was true, brought heaven to witness that all her efforts and expenditures were designed to make him a decent home, give him a wife he would not be ashamed to be seen with in public, bring up his children decently. He hated scenes, especially about money. Deep down he had the feeling that the large sums that had come his way in his career were not rightly his but the work of accident, luck, for doing only the things he would have happily done, anyway, for a pittance. He could not argue about money. Even in business he never dealt directly with contracts but allowed Bryan Murphy in Hollywood and his business manager on Broadway to handle that side of his affairs at all times. Not being able to dicker with a recalcitrant actor about a percentage of the profits of a play or movie, he certainly couldn't stand up to his wife's tears when it was a question of a six-hundred-dollar telephone bill or the cost of a new coat. Still, remembering his early days living in cheap hotels, he wondered by what insidious magic he found himself signing salary checks for two maids who worked in a house in which he rarely ate more than two meals a week and from which he was absent, more often than not, five or six months a year.

Although each time Belinda brought in the checks to sign she put on what Craig had come to recognize as her steadfastly noncommittal face, he found it difficult to meet her gaze and always pretended to be busy and said gruffly, keeping his head down, "Thank you, Belinda. Just put them on the desk. I'll sign them when I have the time."

When he had first met Penelope, she had been a charming young actress of moderate talent who dressed attractively and lived in a pleasant little apartment in the Village on ninety dollars a week. He wondered where that girl had gone. From a frugal young woman who washed her own stockings and underwear each night, she had turned almost immediately into someone who ransacked galleries and antique shops, who patrolled Fifth Avenue like the advance guard of a looting army, who had to have nurses for her children, who could not conceive of living anywhere in New York City except between Sixtieth and Eighty-sixth Street on the East Side. American women, he thought, take to extravagance with all the natural talent of a dolphin to the waves of the sea.

That it was as much his fault as his wife's and that he recognized this did not make the check-signing sessions any the easier for him.

He added up the amounts of the checks he had signed, entered them neatly in the checkbook. The total came to nine thousand, three hundred and twenty-six dollars and forty-seven cents. Not bad, he thought, for a man with two flops behind him.

When he had been working with Brenner on his first play, Brenner had once said to him, "I cannot take the problems of a man who makes more than fifty dollars a week seriously." Brenner had been youthfully extreme then, but he wondered what his old friend would think about him if somehow he had wandered into the office that afternoon and happened to glance down at the repeated signatures on the scraps of paper scattered across the littered desk.

On an impulse he made out one last check, in his own hand, for nine thousand, three hundred and twenty-six dollars and forty-seven cents. He left the space for the payee blank for a moment. Then he filled in the name of a hospital. It was the hospital in which his two daughters had been born.

He wrote a short note to the fund-raising committee of the hospital to go along with the contribution, put the note and the check into an envelope, and addressed it and sealed it.

He had balanced his accounts for the day.

He called through the door to Belinda. He had tried, briefly, installing a buzzer, but its implications had made him uneasy.

When Belinda came in, he gave her the checks and the one sealed envelope and said, "That'll do it for this afternoon, thank you."

Then he went downstairs to the bar next door and had enough to drink so that the evening ahead of him would be a blur.

When he got home, Penelope said, "Do you think I'll ever live to see the day that you'll show up for dinner sober?"

The last guests had just gone. There were empty glasses all around the living room. Penelope was in the kitchen emptying ashtrays. He looked at his watch. One thirty. Everybody had stayed too long. He sank into an easy chair, kicked off his shoes. There had been fourteen at dinner. The dinner had been very good. The company dull. He had drunk too much wine.

Theoretically, his twelve guests were his friends. Of them all, there were only two, Robert and Alice Paine, whom he considered true friends. Robert Paine was a vice-president of a publishing house, on the business side, a portly, solid, highly educated man who spoke slowly, weighing his words, ignoring small talk. Craig had met him when he had been asked to select an anthology of plays for Paine's publishing house, and he had taken an immediate liking to the man. His wife Alice was a child psychiatrist, a large, squarish, handsome woman with mannishly clipped graying hair framing a quiet oval face. Penelope thought they were heavy going, and Craig knew that they had been invited for his sake, so that he wouldn't complain too bitterly about the rest of the list.

There had been nobody at the table who worked in either the theatre or the movies, although two of the men had from time to time invested in plays of his. Bertie Folsom had been there as usual. Since his wife died, Bertie Folsom was at every dinner party. Talking about the stock market. At length. Folsom was a few years older than Craig, a short, sharpfaced, balding, insignificant-looking, meticulously tailored man with a neat, round paunch who headed a big brokerage concern on Wall Street. The farther he went downtown, Craig thought, the more Bertie Folsom must gain in significance. He occasionally gave advice to Craig on stocks. Occasionally, Craig took it. Sometimes the advice was valuable. Since being widowed, he was invited to all dinners at the Craig house. Often he called at six in the evening and asked what they were doing that night. When they weren't doing anything in particular, the Craigs asked him to join them for quiet family dinners. Folsom remembered everybody's birthday, brought gifts for Anne and Marcia. Penelope felt sorry for him, she said. Craig figured that Folsom could not be worth less than two million dollars. Perhaps it was evidence of Penelope's warmth of character that she could find time to be sorry for a man who was worth two million dollars. When they had a party like the one tonight, Penelope invited various ladies for Folsom. They were the sort of ladies, usually divorced, who were always free to come to anybody's house for dinner. When Craig was out of town or working, Folsom escorted Penelope to the theatre and to parties. Somebody had once said Folsom was a useful man, one should always have a widower among one's circle of friends.

The conversation during the evening had been, aside from Bertie Folsom's dissertations on the stock market, about servants, the disastrous quality of the plays on Broadway that season, sports cars, Ferraris, Porsches, and Maseratis, the shortcomings of the young, speculation about the amours, legitimate and covert, of friends who were not present that night, the impossibility of finding a decent place anymore in the Caribbean to spend a holiday, and the comparative virtues of various ski resorts. Somehow, everybody there skied each winter. Except Craig. Penelope spent a month a year in Sun Valley and Aspen. Alone. Sitting at the head of his table in the house on the East Side of New York City, Craig felt that he had become an expert on snow. He had nothing against skiing-he wished he had had the time to take it up when he was a younger man-but he believed people should ski, not talk about it. No one that evening had mentioned his last picture, or any of his pictures, except the Paines, who had come early so as to have a chance to talk to him alone for a few minutes over drinks before the rest of the guests had arrived. The Paines had liked his last picture, although Alice Paine had been bothered by the violence of a scene in a Parisian nightclub in which the hero got involved in a brawl. "Alice," Robert Paine had said affectionately about his wife, "hasn't learned yet how to stop being a psychiatrist when she enters a movie house."

There had been one interlude in the evening during which Craig had listened with some interest. The subject of Women's Liberation had come up, and Penelope, who ordinarily spoke little in company, had been eloquently vehement on the subject. She was for Women's Liberation. Craig had agreed with her. So had the other women at the table. If they had not all been so busy with fittings and arranging dinner parties and observing the schedules of hairdressers and traveling to the Caribbean and Sun Valley, they undoubtedly would have made a considerable impression on the movement.

Craig did not bother with the guest lists for parties. For one thing, he was too occupied with other matters to take the time. Occasionally, he met someone who interested him enough to suggest his or her name to Penelope, but more often than not Penelope would find some reason, usually perfectly valid, why the man or woman or couple would not fit in with the particular evening she was planning.

He sighed, not actually knowing why he did so. He heaved himself out of the chair and walked in his stockinged feet across the thick pale carpet to the sideboard where the bottles were ranged and poured himself a whisky. Penelope came in from the kitchen, glanced at the glass in his hand. When she did that, he always felt guilty. He picked up the bottle and added another ounce to his drink, splashed some soda into it, and went back to the easy chair. He watched Penelope move about the big, comfortable room in the subdued lamplight that shone in soft creamy pools on the polished wood of end tables, the brocade of chairs, the brass pots full of flowers. Penelope would not stand strong light. It was always difficult in any house she inhabited, even houses they rented for a summer, to find a place where it was possible to read.

She was dressed in a long, loose red velvet robe that swung gracefully around her slender, still youthful figure as she touched a bunch of flowers, put a magazine back in the rack, closed the cover of a silver cigarette box. Her taste was sure. Things looked better after she had touched them. There was nothing ornate or showy about her house, but, Craig thought, it was a wonderful place to live in, and he loved it. With the glass of whisky in his hand, he watched his wife move around the warm, welcoming room, and he forgot the dull departed guests. At that moment, admiring her in the midnight silence, he knew he loved her and felt completely married. He knew her faults. She was a liar, extravagant, cunning, often pretentious; she filled his house with second-rate people because she feared the competition of wit, beauty, intelligence; she had been unfaithful to him and at the same time made him suffer from the blackmail of her jealousy; when things went wrong, she invariably found a way to pass the blame onto other shoulders, usually his; often she bored him. Still, he loved her. No marriage was all of one piece. Each partner paid some price. He was sure that in her secret heart Penelope's list of his failings was much longer than the account of his own judgments on her.

He put his glass down, stood up, went over to her, kissed the back of her neck. She stiffened as though the gesture had caught her by surprise.

"Let's go to bed," he said.

She pulled away. "You go to bed," she said. "I still have things to do down here."

"I want to go to bed with you," he said.

She walked quickly across the room, put a chair between them as though for defense. "I thought that was just about over," she said.

"Well, it isn't."

"It is for me," she said.

"What did you say?"

"I said it's over for me. Permanently. I don't want to go to bed with you or with anybody." Her voice was low, even, without emotion.

"What brought *that* on?" He tried to keep his anger from showing.

"You," she said. "Everything. Leave me alone."

He went over and got his glass and took a long drink.

"When you sober up in the morning," she said, "you'll find your passion has been neatly filed away in the back of the vault. Along with a lot of other things."

"I'm not drunk," he said.

"Every night," she said.

"Do you mean what you just said?"

"Yes."

"All of a sudden like that?"

"It isn't so sudden," she said, still behind the barrier of the chair. "You've been bored with me for years. And you've shown it. Tonight you did everything but yawn in the face of all my friends."

"You must admit, Penny," he said, "that it was a drab collection tonight."

"I don't admit anything."

"That Bertie Folsom, for God's sake . . ."

"A lot of people think he's a most intelligent, attractive man." He took a step toward her. He could see her knuckles whiten as she gripped the back of the chair, and he stopped.

"Come on, Penny," he said gently. "Don't let a passing mood make you say things you'll be sorry for later."

"It isn't any passing mood." Her mouth pulled down severely. Even in the soft light she now looked her full age. "I've been thinking about this for a long time."

He finished his drink, sat down, looked searchingly at her. She returned his glance unflinchingly, the enmity plain in her eyes.

"Well," he said, "I suppose this calls for a divorce. And a drink." He stood up and carried his glass to the sideboard.

"There's no need for a divorce," she said. "You don't want to get married again, do you?"

He laughed shortly and poured himself a stiff drink.

"I don't want to get married, either," she went on.

"What do we do—live together just as though nothing had happened?" he demanded.

"Yes. If only for Marcia and Anne. Anyway, it shouldn't be any great hardship. Nothing very much has happened between us for years now. Every once in a while, when you're not bombed to extinction, or you've got a case of insomnia or one of your other girls isn't available, you remember you have a wife, and you come crawling around."

"That's a word I'm going to remember, Penny," he said. "Crawling."

She ignored his warning. "Four or five nights a year," she said, "there won't be any games at home. That's all. I think we both can stand it."

"I'm forty-four years old, Penny," he said. "I don't see myself remaining celibate for the rest of my life."

"Celibate!" She laughed harshly. "There's another word for you. You can do whatever you want. Just the way you always have."

"I think," he said quietly, "tomorrow will be just the day for me to go on a nice long trip. Europe might be just the thing."

"The girls're coming home for Christmas," she said. "The least you owe them is to be here when they come. Don't take it out on them."

"All right," he said. "Europe can wait until after Christmas."

He heard a telephone ringing. Still dislocated in time, he almost called out, "Penny, will you take that, please?" Then he shook himself, looked around, realized where he was, at an ornate, fake antique desk in a hotel room facing the sea, and reached over and picked up the phone. "Craig speaking," he said.

There was a faraway howling over the wires, American voices jumbled and speaking too low to be understood, then, weirdly, a few notes of a piano, then a click and silence. He frowned, put the phone down, looked at his watch. It was past midnight, between three and six in the afternoon on the continent of America. He waited, but the phone did not ring again.

He stood up and poured himself a drink. He felt a wetness on his cheek. He looked disbelievingly at himself in the mirror. He had been weeping. He brushed the tears roughly away with the back of his hand, drank half the whiskey, glared at the telephone. Who had tried to reach him, what message had been baffled in its course to him in midocean?

Perhaps it had been the one voice that could have made everything clear—tell him where he stood, what were his assets, what were his debts, what he owed, what was owed him. On what side of the ledger he might enter his marriage, his daughters, his career. Let him know once and for all if he was morally bankrupt or ethically solvent, announce whether his loving had been a defensible expense, answer the question of whether or not, in an age of wars and endless horror, his preoccupation with fictions and shadows had been a callous waste of honor.

The telephone did not ring. There was no message from America. He finished his drink.

When he had been away from her, Penelope had had the habit of calling him almost every night just before she went to bed. "I don't sleep happily," she had said, "unless I hear your voice and know that you're all right."

The telephone bills had been enormous.

Sometimes he had been irritated by her calls, at other times moved by husbandly tenderness at the sound of the low, familiar, musical voice from a distant city, the other shore of a continent. He had been irritated when he thought that she had been checking on him, testing his fidelity, even though after what had happened between them he felt that he owed her no fidelity, or at least not *that* form of fidelity. He had been unfaithful to her occasionally. Without a sense of guilt, he told himself. Nor did he underestimate the continuing pleasure his indulgence made possible. But he had never allowed himself to become seriously involved with another woman. To that extent, he had felt he had protected his marriage. For the same reason he had refrained from inquiring into his wife's relations with other men. He had never checked on her. She had secretly rifled through all his papers, he knew, hunting for women's names, but he had never picked up a letter addressed to her or questioned her about whom she had seen or where she had gone. Again, without examining this facet of his behavior closely, he had felt that it would have been demeaning to him, a belittling blow to his pride. He had recognized the female cunning in Penelope's late-night telephone calls but for the most part had tolerated them, even been fondly amused by them, flattered by them. Now he knew he had been wrong. He and his wife had avoided candor, and they had drained their marriage.

He had been angry that morning when he had received her letter and had made out the monthly check, and he had reflected on her rapacity and meanness of spirit. But now, after midnight, alone, the memories that had been aroused by passing the house on the Cap d'Antibes that afternoon working within him and the frustrating sounds of the indecipherable voices on the wires still echoing in his ears, he couldn't help but remember better times, gentler encounters.

For Craig, at least, the marriage worked best at times of stress—when late at night, after long hours in the theatre, he would return from the chaos of rehearsals, the savage clash of wills and temperaments whose tensions it was his job as producer to absorb and accommodate, and find Penelope waiting up for him, ready to make a drink for him in the beautifully ordered living room of their house and listen to him pour out his recapitulation of the day's work, the day's problems, the small tragedies, the day's insane comedies, the fears for the morrow, the disputes that remained to be solved. She was sympathetic, cool, understanding. Her intuition and intelligence could be relied on. Invariably, she was helpful, the most reliable of partners, the most useful of advisers, steadfastly faithful to his interests. Out of all the memories of his marriage, all the good times, the summer in Antibes, the deeply satisfying moments with his daughters, even the long-shared pleasure of their lovemaking, it was those countless quiet midnight conversations in which they shared the best of themselves with each other that in retrospect were the real texture of their marriage, the most painful to have to forget.

Well, he had plenty of problems tonight, he could use advice. Despite everything, he knew he longed for the sound of her voice. When he had written her to tell her he was taking steps for a divorce, she had written him a long letter pleading with him not to break up their marriage, with all the reasons, passionate and sensible and homely, for keeping it alive. He had barely glanced as it, afraid, perhaps, that it would sway him, and coldly sent her a note telling her to find a lawyer.

Then, as was almost inevitable, she had become a lawyer's creation, striking for gain, advantage, revenge. Now he regretted not having read her letter more carefully.

On an impulse, he picked up the phone, gave the operator the number of the house in New York. Then, after he had put the instrument down, he remembered from his daughter's letter that Penelope was in Geneva.

Foolish woman, he thought, as he got the operator back and canceled the call, this is one night she should have been at home.

CHAPTER 8

HE POURED HIMSELF a fresh drink, paced the room holding the glass in his hand, angry with himself for submitting himself to the past, torturing himself with the past. Whatever he had come to Cannes for, it had not been for that. Gail McKinnon had a lot to answer for. Well, he had come so far, he thought, he might as well go all the way. Go over all the mistakes, all the wrong turnings, all the betrayals. If masochism was to be the order of the day, enjoy it. Listen to the ghosts, remember the weather of other seasons . . .

He sipped at his drink, sat hunched over at the desk, allowed the past to invade him.

He was in his office, back from three months in Europe. The trip had been neither good nor bad for him. He felt suspended in time, not unpleasantly, postponing all decisions.

There was a pile of scripts on his desk. He leafed through them without interest. Before the breakup with Penelope, or the semibreakup, or whatever it was, it had been his custom to do most of his reading in the small studio he had fixed for himself at the top of his house where he had no telephone and could not be interrupted. But since he had come back from Europe, he had taken a room at a hotel near his office and only occasionally visited the house or slept there. He hadn't moved his clothes or any of his books, and when his daughters were at home, which was rarely, he was there. He did not know how much they knew about the breach between him and their mother, and there were no indications that they had noticed any change. They were so concerned with the problems of their adolescence—dates, school, diets,—that Craig doubted that they would have paid much attention even if their parents had staged Macbeth before their eyes in the living room, complete with bare dagger and real blood. On the surface, he thought, Penelope and he behaved much as they had always done, perhaps a shade more politely than formerly. There had been no further scenes or arguments. They asked each other no questions about their comings and goings. It was a period in which he felt strangely peaceful, like an invalid who is very slowly recovering from a long illness and knows that no great efforts can be demanded of him.

Occasionally, they went out together. Penelope gave him a present on his forty-fourth birthday. They went down to Maryland to see a school play in which Marcia acted a small part. They slept in the same room in a hotel in the town.

None of the play scripts he was offered seemed worth doing, although there were one or two that he was sure would succeed. When they were done by other men and were hits, he felt no sense of loss or opportunity wasted.

He had given up reading the dramatic pages of the newspapers and had canceled his subscriptions to the trade papers. He avoided restaurants like Sardi's and Downey's, which had been favorite places of his and which were always filled with theatrical and movie people, most of whom he would know.

He had not been in Hollywood since the week of the preview in Pasadena. Every once in a while Bryan Murphy would call him and tell him he was sending him a script or a book that might interest him. When they arrived, he read them dutifully, then called Murphy and said he was not interested. After about a year, Murphy only called to find out how he was. He always said that he was fine.

There was a knock on the door, and Belinda came in carrying a playscript with a sealed envelope clipped to the cover. She had a peculiar, wary expression on her face. "This just came in," she said. "By hand." She put the script on his desk. "It's Eddie Brenner's new play."

"Who brought it in?" He kept his voice noncommittal.

"Mrs. Brenner," Belinda said.

"Why didn't she come in and say hello?"

"I asked her to. She said she preferred not to."

"Thanks," he said, and slit the envelope. Belinda closed the door softly behind her.

The letter was from Susan Brenner. He had liked her and was sorry events had made it impossible for him to see her anymore.

He read the letter. "Dear Jesse," Susan Brenner had written, "Ed doesn't know I'm showing you his play, and if he finds out, I'm going to be in for a rough half hour with him. But no matter. Whatever happened between you and him must be ancient history by now, and all I'm interested in is getting the play on in the best way possible. He's been mixed up with mediocre people in recent years, and they've hurt him and his work, and I have to try to keep him out of their hands this time.

"I think this is the best thing Ed has written since *The Foot Soldier*. It has some of the same feeling, as you will see when you read it. The only time any of Ed's plays has received the production it deserved was that once when he worked with you and Frank Baranis, and I'm hoping that the three of you can get together again. Maybe the time has come when you all need each other again.

"I have faith in your talent and integrity and your desire to do things in the theater that are worthwhile. I am sure that you're too reasonable and honorable a man to allow a painful memory to interfere with your devotion to excellence.

"When you've read the play, please call me. Call me in the morning around ten o'clock. Ed rents a little office nearby where he works, and he's out of the house by then. As ever, Sue."

Loyal, innocent, optimistic wife, he thought. As ever. Too bad she hadn't been around that summer in Antibes. He stared at the script on his desk. It had not been typed or bound professionally. Probably Susan Brenner had faithfully typed it herself. Brenner, he knew, could hardly afford hiring a service to do it for him. A painful memory, Susan Brenner had written. It wasn't even that anymore. It was buried under so many other memories, painful and otherwise, that it was like an anecdote told about a stranger in whom he was only remotely interested.

He stood up and opened the door. Belinda was at her desk reading a novel. "Belinda," he said, "no calls until I ask for them." She nodded. Actually, the telephone rang very seldom these days in the office. He had spoken out of old habit.

He sat down at his desk and read the unevenly typed script. It took him less than an hour. He had wanted to like it, but when he put it down, he knew that he didn't want to do it. The play, like Brenner's first one, was about the war but not about combat. It was about troops of a division that had fought in Africa and was now in England preparing for the invasion of Europe. It seemed to Craig that it attempted too much and accomplished too little. There were the veterans, hardened or pushed near the breaking point by the fighting they had already seen, contrasted with the green replacements being whipped into shape, in awe of the older men, uncertain of their courage, ignorant of what to expect when their time came to go under fire. Along with that, and the conflicts engendered by the clash of the two groups, there were scenes with the local English, the girls, British soldiers, families, in which Brenner tried to analyze the difference between the two societies thrown together for a few months by the hazards of war. In style, Brenner varied from tragedy to melodrama to wild farce. His first play had been simple, all of one piece, fiercely realistic, driving in one straight line toward an inevitable bloody conclusion. The new play wandered, moralized, jumped from place to place, emotion to emotion, almost haphazardly. Brenner's maturity, Craig thought, if that was what it was, had deprived him of his useful early simplicity. The telephone conversation with Susan Brenner was not going to be a pleasant one. He reached for the phone, then stopped. He decided to reread the play the next day after he had thought about it for twenty-four hours.

But when he read it the next day, he liked it no better. There was no sense putting off the telephone call.

"Susan," he said when he heard her voice. "I'm afraid I can't do it. Do you want to hear my reasons?"

"No," she said. "Just leave it with your secretary. I'll pass by and pick it up."

"Come in and say hello."

"No," she said, "I don't think I want to do that."

"I'm terribly sorry, Sue," he said.

"So am I," she said. "I thought you were a better man."

He put the telephone down slowly. He started to read another script, but it made no sense to him. On an impulse he picked up the phone again and asked Belinda to get Bryan Murphy for him on the Coast.

After the greetings were over and Craig had learned that Murphy was in splendid health and was going to Palm Springs for the weekend, Murphy said, "To what do I owe the honor?"

"I'm calling about Ed Brenner, Murph. Can you get him a job out there? He's not in good shape."

"Since when have you been so palsy with Ed Brenner?"

"I'm not," Craig said. "In fact, I don't want him to know that I called you. Just get him a job."

"I heard he was finishing a play," Murphy said.

"He's still not in good shape."

"Have you read it?"

Craig hesitated. "No," he said finally.

"That means you've read it and you don't like it," Murphy said.

"Keep your voice down, Murph, please. And don't say anything to anybody. Will you do something for him?"

"I'll try," Murphy said. "But I don't promise anything. The place is reeling. Do you want me to do something for you?"

"No."

"Good. It was a rhetorical question, anyway," Murphy said. "Give my love to Penny."

"I'll do that," Craig said.

"I have to tell you something, Jesse," Murphy said.

"What?"

"I love to get telephone calls from you. You're the only client who doesn't call collect."

"I'm a wasteful man," Craig said. As he hung up, he knew that the odds were a hundred to one against Murphy's finding anything for Ed Brenner on the Coast.

He didn't go to the opening of the Brenner play, although he had bought a ticket, because the morning of the day of the opening he received a telephone call from Boston. A director friend of his, Jack Lawton, was trying out a musical comedy there and over the phone had said that the show was in trouble and asked him to come up to Boston and look at it and see if he had any ideas as to how it would be helped.

Craig gave his ticket for the opening to Belinda and took the plane that afternoon to Boston. He avoided seeing Lawton or anybody connected with the show before the evening performance because he wanted to be able to judge it with a fresh eye. He didn't want to go into the theatre burdened with the complaints of the producers against the director, the director's criticisms of the producers and the stars, the star's recriminations about everybody, the usual cannibalistic rites out of town when a show was doing badly.

He watched the performance with pity. Pity for the writers, the composer, the singers and dancers, the principals, the backers, the musicians, the audience. The play had cost three hundred and fifty thousand dollars to put on, talented men in every field had worked for years to bring it on the stage, the dancers performed miracles of agility in the big numbers, the stars, who had been acclaimed again and again in other plays, sang their hearts out. And nothing happened. Ingenious sets flew in and out, the music swelled in an orgy of sound, actors grinned bravely and hopelessly as they uttered jokes at which no one laughed, the producers prowled despairingly in the back of the house, Lawton sat in the last row dictating notes in an exhausted hoarse voice to a secretary who scribbled on a clipboard with a pencil equipped with a small light. And still nothing happened.

Craig writhed in his seat, breathing the air of failure, wishing he could get up and leave, dreading the moment later on in the hotel suite when people would turn to him and say, "Well, what do you think?"

The thin desultory applause of the audience as the curtain came down was a slap in the face to everyone in his profession, and the fixed smiles of the actors as they took their bows were the grimaces of men and women under torture.

He did not go backstage but went directly to the hotel, had two drinks to restore himself before he went upstairs to the papery chicken sandwiches, the table with whisky bottles, the bitter, pasty faces of men who had not been out in the open air for three months.

He did not say what he really thought while the producers, the author, composer, and scene designer were in the room. He had no loyalty to them, no responsibility. His friend Lawton had asked him to come, not they, and he would wait until they left before he told Lawton his honest opinion. He contented himself with a few anodyne suggestions—cutting a dance here, restaging a song number slightly, lighting a love scene differently. The other men understood that he was not there to say anything valuable to them and left early.

The last to go were the producers, two small, bitter men, jumpy with false nervous energy, rude with Lawton, almost openingly scornful with Craig because he, too, had so clearly failed them.

"Probably," Lawton said as the door closed behind the two men who had come to Boston with high hopes and glittering visions of success, "probably they're going to sit down now and call a dozen other directors to come up here and replace me." Lawton was a tall, harassed man with thick glasses who suffered horribly from ulcers every time he staged a play, whether it went well or badly. He sipped from a glass of milk continually and swigged every few minutes at a bottle of Maalox. "Talk up, Jesse."

"I say, close," Craig said.

"It's as bad as that?"

"It's as bad as that."

"We still have time to make changes," Lawton said defensively.

"They won't help, Jack. You're flogging a dead horse."

"God," Lawton said, "you're always surprised at how many things can go wrong at once." He wasn't young, he had directed over thirty plays, he had been highly praised, he was married to an enormously wealthy woman, but he sat there, bent over his ulcer pain, shaking his head like a general who had thrown in his last reserves and lost them all in one evening. "Christ," he said, "if only my gut would let up."

"Jack," Craig said, "Why don't you just quit?"

"You mean on this show?"

"On the whole thing. You're driving yourself into the hospital. You don't *have* to go through all this."

"No," Lawton said, "I suppose I don't." He sounded surprised at his own admission.

"Then?"

"What would I do? Sit in the sun in Arizona with other old folks?" His face twisted, and he put his hand on his stomach as a new pang gripped him. "This is the only thing I know how to do. The only thing I *want* to do. Even a shitty, dead piece of nothing like this silly show tonight."

"You asked me what I thought," Craig said.

"And you told me," said Lawton. "Thanks."

Craig stood up. "I'm going to bed," he said. "And I advise you to do the same."

"I will, I will," Lawton said almost petulantly. "There're just one or two notes I want to put down while they're still fresh in my mind. I've called a rehearsal for eleven."

He was working on the script even before Craig left the room, jabbing furiously at the pages open before him as though each stroke of his pen was going to transform everything tomorrow by the eleven o'clock rehearsal, make the jokes funny, the music clever, the dances ecstatic, the applause thunderous, as though by his efforts, in his pain, even Boston would be a different city tomorrow night.

When Craig got to his office the next morning, Belinda had the reviews of Brenner's play on his desk. He didn't have to read them. He could tell by the expression on her face that things had gone badly the night before. When he read the reviews, he knew there was no hope, that the play would close by Saturday night. Even Boston had been preferable.

He was in the theatre Saturday night for the last performance. The theatre was only half-full, most of it, he knew, paper. Brenner, he noted with relief, was not in the audience.

When the curtain came up and the first lines were uttered, he had an odd sensation. He had the feeling that something beautiful was about to happen. The actors were intent and fervent and performed with a contagious belief in the value, the importance, of the words that Brenner had written for them to speak. There was no sign that any of them was affected by the knowledge that the play had been discourteously dismissed as boring or confused by the critics only three days before and that when the curtain came down that night that would be the end of it, the sets dismantled, the theatre dark, and they themselves out on the street looking for other jobs. There was a gallantry about their devotion to their profession that brought tears to Craig's eyes even though, as he watched, he saw the faults in casting, direction, and interpretation that had obscured the subtle, multiple intentions of the play and brought down the critics' wrath on Brenner's head.

As he sat in the darkened theatre, with gaping rows of empty seats behind him, watching what he recognized was a flawed and inadequate production, Craig realized that somehow he had been in error in his judgment of Brenner's script. For the first time in a long while his attention was fully awakened in a theatre. Almost automatically, a list of things that could be done to make the play work, bring out its virtues, eliminate its flaws, began to form in his mind.

When the play was over, there was only a thin scattering of applause from the audience, but Craig hurried backstage, moved and excited, hoping to find Brenner, praise him, reassure him.

The old man at the stage door recognized Craig and said mournfully, "Isn't it all a shame, Mr. Craig?" as they shook hands. Brenner, the old man said, was on the stage saying good-by to the company and thanking them, and Craig waited unseen in the wings until Brenner had made his little speech and the actors began to troop off to their dressing rooms, defiantly noisy beneath the drab work light.

For a moment Craig did not move but watched Brenner standing alone in the empty set that was supposed to be the corner of a temporary shabby barracks in wartime England. Brenner's face was in deep shadow, and Craig could not see its expression. Brenner was much thinner than when Craig had seen him last and was dressed in a baggy tweed jacket with a long wool scarf thrown around his neck. He looked like a fragile old man who had to think about every step he took for fear of falling. Brenner's hair was thinning, Craig noted. A bald spot gleamed.

The curtain slowly went up, and Brenner raised his head and stared out at the dark, empty theatre. There was a rustle beside Craig, and Susan Brenner went past him. Susan Brenner came up to her husband, took his hand, and raised it and kissed it. He put his arm around her. They were standing like that, silently, when Craig finally walked out of the wings.

"Hello," he said.

The man and woman looked at him without speaking.

"I saw the play tonight," Craig said, "and I want to tell you I was wrong when I read it."

Still neither of the others spoke.

"It's a beautiful play," Craig went on. "It's the best thing you've done."

Brenner chuckled. It sounded as though he was strangling.

"Susan," Craig said, "you were right. I should have done it, and Baranis should have directed it."

"Thanks for the memory," Susan said. She was wearing no makeup and looked pale and gaunt, depleted in the bare light.

"Listen to me, please," Craig went on earnestly. "You got the wrong production for it, and it came between the play and the audience. That doesn't mean that's the end of it. Wait for a year, work on it, cast it correctly—you never had a chance with all those fancy, overblown sets, with that man in the lead—he's too old, too sophisticated. A year from now we can put it on downtown, off-Braodway—it doesn't belong on Broadway, anyhow—recast it, do it with lights, a structural bare set, use music, it cries for music, get tapes of speeches by politicians, generals, radio announcers, to play between the scenes, frame them in time—" He stopped, conscious that he was rushing too fast, saying more than Brenner could possibly assimilate at this moment. "Do you see what I mean?" he asked lamely.

The Brenners stared blankly at him. Then Brenner chuckled again, the same choking sound. "A year from now," he said ironically.

Craig understood what was going through Brenner's mind. "I'll give you an advance. Enough to live on. I'll . . ."

"Does Ed get another chance to sleep with your wife, Mr. Craig?" Susan said. "Is that included in the advance?"

"Keep quiet, Sue," Brenner said wearily. "I think you're right, Jesse. I think we made a lot of mistakes in the production, a good many of them mine. I agree it should have been done off-Broadway. I think Baranis would know what I was driving at. I think we could make a go of it. " He took a deep breath. "And I also think you ought to get out of here, Jesse. Get out of my life. Come on, Sue." He took his wife's hand. "I left a briefcase in the dressing room," he said. "We won't be coming back, and we'd better get it now."

Side by side the Brenners went off the stage. There was a long run in one of Susan Brenner's stockings that Craig hadn't noticed before.

Alice Paine was waiting in the almost-empty bar for him. He had been surprised when she had called him and said she was in the neighborhood and wondered if he had the time to have a drink with her. He had never seen her without her husband except occasionally, by accident. He had also never seen her take more than one drink an evening, and she was not the sort of woman you'd expect to find in a bar at three o'clock in the afternoon.

She was finishing a martini as he came to the table at which she was sitting. He leaned over and kissed her cheek. She smiled up at him, a little nervously, he thought. He signaled to a waiter as he sat down on the banquette beside her. "I'll have a Scotch and soda, please," he said to the waiter. "Alice?"

"I think I'd like another martini," she said.

For a moment Craig wondered if Alice Paine had been hiding something all these years from him and all of her other friends. She fiddled with her gloves, her strong hands, with no polish on the fingernails, uneasy on the table. "I hope I haven't interrupted something important," she said.

"No," he said. "Nothing much is happening in the office at the moment."

She put her hands in her lap under the table. "I haven't had a drink in the middle of the day since my wedding," she said.

"I wish I could say the same."

"Are you drinking too much these days, Jesse?" She glanced quickly at him.

"No more than usual, he said. "Too much."

"Don't let anyone tell you you're an alcoholic," she said. She was speaking more quickly than ordinarily, her voice a little higher in tone.

"Why?" he asked. "Have you heard anyone saying I was an alcoholic?"

"Not really," she said. "Oh, well, Penelope. Sometines she seems to infer . . ."

"Wives," Craig said.

The waiter came over and placed the drinks before them. They raised their glasses, and Craig said, "Cheers."

Alice made a face as she sipped her martini. "I suppose I'll never find out what people see in these things," she said.

"Courage," he said. "Nepenthe." By now he knew that Alice had not called him merely because she happened to be in the neighborhood that afternoon. "What is it, Alice?" he said.

"Oh, dear," she said, fiddling with her glass. "It's so hard to know where to begin."

He was sure that Alice Paine hadn't said, "Oh, dear," since her wedding day, either. She was not that sort of woman. She was also not the sort of woman who didn't know where to begin.

"Begin in the middle," he said, "and we'll work it around." Her nervousness made him uncomfortable.

"You believe that we're your friends?" she said. "I mean Robert and myself."

"Of course."

"I mean, that's important," she said. "I wouldn't like you to think that I'm a meddlesome woman, or malicious, or anything like that."

"You couldn't be meddlesome or malicious if you tried." By now he was sorry he had been in the office when she had called.

"We had dinner at your house last night," she said abruptly. "Robert and I."

"I hope you had a good meal."

"It was perfect. As usual," she said. "except that you weren't there."

"I'm not home very much these days."

"So I gathered," Alice said.

"How was the guest list?"

"Unbrilliant."

"As usual," Craig said.

"Bertie Folsom was there."

"As usual," Craig said.

She glanced quickly at him again. "People are beginning to talk, Jesse."

"People are always beginning to talk," he said.

"I don't know what sort of arrangement you and Penelope have," Alice said, "but they're seen together everywhere."

"I don't know what sort of arrangement we have, either," he said. "I guess you could call it a large, loose nonarrangement. Is that what you came to tell me—that Penelope and Bertie have been seen together?"

"No," she said. "Not really. First, I want to tell you that Robert and I aren't coming to your house anymore."

"That's too bad," he said. "Why?"

"It goes a long way back. Four years, to be exact."

"Four years?" He frowned. "What happened four years ago?"

"Do you think I could ask for another martini?" she said. She sounded like a little girl asking for a second ice cream cone.

"Of course." He waved to the waiter and ordered two more drinks.

" You were out of town somewhere," Alice said. "We were giving a little dinner party. We invited Penelope. Then, to round out the table, we had to find an extra man. Somehow, it always turns out that the extra man is Bertie Folsom."

"What else is new?" Craig said lightly.

"The trouble with tall men like you," Alice said severely, "is that they never take small men seriously."

"It's true," Craig said, "he's a very small man. So—he sat next to Penelope at dinner."

"He took her home."

"Zounds! He took her home."

"You think I'm a silly, gossipy woman . . ."

"Not really, Alice," he said gently. "It's just that . . ."

"Ssh," she said, and gestured toward the waiter, who was approaching with their drinks.

They sat in silence until the waiter had gone back to the bar.

"All right," Alice said. "This is what happened. The next morning I received a dozen red roses. Anonymously. No card."

"That could mean anything," Craig said, although by now he knew it couldn't mean anything.

"Every year, on the same date," Alice said, "October fifth, I get a dozen red roses. Anonymously. Of course he knows I know who sends them. He *wants* me to know. It's so vulgar. I feel tainted—like an accomplice—every time I go to your house and see him there eating your food, drinking your liquor. And I've felt like such a coward, not saying anything to him, not telling you. And last night, seeing him there sitting at the head of the table pouring the wine, acting the host, staying on after everybody had left—I talked it over with Robert, and he agreed with me, I couldn't keep quiet anymore."

"Thanks for today," Craig said. He leaned over and kissed her cheek.

"I don't know what kind of code we all go by," Alice said. "I know we're not supposed to take adultery seriously anymore, that we laugh when we hear about our friends playing around—I've heard some stories about you, too."

"I'm sure you have," he said. "Most of them no doubt true. My marriage has hardly been a model of felicity for a long time."

"But this particular thing I can't take," Alice said. There was a catch in her voice. "You're an admirable man. A decent friend. And I can't stand that awful little man. And to tell the truth, I've come to dislike Penelope. There's something false and hard about her with all her charming hostessy tricks. If I *do* have a code, I suppose it's that I think that certain people don't deserve what they have to endure, and if they're my friends, I finally have to do something about it. Are you sorry I've told you all this, Jesse?"

"I don't know yet," he said slowly. "Well, anyway, I'll see to it that you're not bothered by any more roses."

The next day he sent a letter to his wife telling her he was seeing a lawyer about a divorce.

Another bar. In Paris now. In the Hotel Crillon, just across from the Embassy. He had fallen into the habit of meeting Constance there when she got through working. It gave a fixed point to his day. The rest of the time he spent wandering around the city, going into galleries, strolling through open-air markets and among the young people of the Latin Quarter, practicing his French in shops, sitting at café tables reading the newspapers, occasionally having lunch with one or two of the men who had been with him on the movie he had made in France and who were sensitive enough not to ask him what he was working on these days.

He liked the room, with its knots of English and American newspapermen arguing at the bar and its shifting population of polite, well-dressed, elderly Americans with New England accents who had been coming to the hotel since before the war. He liked, too, the looks of admiration on the faces of the other drinkers when Constance came hurrying into the bar.

He stood up to greet her, kissed her cheek. Although she had spent a whole day in a stuffy office chain-smoking cigarettes, she always smelled as though she had just come from a long walk in a forest.

She had a glass of champagne, to get the taste of youth out of her mouth, she said. "I'm always surprised," she said, sipping her champagne, "to find you sitting here when I come in."

"I told you I'd be here."

"I know. Still, I'm surprised. Every time I leave you in the morning, I have the feeling that *this* is going to be the day you're going to meet someone irresistibly attractive or hear about an actor or actress in London or Zagreb or Athens you must have to see perform that night."

"There's nobody in London or Zagreb or Athens I want to have anything to do with, and the only irresistibly attractive woman I've seen all day," he said, "is you."

"Aren't you a nice man." She beamed. She had a childish love of compliments. "Now tell me what you did all day," she said.

"I made love three times to the wife of a Peruvian tin tycoon . . ."

"Yeah, yeah." She grinned. She enjoyed being teased. But not too much.

"I had my hair cut. I ate in a small Italian restaurant on the rue de Grenelle, I read *Le Monde,* I went into three galleries and nearly bought three paintings, I had a glass of beer at the Flore, I went back to my hotel, and . . ." He stopped. He was conscious that she wasn't listening to him. She was staring at a young American couple that was passing the table, going toward the back of the room. The man was tall, with a pleasant, open face, as though he had never known doubt or deprivation and that it was inconceivable to him that anybody anywhere could be his enemy or wish him harm. The girl was a pale, tall beauty with dead black hair, wide, dark eyes, something Irish or Spanish in her background, moving with deliberate grace, a dark sable coat rippling about her, smiling at something her husband had just said, touching his arm as they walked between the bar and the tables alongside the windows. They did not seem to see anyone else in the room. It was not discourteous. It was merely that they were so absorbed in themselves that even a careless haphazard glance, the necessity to see or possibly recognize another face, would be a waste, a loss of a precious moment of contact with each other.

Constance kept watching them until they had disappeared in the restaurant section in the rear. She turned back to Craig. "Forgive me," she said. "I'm afraid I wasn't listening. They're people I once knew."

"They're a handsome couple."

"They are that," Constance said.

"How old is that girl?"

"Twenty-four," Constance said. "She was responsible for the death of a friend of mine."

"What?" It was not the sort of thing you expected to hear in the bar of the Crillon.

"Don't look so alarmed," Constance said. "People are responsible for the death of other people all the time."

"She hardly looks like your average murderess."

Constance laughed. "Oh, it wasn't anything like that. A man I knew was in love with her, and he read in the newspapers that she had just been married, and three days later he died."

"What an old-fashioned story," Craig said.

"He was an old-fashioned man," Constance said. "And he was eighty-two years old."

"How did you happen to know an eighty-two-year-old man?" Craig asked. "I know you like older men, of course, but wasn't that pushing it a bit?"

"The old man's name was Jarvis," Constance said. "Kenneth Jarvis."

"Railroads."

"Railroads." She nodded. "Among other things. Many other things. I had a beau who worked with Jarvis's grandson. Don't glower, dear. It was before your time, long before your time. The old man liked to have young people around him. He had a great big house in Normandy. At once time he owned a racing stable. He gave big weekend parties, twenty, thirty people at a time. The usual thing, tennis, swimming, sailing, drinking, flirting, whatever you call it. They were always fun. Except for the old man. When I first met him, he was already senile. He'd drop food all over himself when he ate, he'd forget to button his fly, he'd fall asleep at table and snore, he'd tell the same story three times in ten minutes."

"You paid for your fun," Craig said.

"People who'd known him when he was younger didn't seem to mind," Constance said. "He'd been a charming, generous, cultivated man. A great collector of books, painting, pretty women. His wife had died when they were both young, and he'd never remarried. The man I used to go to his place with said that you had to repay some of the pleasure a man like that had distributed all through his life, and watching him dribble a little on his necktie or listening to the same story over and over again was a small price to pay. Especially since the house and the food and drink and entertainment were exactly as they'd always been. Anyway, only stupid people laughed at him behind his back."

"God spare me," Craig said, "from reaching eighty."

"Listen to the rest of the story. One weekend an old mistress of Jarvis's came down. With her daughter. The girl you just saw pass with her husband."

"God spare me," Craig said, "from reaching seventy."

"He fell in love with her," Constance said. "Real old-fashioned love. Letters every day, flowers, invitations to mother and daughter for cruises, the whole thing."

"What was in it for the mother? Or the daughter?" Craig asked. "Money?"

"Not really," Constance said. "They were comfortably enough off. I suppose they got to know a lot of people they otherwise would never have met—that sort of thing.

The mother had kept the girl on a tight rein. Her only prize. When I first met the girl, she was nineteen, but she acted fifteen. You half-expected her to curtsy when anybody was introduced to her. Jarvis made her grow up. And then it was flattering. To be the hostess at grand dinner parties, to be the center of attention, to escape her mother. To be adored by a man who in his time had known everybody, had anecdotes about everybody, had ordered the lives of thousands of people, had had affairs with all the famous beauties. She liked the old man, loved him in her own way, maybe, was delighted by her power over him. And overnight, he'd changed completely, he'd become young, vital. He never forgot anything he'd said, he walked erectly, where he used to shuffle, his voice sounded robust, where it used to be a wheeze, he dressed impeccably, he'd stay up all night and be spruce and full of energy in the morning.

"Of course, some people snickered. The sight of an eighty-two-year-old man doting over a nineteen-year-old girl as though it was his first love and he was taking her out to her first ball . . . But I saw him once in a while, and I was touched. It was as though a miracle had made time reverse for him. He'd gone back. Not all the way, of course, not to twenty or thirty, but to fifty-five, sixty—"

"He died, you said," Craig said.

"Yes. She met that young man you just saw her with and stopped seeing Jarvis. And he found out that they'd been married only when he saw it in the newspapers. He dropped the paper to the floor and took to his bed and turned his face to the wall, and three days later he was dead."

"It's a nice sensible story," Craig said.

"I think so," she said. "At his funeral a friend of his said. 'Isn't it wonderful? In this day and age to be able to die for love at the age of eighty-two?'"

"In this day and age."

"He couldn't have wanted anything better, could he, the old man?" Constance said. "He'd had a glorious, foolish, lively eight months or so and a noble exit. No oxygen tent, no doctors hovering around, no pipes and kidney machines and transfusions, just love. Nobody blamed the girl, of course. Just envied her husband. And the old man. Both. You have a funny light in your eye."

"I'm thinking."

"What about?"

"If somebody came to me with a play or a movie script based on the old man's story," he said, "I think I'd be tempted to try to do it. Only nobody has."

Constance finished her glass of champagne. "Why don't you take a shot at writing it yourself?" she said.

It was the first time that she had tried to push him in any direction whatever, the first time that he realized that she knew that he couldn't keep going on the way he had been.

"I'll think about it," he said, and ordered two more drinks.

He walked along the sea front of Saint Sebastian in the morning. The rain had stopped. The wind was blustery, the air washed, the big rock far out in the bay a beleaguered fortress, the waves pounding. When he crossed the bridge, the tide in the river was fierce, foaming water, the clash between ocean and land at the land's gates. Half-remembering where he was from other visits, he walked in the direction of the big bullring. Empty now, out of season, immense, it looked like a deserted temple to a forgotten bloody religion. A door was open. He heard the sound of workmen hammering somewhere, the noise reverberating hollowly in the dark caverns under the stands.

He went up through a passageway, leaned against the *barrera*. The circle of sand was not golden, as in other rings, but ash-colored, the color of death. He remembered the matador's words—"It is the only thing that still amuses me. It is my only playground." Too old for the bulls, his friend, sword in hand, blood on his suit of lights, a fixed, rapt smile on his handsome, scarred young-old face, would be facing the horns later that day hundreds of miles to the south. He would have to send a telegram. "Many ears. *Abrazo*."

Opening-night telegrams. Different formulas for different cultures.

He should send a telegram to Jack Lawton, ulcer-ridden, in Boston, to Edward Brenner, his arm around his wife on the dark stage in New York, to Kenneth Jarvis, buying flowers for a nineteen-year-old-girl, all in their arenas, all facing their particular horns, all faithful to their only playgrounds.

A caretaker, dressed in a kind of imitation uniform, appeared on the other side of the ring, waved at him threateningly, shook his fist, shouted with thin authority as though he suspected Craig of being ready to leap into the ring, a crazed, middle-aged *spontaneo* planning to interrupt a ghostly faena, cite a bull who would not appear for another two months.

Craig gestured courteously to him, a lover of the *fiesta brava,* observing its rules, visiting its holy places, and turned and went down under the stands and out into the ragged sunlight.

By the time he had walked back to his hotel he had made a decision.

He drove back to France slowly, carefully, not stopping at the spot where he had nearly been killed the night before. When he reached Saint-Jean-de-Lux, quiet in the preseason lull, he registered in a small hotel, went out and bought a ream of paper. I am now armed, he thought, as he carried the paper back to the hotel, I am re-entering my playground. By a different entrance.

He stayed in Saint-Jean-de-Luz two months, working slowly and painfully, trying to shape the story of Kenneth Jarvis, who had died at the age of eighty-two, three days after he had read in a newspaper that the girl of nineteen whom he loved had married another man. He had started it as a play, but bit by bit it had slid into another form, and he had gone back to the beginning and started it all over again as a film script. He had worked since his first days in the theatre with writers, suggesting changes, whole scenes, the addition of new themes, but it was one thing to work on the basis of another man's ideas and quite another to have a blank page in front of you and only yourself to try to bring it to life.

Aside from two weekend visits from Constance, he kept to himself, spending long hours at the desk in the hotel room, taking solitary walks along the beach and around the harbor, eating alone in the hotel dining room.

He told Constance what he was doing. She voiced neither approval nor disapproval. He didn't show her what he had written. Even after two month's work there would have been very little to show anyone—just a disconnected jumble of scenes, bald ideas, sketches of possible sequences, notes for characters.

By the end of the two months he realized that simply telling the story of the old man and the young girl was not enough. It wasn't enough because it didn't leave room for him, Jesse Craig, in it. Not the actual Jesse Craig, not the recital of the history that lay behind the man who sat day after day at the desk in the quiet hotel room, but his beliefs, his temperament, his hopes, his judgment on the time through which he had lived. Without all that, he came to realize, whatever he finally accomplished would be fragmentary, useless.

So he invented other characters, other pairs of lovers, to people the great house he had imagined on the north shore of Long Island for the summer in which he hoped to concentrate all the action of the film. He had transposed the locale of the story from Normandy. He didn't know enough about Normandy to write about it, and he knew enough about Long Island. He brought in a grandson, aged nineteen, in the first raptures of passion, taken with a promiscuous girl three or four years older than he. And drawing on more recent experience, he involved a comfortably adulterous couple of forty.

Using everything he had learned from his reading, his working on other men's plays and films, on his own observation of his friends, enemies, acquaintances, he tried to intertwine his characters naturally and dramatically so that in the end, without ever speaking in his own voice or in using anything but his characters' words and actions, the final result might be Jesse Craig's statement of what in the second half of the twentieth century in America, it was like to love as a young man or woman, a middle-aged man or woman, and an old man on the brink of death, with all the interplay, the compromising, the wounding, of money, moral stances, power, position, class, beauty and the lack of it, honor and the lack of it, illusion and the lack of it.

After two months the town began to fill up, and he decided it was time to pack and move on. On the long drive north toward Paris, thinking about how he had spent the two months, he knew that he would be lucky if he could get the script written in a year. Maybe lucky if he could ever get it written at all.

It took him the full twelve months. He had written bits and pieces of it in Paris, in New York, on Long Island. Whenever he had come to a point in the script where he couldn't see his way ahead, he had packed and restlessly moved on. But he hadn't once fallen asleep at the wheel on any of his trips.

Even when he had finished it, he showed it to no one. He, who had passed judgment on the work of hundreds of other men, couldn't bear thinking of strangers' eyes reading the words he had written. And any reader, he felt, was a stanger. When he sent it off to be typed, he put no author's name under the title. Merely the legend, Property of Jesse Craig. Jesse Craig, once the boy wonder of Broadway and Hollywood, once known as a keen judge of the dramatic and cinematic art. Jesse Craig, who had no notion whether or not a year of his work was worth anybody's attention for two hours and dreaded to hear either a yes or a no.

When he put the six copies of the script into the valise the day he took the plane to Cannes, there was still no author's name under the title *The Three Horizons*.

The telephone rang. He shook his head dazedly, like a man being suddenly awakened from a deep sleep. Once more he had to remind himself where he was, where the telephone was. I am in my room in the Carlton, he thought, the telephone is on the table on the other side of the big chair. The telephone rang again. He looked at his watch. It was one-thirty-five. He hesitated, almost decided not to answer. He didn't want to hear any more incoherent messages from America. Finally, he picked up the phone.

"Craig speaking," he said.

"Jess." It was Murphy. "I hope I didn't wake you."

"You didn't wake me."

"I just finished reading your script."

"Yes?"

"That kid Harte can write," Murphy said, "but he's been seeing too many old French movies. Nobody's interested in an eighty-two-year-old man, for Christ's sake. You'll never get off the ground with it, Jess. Forget it. I wouldn't even show it around. It'll do you more harm than good, believe me. Drop the option and forget it. Let me work on the Greek thing for you, and we'll keep our eyes peeled for something good for later on."

"Thanks, Murph," Craig said, "for reading it. I'll talk to you tomorrow." He hung up, stared at the phone for a long time. Then he went back to the desk at which he had been sitting. He looked down at the typed list of questions Gail McKinnon had given him, read once more the first question. "Why are you in Cannes?"

He chuckled dryly to himself, picked up the pile of papers and tore them into small bits, dropped them into the wastebasket.

Then he took off his sweater, put on a jacket, and went out. He took a taxi to the casino where he knew the bar would be open all night. He bought some chips, sat down at a chemin de fer table, ordered a double whisky, and played and drank until six in the morning. He won thirty thousand francs, nearly six thousand dollars, mostly from two of the Englishmen who had been in the restaurant with Picasso that evening. It was unfortunate for Ian Wadleigh that he wasn't patrolling the Croisette as Craig walked, almost steadily, through the growing dawn toward his hotel. At that hour Wadleigh would have gotten his five thousand for Madrid.

CHAPTER 9

POLICEMEN WITH FLASHLIGHTS were guiding the cars toward an open field where many cars were already parked. The air was heavy and cold. When Craig turned off the ignition and stepped out, his shoes squished on the wet grass. He walked up the path toward the big, chateaulike house from which came the sound of an orchestra. The house was on a hill beyond Mougins, and it dominated the land around it like a small fortress.

He was sorry that Anne had not yet arrived. She would have enjoyed going into a house like that on her father's arm, to the sound of a French song, attended by policemen who were diligently engaged in lighting the way for you under dark old trees rather than lobbing tear-gas bombs in front of the Administration Building. He had Anne's cable in his pocket. Surprisingly, she had decided to visit her mother in Geneva and would be coming down to Cannes the next day.

Walter Klein, the host, was standing in the hallway greeting his guests. He had rented the house for a month, choosing it because it was large enough for parties. Klein was a small, powerfully built, youngish man with a deceptively easygoing manner. In the turbulent breaking up and realignments of agencies that had been taking place in the last few years, he had walked away from a decaying organization, taking with him a list of stars and directors, and while other agencies and movie companies were collapsing, he had accommodated himself to the new conditions of the industry so shrewdly that a good proportion of the movies being prepared or shot in America or England at any given moment had one or more clients of his in some key spot or were indebted to him in some way for financing or distribution. Where others cried havoc, he smiled and said, "Kids, we've never had it so good." Unlike Murphy, who had grown to affluence in an easier time, and who scornfully kept aloof from the soul-like atmosphere of Cannes during these two weeks, Klein could be seen at all hours talking earnestly in corners with producers, distributors, money men, directors, actors, wheeling and dealing, promising, signing. For his lieutenants he chose soft-spoken and personable young men who had never known the fat, easy old days, who matched him in avidity and amibition, and who, like their boss, hid their honed-down sharpness under a careful display of charm.

When Klein had met Craig in New York some time before, he had said lightly, "Jess, when are you going to leave that old dinosaur Murphy and come to my office?"

"Never, I guess, Walt," Craig had said. "Murph and I have sworn our bond in blood."

Klein had laughed. "Your loyalty does you credit, Jess," he said. "But I miss your name on the old silver screen. If you ever decide you want to come where the action is, give me a call."

Now Klein was standing in the marble front hallway of the mansion talking to some other people who had just arrived. He was dressed in a black velvet jacket, a ruffled shirt, and a bright red bow tie. Beside him was an anxious-looking woman who ran public relations for his firm. It was she who had sent out the invitations for the evening, and she looked pained when she saw Craig standing there in slacks and a blue blazer. Most, but not all, of the other guests were in evening clothes, and Craig could tell by the look on the woman's face that she sensed a small betrayal in his choice of clothing.

Klein shook his hand warmly, smiling. "Ah," he said, "the great man. I was afraid you wouldn't come." He didn't explain why he was afraid Craig would not come but introduced him to the people whom he had been talking to. "You know Tonio Corelli, of course, Jess," he said.

"By sight." Corelli was the beautiful young Italian actor from the Hotel du Cap swimming pool, now resplendent in a jet black, Roman-tailored dinner jacket. They shook hands.

"And if you will introduce the ladies, *carino,*" Klein said. "I didn't quite catch your names, dears," he added apologetically.

"This is Nicole," Corelli said, "and this is Irene."

Nicole and Irene smiled dutifully. They were as pretty and tan and well-shaped as the girls who had been with Corelli at the pool, but they were not the same girls.

He goes in for matched pairs, Craig thought, he must run them in and out on a schedule. Craig recognized envy as easily in himself as in the next man.

"Honey," Klein said to the public relations woman, "take them in and get them a drink. If you want to dance," he said to the girls, "be careful you don't catch pneumonia. The band's outside. I couldn't make a deal on the weather, and winter came up. The merry month of May."

The trio, led by the public relations woman, drifted beautifully away.

"The only thing to be," Klein said, "is Italian."

"I know what you mean," Craig said. "Though you don't seem to be doing so badly." He made a gesture to take in the luxury of his surroundings. He had heard that Klein was paying five thousand dollars for the month he had rented the house.

"I'm not complaining. I go with the flow," Klein said, grinning. He took an honest pleasure in his wealth. "It's not an uncomfortable little pad. Well, Jesse, it's good seeing you again. How're things going?"

"Fine," Craig said. "Just fine."

"I invited Murphy and his frau," Klein said, "but they declined with thanks. They don't mingle with the lower orders."

"They're here for a rest," Craig said, lying for his friend. "They're going to bed early this week, they told me."

"He was a great man, Murphy," Klein said. "In his day. You're still with him, of course?"

"Of course."

"As I once told you," said Klein, "your loyalty does you credit. Is he working on something for you?" He threw away the line carelessly, turning his head as he spoke to survey his guests through the archway that gave into the great living room.

"Not that I know of," Craig said.

"You have anything on the fire yourself?" Klein turned back toward him.

Craig hesitated. "Maybe," he said. He had told no one but Constance and Murphy that he was considering doing a picture again. And Murphy had made his position clear. More than clear. Craig dropped his hint deliberately now. Of all the men gathered for the Festival, Klein, with his energy and his labyrinthine network of contacts, could be the most useful. "I'm playing with an idea."

"That's great news." The enthusiasm in Klein's voice was almost genuine. "You've been away too long, Jess. If you need any help, you know where to come, don't you?" Klein put an affectionate hand on his sleeve. "Anything for a friend. We put combinations together these days that make even *my* mind whirl."

"So I've been told. Maybe I'll give you a call one of these days and we can talk some more." Murphy would be hurt if he heard. He was a man proud of his acumen, and he took it ill if clients and friends didn't follow his advice. Murphy was contemptuous of Klein. "That punk little hustler" was Murphy's description of Klein. "In three years he won't even be a memory." But Murphy these days did not come up with combinations that made the mind whirl.

"There's a swimming pool out in the garden," Klein said. "Come any time you like. You don't have to call in advance. This is one house in which you're always welcome." There was a last affectionate little pat on the arm, and Klein turned to meet a new group that was arriving as Craig went into the salon.

The room was crowded because it was too cold to go outside where the band was playing, and on his way to the bar Craig had to say, "Excuse me," several times to get past guests clustered around easy chairs and small sofas. He asked for a glass of champagne. He had to drive back to Cannes, and if he drank whisky all night, the trip over the winding dark hillside roads would be a tricky one.

Corelli was at the bar with his two girls. "We should have gone to the French party," one of the girls was saying. She had a British accent. "This one is for the dodoes. I bet the average age here is forty-five."

Corelli smiled, offering the room the glory of his teeth.

Craig turned his back on the bar and looked at the room. Natalie Sorel was seated at a far corner, deep in conversation with a man who was lounging on the arm of her chair. Craig knew that she was so nearsighted that she could never recognize him at that distance. His own eyes were good enough to see that no matter what the English girl said, Natalie Sorel was no dodo.

"I used to hear about the parties in Cannes," the English girl said. "Wild. Everybody smashing glasses and dancing naked on the tables and orgies in the swimming pools. The fall of the Roman Empire."

"That was in the old days, *cara*," Corelli said. He had a heavy accent. Craig had seen him in some English films, and now he realized that Corelli's voice had been dubbed. Probably, Craig thought, his teeth aren't his own, either. The thought comforted him.

"This is about as wild as tea at the vicarage," the girl said. "Why don't we just curtsy and say good night and leave?"

"It is not polite, *carissima*," Corelli said. "And besides, it is full of important people here who are not to be offended by young actors."

"You're a drag, darling," the girl said.

Craig surveyed the room looking for friends, enemies, and neutrals. Aside from Natalie there was a French actress by the name of Lucienne Dullin, seated, as though by some unfailing instinct, in the exact center of the room, attended by a shifting honor guard of young men. She was one of the most beautiful women Craig had ever seen, in a simple, bare-shouldered white dress, with her hair pulled back severely so that the feline bone structure of her face and the long elegance of her throat descending to the perfect shoulders could best be appreciated. She was not a bad actress, but if you looked like that, it was unfair if you weren't Garbo. Craig had never met her, and he didn't want to meet her, but looking at her gave him enormous pleasure.

There was a huge, fat Englishman, well under forty, accompanied, like Corelli, by two young women. They were laughing hysterically at some joke he had just made. He had been pointed out to Craig on the beach. He was a banker, and the anecdote about him was that the month before in the bank in the city of London over which he presided, he had personally handed over a check for three and a half million dollars to Walt Klein. Craig understood why the two girls flanked the banker and why they laughed at his jokes.

Near the fireplace Bruce Thomas was standing talking to a hulking bald man by the name of Hennessy whom Craig recognized as the director of a film that was to be shown at the Festival later in the week. Thomas had a picture that had already played six months in New York and was still running, and Hennessy's picture, his first hit, was doing record-breaking business in an art house on Third Avenue. It was already being touted for a prize at the Festival.

Ian Wadleigh, not in Madrid, a glass in his hand, was standing talking to Eliot

Steinhardt and a third man, portly in a dark suit, the face, bronzed by the sun, under a shock of iron-gray hair. The third man looked familiar to Craig, but he couldn't exactly place him. Wadleigh bulged out of his dinner jacket, which had obviously been bought in better and thinner days. He was not yet drunk but was flushed and talking fast. Eliot Steinhardt listened amiably, a slight smile on his face. He was a small twinkly man of about sixty-five, his face sharp and foxlike and slyly malicious. He had made a score of the biggest hits in the business, going all the way back to the middle 1930s, and although the new critics now sneered at him as old-fashioned, he calmly continued to turn out one hit after another as though success had made him immune to defamation or mortality. Craig liked and admired him. If Wadleigh hadn't been talking to him, he would have gone over to say hello. Later, when he's alone, Craig thought.

Murray Sloan, the critic for one of the trade papers, whose tastes were surprisingly avant-garde and whose most intense emotions seemed to be experienced in darkened projection rooms, was seated on a big couch talking to a man Craig didn't recognize. Sloan was a round, mahogany-tanned, smiling man whose devotion to his profession was so great that he had confided one evening to Craig that he had stopped sleeping with a girl he had picked up at the Venice Festival because she didn't appreciate Buñuel sufficiently.

Well, Craig thought, looking over the room, whether Corelli's English beauty is intelligent or not, she's right in saying it certainly isn't the fall of the Roman Empire. It was rich and decorous and pleasant, but whatever cross-currents were flowing through the room and whatever corruption lay beneath the fine clothes, it all was well hidden, the loved and the unloved, the moneyed and the moneyless observing an evening truce, ambition and desolation politely side by side.

It was very different from the old parties in Hollywood when people who made five thousand dollars a week would not invite people who made less to their homes. A new society, Craig thought, out of the ashes of the old. The movement of the proletariat toward Möet and Chandon and the caviar pot.

He saw the man who was talking to Wadleigh and Eliot Steinhardt look in his direction, smile and wave, and start toward him. He smiled tentatively in return, knowing that he had seen the man somewhere and should remember his name.

"Hi, Jess," the man said, putting out his hand.

"Hello, David," Craig said, shaking hands. "Believe it or not, I didn't recognize you."

The man chuckled. "It's the hair," he said. "I get it all the time."

"You can't blame people," Craig said. David Teichman was one of the first men he had met when he first went to Hollywood, and even then there hadn't been a hair on his head.

"It's a wig," the man said, touching the top of his bush complacently. "It takes twenty years off my age. I'm even having a second run with the girls. That reminds me—I had dinner with your girl in Paris. She told me you were down here, and I told her I'd look you up. I just got down here this morning, and I've been playing gin all day. That's some girl you got there. Congratulations."

"Thanks," Craig said. "do you mind if people ask you why you suddenly blossomed out with a mane?"

"Not at all, not at all. I had a little operation on my dome, and the doc left a couple of foxholes in my skull to remember him by. Not a very happy cosmetic effect, you might say. No sense in an old man going around frightening small children and virgin daughters. The studio hairdressing department fixed me up with the best damn hairpiece in the business. It's the only good thing that goddamn studio has turned out in five years." Teichman's false teeth clamped fiercely in his mouth as he spoke about the studio. He had been forced out of control more than a year ago, but he still spoke of it as though it were his personal domain. He had run it tyrannically for twenty-five years, and the habit of possession was hard to break. Bald, he had been a formidable-looking man, his head suggesting a siege weapon, his features fleshy and harsh, half-Roman emperor, half-merchant skipper, the skin deeply weathered all year round as though he had been in the field with his troops or on deck in storms with his crew. His voice had matched his appearance, brutal and commanding. In his palmy days many of the movies that had come out of his studio had been tender and wistfully comic, one more surprise in a surprising town. With the new wig he looked a different man, gentle and harmless, and his voice, too, as if to accommodate to the new arrangement, was soft and reflective.

Now he put his hand affectionately on Craig's sleeve and said as he looked around him, "Oy, Jess, I am not happy in this room. A flock of vultures feeding off the bones of giants. That's what the movie business has become, Jess. Great old bones with little patches of flesh still left on it that the birds of prey are tearing off bit by bit. And what are they turning out in their search for the Almighty Dollar? Peep shows. Pornography and bloodshed. Why don't they all go to Denmark and be done with it? And the theatre's no better. Carrion. What's Broadway today? Pimps, whores, drug pushers, muggers. I don't blame you for running away from it all."

"You're exaggerating as usual, David," Craig said. He had worked at Teichman's studio in the fifties and had caught on early that the old man was addicted to flights of rhetoric, usually to put over a shrewd and well-taken point. "There's some damn good pictures being made today, and there's a whole rash of young playwrights on and off Broadway."

"Name them," Teichman said. "Name one. One good picture."

"I'll do better than that. I'll name two. Three," Craig said, enjoying the debate. "And made by men right in this room tonight. Steinhardt's last picture and Thomas's and that new fellow talking to Thomas over there, Hennessy."

"Steinhardt doesn't count," Teichman said. "He's a leftover from the old days. A rock that was left standing when the glacier receded. The other two guys—" Teichman made a contemptuous sound. "Flashes in the pan. One-shot geniuses. Sure, every once in a while somebody shows up with a winner. Accidents still happen. They don't know what they're doing, they just wake up and find out they've fallen into a pot of gold. I'm talking about careers, boy, careers. No accidents. Chaplin, Ford, Stevens, Wyler, Capra, Hawkes, Wilder, yourself, if you want to include yourself. Although you were a little too special, maybe, and all over the place, if you don't mind my saying so."

"I don't mind," Craig said. "I've heard worse about myself."

"So have we all," Teichman said, "so have we all. We're living targets. But okay, so I made a lot of junk. I'm not too proud to admit it. Four hundred, five hundred pictures a year. Masterpieces don't come in gross lots, and I'm not saying they do. Junk, okay, mass production, okay, but it served its purpose. It created the machinery the great guys found ready to their hand, the actors, the grips, the scene designers, the audience. And it served another purpose, too. It won the world for America. I can see by the look on your face you think I'm batty. No matter what the fancy intellectual critics said, in their dreams the whole world loved us, we were their mistresses, their heroes. Do you think I'm ashamed of having been in on that? Not for a minute. I'll tell you what I *am* ashamed of. I'm ashamed that we pissed it all away. And if you want, I'll tell you the moment we did it. Even if you don't want." He poked a strong finger into Craig's shoulder. "The day we gave in to the yokels in Congress, the day we said, "Yes, sir, Mr. Congressman, Mr. FBI man, I will kiss your ass, you don't like this writer's politics or that actress's morals or the subject of my next ten pictures, yes, sir, by all means, sir, they're out. I will slit my best friend's throat if you lift your pinky.' Before that we were the lucky, beautiful people of the twentieth century, we made jokes the whole world laughed at, we made love the way the whole world wished they could, we gave parties the whole world wanted to come to. After that we were just a bunch of sniveling Jews hoping the guy next door would get killed in the pogrom instead of us. People turned to television, and I don't blame them. In television they come right out and tell you they're trying to sell you a bill of goods."

"David," Craig said, "You're getting red in the face."

"You bet I am," Teichman said. "Calm me down, Jess, calm me down, my doctor would appreciate it. I'm sorry I came to this party. No, I'm not. I'm glad I got a chance to talk to you. I'm not finished yet, no matter how I sound. I'm in the process of putting something together—something big." Teichman winked conspiratorially. "Some men of talent. With old-fashioned values. Discipline. Captains, not corporals. A man like you, for example. Connie told me you had something cooking, I should speak to you. Am I talking out of school?"

"Not really," Craig said. "I have something in mind."

"It's about time. Call me in the morning. We'll talk. Money is no object. David Teichman is not a maker of B pictures. I have to get out of here now, excuse me, Jess. I find it hard to breathe these days when I get angry. My doctor warns me against it constantly. Remember what I said. In the morning. I'm at the Carlton." Rubbing his excellent gray wig, he marched off, defying ruin.

Craig watched the stiff, erect figure, patriot of defeated causes, historian of decay, shouldering toward the door and shook his head. Still, he decided, he would call Teichman in the morning.

Craig saw the man who was talking to Natalie Sorel get up and take Natalie's glass and start toward the bar, threading his way through the crowd. Craig moved away from the bar in Natalie's direction. But before he had covered half the distance, the door from the patio opened and Gail McKinnon came in with a small sallow man whose face was vaguely familiar. He was about thirty-five, with scruffy receding hair and unhealthy, grape-colored puffs under his eyes. He was wearing a dinner jacket. Gail McKinnon was wearing a cheap print dress, the skirt above her knees. The dress didn't look cheap on her. She smiled at Craig, and there was no avoiding her. For some reason that he could not explain, he didn't want her to observe him in conversation with Natalie Sorel. He hadn't seen her since the lunch with the Murphys, but then he had stayed in his room most of the time nursing his cold.

"Good evening, Mr. Craig," Gail McKinnon said. "I see we make the same stops."

"It looks that way, doesn't it?" he said.

"May I introduce . . .?" she started to say, turning to her companion.

"We've met," the man said. His tone was unfriendly. "A long time ago. In Hollywood."

"I'm afraid my memory isn't as good as it should be," Craig said.

"My name is Reynolds," the man said.

"Oh, yes," Craig said. He recognized the name, although he didn't remember ever having met the man. Reynolds had written movie reviews for a Los Angeles newspaper. "Of course." He extended his hand. Reynolds seemed to have to make up his mind to shake it.

"Come on, Gail," Reynolds said. "I want a drink."

"You go have a drink, Joe," Gail McKinnon said. "I want to talk for a minute with Mr. Craig."

Reynolds grunted, pushed his way toward the bar.

"What's the matter with him?" Craig asked, puzzled by the man's open antagonism.

"He's had a couple too many to drink," Gail McKinnon said.

"On all our tombstones," Craig said. He took a sip from the champagne glass he was carrying. "What's he doing so far from Los Angeles?"

"He's been in Europe for a wire service for two years," the girl said. "He's been most helpful." For some reason she seemed to be defending him. Craig wondered briefly if she was having an affair with him. Reynolds was an unprepossessing, sour-looking man, but in a place like Cannes you never could tell what a girl would turn up with. Now he remembered why the man's face had seemed familiar to him. Reynolds had been the man who had sat down at the table with Gail McKinnon on the

Carlton terrace the other morning.

"He's a nut on movies," Gail McKinnon went on. "He remembers every picture that's ever been made. He's a treasure for me. He's seen all your pictures . . ."

"Maybe that's why he's so rude," Craig said.

"Oh, no," she said. "He likes them. Some of them."

Craig laughed. "Sometimes," he said, "you sound as young as you look."

"That lady over there is waving at you," the girl said.

Craig looked at the corner where Natalie Sorel was seated. She was beckoning him to come over. He had come within myopia range. He waved back. "An old friend," he said, "if you'll excuse me . . ."

"Did you get those questions I left at your hotel?"

"Well?"

"I tore them up," Craig said.

"Oh, that's mean," the girl said. "That's the meanest thing I ever heard. I've heard a lot of bad things about you, but nobody said you were mean."

"I change from day to day," he said. "Sometimes from moment to moment."

"Joe Reynolds warned me about you," she said. "I wasn't going to tell you, but now I don't care. You've got enemies, Mr. Craig, and you might as well know about it. You know why Joe Reynolds was rude to you?"

"I haven't the faintest idea. I never saw the man before the other morning," Craig said.

"Maybe not. Although he says you did. But you once said something about him."

"What?"

"He'd written a very good review of a picture of yours, and you said, 'That man writes so badly, I get angry at him even when he gives me a rave.' "

"When did I say that?" Craig asked.

"Eight years ago."

Craig laughed. "There's no animal more thin-skinned than a critic, is there?"

"You don't exactly go out of your way to be lovable, you know," she said. "You'd better leave now. That pretty lady is practically breaking her arm waving to you." Brusquely, she made her way through the crowd toward the bar where Reynolds, Craig saw, was waiting and watching.

How easy it was to make someone hate you for life. With one sentence.

He turned toward Natalie, dismissing Reynolds from his thoughts. Natalie stood up as he approached her, fair-haired, blue-eyed, luxuriously shaped, with dainty legs and feet, all like a lovingly made doll, too pink, white, and curvy to have any true semblance of reality. Despite her appearance and the soft, bell-like tone of her voice, he knew her as a woman of courage, determination, and lust.

"Take me into another room, Jesse," she was saying, stretching her hand out in greeting. "The biggest bore in the world will be back with a drink for me any minute now." She spoke English so well that anybody hearing her without knowing that she had been born in Hungary would only get a little echo of an unidentifiable accent. She spoke German, French, and Italian equally well. She looked no older than when he had seen her last. They had parted more or less by accident, without recriminations. She had had two pictures to do in England. He had had to go back to America. He hadn't seen either of the pictures she had made in England. He heard that she had taken up with a Spanish count. As far as he knew, he and Natalie had never given each other anything but pleasure. Perhaps that was why they had parted so easily. She had never said she loved him. It was another aspect of her character he admired.

She held his hand as they wove through the other guests toward the library. She had a large diamond ring on her finger. When he had known her, she was pawning jewelry, and he had loaned her money.

"As usual," he said, "you're shining tonight."

"If I had known that Lucienne Dullin was going to be here," she said, "I would never have come. Anyone who looks like that should be forced to wear a sack over her head when she comes to parties with older women."

"Never fear," he said. "You're defending yourself very well."

They sat down side by side on a leather couch. They were the only ones in the room, and the noise of the party, the music and the conversation, was pleasantly subdued here.

"Give me a sip of your champagne," she said.

He handed her his glass, and she drank all of the wine. She had avid appetites, he remembered.

She put the glass down. "You didn't answer my call," she said reproachfully.

"I got in late."

"I wanted to talk to you," she said. "And the other night there were too many people around. How are you?"

"Alive," he said.

"There's no news of you. I have asked."

"I've been vegetating."

"That isn't like the Jesse Craig I knew."

"Everybody's too active. If we'd just stand still six months a year, we'd all be much better off. I stepped off the merry-go-round for a while. That's all."

"When I think of you," she said, "I worry for you."

"Do you think of me often?"

"No." She laughed. She had small, very white teeth and a little pink tongue. "Only at obscene moments." In bed, he remembered, just before she came, she often said, "Fock me, fock me." He had found the mispronunciation endearing. She squeezed his hand affectionately. "How long has it been—five years?"

"More like six or seven."

"Ach," she said, "don't remind me. Are you still as bad as ever?"

"What do you mean by that?"

"I saw you talking to that beautiful young girl. Hanging all over you."

"She's a reporter."

"A woman isn't safe anymore," Natalie said. "Even reporters now look like that."

"It would be unseemly," he said. Natalie's teasing made him uncomfortable. "She's young enough to be my daughter. How about you? Where's your husband?"

"He's not my husband yet. I'm still struggling to land him."

"The other night you told me you were getting married."

"I will believe it when he puts the ring on my finger," Natalie said. "Then no more getting up at five in the morning to get my hair done and my face made up. No more being treated like a beast by temperamental directors. No more having to be nice to producers."

"I was a producer," he said, "and you were nice to me."

"Not because you were a producer, darling." She squeezed his hand again.

"Anyway, where is the husband-designate? If I were going to marry you, I wouldn't let you roam loose in a place like this just before the wedding."

"Only you weren't going to marry me, were you?" for the first time her tone was serious.

"I guess not," he said.

"Like a lot of other people," she said. She sighed. "Oh, well, little Natalie has had her fun. Now it's the time for proper behavior. Or should we be wicked and slip off and find out if they still have that room over the sea in Beaulieu?"

"I've never been to Beaulieu," Craig said, straight-faced.

"What a coincidence," she said. "Neither have I. Anyway, it would hardly be worth it. He's arriving tomorrow."

"Who's arriving tomorrow?"

"The husband-designate," she said. "Philip. He was supposed to come with me, but at the last minute he had to stay in New York."

"Oh, he's American."

"People tell me they make the best husbands."

"I wouldn't know," Craig said. "What does he do?"

"He makes money. Isn't that charming?"

"He manufactures things."

"How old is he?"

She hesitated, and the tip of her tongue showed between her lips. He recognized the signs. "Don't lie," he said.

She laughed. "Clever man. As always. Let's say he's older than you."

"How much older?"

"Considerably older." She spoke in a low voice. "He doesn't know anything about you."

"I should hope not. We didn't exactly publish advertisements in the papers." They had had to be discreet. She had had an official lover at the time who was paying some of her bills, and he was still trying to avoid scenes of jealousy with his wife. "And what if he *did* know about me?" he asked. "He doesn't think he's marrying a virgin, does he?"

"No, not exactly." Her smile was a little sad. "But he doesn't know the full extent." She made a wry, childish little grimace. "Not by half. Not by a quarter."

"Who does know the full extent?"

"I hope nobody," she said.

"Just for the record," Craig said, "in the next room here—how many?"

Natalie made a small grimace. "Would you settle for five?"

He grinned and shook his head.

"Six, then," she said. "What do you expect—your little Natalie's been around a long time. And being in the movies is a little like being on an island with the same group of castaways for years and years. A lady is liable to go to and fro—to and fro. A gentleman, too, my friend." She touched Craig's lips lightly with the tip of her finger.

"*Nolo contendere*," Craig said.

Natalie laughed, little white teeth. "Isn't it nice," she said, "I hardly ever had to lie to you."

"And to your husband-to-be?"

She laughed again. "I hardly ever have to tell him the truth." She grew serious. "He's a solid citizen. Very conservative. A Baptist from Texas. He's so puritanical he hasn't even slept with me yet."

"God," Craig said.

"That's it," she said. "God. When he gets here, I'll have to pretend I barely know you. If we meet, don't be surprised if I call you Mr. Craig. If he heard that I was the sort of lady who was known to go off on weekends with married men, there's no telling what he'd do."

"What's the worst he could do?"

"He could not marry me. You will be careful, won't you, Jesse?" There was a pleading note in her voice that he had never heard before. It occurred to him that she was actually past forty.

"If he hears anything," Craig said, "it won't be from me. But I advise you get him out of Cannes as quickly as possible."

"He's only going to stay a few days," she said. "Then we're flying to Venice."

"Haven't you and I ever been to Venice together?"

"Don't you remember?"

"No."

"Then we haven't been to Venice," she said. She looked up and smiled. The man she had been talking to in the salon was standing at the door of the library, two glasses in his hands.

"Oh, there you are," the man said. "I've been looking all over for you."

Craig stood up, and Natalie mumbled both their names. Craig didn't recognize the man's name. He had a small, anxious, easily forgettable face. Arbitrarily, Craig decided that he worked on the distribution end for one of the major companies. The man gave Natalie her glass and shook Craig's hand gravely.

"Well," Craig said, "I'll leave you two kids alone. You've reminded me I'm thirsty." He touched Natalie's shoulder reassuringly and went out of the library and back to the bar, avoiding Ian Wadleigh en route.

In the dining room, where a buffet had been set up, Craig glimpsed Gail McKinnon and Reynolds waiting to be served.

Murray Sloan was standing at the bar, chubby and dapper, staring out at the guests. He was smiling pleasantly, but his eyes were like small, dark computers. "Hi, Jesse," he said. "Join the working press in a free drink."

"Hello, Murray," Craig said, and asked for a glass of champagne.

"This isn't your scene anymore, is it, Jesse?" Sloan said. He was munching contentedly on a small cucumber sandwich that he had lifted from a tray of hors d'oeuvres.

"It's hard to know just what scene this is," Craig said. "The Tower of Babel, the entrance to the Ark, a Mafia meeting, or a prom at a girl's school."

"I'll tell you what the scene is," Sloan said. "It's the ball at Versailles at the court of Louis the Sixteenth, July thirteenth, 1789, the night before the storming of the Bastille."

Craig chuckled.

"You can laugh," Sloan said. "But mark my words. Did you see that picture *Ice* they showed in the Director's Quinzaine?"

"Yes," Craig said. The picture had been made by a group of young revolutionaries and was a deadly serious work about the beginning of armed revolt in New York City in the immediate future. It had some chilling scenes of castrations, murders of public officials, street fighting, and bombings, all portrayed in a flat *cinéma vérité* style that made it very disturbing.

"What did you think of it?" Sloan asked, challengingly.

"It's hard for a man like me to know if it has any validity or not," Craig said. "I don't know kids like that. It might just be a put-on."

"It's no put-on," Sloan said. "It's what's going to happen in America. Soon." He waved his arm to indicate the crowd of his fellow guests. "And all these fat cats are going to be in the tumbrels."

"And where will you be, Murray?" Craig asked.

"In the tumbrels with them," Sloan said gloomily. "Those kids aren't going to make any fine distinctions."

Walter Klein wandered over to the bar. "Hi, boys," he said. "Having a good time?"

Craig allowed Sloan to answer the question. "Loving every minute of it, Walt," Sloan said, observing the ritual.

"How about you, Jesse?" Klein said complacently. "A nice mixture of beauty, talent, and larceny." He laughed. "Look at those two over there." He indicated Hennessy and Thomas, who were talking earnestly near the fireplace. "Bathing in it. On the crest of the wave," he said. "Nice work if you can get it. They're both clients."

"Naturally," Craig said. He took another glass of champagne from the waiter behind the bar.

"Come on over and say a word to the two geniuses," Klein said. It was his abiding rule to introduce everybody to everybody else. As he told his lieutenants, you never know where the lightning will strike. "You, too, Murray."

"I'll keep the duty here at the bar," Sloan said.

"Don't you want to meet them?" Klein asked, surprised.

"No," Sloan said. "I'm going to pan their pictures, and I don't want to be swayed by any false feeling of friendship."

"Have you *seen* their pictures?" Klein asked.

"No," Sloan said. "But I know their work."

"Lo and behold," Klein said mockingly, "an honest man. Come on, Jess." He took

Craig's arm and led him toward the fireplace.

Craig shook Hennessy's hand and apologized to Thomas for not having called him back. Thomas was a slim, gentle-looking man who had a reputation for being unbendingly stubborn on the set.

"What're you two doing?" Klein demanded. "Comparing your grosses?"

"We're crying in our beer," Hennessy said.

"What about?" Klein asked.

"The corruption of the lower classes," Hennessy said. "And how difficult it is to remain pure in an impure world."

"Hennessy's new to the game," Thomas said.

"He can't get over the fact that he had to bribe a sheriff and his deputy when he was shooting in a town in Texas."

"I don't mind a bit of reaming per se," Hennessy said. "But I like it to be a little subtle. At least pay lip service to the notion that the bribery of public officials is somewhat distasteful. But these guys just sat there in my motel room drinking my whisky and saying, "It's three thousand for each of us or don't bother to take the cover off your camera.'" He shook his head mournfully. "And no nonsense like don't you think a big rich company like yours could make a little contribution to the Policemen's Benevolent Fund, or anything like that. Just put the money on the bed, mister. It's tough on a boy who used to be first in his class at Sunday school to shell out six thousand dollars in cash to a couple of cops in a motel room and put it into the budget as incidental expenses."

"You got off cheap," Klein said. He was a practical, empirical man. "Don't complain."

"Then, after that," Hennessy said, "they had the nerve to bust the leading man for smoking pot, and there went another two thousand to get him off. What this country needs, like the vice-president says, is law and order."

"You're in France now," Klein said. "Remember?"

"I'm in the movie business," Hennessy said, "wherever I am. And the thing that drives me crazy in the goddamn business is all the dough that flows out that you never see on the screen."

"Easy come, easy go," Klein said. A man who had recently received a check for three and a half million dollars could talk like that.

"I'm teaching a seminar at UCLA next year in the art of the cinema," Hennessy said. He drawled out *cinema* mockingly. "All this will be in my first lecture. Hey, Craig, how'd you like to be my guest one or two hours and tell the kids how it is in the glamorous world of celluloid?"

"I might discourage them for life," Craig said.

"Great," Hennessy said. "Anything to keep the competition down. I mean it, though. Seriously. You could really tell them a thing or two."

"If I'm not busy," Craig said carefully, "and I happen to be in the States, maybe . . ."

"Where can I reach you?" Hennessy said.

"Through me," Klein said quickly. "Jess and I've been talking about the possibility of his getting back into production one of these days, and I'll know where I can get hold of him."

Klein wasn't exactly lying, Craig thought. He was just shaping the truth to his and perhaps Craig's benefit.

The two directors had glanced sharply at Craig as Klein spoke. Now Thomas said, "What's the property, Jess? Or don't you want to say?"

"I'd rather not say for the moment. It's still all in the dreaming stage." Murphy's dreams, he thought.

There was a small commotion at the doorway, and Frank Garland came in with his wife and another couple. Garland was an actor who had starred in one of Craig's early movies. He was several years older than Craig but looked no more than thirty-five, dark-haired, athletically tall, strong-jawed, and handsome. He was a very good actor and an imaginative businessman and had his own company that produced not only his own films but the films of others. He was a bouncingly healthy, jovial, extroverted man with a pretty wife to whom he had been married for more than twenty years. He had been superb in Craig's picture, and they were good friends, but tonight Craig didn't want to be exposed to that glorious health, that sensible intelligence, that flawless luck, that unfaked and all-embracing cordiality.

"See you boys later," he said to Klein and the two directors. "I need a breath of air." He went out to the patio and down the wet grass of the garden toward the illuminated swimming pool. The band was playing, "On a Clear Day You Can See Forever."

Craig looked down at the bright water. The pool was heated, and a slight mist was rising from the surface. Orgies in the swimming pools, he remembered. Not tonight, Nicole.

"Hi, Jesse," a voice said.

Craig looked up. A man was advancing from the shadows of the shrubbery near the end of the pool. As he came closer, Craig recognized him. It was Sidney Green. The thought occurred to Craig that Green had been driven into the solitude of the cold, wet garden for some of the same reasons as himself. Losers outside, please. Ian Wadleigh would soon appear.

"Hello, Sid," Craig said. "What are you doing out here?"

"It got too rich for my blood in there." Green had a mournful, soft voice, the voice of a man who expects to be treated badly at all times. "I came out and pissed on the expensive green grass of Walter Klein. A man takes what satisfactions he can find in this world." He laughed apologetically, breathily. "You won't tell Walt, will you? I don't want to seem ungrateful. It was nice of him to invite me. With all those people in that room. There's a lot of power in that room tonight, a lot of clout." Green shook his head slowly to emphasize his respect for the potency of the company assembled by Walt Klein that night. "I tell you, Jesse," he went on, "there are men in there who could get a ten-million-dollar production started tomorrow morning just by crooking a finger. They look like me, maybe even worse than me, they're wearing the same kind of tuxedo, maybe we even had our suits made by the same tailor, but God, what a difference. How about you, Jesse? People've been talking about you, wondering what you're doing here. The guess is you've got a picture ready to go and you're here to make a deal."

"There's nothing definite so far," Craig said. Murphy had been definite enough, but there was nothing to be gained by telling Green about that.

"I saw you talking to David Teichman," Green said. "He was something in his day, wasn't he?"

"He certainly was."

"Finished," Green said.

Craig didn't like the bite of the word. "I wouldn't be too sure," he said.

"He'll never make another picture." Green's judgment was final.

"Maybe he's got some plans he hasn't let you in on, Sid."

"If you're thinking of going into business with him, forget it," Green said. "He's going to be dead before the year's out."

"What're you talking about?" Craig asked sharply.

"I thought everybody knew," Green said. "He's got a tumor of the brain. My cousin operated on him in The Cedars. It's just a wonder he's still walking around."

"Poor old man," Craig said. The wig had taken twenty years off his life, Teichman had said.

"Oh. I wouldn't waste too much pity on him," Green said. "He had it good for a long, long time. I'd settle for his life *and* his tumor at his age. At least his worries're just about over. How about you, Jesse?" The dead and dying had had their moment in Walter Klein's rented garden. "Are you coming back?"

"The possibility exists."

"Well, if you do decide to move, remember me, will you, Jesse?"

"I will indeed."

"I'm underrated as a director, I'm enormously underrated," Green said earnestly. "And that's not only my opinion. There's a guy in there from *Cahiers du Cinéma,* and he made a point of being introduced to me and telling me that in his opinion my last picture, the one I did for Columbia, was a masterpiece. Did you happen to see it?"

"I'm afraid not," Craig said. "I don't go to the movies much anymore."

"*Fanfare for Drums,*" Green said. "That's what it was called. You sure you didn't see it?"

"Absolutely."

"If you want, I'll introduce you to the guy," Green said. "I mean the *Cahiers du Cinéma* guy. He's real smart. He has nothing but scorn for most of the people in there tonight. Scorn."

"Some other time, maybe, Sid. I'm going to make an early night of it."

"Just give me the word," Green said. "I have his address. Boy," he said sadly, "I thought this was going to be my big year in Cannes. I had a two-picture deal with options with Apex and Eastern. That's one of those big conglomerates. Three months ago they looked as though they had all the money in the world. I thought I was all set. I took a new apartment in the sixteenth, they're still putting in *boiserie* that cost fifteen thousand bucks that I haven't paid for yet. And my wife and I decided we could afford another kid, and she's going to have it in December. Then everything went kaput. Apex and Eastern is in receivership, and I can't afford orange juice in the morning anymore. If I don't get something down here these two weeks, you can say farewell to Sid Green."

"Something'll turn up," Craig said.

"It better," Green said. "It just better."

Craig left him standing at the side of the pool, his head bent, staring despondently at the mist rising from the heated green water. At least, Craig thought, as he went inside, I don't owe fifteen thousand dollars for *boiserie,* and my wife isn't pregnant.

He spent the rest of the evening drinking. He talked to a lot of people, but by the time he felt he ought to go back to the hotel, all he could remember was that he had looked for Natalie Sorel to take her home with him and not found her and that he had told Walt Klein that he would show him his script and Klein had said that he'd send one of his boys over to the hotel in the morning to pick it up.

He was standing at the bar having one last drink when he saw Gail McKinnon come hurrying in, a raincoat thrown over her shoulders. He hadn't seen her leave. She stopped for a moment at the doorway, scanning the room, then saw him and came over to him. "I'd hoped you'd still be here," she said.

"Have a nightcap," he said. The evening's drinking had made him mellow.

"I need somebody to drive me and Joe Reynolds home," she said. "He hurt himself. Also he's drunk. He knocked himself out falling down the stairs outside."

"It couldn't happen to a nicer fellow," Craig said, cheered by the news. "Have a drink."

"The policeman out there won't let him get into the car" Gail said.

"Astute," Craig said. "The astute French police. Bloodhounds of the law. Have a drink to the noble gendarmerie of the Alpes Maritimes."

"Are you drunk, too?" she asked sharply.

"Not really," he said. "Are you? Why don't you drive the critic home?"

"I don't have a license."

"Un-American. Don't tell any congressman who happens to ask you. Have a drink," he said.

"Come on, Jesse," she said pleadingly. It was the first time, he noticed, that she had called him by his first name. "It's late, and I can't handle the pain in the ass myself, and he's howling and threatening the policeman and bleeding all over the place, and he'll wind up in jail if we don't get him out of here fast. I know you think I'm a pest, but this is an act of charity." She looked around the room. It was almost empty. "The party's over. Take us back to Cannes, please."

Craig drained his glass, smiled. "I will deposit the body safely," he said. He took her arm formally and made her say good night with him to Walter Klein before going out into the drizzly night.

Reynolds had stopped yelling at the policeman. He was sitting on the bottom step of the flagstone staircase down which he had fallen, a nasty gash on his forehead, an eye beginning to swell. He was holding a bloodstained handkerchief to his nose. He looked up blearily as Gail McKinnon and Craig approached him. "Goddamn Frog cops," he said thickly. "Walter Klein and his thugs."

"It's all right, monsieur," Craig said in French to the policeman who was standing politely next to Reynolds. "I'm his friend. I'll drive him home."

"He is in no state to drive," the policeman said. "That is evident to the naked eye. No matter what the gentleman says."

"I absolutely agree," Craig said. He was careful to keep his distance from the policeman. He didn't want to chance the man's smelling *his* breath. "Upsy-daisy, Joe," he said to Reynolds, grabbing him under the armpit and hauling him up. Reynolds let the handkerchief fall from his nose, and a fresh gush of blood spattered Craig's trousers. Reynolds smelled as though he had been steeped, with all his clothes, in whisky for days.

With Gail helping on the other side, they got Reynolds to Craig's car and pushed him into the back seat where he promptly went to sleep. Craig drove out of the parking lot under the dripping trees with exaggerated care, for the watching policeman's benefit.

Except for the sound of Reynold's wet and bubbling snoring in the back of the car, they drove in silence to Cannes. Craig concentrated at the wheel, driving slowly, conscious that the road seemed to have a tendency to blur somewhat in the beam of the headlights on the curves. He was ashamed of the amount of liquor he had drunk that night and promised himself that in the future he would abstain completely when he knew he had to drive a car after an evening out.

When they reached the outskirts of Cannes, the girl told Craig the name of Reynolds' hotel. It was about six blocks away from the Carlton, inland, behind the railroad tracks. When they got there, Reynolds, now awake, said thickly, "Thank you, everybody. Don't bother to go in with me. Perfectly all right. Good night."

They watched him walk stiffly and self-consciously into the darkened hotel.

"He doesn't need any more to drink," Craig said, "but I do."

"So do I," said Gail McKinnon.

"Don't you live in that hotel, too?" Craig asked.

"No."

He felt a foolish sense of relief.

All the bars they passed were closed. He hadn't realized how late it was. Anyway, stained as they were from Reynolds' blood, they would have been a disturbing sight for any late-drinking patrons. Craig stopped the car in front of the Carlton but left the motor running. "I have a bottle," he said. "Do you want to come up?"

"Yes, please," she said.

He parked the car, and they went into the hotel. Luckily, there was nobody there. The concierge, from whom Craig got the key to his apartment, had been trained since boyhood not to change his expression at anything he saw in the lobby of any hotel.

In the apartment Gail McKinnon took off her coat and went into the bathroom while Craig poured the whiskies and soda. There was the pleasant domestic sound of running water from the bathroom, sign of another presence, a barrier against loneliness.

When she came back, he saw that she had combed her hair. She looked fresh and clean, as though nothing had happened to her that night. They raised their glasses to each other and drank. The hotel was quiet around them, the city sleeping.

They sat facing each other on large brocaded armchairs.

"Lesson for the day," Craig said. "Don't go out with drunks. If he hadn't had the good sense to fall down those steps, you'd have probably wound up wrapped around a tree."

"Probably." She shrugged. "The hazards of the machine age."

"You could have asked me to drive you home before the fall," Craig said, forgetting that he had been perhaps just as drunk as Reynolds.

"I had decided never to ask you anything again," she said.

"I see."

"He was raving against you when he made his swan dive. Reynolds." the girl giggled.

"Just for one little nasty crack eight years ago?" Craig shook his head, marveling at the persistence of vanity.

"That and a lot of other things."

"What other things?"

"You once took a girl away from him in Hollywood."

"Did I? Well, if I did, I didn't know about it."

"That makes it even worse for somebody like Joe Reynolds. He hit her, and out of spite she told him how all-round marvelous you were and what other women had told her about you and about how intelligent and sensitive and funny you were. What do you expect him to feel about you? And you were such a big shot out there when he was a pimply-faced boy just breaking in."

"Well, he must feel better about me now," Craig said.

"A little," the girl said. "But not enough. He's given me a lot of the information that's in the stuff I've written so far about you. And he's suggested a title for the piece."

"What is it?" Craig asked, curious.

"The Once and Future Has Been," the girl said flatly.

Craig nodded. "It's vulgar," he said, "but catchy. You going to use it?"

"I don't know yet," she said.

"What does it depend on?"

"You. What you seem like to me finally when I get really to know you. If I ever get to know you. How much guts I think you still have. Or will. Or talent. It would help if you let me read the script you're giving to Walt Klein tomorrow."

"How do you know about that?"

"Sam Boyd is a friend of mine." Sam Boyd was one of Klein's bright young men. "He told me he was coming over here in the morning to pick up a script you owned. We're having breakfast together."

"Tell him to come for the script *after* breakfast," Craig said.

"I'll tell him." She held out her glass. "It's empty," she said.

He got up and carried both glasses over to the table where the bottle was. He made the two drinks and carried them back. "Thanks," she said, looking up at him soberly as she accepted the glass. He leaned over and kissed her gently. Her lips were soft, welcoming. Then she averted her head. He stepped back as she stood up.

"That's enough of that," she said. "I'm going home."

He put out his hand to touch her arm.

"Leave me alone!" She said sharply. She put down her glass, seized her coat, and ran toward the door.

"Gail . . ." he said, taking a step after her.

"Miserable old man," she said as she pulled open the door. The door slammed after her.

He finished his drink slowly, then put out the lights and went to bed. Lying naked on the sheets in the warm darkness, he listened to the occasional rubber swish of a car on the Croisette and the tumble of the Mediterranean on the shore. He couldn't sleep.

It had been a full night. The liquor he had drunk drummed at his temples. Bits and pieces of the evening formed and reformed kaleidoscopically in his brain—Klein, in his velvet jacket, introducing everybody to everybody, Corelli and his two girls, Green pissing forlornly on the expensive green grass, Reynolds' blood . . .

Add to the mixture . . . The game (was it a game?) of Gail McKinnon. Her flickering young-old sensuality. Invitation and rejection. Remember and regret the lushness of Natalie Sorel, try to forget David Teichman, death under the studio wig.

Craig moved uneasily in the bed. It had been like a gigantic Christmas office party. Except that in other businesses they weren't held twice a week.

Then there was the soft, half-expected knock on the door. He got up, put on a robe, and opened the door.

Gail McKinnon was standing in the dim corridor.

"Come in," he said.

CHAPTER 10

HE WAS AWARE that it was light, that he was not yet awake, that there was soft breathing somewhere beside him, that the phone was ringing.

Without sitting up or opening his eyes, postponing the day, he groped for the phone on the bedside table. A faraway voice, through a curtain of mechanical buzzing, said, "Good morning, darling."

"Who's this?" he said. His eyes were still closed.

"How many people call you darling?" the thin, distant voice said.

"I'm sorry, Constance," he said. "You sound a million miles away." He opened his eyes, turned his head. The long brown hair was on the pillow beside him. Gail stared at him, the blue-flecked eyes fixed gravely on him. He was half-out from the sheet that covered her, and he had an enormous erection. He didn't remember ever having seen his cock that size. He had to suppress a ludicrous impulse to grab at the sheet and cover himself.

"You're still in bed," Constance was saying. Distant electronic accusation across six hundred miles of inaccurate cable. "It's past ten o'clock."

"Is it?" he said idiotically. His cock swelled malevolently. He was conscious of the level glance from the next pillow, the shape of the body under the sheet, the neatly turned-down second bed in the room, still unslept in. He regretted having spoken Constance's name. Any name. "This is a late town," he said. "How're things in Paris?"

"Deteriorating. How're things with you?"

He hesitated. "Nothing new," he said.

Gail did not smile or change her expression. The weight of her glance was almost palpable on the insanely stalwart penis towering into the golden morning air like a permanent and shameless feature of the landscape. Gail reached over slowly, deliberately, and ran one experimental finger from its base to its flaming crown. A convulsion racked him as though he had been touched by a high-tension wire.

"Holy man," she whispered.

"First of all," the wavery, mechanical, almost unrecognizable voice was saying in the telephone, "I want to apologize . . ."

"I can hardly hear you," he said, making an agonizing effort to speak calmly. "Maybe we'd better hang up and call the operator again and . . ."

"Is this better? Can you hear me now?" Suddenly the voice was clear and strong, as if Constance were in another room of the hotel or around the corner.

"Yes," he said reluctantly. Desperately, he tried to think of something to say to

Constance that would hold her off, give him time to put on some clothes and go into the living room and wait there for her to call back. But for the moment, he didn't trust himself with anything more ambitious than a monosyllable.

"I said I wanted to apologize," Constance said, "for being so bitchy the other day. You know how I am."

"Yes," he said. Nothing had changed below.

"And thanks for the picture of the lion. It was a nice thought."

"Yes," he said.

"I have some good news," Constance said. "At least I hope you'll think it's good news."

"What's that?" Slyly, surreptitiously, he had managed to cover himself almost entirely from the waist down with the sheet. The sheet still stuck up, though, like a circus tent.

"I may have to be in your part of the world tomorrow or the day after. Marseilles," she said.

"Marseilles?" he asked. For a moment he couldn't quite remember where Marseilles was. "Why Marseilles?"

"I can't say over the phone." Her suspicion of the French telephone system was as strong as ever. "But if things work out up here, I'll be there."

"That's fine," Craig said, his mind on other things.

"What's fine?" Now Constance was beginning to sound irritated.

"I mean maybe we can see each other . . ."

"What do you mean *maybe?*" The tone was becoming ominous.

He felt the shift in the bed beside him. Gail stood up, walked slowly, naked, slender-waisted, pearly-hipped, gently swelling tanned calves, into the bathroom, without a backward glance. "Well, there is a complication . . ."

"This is another damned unsatisfactory conversation, lad," Constance said.

"My daughter Anne is arriving here today," Craig said, grateful that Gail was no longer in the room. The erection went down suddenly, and he was grateful for that, too. "I sent her a cable inviting her."

"Everybody's at the mercy of the goddamn young," Constance said. "Bring her along to Marseilles. Every virgin ought to see Marseilles."

"Let me work it out with her." He withheld comment on the "virgin." "When you know definitely what your plans are, call me. Maybe you could come to Cannes," he added insincerely.

He heard the water of the shower being turned on in the bathroom. He wondered if Constance could here the shower in Paris.

"I hate Cannes," Constance said. "I decided to divorce my first husband there. Christ, if it's too much trouble for you to get in a car and drive a couple of hours to see a girl you're supposed to be in love with . . ."

"Don't work yourself up into one of your rages, Constance," Craig said. "You don't even know if you're going to be in Marseilles or not yet . . ."

"I want you to be eager, she said. "You haven't seen me for a week now. The least you could be is eager."

"I *am* eager," he said.

"Prove it."

"I will meet you anywhere you want anytime you want," he said loudly.

"I suppose that'll have to do, lad," she said. She chuckled. "Christ, it's like pulling teeth. Are you drunk?"

"Hung over."

"Have you been debauching?"

"I suppose you could say that." One stone, at least, in the arch of truth.

"I never liked a sober man," she said. "All right, I'll wire you as soon as I know anything. How old is your daughter?"

"Twenty."

"You'd think a girl twenty years old would have something better to do than hang around with her old man."

"We're a close-knit family," Craig said.

"I've noticed that. Have fun, darling. I miss you. And the little lion *was* a sweet idea." She hung up.

Ignoble, ignobly comic, he thought resentfully as he swung out of bed and began hurriedly to dress. He had on a shirt and a pair of pants by the time Gail came out of the bathroom, still naked, slender and superb, her brown skin glistening with the last drops of the shower that she had neglected to dry off.

She stood with her legs wide apart, her hands on her hips, in a caricature of a model's pose, and grinned at him. "My," she said, "We're a busy little fellow, aren't we." Then she came over to him and pulled his head down a little toward her and kissed his forehead. But when he put his arms around her and tried to kiss her in return, she pulled away abruptly and said, "I'm dying for breakfast. Which bell do you ring?"

He was early when he got to the airport at Nice. The plane from Geneva wasn't due for almost another half hour. His feeling about arrivals and departures had been developed in his marriage. His wife had been a woman who had never been able to get anywhere on time, and his memory of the years with her was composed of a succession of infuriating scenes, his shouting at her to hurry, her tears and neurotic slamming of doors to punish him for his reproaches, and the recurring small agony of apologizing to friends for keeping them waiting, waiting for dinner, planes, trains, theatres, weddings, funerals, football games. Because of that, now that he was rid of her, he allowed himself the satisfaction of getting everywhere with time to spare, his nerves serene. "Leaving your mother," he had once told Anne, who understood what he was talking about because she had developed into a monster of punctuality as a result of her mother's vice, "has added ten years to my life."

He went upstairs and sat on the airport balcony overlooking the runway and the sea. He sat at a little iron table and ordered a whisky and soda. Although it was early in the afternoon, a brisk wind made the air cool and whipped up small curls of whitecaps on the blue water.

Consciously, sipping his drink, he tried to compose himself to greet his daughter. But his hand trembled minutely as he picked up the glass. He felt tense and weary, and when he tried to focus on a plane that was coming in to land but was still about a mile away from the end of the runway in the bright sky, his eyes blurred momentarily behind his sunglasses. He hadn't slept well. And for the wrong reason. Gail McKinnon had come to his room and shared his bed, but she had not permitted him to make love to her. She had offered no explanations. She had merely said, "No," and had gone to sleep in his arms, calm, silken, fragrant, perverse, and sure of herself, abundant and tantalizing in her youth and beauty.

Now, thinking of it while waiting for his child to come down out of the afternoon sky, he was shamed by the absurdity of the night. A man his age allowing himself to be trapped in a silly adolescent game like that! And by a girl young enough to be his daughter. He should have turned on the light, ordered her out of the room, taken a pill, and gone to sleep. Or at least put on a pair of pajamas and gotten into the next bed and slept alone and told the girl he never wanted to see her again when she awoke in the morning. Instead, he had held her close, drowned in melancholy tenderness, wracked by desire, sleepless, caressing the nape of her neck, sniffing the perfume of her hair, listening to her steady, healthy breathing as the light of dawn outlined the shutters of the windows.

And over breakfast, annoyed by the leer, real or imagined, of the waiter, he had told her he'd meet her for drinks that afternoon. And because of her he had offended Constance, lied or half-lied on the phone, risked compromising what he had thought until last night was his faithful love for a grown competent woman who played no games with him, who made him happy, a beautiful, intelligent, useful woman who met him on equal terms, whose affection (why not call it by its proper name?), whose passion for him had helped him in the last two years to get through some of the darkest moments of his life. He had always prided himself on being a man who in good times and bad was in reasonable control of his actions, his fate. And here, in a few drunken hours, he had shown that he was as capable of mindless choice and self-destructive drifting as any romantically brainwashed idiot.

Drunken. He was lying to himself. He had drunk—but not that much. He knew that even if he hadn't touched a drop all night, he would have behaved no differently.

Cannes was to blame, he told himself defensively. It was a city made for the indulgence of the senses, all ease and sunshine and provocative flesh. And in the darkened auditoriums of the town he had delivered himself over to the dense, troubling sensuality of film after film, glorious couplings, the delicious odor of vice, emotion everywhere, the denial of reason, the rites of youth, too heady a mixture for an aging man unanchored and voyaging without a compass across a troubled year.

And now, to make things worse, his daughter was entering the picture. What the hell could have possessed him to have sent that cable! He groaned, then looked around to see if anybody had noticed, pretending that it had not been a groan but a cough. He brought his handkerchief falsely to his lips, ordered another whisky.

He had come to Cannes looking for answers. What he had done in a few short days was multiply the questions. Maybe, he thought, the thing to do is go down to the ticket counter and buy a seat for Paris or New York or London or Vienna. Northern man, at home in a more stringent climate, the white, pagan cities of the south were not for him. If he were wiser, he would leave the complicated, sinister temptations of the Mediterranean once and for all. The idea was a sensible one. But he didn't move. He knew he was not buying any tickets for anywhere. Not yet.

Klein's assistant, Boyd, had telephoned from the lobby during breakfast, and Craig had sent a copy of the script of *The Three Horizons* down with a bellboy. If Klein's reaction was a negative one, he thought, he would get out of Cannes. His decision soothed him. It gave him a fixed point to look forward to, a choice that was mechanical, out of his hands. He felt better. When he lifted his glass, he noticed that his hand was no longer trembling.

The plane came to a halt on the tarmac. The passengers came streaming out, dressed for holiday, dresses blowing in the sea wind. He picked out Anne, bright blond hair whipping around her head, walking quickly and eagerly, looking up at the terrace, searching for him. He waved. She waved back, moved more quickly. She was carrying a bulging khaki bag made out of canvas that looked as though she had picked it up in an Army and Navy store. He noted that she still walked clumsily, in a kind of uncollected slouch, as though she hesitated to pretend to womanly grace. He wondered if he might suggest lessons in posture. She was wearing a wrinkled blue raincoat and drab brown slacks. Except for her hair, she looked dun, self-consciously sober and inconspicuous in her dark clothes among the summery dresses and the patterned shirts and madras jackets of the other passengers. What is she pretending to be *now,* he thought. Irrationally, he was annoyed with the way she was dressed. Back in the time when the money was rolling in, he had set up trust funds for her and her sister. The income from them wasn't extravagant, but it certainly was enough to buy some clothes. He would have to persuade her, tactfully, to shop for some new things. At least, he comforted himself, she was clean and was wearing shoes and didn't look like a Comanche squaw stoned on pot. Be grateful for small favors.

He paid for his drinks and went down to greet her.

As she came out, following a porter trundling her two valises, he arranged his face to welcome her. Childishly, she threw herself into his arms and kissed him, rather inaccurately, somewhere in the region of the throat. "Oh, Daddy," she cried, muffled against him.

He patted the shoulder of the wrinkled blue raincoat. Inevitably, as she pressed against him, he remembered the other young body in his arms that morning, the other kiss. "Let me look at you," he said. She pulled away a little so that he could take stock of her. She wore no makeup and didn't need any. She had a California look about her, clear-eyed, tanned, and blooming, her hair bleached in streaks by days in the sun, a light sanding of freckles across the bridge of her strong, straight nose. He knew from her marks that she was an excellent student, but from her appearance it was hard to believe that she ever bothered to open a book or did anything but spend her time on beaches, surfboards, and tennis courts. If he were twenty years old and was a girl who looked like that, he would not slouch.

He hadn't seen her in six months, and he noticed that she had filled out since their last meeting, that her breasts, free under a dark green sweater, were considerably heavier than before. Her face was fined down, almost triangular, with faint hollows under the prominent cheekbones. She had always been a healthy child, and she was growing into a robust woman.

"Like what you see?" she asked, smiling. It was an old private formula between them that she had hit on when she was still a little girl.

"More or less," he said, teasing. It was impossible to phrase the pleasure, the tenderness, that overwhelmed him, the irrational, warm sense of self-satisfaction she gave him, fruit of his loins, evidence of his vitality and parental wisdom. He took her hand and pressed it, wondering how, just a few minutes before, he could have been dismayed at the thought of her arrival.

Hand in hand, they followed the porter out of the terminal. He helped the porter throw her luggage into the back of the car. The khaki canvas bag was heavy, stuffed with books. One book fell out as he lifted the bag. He picked it up. *Education Sentimentale,* in French. He couldn't help smiling as he pushed the book back into the bag. Careful traveler, his daughter, preparing for a previous century.

They started back toward Cannes, driving slowly in the heavy traffic. Occasionally, Anne leaned over and patted his cheek as he drove, as if to assure herself by the fleeting touch of fingers that she was really there, side by side with her father.

"The blue Mediterranean," she said, looking across him at the sea. "I tell you, it's the wildest invitation I ever got in my whole life." She chuckled at some private thought. "Your wife says you are buying my affection," she said.

"What do you think?" he asked.

"If that's what you're doing," she said, "Keep buying."

"How was your visit?" he asked carefully.

"Average gruesome," Anne said.

"What's she doing in Geneva?"

"Consulting private bankers. Her friend is with her, helping her to consult." A sudden hardness came into Anne's voice. "She's become a demon investor now that you're giving her all that money. The American economy doesn't look strong enough for her, she says, she intends to go into German and Japanese companies. She told me to tell you you ought to do the same. It's ridiculous, she says, for you to get only five per cent on you money. You never had a head for business, she says, and she's thinking of your best interests." She made a little grimace. "In your best interests, she says, you also ought to give up your lady friend in Paris."

"She told you about that?" He tried to keep the anger out of his voice.

"She told me about a lot of things," Anne said.

"What does she know about the lady in Paris, anyway?"

"I don't know what she knows," Anne said. "I only know what she told me. She says that the lady is ridiculously young for you and looks like a manicurist and is out for your money."

Craig laughed. "Manicurist. Obviously, she's never seen the lady."

"Oh, yes she has. She's even had a scene with her."

"Where?"

"Paris."

"She was in Paris?" he asked incredulously.

"You bet she was. In your best interests. She told the lady what she thought of adventuring ladies who took advantage of foolish old men and broke up happy homes."

Craig shook his head wonderingly. "Constance never said a word about it."

"I guess it's not the sort of thing a lady likes to talk about," Anne said. "Am I going to meet Constance?"

"Of course," Craig said uncomfortably. This was not the conversation he had imagined he was going to have with his daughter when he took her in his arms at the airport.

"I tell you," Anne said, "Geneva was just pure fun all the way. I got to have dinner at the Richemonde with Mummy and her friend, along with all the other goodies."

Craig drove silently. He didn't want to discuss his wife's lover with his daughter.

"Little pompous show off," Anne said. "Ugh. Sitting there ordering caviar and yelling at the waiter about the wine and being gallant for five minutes with Mummy and five minutes with me. I suddenly knew why I've hated Mummy ever since I was twelve."

"You don't hate her," Craig said gently. Whatever he was responsible for, he didn't want to be responsible for alienating his daughters from their mother.

"Oh, yes I do," Anne said. "I do, I do. Why did you tolerate that miserable, boring man around the house pretending to be your friend all those years, why did you let them get away with it for so long?"

"Betrayal begins at home," Craig said. "I was no angel, either. You're a big girl now, Anne, and I imagine you've realized quite a while ago that your mother and I have been going our separate ways for years—"

"Separate ways!" Anne said impatiently. "Okay, separate ways. I can understand that. But I can't understand how you ever married that bitch—"

"Anne!" he said sharply. "You can't talk like that—"

"And what I can't understand most of all is how you can let her threaten to sue you for adultery and take all your money like that. And the house! Why don't you put a detective on her for two days and then see how she behaves?"

"I can't do that."

"Why not? She put a detective on you."

Craig shrugged. "Don't argue like a lawyer," he said. "I just can't."

"You're too old-fashioned," Anne said. "That's your trouble."

"Let's not talk about it, please," he said. "Just remember that if I hadn't married your mother, I wouldn't have you and your sister, and maybe I think because I do have you two, everything else is worth it, and no matter what your mother does or says I am still grateful to her for that. Will you remember?"

"I'll try." Anne's voice was trembling, and he was afraid she was going to cry. She had never been an easy crier, even as a child. "One thing, though," she said bitterly, "I don't want to see the woman again. Not in Switzerland, not in New York, not in California. No place. Never."

"You'll change your mind," he said gently.

"Wanna bet?"

Oh, Christ, he thought. Families. "There's one fact I have to make absolutely clear to you and Marcia," he said. "Constance had nothing to do with my leaving your mother. I left because I was bored to the point of suicide. Because the marriage was meaningless and I didn't want to lead a meaningless life anymore. I'm not blaming your mother any more than I'm blaming myself. But whoever's fault it was, there was no point in trying to continue. Constance was just a coincidence."

"Okay," Anne said. "I'll buy that."

Anne didn't speak for several moments, and he drove past the Cannes racecourse, grateful for the silence. The horses of the south. Simple victories, unqualified defeats. The sprinklers were on, myriad arched fountains over the green infield.

"Now," Anne said finally, her voice brisk, "How about you? Are you having fun?"

"I suppose you can call it that," he said.

"I've been worried about you," Anne said.

"Worried about me?" He couldn't help sounding surprised. "I thought it was modern doctrine that nowadays no child ever worried about any parent."

"I'm not as modern as all that," Anne said.

"Why're you worried about me?"

"Your letters."

"What did I say in my letters?"

"Nothing I can pin down," she said. "Nothing overt. But underneath—I don't know—I had the feeling you were dissatisfied with yourself, that you weren't sure about yourself or what you were doing. Even your handwriting . . ." she said.

"Handwriting?"

"It just looked different," Anne said. "Not as firm, somehow. As though you'd lost confidence in how to make an 'e' or a capital 'G.'"

"Maybe I ought to begin typing my letters," Craig said, trying to make a joke out of it.

"It's not as easy as that," she said earnestly. "There's a professor in the psychology department who's a handwriting expert, and I showed him two of your letters. One that I got from you four years ago and . . ."

"You keep old letters of mine?" Extraordinary child. He had never kept any of his parents' letters.

"Of course, I do. Well, anyway, this professor was saying one day that very often, long before anything shows or there are any symptoms or anything like that or before a person feels anything at all, his handwriting sort of—well—*predicts* changes . . . disease, death even."

He was shaken by what she had said but tried not to show it. Anne had always been a blunt, candid child, blurting out everything that crossed her mind. He had been proud and a little amused by her unsparing honesty, finding it evidence of an admirable strength of character. He was not so amused now, now that it was he who was not being spared. He tried to pass it off lightly. "And what did that smart man have to say about your father's letters?" he asked ironically.

"You can laugh," she said. "He said you'd changed. And would change more."

"For the better, I hope," Craig said.

"No," she said. "Not for the better."

"God Almighty," Craig said. "You send your children to a big fancy college for a scientific education and they come out with their heads stuffed with all kinds of medieval superstitions. Does your psychology professor read palms, too?"

"Superstitions or not," Anne said, "I promised myself I was going to tell you, and I told you. And when I saw you today, I was shocked."

"By what?"

"You don't look well. Not at all well."

"Oh, don't be silly, Anne," Craig said, although he was sure she was right. "I've had a couple of rough nights, that's all."

"It's more than that," she persisted. "It's not just a rough night or two. It's something fundamental. I don't know whether you've realized it or not, but I've been studying you ever since I was a little girl. No matter how you tried to disguise things, I always knew when you were angry or worried or sick or scared . . ."

"And what about now?" He challenged her.

"Now—" She ran her hand nervously through her hair. "You have a funny look. You look—uncared for—I guess that's the best description. You look like a man who spends his life moving from one hotel room to another."

I *have* been living in hotel rooms. Some of the best hotels in the world."

"You know what I mean," she said.

He did know what she meant, but he did not admit it. Except to himself.

"I made up my mind when I got your cable that I was going to deliver a speech," Anne said, "and now I'm going to deliver it."

"Look at the scenery, Anne," he said. "You can make speeches any time."

She ignored what he had said. "What I want to do," she said, "is live with you. Take care of you. In Paris, if that's where you want to be. Or New York, or wherever. I don't want you to turn into a solitary old man eating dinner alone night after night. Like . . . like an old bull who's been turned out from the herd."

He laughed despite himself at her comparison. "I don't want to sound boastful," he said, "but I don't lack for company, Anne. Anyway, you have another year to go in college and . . ."

"I'm through with education," she said. "And education is through with me. At least *that* sort of education. I'm not going back, no matter what."

"We'll discuss that some other time," he said. Actually, after the years of wandering, the thought of living in an ordered household with Anne suddenly seemed attractive. And he recognized that he still suffered from the old, unworthy, and by now unmentionable belief that education was not terribly important for women.

"Another thing," Anne said. "You ought to go back to work. It's ridiculous, a man like you not doing anything for five years."

"It's not as easy as all that," he said. "Nobody's clamoring to give me a job."

"You!" she cried incredulously. "I don't believe it."

"Believe it," he said. "Murphy is down here. Talk to him about the movie business."

"People're still making pictures."

"People," he said. "Not your father."

"I can't bear it," she said. "You talking like a failure. If you'd only make up your mind to *try* instead of being so damn proud and remote. I've talked it over with Marcia, and she agrees with me—it's sheer, dumb, shameful waste." She sounded close to hysteria, and he put his hand out and patted her soothingly.

"Actually, he said, "the same idea has occurred to me. I've been working for the last twelve months."

"There," she said triumphantly. "You see! With whom?"

"With nobody," he said. "With myself. I've written a script. I've just finished it. Somebody's reading it right now.

"What does Mr. Murphy say?"

"It stinks, Mr. Murphy says. Throw it away."

"Stupid old man," Anne said. "I wouldn't listen to a word he says."

"He's far from stupid."

"You're not listening to him, though, are you?"

"I haven't thrown it away yet."

"Can I read it?"

"If you want."

"Of course, I want. Can I tell you exactly what I think of it?"

"Naturally."

"Even if Mr. Murphy is right," Anne said, "and it turns out that what you've done isn't good enough or commerical enough or whatever it is they want these days, you could do something else. I mean, the movies aren't the only thing in the world, are they? In fact, if you want to know the truth, I think you'd be a lot happier if you forgot them altogether. You have to deal with such awful people. And it's all so cruel and capricious—one minute you're a kind of Culture Hero and the next minute everybody's forgotten you. And the people you have to pander to, the Great American Audience—good God, Daddy, go into a movie house, any movie house, on a Saturday night and see what they're laughing at, what they're crying over . . . I remember how hard you used to work, how you'd be half dead by the time you finished a picture . . . And for whom? For a hundred million goons!"

He recognized the echo of some of his own thoughts in Anne's tirade, but he wasn't pleased by what she had said. Especially by the word she had used—pander. It was one thing for a man his age who had worked and won and lost in that harsh arena to have his doubts in moments of depression about the value of his efforts. It was another to hear such a sweeping condemnation from the lips of an untried and pampered child. "Anne," he said, "don't be so hard on your fellow Americans."

"Anybody who wants my fellow Americans," she said bitterly, "can have them."

Another item on the agenda, he thought. Find out what happened to my daughter in her native land in the last six months. At our next meeting.

He changed the subject. "Since you've been doing so much thinking about my career," he said with mild irony, "perhaps you have a suggestion about what I should do."

"A million things," she said. "You could teach, you could get a job as an editor for a publisher. After all, that's what you've been doing practically all your life, editing other people's scripts. You could even become publisher yourself. Or you could move to a peaceful small town and run a little theatre somewhere. Or you could write your memoirs."

"Anne," he said half-reproving, "I know I'm old, but I'm not *that* old."

"A million things" she repeated stubbornly. "You're the smartest man I've ever known, it'd be a crime if you just let yourself be thrown into the discard just because the people in the movie business or in the theatre are so stupid. You're not *married* to the movie business. Moses never came down from Sinai saying, "Thou Shalt Entertain," for Christ's sake."

He laughed. "Anne, darling," he said, "you're making a mixed salad out of two great religions."

"I know what I'm talking about."

"Maybe you do," he admitted. "Maybe there's some truth in what you say. But maybe you're wrong, too. One of the reasons I came to Cannes this year at all was to make up my mind about it, to see if it was worth it."

"Well," she said defiantly, "what have you seen, what have you learned?"

What had he seen, what had he learned? He had seen all kinds of movies, good and bad, mostly bad. He had been plunged into a carnival, a delirium of film. In the halls, on the terraces, on the beach, at the parties, the art or industry or whatever it deserved to be called in these few days was exposed in its essence. The whole thing was there—the artists and pseudo-artists, the businessmen, the con men, the buyers and sellers, the peddlers, the whores, the pornographers, critics, hangers-on, the year's heroes, the year's failures. And then the distillation of what it was all about, a film of Bergman's and one of Buñuel's, pure and devastating.

"Well," Anne repeated, "what have you learned?"

"I'm afraid I learned that I'm hooked," he said. "When I was a little boy, my father used to take me to the theatre, the Broadway theatre. I used to sit in my seat, not budging, waiting for the theatre to go dark and the footlights go on, afraid that something would happen and the darkness would never come and the stage lights never come on. And then it would happen. I would clench my fists with happiness and worry for the people I was going to see on the stage when the curtain went up. The only time I ever remember being rude to my father was at a moment like that. He said something to me, I don't know what, and it was destroying that great moment for me, and I said, 'Pop, please keep quiet.' I think he understood because he never said a word again once they began to dim the house lights. Well, I don't have that feeling anymore in the Broadway theatre. But I have it each time I buy a ticket and walk into a darkened movie house. That's not a bad thing, you know—for a forty-eight-year-old man to have one repetitive thing in his life that makes him feel like a boy again. Maybe it's because of that that I make up all sorts of excuses for movies, that I rationalize away the hateful aspects, the cheapness, the thousand times I've walked out disgusted, and try to convince myself that one good picture makes up for a hundred bad ones. That the game is worth the candle."

He didn't say it, but he knew now, had really always known, that the good ones weren't made for the people in the audience on Saturday night. They were made for the necessity of making them, for the need of the people who made them, just like any other work of art. He knew that the agony and what Anne called the cruelty and capriciousness involved in the process, the maneuvering, the wooing, the money, the criticizing and wounding, the injustice, the exhaustion of nerve, was part of the pleasure, the profound pleasure of that particular act of creation. And even if you only played a small part in it, a subordinate, modest part, you shared in that pleasure. He knew now that he had punished himself for five years in denying himself that pleasure.

They were approaching Antibes now, and he turned down toward the road along the sea. "Hooked," he said, "that's the diagnosis. And that's enough about me. Let me say that I'm pleased to see there's another adult in the family." He looked across at her and saw that she was flushing at the compliment. "Now," he said, "what about you? Aside from being sufficiently educated and taking care of me. What are your plans?"

She shrugged. "I'm trying to figure out how to survive as an adult. Your word," she said. "Aside from that, the only thing I'm sure of is that I'm not going to get married."

"Well," he said, "that seems like a promising start for a career."

"Don't make fun of me," she said sharply. "You always tease me."

"People only tease the ones they love," he said, "but if you don't like it, I'll try to stop it."

"I don't like it," she said. "I'm not secure enough to take it."

There was a rebuke there, he realized. If a girl of twenty was not secure, who but her father was to blame? He had learned a great deal about his daughter between Nice and Antibes, and he wasn't certain that it was reassuring.

They were going along the outside road of the peninsula and approaching the house he had rented for the summer of 1949, the house in which Anne had been conceived. She had never been here before, but he wondered if some prenatal memory would make her look up and notice the tall white building in the garden above the road.

She did not look up.

I hope, he thought as they passed the house, that at least once she has three months like the three months her mother and I had that summer.

CHAPTER 11

GAIL MCKINNON WAS just coming out of the hotel as they drove up, and there was no avoiding introducing her. "Welcome to Cannes," she said to Anne. She stepped back a pace and examined Anne coolly. Insolently, Craig thought. "The family is getting handsomer as it goes along," she said.

To stop any further discussion of the progression toward perfection of the Craig family, he said, "What's new with Reynolds? Is he all right?"

"I imagine he's alive," Gail said carelessly.

"Didn't you go to see him?"

She shrugged. "What for? If he needed help, somebody would call. See you around," she said to Anne. "Don't walk alone at night. See if you can't convince your father to take us to dinner sometime." She hardly looked at Craig and went striding off, her bag swinging from her shoulder.

"What a peculiar, beautiful girl," Anne said as they went into the hotel. "Do you know her well?"

"I just met her a few days ago," Craig said. The truth, as far as it went.

"Is she an actress?"

"Some kind of newspaperwoman. Give me your passport. You have to leave it at the desk."

He registered Anne and went over to the concierge's desk for his key. There was a telegram for him. It was from Contance.

"ARRIVING MARSEILLES TOMORROW MORNING STAYING HOTEL SPLEN-
DIDE STOP DEPENDING UPON YOU MAKE GLORIOUS ARRANGEMENTS
STOP LOVE C."

"Is it important?" Anne asked.

"No." He stuffed the telegram in his pocket and followed the clerk who was going to show Anne her room. The manager had not been able to free the room connecting with Craig's apartment, and Anne would be on the floor above him. Just as well, he thought, as they got into the elevator.

The short man with the paunch he had seen once before in the elevator with the pretty young girl went in with them. The man with the paunch was wearing a bright green shirt today. "It'll never go in Spain," he was saying as the elevator started. He looked appraisingly at Anne, then across at Craig. Was there a kind of conspiratorial smile at the corner of his lips? In a simpler world Craig would have punched him in the nose. Instead, he said to the clerk, "I'll stop at my floor first. You take my daughter to her room, please. Anne, come down as soon as you're settled."

The man in the green shirt dropped his eyes. He had been holding the pretty girl's elbow. Now he took his hand away. Craig smiled meanly as the elevator came to a halt and he went out.

In the living room he looked at the schedule of movies that were being shown that day. At three o'clock there was an Italian film he wanted to see. He picked up the phone and asked for Anne's rom. "Anne," he said when she answered, "there's an interesting movie this afternoon. Would you like to see it with me?"

"Oh, Daddy," she said, "I'm just putting on a bathing suit. The water looks so marvelous . . . "

"That's all right," he said. "Have a good swim. I'll be back a little after five."

When he had put the phone down, he reread Constance's telegram. He shook his head. He couldn't refuse to meet her in Marseilles. And he couldn't take Anne with him. There were limits to the frontiers of the permissive society. But leaving his daughter alone in Cannes immediately after she had flown five thousand miles to be with him could hardly add to her sense of security. He would have to work something out with Constance so that at most he would be gone only a day or two. *Glorious arrangements.*

Dissatisfied with himself, he went over to the mantelpiece and stared at his reflection in the mirror hanging there. Anne had said that he didn't look well. It was true there were unaccustomed deep lines under his eyes, and his forehead seemed fixed in a permanent frown. His complexion now seemed pale, almost pasty, to him, and there was a slight film of sweat above his mouth. It's a hot day, he thought, summer is coming on, that's all.

The psychologist in California had said that there were secret predictions buried in the way your hand shaped a word on paper. Change, Anne had said, disease, death even . . .

His throat felt dry, he remembered that he sometimes felt slightly dizzy these days when he got up from a chair, that he had little appetite for his food . . . "Fuck it," he said aloud. He had never talked to himself before. What sort of sign was that?

He turned away from the mirror. *He has a certain dry elegance,* Gail had written about him. She had not consulted Anne's professor.

He went into the bedroom, stared down at the bed, now neatly made, which he had shared, if you could call it that, with the girl the night before. Would she share it again tonight? Would he be fool enough to open the door for her once more? He remembered the silken feel of her skin, the fragrance of her hair, the clean swell of her hip as she lay beside him. He would open the door if she knocked. "Idiot," he said aloud. It might be a symptom of some obscure aberration, a warning of eventual senescence, but the sound of his own voice in the empty room somehow relieved him. "goddamn idiot," he said, looking down at the bed.

He bathed his face with cold water, changed his shirt, which was damp with sweat, and went to see the Italian movie.

The movie was disappointing, plodding, and serious and dull. It was about a group of immigrant anarchists in London, led by a Sicilian revolutionary, in the beginning of the century. It was probably as authentic as the writer and director had been able to make it, and it was plain that the people who were responsible for the film had a laudable hatred for poverty and injustice, but Craig found the violence, the shooting, the deaths, melodramatic and distasteful. So many of the other films he had seen since he arrived in Cannes had dealt with revolution of one kind or another, millions of dollars handed over by the most Republican of bankers to be invested in the praise of violence and the overthrow of society. What motivated those neat, prosperous men in the white shirts and narrow suits behind the wide, bare desks? If there was a dollar to be made in a riot, in the bombing of a courthouse, in the burning of a ghetto, did they feel that they, honorable accruers, owed it to their stockholders to offer the fortunes from their vaults, regardless of the consequences? Or were they more cynical than that? Wiser than lesser men, with their hands on the levers of power, did they know that no movie had ever brought about public upheaval, that no matter what was said in a theatre, no matter how long the lines were in front of the ticket offices for the most incendiary of films, nothing would change, no shot would be fired? Did they laugh in their clubs at the grown-up children who played their shadowy celluloid games and whom they indulged with the final toy—money? He himself had never gone raging out into the streets after any film. Was he any different from the others?

Was it a sign of age that he was unconvinced, that he believed these reckless calls to action could only lead to worse abuses than the ones they sought to correct?

If he were twenty, like Anne, or twenty-two, like Gail, would he be encouraged to revolt, would he not glory in plotting the destruction of cities?

He remembered Murray Sloan's tumbrels, Versailles the night before the fall of the Bastille. Whose side would he be on the day the tumbrels rolled down his street? Where would Anne be riding? Constance? Gail McKinnon? His wife?

The Italian film was a bad one for a man to see just after he had told his daughter he was hooked on making films. It was stillborn from the beginning, worthless or evil as art, finally boring. It didn't even have the true tragic advantage of reducing his own predicament to scale, of making his own small, private concerns, his entanglements with women, his professional drifting, seem picayune or comfortingly inconsequential.

He left before the end, and as he went out of the theatre to restore himself, he tried to remember, frame by frame, the films of Buñuel and Bergman he had seen that week.

The sun was still high over the horizon, and on the chance that Anne hadn't gone in yet, he went down the steps to the Carlton beach to look for her. She was at a table near the bar in the briefest of bikinis, broad-shouldered and opulently shaped. As father, he would have preferred a less revealing costume. Seated next to her was Ian Wadleigh in swimming trunks. Across the table from the two of them was Gail McKinnon, wearing the scant, pink, two-piece bathing suit she had worn at the Murphys' cabana. Craig felt guilty for allowing Anne to go off on her own, not providing her with other company.

Wadleigh had obviously not been wasting his time seeing too many films. He was as brown as the two girls. In his ill-fitting clothes he had seemed ungracefully shaped, almost tumescent, but stripped for the beach as he was now, his flesh was solid, and he looked powerful and dominating. He was laughing and gesturing with a glass he held in his hand. None of the three noticed Craig for the moment, and he half-resolved to turn and walk away. There was something too reminiscent in the group for him, it was too much like the Italian actor on the beach showing his teeth in a smile, the two girls listening to him.

But he fought down the impulse as bad-tempered and childish and went up to the table. Gail was fiddling with her tape recorder, and for a second Craig was seized by the uneasy thought that she had been interviewing Anne. He had neglected to warn Anne to keep her mouth shut. But as he came up to the table, he heard Gail saying, "Thanks, Ian. I'm sure they'll like it back in the states. I'm not so sure that you'll ever be allowed back in Cannes again, though."

"Down with double talk," Ian said. "Screw *politesse*. Name the whores and their works, that's my motto."

Oh, Christ, Craig thought, he's still on that kick. "Good evening, folks," he said.

"Hi, Jess," Ian boomed out, his voice as imperial as his bronze body. With an audience of two pretty girls, he was transformed. "I was just instructing these charming young women on the inner workings of film festivals," Wadleigh said. "Who sells what, who buys whom, in what sweat and slime Golden Palms are traded across secret counters. Sit down, Father. What'll you have? Waiter. *Garçon!*"

"Nothing, thank you," Craig said. Wadleigh's "Father" had a derisive ring to it. He sat down next to Gail, facing Anne. "What are you drinking?" he asked Anne.

"Gin and tonic," she said.

He had never seen her drink before. When he had offered her wine at meals, she had refused, saying she didn't like the taste. Gin, perhaps, was more suitable to youthful palates.

"It's awfully good of you, Father,' Wadleigh said, "to import admirers, at great personal expense, across continents and oceans."

What're you talking about?" Craig asked.

"I read his novels," Anne said. "they were assigned in a Modern Lit course."

"Hear that," Wadleigh said, "I am a fixture in Modern Literature. Nubile scholars from coast to coast burn the midnight oil in honor of Ian Wadleigh. Imagine, on the bleak and desperate shingle of Cannes, I have found a reader."

"I've read a couple of them, too," Gail said.

"Praise them, dear, praise them," Wadleigh said.

"They're okay," Gail said.

"My poor girl," Wadleigh said jovially, "I'm afraid you've flunked the course."

Wadleigh was being obnoxious, but Craig couldn't help being offended by Gail's offhand dismissal of a man's life's work. "I think perhaps you ought to reread his books, Gail," Craig said. "When you grow up." For once he could take advantage of the difference in their ages. "Perhaps you'll make a more enthusiastic judgment."

"Thanks," Wadleigh said. "A man needs all the protection he can get from the young."

Gail smiled. "I didn't know you were such close friends, you two," she said. "Now, Jesse, there're a couple or so more questions I have to put to the maestro, and then you can have him all to yourself . . . "

"I'm sorry," Craig said, standing. "I didn't mean to interrupt. I just came down looking for Anne. You ought to go in now," he said to Anne. "It's beginning to get cold."

"I'd like to listen to the end," Anne said. "I'm not cold."

"You stay, too, Jess," Wadleigh said. "I'm at my most eloquent before my peers."

Unwilling, for no sensible reason, to leave Anne there with Gail McKinnon, Craig said, "Thanks for the invitation," and sat down again. "As long as I'm here," he said, "I'll take a whisky."

"Two more," Wadleigh said, holding up his glass to a passing waiter. Then to Gail McKinnon, "Shoot."

Gail turned her machine on. "Mr. Wadleigh," she said, "earlier in this interview you said that the position of the writer for films is being steadily eroded. Would you care to enlarge on that?"

Craig was conscious of Anne's close, admiring attention to Gail as she worked. He had to admit that her manner was professional, her voice pleasant and unaffected.

"Well," Wadleigh was saying, "in one way, the writer for films is more powerful than ever. I'm speaking of the writer who directs his own stuff and because of that controls the final result, the man who gets the critical attention and reaps the financial rewards. On the other side of the coin, however, the writer who is only a writer is lost in the shuffle." He was speaking seriously now, not trying to amuse or play the great man before the two girls. "For example—at this Festival—there are rewards for actors, directors, composers, cameramen, etc., but not one for writers. This is a recent development, and it's been brought about largely by the critical acceptance of the *auteurist* theory of film making."

Now Craig was sure Wadleigh had written all this before, probably for an article that had been turned down by a dozen magazines.

Gail flicked off the machine. "Remember, Ian," she said, "this is for American listeners. You'd better explain, don't you think?"

"Yeah, you're right," Wadleigh said. He took a gulp of the fresh whisky the waiter had put down in front of him.

"I'll ask you the question," Gail said. She started the machine again. "Would you like to describe that theory for us, Mr. WAdleigh?"

"The *auteurist* theory of film making," he said, "is very simple. It rests on the conviction that a film is the work of one man—the director. That in the final analysis the man behind the camera is the real author of the work, that the film, in essence, is written with the camera."

"Do you agree with that theory?"

It's like a charade, Craig thought, little girl wearing Mummy's dress, or in this case, Mummy's bikini, and going down to Daddy's office and sitting at his desk and talking into the intercom.

"No," Wadleigh said. "Of course, there are directors who are in fact the authors of their films, but all that means is that as well as being directors, they are also writers. If they deserve a prize for their work, they deserve two prizes—one for the script and one for the direction. But the truth is that in America, at any rate, there are only five or six men who are really both. Of course, directors being the self-deluding beasts they are, there are plenty of them who *think* they are writers and impose their written efforts on the audience."

The same old whine, Craig thought.

"We are fortunate enough," Gail said calmly into the microphone, "to have Mr. Jesse Craig, the eminent film producer with us here on the beach in Cannes. I wonder if I could ask you, Mr. Craig, if you agree with Mr. Wadleigh. Or if you disagree, why?"

Craig's hand tightened on his glass. "Cut out the jokes, Gail," he said.

"Oh, Daddy," Anne said, "go ahead. You were talking to me for half an hour about the movies in the car. Don't be sticky."

"Shut the damn machine off, Gail," Craig said.

Gail didn't move. "There's no harm done. I splice together what I want later and throw out the junk. Maybe," she said, smiling agreeably, "if I can't have you, I'll put Anne on the air. The confidences of the daughter of the abdicated king, the Life and Loves of the one after the last Tycoon, as seen through the clear young eyes of his nearest and dearest."

"Any time you say," Anne said.

"I'm sure your listeners in Peoria," Craig said, making an effort to keep his temper and sound off-hand at the same time, "are waiting with bated breath for just that program." I'm going to wipe that dancing smile off your face, lady, he thought. For the first time in his life he understood those writers who regarded the penis as an instrument of revenge.

"We'll just keep it in mind, Anne," Gail said. "Won't we? And now Mr. Wadleigh—" She resumed her professional voice. "In a conversation with Mr. Craig some days ago on the same subject, when I asked him why he had not directed any of the films he had produced, he replied that he didn't think he was good enough, that there were perhaps fifty men in Hollywood who were better at the job than he thought he could be. Similarly," she went on, staring coolly at Craig as she spoke so that it was evident to him, if not to the others, that she was maliciously playing with him, using their presence to ensure that he suffered in silence, "similarly, is it an equally admirable modesty on your part that prevents you from working behind the camera?"

"Shit," Craig said. "Shit, shit. Send *that* out to the homes of America."

"Daddy!" Anne said, shocked. "What's the matter with you?"

"Nothing. I don't like to be trapped, that's all. When I want to give an interview, I'll give it. Not before." He remembered the title Gail had said she was going to use on the piece about him, "The Once and Future Has Been," but he couldn't tell that to Anne. He also couldn't tell Anne that he had slept with that cool, smiling girl in the pink bathing suit the night before and that if he could, he would sleep with her in the night to come.

"If you recall my question, Mr. Wadleigh," Gail said, "has it been due to modesty, as in the case of Mr. Craig, that you have not directed any of the scripts you have written for films?"

"Hell, no," Wadleigh said. "If I couldn't do better than ninety-nine per cent of those bums out there, I'd shoot myself. It's just that the bastards in the front offices won't hire me."

"I think that brings us to the end of this program," Gail said into the microphone. "Thank you very much, Mr. Wadleigh, for your frank and enlightening discussion of the problems of the writer for the motion pictures. I am sorry that Mr. Craig was unexpectedly called away so that we were denied the benefits of his long experience in the field. Perhaps we shall be lucky enough in the near future to have Mr. Craig, who is an extremely busy man, with us at greater length. This is Gail McKinnon, broadcasting from the Cannes Film Festival."

She flipped off the machine, smiled brightly and innocently. "Another day, another dollar." She started to pack away the machine. "Isn't Daddy the *funny* one?" she said to Anne.

"I don't understand you, Daddy," Anne said. "I thought you and she were friends."

There's a description, Craig thought.

"I don't see what harm it would do to say a few words," Anne persisted.

"What you don't say can't hurt you," Craig said. "You'll find that out eventually, too. Ian, what the hell good do you think you did yourself just now? Can you figure out why you did it?"

"Sure," Ian said. "Vanity. A trait not to be taken lightly. Of course, I know you're above such human failings."

"I'm not above anything," Craig said. He wasn't arguing for himself but for Anne, for Anne's education. He didn't want her to be taken in by the American craze for publicity, for self-congratulation, for flattery, for the random, glib chatter on television whose real, dead serious purpose was to sell automobiles, dedorants, detergents, politicians, remedies for indigestion and insomnia. "Ian," he said, "I know why Gail goes through all this nonsense—"

"Careful, careful," Gail said mockingly.

"She makes her living out of it, and maybe it's no more discreditable than the way you and I make our living . . . "

"Blessings on you, Daddy," Gail said.

I'm going to lock the door tonight, Craig thought, and stuff cotton in my ears. With a wrench he made himself look away from the lovely, teasing face and talk to Wadleigh. "What possible good did babbling away here this afternoon do you? I'm serious. I want to know. Maybe you can convince me."

"Well," Ian said, "first of all, before you came, good old Gail plugged my books. Gallant little liar, she had a good word to say for all of them. Maybe her program'll get one person to go into a bookstore to buy one of them or two or all of them. Or since they're out of print, maybe it'll get a publisher to bring out my collected works in paperback. Don't be holy, Jess. When you make a picture, you want people to see it, don't you?"

"Yes," Craig admitted.

"Well, how does that make you different from me?"

"Do you want me to use the machine, Jesse?" Gail said. "It'll only take a minute. We can start the interview right now."

"I'm not selling any pictures at the moment," Craig said. "Leave the machine alone."

"Or some producer or director might happen to tune in on the program," Wadleigh continued, "and say, "Hey, I thought that guy was dead. If he isn't dead, he might be just the guy to write my next picture.' We all depend on luck, you, I, Gail, even this beautiful young girl who has turned out to be your daughter. A switch of the dial on the radio might mean the difference in life or death for somebody like me."

"Do you really believe that?" Craig asked.

"What do you think I believe in?" Wadleigh said bitterly. "Merit? Don't make me laugh."

"I'm remembering all this," Gail said. "I'm sure it's going to be useful for something. For the piece I'm doing about you, Jesse, for example. The public figure who refuses the public role. Is it for real, I'll ask my readers, or is it a clever play to titillate, to invite while seeming to reject? Is the veil more revealing than the face behind it?"

"Mr. Wadleigh is right," Anne broke in. "He's written these wonderful books, and he's being neglected. And I listened to the whole interview. He said a lot of things that people ought to hear."

"I've told Anne," Gail said, "that you're being difficult about cooperating."

"You two girls seem to have managed to cover a lot of ground in two hours," Craig said sourly.

"There was an instant bond of sympathy," Gail said. "We bridged the generation gap between twenty and twenty-two in a flash."

"People your age, Daddy," Anne said, "are constantly complaining the young don't understand you. Well, here you have a perfect chance to get whatever it is you want to say to *hordes* of people of all ages, and you turn the chance down."

"My medium is film," Craig said, "not indecent public exposure."

"Sometimes, Mr. Craig," Gail said with a straight face, "I get the feeling that you don't approve of me."

Craig stood up. "I'm going in," he said. He pulled some bills out of his pocket. "How many drinks did you have, Anne?"

"Forget it," Wadleigh waved grandly. "I have it."

"Thanks," Craig said. On my three hundred dollars for Spain, he thought. "Coming, Anne?"

"I'm going to have one last swim."

"Me, too," Gail said. "It's been hot work this afternoon."

"I'll join you girls," Wadleigh said. "You can save me from drowning. Oh, by the way, Jesse," he said as he finished his whisky and stood up, "I suggested we all have dinner tonight. Shall we say eight o'clock at the bar?"

Craig saw Anne looking appealingly at him. Anything, he thought, rather than have dinner alone with Dad. "Don't you have to see the picture tonight for your article?" he asked Wadleigh.

"I read the synopsis," Wadleigh said. "It's something about raising hawks in Hungary. I think I can skip it. My fairies in London aren't made about Hungarian hawks. If it's any good, I can quote from *Le Monde*. See you at eight?"

"I'll see what my schedule is," Craig said.

"We'll be there," Anne said. "Come on, let's hit the water."

He watched the two girls, one tall, one short, both swift and young, silhouetted against the evening light, run down the beach and dive into the water. He was surprised that Wadleigh could run so fast as he followed and plunged into the sea in a huge splash of foam.

He climbed up from the beach slowly. As he stepped off the curb of the Croisette, a car nearly ran him down. There was a squeal of brakes, and a policeman shouted at him. He smiled politely at the policeman, apologizing for almost having been killed.

In the lobby, when he picked up his key, he asked for messages. There were none. Klein hadn't called. Of course, he told himself, it's too early. In the old days when Jesse Craig sent anybody a script, there was a call withih three hours.

Going toward the elevator, he met Reynolds. Reynolds had a big fresh bandage on his forehead, a huge lump, yellow and green, over one eye, and his cheek had jagged scabs on it as though he had been dragged through broken glass.

"I'm looking for Gail," Reynolds said without saying hello. "Have you seen her?"

"She's swimming in the direction of Tunis," Craig said. "How do you feel?"

"About the way I look," Reynolds said.

"You can't be too careful in the movie business," Craig said, and went into the elevator.

CHAPTER 12

IN EVERY GROUP, however small, there is one person who is its center of gravity, its reason for existence as an entity and not merely a collection of unconnected egos. For this night, Craig thought, it was Gail McKinnon. Anne was clearly fascinated by her, reacting openly to every word she spoke, addressing herself more often to Gail than to any of the others, and even when talking to Craig or Wadleigh, looking for approval or criticism in Gail's direction. On the way over from the hotel to the restaurant Craig had been half-amused, half-irritated when he noticed that Anne was subtly imitating, consciously or unconsciously, Gail's striding, brusque manner of walking. Still, it was an improvement on Anne's habitual, over-modest, childish slouch.

For Wadleigh, Gail represented an audience. In recent years he had had no surfeit of audiences, and he was making the most of it.

As for Craig, he would not have been there tonight had it not been for Gail. It was as simple as that. Watching her across the table, he knew that the movies were not the only thing he was hooked on. I am here, he thought, to unhook.

He let the others talk most of the time. When Gail spoke, he listened secretly for a hint, a signal from her, a guarded promise for the night, a tacit refusal. He found neither.

I will forget her tomorrow, he told himself, in Constance's arms.

Wadleigh insisted on acting the host, ordering the wine and suggesting what dishes the girls should choose. They were in the restaurant on the old port in which Craig had seen Picasso at dinner. If Wadleigh was going to pay the bill tonight, Craig thought, he'd be lucky to get as far as Toulon, let alone Madrid.

Wadleigh was drinking too much but up to now wasn't showing it. For once he was dressed well, in a gray suit and oxford shirt with a collar that was buttoned neatly below the heavy throat and a new striped tie.

Gail was wearing rose-colored, tight-fitting shantung slacks and a soft silk blouse. She had swept her hair up for the evening, and it made her head seem charmingly and incongruously mature over the slender youthful column of her neck.

Anne, poor girl, was wearing a disastrous billowing yellow organdy dress, too short for her long legs, making her look gawky, like a high school junior dressed for her first prom.

The restaurant was not yet full, but Craig could see by the little signs on the vacant tables that the room would be crowded before long. He hoped, for Anne's sake, that one of the tables was being kept for Picasso.

Two young men, one with a lion cub, the other with a Polaroid camera, whom Craig recognized as one of the teams that worked the Croisette and the cafés, came into the restaurant. As they approached the table, Craig tried to wave them away. "At these prices," he said, "we ought to be protected from lions."

But Wadleigh took the cub from the man who was holding him and put him on the table between Gail and Anne. "I want a picture of them with the king of the beasts," he said. "I've always had a weakness for lady lion-tamers. One of my fantasies is making love to a woman in tights and spangles, with a chair, inside a cage."

Depend on Wadleigh, Craig thought, to make you uncomfortable with your daughter.

The photographer, using a flash, which made the cub snarl, snapped one picture after another. Gail laughed at the show of infant ferocity, stroked the animal. "Come around when you've grown up, Sonny," she said.

"I heard someplace," Craig said, "that most of them die in a month or so. They can't stand the handling."

"Who can?" Wadleigh asked.

"Oh, Daddy," Anne said, "don't spoil the fun."

"I'm devoted to ecology," Craig said. "I want to keep the population of lions in France in balance. So many lions eating so many Frenchmen a season."

The cameraman developed the photographs swiftly. They were in color. Anne's bright hair and Gail's dark pile made an effective composition with the tawny cub snarling among the wineglasses. On the shiny print, except for the blonde hair, Anne looked disturbingly like her mother.

The cameraman's helper picked up the lion, and Wadleigh paid, extravagantly. He gave one of the photographs to Gail, the other to Anne. "When I am old and gray and full of sleep," he said, "and having a bad day, I will summon one or the other of you to my rocking chair and order you to produce this picture. To remind me of a happy night when I was young. Did you ask for the wine, Father?"

Wadleigh was pouring when Craig saw Natalie Sorel come through the door of the restaurant with a tall, beautifully dressed man with silvery hair. Fifty-five, sixty, Craig thought, with everything that a barber and a masseur and the best tailors could do to make it seem like less. Natalie, in a dress that was designed to show off her slender waist, her graceful hips, looked fragile and dependent beside him.

The woman who owned the restaurant was leading the couple toward the rear, and they would have to pass Craig's table. Craig saw Natalie glance at him quickly, look away, hesitate for a moment as though she meant to go by without stopping, then decide differently.

"Jesse," she said, halting at the table and putting her hand on her escort's arm. "How nice to see you."

Craig stood up, and Wadleigh followed. "This is my fiancé, Philip Robinson," Natalie said. Only Craig, he hoped, heard the warning clarity of the word "fiancé." "Mr. Jesse Craig."

Craig shook hands with the man and introduced the others. Anne stood up. Gail remained seated. Craig wished Anne were wearing another dress. The man's hand was dry and smooth. He had a slow, warm, Texas smile, an outdoor complexion. He didn't look like a man who manufactured things, as Natalie had described him.

"It seems as though Natalie knows everybody in this town," Robinson said, touching Natalie's arm affectionately. "I'm having trouble keeping all the names straight. I've seen your pictures, haven't I, Mr. Craig?"

"I hope you have," Craig said.

"*Two Steps to Home,*" Natalie said quickly. "That was his last one," She was protecting everybody.

"Of course," Robinson said. He had a deep, self-assured voice. "I liked it very much."

"Thank you," Craig said.

"And did I hear correctly?" Robinson said to Wadleigh. "You're the writer?"

"Once upon a time," Wadleigh said.

"I really admired your book, sir," Robinson said. "Immensely."

"Which one?" Wadleigh asked.

Robinson looked a little flustered. "Well," he said, "the one about the boy growing up in the Midwest and . . ."

"My first one." Wadleigh sat down. "I wrote it in 1953."

"Please sit down," Natalie said hurriedly. "Everyone."

Anne sat down, but Craig remained standing. "Are you having a good time in Cannes, Mr. Robinson?" he asked, steering the conversation away from the dangers of literature to the safer banalities of tourism.

"Well, I've been here before, of course," the man said. "But this is the first time I've seen it from the inside, so to speak. Thanks to Natalie. It's a whole new experience." He patted her arm, a fatherly pat.

You don't know how much on the inside you are, Brother, Craig thought, smiling socially.

"We'd better sit down, dear," Natalie said. "The lady's waiting for us."

"I hope I see your fine folks again real soon," Robinson said. "You and your pretty daughter, Mr. Craig, and you, Mr. Wadleigh, and your . . ."

"I'm not anybody's daughter," Gail said, chewing on a piece of celery.

"She defies description," Wadleigh said. His tone was hostile. Robinson obviously was no fool, and his face hardened. "Enjoy your meal," he said, and allowed Natalie to lead him to the table that the owner was pulling out for them.

Craig watched Natalie as she passed, in the lightfooted, slightly swaying dancer's walk he would always remember, between the rows of tables. Frail and elegant and carefully prepared to please men's eyes, rouse men's desires, courageous, and full of guile.

In a place like this you had to expect bits and pieces of your past to float by, to exert the power of nostalgia, to become again, for a little while at least, part of the present. Staring at Natalie Sorel, lovely and memorable, walking away from him on another man's arm to the rear of the restaurant, he wondered what perversity of chance had ruled that the part of his past embodied in Ian Wadleigh was claiming him tonight instead of Natalie Sorel.

As he sat down, he was conscious of Gail's looking at him quizzically, knowingly.

"Did I hear correctly?" Wadleigh was saying, mimicking Robinson's slight Texas drawl. "Are you the writer?"

"Keep it low," Craig said. "This is a small restaurant."

"I really admired your book, sir," Wadleigh said. Then, bitterly, "I've been writing for twenty years, and I've got eight books to show for it, and he liked my book."

"Calm down, Ian," Craig said.

But the wine was beginning to work. "And it's always the first one. The one I did when I hardly knew how to spell my own name. I'm getting so tired of that book I think I'm going to burn it in the public square on my next birthday." He poured himself a full glass of wine, spilling some on the tablecloth.

"If it'll make you feel any better," Anne said, "my English professor said he thought your second book was the best one you've written."

"Screw your English professor," Wadleigh said. "What the hell does he know?"

"A lot," Anne said defiantly. Craig was glad to see that his daughter had that most difficult of virtues, courage among the teacups. "I'll tell you another thing he said . . ."

"Do, do!" Wadleigh said. "I can't wait to hear."

"He said that the books you've written since you've moved abroad are comparative failures," Anne said. Craig recognized the way she lifted her chin, a habit she had developed as a child when she decided to be stubborn and willful. "That you're not really exploring your talents to their utmost, that you ought to come back to America . . ."

"Did he say that?"

"Yes, he did."

"And you agree with him?" Wadleigh asked, icy and calm.

"I do," Anne said.

"Screw you and your English teacher both," Wadleigh said.

"If you're going to talk like that," Craig said, "Anne and I will be going home." He knew that the drink had made Wadleigh reckless, that he was ripe for torture, and that he had been touched on his sorest point, but he didn't want to expose Anne to Wadleigh's agonized thrashing about.

"Cut it, Ian," Gail said crisply. "We can't all be loved by the whole world every minute of our lives. Be a big grown man, for God's sake. Be a writer, a *professional* writer, or go do something else for a living."

If Craig had said that, he knew there would have been an explosion. But Wadleigh blinked, shook his head as though emerging from a wave, grinned at Gail. "Out of the mouths of babes," he said. "Forgive me, folks, I hope you're having a good time in Cannes. I want some more fish. Waiter . . ." He waved, but politely, to the waiter who was hurrying past him with a tureen of steaming soup. "Should we order a soufflé for dessert?" Wadleigh said, the perfect host. "I understand they do them very well here. Grand Marnier or chocolate?"

Craig saw Murphy come rolling through the door, looking, as usual when he entered a room, like a bouncer hurrying to break up a fight. Behind him was Sonia Murphy and Lucienne Dullin and Walter Klein. The tribes are on the move, Craig thought, the princes are meeting at the summit. He had lived in Hollywood too long to be surprised at seeing men who at other times denounced each other in the bitterest terms dining cordially together. In that tight, competitive world the lines of communication had to be left open at all times. He was sure that Murphy would not tell Klein that he had read *The Three Horizons* and that Klein would not tell Murphy that the script was on his desk. The princes were discreet and made their dispositions under cover of night.

Even so, he was relieved to see that the owner was seating the group near the entrance, well away from their own table. A long time ago, when Wadleigh was in fashion, Murphy had been his agent. When Wadleigh's bad years began, Murphy had dropped him, and Wadleigh, as might be expected, bore him no great love as a consequence. If the two men were to be seated near each other, with Wadleigh as far gone in drink as he was, the atmosphere would be less than friendly.

But Murphy, who scanned each room he entered like a ship's radar, spotted Craig, and while the others settled themselves at the table near the door, came rolling down the central aisle of the restaurant to greet him. "Good evening, everybody," he said, smiling at the girls and somehow excluding Wadleigh from the greeting. "I called you five times today, Jess. I wanted to invite you to dinner tonight."

Translated, that meant that Murphy had called once, had heard the phone ring twice, had nothing of importance to say to him, and had hung up, too impatient to get the operator back to leave a message. Or it might even mean that Murphy hadn't called at all.

"I had to go to Nice," Craig said, "to pick up Anne."

"God," Murphy said, "this is Anne! I wondered where you'd found the beauty. Turn your back for a minute on a scrawny little freckled kid and look what happens."

"Hello, Mr. Murphy," Anne said gravely.

"Sonia'd love to see you, Anne," Murphy said. "I tell you what. Why don't you and Miss McKinnon and your father come over to Antibes for dinner with us tomorrow night?"

"I won't be here tomorrow," Craig said. "I'm leaving Cannes." He saw Anne's questioning look. "Just for a couple of days. We'll do it when I get back."

"I'm not leaving Cannes, Murph," Wadleigh said. "I'm free for dinner tomorrow night."

"Isn't that interesting?" Murphy said flatly. "See you later, Jess." He turned and went toward his table.

"The gracious benefactor of the rich," Wadleigh said. "Bryan Murphy, the walking Who's Who. Gee, Jesse," he said with mock innocence, "I sure am glad you're still in there in the current issue." He was going to continue but stopped because Murphy was coming back.

"Jesse," Murphy said, "I forgot something. Did you see the *Tribune* today?"

"No," Craid said. "Why?"

"Edward Brenner died yesterday. A heart attack, the story said. It was short, the obit, I mean, but not too rough. The usual—After an early success, he faded away from the theatrical scene, etc. They mentioned you."

"What did they say about me?"

"Just that you did his first play. Pick up a copy of the paper and read it yourself. Do you have his address? I'd like to send a cable to his family."

"I have an old address," Craig said. "I'll give it to you in the morning."

"Okay," Murphy said. He went back to his table.

"Was he a friend of yours, Daddy?" Anne asked. "Edward Brenner?"

"Not recently." He was conscious of Gail's eyes fixed on him, searching his face.

"Wipe away a tear," Wadleigh said. "Another writer gone. Waiter," he called, "*encore une bouteille.* Let's drink to the poor bastard."

An old friend, an old enemy, now just a name in an obsolete address book, was dead across the ocean, and some ritual, some grave marking of the moment, was in order, but Craig contented himself merely with bringing the wine glass to his lips when Wadleigh raised his glass and said flippantly, "To dead writers everywhere."

Observing himself as though from outside himself, Craig noted that he ate his meal with relish and enjoyed the soufflé when it came. Brenner, he thought, would have been more demonstrative if it had been Craig's name in the obituary column.

He wondered if some months before he died, Edward Brenner's handwriting had changed.

By the end of the meal Wadleigh was very drunk. He had opened his collar, complaining that the restaurant was too hot, and had added up the check slowly, three times, and fumbled with the crumpled hundred-franc notes he pulled out of his pocket to pay the bill. As he stood up, he knocked over his chair.

"Get him out into the open air quick," Craig whispered to Gail. "Anne and I have to stop and say hello to Sonia Murphy."

But when they came to the Murphy table, even though Gail kept tugging at Wadleigh's sleeve to get him to move, he planted himself behind Murphy's chair as Sonia greeted Craig and Anne and Klein introduced Miss Dullin, who said, with a lilting French accent, that she had long wanted to meet *Monsieur* Craig. While Sonia Murphy was telling Anne how happy she was to see her again after all these years and to make sure to come over and use their cabana at the Hotel du Cap any time, Wadleigh, rocking gently back and forth on the balls of his feet behind Murphy's chair, began to hum loudly, "Hail to the Chief."

Klein, diplomatically, pretended to be amused. "I didn't know you were so musical, Ian," he said.

"Among my many talents," Wadleigh said. "Mr. Murphy is going to book me into La Scala next season, isn't he, Mr. Murphy?"

Murphy ignored him. "Give me a ring in the morning, Jess," he said, and turned back to his dinner.

"Come on, Ian," Craig said.

But Wadleigh refused to budge. "Mr. Murphy is a great little old booker, isn't he, Mr. Murphy? All you have to do is have a number-one best seller for a year and a picture that has just grossed forty million dollars and Mr. Murphy is almost a sure thing to get you a job writing a Lassie picture or a television commercial for aspirin. Don't you wish you were as successful a flesh-peddler as Mr. Murphy, Mr. Klein?"

"Indeed I do, Ian," Klein said soothingly. "And you can call me Walter."

"Cut it out, Ian," Craig said sharply. Wadleigh was talking loudly, and the people at the surrounding tables had all stopped eating and were watching him.

"I'll give you a hint, Mr. Klein," Wadleigh went on, still rocking gently and dangerously back and forth behind Murphy's chair. "I'll tell you the secret of Mr. Murphy's great success. You, too, can be rich and famous and invite girls to your cabana any time. It's not whom you represent that counts, it's whom you drop. You have to learn how to drop the deadwood, Mr. Klein, and drop them fast, before anyone else even knows they're droppable. One bad review and you drop. You'll never get as expert at it as Mr. Murphy, Mr. Klein, because he's got it in his blood, he's the genius of the age for dropping, he lets nothing stand in the way of his craft, not friendship or loyalty or talent, he's like the war-horse in the Bible, he sniffs failure from afar. The telphone rings, and he's not in. See, that's the secret. When the telephone rings and you know it's me, you're not in. The fact that you made thousands and thousands of dollars on me doesn't make any difference. You're not in, see. Remember that simple rule, Mr. Klein, and you'll go far, very far. Won't he, Mr. Murphy?"

"Take him away, Jesse," Murphy said.

"Come on, Ian." Craig tried to lead Wadleigh away. "Everybody gets the point."

But Wadleigh pushed away his hand. "I can't get to talk to Mr. Murphy on the telephone," he said, "so I talk to him in restaurants. I like to talk to Mr. Murphy about his profession—about all the jobs he could have suggested me for that he didn't suggest me for . . ."

Finally, Murphy turned around. "Don't make me laugh, Wadleigh," he said calmly. "With the way you've been going for the last ten years, I couldn't sell you for dog meat."

Wadleigh stopped rocking. His lips twitched. The entire restaurant was silent. Sonia Murphy was sitting with her head bowed, staring down at her plate. Lucienne Dullin was smiling slightly, as though she were being amused. The chances were that she couldn't follow Wadleigh's drunken English and probably thought it was a friendly, if rather boisterous, conversation. Klein was playing with his glass, not looking at anybody. Anne was the only one who moved. With a gasp, she bolted out the door. Wadleigh took a step as though to follow her, then suddenly turned and hit Murphy. The blow was aimed at Murphy's head but slid off and landed on Murphy's shoulder. Murphy didn't move as Craig threw his arms around Wadleigh and pinned his arms.

"Get that bum out of here, Jesse," Murphy said, "before I kill him."

"I'm going home," Wadleigh said thickly. Cautiously, Craig released him. Wadleigh walked stiffly out the door.

"I'll get a taxi," Gail said, "and take him to his hotel." She hurried after Wadleigh.

"I do like your friends," Murphy said to Craig.

"He's drunk," Craig said inanely.

"So I gathered," Murphy said.

"I'm sorry for everything," Craig said to the others.

"It's not your fault," Sonia said. "It's just too bad. He used to be such a nice man."

The noise in the restaurant was rising to its normal pitch as Craig went out into the street.

CHAPTER 13

WADLEIGH WAS ON the quay puking into the harbor. Gail was standing near him, ready to grab him if he started to teeter toward the black water. Anne was a few yards away from Gail, making a point of not looking at Wadleigh. Drunk as he was, Wadleigh, Craig was sure, was not vomiting because of the wine he had downed.

Watching Wadleigh bent over the harbor edge, his shoulders heaving convulsively, Craig felt his anger cool. He put his arm around Anne to comfort her. He felt her shiver minutely. "I'm sorry, Anne," he said, "to have let you in for something like that. I think that's the last dinner we'll have with Mr. Wadleigh for some time."

"The poor, poor, desperate man," Anne said. "Everybody is so hard on him."

"He asks for it," Craig said.

"I know," she said. "But even so."

Wadleigh stood straight, turned around, dabbing with a handkerchief at his mouth. He tried to smile. "There goes a hundred-franc meal," he said. "Well, it's been a nice party. Worth every penny of it. All right, Jesse, say what's on your mind."

"Nothing's on my mind," Craig said.

Gail hailed a taxi that was making a U turn in front of the restaurant. "I'll take you to your hotel, Ian," she said gently.

Docilely, Wadleigh allowed himself to be led to the taxi. The door closed behind him, and Gail and the taxi spurted off. No hints, no signals.

"Well," Craig said, "that's that."

Then Anne began to cry, hard, wracking sobs. "There, there," he said helplessly. "Just try to forget it. He'll probably forget the whole thing by morning."

"He won't forget it," Anne said between sobs. "Not for his whole life. How can people be so ugly to each other?"

"They manage it," Craig said dryly. He didn't want to show too much sympathy for fear of further tears. "Don't take it so hard, darling. Wadleigh's survived a lot worse things than tonight."

"You never imagine a man would behave like that," Anne said wonderingly as the sobs subsided. "A man like that who can write so beautifully, who seems so sure of himself in his books . . . "

"A book is one thing," Craig said. "The man who writes it is another. More often than not a book is a disguise, not a description."

"When the telephone rings, and you know it's me, you're not in," Anne said. The tears had stopped, and she rubbed her eyes with the back of her hand like a little forlorn girl. "What a terrible thing to know about yourself. I hate the movie business, Daddy," she said fiercely. "I just hate it."

Craig dropped his arm from her shoulders. "It's no different from any other business," he said. "It's just a little more concentrated."

"Can't anybody do anything for him? Mr. Murphy? You?"

Craig was surprised into laughing. "After tonight . . . " he began.

"*Because* of tonight," Anne insisted. "On the beach today he told me what good friends you'd been, what great times you'd had together, how marvelous he thought you were . . .

"That was a long time ago," Craig said. "The good times we had together. People wear away from each other. As for his thinking how marvelous I am—that comes as news to me. If you want to know the truth, I'm afraid it's something of an inaccurate statement about your father."

"Don't *you* run yourself down, too," Anne said. "Why should it only be people like Mr. Murphy who are sure of themselves?"

"Okay," he said. He took her elbow, and they started to walk slowly along the quay. "If there's anything I can do for him, I'll try to do it."

"You drink too much, too, you know," Anne said, walking beside him.

"I suppose I do," he said.

"Why do people over thirty try so deliberately to ruin themselves?"

"Because they're over thirty."

"Don't make jokes," she said sharply.

"If you don't have the answer to a question, Anne," he said, "you're liable to make a joke."

"Well, then, don't make them in front of me," she said.

They walked in silence, her rebuke between them. "God," she said, "I thought I was going to have such a wonderful time here. The Mediterranean, this great city, all these famous, talented people . . . " Being with you." She shook her head sadly. "I guess you shouldn't expect *anything* in advance."

"It's only one night, Anne," he said. "It's bound to get better."

"You're leaving tomorrow," she said. "You didn't tell me."

"It came up suddenly," he said.

"Can I come with you?"

"I'm afraid not."

"I won't ask why," she said.

"It's only for a day or two," he said uncomfortably.

They walked in silence, listening to the lapping of the harbor water against the boats tied up along the quay.

"Wouldn't it be nice," Anne said, "to get on one of these boats and just sail off?"

"What have *you* got to run away from?"

"Plenty," she said quietly.

"Do you want to talk about it?"

"When you come back," she said.

Women, at all ages, he thought, have the knack of making you feel you are deserting them even when you are only going down to the corner for ten minutes for a pack of cigarettes. "Anne," he said, "I have an idea. While I'm gone, why don't you move over to Cap d'Antibes? The swimming's better, and you can use the Murphys' cabana and . . . "

"I don't need any chaperone," Anne said harshly.

"I wasn't thinking of chaperones," Craig said, although he realized now that she had used the word that was exactly what had been at the back of his mind. "It was just that I thought you'd enjoy it more there, you'd have someone to talk to . . . "

"I'll find somebody to talk to right here," she said. "Anyway, I want to see a lot of movies. It's funny, I love to see movies. I just hate what it does to the people who make them."

A car with two women in it came up alongside the quay and slowed down. The woman nearest them smiled invitingly. Craig ignored her, and the car moved off.

"They're prostitutes," Anne said, "aren't they?"

"Yes."

"In the temples of ancient Greece," Anne said, "they prostituted themselves to strangers before the altars."

"The altars have changed since then," Craig said. Don't walk alone at night, Gail had told Anne when they had met on the steps of the hotel. Don't walk with your father, either, she should have added. Even whores, he thought angrily, should observe *some* rules.

"Have you ever gone with one of them?" Anne asked.

"No," he lied.

"If I were a man," Anne said, "I think I'd be tempted to try."

"Why?"

"Just once, to see what it was like," she said. Craig remembered a book he had read when he was young, *Jurgen,* by James Branch Cabell. He had read it because it was supposed to be dirty. The hero kept saying, "My name is Jurgen, and I will taste any drink once." Poor Cabell, who had been sure of his fame ("Tell the rabble/My name is Cabell," he had announced from what he had considered his enduring and disdainful eminence), poor Cabell, dead, discounted, forgotten even before his death, might now find consolation in the fact that a whole generation so many years later was living by his hero's disastrous slogan, was tasting any drink once, trying any drug once, any political position, any man or woman, once.

"Maybe," Anne said with a gesture of her head for the disappearing red lights of the whores' car, "maybe it would help define things."

"What things?"

"Love, maybe."

"Do you think that needs definition?"

"Of course," Anne said. "Don't you?"

"Not really."

"You're lucky," she said. "If you really believe that. Do you think they're having an affair?"

"Who?" Craig asked, although he knew whom she meant.

"Gail and Ian Wadleigh."

"Why do you ask?"

"I don't know," she said. "The way they behave together. As though there's something between them."

"No," he said. "I don't think so."

Actually, he thought, I refuse to think so.

"She's a cool girl, isn't she, Gail?" Anne said.

"I don't know what people mean by cool anymore," he said.

"She goes her own way," Anne said, "she doesn't depend on anyone. And she's beautiful, and she doesn't make anything of it. Of course, I only met her today, and I may be way off base, but she gives you the feeling that she makes people live up to the way she wants them to be."

"Do you think she wanted Wadleigh to end up the night puking his guts out because he behaved like a fool?"

"Probably," Anne said. "Indirectly, she cares for him, and she wanted him to see for himself what a dead end he'd reached."

"I think you're giving her more credit than she deserves," he said.

"Maybe," Anne admitted. "Still, I wish I could be like her. Cool, above things, knowing what she wants. And getting it. And getting it on her own terms." She paused for a moment. "Are you having an affair with her?"

"No," he said. "Why would you think so?"

"I just asked," Anne said offhandedly. She shivered a little. "It's getting cold, I'd like to go back to the hotel and go to bed. I've had a long day."

But when they got back to the hotel, she decided it was too early to go to bed and came up to his apartment with him for a nightcap. She also wanted to get a copy of his script, she said.

If Gail knocked on the door while Anne was there, Craig thought ironically as he poured the whiskies and soda, they could have a nice little family get-together. He could start the evening off on the right foot by saying, "Gail, Anne has some interesting questions she'd like to ask you." Gail would probably answer them, too. In detail.

Anne was staring at the title page of the script when he brought her her drink. "Who's Malcolm Harte?" she asked.

"A man I knew during the war," Craig said. "He's dead."

"I thought you said you wrote the script yourself."

"I did." He was sorry that he had been so careless on the trip back from the airport and had told her he had done the writing himself. Now he would be forced to explain.

"Then what's another man's name doing on it?"

"I guess you could call it my *nom de plume,*" he said.

"What do you need a *nom de plume* for?"

"Business reasons," he said.

She made a face. "Are you ashamed of it?" She tapped the script.

"I don't know. Yet," he said.

"I don't like it," she said. "There's something shady about it."

"I think you're being a little too fine." He was embarrassed by the turn the conversation had taken. "It's in an old and honorable tradition. After all, a pretty good writer by the name of Samuel Clemens signed his books Mark Twain." He saw by the set of her lips that this had not convinced her. "I'll tell you the truth," he said. "It comes from uncertainty. Put it more bluntly. From fear. I've never written anything before, and I haven't the faintest notion of how good or bad it is. Until I get some opinions on it, I feel safer hiding behind another man's name. You can understand that, can't you?"

"I can understand it," she said. "But it still strikes me as wrong."

"Let me be a judge of what's right and what's wrong, Anne," he said with a firmness he didn't feel. At this stage of his life he was not prepared to live up to the dictates of his twenty-year-old daughter's stainless-steel conscience.

"Okay," Anne said, hurt, "if you don't want me to say what I think, I'll shut up." She put the script down on the desk.

"Anne, darling," he said gently, "of course I want you to say what you think. And I want to say what *I* think. Fair enough?"

She smiled. "You think I'm a brat, don't you?"

"Sometimes."

"I guess I am," she said. She kissed his cheek. "Sometimes." She raised her glass. "Cheers."

"Cheers," he said.

She took a long swallow of her whisky. "Mmmm," she said appreciatively. He remembered watching her drink her milk before bedtime when she was a little girl. She looked around at the large room. "Isn't this awfully expensive?"

"Awfully," he said.

"Mummy says you're going to wind up a pauper."

"Mummy is probably right."

"She says you're wildly extravagant."

"She should know," he said.

"She keeps asking me if I take drugs." Anne was obviously waiting for him to ask the same question.

"I take it for granted, from all I see and hear," he said, "that every student in every college in America has smoked pot at one time or another. I imagine that includes you."

"I imagine it does," Anne said.

"I also imagine that you're too smart to fool around with anything else. And that takes care of that," he said. "And now let's call a moratorium on Mummy, shall we?"

"You know what I was thinking all through dinner, looking at you?" Anne said. "I was thinking what a handsome man you are. With all your hair and not fat and those lines of wear and tear in your face. Like a retired gladiator, a little delicate now from old wounds."

He laughed.

"*Noble* wear and tear," she said quickly. "As though you'd learned a lot and that's why the lines were there. You're the best-looking man I've seen since I came here—"

"You've only been here a few hours," he said. But he couldn't help sounding pleased. Fatuously pleased, he told himself. "Give yourself a couple of days."

"And I wasn't the only one," she said. "Every lady in that restaurant looked at you in that certain way ladies have—that little butterball, Miss Sorel, that fabulous French actress, even Sonia Murphy, even Gail McKinnon."

"I must say, I didn't notice it." He was being honest. He had had other problems to think about during and after dinner.

"That's one of the great things about you," Anne said earnestly. "You don't notice it. I love coming into a room with you and everybody is looking at you like that and you not noticing it. I have a confession to make—" she said, sinking back luxuriously in an easy chair. "I never thought I'd grow up enough to be able to talk to you the way I've done today and tonight. Are you glad I came?"

For an answer he went over and leaned down and kissed the top of her hair.

She grinned, looking suddenly boyish. "Someday," she said, "you're going to make some girl a good father."

The telephone rang. He looked at his watch. It was nearly midnight. He didn't move. The telephone rang again.

"Aren't you going to answer it?" Anne asked.

"I'll probably be happier if I don't," he said. But he went over and picked up the instrument. It was the concierge. He wanted to know if Miss Craig was with him, there was a call for her from the United States.

"It's for you, Anne," he said. "From the United States." He saw Anne's face become sullen. "Do you want to take it here or in the bedroom?"

Anne hesitated, then stood up ad placed her drink carefully on the table beside her chair. "In the bedroom, please."

"Put it on the other phone, please," Craig told the concierge.

Anne went into the bedroom, closing the door behind her. A moment later he heard the phone ring there and then the muffled sound of her voice.

Holding his glass, he went to the window, opened it, and stepped out onto the balcony to make sure he didn't overhear Anne's conversation. The Croisette was still full of people and cars, but it was too cold for anybody to be sitting on the terrace. There was a long swell coming in, and the sea was breaking heavily on the beach, the white of the foam ghostly in the reflected lights of the city. *Sophocles, long ago,/ Heard it on the Aegean,* he recited to himself, *and it brought,/Into his mind the turbid ebb and flow of human misery.* What ebbing and flowing and turbidity would Sophocles be reminded of listening to the sea in Cannes tonight? Who was ebbing, who flowing? Was Sophocles his real name? Or did he, too, use a *nom de plume? Oedipus at Colonus,* by Malcolm Harte, now dead.

He wondered if Penelope had also read the *Tribune* that day and what she had felt, if she had felt anything at all, when she had come across the name of Edward Brenner, another dead writer.

He heard the living-room door open and went in from the balcony. Anne's face was still sullen. Without a word she picked up her drink and finished it with one swig. Maybe, he thought, I am not the only one in the family who drinks too much.

"Anything serious?" he asked.

"Not really," she said, but the expression on her face didn't match her words. "It's a boy I know in school." She poured herself another drink. With very little soda, he noted. "Ah, Christ," she said. "Nobody leaves you alone."

"You want to talk about it?"

"He thinks he's in love with me. He wants to marry me." She plumped herself down despondently in the easy chair, cradling her drink, her long brown legs stretched out in front of her. "Prepare for visitors," she said. "He said he's coming over. Air fares're ridiculously cheap these days, that's the trouble. Anybody can follow anybody. One of the reasons I asked you to let me come here was to get away from him. You don't mind, do you?"

"It's as good a reason as any," Craig said noncommittally.

"I thought I was in love with him, too," she said. "For a hot month. I liked going to bed with him, maybe I still like going to bed with him. But marriage, for God's sake!"

"I know I'm being old-fashioned," Craig said, "but what's so awful about a boy wanting to marry a girl he's in love with?"

"Everything. You don't see Gail McKinnon rushing off and getting married to any half-baked jock college boy, do you? You don't see *her* sitting at home and popping television dinners into the oven, waiting for dear little hubby to come home from the office on the five-thirty commuters' train, do you?"

"No, you don't," he said.

"I'm going to be my own woman first," Anne said. "Like her. And then if I want to get married, my husband'll know what the rules are."

"Can't you be your own woman, married?"

"Not with that stupid jock" she said. "He's not even a good jock. He got a scholarship to play football, he was all-state in high school, or all-idiot, or something like that, and the first week in practice with the varsity team, he tore his knee to bits, and he can't even play football anymore. That's the kind of fellow he is. Ah, maybe I *would* marry him if he was smart or ambitious, if I thought he was going to amount to something. His father owns a grain and feed business in San Bernardino, and all he wants is to go into the grain and feed business in San Bernardino. San Bernardino, for God's sake! Bury me not on the lone prairie. He says he's not against women working. Until they have children, of course. In this day and age! With all the things happening in the world, wars, revolutions, crazy men with hydrogen bombs, Blacks being gunned down, women finally standing up and asking to be treated like human beings. I know I sound adolescent and naïve, and I don't know what the hell I expect I can do about any of it, but I know I don't want to wind up teaching kids the multiplication table in San Bernardino just because some big California lunk has got a fix on me. I tell you, Daddy, sex is the biggest goddamn trap ever invented, and I'm not having any of it. The worst thing is, when I heard his voice on the telephone saying, 'Anne, I can't bear it,' I felt as though all my insides were melting into one big stupid syrupy lump. Ah, shit! I wouldn't care if he didn't have a penny, if he walked around barefooted, if he only wanted to *do* something, join a commune and bake organic bread or run for Congress or be a nuclear physicist or an explorer or anything. I'm not all that freaked out myself, but I'm not all that square, either." She stopped, stared at Craig. "Am I? Do you think so?"

"No,' Craig said. "I don't think so."

"I just don't want to live in the nineteenth century. Ah, what a day," she said bitterly. "He had to come over and sit next to me in the library. Limping from his goddamn knee. With long hair and a blond beard. You can't tell what people are like from the way they look anymore. And now he's coming over here to moon away at me with his big baby blue eyes, flexing his goddamn biceps and walking around the beach looking as though he ought to be on a marble pedestal somewhere in Thrace. What do you think I ought to do—run away?"

"That's up to you," Craig said. "Isn't it?" So that's what had happened to her in the last six months.

She put her glass down roughly. Some of the drink spilled over on the table. She stood up. "Don't be surprised if I'm not here when you get back from wherever you're going," she said.

"Just leave word where I can reach you," he said.

"Have you got any pills?" she said. "I'm all jangled. I'll never get any sleep tonight."

Modern father, after having plied his daughter with drink during the evening and having listened without comment or demur to her description of her carnal relations with a young man she scorned to marry, he went into the bathroom and returned with two Seconals to assure her night's rest. When he was twenty, he remembered, he had slept undrugged, even under bombing and occasional shellfire. He had also been a virgin. Insomnia began with liberty. "Here," he said, handing her the pills. "Sleep well."

"Thanks, Daddy," she said, taking the pills and throwing them into her bag. She picked up a script. "Wake me in the morning before you leave and I'll come down and have breakfast with you."

"That would be nice," he said. He did not mention the possibility that there might be other company present for the same meal. Or that she might expect the waiter to look at her oddly. He took her to the door, kissed her good night, and watched her go down the corridor toward the elevator with her pills and her problems. Even now, he noticed, she was imitating, just a little, Gail McKinnon's way of walking.

He didn't feel like sleeping. He fixed himself a fresh drink, looked at it thoughtfully before taking the first sip. Was it possible that he did drink too much, as Anne had said. The censorious young.

He picked up a copy of *The Three Horizons* and began to read. He read thirty pages. They didn't make much sense to him. I've reread it too often, he thought, it's gone dead on me. He couldn't tell whether he should be ashamed of it or not. At that same moment, perhaps, Walter Klein in his castle and Anne upstairs in her single room were reading the same pages. He was being judged. The thought made him uneasy. He noticed that he had finished his drink as he read. He looked at his watch. It was nearly one o'clock. He still wasn't sleepy.

He went onto the balcony and looked out. The sea was higher than before, the noise of the waves greater. The traffic on the Croisette had diminished. American voices floated up, women's laughter. Women should be forbidden to laugh outside your window after midnight, he thought, when you are alone.

Then he saw Anne coming out from under the porte cochère. She was wearing her raincoat over the yellow organdy dress. He watched as she crossed the street. Two or three men who were passing by glanced at her, he saw, but kept on walking. Anne went down the steps to the beach. He saw her shadowy form moving close to the water's edge, outlined against the luminous gleam of the breakers. She walked slowly, disappeared into the darkness.

He checked an impulse to hurry after her. If she had wanted to be with him, she would have let him know. There was a certain point at which you no longer could hope to protect your child.

The young spoke candidly, endlessly, shockingly, about themselves to you, but in the long run you didn't really know any more about them than your father in his time had known about you.

He went back into the room, had his hand on the whisky bottle, when the knock came at the door.

When he awoke the next morning in the tumbled bed, he was alone. There was a note for him in Gail's handwriting on the desk in the living room. "Am I a better lay than my mother?" she had written.

He called her hotel, but the operator said Miss McKinnon had gone out.

All those big masculine writers were wrong, Craig thought, it was actually the vagina that was the instrument of revenge.

He picked up the phone again and called Anne's room and told her to come down for breakfast. When she came down, in her bathrobe, he didn't tell her he had seen her leave the hotel the night before.

When the waiter came in with the two breakfasts, he looked at Anne the way Craig had known he would look. He didn't tip the man.

CHAPTER 14

ON A CURVE, a Peugeot loaded with children and going ninety miles an hour nearly hit him head on. He swerved, just avoiding the ditch alongside the road. He drove slowly and carefully after that, wary of all Frenchmen on wheels and not enjoying the views of the vineyards and olive groves through which the road ran or the occasional glimpses of the sea off to his left.

He was in no hurry to get to Marseilles. He had not yet decided what to say to Constance. If he was going to say anything. He wasn't sure that he was a good enough actor to be able to pretend successfully that nothing had happened. He wasn't certain that he wished to pretend that nothing had happened.

The night had shaken him. This time there had been no coquetry or refusal. Wordlessly, in the dark, with the sound of the sea outside the window, Gail had accepted him, gently, gravely. Her hands were soft, her mouth sweet, her touch delicate and slow. He had forgotten the skin of young girls. He had expected avidity, or if not that, brusqueness, or even resentment. Instead, she had been . . . Well, he thought, the best word he could find was welcoming, profoundly welcoming. At the back of his mind a thought flickered at the edge of consciousness—*This is better than anything I've had in my whole life.* He recognized the danger. But some time during the night he had said, "I love you."

He had felt tears on her cheek.

And then in the morning there had been that harsh joke, the note on the desk. Who the hell could her mother have been?

As he approached Marseilles, he drove even more slowly.

When he got to the hotel, there was a note from Constance. She would be back some time after five, she had reserved a room adjoining hers for him, she loved him. And there was a message at the concierge's desk. Mr. Klein had called and would like him to call back.

He followed the clerk up to his room. The door between his room and Constance's was standing open. When the clerk had left and the porter had put down his bag, he went into Constance's room. Her familiar comb and brush were on the bureau, and a linen dress that he recognized was hanging outside a closet door to shake out the wrinkles. The rooms themselves were dark and hot and heavily furnished. There was a great deal of noise coming in from the street, even though the windows were closed.

He went back into his own room and sat on the bed, his hand on the telephone. When he picked it up, he started to give the number of Gail's hotel to the operator, then corrected himself and asked for Klein's number.

Klein answered himself. He was a man who was never more than five feet from a telephone. "How's the great man?" Klein asked. "And what is he doing in Marseilles?"

"It's the heroin center of the world," Craig said. "Haven't you heard?"

"Listen, Jesse," Klein said, "hold on a minute. I have to go to another phone. There're a lot of people in here with me and . . . "

"I'll hold," Craig said. There were always a lot of people in there with Klein.

A moment later he heard the click as Klein picked up the other phone. "Now we can talk," Klein said. "You're coming back to Cannes, aren't you?"

"Yes."

"When?"

"In a couple of days or so."

"You'll get back before everybody breaks camp, won't you?"

"If necessary," Craig said.

"I think it'll be useful," Klein said. "Look, I read that Harte script you sent me. I like it. I think I may be able to put something together. Right here. This week. Are you interested?"

"It all depends."

"It all depends on what?"

"On what you mean by putting something together."

"I think I may have a lead," Klein said. "With a director. I won't tell you his name because he hasn't said yes or no yet. But he's read it. And nobody's said a word so far about money. And there's many a slip et cetera . . . You understand."

"Yes," Craig said. "I understand."

"What I mean," Klein said, "is that I think it'd be worth your while to get back here as soon as possible. But there's no promises. You understand that, too, don't you?"

"Yes."

"Another thing," Klein went on. "I think the script needs work."

"I never heard of a script that didn't," Craig said. "If Shakespeare showed up with the manuscript of Hamlet, the first man he showed it to would say, 'I think this script needs work.' "

"I don't know who this fellow Harte is, but he's no Shakespeare," Klein said. "And I have the feeling he's shot his load on this draft. I mean, I think whatever director agrees to do it would want to bring in another writer for a second version. Before I talk to the director, I have to know what you thing about that."

Craig hesitated. Maybe, the thought, this was the moment to announce that there was nobody named Malcolm Harte. But he said, "I'd have to talk it over with whoever was finally going to do it. See what his ideas are."

"Fair enough," Klein said. "One more thing. Do you want me to tell Murphy I'm handling this, or will you? He's bound to hear. And soon."

"I'll tell him," Craig said.

"Good," Klein said. "It's going to be a rough ten minutes."

"Let me worry about it."

"Okay. Worry. Can I reach you at the Marseilles number if something comes up?"

"If I move," Craig said, "I'll let you know."

"I don't know what's so great about Marseilles, for Christ's sake," Klein said. "We're having a ball here."

"I bet."

"Keep your fingers crossed, kid," Klein said, and hung up. Craig looked at the telephone. He who lives by the telephone, he thought irrelevantly, dies by the telephone. He supposed he should have been elated by Klein's reaction to the script. Not wildly elated but cautiously, quietly elated. Even if nothing ever came of it in the end, here was some proof that he hadn't been wasting his time entirely.

He picked up the phone again and asked for the Carlton. Anne must have read the script by now, and it might help to know what she thought of it. Also, good father, having left her with the problem of the young man arriving from California, perhaps he could offer some useful advice. If she asked him for any.

While he was waiting for the operator to reach the Carlton, he shaved and took a shower. He should look and smell his best for Constance. It was the least he could do.

He had to climb out of the shower when he heard the telephone ring. As he stood dripping, waiting for the operator at the Carlton to connect him with Anne's room, he looked at his wet, high-arched footprints on the worn carpet. At least I'm flatfooted, he thought. A man could be vain about the most idiotic things.

There was no answer from Anne's room. If she needed advice, she was getting it elsewhere. From Gail, most likely. He wondered what Gail would have to say to his daughter, how much she would tell her. What if she told her everything? And what, exactly, was everything? Cross that bridge when you come to it.

He went back into the bathroom and stood under the cold water rinsing the soap off.

He dried himself and dressed quickly. He needed a drink, he told himself. He hadn't brought a bottle along, and he would have to go to the bar. There was a certain amount of cowardice involved there, he acknowledged to himself. He didn't want to greet Constance in their rooms. Where she might expect him to get into bed with her immediately. Immediately was not for today.

The bar was dark red, blood-colored. There were two small Japanese men in identical dark suits looking over a thick bundle of mimeographed sheets of paper and speaking Japanese earnestly, in voices just above a whisper. Were they planning to bomb the harbor of Marseilles? He wondered how he could have hated small neat polite men like that as much as he had when he was a young man. *Banzai.*

He was on his second Scotch when Constance came into the bar. Red was not her color. He rose and kissed her. Her hair was a little damp from the heat. He should not have noticed. "You look beautiful," he said. Everything else could wait.

"Welcome, welcome," she said.

The word had an echo he would have preferred not to hear.

"I need a Tom Collins," she said. "He knows how to make them." She gestured toward the barman. She had been there before. With whom? Had there been tears on her cheek recently?

He ordered the Tom Collins and another Scotch for himself. "How many does that make?" she asked lightly.

"Only three," he said. Anne was not the only one who was concerned about his drinking. Next month he would go on the wagon. Just wine.

"I knew I would find you in the bar," she said. "I didn't even bother to ask the concierge."

"I have no mystery left for you," he said. "It's a bad sign."

"You have plenty of mystery," she said. "Never fear."

They were uneasy with each other. She picked up her bag and put it down, her fingers fiddling with the clasp.

"What're you doing in Marseilles, anyway?" he asked. Klein had asked him the same question. Was it possible that all the million inhabitants of the city asked each other every morning, "What are you doing in Marseilles?"

"One of my darling Youths is in trouble," she said. Verbally, she always capitalized Youth. The police picked him up in the Vieux Port with two pounds of hash in his rucksack. I pulled some wires, and they told me in Paris that if I came down and flung my charms around liberally, I might be able to get the idiot out of the French pokey some time before the end of the century. I've been flinging my charms around liberally for the whole afternoon. The Youth's father has also promised to cable an interesting selection of money for the support of the French narcotic squad from St. Louis. We'll see. I'll have to hang around at least two days. God, I need a drink. And God, I'm glad to see you." She reached out and took his hand, squeezed it. She had strong fingers, smooth palms. Delicately made, she was a strong, smooth woman. Damp hair and all. Bold, intelligent, inquisitive features, direct, humorous green eyes, dark now in the red light of the bar. Much sought after by men. He had been told that by friends. Also by her. Active in the service. She had a bad temper, a sunny smile, was easily hurt, quick to hurt in return. Always something for a man to think about. Take nothing for granted. How many men had she abandoned? He would have to ask some day. Not in Marseilles.

They touched glasses before they drank. "I needed that," she said after the first long draft. "Now tell me everything."

"I can't," he said. "We are surrounded by Japanese spies." Postpone with a joke.

She grinned. "Glad you came?" she asked.

"All my life," he said, "I have dreamt of meeting a girl in Marseilles. Now that I've done it, let's go someplace else. If you've got to hang around a day or two, anyway, there's no sense in staying here. If the money comes from St. Louis, they can call you."

"I suppose so," she said doubtfully.

"This hotel is death," he said. "And there's so much noise outside, we won't sleep all night."

"I didn't know you'd come here to sleep," she said.

"You know what I mean."

She smiled. "Where can we go? No Cannes."

"Forget Cannes. There's a place I've heard of," he said, "in a village called Meyrague. Somebody told me about it. It's a converted chateau on a hill. We can get there in under two hours."

"Have you ever been there with anybody else?"

"No," he said truthfully.

"On to Meyrague," she said.

They packed hurriedly, no time for love. It would be dark before they got to Meyrague as it was. He was afraid the telephone would ring before they got out of the room. The telephone didn't ring. The clerk at the cashier's desk was sullen but resigned. He was used to guests leaving his hotel suddenly. "You understand," he said in French, "I am obliged to charge you for the full night."

"I understand," Craig said. He paid both bills. The least he could do for an American Youth in the hands of the French police.

The traffic was bad as they started out, and Craig had to pay attention to the driving, and there was no chance for talking until they were outside the city limits, going north in the direction of Aix-en-Provence.

He sorted out the subjects in his head as they drove. Fidelity, parenthood, career, his wife, his daughter, Klein, Gail McKinnon. The mother of Gail McKinnon. Not necessarily in that order.

Constance sat beside him, her short hair blowing in the wind of their passage, a small contented smile on her lips, the tips of her fingers on his leg.

"I love going on trips with you," she said. They had been to the Loire Valley together, to Normandy and to London. Small, delightful voyages. Simpler than this one. He wondered if he was glad or sorry she had refused to come to Cannes with him.

"Did you talk to David Teichman?"

"Yes," Craig said.

"Isn't he a nice man?"

"Very." He didn't tell her what he had heard about the old man. Keep death out of the conversation on the road from Marseilles. "I said I'd be in touch. His plans're vague." He hurried past the subject of David Teichman. "Actually, somebody else may be interested in the script. I'll probably know when I get back to Cannes." He was preparing for departure. Constance took her fingers away from his leg.

"I see," she said. "What else? How's your daughter?"

"It would take all night to tell you," he said. "She's after me to quit the movie business. Altogether. She says it's cruel and capricious and the people're awful."

"Did she convince you?"

"Not quite. Although I more or less agree with her. It *is* cruel and capricious, and most of the people *are* awful. Only it's no worse and probably better than most other businesses. You get more bootlicking and lying in one day in any army, for example, than in a year in every studio in Hollywood combined. And there's more throat-cutting and double-dealing in politics, say, or selling frozen foods than there ever possiby could be on a movie set. And the end product, no matter how bad it is, can't do any more harm than generals and senators and TV dinners."

"I take it you told her you'd hang in there."

"More or less. If they let me."

"Was she happy about it?"

"At her age I think that she believes the idea of being happy is a betrayal of her generation."

Constance laughed ruefully. "God, I have it all ahead of me with my kids."

"So you do," he said. "Another thing my daughter told me—she's been to see her mother." He could feel Constance tense slightly beside him. "Her mother told her she'd been to see you."

"Oh dear," Constance said. "You don't have a bottle stashed away in the car somehwere, do you?"

"No."

"Should we stop somewhere for a drink?"

"I'd rather not," he said.

Constance moved a little toward her side of the car. "I hadn't planned to tell you," she said.

"Why not?"

"I thought it might disturb you."

"It does," he said.

"She's an attractive woman," Constance said. "Your wife."

"She did a very unattractive thing."

"I suppose you could say that. The Youths in the office got an earful." Constance shrugged. "I don't know what I would do if I'd been married to a man for over twenty years and he left me for another woman."

"I didn't leave her for another woman," Craig said. "I left her for her."

"It's hard for a woman to believe that," Constance said. "When you reach her age, in a situation like that, you're not likely to be completely reasonable. She wants you back, and she'll do everything she can to get you back."

"She's not going to get me back. Did she insult you?"

"Naturally. Can't we talk about something else? This is holiday time."

"My lawyer says she's threatening to name you in the suit for divorce," Craig said. "In the end she probably won't because I'll pay her off not to do it. But I thought you'd better know."

"Don't pay her off on my account," Constance said. "My reputation will survive."

He chuckled dryly.

"Isn't it dreary to think of—a poor little French detective standing outside my window all night while we tossed and turned in the steamy raptures of middle-aged passion?" Her tone was mocking and bitter. His wife, Craig realized, had accomplished at least part of her mission in the scene with Constance.

"You're not middle-aged," he said.

"I don't feel middle-aged," she said. "Tonight." They were passing a roadside sign. "Aix-en-Provence," she said. "Minstrels at the court singing to the sound of lutes. Tournaments of Love."

"I'll tell you if anything happens," he said.

"Do," she said. "Keep me posted."

Unreasonably, he felt, she was blaming him. No. Reasonably. After all, it was his wife. He had had more than twenty years to train her to behave politely to his mistresses.

A car came in from a side road, and he had to jam on the brakes. Constance put out her hand to brace herself against the glove compartment. "Would you like me to drive?" she said. "You've been driving all day, and you must be tired."

"I'm not tired," he said shortly. He stepped on the accelerator, although he knew he was driving too fast. For a while in the car, it was not holiday time.

The hotel was a chateau on top of a wooded hill, and it was warm enough to eat outdoors, by the light of candles, on a flagstone terrace overlooking the valley. The food was very good, and they had two bottles of wine and finished off the meal with champagne. It was the kind of place and the kind of dinner that made you understand why, for some part of your life, it was imperative to live in France.

After dinner they wandered down the road through the little forest, through patches of moonlight, into the village and had coffee in a tiny café where the proprietor had the week's football scores chalked up on a slate.

"Even the coffee is good," Craig said.

"Even everything," Constance said. She was wearing the blue linen dress because she knew he liked her in blue. "Happy you're here?" she asked.

"Uhuh."

"With me?"

"Well," he said slowly, as though he was considering the question very carefully, "I suppose if you have to be in a place like this with a girl, you're as good a choice as any."

"Why, that's the nicest thing anybody has said to me all day," she said.

They both laughed.

"Spell Meyrague," he said.

"J-e-s-s-e C-r-a-i-g."

They laughed again. She looked at the slate with the scores on it. "Isn't is wonderful that Monaco won?" she said.

"It makes my week," he said.

"We've both had too much to drink," she said. "Wouldn't you say?"

"I would say." He gestured to the proprietor behind the bar. *"Deux cognacs, s'il vous plaît."*

"Aside from everything else," she said, "it speaks French."

"Among its many accomplishments," he said.

"Tonight," she said, "you look twenty years old."

"Next year," he said, "I'm going to vote."

"For whom?"

"Muhammad Ali."

"I'll drink to that," she said.

They drank to Muhammad Ali.

"Whom are you going to vote for?" he asked.

"Cassius Clay."

"I'll drink to that," he said.

They drank to Cassius Clay. She giggled. "Aren't we being foolish?" she said.

"I'll drink to that," he said. He gestured toward the bar. *"Encore deux cognacs, s'il vous plaît."*

"Eloquent, eloquent," she said. "In several Romantic languages."

He stared across the table at her. Her face became grave, and she reached across to grip his hand as if for reassurance. He was on the verge of saying, Let's stay here all week, all month. And after that we'll take a year to cross the roads of France in the sunshine. But he didn't say anything, just gripped her hand a little more tightly.

"Did I spell Meyrague correctly?" she said.

"It's never been spelled better," he said.

On the way up the hill he said, "Walk in front of me for a while."

"Why?"

"I want to admire your glorious legs," he said.

She walked ahead of him through the woods. "Admire," she said.

The bed was huge. The moonlight came in through the open windows and the smell of the pine forest. He lay on his back in the silvery darkness listening to Constance moving around in the bathroom. She never undressed in front of him. It was a good thing, he thought, that Gail was not one of those girls who raked a man with her nails in the act of love. He had been marked in his time. Then he was displeased with himself for thinking of it. The treachery of memory, eroding the body's pleasure. He was determined not to feel guilty. Tonight's choice was not last night's choice. Each night to its own innocence. He had never sworn fidelity to Constance or she to him.

She glided across the room, a pale shadow, slipped into the bed beside him. Her body was precious to him, generous and familiar. "Home again," he whispered to her, erasing other memories.

But, later on, lying still, side by side, she said, "You didn't really want me to come to Cannes."

He hesitated. "No," he said.

"It wasn't only because of your daughter."

"No." He had been marked. Somehow.

"There's somebody else there."

"Yes."

She was silent for a moment. "A serious somebody else or an accidental somebody else?"

"I would say accidental," he said. "But I'm not sure. Anyway, it *happened* accidentally. That is, I didn't go to Cannes to meet her. I didn't know she was alive until a few days ago." Now that she had broached the subject, he was relieved that he could talk about it. She was too dear to him for lying. "I don't really know how it happened," he said. "It just happened."

"I didn't stay home alone in Paris every night since you were gone," she said.

"I won't ask what you mean by that," he said.

"It means what it means."

"Okay."

"We're not bound to each other," she said, "by anything else but what we feel for each other at any given moment."

"All right."

"Do you mind if I smoke a cigarette?"

"I always mind if anybody smokes a cigarette."

"I promise not to come down with cancer tonight." She got out of bed, put on a robe, and went to the dresser. He saw the flare of the match. She came back to the bed and sat on its edge, her face from time to time lit by the glow of the cigarette tip when she inhaled. "I have some news for you tonight, too," she said. "I was going to save it for another time, but I'm in a chatty mood."

He laughed.

"What're you laughing at?" she asked.

"Nothing," he said. "Just laughing. What's the news?"

"I'm leaving Paris," she said.

Unreasonably, he felt that this was a blow aimed at him. "Why?"

"We're setting up a branch in San Francisco. There's been a big movement of the Youth back and forth to and from the East. Exchange scholarships—stuff like that. We've been negotiating with an organization in California for months, and it finally came through, and I'm elected. I'm going to be our private Window on the Awakening Orient."

"Paris won't be the same place without you."

"I won't be the same lady without Paris," she said.

"How do you feel about it?"

"About living in San Francisco? Curious. It's a pretty city, and I hear it's seething with cultural aspiration." Her tone was mocking. "It'll probably be good for my kids. Improve their English. A mother has to think about improving her children's English from time to time, doesn't she?"

"I suppose so," he said. "When are you going to make the move?"

"Sometime this summer. A month or two."

"I have lost another home," he said. "I will wipe Paris off my itinerary."

"That's loyal," she said. "Will you add San Francisco? They tell me there are some good restaurants."

"So I hear," he said. "I'll be there. From time to time."

"From time to time," she said. "A girl can't ask for everything, can she?"

He didn't answer her. "Foundations keep shifting," he said.

Then, much later, she said, "I don't pretend I'm wildly pleased by what you told me tonight. But I'm no child, and neither are you. You didn't expect me to make a scene, or throw myself out the window, or anything like that, did you?"

"No, of course not."

"As I said, I'm not wildly pleased," she said. "But I *am* wildly pleased about a lot of other things about us. Will you do me a favor?"

"Of course."

"Say, I love you."

"I love you," he said.

She stubbed out the cigarette, took off the robe, dropping it onto the floor, and got into the bed beside him, her head on his chest. "And that's enough talk for tonight. I'm not in a chatty mood anymore."

"I love you," he whispered into her tumbled hair.

They slept late and woke to sunlight and birds singing. Constance called Marseilles, but the money from St. Louis hadn't arrived yet for her Youth, and the narcotics man would not be in until tomorrow. They decided to stay in Meyrague another day, and he didn't call Cannes to let anyone know where he was. The day was going to be only theirs.

Then, the next morning, the money still hadn't come, and it was too nice to leave, and they stayed another twenty-four hours.

When he left her at the hotel in Marseilles the next morning, he told her he would take her to lunch in Paris on Monday. It looked, she said, as if she had a good chance to spring the Youth by nightfall. If she failed, she'd go back to Paris, anyway, and leave him to his fate. She had spent enough time in the south, she said. She was a working woman.

CHAPTER 15

"DAMN IT, JESSE," Klein was saying loudly over the phone, "I tried to get you ten times. Where are you now?"

"Cassis," Craig said. He had stopped off for lunch on the way back from Marseilles. He was calling from a restaurant on the harbor. The harbor was blue and toylike. The season hadn't begun yet, and there was a sleepy, tranced look about it, the boats all closed up under their winter canvas and everybody away for lunch.

"Cassis," Klein said. "Just when you need people, they're in Cassis. Where the hell is Cassis?"

"In between," Craig said. "What did you want to talk to me about?"

"I think I have a deal for you. That's what I want to talk to you about. When can you get here?"

"Three, four hours."

"I'll be here," Klein said. "I won't move all afternoon."

"Will you do me a favor?" Craig said.

"What?"

"Will you call Murphy for me and ask him to be at your place at five o'clock, too?" He could sense Klein's hesitation at the other end of the line, an intake of breath, an almost-cough.

"What do you want Murphy here for?" Klein asked.

"I want to spare his feelings as much as possible," Craig said.

"That's a new one, a client wanting to spare an agent's feelings," Klein said. "I wish I had some like that."

"I'm not sparing an agent's feelings," Craig said. "I'm sparing a friend's feelings."

"Murphy's read the script, of course," Klein said.

"Of course."

"And he said he didn't want to handle it."

"Yes."

"Well," Klein said reluctantly, "if you insist."

"I think it would be better all round," Craig said. "But if you don't want to do business with someone looking over your shoulder . . . "

"Hell," Klein said, "I'll do business with the Pope looking over my shoulder. I'll call Murphy."

"That's a good fellow."

"That's me," Klein said. "Despite all rumors to the contrary."

"I'll be there at five," Craig said. He hung up. While it was a fact that he was asking for Murphy out of affection for his old friend, he also wanted him in on the beginning of the talks about the deal. He knew that he himself was a poor dealer for himself, loath to press for advantage, and Murphy had always protected him in all the contracts he had signed. And this contract promised to be a complicated one. It was true that he had written *The Three Horizons* for other reasons than the money he might eventually make out of it, but he had been around the movies long enough to know that the more money you were paid, the easier it was to get your way in other matters. While the old formula, Money versus Art, often held, he had found that in the movie business, in his case, the formula, Money multiples Art, was likely to be the more valid one.

Craig went out and sat at a table overlooking the harbor. He was the only customer. It was restful, being the only customer, looking out at the sunny little blue body of water, thinking of lunch and Klein not moving for an entire afternoon. He ordered a *pastis* in honor of the fishermen and vintners of Cassis and leisurely examined the menu.

He ordered a dorade and a bottle of white wine and sipped at his *pastis*. The liquorice taste made the Mediterranean richer for him, brought back the memory of a hundred lazy afternoons. The time with Constance had been good for him. He thought of her fondly. He knew that if he ever used the word in her presence, she would be enraged. No matter. It was a fair enough word. People were not fond enough of each other. They said they loved each other, but what they meant was that they wanted to use each other, patrol each other, dominate each other, devour each other, weep for each other. Constance and he enjoyed each other, at least most of the time, and fond was as good a word as any for that. He postponed thinking of San Francisco.

He had said, "I love you," to Constance, and he had said, "I love you," to Gail McKinnon, and he had meant it both times, and perhaps he meant it simultaneously. In the sunlight, alone over a milky cold southern drink, it seemed easily possible.

He also did not deny to himself that it was pleasant to sit idly by the side of a deserted harbor and know that a man as involved in important affairs as Walter Klein had called him ten times the day before and was even now waiting impatiently for his arrival. He had thought that he had given all that up, but he realized now, with some satisfaction, that he was not immune to the joys of power.

Well, he thought, with everything that has happened, it wasn't a bad idea coming down to Cannes after all. He hoped that when he arrived in Cannes that evening he would discover that Gail McKinnon had left town.

When he reached Klein's house just a little after five, he saw a car with a chauffeur parked in the courtyard and knew that Murphy was already there. Murphy didn't like to drive himself, He had been in three accidents and had, as he put it, gotten the message.

Murphy and Klein were sitting by the side of the heated swimming pool, Murphy drinking. The last time Craig had been there, the night of the party, it had been Sidney Green, the director who had been hailed by *Cahiers du Cinéma* and who couldn't get a job, who had come out of the bushes to greet him after pissing on the expensive green grass of Walter Klein. For losers only, Craig remembered thinking. Today he didn't feel like a winner, but he didn't feel like a loser, either.

"Hi, boys," Craig said as he came up to the side of the pool. "I hope I haven't kept you waiting." He sat down quickly so that they wouldn't have to decide whether or not to stand up to greet him.

"I just got here," Murphy said. "A half ounce of Scotch ago."

"I explained a little of the situation over the phone to Murph," Klein said.

"Well," Murphy said gruffly, "if there's somebody damn fool enough to put up a million bucks for that script on today's market, more power to him."

"Where did you get that amount?" Craig asked. "A million dollars?"

"That's what I figure it'll cost to make," Murphy said. "Minimum."

"I haven't discussed money yet with anyone," Klein said. "It's all according how you want to make it and with whom."

"You told me a director had read it," Craig said to Klein. "Which director?"

"Bruce Thomas," Klein said. He looked quickly from one to the other of the two men, enjoying his moment of triumph.

"If Bruce Thomas wants to make it," Murphy said, "you can get all the money you need." He shook his head. "I would never have guessed Thomas. Why he would want to do something like this. He's never done anything like this before."

"That's exactly why," Klein said. "That's what he told me. Now," Klein said to Craig, "Thomas agrees with me, the script needs a lot of rewriting. What do you think, Murphy?"

"Yeah. A lot," Murphy said.

"And Thomas would like to bring in another writer," Klein said. "To work on it alone, preferably, or if there's a hitch, to work with this fellow Harte. Just what sort of deal do you have with Harte, Jesse?"

Craig hesitated. "No deal," he said.

Murphy made a startled noise. "What do you mean by no deal?" Klein asked. "Do you own the script or don't you?"

"I own it, all right," Craig said.

"So?" Klein asked.

"I wrote it," Craig said, "with my own little old fountain pen. There is no Malcolm Harte. I just picked a name at random and put it on the script."

"What the hell did you do that for?" Murphy said angrily.

"It's too complicated to go into now. Anyway, there we are," Craig said. "Let's move on from there."

"Thomas is going to be surprised when he hears," Klein said.

"If he likes the script with the name Malcolm Harte on it," Murphy said, "he's going to like it with the name Craig on it."

"I suppose so," Klein said doubtfully. "But it's bound to change his thinking somewhat."

"How?" Murphy asked.

"I don't know how, but somehow," Klein said.

"Where is Thomas?" Craig asked. "Why don't we call him up and have him come over?"

"He had to leave for New York this morning," Klein said. "That's why I was calling you so frantically. God, I hate it when people drop out of sight."

"You're lucky," Murphy said. "You only lost him for one day. I sometimes lose him for three months at a time."

"Well," Klein said, "I might as well give you the whole thing. First, as I said, he wants another writer. Now, hold your hats, boys. The man he wants is Ian Wadleigh."

"Oh, shit," Murphy said.

Craig laughed.

"You laugh," Murphy said angrily. "Do you see yourself working with Wadleigh?"

"Maybe," Craig said. "Probably not. What made Thomas pick on Wadleigh, of all people?"

"I asked him that myself," Klein said. "He just happened to see Wadleigh around, you know how it is down here. He talked to the guy by accident once or twice, and Wadleigh gave him a copy of his last book. I guess he couldn't sleep one night, and he picked it up and looked through it, and something caught him."

"Wadleigh's last book!" Murphy snorted. "It got the worst reviews since Hiawatha."

"You know Thomas," Klein said. "He doesn't read reviews. Not even his own."

"The perfect reader," Craig murmured.

"What did you say?" Klein asked.

"Nothing."

"Well, anyway," Klein said, "Thomas thinks Wadleigh's just the man to bring out the feeling he's looking for in the script. Whatever that means. Don't blame *me*, Jesse. I had nothing to do with it. It wouldn't occur to me in a million years to read a book by Ian Wadleigh. You know my position—my client wants him—I try to get him. How the hell was I to know that you're Malcolm Harte?"

"I understand," Craig said. "I don't blame you."

"The question is, What am I going to tell Thomas? Will you talk to Wadleigh at least? Let him read the script and see what his ideas are?"

"Sure," Craig said. "I have no objections to talking to him." While Klein had been talking, the idea of collaboration with Wadleigh had begun to seem attractive. The uncertainty that had made him put a *nom de plume* on the title page of the script had not been dispelled by Thomas's approval. The thought of sharing final responsibility was not unwelcome. And Wadleigh's talent, however tarnished, was a real one. Finally, he knew, there almost never was a screenplay that was completely the work of one pair of hands. "I don't promise anything," Craig said, "but I'll talk to him."

"There's another thing," Klein said. Now he looked embarrassed. "There's no sense in not putting it all on the table right from the beginning. You know, Thomas has produced his last two pictures himself. He doesn't need another producer and . . . "

"If he wants to do this picture," Craig said crisply, "he needs another producer. And that producer is me."

"Murph . . . " Klein looked appealingly to Murphy.

"You heard what the man said," Murphy said.

"Okay," Klein said. "There's nothing I can do about it, one way or another. I think the best thing we all can do is get on a plane to New York and talk it out with Thomas. And take Ian Wadleigh along with us and see if we can fit all the pieces together."

Murphy shook his head. "I'm due in Rome next week and London the week after that. Tell Thomas to wait."

"You know Thomas," Klein said. "He won't wait. He's got another commitment starting in January, and everybody'll have to work day and night to get this one in the can before then. One of the things he likes about your script, Jesse, is that it's easy to do and he can fit it in."

"Jess?" Murphy said. "You're really the one who has to do the talking. I can come in later."

"I don't know," Craig said. "I'll have to think about it."

"I'm going to call Thomas tonight," Klein said. "What should I tell him?"

"Tell him I'm thinking about it," Craig said.

"He'll love that," Klein said sourly. He stood up. "Anybody want a drink?"

"No, thanks." Craig stood up, too. "I have to get back to Cannes. I appreciate what you've done so far, Walt."

"Just out to turn an honest dollar for me and my friends," Klein said. "I don't know why the fuck you didn't use your own name."

"I'll tell you some day," Craig said. "Murphy, why don't you drive with me to Cannes? Tell your chauffeur to pick you up at the Carlton."

"Yeah." Murphy looked strangely subdued.

Klein walked out with them to the courtyard. They all shook hands ceremonially, and then there was the ringing of the telephone from inside the house, and Klein hurried in as Craig and Murphy drove off, the chauffeur following in Murphy's Mercedes.

Murphy was silent for a long time, staring out at the wild green countryside, the trees throwing long shadows in the evening light. Craig didn't speak, either. He knew that Murphy was troubled and was preparing himself for the conversation that had to take place.

"Jess," Murphy said finally, his voice low. "I want to apologize."

"There's nothing to apologize for."

"I'm a horse's ass," Murphy said. "An old horse's ass."

"Cut that," Craig said.

"I've lost my touch. I'm just no good any more."

"Oh, come on, Murphy. Everybody makes mistakes. I could tell you about some of mine." He thought of Edward Brenner in the empty theatre on the night after the final performance of Brenners' last and best play.

Murphy shook his head sadly. "I had that script in my hand, and I told you to forget it, and that little punk Klein got you the hottest director in the business for it with one telephone call. What the hell do you need me for?"

"I need you," Craig said. "Is that clear enough? I should have told you I wrote it myself."

"That makes no difference," Murphy said. "Even though it was a crappy thing to do to me. After all these years."

"I have my own problems," Craig said. "You know some of them."

"Yeah," Murphy said. "There's one big problem I could have helped you with—should have helped you with—a long time ago . . . And I didn't."

"What's that?"

"Your goddamn wife."

"What could you have done?"

"I could have warned you. I knew what was happening."

"So did I," Craig said. "In general. And late in the game. But I knew."

"Did you ever figure out why she did it?" Murphy asked. "I mean, she wasn't a nymphomaniac or anything like that. It wasn't as though she couldn't control herself. She isn't one of those women who throw themselves in bed with the boy who delivers the groceries, for Christ's sake."

"No, she isn't."

"Has it ever occurred to you how she made her choices?"

"Not really."

"If this is painful to you, Jess, I'll shut up."

"It's painful," Craig said, "and don't shut up."

"She always picked your friends," Murphy said, "people who admired you, people you worked with, people *you* admired."

"I can't say that I'm wild with admiration for her last choice," Craig said.

"Even him," Murphy inisisted. "He's a successful man, successful at something that you're lousy at, that you're ashamed you're lousy at. You went to him for advice. You trusted him with your money. Do you see what I mean?"

"In a way," Craig said, "yes."

"And all these people always wanted to see you, listen to you, you were the center of attraction. She was always in the background. There was one way she could stop being in the background. And she took it."

"And she took it." Craig nodded.

"I saw it a long time ago," Murphy said. "So did Sonia. And while there was still time to do something about it, I kept my mouth shut, I left you with your problem. And how do I make up for it?" He shook his head mournfully again. "I became another one of your problems." He looked tired, somehow diminished, sitting in the small car, his bulk slack in the flimsy bucket seat, his voice weary, his face sorrowful in the moving shadows from the trees that lined the road.

"You're not a problem," Craig said sharply. "You're my friend and my partner, and you've done wonders for me in the past, and I expect you to do wonders for me in the future. I wouldn't know what to do without you."

"Being an agent is a joke," Murphy said. "I'm a sixty-year-old joke."

"Nobody thinks you're a joke," Craig said. "Not me and certainly not anyone who has to do business with you. Snap out of it." He hated to see Murphy, whose style, whose reason for living, even, was to be robust, assured, overriding, in a mood like this.

"If you want, Jess," Murphy said, "I'll cancel Rome and London and fly to New York with you."

"Unnecessary," Craig said. "You'll come on stronger when they know they have to wait for you."

"Don't make any concessions before I get there." Murphy's voice was stronger now. "Don't give a fucking inch. Let me think about it overnight, and tomorrow you tell me exactly what you want and we'll figure out just how much of it you can get and how you can get it."

"That's more like it," Craig said. "That's why I told Klein to ask you to be there when I saw him."

"Christ," Murphy said loudly, "how I hate to have to split a commission with that little punk."

Craig laughed. Then Murphy laughed, too, sitting up straighter in the bucket seat, his laughter resounding in the little car.

But when they reached the Carlton, he said, "Jess, do you have an extra copy of the script? I'd like to read it again, just to see how stupid I can be."

"I'll have it for you tomorrow," Craig said. "Give my love to Sonia."

When Murphy got out of the Simca and walked over to his own car, he was striding imperiously, huge and dangerous, a terrible man to cross. Craig couldn't help grinning as he saw his friend hurl himself into the big black Mercedes.

The lobby of the hotel was crowded. There were already people in dinner jackets and evening gowns, dressed for the showing in the Festival Hall that night. Automatically, as he made his way to the concierge's desk, Craig looked around the lobby to see if Gail was there. There were many familiar faces, Joe Reynolds' among them, but no Gail. Reynolds' bruises had turned a streaky yellow. It didn't help his looks. He was talking earnestly to Eliot Steinhardt. A large young man with a blond beard was standing near the elevator, and Craig felt him staring at him. While Craig was collecting his mail and his key, the young man with the beard came up to him. "Mr. Craig?" he said.

"Yes."

"I'm Bayard Patty," the young man said.

"Yes?"

"I mean I'm Anne's friend. From California."

"Oh, how do you do?" Craig extended his hand, and Patty shook it. He had an enormous, crushing hand.

"I'm very pleased to meet you, sir," Patty said. He sounded mournful.

"Where is Anne?" Craig said. "Let's get her and have a drink."

"That's what I've been waiting to talk to you about, Mr. Craig," Patty said. "Anne's not here. She's gone away."

"What do you mean, she's gone away?" Craig said sharply.

"She's gone away, that's all," Patty said. "This morning. She left me a note."

Craig turned back to the concierge. "Has my daughter checked out?" he asked.

"Yes, *monsieur,* the concierge said. "This morning.,"

Craig looked through his mail and messages. There was nothing there from Anne. "Did she leave a forwarding address?" he asked the concierge.

"No, *monsieur.*"

"Patty," Craig said, "did she tell you where she was going?"

"No, sir," Patty said. "And please call me Bayard. She just vanished."

"Wait here for me, Bayard," Craig said. "Maybe there's a note from her in my room."

But there was nothing from Anne in his apartment. He went downstairs again. Patty was waiting near the desk like a huge, faithful, shaggy Newfoundland.

"Was there anything?" Patty asked.

Craig shook his head.

"She's a peculiar girl," Patty said. "I just got here yesterday. I flew over the Pole."

"I think we both could use a drink," Craig said. He felt very small walking beside the enormous young man along the corridor toward the bar. Patty was dressed in blue jeans and skivvy shirt and a light brown windbreaker. He limped a little, too, which made him even more conspicuous among the dinner jackets and jewelry.

"I see you're still limping," Craig said.

"Oh, you know about that." Patty sounded surprised.

"Anne told me about it."

"What else did she tell you about me?" There was a childish bitterness in the way Patty asked the question that was incongruous in a man his size.

"Nothing much else," Craig said diplomatically. He was certainly not going to repeat Anne's judgment on the bearded boy from San Bernardino.

"Did she tell you I wanted to marry her?"

"I believe she did."

"You don't think there's anything so all-out horrible or depraved about a man wanting to marry the girl he loves, do you?"

"No."

"It cost me a fortune to fly over the Pole," Patty said. "I see her for a few hours—she wouldn't even let me stay in the same hotel—and then, bang, there's a note saying she's leaving and good-by. Do you think she'll be coming back here?"

"I have no idea."

All the tables were full, and they had to stand at the crowded bar. More familiar faces. "I'll tell you," a young man was saying, "the British film industry has signed its death warrant."

"Maybe I should have put on a suit," Patty said, looking around uneasily. "I *own* a suit. In a fancy place like this."

"Not necessary," Craig said. "Nobody notices how anybody dresses anymore. for two weeks here you have a really open society."

"You can say that again," Patty said sourly. He ordered a martini. "That's one good thing about my leg," He said. "I can drink martinis."

"What's that?"

"I mean I don't have to worry about keeping in shape and all that crap. I'll tell you something, Mr. Craig, when I heard my knee go, I was relieved, mightily relieved. You want to know why I was relieved?"

"If you want to tell me." Craig sipped his whisky and watched Patty knock off half his martini in one gulp.

"I knew I didn't have to play football anymore. It's a game for beasts. And being my size, I didn't have the guts to quit. And another thing—when I heard it snap, I thought, 'There goes Vietnam.' Do you think that's unpatriotic?"

"Not really," Craig said.

"When I got out of the hospital," Patty went on, wiping the martini-damp beard with the back of his hand, "I decided I could finally ask Anne to marry me. There was nothing hanging over us anymore. Only her," he added bitterly. "What the hell has she got against San Bernardino, Mr. Craig? Did she ever say?"

"Not that I remember," Craig said.

"She's given me proof that she loves me," Patty said belligerently. "The most convincing proof a girl can give. As recently as yesterday afternoon."

"Yes, she mentioned something about that," Craig said, although the yesterday afternoon surprised him. Unpleasantly. Most convincing proof. What proof had *he* given yesterday afternoon in Meyrague? The boy's vocabulary had not yet emerged from the Victorian era. It was somehow touching. Anne had not been circumspect in her choice of words when she had spoken on the subject.

"I've *got* to go back to San Bernardino," Patty said. "I'm the only son. I've got four sisters. *Younger* sisters. My father worked for a lifetime to build up his business. He's one of the most respected men in the town. What am I supposed to say to my father—'You did it all for nothing'?"

"I find your attitude refreshing," Craig said.

"Anne doesn't," Patty said dolefully. He finished his drink, and Craig motioned for two more. He wondered how he was going to get rid of the boy. If music was the food of love, Patty was a high school band playing the school anthem between halves of a football game. He couldn't help grinning slightly at the thought.

"You think I'm foolish, don't you, Mr. Craig?" Patty asked. He had noticed the twitch of Craig's lips.

"Not at all, Bayard," Craig said. "It's just that you and Anne seem to have two different sets of values."

"Do you think she'll change?"

"Everybody changes," Craig said. "But I don't know if she'll change in your direction."

"Yeah." Patty hung his head, his beard down on his chest. "I don't like to say this to any girl's father," he said, "but the truth is I'm a shy man, and I don't make advances to anybody. Your daughter led me on."

"That's quite possible, Craig said. "You're a handsome young man and, as far as I can tell, a very nice one . . ."

"Yeah," Patty said without conviction. To cheer him, Craig said, "She even told me that when you walked on the beach, you looked as though you belonged on a marble pedestal in Thrace."

"What does that mean?" Patty asked suspiciously.

"It's very flattering." Craig handed him his second martini.

"It doesn't sound so damned flattering to me," Patty said, taking a gulp from his drink. "Actions speak louder than words, I always say. And your daughter's actions are mystifying, to say the least. Ah, what the hell—I know how she's been brought up . . ."

"How do you think she's been brought up, Bayard?" Craig honestly wanted to know.

"Fancy school in Lausanne. Speaking French. Famous father. All the money in the world. Talking to high-flying people all her life. I must look like a big Mr. Nobody to her. I suppose I ought to have more sense. Only when I think about her, I don't have any sense at all. You must have *some* idea, Mr. Craig—do you think she'll come back here or not?"

"I really don't know," Craig said.

"I have to be back in California in a week," Patty said. "They're operating on my knee again. They promise me I'll be able to walk okay in three months. So it's not as though she'd be marrying a cripple or anything like that. One year ago, if anybody'd told me that me, Bayard Patty, would fly six thousand miles across the Pole to come to France to see a girl for one week, I'd have told them they were crazy. I tell you, Mr. Craig, I don't think I can live without her." There were tears in the bright, clear blue eyes. "I sound dramatic, don't I?" he said, pushing an enormous hand at his eyelids.

"A little."

"I mean every word I say," Patty said. "She's got to get in touch with you, doesn't she?"

"Eventually."

"Will you tell her that she's got to phone me?"

"I'll pass on the word."

"What do you think of me, Mr. Craig? Honestly. You've lived through a lot. You've seen people come and go. Am I so bad?"

"I'm sure not."

"I'm not the smartest guy in the world. But I'm not the dumbest, either. It's not as though I'd be dragging her down. I'd respect her tastes. I'd be happy to respect her tastes. You've been married, Mr. Craig. you know. It isn't as though marriage has to be a prison, for God's sake. That's what she said, Anne, prison."

"I'm afraid my marriage hasn't given my daughters a very encouraging example," Craig said.

"I know you're separated," Patty said, "and I know you and your wife aren't on very good terms . . . "

"That's one way of putting it," Craig said.

"But that doesn't mean *every* marriage has to break up," Patty said doggedly. "Hell, my father and mother have had some pretty rough times. Still have. You should hear some of the arguments around my house. But that hasn't scared me off. Even having four sisters hasn't scared me off . . . "

"You're a brave man, Bayard."

"I'm not in the mood for jokes, sir," Patty said.

"I wasn't really joking," Craig said soothingly. It occurred to him that if Patty ever got angry he'd be a ferocious man to deal with.

"Anyway," Patty said, partially placated, "if you'd put in a good word for me with Anne when you hear from her, I'd deeply appreciate it."

"I'll put in a word," Craig said. "Whether it will be good or not only time will tell."

"It helps me to talk to you, Mr. Craig," Patty said. "It's a, well—a kind of connection with Anne. I don't like to impose, but I'd be honored if you'd allow me to take you to dinner tonight."

"Thank you, Bayard," Craig said. He felt he had to repay some devious family debt. "That'd be very nice."

There was a tap on his shoulder. He turned. Gail was standing there in the same print dress she had worn at Klein's party. They stared at each other for a moment in silence. "Buy me a drink," she said.

"Do you know Bayard Patty?" Craig said. "Gail McKin—"

"Yes, we've met," Gail said. The man who was sitting next to Craig got up from his stool, and Gail swung up and sat down, putting her bag on the bar.

"Good evening, Miss McKinnon," Patty said. "Anne introduced us," he explained to Craig.

"I see." Craig wished that Patty would disappear. "What are you drinking?" he asked Gail.

"Champagne, please," she said. She looked fresh, demure, as though she had never drunk a glass of champagne in her life or was ever capable of asking a man if she was as good a lay as her mother.

Craig ordered the champagne. "Bayard tells me that Anne left this morning. Do you happen to know anything about it?"

Gail looked at him queerly. She didn't speak for a moment but shifted her bag on the bar. "No," she said finally. "Nothing. Did you have a good time in Marseilles?"

"How did you know I was in Marseilles?"

"All movements are charted," she said. "Walt Klein was spastic because he couldn't reach you."

"It's a charming town, Marseilles. I recommend it to you," Craig said. "Yes, I had a good time."

Gail sipped at her champagne. "Are you staying on here in Cannes, Mr. Patty?"

"Call me Bayard, please. I'm not sure. I'm not sure of anything."

"We're having dinner together, Bayard and I," Craig said. "Would you like to join us?"

"Sorry," she said. "I'm waiting for Larry Hennessy. They're showing his picture tonight, and he's too nervous to sit through it. I promised I'd have dinner with him and hold his hand. Some other night, perhaps?" Her tone was flat, deliberately provocative.

"Perhaps," Craig said.

"There's going to be a party in his rooms after the showing," Gail said. "I'm sure he'd be delighted if you two gentlemen came along."

"We'll see how we feel," Craig said.

"I'm doing a piece on him," Gail said. "the other piece I was doing seems to have fallen through. He's a sweet man. And wonderfully cooperative." She sipped her champagne. "With other people it's so uphill. Ah, there he is." She waved toward the door. "Oh, dear, he's being waylaid by bores. I'd better go and rescue him. Thanks for the wine." She slipped off her stool and strode toward the door where Hennessy was talking volubly to two women and not seeming bored at all.

"I don't like to say this, Mr. Craig," Patty said, "and I only met her yesterday, but I have the feeling that girl isn't a good influence on Anne."

"They hardly know each other," Craig said shortly. "Look, I have to go up and shower and change. I'll meet you in the lobby in half an hour."

"Do you think I ought to put on my suit for dinner?" Patty said.

"Yes," Craig said. Let him suffer, too, that evening, with a tie around that bull neck. Craig paid for all the drinks and went out through the terrace entrance so that he wouldn't have to pass the door where Hennessy stood talking jovially, his arm around Gail McKinnon's shoulders.

It was almost an hour later that he went down to the lobby. Before starting to get dressed, he had picked up a copy of *The Three Horizons* and had glanced through it. Knowing that other people had read it, had liked it well enough to start the whole intricate and exhausting process of bringing it to life on the screen, made him review his work with fresh eyes. Despite himself, he felt the old excitement run through him as he read the pages. They were not dead to him anymore. Ideas for casting, for changes in the writing, for using the cameras, for the kind of music for specific scenes, flooded through his mind. He had to wrench himself away from the script to shave and take his shower and dress. He couldn't leave poor Bayard Patty standing in the lobby all night, bereft and pitiful in his suit, waiting for him.

He was annoyed with Anne's behavior but not much more than that. He wasn't really worried about her. She was a grown girl and could take care of herself. She had been cruel to Patty, and not being cruel himself, he disapproved. When he saw her, he would make that clear. Going to bed with the boy and then disappearing the next morning was a monstrous thing to do, but she was not the first girl to waver, then run away from a problem. Nor the first man, either. Nor the first member of the Craig family, if it came to that.

He called Klein and got Bruce Thomas's address in New York. Pleased with his own impatience, he told Klein that he would take the plane the next day.

"That's what I like to hear," Klein said. "Get the wheels moving. This Festival has run out of gas, anyway. You're not missing anything." There was the babble of many voices over the telephone. Klein was giving a cocktail party. He was getting his money's worth out of his five-thousand-dollars-a-month rent. Craig felt benevolent and unwontedly friendly toward the man. The world was full of useful people, and Klein was one of them. He would have to get Murphy to stop calling him that little punk.

He wrote out a cable to Thomas telling him he was arriving in New York and would call as soon as he landed. He thought of sending a telegram to Constance canceling their lunch date on Monday, then decided against it. He would call her in the morning and explain. He knew she'd understand. And approve. And New York was closer to San Francisco.

In the lobby, with Bayard Patty, standing next to him in a dark blue suit and necktie, he gave the cable to Bruce Thomas to the concierge and asked him to reserve a seat on a plane the next day from Nice to New York.

Patty looked forlorn as he listened to Craig's conversation with the concierge. "You're leaving so soon?" he said. "What if Anne comes back?"

"You'll have to take care of her," Craig said.

"Yeah," Patty said without conviction.

They got into the car, and Craig drove to Golfe Juan where they ate in a seafood restaurant built right on the beach. The sea was rough and growled at the pilings on which the restaurant was built. Patty drank more wine than was good for him and was garrulous. By the end of the meal Craig knew all about his family, his politics, his ideas of love and student revolt. ("I'm not a typical jock, Mr. Craig, I'll tell you that. Most of the things the kids are complaining about, they're right. But I don't go along with taking over buildings and bombing banks and crazy stuff like that. At least that's one thing Anne and I agree about. My father thinks I'm a wild-eyed Red, but I'm not. And there's one thing about my father—you can stand up to him like a man and he listens to you and tries to see your point of view. When you get out to California, you've got to meet him. I'll tell you something, Mr. Craig, I'm a lucky man to have a father like that.") At no point did he say that Anne was a lucky girl to have a father like Craig. He had seen two of Craig's movies and was polite about them. He was a polite young man. By the end of the meal Craig was certain that, politics or no politics, it would be disastrous for Bayard Patty if his daughter married him, but he didn't think he had to tell the boy that.

By the time they had had their coffee, it was still too early to go to the Hennessy party, which wouldn't begin until around midnight. And Craig wasn't sure that he wanted to go to the party or that Patty would be at ease there.

"How old are you?" he asked as they went out of the restaurant toward the car. Patty had insisted on paying for the dinner.) "Over twenty-one?"

"Just," Patty said. "Why?"

"Have you got your passport with you?"

"What do you want me to do?" Patty asked in a flare of belligerence. "Prove it to you?"

Craig laughed. "Of course not. I thought we might take in the casino. You ought to see some of the sights, anyway, as long as you're here. And you need your passport to get in." At the gambling tables he would be spared the boy's dejected confidences for an hour or two.

"Oh, I'm sorry," Patty said. "Sure. I have it in my pocket."

"Would you like to go?"

"What have I got to lose?"

"Money," Craig said. "That's all."

In the casino, Craig explained briefly about roulette and put Patty next to a croupier to help him out. He himself sat down at a chemin de fer table. He had only played the one time since coming to Cannes, the night he had loaned Wadleigh the three hundred dollars, the night Murphy had told him to forget the idea of putting on *The Three Horizons*. He chuckled to himself, remembering Murphy on the phone. As he sat down at the table, he thought comfortably, I'm thirty thousand francs ahead, I can afford to fool around.

From time to time, when they were making up a new shoe at his table, Craig went over to where Patty was playing. There was a sizable pile of chips in front of Patty and an intent and fascinated glint in his eyes. I have introduced him to a new vice, Craig thought. But at least, putting his money on the numbers and on the red or black, he wasn't mooning about Anne.

A place fell vacant at his table opposite his, and a woman sat down at it. She was a buxom woman in a bare-shouldered white silk dress that left a good deal of craftily engineered bosom showing. Her hair was marvelously set, and there was a considerable amount of heavy eye shadow. Thin, incongruous lips in the round, lacquered face were filled out dramatically in gleaming red. The deeply tanned skin of shoulders and bosom shone as though it had been oiled. Her fingers, armed with long curved crimson nails, were heavy with diamonds, which Craig, who was not expert at such matters, took for authentic. She had carried a pile of big chips from another table and placed them geometrically in front of her, tapping possessively on them with the long painted fingertips. She looked across at him and smiled cunningly, without warmth.

Now he recognized her. It was the plump woman who had been sunning herself when he and Murphy had passed on the way to the bar at the Hotel du Cap. He remembered the sweaty makeup, the naked, spoiled expression, the marks on the ill-tempered, self-loving face, he had thought, of grossness, devouring lust. The other side of the sensual coin. He was sorry she had come to the table.

He was sure she would win. She did. After a few hands he got up from the table, carrying his winnings. The pile of chips in front of Patty had grown somewhat, and Patty was hunched over the table in deep concentration on the spinning wheel.

"I've had it, Bayard," Craig said. "I'm cashing in. How about you?"

Patty seemed to come back from a long distance as he turned at the sound of Craig's voice. "Yeah, yeah," he said. "I might as well quit while I'm ahead."

At the cashier's desk Craig saw that Patty had won a little over a thousand francs. "How much is that in dollars?" Patty asked.

"About two hundred and fifty."

"What do you know," Patty said wonderingly. "As easy as that. Well, like they say, lucky in love . . . "

"Oh, come on now, Bayard," Craig said.

"Anyway," the boy said, "it helps pay for the trip." He folded the bills neatly and put them into an ostrich-skin wallet with gold corners. He stared mournfully at the wallet. "Anne gave this to me," he said. "In better days. It has my initials on it."

They walked back to the hotel. They were solicited several times by whores. "Disgusting," Patty said. "Open like that." He said he didn't want to go to the Hennessy party. "You know as well I do, Mr. Craig," he said, "parties like that aren't for me." He went into the lobby of the hotel with Craig just in case there was a message from Anne. There was no message.

"If I hear anything before I leave, I'll let you know," Craig said. He felt uneasy in the boy's presence, as though he were deserting him.

"You're a friend," Patty said. "I regard you as a real friend, Mr. Craig."

Craig watched the enormous form of his daughter's lover limp forlornly out into the night through the lobby doors.

I have done my duty as a father, Craig thought, as the boy disappeared. Or part of my duty.

The door to Hennessy's apartment was open, and the noise of the party could be heard all the way down the hall. It was the unmistakable noise of success. Hennessy's movie must have been very well received that evening. There was also the equally unmistakable smell of marijuana floating out through the open door.

In my day, Craig thought, we just got drunk. Was there what the professors of sociology called a value judgment there?

The room was crowded as Craig pushed in. Murray Sloan, the critic from the trade paper, was standing next to a big table ranged with bottles. He was not smoking marijuana. Faithful to an older tradition, he was loading up on free whisky. On a big couch against the wall on the other side of the room Gail was sitting next to the hero of the evening. Hennessy was in his shirt sleeves, in suspenders, beaming and rosy and sweating. He was sharing a joint with Gail, who looked remote and cool, beyond the noise and celebration.

"How did it go tonight, Murray?" Craig asked Sloan.

"As you can see." Sloan waved his glass at the chattering guests. "They slobbered over it."

"Is that what you're going to write?"

"No. I'm going to write that it was full of genial, rough American humor and that the audience reaction was all that the producers could hope for. It is a candidate for the highest honors." Sloan teetered a little, decorously, and Craig could see that he had done his drinking diligently. "Another thing that I am not going to write is that the money spent on hash tonight would have financed a small-budget pornographic film. Another thing I am not going to write is that if it wasn't for the free liquor, I would never go to another festival. And how are you, my friend? Is there any news of you I ought to put on the telex?"

"No," Craig said. "Have you seen Ian Wadleigh around?"

"No," Sloan said. "Old drinking companion. Notable by his absence. I heard about his big night with Murphy in the restaurant. He's probably crawled into a hole in the basement and pulled it in after him."

"Who told you about that?" Craig asked sharply.

"The wind speaks," Sloan said, teetering and smiling. "The Mistral mutters."

"Have you written anything about it?" Craig asked.

"I am not a gossip columnist," Sloan said with dignity. "Although others are."

"Has there been anything in any of the columns?"

"Not that I know of," Sloan said. "But I don't read the columns."

"Thanks, Murray." Craig moved away from the critic. He hadn't come to the party to spend his time with Murray Sloan. He made his way across the room toward Gail and Hennessy. Corelli, the Italian actor, was there, sitting boyishly on the floor, showing his teeth, with his inevitable two girls. Craig couldn't remember whether he had seen these particular two girls before or not. Corelli was sharing his cigarette with the girls. One of them said, "Pure Marrakesh heaven," as she exhaled. Corelli smiled sweetly up at Craig as Craig nearly stumbled over his outstretched foot.

"Join us, Mr. Craig," Corelli said. "Please do join us. You have a *simpatico* face. Doesn't Mr. Craig have a *simpatico* face, girls?"

"*Molto simpatico,*" one of the girls said.

"Excuse me," Craig said, being careful not to step on anyone as he made his way to Hennessy and Gail McKinnon. "Congratulations, Hennessy," he said. "I heard you killed them in there tonight."

Hennessy beamed up at him, tried to stand, fell back. "I am immortal tonight," he said. "Move over for the new Cecil B. DeMille. Isn't this a nice party? Booze, hash, and fame, with the compliments of the management."

"Hello, Gail," Craig said.

"Why, Malcolm Harte, as I live and breathe," Gail said. Craig couldn't tell whether she was drunk or drugged.

"What's that, what's that?" Hennessy said querulously. "Did I invite anybody else?"

"It's a private joke," Craig said, "between Gail and myself."

"Great girl, this kid," Hennessy said, patting Gail's arm. "Drank me drink for drink all night long while my fate was being decided on the Côte d'Azur. Interested in my early life. Up from slavery. Amateur boxer, truck driver, stunt man, pool hustler, bartender, publicity man . . . What else was I, dear?"

"Garage mechanic, farmhand . . . "

"That's it." Hennessy beamed at her. "She's got me down pat. Perfect American banality. I'm famous, and she's going to make me famous, aren't you, dear?" He passed his cigarette to Gail, and she drew in a long draft, closing her eyes as she did so.

This isn't any party for me, Craig thought. "Good night," he said as Gail opened her eyes and slowly let out the sweetish smoke. "I just wanted to tell you I'm leaving for New York tomorrow."

"Traveling man," Gail said, giving the cigarette back to Hennessy. "Good night, traveling man."

He was awakened by the ringing of the telephone. It seemed to him that he had never been asleep, that he was in the middle of one of those dreams in which you feel you are really awake but are dreaming that you are asleep. He fumbled for the telephone in the darkness.

"I knocked and knocked," Gail said, "but nothing happened." Her voice sounded as if she, too, were in his dream.

"What time is it?"

"Three A.M.," she said, "and all's well. I'm coming up."

"No, you're not," he said.

"I'm floating, floating," Gail said. "And I'm horny. Beautifully horny for the touch of my true love's lips."

"You're stoned," he said.

She giggled. "Beautifully stoned. Beautifully horny. Leave the door open."

"Go home and go to bed," he said.

"I have a joint with me. The most beautiful Moroccan kif. Leave the door open for me. We'll drift away together into the most beautiful Moroccan heaven."

He hesitated. He was fully awake now. the familiar dreamy caressing voice troubled him, traveled insinuatingly along the electric circuits of his nerves.

Gail giggled again. "You're crumbling," she said. "My true love is crumbling. I'm on my way up." There was the click of the telephone.

He thought for a moment, remembering what it had been like to make love to her. Young girl's skin. The soft, bold hands. It would be the first and last time he would ever know what the rest of the world seemed to know about drugs. Whatever else Gail was at the moment, she was certainly happy. If he was to share that secret and delicious happiness for an hour or two, who would be the loser? He was going to be on another continent in twenty hours. He would never see her again. Another ordered life was to begin for him tomorrow. He had one last night to enjoy the pleasures of chaos. He knew that if he kept the door closed, there would be no sleep for him that night. He got out of bed and went to the door, unlatched it. He was naked, and he stretched out on top of the bed sheets and waited.

He heard the door open, close, heard her come into the room. "Sssh, sssh, my true love," she whispered.

He lay still, heard her undress in the darkness, saw her face briefly in the flare of the match as she lit up. She came over to the bed, got in beside him without touching him, moved a pillow, sat up cross-legged, propped against it, the pinpoint of light glowing and getting larger as she pulled at the beautiful Moroccan kif. She handed him the cigarette. "Keep it down as long as you can," she said in her dreamy, remote voice.

He had given up smoking, from one day to the next, more than ten years ago, but he remembered how to inhale.

"Beautiful," she whispered. "Beautiful boy."

"What was your mother's name?" he asked. He had to ask quickly before the smoke began to take effect. Even the first lungful was already at work.

She giggled. "Full fathom five my mother lies," she said. She reached for the cigarette, touched his hand. He felt as though his body was being swept by a soft, warm wind. It was too late for questions.

They finished the joint slowly, alternating it from hand to hand. The room was misty with smoke. The sound from the sea outside was musical, a rhythmic, soothing resonance, an organ in a cathedral. She slid down beside him, touched him. they made love timelessly, tracklessly. She was all the girls, all the women of that southern coast, the plump, lustful woman stretched out on her belly in the sun with her legs apart, the blonde young mother at the pool, all of Corelli's bread-brown, bread-warm girls, Natalie Sorel, white-bosomed and dancing, Constance spelling Meyrague.

After, they did not sleep. Nor talk. They lay side by side in what seemed like an endless, perfect trance. But when the first light of dawn slanted in through the shutters, Gail stirred. "I must go now," she said. Her voice was almost normal. If he had had to speak, his voice would come from miles away. It made no difference to him whether she went or stayed, whether anyone went or stayed. Through a haze he watched her dress. Her party dress.

She leaned over him, kissed him. "Sleep," she said. "Sleep, my true love."

And she was gone. He knew he had a question to ask her, but he didn't know what the question was.

CHAPTER 16

HE WAS ALMOST finished with his packing. He moved with a minimum of luggage, and he could pack for anywhere in a quarter of an hour. He had a call in for Paris, but the operator had reported that all lines were busy. He had told her to keep trying.

When the phone rang, he picked it up without enthusiasm. He didn't relish having to explain to Constance that he wasn't going to take her to lunch on Monday, after all. But it wasn't Constance. It was Bayard Patty speaking in a voice that sounded as though someone had him by the throat. "I'm in the lobby, Mr. Craig," Patty said. "And I have to see you."

"I'm in the middle of packing and . . . "

"I tell you I have to see you," Patty said in that strangling voice. "I've heard from Anne."

"Come on up," Craig said, and told him the number of his apartment.

When Patty came into the room, he looked wild, his hair and beard disheveled, his eyes red-rimmed as though he hadn't slept in days. "Your daughter," he said accusingly. "Do you know what she's done? She's run off with that fat old drunken writer, Ian Wadleigh."

"Wait a minute," Craig said. He sat down. It was an automatic reaction, an attempt to preserve at least the appearance of reasonableness and convention. "It can't be. It's impossible."

"You say it's impossible." Patty stood over him, his hands working convulsively. "You didn't talk to her."

"Where did she call from?"

"I asked her. She wouldn't tell me. All she said was she was through with me, for me to forget her, she was with another man. That fat old drunken . . . "

"Hold on a second." Craig stood up and went over to the phone.

"Who're you phoning?"

Craig asked the operator for Wadleigh's hotel. "Calm down, Bayard," he said while waiting for the call to be put through.

"Calm down, you say. You're her father. Are *you* calm?" Patty strode over and stood close to him as though he didn't trust any message that Craig might give or receive and wanted to hear everything that was said with his own ear.

When the operator at Wadleigh's hotel answered, Craig said, "*Monsieur* Wadleigh, *s'il vous plaît.*"

"*Monsieur* Wadleigh *n'est pas là,*" the operator said.

"What's she saying?" Patty asked loudly.

Craig waved him to be quiet. "*Vous êtes sûre, madame?*"

"*Oui, oui,*" the operator said impatiently, "*Il est parti.*"

"*Parti, ou sorti,* madame?"

"*Parti, parti,*" the operator said, her voice rising. "*Il est parti hier matin.*"

"*A-t-il laissé une adresse?*"

"*None, monsieur, non! Rien! Rien!*" by now the woman was shouting. The Festival was abrasive for hotel operators' nerves. The line went dead.

"What was all that about?" Patty demanded.

Craig took a deep breath. "Wadleigh checked out yesterday morning. He didn't leave any forwarding address. There's your French lesson for the day."

"Now, what are you going to do?" Patty demanded. He looked as though he was going to hit something. Probably me, Craig thought.

"I'm going to finish packing my bags," he said, "and I'm going to pay my bill, and I'm going to drive to the airport, and I'm going to take a plane for New York."

"You're not going to look for her?" Patty asked incredulously.

"No."

"What kind of father are you, anyway?"

"I guess I'm the kind of father it's necessary to be these days," Craig said.

"If I was her father, I'd track him down and kill the bastard with my bare hands," Patty said.

"I guess we have different notions about fatherhood, Bayard," Craig said.

"It's your fault, Mr. Craig," Patty said bitterly. "You corrupted her. The life you live. Throwing money around as though it grew on trees. Running after young girls—don't think I don't know about that Gail McKinnon chick—"

"That's enough of that, Bayard," Craig said. "I know I can't throw you out of here personally, but I can get the police to do it for me. And even a very small French policeman can make things very uncomfortable for a very large young American."

"You don't have to threaten me, Mr. Craig, I'm going. Don't worry about that. I'm disgusted. With you and your daughter." He started to leave, then wheeled around. "I just want to ask you one question. Are you *happy* she's gone off with that old fart?"

"No," Craig said, "I'm not happy. Not at all happy." At the moment he didn't think it was necessary to remind Patty that Ian Wadleigh was quite a few years younger than Jesse Craig. "And I'm sorry for you, Bayard. I really am. And I think the best thing for you to do is take Anne's advice and forget about her."

"Forget about her." Patty shook his head sorrowfully. "That's easy to say. Forget about her. I'm not going to be able to do it, Mr. Craig. I know myself. I just won't be able. I don't know if I'll be able to *live* without her." His face contorted, and was shaken by an enormous sob. "How do you like that," he said in a small voice. "I'm crying." He almost ran out of the room, slamming the door behind him.

Craig passed his hand wearily over his eyes. He had looked at himself closely while shaving, and he knew that he didn't look much better thatn Patty this morning. "The son of a bitch," he said aloud. "The miserable son of a bitch." He was not speaking of Bayard Patty.

He went into the bedroom and resumed his packing.

His plane would be an hour late in leaving, the man at the check-in counter told him. The man said it graciously, as though he were bestowing a gift on Craig. Sixty minutes extra of the civilization of France. Craig went over to the telegraph desk and sent an apologetic telegram to Constance. He was writing out a cable to his secretary in New York telling her to meet him at Kennedy and get him a hotel reservation when he heard Gail's voice saying, "Good morning."

He turned. She was standing beside him. She was wearing the blue polo shirt, the white, hip-hugging jeans. Her face was hidden behind dark green sunglasses, uselessly large, like the ones she had worn the first morning and then thrown out of the car on the way back from Antibes. Perhaps she bought them by the dozen.

"What are you doing here?" he asked.

"Seeing a friend off," she said, smiling. She took off the sunglasses, twirled them carelessly. She was fresh and clear-eyed. She might just have come from a dip in the sea. She was a perfect advertisement for the benefits of marijuana. "The concierge told me when your plane was leaving," she said. "You don't have much time."

"The concierge was wrong. The plane's an hour late," Craig said.

"One precious hour." Her tone was mocking. "Good old Air France," she said. "Always time for farewell. Do we get a drink?"

"If you want," he said. Leaving was going to be more difficult than he had expected. He fought down the impulse to go over to the check-in counter and reclaim his luggage and tell the man there had had changed his mind about traveling. He gave the cable to the man behind the desk and paid. Carrying a leather envelope with the script of *The Three Horizons* in it and with a raincoat over his arm, he started toward the staircase up to the bar. He was sorry Gail had come. Seeing her there after the scene with Patty eroded the memory of their night together. He walked swiftly, but Gail kept up with him easily.

"You look funny," Gail said.

"I had an unusual night."

"I don't mean that. It's just that I've never seen you with a hat on before."

"I only wear a hat when I travel," he said. "It always seems to be raining everywhere when I get off a plane."

"I don't like it," she said. "It adds other facets to your character. Disturbing facets. It makes you look more like everybody else."

He stopped walking. "I think we said good-by last night better than we can possibly do this morning," he said.

"I agree," she said calmly. "Ordinarily, I hate fraying away from people in waiting rooms and on train platforms. It's like old tired rubber bands stretching and stretching. But this is a special occasion. Wouldn't you say so?"

"I would say so." They started walking again.

They went out to the balcony overlooking the field and sat at a small table. He ordered a bottle of champagne. Just a few days before he had sat on the same balcony waiting for his daughter to arrive. She had arrived. He remembered the copy of *Education Sentimentale* falling out of the canvas bag. He remembered being annoyed at the unattractive way she was dressed. He sighed. Gail, sitting across from him, did not ask him why he sighed.

When the waiter came with the champagne, Gail said, "That should do us for an hour."

"I thought you didn't drink until nightfall," he said.

"It looks pretty dark out there to me," she said.

They drank in silence, looking across the concrete to the blue sea at the field's edge. A ketch, heeling over the wind, all sails taut, foamed through its bow wave on its way toward Italy.

"Holiday country," Gail said. "Will you sail away with me?"

"Maybe some other time," he said.

She nodded. "Some other time."

"Before I go—" He poured himself some more champagne—"you have to answer one question. What was all that about your mother?"

"Ah, my mother," Gail said. "I guess you have a right to ask. My mother is a woman of many interests." She twirled the stem of her glass absently and stared out at the white sails beyond the landing strip. "She went to art school for a while, she dabbled in pottery, she directed plays for a little theatre group, she studied Russian for a year, she took a Yugoslav ballet dancer as a lover for six months. One of the things that she *wasn't* interested in was my father. He had a merchant's soul, she told him, whatever that is. Another thing she wasn't interested in, it turned out, was me."

"She sounds like hundreds of women I've met in the course of my life," Craig said. "What did she have to do with *me?* I was never a Yugoslav ballet dancer."

"May I have some more wine please?" Gail offered her glass. He filled it. The smooth muscles of her throat moved almost imperceptibly as she lifted her chin. He remembered kissing her throat. "She worked for you once. A long time ago. If I know my mother, you went to bed with her."

"Even if I did," he said angrily, "don't make it sound like incest."

"Oh, I didn't think of it that way at all," Gail said calmly. "I thought it was just a private joke. Between me and me. Don't worry, dear, I'm not your daughter."

"It never occurred to me that you were," he said. On the tarmac below a group of mechanics were working omniously on the undercarriage of the plane that was to fly him to New York. Perhaps he would never leave French soil. Or die on it. Gail sat across from him, lounging, aggravatingly at ease. "All right," he said, "what was her name, and when did she work for me?"

"Her name was Gloria. Gloria Talbot. Does that mean anything to you?"

He thought hard, then shook his head. "No."

"I suppose not. She only worked for you for a month or two. When your first play went on. She was just out of college, and she was hanging around the theatre, and she got a job in your office doing the scrapbooks, pasting up reviews and publicity stories about you and the poeple in the play."

"Good God, Gail," Craig said. "I must have hired and fired five hundred women since then."

"I'm sure," she said calmly. "But you seem to have had a special effect on dear old Mums. She just happened never to stop the good work. I don't imagine any of the other five hundred ladies got married and then continued to keep a scrapbook with every word written about you and every picture ever printed of you from 1946 to 1964. '*Jesse Craig to present new play by Edward Brenner this season. Jesse Craig signs one-picture deal with Metro. Jesse Craig to be married tomorrow. Photograph of Jesse Craig and wife leaving for Europe. Jesse Craig to . . . '*"

"Enough," he said. "I get the idea." He shook his head wonderingly. "What would she want to do that for?"

"I never got a chance to ask her. Her loyalties were tangled, perhaps. I only came across the clippings after she'd run off. When I was sixteen. With an archaeologist. I get postcards from Turkey, Mexico. Places like that. Twenty-two volumes bound in leather. In the attic. She was in such a hurry, she only packed an overnight bag. My father was only away for two days, she had to move fast. I was cleaning out the attic—my father decided he didn't like the house anymore, and we were moving—when I came across them. Many's the happy hour I spent after that rummaging through the history of Jesse Craig." Gail smiled crookedly.

"That's how you knew so much about me."

"That's how. Do you want to know where you spent the summer of 1951? Do you want to know what *The New York Times* said about you on December 11, 1959? Ask me. I'll tell you."

"I'd rather not know," Craig said. "So you took it for granted that I'd had an affair with your mother because of all that?"

"If you knew my mother," Gail said, "you'd know it would be natural to take it for granted. Especially for a romantic sixteen-year-old girl sitting in an attic with her mother off in the wilderness someplace with an archaeologist. If you want, I can send you a picture of her to refresh your memory. People say I look like her when she was my age."

"I don't need any picture," Craig said. "I don't know what sort of life you think I led as a young man . . . "

"You led an enviable life. I've seen the expression on your face in the photographs."

"Perhaps. But one of the enviable things about me at that time was that I was in love with the woman I later married, and I believed she was in love with me, and I never looked at anybody else all that time. And no matter what it may seem like to you after this week, I've never been a promiscuous man, and I certainly remember the names of all the ladies I've ever . . . "

"Will you remember mine in twenty years?" Gail asked, smiling.

"I promise."

"Good. Now you know why I was so keen on seeing you when I found out you were in Cannes. I'd grown up with you. In a manner of speaking."

"In a manner of speaking."

"It was a sentimental reunion. You were a part of my family. Also in a manner of speaking." She reached over and poured some champagne for herself. "Even if you never touched my mother and never even knew her name, you had some sort of weird permanent effect on her. She was obviously fascinated with your life. And just as obviously dissatisfied with her own. And in some foolish way one thing was connected to the other. You can't really blame me if I began to look on you with some disfavor. And curiosity. Finally, I knew I had to meet you. Somehow. Remember I was only sixteen."

"You're not sixteen now."

"No, I'm not. I'll tell you the truth— I was *offended* by you. You were too successful. Everything turned out too well for you. You were always in the right places. You were always surrounded by the right people. You lived in a bath of praise. You never seemed to say the wrong thing. As you got older, you never even got fat in your pictures . . . "

"Newspaper handouts, for God's sake!" He gestured impatiently. "What could that possibly have to do with reality?"

"That's all I knew about you, remember," she said, "until I walked into your room. It was all such an awful contrast with my foolish mother, with her pottery and her Yugoslav and my father, scraping away at a miserable living in a dingy office in Philadelphia. First, I wanted to see what you were like. Then I wanted to do you as much harm as I could. I made a pretty good start, didn't I?"

"Yes, you did. And now . . . ?"

There was the silvery tinkle of the public address system and a woman's voice announcing that passengers were to board immediately for the flight to New York. Miraculously, the group of mechanics around the plane had disappeared. Gail reached over and touched the back of his hand lightly. "And now I think you'd better go down and get on your plane."

He paid, and they walked past the bar and down the steps to the main hall. He stopped as they came up to the passport control booth. "Am I going to see you again?" he asked.

"If you come to London. There will be complications, of course."

He nodded. "Of course." He tried to smile. "Next time you write to your mother," he said, "give her my regards."

"I'll do that," she said. She dug in her bag. "I have something for you." She pulled out a thick envelope. "The concierge gave it to me when I said I was going to see you off. It came just after you left."

He took the envelope. He recognized Anne's handwriting. The letter bore a Nice postmark. He looked up at Gail as he stuffed the envelope in his pocket. "You know about Anne?"

"Yes," she said. "We had a long discussion."

"Did you try to stop her?"

"No."

"Why not, for Christ's sake?"

"I was hardly in the position to."

"I suppose you're right." He put his hands on her arms, pulled her toward him, kissed her briefly. "Good-by," he said.

"Good-by, my true love," she said.

He watched her stride brusquely toward the exit of the terminal, her bag swinging from her shoulder, her long hair streaming brightly behind her and every man she passed looking hard at her. He saw that she took out the sunglasses and put them on as she approached the door. He felt bruised and old. They were announcing the departure of his plane as he went through the passport gate. He touched the bulk of Anne's letter in his pocket. Reading matter for the Atlantic.

A decorously dressed tall African with tribal scars and his pretty buxom wife, swathed in gorgeously colored silks, were the only other passengers in first class with him. Craig always felt guilty about paying for first class on airplanes and always paid. The African and his wife were speaking in a language he couldn't understand. He hoped they spoke no English or French. He didn't want to talk to anyone before he reached New York. The man smiled politely at him. He half-smiled in return, a rigidity of the lips, and looked out the window. It was not beyond the bounds of possibility, he thought, that twenty years from now they would meet again, perhaps in the final confrontation between the races, and the man, or his son or daughter, would say, "I remember you. You were the white traveler who refused the smile of friendship offered in the plane at Nice. You are a racist colonial, and I condemn you to die."

You were the helpless addition of the accidental and unconsidered moments of your history. Unknowing, you impinged upon the population of your past. Carelessly, you made a joke about a man you had never met—oblivious of his existence, you took his mistress to dinner—for the rest of his life he did what he could to harm you. A silly, stage-struck girl wandered into your office and was hired by your secretary and was a vague, nameless presence in the background for a month or two when you were a young man. More than twenty years later you suffered—profited from?—the consequences of the acts, or the nonacts, of your early manhood. Nothing was lost, nothing forgotten. The man who had devised the first computer had merely organized the principle of inexorable memory into a circuit of wires and electrical impulses. Unnoticed passers-by noted your orbits, punched their private indestructible cards. For better or worse you were on file, the information was stored for eventual use. There was no escape. The process was perpetual. What would Sidney Green say about him among the unpaid-for *boiserie* in the Sixteenth Arrondissement? What would David Teichman's final instructions be concerning Jesse Craig before he died? How would Natalie Sorel refer to him in the mansions of Texas? What would be the reaction of Gail McKinnon's daughter upon hearing his name when she was twenty?

He looked hopefully toward the tall African across the aisle, but the man's face was averted. The engines started up, the demonic howl luxuriously muted by the sound-proofed hull. He took two Miltowns before the plane started to taxi. If he was going to crash, he was going to crash tranquilly.

He waited until after lunch was served before he opened Anne's letter. He knew that whatever she had to say would not improve his appetite.

There was no date on the letter and no address. Just "Dear Daddy . . ."

Dear Daddy put on his glasses. Anne's handwriting was difficult to decipher, and this was worse than ever. It looked as though it had been written while she was running down a steep hill.

"Dear Daddy," she wrote, "I'm a coward. I knew you'd disapprove and argue, and I was afraid you'd try to convince me and afraid you *would* convince me, so I'm taking the coward's way out. Just forgive me. Just love and forgive me. I'm with Ian. I thought a long time about it . . ."

How long was it, he thought. Three days, five? Well, perhaps when you're twenty years old, five days are a long time to figure out how to waste your life. He didn't remember.

"I won't go into the details," she wrote. "I'll just tell you that that night in the restaurant when Ian was treated so horribly by Mr. Murphy, I felt something that I'd never felt for anybody else in my life before. Call it love. I don't care what it's called. I felt it. Don't think it's just hero worship for a writer whose books I admire. And it's no schoolgirl crush. No matter what you may think, I'm past stuff like that. And I'm not looking for a father figure, which I'm sure you would have said if I had stayed to tell you. I have a perfectly good father. Anyway, Ian's only forty, and look at you and Gail McKinnon."

I am served, he thought, and well served. He asked the stewardess for a whisky and soda. It was a letter that needed alcohol. He looked out the window. The valley of the Rhone was hidden by cloud. The clouds looked so solid that you were tempted to believe that you could jump out and swim through them. He sipped at his whisky when the stewardess gave it to him and went back to the letter.

"Don't think for a minute," he read, "that I'm against anything you've done with Gail. I'm absolutely pro. After what you've gone through with Mummy, I wouldn't blame you if you took up with the bearded lady in the circus. And, good God, Gail is one of the best people I've ever met in my whole life. What's more, she told me she was in love with you. I said, of course, everybody's in love with him. And that's almost true. What you're going to do with the lady in Paris is your own business. Just like Ian is my own business.

"I know the arguments, I know the arguments. He's too old for me, he's a drunk, he's poor, he's out of fashion, he's not the handsomest man in the world, he's been married three times." Craig grinned sourly at the accurate description of the man his daughter was in love with.

"It's not as though I haven't taken these things into consideration," Anne wrote. "I've had long serious discussions with him about it all."

When? Craig wondered. The night he saw her leave the hotel and walk down the beach? On getting out of bed after having offered her convincing proof to Bayard Patty? He felt a pain at the back of his head, thought of aspirin.

"Before I told him I'd go away with him," Craig read on without aspirin, "I laid down conditions. I'm young, but I'm not an idiot. I've made him promise to quit drinking, first off. And I made him promise to come back to America. And he's going to keep his promises. He needs someone like me. He needs *me*. He needs to be esteemed. He's a proud man, and he can't go through life being derided, deriding himself, the way he's been doing. How many scenes like that one in the restaurant can a man go through in one lifetime?"

Oh, my poor daughter, Craig thought, how many women through the ages have ruined themselves under the illusion that they, and only they, can save a writer, a musician, a painter? The dread hold of art on the imaginations of the female sex.

"You're different," Anne wrote. "You don't need anyone's esteem. You're twenty times stronger than Ian, and I'm asking you to be charitable toward him. In the end, knowing you, I'm sure you will be.

"Sex is a big tangle, anyway, and you should be the first one to admit it." Craig nodded as he read this. But it was one thing to be forty-eight and come out with a truism like that, another to be twenty. "I know that I was mean to poor old Bayard, and I suppose he's got to you by now and has been crying on your shoulder. But that was just flesh . . ."

Craig squinted at the word, stopped on it. Flesh. It was a strange word for Anne to use. He wondered for a moment if Wadleigh had helped her write the letter.

"And flesh isn't enough." The scrawl dashed on. "If you've talked to Bayard, you must know that was impossible. Anyway, I never asked him to come to Cannes. If I'd married him, as he kept asking me to do (I nearly screamed, he was so insistent), in the long run I'd have been his victim. And I don't want to be anybody's victim."

Some day, Craig thought, I am going to make up a list for her. One thousand easy ways to be a victim.

"Don't be down on poor Ian for our sliding out the way we did. He wanted to stay and tell you what we were doing. I had the hardest time convincing him not to. Not for his sake but mine. He's in something of a daze for the time being. A happy daze, he says. He thinks I'm something extra-special, and he says he fell in love with me that first day on the beach. He says I'm so absolutely different from all the other women he's known. And he says he never dreamed I'd even look at him. He hasn't touched a drink in two days. Even before we left Cannes. He says it's a world record for him. And I read the part of the book he's working on that he has finished, and it's just wonderful, and if he doesn't drink, it'll be the best thing he's ever done. I'm convinced. And don't worry about money. I'm going to get a job, and with the money from the trust fund we can get along all right until the book is finished."

Craig groaned. The African with the tribal scars looked over at him politely. Craig smiled at the man, to reassure him.

"I'm sorry if I'm causing you any pain," Anne went on, "but later on I'm sure you'll be happy for me. I'm happy for myself. And you have Gail. Although it's more complicated with Gail than you think."

That's what *you* think, Craig almost talked back aloud to the page.

"There's a long story about her mother," Anne wrote, "that she told me but I haven't the time to go into now. Anyway, she told me that she was going to explain everything to you. Whatever it is, I'm sure it can't do you any discredit, no matter how it looks on the surface. I really am sure, Daddy.

"I'm still cowardly enough, even now with Ian at my side, not to tell you where we're going. Just for the moment I couldn't bear the thought of seeing you and having you disapprove of me in that reasonable, austere way you have. But as soon as we're settled in the States, I'll get in touch with you, and you can come and visit us and see for yourself that all is well. Please love me, Daddy, as I love you, Anne.

"P.S. Ian sends his best regards."

Best regards. Out of consideration for the African couple Craig refrained from groaning again. He folded the letter neatly and put it in his pocket. It would bear rereading.

He thought of Ian Wadleigh in bed with his daughter. "Miss," he said to the stewardess who was walking down the aisle, "do you have any aspirin?"

CHAPTER 17

BELINDA EWEN, HIS secretary, was waiting for him when he came through customs. He saw that she had not lost her disastrous taste for loud colors in her clothes since he had seen her last. She had been working for him twenty-three years, and it seemed to him that she had always been the same age. He kissed her on the cheek. She seemed happy to see him. He felt guilty because he hadn't answered her last two letters. If a woman has spent twenty-three years of her life working for you, how do you avoid feeling guilty when you see her?

"I have a limousine waiting for us," she said. She knew better than anyone that the money wasn't coming in as it had done for so long but would have been shocked if he suggested that a taxi would have done just as well. She had a fierce sense of their joint status. She screamed over the phone at agents when she discovered that scripts they had sent to the office had first been offered elsewhere.

It was a muggy, oppressive day, and it began to drizzle as they waited for the limousine to be brought around. He touched his hat grimly. The voices of the travelers piling into cars and taxis seemed harsh and angry to him. A child's screaming grated on his nerves. He felt tired, and the aspirin hadn't helped much.

Belinda peered at him anxiously, scrutinizing him. "You don't look well, Jesse," she said. He had been so young when he hired her that it had been impossible to ask her to call him Mr. Craig. "At least I thought you'd have a tan."

"I didn't go to Cannes to lie on the beach," he said. The limousine drove up, and he sank gratefully onto the back seat. Standing had been an effort. He was sweating, and he had to mop his face with a handkerchief. "Has it been as warm as this all along?" he asked.

"It's not so warm," Belinda said. "Now will you tell me why in the name of heaven you asked me to put you into the Manhattan Hotel? On Eighth Avenue, of all places !" He usually stayed at a quiet, expensive hotel on the East Side, and he could tell that in Belinda's eyes the change represented a demeaning attempt at economy. "I thought it would be more convenient," he said, "to be closer to the office."

"You're lucky if you're not mugged every time you go out the front door," Belinda said. "You don't know what Eighth Avenue is like these days." She had a sharp, aggressive voice. She had always had a sharp, aggressive voice, and for a while he had toyed with the idea of suggesting to her that she might go to a speech teacher. He had never quite had the courage. Now, of course, it was too late. He didn't tell her he had decided to go to the Manhattan only at the last moment, as he was writing out the cable to her in the Nice airport. The Manhattan was a brassy commercial hotel that he would ordinarily avoid, but he had suddenly remembered that he had lived there while he was putting on Edward Brenner's first play. With Edward Brenner. Now no longer writing plays. It had been called the Hotel Lincoln then. Presidents everywhere were being downgraded. He had been lucky at the Hotel Lincoln. He wished he could remember the number of the room. But he couldn't tell any of that to Belinda. She was too sensible a woman to pamper her employer's superstitions.

"You certainly didn't give me much warning," she said, aggrieved. "I just got your cable three hours ago."

"Something came up suddenly," he said. "I'm sorry."

"Anyway—" she smiled forgivingly. She had sharp little teeth, like a puppy's. "—anyway, I'm glad to have you back. The office has been like a morgue. I've been going mad with boredom. I even have taken to keeping a bottle of rum in my desk. I nip at it in the afternoons to keep sane. Don't tell me you've finally condescended to go to work again."

"In a way," he said.

"Hallelujah," she said. "What do you mean, in a way?"

"Bruce Thomas wants to do a script I own."

"Bruce Thomas," she said, impressed. "Oo, la, la." This was the year when everybody spoke the name of Bruce Thomas in a certain tone of voice, he noticed. He didn't know whether he was pleased or jealous.

"What script?" Belinda asked suspiciously. "I haven't sent you anything in three months."

"It's something I found in Europe," he said. "In fact, I wrote it myself."

"It's about time," she said. "It's got to be better than the junk we've been getting. You might have let me know," she said. She was hurt. "You might even have sent me a copy."

"Forgive me," he said. He reached over and patted her hand.

"Your hand is icy cold," she said. "Are you all right?"

"Of course," he said shortly.

"When do we start?" she asked.

"I'll know better after I see Thomas," he said. "There's no deal yet." He looked out the window of the car at the heavy clouds weighing on the flat landscape. "Oh," he said, "I wanted to ask you something. Do you remember a woman by the name of Gloria Talbot? I think she worked for us."

"Just in the beginning, for a couple of months," Belinda said. She remembered everything. "Absolutely incompetent."

"Was she pretty?"

"I suppose men thought she was pretty. My God, it was nearly twenty-five years ago. What made you think of her?"

"She sent me a message," Craig said. "Indirectly."

"She's probably on her fifth marriage," Belinda said primly. "I spotted the type right off. What did she want?"

"It was hard to say. I imagine she just wanted to communicate," he said. Talking, somehow, was a great effort. "If you don't mind, Belinda," he said, "I'm going to try to nap a little. I'm absolutely bushed."

"You travel too much," she said. "You're not a baby anymore."

"I guess you might say that." He closed his eyes and leaned his head back against the cushions.

His room was on the twenty-sixth floor. It was misty outside, and drops of rain slid down the window panes. The towers of the city were glints of glass, dim tiers of light in the wispy late-afternoon grayness. The room was hygienic and impersonal and had not been furnished for Russian nobility. He could hear horns from the Hudson River a few blocks away. There was nothing in the room to remind him of the lucky time with Brenner's play. It occurred to him that he ought to find out where Brenner was buried and lay a flower on the grave. Unpacking was an effort. The light clothes he had worn in Cannes seemed incongruous in the rainy city. There were many people whom he would call, but he decided to put it off to another day. Still, there was one call he had to make, to Bruce Thomas, who was expecting him.

He gave Thomas's number to the operator. The brisk, cheerful American voice of the operator was welcome after the shrill, harassed voices of the *standardistes* of Cannes. Thomas was cordial when he came to the phone. "Well, now," he said, "that was a surprise, your writing a script like that. A pleasant surprise." Klein had spoken to him. "I don't know exactly what we can work out, but we'll work out something. Are you busy now? Do you want to come over?"

Thomas lived on East Seventieth Street. The thought of trying to traverse the city was fatiguing. "Let's do it tomorrow, if you don't mind," Craig said. "The jet lag's got me."

"Sure," Thomas said. "How about ten in the morning?"

"I'll be there," Craig said. "By the way, do you happen to have Ian Wadleigh's telephone number in London?"

He could sense Thomas hesitating. "You know," Thomas said, "I suggested Wadleigh before I knew you'd written the script."

"I know," Craig said. "Have you talked to him yet?"

"No," Thomas said. "Naturally, I wanted to find out what you thought about it. But after Klein told me you didn't mind discussing it, I tried to get in touch with him. He's not in Cannes, and there's no answer at his London address. I've sent him a cable asking him to call me here. Wait a minute, I'll give you his number."

When he came back to the phone and gave Craig the number, Thomas said, "If you do find him, will you tell him I've been trying to reach him? And would you mind if I sent him a script? I've had some copies Xeroxed. There's not sense in his coming over here if for some reason or another he doesn't want to work on it."

"I think I heard somewhere that he's planning to come back to the States to live, anyway," Craig said. Somewhere. Flying over France, heading toward the English

Channel, the brave New World. *Dear Daddy.*

"That's interesting," Thomas said. "Good for him. See you in the morning. Have a good night." He was a nice man, Thomas, polite, thoughtful, with delicate manners.

Craig asked the operator for the London number and lay down on the bed to wait for the call. When he moved his head on the pillow, he felt dizzy, and the room seemed to shift slowly around him. "You travel too much," Belinda had said. Wise woman. Twenty-three years in the service. He was terribly thirsty, but he couldn't make himself get up and go into the bathroom for a glass of water.

The phone rang, and he sat up, having to move slowly to keep the room from spinning around him. The operator said that there was no answer at the London number and asked him if he wanted her to try again in an hour. "No," he said, "cancel the call."

He sat on the edge of the bed until the room steadied, then went into the bathroom and drank two glasses of water. But he was still thirsty. He was cold now, too, from the air conditioning. He tried to open a window, but it was nailed shut. He looked at his watch. It was six-thirty. Twelve-thirty tomorrow morning in Cannes. He had been up a long time, journeyed a great distance. He didn't remember ever having been so thirsty. An ice-cold glass of beer would do wonders for him. Maybe two. The next time he crossed the ocean, he decided, he would go by boat. America should be approached cautiously, in slow stages.

He went downstairs to the grill room, which was decorated with posters from plays. I am in a familiar arena, he thought. He remembered horns, the color of the sand in Saint Sebastian. He sat at the bar and ordered a bottle of beer, drank half the first glass in one gulp. The ache at the back of his throat subsided. He knew he should eat something, but all he wanted was more beer. He ordered another bottle, treasuring it, drinking slowly. By the end of the second bottle he felt pleasantly lightheaded. The grill room was filling up now, and he balanced the possibility of running into someone he knew and having to talk to him against the joy of one more bottle of beer. He decided to take the risk and ordered a third bottle.

It was nearly eight o'clock by the time he got back to his room. He hadn't had to talk to anybody. It was his lucky hotel. He undressed, put on pajamas, got into bed, and turned out the light. He lay there listening to the muted hum of the city far below him. A siren screaming past reminded him that he was in his native city. Ah, he thought regretfully as he slipped off to sleep, there will be no knock on my door tonight.

He awoke in pain. His stomach was contracting spasmodically. The bed was soaked in sweat. The pains came and went, sharp and stabbing. Christ, he thought, this must be something like what women go through in childbirth. He had to go to the bathroom. He put on the light, swung his legs carefully over the side of the bed, walked slowly into the bathroom, sat on the toilet. He could feel what seemed like gallons of hot liquid gushing out of him. The pain went down, but he wasn't sure he would be strong enough to get back to bed. When he finally stood up, he had to hold onto the shelf over the basin for support. The liquid in the toilet bowl was black. He pulled the chain. He felt a hot wetness dripping down the inside of his legs. It was blood, blackish red. There was no way in which he could control it. He wrinkled his nose in disgust. He knew he should be afraid, but all he felt was disgust at his body's betrayal. He got a towel and stuffed it up between his legs. Leaving his stained pajama bottoms on the bathroom floor, he made his way back to the bed and dropped on it. He felt weak, but there was no pain. For a moment he thought that he had dreamt it all. He looked at his watch. It was four-thirty in the morning. New York time, he remembered. Zone of blood. It was no hour to wake anyone. If he was still bleeding by eight o'clock, he would call a doctor. Then he realized that he didn't know the names of any doctors in New York. The penalty of health. He would figure it out in the morning. He put out the light and closed his eyes and tried to sleep. *If I die before I wake, I pray the Lord my soul . . .* Childhood formulas.

Anne's psychology professor had seen something in his handwriting. Had he seen this night in New York?

Then he fell asleep. He slept without dreaming.

He was bone-tired when he awoke, marrow-tired. But there was no more bleeding. It was almost nine o'clock. There was pale, smog-diluted sunlight outside the window. The city shimmered in a haze of heat.

He took the towel out from between his legs. He had obviously bled for a while during his sleep, but by now the blood was caked and dry on the towel. Old, unsolved, interior murders. He moved with care, showered for a long time but did not have the courage to turn the water cold. As he dressed, his body felt broken, as though he had fallen from a great distance.

He went downstairs and had breakfast among the tourists and traveling salesmen in the coffee shop. The factory taste of frozen orange juice. No Mediterranean outside the window, no daughter, no mistress across the table, no leer from the waitress. The coffee of his homeland was like dishwater. He made himself eat two pieces of toast for strength. No croissants, no brioches. Had he come to the wrong country?"

He read *The New York Times*. The casualty count was down in Vietnam. The vice-president had made a provocative, alliterative speech. A plane had fallen. He was not the only one who traveled too much. A critic he had never heard of scolded a novelist he had never read. Teams that had not been created when he still went to baseball games had won and lost. A pitcher who was nearly as old as he still made a living throwing the knuckle ball. The men and women who had died the day before were people he had not known. Informed now, he faced the day.

He went from the world of air conditioning out into the climate of New York. He winced on the sidewalk. Remembering his secretary's warning, he was wary of muggers. If he announced, I have bled this night, would a boy scout find him a taxi? He had no quarter for the doorman, so he gave him a dollar bill. He remembered when doormen were grateful for dimes.

Getting into the taxi was like climbing a cliff. He gave the address on East Seventieth Street. The taxi driver was an old man with a greenish complexion who looked as though he were dying. From the permit on the back of the driver's seat, Craig saw that the man had a Russian name. Did the driver regret that he, or his father before him, had left Odessa?

The taxi inched, spurted, braked, missed other cars by inches on its way across town. Near death, the driver had nothing to lose. Forty-fourth Street, going East, was his Indianapolis. He was high in the year's standings for the Grand Prix. If he survived the season, his fortune would be made.

Bruce Thomas lived in a brownstone with newly painted window frames. There was a little plaque near the font door that announced that the house was protected by a private patrol service. Craig had been there several times before, to big parties. He remembered having enjoyed himself. He had wandered once into Bruce's study on the second floor. The shelves of the study had been laden with statues, plaques, scrolls, that Thomas had won for his movies. Craig had won some statues, scrolls, and plaques himself, but he didn't know where they were now.

He rang the bell. Thomas opened the door himself, dressed in corduroy slacks and an open-necked polo shirt. He was a neat, graceful, slight man with a warm smile.

"Bruce," Craig said as he went into the hallway, "I think you'd better get me a doctor."

He sat down on a chair in the hall because he couldn't walk any farther.

CHAPTER 18

HE WAS STILL alive after three days. He was in a bright room in a good hospital, and Bruce Thomas had found him a soft-voiced old doctor who was soothing and taciturn. The chief surgeon of the hospital, a cheerful round man, kept dropping in as though he just wanted to chat with Craig about the movies and the theatre, but Craig knew that he was watching him closely, looking for symptoms that would mean that an emergency operation might be necessary at any moment. When Craig asked him what the chances were after an operation like that, the surgeon said flatly, without hesitation, "Fifty-fifty." If Craig had had any relatives the doctor could talk to, the doctor would probably have told him instead of the patient, but the only people who had come to his room so far were Thomas and Belinda.

He was under light sedation and suffering from no real pain except for the bruised places on his arms where the needles had been placed for five transfusions and for the varying intravenous feedings of glucose and salt. For some reason the tubes kept clogging, and the needles kept falling out. The veins in his arms had become increasingly difficult to find, and finally the hospital expert, a lovely Scandinavian girl, had been called in to see what she could do. She had cleared the room, even shutting the door on his private day nurse, a tough old ex-captain in the Nursing Corps, a veteran of Korea. "I can't stand an audience," the expert had said. Talent, in a hospital as elsewhere, Craig saw, had its imperious prerogatives. The Scandinavian girl had pushed and prodded, shaking her neat blonde head, and then with one deft stroke had inserted the needle painlessly into a vein on the back of his right hand and adjusted the flow of solution to it. He never saw her again. He was sorry about that. She reminded him of the young Danish mother by the side of the pool in Antibes. Fifty-fifty, he marveled, and that's what a man thinks of.

The worst thing was the headaches that came after the transfusions. That was normal, he was told. Naturally, in a hospital, pain must seem normal to the people who work there.

Thomas had been perfect. He visited the room twice a day, not overdoing his concern. "There's a good chance," he said on the third day, "that you'll be out of here in less than two weeks, and then we can get to work." He had not wasted any time. He had secured an O.K. from United Artists, and they were talking of a budget of a million and a half dollars for the picture. Thomas had already found a great old mansion in Sands Point where they could shoot on location. He took it for granted that Craig would be the co-producer. If he had heard the surgeon's fifty-fifty estimate, he gave no hint of it.

He was in the room on the third day when the door swung open and Murphy strode in. "What the hell is going on, Jesse?" Murphy asked loudly.

"What the hell are you doing here?" Craig said. "I thought you were in Rome."

"I'm not in Rome," Murphy said. "Hi, Bruce. Are you two guys fighting already?"

"Yes," Thomas said, smiling. "Art is long and ulcers fleeting."

Craig was too tired to inquire how Murphy had found out that he was in the hospital. But he was happy to see him there. Murphy would arrange everything. He himself could just drift into his doped and not unpleasant dreams in which night and day blended, pain and pleasure were impersonal abstractions. Knowing that all was now in safe hands, he could concentrate merely on dominating the rebellion of his blood.

"They told me I could only stay five minutes," Murphy said. "I just wanted to see if you were still alive. Do you want me to fly in my guy from Beverly Hills? He's supposed to be the best in the country."

Everything that Murphy touched was the best in the country. "No need, Murph," Craig said. "The men I have here are fine."

"Well, you just don't worry about anything but getting better," Murphy said. "By the time you get out of here, I'll have a contract ready for you to sign that'll have United Artists screaming in anguish. Come on, Bruce. We have things to discuss that are not for invalids' ears." Murphy patted Craig's shoulder roughly. "You mustn't scare your old friends like this," he said very gently. "Sonia sends her love. All right, Nurse, all right, I'm going." The ex-captain in the Nursing Corps was glowering blackly at him and looking dramatically at her watch.

The two men went out. The nurse fussed a little with a pillow. "Business," she said, "kills more men than bullets."

For a man who has begun his working life in the theatre, Craig thought, a hospital room is a fitting place to end it. It is like a stage. The hero is in the center with all the lights upon him. The doctor is the director, although he doubles by playing one of the parts. He watches mostly from the wings, preparing to intervene when necessary, whispering to the other actors that they can go on now, that they must enter smiling, that they are not to prolong their scenes unduly. The nurses, like stagehands, move the props around—hurry on with thermometers, trays, bedpans, syringes, instruments for the taking or infusion of blood.

The hero has a long part to play—the work is constructed around him, he never leaves the stage, he has a run-of-the-play contract. Ungratefully, he sometimes grumbles at his prominence, is quick to criticize the manner in which other actors play their scenes with him, would replace them or cut them if he could.

The first one he would have eliminated, if he could, was Belinda Ewen. By the fourth day in the hospital she had decided that he was going to recover and that his recovery would be speeded by forcing him to stop brooding, as she described it, and occupy himself with the business of everyday life. She reported that she had checked him out of the hotel and packed his things. His suitcases were now thriftily stored in the office. Mail and messages were to be forwarded. People had been notified. She had called the *Times*. When he protested weakly about this, she said, firm in her concept of orderly, civilized behavior, that friends and family and the public had a right to know. He refused to ask her what friends and family she had selected. The telephone in the office rang all day. He'd be surprised how many people were interested in him. With her efficiency it was likely that hundreds of well-wishers would soon be thronging through his room. He pleaded with the doctors for release, plotted escape.

In fact, by now he felt strong enough to see people. They had removed the needles from the battered veins, there were no more transfusions, he could sit up and take liquid nourishment. He had even shaved. His face in the mirror had shocked him. It had the same greenish pallor as the Russian taxi driver's. He resolved that until he left the hospital he would allow Miss Balissano, his military day nurse, who had offered to do so, to shave him.

The mail Belinda brought him included a bill from his wife's lawyer for five thousand dollars. On account. He had agreed to pay her lawyers in the first burst of generosity and relief when he had finally made the decision to get a divorce and realized that, with money, it was possible to obtain one.

A letter from his accountant reminded him that he had to make up his mind about what he wanted to do about the seventy thousand dollars that the Internal Revenue Service was demanding from him. They were becoming menacing, his lawyer wrote.

Belinda had found the copy of *The Three Horizons* in his hotel room and had read it. She was favorably impressed by it and brought over large casting books with the photographs of actors and actresses in Hollywood and New York for him to glance through and think about who might play which part. He fingered through the books languidly to please Belinda.

She had brought over his checkbook. There were bills to be paid. He had no Blue Cross or Health Insurance, and the hospital had asked her discreetly for an advance. She had made out a check for a thousand dollars. Obediently, he signed it. He signed checks for office rent, telephone and telegraph bills, the Diners' Club, the Air-Travel Card. Dead or alive he must maintain his credit rating. He hoped Anne's psychology professor would never see his signature.

Now that he was back in business, Belinda said, she had brought over the scripts of two plays by prominent authors that had come into the office in the last week. She had read them and hadn't thought much of them, but the prominent authors would expect a personal note from him. She would bring her pad the next day, prepared to take dictation. He promised to read the plays by the prominent authors. She admired the flowers that the Murphys and the Thomases and Walt Klein had sent, all lavish displays from the most expensive florist on Fifth Avenue. She was shocked when he said, "They make me feel as though I'm on my own bier. Send them down to the children's ward."

She warned him darkly about Miss Balissano. The woman was callous, she said, and at the same time maniacally overprotective. She practically had to fight her way with physical force to get into his room each time she came. Fanatical overprotectiveness was dangerous. It was negative thinking. He promised to indulge in no negative thinking, to consider replacing Miss Balissano.

Miss Balissano came in at this point, and Belinda said, "I see my time is up," her tone suggesting that she had been struck across the face with a weapon. She left, and for the first time since Craig had met Miss Balissano, he was glad to see her.

Miss Balissano took one look at the manuscripts and casting books piled on his bedside table and picked them up and put them on the floor out of sight. She had learned something in Korea.

He was lying in his bed with a thermometer in his mouth when Anne came in. It was a gray day, almost evening, and the room was dark. Anne opened the door tentatively, as though ready to flee at the first word from him. He waved a dumb greeting to her, indicating the tube in his mouth. She smiled uncertainly, came over the the bed, leaned over and gave him a little nervous peck on the forehead. He reached out his hand and held hers. "Oh Daddy," she said. She wept softly.

Miss Balissano came in, turned on the light, took the thermometer, made a notation on his chart. She always refused to tell him what his temperature was.

"This is my daughter, Miss Balissano," Craig said.

"We've met," Miss Balissano said grimly. But then she said everything grimly. She took no notice of the girl's tears. She fussed with his pillows, said, "Good night. Sleep well. Don't be long, miss." She marched out, the sound of guns over the horizon. The night nurse would be in soon. The night nurse was a Puerto Rican young man who was a student at City College. He sat in a corner of the room all night reading textbooks in the glow of a carefully shaded lamp. His only duty was to call the intern on the floor if he thought Craig was dying. So far, he had not called the intern.

"Oh, Daddy," Anne said, her voice trembling. "I hate seeing you like this."

He had to smile a little at the youthful egotism of her first words to him. I, I, I.

"It's not my fault, is it, Daddy?" she said.

"Of course not."

"If it's too much trouble to talk, don't talk."

"I can talk," he said irritably. He was irritated with his illness, not with Anne, but he could see that she thought his temper was directed at her.

"We came as soon as Ian got Mr. Thomas's cable," Anne said. "We were in London."

Craig wondered from whom Wadleigh had borrowed the money for the voyage. But he didn't ask the question. "It was good of you to come," was all he said.

"You're going to be all right, aren't you?" Anne asked anxiously. Her face was pale. Traveling didn't agree with her. He remembered all the times he had had to stop the car on trips when she was young and prone to carsickness.

"Certainly, I'm going to be all right," he said.

"I talked to Dr. Gibson yesterday, I came right to the hospital as soon as we got in, they said I should wait a day to see you, but Dr. Gibson wouldn't say yes or no when I asked him about you. 'Only time will tell,' he said. I hate doctors."

"He's very good," Craig said. He felt a great affection for Dr. Gibson, quiet, efficient, modest, lifesaving man. "He just doesn't like being asked to be a prophet."

"Well," she said childishly, "he might at least try to be a little bit encouraging."

"I guess he doesn't think that's his business," Craig said.

"You mustn't try to be too stoical," Anne said. "Ian says that that's what you are—stoical." She was already quoting her lover, Craig noted. "He says it's an unprofitable attitude in this day and age."

"Will you pour a glass of water for me please, darling," Craig said. He wanted no more quotations from the accumulated wisdom of Ian Wadleigh. He wasn't really thirsty, but Anne seemed embarrassed and uneasy with him, and asking for a small service from her, even one as minute as pouring water out of a thermos, might make a dent in the painful barrier between them. He saw that the "darling" had pleased her. He sipped a little from the glass she offered him.

"You're going to have more visitors," she said. "Mummy's arriving tomorrow and . . ."

"Oh, God," Craig said. "How does she know?"

"I called her," Anne said defensively. "She was terribly upset. You don't mind that I told her, do you?"

"No," he said, lying.

"It's only human," Anne said.

"I agree," Craig said impatiently, "I agree. It's only human."

"Gail is on her way, too," Anne said.

"You called her, too?"

"Yes. I only did what I thought was right, Daddy. You're not angry at me, are you?"

"No." Craig put the water tumbler down and lay back resignedly, closing his eyes, to show Anne that he was tired and wished to be alone.

"I have something to apologize to you about," Anne said. "In my letter I was too much in a hurry to say anything about your script. I don't know whether it means anything to you or not, but I love it, and I should have told you . . ."

"You had other things on your mind," he said.

"I suppose you have a right to be sarcastic with me," Anne said humbly. "But, anyway, I love it. So does Ian. He wanted me to tell you."

"Good."

"He's talked to Mr. Thomas already. He and Mr. Thomas agree on a lot of things about the script. They're both wildly hopeful."

"Good," Craig said again.

"Of course, Mr. Thomas doesn't know anything about me yet," she said. She hesitated. "Ian is afraid that because of me you're going to be against him. About working on the script, I mean." She waited for Craig to speak, but he kept silent. "I told Ian you're too big a man to stand in his way just because . . ." She trailed off.

"I'm not quite as big a man as I was last week," Craig said.

"Ian needs the job badly," Anne said. "It'll get him off the ground, he says. He's been having such a bad time . . . You're not going to say no, are you, Daddy?" She was imploring now.

"No," he said, "I'm not going to say no."

"I knew it," she said. She was his happy little daughter now, being promised a treat, oblivious of the world of hospitals, pain, blood. "Ian's downstairs," she said. "He'd love to come up and say hello. He's terribly worried about you. Can I tell him to come up? Just for a minute?"

"Tell Ian to go fuck himself," Craig said.

Anne took in her breath sharply. It was the first time, as far as he could remember, that he had ever said the word in front of her. "Oh, Daddy," she said. "How can you be so unjust!" She turned and ran out of the room.

She's a big girl now, Craig thought as he sank deeper into the pillows. She knows all the words. I'm going to move into a public ward. Where they don't allow visitors.

They operated on him that night. There was no enormous hemorrhage like the night in the hotel, but the tests had shown that he had begun to bleed again, as slow, steady seeping away in his gut whose source they couldn't locate, dangerous and life-sapping.

Before he was given the preoperative shot of morphine, while they were shaving his chest and abdomen, he realized that he wasn't afraid. Fifty-fifty, the doctor had said. A man couldn't ask for fairer odds.

Faces came and went, briefly, silently, seen obscurely, through haze—Murphy, Thomas, Dr. Gibson, noncommittal, no warnings or encouragement, his wife, his daughter Marcia, grotesquely plump and weeping, Gail McKinnon, sea-fresh, Constance, almost unrecognizably stern, Edward Brenner . . . But Edward Brenner was dead. Were they all a dream? He spoke only once. "Marcia," he said, "you're a good size."

He was in great pain, but he kept from groaning. The African with tribal scars in first class would not understand. The White Man's burden. He was stoical and waited for the morphine every four hours without asking for more. Who had said that stoicism was an unprofitable attitude? No friend of his.

The stagehands, in white, brought on the props—the syringes, the blood. The lighting stage center was rearranged. There was the sound of surf in his ears. He woke. He slept. The faces came and went, with their several claims. Where was Ian Wadleigh, that loose, deceitful man? Belinda Ewen, in electric blue? What checks did she have for him to sign?

Other doctors. The best man in the country. Soft medical voices, whisperings offstage. The Scandinavian blonde with the expert hands did not reappear. Alas.

How many days ago had he left Meyrague? What drink had he ordered on the *terrasse* of the little restaurant overlooking the harbor of Cassis? What had that girl said about her mother?

He could sit up in bed and even eat a little, but the fever persisted. In the morning it was around a hundred and one, in the evening it went up to one hundred and three and a half. The plastic bag hung on a stand above his head dripping antibiotics into his veins day and night. Either the fever or the antibiotics, or both, kept him in a heavy-lidded daze, and he began to lose track of time and not remember how long he had been there. Nobody mentioned it, not he nor any of the doctors, but he knew that they were afraid that he had picked up one of those new hospital-bred wild strains of bacteria for which no treatment had yet been found.

Dr. Gibson had forbidden any visitors, and he was grateful for that. Dr. Gibson had told him that when he had been free of fever for three whole days, he would be discharged. In the meanwhile, he sleepily watched the television set that had been wheeled into his room and placed at the foot of his bed. Mostly, he just watched the baseball games. It gave him pleasure to watch young men running swiftly across green grass in the sunshine, clearly winning and distinctly losing. He remembered having read about the condemned murderer in Massachusetts who also had watched the baseball games on television in his cell and whose only regret was that he would never know whether or not the Dodgers had won the pennant.

He wondered if he would know who won the pennant this year.

Finally, Murphy convinced Dr. Gibson that he had to see Craig. Craig had had two good days. The fever had gone down to ninety-nine in the morning and one hundred and two at night. Miss Balissano still refused to tell him what his temperature was, but Dr. Gibson was more lenient.

Murphy's face when he saw Craig told him as accurately as any mirror how bad it was. He hadn't looked in a mirror since the operation.

"I had to see you, Jess," Murphy said. "I have to leave for the Coast tomorrow. Things're piling up, and I just have to be there."

"Sure, Murphy," Craig said. His voice sounded thin and old in his ears.

"Three weeks in New York is all I can manage," Murphy said.

"Is that how long I've been here?" Craig asked.

Murphy looked at him queerly. "Yes," he said."

"A long time," Craig said.

"Yes. And the doctors won't give me an estimate about when you'll get out."

"They don't know."

"Gibson tells me you won't be able to work—at anything—for at least six months even if you get out tomorrow."

"I know," Craig said. "He told me."

"Thomas can't wait," Murphy said. "He's got to start shooting in a month if he wants to do it this year. For the weather."

"For the weather," Craig nodded.

"He and Wadleigh have been working eighteen hours a day. Thomas says Wadleigh is really panning out. He says you'll be crazy about the final script."

"I'm sure."

"Do you want me to tell you about who they've got to play it?"

"Not really, Murph."

Again, Murphy looked at him queerly. "Don't worry about the money," he said. "You've got a big chunk up front and five per cent of the profits."

"Tell me some other time," Craig said.

"Thomas has been a real gent about everything."

"I'm sure." Craig closed his eyes. Murphy seemed to be far away, at the other end of a long hall, and it disturbed him.

"You're tired," Murphy said. "I won't bother you anymore. Just call me if you need anything."

"I'll do just that." Craig didn't open his eyes.

"Sonia sends her love."

"Thanks Murph."

"Take it easy, kid." Murphy went softly out of the room as Miss Balissano came in.

"Turn on the television, please," Craig said.

When he heard the noise of the crowd, Craig opened his eyes. It was sunny in St. Louis.

On the day that his temperature was normal for the first time, Dr. Gibson allowed his wife to visit him. As far as he knew, Dr. Gibson hadn't been told that they were in the process of getting a divorce, so it was natural for him to let her in. Dr. Gibson hadn't warned Craig that his wife was coming to see him. He probably thought it would be a salutary surprise.

Penelope was smiling tremulously as she came into the room. She had had her hair done, and it hung youthfully down to her shoulders. She was wearing a navy blue dress. He had once said that it was the color he liked best on her. A long time ago.

"Hello, Jess," she said. Her voice was soft, shaky, her face drawn. The last time they had met it had been in a lawyer's office. He couldn't remember how many months ago. She bent over and kissed his cheek. The ten thousandth kiss.

"Hello, Penny," he said. "How's the web going?" It was an old joke between them.

"What?" she asked, frowning. "What web?"

"Never mind," he said. She had forgotten.

"How do you feel?"

"Fine," he said. "Can't you tell?" He thought about her lawyers to keep from thinking about her.

He saw her lips set, then soften. He knew she was trying to restrain her anger. "Dr. Gibson says there are encouraging signs. Very encouraging."

"I'm very encouraged," he said.

"You don't change, do you?" she said. Anger had momentarily gotten the better of her.

"I'm a faithful man," he said. He was fighting against her pity. What she probably would call her love. What might very possibly be her love.

"Dr. Gibson says you will have to rest for a long time after you get out of here," she said. "You'll need someone to look after you. Do you want to come home?"

He thought about the broad brick house on the quiet, tree-lined New York street, the small back garden, now a dusty green, the desk in his study, his books on the shelves. They had agreed to divide the furniture, but they had not yet done so. There was no place he could put it. He couldn't carry his desk from hotel room to hotel room. She waited for his reply, but he said nothing. "Do you want to call off the divorce?" she said. "I do."

"I'll think about it." He wasn't strong enough to struggle with her now.

"What made you do it?" she asked. "Out of a blue sky. Writing me that awful letter asking for a divorce. After all, we were getting along. You were free to come and go. For months at a time I didn't even know whether you were in the country or not. I never asked you about your other—whatever they were. Maybe we weren't love's sweet young dream, but we were getting along."

"Getting along," he said. "We hadn't slept with each other for five years."

"And whose idea was that?" Her voice grew harsher.

"Yours," he said. She had a convenient memory, and he waited for her to deny it and believe her own denial. Surprising him, she said, "What did you expect? You'd been making it plain for years that I bored you. You'd invite anybody in the world to keep from having a meal alone with me."

"Including Bertie Folsom."

She flushed. "Including Bertie Folsom. I suppose that slut daughter of yours told you about Geneva."

"She did."

"At least he paid attention to me."

"Bully for him," he said. "Bully for you."

"There's another victim you can add to your score," she said, all holds barred now, the hospital room, the plastic bag dripping ineffectual remedies into his vein from its chromium stand, all ignored. "Driving her into that drunkard's arms."

"He's stopped drinking." Too late, he realized how idiotic it sounded.

"He hasn't stopped doing anything else," she said. "Married three times and looking around for more. I'll never talk to that girl again. And your other daughter. Poor Marcia. Flying here all the way from Arizona to comfort her father. And what did you have to say to her? The one sentence that crossed your lips. 'Marcia, you're a good size.' She cried for days. You know what she said? She said, 'Even when he's bleeding to death, he makes fun of me. He hates me.' I tried to get her to come up here with me, and she wouldn't do it."

"I'll make it up to her," he said wearily. "Sometime. I don't hate her."

"You hate *me*."

"I don't hate anybody."

"Even now you have to humiliate me." Coldly, he noticed the old false melodramatic tone that came into her voice when she recounted her trials. "Right now that woman is shamelessly parading herself downstairs, waiting to come up here as soon as you've thrown me out."

"I don't know any 'that woman,'" he said.

"That whore from Paris. You know her all right. And so do I." Penelope paced around the room, obviously trying to regain control of herself. He lay with his eyes closed, his head back on the pillow. "I didn't come up here to argue, Jesse," Penelope said, switching to her reasonable voice. "I came up here to tell you you are welcome to come home. More than welcome."

"I told you I'd think about it," he said.

"Just for my own satisfaction," she said, "I'd like to know once and for all why you thought you had to have a divorce."

Well, he thought, she's asking for it. He opened his eyes so that he could see her reactions. "I met Alice Paine in New York one day," he said.

"What's Alice Paine got to do with it?"

"She told me a peculiar story. Every October fifth she gets a dozen roses. Without a card. Anonymously." He could tell by the sudden rigidity of her face, her shoulders, that she knew what he was talking about. "Any woman," he said, "who has anything to do with a dozen roses on October fifth, year in, year out, is not ever going to get me—alive or dead." He lay back and closed his eyes once more. She had asked for it, and he had given it to her, and he felt a great relief that he had finally gotten it out.

"Good-by, Jesse," she whispered.

"Good-by," he said.

He heard the door closing softly behind her. Then, for the first time, he wept. Not from anger or loss but because he had lived more than twenty years with a woman and had had two children with her and he didn't feel anything when he said good-by, not even rage.

After a while he remembered that Penelope had said that Constance was in the building. "There's a lady downstairs waiting to see me," he said to Miss Balissano. "Will you ask her to come up, please? And let me have the comb and brush and a mirror."

He brushed back his hair. It had grown very long in the three weeks. Vigorous. His hair had rejected his illness. There was no more gray in it than before. His eyes looked enormous and overbright in his thin face. Losing weight had made his face look much younger. He doubted that Constance would appreciate his new simulation of youth.

But when the door opened, it was Belinda who came in. He hid his disappointment. "Belinda," he said heartily, "I *am* glad to see you."

She kissed his cheek. She looked as though she had been crying, the small sharp face made more womanly by her sorrow. She was still in electric blue. It was her costume for deathbeds.

"They're monsters in this hospital," she said. Her voice was softer, too. My illness had improved her, he thought. "I've been here every day this week," she said, "and they wouldn't let me see you."

"I'm sorry about that," he lied.

"I've kept track, though," she said. "I've talked to Mr. Murphy, too. You're not going to work on the picture."

"I'm afraid not."

She pulled on her hands. They were small and harsh. Twenty-three years at the typewriter. Her nails were painted blood-red. She had an unerring eye for the wrong colors. She went to the window, pulled the shade down a little. "Jesse," she said, "I want to quit."

"I don't believe you."

"Believe me," she said.

"Have you got another job?"

"Of course not." She turned away from the window, her face hurt.

"Then why quit?"

"You're not going to be able to work when you get out of here," she said.

"For a while."

"For a long while. Jesse, let's not kid ourselves. You don't need me or that office. You should have closed the office five years ago. You kept it open just for me."

"That's nonsense," he said, trying to sound sharp. She knew he was lying, but the lie was necessary.

"I've just been going through the motions," she said quietly. "Thank you and enough. Anyway, I have to get out of New York. I can't stand it anymore. It's a madhouse. Two of my friends have been mugged just this month. In broad daylight. My nephew was stabbed in the chest for a pack of cigarettes, and he nearly died. I don't dare leave my apartment at night. I haven't seen a movie or even a play in a year. I have four different locks on my door. Every time I hear the elevator doors open on my floor, I tremble. Jesse, if they want this city so much, let them have it."

"Where are you going to go?" he asked gently.

"My mother still has our house in Newtown," she said. "She's ailing, and I can help her. And it's a beautiful quiet little town, and you can walk in the streets there."

"Maybe I'll move there, too," he said, only half-joking.

"You could do worse," she said.

"What are you going to do for money?" Finally, you always had to come down to this question.

"I don't need much," she said. "And I've managed to save quite a bit. Thanks to you, Jesse. You're a marvelously generous man, and I want to let you know that I know it."

"You worked."

"I loved working for you. I was lucky. It was better than any marriage I've seen around."

Craig laughed. "That doesn't say very much, does it?"

"It says a lot to me," she said. "The lease for the office is up for renewal this month. Shall I tell them we're not signing?" She waited for his response, pulling at the blood-red fingernails.

"We've had a nice long run, Belinda," he said softly, "haven't we?"

"Yes, we have," she said. "A nice long run."

"Tell them we're not renewing," he said.

"They won't be surprised," she said.

"Belinda," he said, "come here and give me a kiss."

She kissed him, decorously, on the cheek. He couldn't embrace her because of the tube in his arm. "Belinda," he said as she stood up straight again, "Who's going to write out the checks for me to sign now?"

"You can write them out yourself," she said. "You're a big, grown man. Just don't write out too many."

"I'll try not to," he said.

"If I stay here one more minute," she said, "I'm going to bawl." She fled from the room.

He lay back in the bed staring at the ceiling. There goes twenty-three years, he thought. Add to that the twenty-one years of his wife. The sentences having been served concurrently.

Not a bad day's work.

He was asleep when Constance came into the room. He dreamt that a woman whom he couldn't quite identify was kissing him. When he opened his eyes, he saw Constance standing near him staring gravely down at him.

"Hello," he said.

"If you want to sleep," she said, "I'll just sit here and watch you."

"I don't want to sleep." She was on his good side, the one without the tube, so he could stretch out his hand and take hers. Her hand was cool and firm. She smiled down at him. "You really ought to leave your hair long," she said. "It's very becoming."

"Another week," he said, "and I'll be able to play at the next Woodstock Festival." He would have to try to maintain the light tone. Constance wasn't his wife or Belinda Ewen. They had to avoid hurting each other or reminding each other of different moments they had spent together.

She drew up a chair and sat next to the bed. She was wearing a black dress. It didn't look funereal on her. She looked serene and beautiful, the hair brushed back from her broad, fine forehead.

"Spell Meyrague," he said. Then he was sorry he had said it. It had just come out automatically.

But she laughed, and it was all right. "Obviously you're getting better."

"Rapidly," he said.

"Rapidly. I was afraid I wasn't going to get the chance to see you. I have to go back to Paris tomorrow," she said.

"Oh."

There was silence for a moment. "What are you going to do when you get out of here?" she asked.

"I have to take it easy for a while," he said.

"I know. It's too bad about the picture."

"Not so bad. It's served its purpose. Or most of its purpose."

"Are you coming back to Paris?"

"Are you leaving Paris?" he asked.

"I'm supposed to leave in two weeks."

"I guess I'm not coming back to Paris."

She was silent for a little bit. "They've rented a house for me in San Francisco," she said. "You can see the bay, they tell me. There's a big room at the top of the house where a man could work. You wouldn't hear the kids yelling. Or hardly."

He smiled.

"Does that sound like a bribe?" She answered herself. "I suppose it does." She laughed, then became serious. "Have you thought about what you're going to do after you get out of here, where you're going to go?"

"Not really."

"Not San Francisco?"

"I think I'm a little old for San Francisco," he said gently. He knew it really wasn't the city he was thinking of, and she knew it, too. "But I'll visit."

"I'll be there," she said. "For a while, anyway." The warning was clear, but there was nothing to do about it. "Sweep the town by storm," he said.

"I'll try to take your advice." She was grave again. "It's too bad," she said. "Our times didn't really coincide. Anyway, when you run out of hotel rooms, think of Constance." She reached out and stroked his forehead. Her touch was pleasant, but there were no sexual stirrings in him. The ailing body devoted all its time to its ailment. Illness was the supreme egotism.

"I've been doing something that I abhor these last few days," she said, taking her hand away. "I've been adding up love. Who loves whom the most. My accounts came out cock-eyed. I love you more than you love me. That's the first time it ever happened to me. Well, I suppose it had to happen once."

"I don't know . . ." he began.

"I know," she said harshly. "I know."

"I haven't added up any accounts," he said.

"You don't have to," she said. "Oh, that reminds me—I met your pretty young friend from Cannes. Dr. Gibson introduced us one night. We became very chummy.

We had lunch together several times. She's very bright. And very tough. Enviably tough."

"I don't know her that well," he said. Surprisingly, it was the truth. He didn't know whether Gail was tough or not.

"She knew all about me, of course."

"Not from me," he said.

"No, I'm sure not," Constance said, smiling. "She's going back to London, did you know?"

"No, I haven't seen her."

"Poor Jesse," Constance said ironically, "all the working ladies are running out on him. In the future I suggest you stick to one town and pick on women of leisure."

"I don't like women of leisure," he said.

"Neither do I," Constance said. "Here—" She rummaged in her bag and brought out a slip of paper. He recognized Gail's handwriting. "I promised her I'd give you her telephone number if I saw you before she did. She's in Philadelphia, staying with her father to save money. She's flat broke, she told me."

He took the slip of paper. There was an address, a telephone number. No message. He put the slip of paper on the bedside table.

Constance stood up. "Your nurse told me not to tire you," she said.

"Will I see you again?"

"Not in New York," she said. She began pulling on her gloves. "You can't keep gloves clean more than an hour in this city." She brushed the back of one glove with an annoyed gesture. "I won't pretend I enjoyed New York this trip. A kiss for good-by." She leaned over and kissed him on the mouth. "You're not going to die, darling, are you?" she whispered.

"No," he said. "I don't think so."

"I couldn't bear it if you did," she said. Then stood erect and smiled. "I'll send you a card from the Golden Gate," she said, and was gone.

She was the best girl he had ever known, and she was gone.

He didn't call the Philadelphia number until the next morning. A man who answered the phone and who said he was Miss McKinnon's father asked him who was calling. When Craig gave him his name, Mr. McKinnon's voice grew icy, and he seemed to be delighted to be able to tell Craig that Miss McKinnon had left the day before for London.

Fair enough, Craig thought. He himself would have been no more polite with Ian Wadleigh.

A week later they let him out of the hospital. His temperature had been normal for three days in a row. The evening before he was discharged Dr. Gibson had a long talk with him. Or what passed for a long talk with Dr. Gibson. "You're a lucky man, Mr. Craig," Dr. Gibson had said. He sat there, a spare, ascetic old man who did a half-hour of exercise every morning and swallowed ten yeast tablets a day, laying down the law. "A lot of people wouldn't have pulled through the way you did. Now, you've got to be careful. Very, very careful. Stick to the diet. And no alcohol. Not even a sip of wine for a year. Maybe forever." Dr. Gibson was a fanatic teetotaler, and Craig thought he detected a steely pleasure in Gibson's voice as he said this. "And forget about working for six months. And you seem to be a man who leads a complicated life—most complicated, I would say." It was the first time that Dr. Gibson had suggested that he had drawn any conclusions from the list of people who had come to visit his patient. "If I were forced to make one single diagnosis of what produced your attack, Mr. Craig," the doctor said, "I would hazard the guess that it was not a functional accident or malformation, or some hereditary weakness. You understand what I mean, I'm sure, Mr. Craig."

"I do."

"Uncomplicate yourself, Mr. Craig," Dr. Gibson said. "Uncomplicate yourself. And eat yeast."

Eating yeast, Craig thought, as Dr. Gibson stalked out, eating yeast would be easy.

He shook hands with Miss Balissano at the hospital door and stepped out into the street. He had told Miss Balissano that he would have somebody pick up his things. He walked out into the sunshine slowly, blinking, his clothes hanging loose around his body. It was a clear, warm day. He hadn't let anyone, not even Belinda, know that today was to be the day. Superstition. Even as he went out the door, he was afraid that Miss Balissano would come running after him and say that a terrible mistake had been made and that he was to be rushed back into bed and the tube stuck once more into his arm.

But nobody came after him. He walked aimlessly on the sunny side of the street. The people he passed seemed beautiful. The girls were lithe and walked with their heads up, half-smiling as though they were remembering innocent but intense pleasures of the night before. The young men, bearded and unbearded, walked with a purpose, looking everyone in the eye. The little children were clean and laughing, dressed in anemone colors, and darted past him with immortal energy. The old men were neat and sprightly, philosophic about death in the sunshine.

He had made no hotel reservation. He was alone, alive, walking, each step stronger than the one before it, alone, with no address, drifting down a street in his native city, and no one in the whole world knew where he was; no friend, enemy, lover, daughter, business associate, lawyer, banker, certified public accountant, knew where he was going, had any claims on him, could reach him or touch him. For this moment, at least, he had made a space for himself.

He passed a shop in which typewriters were on display. He stopped and examined the window. The machines were clean, intricate, useful. He went into the shop. A soft-spoken clerk showed him various models. He thought of his friend the matador making a selection of swords in the shop in Madrid. He told the clerk he would be back and leave his order.

He left the shop, the future, comfortable clatter of the machine he would eventually buy tapping in his ear.

He found himself on Third Avenue. He was in front of a saloon he had once frequented. He looked at his watch. Eleven-thirty. Time for a drink. He went in. The saloon was almost empty. Two men talking at the other end of the bar. Male voices.

The bartender came up. The bartender was powerful, pink and fat in his apron, and had an old fighter's broken nose, scarred eyebrows. The bartender was beautiful. "A Scotch and soda," Craig said. He watched with great interest as the bartender poured the whisky into a jigger, splashed it over ice, opened a bottle of soda. He poured the soda himself, carefully, enjoying the cold feel of the bottle in his hand. He stood looking thoughtfully at his drink for a full minute. Then he drank, with truant joy.

From the other end of the bar a man's voice said loudly, "Then I told her—you know what I told her—'Fuck off!' I told her."

Craig smiled. Still alive, he took another sip of his drink. He didn't remember when a drink had ever tasted as good.